Fiona Shaw is the author of *The Sweetest Thing*. She lives in York.

THE PICTURE SHE TOOK

In a bombed-out village on the Western Front, Jude nurses the wounded in her cellar hospital. War is the making of her, and she records all she can, taking photographs of everything, capturing life in the midst of death . . . Survivor of a different conflict, Daniel has come home from Ireland a haunted man. Signed up to the hated Black and Tans, he is disfigured by a campaign he fought in but didn't understand . . . A few years later, an innocent photograph exposes an extraordinary tale. A snapshot, showing two soldiers sharing a cigarette, brings together Jude and Daniel and propels them on a strange journey. People travel a long way from themselves in battle and some never return.

Books by Fiona Shaw
Published by The House of Ulverscroft:

THE SWEETEST THING

FIONA SHAW

THE PICTURE SHE TOOK

Complete and Unabridged

CHARNWOOD
Leicester

First published in Great Britain in 2005 by
Virago Press
an imprint of
Time Warner Book Group UK, London

First Charnwood Edition
published 2006
by arrangement with
Time Warner Book Group UK, London

Lines by T. S. Eliot from 'Little Gidding'
(Four Quartets) in the *Collected Poems 1909 – 1962*
reproduced by kind permission of
Faber and Faber Ltd

British Library CIP Data

Shaw, Fiona
    The picture she took.—Large print ed.—
Charnwood library series
    1. War—Psychological aspects—Fiction
    2. Large type books
    I. Title
    823.9′2 [F]

    ISBN 1–84617–428–7

Published by
F. A. Thorpe (Publishing)
Anstey, Leicestershire

Set by Words & Graphics Ltd.
Anstey, Leicestershire
Printed and bound in Great Britain by
T. J. International Ltd., Padstow, Cornwall

This book is printed on acid-free paper

For Hugh

And the end of all our exploring
Will be to arrive where we started
And know the place for the first time

T. S. Eliot

MISTER ICARUS

1

The day being bright made a difference. Having paid the tuppenny entrance, virtue was rewarded if the sun also shone, and so the visitors doffed their hats in tribute and allowed themselves the leisure of sitting a moment on the benches between the columns.

The girl at the desk, her head ducked to her knitting, would look up as if surprised at each new person, then find her smile, tear a ticket off and make change.

'There's nothing too . . . ?' a lady might say, and the girl would shake her head, reassuring.

'No, nothing like that. I'd even bring my grandmother. And besides, you can sit down in between, if you want. The benches are quite comfortable.'

So they paid their 6d, 3d for ex-servicemen and children, and walked in, their step apprehensive despite the aspidistras.

It was the lunch hour and the room was quite full. Although the ceiling was high and the windows open, the air was warm and people were caught at the door for a moment by the smell. It was nothing more than the fading perfumes and colognes and the half-day's sweat of so many bodies, but it checked them until they found that the girl was right; there was nothing to fear, and their noses became accustomed.

'Our Brave Men who Battle On', the poster said outside.

The first photographs showed soldiers just out of battle. Torn and dirty uniforms, bloody bandages. Some were on stretchers, some on the ground, others in ambulances and lorries and tents. Their eyes were wide and dull with injury, their bodies looked heavy. The visitors stood before the blood and mayhem, and quickly understood the crueller tones of blacks and greys. If they could, searched out the smaller details: the laces on a boot undone, the stretcher handles which reminded them of the rake left in the garden, that the man wore a wedding ring.

The next set were easier, everyone ordered once again. Lines of white beds, nurses in white uniforms, smiles, everything tidy and covered over. Even in the makeshift places, which looked little more than a cellar or a rough tent, the blanket corners were neat and the men held out cigarettes or mugs of tea.

The visitors stepped in closer, sometimes peering right up. It would be all right to recognise a face now. Women exchanged smiles and could wonder safely about the injuries beneath. Conversations started up, and they thought they felt again something of that spirit so remarked upon at the time.

The men stood more alone, and they didn't dawdle or catch each other's eye. They moved round the little knots of women with abrupt, careless steps, affecting not to notice the images pinned to the wall, and they glimpsed up through the windows at the blue sky, tugging at their collars as if more air were needed.

In the last photographs, young men seated on chairs outdoors in smart, double-breasted suits, arms across one another's shoulders, faced the camera with serious, intent expressions. They were like members of a sporting team, a proud nurse to one side instead of a coach. And where their legs should have been there was only air, their tucked trousers the trophy of their sport. A young man held a life mask up close to where his face used to be, his hair slicked back and shiny, his eye socket puckered tight. And men with pinned sleeves were painting signs, one foot crossed beneath them, the other extended, toes pointed like a dancer's, the paint-brush just visible between. A poster on the wall behind read 'Men Made Here', and showed men with calliper hands sat at a table of metal parts.

'What they can do now,' a young woman whispered.

'Marvellous,' her companion said.

It seemed to be understood among the visitors that one must behave dispassionately; that it was all to the good, what one was seeing, the men leading useful lives. The lunch hour pressed on and the air remained warm. Sandwiches could be eaten in the park, if one was quick, and anyway it wasn't the thing, to linger.

The exhibition was still busy when the young man with the limp bought his ticket from the girl at the desk. She didn't need to say that a limp wasn't unusual in here, and besides, beggars couldn't be choosers.

'I could come round to a bit of arm or leg

gone,' she told her friend on her lunch break. 'It's funny what you get used to.'

He was a nice height, not too thin like lots were. Plenty of hair, ordinary colour, somewhere between brown and fair. And well-dressed. Bespoke suit, not a thirty shilling number. He didn't smile.

'They often look fierce,' she'd added to her friend. 'It's these pictures. Takes them back.'

The girl sold the man his ticket with a smile, 3d rate like she'd guessed, and watched him go in.

Daniel Brown hadn't meant to come here. He'd thought he could get back to the office, but it was too far.

'Bloody vanity,' he said to himself. 'Bloody fool.'

He sat down on a bench and stretched his right leg out before him. He didn't know why it should be so sore today, but the pain cut up through his body, hard into his skull. He closed his eyes and waited for the pulse to ease. He sat with his fists on his thighs, thumbs tucked in, back straight, his eyes closed. Once the pain relented, he'd leave. But for now, he must just sit still.

He knew people would be looking. There were plenty like him and worse around, and most people didn't give you the time of day any more. But there'd be the women his mother's age who'd want to ask him was he all right, bending and putting their faces to one side, which only made him want to shout at them. And the girls who'd think he was a hero, always standing off a way and looking him up and down to see whether he was all there. And the men with tired eyes who didn't want reminding.

The colours behind his eyes were sharp, jagged. Lines of orange and black firing off, figures running off and beyond his sight. And when finally the colours had died down and he opened his eyes, the room had emptied and he was almost on his own.

'Going to be late back?' the girl said.

She must have been watching him. He picked up his hat, then got to his feet. He walked up close to the frames of wounded men. This one wasn't his war. He'd never been in a trench, never got shelled. He didn't want to look at them, but he was damned if he'd hurry in front of the girl. He walked slowly, listening to his awkward step on the marble floor, letting the images brush over the top of his mind. He set his thoughts on the afternoon, the tasks that waited back in the office. She was still watching him. Why didn't she pick up her knitting again? He went on looking, more closely than he wanted, but only half-seeing the pictures before him.

What a joke, he thought, him ending up looking at these.

'What a joke,' he said out loud, and with a final glance at the men, all bloody with arms round one another's shoulders, he left.

The wounded men. They didn't know how lucky they were, bloody innocents. It was enough for him to go about his life now. The pavement felt very hard as he walked towards the office. He measured his steps. It used to be a stride and a half to cover these city slabs, but now it took him over two, first his left foot and then his right, catching the bears between the cracks, which he had never done as a child. Head down, he watched his feet, his shoulders hunched with the habit of it.

Daniel had been at his desk no more than a few minutes before his father walked in. Mr Brown was taller than his son. His suit was impeccable and his shoes never grew dusty. His natural movements were precise, clipped, and he crossed the office floor in less than two strides. He set some papers down on Daniel's blotter.

'Your signature's as good as mine,' he said.

Daniel uncapped his pen.

'Good lunch?'

Daniel nodded. 'Lamb chop.'

The tickety-tick from the secretaries' desks in the room next door ebbed and flowed. Right now they were quiet and Daniel could hear his father's breathing.

'And you've just got back in?'

'I stopped in the park. Forgot the time, watching the boys and boats.'

'Home as usual?'

'I expect so.'

'Good,' his father said. 'I'll see you downstairs at five-thirty-five.'

He left the room, shutting the door with such care you might have thought he was visiting an invalid in hospital. Daniel got up and stood at the window. The sash was open at the top and he could tell, from the spill of cool air down the glass, that there was quite a strong breeze. Two pigeons were necking on his window sill, Renaissance ruffs of feathers round their necks, their toes shuffling in the dirt. City pigeons, running the gauntlet of motor cars and trolley buses, they were used to his body behind the glass and didn't pause or fly when he appeared, just carried on with their wistful song. He stared out beyond them at the walls and windows opposite. You couldn't see anybody from here. No people. Only stone and brick and these resolute birds.

Doesn't stop the pigeons, a duff leg, he thought. He should be getting down to his work, reports to write, invoices to send, but something was nagging at him and he stood on at the window, hoping it would surface where he could see it.

Daniel took the lift down to meet his father. His leg was easier after the hours at his desk, and he opened the lift door with force, relishing that snap of metal closing on metal. His mother had always been sure he would trap his hand in one of these doors when he was a child, concertina'd between the bands of steel. He still didn't like to touch the criss-cross of metal, but in defiance of his mother, he traced his finger along the shiny, polished tracery of leaves that decorated the doorway.

He thought he had the lift to himself, but several girls from the secretarial division arrived as he was about to press the button for the ground floor.

'If you don't mind, sir,' one of them said.

He inclined his head and made a show with

9

the folding metal door, opening it gently this time so there was barely a click. Waiting for them to chivvy in with all their clutter, then sliding it shut again. They smiled and chirruped thanks to him, but he kept his face stern. They saw his limp. Even before they saw him as the boss's son, they saw his limp, he knew they did.

Four storeys down they stood closed-in together, and as the lift descended Daniel watched the metal leaves and vines rise up from below, the top of each leaf curve soft with thick, white dust.

'Your leg is worse tonight,' Mr Brown said as they walked across the river.

With the warming weather, Daniel could smell the water. Something ached at the base of his skull, like the beginning of a headache, like the weight of something forgotten and nearly remembered.

'It's worse,' Mr Brown said again.

The water shone in the late sun. It shone and it smelt.

'Just tired,' Daniel replied.

He'd been proud the day his legs were long enough for him to match his father's pace. For years he'd marked his stride when they were out walking the dog along the river or in the park, his two quick steps to his father's one, the skip he'd put in to come up level again. His father's irritation if Daniel, his attention straying, fell too far behind. And then one day he didn't need to try and he wondered that he'd ever had to.

Mr Brown checked his watch.

'We'll catch the slow train,' he said, his irritation hobbled.

The carriage was warm and Daniel reached up for the window cord. Mr Brown opened the evening paper. The train moved slowly out of the station into the evening light and Daniel fought with his reflection to see out, the sun lighting the streaks of soot into patterns on the glass, raddling the air. Out through the sidings, black bricks and grubby weeds. Buddleia bloomed, purples, whites. He remembered Johnnie telling him it would grow anywhere, on a coal tip even. Butterflies, tortoiseshells, orange tips, fritillaries, went about their business in the flowers. He watched their wing flicker, their jerky elegance. Two painted ladies, flirting in the air, kept pace with the train a few seconds, then dropped away.

Daniel turned back into the carriage. His father wore his newspaper like a shield. Another man slept and a woman read a book in the corner. He shook his head. Still watching butterflies, fiddling, and Rome already burnt.

The sidings widened and the train made its slow way out and through the city. Sounds came in like memories of themselves: a blackbird's song, motor cars, a horse's bray, another train's whistle. There were high tenements outside, washing hung like bunting, open windows making holes to their insides. In the winter the darkness let you in for a glimpse, a peep show. And tonight, when the summer light kept him at bay, people still held things out of the windows for him to see. A boy with a puppy; a woman stretched forward, her mouth wide in a yell; an

11

arm flung out several floors up, the fingers fisted round a cigarette.

Then there was a high street crossed over, motor cars, carts, advertising hoardings, beaming faces eating mustard, drinking ginger wine, the bric-a-brac of small shops, two cats on a wall, a boy running round a corner, an old woman with a basket on wheels, stumbling at the kerb. A smell too, something frying. He leaned back in his seat. There it was again, the pressure at the back of his skull, as if someone were pressing their fingers in. The smell reminded him of the breakfasts they'd had in Ireland. They were different from England, the bacon tasted different, and the tea. There was something in the day he needed to remember, if it would only rise higher. He took out his novel, refuge for a short while.

There were boys at cricket on the green, over at the far side near the theatre, where the grass was longer and they wouldn't be yelled at. Walking down Duke Street, Daniel could already hear them, the nippy shouts, the keen dull sound of a bat striking a ball. And he saw Mr Brown forget him and lengthen his stride, eager to round the corner and see the lads at play. Daniel stopped and leaned against the railings outside the Baptist chapel. It was Johnnie who'd played. He'd been good.

A man was rolling barrels onto a wagon. His horse, a heavy, white dray with dirty fetlocks, had his head in a bag of feed. Each time, at the top of the ramp there was a moment of suspense, the man's strength, arms crooked to take the barrel's weight, the lines of muscle picked clear, braced against the curved wood, each perfectly weighted as if they could hang there together for good, before the man gained the edge and tumbled it in. Daniel watched with narrowed eyes, the man's grace, his economy of gesture, as if he could gather in the secret, recover it for himself again.

Daniel could still have sat on a cart and pulled on the reins. It wasn't *that* that he envied. It was the man's ease, his physical competency, known and unquestioned. Daniel had been a better horseman than his brother, a better horseman than most people. It had been as natural to him as breathing and now all that was gone.

The light was flattening, as if the end of the day sucked out perspective. The cricket game had slowed. The boys couldn't trust their eyes quite any more, the ball lost in the air until it was upon them. Mr Brown still watched, a hand raised as if shielding his sight though the sun had long dropped away. Lights had gone on in houses, but too much of the day remained as yet, and they kept themselves to themselves, threw out no glowing pools.

Those people still returning home felt excluded, left outside things, and hurried now. Even the men standing outside the pub drank their pints down quickly and excused themselves, or slouched back inside to find some light and human jostle again.

Mr Brown checked his watch. 'She'll be worrying,' he said.

'It was only a bit of cricket,' Daniel said. 'She

won't mind a few minutes.'

They walked down Old Palace Lane and on to the towpath. Fishermen were setting up, the glow of their cigarettes, the dull glint of a thermos, their lines tipping the water, invisible in the dusk. A mallard trailed her brood towards the bank. Daniel counted more than half a dozen ducklings, a long, straggly line. The last duckling had become distracted by some river plant, tugging at it with its beak.

'They've no eye for detail,' he said.

'What?'

'Look. The mother hasn't noticed. She's just paddling on.'

'Come on, Daniel,' Mr Brown said.

'Win some, lose some.'

Daniel squatted down to see the duckling better, his trouser cuffs lost in the river weeds. The mother was almost out of sight, her flotilla zig-zagging behind her.

'We used to watch for hours when we were boys,' he said. 'Coots and moorhens are careful, they count them up. One's missing, they send out a scouting party. But not the mallards.'

'Your mother will be waiting at the window,' Mr Brown said.

'We saw a rat take a duckling once.'

'She can't see us from the window this time of year, but she'll still be standing there,' Mr Brown said.

'We'd been crouched for ages, watching something, but I can't remember what. I do remember that Johnnie had a nettle stroking his leg and didn't dare move, and you could still see the white bumps the next day. And we saw a rat, sleek, pretty, slip into the water, just its head visible. It swam without a ripple straight to a stray duckling — the mother mallard was way ahead — and carried it gently by the neck back to the shore.'

'I'll wave from the bridge, anyhow,' Mr Brown said.

★ ★ ★

It was the time beyond their return that Daniel dreaded. Once the bustling was done — the shedding of coats and baggage, the washing of faces and hands, the enquiries over the journey, his leg, the office, the traffic, the pouring of sherry — then his mother would take off her apron and allow his father to sit her down before the fire with her drink. Daniel knew she couldn't help the look on her face. It was as if she hoped, despite herself, that he would somehow be more than he was.

When he was younger, he told jokes for her. To distract her, especially when she was fed up, or there was an argument.

'Come here my little fellow,' she'd say, before he was even finished, and he'd let her put her arms around him, or place her hands, flat, on either side of his head and she'd stare at him so that he'd be too abashed to finish.

It was a private game of theirs, hers and Daniel's, a conspiracy. But when Johnnie was killed, their game was over.

'We stopped to look at the cricket,' Mr Brown said.

Mrs Brown nodded. She'd been watching the road for them and now she held the front door to her like a lover, as they walked up the path. Mr Brown took her hand and kissed her on the cheek.

'The green was nice with the sun going down,' he said. 'People outside in shirtsleeves, you know. Pigeons.'

Mrs Brown laughed, an abrupt, uncertain laugh, new to Daniel since his return.

'You needn't have worried,' Mr Brown said and she shook her head and looked at Daniel coyly, and at the ground.

'Just you dawdling,' and she tapped the back of her hand as if in rebuke. 'I know.'

'Sherry,' he said, leading her back indoors.

'Dinner will be ready soon,' she said.

Daniel followed his parents into the house and went to wash his hands in the cloakroom. He could hear his mother asking after him, her voice lowered so he couldn't hear.

'He's very pale,' she said. 'Is it hurting?'

'It's the end of the day. We're all tired.'

'Is that why you stopped on the green? So he could rest?'

The house was muggy with old air and the smell of cooking. Daniel dipped his face into the basin, held it there. The cold water made the skin on his neck tighten. He'd have liked to sink his ears into the water, but the basin was too shallow. He loved it, in the sea, to lie back and float, let the water fill his ears so that all he could

16

hear was the shift and crunch of the pebbles at the edge of the tide as they were lifted and turned. He'd float until his head ached with the cold.

'Is it hurting?' Mrs Brown asked him as they sat down to dinner.

Daniel shook his head. 'It's all right.'

And she nodded, and gestured to the maid to bring in the soup.

Mr Brown began to talk about his day, meetings, sales figures, northern contractors. Daniel ate his soup and watched his mother. She appeared to be listening, but she wasn't really there. They both knew it, he and his father.

Although it looked out onto the garden, the room was airless, the windows closed tight. Too late to see any birds now, but there were bats through the glass, little more than dancing shades in the twilight. Usually he didn't ask, just waited till the meal was over and then slipped outside. But tonight something was pressing on his mind and his patience, even with his mother, was wearing thin.

'Could I open a window?'

Without waiting for an answer, he pushed back his chair and got to his feet.

Mrs Brown put down her soup spoon.

'It might let in a draught,' she said.

Daniel pushed the sash upwards. The garden air was like balm, cool now, and fresh. Leaning out, he breathed deep, the stale behind and the sweet before him, and reeled, putting a hand out for balance.

'Daniel?' His mother's voice was pitched high,

and he turned back to the table to reassure her.

'Needed some air,' he said.

He couldn't bear his mother's face, her soup spoon gripped like a talisman.

'Don't, Mother,' he said. 'I just wanted some air.'

'Charlotte,' Mr Brown said, his voice stern.

They had slipped into old roles, Daniel and his parents, since his return, as if to make for themselves a cocoon against the recent years. The very things that should have changed his birthright — his brother's death, his own heroic wounding — had left them now in thrall within an earlier kingdom. And just as his mother couldn't help herself but feed him milksop and warm his bed with a hot jar at night, so Daniel found a certain old childish incontinence returned. He knew, because his mother had told him, that when she looked at him, she saw Johnnie, and now he spoke quickly, the first thought, to distract her.

'I went to an exhibition at lunchtime,' he said.

He hadn't meant to speak of this, and immediately he regretted it.

'You didn't tell me that,' Mr Brown said. 'You just said something about boys and boats.'

'I only went in because I needed to sit down,' Daniel said. 'The walk back from the pond was harder than I'd expected.'

He took a mouthful of soup. It was tepid, coating the back of the spoon like some viscous medicine. He was tired. The shake began in his hand and he set down the spoon quickly.

18

'You've been biting your nails again,' Mrs Brown said.

Daniel looked across at her. 'The soup's good.'

'So what was it about? The exhibition?' Mr Brown said.

'Just some photographs.' He shouldn't have let it slip. 'Anyway, tell Mother what you were telling me. About the bearings, and northern sales.'

'But we'd like to hear about the exhibition that left you so late back to work, wouldn't we?' Mr Brown said, turning to his wife, who was still looking at her son as if his face held something she had lost. So, feeling caught out by himself just as he used to as a child, Daniel was forced to tell them. He said as little as he could, but it was enough for Mrs Brown.

'Injured soldiers?' she said.

'Yes.'

'On the front line?'

'Some, yes.'

'Did you look closely?'

'Mother, please,' Daniel said.

'Did you?' she said again, her voice fierce.

'He wasn't there. Just strangers.'

'Tell me about them then, the strangers,' she said, and she carried on eating her soup, her knuckles still white around the spoon.

'I didn't mean to go, and I wasn't going to tell you,' Daniel said.

Mrs Brown continued with her soup. It wasn't her fault, he knew that, but her grief was like a diviner's rod. It drew a fury from him, dragged his rage up through his body till it seeped out of his skin.

'All right,' Daniel said. 'One of the soldiers, you can see the bone coming out through his thigh. His head is slumped down and two others are dragging him through the mud. There's a dead horse behind him. Another picture, a lad is on a stretcher, bloody bandage round his head. They've put a blanket over him, but he still looks so cold, pinched. And another, it's a soldier sitting on the ground, one leg out before him, boot off. His mouth is wide open and you can see he's got a tooth missing at the side. He's being given a drink, tea, in a mug, and they're doing something with bandages to the foot. But it's his face — that blank look they get.'

Daniel would have gone on, he was finding his stride now, his recollection of the photographs collapsing in with other memories. Mrs Brown sat perfectly still, her hands on her lap, her face bleached in the growing dark and pared down to elements: cheekbones, nose, chin, brow.

But Mr Brown pushed back his chair and spoke to his wife now, and his voice was so gentle, the thought crossed Daniel's mind that this must be how he'd made love to her when they'd first met, with these soft tones.

'I think we've heard enough, Charlotte, don't you.' He took her hands and drew her to her feet. Then he turned to Daniel. 'For God's sake.'

Daniel watched his father lead his mother from the room and the maid come in and clear the soup bowls. He nodded his head when she asked, would she put the meat and vegetables in

20

the warming oven. And he sat on at the table.

Except for the windows to the garden, he'd never liked this room. They ate their meals in here every day, and yet it still felt unlived in, with its heavy furniture, its smell of polish, the dark-leafed plants in the cold grate. When they were little, it was the place Johnnie went, playing hide and seek, if he didn't want to be found, because Daniel wouldn't go in there.

'Cowardy custard,' Daniel sang under his breath. 'Cowardy custard.'

Johnnie had set the rules in their games. He was older, and it went without saying. But Daniel nearly always won them. Hide and seek or grandmother's footsteps. He was shrewder about how not to be noticed, more furtive. Daniel had demanded that the dining room be off limits, threatened not to play otherwise, so it was only when Johnnie broke the rules that he won.

Johnnie had broken the rules to enlist, upping his age by a year. The last photograph they had of him was from the day he went to war. He stood on the doorstep, his haversack beside him. Daniel had watched his brother in the bathroom with his new shaving tackle, teased him over his smooth chin. And in the photograph he could see the chafing on his brother's skin, darker patches in the black and white.

Of course he'd looked for his brother in the exhibition photographs. You always did that, couldn't help it. But it wasn't to do with Johnnie, whatever it was that hung, like a tiny lead weight, at the back of his mind. It was to do with somebody else. And the lead weight had been there for years. It was just that he'd forgotten it for a while till today.

★ ★ ★

The girl was there with the same bit of knitting. She greeted him like a friend, wouldn't take his threepenny payment.

'Forget something?' she said.

'Something like that,' he said.

'Well, we're all still here,' she said.

'Yes. Thank you,' and he turned to go in.

'Nobody's got any worse since yesterday,' she said with a little laugh. 'No new casualties.'

As soon as he saw the photograph, the lead weight dropped, a plumb line into his past. It had been taken in what looked like a cellar — a low-ceilinged room with a small stove and some rough shelves visible on rusty gallows brackets holding boxes and bottles. One of the boxes said OXO. Trestles supported a stretcher and on the stretcher lay a wounded man, an officer. Beside him stood another officer who was feeding the wounded man a cigarette. Daniel could see that his tunic was torn and his boots were thick with mud. A nurse dressed in breeches, boots and a man's overcoat stood to one side. They were all smiling for the camera.

'Colonel Whittam,' Daniel said.

Colonel Whittam was dead now. He'd walked away from the path near the White Lodge in Richmond Park three years ago and been found face down in the bracken two days later by a woman walking her dog. When Daniel first read about it, it was the two days that he wondered about. He imagined a spider starting its web across the colonel's ear lobe, stretching its silk between the cold velvet skin and a blade of grass. He wondered whether the deer had been frightened shy by the smell of the body, and whether the crows had been lured down to peck.

Daniel had admired Colonel Whittam. He respected him and knew that he'd done his best by his men and that the ambush hadn't been his fault. He'd been wounded himself, hadn't he? A shoulder wound, Daniel remembered. But he hadn't been surprised to hear the news. The obituary had said that he'd served with distinction at the Western Front during the Great War and in Ireland, that he'd had a fatal accident while out shooting rabbits and that he would be sadly mourned by his wife, family and regiment. But Daniel knew differently. He knew Whittam had never recovered, never forgiven himself, though there was nothing he could have done. He'd heard that Whittam's wife had stopped him once before when she'd found him with a pistol, so this time Whittam had made sure he was safely alone.

Daniel stood in front of the photograph for a long time. It showed the other officer, smiling, holding a cigarette delicately between thumb and forefinger for the wounded man to smoke. They were clearly friends. It was something about the way the officer's other hand rested behind Whittam's head, as if he were cradling or shielding it. Daniel had brought his notebook with him this time, and flicking over the bird drawings, he found a blank page and sketched out what he could. He did it quickly, only taking his time over the faces. Then hc stood looking again. The other man had the kind of face you might think you knew, but that would be too much of a coincidence. He looked a little while longer, until the ticket girl gave a little cough.

'You all right? Only there's a couple of ladies would like to look at that picture,' she said. 'Really I think they're curious to see what you've been stood staring at for so long.'

'Fine, thank you,' he said.

'Daydreaming,' the girl said with the wisdom of weeks in this job. 'You're not the first. Lots do it, get lost like that. Though maybe dreaming's not the right word, because I don't suppose it was very nice, was it?'

'Thought I recognised somebody,' Daniel said, and then regretted it when her face opened with curiosity. 'Thank you, anyway,' and he left.

It was over two years since he'd left the hospital. When he arrived, the nurses were glad of him with so many other men going. The early weeks he was too ill to notice much. It was his leg that was hurt, as he observed in those first, lucid hours after it happened. But once he stopped pretending that he could keep himself separate from the pain, then it occupied the whole of him. He lay in a bed, his body braced, and when it rode him, he bared his teeth and clenched his fists, bit his lips, his cheeks to bleeding not to let it out beyond. He knew that if he gave it voice, it would take over everything, and then nothing — not the bed or the nurses, or the window above him or the strip of sky, which seemed to have a colour for each day of the week, or the tree he could sometimes see, upside down, its roots blossoming — nothing would be outside it. Sometimes, despite his efforts, it escaped him and then he roared and moaned, the sweat breaking out on his forehead.

The nurses gave him little rubber balls to squeeze, a gag to bite on. They gave him tea in a cup with a lid and a spout, coloured blue for a boy. They washed him and changed his bed and by the time he was getting better, he'd have married any of them.

'You wouldn't, would you though,' he said to one nurse. 'Marry a man who wasn't whole, a broken doll,' and he sang the last phrase, like the song.

'Course I would if they were my chap,' she said. 'But I've already got mine and so it won't be you, sweet young Mr Brown.' But she didn't take her arm away and he continued stroking it. 'Anyway, haven't you got a girl?' she asked.

'No,' Daniel said. 'Just as well, probably,' and she rolled her eyes at this.

'I've seen plenty a lot worse off than you,' she said. 'And their girl by their side, often as not.'

But Daniel hadn't meant it for self-pity. More that since Johnnie's death something had drawn itself in inside him. Something that was turned away from people, rolled up on itself. Like a woodlouse. Curled up, every soft part tucked away.

'I did, before the army,' he said, 'have a

25

girlfriend, but it didn't work out. She's married, got a baby now, my mother said.'

'You'll find yourself another, when you're out of here,' she said, 'handsome chap like you.' Daniel didn't reply. He couldn't bear much curiosity, even from himself.

★ ★ ★

Something was still bothering Daniel about the photograph. He'd find himself standing stock-still, in his bedroom or the kitchen, even on the street, as if stopping all movement might clarify something. Once they went camping on Dartmoor, he and Johnnie, and when he dipped his mug into a stream, it filled with icy brown water that smelt of the rocks and the peaty ground. He watched the water swirl, then grow still and clear itself, so that after a couple of minutes he could see down through it to the sediment covering the white tin. Now he felt that something similar should happen to his mind, that if he stopped his bustle, something would clear and he'd be able to see straight down into the back of his own memory.

Mr Brown read things out of the newspaper. He read them slowly, steadily, and without any inflection so that to his listeners the price of eggs sounded as grave as news of the Bolshevik Revolution. There had been a time when this drove Daniel nearly to distraction, but by now he had learned to block out the sound. He heard the words but they didn't go in. His soldiering had helped, the noise of the mess hall. And now his father's steady drone was like a filter for Daniel's thoughts and his mind kicked free of the dining room and the breakfast things, of his mother's blank face and his father's voice.

Instead he could hear a different man's voice, his own at first, hard and angry. Then it was someone else's shouted over him, words and half-words dropping, making sense and no sense. And the smell of the cigarette. The cigarette. It looked like it was cut into his lip from below, then in his fingers and the ash dropping down to Daniel, on Daniel, the man not noticing because why would he?

Mr Brown liked to finish on something cheerful. Then he could leave for work feeling he had given his wife something uplifting to take into her day about the house. He began with the new Noël Coward play, then moved on to the Egyptian excavations.

Daniel could feel the pain in his leg and across his shoulders, could feel it rising to his lungs and up his throat into his mouth, and then, through the pain, the man's voice again and a gun being fired, sharp, efficient, and somehow Daniel kept the pain in, gave it no voice. Lay doggo. He didn't want to remember, but the memory wouldn't leave, and always there was something there that he couldn't name and that he didn't understand.

But that was who it was. That was the man he'd seen in the photograph. The man holding the cigarette for Daniel's wounded colonel.

⋆ ⋆ ⋆

When he'd stood before the girl for the third time, he saw anxiety cross the girl's face.

'It's only something I need to know,' he'd said. 'I'm not wanting to look.'

It took him a week to telephone the Crystal Palace number printed on the card she gave him. He'd been rolling the marble for ten minutes, from one side of the blotter to the other, to and fro across the inky map. It didn't roll smoothly, got caught on the roughened pink fibres.

'I'll dial the number the first time it runs straight,' he said.

But they are foolish pledges, those made against the spirit, because when the clear run came, he still couldn't nerve himself to it, and in the end he put the marble in his pocket, slapped himself on the cheek, held his breath and put his finger to the dial.

'Don't know that we have that information,' the voice said. 'Call again in half an hour.'

Daniel waited and ran his marble again. He watched the pigeons. They were beyond courtship now. He wondered how they balanced, heaped on top of one another on the window sill. Curtains of feathers rubbing up against the glass. The voice was more forthcoming when he called back.

'You'd be surprised, what we get asked,' it said, when Daniel explained once again what he was looking for. 'There's some think they can see a loved one in a picture. Not the real figures but, you know, their ghost in a corner or something. And others say we shouldn't be showing them at all because they're bad for morale when the country's got to be looking ahead. And you get them that can't speak at all, only cry. That's tricky, not wanting to hurt their feelings, but a job to do and so on.'

The voice was getting into its stride. The marble made another clear run and Daniel cleared his throat.

'Did you find a name for the one I mentioned?' he said, pitching his voice in at a pause.

'The two men with the cigarette, and the nurse?' the voice said.

'Yes.'

There was a long pause, so long that Daniel wondered if the telephone had gone funny. He noticed out of the window that the pigeons had finished. One was pecking at a piece of weed that had somehow found its way to this third floor window sill, while the other, as Daniel watched, flew out into the sky, its heavy body rising, soaring up. He was about to put down the receiver and dial up again when the voice returned.

'There's a letter of assurance here from a J. Hursten. It's definitely about that photograph, got the red tally number in the corner. Telling us we can go ahead and use it. We try to get them from all the private donors. Some of the photographs are official, but lots are taken by soldiers, nurses, what have you. They've sent them in to us.'

'Is there an address for him?' Daniel rolled the marble beneath his hand, its hard curve pressing into his palm.

29

Another pause, the sound of papers shuffled, and then the voice read it out, three lines, and Daniel pocketed the marble.

★　★　★

When his mother woke him, her fingers resting on his arm, Daniel flailed out, catching her on the cheek with the back of his hand.

'Don't touch me! . . . Johnnie!' he yelled, or dreamed he had.

He was awake the second after and saw his mother's eyes wide, her hand to her cheek.

'Did I do that?' he said.

'You were dreaming. You said something, but I couldn't hear the words.'

'What time is it?'

'Your father is listening to the news. I have cocoa done.'

Daniel sat up, his body heavy with the dream. He nodded.

It was the dream he often had, never exactly the same, but near enough. He was standing at the end of a road, facing a hill. It wasn't raining, but the air was heavy, so dense that his shoulders were weighted down with it. Though he couldn't see what it was, he began striking down on something, a block of wood or a mound of earth, with an implement, perhaps a spade. As he struck, he could feel the impact through his arms and his shoulders. The spade became a rifle and he was striking a man while women and children watched him silently, and as Daniel beat down, the man stared up at him.

Then he was in a ditch which was also a truck somehow, and Johnnie was there (he was always there), and Will Savage and Cadet Charters, whose name Daniel had never even known before it was over, and George Spring. It was foggy, always foggy. Others too, but their faces slipped away from him as he woke. They were wounded, dying, and he wasn't, but he couldn't move, couldn't help them. He could see them all, their wounds, and the yellow gorse, the rocks behind. There were women holding the guns, two older and a younger one with a small child at her skirts and a bigger, silent boy. They'd done the shooting. They stared at Daniel and as long as they looked at him, he couldn't move. One of the children was crouching near, arm reaching towards him, when his mother woke him.

Her fingers touching her face, Mrs Brown walked to the door.

'Did I hurt you?' he said.

She shook her head.

Downstairs, his father had lit the fire. It had rained hard in the day and now the air was sweet and cool and the sky clear to the stars.

'Fall asleep?' Mr Brown said.

Daniel nodded.

'Ought to get out more. Join a club. You'll never meet a girl, or anyone, always on your own. And we won't be here forever.'

Mrs Brown brought in a tray with three cups and saucers.

'Daniel had a nightmare,' she said.

'You could enquire at the library. We'll stop off

31

on the way home. Debating society, philosophical society, something like that. They'll have information.'

'It might need more sugar,' Mrs Brown said, passing Daniel a cup and saucer.

'You used to like the tennis club, didn't you?' Mr Brown said. 'And the riding? All those friends you had? It wasn't only the sport.'

'I've forgotten the teaspoons,' Mrs Brown said.

Daniel hadn't told them about his telephone call. He had never properly talked about what it was like over there and they'd never properly asked him. He could imagine his mother. She wouldn't believe him. She'd want to take his part. And his father, shaking his head as if to keep out the sounds he didn't like. He'd say it was what happened in a war, though he'd never had to fight in one.

Opening the cutlery drawer, Daniel took out the teaspoons. He put one in his mouth and bit down. It was cold and hard against his teeth and a nerve sang through his jaw. He'd gone beyond the bounds and he didn't know how to think about it. He'd been broken, but there was nobody to tell, and no way to get away from it. He took the teaspoons in to his mother.

When he had returned, before he said anything else, he'd told them they were not to ask what had happened, nor were they to tell anyone else anything they might learn. Most especially they were to say nothing to anyone in Ireland. It was a motor-lorry accident, and that was all. So they had never asked him. Instead they'd all busied themselves. Hidden like crabs in the sand, digging and shimmying, covering themselves over with the practical questions till after two years all that could be seen was hard shells.

How long would he be in hospital. Would he walk again. Who was the best doctor for his leg. For his shaking arm. Was swimming good. Was walking. Cycling. Which were the best crutches. Which the best stick. He'd need a steady hand in the family business. Of course, they knew he couldn't ride a horse. A good hand with a pen was important for business. A firm signature. What to do for the pain. And by the time it was safe to talk, and Daniel knew it was safe by now, it was too late. His parents didn't want to know.

Sometimes, passing other young men in the streets, he'd wonder whether they were all silent too, about what they'd seen, and done.

He waited till his parents were asleep before opening the front door. The moon was full, but still he had to take care, walking in the dark, the jolts and fissures in the paving stones seeming to rise and meet his feet. He lifted his stick from the umbrella stand at the last minute, and now, with so much else pressing, he was glad it could take some of the weight.

The river was up. You could smell it before you could see it. Even a few steps away, it looked still, unmoving, pools of shining dark under the gaslights. But leaning close over the railings, Daniel could see its force, its pull towards the sea. It was a spring tide and the water was very high. Daniel knelt and put his hand in, held it there till it was cold. When he lifted it to his face, it smelt of somewhere else. He went across the lock-bridge. No toll. This late at night you could cross the river for free.

He walked for a while towards Kew. Somewhere there were lovers. Their voices hung over the water, ripples of laughter and soft noises fading as they reached his shore. The 'hooo, hooo' cry of a tawny owl ahead of him, and behind him the last train crossing the river towards St Margaret's.

Johnnie dared him once to cross the river on the railway bridge. Walk along the rails in the wake of a train. If another train came, you'd have to jump up on to the balustrade and dive into the river. They shook hands on it, 'a firm shake', Johnnie called it, which meant you had to go through with it. But when they pulled open the heavy cast-iron gate and crossed the grass, climbed over the wall and squatted just out of sight, waiting, fingers clutching tussocks of weed while a train went past them, then stood at the top, the rails still purring, and looked along the line of the track, the sleepers stretched out, away, like an endless ladder, then he didn't mean to, but his head went faint. And if Johnnie hadn't held on to him, he'd have run away through the thistles and nettles and dirty yellow flowers.

He held him just long enough for Daniel to find his feet again, and then Johnnie climbed onto the track and did it for him, his legs steady in a jerky half-run over the sleepers.

Daniel wondered whether Johnnie would have done the things he had over there. He wondered whether some of those things hadn't also happened in the trenches, though the men came back from that war as heroes.

Daniel walked as hard as he could on into the night, daring his leg to fail him, daring himself to go further. The tow-path was soft and quiet under his feet after the rain. Across the water, the herons hunched high on their island were silent. The night gathered and thickened around him. He had the piece of paper in his pocket with the address written on it and, as he walked, he knew that somehow he must set off along the sleepers and go there.

★ ★ ★

The sky was grey as the train left London and Daniel looked out through a window slashed by rain. As the train gathered speed, the drops were driven faster across the glass, chivvying each other. His father was surprisingly amenable when he asked for the holiday.

'I might be back in a day or two, might be longer,' Daniel said.

'Take as long as you want,' Mr Brown said. 'It's slack right now and the break would be good for you. Just check out the contractor for me while you're there.'

'I'm not ill.'

'No, but it's hard work, the business, and what with your leg.'

'And my leg is fine. It's just . . . ' Daniel stopped himself. 'My injury,' he said. 'The day I was injured . . . '

'You offered yourself up,' Mr Brown said.

'Nobody could ask more.'

Daniel shivered. His father had no idea. Daniel didn't even know who was hurting whom. 'But what happened that day, what I told you wasn't . . . '

Again Mr Brown interrupted.

'Just don't go over it with your mother. More than she could take.'

So Daniel didn't try to say any more. And there was no point in being angry.

'Only thing might be,' Mr Brown said, 'to give her a call every now and then.'

'I was going to write.'

'Better for her to hear your voice,' his father said.

'Since I don't know that I'll find a telephone easily.'

'She doesn't trust letters much these days,' Mr Brown said.

'Of course,' Daniel said, and he bit his lip hard at his stupidity.

★   ★   ★

He heard the post arrive that day and went to the front door for it, shuffled together the letters, not looking at them, and returned to the sitting room. He handed letters and paper knife to his mother and she began to slit the envelopes. It was a habit of hers, to open all the letters in the pile before she began to look at any. She did it by feel, finding the envelope's top edge with her fingers and easing the tip of the knife under, then a swift pull to cut the paper. Usually she was talking as she did it, to Daniel or his father, or to the maid. Or she was reading, one of her library novels. Today, however, she wasn't talking. And though her eyes were open, she had the appearance of someone who is looking at another place entirely. Mr Brown was at the desk on the far side of the room with various pieces of official correspondence before him. His pen was uncapped and he had clean notepaper ready to use, but for the last half-hour he'd been reading the same piece of paper, his fingers tugging at his shirt cuffs, his right shoulder hitching every now and then with the slight tick that surfaced when he didn't know what to say. Except for the small crackles and shuffles of the coal in the fire, there were no sounds in the room. The clock was not wound, and it felt as if everything was suspended, like a breath drawn in that you daren't let out, lungs tight to bursting. And although it had only been two days, Daniel couldn't imagine how they would ever breathe again.

It was the third or fourth letter in the pile and Mrs Brown was putting the knife to it, her gaze still elsewhere. Daniel was watching her and as she let the letter drop onto the pile, it caught his eye. Mrs Brown reached for another, and Daniel picked up the dropped letter. He held it flat on his palm. It weighed so little. He knew his brother's writing as well as his own. Despite the masters' fierce efforts at school, Johnnie still wrote with his left hand and his writing was as unkempt and changeable from day to day as Daniel's was regular and precise. Although he

37

didn't want to, although it was the last thing he wanted to do, Daniel could see Johnnie now, his arm caught tight in against his ribs and the paper turned sideways in the effort to avoid smudging. He imagined him seated, hunched, on a crate perhaps with the product stencilled on the side, 'Capstan' or 'Cadburys', his hands over his ears to concentrate, to block out the booming, battering noise he wrote was so hateful, so oppressive. He saw him pick up his pen and dip the nib, the ink bottle pushed into the mud at his feet, stroke the nib against the side. Then the quick rush of words, dipping the nib impatiently now, blotting the smudges with his handkerchief. Daniel could see Johnnie's bayonet leaned up against the side of the dugout, could see him tap a cigarette from his case, hitch it into the side of his mouth, just as Daniel would learn to do, cup his hand around the match and suck in the flame as if his life depended on it. Then pick up his pen again and write the address in capitals.

Daniel chuckled at that thought. He would bet that Johnnie had laughed as he wrote it. It was an old joke between them, that even Johnnie's capitals were illegible.

'Daniel?'

His mother's voice startled him and he was there once more, in that room that could never be warm again, his father standing at the desk, his mother with a pile of letters she couldn't bear to read.

'What are you laughing at?'

He held out the hand with the letter.

'It's from Johnnie,' he said. 'Isn't that funny?

He's dead for two days and here he is, alive again.'

★ ★ ★

It was afternoon by the time Daniel arrived at his destination. He'd enjoyed the journey. It had been a suspension, like time out of place. He hadn't read the newspaper nor either of the books he'd brought. He'd barely even looked out of the window, as if just for now he would take nothing in, and he seemed to have passed much of the journey in a trance.

The air was colder up here, and fresh. The train had shrugged off the rain long before and now the sky was streaked with high cirrus cloud and the sun made long, late-afternoon shadows of the passengers on the platform. The station-master suggested a good inn and, once he'd seen Daniel's limp, drummed up a man with an Austin 7 to take him there.

'You're too late to see the best,' the Austin 7 man said. 'From the south?'

Daniel nodded.

'We start earlier up here,' the man said. 'Always have had the jump on you, doesn't matter if it's royalty or sheep.'

Daniel wondered whether the man was joking, or looking for a rise, but there was no change of expression, no sly look.

'What did I miss?' Daniel said.

'Best livestock this country can find.'

'I don't know very much about animals,' Daniel answered.

'Though I did use to ride before . . . ' He gestured towards his leg.

'Except for birds. I know about birds.'

'So, what are you doing in town on market day, then?' the man said, but went on with a nod before Daniel had to find an answer.

'The Green Man,' he said. 'Rooms are reasonable and they'll do you a good tea, but you'll want to be careful of the smell,' lifting a finger to the side of his nose. 'They bring the cattle to the pens down the ginnel one side of the inn and the dung won't be cleared till the morning.'

The room smelt of beer and pipe tobacco and it looked out over the banked cobbles of the town square. Knots of men still stood about, cap brims touching, talking, Daniel supposed, about the price of sheep. Beyond, he could see the first rise of the moors, mauve and orange in the late sun, and the last swifts playing havoc in the sky.

A red and white quilt covered the bed and rag rugs were spread over the boarded floor. It was like somewhere else he knew, somewhere good. Daniel lay back on the bed, shoes kicked off, arms and legs spreadeagled, and listened to the bar below, people's voices rising muffled through the rugs. The man had been right about the tea. He'd eaten a vast plate of beef and potatoes, peppery swede, rhubarb and apple pie. Running his fingers across the quilt, he could feel the seams between the colours, and how, in alternate strips, one colour was more worn than the other, the fabric rubbed to strands in places. He remembered. It was Coolderry. The rug and the quilts reminded him of Coolderry.

He thought he'd walk downstairs and sit elbows out and friendly at a table and strike up easy conversation, buy a round, admire the local beer. Make believe he was the person he used to be and maybe it would happen. But his limbs were heavy and the bed was soft, and before he could prevent himself, he was wrapped like a caterpillar in a cocoon of quilt and asleep, rocked deep in anonymous ease.

The house was near the square, past the game butchers with its proud flock of dead ducks hanging line upon line outside, left at the auction house and up the hill, beyond the livestock pens, where men were still busy with brushes and water, making the road run brown, and past a terrace of polished front steps. Daniel had scrubbed the night's lethargy from himself and he felt sure and sharp.

As he walked, he rehearsed what he would say. How he would explain that he'd travelled over two hundred miles to ask a question about two men in a photograph taken during a war that ended eight years ago. He had his sketchbook in one hand, ready to show.

'Keep as close to the truth as you can,' he told himself. 'Much easier that way.'

He was nervous, dry-mouthed, when he reached the house and he hesitated before walking up the path and pulling the bell.

He noticed the size of the house, its rough golden stone, the rise of windows high up to the dormers in the roof; the child's pram and the tricycle, abandoned on the front lawn; the flower

41

beds full of stocks and lavender; the drive down one side and, just visible, a motorbike and sidecar. And later he would recall all this and think upon it. But right now the only thought he had in his mind was to ask his question.

He pressed the brass button and bells rang in different places. A dog barked. A moment's silence, voices far off, then footsteps. A maid opened the door, frowning, brushing off her skirts. Daniel could see a wide hall behind with chequerboard tiles, a table with a jug of flowers, and what looked like a train set half set out on the floor.

'I'd like to speak to Mr Hursten.'

'Mr Hursten is out at the moment.'

'I'll leave my card and call back later then,' Daniel said. 'Daniel Brown, if you could say that I called. What time is he likely to return?'

Sucking the air in through her teeth, the maid considered. 'Won't be till late in the day, I wouldn't think,' she said. 'And tomorrow being Sunday . . . ' She began to push the door to.

Daniel wasn't sure why he shouldn't call on a Sunday, whether there might be some impropriety. It wasn't, after all, a business call, but perhaps Mr Hursten had religious convictions that made it difficult. He turned and walked back down the path.

'Janey, who is it?'

Daniel heard the voice before he saw its owner.

'It's just a man,' the maid said.

'Just a man for what?'

'Wants to speak to Mr Hursten.'

'Perhaps I will do instead,' and the door was pushed wide open again by a young woman with white hands raised before her, as if in surrender.

2

It started deliberately, Jude's finger framing. She'd set her fingers around what she saw: her bicycle, the dog, a man selling chestnuts, a woman with a pushcart. She'd make a rectangle, then draw them in closer, see how it altered things. When something caught her attention, she'd try to make a memory of it and she'd tell herself that when she had a camera, she'd take a picture of it.

Leo teased her at first, and her parents told her it looked peculiar, this girl too often with her hands before her face. But they became accustomed to it and then they stopped remarking.

She'd been an accident, an afterthought. She knew this from listening at the door. She hadn't meant to, but she'd heard her name spoken, her mother's voice in a room with the door nearly closed. Her mother had laughed. She'd been talking to Jude's aunt who had come to stay from her farm, bringing eggs and raspberry jam, and smelling of damp wool and the air beneath the trees.

'The last thing on my mind,' Jude's mother had said. 'A precious mistake. At my age, for heaven's sake,' and Jude, kneeling on the cold hall tiles, had heard her mother chuckle, and her aunt, who had no children, join in.

She went to find Leo then, and asked him

what their mother meant, and he told her it served her right for listening at keyholes.

'Is that why she's so wrinkled?' Jude said. 'More than the other ladies?'

'What?'

'Because of the worry. At making such a mistake?'

'No, silly.'

'But other girls, their mothers aren't.'

'It's because she's older,' Leo said, with all the authority of the newly grown, and he stood up, tall above his ten-year-old sister and did his growl to make her laugh.

'And now I'm going to eat you,' and he bent down, put his hands around her waist and lifted her high so that she shrieked with pleasure.

⋆ ⋆ ⋆

Leo had given Jude the Kodak for a going-away present. A running-away present, he called it. And she shot everybody with it, unless they looked about to die.

In Belgium the men liked the camera. They'd lean up on a shoulder if they could, or grin and lift a fag to their mouth, or give the 'V' for Victory. 'Send it to the wife as proof,' they'd say, winking. Or 'Be sure and get my right side, it's the better one.' One man told her this as she pointed the Kodak and she couldn't tell whether he knew that his right cheek was only a bloody hole, whether he was joking.

But mostly it wasn't the men she photographed. It was herself, and Kate, and their

Poste de Secours, their first-aid station. It was the ordinary that she wanted to capture. How they made their own particular ordinary in the middle of that particular horror. Still lives.

They'd fought their own battle for this place. When they first walked in, the village seemed little more than rubble with a church tower that stood incongruously alone and a bell hanging silent. Nobody wanted to be there, the war going on only yards away. They found themselves a carcass of a house, the enamel number plate still stuck on: 26. It had a dry, vaulted, brick-floored cellar, jars of jam and chutney still safe on the shelves. And in the parlour they found Christ still hung bleeding from the wall, which seemed apt, and so they left him there, safe right until the end.

There was a meal on the kitchen table, or what had been a meal before the rats had it. Plates, cutlery, glasses still in their places on the table, and spilt salt. Jude tossed some over her shoulder. Kate opened cupboards.

They occupied the house within the hour and often Jude came across something — a piece of ribbon, a spirit level, a child's bonnet — that made her stop and wonder.

The first days they had no more than they'd carried with them. A tin of cocoa, a box with bandages, swabs and dressings, some iodine, Lysol, a bottle of brandy, some morphine and syringes Kate had badgered from a doctor, two slabs of navy chocolate, some bread, tins of corned beef, crackers, a hurricane lamp, sleeping bags, bed rolls, disinfectants and a box of sanitary towels.

'Might have to use them as dressings if the other stuff doesn't arrive quickly,' Kate said.

They put their bedding in an upstairs room. Jude brushed the floor, laid out the bed rolls, put a candle in a pot and a mug of water at the head of each and their haversacks at the base. Kate mixed something in a bucket.

'Against the rats,' she said. 'Dettol and Keatings powder.'

'It doesn't look so dirty,' Jude said, as Kate soaked a rag in the mixture and made a ring around the bedding, trailing the wet rag across the floorboards.

Jude laughed. 'Our desert island.'

But that night it was Kate who slept soundly while Jude lay awake and very still, legs together, arms tight to her sides, and listened to the heavy scurrying. And in the morning it was Kate who was laughing.

'You look like a convent girl, laid out like that,' she said. 'No touching. The nuns would be proud.'

From then on, until the rat traps arrived, it was Jude who painted the magic circle, swabbing the mixture on to the floorboards as if her life depended on it.

Peter walked into the kitchen on their second day, stooping in the doorframe, their slender fairy-tale prince. He'd been seconded to them by a kindly major because of his nerves. He wasn't allowed to go home, he wasn't far gone enough for that, but he was more use to them in their

47

house than he was in the trenches. So while Kate and Jude unpacked, sandbagged the front door, checked their medical supplies, Peter lit the stove. He found a kettle, and a black pot and then he was away for slates. He never seemed to rush, but the pot was never empty, or so it seemed, and he was its tattered Cinderella.

With every pump smashed and every well blocked with rubble, for the first two weeks they took their buckets to fill from the ditches. The long ditches where, however often they were cleared, still the dead men lay.

'We're as good as taking our water out of dead men's bellies,' Kate said, and despite all she had seen already, the thought made Jude shiver.

She would scan as far as she could, to left and to right, searching out the signs of a body, a limb flung up the bank, the hump of a man's tunic, and then she would let her buckets fill and pray. And she thought that perhaps the gods heard her, because none of them fell ill with it. But though they boiled and re-boiled the water, still the taste remained, and the day that Peter cleared a well and gathered the first bucket of clear water, they toasted him with it.

There was wood everywhere for the burning. No shortage of fuel. Log piles, neatly stacked, at the side of most houses. And once these were exhausted, there were the broken houses to plunder. Chairs and tables, beams hanging from ceilings, crushed beds, some covered in rubble but with their counterpanes still folded, ready for the night. But it was strange, discovering the things they baulked at, and while Jude was happy

48

to carry logs and pull down fences, she couldn't bear to split the broken legs from chairs; or tug the shelves from a kitchen cupboard; or wrench the boards apart of some old table, its heart already damaged by the shelling. Her fingers would rub rough on some grains of spilt sugar, or she'd see where a child had carved some letters or where some wine had spilt, and find herself close to tears. So she left this gathering to the others.

They found saws, their teeth oiled, and axes hung up on nails in abandoned outhouses. These peacetime tools were sharp, precise. Kate cut her thumb, testing an axe blade. Jude would have liked to have sawn wood and chopped logs, but it quickly became clear that, together with the pot, this was Peter's province, and it wasn't long before he always had some handsome soldier, sufficiently recuperated, to help him in the long hours chopping and sawing in the outhouse.

Jude had been so young at the start and so ignorant, that she wondered at first why Kate had been willing to set this all up with her and not somebody more experienced. She could do very little by comparison. The motorbike was Kate's, though Jude rapidly learned both to ride and repair it. And although Jude had been to VAD training camp, she wasn't a trained nurse like Kate. When they met, Jude had been in Belgium for little more than a month, frustrated that she couldn't get closer to the action, frustrated with watching men die, not from their wounds but from the trauma of their journey away from the trenches, cold, exhausted, hungry, shocked. So when Kate suggested they do something about it, Jude leaped at the chance, and a month later they were there, in sight of no man's land, in the house that was to be their home for over three years.

Jude raised her age to get to the war, just like the boys she knew. Leo tried to stop her, and when he couldn't prevent her with argument, they tossed a coin over it. Heads she'd stay, tails she'd go. He tossed the coin, she picked it up. He should have known better, she told herself.

She took his old motorcycle jacket over with her and wore it all through. She said afterwards that she must have known, had some mysterious insight that she'd need it. It was too big, always sitting on her stiffly, a beetle carapace. But it didn't take long, over there, for the black sheen to rub away and soon there were cracks, fault lines, in the creases of the arms. Sometimes, at the end of a day and exhaustion riding pillion with her, the weight of it felt nearly too much. But if she opened the jacket and buried her face in the lining, through the dirt and the sweat she could smell home, so she wore it always, her familiar skin.

★ ★ ★

The farmhouse had been part of their inland sea, the nearest island on their watery horizon. Kate and Jude could see it, walls and roof, from their upstairs room. And when the waters were still and the sun shone, it rose out of its own reflection. But as the flooding finally drew back, a track appeared, first like a shadow and then, more substantial, lifting like a rift in the water's seamless cloth, linking farmhouse and village.

It was Peter's idea to go out there.

'See what remains,' he said.

'We know what will have remained,' Kate said. 'We've seen it dozens of times.'

He shrugged. 'I'd still like to see. It's eerie, having it out there unvisited. It deserves a bit of human sympathy.'

Jude laughed at that. 'I'll come with you,' she said, so, a week or so later, when they judged that the track would have dried enough, the two of them walked out there, Jude with her camera, empty haversacks on their backs, because, as Jude said, who knew what you might find, even in a house that had been all at sea?

On their way out, she took a photograph of the farmhouse, four-square in its watery domain, and much later then it was Elsa who asked, was this how Noah's ark had been?

A high tideline was visible round the outside of the house higher than Jude's waist, and the bricks were damp above it and still wet below. The windows and the doors were swollen and the paint was crawling off. Mud pressed itself up to the walls and rotted vegetation languished. Peter managed to open the kitchen door, and the two of them went in.

Little remained in the downstairs rooms. The furniture was gone, taken off, Jude imagined, on a cart like one of those she had seen so often at the fringes of this war, piled beyond hope with objects and people. Despite the flooding, squares of shade were still visible on the walls where pictures had been, and on a nail beside the door, two keys. A filter of silt lay over all.

They went upstairs, Peter into one room to exclaim at the view back, across the strange sea, she into the other.

'I can see our place,' he called out. 'Come and get a picture of it. The roof. Your white cross. It's clear as day. I love it that you can't paint straight.'

Jude laughed and stepped further into a room with a small gilded mirror and a bed, all curlicues and little painted flowers that must have been unwillingly left behind. She walked past the mirror, catching a slice of herself, her jacket, her hands around the camera. They looked like a man's hands, strong-fingered, the nails clipped almost to the quick. Stepping back, Jude bent a little. She hadn't seen her face in a mirror for weeks, except in the tiny compact Kate had tucked into her kitbag, and you could only see one thing at a time in that, an eye, a cheekbone, your mouth. She stared at herself and wondered at how young she still seemed. She looked as young as the boys she nursed. Then she grinned at her own foolishness.

Jude took out her camera and stepped closer to trace the painted patterns and then, despite herself, despite all she had seen, she exclaimed, so loud that Peter came running.

'What is it?' he said.

In the centre of the mattress, her spine curved round, protective, lay a cat, dead for so many months, the skin of her jowl stretched tight against her jaw, her tabby belly fur dipped, hollowed out, her eyes two tiny raisins. And nestled in to her, three balls, one black, one tabby, one fiercely striped in grey.

'I don't cry at the men,' Jude said, 'but these.'

★   ★   ★

'If you don't know your arse from your elbow, then get out of the bloody kitchen.' Kate lifted the lid on the pot and the steam billowed up, blanched her face. 'Christ,' she said, stepping back.

'Mind him!' Jude shouted.

Kate gave a cursory look at the shape on the stretcher. 'He's dead to the world, not going to feel a thing. Come on, you stir it. Burn your own lips.'

Cautiously, Jude looked into the pot. 'Peter said half the liquid should have gone, and it should smell peppery.'

'And?'

'It does smell peppery. But maybe we ought to add a bit more water. There's only a few inches.'

'He'll murder us if we've ruined his stock.'

'Kate, we were busy.'

'I was busy. You were just doing what I told you to.'

'And you'd have thanked me if I'd been stirring the pot instead of passing you the swab?'

Kate made her way round the unconscious soldier and peered into the pot. She turned to Jude. 'I can't tell. Will he know, if we add more water?'

'He said to take the bones out, once it was done.'

'But if we put more water in?'

'What is it about you?' Jude said. 'Completely calm taking out shrapnel, stitching a wound, cleaning mud out of flesh, deciding what you can do to save a life, but when it's Peter's stock pot, you go to pieces.'

'Well, do we or don't we?'

'What?'

'Add the water, for Christ's sake. God, you'd think I'd have known better than to get stuck away in this hole with someone who conjugates Latin, rides motorbikes at daft speeds, isn't afraid of death and can't do a lot else.'

They'd been in the house four months and exhilaration had given way to exhaustion. Food was their calling card, and it had taken only days for word to spread amongst the soldiers. So every day now they fed soup and hot chocolate to a stream of men queuing with mugs. And every night, carrying heavy, steaming jugs, they made their way to the sentries in their dug-out outposts at the end of the world, looking out into the darkness, over the mist, over the floods. They'd hear no sounds except their breath, their footfalls. The quiet bark for the password, then a hand would appear and take the jug. They'd hear tin mugs being filled and after a few seconds the jug would be handed back empty, no word spoken, and they'd return. Sometimes a star shell would break above them and they'd have to stand stock-still and watch its cold light harden over the blank fields and dead water, the ruined buildings, then fall to the ground around them, before they moved on.

Sometimes by day the village was still shelled and you had to listen to the skies. But at night the ground was more treacherous than the air, darkness hiding the slurry and the shell holes. Still, Jude liked the night walk back through the village. It seemed less ruined when she couldn't see behind things. And she came to know the craters and the gashed walls, the piles of masonry and where the water spilled, and felt a growing ease with this shattered place. There was a single plane tree surviving on the main street, a strange, lopsided thing, but she noticed that it had managed some leaf buds ready for spring, and passing in the night, sometimes she'd put a hand out to touch the trunk, as if by accident, not wanting Kate to see her do it.

If the food was their calling card, then the cellar became their salon. They received all comers, day or night, the wounded and the dog-tired and the scared. Mostly the wounded came to them, but sometimes Jude and Kate would go out and help retrieve them, laying their stretcher down on the mud, and lifting the man on. At first Jude would apologize, each time the man cried out or jerked with the pain, 'Sorry. So sorry,' till Kate took her to task.

'If you say that once more, you can carry the damn stretcher on your own,' she said. 'Tell them something useful. That you love them, that you're their mother, whatever you like, but not sorry.'

The first wrench from the ground was the

hardest, with the mud fighting them, gravity fighting them, with the sniper waiting for them to stumble into his sights, with the man's cries of pain to be left still, left alone, and always under their boots the horrid slush of war. Then they'd have the stretcher up to waist level, the handles rubbing into their blisters, pressing the blood from their fingers. And the weight of the man, and his boots and rifle, his uniform and tin hat, of the unsent letter and the dog-eared photograph in his pocket, the weight of all that expectation that gathers itself into staying whole, being alive, pulled their arms from their shoulders, bent them down, as they made their way over the cratered ground. And though there were times Jude's arms were shrieking with the strain of it and she thought she couldn't make another yard, still they never dropped a man.

Jude took the bones out of the stockpot and put them in a pail. Outside, the air was cold and the bones steamed. If you touched them, they felt like velvet after so much boiling. You could press your nail in.

With so many dead horses, there was no shortage of meat. You saw them everywhere. Sometimes a couple of dogs nuzzling at them or, at twilight, rats. Peter would go out with his axe and his knife when the shelling had been bad. Wait till the sky was quiet. He had an old tarpaulin with him and he only came back with the very fresh.

'Too risky otherwise. Don't know what else the rats have been in,' he'd say.

The Belgians were impressed. He cooked as

well as a native. But he stopped telling the British soldiers what it was in the stew after one refused to eat a 'man's best friend'.

'You'd think we were cannibals, the way he carried on,' Kate said.

'What the eye doesn't see, the heart won't grieve over,' Jude said. And after that the men ate ravenously and only ever asked for more salt.

Jude picked her way down across where the garden used to be to the shell hole they were using for their rubbish, and tipped the bones in. She liked this chore. Except for these short times, carrying rubbish, or going for the turnips or potatoes, or spotting planes, she could rarely be on her own.

The first time she'd climbed onto the roof, it was to put back some tiles. Peter had no great head for heights and Kate was away with the ambulance. What with the shelling, there had been leaks since they arrived and they'd become canny with the buckets, but it was getting worse, so when Peter found a stack of unbroken tiles, the short straw fell to Jude.

They were red pantiles and they reminded her of home. She'd slung a satchel across her shoulders, leaving both hands free, and Peter had loaded in a half dozen. The ladder took Jude up to the gutter and then she had to hitch one foot up, wedging her boot toe against the gutter edge for purchase, and pull herself onto the roof. The roof pitched steeply and she had to be careful not to dislodge the tiles as she climbed. Keeping her weight forward and her hands out above her, bracing her legs and shoulders against the slip of gravity, she clambered up to the ridge where the worst hole was.

She looked down once and felt her muscles tighten. Then she thought of the cliffs she loved, the birds making their nests on the edge of nothing, and that steeled her. Replacing the tiles took only a few minutes and she was back down to collect some more. Peter stood at the base of the ladder, his hands gripping the sides, his face scrunched with anxiety.

'Stop standing there like some mother,' she said. 'Least nobody's trying to kill me.'

Peter shrugged.

'Have you always been like this?' Jude said.

'Yes, but it's worse when there are children around. I think you count as a child, though. God knows what'll happen if I have a child of my own one day.' He grinned. 'Though that is a bit unlikely.'

'You'll be a Nebuchadnezzar. On all fours.'

The next time up, her body was easier with it and she allowed herself more time, straddled the roof ridge and looked around. After all the rain it was a clear day, ribbons of cloud strung across. Near to, the village was laid out, houses with their insides showing, pieces of wall with tatters of wallpaper strung like bunting, rafters pointing all ways but across where the roof had been, mad spokes, all the savage work of the war exposed. In the far distance baubles of smoke hung rounded in the blue sky like decorations. And in between, she could see water and the lines of war. All was quiet.

'You can see everything from here,' she called.

58

'Come down,' she heard in return. And though she recognised the urgency in his voice, it was diluted and came up to her light, insubstantial.

The front line had shifted several times since they'd arrived. Now it stood farther off, but up here she could see right across the awkward criss-cross of trenches and earthworks, strange lumps and ridges from where she stood, over the coils of barbed wire and into no man's land. It seemed as if the land stood waiting, awaiting. Nothing moved there, no man, no animal. Even the wind seemed to have given up the ghost. She knelt down, her back against the chimney. The river ran across the bottom of her view, only a stubble of trees left to mark its course now. A heron crossed the sky towards it, the heavy tread of its wings. When it flew too close to the church tower the rooks came out to see it off, flapping their black cloaks, pitching in sharp to harry it. The heron lifted its heavy chest, turned a few degrees, and flew on, steady, unhurried.

When Jude first heard the plane, it was a distant whine, high-pitched, irrelevant. Sometimes they watched dogfights in the sky here, planes wheeling high up, flimsy, like dancers, as if they had nothing to do with the dirty mess on the ground. The plane came closer. Jude stood up, tall, straight-backed, her arms around the chimney. She couldn't see the markings yet, but it seemed to be on its own, and it was trailing smoke and losing height.

'Get down,' Peter shouted. 'You've no cover.'

She shook her head. It was close enough now

for her to see the markings. The plane was German and it would pass dangerously near to her roof. She had no camera up here to put between herself and this plunging metal bird. The whine had grown to something ghastly, a sound that cut through the roof and shivered the chimney bricks. Now she could see the pilot, his face white, unseeing, locked in concentration, in the effort to fly.

The plane must have passed only twenty feet from the house and Jude watched on, just long enough to see where it would end.

'Get the bike,' she shouted to Peter, who had come out again and, with a last look, she came down the ladder.

It had landed in no man's land, in full view of the German gunners, but they knew by now what Jude did, they were familiar with the red crosses on her Matchless, her sidecar. And besides, he was one of theirs. That first time the pilot was dead before she reached him. He'd managed to make a landing of sorts, but the impact had pushed the joystick too far into his chest. He was so fresh, in his pilot's uniform, so unmuddied, unsullied, she thought he looked like one of Leo's friends come to call, still barely shaving, a boy of nineteen or so. They buried him in the German corner of the churchyard.

From then on they kept the ladder handy for the roof. The German snipers never fired at them up there. And it became another place where Jude could be alone.

Since childhood, Jude knew she had never stood at the heart of things. At high school, she saw how it was done, the belonging, the groups and games, but she was one of those who stayed on the outside, unnoticed. At break times the other girls would glimpse a tall, slight figure with unruly dark curls at the edge of the view, her mackintosh half-buttoned against the wind, her tam-o'-shanter crooked as she walked around the playing field, or stood against the school wall, her shoulder blades in two points against the brick, and made pictures with her fingers. She only swam into full view if they were a girl short, when they might demand that she joined in with the game of tag, or held a rope for their skipping. And she would do so, but as soon as she could, she'd slip away again to the shadow of the wall.

'Take your fingers down,' Miss Bude, who taught history, would tell her when she came across Jude framing things, and she would whip her knuckles across Jude's hands so that they smarted. 'We must take part, Judith, as best we can.' And Jude would try her hardest for Miss Bude, who wept at the fate of Anne Boleyn and Lady Jane Grey and all the other lady victims of history.

Jude liked Miss Bude and she liked Miss Cupinall, who taught French, and most especially she liked the botany teacher, Miss Butterling, who took the girls deep into meadows of tall grass so that they could see for themselves trembling couch and rye, rattle, mare's tail, timothy and willow, and learn how various even the fields above their own town

61

were. She laboured hard to remember the difference between St John's wort and saxifrage, or between loosestrife and creeping Jenny, propping her exercise book behind Leo's plate of breakfast so that he could test her as he ate his eggs.

But often, at school, her thoughts took flight. Seated at her desk in a classroom intent upon calculus or the Roman conquest, Latin conjugations or the fate of the soul after death, Jude's mind would skip a beat and hang with the buzzing fly above the gas lights, or wriggle its way through the slit of open window and become lost in the toss of the leaves in the beech trees beyond the tennis courts. And when a question came her way, she found herself stranded, like the porpoise she had read of, lost up the river Thames, her body in one place and her spirit in another.

'But you're a clever enough girl,' her father would say perplexed, Jude's school report on the desk before him. 'I wish your mother were here to advise me.'

And he'd put a hand to his head and stroke his shiny, liver-spotted skull. Then, when she made no reply, he'd reach for his bowl of pipes and Jude, watching, would think how much she'd like to take a photograph, the angle of his head, the line of the pipe stem.

★　★　★

When Jude had first returned from the war, she couldn't bear to live in a house. Not Leo's, not anybody's. She didn't trust their steady walls. At the end, the hospital was tents. Solid, large, but still tents, which she'd been glad of. Then there were the trains, crammed, euphoric, and all the time, outside, the platforms with cheery people who only wanted to know you were alive.

Leo and Sally were on her platform, and their children, a baby in Sally's arms, a child with one hand tight in Leo's. Jude stood still as the train pulled out and away and wished she was not here.

Leo walked towards her, his small son tugging back, reluctant. The boy had Leo's hair, his walk.

'Jude,' Leo said, his face unsure.

'The journey was all right,' she said. She smiled at him. 'You've come with everybody.'

Leo looked down at the little boy, and over at Sally, holding the baby.

'They're the family,' he said.

She nodded.

'You look . . . ' Leo said.

'It doesn't matter how I look,' she said.

Leo put his hand to his cheek, as though she had slapped him. Jude shut her eyes, watched the flash and dazzle of her own darkness. When she opened them, Leo was still there, and the little boy was on his way steadily back towards his mother further down the platform. Leo moved closer to Jude and lifted the haversack from her back.

'I didn't know Father was that bad,' he said. 'He didn't tell me. Didn't tell anybody.'

'Why?'

Leo shrugged. 'Maybe because of the war, all

the young men dying. I don't know.'

'Was he in pain?'

'No. Just terrible fatigue. And of course he wouldn't listen to my suggestions, but then I didn't know how ill he was. Father had told the doctor not to tell me. I wrote as soon as . . . '

'Yes,' Jude said.

Leo put his arm around her, and standing on the platform, she let herself cry at last.

'You're home now,' Leo said, and his shoulder, where it was wet with her tears, smelt of milk, smelt of the baby over there in its mother's arms, waiting for its father.

They tucked her into their house, covered her with comfort, their questions hanging silent fire in the movement of their arms, their heads angled to listen better. But she couldn't tell them anything, not even that she was all right. She didn't want to, and so she left after two nights.

'You're not yourself,' Leo said to her. 'Jude?'

She shrugged. 'I have been,' she said. 'Be patient.'

She took a train and then a slower one, and a third, and walked the four miles to her Uncle William's farm. The short cut above the road was wet with rain, so that treading through the grasses and the buttercups, her boots darkened and she could feel the slink of her toes. Years back, she'd have taken the boots off, knotted and hung them from her neck, laughed when her aunt chided her for her bare feet. But she knew better than that now. You don't take off your boots, not unless you have to.

Her uncle offered her a cottage, empty until

harvest time. But she didn't want anything so strongly fixed. She didn't know how he'd come by the caravan. The wheel axles were rotten, so it wasn't going anywhere, but still it wasn't rooted in. William said he'd fix it up for her, find her a horse even, if that was what she wanted. But she wanted only to be left there, and he did so.

They gave her food, William and his wife Joan — eggs, bread, meat, milk, vegetables — and every so often she'd go down to the farm for a bath.

'Let her be,' William said when she arrived. 'She won't let you be her mother. Nor me her father.'

There were the sores and scabs and her hair was cropped like a boy's. She liked to put her hand over it, the tickle on her palm. They didn't touch her, not even a stroke to the cheek, and her hair grew and the scabs became scars, some of them.

She knew that they wondered what had become of her. She could see them at it. She knew the girl they'd lost, the girl that they could wrap themselves around. The girl who'd visited them every holiday, copying them in their tasks, making a game in the midst of their labour. She'd seen her go, and somebody else grow up in her place.

That girl was a fairy-tale creature now, a mischievous will-o'-the-wisp who crept out of the mist and tugged William's arm as he walked to the cowshed in the early morning, or plucked at Joan's scarf as she bent to cut sweet peas. She haunted the place. They heard the odd tuning of her whistle in the distance, caught a glimpse of her dance, were sure they saw her disappear into the hay barn or heard the creak of her footstep on the stairs, tousled from a nightmare. But she wasn't there.

She was too tall for her aunt's, so she went about in her uncle's clothes, having brought nothing of her own beyond what she stood up in: his corduroy trousers, pulled in with a belt, his shirts, the cotton soft with age, the collars turned and bare, his ancient pullover darned in the elbows, his old boots when hers got a hole. She was at ease in these things.

A cat joined her in the caravan, a wild streak of a creature, as unwilling to be touched as she was. It ate the same food she did — meat, scrambled egg, bread soaked in milk — and slept at her feet, but it wouldn't be touched.

The first time she noticed it behind her, a mile from the farm, she thought it was chance that had brought her haphazard walking and the cat's hunting to the same place. But when it happened again, she knew it must be deliberate. The cat became her only company, stalking her at an angle, as though it wished to persist with the illusion that their proximity was accidental.

She walked for miles each day, her journeying sometimes taking her so far off that she would stumble her way back in the dark, and more than once she was forced to sleep the night curled into the corner of a barn. She carried her Kodak with her and took photographs of the long views, the horizon, the hills rising on the skyline. Her father was dead, her lover was dead, her closest friend. And all the others. With so many gone, she needed to walk in an empty landscape, needed to take her mind's eye as far away as she could.

For a time, while she was in Belgium, Jude had taken photographs of hands. Her own, Kate's, Peter's, other soldiers', trying to capture them in a gesture or going about some habitual movement, peeling potatoes, lighting cigarettes, playing cards or rolling bandages, their precision, their delicacy. But there had been one young soldier brought in, she could still see him come through the doorway, and he'd changed that. It was winter and very cold. The soldiers were suffering badly from chilblains, their hands and feet swollen and painful, and some had frostbite, so that at first she thought that was this man's trouble. He stepped forward, eyes wide, shocked, and held his gloved hands out to Jude, like an offering, and if she hadn't caught him, he would have fallen to the ground.

The soldier behind him told her that it was the left one that had been hit, but that the young fellow wouldn't look at it even.

'He's too frightened,' he said.

Jude got the man on to a stretcher and gave him a slug of brandy. Still he hadn't spoken a word. As gently as she could, she began to cut away the woollen glove, and for a short moment she thought the injuries might be superficial. Then she saw that the darkness of the glove was made up as much of blood as of the dark blue wool. As the hand was uncovered, it became a mess of bone and blood. Two fingers were severed, the knuckle bones sharp white even in the cellar's poor light, and the flesh on the hand was macerated, raw. Woollen fibres were tangled into the mess of it all, so deeply threaded into the flesh, it was almost as though God had made it that way. The doctor would be here later, but she knew there was nothing he could do with this.

She was exhausted by the time she'd finished and though he was conscious, staring at the ceiling, still the soldier hadn't flinched, still he hadn't spoken.

'It's serious,' she said, 'but you should make a good recovery. I've cleaned it up pretty well. We'll get you back to the hospital tomorrow, and you'll be strong again before you know it.' And because he wouldn't speak and because she was so tired, she said, 'You're not left-handed, I hope?' and still he didn't speak, but when Jude saw that he was crying, she was sorry for her facetiousness and she went and found the one who'd brought him in.

'He's not left-handed, is he?' she said to the soldier, who looked up at her over his mug of soup, and he shook his head.

'He's a pianist,' he said.

So later, in all her time on her uncle's farm, Jude never shot people. No bodies, no limbs. And when finally she came to leave the caravan, she threw away all the landscapes on the rolls of shot film, as she'd known she would.

Jude never found out how they recovered the motorcycle. She hadn't mentioned it. But one day William came to her door, waving a slip of paper.

'It's at the station,' he said. 'We'll go for it this afternoon.'

She waited for him to explain, and he handed her the slip.

'Matchless arrived 0600 hours. To be collected, Mr Emerson.'

'My motorcycle?' she said.

'We'll set off soon as dinner's done,' he said, giving a nod as if to confirm it to himself. And maybe she clenched her jaw and he could see that she was close to something, because he turned and walked away.

Kate's motorcycle. It was very dirty. It hadn't been ridden since. Mud, grit, oil, crud caked hard over wheels, forks, footboards, handlebars, sidecar. The same mud and grit. She didn't touch it. Just looked. When they got back, William wheeled it down from the trailer and into the yard. Strange, to see it there in the sunshine. As much as her, it had lost its place in the world.

The dogs sniffed it, though they didn't lift a leg, didn't mark it out as theirs, and the hens pecked around it, odd inconsequential birds. Sparrows sat on the saddle, chivvied around the sidecar. She waited, still didn't touch, and only at last when they'd gone elsewhere, when everything seemed to have gone elsewhere, did she go close and grip the handlebars, and allow herself to straddle the bike, and remember.

She'd ridden pillion for the first lesson, Kate yelling instructions to the wind and Jude nodding blindly, her eyes streaming without goggles. But there had been little time beyond that for the luxury of learning and already the following day, Jude had had to set off on the bike for supplies with Kate's injunctions still burning in her ears.

'For God's sake gently with the throttle,' Kate yelled after her, and then something that began, 'If you bring her back . . .', but by then Jude was beyond earshot, and looking in the mirror she could see that Kate had already turned back towards the wounded men in the cellar below.

'It's enough now,' Jude told herself in her uncle's yard, climbing off the saddle, and though she didn't know what she would do, she knew that she would ride the bike again.

*   *   *

She stayed longer on the farm than she could have believed, out and away from the returning world, and it took her a long while to get used to living in a house, to get used to streets and motor cars and drays and lorries. People, sounds, buildings seemed to press in very close and her reflexes, still strung along war wires, made her start and duck, so that she began to take her camera out with her again as a way of keeping her distance, as defence. Leo and Sally never pressed her about money, never asked her to find a job, but she knew before she was ready to that she must.

'But not nursing,' she said.

'Not nursing?'

70

Jude and Leo were sitting on the lawn in the garden, keeping watch over Elsa on the swing.

'No.'

'Because?'

She was fiddling with a blade of grass, stretching it between her thumbs, blowing at it.

'Kate taught me to whistle,' she said. 'She told me it didn't work with garden grass, but I didn't believe her.'

'Why not nursing?' Jude could see Leo's hand twitch. Seven years earlier and he'd have snatched the grass from her fingers. Seven years earlier and she was still a child and wouldn't have been able to answer his question. Jude rolled her shoulders. She could feel the muscles bunched tight.

'Because I couldn't do it like before. Matrons are much worse than generals. I couldn't obey all the rules. Couldn't stand being humble.'

Leo laughed. 'You could learn.'

'No.'

'And not teaching?'

'No,' her voice impatient.

'So, what then? There isn't much, not even factory work, now the men have returned.'

'I want something I don't need to care about,' she said. 'Do it and leave it.'

'Father thought you should be a photographer,' Leo said.

She shook her head. 'I couldn't be the kind I wanted to be.'

'You don't know that.'

'I do,' she said.

At the edge of the flower bed, missed by the

lawnmower, she found a piece of rougher grass and holding it between thumb and forefinger, carefully she pulled it free of its sheath. Running her thumb down its edge, its bristles caught at her skin. She laid the blade flat against the side of one thumb, married her other thumb tight on top, lifted them to her lips.

The sound was oily and coarse, like a strange bird cry, and it took her back. She blew again.

'I know you've always said no before, but I could try to get you a job,' Leo said. 'In my company. Pay would be very low to start with, while you were training.'

'What kind of training?'

'It's mainly on the job, and some evening classes. Typewriting, shorthand.'

'So I'd be a shorthand typist?'

Leo nodded.

'They'd have known Richard.'

'Yes.'

Jude twisted the grass around her finger like a tourniquet, watched the skin whiten.

'Would they know I was your sister?'

'I could only get you an interview. They won't do favours. It'd be up to you, if they took you on.'

'I don't think they'd like my other skills,' Jude said.

'I don't think you should tell them. In fact you'd need to bite your tongue. You know that now, anyway. Yes, sir, and no, sir. And your hair. They'll probably ask you to keep your hair longer.'

Jude unwound the grass.

'But I want it shorter.'

'Why?'

'D'you remember when I got back, after the war?'

Leo reached over, put his hand on Jude's hair, the tight black curls, like his.

'That was because of the lice. You told me.'

'I liked it, too.'

He shrugged. 'Long hair dressed in a bun, or back with ribbon. Dark ribbon.' He pointed at Elsa, swinging, humming to herself. 'That length. And no rings.'

'Not even a wedding ring?'

'Only single women, you know that.'

'For God's sake,' Jude muttered, but not at Leo's words because he was right, she did know that. 'It took me half an hour once,' she said a minute later, in a different voice, 'and the brother standing by me, to pull the wedding ring from a dead man's finger.'

'Jude?' Leo said, uncertain, and Jude shook her head.

'Cobwebs,' she said, her voice breezy now, implausible. 'Anyway, how do you know so much?'

'I used to interview them,' he said.

Jude was silent, brooding.

'I don't much mind what I do,' she said at last. 'It'll be dull, won't it?'

'But you don't want . . . '

'No, dull is fine. What about the motorcycle?'

'To work?'

Jude nodded.

'No. Recreation only. Train to work. Besides,

it'd be dangerous in a skirt.'

'You won't see me for dust at the weekends, then,' she said, flicking the grass away.

★ ★ ★

What shocked Jude most was that she got used to the office. At the end of the first day she was ready to leave, and again at the end of the week, and certainly after a month, and still after six, then a year, and so on. She couldn't quite believe that she had to keep going there. She felt like Elsa after her first week of primary school. Couldn't she stop now and go back to her play? But Jude didn't leave. She bit her tongue and kept her place.

Each morning she would tug the blue worsted suit from its hanger, put on the white silk blouse, the lisle stockings and sensible shoes, drink a quick cup of coffee and take the train into the city with Leo. She stood on the platform looking like anyone else while Leo flicked the pages of *The Times*. They didn't walk together beyond the station. You couldn't do that to work, even brother and sister.

The weather was hot those first weeks and by the time she reached the office Jude's skin was sticky and she could feel the sweat beading under her hat and she was longing to pull off her gloves. Crossing Boar Lane, she'd walk up Park Row to George Street, one of such a stream of girls. She'd never have imagined there could be so many.

When she was a child and visiting her father,

Jude had been scared of the revolving door. The way it seemed to suck people in, usher them secretly, never opening except when it was already closing. You might be squashed if you timed it wrong, or you might twirl and twirl, go faster and faster, be caught in the blur of wood and glass, and never escape. She'd always let her mother go first, and then wait for an age to go in, terrified. She'd wait so long that often enough her mother or her father would be spat out again to find out what had happened to her.

The room was large and bleak. High windows, which Jude was glad about, through which you could just see the tiling on the mansard roofs, a bank of filing cabinets along one wall, and trestle tables along the others. Twenty girls sat at twenty typewriters and now Jude was one of them.

★ ★ ★

The sea was like another field. A rising stain of green, thin-lined below the sky, tugging her eyes from the road. Leo had his arm out, signalling to stop, and Jude pulled into the side of the road behind him. She stepped away from the Matchless, the dew coating her boots. The air was still. She could hear the birds again. She pulled off her gloves and put her hands to her face, her cheeks cold and hard from the wind, her eyes still dazed. Her arms and legs were stiff and she teetered for a minute before shaking out the motion.

'You're determined to go up there?' Leo said.
'Yes.'

75

'If you wait, I can leave them on the beach and come with you.'

'I'd rather be on my own.'

'And if . . . ' he fell silent at the thought they both had.

'Leo,' Jude said, a plea in her voice.

'I've made as much room for you as I can,' he said. 'I know you need it. But I can't stand and watch, if I think you're going to . . . '

'That's not what I want,' Jude said.

She could see his fists clenching. She knew that anxiety was seeded in his belly like a scatter of pearls, his muscles gathering around them. But she must go. She waited, and finally he undid his fingers and gave her a hug.

'You'll find us on the beach, then?' he said.

'Will you swim?' And her question made him smile. It was an old joke from childhood, when Jude was fearless and he was scared. 'Keep me some beer,' she said, 'and don't let the children out too deep.'

'I'll be watching for you,' he said. 'Remember.'

He blew a dandelion. 'She loves me, she loves me not,' but she wouldn't play that far.

'I'll find you by lunchtime,' she said and she started up the motorbike and there were no other rhymes in the world.

She was safe, watching the birds. Safe as houses, if she could face out her fear. She turned into the wind, the sharp, ammoniac air, and walked towards the cliff.

When they had come here as children, Leo would hold Jude by the wrist to stop her going too close to the edge. He'd plant his feet squarely, one hand holding her, so tight it hurt her bones, and the other clamped against one ear because of the din. There was the smell too, so he'd breathe through his mouth. Then it'd be a tug-of-war, she bracing her slight weight against him, trying to unbalance him and inch towards the cliff edge, and him with the bulk, standing stock-still. She didn't see the danger then, any more than his children could see it now, kept safe by his caution. But Leo didn't need to hold her away any longer, or even warn her.

The ground was uneven, humped up, so that Jude had to watch her steps, though there'd be nothing worse than bird shit to fall into here if she lost her footing. She left no footprints in the wiry grass, and the tiny cliff-top flowers — thrift and saxifrage, tormentil's fierce yellow, the purple pinheads of wild thyme — remained untouched by her boots, impeccable.

The noise was getting louder, a shrieking swell rising from the line where the land stopped. Birds turned above her and she could sometimes pick out their single cries before they dropped and dived down beyond her sight. The stench of birdlime burnt her nostrils. Far away on the sea, easy in the swell and break of the waves, clusters of razorbills and guillemots, puffins and kittiwakes sat high. And now she was close enough to see the cliffs, the smeared white of the rock, busy with the business of thousands of nesting birds. Close enough to see how far away down the sea was.

Before the war she had often come here with Leo. But since returning she'd been out only once. It was winter and she was on her own, wanting just to see the cliffs. But she was too scared to stay. The sweat poured from her even before she got close, and her heart pounded so that it hurt. That day she stopped fifty yards off and stared down across the meadow to where the land ended, terrified that if she moved forward another step, she would run and not stop, that she would have her last fling with the air.

'Richard,' she whispered, 'please don't make me,' and she stood, unable to move, until at last some cattle, unafraid of this stationary figure, grazed their way across her vision and she was able to turn and walk away.

Jude had no idea how Leo had known. She hadn't told him, but that evening he came and found her in her dark room.

'Things take a lot of time,' he said, 'especially these hard griefs. Don't hurt yourself, please.'

This second time, Jude was sure that she'd be able to manage it. Leo would be below, on the beach, and though he could prevent nothing, she'd be in his view. And far from being empty, the cliffs were so densely inhabited at this time of the year, she couldn't imagine tumbling over, into all those bird lives. Of course she didn't know if she could, but she was determined to keep her nerve if possible, at least for long enough to take some photographs.

She knew a place she could stand away from the edge, from where she could see a piece of the cliff face and the sea below, and she walked there slowly, keeping pace with her fear, marking the charge of her heart. When she arrived, she spent a few minutes getting her camera ready. Then, putting it down for now, she took out her binoculars and dared herself to look.

The relief was as palpable as the fear. She could feel it in her arms, in her stomach. She had survived and now she could let herself go.

At first, watching them, the birds looked chaotic, their flight random. As if they were caught in the sky together just for the hell of it, just to be suspended high above the water and in the face of the cliffs. But if she picked out a bird and kept her eye on it, refused to let her attention be drawn by another gull's fancy flightwork, or by another bird's sure fire pitch into the cliff, then she'd quickly see how concerted each was, how focused, so that they reminded her of the eight-fifteen city rush off the morning trams for work, except they were climbing the skies instead of treading the pavements.

★　★　★

In the war she'd taken photographs as still lives, intimate things to set against that vast, awful energy: their truckle beds, hers and Kate's, the lanterns on nails behind, Kate's diary on her pillow, the shelf with binoculars, photo frame with heads visible, an apple; or the kitchen stove, herbs drying above as if all were well, bottles and tins, tin spoons in a pot, a pan with steam. And she'd taken portraits. Kate mainly: reading, bandaging a man's hand, stroking the cat; or

Peter at the stove, peeling vegetables, turning to the camera, grinning. And the wounded men, of course. Other, grimmer things too, sometimes. A skull in a ditch, two dead horses, a single flower in the rubble, the land besieged.

Now, Jude wanted to capture movement. To hold something still in the lens when all its impetus was to be away and gone.

Sometimes at home she looked at the pictures she took before the war, before she needed to try to keep things still. Not the ones in the albums, but those left loose. Took the box out from under her bed and carried it downstairs to the drawing room where the light from the windows was strong. She lifted off the lid and drew out an unruly pile, sharp corners pricking her fingers. Tom and Elsa joined in if they could, closing their eyes tight and shuffling down in with their hands, playing lucky dip with the past.

They picked out photographs one by one and asked different questions of her.

'Why has the boy got his hat on? Whose dog is it? Why are they running away? Is it Grandma making stew? Who won the marbles? Did you comfort her, the girl crying?'

Most of the photographs she knew immediately, where she was, what the light was like, even sometimes what she'd wanted to capture. Though she wouldn't know what the dog was called or remember why the girl was crying, so she had to make that up. But there was one that Tom found one day, deep in the box, that she couldn't bear to speak of.

'Jude, why's the boy leaping?'

Tom was leaning over the photograph as if to interrogate it, and his voice was puzzled.

'And you've missed off his arms. And his head.'

Elsa looked up from her crayons, forehead pinched at the interruption, and leaned to look.

'It's not Daddy,' she said. 'He was never like that.'

And despite herself, Jude laughed.

'He was as thin then,' she said, 'but he could never jump that high, no.'

'That's our leaping rock, isn't it? He's doing it from there.'

'Yes.'

'I like this one specially. Who is it?' Elsa said, and before she thought to say nothing, Jude answered her.

'It's the boy who flew too close to the sun,' and she turned the photograph over so they could see the inscription.

'*Icarus, 1912*,' Tom read out.

There was so much more she could have told them. That he'd been a friend of Leo's, for example. She could have told them that. Or that he'd worked in their father's firm. Or that he'd worn a suit to work and was as slender as a reed, supple as a fish. She could have told them how he laughed and larked, told them his pranks. That he let her take photographs of him. Or that he'd shot his share of the enemy, sometimes because they were shooting back and others because there were only so many prisoners you could take and what else were you to do. She could have told them that he couldn't weep at

81

what he'd done, and that his letter to tell her of this had taken five weeks in the writing, each new start beginning with the words, 'I am still here'. She could have told them that he never got the letter she wrote in reply.

She could have told them that she loved him. And that it was only when he was gone that she knew how far from himself he had had to go.

She could have told them that when the wax melted and he fell, down onto the barbed wire, his face and leaping legs torn, and then fell still further into the mud and the filth, that then it seemed a terrible thing ever to look at him soaring so high, so that when she came home from the war, she took the photograph down and put it away in the box.

'Go on out now,' she said. 'Enough of the photographs.'

'But I haven't finished my picture,' Elsa said.

'Go on.'

'And I'd only looked at a few,' Tom said.

She picked up Elsa's picture and the box of crayons and put them in her arms.

'No,' she said, and they heard her voice, and went.

★   ★   ★

If Leo had been up here on the cliff, he'd have been telling her what kind of fish each bird favoured. How the black guillemots dive for molluscs and worms whereas the common guillemots eat sand-eels and sprats like the puffins. Or how the bigger gulls cruise the cliffs for other birds' eggs and chicks. Or how the biggest of the gulls had a wingspan of more than five feet and could swallow a rabbit whole. But he was on the beach, a tiny speck, and she was alone.

She'd been given these binoculars when it was all life or death. When she lifted them to her eyes, there'd be a few seconds, not more, when all she could see were the black rims of the lenses, everything blurry beyond. And now, years after her war's end, she could lift them and look and for a moment it wasn't the cliff, or the sea, or the children running far off, that she'd see drawing into focus. It was the mud and duckboards, and the grey pan of the sky, and the distant figures weren't moving, but too still. Then she'd focus and the squall of the birds would be back, veering into sight, and the cliff and the sea.

The birds dinned into her skull. There was no room for other sound or thought. There must have been a mackerel shoal close in to the shore, because suddenly the gannets were diving closer than usual, slicing into the water like bullets, worrying the sea to a froth, tugging the fish free. They dropped as fast as a stone. It was how they lived. Putting down the binoculars, she took up her camera. Usually they were too far out, but maybe she could shoot them today. The long, lazy beat of their wings, the arc of their flight, turning above the water, then dropping lower, circling tighter until finally the half-tuck of their wings, sharp-angled, and the drop. They were virtuosos of the dive.

But the trick was to catch the bird before it dived. It was like that half-moment before a man jumped from a wall, or ran between sniper fire, when his soul had already gone and it only remained for the body to follow. A moment when action and suspension were the same. But she couldn't get the timing right today, so instead she picked a gannet returning, watched as it hung in the air with its sliver of silver before dropping to its nest, running the gauntlet of hostile beaks. She followed the bird with her camera so it became the still point, its long, black-tipped wings caught in an upbeat, the world around a blur.

*   *   *

'Daddy saw you,' Elsa said. She looked like some kind of sea elf, a creature that lived in the seaweed and only came out at low tide, her slender child body pale and goose-fleshed, her long hair caught, salt-sticky, across her shoulders. She was dressed in a cast-off swimming costume of Tom's, which would always be too large for her slight form, and as she ran across the sand, the wet knitted wool dragged in the wind, so that she seemed to be trying to leave its clumsy weight behind her.

'He's cross, but if you look after me near the waves he'll be better,' and she took hold of Jude's hand and tugged towards the water.

Jude looked over at the cliffs, the birds only slight lines in the sky from here, then over towards Leo and Sally's windbreak, set up far behind at the back of the beach. Leo was pouring from a thermos, Sally was taking things out of a bag and Tom was heaping sand nearby, busy with barricades.

'He could barely have seen me from that distance,' she said.

Elsa shrugged. 'But you were too close. He said so,' and letting go of Jude's hand, she set off towards the sea, running and jumping, high-stepping and awkward on the hard, rippled ridges of sand.

So Jude took off her boots, slung them up the beach and followed, slow with her photographic lumber. Elsa was only knee-deep, jumping the wave frills as best she could. The water was warm and clear, rising over the sand. She turned.

'No crabs?' she said.

Jude shook her head. 'Not here. Too much sand. They like the rocks,' and Elsa nodded, and turned back.

The waves reached up, darkening Jude's rolled trousers. Elsa was crouched low, peering down, one hand cupped to her eyes as if she could see more clearly through the waves that way.

Jude looked across the sea to the horizon. The boats out on that line. If you were standing on their decks, there'd be noise and motion, the sea alive beneath and the wind loud, raucous in the sails. But from here they were motionless. And if her photographs were good, the birds would be caught there, impeccable, suspended in their fierce movement. It wasn't so hard to hold things still, and the water was gentle round her legs. The boats weren't moving and the sun was warm. She could stand here a while, it wouldn't hurt. She shut her eyes. Elsa had moved a little further off, body still hunched, still intent on looking. She was making noises, small sounds of pleasure. The sun was bright on Jude's eyelids, hot in her hair, and the water was smooth, a caress against her calves. She could be lost in here for now.

But then the dizziness came. With her eyes closed, her body began to lose up from down, to confuse sky and sea. And Elsa's noises became louder till suddenly Jude knew it was not pleasure. She opened her eyes. Elsa was screaming, shouting something, but not at Jude. She was shouting at the sea, standing motionless, her arms caught tight below her chin, hands over her ears, eyes staring out towards that same horizon.

'Elsa,' Jude called. 'What is it?'

But she didn't answer, didn't move her hands from her head, didn't stop her screaming. Jude waded towards her, the sea dragging at her, now that she wanted to move faster. As she came close, she slowed, and then it was that she felt the tickling on her feet. She looked down and even through the waves and flurry she could see them. Dozens of little crabs, skittering sideways on their way elsewhere.

Jude lifted up the little girl and carried her towards the shore.

'It's all right now,' she said. 'You're out of the water.'

Elsa made no sound.

'They couldn't have hurt you, Elsa,' she said.

'They were barely big enough to tickle.'

Still Elsa made no sound, only hung from her in a limp fury, and when they reached the dry sand and Jude set her down, she ran from her up the beach towards the windbreak and her parents.

Jude followed behind slowly with her boots and bag, and watched Elsa climb into her mother's arms. Sally had made a castle of her groundsheet. Towel heaps made boundary stones and Tom's sandworks formed the outermost defensive wall. Inside, she was surrounded by the clutter of the picnic and neat piles of discarded clothes, mackintoshes, books, hats, a cricket bat, the newspaper weighted with a stone, Leo's glasses.

Jude had reached the highest of the tide lines by the time Leo met her. The bladder wrack was brittle and sharp under her feet. Swarms of tiny flies settled like bloom. Setting down her burdens, she picked up a piece of driftwood, smooth and light, took the weed from it. Leo stood before her as if facing her down over something.

'She was terrified,' he said.

'I know.'

'You shouldn't have said . . . '

'I wasn't trying to deceive her,' she said. 'Crabs don't live in sand.'

'You always act as if you're the only one in the landscape,' he said.

He was angry with her.

'What shouldn't I have done, Leo?'

'You take things too close,' he said. 'I saw you

up on the cliff. And then Elsa running back so scared.'

'I'm going back,' Jude said. 'I'll see you tonight,' and she turned back towards the path inland.

Leo followed.

'But you haven't had any lunch,' he said.

And she shrugged, and left the beach.

★ ★ ★

Jude took the thin road away, high over the wolds. She held the motorbike tight to the road, taking the corners sharp on the inside, accelerating out of the bends. This she could do. First she rode the eight miles to Rudston where she stood before the megalith in the churchyard. High as a house, like a vast spearhead, nobody knew how it had got there in a time when they had no wheels, no iron, no machinery for such grand display. An old woman was bringing flowers to the church. Seeing Jude, she came up and whispered to her.

'It goes down into the earth as deep as it goes high into the air,' she said.

Jude stood up close and pressed her hands against the rough grey stone, traced the carvings of the weather. Then she was back on her bike and into the hills, dipping into villages, Wold Newton, Foxholes, Butterwick, Helperthorpe, through East Lutton and turning across Thirkleby Wold to Sledmere.

The memorials were close to each other, within shouting distance. The one on the village green, needle-sharp, pointed to the heavens. Its brassy armoured saints, facing out from the panels, knew nothing of what had gone on. The other one stood beside a coppice of beech trees, as sturdy as the men it remembered, or sturdier, since they had died so easily. From a distance it looked like a core of ancient column, like something found in Rome, raised up on stone steps, guarded by four smaller pillars, and point-capped with a great stone bullet head. Up closer and its carving told a tale, spiralling down. First there were the farm labourers, men from this place, high up on the column, steady with their rakes and pitchforks, bringing in the harvest; stooks of corn, wagons high with bales. Then enlistment and farewells, the journey to the war in boats. There was the battle with the ugly Huns, their bayonets lanced towards the sturdy waggoners, bullets like large bees in lines above their heads, and still the waggoners stood firm, as unyielding in the storm of battle as they had been beneath sun and rain. And at last their return, to take up their rakes and womenfolk again, though in truth few of them returned.

Maybe it was a good thing, to mark it down like this, carve it in stone, even if it was nothing like. Something to stand in for it all, something you could come to and look at, trace with your fingers: the wagon wheels, the little dog chasing after, the scowling enemy, the neat bullets. Except it didn't do for Jude.

She sat on the grass and thought to herself that she should go home. The sun was hot, and she took off her jacket, laid it beside her like a torso, arms flung out. The smell of the warm leather was comforting. An old man came and stood before the memorial. He carried a vast horse mushroom in his arms, cradling it as if it were a baby. Putting it down gingerly on the grass, he stood. Or maybe he wasn't that old, but he had had a son die; she knew that. One of those sturdy young waggoners who had taken the bee-bullet into himself. Or it could have been the bayonet's jag, the Hun thrusting so hard that he'd made a hole in the boy's chest, and the father in his fields still sowing his crops for his son's return. The old man stood before the column of stone, not seeming to look at it, his cap pulled down on his brow, eyes to the ground. Then he walked around it once and turned to Jude and nodded and made a noise that was maybe a cry, or a greeting, picked up the horse mushroom, nursing it again, and went on his way.

The sky was clear as day, no clouds to cover the sun. She rode home and in the evening lay on her bed and watched her square of blue darken, and the swifts' mad flight give way to the jagged dance of bats.

3

It was a week after the trip to the sea and Jude's hands were white with flour when the doorbell rang. The bread got delivered during the week, but on Saturdays, while Leo and Sally went into the city on errands, Jude liked to make it with Tom and Elsa. It had become a habit with them and sometimes they would experiment with different shapes, cottage buns, plaits, little knots, and sometimes it would be just loaves.

Jude always had the children roll up their sleeves when they helped her make bread, and, making a pile of her watch and signet ring at the end of the table, she warned them about getting dough stuck in watches and rings when they were older.

''Specially you, Elsa. If it's an engagement ring, imagine. Dough in the diamonds.'

As she kneaded the dough, she rolled her shoulders. 'Like this, remember?' she said, exaggerating for the children, playing the fool, so that they giggled together, but under the heels of her hands they saw the dough become shiny, elastic, and so they copied her. Then she'd gather the different pieces together and knead them into one, put the dough in the large bowl, cover it with a dish towel and put it in the airing cupboard to rise.

When the doorbell sounded, Jude crossed the kitchen to the scullery steps.

'Janey,' she yelled down. 'Can you get the door? My hands are . . .', and Janey came up the steps, her face red with the steam from the washing, pulling off her old apron, rolling down her sleeves, wiping her brow, taking her time.

'Sorry, Janey, it's only that,' and Jude rolled her eyes at the children, their hands deep in dough.

But when Janey opened the front door, Jude could hear the colour of her voice, its sullen irritation, and so, with her hands still white, she left the children in the kitchen and went to see who it was.

'Probably a tradesman,' she said to them. 'So he'll need rescuing. I think Janey was out of bed on the wrong side.'

She stopped and turned around before going out of the kitchen door, doing it slowly to give them time, but still she caught them both.

'I told you not to,' she said, her voice mock-ferocious, which had Tom smirking, his fingers still in the dough, but Elsa near to tears, the white gobbet sticky between her fingers. 'Your mother will not forgive me, she says it gives you a bad stomach,' and then she winked at them and allowed herself the pleasure of Elsa's smile.

'Janey, who is it?' Jude called.

'It's just a man,' Janey said, her face sullen.

'Just a man for what?'

Janey had almost shut the door on him by now.

'Wants to speak to Mr Hursten.'

'Perhaps I will do instead,' Jude said, and she

pulled the door open again.

The man was walking away down the path and Jude noticed that his right leg pulled slightly. He was young, not more than twenty-two or three she guessed, quite tall and slightly built, and smartly dressed.

'Can I help you?' she said, her white hands up before her.

He turned back, his steps first uncertain, and then, as if he'd made a decision, bold. His limp didn't sit easily with him. It looked like something he was still reluctant to give way to. He had his hat pulled forward so that it wasn't until she spoke again, and he lifted his head, that she could see him.

'Excuse the flour,' she said.

Her first sight of his face, she had to look away, pretend that something, a bird, a dead flower, had caught her eye. She bent and peered down at the flower bed, then stood, the blush still full in her cheeks.

It wasn't that she mistook him. She could see he was different. Not Richard. But he was the same height, the same build, and, she didn't know why, but there was something about the way he had lifted his head that reminded her so strongly, she felt as if someone had punched her in the gut.

Jude thought that this was a man who never rested. He didn't seem agitated, it wasn't that, but it was as if he couldn't see enough. She watched him look at her, his eyes, which were, as she knew they must be, the deepest blue, probing, enquiring, seeking out the details of her face, glimpsing down at her trousers, her shoes, taking in her clothes, her hair, her floury hands. He noticed her scratch at a scrap of dough on her thumb, he saw the curls of hair escaped from her scarf, saw how one of them tickled her cheek, making her twitch her shoulder against her face, then tuck it behind her ear, leaving a dab of flour on her ear lobe. She knew that he saw all these things, even as he took the step forward, even as he spoke to her.

'I was hoping to speak to Mr Hursten,' he said.

He spoke tentatively, but also with determination, as if this wasn't easy, but he would do it anyway. She noticed now, because he was patting it, that he held a small, leather-bound notebook in one hand.

'He won't be in till later,' she said, and she hoped he didn't want to sell something to her, because she didn't want him to take his leave.

'Perhaps I could explain to you, then,' he said, and she nodded. She liked his voice. It was deeper than she'd have expected, from such a slim figure. 'I won't take more than a minute of your time. It's about a photograph.'

He opened the notebook, flipping the pages over as he spoke. There were pages full of birds, pencil-sketched. Some pages seemed to be given over to details: wings, beaks, feathers, claws; and on others she glimpsed birds in flight, or plucking at a worm, or perched in a tree. The drawings were rough, often partial. Sometimes there would be a landscape added, some water, once she glimpsed part of what looked like a low cottage, all a matter of a few line strokes.

'Just a moment,' he said, flipping through. He held the notebook out for her to see. 'It's only a sketch,' he said. 'I got down what I could. I know it's a long shot, but I discovered that it was Mr Hursten who took the photograph, and I'm hoping he might be able to remember more about it.'

Jude looked at the sketch. It was nothing dramatic. One man lying on a makeshift bed, another in officer's uniform giving him a cigarette, and a woman in man's clothes with a scarf over her hair, standing to one side. She noticed that he'd drawn in the medal one man wore on his chest and that he'd put in the shelf behind, with the OXO box and the bottles. They made a pleasing shape. She'd seen that too. And though he had only drawn the bodies in roughly, he must have been at pains with the faces because she knew them for real people.

The man was still speaking, explaining that it wasn't that he'd been there himself, but that he'd met one of the men afterwards, telling her that he'd been too young for the war though his brother had gone, saying he was sorry if he'd intruded at a weekend and could he call back later to see Mr Hursten. And Jude was going through all the motions of listening, still holding her white hands out from her sides, stiffly, like one of Elsa's dolls, till finally he stopped and she could tell him that it wasn't her brother Leo's photograph at all and that, in fact, Leo was here all through the war, on account of his chest.

'Oh,' he said, and it seemed as if all his energy

left his body in that small sound and he was reduced, caved in. For a moment it looked as if he might fall, and reflexively, she put her hand on his arm to steady him, which he bridled from and she cursed herself for her clumsiness. She was out of practice. She had been about to say something else, but she checked herself and asked instead whether he wouldn't like a cup of tea. The unsaid words burned like a hot branch in her stomach.

'If you don't mind the children and the dough. And please do tell me your name.'

'Daniel Brown,' he said.

'Jude Hursten,' she said, putting out her floury hand. They shook hands, which seemed to Jude a little after the event by now, and the flour made Daniel's dark cuff cloudy. She noticed him brush it off and she noticed him smile.

The children had grown tired of kneading. Elsa was shaping little snakes and hearts, and Tom had made a battlefield, two dozen knobs of dough in pitched warfare. At first they didn't see Daniel, intent within their games. Not until Jude lifted the kettle onto the hob and asked Daniel whether he'd like to sit down. They looked up then, at the strange man in the kitchen.

'Is he Mister Ictharus?' Elsa asked.

Daniel raised one eyebrow at Elsa and she giggled. Jude laughed. 'This is Mr Brown,' she said. 'He's come to look at a photograph.'

Elsa nodded and went back to coiling snakes, but Tom watched as the strange man pulled out a chair, sat down. Tom looked at Jude, as if for

96

direction, and she shrugged, turned to find cups and jug.

'Why are you limping?' Tom said.

Daniel picked up a piece of dough. It gave beneath his fingers. He rolled it into a marble, placed it on the table before him.

'An old injury,' he said.

'In the war?'

'No.'

'So you weren't a soldier?'

'No, I was. But not in the Great War.'

'So you didn't know Jude?' Elsa said. 'Or Mister Ictharus?'

'Here, tea,' Jude said. This man had some mystery behind him, and she was intrigued. She put the cup down in front of Daniel and picked up the flour dredger, shook it into the bread tin. 'Tom, finish the game. If you knead the bits together and put them in the tin, your parents will never know they're eating a battlefield. And we can bake your hearts,' she said to Elsa. 'Maybe wrap the snakes around themselves, make coil buns?'

She sent the children out into the garden with biscuits and milk, then sat at the table. Her visitor had bitten nails, and a signet ring on his right hand. He was still rolling the lump of dough beneath a finger.

'You were in the war?' he said.

'I was a nurse. I took the photograph,' she said.

He didn't look up. Didn't lift his eyes from the dough.

'I'll have the negative somewhere,' she said. 'I

97

could probably find it and make you a print. I might remember more, too, if I saw it again myself.'

He didn't answer her at first, only drank the tea down like a man with a thirst. He didn't lift his eyes from the cup, wouldn't catch her glance. Jude looked down at the table, noticed a scurf of dough she'd missed with the cloth. If Leo were to return now, he'd be angry with her for asking this man in. She could imagine what he'd say to her, privately, not in front of anyone. He'd ask her if she'd thought of the danger. He'd remind her of the stories you heard, about war injuries and shell shock leaving men changed. Aggressive and violent in their moods where they used to be calm and gentle. He'd ask what if this stranger had attacked the children, or herself? And she wouldn't have anything to say in her defence, except that he reminded her of his friend, whom she'd loved.

'Could I have some more tea?'

Jude looked up at his voice.

'I seem to be parched,' he said.

★   ★   ★

Before Jude's return, the side shed was the place they stored the apples. They laid them out on the *Leeds Mercury* in September, a little air between each to prevent decay spreading, and the apples would last till the spring. When she was little, Leo used to tease her that those last, wizened apples, with their liver spots and dense, soft flesh, were really old people, enchanted by a wicked witch, so that even now, as an adult, she found it hard to eat them.

They'd picked apples in Belgium, too. Somehow, in that blasted place, the grass was still green beneath the two surviving apple trees. Kate found a wide basket, like a cradle. The apples were small red globes, not like the ones Jude knew from home. She sat down, leaned back on her hands. The grass was cool, scratchy. It held tiny wild blue flowers, not violets or speedwell, ones she didn't know.

'Get picking,' Kate called, and so Jude picked up an apple. It was rotten, and black, where she hadn't seen, with ants. Parting the grasses, she tracked them, a wavery, determined filament, to their hole, the earth bunkered up in grains around it. The ants processed in, tugging their particles of rotten apple, storing up their future.

Kate was in a tree, her weight making the branch creak. It was old, its bark hoary and knobbled, dappled green with lichens.

'Catch,' she said, but the apples were raining, so many small worlds coming down on Jude's head, and she scurried about, with none of the ants' steady composure, to gather them in.

The photograph Jude sent back home showed Kate standing in the sun, the basket at her feet piled with shiny fruit.

'They'd never guess,' she said.

The shed was Jude's darkroom now, and still beneath the chemicals she could often catch the mulching smell of old fruit, old vegetables. She'd promised Daniel Brown that she would do her best to find the negative that day and have a print ready by tomorrow, so after she watched his tilting figure off down the path, and without allowing herself to think about what she was agreeing to, she went there. She could hear the children far down the garden and through the trees she could see the flash of the swing rope.

★ ★ ★

On Jude's fourteenth birthday her father had given her a camera, a Leeds plate reflex camera. Not a point-and-shoot Box Brownie, which a few girls at school had, but a proper camera where you had to make the picture.

'We'd decided years ago it should be now,' he said. 'At this age.'

'Even before Mother was ill?' Jude said.

He nodded. 'Even before then.'

It came with instructions which she memorised that same day and which even years later she could recall verbatim. The camera had black bellows with chamfered corners, a twelve-plate plate-holder and a square back. The plateholder could go in either way: vertically for upright or horizontally for landscape pictures, and there were lines marked out on the viewfinder for both. Behind the lens there was a mirror at forty-five degrees, which reflected the view back on to the focusing screen so that when you looked through the viewfinder, the picture was the right way up.

Jude pressed her head in on her father's shoulder, the heat rising to her face, her eyes.

'Now it'll be a box in front of your face, and

not just your fingers,' her father said.

She couldn't trust herself to speak. So she lifted the camera up and looked down through the viewfinder. She didn't know how to use it, but that first movement was enough. She knew in her bones, in her arms and shoulders, in her neck curving down and her fingers braced with the weight, in the pressure of the darkness on her eye, that she needed this for herself.

Mr Hursten bought *Photography for Novices: The Primus Handbook* by Percy Lund and they followed his instructions to the letter to make a darkroom. They made a screen, edged with green baize and covered with canary and brown paper for the bathroom window, and a developing table to sit on the wash basin. A cylinder of canary paper placed over a candle was a darkroom light. Then there were dishes, trays and tanks, racks, scales and solutions, printing tray and papers, and a stool to sit on.

At first Jude lost more photographs than she made. She used too long an exposure and the image was fogged, or too short and the shadows had no detail, or her hands were too shaky, or she cut off the head, or the feet, or the tail of the dog. So she read up in *Photography for Novices* on how to prevent flare, or to avoid 'soot and whitewash' and sat on her stool into the small hours and brushed and immersed, soaked and blotted till the prints were hung, like smalls, to dry. And soon what she took was good, and something very different from the pleasing views, or well-balanced portraits, or harmonious landscapes that Mr Lund thought suitable.

She took people unawares. Her aunt's hands on the kitchen table, the skin loose with age and dusty with flour from bread-making. Her father, stripped to the waist, working in his garden, though it was his back that caught her eye, shiny with sweat, the muscles still ridged up like plough lines. Leo and his friend Richard playing chess, neither young man aware of the fifteen-year-old girl watching.

From her bedroom window she photographed the street below, the children playing out, as she and Leo were never allowed to do, their games between the gas lamps and the kerbs. The line of the rope in its high arc over a girl skipping; a boy after a ball, one leg stretched out, elbows wide for balance; a girl with a kitten, holding it high by the tail, its body twisting. She began to learn the geometry of captured lines. And she loved the alchemy of a world changed to black and white.

She found she could be invisible with her camera. She could be seeing, but not seen. Like an insect which impersonates its surroundings to fool predators, she could become the bark and leaf, the stick and the shade of the place, so that where before she had been timid, now she could be fearless. It was true, if she stood in the street for too long, people would start to ask her what she was up to, and little children would pester. But only for a moment, only till the adults checked their watch and hurried on; and the puppy, or the loose ball, or the muffin man, caught the children's eye, and then she'd be unnoticed again.

★ ★ ★

Daniel Brown was just a man asking about a photograph, Jude told herself. And all she was doing was making him a copy. It was generous of her, but nothing more. Anybody would have done it in her place. With the children's voices in her ears, still arguing over the swing, she went to open the darkroom door. A spider had spun its way across; the web was so fine it left no shadow in the sun, and no flies yet, or none that Jude could see. She thought at first that the spider was basking, but when she looked closer she saw that it was braced, legs tense. As she watched, it plucked at two spokes of web, waited a second, then turned and plucked the next two, waited, and turned again. It had made almost a complete circuit and she could see no flies caught yet to shiver at its tug, but on the sixth, the spider knew otherwise. It plucked again at the web and then, too quick for Jude's eyes, it pounced.

The fly was a small one, its agitation barely visible, but the *coup de grâce* was performed with the aplomb you might expect for something more resplendent, a bluebottle or a bee. The fly was trussed and dragged to one side, tight into the joint of the door. Jude watched it all through, no corners cut by the spider in securing its dinner, before she opened the door, broke up the spider's pattern.

4

Daniel returned to the house the next morning. He rang on the bell and this time a tall, big-boned man came to the door, stooping as if trying to be smaller. He put out his hand.

'Leo Hursten,' he said. 'I know who you are. It's been explained,' and he ushered Daniel in.

There was the smell of roasting meat, and he could hear a child's voice somewhere chanting a rhyme.

'If you could wait a moment,' Leo said, leaving Daniel in the hall.

The child's rhyme came closer. On the wall there were prints of Fountains Abbey and York Minster. The day before, at a loose end after his visit to the house, he'd taken a train to the moors and walked across the heather, found a stream and dipped his feet as he used to as a boy. So that today, after all that walking, his leg was very sore and he leaned heavily on his stick.

When the child appeared — he couldn't remember her name — she stopped her singing and looked hard at him, his stick, the angle he was leaning at.

'Why don't you sit on the chair?' she said, and when he had sat down, she nodded, like a job well done, resumed her rhyme and went on her way.

He heard doors open and close, felt the brush of a draught against his trousers, and Jude appeared. She walked into the room as though it were the place above all she needed to be. She wore a blue print cotton dress that caught and drifted at her hips, and the dark curls of her hair were loose, corkscrewing to her shoulders. She flicked it from her face in a way that reminded him of a horse flicking its tail, something habitual and yet graceful. She was holding two envelopes.

'I've made your print,' she said without preamble. 'It's a good one.'

They sat in silence at the dining-room table with the photograph between them and Daniel wondered how to ask the questions in his mind.

'It is the one you were looking for?' she said.

He nodded. 'Yes.'

'And you know one of the men?'

'Yes. I know one. And the other, I think I've seen the other man, too.'

'Is he still alive? The one you know?'

Daniel shook his head. 'But he didn't die in the war. Not there.'

'And the woman? Do you recognise her?'

Daniel shook his head again. 'She's a nurse?' he said, a little unsure, because she wore no uniform.

Jude's questions had come thick and fast to here. She wasn't aggressive, but she wasted no time. Now she stopped, brought up short by Daniel's query. He recognised the look in her eyes and he waited.

Finally Jude nodded. 'I knew her very well.'

Daniel shifted in his chair. He leaned back and looked around the room. Strange, that his visit to the exhibition should have brought him here, to Yorkshire, to this room in a house in a place he didn't know. To this woman who was beautiful, but who either didn't know or had forgotten it. The room was hot, and he took off his jacket, pulled up his sleeves till the cufflinks were taut.

'So,' he said. 'Can I ask you? I know it's a few years back, and the war was its own time, but . . . '

Jude made no answer immediately. Daniel shut his eyes. He hadn't slept well the previous night and he felt bone-tired. It was a wild goose chase, this. Probably he should put away his boldness, take his leave and go back home.

When Jude started speaking, he thought at first she was talking about the children.

'They'd been playing on the see-saw earlier that same day, those two,' she said.

He opened his eyes, looked at her. She was still staring at the photograph.

'The see-saw?'

'We'd put it up beyond the house, on a bit of clearer ground. Peter's doing. He'd used a long, long plank, so you could go very high, and cobbled two saw-horses he'd come across. It was madness really, except no one ever did get hurt. Bruises, but nothing else. The newspapers wouldn't publish my photographs of the see-saw. It gave the wrong impression, they said. Leo sent them out to several. The Germans had a game with us sometimes, taking pot-shots at the man at the top. That's how close to the front line we were.

'So these two and a couple of others had been

trying to bounce each other off. They had a fine game, and then it was back to the trenches, and later on it was the one brought the other in wounded. He was leaning for Pisa and his blood all over the other's uniform. He had caught some shrapnel in the stomach, the worst place, been stuck in no man's land a while. So we took it out and dressed the wound. And he kept on about the officer rescuing him and could we rinse his tunic.'

'Colonel Whittam,' Daniel said. 'He was the man injured. Except he wasn't a colonel then. So did you take the photograph that day?'

'The next, I'd guess. The fellow, Whittam, looks too perky, and he wouldn't have been good for much the same day.'

'Did you find out how he was rescued?' Daniel leaned forward over the photograph as if to see inside.

Jude pushed her chair out and walked to the window. Daniel looked at her. He tried to remember how she had looked the day before, but all he could conjure were her hands covered in flour, and an apron. And her hair. Those tight black curls.

'What exactly do you want?' She was up close to the window and her voice was muffled by the glass, so that Daniel couldn't tell her tone. 'I don't know what I think about you,' she said. 'Or only that it's strange, having you in my home when I know next to nothing about you. Or even why you're here. I didn't know quite what to say to my brother and his wife last night. And there are the children. It's not as if you're asking for something easy, is it?'

She turned from the window and looked at him, one hand in her hair as if wrestling with the dark mass of curls. He looked down at his knees. He didn't know how to answer her.

'Ha!' She was grinning now. 'There's a speech for you,' she said.

'You're right,' Daniel said. 'A strange man with a strange request. I might have done anything.'

'You might,' Jude said, 'though it wasn't that that was bothering me.'

'But you don't know. You can't tell from the outside what somebody might be. I know now the thing that I was dreading, the worst thing of all. That they knew each other, were even friends.'

Jude laughed. 'There's a problem with friendship? Anyway, I'm not about to start thinking you're a murderer or a kidnapper, if that's what you mean.'

'I should go,' Daniel said. 'Go back home and leave you be.' Jude looked at him nonplussed as he started to get to his feet. 'You've been very generous. Before I leave, could I buy . . . ' and he nodded in the direction of the photograph.

'I didn't mean the conversation to take such a turn,' she said. 'I was only asking to know a little more about you. And you can't buy it, though I will give it to you.'

'Is that what you do?' he said. 'For a living?'

'I'm a typist,' she said.

'A typist by day, and . . . '

'What?'

'And in the war? What kind of a nurse were you, to be so close to the front line, and the see-saw?'

'We set up a first-aid station.'

'Who?'

'Me, and another nurse. Kate.'

'Is she a typist now, too?' Daniel's tone was facetious.

'No.'

Daniel paused before speaking again.

'You shouldn't be tapping keys all day. Not when you can take photographs like that.'

Jude put the photograph and the clipping back in their envelope. Then she opened a cigarette box, offered it to Daniel, who shook his head. 'No manners,' she said. 'I haven't even offered you a glass of sherry. Nearly noon on a Sunday.' She lit a cigarette and drew deeply.

Jude held the cigarette loosely. She'd smoked only half of it and Daniel watched the glow travel up towards her fingers.

'But you must explain more,' she said, 'if you don't leave.'

He wondered if the little girl had been listening at the door, to knock at this moment.

'Mummy wants to know, will your visitor be staying for lunch?'

'Thank you, Elsa,' Jude said. She turned to Daniel. 'Will you?'

* ★ ★

Jude had no appetite for lunch and she watched the conversation around the table as if from another room, the voices — Leo's, Daniel's, Sally's — sounding far away and unconnected. Her mind was snagged somewhere in the photograph, caught on something, and she couldn't pull it free. From a distance she watched Leo carve the joint and count out the potatoes. He had the same way of doing these things as she did, she knew this without thinking. Steadying his feet and dipping his head as if to block out the world while carving, just as she had done over the live bodies jolted down into her cellar. To focus so that nothing else existed. Whereas this stranger at their dinner-table with his eyes that never rested, she would guess that his glance always went wide. He was talking with Sally now. She was questioning him. Safe questions: Where did he come from? Did he like the suburbs? Had he any brothers or sisters?

She watched him as he ate. One hand was tucked below the table, but the other, his left, had escaped and fidgeted with his fork, turning and turning it. She could see the muscles in his forearm shift, like lines of current in the sea. He had a high brow, the hair drawing back already, and more on one side than the other. That would impress Leo, she thought, who had a theory she didn't believe in about intelligence and the size of your forehead.

'Jude, please, would you mind?' Leo was handing her a spoon. 'Make sure you give them both plenty of beans.'

'And what do you do for a living?' she heard Sally asking bluntly, and his pause.

'He's a soldier,' Elsa said. 'It's why he's got the stick.'

Tom put his hand to his forehead. 'Stupid, the stick's why he's not a soldier.'

'Don't call Elsa stupid,' Sally said. 'And eat your beans.'

Jude noticed Daniel's small smile.

'They're delicious beans,' he said.

'They're Father's,' Tom said, and now Elsa rolled her eyes.

'They're not his. They don't belong to him.'

'He knows what I mean,' Tom said.

Jude heard Sally's voice grow stern, noticed Leo's brow, watched Daniel's polite ignoring of the family argument. She saw her plate of food, the meat and potatoes, the slight skim on the cooling gravy, the sliced beans. She saw the shape of her lip where the sunlight struck through her glass, the smear on her knife from the meat. She didn't want to be in the house, in amongst the family, any longer, and she thought that she would go somewhere after lunch where the light was sharp, somewhere which belonged to no one.

'I'm going to take Daniel up to the Rocks after lunch,' she said. 'He'd like to see them.' She looked at Daniel. 'You'll be all right, in the sidecar? Being tall, I mean?'

'Fine, yes.' His face was bemused, but he didn't ask anything.

'Can't we come too?' Elsa's voice was shrill. 'Daddy? Can't we go too? You could take us in the motor car?'

'Not today,' Leo said.

111

'But please. I want to show him the hermit cave.'

Leo shook his head and Elsa hunched over her plate and scowled. Jude wished the meal were over. Tom was lining up the food around his plate. She set her eyes on the far wall.

'Tom, please eat your beans.' Sally's voice was fiercer than the beans warranted. Tom put some in his mouth. He sat suddenly straight and tapped Daniel on the shoulder.

'And the leaping rock,' he said, his mouth a mash of green. 'Did she tell you about the leaping rock?'

'Tom, please,' Jude said.

'Did she tell you?'

'It wouldn't be something he could do,' Jude said.

'It's in her box of pictures,' Tom said. 'A man leaping from it.'

'Barely more than a boy,' Jude said quietly.

'But he died in the war,' Elsa said, cutting vainly at her meat.

'Mr Icarus?' Daniel said, but he didn't look at Jude, and he didn't ask her to explain.

★　★　★

It had only been at the last minute that Leo couldn't come too. Some business at home, he told Jude, and she and Richard should go on anyway, he'd squared it with Father. She was disappointed, but relieved, because she had something in mind that she wanted and she couldn't bear to wait for longer to try to achieve

112

it. So she groaned for him, and felt glad for once to be a girl, whom business never detained. And it was only later she saw that it must have had to do with their father's last illness. That he would have known by then, though he hadn't told his son. So she had packed her picnic and her camera bag and gone to meet Richard.

'Leo can't come,' she said. 'So it's just me, unchaperoned, and my camera.'

'Of course, your camera,' Richard said.

They had taken the train as far as they could, and then walked. High cloud flattened the light. The landscape seemed subdued, suspended, as if the fields and the hedgerows were waiting for something to bring them to life. The camera bag was heavy and the strap cut into Jude's shoulder. On the train, seated beside one another, their hands on their laps, they had talked of anything. Of the *Titanic* and Home Rule for Ireland and votes for women. About war with Germany and Scott reaching the South Pole. But now, on the empty road, walking into the moors, everything seemed used up and so Jude was silent, at a loss, and Richard whistled a tune she didn't know.

They were nearly to the Rocks before either of them spoke. Jude glimpsed them through a break in the hedge a half mile ahead.

'So what's it to be this time?' Richard said. He had cut some grass from the hedgerow and now he draped it over his head. 'I'd be very fetching as a girl,' and he posed so that Jude couldn't help herself but laugh.

'A pity Leo won't let you take him,' he said. 'He hasn't given in?'

She shook her head.

'He was cross when he saw I'd shot him unawares.'

'So you'll have to make do with me. I'm glad I'm useful for something. Thank God I can strike such good poses,' and he affected to walk a tightrope before dropping the picnic basket and turning a cartwheel into the ditch, his body seeming to be all angles, elbows and knees, yet oddly graceful.

Jude laughed. 'I want to take you in flight,' she said. 'That's why Leo suggested the Rocks.'

'In flight?'

'Leaping. Close as we can get.'

He flapped his arms. 'No wings. So I'll be falling.'

'It depends,' Jude said. 'Whether you think you're falling as soon as you leave the ground. Even at the moment you're jumping up.'

'Like dying, then,' he said. Jude looked at him. 'As soon as we're born, we're on our way to it,' and he grinned, as if to disarm her, then set off striding on.

Later Jude wondered how it was that somebody who was just one part of your landscape could, so suddenly, fill the centre of your eye. She stood absolutely still on the road and, as though her gaze might consume him, she looked away from Richard's back, and down. An ant pulled an ear of grass over a twig and a moth paid homage to the ground, its yellow wings spread like a favour. Jude closed her eyes. The feeling in her chest was more like a fury than a pleasure and she clenched her fists, then followed after the slender form of the man she would have fly.

Four times Richard leapt, his feet bare, his shirt pressed tight to his chest in the wind, and Jude photographed him, his body high above the rocks. Each leap, he seemed balanced in air and there was time enough and more. But when Jude developed the negatives that night, setting the four plates to drain in the rack, she saw that she had caught him only once. She made the print, then knocked on her brother's door.

'Look,' she said, handing him the print, and Leo looked at the figure, no arms, no head, who seemed to be leaping at the sun. She watched him and saw that she had told more than she meant to of her feelings.

'Like Icarus,' he said. 'Be careful, Jude.'

* * *

Jude gave Daniel a pair of goggles and one of Leo's old sweaters, slipped her bag down by his feet and fitted the tarpaulin over him. He was embarrassed, she knew, by the intimacy this demanded, her fingers tugging the loops over the hooks beside his hips, her breath close to his face.

'It can be cold in that sidecar, even on a day like this,' she said. 'Especially with a strong wind.'

'Do you often do this with strangers?' Daniel said.

'I usually ask them to be wounded first,' she said with a laugh.

115

Away from the town, and even with the wind, the landscape looked slick with heat. Cattle swam in the grass and the sky was bleached of colour. The rocks were an island rising high above them until, at the last, the road dipped its head before turning and climbing to reach them.

Jude knew from Daniel's face, when he took off his goggles, that the ride had left him free, as it had her. She unhooked the tarpaulin, folded it to carry, and offered him an arm for climbing out.

'I used to feel like this, riding a horse,' he said.

'We can walk round to the top,' she said. 'There's a stile.'

Daniel nodded, and she wondered what it was she hoping for, bringing him here. They walked slowly round the lower rocks and Jude pointed out 'The Eagle' and 'The Camel', 'The Dancing Bear' and 'The Yoked Man'. They passed the rock she had stood below that day, waiting, with her camera ready, for the figure leaping at the sun. But she didn't name it to Daniel.

The wind was loud and warm around them, and the tossing air smelt of gorse and honeysuckle.

'There was a place in Ireland that I loved, made me feel like this,' he said. 'They were high up on their hill. Three stones only, and man-made, but ancient. You could feel apart, standing there beside them.'

'I saw a kite here,' she said.

'A red kite?'

'Thought it was a buzzard, that 'wheeo' sound. But when I looked up, there it was. That forked tail. It was a day like today, and I watched it swing across the wind.'

She saw that he was flagging, leaning harder on the stick, studying the craggy ground carefully at each step.

'The other side of that rock,' she said. 'Tom's hermit cave.'

The ground was worn to dust, littered with sheep droppings. Jude spread the tarpaulin and Daniel sat down heavily, one leg out straight before him, the other bent up, and he looked out at the hill rising behind, the bent trees, the straggle of sheep, the gorse's sweet yellow. His fingers found a small smooth stone in the dust, and without even looking at it, he slipped it into his pocket. Jude squatted the other side, her boots flurrying the dust into heaps and troughs for a moment. She looked across at Daniel, this stranger she'd brought up here.

'That photo,' she said. 'What are you after?'

Daniel had moved barely a muscle, only his eyes blinking in the wind. She licked her finger, dipped it in the dust, a smooth grey oval, rubbed it away and settled down to wait. She didn't look across at him, but set her eyes to the hill. A flurry of little birds worried the gorse away in the middle distance, the size of sparrows, though they weren't. This time tomorrow she'd be at a typewriter in that high-up room, typing away as if her life depended on it, taking her lunch in a tea-shop with the other girls, boiled egg, treacle roll, scrubbing the ink from her fingers at night. That's something Sally wouldn't believe, what a dirty job it is, being a typist. Somewhere,

117

thunder rolled and she noticed that the wind had dropped.

'We weren't allowed secrets when we were small.' Daniel's voice was quiet and steady. Jude looked over to him. Although she knew he was speaking to her, it was as though he were speaking to himself, his eyes focused on the grey rock. She waited for him to go on.

'It wasn't done. Mother told us that very clearly. Not if you were a little boy. And to be caught with one, it was worse than being caught with your hand in the biscuit barrel.'

'But I'm not your mother,' Jude said. 'And anyway the biscuit barrel loses its gleam once you grow up.' She stood up. 'I'm not leaving, it's only my feet are going numb.'

He smiled and looked down at his leg stretched before him, rubbed it absent-mindedly. She hoped he wouldn't go on with the childhood memory because she didn't feel very patient.

'All right,' he said, and now his voice was resolute, as if he'd come to a decision, and he looked straight across at Jude. 'I don't know what I know.'

The air hung very heavy and the clouds were banked high and rimmed with coarse purple. The sheep had gathered themselves into a corner and the air seemed suddenly full of tiny, haranguing flies. Jude shook out a cigarette packet, offered it across. Daniel shook his head.

'Against the bugs,' she said, lighting up.

'Ireland wasn't like the trenches. You never knew who the enemy was,' Daniel said. 'Or

118

where. It was all hell let loose but you couldn't see it.'

'And Colonel Whittam?' Jude said.

'He was my commanding officer. He'd had a good war, though it didn't count for much over there. Maybe made things harder, though he was very clear to us. We were to obey orders, stick together, and let the politicians do the thinking. If we did that, we'd be doing nothing wrong, clean consciences. But it wasn't true. The men who thought it was important for the cause, what we did, maybe they've had a better time with it. But those things you do, the dirty things, they come out of you, but they still stay inside. And they're in no cause, that's what's terrible, and afterwards all you can do is hide. Maybe that's what I've been doing.'

'You wouldn't be the only one,' Jude said.

Daniel looked at her. She had her head turned away. He rubbed his face. She was such a mix to him already with this reluctant vulnerability and her fierce directness.

'And the day I was injured, there's a thing that still troubles me, but it's the other fellow, the standing one. There's something about him. Though if I look at him full on, then it goes.'

'Where were you then?' Jude's voice was quiet, low.

'Cork. County Cork. For a year, just over, back before the Truce.'

'I don't know a lot about Ireland,' Jude said. 'But it didn't sound like an easy war to be fighting.'

'No.'

Jude turned and looked at him. He was defiant now, as though she'd said something to attack him, but his face, his cheeks and his eyes, looked hollowed out, emptied of something. She looked at her cigarette. She could draw one more lungful, and she shut her eyes, breathed in deep, felt her lungs fill with smoke. Sometimes she wanted to go back inside her old shell, become a snail again and look at the world from a distance, her eyes outside her.

'It was a bloody horror,' he said, 'and nobody over here knows a thing or gives a damn. And so far nor do I, except in my dreams.' He shifted his leg. 'Which is maybe just as well.'

Jude wondered what it was he knew in his dreams that he couldn't know when he was awake. She wondered whether Richard had had dreams like that. She flicked her cigarette butt into the dust.

'And now you've come all this way north to look out of the corner of your eye?' she said. 'You don't do that just because somebody looks familiar.'

She saw him pause and then decide something before he replied. She could see it in his face and the thought went through her head that she was noticing a great deal about someone she'd only met the day before.

'It's funny,' Daniel said. 'We used to call him 'The Trout', Colonel Whittam. Not to his face, but he knew it anyway. Partly it was because of his fishing, and partly his face. And now I'm on his hook and I can't get free.'

Jude knew then that he wasn't going to tell

120

her. She didn't know what, only that he'd come to a decision and was giving her the easy story. She'd heard plenty of men doing that. It was a necessary part, an awkward part, of surviving. And if he wasn't telling her, she would do the same. She knew more than she would say to him about those two men.

The rain had started, coming straight down, steady, putting a veil beyond the rocks. Daniel looked out from inside their cave. The world beyond had gone dim.

'I came up here on a whim, I suppose,' he went on. 'Hoped that if I found the photographer, they'd remember something. Anyway, it's been a good excuse to get away from home.'

'Were you injured over there?'

'Motor lorry accident in the fog,' he said, too quickly she thought. 'Bloody Crossley! Invalided out, thank God.' Then he laughed.

'What is it?' Jude said.

'Actually, it wasn't an accident,' he said. 'It's just what I've always said. Got used to saying. Had to at first, and then it was just easier. A bit ignominious, if you're a soldier, but easier.'

Jude waited.

'It was an ambush. First time I've told anyone.'

'Even your family?'

He nodded. 'We were ambushed, and I was the only one, nearly, who came out alive. They left me for dead and they'd have hunted me down if they'd known I wasn't.'

'But not any more?'

'No. They've got better things to do over there

now. But the letter that arrived nearly did for my mother. She thought it was to say I'd been killed. Couldn't open it, left it in the hall all day till my father came home. It's all she expects, all she's waiting for, since Johnnie died.'

'Johnnie?'

'My brother.'

'He was killed in the war?' Jude said, and Daniel nodded.

'So what will you do now?' she said.

He shrugged. 'Go home. And die for lack of air.' He laughed. 'I've got a bit of work to do for my father. And I'll get a train south on Tuesday.'

'A wild goose chase.'

'Dead end.'

She drove him back to The Green Man. He took off Leo's sweater.

'I'll send you my address,' he said, 'in case.'

Unsure how to take their leave, they shook hands on the pavement. Jude took an envelope from her bag.

'The photograph,' she said, giving it to him. And not knowing how to tell him that she'd known men like him, that she knew things went wrong in war, not knowing how to say that it wasn't something she usually did, taking men up to the Rocks, showing them photographs like that, not knowing what to do with the urge she felt to put a hand to his face, or his hair, to stand near to him and feel the length of his body against hers, not knowing what to do with the thought that she liked this man powerfully and the wounds and scar-tissue did nothing to diminish this, not knowing what else to do, she

122

climbed back onto the motorcycle and was gone.

In the weeks that followed, nothing seemed to happen to Jude. Daniel sent his address, as promised, and his thanks. He made no mention of any photograph. It was a dull, formal note. He might more likely have been thanking her for her contribution to some charity drive, she thought, than for the time they'd spent, but she put the letter away carefully in a drawer in her room, pushing it back into its envelope, tucking it in under her writing paper. It seemed unlikely she would ever have reason to contact him again and the thought made her feel hopeless in her life.

The weather remained quite warm and she was exercised by the difficulty of not appearing at work with sweat rings under her arms. A girl had been dismissed the previous year for this. She had begun to take more dictation, now they had found out about her French, and this made the job slightly less irksome. But still, if she stopped long enough to think, she couldn't believe that this was what she was doing.

At home she fended off the questions about Daniel, which wasn't hard since nothing had gone on, but still they made her very cross. It was an odd mission he'd been on, she told them, she couldn't help him further, and he'd gone home to his life in London. That was all there was to it. And having sent Tom off with a flea in his ear, made Elsa cry and snubbed Sally and Leo into silence over dinner, Jude thought that surely there would be an end to it. She even told herself that it was all no more than a curious quirk, a brief postscript to her war time.

Whatever it was that had brought Daniel Brown to find her, she knew it was something grave, even if he was telling her the truth and didn't yet know what it was himself. She knew the sound of it, recognised it. Richard's last letter had had something of the same quality. He had shot unarmed men, prisoners of war, men whose arms had been raised in surrender. He'd been under orders, he should have disobeyed and now he must live with it. But then he had died on the wire and she would never know how he might have lived with it, or how she might have done.

It wasn't just natural curiosity that made her hope she'd see Daniel again. Nor, oddly, was it only that she liked him, or pitied him. She had been let off the hook, spared something with Richard's death, despite her grief, and she didn't want to be. She didn't know what had happened to Daniel, or how far he had gone beyond the bounds of war. But she wished, whatever it was that had gone on, that he would break the silence.

5

Some weeks went by and Jude's life settled again. It was Friday evening and she was going out. Elsa sat on the bed, swinging her heels. Jude sat beside her in her slip, unpinned her hair and started to brush it out. It spat and crackled.

'Can I do it?' Elsa said.

'If you're gentle.' Jude gave her the brush. With one hand on Jude's head, Elsa began to brush. Jude shut her eyes. It was an age since anyone else had done this for her.

'Who is he?' Elsa said.

'Martin Dawes. You've seen him before.'

'Is he your boyfriend? Will you marry him?'

'Elsa, for goodness' sake.'

'Does Daddy know him?'

'I've known him since I was five and we played tea-parties together on the lawn.'

'Did Daddy play too?'

'No. He broke up the party. And we went crying to our mothers and Leo got told off.'

'Is he coming here to get you? Will I see him?'

Jude wagged a finger. 'Don't mention the tea-party.'

Elsa giggled. 'What if I do? What if I say it to him when he comes in?'

'Then I'll do the same to you when you have a boyfriend.'

'So he *is* a boyfriend.'

'No. He's not.'

'He's Mr Ictharus's brother, isn't he?' Elsa said.

Jude turned towards Elsa, so that the brush caught at the fine hair on her nape.

'Ouch!'

'You moved. Anyway Mummy told us. She said he was very kind.'

'What exactly did she . . . ' Jude said, then checked herself. 'Will you fetch the pins? On the shelf.'

Elsa had arranged Jude's clothes on the bed. Blouse with its arms out, skirt, stockings stretched like snake skins, wrap over the shoulders, paste-pearl necklace over the hollow of the neck, earrings each side of the pillow, shoes like clown's feet at the bottom.

'Now you can climb inside,' she said. 'Like a ghost, putting on a body.'

'Thank you,' Jude said, amused, disconcerted.

'Are they real pearls?'

'No. Paste. But pretty still.'

'Don't the earrings hurt, clipping on?' she said.

'Try them.'

Jude laughed as the little girl attached the first, wincing, solemn-faced.

'Pretty,' Jude said. 'Look in the mirror.'

The second earring tumbled from the bed and rolled underneath.

'I'll get it,' Elsa said.

She came out swimming, dust balls gathered in her hair like weed. She had the lost earring in one hand and something square and tarnished in the other.

'Look!' Elsa's voice was breathless. 'Buried treasure. What is it?'

'Let me see,' Jude said, stepping towards her. Elsa held her hand tight round the object and Jude smiled at the little girl's conflict, the right of possession at war with her curiosity.

'If you'll let me see, then maybe I can tell you.'

Elsa put the object down on the table. She rubbed at it, solicitous, and wiped the blackened finger on her dress.

'So?' she said, peremptory, and Jude stepped over to the table.

Where Elsa had rubbed, the metal gleamed and the beginnings of a pattern showed through. Jude looked and felt a small punch to her stomach. She picked it up and rubbed at the tarnish.

'You'll have your hand mucky for going out,' Elsa said, disapproving.

'Do you see now what it is?'

Elsa shook her head. Jude flipped open the lid.

'Oh!' Disappointment had winded the little girl. 'It's not gold then.'

'No. It's a . . . '

'I know. It's a cigarette lighter.' Elsa walked to the door.

'What about my clothes?'

'I'm bored. I'm going in the garden.'

'Leave me my earring then,' Jude said.

Zig-zags cut across one side of the tarnished brass, and there was a date, 1916. She turned it over, and on the other side were two clasping hands and a four-leafed clover.

'I know you,' Jude said, turning the lighter in

127

her hand. 'And I'd forgotten you.'

So many men had made these things, she'd seen dozens of them: lighters and vases, cigarette cases, ashtrays. Peter had made a paper knife out of a piece of shrapnel and a lighter from German belt buckles, '*Gott Mit Uns*' carved around the edge, and he'd taken home a dinner gong made out of a howitzer shell, though Jude couldn't imagine him using it in the little flat he'd described. But this lighter had been Kate's first, a gift from a wounded soldier, carved from a shell casing.

She should be dressing. She should be making her face up ready for the evening, preparing to smile, to be grateful.

Jude flipped it open and struck the flint, felt its soft grind. Kate didn't smoke, but she'd always carried a lighter for the men's cigarettes. Jude smiled. There had been a way Kate had of reaching forward with it, eyes almost averted, as if she were embarrassed at being brought so close to another person's mouth. And then she'd shut it off too soon, before the cigarette was lit, and have to start again.

'Don't whip it away so fast,' Jude told her. 'Let them get a proper drag.'

'I keep forgetting.'

'So take up smoking,' Jude said. 'Then you'd get the hang of it.'

'I don't like the smell.'

'It's better than most of the smells here.'

'But you don't stick them in your mouth and suck,' Kate said.

So Jude had had her practise. She'd lean

across from her camp bed, cigarette between her lips, leering, and Kate, face set, stern, would try to hold the lighter steady, try not to jerk it away as Jude's face loomed in closer.

Jude stood the lighter on the table. 'Let's see if you still work,' she said, and found her lighter fluid, refilled the tank. She struck the flint again and the spark caught, almost transparent in the early evening sun. Turning her back to the sunlight, she cupped her hand around it and watched the steady flame.

She put the lighter in her bag. Checking her face in the glass, she went downstairs. Martin Dawes was waiting, smoking a cigarette with Leo in the garden. The evening was warm and both men were in shirtsleeves. Jude thought how solid Martin looked, how confidently he stood there, feet planted apart, one hand in a pocket, tipping the ash onto the lawn.

Martin offered Jude a cigarette, lit it for her, and she kissed him on the cheek, and remembered that he wore the same eau de Cologne as his brother used to, and then remembered, blushing, how his brother's cheek felt.

The men talked on for a few minutes, trading local business news, opinions on house building schemes. Jude watched Martin scuff up the gravel with his toe, brush the dust from his shoe. He had been kind to her after Richard died, Sally was right to tell Elsa that. The two brothers had gone to the war together and only he had come back. She'd never told him about Richard's last letter to her.

But it wasn't kindness that she wanted. When he turned to her, she smiled and nodded.

'We must go, or we'll miss the start of the picture,' she said.

'What is it?' Leo said.

Martin shrugged. 'What are we going to see, Jude?'

'*Safety Last*. A Harold Lloyd picture.'

'Enjoy yourselves,' Leo said, and waved them off as if they were going on a journey rather than a date.

The difficulty started at the cinema. They'd been to films before, sat side by side, knees together, hands in laps, only the accidental brush of an elbow or the passing of the chocolates to connect them, and Jude had been quite content with it. She hadn't minded the courting couples on either side, the shifting and shuffling, the rustle of petticoats as hands reached over the arm-rest and under the skirt; the heads caught kissing in the glow of the film romance. But tonight she did mind, though she couldn't have said why, and she was twitchy, uncomfortable in her seat.

'Do you want to leave?' Martin put his hand over hers on the arm-rest.

She shook her head and took her hand away.

'I hate leaving the pictures early.'

So they stayed till Harold Lloyd was down on the ground again and had Mildred Davis in his arms, then Jude was up and out, before the lovers around them surfaced.

'Where'd you get it?' They were at a corner table in Giacomelli's. Jude would have liked to go somewhere bigger, noisier, somewhere more impersonal, but it hadn't been up to her. Martin reached across the table for the lighter. He flicked it on, the flame lighting up his fingers. And off, and on, and off. 'Somebody else taking you out to the pictures? Man from the office, maybe?'

'You'll use up the fluid. I don't think there's that much in it.'

He turned it over in his hand. 'Not a bad piece of work. Though I did see better when I was over there. This one, it looks like it was done by an amateur.'

'I don't know who made it. Let's choose some food.' Jude put her hand out for the lighter.

Martin opened his menu.

'Rack of lamb for me, and why don't you have the sole,' he said and he flicked her menu shut and turned, his fingers raised, to catch a waitress.

'Martin,' Jude said, and he didn't answer, but perhaps he didn't hear her with his head turned.

'Martin,' she said, louder. 'I haven't chosen my food yet.' She opened the menu again. 'Give me back my lighter.'

He turned back to the table and, looking hard at Jude, put his hand out, palm flat. Jude took the lighter, put it on the table, and looked back at him.

'What's possessed you?' she said.

'You loved my brother,' he said, 'but it was me who came back.'

'And so?'

'And so maybe . . . ' He tapped a finger on the table. 'I lost him too.'

'I know, Martin. I know it isn't only me. I'm sorry. I don't mean to sound as if . . . '

'So cut me a bit of slack, then. I know I'm not the same as Richard, but you could do a lot worse, so maybe . . . '

'I'll have the steak,' she said.

'You might love me instead,' he said. 'Perhaps we could comfort each other, that way,' and then he asked again, but quietly, as if to distract her from these words, 'Who gave you the lighter?'

'It wasn't Richard,' Jude said.

'I know it wasn't Richard. He couldn't carve his name on a tree, let alone . . . But your mind's elsewhere. You haven't been with me all evening.'

'We're friends, Martin. But I'm not in love with you, and even if I were, I wouldn't want you choosing my food.'

'And the lighter?'

'Kate's.'

Martin's face looked heavy in the shadows of the restaurant's half-light, his mouth dragged down, his eyes dull, though Jude couldn't tell if it was with mistrust or disappointment. He didn't look angry now, thank God, but she didn't know how to fend off his dismay. The waitress came with drinks and took their order.

'I was watching gulls and picking up pebbles.'

'You were what?'

'When she got gassed. I was on a beach. Photos to prove it. Seagulls like army majors, strutting on the tide line. Pebbles in the sand. I brought one back for Kate.'

'Why were you on a beach?'

Jude gave a sharp laugh. 'It was a gift. Kate

made me a bet for my birthday, that she could fix the visit. 'A bit of sea air,' she said. So there I was breathing the sea breeze when there she was gasping for her breath.'

'You need a cigarette,' Martin said, holding out his packet. He reached over for the lighter, held out the steady flame.

But Jude, drawing fiercely on the cigarette, no longer saw him, or the restaurant.

★   ★   ★

Jude had been awake since the dawn. No need to be up early, it was a Sunday, but the routine was dug in too deep. She'd been staring at the cracks, a left-over habit.

The room they had had, she and Kate, had been on the first floor. Not as safe as the cellar, but that was always full of wounded men. Although they had sandbagged the house and stuck a large white cross onto the roof, it had been shell-damaged before they ever arrived and when the barrage began each dusk, the shells came very close. So they had put strips of brown paper over the worst of the cracks and each morning they would check to see if the paper had torn. It was a bit of a genteel farce, as Kate called it. Because there was nowhere better to go, and even if you could drive a coach and four through the cracks, they'd still very likely be sleeping in there.

The cracks on Jude's attic ceiling now didn't change. The three that made the boat, high-prowed, straight line for mast. And the sail, a stain where a tile had fallen two winters past and the rain had come through.

Jude could reach her boots with one hand, tied to the bedstead behind her head. Even up here, even these years later, she didn't trust them on the floor. Too many men had lost their heads with no boots on.

Over there she had been living so close to the front line, they had called her skywatcher and given her the duties of it: a pair of Zeiss binoculars and a field telephone to mark out the progress of their planes. Up here in the attic was a square of blue. A safe sky, a cut-out square, no elbow-room any more for playful gods. There were only swifts this high up, their crazy shrieking, their mad speed. They made her gut tumble sometimes, they cut so close, but they never hit and they never fell, and she loved them for that.

She went downstairs quickly, in twos, then the three around the corner and a final two and two and one. Round the landing, listening for the family's sleeping sounds, and down again.

In the kitchen, the stove was warm still. She fed it, lifted on the kettle, squatted close, lit a cigarette and watched the steady stumble of the glow. The dog knew not to shift. Only let his tail bang twice on his basket and watched her with one eye. She walked across to the pantry, unlatched the door with its diamond peepholes. Such dull gleams inside. Such cool. No colours to surprise. Jars of Leo's jam and chutney, pickled onions lined the higher shelves, the marble slab so cold under her palm, it sent a chill along her arm. It kept the meat nice, kept the blood sweet, too.

Remembering was a strange affair. Jude made it a habit not to linger any more, but so much was inadvertent. She couldn't help it when her ears or fingers found echoes. Rummaging amongst the tins and packets, she found the bag of coffee beans and closed the pantry door. In Belgium they kept the coffee in the meat safe that Peter had devised. And in the winter months, they found a spot for it outside. She'd keep it in the refrigerator now, but Sally said it took up too much space. She spooned the beans into the coffee mill and turned the handle. The smell rose like a dream. Scooping the ground coffee into a small jug, she lifted the kettle from the hob and waited till it was off the boil before pouring the water in, just enough to cover the grounds. She found the strainer and a small cup, adding two spoons of sugar. Then she sat, head sunk over the cup, and breathed deep.

Once Jude had had a pile of different futures planned: scientist, photographer, aviator, explorer, journalist, doctor — she wasn't sure which would suit her best, and she'd talk them over with her friends on the train home from school, her mind alive with possibilities, her fourteen-year-old determination like a willow branch, green and pliable, whippy and strong. Nowadays, when she saw girls dressed in that familiar uniform — the green gabardine tunic, black stockings she knew to be buttoned up high to a Liberty bodice, square-necked tussore blouse, hat and gloves, even in summer — she wanted to warn them, plead with them: be unrelenting and ruthless with your heart and with your mind; think only of yourself.

'But your heart wasn't broken over there,' she said to herself. 'It was the best time.'

Jude wished the children were awake and down, wished their noise and demand would keep her from thinking. But it was still not seven o'clock and, no need to wake them for school today. Somewhere outside she could hear a bell, like the muffin-man's, only it was too early. The day looked bright, clear. She'd take her camera and ride up into the moors instead, catch the light breaking over one of the small high lakes maybe, or ride into the city. She got out the bread and was parcelling some slices up in brown paper when Sally came in, dressing-gown wrapped around her.

'You're up very early,' Jude said.

'He's snoring again,' Sally said. 'I stood it as long as I could.'

Jude laughed and took down a mug, poured Sally a coffee.

'Thanks.' Sally slumped into a chair near the stove. 'You going out?'

'I woke before the crack. Thought I might take an early ride out.'

Sally took a sip, shuddered. 'God you make it strong.'

'Be back later in the morning.'

'Sit down a moment, have another coffee,' Sally said. 'Cigarette.'

'Now you've got me,' Jude said, smiling, and

she poured out the last of the jug, and lit up.

'How was Martin? The film?'

'The first became tedious, the second was good.'

'Poor Martin,' Sally said with a grin.

'Poor Martin!'

'How's the job going?'

Jude shrugged.

'I see you going off each day, coming back, but I still can't think of you doing that, even after all this time.'

'It's work,' Jude said. 'It pays me my pin-money. It pays you something, at least.'

'You don't have to do it,' Sally said. 'At least not for that reason. We'd all survive.'

'I can't allow myself to stop,' Jude said. 'Even though typewriting is deadly.'

'You've learnt shorthand as well, though.'

'Nearly as bad. I knew it after the first day and here I still am.'

'Maybe you'll have an adventure,' Sally said. 'Like in the romances.'

'You're still half-asleep,' Jude said, 'if you can talk about romance and typewriting in one go. Though I suppose I could use my gauntlets. Instead of wearing them to protect my blouse from typewriting ink. I look like some emasculated knight.'

'They're quaint.'

'Closest I get to an adventure.'

'What about a noble insurance manager,' Sally said. 'You know. You're called in to take down a letter and one look from those eyes, or on the stairs, you're walking up, gaze a little averted, demure, and he's rushing down and knocks you flying.'

'Did Leo ever behave like that?' Jude said laughing. 'Or havc you taken to reading those novels. *Love's Ecstasy*, or *The Enamoured Virgin*, that kind of thing?'

'I read in a magazine that more couples are meeting in the workplace these days than ever before the war,' Sally said.

'We don't even use the same staircase as the men, Sally.'

'In case of what?'

'In case of God only knows. Spontaneous pregnancy, perhaps.'

'That's why you never bump into Leo.'

'I'm as fast as anybody, and I've been doing the French documents for a while, which is a bonus. But I'm not going to meet a husband there. I feel like I'm treading water. Three years of it now. Just keeping my head afloat with as little effort as possible.'

'But you mustn't let it be the death of you,' Sally said.

A thin ribbon of sunlight struck the far wall. If she put her hand up, Jude could break it, make a shadow jump on the wallpaper.

'I don't press you about things because I don't think you want me to,' Sally said. 'But I'm anxious about you. And you know what Leo is like. I don't learn anything from him.'

Jude stood. 'I'm going to go, while there's this early light.'

'Thanks for the coffee.'

'Thanks for putting up with me,' Jude said.

'Not easy, I do know.'

She left the house quietly and pulled her helmet close around her head. She would ride into the city, an act of defiance, not in her skirt and stockings and cardboard gauntlets this time, but in her britches, on her motorbike. It would be empty this early, the streets all hers.

Without the people, City Square seemed wide and free. The wind blew. The pigeons were still asleep on the statues, heads beneath their wings, like so many small grey boats. The air was so clear, Jude was sure she could smell the heather from the hills that rose behind. She walked across, exhilarated by the space and the light, by how different it all looked without people. She photographed the slender classical figures carved in bas-relief above the pilasters of the Union Life building and caught Time with his gilded scythe in her lens as the quarter hour rang out from the clock on Colonial Sphere Importers. The sun, still rising, cut between the buildings and across in a single narrow stroke, and standing in the bright line, Jude stared at her shadow. Crouching low she looked through the viewfinder, but the shadow was too long and she lost her head, or her feet, however she tried.

She felt like a child let loose in a sweet-shop, as if somehow the square, and all this space and air, had been given over just for her to see for these minutes, a reward for something. The blade of light stretched beyond her shadow over the far pavement and up the brick façade of Rathbone's Temperance Hotel. Through the ground floor window a figure was visible, a

139

waitress laying for breakfast, and as Jude watched, a man in sober suit opened the front door of the hotel and stood looking out at the day.

Lifting her camera, she followed the light line up the building, across three windows, their curtains drawn, to the fourth floor where the sash was open wide and the net curtains were gusting out across the brickwork. She wondered why anybody needed net curtains up there, what on earth they feared might look in. The light on the hotel looked sculptural, and Jude wanted to photograph it. Setting her shutter speed and aperture, she smiled at the memory of Mr Lund, her first mentor, and his *Photography for Novices*. He would not have approved her subject or technique.

When she looked again at the hotel, a female figure had placed herself in the window on the fourth floor, head and shoulders visible, as if expressly for Jude's photograph. She readied her camera and was about to take the shot, when the woman moved, disappearing. Jude waited to see if she would reappear, and perhaps a minute later she did, this time with a white bandanna around her head. But before Jude could take the shot, the woman leaned forward, chin on the sill, and pulled herself up, so that now she was crouched there, hunched over her knees four floors up, the curtains blowing out like wings on either side, her skirts hitched to her thighs, the patent toes of her shoes glinting.

Jude breathed in sharply. The sight made her dizzy. She felt her heart thump in her chest. All was so quiet. The woman made no sound. Jude looked around, but the square was still empty. Breathing deeply, steadying herself, she lifted her camera again.

Gingerly, the woman stood up on the sill, one hand on the raised sash for balance. She brushed off her skirts, pulled her cuffs down straight, put a hand to her hair. And then she jumped.

'No,' Jude whispered.

For a split second, she didn't look like she was falling, but seemed to hang. Jude could see her mouth, painted red, and wide as if surprised. Then she dropped, catching a heel on the sill as she fell, so that she tumbled head over heels, her smoothed skirt, her petticoats rucked up with the speed of her fall, limbs akimbo, like a rag doll flung away by a child.

Jude took one photograph before she hit the ground.

Her bandanna, which had come loose from her hair, fell more slowly, dropping like a wreath.

In a trance, Jude walked closer. It reminded her of a battlefield, when the noise has stopped, figures making slow, tentative movements in this changed landscape. She took a couple more photographs: the waitress standing at the restaurant window, her face pressed to the plate glass; the man at the door peering round from his spot on the step, hand to his head scratching like Stan Laurel. The woman, fallen to the ground, seemed little more than a heap of clothes, and Jude was about to take another photograph when the man in the doorway yelled something out. She stopped, suddenly horrified at herself, and turned and ran. She knew that there were lots of things you shouldn't see, and one of them was a body falling through so much air.

6

It was Monday, early evening, when the telephone rang. Daniel was doing some work on the dining-room table.

'Hello, Twickenham one oh nine?'

'I've changed my mind. I know who the other man was.'

'What?'

'No question. It's probably not enough, but I'm completely sure.'

Daniel frowned. The voice was familiar. He waited for it to introduce itself, explain what it was talking about.

'Daniel?' It sounded both impatient and anxious, and now he recognised it and found his stomach leaping.

'You don't go for preamble, Miss Hursten,' he said, smiling.

'Mr Brown, I phoned to tell you something important. Given that you travelled over three hundred miles north in pursuit of my recollections, it doesn't seem particularly odd that I should get straight to the point in a telephone call. And if you persist a minute longer in calling me Miss Hursten, I shall put the receiver down.'

There was a small notebook next to the telephone, and a pencil. Daniel flipped the notebook open, ran his eye over a list in his mother's hand: A.M.: Change bedding. Flowers for John. Coffee. Letters. Sandwich lunch.

Groceries, usual. P.M.: Rest. Tea with Marcia. Prepare dinner.

'Could you repeat what you said first?' he said. 'I wasn't entirely ready for it.'

There was a sigh at the other end, and then Jude's voice, speaking slowly, clearly, so that he could imagine her mouthing the words as if to a simpleton.

'The man in my photograph,' she said, 'the one not wounded.' Already she'd forgotten about speaking slowly, her voice back to its usual pace. Daniel could feel the fear blooming in his stomach. He barely knew this woman. Did he trust her?

'He was from Cork. I don't know any more about him. But I do know he was from County Cork. I remember that because Kate made a joke about a wine bottle.'

'Not a very funny joke,' Daniel said.

'It didn't much matter,' Jude said. 'Any joke would do, there.'

The trip to Yorkshire had made Daniel's nightmare worse, and it had unlocked other things. He supposed they were memories, though to begin with most of them weren't things he even knew he'd noticed. There was the noise of the bees in the fuchsia hedges, so loud in the summer that he'd wanted to block his ears in the narrow country lanes, 'the boreens' they called them. Then, walking over the bridge to the station a few days ago, it had been the mud. The tide had been out and the estuary mud gleamed, swollen, smooth, the birds already busy in it. Always if he had a minute, Daniel would look to see what was there, the different birds dipping their beaks, and once he'd seen a dunlin far away from its beach and once a green sandpiper. He'd always liked the smell of it, sulphurous, slightly rank, touching the back of his nostrils. It was its own element. But last week it had made his heart race to smell it and he had hurried past, blocking his ears to the sound of his memory, giving some poor explanation to his father for his haste. The roar of lorries in the street, a cat wailing in the night, the flare of a gas lamp, the single clip of somebody's shoes walking past the house at night, the smell of kippers, or beer, boys pushing by him on his way home, the gardener's bonfire flaring late in the twilight — it seemed that almost anything could catch him out now so that he felt hunted by his own thoughts, on the run.

Daniel knew the nightmare well. It was always the same, more or less. Of attacking, then being attacked. Of striking hard, beating. His brother Johnnie. Then women and children with guns, and the boys he knew, Will, hurt, dying, and him powerless. Always the colours of the heather and gorse, the nubbly hills, rocks, mist, the air heavy with moisture. He'd been having this dream ever since he returned. Some weeks it would be night after night, other times he'd be free of it for a month or more. He knew his mother had heard him crying out, though she always claimed she couldn't make out what he said, and this worried him as much as the dream itself, which he'd almost grown used to.

But these other things, these memories, slipping into his waking mind, leaching like a dye into the fabric of his life, these were worse, these he couldn't prevent or wake up from.

He put the telephone earpiece down on the table, took a step back. He felt the coldness of the hall tiles under his shoes. Jude's voice went into the polished wood, tinny and incoherent, then stopped. He stared at the earpiece through narrowed eyes. It looked like a rat, the coil of its connection lying quiet across the table. Something hung in the balance. He had asked Jude to tell him if anything came back to her, sent her his address, his telephone number, and here she was doing so. He could either ignore what she had to say, or he'd have to do something.

When Jude started speaking again, her voice was so loud, she made Daniel jump.

'If — you — don't — reply — I — shall — replace — the — receiver — and . . . '

Reflexively he reached for the telephone again.

'Hello,' he said.

'I'm in the sitting room lighting a cigarette, and when my brother is angry, because he doesn't like the smell and he hates me smoking, I shall blame you.'

Despite himself, despite his fear, Daniel laughed. Something had been bridged, broached, since their meeting. Or maybe it was by virtue of their having met before, so that now they talked with greater familiarity than they properly possessed, and this surprised him. It pleased him.

'But there can't be many bugs in your sitting room,' he said, and she laughed, so he knew she remembered the Rocks.

146

'Bugs and nerves,' she said. 'Two of the best reasons for a cigarette.'

'Nerves? You didn't strike me as . . . '

Her voice broke in like rapid fire.

'Look, is what I'm telling you helpful or not?'

He didn't know what to say. Because if he told her yes, it was helpful, he knew he'd have to act, go over there, and he didn't know if he dared. But if he told her no, then she would replace the handset and that would be that, and he'd be standing in the hall on the cold tiles, his parents drinking their morning coffee on the terrace and his head silting up further every day with these memories and nothing in the world to keep them in there even, but his life becoming like an echo chamber.

She didn't try to hurry him and he thought he could hear her waiting in this shared telephone silence. He pictured her, seated in a hard chair against the sitting room wall, the telephone on the floor beside her. She'd have her elbows on her knees and she'd be looking out, her body very still, brown eyes focused on something beyond the room, into that long, unkempt garden he'd only glimpsed. He imagined one of the children coming in, Elsa. He wondered whether Jude would brush her off, impatient with the interruption. Or whether she mightn't lift the girl onto her lap, almost absently, put her hand round Elsa's middle to keep her from slipping as she carried on the conversation. Because it was those two children, he thought, more than anybody else, except perhaps her dead lover, who held Jude's heart.

'What you've told me,' he said finally, 'the men that are dead aren't going to come back to life because of it. It won't make any difference to what's gone.'

He paused, and she waited. Then she asked, in a gentler voice than he'd heard so far, 'But will it make a difference to you?'

* * *

Jude wondered later whether Leo didn't know better than she did, what would come out of her trip south the weekend after. Daniel's request had taken her by surprise and she'd answered him before she had time to think, then written to confirm it, needing to send the letter as much for her own certainty as for his.

'In the spirit of enquiry,' Daniel had said, and when she told this to Leo, she didn't know whether or not she was offended by his roar of laughter. She'd found him in the vegetable garden, crouched down, picking the lowest runner beans, and when he'd straightened up to listen to her, she thought he looked like a green man, something wild, the last red flowers on the beans like a garland on his hair.

'I've never heard it called that before,' he said, and she would have taken offence, except that somewhere she knew the justice of his remark.

'I'm meeting him in Kew Gardens, which is near his home. And I'll stay with Peter, be back on Sunday in time to press my blouse for Monday.'

'You've spoken to Peter already?'

'He was intrigued. Wants to make it all into a detective story. Put me in some sleuthing hat and pipe.'

Leo picked up the trug, full of beans, and stepped carefully out, lifting each foot high.

'I need to do this,' Jude said.

'Whatever it is.'

'Yes.'

'We'll tell Sally it's an old school friend,' he said.

'Why?' Jude raised her eyes to his in question. 'Why not say who it is?'

'Daniel Brown worries her. She thinks he needs too much.'

'That's absurd. All he did was sit and eat her Sunday lunch. She seemed to like him.'

Leo put a hand up, stopped Jude's noise of protest.

'It's what she thinks.' Leo shrugged. 'And you like him, don't you?'

Jude took a bean from the trug and bit into it.

'He seems like a nice enough fellow,' Leo said. 'Clever. And troubled, but then who isn't after such times? Certainly a match for you, which is important. You'd never be able to bear someone too easy.'

'I'm going down there to try to help him with something,' Jude said. 'Not to make love to him.'

'Something's happened, Jude. Is it just because of this man turning up on the doorstep?' He shook his head. 'There's something very urgent about you.'

Jude didn't reply. She hadn't told Leo about the falling woman. She hadn't told anyone.

When she'd come home afterwards, she'd pleaded a headache and kept to her room till late into the day. She hadn't thought much about what she was doing, but she'd found herself staring at the photographs from the war; at that desecrated landscape where she had been so powerfully alive, at Peter, at the wounded soldiers, and most of all at the friend she so loved.

'I know there doesn't have to be only one reason,' Leo said, 'and that sometimes you're the last person to know something about yourself.'

Jude tossed the bean away and spat the coarse, milky fibre into the grass. 'Anyway, needs too much what?' she said.

'You'll find out, perhaps,' Leo said and he got up and walked away back up the garden, swinging the trug and its lanky green load, calling up to the two children who were playing by the pond, and Jude watched him and envied his contentment.

She had her camera and a newspaper for the train south. Also a book. Jude wasn't much of a reader, but this would be a long journey, and Sally had persuaded her to bring it.

'It's about a girl called Ann Veronica,' Sally said. 'More your kind of thing than mine. She's quite determined to have her own way.'

Leo had lent her a book about war by George Bernard Shaw, but she'd left that one on her bed.

Jude opened the novel first, but the girl's gusty eagerness was oppressive and she put the book away. The newspaper told her that England had beaten Australia in the cricket, that you could see movies with sound now, 'talkies', and that the coal miners were giving the government a hard time. She folded the newspaper and looked out of the window.

It was hard today, sitting still for so long and she felt a terrible impatience brewing. The muscles in her calves and her arms were twitching and she couldn't let her eyes settle. Her gaze rested in some middle distance and the landscape passed beneath it. She saw the cropped fields shearing away under the hard summer light, the pools of cattle under trees, tiny men with carts and heavy-legged horses, the long, colourless sky. Kestrels hunched small on telegraph poles and rooks scattered, their messy black rise and fall like so many scraps of litter, and Jude wondered whether you could ever catch that motion in a photograph.

What was she hoping for? She didn't know, except to stave off the panic that beat against her ribs whenever she thought that her life might have settled now for good. She wouldn't think, tried not to think, about Daniel and the tall line of his body standing outside her door, or his face against the rocks, or his voice, thick with uncertainty, asking for her help.

She took the Underground from King's Cross. When she had told the children of her trip to London, Tom had been uninterested, except on one point, which was that she might find herself taking an escalator. It was one of his four greatest ambitions, to take an escalator, and he managed his envy by requesting Jude to note down everything there was to tell about it. How high it was, how many steps there were, was there any visible machinery, and was a man with a wooden leg on the up as well as the down part?

'They'd need a lot of men by now, if they did that,' said Jude. 'Lots of the stations have escalators.'

'But there's loads without legs. And they might lots of them be glad of a job. And it's indoors, and no walking. Only standing.'

'Where did you pick this up? In the *Boys' Own*?'

'But it's true, Jude. They do pay men with wooden legs.'

'Why?'

'So as people aren't frightened, going on.'

Jude didn't press him further. And being in good time at King's Cross, she took the escalator down and then up and then down again, pausing after the second descent to write some notes for Tom and to try a photograph. She held the camera as steady as she could on a long exposure, but the ground shook with the rumble of the trains and the light was very poor, so she didn't hold out much hope.

She took the Piccadilly Line down to Earl's Court and changed there on to the District. The tube was crowded and she had to stand, her hand on the rail for balance. She looked along the rail at the half a dozen others gripping on and she wondered for a moment what had become of the young pianist.

The slender-fingered female hand, engagement and wedding rings dull in that light, nails manicured for battle, gripped close to the rough, broken nails and coarse skin of the labourer's; long, brown-skinned fingers made close companionship with the broad reach of freckled, ginger-haired fingers. Her own hand with its wide knuckles and nails cut short for typing, still a trace of engine oil beneath one, found common cause with an ancient fist, its knuckles swollen and pushed about with arthritis. Incongruous couples, and she wished she could have caught them in her lens.

Jude hadn't known she was holding her breath, but when the train surfaced, first at Baron's Court, and then properly after Hammersmith, she let out a tremendous sigh, and she felt as she used to after huddling in the cellar while the Germans sent their shells whistling around, which was a bit light-headed, breathy. Coming out at Kew Gardens, she fished a piece of paper from her pocket with Daniel's instructions scribbled down. She was to make her way to the entrance at the end of Kew Green and he'd meet her there.

Jude had no idea what she was walking towards. But what she did know, what had painted itself across the inside of her eyes on the journey south, was that she would do anything to break the toppling inertia of her life now. In the war she'd done this every day, walked blindfold towards things. Sometimes because she couldn't see how dangerous it might be, and sometimes because if she'd pulled the scarf from her eyes and looked straight out, she'd have been too scared to step forwards. Better not to see.

The war had been a very big adventure and she'd been at the top of the list. Better than in Tom's *Boys' Own* with its bareback riding and rafting and shoot-outs, she'd rescued men and saved lives. And today, although the adventure didn't look so likely, walking towards the Royal Botanic Gardens along the pavements, past the quiet, tidy houses with front gardens and railings to keep things in, she pleaded with the gods to intervene.

He was waiting by the turnstile, leaning against the Opening Times board, watching the people file up and ratchet through. He didn't seem to be looking out for her, his head half-turned from the road, but when she was within a few yards, he stood tall and raised his hand. And though she had seen him from a distance, known it was him, still when he turned towards her, she felt that shock of the actual, a single pulse through.

She noticed how he moved, as though his limbs were connected at the joints with pins. Rusted pins, pushed in at an angle. So that his hand, raised in greeting, seemed ill at ease with his arm, and his arm moved oddly from his shoulder. She was moved by the sight of him, and taken aback by the range of her own feelings.

'So,' he said. 'You have come.'

'Did you think I might not?'

'It's a long journey to make, and . . . '

Jude shrugged. 'What would be good to see?'

'My mother says the lavender beds at this time, and the roses.'

'My grandmother kept lavender,' Jude said. 'Against a wall, south facing. A great bank of lavender, high up in Yorkshire. She'd cut it about now, put a vase in every room to keep the flies away.'

'Flies?'

'They don't like the smell. We used it in Belgium too. It's good for wounds.'

'Do you need to drink tea first?'

'No.'

They walked beside flower beds heavy with the day's scents, silent, both awaiting. The paths were busy with Saturday afternoon people. Fathers with little figures hoisted on shoulders, old women with bread for the birds, children bickering over hoops and ice creams, feeding squirrels, chasing squirrels, mothers wiping noses and mouths, couples wandering, fingers intent in one another's palms, oblivious or arguing. Daniel watched them, all the ordinary motions, all the ordinary pleasures and quarrels, and fought with the fear that cut like a band across his chest. The fear that these things were closed to him because he'd smashed them somewhere else, that he'd stepped beyond them.

He watched a boy peg a pebble at a squirrel and the father in his Sunday best cuff his son so hard across the ear, the boy stumbled. He watched a girl snap the heads from a line of proud daisies and felt his skin shiver. Jude bent to smell a flower and he looked at her, her elbows out, her dark curls tickling over her face so that she put a hand up to wash her skin clear.

She was someone more at ease, he guessed, with larger movements.

Jude looked round at him and he saw her expression acquirc that cast she must have learnt in the war, of solicitude, professional concern. And he knew then, somewhere behind his fear, somewhere behind the horror of what had gone on, that he wanted to know this woman when that guard was down.

'Let's go and talk,' he said. 'Sit down somewhere, under a tree where it's private.'

'The lavender?'

He shook his head. 'The perfume's too bloody strong.'

'Your leg's hurting,' Jude said. 'You should have said.'

Daniel stopped dead and faced her, very upright. 'No, it's not,' and he said the words so loud he made her flinch. 'My mother does that,' he said.

'Does what?'

'She tells me what's hurting.'

'My apologies,' Jude said, her voice clipped tight. 'I won't again. You can yell and scream all you want and I'll say nothing. I've heard enough men screaming in my time, for God's sake. It's nothing new.'

She didn't walk away, or cross her arms, but Daniel knew from the edge of her shoulder, from the fierce forwardness of her gaze, that he'd angered her. Things were pushing out from inside and he didn't know the limits of his own restraint. He must speak his mind to her soon, before the echoes got the upper hand.

'I suppose it is less than clever to compare a woman to one's mother,' he said, finding from somewhere a lighter tone, and Jude turned away to hide her grin.

'Especially,' Daniel went on, wondering whether she would baulk at his tone, 'when that woman has journeyed hundreds of miles to help one, and is so entirely unlike one's mother.'

'There's no need to become extravagant,' she said, still smiling. 'But let's talk.'

They had stopped in the middle of the path and people skirted them like a river round an island. They stood in a diamond of space. Daniel searched for a likely place to go. A little stand of trees ahead and to the right looked good, nobody near. He pointed to it.

'We could sit there.'

They walked past beds of red hollyhocks and blue cornflowers, past yellow sunflowers and stocks in every colour, and perhaps this blaze, which battered the eyes, explained why Daniel didn't notice the fuchsia until it was nearly upon them.

'Listen,' Jude said, walking closer, 'the bees. We had this in the garden, my mother loved it. Leo and I, we'd spend ages pulling off the flowers. There'd be this pinprick of sweetness if you sucked. He got stung once, doing it.'

She turned, but Daniel hadn't heard her. He had moved away and was leaning hard with one hand on his stick, the other clapped to his ear, like a man beyond his years, his eyes on the ground.

'Daniel?' she said.

'It's everywhere in Ireland, in the west,' he said. It grows wild there, the hedges are made of it. So loud. It crowds in on you from every side. They hack it back and it just grows bigger and bigger.'

He looked up and his eyes were scared.

'And you didn't ever suck the flowers,' Jude said, trying for lightness.

'I don't want to see it,' he said and, hearing his voice, Jude said no more.

They sat in silence beneath the tree, Daniel with his eyes on the ground, Jude looking out from beneath the heavy canopy. A woodpecker dipped between trees, laughing hard. Two stag beetles fought it out in brittle dance in the dust at Jude's feet, till one was tipped over onto its shiny back, legs jerking in the air. High and tiny, an aeroplane made loops, and in the distance, on the path they had left, people watched, a child tracing the O's with its finger to the sky.

7

Jude waited, and when Daniel finally started to speak, she leaned back against the rough bark and shut her eyes to the Saturday world strolling past. She'd come a long way to listen.

'I only just got to the war,' he said. 'By the skin of my teeth I made it. Got my commission, like Johnnie, was gazetted, did my training and got over there. My mother crying at the door, tugging at my damn coat.'

Despite the warmth of the day, Daniel pulled his jacket round him as if, even now, he could feel his mother's hands. Jude looked away. She felt as if she were witness to something private.

'So you went to France,' she said, 'you went into the trenches,' making her voice loud and solid.

'I couldn't stay, not with Johnnie dead. Every time my mother looked at me, she saw a ghost. I was in flight, for God's sake. I had to get away.'

Jude dug her toe into the dust, watched an ant divert its course away from the mountain of her shoe. She looked round at Daniel. He was staring straight out across the grass, for all the world, she thought, as if *he* had seen a ghost.

'But that's normal now,' she said. 'There are millions of men dead all over Europe, millions and millions of mothers, and wives, and sweethearts, and half of them seeing ghosts.'

'I wasn't frightened,' Daniel said. 'Not a bit. If

anything I was stronger after Johnnie's death. Determined. I was going to be all the things he was. I'd got myself stronger, been lifting weights. And now I was going to go to the Front and come home again. Not a telegraph for my mother this time.'

'So you did fight?'

Daniel shook his head. 'Got packed off to the front line and it was over. I never fired a shot, never even got to stand in a trench.'

'And then you left the army.'

'We had to wait for ever to be demobbed. Last in last out, and no war fought. It made some of the men murderous. I came home, and that seemed to make it worse for my mother than before. Johnnie had never come home. So now it was as if I was a ghost, but the wrong one. We did look alike, same brown hair, same physique, height almost, mannerisms of course. I'd see her staring at me, and ask if anything was wrong. Had I got a smut on my nose? Was my parting crooked? And she'd never answer, I don't think she heard me, but sometimes she'd come close and touch my eyebrows, or run her fingers through my hair, and it wasn't me she saw then, it was Johnnie.'

Daniel paused. He wondered, did she know she was the first person he'd ever spoken to of this, and he turned to look at her. She returned his gaze, made no effort to speak, and he thought that probably she did know. Somewhere far off behind them, it seemed infinitely far, he could hear a child's call, 'Catch me.' He gripped his arms tight, feeling the print of his fingers against

160

bone. He was doing this well, telling it. He could do this, and he'd go on now.

'My friend, Will Savage, he'd got decorated in France, seen everything and was still alive. He was demobbed before me and we lost touch. Don't remember how we got to be friends, but anyway I bumped into him, in a pub off Oxford Street. I was in a suit, working for my father by now, and he, I don't remember, but he told me he was going to Ireland. They had problems there, violent rebels who'd stop at nothing and they were murdering policemen, causing havoc. So they were recruiting for a special force.

'We got to talking and he said to me why didn't I sign up too? Since I'd missed the action first time around. He said had I seen the adverts? They were offering a pound a day — a very good wage — and they wanted ex-officers. They wanted them experienced, but seeing as they were hungry for men, he was sure he could talk them round to me. So I joined.'

'When was this?' Jude said.

'1920. Summer of 1920. I became a temporary cadet in the Auxiliary division of the Royal Irish Constabulary, but a soldier, as near as damn it. They gave us some training, six weeks in the Curragh, and a uniform, tam-o'-shanter beret with a little golden harp badge, and plenty of guns, and then they sent us south in our big lorries and none of us, not even Will, had a clue.'

'Was it like a war?' Jude said.

Daniel shook his head. 'We didn't know who the enemy was. We were meant to protect people.

161

We were meant to make Ireland hell for the rebels to live in. That's what it said in the *Dublin Police Journal*, and so somebody wrote it out large on a banner and put it in the mess: 'Make Ireland Hell for Rebels'.

'I thought the enemy would wear a uniform. So you didn't shoot the wrong person. But you'd drive out of the barracks and there would be people in the town going about their business, men and women standing about on corners, and you wouldn't know what they were. Not even the children. Some of the women were friendly enough, lots weren't. But then you found out it was the friendly ones were carrying the messages for the men, or the weapons, and so you started not to trust anyone. You'd hear those voices, that accent, and think that if they spoke like that, they'd be bound to be out for you one way or the other. Men, women, children, priests, all of them. Christ, one fellow, he started searching the dogs for stuff.

'It made us scared, angry, feeling like that, and then you start seeing things differently, drinking to get your courage up and so things happen when you go out on patrol that oughtn't to. Things I wouldn't do, but I did them. And afterwards nobody says you shouldn't have, nobody punishes you. Everyone says it's what they deserve and we're only here to help them in this godforsaken place, or they say that they were the enemy and they had it coming to them, and so you say it too, and believe it even though you know it's not true. Not really. And then you do it all again, and again.'

'So you were a . . . ' Jude hesitated.

'Black and Tan. Yes,' he said. 'More or less.'

Jude stood up. She walked away from the tree, elaborately stretching, and then back to it again.

'I never understood the nickname,' she said.

Daniel shrugged. 'Nothing special about it,' he said. 'It was the uniform — dark green and khaki. A bunch in Limerick went on a drinking spree early on, smashed things up, and they got named 'Black and Tans' after a pack of hounds that went by that name there, and because of the colours they wore. And then the name stuck for all of us.'

'So you were one of them, and you got wounded over there,' she said.

'Yes.'

'And in between?'

'I'd like to say we were a little mad over there, some of the time. But that would be making excuses. It was horrible, what went on sometimes, and we were being told to do it, ordered, so we laughed and laughed. Harder and harder.'

'I know what men do in wars,' Jude said. 'I saw it for myself.'

'Saw it?'

'As near as damn it, yes.'

Daniel put his hand on his leg, felt with his fingers through the cloth of his trousers to where the skin was puckered, to where the ridges of scar tissue crossed his leg like so many fortifications. He'd kept it going up to here, but it was slipping, he could feel it slipping.

'And us meeting, it all has something to do

with the photograph of two men sharing a cigarette that I took in Belgium in the Great War.'

Daniel looked up at her. She was staring at the tree trunk, one finger prising at the thick bark. He noticed how she lifted her eyebrows, when she said something that was especially important.

'It's strange, don't you think?' she said, raising her brow again.

Daniel didn't answer her question, if it was one. He looked away.

In the distance two boys, brothers from their matching clothes, were playing some kind of tug-of-war with a branch. The branch was slender and Daniel could see the white grazes where they had cleaned it of its shoots.

First, one boy would grasp it, both arms outstretched, hands placed firmly round the wood, and the other boy would try to twist and tug it from him, and then they would swap around. From this distance they looked like dancers. There seemed to be a rule to do with how far along they could hold the stick, so that more than once one of them overstepped the mark and they swapped. But then a dispute arose which neither had the will to resolve. They grappled for a time, then the larger boy let go of the stick and pushed his brother to the ground and the game was over.

'Things taste different there, the same things we eat here. Like the bacon except they call it rashers and bacon's something different. And the milk. And brown bread like a cow pat and a cross in the middle, which isn't like ours and not even made with yeast at all. One of the kitchen boys told me. The place is like that, things looking like they should be the same, but they're not, so you don't know where you are and you sit down to breakfast and it all looks about right and you pick up your knife and fork and cut something, put it in your mouth and it's nearly there but not. Except for Coolderry, and Horse Island.'

'Horse Island?' Jude said, but he didn't seem to hear her.

'At least they were good places. Places you could be in properly.' He traced the names on the grass, then tapped his head. 'That's where I try to go back to in here, every day nearly.' He paused. 'It's not nicer or nastier, the bacon, or the bread. It's just different. Foreign.'

Jude was looking at the bark she'd picked from the tree, how on the inside it was smooth and damp. Daniel put his hands down on either side of him, and rolled his shoulders round. Tension cut like blades down his back. Dropping the bark, Jude sat down. She didn't know what the names meant, and it wasn't the time to ask. She needed him to tell her about the photograph.

'Stop telling me about the bacon,' she said. 'And tell me what you need me to know.'

Daniel breathed in deep, making his head swim. He couldn't speak about the things he'd seen, the things he'd done. He wanted to, he hoped she'd ask him, demand to know, suspect him and interrogate. It was her fault if she didn't ask, because then how could he tell?

165

'What did you think when the journalists wrote about the Boche nailing babies to front doors? Did you believe it? Since you were there?' he said.

'No more than I'd believe it of our lot, no. I saw plenty of horror, but never anything like that.'

'But people go too far in war, that's what they do.'

'Killing other men is going too far,' Jude said.

'Yes, but not just that.'

'I didn't come down here to discuss the morals of war,' Jude said, because she couldn't bear to take it further now. She knew what he was asking her to do, but she couldn't be the bearer of his conscience. Only she wondered where his own revulsion was.

'All right,' he said, though he knew she was wrong. Absolutely wrong. And then like a man plunging from the rocks into an unknown sea, he began again.

'The man in your photo, the Irish man, he was a soldier in the British army, an officer. I know this because there it was in the exhibition, 'Our Brave Men who Battle On'. I saw it, and the camera doesn't lie. I stood and looked at him a month ago, and everyone else saw him too, arm around his wounded brother soldier, and I recognised him. And the old ladies went 'Ah' because, look at that, they're sharing a cigarette and there's a smiling nurse standing behind and it's all like it should be and doesn't he deserve her smile, after all he'd done for his country . . . '

He paused. He was beginning to shout and he

could feel the rage rise inside him, the mad rage in which you could do anything, to anybody. He paused. He must try to be calm. He was speaking too quickly and forgetting to breathe. His hand was a fist and something sharp was pressing into his palm. Slowly he breathed in through his nose and out through his mouth, like Will had shown him when they were on a raid. Opening his hand, he found a sappy piece of twig on his palm, its shoots making their prints on his skin, and he put it in his pocket.

He barely knew this woman but he needed her to hear him out. He mustn't scare her away, or not scare her exactly, because he knew already she wasn't the scaring type. But he mustn't revolt her either. He could feel his fingers tightening and his lips drawing back and the saliva becoming thick in his mouth and he didn't want to gouge at the earth or bare his teeth or become one of those figures you passed in the corners, flailing and spitting at the world. He looked up. He must remember. Here he was in Kew Gardens on a sunny Saturday afternoon with a pretty girl beside him, and over there families were promenading, and courting couples were looking at the flowers and each other.

'This is what makes me . . . ' he said, and he spread his shaking hands out for her to see, palms towards the sky. 'It's like the duck rabbit picture. You look and it's a duck, you look again and it's a rabbit. It's both, but never both at once. One is the outside of the other and the other is the outside of the one. It's why I'll have to go back and find out, is it a duck I'll be shooting, or a rabbit? I saw him last month on the exhibition wall and he was a British soldier from the trenches. And before that I saw him, in Ireland, in the flesh, and he was dressed like a soldier then too.'

Daniel stood up. For some reason he couldn't say any more, and he rummaged in his mind for why. He wiped his mouth on his sleeve.

'My mouth is dry. I must find some water.'

He started walking towards the path. Jude sat watching him, unsure what was happening. Then she picked up her bag and camera and followed.

★   ★   ★

Later, that evening, telling her tale to Peter, Jude found it hard to describe what had happened.

'It was as if I wasn't there any more,' she said. 'As if he didn't see me, or the gardens, or the people walking about, or the birds, or ducks, or flowers. He didn't seem to see any of it, or only when it fitted to some other place that was in his head. As though he was in a different landscape. Different weather. He was walking that lopsided walk fast as he could, urgent, stick in one hand, and buttoning his jacket with his other, pulling up the collar as if the day had gone cold, and around him people were basking in the sun.'

Peter nudged Jude's cocktail with a finger. 'Drink, lady. Best Manhattan in town.'

Jude took a sip, looked around her. 'Classy bar. Is this your usual?'

'It is for now, till I get a better offer,' he said,

smiling over behind her. Jude turned her head to see, and caught the barman's bow.

'Very nice,' she said and took another sip. She grinned, remembering the first time she'd met Peter, how cross she'd been when she thought he was making up to her.

'How did he get his leg injury?'

'An ambush,' Jude said. 'He told me that before. Said he'd never told anyone else before.'

'So you followed him?' Peter said.

'Of course I followed him, though I didn't try to catch him up. I thought he was making for the path, maybe going to the tearoom, because he'd said he was thirsty. But he crossed the path, people staring at him because he's going so fast, his head down, and muttering, though I couldn't hear what at first. There was a woman standing there and he brushed her face with his arm as he went past, didn't seem to see her.

'He was walking in a straight line towards these bushes. He could easily have gone round them, but he didn't, as if he didn't see them either. I was close to him now, almost as close as I am to that next table, and when we got into them, I could hear him fairly clearly and he seemed to be saying something about them. 'Bloody bushes,' he said, more than once, but as if he'd only just seen them, as if they'd jumped up and hit him.'

'Bloody bushes?' Peter said.

'Yes. And something about getting caught in the bush, I wasn't quite sure. He might have meant the ambush, I suppose, or the bushes he was pushing through.'

'But you weren't frightened of him?'

'After what we went through,' Jude said, 'you and me?'

'People losing their marbles is more frightening than them losing an arm or a leg. And it sounds like he came quite close. Though we did see some like that too, of course. And God knows what he'd got up to in Ireland.'

'It was as though his wound was still raw, still filthy from battle. As if nobody had taken a piece of lint and some iodoform and cleaned it yet. But no, I wasn't frightened. I was very curious. And cross. He'd stood me up, so to speak. Got me all the way down here and then walked out on me. And he was sane when he walked out, I'm sure of it.'

'Jilted lover, then,' Peter said. 'Is he handsome? Tall? Dark? Sharp cheekbones? Broad shoulders?'

Jude gave him a look. 'Not your kind of handsome.'

'So, tell me something.'

'He's quite tall, very slim, hair brown on the way to fair. The kind of hair that gets streaked by the sun. And eyes that change depending on the light. Green almost, indoors, but then blue outside.' She looked down at the table. 'Anyway, this is ridiculous because I barely know him.'

'So? I barely know him,' Peter said, tipping his head towards the barman.

'He gives you Manhattans. Daniel Brown has given me nothing but trouble. I can already hear Leo saying, 'I told you so.' And Sally being quietly right behind him.'

'So, he might be handsome,' Peter said, nodding to himself. 'And you don't really know how hurt, do you? You don't know how much he'd take.' He paused, thinking a moment. 'So, tell me the rest. After the bloody bushes.'

Jude put a hand to her neck. She was very tired.

'Cigarette,' Peter said. 'What you need now,' and he pulled two from a packet and stuck them between his lips.

Jude found her lighter for him. He lit them and passed hers across the table.

'Recognise it?' Jude said.

Peter turned the lighter over in his palm. 'It is familiar, but I've seen so many of them. Just about every soldier, every sailor I meet,' and he shrugged his shoulders. 'Kate's?'

'Yes.'

'And she didn't smoke.'

'No.'

Jude knew Peter was waiting, that he'd take his cue from her. But she didn't want to talk about Kate now, only to say her name out loud, remember her for a moment.

'Do you want to finish your story?' he said.

'There's not much more to tell,' Jude said. 'He was walking through some oak trees, me still just behind, and he stopped short, turned and looked at me. He'd seemed very nearly mad in all this, but when he looked at me, the madness was gone and he was absolutely sane. He said, 'I have to go now and I'm sorry to have led you such a poor dance. Perhaps if we'd met at another time . . . ' and then he walked away.'

'And you didn't try to follow him?'

'No.'

'That's not like you.'

'It was clear he didn't want me to. And he seemed very sane then. So I just walked round the gardens for another hour or more, and then I came to meet you.'

Peter stirred the last pale dregs in his glass, drank them off, more as if it were a pint of beer than a cocktail, Jude thought, and set the glass down. He looked over to the bar, but the barman was busy flirting with another customer, a thick-set man in a smart suit.

'He'll want to be careful,' Peter said in a low voice. 'They have them undercover in places like this.'

'Can we go back to your flat?' Jude said. 'I'm very tired.'

Peter threw another look towards the bar.

'And I want your full attention,' she said. She pushed her glass towards him. 'Finish mine for me?'

⋆　⋆　⋆

They could hear the telephone bell ringing as they came up the last flight of stairs, but by the time Peter had the door open, it had stopped.

'They'll try again if it's important,' he said. He sat her down on a chair in the kitchen, put on the kettle and took out the cocoa tin.

'In memory,' he said, holding up the tin. 'Also, you look done in. When you've drunk it, I'll make up your sofa.'

The cocoa nearly made Jude cry, so she held her face just above the mug and made something of a dance about the steam from the mug scorching her face, to hide the flush that tears brought. They sat either side of the red oilcloth, hands clasped round mugs almost as if in prayer.

'Do you remember Kate working out one day how much cocoa we'd made? How many gallons, and then how many bathtubs, and then a swimming pool, and so on,' Peter said.

'I told her she was making it up, and she got cross.'

Peter laughed. 'You were like a couple of sisters with your squabbling. Always nit-picking down in that cellar. Real nits too.' He got up and went out, came back carrying a small hinged leather photo frame, which opened to show three photographs.

'I have this on my bedside table,' he said, passing it to Jude.

She opened it and smiled. Peter had taken the middle photograph. She remembered him doing so. It was her birthday, nineteen years old, and they had had a picnic. She was lying on a piece of tarpaulin, and next to her was Kate. They were laughing at something. Kate had a wine bottle in her hand, and Jude had her arm round Kate's shoulder. They looked so young and so carefree, and in the distance behind them, just visible, was the outline of the broken church tower.

Flanking this was a photograph of Peter at the stove, head turned towards Jude's call, caught by surprise, wooden spoon in his hand, his mouth open for retort. And on the other side a photograph Jude hadn't known of. It showed her in profile, Kate's greatcoat wrapped around her, britches and boots, white headscarf gathered and tumbling down her back like water in spate, binoculars raised towards who knew what.

'You look so beautiful,' Peter said.

Jude laughed. 'In the greatcoat and boots?'

'Then and now. You should be in love.'

'Perhaps I am. Perhaps I have been,' Jude said, a finger to her lips so he wouldn't ask more. 'Anyway, what about you?'

Peter started to wash out the saucepan. She watched him, his economy of gesture, his grace.

'I used to love watching you cook,' she said, rolling her head forwards, trying to ease the tension in her neck.

'Do you want a bath? Plenty of hot water here. I've got some lovely bath salts.'

Jude laughed. 'That bath,' she said.

'Four of us to get it into the room.'

'The two inches was heaven, and us so prudish. Funny, the pair of us dealing with wounded men all day and night, we must have seen everything there is to see. But it's not the same, the other way around. And then you brought us champagne. There was more champagne than there was hot water.'

'Champagne in tin mugs.'

'I hadn't been in a bath with someone else since I was too young to remember.'

'Somebody to soap your back.'

Jude looked down into her cocoa mug, her throat suddenly tight again.

'Jude?' Peter's voice was tender, soft.

'That's why I keep the photographs at the bottom of the box,' she said. 'And why I haven't been in touch very much.'

'So as not to be reminded.'

'Yes.'

'So many deaths,' Peter said.

'It's just the two that I can't bear.'

'Kate would understand.'

'I was picking up pebbles at the seaside and she was drowning in her own lungs.'

'You couldn't have saved her.'

'I know,' she said.

'The people we love die. And in the war, too many of them die, for all of us.'

'I know, but she was one of the people I knew. Me especially.'

'I never met Richard, but I remember the letter arriving,' he said. He covered her hand with his, stroked her fingers. 'That's when you stopped sky-watching.'

'I lost my head for heights. It just happened.'

'That still the same?'

Jude nodded.

'I think you need to do something differently,' he said at last. 'This new friend of yours, what's his name?'

'Daniel Brown, but he's not a friend. Not yet.'

It was getting dark, sapping the colours from the kitchen. Jude saw Daniel crossing the grass, moving away from her, his hobbled walk, his blind distress.

'You think that there's something about him. Something beyond his madness, or sanity, illness, whatever it is,' Peter said.

Jude nodded again.

'What does he look like? Will you tell me now?'

'He reminds me of Richard. Same way of moving, despite the limp. There was something awkward about Richard, and yet he was so athletic.' She thought a moment. 'He was like a colt. Barely grown when he died.'

'And you like him, don't you? This Daniel?'

Jude shrugged.

'I thought so,' Peter said.

'I like the way he listens. And I want to hear what he will say. And he looks like a man who wants to be freed,' Jude said.

'From his body? His hurt leg?'

'From his mind.'

'So is that what made you come down and meet him? Because it wasn't just the colour of his eyes.'

'I needed a change.' Jude gave a rueful grin. She couldn't answer him, not tonight, not quite yet.

Peter shrugged. 'All right then. What will you do if he contacts you?'

'I don't know,' she said.

'Which is unlike you. The whole thing is very cloak and dagger.' Peter put his arm around Jude's shoulders. 'That's enough now. You're exhausted, and I'm going to tuck you up like I used to. We'll talk in the morning.'

She was so tired, Jude barely took in Peter's flat, its high ceilings and battered cornices. She didn't know why she'd left the sitting room door ajar, but last thing before she slept, her eyes drifted over the slender slip of light, like a soft searchlight, that threw itself in from the hall and she thought how simple it would be to close the door against it, and how hard.

★   ★   ★

Jude had told her boss she had to come to London for the final illness of an elderly uncle and so could she please have Monday off in lieu. An elderly uncle, even a very ill one, wouldn't usually have been enough to gain the day, but when Jude mentioned the will, they were very understanding. And she'd never missed a day before, not in the four years she'd been working there.

'So is it me or Daniel Brown who's the uncle?' Peter said when she told him this.

'Well, there'd be no point touching you for any pennies, would there?' she said. 'And frankly, after yesterday, I don't know whether I'll ever see Daniel again.'

'You might be glad of that,' Peter said.

'No,' she said.

★   ★   ★

They had a leisurely Sunday, beginning with a slow breakfast and, after a short discussion which took them nowhere, an agreement to avoid, if possible, contentious conversation. So instead they walked through the Sunday city talking of plans and aspirations, of Peter's hopeless romances and Jude's dream of travelling round Europe on her motorbike with her camera, of leaving one life and beginning another. They remembered the funny and the terrible times in the war, and they didn't talk about Daniel or Kate.

Jude was exhilarated by the empty city, and, determined to walk free from her ghosts for this short time, she began to photograph the Sunday figures: women in hats returning from church, a wandering dog, a man on his own with a placard, railing against the secular hordes who were nowhere to be seen, a figure visible through an open window sipping from a glass. But she hadn't noticed how her eyes were drawn upwards until Peter spoke.

'What's so fascinating about the tops of the buildings?' he said. 'That's all you've been looking at this last half hour.'

And as he said it, she saw again the woman crouched there, saw her lean into the air and jump.

'It's something,' she began, and then she stopped. She didn't want to talk of it now. 'It's a bad habit,' she said. 'Something I'm trying to stop doing. Let's walk in a park now instead. I won't be tempted then.' And shaking her head at his raised eyebrows, she packed her camera away into its bag, took his arm and tugged him into a stride, till he laughed and rolled his eyes, and he didn't ask her more.

After lunch, they went to the movies, bickering all through *The Thief of Baghdad* about Douglas Fairbanks' costumes, which Peter coveted, his body, which Jude thought handsome and Peter did not, and his swordplay, which neither were that excited by. So that by suppertime Jude was feeling much more relaxed, as Peter had predicted, but also as if something important might be slipping by.

'Perhaps I should telephone Leo,' she said. 'See whether Daniel has been in touch.'

'Don't,' Peter said. He opened the oven door, peered in and shut it again. 'Rice pudding's ready.'

Jude looked at him amazed. 'Yesterday you were the one saying I should have followed him in Kew Gardens.'

Peter put his finger to her lips. 'But you needed the rest today. And if you telephone now you'll undo all that, whatever Leo tells you. Anyway, there's nothing you can do between now and then.'

'Then?'

'Tomorrow, once you're back home.'

Jude groaned. 'I hate having pipe dreams. Makes going home harder.'

Peter opened the oven door again and the kitchen was filled with the smell of cinnamon and nutmeg. Jude took two spoons out of the drawer and they set to, breaking the thin skin of the pudding, then dipping their spoons deep.

'You mustn't stay a typist,' Peter said.

'But I can't do anything else that pays.'

'Nursing?'

'God, no! I've been spoilt for that. I couldn't bear being told what to do by one of those starchy buggers. They wouldn't accept any of what I did in the war, I'd have to start and train from scratch.'

'You sure of that?'

Jude nodded. 'I checked a few years back.'

'And why not photography?'

'That's something I would love to do.'

'You know you're good at it, all the pictures you took in the war. So?'

'So the war was a unique thing. Terrible. But women did all kinds of things they'd never been allowed to do before, and then the war stopped and that was it.'

'But it's not like being a train driver or an engineer. You don't have to stop taking photographs just because the war's stopped, do you?'

He looked at Jude, waiting for an answer. Abruptly she stood up and, going into the hall, she rummaged in her bag. She came back into the kitchen holding a manilla envelope and pushed it across the table.

'I saw this happen. I took this, and I don't know why, but it's what made me call Daniel Brown.'

Putting aside his bowl of rice pudding, he opened the envelope and pulled out a photograph. Smoothing the crumbs from the table, he put the photograph down before him.

Slowly, beginning at the bottom edge, he moved a finger, tracing over the black band of border until it reached the falling woman: her diving arms, the flounce of her petticoats caught upwards in the fall, her face, eyes shut, mouth tight, her hair. Then it moved on, so slow now that he might have been marking out each brick on the building, till it reached the window where the waitress stood, just out of focus, staring out, while just above her, beyond her sight for just a split second longer, a woman is falling to her death. His finger stopped, and he circled the waitress's head.

'Almost my first action photo,' Jude said.

'You being sarcastic?'

'Am I ever sarcastic about myself?'

'You wouldn't want to be her, would you?' he said, and though his tone was light, she saw that his eyes were worried.

'No,' she said. 'I wouldn't.'

'That's all right then.'

'I want to be the one with the camera,' Jude said.

'You caught her in flight,' he said.

'But not like taking birds.'

'It's extraordinary. Terrible.'

'It was just chance, my being there. I was looking for something different, but then she climbed out and . . . '

'What made her jump?'

Jude shook her head. 'I only took the photograph.'

'So do it again. And again. Become a photographer.'

'But I don't want to take pictures of children, or dogs, or newly-weds. And that's what women photographers do if they're lucky, that's what's considered suitable, not women caught plunging to their deaths. Oh, and the royal family, and military occasions, strangely enough. Over here, anyway. I couldn't be a photo-journalist, though that's what I was in Belgium. At least not with an agency.'

'So break the mould. Be the first.'

'And all the time I'm trying to break the mould, what do I live on?'

'Be the waitress too. Get a job in a restaurant. You could share with me, here,' and he waved his arm with what struck Jude as touching largesse.

'On your sofa?'

'It'd be fine.'

'And if you had a friend back?'

'As long as you didn't try to pinch him.'

Jude laughed. 'And if I wanted to have a friend back?'

Peter threw up his hands. 'Well, don't smoke a pipe then. No dreams. But anyway come back and visit me sooner,' and he reached across the rice pudding, tugged Jude's hand across the table and lifted it to his lips.

'If I weren't . . . you know,' he said. Almost coyly, Jude thought.

'Except you're not my type,' she said with a grin.

Lying on the sofa that night, Jude thought about the conversation and wondered if Peter was right. That it was better not to have the pipe dream, if you never did anything with it. Still, his was the easier one she thought, as her mind stumbled into sleep, the right man rather than the right life.

Peter's voice woke Jude. He was speaking to somebody, and she realised that the telephone bell in her dream had been real. It was the middle of the night and he was standing by the hall table in his pyjamas, his body still hunched over with sleep but his voice with a note to it that had Jude entirely awake even before she'd fully remembered where she was. She'd heard this accent before, when they'd received casualty warnings before a bombardment. Then, too, Peter's voice would become clipped so that you might almost mistake it for hostility if you didn't know him.

'Yes . . . yes, I understand. She did see him, yes. I'm not in a position to answer that. No. She is, yes. No, I can't do that now, but if you give me your telephone number, she will speak to you in the morning.'

Her eyes narrowed against the light, Jude pushed open the sitting room door.

'Leo?' she said.

Peter put a hand over the receiver. 'It's his father,' he said. 'He's disappeared.'

'Who's disappeared? Whose father?'

'Daniel Brown's father.'

Jude shut her eyes, shook her head to clear it. She put her hand out for the telephone receiver. 'Let me talk,' she said.

Peter handed it to her, disappeared to the bedroom and returned a moment later with a dressing-gown, which he draped around her shoulders, and a sweater for himself.

Jude leant down to the mouthpiece. 'Hello, this is Jude Hursten.'

It might have been Daniel speaking, the voice was so like his, urgent, desperate in tone.

'Our son went to meet you on Saturday? He

said he was meeting you?'

'Is that Mr Brown?' Jude said.

'Yes, yes. Daniel's father. We don't know what's happened to him.'

Jude looked down at the floor, at her feet pale and distant. She shivered and crossed one foot on top of the other for warmth, feeling the floor dust rub across her skin.

'I met him in Kew Gardens on Saturday afternoon, and he left me there at about half past four.'

'He wouldn't say anything to us afterwards. Not a word. Only packed up a few things and left.'

'What things?'

'His passport, and some money. I don't know what else. He took a small suitcase.'

The thought crossed her mind that this wasn't usually how you met the parents, and she swallowed a smile. She looked over at Peter, squatted down, his back against the kitchen door, his head slumped. She watched him put a fist to his sleepy eyes and was struck by a wash of affection. At that moment he looked to her just like her little nephew Tom and she wanted nothing more in the world than to put her arms around him and take him back to his warm bed. The telephone earpiece was hard against her ear.

'How did you get this number?' she said.

'He's not with you then?'

'I haven't seen him since I left Kew Gardens, but it was only on Saturday.' Jude looked at her watch. It was one o'clock in the morning. 'A day and a half ago. How did you find me here?'

'We telephoned your brother. Woke him up, I'm afraid. Please, Miss Hursten, Daniel has never gone like this before, even in the worst times after Ireland. We're beside ourselves.'

Jude could hear another voice weeping in the background, Daniel's mother she supposed. She put her hand over the receiver and looked across at Peter. 'What should I say?' she whispered.

He looked up at her, his eyes alert. 'You could meet them tomorrow?'

'But I don't know what's happened to him.'

'Perhaps you could find out.'

'I have to get a train north.'

Peter looked at her again, not speaking.

Jude took her hand off the receiver. 'I don't know that there's anything I can do to help,' she said, 'but . . . '

There was silence at the other end of the line, a breathing, waiting silence.

'I could visit you tomorrow morning, perhaps? He might have returned by then anyway, and if not . . . ' Jude left the sentence unfinished.

'Thank you, yes,' the voice said. 'Thank you. Perhaps ten o'clock? We're at the end of the District Line. Richmond. If you take a cab from the station?' And as if anxious to finish the conversation before Jude could change her mind, Mr Brown gave out an address and said goodbye.

★   ★   ★

They were waiting for her, the front door opened, ready before she was through the gate,

185

so that she had to push away the feeling that she was in some sinister folk tale from which she'd never emerge. Mr Brown was tall and slender like Daniel, and dressed with more care than his son. He shook Jude's hand and showed her into the drawing room. Once again it was a sunny day, but a fire was burning in the hearth and the room was sweltering.

'She feels the cold so easily now,' Mr Brown said as Jude sat down. 'She's just going to bring in some coffee. You would like some coffee?'

'Thank you.'

Mr Brown nodded.

'You haven't heard from him then?' Jude said.

Mr Brown shook his head.

'And friends, family, nobody else has?'

'We don't see very many, we're quite private, cosy I suppose. Just the four of us, three now since John.'

'Daniel told me of his death. I'm very sorry for your loss,' Jude said. She waited for Mr Brown to ask her how she'd met his son, where she lived, anything, but he said nothing more, only walked to the door.

'I'll just help her in with it. Sent the maid home today. Easier if we do it ourselves, these awkward times.'

Left alone, Jude looked around. The room had all the usual paraphernalia — easy chairs, a sofa, rugs, mantelpiece with clock, photographs, some ornaments. Jude looked at the photographs, Daniel in his family, his dead brother. The last showed John, smart in army uniform and proud as punch. There were a few pictures on the wall

186

and a newspaper and a couple of magazines on the side table, just what might be expected. But there was something about it all that at first Jude couldn't put her finger on, something which, despite the blazing fire, left her spirit cold. She sat down on the sofa and narrowed her eyes like she did when sizing up a photograph. Sometimes it made things clearer, brought them out of the shadows. Now it made her see how carefully the room had been arranged, everything lined up, from the objects on the mantelpiece, each equidistant from the next, to the pictures, to the armchairs which were at matching angles before the fire. Even the hearthrug fronds reached to exactly the same place beyond the fireplace. The curtains were tied so that each had the same number of folds in the hanging, and the books in the shelves looked as if they had been arranged by height.

Sitting still in the midst of it all, Jude felt her skin flinch and she got up and went to the window, looked out at the garden, at the trees and the shrubs, at all there was to see that was alive and unruly, till the door opened again and Mr Brown came in with the coffee tray, followed by his wife.

If Daniel had his father's voice, he had his mother's eyes, the same blue, the green blue of the sea before a storm. But unlike her son, who looked around so restlessly, Mrs Brown seemed like someone who couldn't afford to see anything more. Her eyes were cast down, as if the pattern in the carpet held some solution, so that apart from the brief glimpse Jude had on shaking her hand, all she could see of Mrs Brown's expression was the slight movement of her mouth as she opened it to drink the coffee and, in the end, to speak.

'Thank you for coming,' Daniel's father said.

Jude gave a slight nod and sipped the weak coffee and waited.

'My wife doesn't agree with me, doesn't think you could help, feels we should keep it in the family. And maybe she's right, I don't know, but if there's the slightest chance . . . '

'What makes you think Daniel might need helping?' Jude said, keeping her voice impartial as best she could. 'He's only been gone since Saturday afternoon, and he is an adult.'

Mr Brown looked over at his wife, but she kept her eyes on her lap and said nothing.

'I don't know what he has said to you,' he said. 'I don't know what it is he thinks he's seen in your photograph. But lately he's been having dreams, violent, disturbing dreams, about his time abroad.'

'In France?' Jude said.

'In Ireland. And not only in his sleep. Talks about people not being what they seem, about needing to know things, needing to go back. And when he's not speaking like this, or muttering rather, he's more and more withdrawn. You ask him a question and he doesn't answer. And he can't bear being in the house.'

'He was a little jumpy in Kew Gardens,' Jude said carefully.

'He wouldn't speak to us afterwards. Twenty

minutes, and then he left, not uttering a single word.'

'So, where do you think he might have gone? What might he have done?'

And when Mr Brown looked at her, Jude knew his worst fear.

'But he took a suitcase,' she said, and suddenly she had an idea as to where Daniel might have gone. It was just the germ of an idea and she said nothing aloud. She didn't want to raise their hopes or fears, nor her own.

So far Mrs Brown had sat motionless, but now she raised her head and stared at Jude.

'What did you say to him? To my son?' she said quietly.

'I didn't . . . ' Jude said.

'It's your fault,' she said, very calmly, just as if she'd said it was a fine day, her hands gathered on her lap, though Jude could see that her fingers were white in each other's grip. 'He was doing quite nicely till he met you, you and your picture.' She turned to her husband. 'We had everything nicely set up, didn't we, for him? Really quite nicely, all the wars over with.'

'My dear, I don't think we can blame Miss Hursten,' said Mr Brown. But Mrs Brown seemed not to hear him, or at least not to heed him. Standing up, she set her cup and saucer on the tray and left the room, shutting the door behind her.

Mr Brown walked to the window, stared out.

'Did he say anything, in Kew Gardens, that might have led you to think that he wasn't well? Or did you have any kind of disagreement? I'm sorry my wife spoke to you like that, it's just that we are at our wits' end. I need to be calm, not least for her sake, but we don't know what to do.'

'What about the police?'

'We thought about that, but unless we think Daniel's done something wrong, broken the law, or . . . ' He tapped at the window glass. 'The river's just behind us. They pull people out every year. Not usually up here, usually further in to the city.'

'He didn't say anything to me that made me think that,' Jude said.

'But what did he talk about? You were the last person to see him.'

'He did say a bit about Ireland, about the food tasting different.'

This made him laugh, and Jude had a glimpse of a different man.

'He had my wife cook him bacon every day for a week when he got home,' he said. 'He couldn't get enough of the taste of it. Even staying with the Murrays, the food didn't taste like home.'

'Irish friends?'

'Not exactly, no, but they were very kind to Daniel. My wife's sister, Daniel's aunt, was at school with Moira Murray. She said they'd be happy to have him visit during his time there, if he was stationed near enough.' Mr Brown fell silent.

'And he was? Stationed near enough?' Jude said after a minute, prompting.

'Yes. They live in a place called Castletowne, which I gather is in a pretty corner of the west.

190

And Daniel stayed there quite a bit. Coolderry House.'

And Jude nodded, and kept her face still.

Mr Brown's suggestion that she look in Daniel's bedroom took Jude by surprise.

'How could that help? I don't know him very well,' she said, uncomfortable with the thought of such unsolicited intimacy.

'I know it's a strange thing to ask. Snatching at straws really. It's only, we don't have people into the house, and nobody who knew him, maybe you might notice something we've overlooked.'

So, for the sake of his desperate father, Jude agreed. She stood in the middle of the small room and looked at Daniel's neat white bed, pyjamas laid out at the foot, his wardrobe, his bookshelf with its books, not arranged by size, his writing desk, the half dozen school photos on the wall. She looked for the disturbed, desperate man she had met and she looked for the man, still mysterious to her, that she found so compelling. But the room gave nothing away.

Mr Brown pulled open one of the desk drawers. 'I'm afraid that I've had a look at the letters,' he said. 'Didn't like doing it, but, anyway, there was nothing recent, apart from your letter of course. That's where we got the telephone number from. I hope you don't mind.'

Jude inclined her head in a way she hoped signified neither offence nor acquiescence.

'So, you never found out what happened to him in Ireland? Contacted the Murrays, perhaps, in case they knew more?'

Mr Brown shook his head.

'Daniel was very clear about that when he got back. He was all those months in the hospital, you know. He couldn't tell us anything for military reasons, and we were to say nothing to anybody else, even if they asked, and especially if they were Irish. So when the Murrays wrote, concerned as to Daniel's well-being, we didn't reply. Terrible, not to reply to such a letter. But Daniel had been adamant. So fierce.'

Mr Brown fell silent. Jude pointed at the drawer of letters.

'There was nothing in there that might help you?' she said.

'They were mainly letters from John. A couple from us, when he was in Ireland. Some postcards from school friends. Nobody he has seen for years. But you could look at them, if you wanted.'

Jude was beginning to regret coming. Despite her deepening conviction about where Daniel might have gone, there was nothing she could do in this house, and she was seeing too much, too much of these people's pain.

'I think probably you'd have found anything important,' she said. 'I should go now.'

They stood uncertain, neither quite sure how to take their leave, Mr Brown rolling gently on to the balls of his feet and then off again. He put his hand out, and Jude, thinking that it was probably more appropriate to shake hands here, in Daniel's room, than on the doorstep of a house that could bear to let nothing in, and noticing how well-kept his fingernails were, was lifting her hand in response when there was a scream downstairs, and the sound of breaking glass.

Jude had a thorough acquaintance with breaking glass and this sound, she knew, was of something small, a glass probably. But what was disconcerting was that the scream had come first. She watched Daniel's father rock backwards and turn towards the door in a single fluid motion, the sounds tugging him as a magnet tugs at iron filings.

'Don't go before I return,' he called back to Jude.

'No,' she said, because under the circumstances she couldn't very well say anything else.

Sitting down on Daniel's white bed, the door pulled to, and though she could hear sobbing below, Jude felt calm, dispassionate. Her disquiet at being so close to this family's grief dropped away, rushed down the stairs with Mr Brown, and she looked around the room as if for the first time.

'There must be something to find,' she said, and she went to take a closer look at the desk.

But Daniel's father had been right. Old letters from other people held no clues, and there was nothing else in that drawer. She pulled open the others, but they had little in them beyond the usual detritus: old fountain pens, a cricket ball, writing paper, school fixtures diaries, penknife, feathers, a few toy soldiers, an old school timetable.

She went over to the wardrobe, opened the door, her reflection swinging away in its mirror. A few suits hung hollowly, below them several pairs of shoes, so that they looked together like puppets with no strings. There were four broad shallow boxes stacked beside the shoes. Jude lifted one out and its lightness surprised her till she lifted the lid. Inside were birds' eggs, each caught in its own false nest and neatly labelled.

At the back of the wardrobe, braid catching the light, Jude could see an officer's uniform. A string of ties hung across the door, and as she pushed it to, they swung in easy motion, several getting caught in the lock.

She wandered over to the bookshelf and glanced at the titles. An abridged Gibbon, some Greek philosophy, Nietzsche, a few novels: Dickens, Henry Dana, Kipling, Rider Haggard. In the centre of the shelf were the two volumes of Coward's *Birds*, a book Jude knew of but did not own. At a loss in this room, she reached and pulled out Vol. I. Opening it randomly, she glanced through the pages. There were dates and locations written in beside some of the bird descriptions: Mothercombe, Aug 24, 1920. South Downs, Feb 16, 1924. Timoleague, Dec 12, 1920, and occasionally the comment, 'sketch made', and she remembered their first meeting, Daniel's notebook, full of wings and feathers. It was in putting the volume back that Jude noticed the diary. She had to push Nietzsche and Plato hard up against Kipling to make space again, and as she was slanting Coward's *Birds* Vol. I back in to the shelf she noticed what at first she thought might be a sketchbook, placed flat to the wall, as if in hiding.

It was a slender volume bound in imitation red

morocco, and inscribed on the first page in careful hand.

Occasional Diary
Belonging to Daniel Frederick Brown
June 1920

Turning the page, there was a drawing of a wading bird, and behind it, barely sketched in, a ruined tower. Beneath this: Castletowne, Jan, 1921. She flipped to the end of the diary. It seemed to break off and the last pages were empty, but at the back there were lists of birds and plants, some with place names and dates beside them. Jude was about to read the first entry when she heard Mr Brown's footsteps on the stairs and, without a qualm, she slipped the book into her bag.

He came in, diffidently, almost as though it were her room.

'I'm sorry,' he said. 'It was only a small breakage.' He was silent a moment, rubbing absently at his right hand. 'There can't be anything really that you . . . '

'I can't promise anything,' she said, 'but . . . '

He put his hand to his head and Jude watched a thread of blood well up and trace itself across the knuckles of three fingers.

'You've cut yourself,' she said.

He nodded.

'Have you got some disinfectant?'

'It's only that I don't know what to do, and if you were to think of anything?' and Jude nodded, then shook her head.

195

8

Telling Peter, Jude didn't know where the decision had come from, except that she knew she had made it with absolute certainty, that this was what she was going to do. When she got on to the tube at Richmond, she hadn't known, but by the time she reached Regent's Park, she had come to a decision.

'You barely know this man from Adam,' Peter said. 'He's disturbed, shell-shocked very likely, maybe violent, and he's been a Black and Tan. I'm not even sure that you're in love with him. Not with the man himself. And now you're proposing . . . '

'Not proposing. I am going.'

'All right, at the drop of a hat you're going on your own to a country you don't know, that's just come out of a war with England, to rescue him. A bloody tricky needle in a dangerous haystack.'

'Yes. That's about it, except for the rescuing.'

Before negotiating her way into the hotel kitchens to find Peter, Jude had used one of the telephones in the lobby to make a call. The telephone booth had a door with glass panels that folded shut, so that you could see the comings and goings, but not hear them, and it had a gilt chair upholstered in maroon velvet. Jude sat down, sinking into the plush, and shut her eyes. This softness was seductive and for a moment she imagined never getting up, but the telephone rang. Her call had been put through.

She would have preferred to speak to Leo, but he was at work and hard to get hold of. So she was telephoning home to Sally instead.

'It's Jude here,' she said. 'I'm still in London.'

Sally's voice was anxious. 'You're not ill?' she said.

'No, I'm well, but I won't be back today. And I've decided to leave my job.'

Jude was glad she was sitting down to say this. She felt her legs go shaky. She'd decided what to say and rehearsed the words on the tube, but still it was different speaking them out loud, to someone else.

'You've decided to do what?' Sally's voice sounded rushed and impatient.

'Could you tell Leo I'm leaving my job. I'll write properly when I get back, but if he could please send in a note for me tomorrow.'

She could hear Sally breathe in deeply, but she said nothing.

'I'll be coming home, probably tomorrow, for a short time anyway. I'll explain as best I can then,' Jude said.

'Is it that man?' Sally said.

'It's not what you'd expect.'

Sally sighed. 'No,' she said, 'of course it isn't.'

'Sally,' Jude said. 'Would you?'

'I don't want to be picking up your pieces again,' Sally said, and Jude hung her head as if she were a child, although Sally, hundreds of miles away, could have heard only the silence.

Eyes straight ahead, walking confidently and

quite as if she knew her way and had an appointment, Jude bluffed her way through five sets of double doors to reach the kitchens. Peter's kingdom. She stood inside the last set, winded for a moment by her own decisiveness. The room before her seemed to stretch forever, a domain of scrubbed wood and marble, black ovens squatting like chiefs, shelves full of pans, bowls of vegetables, tubs of herbs, pots of spices, things waiting for their moment under tea towels, and all around figures wrapped in white aprons ministering, pouring, stirring, chopping.

The air was warm and moist, and as Jude crossed the kitchen, scouting for her friend, different smells gusted across her, garlic sautéing, bread dough, rosemary, cinnamon, charging her taste buds, making her mouth water. A boy swabbed at the quarry tiles with a mop, and Jude tapped him on the back.

'I'm looking for Peter Davis?' she said. 'He's a chef de partie.'

'Sauces,' the boy said, pointed Jude across to one side and put his head down to his swabbing again.

Peter had his little finger in a small pan when she found him, a young commis chef standing anxiously beside him. He looked like someone tasting wine, rolling the flavour round his mouth, sucking in air, before nodding.

'Butter needs to be a fraction browner,' he said, 'otherwise good.' Then he turned and saw Jude. She saw the surprise in his eyes, but he didn't say anything. Instead, after taking a long look, he asked her whether she'd eaten anything since breakfast.

She shook her head and would have spoken, but he put his hand up.

'After I've fed you,' he said. 'Tell me then. If it's this important, you need fuel first.'

He took her over to the ovens and lit the gas under the smallest burner.

'Omelette,' he said, and she leaned back against the chopping block and watched him in his element, just as she'd watched him in the cellar years ago, his movements, then and now, both fluid and utterly efficient.

'I'm on an early shift today,' he said. 'Once I've finished prepping, we can talk. And I'm not on tonight.'

Reaching for a bowl on the shelf, he took a pinch of fresh herbs and sprinkled them over the frying pan.

'Cheese?' he said, and she shook her head. 'Good girl. It's often what they want out there, but it buggers up an omelette, I think,' giving a shrug and a grin.

Pulling a plate off one of the piles stacked below the prepping tables, he folded the omelette over on itself and slid it onto the plate. Shouting out some instructions to the commis, he signalled to Jude.

'The vegetable store,' he said. 'We can sit in peace there,' and he led Jude over to a door in one corner.

It was cool and smelt of earth. They sat on sacks of potatoes, and when Jude had finished the omelette Peter set the plate down on one side and crossed his arms.

'So?' he said.

'So,' Jude said, and she told him everything, and then she told him of the decision she'd come to. 'These places. Horse Island. Coolderry, which is a house. They were important to him, and he spoke as if they were connected. And then, when Mr Brown mentioned this place, Castletowne, of course I don't know, but if I had to guess, I'd say that wherever they are, these names, that's where he'll have gone.'

'Why?'

'Because he spoke of them as good places, refuges. In Kew Gardens he talked as if in the grip of something terrible that had happened over there. Not being ambushed, and not his injury. Something that gave him nightmares, that was still pulling him in. And set against the nightmare were these places. Coolderry House, Horse Island, that he tried to return to in his head instead.'

'That was talk,' Peter said.

Jude shook her head.

'I think he will break out of his mind, whether he goes there or not. And I'm sure he's gone there for real.'

Peter took her hand, squeezed it. 'Why do you want to do this?'

Jude looked down at the cool, dark floor. 'I don't know. Superstition, maybe. There were things Richard wrote about to me, I don't know what to do with them, and he died before I could find out. Daniel Brown's a haunted man too. Perhaps I don't want to find out too much about his ghosts before I have to, in case it stops me doing something.'

'I think you should let it go. I know you're drawn to him. Whatever you say, you are, and it's great to see you so alive, but it might be very dangerous. He's in a pickle and you barely know him. You made no promises. And you've got your own life to live.'

'That's exactly why I can't let it go.'

★　★　★

He argued at her nearly all the way back to the flat, telling her she didn't know what she was going into, that Daniel was a virtual stranger, that he might be violent, crazy, impossible to find. That her guess might be wrong, and he might turn up at his parents' house tomorrow, that she would do better to forget all of this, that it was a mad quest, a piece of folly, that she was only doing it because she was frustrated with her own life.

Jude listened as they walked through the commuter crowds, jostled for space in the underground lift, stood sardined on the tube, elbows in one another's faces, and mostly she agreed with him. And by the time they reached Peter's flat, he knew he couldn't dissuade her.

'It's for myself as much as for any thought of rescuing,' Jude said. 'Same as in the war. I'm not pretending to much virtue.'

Three storeys up, she looked out of Peter's kitchen window, beyond the patch of garden belonging to downstairs, beyond the garden wall, to the cemetery. They'd be shutting the gates soon, but she could see a few people still wandering under the angels' long, stony shadows. Peter put a sheet of paper and a pencil on the table.

'Since I can't dissuade you,' he said, 'make a list, and I'll make toast.'

They covered everything they could think of. What clothes to take, money, travelling as a woman, priests, the journey to Holyhead, the IRA, what story to tell, what to do in an emergency.

'Send me a telegram, or call me. Doesn't matter what time. Reverse the charges.'

'I'm going to go as soon as I can,' Jude said. 'By the end of the week, I hope.'

'Can you get the money released that quickly?'

'Leo will loan it to me if necessary. He's got the same legacy.'

Peter raised his eyebrows. 'Even if he doesn't want you to go?'

'I think so. No point in making bad blood between us.'

'Even though it could be dangerous.'

Jude rolled her eyes. 'It won't be the first time. I'm very well used to bullets and bangs.'

Peter sat down opposite and buttered some more toast. 'Don't be flippant. You know I don't mean bullets and bangs.'

'Well, I'm probably safer as a girl than as a boy.'

'I bet you don't know any more than I do what it's like in Ireland now or what he's like over there, if he is. But if he was a Black and Tan he can't have been a very gentle chap, and they won't be best pleased to have him back.'

'Which I'll find out soon enough.'

'Sherlock,' Peter said, knocking a cigarette from his packet and passing it to her. 'So bring me back some Powers, since you won't be stopped. A big bottle.'

★   ★   ★

More than anybody else, Tom knew why she was going. She hadn't told Tom and Elsa much, only that she was going to go to Ireland on her motorbike to search for someone whom she thought had got lost there.

'So why don't they ask somebody the way?' Elsa said.

'It's not that kind of getting lost, stupid,' Tom said.

'Tom,' Jude said, 'she's younger than you.'

'But it isn't,' he said, and then seeing his sister near to tears, he sighed and tried to explain. 'You know Elsa, it's like playing cowboys and Indians and you're lost in the desert and I know where you are really, you're up on that bit of wall in the corner, behind the greenhouse. But in the game I have to make up clever ways for you to come down all by yourself and get to the stockade.'

'But who is it that's got lost?' Elsa said. 'Not any of us. Not Daddy 'cos he's at the office, and Mummy's gone to buy some muslin. And not Martin because we saw him yesterday.'

Tom shook his head in exasperation.

'What about Grandma and Grandpa then?'

Elsa went on. 'Or the man Jude took to the Rocks, with the stick?'

'Or Elsa's Mister Ictharus?' Tom said. 'Are you going to say everybody we know who it isn't? What about Father Christmas, or the Hound of the Baskervilles?'

Elsa's lip began to quiver again.

'Actually you're right, Elsa. It is the man with the stick,' Jude said.

'He was called Daniel,' Elsa said.

'Why does he need to be found?' said Tom.

'I won't know that till I find him,' Jude said, and both the children seemed to think that that was enough of an answer, or at least they didn't ask any more.

⋆   ⋆   ⋆

Jude stood against the ferry rail and watched the gulls pitching and scavenging in the wake. Her camera was packed away deep in the sidecar down in the hold of the boat, so she couldn't step aside behind the camera's eye, and she had just to look. She had sat in the saloon for a time, but there seemed to be a great many commercial travellers tucking into their dinners and the smell of the lamb chops became too much. She was better off outside, watching the wind suck at her cigarette and the light drop out of the sky.

Leaving had been easier than she'd anticipated, except with Leo. He didn't try to argue her out of it, as Peter did. Instead he sulked, more as though she were his eldest child than his sister.

'But we've made every allowance for you,' he said. They were picking raspberries for supper, and all Jude could see of him was the top of his old straw hat. 'The darkroom, your comings and goings, not expecting you home for meals.'

'You have,' Jude said, 'and I'm very grateful for all you've done, making your home mine too.'

'I don't want gratitude,' Leo said, 'but I do expect you to have the same consideration for us as we have for you.'

'Leo,' Jude said, 'this has nothing to do with you or with how you've been. It's nothing to do with all of this, the house, Sally, the children. It's separate,' and even as she spoke, she knew that that of course was what he resented.

'We do everything for you and then you go and you shove it back in our faces,' he said.

Jude said nothing.

'I don't expect there's anything I can do to stop you going.'

'No, there isn't.' She put down her bowl of raspberries and walked round the canes to his side. 'But you are my family. You know that. You've been father and mother to me since they both died. I'm not shoving anything back in your face, and without you, God knows.'

She sat down on the grass.

'Please?' she said, patting the place beside her, and after a moment of hesitation, Leo sat down, arms folded over his chest.

'I have to do this,' she said. 'Not only to try to help Daniel Brown, wherever on earth he is, but also for Richard, and most of all for myself.'

'You can't bring Richard back by saving Daniel,' Leo said.

'I know.'

'Then . . . ? Leo looked round at her, a question on his face, but she shook her head.

'Don't ask me now, because I can't say. But I promise I'll explain when I come back.'

They sat on in silence till Elsa came with a message from the kitchen requesting raspberries.

After this conversation, Leo fussed around Jude like a mother hen, which she was glad of, bringing back purchases of maps, waterproofs and warm socks, all a girl could need, even helping her concoct a story about what she was doing, travelling in Ireland alone.

★　★　★

Jude wondered whether Daniel had been on this boat, or whether he'd taken a different route back. If, that was, she was right about his returning. But her hunch was strong. She was certain she would find him in Ireland. She put a hand to her breast to feel the diary, tucked away safely in an inside pocket. Though she had a Baedeker in her bag, who knew but that this little book might be her most important guide.

The sky was overcast and it was nearly dark on the deck by now, and getting cold. Looking down a last time over the rail, Jude could see only sharp glints from the sea, all else black. She turned towards the light and looked in at the saloon.

The chops had been despatched, the glasses of porter refilled, sluicing and slopping with the slant of the boat, and there was an air of thrusting bonhomie, visible even from the other side of the porthole. A band of exhaustion tightened across Jude's shoulders. Though soon she would have to be a gregarious and affable self, and she would do it very well, for now she wanted nothing more than to nurse her solitude, so drawing back from the glass, she went to find her cabin.

The lower berth was already filled, its occupant lying with the blanket pulled high to her chin, eyes tight shut, dark hair tethered in a net like a separate creature, Pierrot face in the night cream. Jude got ready for bed as quietly as she could, and was climbing up to her berth when the Pierrot spoke.

'I have the cotton wool taken out now, so I'll be hearing you better.'

'I had hoped not to have woken you at all,' Jude said, stranded on the ladder.

She took a step back down, because it seemed uncivil to carry on climbing up.

'Ah, I was only just in myself,' the Pierrot said. 'Catherine Whelan. Pleased to meet you.' She waved the cotton wool. 'Against the engine noise,' she said. 'Would you want some yourself?'

'Jude Hursten,' Jude said nodding. 'Cotton wool?'

'Yes.'

'Thank you, but I like the engine noise. It soothes me. Sorry to have woken you. Goodnight.' And retreating up the ladder, she grappled with the sheets, which seemed maliciously tucked so as to prevent entry, and finally slid between them and slept.

FLIGHT

9

Daniel sat on the tube to Paddington staring at the map, staring at the lines reaching out this way and that, to Bow Road and Hounslow Barracks, Finsbury Park and Golders Green, as if they were straining to leave the centre, to unravel.

It was so different, going to Ireland without a gun, as if really he were in disguise.

He knew that the Murrays couldn't solve his problem, but he needed a safe place to go to, and their house, Coolderry, above that stretch of sea was as safe a place as he knew. Probably he should have telegraphed them, made sure his visit would be all right, made sure they were still there, but he had decided that he should just act now, no prevarication, no forward planning. And if, when he arrived, they had left and their house had gone up in the Troubles, then he would walk in the rubble and cold ash, with the rooks behind in their stand of pines and the herring gulls shouting above the sea and his next move would come to him.

He wondered what Jude had done, after he'd left Kew Gardens. He was sorry he'd left her like that, but he'd walked very fast until he was sure she wasn't following. It made things harder that he liked her, though what on earth she thought of him he couldn't say.

When she'd come towards him at the

turnstile, he'd felt proud that this beautiful woman was coming to meet him, and even with everything else crowding in, he'd wondered whether people might think shc was his girl, fiancée even. She moved so surely, as if everything she did rose from a clear decision. The way she walked, turned her head to look around, even the way she fished in her bag for something, and it wasn't that she was entrenched, only that she knew what it was she was moving towards.

If his mother were to meet Jude, he knew she'd say afterwards that she was a man's woman, which was a way of saying she was too forward in her own bearing. And his father would talk even harder than usual, about world affairs or cricket, or the state of the roads, to veil his unease in the face of such strong definition. Daniel knew all too well where Jude had gone since her war and, standing there in Kew Gardens, waiting for her to see him, and even in the midst of his own confusion, it crossed his mind that he'd like to be there when she walked back in from outside again. He'd watched her smile when she saw him and it had made his skin jump.

On the train from Cork a couple sat opposite Daniel, a woman in a blue cloak and an older man. The man had mud on his boots, and his hands were resting flat on his thighs as though he had been taught to sit that way in public places. The woman was crying a little, wiping her eyes on a corner of the cloak. The man leaned forward, tapped Daniel on the knee.

'No basket,' he said, pointing to the woman.

'No?' Daniel said.

'He was the last, we've just seen off. We didn't take the train with the others, but he was our last, so we've been to see him off at Cobh. We watched him into the ship, and he was holding the basket, waving to us with the other hand, just as if he was off to Cork for some business.'

'Oh,' Daniel said, unsure what response the man wanted.

'They said it would be better with the war over.'

'The war?'

'Against your lot.'

Daniel looked down at the floor. The boards were scuffed. If you ran your hand along them, you'd fetch up with a splinter. The man doesn't know, Daniel told himself.

'And it isn't? Over?' he said.

'It's a great thing to have the British gone, no offence, and to have the next madness over, thank God. But there's still nothing to be done for work, and so the young ones, they've no choice but to leave. Always the emigration.'

'I'm very sorry,' Daniel said, but as he spoke, he knew the apology was for something more, something that he'd never yet dared face. And he felt the fear rise, because he had breached his own defence, coming back here.

The man shook his head. 'No, no. I'm only telling to explain about the basket . . . '

'I am very sorry,' Daniel said again, and he thought, I have kept this from me, kept it away with my injury and my fury. Now what will I do?

'Because you might be wondering, otherwise, though maybe not, being from over the water and things done differently there,' the old man said, and from the way that he stopped talking, Daniel saw he was expected to answer.

It went through his head that he would go mad. He knew that a terrible thing had been done to him, and he had come back here because of it. But there was something else looming, that he'd kept his eyes averted from all these years till now, and sitting opposite this old couple and riding across this landscape, he couldn't do so any longer. He'd done nothing to injure these two particular people, nothing to harm them, but it might as well have been the old man he'd arrested; it might have been their son he'd pistol-whipped or their daughter he'd burnt out; it might have been their family he'd looked away from as the boys obeyed orders. In the name of another man's order, he had done what no man should and he didn't know how to stand before it now.

The woman had dried her eyes by now and was staring out through the window.

'Be quiet, Dennis, for pity's sake,' she said. 'Going on about the basket. It's a wonder I haven't sent you over the water too,' and she turned her head and looked at Daniel gravely.

'From England,' she said, a statement and not a question, and Daniel nodded. 'Whereabouts?'

'London.'

'We've relatives in London. In the north of the city. Kilburn.'

'I'm from the south. Twickenham.'

'So it's your first time over here, is it?' the man said.

'Is it so obvious?' Daniel said, bringing out a hollow laugh from somewhere, for it felt to him as if his guilt must be written on his skin.

The man tapped himself on the chest. 'I've an eye for such things. Are you going a long way?'

'Castletowne,' Daniel said, and the woman nodded as if he'd just confirmed something she already knew.

'And then home to your mother?' she said, the words tugged from her as if she couldn't help herself but ask, and when Daniel nodded, she turned her face to the window again.

The man had been filling his pipe, tamping down the tobacco. 'Is it family you've got here?' he said.

Daniel could smell the tobacco, its sweetness filling his head, familiar, conjuring something.

'I don't know,' he said, and maybe it was the look he had, but they didn't ask him more after that. The woman looked on out of the window, the man attended to his pipe, and Daniel shut his eyes and pretended sleep.

The train ran across rough land. There was Cork city; there were small towns, Crookstown, Macroom, Bandon, Dunmanway; villages occasionally, a string of buildings and a creamery; sometimes a smallholding, dogs chasing the train, wild-haired children waving, shouting, their mouths wide in silent cries, the smell of turf in the carriages. But always the land threatened, rough bog, rocks, hills dense with gorse and heather, the metal gleam of surface water catching the shadow of the train as it went past.

Daniel sat, eyes closed, and clutched at the straw of his sanity.

The weather had darkened by the time the train reached Skibbereen, a soft rain gentling the edges of buildings. Before leaving the train, the woman found an umbrella and the man buttoned his jacket high into his neck. Relieved to have something to do, Daniel took out his cape and pulled on his hat. He thought it was about five miles to Castletowne, and he'd already decided to walk, ignoring the ache in his leg, always stronger when it rained. Stepping down from the train, Daniel turned to the woman.

'Where would be best for something to eat?'

She seemed to look him up and down before answering, as though they hadn't already met.

'You'd better try Becher's,' she said.

Daniel put out his hand. 'All the best then.'

And she nodded, her lips in a tight line, and maybe it was just his mood, but Daniel thought something in her eyes had gone hard. He turned to her husband, but he had his back to them and was deep in conversation with a man in an overcoat. So Daniel left them and went on his way.

He ate dinner at the hotel in the plainest of dining rooms, its walls a pale yellow at the wainscot rising to a deep brown near the ceiling, the air very slightly rancid with the decades of tobacco smoke, a single glassed-in trout — fifteen pounds in weight and caught in the Ilen river on 29 February, 1904 — eyeing him as he ate the food quickly, cutting the meat up into equally-sized pieces, breaking his knife through the potatoes' coarse skin into the floury flesh, scooping it up with his fork. He had forgotten these potatoes till now. They didn't exist in England, and if he hadn't been so hungry, he would have left them on his plate.

'I must be crazy, to be coming back,' he thought, and his heart began to race and his palms became sweaty. He had to do this and it made him very scared.

It was still raining when he left Becher's. He shook out his cape and was about to fasten it around his shoulders when he looked at it with horror.

'Christ almighty!' he said below his breath.

Pulling the cape off and gathering it in his hands, he stared about him, but nobody seemed to have noticed, and he opened up his suitcase and stuffed it inside.

'Bloody fool!' he said, because it was his Auxiliary cape he'd been wearing, as clear a badge of office as pulling on the beret and pointing a pair of revolvers. Perhaps that was why the woman on the train had gone cold and the old man turned away with no farewell. And if that were so, he'd been lucky to get away with nothing worse than a woman's contempt.

Leaving the town with its Weeping Maid of Erin and its grey, weeping houses, his spirits calmed and he set his mind to the road and the effort the walk demanded. He would not think for now. Twice, carts slowed to offer him a lift; one stacked high with turf, the other with two milk churns, some hens in a basket and two sheets of corrugated iron. And both times Daniel returned their gestures and smiled and waved them on saying thanks, but he could do with the air, and both times it brought a laugh and an exclamation about the weather, then a flick of the whip, the donkey's reluctant hooves striking up a quicker pattern and slowly the cart would pull away from him.

Now he was back here, on a road like the road in his dreams. Rough banks of hedge with swags of mombretia, ditches full with clear ochre bog water and dense with tiny yellow flowers and wild watercress; fuchsia in its violent red and the endless, heavy hum of the bees; the coarse fields with their boulders and yellow blaze of ragwort, and the rain falling through the still air so that he could smell the damp wool of his jacket, so that his shoes squeaked. But it was better, this, to be able to see and touch and smell it than have it slip around him like vapour. So as he strode on, his suitcase clutched as tight as any weapon, though he was frightened, he felt clearer in his mind and he was sure he'd been right to come.

He passed cabins and farmhouses where dogs barked to kill, a shrine in pastel blue and chipped shells, the Virgin reaching out her arms, prayers tied to her wrists, her elbows, and cold candles guttered out on stones. And after a couple of miles, above the smell of burning turf, he could smell the sea. He wouldn't see it until he was almost there, but the brine in the air was enough to lift his head. Things steadied with the thought of it. The road turned and twisted as if reluctant to arrive and then he saw ahead the

218

plain, straight steeple of the Catholic church on the crossroads. It was only another mile or so to the village, another half mile beyond that to the house. A flock of sheep came wailing and bleating towards him, two boys and a dog chivvying. Daniel stood still while the sheep shoved their way by him, their wool pungent, mud-smeared, baubled on their rumps with droppings.

The sheep past, the boys were close in their ragged trousers, shirts and grubby waistcoats. One lifted arm and stick in greeting. But before he'd said more than a word Daniel was reaching round to his shoulder, pulling for where his rifle should be, the suitcase hitting against his legs so that he stumbled and fell on to the wet tarmac, his hands still grabbing air, thunder in his ears, a shout swallowed in his throat, till suddenly everything went still and he heard the sheep again and above him stood just a boy in torn trousers.

'Yous all right?' the boy said, putting out his hand.

'Lost my balance,' Daniel said, and the boy nodded, raised a finger in farewell and turned back to his flock.

He didn't let himself think about falling, about losing his footing on a wet Irish road, about what he'd seen in the boy's raised arm. Instead he set his mind to the house on the hill and the path down to the beach, to the little boat, to those two people who, he was sure, could help him somehow.

Passing the church, Daniel soon came to the

long hill down into the village. His leg was sore and he winced, walking carefully. He recognised the tumbled gate that led up to the standing stones on the crest of the hill. Mr Murray had taken him there, and to the hill fort opposite. You could see the whole of the peninsula from it. They'd stood there in the long shadows of early evening and Daniel had joked that he could hide out in the fort and never go back.

Down past the long wall, then he'd turn off to the right and though he was going slowly, it would only be another ten minutes' walk.

You couldn't see the house from the road. There was a short, winding drive dipping down in amidst the rhododendrons, oak trees behind, and then, magically, a glimpse of the sea, before you saw the house. It was nearly teatime by now. The rain had stopped and there were breaks in the cloud letting lines of sunlight through. Daniel turned through the gateposts. The gate had been painted since he'd last been here, and the hedge had been clipped recently. He made himself walk slowly. Wild strawberries grew on either side and he stopped and gathered some, carrying them in his cupped palm. As he came around the corner, though he knew it would be there, his heart leaped at the thin lip of blue beyond the green of the lower meadow, before it was hidden again by the outbuildings and then by the house.

It looked just the same. Except it was summer now and it was almost too pretty. Old roses flowered up the walls, the beds on either side were full of blues and yellows and in front of the house nasturtiums tumbled in a riot of orange and red. A black Labrador lay in front of the house. It got up and wagged its tail. A woman in a faded dress and wellingtons, her greying hair slipping from its pins, bent in front of them with scissors, snipping, and she stood and turned as Daniel approached.

'Daniel! My God!' the colour draining from her face, and he saw her drop the scissors which bounced on their points like a dancer, before lying, legs akimbo, on the ground.

'I'm sorry, I should have telegraphed, or written, but it all happened so fast.' Daniel put down his suitcase and put out his hand. 'I'm glad to see you again, Mrs Murray.'

She took his hand, and then drew him closer, gripping him by both arms, holding him.

'We thought you were dead,' she said at last. 'No word, ever. I wrote to you, and your parents, and your aunt. And Joe spoke to the police in Cork, and the barracks, and nobody would tell us anything.' She shook him again, as if for good measure. 'And now, here you are, in the flesh.'

'I couldn't . . . ' Daniel began.

Mrs Murray put a hand to his lips. 'Later. Come inside. I must find Joe.'

★ ★ ★

They gave him tea and buttered barmbrack, sitting on the terrace looking out to the sea, and talked of the weather and what the farmers were saying, and how the fish were running. The sky had cleared and there was no sign of the earlier rain clouds, only wisps of high cirrus streaked across the blue. The air was warm and the sea was calm in the estuary, smooth except for the wash of a couple of boats making their way out to fish, or gather in lobster pots. Though he knew from their faces that they were worried about him, Daniel was relieved and grateful that they didn't demand any explanations. Not yet at least. And when he spoke finally, he didn't try to explain anything, but only asked if he could stay with them a while.

'There's something I have to do. I'm not safe from things, but I believe I'll be safer here than anywhere else.'

'We've already discussed it, and you can stay,' Mr Murray said.

Daniel breathed out. He hadn't known he'd been holding his breath. 'Thank you.'

'Only thing is, if you want any supper, you're going to have to get out and catch it,' Mrs Murray said.

'It's still a rising tide, so we've a good chance with the mackerel.' Mr Murray pointed. 'You see where the water's ruffled? That'll be a mackerel shoal, on the hunt for sprats. Sometimes the sprats are so desperate, what with the mackerel all around them like tigers, that they'll throw themselves up on the beach.'

'How many did you find inside one that time?' Mrs Murray said.

'Last year it was. I was over a shoal and caught ten in about five minutes. No point taking more, we can't use them. And I was gutting them in the boat, throwing the heads and bits over the side, and the largest of them had fifteen sprats inside him. None of them eaten yet, lying there end to end. Like sardines.'

★ ★ ★

Daniel had been in the boat before, though not in the summer. He knew nothing about sailing, little about the sea, but Mr Murray had taught him which sheet to pull when he shouted out and Daniel had loved getting lost to the wind and the water and the demands made by the sails. This time Mr Murray took them across and beyond Horse Island before letting the sails flap and handing Daniel a spool wound round with fishing line, and knotted on the last length with a series of hooks, small weights and spinners that fractured the sunlight as the two men unpicked the sharp points from one another, then unwound the lines over the side of the boat.

'Let out most of the line and keep it taut against your finger,' Mr Murray said. 'So you can feel if there's a tug. And pull it gently every couple of minutes, to keep the spinners moving. It's the light they're drawn to, they gulp at the spinner and then they're hooked.'

It was just as Daniel thought nothing would happen that his line began to jerk.

'It's tugging,' he yelled.

'Wind it in then.'

Watching the surface of the water as he wound, the point where the line dipped down and out of sight, Daniel waited to see what he had hooked, and when he reached the end of the line and there were four floundering bright-eyed fish, their bellies iridescent green and blue, he felt his eyes fill with tears and he turned back to the water and peered at its sheer surface and let the spray wet his face so the one salt was like the other.

The fish gasped and bled for air on the floor of the boat, tossing and flipping and staring, till Mr Murray cleaned them with his penknife. Two sharp strokes into the gills and he flung the head high to a waiting gull. Then another stroke to open the belly, tugging the guts out quickly with his fingers, dragging his hand over the side of the boat to wash them free. When the fish were safely in a basket, lidded against the hovering gulls, he turned for home.

'Four's enough for tonight.'

That evening the Murrays talked about many things: their daughter Isobel, Mrs Hewetson and the St Barr's Flower Committee, the old dog, and the kittens born in the hot press. And Daniel caught the look that Mr Murray gave his wife at least twice in the evening, and he caught her slight shake of the head, so that still they didn't ask him why he'd walked down the drive that day.

Daniel ate and drank like a man not knowing where his next food would come from. The mackerel was good, and the cabbage. Mrs Murray brought in a glass bowl of gooseberries and another of whipped cream. Mr Murray talked a little about the hotel trade, that it was picking up, now their own wars were over.

'Thank God you'd retired before it got really

bad,' Mrs Murray said.

'And I'm hopeful. More visitors again, the new government being seen to govern.'

Mrs Murray rolled her eyes. 'Though we can't expect them to do anything for the likes of us. Most of them are IRA men. They'd rather see us burned out than help us out.'

'That's not quite fair,' Mr Murray said, patting his wife's hand. But she pulled it away, and Daniel could see the rage far back behind her eyes.

'We're as Irish as they are,' she said. 'But they'd be rid of us if they could. They've been rid of a fair few already.'

'There've been terrible things on both sides,' Mr Murray said. 'And now . . . '

'And now they have it that we've only been out for ourselves. They tar us all with the same brush. If you're a Protestant, you're the enemy.'

'Come on love, the people who know us think no differently than they've ever thought.'

Mrs Murray looked round at her husband. 'I was in Mr Moriarty's last week and I'd to wait a while for my order, and Mrs Moriarty was cutting a ham. Mrs Moriarty, whom I've known since before this century began. She asked after Isobel and I said how they weren't so happy in England and were thinking of moving to Canada. And she said, all tears and sympathy, how it must be sad, people not wanting you wherever you went. Then she said, was it enough ham she had cut.'

'Darling . . . ' Mr Murray said.

'Don't darling me. I've never done a thing to

hurt Mrs Moriarty. Any of them. They're no better than peasants, treating us like that.'

'Moira!' Mr Murray's voice was severe. 'We have a guest at our table.'

After a pause, she shook her head and nodded. 'Hard times, and you don't want to be hated.'

They ate in silence for a few minutes, before Mr Murray spoke again, and he must have had a different kind of nod from his wife, because this time he asked Daniel a question.

'What about you?' he said to Daniel. 'We thought . . . we guessed you'd been injured over here, and when we didn't hear, no answer to our letter, we assumed the worst. Is that where you got the injury to your leg?'

All the way here — on the train, and the boat across the water, and the next train, and walking, and then arriving — all the way he'd thought he might not be able to do the next thing. But he had, and he'd arrived here. As fiercely as he could, he'd kept his mind on this place — sea, trees, birds, these two people — and kept at bay the fury tied inside him like a knot. But something else was lurching in his gut now, something he could control even less than the fury. He put his hands to his head, over his ears, he hunched his shoulders, as if he could shrink, as if he could make himself disappear.

'An accident,' he muttered, 'motor lorry accident.'

'Don't ask any more,' Mrs Murray mouthed at her husband, and he nodded.

'How are your parents?' he asked, and Daniel

told them how his mother was and they nodded and looked sorry.

'Do they know you're here?'

'I'm going to write. Tomorrow.'

'It must be hard, being the only one,' Mrs Murray said.

'That's why I went to Ireland, partly,' Daniel said, still speaking as if from behind some barricade.

'But not why you came back?' Mr Murray said.

'No. Not why I came back.'

'That was the motor lorry accident.'

For a minute, Daniel didn't answer. Something was unravelling, and he didn't know if it was inside him, or, like some white, swaddling cocoon, outside.

'No,' he said at last. 'It wasn't an accident. It was an ambush. And I couldn't tell you then, even that I was alive, because it was too dangerous. And maybe it is now, too. But I can't hold things in any longer now. The worst of it, do you know the worst of it?'

The two people either side of him waited, their faces still.

'It's Johnnie, and Will and . . . ' Daniel shrugged. 'Can we talk of something else now?' he said, his voice, to his surprise, sounding calm. So they changed the subject then, and the three of them laughed at the dog, sleeping with her paws over her eyes, and after a few minutes Daniel uncoiled and picked up his spoon.

'So how's your father's business?' Mrs Murray said at last.

'I'm working for him now,' Daniel said.

'I remember you were in several minds about that.'

Daniel nodded. 'My leg . . . well, it put paid to the other minds. And now.' He stopped. The gooseberries were green in their bowl, the cream was white. The two people looked at him, waiting. He could see their faces, and beyond their faces the window and the darkening summer light. The sun had dropped beyond the line and the colour was gone from the day, things changed to black and white. He had to speak to them, but he was so tired, and it was so hard to get his tongue to make the right movements. Words were beginning to come out wrong and he feared what he might say.

'I will have to,' he said, and even this took the most terrible effort.

'You need to rest,' Mrs Murray said. She turned to her husband. 'It was too much, taking him out in the boat today.'

She went round to Daniel and squatted on the floor beside his chair.

'I'll take you to your bedroom. You should sleep now. Whatever we all have to say will wait.'

The room they gave him faced the hill. She told him that as she led him up the stairs. 'It's like being in the trees,' she said.

'I might dream loudly.'

'Do you want us to wake you?' she said, understanding.

He nodded. 'If you can.'

The Murrays agreed between themselves that

for now they would try to keep Daniel's presence in the house quiet.

'He is so changed,' Mrs Murray said.

'What if he needs a doctor?'

'If he needs a doctor, then we'll have to trust Dr Ross. He met him of course, the first time. But otherwise, let's wait till we know why he's come here.'

'Lizzie will be tricky. We don't want the wrong people knowing about him. It could be dangerous.'

Mrs Murray thought for a moment. 'We'll send a message saying we've come down with something. Flu.'

'She'll still want to do the laundry.'

'So we'll leave it in the porch. For her well-being. And we'd better cancel bridge, and the Mahonys. They were coming on Saturday.'

'You don't think it's a girl, do you? Daniel's problem.'

Mrs Murray shook her head. 'I wish it were, but I think it's a different kind of pain. I'm not sure he knows it all himself.'

'It's the Troubles, isn't it? That's why he's come back. It's something to do with that, with his injury maybe, something to do with over here.'

'He'll tell us when he can because it's burning a hole.'

He was quiet that night, and still into the morning he slept. He slept throughout that day, rousing somehow only to drink some water, and the Murrays kept watch. He was, for the time being, safe to surrender.

10

Catherine Whelan was still sleeping the next morning, a gentle chug of a snore slipping between her lips on each breath, when Jude shut the cabin door behind her. She'd been woken by the change in the engine sound, and when she stepped out on deck, she knew why. The ferry was turning away from the sea, turning into smooth-skinned water, past two hulking forts high on the headlands and into another country. Jude shivered. The sky was pale and clear, the sun still a small flat unremarkable circle. Mist hung above the water and she could hear the plash of oars in the water somewhere, though she couldn't see the boat. The shores were wooded, here and there a break in the trees and a low cottage, a thread of smoke from the chimney, or the glimpse of something much larger. A couple of men huddled at the rail, their hat brims touching, muttering important things to one another and not looking at the scenery, or noticing Jude in her britches and her boots. Otherwise Jude was alone. Soon she would have to decide what on earth to do next, and somehow keep faith with herself that this was not all a piece of folly. She turned away from the waking landscape and pushed open the deck door.

She was on to her third cup of coffee by the time Catherine found her.

'You're visiting Cork, then?' Catherine said, sitting down opposite.

Jude nodded. Catherine Whelan was younger than she'd first thought, now her mask was removed, barely a woman yet.

'Family?'

'Work,' Jude said. She'd thought by now about what she'd say to this young woman. 'Photographs. Birds, chiefly. I'm a photographer. Started during the war. I'm on an assignment for some magazines.'

'Oh,' Catherine said, her voice rising with curiosity. 'The Irish birds'll be different from the English ones, then?'

'It's more to do with the landscapes,' Jude said. 'They're keen for me to show off the Irish countryside, remind people what a beautiful country it is, especially after . . . '

'It'll take more than a few photographs to do that,' Catherine said, her voice suddenly sounding older than her face seemed. Then, like a clown, she buttoned on a different expression. 'Anyway, you'll have to come and have something to eat with my family,' she said, 'and I'll show you the sights. I'll write you out my address.'

'It's very kind of you, but . . . I'm not sure of my schedule,' Jude said, but Catherine waved her down.

'No, you must,' she said. 'We have the best cook in Cork, and I'll be offended if you refuse. Anyway, are you not eating now?' she said, sitting down opposite.

'I've eaten,' Jude said. 'You?'

Catherine shook her head. 'I'll wait for the solid land.' She looked hard at Jude's sweater, at the leather jacket bunched over the seat beside, then up at Jude, her forehead creased in a question.

Jude smiled. 'My motorbike's down there with the motor cars,' she said. 'Hard to ride it in a dress.'

Catherine leaned over, glimpsed Jude's britches and her eyes widened.

'Of course it is,' she said, and she looked down at her own clothes. 'I can see that would be something of a problem.' She thought for a moment. 'So it's for getting around to see the birds you have the motorbike, is it then?'

'That's right.'

'They'll be all over it when you bring it onto our street,' Catherine said. 'And I'll be splitting myself looking at their faces when they see you're a girl.'

'Have you been away for long?' Jude said.

'It was my sister's lying-in. She has a nurse with her, but she wanted someone from home. So I've been over helping. Her first.' She opened her handbag, fished out an envelope and passed it to Jude. 'Such a dote,' she said.

Jude took out a small photograph. It was slightly out of focus, which, having no passion for babies herself in general, she thought helped endear, and the baby was so swaddled that its eyes were only just visible below its bonnet. She nodded and smiled.

'Sweet,' she said. 'Where does your sister live?'

'London.'

'And she's well?'

Catherine nodded. 'It's a girl, a strong one. Esther they're calling her, and both of them fine. Three weeks ago today.'

She stared out of the window, then pointed. 'Spike Island,' she said, her voice suddenly lower and darker.

'What's that?'

'A cousin of mine was in there for a while. Possession of a firearm, enough to put a man away then.'

Across the water Jude saw a series of low grey buildings. 'It's a prison?'

'A military prison. Your lot still have it.' Catherine got to her feet. 'Let's go outside, I'll point you out a few things.' And without waiting, she was weaving through the tables and pushing open the saloon door. So Jude followed.

'Now enough of all that,' Catherine said in a breezy voice. 'That's Cobh, used to be Queenstown,' pointing. 'The *Titanic* set off from there. And it's where we do our emigrating from.'

Jude saw a town of grey stone rising steeply up the hillside above the water, lines of tall terraces, and in its midst a great church with a vast tower high above the roofs.

'St Colman's cathedral,' Catherine said, pointing. 'You'd be a Protestant, wouldn't you?'

'I haven't been to church for years,' Jude said. 'I don't think I believe in anything very much.'

'Then you'd be a Protestant.'

'Yes, I suppose so.'

Catherine nodded, something confirmed, and

pointed towards the shore.

'We're headed up the Lee at last. We'll be in soon enough now and I'll be on the tram and home. Are they putting you up somewhere proper, your assignment people?'

'My assignment people?'

'The ones who want the birds.'

'Oh, yes. Yes they are, for a night at least, though I don't remember the name of the hotel.'

Catherine looked at her doubtfully. 'But you're sure now? You've somewhere to be going to?'

'Yes, sure.'

'Well so, here's my address. It's in Sunday's Well, north of the river, but it's near in. Anyway, you have your motorbike to be getting about on. You'll come and have some supper with us tonight. My mother will be delighted.'

If a tall man in a heavy tweed suit hadn't come up at this point, Jude thought later, she'd have had to have made up an excuse very fast to get away. She needed to collect herself, and she couldn't with Catherine pointing out every bend in the river. She'd have been getting her to go to Mass next thing.

'Why, Catherine! Such a thing to meet you here. I spotted you over my fried eggs,' he said, pointing back towards the saloon window. 'Whatever are you doing, so far from your mother's apron strings?'

'Dr Kelleher!' Catherine said, turning to the figure bearing down on them. 'This is my new friend, Miss Hursten. Dr Kelleher. Our doctor, before he moved on to grander pastures.'

Jude looked up at a face whose ruddy

complexion looked more like a farmer's than a doctor's, but whose broad smile didn't conceal the sharp quiz that was in his eyes.

He held out his hand. 'She's always a one for the flattery. You'd want to watch her if you were a fellow,' he said.

'She's here to take photographs,' Catherine said. 'They want to see our birds now back in England.'

Jude gave a laugh and nodded. His handshake, like his smile, was both firm and somehow interrogatory.

'Well, good,' Dr Kelleher said. 'So whereabouts are you headed for?'

'Tonight, no further than Catherine's house and supper,' Jude said, matching his jolly tone with her own. 'The Irish living up to their reputation for hospitality, and I'm not even off the boat. If you'll excuse me, though, I ought to check my equipment,' and she was walking towards the saloon door before she'd even finished her sentence.

'Come at six, then,' Catherine called. 'And watch out for the Cork drivers. They're the devil. Specially the ones with a donkey.'

* * *

Two hours later Jude lay sprawled on a pale green needlecord counterpane and marked out the cracks on the ceiling. Daniel's diary was beside her, but her thoughts were rushing and she told herself that she needed to steady them before she opened it again. It had been so straightforward, getting to here, as if some powerful external momentum had been driving her forward. But now, lying on this bed in the middle of this noisy, foreign, unknown city, she felt beached.

A travelling salesman in the ferry hold had recommended the hotel just as the boat was docking.

'Try the Victoria. Clean, very reasonable. Bang in the middle of the city. You can put your motorbike in their yard, too. It's full of hens, but safe from little fingers. Patrick Street, opposite the Ulster Bank, perfectly safe these days. Ask for a room at the back though. It's noisy at the front.' And then, looking at her in her britches and her boots, he'd said, 'But you want to be careful what you get up to over here, you know. The Pope might not like it.'

And she was going to ask him what he meant, but then they opened the hold doors, he started up his van and it was too late.

There were no vacant back rooms in the Victoria, but Jude didn't mind being at the front, all the bustle of a city at its business below. She listened to the sounds: tram bells, the clip of heels and horses, motor cars, women's voices, a child wailing. It was so close to home, almost like England, and yet so foreign. The voices had a different rhythm, different tune almost, and though she'd barely spoken to anybody here yet, hers felt a heavy, blunt thing beside this other, quick music.

She wondered now whether this was a fool's errand, a mad journey she was making. And to busy herself, and stop herself wondering further, after writing out a list of errands — maps, provisions, postcards, telephone call to Leo — she packed the diary into a bag and went out into the city.

An hour later and she was done. Three postcards lay stamped and ready on the table in front of her. Peter's with a stout Irish man in tailcoat, worsted stockings and knee-breeches, puffing a clay pipe and making eyes at a pretty Irish girl in a shawl; Tom's showing another stout Irish man driving a jaunting-car over boulders and upsetting his tourist passengers; and Elsa's with the same figure again leaning over a pigsty and a bubble over the pig's head saying, 'Oh no, not that old tale again'. Leo had been called and her bag was heavy with provisions and camera film.

She sat by the window in the Pavilion restaurant and looked out at the people on the street, her gaze catching on different figures: the black-shawled woman staring in through Lipton's window at the bacon cuts; the young men heading in beneath the Bar Billiards sign; the mother with her daughters in hats and gloves; the boy peddling string with a grin; the man up a ladder pasting 'Wolsey Underwear' to a billboard; the old man filling a clay pipe leaning up against a cart, cap pulled low, fingers shaking. And all around them, the crowds busy about their day.

A waitress brought her a huge lobster salad. Finding herself in something of a holiday spirit, Jude brandished the nutcrackers and broke open the thick shell of the claw, laying bare the soft pincer within. The lobster had come with bread and butter, thick slices, different from any bread she'd had before. It had a rough brown crust and a soft, moist, yellow crumb. It was delicious. As she buttered it she remembered Daniel telling her how different the food was here, so that he had craved the tastes he knew. She drew out the flesh and dipped it in the mayonnaise.

Jude hadn't opened the diary since the day she found it in Daniel's room, and though it was less than a week ago, it seemed like a lifetime. She'd told herself she had enough else to organise, and till she got there, there was nothing she could do anyway. Now, though, she knew she'd been putting it off. She needed to face out her fear of what she would find in there. She wished Peter was with her, to offer up sardonic asides if it got too much. But she was here alone and she needed to find any clues she could about where Daniel might be and why. So she took the diary from her bag and put it on the table. She'd open it once she'd finished the lobster.

They were building something huge across the other side of the broad street, she could see it in between the trams. Men with winches lifting great blocks of stone, others hunched over holes, a crane swinging out over the Tivoli restaurant, over the busy pavement, another over boards for 'Paddy's whiskey' and 'Jacobs biscuits', and a clutch of little boys, all knees and elbows, agog at it all, who made her think of Tom.

'What are they putting up?' Jude asked the waitress.

'They say it'll be the grandest shop in Europe,' the waitress said.

'Who's building it?'

'So my da swears, there's money gone in from over the water, though I don't believe a word of it.'

'Over the water?'

'Guilt money from your lot, but very hush-hush. It's a fellow he knows in the pub works on the site and he overheard the foreman, you know how they make them travel, those stories,' and Jude nodded. 'Says it's your government in England has put it up, but he doesn't say it in the kitchen or my ma'd have him. She says she's had her fill of the Troubles and there's to be no more mention in her house. Now, will you have anything else?'

And lifting the plate of lobster shell from the table, the waitress swung away. Jude looked again out of the window, taken aback by her own forgetting. She'd seen the photographs in the papers, it couldn't have been much more than four years ago, 'Cork city ablaze'. She even remembered having an argument about it with Martin.

'Good propaganda for the IRA,' he'd said, facetious, grinning, but still, and she'd been outraged, which was what he'd wanted.

'Lloyd George sent the Black and Tans over as thugs. They've been burning homes ever since they started. And now this, now they're burning cities.'

'The photo could be of France or anywhere,'

he'd gone on. 'Piles of rubble and burned-out buildings. And anyway there are some saying the Black and Tans didn't light the fires but were trying to put them out.'

Jude wanted to ask the waitress, did she see the burning? And the Tans? Was her family involved? She wanted to ask this young girl in her pinny and starched cap, who was just then walking so carefully to the table in the corner, her tray heavy with plates of oysters and pots of tea, what she thought of it all, and did she hate the young English men who burned her city and terrified her people, one of whom Jude had come to find.

She sat back in her chair and checked her watch. It was two o'clock. She had as long as it took. Weighting the diary open with the sugar bowl on one side, salt cruet on the other, she started reading, writing down notes in the 'Bells of Shandon' notepad she had bought for the purpose: names, places, important events, questions as they occurred to her. She didn't notice the waitress returning.

'Will you have something else? Tea maybe, or coffee? We do lovely coffee.'

Jude started and shut the diary, tipping over the salt cruet as she did so. Pinching up some spilt grains, she flicked them over her shoulder.

'Superstitious,' the maid said, smiling.

'Doesn't work though,' Jude said.

And only once the coffee had arrived and the waitress had gone did Jude begin her reading again.

<u>Feb 21st, 1921.</u>

5.30 a.m. Rain still. Very dark inside barracks, what with shutters and shell boxes. I
think it makes men worse. You can feel the
pressure building, especially when
you can't see the sky. Two or three of the
lads very nervy, out for blood. I don't
think they've slept much. They say they
know who the Shinners were. They say
Smith was shot in the back. I saw his
body when they brought him in last night.
I couldn't say for sure.

There'll be a fishing trip.

Jude looked up from the words, at the bustle,
the people eating and drinking. Daniel might
have sat next to any of these, might have
passed the time of day. She was glad she was
reading this in a place where people were
doing ordinary, busy things, and not on her
own. Looking back down at Daniel's small,
neat script, she thought how innocent the
words would look from a distance, to a
passer-by. Their tidy sentences and paragraphs,
all the dates underlined, no crossings-out,
proper punctuation. She sat up straight and
rolled her shoulders, tried to ease the tension,
then went on reading.

It certainly makes you angry, and when you
thought you were trying to help them. Not
the out and out Shinners, they're the enemy,
but the women, and the little boys that sit on
the walls watching. Because they're as likely

241

to be up to something as the men. Duguid came in shouting about how he was going to shove his hands up the next lot of skirts he came to, orders or no orders, and then about what he was going to do with what he found.

They're signing out ammo, so we'll have to go into the town and let them know what's what. Col. Whittam ordering us to use restraint, but you can see he doesn't believe it. Reminding us about firing in the air, firing at windows. A child was injured last month, and some cows. Those Shinners will have gone by now, they'll be in the fields or the hills, or gone to the city. So we'll have to bring in others.

1.00 p.m. What a fishing trip. I was right. There were only the women left. We searched the places pretty thoroughly, O'Connor's house and shop, the other fellow's farm, and only found a cousin, a boy about fifteen, hidden out in the pigsty. All the men had gone, both the fathers. A few bits got broken, some windows of course, whatever Col. W says. Behave like pigs, treat them like pigs, Will said, which I was surprised at. It's a sign of the pressure, I suppose. It gets to all of us. Still, for corner boys and rustics who barely know a rifle from a hurley stick, they do enough damage. It's no wonder our boys retaliate.

I'm in the mess upstairs, in my corner. Jumbo is sprawled on the table next to this diary, his tail flicking at my pen as if it were some aggravating insect. He's my favourite of the barracks cats.

The boy is downstairs, he's Col. Whittam's, so he should be safe enough. There's a couple of others brought in who are already on our lists, so they're bound to know something. He's got them downstairs too. I can hear them when somebody opens the mess door. He's not being very gentle, but then they weren't very gentle with Smith.

Jude put her hand over the page and shut her eyes. This had been written by a man she thought she liked, by the man she was searching for. He had sat at a table, stroked a cat and written paragraphs describing what amounted to torture. Torture he was justifying as tit-for-tat. Jude's heart raced, and she made herself breathe deep and slow. A girl was discussing her trousseau at the next table, how many nightgowns, how many handkerchiefs she would need, and Jude listened in for a few minutes before opening her eyes and making herself return to the page.

Col. Whittam has sent notice to both families to vacate their premises. I don't want to be on burning duty, I hate it. You get drunk on it, shouting and roaring with the others, and these pathetic figures standing there in the street, watching their home burn, women and children again usually, and you loathe them and their men who've run and hidden, and then afterwards you're left with a horrible

243

taste in your mouth. Maybe everybody else feels like that too, but you don't talk about it so I don't know, even about Will. The enemy does it back, of course, but still it doesn't seem right.

There's been stuff at home in the papers again about over here, but they should come and see for themselves. I don't know where they get their information from, but it's not from us. It's enough to drive a bloody conchie to violence.

I'm 4-1 up over Will at billiards. I've got the hang quicker than he has of playing the tears in the felt. No word on when it will be replaced, but we've got the glass back in the windows, so better light, which makes the shots easier.

Nothing from home still. I'm worried about Mother.

Passes out are cancelled for now, so no fish and chips, even if they do taste like they're fried in engine oil. Will said they wrapped his in the IRA propaganda paper one time. It's written *An t'Óglach*, but I don't know how to say it. So he says he read all this IRA propaganda, made-up victories and arms hauls, but I don't believe him. Too risky. The shopkeeper would've been shut down, gaoled for it at the least.

Everyone's getting more pent up. It must have been easier in the Great War. A proper enemy, and the women and children properly innocent.

Except for the Murrays and Coolderry and

Horse Island, the sea, the birds, I wish I was out of this godforsaken country.

This latest mess makes real fishing look more unlikely. I was hoping to go there in three weeks. But even Castletowne might be too dangerous now. For me and for the Murrays. Prods are fair game for the Shinners anyway, though Mr Murray said not a single person in their vicinity had been attacked so far. If I go I'll have to be incognito somehow.

There are stories of IRA reading all our mail. One Auxie being told by a Shinner on the street that his mother had died before he even knew it himself. Don't know whether to believe it, except that worse has happened that I know to be true, so why not.

Some of our boys very keen on confetti at the moment. That's what Will calls it. Getting blind drunk then driving through town shooting off at the bushes, trees, bog, spraying bullets at everything. There are accidents of course. Lots of damage to property. A little girl with two bullets in her leg, a man killed working in a field. He only had a spade. They've had a dressing down for it, but Col. W will do what he can for them.

For as long as she was reading it, if she pretended the diary was nothing to do with her, treated it like a novel, or a newspaper, written by somebody she had no knowledge of, Jude could read the entries through. The lists of food, the numerous so-called fishing trips, the burnings and brutality, the anecdotes, the searching for

Shinners, the broken 'bits', as he liked to term Irish property. But as soon as she stopped, the horror came in and she felt her bile rise. Who was this man? This callous figure who could write about bullets as confetti and children as less than innocent. Jude didn't recognise him, didn't know how to put him together with the man she'd taken to the Rocks, or even with the haunted man she'd met in Kew Gardens.

She became quite ruthless to get through it, banished her thoughts, her fears, and in this way she read it all right through.

The waitress brought her another pot of coffee, and then one of tea, so that by the time she was finished, Jude felt awash. Outside, shops were beginning to close, tired shop girls rolling down shutters and lifting grilles into place, and the water wagon was laying the day's dust to rest. 'Wolsey Underwear' gleamed out whitely opposite, its glued seams smoothed, and there was a new trickle of young men, still in working clothes, disappearing under the Bar Billiards sign.

Jude looked at her watch. It was nearly five o'clock. Catherine had asked her for supper at six. She was numb, unable to take in what she'd read. Even within the diary she couldn't connect one Daniel with another, he seemed so different at different times. And the man with blue eyes that were also green, with his twitches and his lame leg who had knocked at her door, it seemed an age ago, though it wasn't more than a couple of months, he was somebody different again. She remembered Richard's letter. He'd shot defenceless men and he couldn't weep. Closing the diary, she put it in her bag and, one hand on the table to steady herself, she got to her feet to go.

11

The hotel yard was locked and the man with the key, having fed the hens in the yard, had gone to feed his own when Jude went to retrieve her motorbike. So she took the tram to Catherine's house in Sunday's Well. She had posted her mail in the pillar box on the corner. A scratch in the green showed the old British red through, and the 'V R' and its royal insignia was painted over but still clear to see.

The sun was setting and the river had turned black, slick as oil. Jude sat and shut her eyes. Exhaustion hit her, piled itself on, pulsing through her skull, pressing at her eyes, crushing her shoulders, turning her stomach over. She should look out of the window, watch the scruffy boys at their errands and the girls in their layers of skirts slowing their step at last for the young men who hung about the quays, and the women tugging barrows and the men walking home from she didn't know where. She should look up at the city, at Shandon's steeple high and white above. The busboy in the Victoria had already told her about the bells.

'It's a Mr Meredith you'll want to find,' he told her. 'He's the bell-ringer. He'll do just about anything you'd want, 'The Harp that Once', 'Oft in the Stilly Night', 'The Last Rose of Summer'. You can hear them across the city.'

'What would you ask for?' Jude said, and the

boy replied that he'd ask for 'The Croppy Boy', though he'd never heard it played on the bells, and Jude said she didn't know that song, at which the boy nodded as if he knew that.

But now it was evening and too late for the bells and anyway Jude's eyes were closed as the tram made its way, her thoughts drifting away from Cork city and the busboy and the bells of Shandon. She was horrified by what she had read. But the harder thought, the one she was keeping at bay, would push from her mind for the evening, was what on earth she was doing here, pursuing the man who had written those things.

She'd asked the tram conductor to let her know when they had reached the nearest stop to Catherine's address, and it was now that he tapped her gently on the shoulder.

'There's the convent there, and beyond is the gaol. You'll be somewhere near the two of them.'

The Shandon bells struck the quarter as Jude climbed down from the tram. The steeple reminded her of some building blocks Tom and Elsa used to play with. You could stack them, each one smaller than the one before, the yellow on the red, red on green, green on white and so on up, and make a steady tower.

She could smell roses somewhere in the air, though none were visible, and horse dung, familiar smells, but not enough to reassure. She'd give her eye teeth right now to be stacking building blocks, or anything that went one upon the other upwards.

Jude wished Kate were here, or Peter. She felt

very much alone on this hill above Cork city, all high walls and secrets, the night coming on, on some crazy adventure to find a man she barely knew who'd been involved in God knew what, and in a country she didn't understand.

Five minutes later and Jude had found Catherine's house. It stood at the end of a tall, grey-plastered terrace, long thin gardens sloping away down the hill towards the river far below. Through the front window she could see somebody at the piano, and a somewhat thumping rendition of 'Für Elise' made its way through the window.

The door was opened almost before she'd knocked on it and a diminutive version of Catherine in a faded print dress and bare feet stood before her, grinning.

'You'll be Catherine's English friend from the ferry boat,' the girl said. 'The one with the motorbike,' and she peered out into the street.

'I came on the tram,' Jude said.

'They'll never believe me now,' the girl said, her face glum as quickly as it had been bright.

'About what?'

'That girls can ride motorbikes, they'll never believe me, Frank and Dermot. You have got one?' and her tone was both questioning and accusatory.

'Next time, I promise,' Jude said. 'And you can have the first side-car ride, if your mother allows.'

'Really?'

'If your mother allows.'

The girl nodded, grinning, and took Jude's

hand. 'I'm Martha Whelan.'

'Jude Hursten.'

A square woman bustled up at this point and gave a rough curtsey to Jude and ttched at Martha, pointing at her bare feet.

'It's our guest, from England,' Martha said. 'With the motorbike, only she hasn't it with her now. Will I go on and tell Mammy?'

The woman patted the small girl on the head.

'Put your sandals on and take our guest in. I'll go and tell the mistress,' and still without saying a word to Jude, she was gone.

'Catherine's been in such a tizzy, with having you to supper, we've hardly heard a thing about Daisy's baby. Mammy had to have a word,' Martha said, taking Jude's hand.

'I'm sorry,' Jude said.

'No, no. Mammy's very glad. She loves to have guests. It's only with Catherine back from England and sounding like she knows a thing or two above. It's a stir to her. She says she's been boiling bacon since before Catherine was even a spark in the eye, and if Catherine would like to do something useful she could go and lay the table, which is already seven, and then Dr Kelleher coming, though he might be late, with his house calls. Catherine said you'd met him on the boat.' She paused for breath, then finished up. 'Of course, it's the cook who boils the bacon, but I suppose it's Mammy tells her to.'

Listening to this little girl's chatter, Jude felt a dart of homesickness. Martha must be about Elsa's age and for a moment she would have given anything to be back at home with Elsa and

Tom, and not heading off on this strange pursuit, even in the company of such small and charming strangers.

Martha's speech had brought them through a hall, which seemed only just to contain the hats and coats, cricket bats, hockey sticks, umbrellas, skipping ropes, hoops, school satchels and bowls of flowers that were hung, leaned, hooked and piled, and past two steps down to the kitchen. Even with the door closed, a delicious steam, sweet with cloves, issued from in here.

Martha pushed open the sitting room door and Jude followed her in. The room was high-ceilinged, papered in a Japanese style, with windows showing onto a long garden bounded on each side by a high wall. Far down it Jude could see fruit trees, and nearer to, a boy, older than Tom, intent with a stick of some kind. Although it was summer, a fire was burning in the hearth and a woman sat on a sofa before it, darning, a heap of stray socks in a basket at her feet.

She got up as they approached, wiping her hands on her skirts as though she had been cooking, and put a hand out to Jude, meeting her with a strong smile.

Jude's first thought was that Mrs Whelan looked like a woman who was used to meeting her troubles face on. Something to do with the way she squared her slight body as if making herself ready, balanced like a dancer.

'Welcome,' Mrs Whelan said. 'I see you've had a somewhat formal introduction to the household.'

Jude laughed. 'It's very kind of Catherine to invite me, but I hope it hasn't been a trouble to you.'

'Not at all. Will you have a glass of sherry?' She beckoned to Martha. 'Be a great girl and bring us some sherry. Very carefully.'

The little girl nodded slowly, importantly. 'Which glasses is it?' she said. 'The ones are all jagged, or the ones like the communion cup?'

'Like the communion cup, but little,' Mrs Whelan said, showing with her fingers how tall, and Martha nodded and was off.

'Catherine says you've an interesting job to do over here,' Mrs Whelan said, 'photographing our birds and such like.'

Jude nodded.

'And that you've come on a motorbike?'

'I have. I've ridden it since the war.'

'The European war?'

Jude nodded again. 'Actually, I wondered, would you have any objection to my giving Martha a ride in the sidecar another time? I promised I'd ask.'

Mrs Whelan studied her guest. 'Is it safe? Have you had any accidents ever?'

'None on the motorbike,' Jude said. 'It's as safe as a bicycle.'

Martha returned with the sherry and glasses, slow-stepping into the room, craning her head over the tray to avoid tripping, picking her feet up elaborately high. Jude watched Mrs Whelan pour the sherry. Though her daughters were dark, she was red-haired and in that evening light her skin seemed translucent. Her face was angular, pale, cutting different planes as she moved and the shadows around it shifted. Something in the way she moved reminded Jude of Kate.

'I'd love to take your photograph,' she said, the words coming out before she had time to consider them, and for a moment Jude felt a pang of guilt. As if, even though Kate had died all those years before, this new adventure broke an old pact of intimacy that Jude had kept in trust all this time.

'My photograph?' Mrs Whelan sounded taken aback, and Jude was annoyed at herself, because perhaps professional photographers didn't say things like that.

'I'm sorry. That's very rude.'

'No, no, it's not rude. Just surprising.'

'The light at this time, in this room. It'd be good for it. Perhaps when I'm back in Cork?'

'It might be raining then,' Mrs Whelan said. 'But I'm flattered. I'd be curious, to see what you made of me. So you've been here a quarter of an hour, and you're going to take my photograph and give my children rides on your motorbike. Tell me this isn't how you usually meet strangers?'

And Jude couldn't begin to answer her, because Mrs Whelan was right, and she didn't know how it was that this strange quest to find a missing man should make her so forthcoming, and she put the thought by, as something she should think about when she was on her own later.

'So it's your first time over here?'

'It is,' Jude said, and after a little more small talk and with the sherry drunk, Jude was despatched with Martha to the parlour while Mrs Whelan checked the progress of the dinner arrangements. The pianist, a girl a fraction taller than Martha, had moved on to somewhat frantic scales. Catherine came in, proprietorial, with fresh lipstick, and kissed Jude on the cheek. Then she turned to the pianist.

'If you play them slower you'll learn them faster, that's what Ma says, and could you stop now, so our guest can sit till supper.'

The little girl stopped playing dead, mid-scale, slid down from the stool and without a glance at Jude, stalked from the room.

'That's Mary,' Martha said. 'She's a year and twelve days older than me, and very good at the piano playing, but she's the worst of the tempers, and she hates to be commented on. D'you know who they are, though?' and Jude was nonplussed till she saw that Martha was looking at the pictures above the piano.

Jude walked up closer. There were some nondescript water-colour landscapes — the Italian Alps, the Killarney Lakes, the Lake District — and a couple of horse races, together with some photographs of young men in teams, a rugby ball sitting proudly between the legs of the captain. Somewhere in all that burly good cheer, Jude thought, must be their father. There was another photograph of men in lines, this time in police uniform, their buckles catching the sun, and flanking the lot, one on each side, were two portraits of historical-looking men.

'So do you know who they are?'

'Do I know who which are?' Jude said.

'There's our papa,' Catherine said, pointing to a figure sitting smart in his police uniform.

'Now you have to find him in the rugby,' Martha said, 'and no help from us,' and Jude did so easily, struck by the girls' likeness to their handsome, dark-haired father.

'But do you know who those two are?' Martha said then, pointing at the small portraits.

Jude looked at them, not allowing herself to look at their names, then shook her head.

'You don't know?' Martha said. 'Truly?'

'No,' said Jude.

'So then, that's Daniel O'Connell, and that's Robert Emmet and they are both Irish heroes, but I don't remember which came the first.'

Between the two of them, the two girls told Jude all she could possibly need to know about the family before the bell was rung for supper. And Jude listened as it was spilled out before her, and it filled up her head and, for now, kept at arm's length the dark material of Daniel's diary.

'Our papa was in the Force,' Martha said.

'That's the RIC,' Catherine said, 'except it isn't called that any longer. It's the Garda now.'

'Anyway, he was a policeman.'

'He was a District Inspector,' Catherine said grandly.

'But he died,' Martha said. 'How long ago was it he died, Catherine?'

'Five years,' Catherine said.

'I'm sorry,' Jude said. 'That's very hard, to lose

your father so young. Do you remember him well?'

'I helped him put on his uniform,' Martha said. 'That was my job. And I got to put his cap on him.'

'Quite a responsibility,' Jude said, thinking the little girl couldn't have been more than three years old.

In the silence, Jude could hear the boys arguing outside the door, then just thuds as they fought.

'And once when I'd the fever, it was in the night and I was allowed to sit up with him while he had chops and tea and then he went out. Mama didn't like him having chops and tea because it's what the constables ate and he wasn't one, he was higher up. But he said it was what he liked and he should be the one to choose.'

'Martha,' Catherine said, 'there's no need to be saying all of that.'

'And he didn't die in the Troubles,' Martha went on, and as she spoke, she hit a piano key again and again. 'And it wasn't the IRA that killed him. He had a weak heart and he was after chasing somebody one night and in the rain, and it shouldn't have been him doing it. It's the wet that did for him, and Dr Kelleher won't deny it either, and he should know.'

'I'm sorry,' Jude said.

Martha jigged on the sofa next to her. 'Play something, Catherine, please? Like Ma said, to entertain.'

And Catherine turned to the piano and played till the bell sounded.

Jude enjoyed supper. It was loud and genial and she was treated both as an honorary member of the family and as somebody who needed to be looked after, not understanding the customs of the place, especially by Martha.

'You should eat the cabbage with the bacon,' Martha had instructed her, 'it's how God intended, is what our papa told us.'

There were arguments between the boys about cricket and hurley, whatever that was, until Catherine rounded on Dermot.

'The way you go on, you'd think there was nothing in the world but hurley,' she said, rolling her eyes. 'You'd think the Holy Father played it the way you go on.'

And then Mrs Whelan intervened, and Jude sat back and enjoyed it all and missed Tom and Elsa in equal parts, until the door bell rang.

The table changed with Dr Kelleher there. It wasn't that he demanded anything, as far as Jude could see, or that he expected anything particular from the children. But she noticed how each of them tried to impress him in their different ways. So Dermot sat straighter and finished his vegetables and Frank announced that he knew how to do long division and that he'd come nearly top in the Latin test. Martha had taken Dr Kelleher's jacket from him and Jude could see her trying to hang it on a peg in the hall, jumping with the jacket above her head, till Mrs Whelan sent Frank to do it for her. And Mary, seated next to him, got him salt and pepper and the mustard pot, chivvying up the table to have them passed along quickly.

Mary and Martha especially, the youngest of the children, seemed not just anxious to please the doctor, but wanted to press in on him, get as close as they could. More, Jude thought, as if he were a father returned, rather than a family friend.

'Your first day in Ireland began fine on the ferry this morning. I hope it has continued that way,' Dr Kelleher said.

'Yes, thank you.'

'Not so many birds in these parts for you to snap, though.'

'It's not only birds I'm wanting. But anyway I plan to head off into the countryside tomorrow.'

'Ah.'

There was something in Dr Kelleher's tone that Jude couldn't make out. Not that he didn't believe her exactly, but certainly some element of suspicion.

'And tell me again what you're taking them for?'

'It's a commission from a picture magazine. They want to run a piece on the landscape of the British Isles. So landscapes and some animals.'

'You must be a very good photographer. Can't be an easy world for a woman to make her way in.'

'No, it isn't. But I've known it's what I want to do from very young, and then I took a lot of photographs during the Great War, just as an amateur, I was nursing in Belgium, but it still helped, I think. My name got around a bit, I made some contacts. One of the very few for whom the war brought good fortune amongst the bad.'

She felt dizzy, tipsy almost, as though she had drunk far more than the one glass of sherry. What was strange was that it felt so easy, to make up this story, exhilarating. As though by saying these things, she was making them so. As though she were making up for herself someone else to be in the world. 'But be careful,' she told herself, 'or he will find you out.'

'I don't suppose you've any with you, though,' Catherine said. 'Magazine photographs, I mean?'

'No, I haven't.'

She had Daniel's photograph in her bag, though. What she thought of as Daniel's photograph, of the two men sharing a cigarette and Kate standing behind. And a few others from the war, and a couple of birds in flight she'd taken recently, that she'd stuck in the envelope too, she didn't quite know why. Old times' sake, maybe, the war ones, though she winced at the thought. So on the spur she decided to show these around the table. After all, Daniel had been stationed in County Cork, and if his Irishman, as she thought of him, if he'd been important, he might be well known. His photograph might have been in a newspaper. Somebody might recognise him. She opened her bag and took out the envelope.

'But I have got a few other photographs. A couple of birds, gannets, I took recently, and a few that I took in the war.' She passed them to Catherine. 'The war ones are snaps really, amateur things,' she added, swallowing with pleasurable ease the small bubble of embarrassment she felt at her white lie.

'You were nursing over there? In the European war?' Catherine's voice was sharp with excitement.

'I was.'

'Your mother let you go and do that?' Catherine said.

'My mother died while I was still at school. And my father couldn't really stop me, not when so many young men were joining up to fight.'

'Girls get up to all sorts these days,' Dr Kelleher said, looking at Mrs Whelan, and Jude was conscious of another conversation going on at the table, one she was not privy to.

Catherine glanced for a second at the gannets and then pored over the wartime shots as though if she studied them hard enough, they might yield up the key to her ambition.

'Come on and let the rest of us have a look,' Dermot said, and reluctantly, Catherine passed them round, the bird photos first, and then, one by one, the others.

Jude sat watching. It was uncomfortable, being viewed like this. But if she was to play her part properly, she supposed it was something she would have to appear used to, so she tried to look relaxed and bit her tongue. Sat on Catherine's left, Dr Kelleher was the last to see them. Frank had wanted to know what kind of rifle the soldiers carried, which she couldn't answer, and Catherine asked whether she'd seen men die, to which she said she had, and women

261

too. Dermot asked her how fast she rode her motorbike and she explained that it depended. That if you had a wounded man in the sidecar, you went slowly so as not to bump him, whereas if it was just you, and you were trying to avoid being shelled, you went a good deal faster. She told him that she'd had to ride across the fields once, the road being blown up, and that some of the shell holes were so big, half the size of this room, and filled with water, that you might disappear for ever at night if you weren't very careful.

'Like Doctor Foster who went to Gloucester,' she said. 'We were forever stepping in puddles up to our middles.'

Dermot listened gravely. 'That's nothing,' he said. 'We've those all over in Ireland. Isn't that right, Dr Kelleher?'

'Well, there are still holes in the roads, certainly,' Dr Kelleher said laughing. 'I don't think we'll have them smoothed over in a hurry. But they're not the kind from the Tan war any more. Those have been mended now, and they weren't shell holes. Trenches more often, and made on purpose. Miss Hursten wouldn't have been able to skirt round those on her motorbike. That was the point of them.'

The photographs had reached Dr Kelleher by now, and Jude, her thoughts drifting back over that drowned Belgian landscape, was only half-watching. She could smell it again, riding on the road to the village, where, even in the cold air, behind the water there was the sweet, rank smell of rot. She saw the pale light over the flooding, ruined farmhouses like islands in the watery plain. Cows like floating balloons, dead fish breaking the surface, their white bellies to the sky, and sometimes a dead soldier lifting the flat line of the strange inland sea. Occasionally there was a burned-out motor car, the passengers still sometimes seated, unrecognisable, unmistakable, or the humped-up body of a horse or a sheep, clumsy in death. And if the sun broke through and the light sharpened, then visible on the horizon was the low line of trees that hid the German guns. Jude could see their tongues of fire across the flood waters, and the shells digging geysers, throwing columns of water into the air, the filthy spray falling like stones, hurling fish on to the sodden land.

'You look as if you've seen a ghost.'

Jude started from her reverie. It was Mrs Whelan speaking, but not to her. Mrs Whelan leaned across the table and tapped the doctor's hand. He looked back at her blankly.

'Dr Kelleher?' she said.

He turned abruptly, and stared at Jude.

'You're not staying long here?'

'I'll be off tomorrow,' she said, waiting, wondering if he had more to say, if perhaps he had recognised somebody.

'Not planning any photographs of the city then?'

'She's going to take Mammy's photograph,' Martha chirped and Jude felt herself blush, though she didn't know why.

'I am,' she said, 'but that'll be on my return through Cork. I did think I'd take a few of the

263

city early tomorrow, before going,' Jude said, unsure of his tone, unsure what he wanted.

'In which case, perhaps you'd let me be your guide,' he said, in a tone that had more aggression than courtesy in it. He shuffled together the photographs and handed them back, his eyes all the time on Jude, not giving them another look.

'I was going to go out at about seven-thirty,' Jude said.

'That'll be fine. We'll meet underneath Father Mathew.' Jude looked blank. 'It's a statue further down Patrick Street, near the river.'

'So who was he?' Jude said.

'A big temperance fellow,' Catherine said, 'and the statue was put up as a reminder.'

'And does it work?' Jude said.

'Not at all,' Frank said. 'As Father always said, the statue is a beacon to the porter drinkers of Cork,' and Catherine scowled and everyone else laughed.

'All right,' Jude said to Dr Kelleher, 'seven-thirty tomorrow.'

'Could I come too?' Catherine said, grinning, perky.

'No,' the doctor said, so abruptly that Jude saw Catherine's chin quiver, and the girl said nothing more. Something had altered his mood, but Jude could see that he wasn't going to say what. He got to his feet.

'I'd better be going.'

'But you never go till much later,' Mary said. 'And I'm to show you my piano piece, and Dermot, he's . . .'

The doctor shook his shoulders, as if to shrug the children from him.

'No, it's bedtime for me now, if I'm going to be on my toes first thing tomorrow.'

'But you've not had any pudding,' Martha said, tugging at his sleeve. 'You never go without pudding.'

'Let go, Martha,' he said.

'Martha, go and get ready for bed,' Mrs Whelan said severely, and Martha did so without another word.

12

Daniel had made a flag for himself on Horse Island. A spindled, bleached branch as the pole, bark worried off by the sea, knots standing proud, and on top his shirt, though it didn't blow out much that day, there being so little wind. He didn't put it up on the beach because nobody must know he was there. But if he climbed up the rocks at the back of the beach, he could follow a sheep path through the bracken and broken stone walls to the middle of the island. So he'd carried the flag in and stood it where it couldn't be seen, anchored with stones.

The sheep were in a sorry state, their torn wool hanging like bandages beneath them. They didn't like to go down to the beach either. They were anxious. Daniel tried not to look at them, always turning this way and that, jutting their heads, rushing off one after the other through the bracken.

If there'd still been horses, then he could have caught one and ridden it bare-backed when danger came. But there were no horses on the island any more. Mr Murray said it was the good herbs they used to bring them over for. Good herbs for sick horses. They'd leave them here a while, then fetch them back. Daniel wondered what a horse would look like in a boat, Mr Murray's boat for example. It would look too tall.

He stood up on a piece of wall and looked out across the channel. Birds hung above the woods and he could hear a cuckoo. The fishermen were long gone on the early tide, he'd watched them leaving when he woke. But he counted three yachts moored, nobody visible on them, and a few sailing boats. Near the mainland, a dinghy with some boys larking about. He imagined boats tip to tail across the sea, from there to here, a sick horse in each and a man pulling the oars.

They'd wanted to make the Irish horses sick. Will had shown him a sheet of paper.

'Don't ask where I got it,' he said. 'Read it.'

Glanders in Horses: Propaganda Directive No. 16. He remembered the number. He hadn't known what glanders was. But Will had known. The island herbs wouldn't have been enough for those sick horses. He'd told Daniel about abscesses and ulcers, the skin swelling and bursting with pus, suppurating, and then the muscles and the joints and finally pneumonia.

'Most don't survive,' Will had said, 'it's a horrible death. Two weeks or so it takes. And it's very contagious. Even humans sometimes.'

Directive No. 16 had been very practical. How to doctor a bag of oats with a hollow stick and microbes, and how it might help to turn the war for the British.

'Turn the war how?' Daniel had said, and Will had looked at him scornfully.

'Because of their passion for horses. To break their spirit.'

At the far end of the island the watchtower on

267

its cliff faced out to sea. It was round and had no roof now. He stood in the middle of the circle and looked up at the blue sky. A blackthorn bush was seeded up at the top, its trunk making a loop around the stones, and there was ragwort in the window-hole. The light was very clear and Daniel could stand inside the doorway and look far out over the water. That's where the Spanish ships had come from, the Armada. They'd been fleeing, at their wits' end. But it wasn't out there that the danger would come from now. If Johnnie had been here, and not dead in France somewhere, they could have split the lookout and one of them fished or slept while the other watched. It was easier having Johnnie in his mind when he was on the island. He could imagine him here. Johnnie would have understood this place.

He made a den inside the bracken so nobody could see him, and slept. In his dream everybody was a horse except him. Will was, and Colonel Whittam, and there were horses with glengarries on their heads, and others with slouch hats and overcoats. Then the shooting started and there were horses wounded and dying all around him, his friends. And other horses, foals and fillies, looking on, holding the guns. Then a piebald foal lifted a hoof towards him and raised a rifle, and Daniel sat straight up, back tight away from the foal, hands to his face for protection, because everything was touching him, his neck, his hands, ankles, arms, scratching, tickling, and the air was murmuring. He opened his eyes and the air grew green and quiet. He sat till his heart had calmed, then crawled out of the bracken and lay on the grass above the rocks.

'I am awake now,' he said. He was thirsty and took out the thermos of water Mrs Murray had packed for him. Then he ate a sandwich and three plums.

He had brought nothing to Ireland for the birds, so Mrs Murray had found him a notebook and soft pencil and he had Mr Murray's binoculars for the day. He was careful with the binoculars. If the lenses caught the sun, the dazzle would betray him. A flock of choughs wheeled above the woods across the water, their 'keeow' calls soft at this distance, then scattered as a peregrine winnowed its way high into the sky before making a lazy glide across the canopy. Sitting far back on the beach, he watched the oystercatchers, their red bills and red legs, as they hammered limpets from the rocks and dug in the sand for worms. They stood in lines at the low tide, facing out to sea, waiting for the water.

The water was cold and very clear. At one end of the beach there were sea urchins in the deeper pools. Daniel saw a small starfish. If he needed to, he could fish for mackerel off a rock, or collect winkles and boil them in sea-water over a fire, pick out their insides with the hoof pick on his penknife. Johnnie should be here too, but he wasn't.

Daniel stood very still in the shallows and after two minutes or so small fish began to nuzzle round his shins.

The tide had gone right down and begun to rise again and the wind was rising when he saw the boat coming to get him. He crouched behind a rock until he could see the colour of the hull. Mr Murray's boat was painted green. Once he knew it was green, he rolled his trousers up and stood up to the knees, waiting for Mr Murray to come and take him off.

13

Jude was woken early the next day by the sound of the water pipes, which groaned and rattled under the floor like hard-done-by ghosts. She surfaced from sleep slowly, remembering where she was. The day was bright. She could hear the rattle of carts, the occasional shout, something foreign in the rise and fall of the voice.

She found that one of her arms was above her head, dead to the world, and until she put her other hand up and felt it there, fingers caught between the bars of the bed head, she couldn't work out where it had gone to. Easing the hand free, she lifted the arm down to her side. The blood surged back so that she wanted to clench and grip, clutch against the feeling returning. She'd woken like this so often, she should be used to it by now, but she still found it strange. She would go to sleep lying on her side, legs drawn up, arms between her knees, wrapped around herself, and wake to find herself undone, reaching away.

As the feeling returned, Jude caught up with the waking day. She remembered now and her stomach clenched. She was meeting Dr Kelleher this morning.

She took pains with her hair, and put on her prettiest blouse and a skirt, though she would change out of both before the journey. For half a minute she wondered at herself. This wasn't a date, for God's sake, so why was she dressing up? And it occurred to her that it wasn't so much the doctor she was dressing up for as herself. As though she wanted to give herself the pleasure of her own beauty.

'You need some air,' she told herself then. 'Clear the cobwebs,' and she shook her head at the thought and lifted the heavy sash open to the day.

Jude was early to the statue. She had paid her bill at the hotel and packed her things. The motorbike was ready, she had checked the tyres and the oil, and as soon as this meeting with the doctor was over, she'd be away.

★ ★ ★

The morning light was grey and the sky low, the air was heavy and damp. She had her camera bag slung on her shoulder, but the light was too dreary even to pretend to be a photographer. She'd thank Dr Kelleher for his offer to show her around and then she'd take her leave. Politely, but definitely. The Whelans had been wonderfully hospitable, just what she'd always heard about the Irish, but she was less sure of the doctor. He wasn't being hospitable, and she didn't think he particularly wanted to show her the sights of his city. He made her uncomfortable, aware of herself, though she couldn't say why.

She looked down the empty street. A few boys were unlocking grilles from the shop fronts. It was nearly seven-thirty. Father Mathew held out his hand in bronze benediction above her and the pigeons slept on between his feet, heads curled into their chests. She sniffed the air and remembered the ditty Dermot had come out with last night.

The smell from the river is something wicked, how do Father Mathew stick it?
Here's up 'em all says the boys of Fair Hill.

The song was right, Jude could smell the river this morning. She looked over across the bridge and up towards Patrick's Hill. There was one figure walking towards her and before he reached the far side of the bridge, she knew it for Dr Kelleher.

He walked with his head down as if deep in thought, nearly bumping into a woman pulling a barrow over the bridge, and when he was close enough for Jude to see his face, she thought he looked tired, as if he hadn't slept. He had his jacket buttoned against the early morning chill, but she was fairly sure he was dressed in the same clothes she'd seen him in at the dinner table the previous evening.

She felt a rush of pity, like the prick of so many pins against her neck, across her skull, and she could smell from nowhere her father's study. Her father had retreated there when her mother died and she would come to find him, to bring him to the dinner table or tempt him with a piece of warm toast, stepping into a fug of pipe-smoke, old tweed and the aniseed balls he had her buy for him by the pound at the grocer's shop. Now she felt it, obscurely, for Dr Kelleher, but as a woman, not as a child.

Ignoring Jude, the doctor lifted his arm wearily and saluted Father Mathew.

'I swear I haven't taken a drop in days,' he said.

Then he turned towards Jude and nodded a greeting. 'Good day,' his tone curt, his lip curled in something between a smile and a grimace.

'Good morning.'

'Ready to snap?'

'It's kind of you to meet me. I'd have telephoned you if I'd been able.'

'Why is that?'

'Well, the light's very poor this morning, not good for the kind of photographs I want. I haven't that much time so it'd be better for me to be on my way and I'll try to get the photos on the way back.'

Dr Kelleher made no immediate reply. He had taken Jude's elbow while she spoke and walked her down towards the bridge. She hadn't tried to break his grip, but his fingers were pressing into her arm. It wasn't aggressive, but it was very definite. When they reached the edge of the river, he stopped and they stood, unspeaking, staring at the grey water. Jude watched a crate float towards the bridge on the tide. Two gulls sat on the lettering, the remains of which read 'RY'STEA'. As the crate slipped beneath the bridge, the gulls lifted from it, wheeled high and dropped down to perch on the limestone posts that ran, joined by an iron rail, along the river's edge.

'You'll walk with me a little way because I'm going to show you something,' Dr Kelleher said, and as he spoke, he pulled at her arm. Jude looked at his face. It was stony, his eyes hard, his mouth in a thin line.

'You're holding me too tight,' she said, and the doctor loosened his grip, but he didn't let go.

A tram rumbled over Patrick's Bridge, sleep-eyed people staring out at the couple walking by the waterside. Across the river, above the blue-slated roofs and the threads of smoke, the bells of Shandon tower rang out the quarter, and elsewhere other bells clanged and echoed.

Steps cut down to the water, a flight and a landing and another flight, and two boys hunched over a fishing line halfway down, heads intent. They passed an old woman with a basket of cabbages and two younger women hurrying. One of them muttered something to Dr Kelleher and tugged at her skirts in a kind of half-curtsey, and he gave a curt nod in return. They were approaching a large building which Jude thought must be a church, the curve of a chapel facing towards her.

'The Opera House,' Dr Kelleher said, and Jude saw that the near end was a box office, posters pasted up on the wall for *The Scarlet Pimpernel* and *Macbeth*. A little further on and he stopped, letting go of Jude's arm. Stepping away, she watched the gulls gyring, arguing in the sky. Dr Kelleher paced behind her, chinking the money in his pocket. She wondered whether she was frightened by him, and couldn't decide. Turning back she looked up at the Opera House, its bulk, its Doric columns and high balustrade.

'You brought me to see this?' she said, because although it was an imposing building, she couldn't believe he had gripped her arm so tight to bring her here, and she was bewildered.

The doctor looked pale, but she couldn't tell if it was just the early light. And his bigness, his bulk, which she had found overbearing before, now seemed hollow. As if somewhere inside that large suit a much slighter man was camping out.

'You don't get much of our news over there,' he said, gesturing with a thumb down the river, towards the sea. 'Your newspapers have got more important things to write about, of course. A whole empire. We're just the nearest scrap of it. Most of them think we should be cut off and pushed far out into the Atlantic, and of course I don't agree with them, but I can't say I'm surprised. Not when you look back at it. They've always thought of us like that.'

'But you've got your own government now,' Jude said. 'And the British troops have gone, most of them. You won in the end, didn't you? More or less?'

Dr Kelleher shook his head. 'I shouldn't have begun like this. Stupid of me. You'll read the *Manchester Guardian*, I'd bet.' Jude nodded. 'Which is better than nothing. But anyway I'm getting off the point. I have a story to tell you. It came to mind when you showed us that photograph of the wounded man yesterday evening.'

'You know the men in the photograph?' Jude couldn't keep the excitement from her voice.

'I didn't say that.' Dr Kelleher crossed his arms and, leaning forward into the iron rail that ran along the river's edge and staring down at the water, he began.

'It was a winter evening, not late, but dark. About five years ago, that'll be all, but it was just before the Auxies, the Auxiliaries, burnt Cork.' He looked at Jude. 'You knew about that?'

'I read about it in the newspapers. We were shocked.'

'And did you read about the Secretary for Ireland, Hamar Greenwood, claiming in your House of Commons that the citizens had started the fires? That it was nothing to do with the Forces of the Crown? Even suggesting that the fire leapt over the river on its own to set the town hall ablaze?'

'Did you see the fires?'

'You couldn't not. The sky red and the noise of the blaze. The smoke. Terrible. And Greenwood, a Canadian, for the love of God. You'd think he'd understand a bit more than the rest of them.' He gave a short laugh. 'There's an expression over here now about tall tales: 'Don't tell a Greenwood'. But you won't have heard that one.'

'No,' Jude said. And then she asked: 'Did they arrest any of the men, the Auxies?'

Dr Kelleher snorted. 'Did they fly and go to heaven? Of course not. They just moved them up to Dublin. And a friend up there wrote me that he'd seen them patrolling on Patrick's Green with burnt corks in their glengarries, boasting of it.

'But anyway, this night was before the burning. I'd been working all day, my surgery off Paul Street, people with nothing except a pile of poverty and illness. My housekeeper was gone home. She was always gone early those days, to be back before the curfew, my dinner left in the oven ready. I'd just set it on a tray with a glass of stout, to eat in front of the fire. I'd turn on the wireless, shut out the day. I remember it was lamb chops. Then there was a knock on the door.

'A certain knock, two raps, then three, I'd know what it was about. There wasn't a week went by at that time without me opening the door at night twice, sometimes three times. The woman on the doorstep was a messenger. Moira Sullivan. I knew her face, she was part of the Sullivan clan from around Grattan Street, the 'Marsh'. She said could I come at once, and sure enough it was an address over there. Broad Lane, the other side of the river. She was to take me. I told her to come in a moment while I found my shoes and bag. She stood in the hall, and I could see she was shaking.

'They always wore long coats, those women, and you didn't ask what they carried underneath. But the Black and Tans and the Auxies weren't allowed to search women, or priests, so they were the ones could act best as couriers, weapons and messages. As dangerous a work as anybody's.

'I asked her if she'd met anyone and she said no, but she'd heard a patrol over near North Gate Bridge. She thought they were heading across towards Blarney Street. I asked her, could she tell me the problem, and she said it was two men shot. One in the face, alive when she left, the other a wound to the shoulder but bleeding badly. She asked for a drink of water, which I got her, and then we went.

'We crossed Patrick's Bridge fine. The night was dark but clear and there was quite a moon. It would have been better if it had been raining. It would have put the Tans off their roaming and maybe this would be a different tale. Anyway, we turned onto the quays and there was nobody about, not even a dog. We'd got as far as the Opera House, just where we're standing now, when a band of Black and Tans appeared. They must have come down Half Moon Street, and normally you could hear them a mile off, but this lot were quiet as mice. Five of them.'

Dr Kelleher stooped and picked up a pebble. 'I don't suppose you've ever met a Black and Tan,' he said.

Jude had been listening so intently, the question made her start. She didn't want to answer it. She remembered Daniel telling her in Kew Gardens and how she'd walked away for a moment. Dr Kelleher threw the pebble far out into the water where it disappeared without a ripple and she realised that the question was near enough rhetorical. That he certainly wasn't expecting her to say yes. She shrugged, hitched up her camera bag, which was beginning to weigh heavy.

'What did they look like?' she said.

'Brutal. Hung about with weapons, sneering. Revolvers on each hip, bandoliers of ammunition

279

slung across their chests, muskets, hand grenades in their pockets, as they liked to let you know given a half chance. Less than half.'

Jude nodded. She couldn't imagine Daniel dressed like that, couldn't imagine him pointing a rifle or pulling the pin on a grenade. There were a dozen things she'd have liked to say, to ask, but she bit her tongue.

'And this lot,' the doctor said, returning to his story, 'soon as they saw us they started singing, just quietly.

> We are the boys of the RIC
> As happy as happy can be.

'I tell you, that singing was far more frightening than any roaring, and I'd heard them do that too.'

The pantomime English voice Dr Kelleher sang the words in made Jude's skin crawl. She could hear Daniel's accent, and her own, inside it. But surely Daniel Brown couldn't have done this kind of thing?

'Then my messenger started to panic,' Dr Kelleher said. 'I could hear her, her quick, short breaths. I could see her hand clutching at the front of her coat. So I took her arm, told her to breathe deep and slow, told her I'd do the talking, and by the time the Tans were close, she had calmed down. I told her it'd be a night in gaol at the very worst, fool that I was.'

The camera bag had become too heavy. Jude set it down on the cobbles and put her hands on one of the posts. It was cold and stony under her palm, soothing. She turned away from the doctor and stared up the river. The sun warmed her back and cast a long, slender shadow before her. He was silent for what felt like an age but Jude knew it was probably no more than a couple of minutes. It was extraordinary, to be standing by the river Lee in the middle of Cork city early one weekday morning when she should be jostling her way to work. Standing there listening to a tale that made the hair on her neck rise as if it were the most normal thing in the world.

When the doctor began to speak again, she was sure she heard a catch in his voice.

'I could have told you any number of stories,' he said. 'Terrible things. I saw terrible things. You do as a doctor, and in a war . . . ' He spread his hands on the rail, pressed them down. 'You'll know that. But this was one of the worst, and I didn't even see it happen, and anyway I couldn't prevent it.'

Jude turned back towards Dr Kelleher. It had taken her by surprise, seeing him like this. She had guessed him for a grimmer man last night at the Whelans', someone more inured to human suffering.

'I always found it easier to be in the thick of it,' she said. 'At least then I could see where things began and ended. Wounds, pain. If you're not there, if you only hear about it, then your imagination can pick up and run off with you.'

Dr Kelleher looked at her and then he smiled, as though, in the middle of his tale, she'd reminded him of something.

'You must have been so young,' he said.

'No more than the boys. And it was a very different war,' Jude said. 'But you were going to tell me a particular story.'

He clenched his eyes shut, and opened them again. 'Yes. The Volunteer, the one with the shoulder wound, that's what I had to tell you about.'

'But what about the woman? And the Black and Tans?' Jude said.

'You see, that's so often how it was. All the people who suffered by the by. Not the Volunteers, I don't mean them, though they did of course, they got shot and wounded, tortured, imprisoned and killed, but they were soldiers, IRA men, they expected it. But the women who knocked on your door after curfew, they'll never make the history books.'

'What happened to her?' Jude asked, trying to keep her tone gentle, but she had to know now.

'They walked up to us like a posse of tomcats, those Tans. That swagger.' He almost spat the words. 'Said what were we doing out after curfew, did we know the penalty, sneered at us. They were drunk, of course, I could smell it on them even before they got close. I kept my voice calm, explained that I was a doctor and that the woman had come for my help, someone in her family was ill. I think I said suspected scarlet fever, something catching anyway.'

'Did they believe you?'

'They wouldn't let Moira Sullivan come on with me. That was the thing. And they wouldn't let me stay with her. There was an argument between them about who was staying and who going, so that for a moment I thought maybe we'd be able to get away, if they all started fighting. But then one of them fired his revolver in the air and that quietened them.

'She was shaking like a leaf now. I think she knew much sooner than I did what was going to happen.

'Two of the Tans came up and shoved me away from her, demanded to know where was I going. So I had to think fast and give a false address. Someone I could trust to guess what I might be up to and to play along. I told them the number of a house on Henry Street, just off Bachelor's Quay, near Broad Street, and they marched me away. The last I saw of Moira Sullivan that night, she was standing with the Tans around her, her arms wrapped around her coat, her face white under the moonlight.'

'And afterwards?' Jude said.

'I saw her afterwards, but she couldn't bear to look at me.'

'They'd beaten her up?'

'They hadn't touched her face. Left her unmarked, the bastards.'

Dr Kelleher bent and picked up Jude's camera bag, toted the strap on his hands like a man playing 'Guess the Weight' at a fair, swung it gently to and fro.

'By the time I got to them, one of the Volunteers was dead. The other one, I patched him up and he survived. Went on to fight another day, as they say. He's a bit of a famous fellow in Ireland now.'

Dr Kelleher looked hard at Jude. He still held

the camera bag but he was swinging it violently, the strap flat across the pads of his fingers. Any minute, the momentum would take the bag beyond his control, it would drop onto the cobbles and her lenses and maybe the camera itself would be smashed.

'Please put the bag down,' Jude said.

'Tell me what you're really doing over here. Because I don't think you've come over for the birds and the bees, not really, have you?'

'It's not the whole story, no,' Jude said.

'It's got something to do with that photograph you passed around last night.'

Jude nodded.

'I think we should go and sit down somewhere and order tea, maybe some toast, be civilised about it, and then you can tell me what exactly it is that you're after,' Dr Kelleher said, and he hitched the camera bag over his shoulder.

So Jude ended up in the Pavilion restaurant again, making small-talk with the doctor while the waitress, a different one, brought tea and a shiny silver-covered dish to the table.

'I love being served toast,' Dr Kelleher said, lifting the lid on the dish. He seemed less angry here, but perhaps it was just because he was seated, and no longer swinging her camera close to oblivion.

'Do you see?' he said, and easing his butter knife below the piled slices, he prised up the base and gestured to Jude to look. 'To keep them warm. A *bain* of hot water.'

They ate several pieces in a silence Jude found to be strangely companionable. Sipping tea and spreading jam, the doctor seemed more like a bluff, genial uncle who might be enquiring after her well-being, than the steely adversary she knew he was. But then he put down his teacup and wiped his mouth with the napkin and she knew the interval was over.

'So?' he said.

Jude gathered her thoughts and decided she'd counter his question with one of her own.

'Was one of the men in the photograph the man you went to help that night? The man with the shoulder wound?'

'And what do *you* know of him?'

'You said he became a hero. If he's still alive, then it's very important that I find him.'

'Why? How could it be so important when you don't know a thing about him? Not even his name?'

There was no trace of the uncle about Dr Kelleher now. He sat back, arms crossed, ready to wait for as long as it took, and he didn't take his eyes off Jude. She was pinioned to her seat. She decided there was nothing for it but to tell him as much as she could and hope to God she hadn't misjudged this fierce man.

'Perhaps I could tell *you* a story now,' she said, putting away the photograph.

The doctor refilled her teacup, and then he nodded.

Jude fished her cigarettes and lighter from her bag. 'Do you mind if I smoke?'

'They'll make you cough,' he said. 'But go ahead.'

She lit up and took a pull, enjoying that first

full tug in her lungs.

'May I have a look?' Dr Kelleher said, pointing to the lighter. Jude passed it to him. 'Where did you get this?' he said, tracing the four-leaf clover with a finger.

'All right,' she said. 'My story. I was in Belgium nursing for nearly four years. Set up a first-aid post with another nurse. Hundreds of soldiers came through it, Belgian and British mainly, most of them so young, many of them horribly wounded. Those with minor injuries, if we could patch them up and send them back into the trenches, we did. And they'd take whatever we could send them back with, pathetically grateful, a slab of chocolate, a new pair of mittens, or just a full belly. They didn't hate the enemy, most of them. There was far more resentment against the top dogs, Haig and his cronies. They were the ones carrying on this war. They were keeping the men in the mud and the horror.

'But not all of them were wounded. Some we just fed, we had Peter for that, a wonderful cook, or they came and slept like the dead in our cellar. Lines of palliasses. Kate, she was the other nurse, and I, we had our camp beds in our own room but as often as not we never made it into them. We had fifty hot water bottles to fill some nights. Soup and cocoa to an endless stream of men. I must have taken hundreds of photographs, of anything and everything. Kate at every kind of task: brushing her hair, changing a dressing, winding bandages, digging potatoes, on her motorbike. And Peter, cooking, grinning usually.

'I took a photograph of two officers in a British regiment, one wounded, the other a friend, sharing a cigarette. For me that's all it was. A photo of two friends in wartime. There were piles of others. This one was nothing special.

'I did know one of the men a little, enough to say hello to in the street, if there had been a street. That was because he and Kate, they flirted a little over the dressings till his friend was patched up, and so I remember him. I knew he was Irish, and there was a joke about a wine bottle so I remember that he was from Cork, but that was all.'

'What happened to Kate?' Dr Kelleher said. Jude looked across at him. The question had surprised her.

'Kate?' she said.

'You mention her a lot.'

'She died. Gassed.'

The doctor nodded. 'Not your fault then.'

'No.'

'So go on about the photograph,' he said.

'An acquaintance of mine saw it in an exhibition a month or so ago, and it meant something very different to him, and that's what I'm trying to understand. He didn't explain it to me properly but it was obviously important. The last time I saw him he was very agitated, and now he's disappeared. But I think he's come to Ireland, and the photo is all I have to go on.'

'I'd like to see it again,' Dr Kelleher said.

Jude opened her bag and took out the photograph, passed it to him. 'It's like looking at a riddle,' she said.

He studied it, then set it down on the table.

'Your acquaintance,' he said, 'what does he have to do with the man in the photo? Why do you think he might have come here?'

Jude lifted out another slice of warm toast. She needed to steady herself, do something ordinary, and the only thing available was spreading jam. She took her time, bit and chewed, sipped at the tea, which she noticed now was the deepest brown.

'You make it very strong over here,' she said, swirling her teacup. A few dark grains eddied to the surface and sank again.

'It'll be Barry's, the tea. Best tea in Ireland. Anywhere.'

A man in a double-breasted suit came over to the table and greeted Dr Kelleher. Introductions were made, 'Miss Hursten, photographer from England, Mr Flynn, my friend and lawyer,' the men exchanged a few hurried sentences, agreed a time for a meeting, and with a brief nod of departure, Mr Flynn was gone. Dr Kelleher looked across at Jude again.

'So?' he said.

Jude didn't want to mention the diary.

'He spoke about a place in Ireland that he loved, Coolderry, in Castletowne, and an island, Horse Island, places where he felt more at ease than in his own home, and something he said makes me think he may have gone there now.'

Dr Kelleher sat perfectly still, waiting.

'He came to know these people a few years back,' she said.

'During the Troubles?'

Jude nodded.

'So he was here during the Troubles.'

'Yes. And that's when he met the man in the photograph, though I don't know what went on between them.'

She knew so little. Only that Daniel had been injured in a motor lorry accident over here, that he still walked with a limp and that the sight of that photograph had driven him to strange and disturbing lengths. She was sure he had come to Ireland, sure he'd gone to Castletowne and Coolderry house, and that if she could find him, she could help him.

'If it was during the Troubles and your man is English, then whatever went on, it won't have been very pretty.'

'No,' Jude said.

'He was a Black and Tan, wasn't he? That's what you're finding so hard to tell me.'

'He told me he was an Auxiliary.'

The doctor chuckled. 'An Auxie. Worse and worse.'

'What's the difference?'

'Not much. The Auxiliaries had to have been officers. There's many thought they were worse than the Tans. What was his name?'

'Daniel Brown. I don't believe he's done the kinds of things you described.'

The doctor shrugged. 'Are you in love with him?'

'No,' Jude said, too quickly, she knew at once.

The doctor gave her a long look. 'So why the mission? It's a big thing, to drop your life and come looking for a stranger in a foreign land.'

'Nobody else can come looking for him, and I've nothing to lose. I'm worried for his safety.'

'With good reason,' Dr Kelleher said. 'An ex-Auxiliary wandering the Irish roads. He won't find many friendly faces if they know what he's been up to, and they'll probably guess soon enough, and once they do, he'll find worse than scowls coming his way.'

'So I'm realising.'

'And you're over here as his Don Quixote.'

The waitress came over and Dr Kelleher ordered another pot of tea. 'If you're going off into the wilds later, you should build up your strength,' he said. 'What about joining me in a full breakfast? You've told me the worst, so your stomach should be calmer.'

Jude grinned and nodded to the waitress.

'Will you be wanting them fried, poached or scrambled?' the waitress asked.

'Poached, thank you.'

Once the waitress was gone Dr Kelleher resumed. 'So will your man be looking for this fellow?' he said, pointing to the standing soldier, leaning over with the cigarette.

'Would he be hard to find?'

'I'd say not. He's a bit of a hero in these parts.'

'Can you tell me his name?'

Lifting his hands to his head, the doctor rubbed across his face, as if to wake himself from something.

'If I hadn't met you on the boat with

Catherine, then we wouldn't be here now. You'd have gone off happy this morning to find your friend, and I'd have got up and sat with the *Examiner* and a pot of tea for half an hour and then sauntered out to open my surgery and greet the first of my ill flock. None of this would have been brought up today and I've only myself and my fierce curiosity to blame.'

'I'll be gone from the city very soon,' Jude said. 'And then you can put me from your mind.'

'Maybe,' he said.

The waitress came with their food and for a few minutes they welcomed the distraction that the eggs and rashers, sausage and tomatoes brought.

'There's no point my not telling you his name,' Dr Kelleher said finally, 'because you could find it out soon enough. You could stand on the pavement in Patrick Street waving that damn photograph about and somebody would tell you within five minutes that the Irishman in the British army uniform is Matt Walsh. They might think he was in fancy dress, but they'd know the man.'

'Matt Walsh,' Jude said. 'I've never heard of him.'

'But then you don't know much about Ireland across the water, do you.'

'So what's he famous for?'

'Well, not for serving in the British army. There'd be quite a few would be surprised to learn about that, though I'm not, and he's not the only one in the IRA by a long shot.'

Dr Kelleher wiped a last piece of brown bread

around his plate and gathered his knife and fork.

'Not that he'll have hidden it, but sure, I didn't know about it till yesterday when I was passed your photograph. Gave me a bit of a stir, even so,' he said, putting a hand to his chest. 'And he's a wellknown figure in County Cork now. A business man. Building business. Respected. And still a fearless Republican. Fought the British and opposed the Treaty. Was gaoled by everybody. It'd do him no good if this picture was put about. I'd be wondering what was going on myself, if I hadn't heard the tale from you.'

Jude drew on her cigarette. 'Fought against the British,' she said. 'After fighting with them. Does he hate us then?'

'Have you noticed us hating you since you arrived?' Dr Kelleher said sharply.

Jude felt her colour rise. 'No, of course not. Stupid of me,' she said.

'He's famous for an ambush,' he said flatly. 'He fought all the way through, like Dan Breen or Tom Barry or O'Malley. You wouldn't know who they were. But it was the ambush put his name up in lights.'

'What happened?'

'An IRA flying column took out an Auxiliary patrol, two lorry loads, sixteen or so men, in West Cork. All the Auxies were killed except the Commanding Officer. He was wounded as I remember, and shipped back to England smartly, else the IRA would have finished him off. He'd seen too many of them. Anyway he killed himself not that long afterwards.'

'And Walsh?'

'Walsh was the commandant of those boys. The brains behind it all.'

The waitress came to clear the plates, and Dr Kelleher fell silent. Jude reached into her bag for another cigarette. She put it between her lips and struck the lighter, holding it before her and watching the pale flame. The pulse beat in her neck, and her scalp prickled with apprehension.

Dr Kelleher's voice took her by surprise. 'If you're going to light that nasty bit of tobacco, do so. Or have you hypnotised yourself?' he said.

She started, jabbing the lighter away from her, extinguishing the flame.

'Did nobody else survive?' she said.

The doctor shook his head. 'Which is quite something when you think that the Auxies were all armed to the teeth as usual. The Column had two killed and several wounded. One of the lads killed, I know his family. He was the eldest son, a good boy.'

Jude lit her cigarette. 'A good boy?'

'Your Auxie friend was probably not so very nice when he was over here,' Dr Kelleher said. 'Why don't you ask him a few questions when you find him, about what he got up to in our country.'

'So the man you went to help that night in Cork, the one with the shoulder wound,' Jude said, ignoring his last remark, 'that man was Matt Walsh.'

'It was.'

'It's been quite a piece of luck, meeting you, then.'

293

'Why?'

'Because it turns out you know one of the men in the photograph.'

'Luck has a smaller pond over here. Sure everybody knows everybody. Still, I'm sorry I haven't shown you the sights of Cork. Though it hasn't been an utter surprise to me that sights aren't your first reason for coming over here.'

Jude laughed. She put a hand down to her camera bag. 'Since I've got my camera with me, could I take your photograph? It's not only a front, the camera story. Outside, beside Father Mathew perhaps, or the river?'

Dr Kelleher tugged at his collar, brushed at a crumb on his waistcoat. He smiled.

'Next time, maybe,' he said. 'And if you're going to go searching people out,' he said, 'you'd maybe want to broaden your story. Make yourself more of a journalist, wanting to write stories about what's become of the heroes perhaps. And have yourself working for an American outfit. We love America here, and they love us. And they've buckets of money to spend sending ignorant young new women journalists over the water with.'

'You're out to help me now?' Jude said.

'I'm not going to stop you, am I?' Jude shook her head. 'So then, I might as well give you some tips on surviving.'

Jude put her hands on the table. 'Thank you,' she said, grinning. 'And I'll work on my story.'

'I'm old enough to be your father,' the doctor said.

'My father is dead,' Jude said.

'Well, maybe that is a small mercy for him, God rest his soul. Here's another tip. My last for today. The ex-Auxie fellow you're wanting to find, he might be sorry now for what he did then, and you might be the judge of that. For me, I'll leave God as judge. Forgiveness is hard when you've seen what they did, though I'll do my best if I have to. But even if the fellow is sorry, truly sorry, be as careful as you know how. Because what happened over here, it'll have found out a danger in him and that won't ever leave.'

Jude stared at her fingers. The doctor's words took her back to the afternoon in Kew Gardens, and the terror, or violence, that loomed behind things for Daniel, and she knew he was right.

'Now, my guess is you've a last favour to ask me,' Dr Kelleher said. 'So I'm going to make mine first. If you've the time down there in West Cork, would you be able to take me a few photographs?'

'Of course,' Jude said. 'What of?'

'It'd be for my pleasure, nothing more serious, a hobby I have. Ancient stones.'

'Ancient stones?'

'Stone circles, chamber tombs, wedge tombs, ring forts. Ireland's full of them.'

'You want me to photograph any I see?'

Dr Kelleher laughed. 'No. There's a particular stone circle called Drombeg. I've been there, but without a camera. You should go there anyway, it's an extraordinary place. Two miles east of Glandore.'

'I'd be delighted,' Jude said. 'I can include it in

my photo-essay of Ireland.'

Dr Kelleher nodded briskly. 'Now you have got a last question, haven't you?' he said, in that cheery voice Jude associated with doctors who, having given the gravest news, finish off by asking if you've been to the pictures lately.

'Yes,' she said.

'So ask away,' he said.

'If I needed to contact Matt Walsh, where would I find him?'

'And you don't know yet if you do need to, because it depends on your friend?'

'Yes.'

The doctor looked at her and she met his gaze. Reaching down to his jacket on the back of the chair, he tugged a prescription pad and pen from the breast pocket. Although his hands were as big as the rest of him, his fingers were deft, their movements elegant as he opened the pad, uncapped his pen. She noticed the pale hairs along his finger, and his broad, scrubbed doctor's nail. When he held the pen, Jude saw that the middle finger of his right hand lifted crookedly above the others. It must have been broken at some point. He wrote down two addresses and the name of a town, Liscool, on one sheet.

'This is mine,' he said, pointing to the first address, 'and this one, if you go to Liscool and find Paddy McCarthy, he'll take you to Walsh. McCarthy's the man you need. A draper now. A draper then, come to that. Lives up the hill.'

Tearing the sheet out, he handed it to Jude,

and on a second sheet he wrote a note of introduction.

'I have met the bearer of this note, and I trust her. Please answer her questions if you can.' And he signed it Dr Frank Kelleher.

'I've given my name,' he said. 'But go carefully! There's a lot you'll be treading on.'

14

Daniel returned to the island each day, going out in the morning and coming back before the sun went down. It was a good place to keep things at bay, better than the mainland. And he could take precautions, now he knew its topography. Be master of it. The weather had been steady, with some sun and no rain. But when he woke on his fourth morning, the sky was black and heavy and the wind rising. He knew that he must have had the dream again, he could feel it in his limbs. Beyond the window the trees were flailing, as if something was beating at them again and again and they were trying to get away.

Down beyond the garden, the sea was grey and coarse. The seagulls flew into the dark sky like bright, white scissors, cutting the air to shreds. He saw a hare cross the corner of the lawn, lean-limbed, its hind legs lifting high, loping slowly, then stopping to tug at some green delicacy.

The last time he had been here, on a weekend pass out from the barracks, he had come in towards the kitchen one day to find both dogs, shut out, standing faces up to the back door, tails still, noses quivering. Inside, Mr Murray was skinning a hare, peeling the fur from its haunches. A white bowl of blood was at one end of the table and the air was thick with the smell of it. Daniel had watched for a minute, though the smell made him nauseous. Something about the creature's limbs seemed too human. He had nudged the bowl of blood so that it swilled slightly, leaving a filter of pink against the white sides.

'It's very red,' he'd said.

'Of course it's red,' Mr Murray had said, snipping the fur from the ankles with scissors.

'No, but redder than a rabbit's. More like a man's,' he'd said, and Mr Murray had stopped snipping and looked up at Daniel. 'I mean it looks more like a man's than an animal's,' he'd said, and then the smell had been too much and he'd left the room.

This fourth day, Daniel found Mrs Murray in the scullery, putting some roses in vases.

'I want to go to the island today,' he said. 'Take a tent, food, stay a night or two.'

Mrs Murray shook her head. 'It's going to pour, and there's no shelter.'

'But I need to go,' Daniel said.

'Why?' Her voice was curious.

'Well, there's the bracken, which is good and deep, and the watchtower, though it doesn't face the right way any more.'

Mrs Murray snipped the rose stems at an angle and trimmed the lower leaves. 'Doesn't face the right way?' she said carefully.

'And there are fish of course, if I took a line. Water might be a problem though. I'd have to take a few bottles. I didn't see any springs.'

'Have you had some breakfast?' Mrs Murray said.

'I'll eat a lot. Stock up.'

299

Mrs Murray cooked him up a big breakfast, and she must have called Mr Murray in from somewhere, because they were both at the table as he ate, just drinking tea. They didn't say much, didn't look at him much, but he had the feeling they were watching him more than they were doing anything else.

'The hare on the lawn this morning? It wasn't like the last one,' Daniel said, in what he thought was a conversational tone. 'I couldn't bear the smell of that one, do you remember? And the colour of the blood? But the hare today was alive so I could only smell the air.'

'I don't remember the dead hare,' Mr Murray said.

'Well, it doesn't matter.'

'Daniel,' Mr Murray said, 'you've come here straight from England. That's right, isn't it?'

'Took the first train from Cork,' Daniel said, smiling.

'And you've been working in the family business till just the other day.'

Daniel nodded. 'I've been doing quite well. I think my father's pleasantly surprised.'

'Not recuperating recently? Or resting? Or . . . '

'No. Did a deal last week, and the pigeons just beyond the window, then the lift down, with the concertina doors and the soft dust, and the girls with their able bodies and umbrellas, to meet my father.'

'But when you left Ireland the last time, you were badly wounded?'

Mr Murray's brow was very creased, and there was something about his tone that bothered

Daniel. As if he was listening, but hearing different words. Daniel picked up his teacup and took a sip. His mouth was dry. He would try to be very clear.

'I was months in hospital and by the time I came out they'd stopped fighting the British and turned on each other. But I couldn't talk about it. It was too dangerous.'

'Even in England?'

'Yes.' Daniel thought a moment. 'It's all right now, I think, and that's why I've told you, but then, it was too dangerous. And it was easier for my parents that way. After Johnnie's death, my mother couldn't bear to hear about the war. Any war. And I didn't want to think about it either. So I never told them what happened, and they don't want to know any more.'

'And you?'

'Look at me, still can't walk properly,' Daniel said, and he did another smile. But he didn't like this conversation very much, so he asked them about something that had been puzzling him.

'It's much quieter here. What's happened to your pretty maid? And your friends calling in? You haven't had arguments? Fallen foul of something?'

Mr Murray laughed and shook his head. Then Mrs Murray put her hands on the table, as if, Daniel thought, to show that she wasn't holding a gun.

'You're going to have to tell us why you've come back here,' she said. 'For your own safety, and maybe for ours, you're going to have to tell us.'

A cold wave spread beneath Daniel's skin. He'd been careful, he thought, he hadn't seen anybody, not anybody he knew, coming here.

'Has somebody asked for me?' he said, and he saw a look pass between the Murrays.

'No,' Mrs Murray said. 'Nobody. But we're worried. Your distress. The dreams, the sweats, that you want to hide away from everything. We're going to ask Dr Ross to come and see you.'

Daniel shook his head. He picked up his teacup, but his hand was shaking, making ripples, so he put it down again.

'You haven't sent the letter to your parents yet, have you? Telling them you're here. Safe.'

'I'm going to,' Daniel said.

Mrs Murray shook her head. 'That's what you said the first time we asked, but you still haven't. We'll post a letter tomorrow. Either the one you'll have written by then, or one of our own if you haven't.'

One hand resting on the table, Mrs Murray carved an endless figure of eight into the tablecloth. She looked across at Daniel. He watched her fingernail circle and circle. She was waiting. He wondered how much it mattered what he said next.

'Why on earth have you come back?' she said.

'My parents never replied to you because I told them not to. I told them it would have put me at risk. That the IRA would have come and found me if they'd known I was alive.'

'And would they?'

'Perhaps in those first months, I don't know.'

302

'Why have you come back, Daniel Brown?' Mrs Murray said again, her voice hard. 'Because your story isn't clear. You don't have your facts straight.'

'There's a question in my head, it's been there since that day, only mostly it's been like a spirit or a mood, taken the form of something else, so that I've thought I was going mad at times. But now I know that it's a real question about a real man.'

'So keep it in your head.' Mrs Murray's nail pressed hard into the cloth. 'And go home.'

'I can't. And since I got here, other things keep pushing in at me. Things I have to answer to. Things I've kept at bay these years, never let in.'

'People won't want to know about your past here,' Mr Murray said. 'And for your own safety, it's better they don't.'

'They don't want to know in England,' Daniel said, 'and I don't want to tell them.'

'In England it's because they're ignorant,' said Mr Murray. 'But over here it's because they're exhausted with it. There are too many wounds. Ones you can see and ones you can't. First fighting the British, then turning inwards and two years of civil war. Brother fighting brother, towns and villages torn apart, so much hatred, bitterness.'

Mrs Murray's finger stopped. 'You're too soft, Joe. Too soft to say what it's like, seeing your country turned over to thugs and corner boys. Because that's what's happened. We know people whose families have been here for hundreds of years. They're Protestants, but they're as Irish as anybody is, and they've been burned out of their homes, turned off their own land by a small bunch of bully boys carrying hurley sticks and shotguns. We know people shot in their beds for nothing more than being a Protestant. I don't say that Daniel's lot always behaved as they should, but to make out that the IRA always had right on their side.' She shook her head. 'We'll see if you're right, Joe, or whether we don't end up like so many, and have to throw in our lot here, in this country that we love.'

Daniel put a hand to his collar. It was chafing. Mrs Murray's speech was confusing. He didn't want to think about all the other people. He didn't even want to think about the Murrays. It was too much already just thinking about himself, about what he had done, what had been done to him.

'Does it matter as much, if you didn't mean to do something?' he said.

There was a long pause before Mrs Murray answered him.

'What do you mean?' she said, her voice careful, alarmed.

Daniel shook his head slowly and fiercely from side to side, as though trying to shake something free inside it. 'I'll go out to Horse Island,' he said. 'Clear my head.'

Mrs Murray didn't answer, only put a tray on the table and cleared his breakfast things. He saw that her hands were shaking.

'It was warning shots, when we fired in the air,' Daniel said. 'Let them know we were there.

We were always out in the open, you know. Not like their lot. But the women would be squawking, like the hens, and the kids with their wide eyes. They made you angry, looking at you like that. Waiting for you to be angry and so you were. And the men. You didn't trust a man with his hands in his pockets. They want us to believe them, they can walk with their hands out.' Daniel pulled his cuffs up his wrists. 'Look, see? Nothing. Simple, isn't it. Keep your hands empty in the day, go to bed at night, and then we'll believe you.'

Mr Murray had stood up too now, and he walked round the table. He was walking slowly, as if he were in the woods and stalking something, Daniel thought. He stood behind Daniel's chair and Daniel felt his hands, very light, on both his shoulders.

'Come on,' Mr Murray said. 'We'll get some air.'

'But what happened when my leg got hurt, we didn't hurt the kiddies and the girls and the women like that. They didn't need to do it.' Daniel stopped and put his hands to his ears. 'Oh, God! Oh, Jesus! The Trout, Mr Murray. I have to fish. It's what I've come for. To fish for the fish. I'll have to do it soon.'

He felt Mr Murray's hands under his arms, holding him firm, lifting him up.

'Fishing's a good idea,' Mr Murray said, 'the weather looks right with the rain coming. I think the wind will drop. We'll go inland, take rods.'

Daniel turned towards the door. Mrs Murray stood there.

'I wouldn't tell my own mother,' he said.

She moved aside to let him by.

'I'll find you an oilskin,' Mr Murray said, 'and boots. It's going to be wet.'

Daniel went up the stairs. He heard their voices below.

'If you wait ten minutes I can hard-boil eggs. There's some cold meat, apples fresh off the tree, a bit sharp, but very tasty, thermos, fruit cake.'

'Sallin Lake, not a half hour's walk away.'

'But if you're not back by four, I'll telephone Dr Ross, or the Guards.'

'Is he safe?' Mr Murray said.

'Do you think he should be?'

'What he's saying? It's frightening. I don't understand what's gone on.'

'Nor does he,' Mrs Murray said. 'He might be in more danger if he did.'

When he heard both of the Murrays go into the kitchen, Daniel came down the stairs again. The dog lay on the rug in the middle of the hall floor, legs outstretched as if she were running lying down. She thumped her tail, but Daniel made no gesture towards her. He didn't want the dog following. He opened the front door.

Outside, the rain had begun. The wind had dropped. Daniel walked up the drive and out on to the road. He would go in a straight line from here.

He climbed the wall opposite into a field. Cows stood in one corner under a small tree. They didn't move except to turn their heads and watch him walk across. He crossed another wall, dislodging stones. It was raining steadily. The ground was hard after the days of sun but already it smelt of the wet. He walked across two more fields and then the ground rose, awkwardly, as if it had been heaved and piled. His straight line took him up, so he climbed. The thistles grew to four feet and the ground bucked and split invisibly beneath the coarse thick grasses, so that several times he had to brace himself from falling, making his bad leg ache and throb. More than once he nearly turned an ankle. Larks taunted him, singing high in the air as he stumbled near their souls. He had found a lark's nest once in the ground, its dappled brown eggs nestled in a hoof print, and seen one high bird dip away in the sky and stop its song. Linnets sang in the gorse, finches flashed and stonechats jigged and jerked their warning dance, *tsak tsak, tsak tsak*, pleading.

The Trout had swum in a straight line out of the ditch. Daniel had seen him. He'd risen to his feet and climbed up out, trailing weed from his greatcoat, walked through the fog and straight at the hill, just as if he knew where he was going. After that Daniel had shut his eyes, because you couldn't play dead if you were blinking, though everyone was gone by then. But anyway it was easier to shut them against the burning in his leg.

There had been the marching and the songs before, some of those men their voices shaking, as whose wouldn't be after what they'd done.

He'd recognised one of the songs. They'd found a copy of it under the floorboards during a house search and they'd made the lad in the house sing it. He'd had a lovely voice, which Will said was proof of him being a rebel.

Remember Comrades of Ireland,
As forward to Victory we go,
That England, the Tyrant of Tyrants,
Has Mercy ne'er shown to the Foe.

They'd taken the boy in for knowing the song. They hadn't found anything else, no guns or grenades. Not even a pitchfork out of place. But he'd known the song and it was enough.

'Bloody corner boy,' Will had said, just like Mrs Murray. 'That's what they all are. Thugs. Never done a full day's work. Spend all their time scheming against us and practising their bloody songs. Pretending to be soldiers.'

But the corner boys had got Will. Shot him clean in the head, Daniel found that out later, while the Trout swam away.

Daniel stopped climbing and stood up straight. Behind him he could see over the land to the sea. The rain was coming down steadily and you could barely see where the sky ended and the sea began.

15

When Jude went to retrieve her motorbike from the hotel yard, she found hens pecking around the tyres and a skinny boy, all knuckle and knee, in an old cloth cap, and a filthy waistcoat, leaning over the sidecar. He was fiddling with something and after the conversation with Dr Kelleher, crazy fears ran through her head.

'Leave it alone,' she shouted. 'What the hell are you doing?' and she tried to pull him away. But the boy seemed unperturbed and for an answer only wriggled from her grasp and leaned further over. Then he reached both his hands in to a dipped corner of the sidecar tarpaulin, drew them out full, and stood up triumphant.

'See,' he said and showed Jude a clutch of eggs.

The boy kept one egg, and the others he wadded round for her in a piece of old cloth and they were stowed now in a corner of the sidecar. It was something she'd learned to do in France, drink raw eggs. Even better when Peter had whisked them with brandy and sugar. She smiled at the memory. Kate's agonised gargle, her throat gagging at the texture. And though she knew it was absurd, she felt that the eggs were intended.

The journey demanded all Jude's attention. She knew she would have to stop and think about things, make some decisions, decide how to approach Daniel, if she found him. But for now it was a relief to have to concentrate on the road. She took the long straight road west out of Cork. It ran close to the river. The rain was still holding off, and away from the city, under the high grey sky, the surface of the river was smooth and very green. Swallows dipped and men fished, the curve of their mackintoshed backs visible above the water. There were a few clutches of buildings flanking the river on the far side: a waterworks with tall tower in pretty lines of red and white brick, and then a long line of grey buildings, all turrets and gables and hundreds of mullioned windows, which Jude assumed must be a hospital. Then she thought that over here it might equally be a convent.

Two miles out and the city was behind her. There were fields with cattle and cottages, single-storey, white-washed, occasionally a house with a few sycamores or poplars on either side. Jude felt her body ease against the bike. It was a relief to be doing something she understood so well. This she knew how to repair.

Jude stopped in Ballincollig to check her map. The long grey wall of the military barracks ran down the right side of the town, and she noticed the young soldiers keeping guard at the gate in their Free State uniform, and the tricolour flying above. It would have been only a few years before, when Daniel was here, that it would have been a Union Jack and English troops, lads with broad Derbyshire or Yorkshire accents perhaps, and now they were Irish boys. Passing them on her bike she gave a half salute, and one didn't move a muscle and the other grinned.

The motorbike was a good place for thinking. In Belgium she'd found solutions to all sorts of difficulties while bringing in wounded men or collecting supplies, and now Jude's thoughts went back to Daniel.

His diary, and Dr Kelleher's words, had sickened her. But she saw before her again the stranger who had come to her door that day and smiled when she'd dusted him with flour, the slender, nervy figure who had eaten Sunday lunch with her family just as if he were her beau, the first man since Richard she could imagine saying anything to, who had sat with her in the shelter of the Rocks. The same frightened, wounded figure who had walked away from her in Kew Gardens.

The road became rougher as Jude rode further away from the city, and it took all her concentration to avoid the worst of it. She passed men with hoes and forks on their shoulders, an occasional cart or a bicycle, women who stood to watch her, hands on hips. They'd lift a single finger in greeting as she went by, and she quickly learnt to return the gesture. Children shouted out and dogs ran behind the motorbike, yelping wildly, grey ghosts in the dust thrown up by her wheels. Deep ditches shaded into the sides of the roads, brown with bog water and edged with green plants Jude didn't know the names of.

She rode on to Macroom, some twenty-five miles out of Cork, and found a garage on the South Square. The man who came to the pump was singing something. Jude couldn't hear the words, but it sounded like a ballad.

'Lovely day,' he said to her as he unscrewed the petrol cap. 'You on your way somewhere else?'

'Yes,' Jude said. 'You have a handsome town here.'

'It is,' he said. 'And more so with its ruins. Picturesque, you might say,' and he looked at her quizzically. 'English?'

'Yes,' Jude said. 'What are the ruins?'

The man nodded to the left. 'Go on up there and you'll see, through the gate, the far side of the town hall.'

Although she was anxious to get on, Jude was curious about what the man had said. She rode slowly up one side of the square. Ahead of her was a turreted, castellated lodge. Leaving her bike outside O'Leary's Hardware, camera over her shoulder, Jude walked up to the broad gateway beneath. She ignored the old woman who had set down her basket of tinned pilchards and cabbages the better to stare, and the inevitable small boys appearing as if from nowhere to gaze at the motorbike.

Beyond the gateway was the blackened shell of what must have been a forbidding castle. Jude walked up close and rubbed a finger on the wall. It fetched up soot. This wasn't an ancient ruin, the kind you find in history books. It was a recent ruin. She looked through a window cavity. There was a damp mass of stone and rotted plaster and tangled metal which must once have been balustrades. No roof left, only sky. Wild plants had begun their travels, but the castle could only have been burned a few years before.

312

Jude thought back to the petrol man, his words and his manner. She saw that they were meant, however courteously, as a lesson to her. This would have been an English castle, and it must have been burnt by the IRA. She took a few photographs of the eyeless hulk, of the slender green snaking its way round the twisted ironwork, and then returned to her bike.

Ten miles on and the road was rougher still and muddy. She stopped to clean her goggles, cutting the engine, and the quiet filled her head. It was still one of the moments she liked the best, disconcerting and exhilarating, when the blast of her own noise stopped and slowly, as her ears adjusted, the rest of the world came in again. From somewhere she heard the sounds of a cart, and otherwise nothing but the wind pressing against the gorse. The road ran straight here, through the bog. Jude looked back towards the ruins of a house just passed. Some words had been painted on to the gable end, white lettering dashed on in slanted capitals:

REMEMBER THE DEAD.

Finding her camera, Jude took a photograph. It began to rain, softly and thoroughly, and Jude stowed the camera quickly and climbed back on her bike. Soon the dust was exchanged for mud.

The route had looked straightforward on the map, but Jude discovered that signposting, even on main roads, was very intermittent. Several times she had to ask the way. Nor was it an easy matter, once she had found someone in this empty country, to understand what they said. Although they seemed to speak in the same accent as Dr Kelleher or Catherine, it was so much faster and in such an intense singsong that she didn't know where the important words fell.

The rain had been unrelenting and Jude was soaked. Her face was cold and her hands were stiff, fumbling with the tarpaulin rope to find the eggs. The road had been climbing for a few miles and she could see that it dipped down ahead. There must be a view, but with the rain driving across like mist, she could see nothing beyond. Dirty sheep knelt at the roadside like supplicants.

Jude picked up a small stone and, very carefully, cracked the top of the first egg. She put it to her mouth, and prising the shell open, she drank down the egg white before it spilt. The yolk lay alone in the curve of the shell, a deep orange. Jude stared down into it, this piece of dense colour in a landscape washed into greys and dull browns, then lifted the shell to her lips and felt the yolk slip across and break over her tongue.

She felt better. Making a rudimentary shelter with the tarpaulin, she unfolded the map and checked her position. She was less than ten miles from her destination, she thought. There was a lake marked very near, virtually reaching to the road, and though she couldn't see it from where she stood, she decided to look for it before going on.

'It'll warm you up, at the least,' she said to herself. 'Even if you don't find it.'

314

Tucking the map away, Jude leaped over the ditch and clambered down the bank. She could just make out a line of rushes about forty yards away. The lake would be there. Stepping down, she thought onto solid ground, a cushion of bright green mosses and tiny flowers, she found herself ankle deep in brown water. She pulled her boot free from the suck of the bog and managed to plant it on one of the coarse grass tussocks that grew proud of the moss. Then, keeping her arms wide for balance, she stepped from hummock to hummock towards the rushes.

'Miss Barnstaple would be proud of me,' she muttered, remembering the broad calves and the long suffering of her school gym teacher.

The lake was like a haunted place. Rain stippled its surface but otherwise nothing moved. A bird cried out like a lost soul somewhere in the reeds. Bulrushes stepped their way into the deeper water, haughty, erect. Jude stood still and stared, waiting for something, some motion, some action. But nothing came and suddenly she was unnerved and turned, leap-frogging the bog back to the road and her motorbike.

By the time she reached Skibbereen, Jude was cold. The rain was still falling steadily, her jacket and britches were heavy and wet, and, despite her balletics, the bog water had seeped in through the lacing on her boots. When she stood down from the bike again, she couldn't feel her toes. Two raw eggs had been fine for nourishment but they had done nothing to warm her, and she went in search of hot tea.

The rain had stopped when she came out of

the tea room. Thin beads of sun made the wet streets gleam. She walked back towards the bike to see a group of boys gathered around it, laughing and daring the tallest of them, who was straddled over the saddle, leaning into the handlebars, vrooming like someone half his size. As Jude approached, swinging her hips, he started up and swung off.

Pretending she hadn't seen him on the bike, she took out her helmet from the sidecar and laced the tarpaulin tight.

'Mother of God, it's ridden by a girl,' one of them said.

'And a pretty one,' the tall boy said, not quite below his breath, and Jude felt herself blush with pleasure.

'Could you tell me if there's a garage near here where I can fill up with petrol?' she asked him.

His bravado crumbled into incredulity.

'It's not ever yours,' he said, and when she nodded, his mouth dropped.

'And you a lady,' he said, shaking his head, and the other boys followed suit. 'English though,' he added, as if this explained something, and they all nodded with him.

'I'll give you a ride if you'll direct me to the garage,' Jude said, and she watched his face break into a grin.

With the boy on behind her and wearing her helmet, his hands gentle round her waist, Jude rode through the town, turning left or right at the tugs on her sleeve. He was, she suspected, taking her on the long route to the garage, down any number of tiny streets with streams running by and old women in black and children scattering at the sound of the bike. But that was fine. Now she'd got this far she found she was nervous, and happy for any excuse to delay the last leg of the journey.

The other boys were already there, out of breath, waiting, by the time they reached the garage, and they greeted their friend with claps around the head and punches. When she set off, they saw her away with shouts and laughter.

She thought how strange it was that she'd come to a foreign country and found herself more at ease with people than she often felt at home. These boys, met for five minutes, the Whelans, even Dr Kelleher. But maybe that was why it was like that over here. Because nobody knew her, not even Daniel, if she ever found him. She had no history. Nothing was assumed, and for now she could leave behind the warring in her own heart.

And something more she felt too, which was more like the dawning of some new sense — and it came back to her in the strangest flood of emotion how she had felt that afternoon alone with Richard and him leaping. She had felt herself stretch and unfold then, and this now was something like it again.

The road to Castletowne gave nothing away, not even a sight of the sea. Although the tea had warmed her, Jude found the five miles or so exhausting. Her muscles ached and she could feel the pressure in her neck rise. She longed to be off the bike. Every pothole, every stone jarred and it seemed a miracle she'd had no puncture on these rough roads.

She kept her eyes forward. She wouldn't let herself think about what might happen next. What, for example, she would do if Daniel were not there? Or what she should say to him if he were? She'd never been good at prepared speeches, always come last in school debates. So she'd have to trust to her native sense now.

There was a steep hill down into the village and finally, churned and frantic, the sea beyond. Leaving the motorbike at the top of the hill, Jude walked down. She didn't have an address for the Murrays, but she guessed from Daniel's diary that the word Coolderry, his good place, was probably the name of their house, and she knew they had a dog and a daughter, and that they'd owned a hotel before retiring. Somebody would know them.

Twenty minutes later she had address, directions and quite a lot of information about Mrs Murray's deficits as a flower arranger, the unruly nature of their dog and the more interesting fact that they had reportedly come down with flu, or so their girl had said.

'My God, you're such a good liar,' Jude told herself. 'Who'd have thought you'd find so much to say about roses, let alone the ecclesiastical virtue of the chrysanthemum?' and she muttered her thanks into the damp air for all those times when Leo had bored her silly with his flower talk.

The house was a short distance outside the village. Fifteen minutes walk, her informant, Mrs Hewetson, had told her, but which Jude reckoned for ten, if you weren't carrying quite so much weight forward as Mrs Hewetson. Anyway, after some deliberation, she decided to ride there. She didn't know why, but she wanted to be sure she could get away quickly if she needed to.

Jude found the house easily. The name Coolderry was carved onto a piece of slate beside the gates. She coasted down the drive, then cut her engine and sat in the silence. Now she was here, she realised she had no plan or thought as to what she would do next. A Labrador came round the side of the house barking, tail out high behind. It stopped a few yards from the motorbike and threw out short, aggressive yelps. Jude swung her leg over the saddle and stood away from the bike.

'Hey, come on now, boy. You're not so different from Rex.' Jude put her hands out flat towards the dog. 'Only you're a girl I see now. Didn't notice that at first. Shouldn't make those assumptions.'

Reluctantly, as if being coerced, the dog walked towards her, gingerly, as if the gravel was glass. Jude stroked down between the dog's ears and along her back. Her fur was warm and smooth. When the dog leant her weight against Jude's legs, she accepted the invitation and gently scratched the dog's ribs. Just now she missed home powerfully. Leo and Sally, her high bedroom, Rex, and most of all the children. She didn't hear the man approach.

'Who the hell are you?' he said, and Jude jumped, as if she'd been caught out at something. He called to the dog, who slunk straight to him, tail between her legs.

Jude straightened up. He was a tall, thin man dressed in old corduroy trousers, a gingham shirt, sleeves rolled up to the elbows, and a sleeveless Fair Isle sweater. His hair, still thick on his head, was white though his broad moustache was still black, and his arms and face were weather-beaten and freckled. He had the bearing of an army major and she was tempted to click her heels and salute, but she checked it and introduced herself. If this is Mr Murray, she thought, and if Daniel is here, he might have mentioned me, and she watched to see if his expression changed with her name. But he showed no sign of recognition, only folded his arms and stood waiting.

Jude thought of making something up, some other reason that had brought her to this corner of this country and down this particular steep drive. 'Landscape photographer' seemed thin, now she was in the landscape.

'I'm looking for someone,' she said.

His expression didn't change, but Jude saw that he became very still.

'You're looking for someone?' he said back, and she knew that he was buying time.

'Yes.'

'Well, I'm afraid there's only my wife and me here. The O'Connors are further on, a hundred yards or so, and there are the Rourkes. They're another half mile. But as you can see, we're very out of the way', and he waved an arm around abruptly as if the trees and rhododendrons could demonstrate how far out of the way it was.

Now it was Jude's turn to pause. The dog stood between them, her velvet ears twitching, wagging her tail in a desultory, uncertain way, as if unsure where to bestow her favours. Whether with her master who was clearly out of temper, though not usually a jealous god, or with this stranger who had arrived so loudly but stroked her so gently.

'Excuse me,' Jude said, 'but you are Mr Murray?' and when he nodded, she said, 'I'm looking for Daniel Brown.'

When she looked back on it that night, she couldn't remember Mr Murray ever saying out loud that Daniel had been there. It was as if it became a known fact between them without being spoken. The dog made up her mind and picked her way across to Jude, who stroked her absently and waited. Mr Murray put his hands to his head, then dropped them to his sides.

'You'd better come in.'

16

There was a large brown pot of hot tea already at one end of the kitchen table and two cups poured, and at the other end two mackintoshes flung across, and a torch, a package of sandwiches, apples, a thermos and a haversack. Mr Murray pulled out a chair for her.

'My wife will be here in a moment. I know she'll say you should eat something before we set off.'

He poured another cup of tea and put two eggs in a saucepan.

'Set off?' Jude said.

'To look for Daniel.'

'Oh?'

'You're right, he has been with us, it must be a week now. Just arrived here one afternoon, on foot for God's sake, with his leg ... ' He shrugged, and Jude nodded.

'But he's not here now,' she said.

'No. The last few days, he's taken to walking off,' Mr Murray said. 'And of course he's a grown man, but ... ' and so much hung in the 'but'.

'I know,' Jude said.

'So, I must find my wife, explain things,' and he left the kitchen.

The dog sat beneath the table with her head on Jude's lap but Jude wasn't fooled by cupboard love. She stared ahead, her eyes resting on the canvas of the haversack, seeing nothing. She should be looking around, getting a gauge, but just now she was too tired. She could hear Mr Murray's voice in the hall, and another voice that must be his wife's. There were footsteps, and Mrs Murray came in.

She nodded a greeting to Jude, put her hand on her shoulder, as though they were old familiars.

'Joe says eggs are needed,' she said, and Jude warmed to this woman immediately, and she understood. That there was too much to be explained, that, at least for now, just this time in the kitchen perhaps, much must be taken on trust. She liked this woman, she liked her sureness.

Mrs Murray boiled up two eggs and cut bread.

'Irish eggs are very good,' Jude said, remembering her earlier two.

'It'll be the moisture in the air,' Mrs Murray said, and Jude couldn't tell if she was joking. 'You'll be tired. It's a devil of a road in spots, from Cork. Maybe you'd be better waiting here, while we go?'

'No, I'm fine.'

Mrs Murray found her some dry clothes.

'You won't mind trousers, what with the motorbike?' Jude shook her head. 'Only they'll be more comfortable.'

Mr Murray was to go up the hill behind the house, and Mrs Murray and Jude would head off towards the standing stones. They'd all get back by seven latest, they agreed, and if they hadn't found him, then they'd set out and search again.

The two women walked in silence at first, finding a shared pace, eyes to the ground to keep their footing. The clouds had cleared for the late afternoon and the sun sent long slender shadows out from the walkers. Jude wished she had her camera with her. They crossed several fields, scrambling over the walls, avoiding the brambles and gorse as best they could, stopping every while and scanning the landscape, searching.

'Perhaps we should call out?' Jude said at last, staring across the rough country. 'You could hide for ever out here.'

'No,' Mrs Murray said. 'It makes him dig in deeper. We've discovered that already.'

'Has he been gone long?' Jude said a minute later.

'About six years.' Mrs Murray laughed abruptly. 'No, since breakfast,' she said then. Mrs Murray walked on more quickly now, and despite being at least thirty years younger, or so she guessed, Jude had to work to keep up.

'Has he . . . ' Jude stopped. 'How is he?' she said then.

Mrs Murray halted mid-stride and looked at Jude, hands on her hips, breathing deeply. For a minute or so she didn't speak, only fixed Jude so intently, that Jude had to stare back. It was the first time she'd had opportunity to look properly at Mrs Murray, so quickly had things gone since she'd arrived there. Her face was as weathered as her husband's, perennially brown, Jude guessed, and lined. But whereas his seemed cut into by the natural elements, sun, wind, rain, hers was the face of someone who had worn her emotions close to her skin. Even as they stared, Jude watched mistrust, fear and curiosity cross the older woman's face.

'Perhaps you should tell me,' Mrs Murray said at last. 'Perhaps I'd like to ask you a thing or two,' catching her breath, her voice rough. 'You've arrived out of the blue at our house on a motorbike looking for Daniel. Who are you? We don't know anything about you, or what you are to him. Why on earth should we trust you?'

Despite her efforts, Jude had caught her hand on a bramble a little way back, and she picked at a thorn in the side of her thumb. She could see the black nub of it, but it was in deep. She wondered how much she should say. Mrs Murray waited, her eyes never leaving Jude's face. Jude pressed her teeth against the thumb and squeezed it till it ached. She could feel the thorn with her tongue tip, but it wasn't coming proud. Letting go, she made her decision and for the second time in as many days she told a virtual stranger the story of her photograph. Even as she spoke, it crossed her mind that she had left behind more than she knew when she crossed the water, and for a moment she felt light-headed with exhilaration.

When she had finished her tale, Mrs Murray didn't say anything for a minute. Then she nodded.

'We're nearly to the Three Fingers,' she said. 'Let's climb up to them first, in case,' and Jude understood. Daniel might be there, and if he were, then things would go another way for now.

The fingers stood in a line on the crest of a

hill, slender, tall and rudimentary-looking. On one side the hill sloped down and away, and looking across Jude could see over to the peninsula, right out to where the ocean met the sky. There was no sign of Daniel. She put a hand to the middle stone. It was cool and coarse against her palm, the lichen tickling slightly.

'They make you want to stand as tall,' Jude said, 'or to hold on to them. Put your arms round,' and she reached her arms out around it.

'They've been here for over three thousand years. There used to be four, but our local lady of the manor, she fancied it for her rockery.'

Jude laughed. 'I can imagine Daniel here.'

'It's where I first met him,' Mrs Murray said. She leaned back against one of the stones. 'I knew Daniel's aunt, Charlotte's sister, though we hadn't seen each other for years. It was Christmas letters, that kind of thing. Then in the midst of these troubles, Charlotte wrote asking if her son could look us up, if he had opportunity. He was coming over to be part of the new police force. And we wrote back and said that he could, if he was careful. But we didn't hear anything from him, and to be honest, it was relief. The more we heard about these Black and Tans and Auxiliaries, the worse they sounded. No better than the IRA lot, and many were saying worse.

'So one day I'd come up here, just for a walk. It was a day a bit like this, the clouds clearing near the evening. Joe didn't like it, me going for walks then. He said it was too dangerous. But I couldn't bear not to, and besides, he was being over-protective, which always brings out the bloody-minded in me.

'I was standing here, right by the stones, so I saw him coming. He had a lovely bearing on the horse, that's what I noticed first, so fluent. And I think I knew before he reached me who he was.

'When he asked, very politely, for directions to my own house, but as though we were standing on Patrick Street, or Stephen's Green, I couldn't help laughing, and then he laughed too.'

'What chance. What a strange meeting,' Jude said.

'In the middle of the Tan war. One of the worst times. And you didn't mix with people like him, Auxiliaries and Tans. Or the military. You didn't even give them directions, not if you could help it. Even in a place like Castletowne which has more than its fair share of men who've given their best to protect the British Empire, and where you'd never hear the Angelus bells ring, even here people had been shot for less. Found in a field, or under a bridge, a card around their neck, 'Convicted spy'. It was different elsewhere, maybe in Wicklow or Galway, Sligo perhaps, but not around here. Besides which, most of the Black and Tans were ruffians. They were as bad as the other lot. Thugs. They'd come over here for a free-for-all, courtesy of the British Government. So it wasn't a good idea, us meeting Daniel.

'He was joy-riding that day. Shouldn't have taken the horse, though he said he was given the wink by his superior, and he got lost. Then finding he was close to Castletowne, he'd remembered our invitation. It was a bloody stupid thing to do, and he knew it. He wasn't in uniform, but it wouldn't have taken more than a few words for anyone to guess what he was up to over here.

'I can still see Joe's face before I introduced them. He was angry enough to hit me, bringing a Tan into the house. But then I told him who this was, and Daniel asked him something about fishing, he'd noticed the rods in the corner of the hall, and that was that. So simple. There was no question after that but that we'd be friends. Joe and Daniel had a way of understanding one another, it was more like father and son. Joe would have loved a son. And Daniel was so affectionate with me. Always found something to bring me, a little gift.'

She looked over towards the sea, her eyes reaching back.

'It was Turkish Delight one time, from Hadji Beys, and chocolates another. Then he started bringing me things he'd found. From anybody else I'd have been offended. Strange gifts. Bunches of flowers, not garden flowers, wild flowers. A smooth stone, a robin's egg, grasses one time. I asked him what their names were, but he didn't know. Only things he did know about were birds.' She paused. 'And you think you can rescue him?' she said.

Jude blushed. 'Or myself. I don't know, or both.'

'It's better if you're not here only for him,' Mrs Murray said. 'Or else he might take too much.'

Jude nodded.

Mrs Murray laughed. 'He used to eat me out of house and home. Never seen anyone eat so much. Only having had a daughter, I'd never met ravenous boys.'

'They were like that when I was nursing,' Jude said. 'Once they began to recover, we couldn't give them enough to eat.' But she wanted to hear the rest. 'So it was dangerous then, having him to stay?' which was disingenuous, because she knew the answer.

'Terribly risky, we all knew that. Even in our house, which is fairly isolated. Surrounded by woods. You might get men, armed men, at your door at any time. They'd demand food, shelter, guns even. And there was a levy made, a gunpoint levy, especially on Protestants, and most of us paid it. Stupid not to. We did, certainly. A man not two miles away refused. He was warned twice. Then they burnt him out. He's living in Berkshire now, I heard.

'Anyway, Daniel would come, not that often, every month, six weeks or so, and stay overnight. And right from the start, we had an unspoken agreement. As long as he was with us, we'd none of us mention the Troubles. He'd be distressed when he arrived sometimes, abrupt, black-browed, but we never crossed that line. It was the only way we could all keep it going.'

'You never asked him what he was doing, when he wasn't with you?' Jude said, and after all she'd heard from Dr Kelleher, she couldn't keep the incredulity from her voice.

Mrs Murray looked up, stony-faced. 'We should be getting back,' she said. 'If Joe hasn't found him, we'll have to be out again.'

'I'm sorry,' Jude said. 'I'm coming to all of this fresh. It's only after what I heard in Cork. About the Auxiliaries, and the Black and Tans.' And Daniel's diary, she thought. There's enough in that to sink a strong man. They couldn't think his hands were clean, surely.

Mrs Murray stared at her, such fierce scrutiny, Jude felt as if the older woman was sucking out and testing her very marrow.

'You don't know any better, do you?' Mrs Murray said at last, and Jude breathed out with relief, as if she'd been allowed to live after all. Not waiting for an answer, Mrs Murray went on. 'This is an exhausted country,' she said. 'Things have been done, terrible things, that nobody can think are right, and by all sides. I could tell you some tales, true ones, to set against whatever you've been told about the Tans.' She shook her head. 'Though what you heard was probably no more than the truth.' She paused. 'If you know Daniel — which you must do surely, to come all this way — do you think he's a brute?'

Jude ducked the question. 'Tell me what happened next,' she said.

The light was closing in, collapsing and confusing distances. An owl started up, and only the swifts were left, high up in the last of the sunlit air. The two women set off back, walking in silence for a time, and then Mrs Murray told the rest.

'I think it was his visits with us that kept him sane. Towards the end, for sure.'

'The end?' Jude said.

'We never knew what had happened to him. He just didn't turn up again. He'd arranged to come, and he never appeared and he never called. It happened once before, and he managed to send us word. They were sent out on a last minute patrol that time, all leave cancelled. But no word this time. Then we read about the ambush in the *Irish Times* and it was his division, and put two and two together. There'd been a lot killed and they gave numbers and no names, so we couldn't be sure, but he had to be one of them, it was the only explanation. We wrote to his parents, and his aunt, but never heard back, though now he's explained why that was.'

'And then he turned up again last week,' Jude said.

Mrs Murray nodded. 'Looking like a ghost. A limping, hunted ghost. I can't bear it, seeing him. I'm worried he'll do something terrible.' She looked at Jude. 'And I tell you, when we find him, if I think you're making it worse, or putting him in any further danger, or distress, I'll see you out of my house, whether I like you or not.'

And she strode on, not waiting for Jude's reply.

Mr Murray had already returned when they arrived back at the house, and he shook his head when he saw them.

'We'll have something to eat first,' Mrs Murray said. 'We'll need the energy. No point in getting exhausted.'

'And then?' Jude said.

He told Jude about Horse Island.

'It didn't occur to me earlier, God knows why not, but he might have taken somebody else's boat and rowed out. I checked and ours is still there. Or swum even. It's not so far if you walk round a way first, though with his bad leg, God knows, and it's a falling tide and there is a bit of a current.'

Mrs Murray cooked an omelette, and after they'd eaten, they gathered lanterns and walked down from the house and round the headland before dropping to the beach and searching out the darkness where the island lay, peering for any sign of a fire. But there was no sign. Only the sound of the water sipping at the shore and the whistle and spit of beached seaweed.

'Can't we go out there?' Jude said.

'Not in the dark. It'll have to be first light tomorrow.'

And so they were making their way up the path when they heard the dog. She'd been with them down on the beach, dragging out driftwood branches even in the dark. But now she was somewhere beyond and below, giving long yelps that echoed over the water, then silence, then yelping again.

'Would you ever tell that dog to be quiet,' Mrs Murray said. 'Call her, Joe.'

But she wouldn't come, and only carried on with the barking.

'She couldn't be chasing rabbits this late,' Jude said.

'She's down by the water. Near the tower, I'd say. Sounds like something's alarmed her,' Mr Murray turned to his wife. 'Why don't you go on up, and I'll get her.'

'I'll come with you,' Jude said, and so she and Mr Murray made their way down again, all the while the dog's yelps getting louder.

'What's the tower?' Jude said.

'It's ruined. Part of the lookout system going back to the time before the Protestant plantations. To keep out the French, or the Spanish, or the pirates, which I suspect often came to the same thing. There's one on almost every headland around here.'

They came out of the woods on to another beach. The sky had cleared of all cloud and the moon shone down on the water, its thin silver light cutting across the black sea towards them in a fading arc. They trod through the dark mass of the tide line and out on to sand. The dog was visible now, standing at one side of the beach, barking at nothing, Jude thought, or nothing she could see. Small rocks and stones skirted with seaweed littered the beach, and Jude walked carefully. It would be easy to trip here and turn an ankle. She thought it must be the effect of the moon, but sometimes as she stepped, the beach seemed to glisten for a moment.

Mr Murray went off to the right, towards the tower, and Jude walked towards the dog. At first she thought the dog was barking at a rock. But as she walked past and on, she saw it was no rock but a man. And as she drew closer still, she knew that it was Daniel. He was crouched down, sleeves pulled up to his elbows, scrabbling in the sand. This time she was sure, there were sparks, like light, where Daniel's hands disturbed the sand, and as she watched, he tugged at some seaweed and flung it away, and it shimmered in the darkness.

As if relieved of responsibility once Jude was there, the dog gave up her noise and trotted over towards Mr Murray, and now Jude could hear that Daniel was breathing heavily. Coming close with the lantern she bent towards him, slowly, not wanting to alarm him. As she watched, he picked out what looked like a small flat piece of shell or stone. Rubbing the sand from it, he put it into his pocket, then started scrabbling again. He didn't seem to have noticed her.

'Daniel,' she said softly. 'Daniel.'

He paused, fingers in the sand, and looked up. 'Hello, Jude,' he said, and she had a strong sense of *déjà vu*.

'If you shut off your light, you'll see the phosphorescence,' he said.

'What are you doing?' she said, and he put his hand in his pocket and brought out a piece of broken china, white in the lantern light.

'Feel,' he said, holding it out.

She took it. It was smooth, edges worn by the sea.

'You can't see the patterns in the dark,' Daniel said. 'They throw them into the tide once they're not wanted. But at least the sea is softer with them than the earth. Better than the bottom of the garden.'

'Not wanted?'

'Damaged, chipped. Limping a bit,' he said.

Jude couldn't see his expression in the darkness. She couldn't tell whether he was joking or serious, or even how far he knew what he was saying.

'It's dark, Daniel,' she said. 'Night-time. The Murrays, me, we've been very worried.'

'They're all over the place,' he said. 'Everywhere. Like cockles. If you know where to pray, you can dig and find them.'

'Pray?'

'To the Crom Dubh. An Irish god.'

She heard Mr Murray approach, the dog at his heels.

'Jude?' he said.

'Daniel's here.'

17

Daniel knew it must be drawing close, the end to all this, because Jude arrived. He didn't know how she could be here, but it didn't surprise him.

When she found him on the beach, he showed her a piece of the china, but he wasn't sure whether she liked it or not, because it was dark.

He wanted to talk to her, explain himself, tell her about the island, but Mrs Murray insisted on everybody going to bed. She was fierce about it. It would all wait until the morning, she said. Before he fell asleep, he thought he heard their voices downstairs, and his name spoken several times. But the day had been long, and he was very tired, and he fell asleep very quickly.

In the morning the sun made the edges of the curtains sharp and drew a line up the rag rug and across the quilt on his bed, catching the white then the red then the white. Daniel's leg ached. He would go out to Horse Island today and take Jude with him. Next best person since he couldn't be there with Johnnie. At least you went in a circle if you tried to walk away there, and the bracken and tumbled walls slowed you down, not like the grass in Kew Gardens. And though he didn't know how, he was determined to call a halt to his travels. His head was weary. He longed to make a peace.

Downstairs, Mrs Murray had her arms full of

flowers, tall flags of irises, delphiniums. Outside Mr Murray was sitting astride the bike and Jude was crouched beside. They were deep in conversation about camshafts, gearboxes and internal expanding brakes. Leaving them to it, Daniel went and sat on the terrace, his back to the wall of the house, and waited. The pulse of pain in his leg was strong today, a sign of tiredness. He sat very still, turning his piece of china between his fingers, and watched black-birds tug worms from the lawn. They were like magicians, he thought, with their silks.

Mrs Murray brought out a jug of coffee and then he watched her bend to her roses, her secateurs like angels of mercy, cutting the dead from the quick. The air was so still, not a breath of wind, it would make hard work of their sailing later. Beside him, a butterfly clipped to the wall on the threads of its toes felt the sun on its back at last and shook itself awake, opening its wings coyly like a courtesan with her fan. Daniel shut his eyes against it. He could see too much today. Listening to the soft, clean cut sound of the secateurs, something became clear to him. Perhaps it was his exhaustion that freed him, perhaps it was the butterfly's spread, perhaps it was the secateurs, or perhaps it was just that it was time now. He wondered a little behind his shut eyes, feeling the gentle sun on his eyelids. And when they were all seated finally, Mr Murray twitching his old panama against the sun, Jude wiping at the oil on her hands with a rag, each drinking their coffee, Mrs Murray's secateurs laid on the ground beside her, Daniel

337

opened his eyes and stared across the garden to the sea beyond. If you painted it now, he thought, it would be the thinnest line of paint, not even enough for a bird to dive into. Then he spoke.

'I don't know what happened in the ambush,' he said. 'But it is what I need to know. And I don't know, coming here, whether I'm running away from something or towards something, right into it, full-face, not even a hand up to protect.'

There. He had begun it.

'You want to talk about it now?' Mrs Murray said, and Daniel nodded.

'It was the photograph that set it all going?' she said. 'The one in the exhibition, that Jude took? Because it showed two men sharing a cigarette?'

He nodded. She said it so bluntly. 'Those two men,' he said, and now he felt cold, so cold in the sun.

'Daniel.' Jude's voice cut in. He took his eyes from the line of the sea and looked across at her. She wanted to rescue him, but he couldn't help. He wished he could hold on to her voice, keep it right there in his head, this good voice. He was falling in love with her, which wasn't why she was here at all.

'Tell us what you did over here,' she said. 'What happened that day.'

Daniel's stomach clutched. These were the wrong words for her voice. He turned his head, put her out of his sight, but she went on speaking.

'Don't run away.'

'It wasn't me who ran,' he said.

'But it was somebody else?'

'Can you imagine a fish running?' he said, and he turned in his chair and looked over his shoulder at the wall. The butterfly was gone. He put a finger to the plaster. It was a bare place to sleep away the night.

They were talking about him, over his head, behind his back, the Murrays, Jude. He turned back to them and he made his voice light, like the shiver of wind on water, like the flour from the dredger sifting down the first time he'd met her.

'What do you want to know?' he said.

'What do you mean, about the fish?' Jude said.

'I told you that, or I told somebody. It's what we called him, the Trout. Colonel Whittam.' Daniel looked back at the butterfly's wall. 'Well, it was because of him, I suppose, that we called the actions fishing trips.

'He liked to go fishing. Fly-fishing. So we got to calling it fishing, what we all did. Fishing. We had to be fierce. Keep down the natives,' he said with a laugh. 'Fishing.'

Mrs Murray picked up her secateurs and went to the roses again. Jude watched her, her movements brusque, jagged.

'I'm going to go and meet someone who was there, at the ambush,' Jude said.

Daniel shook his head. 'Everyone's dead. My brother Johnnie first, in his war, and then everyone else in mine. Whittam was the only other one to get out, and he killed himself three years back. I told you that already.'

'I'm going to meet somebody from the other side,' Jude said. She waited, but he said nothing. 'Matt Walsh. The man in the photograph. The Cork man.'

'I'm very cold,' Daniel said. 'Let me go in.'

'I looked after him. He brought his friend, Whittam, in wounded and I fed him hot tea and wrapped a blanket round him and kept him from the war for a few hours.'

'I'm against the wall, aren't I? Not warming my wings at all.' He rubbed his hands together.

'Please, Daniel. I need to know what happened,' she said.

Mr Murray got up and went inside. Jude picked up her coffee cup. Her hand was shaking. Mrs Murray stood, staring at a rose bush. Daniel rubbed at his leg. His skin was in pinpoints. Mr Murray came back outside with a rug, and he put it over Daniel's lap, put his hand for a moment on Daniel's shoulder before sitting back down.

She knew it was her imagination, but Jude could have sworn that everything stopped in the minutes that followed. Not just the people, but the whole world. Trees, wind, birds, bees. That they all stopped what they were doing and turned to Daniel, waiting.

When he began to speak again, it was in a different voice, a practical, matter-of-fact voice, as if the words weren't really coming from him, but from someone else, someone speaking through him. He stared out from his chair towards the roses, but Jude didn't know what he was seeing. His hands rested flat on the rug, fingers still, no twitching.

'There'd been a burning,' he said. 'A farm and all its buildings. An official reprisal, I don't remember for what, but we went a bit wild. You know how the IRA used to cut off a girl's hair, hack it from her head, if she was thought to be walking out with one of us? That was the first warning. Will had been seeing a girl in the town and they'd done it to her, and the night of that particular burning he was still very angry about it.

'The family was in bed when we arrived and we hammered at the door, then opened it and marched in. A man came down to us already pulling on his trousers, and when Will read off the order, he didn't say a word, only disappeared and was back again with two sons. They went past us and outside and were rushing to the livestock. We didn't bother to tell them we'd be taking the livestock too. Instead we went on in to the house, had a look around. It was cleaner than most, and there were some nice things.

'The girl must have been seventeen, eighteen years old, pretty. She came down still in her nightdress while we were rummaging. She started pleading with us. Her grandmother was upstairs, and frail and ill. Couldn't we wait till tomorrow? Or let them bring a cart for the old woman and take her somewhere else? But we had our orders, and you couldn't trust them, not even the young ones. We'd been tricked like this before. So Will told her no, the house was to be burnt in fifteen minutes and everyone was to be out by then.'

'It was official, this kind of thing? You had orders to do it,' Mrs Murray said, 'official orders?'

Although Daniel didn't respond and went on with his account, hands still flat to his lap, Jude saw his index fingers start to twitch, as if jerked up and down on a string.

'It was easy for my brother, stuck in his trench. Easy. No girls or old women. His fault I ended up here. If only he hadn't died.' He paused, then went on. 'The girl got angry then. She was abusive. The language coming out of her was shocking.

'I think it was the foul language that did it for Will, because one minute he was listening, and the next he'd gone and found a kitchen knife, a blackened ugly thing, and he grabbed the girl's hair and started slashing at it. What with her struggling, it's a miracle he didn't catch her on the neck, but me and Duguid managed to restrain her and then Will did his business. When we let the girl go, she rushed back upstairs and we followed her and there was the grandmother, just as she had said. And when Will saw her, he started yelling again, over and over. 'Out! Now! Out!' And the old woman didn't say anything, didn't move from the bed, just stared at him. Then there was this smell and she'd wet herself and worse. The girl was sobbing, trying to get a sweater, a coat on her. But what with the hair cutting and so forth, there was no time left for niceties and in the end we had to drag the old woman out, because she wouldn't let us carry her, the girl sobbing behind. I don't know what happened in the yard because I was busy with the petrol by then, but Will says the old woman had a fit. Anyway she died.'

Jude heard Mr Murray's gasp, the exclamation swallowed in the throat, and she kept her eyes on the sleeping dog, its paws running to nowhere inside a dream.

'It was quite a job to throw everything into the fire. Feeding troughs, horse harnesses, tackle, plough, scythes, hay rake, even the milk churns. But our orders were for everything, so everything went in. Then some of us went off searching for the men. I was relieved to be away from the blaze. We found them quite easily and Duguid and Charters took them off to the barracks for questioning and I was left with a couple of others to bring the cattle back. The horses were gone.

'Some of us thought it was a good sign, things going so quiet those next weeks. That they were frightened at last. But we should have known. So it must have been a couple of weeks later that we were on the road between Dunbeg and Clonnacook, two lorry-loads of us, eighteen men. It was dusk, teatime, and foggy. That's what I was thinking about when it happened, I was thinking about a cup of tea. We'd been out on patrol since before dinner and nothing found, nobody sighted, and nearly back at the barracks. Another quarter of an hour and I'd have my mug of tea. Will Savage was seated next to me and George Spring across. Colonel Whittam was up in the front, in the cab with the driver. You couldn't have much of a conversation in those Crossleys. They were too noisy, what with the wind. And that day we were all cold and weary. There was a fine rain dropping, like a mist, and our mackintoshes were saturated, our britches sodden and heavy on the legs.

'We turned a corner and there ahead, in the middle of the road and waving his arms up and down, was a British soldier. I didn't notice him because of the mist, till the lorry slowed.

'There was nothing we could have done. You couldn't tell him for a rabbit, or a duck, and nobody even raised their rifle. He was a soldier, dressed as one of ours, as far as you could see in that light; khaki trench-coat, steel helmet. And when we were twenty, maybe thirty yards away, he lobbed a Mills bomb into the cab.'

Daniel stood up, the rug falling to the ground, then reached down and picked a small stone off the terrace. The others watched in silence. Swinging his right arm, he threw the stone in a high arc over on to the lawn.

'Like that,' he said. 'That's how you're taught to throw them. As if you were an off-spinner. That's what they told us.'

'A what?' Jude said.

'An off-spinner,' Mr Murray said. 'Slow bowler. Cricket.'

'And it must have happened in a split second,' Daniel went on, 'but I had this thought. Which was what a good cricketer he must be, because he had a lovely action with that Mills bomb.'

Daniel stopped talking again. He picked up another stone and threw it, then another, his face blank, giving nothing away. Jude could hear the wind in the yew tree and she could feel the blood banging in her fingertips, she had them gripped so hard around the struts of her chair. She hadn't noticed it before, but now she could smell Daniel's cologne, and something else, something she knew from the war, which was fear: an acrid, sharp sweat smell.

'Sit down, Daniel,' Mrs Murray said. 'Don't throw the stones any more.'

And he sat down again, gathered the rug across his lap, and went on with his story.

'He lobbed the Mills bomb into the cab and it exploded. I found out afterwards they did the same to the other lorry. We swerved and the Crossley nose-dived into the ditch, its back end reared up, and next thing I'm scrambling out over somebody who isn't moving, I don't know who it was, trying to find my feet, my boots sinking into the bog, the gorse up against my cheek, and brambles, so that I was finding thorns in my skin weeks later. And finally I made it up on to the road and took cover round one side of the lorry. It's all hell let loose there, men firing down on us from both sides, they're high up on the hill, behind rock outcrops, behind the wall on the far side of the road. Some of us are injured. Freddie Charters screaming blue murder. His neck is spouting blood so that I get a mouthful as I lift my rifle. I don't know how many of us are wounded, or dead.

'It reminds me of those playground games of tag we played at school. I was often the last boy left in then too, because I was quick on my toes.

345

Nimble. Anyway, they were putting out some stiff fire from the other lorry, which was skewed across the road, but from where I was, I couldn't see how many men. I got down behind the Crossley and shot at the figures on the hill as best I could, and there were a couple of others with me, three at first. Colonel Whittam, who'd made it out of the cab, and Will. He was with us. And Springer, but he caught a bullet quickly and I took his rifle.

'It was the first proper action I'd seen over there, that wasn't raids and old women. I was firing like the blazes, wild with it, yelling. One of theirs fell forward wounded, and before they could pull him off the heather, I got him in my sights and finished him. But there were far more of them and it was obvious they'd got the better of us, they were gaining ground. So Colonel Whittam shouted at us to surrender. He threw down his rifle, and we did the same, me and Will, put down our rifles, put our hands up. Four sets of hands went up in the air from behind the other lorry. We counted them.

'The rain was falling harder by now, stair-rods, and we stood there, our hands in the air, while they scrambled down towards us, fifteen or twenty of them, rifles pointed, but not firing. The hardest thing I've ever had to do. Stand like that. Seven of us, with our arms in the air, and the rest groaning, writhing on the ground, or still. The leader, and I knew by his dress he was the man who had flagged us down, shouted to his men to take our weapons. The light was getting bad by then, so it was hard to make out the faces you knew, let alone theirs.

'They put all the weapons in a pile on one side of the road. The man who took mine, he must have been about my age and he wasn't wearing any kind of uniform. He had a cloth cap and a heavy farming jacket, a thick scarf wrapped around and tucked inside, and when he checked my pockets for bombs, I could smell the wet wool of the scarf. His hands were scratched from the hillside, like mine.

'They had us disarmed and the main man was yelling at us to stand all together. They were prodding us into a group with their bayonets and rifle points, just like my man must have prodded his cattle. We were scared to hell by now, some of us crying, it might have been me, it's hard to know what I was doing and what I wasn't. Colonel Whittam was standing stock-still, mouth open. Will was muttering over and over, 'Christ, not me, Christ, not me, Christ, not me.' '

Daniel's fingers were dancing as he spoke now, jerking, and then it was his hands, pattering on the rug in a muffled tattoo. Jude got up and crouched beside him. She put her hands over his. His fingers were cold, white below the nails.

'My dream is about this. It comes back again and again. The stretch of road, the corner, the rocks and gorse, the lorries. It's never exactly the same, and it's not how it really happened. There are women and children there, and my brother, Johnnie. And each time when I wake up I think that if I could only remember properly what did happen, then I could be rid of the dream. But it's all so confused.

'Anyway, it was certainly quiet suddenly. After all the noise, grenades and firing, men shouting. We were surrendered and it was quiet. Even the men on the ground were quieter, not groaning so much and I loved it. I stood there, my comrades wounded, dead, around me, and I fell in love with that silence. I didn't ever want to move. Saying it now, just thinking about it, I can feel it again.'

His hands were still under Jude's, and she could feel them relax, his fingers unclench.

'It was quiet as the grave, and then all hell let loose. Suddenly the Shinners were firing at us. Taking aim and firing. For a moment I didn't understand what was happening. They'd just disarmed us, so we hadn't any weapons. I must have looked daft down their sights, my mouth hanging open amazed. I can see one of them now, he had the shakes badly and he was firing his pistol into the air like a mad thing, laughing wildly. Then I got shot.

'One minute I was on my feet, and the next I didn't know where I was or what had happened. I thought my leg had caught fire. There was water seeping in under my collar and my face was pressed into the bog earth. I managed to turn over, so I was looking up, my leg screaming with pain, my mouth screaming with pain, except that I must have been silent, because otherwise I wouldn't be here now. The shooting went on, the noise, and I shut my eyes. Can't have gone on for long though, minutes, not more, because the Shinners were always so short of ammunition, they wouldn't waste it. But it might have been for hours for all I could tell. Then it stopped. It was quiet again, only I was in pain inside it this time.

'A man was standing above me. I knew he must be on the road, which meant I was in the ditch. So what I could just see beyond, because it was very misty, was the hillside opposite. I could hear his voice, it dropped down to me in bits and pieces, and some bits I understood and others I didn't. And I could smell his cigarette. He was laughing. It was a hard bark of a laugh. And yelling. Yelling at somebody, telling him to get on and shoot him, not to be a coward, and he'd match the shot with one of his own, so I knew he was the commandant. I opened my eyes and looked up. He wasn't looking at me. His cigarette stood out from his lip and his pistol hung from his fingers, its nose pointing, aimless, straight down at my head. He had a wound on his hand, because I got drips of his blood on my face and they tickled. I knew then, as if it was the only thing I understood in the world, that I must play dead. Not move. Keep my eyes shut, keep still, despite the fire from my leg pushing up through me, despite his blood.

'I heard a shot and the commandant above me shouted out 'Yerra, boy' and laughed, and then kicked at my ribs with his foot. I didn't move, didn't shout out. 'This one's gone,' he said. 'Only the boss left, and he's mine.'

'I could hear Whittam somewhere close to me. It was his voice whispering. 'Get in the ditch,' the commandant said to him. He told him to face him with his left shoulder. Then he said, 'Play dead when I've shot you,' and he whispered something, which I couldn't hear. It seemed a sick kind of joke to tell a man you're about to kill to 'play dead'. There was a shot, loud, close to me, and I felt Whittam slump in the ditch, some part of him pressing against my leg, so that I wanted to scream out with the pain. He didn't move then.

'That was his parting shot, the last one fired. He had them drilling and singing before they left, and there was his laugh in between it all. I was in and out of things, what with the pain and loss of blood, but I still remember the song,' and staring ahead, Daniel intoned it:

"Remember Comrades of Ireland,
As forward to Victory we go,
That England, the Tyrant of Tyrants,
Has Mercy ne'er shown to the Foe.'

They were singing and marching and wheeling, their boots crunching close, and away again, and close again. One of them was sick nearby me, I could smell it. Then they were gone and it was all very quiet, not even any groaning left.'

Daniel fell silent, and Jude, her hand still over his, felt his body slump, felt his exhaustion.

'But he wasn't dead,' Mr Murray said. 'Whittam.'

Jude glared at him. 'Give him a moment, for God's sake,' but Daniel cut across her, shrugging off her hand.

'No,' he said. 'He wasn't.'

'So?'

350

'The ravens made him move.'

'The ravens?'

'They were there so quickly, but then they like their meat warm. Johnnie used to write home about the French ravens. He would watch them hopping about beyond the wire amidst their spoils. He said it made him murderous.' He laughed.

Jude nodded. She remembered the ravens, and the rats, and the dogs. It was men who had done the killing. The animals were only going about their ordinary business. But it was repulsive when that business was the flesh of dead soldiers.

'That croak,' Daniel said. 'You can't mistake it. I opened my eyes and one was standing just above me, jutting out its beard, giving me the eye.' Daniel stuck out his chin. '*Cruck, cruck,*' he said, making his voice deep, hoarse. 'Like that. It hopped out of my sight, towards Whittam, and that's when I knew he wasn't dead. Maybe it even pecked at him, I don't know, but he cried out. 'Off me, off me,' something like that. The raven flew away, the lovely black green of its feathers. Colonel Whittam began muttering and sobbing.

' 'Everybody dead,' he kept saying, 'everybody dead', and then all our names, our full names, like a roll call, reciting them. He was shaking, I could feel it. Then he got up. 'Go straight, just go straight,' he kept saying. When he started climbing out of the ditch, I opened my eyes. He was holding his shoulder, the blood pushing between his fingers. He walked across the road

351

and up the hill opposite in a straight line, into the mist, then he was gone.'

'Why didn't you tell him you were alive? Call out to him, something?' Mr Murray said.

Daniel shrugged. 'I don't know. Something spooked me. And the next time I saw him was on the boat to England. I was on a stretcher bed. He came to see me, with his shoulder strapped. He told me I'd been very brave. He said it was a relief to think I'd been unconscious once I was wounded at the ambush. He'd thought I was dead. And I said I had no memory of it.'

'Why?'

'Because I didn't want to, I didn't want to remember. But it hunts me, and now I think I know why.'

'And did he believe you?' Mr Murray said.

'It doesn't matter whether he did or not,' Daniel said, 'because what matters is what I saw in that photograph.'

'What did you see?'

Daniel was shaking. 'I saw him sharing a cigarette. I saw an Auxiliary sharing a cigarette with a Shinner.'

'The man with Whittam is Walsh, the commandant,' Jude said in a low voice.

'But it wasn't in the Irish war,' Daniel said. 'That hadn't even happened. They were still in France. So he knew that man before he ever got here. Ask Jude,' he said, his voice rising. 'Ask her about the two of them.'

Mrs Murray stood up. 'It's enough for now,' she said. 'Joe? Jude?'

Jude hadn't felt it before but suddenly she was

exhausted, and the task before her seemed very heavy, and for the first time she was scared. She walked off a little way, down onto the lawn. The grass was deep. She stood and stared across the garden, its colours coming in like balm. She tried to stop thinking, to let her mind rest.

The Murrays were talking behind her, their voices just sound from where she stood.

What do they think I'm doing? she asked herself. What do I think I'm doing? I'm not some bloody knight on a white charger. Crouching down, she laughed at the thought, and laid her hands out flat on the grass, felt the blades tickle her palms.

'Jude,' Mr Murray called down, 'we thought we'd take you out to see Horse Island, Daniel and I.'

'Where?' she said.

'It's only ten minutes in the boat,' he said. 'Before anything else happens.'

18

They all knew it to be a reprieve, the trip to Horse Island, and already, walking down to the boat, there was a mood amongst them which reminded Jude of the end of school examinations. Something had been faced by them all, the consequences couldn't be known yet, and in the short meantime, they would go to a place apart from their troubles, not quite a dreaming place, but not the hard day either.

Daniel was sure that Jude understood about the island. Crossing to it, she did look a bit green about the gills, as his father would say, the little boat lurching across the water. But once they were there, she was in her element. The way she crouched to the shingle when they arrived and ran her fingers through, and below into the finer sand, and picked between the stones and put one in her pocket. He liked the way she used her hands, and then, when the thought crossed his mind that he'd like her hands to touch him, he didn't banish it, as he might.

Mrs Murray had offered Jude a pair of boating pumps, but she said she was happy to go barefoot and Daniel stood in the shallows, his stick sinking into the sand, and watched her, arms around her camera bag, dance up the beach, where the rocks had gathered all the heat of the Irish sun, up towards the tideline and into the shade.

Jude and Mr Murray pulled the boat up high and Mr Murray secured the painter beneath a rock. He sat down.

'I'll stay with the boat,' he said. 'Perfect opportunity for some peaceful reading,' and he pulled a book from his pocket.

'So you'll have to show me the island then,' Jude said to Daniel, and he smiled and took her hand.

'Just to steady me,' he said.

They climbed high over the rocks behind till they reached a plateau of wiry grass, and then they sat for Daniel to rest his leg. Jude watched Mr Murray turn a page, watched him rub his fingers over the smooth silver curve of his rock. She watched as three oystercatchers gathered their wits on the wet slope of sand beyond, and she took a shot of them before some unseen danger caught their eye and they rose with a cry and cut low and straight between the waves for another shore.

The clouds drove across the sky and the sun was fierce between them. She photographed Mr Murray and the boat, then turned towards Daniel.

'Tell me about something,' she said, and as he began to speak, she photographed his face.

'I know the names on the island,' Daniel said. 'All the names. The flowers, the ferns, the herbs for the horses. They all still grow here. Mr Murray told me and I wrote it down. Tormentil and lousewort, bird's foot trefoil, silverweed and tufted vetch, thrift and lady's bedstraw, spear-leaved orache and samphire.'

Jude smiled. He sounded like Tom, like a child, eager to show off his knowledge. Then she remembered the lists of plants and birds at the back of his diary.

'The herbs?' she said.

'They used to bring sick horses here. Bring them and leave them for a while. The herbs made them well again.'

'Do they still bring them?'

Daniel shook his head. 'Too much other sickness now. It's no time for horses.' He got to his feet. 'Come on and I'll show you.'

They followed a narrow trail through hummocky grass and high bracken, crossing crumbling drystone walls, and every so often Daniel stopped to point out some fronded stem, or a small flower, or he picked a leaf and placed it on Jude's fingers, telling her to rub it and smell.

'Sorrel,' he said. 'Thyme. So close to the ground, you only know it when you've trodden on it. Yarrow. Scabious. Sheep's bit scabious with the little flower, and devil's bit with its jagged root.'

And all the names gathered in Jude's head like a strange song.

Daniel walked slowly, securing the ground with his stick before each step. Walking behind, Jude watched the injured stoop of his shoulders, the burden of his past leaving his body awkward, uncomfortable. And yet when he lifted his head and looked around him, or stopped for something particular growing, she glimpsed a different figure. Someone alive to the world, someone sure and eager, fiercely curious.

She thought that they were not so unlike in that way. She too was trying to lift her head and look around her again, to let go of a piece of her past so she could walk in the present.

They walked along the dipped spine of the island. It was warm beneath the sun, protected from the wind, with its own gathered perfumes from the gorse and the bracken, the heather and thyme. Jude felt protected here, as if for this brief time she could leave her journey behind, and Mr Murray, stroking the rock, deep in his book, would be gatekeeper, holding all beyond at bay. She felt her shoulders lift and she breathed deep into the briny, sweet air.

'Look here,' Daniel said holding his hand out, and there was a fine, white, bleached bone, curved into different planes so that however he held it, it tipped on his palm between points. Jude took the bone between her fingers. Its edges were like pinpricks, and it was very light. It was hard to imagine something this delicate clothed in flesh and fur. She lifted the bone to her face and stroked her cheek with it, very gently. A sharp line of sensation made her scalp quicken. She gave it back to Daniel and he put it in his pocket.

'Only a rabbit,' he said.

Cliffs rose steep at the island's end, the black rock, cut in vast diamonds, shouldering itself against the dint of the sea. As the island turned away from such exposure, the cliffs gentled themselves a little, allowing small ledges for seabirds and rifts and gullies for plants and lichens in grey and green and yellow. Up here, out of the island's protection, the wind beat in fiercely, barracking Jude's ears. Though she had stopped a safe way from the edge, still she crouched down. She didn't take her camera out.

It was easier, close to the ground. She looked over to Daniel. He too was crouched, but she saw that he had gone further than her and that now he was up at the edge, close to it, reaching his hands out to where the grasses gave way, and as she watched, he leaned into the sheer air.

Ice covered her skin and she saw the woman at the window, the woman climbing out and stepping forward, stepping off, she felt herself lifting the box to her eyes, framing it, her arms like lead, and she closed her eyes against the pit in her stomach, against the tumble of her heart, but she couldn't bear it, and she opened her mouth and yelled across the wind.

'Daniel! No!'

When she opened her eyes, he was turning back to the land, smiling, beckoning. She shook her head, and so he stood and walked across to her.

'All right?' he said.

'You were too close.'

He frowned, not understanding.

'To the edge,' she said.

'I was quite safe,' he said. She didn't answer. 'There's samphire growing on the cliff. I wanted you to see it.' He knelt down and looked at her more closely. 'You're sweating.'

'It's a hot day,' she said.

'But it's not that,' and he reached out and

touched her brow. She didn't pull away. 'What are you afraid for?'

She stared out over the water. Unobserved, Daniel looked at the profile of her face. He noticed the small mole below her ear, and the dent of a scar above her chin, perhaps from chickenpox. He noticed that she had a slight bump on the bridge of her nose, which he had thought entirely straight. He wanted to touch her face with his fingers again, trace it, and the thought came to him that his looking at her now was as a lover might look and he felt a blush wash across him. He turned away and looked at the spread of the island.

'We must go to the tower before we leave,' he said.

Jude faced back in towards him. Two tears were scudded across her face, but he couldn't tell if it was the wind or some grief that had drawn them from her. He touched her cheek lightly.

'Your skin is gone rough with the salt,' he said.

'I'm glad you brought me here,' she said, getting to her feet. 'Thank God we don't have to deserve somewhere like this.'

Although Jude had glimpsed the tower from the boat, up close she understood why Daniel had insisted they must go right to it.

'Mr Murray said it was built as a beacon for boats,' Daniel said. 'But I'm sure it was in case of a marauding navy too. A watchman would be stationed here and he would send a signal — light a fire perhaps. You'd see it for miles.'

Jude stood at the centre of the tower and

looked up at the walls, rising to the circle of blue above. She laid her hands on their stone.. The pieces were roughly cut, bedded in crudely. A swallow dipped in and down from the sky and pecked at the mortar before winging away again. She could still feel the touch of Daniel's finger on her cheek, and she knew she didn't only want to rescue this man. She saw how the lichen had gathered on one side only.

'You've been out here often?' she said.

'As often as I can.'

'Perhaps we'll come back here afterwards,' she said.

'After what?'

'I'm sorry about before,' she said. 'My shouting, on the cliff. I used to go to great heights, but not now. And other people, unless I am caught out, I can't watch other people.'

She could say nothing directly. She feared for too much. This man had woken her to herself as nobody had since Richard, since Kate. And yet the story that was unfolding around him was so horrible, she didn't know, at the end of it all, what she would be able to bear. Whether she would be able to bear the loving of him.

She looked out across the water. The current lines twisted away and the cloud shadows chased across, and it struck her, what an extraordinary point she had come to in her quest for the dragon. An insect crawled across one foot and the sun warmed her shoulders. She lifted her camera to the view.

'Queen of all you survey,' Daniel called to her. She looked over at him. He had walked forward from the tower towards the cliff. A safe distance from the edge, he put down his stick and stretched his arms out on either side.

'Mister Icarus,' she called back, smiling.

'The photo,' he said. 'I remember. I don't think Elsa would let you call me that. Anyway, I'm a cripple,' he said, grinning back.

'I don't mind about your leg.'

'I don't mean my leg.'

'Well, I can't fly either,' she said, and she turned and walked back towards Mr Murray with his book and the beach.

★ ★ ★

That evening, they made a plan. It wasn't complicated, and it couldn't be hard and fast, because they had no idea what would happen. But in two or three days' time Jude and Daniel would set off for the town of Liscool. Jude would have Dr Kelleher's letter of introduction in her pocket and, though only he knew it, Daniel would have a knife in his.

'There'll be a Protestant church in the town,' Daniel said. 'Drop me there and we'll agree a time to meet up.'

'What'll you do while I'm trying to find him?' Jude said.

Daniel laughed. 'A few more hours to kill won't hurt. Read the gravestones, count the dead. And if you do find him and he talks about the ambush, ask him whether they killed us all. Every last man. You must ask him that.'

And after they had discussed a little more

361

what Jude should say, Daniel took his leave, exhausted by the day, leaving Jude and the Murrays still talking by the fire. The murmur of their voices came up to him, and he was comforted before he slept.

He woke without dreams, feeling calm, a still point. He mustn't allow his feelings in now. Mustn't allow himself to think about Jude, for instance. About the way she raised her eyebrows when she was saying something important, or about the curves her body made, or about how she twisted a strand of hair in her fingers when she was listening to someone, and then, before replying, would tuck it behind her ear. He made his thoughts narrow.

It was then that he went and found Mrs Murray's knife. He took it from the shed. It was the one Mrs Murray used on her plants. He sharpened it on the whetstone outside the back door and wrapped a handkerchief around the blade. It fitted his pocket nicely. But he didn't mention it to anyone, reasoning to himself that it was no different to carrying a penknife, and he'd left his penknife in a drawer in Twickenham.

After that he walked on the beach, nodding a greeting to the man further out with his fork and his bucket, but he kept his hands clean, away from the stones and the weed.

Soon he would see if it was a duck in the picture, or a rabbit. He would have liked to have had a gun in his pocket. The Webley .45 would have been best, like he'd had with him that day. But the knife would have to do. He stroked the handle with his thumb. The wood was smooth, warm. He'd keep it with him till the time came.

★ ★ ★

Jude set off that day to find Dr Kelleher's stone circle, determined to get him the photograph he'd requested of her. She was glad to be on her motorbike, glad to be on her own. The day was overcast, not what she wanted, but Mr Murray had said the cloud would break later. Her route took her along narrow lanes cut down into the riddle of tiny fields, which would open out like magic to reveal deep, wooded estuaries and, the tide out to sea, an expanse of mud shining beneath the cloud. The journey was short and she stopped only once, to photograph a man at work digging worms, solitary in the mud sheen. She was glad of this task, that had nothing to do with her, that demanded her skill, and that left her alone. She brooded as she rode. The typewriting offered that, she supposed, but she so hated the work, whereas this she loved, catching things in her camera, and she could do it.

Dr Kelleher had told her no more than the name of the place, Drombeg, and the Murrays, busy with other things, had simply given her directions, and she'd no idea of what would be there. So to find a perfect circle, a crown of fourteen ancient stones high on a ridge, with the sea beyond and the hills behind, took Jude's breath away. A flat stone lay recumbent at the heart of it, and Jude sat here and waited for the sun. Her thoughts drifted, not along the ferocious currents of yesterday, nor into the life she'd lived in the war, but back to a conversation with Peter in London. Break the mould, be the first, he'd told her. Do what is necessary to make the life you want. And it came to her, sitting here, that she would, now. That this photograph for Dr Kelleher would be the first she took not just pretending to be a professional photographer.

When at last the sun came out, Jude took her shots and she knew they were good. Then she stood a last time at the centre of the circle and made her own pledge. She would not forget the past, nor ignore the needs of the present, but she would risk making her own future. The bike was hard to start, it began to rain and Jude surprised herself by coming close to tears. Then she reminded herself of her new resolve and she grinned at the drops and kicked the bike, which sputtered into life and she rode back in.

19

The town was grey and the sky was grey. Grey stuccoed houses with empty windows and dirty fan-lights. There was nothing to lift the spirits, no hills, no sea. No children even, being still in school. The streets were quiet, only a few women here and there, and a few dogs arguing the toss in a corner.

The Protestant church stood at the bottom of the town, near the river. It might as easily have been in Yorkshire as in Ireland, Jude thought, as she watched Daniel through the lych-gate, Mrs Murray's packet of sandwiches tucked under his arm, her camera bag over his shoulder. All being well, they would meet here again in two hours' time. Then she turned her attention to her task.

Dr Kelleher had been clear in his instructions: she was to find Paddy McCarthy first, and he would take her to Matt Walsh.

She left her motorbike outside the Catholic church in the town square. As she dismounted, a priest appeared at the top of the church steps, arms folded comfortably beneath a substantial belly. She nodded a greeting, murmured a 'Good morning Father,' which she thought was the right thing to say, but which was not returned, and she walked away with his eyes burning a hole in her back.

'Another bloody raven,' she said below her breath.

After some wandering and a few enquiries, Jude found McCarthy's Drapers, white lettering on a chipped red board. It was between O'Halloran's Bar, with its two bottles of Murphys and several tins of fruit in syrup in the window, and a shop called Leahy's, which gave no sign away as to what it might contain. The street led straight up the hill from the square and ended, as far as she could see, in a field. She wished she had her camera with her, though she knew she was right to have left it behind with Daniel. She mustn't let herself look away from people's words today, and the camera lens would have tempted her.

A faded poster propped up in the shop window showed a line of little girls in white frocks and behind them a smiling nun. An ancient mannequin, gender indeterminable to Jude, modelled something that might be a summer dress, one arm flung upwards, the other adrift on the floor.

Pushing open the door, she stepped down and into a small room. The walls were lined with bolts of cloth — different degrees of grey, black and brown — that reached high into the gloom. A long wooden counter, the brass yards inlaid, stretched across the width of the shop. More bolts of cloth lay on shelves at the back, and a tall ladder stood ready for climbing. Nobody was visible, but there was a large bell on the counter. Jude rang it, and listened.

From somewhere distant she heard the sound of doors opening and closing, then footsteps, and as they came closer, a voice calling out.

'Just give us a minute, for the love of God. It's not you already, Nellie, is it?'

A head came around the door, mouth wide in a smile, blue eyes bright with anticipation. Catching sight of Jude, the mouth, open ready to speak, clamped shut.

'Good day,' Jude said.

'So it's not Nellie,' the head said. 'Excuse me,' and disappeared.

Jude ran her fingers through a bowl of buttons that stood like sweets on the counter and waited. A minute more and the door opened again. This time the man stepped into the room, sleeves rolled up, measuring tape around his neck, shifting his shoulders beneath his braces. Even under the yellow gaslight Jude could tell he was blushing.

'They were twisted,' he said apologetically. 'And I couldn't reach around to them. If you'd been Nellie now, I'd have had you tweak them for me. But you being a stranger, I couldn't very well . . . '

'Nellie?'

'My daughter,' he said, as if that were obvious. 'But she's a while before she should be home for her dinner. You're not from these parts though? And I'd say you weren't here to buy some yards of cloth?'

'No.'

'So have you lost your way, maybe?'

'No, not exactly . . . ' Jude said. 'I've been sent by a magazine, an American magazine, to write an article. It's going to be called, 'Where are they now? The Heroes of the Irish War of Independence.''

'Oh,' he said, 'all the way here to Liscool,' and something in his demeanour changed and he seemed to grow several inches. 'So you're a lady journalist, then?' Jude nodded. 'That's a new one on me. Haven't met one of you before.' He looked her up and down. 'Is that why you're dressed . . . '

'In trousers?'

'That, and the rest.'

'I came here on a motorbike,' Jude said. 'Not safe to ride one in skirts.'

He shook his head. 'No, no, I see that,' he said. 'Did you leave it somewhere, then?'

'Outside the church.'

'And the priest. He didn't happen to catch a sight of you, did he?'

'As a matter of fact he did.'

He ran his fingers over the top of his head, as he must have done when he'd had hair there to run them through. 'He won't have given you a smile then, I'll be guessing.' Jude laughed, and shook her head. 'That'll be us done for the next two Sundays. Three even. We won't hear the end of it, a lady in man's dress.'

Jude put out her hand. 'Judith Hursten. Pleased to meet you.'

'Paddy McCarthy,' the man said, putting out his, and they shook. 'Pleased to meet you, Miss Hursten. And the magazine is paying you?'

'Yes.'

'All right so. But it's just writing is it, for the magazine? No pictures?'

'I was going to come to that later,' Jude said.

'I've arranged to meet up with my photographer later on.'

McCarthy nodded, and was about to speak again when something made him pause. Picking up a pencil, he jabbed it at the counter. 'This is what I don't like,' he said.

'I'm sorry?'

'This mistrusting of people. I'm no earthly good at it, but I've to do it or where would we be?'

Jude waited while McCarthy made a few more desultory jabs. Then he looked at her in what she took for a stern expression, because he pursed his lips and narrowed his wide blue eyes.

'How do I know you're telling me the truth?' he said, pointing the pencil at her, and a moment later, as if embarrassed by his suspicion, added, by way of explanation, 'You weren't here in the bad times, you see, and they're not long over.'

'You mean the Tan war?'

'No. That was bad, very bad. But it was worse afterwards. Not just in Ireland, but in this place, Liscool, this very town, and Nellie only a tiny creature. We had men take up arms against their own brothers. Blood against blood, can you believe it.'

'And now?'

'And now there are men won't come to me for the cloth for their Sunday suits, and no more will their womenfolk. But Nellie plays with their daughters, so . . . ' He laid the pencil down. 'So that's why I must be careful of you,' he said. 'Because it would take less than a poke to stir up the hornets' nest again.'

Jude reached into the inside of her jacket and brought out the note of introduction Dr Kelleher had written for her what seemed a lifetime ago. She put it on the counter.

'I met Dr Kelleher in Cork last week.'

McCarthy picked it up and read it, then he smiled again.

'And he's done it on his own prescription pad, so it must be bona fide,' he said, shaking his head admiringly. 'He's a clever man, that Doctor.' He handed the note back to Jude.

'So ask away,' he said.

'Dr Kelleher gave me two names,' she said. 'Yours and Matt Walsh's.'

In the pause before he replied, Jude thought how much hung now upon this name. And yet when she took that photograph, he'd been nothing more than another young soldier, barely more than a boy. A smile for the camera and then the temporary comfort of her cellar retreat: a blanket and hot soup and the brief reassurance of a woman's arm around his shoulder. He'd been no revolutionary then, no violent figure in another man's horror, no hero.

'Your man saved Matt's life,' McCarthy said. 'Did he tell you that?'

Lost in recollection, Jude started, then nodded.

'He said he'd patched him up.'

'Risked his own life to do it,' McCarthy said. 'They had Kelleher in their sights, the Tans, and a doctor could be arrested, not reporting a gunshot wound to the police. But if he hadn't got to Matt, Matt would have died. And if he'd died . . . '

During the journey Jude had brooded on how to come to the point. Whether to break in slowly or go straight for it. But McCarthy had done it for her.

'Tell me about the ambush,' she said. 'In your own words.'

'The Clonnacook Ambush,' he said.

'Is that how it's known?'

'It's famous across Ireland.' His voice was thick with pride. No shade of doubt that Jude could hear. 'Eighteen of theirs dead against one of our fellows, died of his wounds, God rest his soul, and three others injured. But they're right as rain now.'

'And Matt Walsh was your leader?'

'Our commandant, that's right. One of the best men you'll ever find. It was his plan, and it was him got us out afterwards. A bloody hero, he is.'

'So he's famous in these parts then, is he?' Jude said, remembering again the exhausted, frightened boy she'd seen him as in Belgium, neither hero nor villain, just alive.

'He is. And a big man still. A TD. We call him the Boss around here. He has a building firm now. Finger in all the pies, looks out for his own, too. He'd never let me go without, or any of the boys, not if he could help it.'

'What's a TD?'

'A Teachta Dála, a Deputy of the Dail. Like your MPs in Parliament.'

'Why did Kelleher send me to you first?'

'Liaison officer,' he said proudly. 'He's a very busy man. I'll vet a person, and sometimes they won't get to meet him.'

'You censor thcm?'

'I do. If I don't trust their motives.'

Jude thought it better not to pursue this, and she returned to the ambush.

'So what happened at Clonnacook, what was it like?'

'Did you not read about it before you came here? Look it up or something, whatever it is your lot does?'

'It is what I'd usually do, you're right. But when they gave me the assignment, they said: 'Just go and find those men. No homework first.' That way, it'd be fresh to me, I'd hear it all for the first time straight from the horses' mouths, if you'll excuse the phrase.'

McCarthy laughed. 'Horses is fine. The life of Ireland, they are.'

'So, will you tell me about it? In your own words?' Jude said.

McCarthy looked down at the ground and Jude waited. Finally he looked up, and shook his head.

'You should hear it from the Boss,' he said. 'He knows how to tell it straight. I'd misremember anyway. I'd be making mistakes. It was very foggy that day. Besides, it's him you've come for,' and he got to his feet, as if to end all discussion. 'I'll take you to him now,' he said. 'Then I can show you something of the place. It should be a good time of day to catch him.'

They set off at a brisk pace, not back into the

town, but up the hill towards the fields. Jude could feel her pulse quicken. She was getting very close now. For a minute or so McCarthy didn't speak. But once they had reached the top house and rounded the corner, he slowed down.

'Father Lynch never comes this high up the town,' he said. 'His heart.'

'The priest?'

He nodded. 'It was a queer time,' he said.

'During the Tan war?'

'It's funny still, hearing it called that. And there's even some calling it the Revolution now as well. So I heard, anyway.'

'Why funny?' Jude said.

'We'd call it 'the scrap', if we had to call it anything, or the Troubles, sometimes. By way of a joke, I suppose, whoever said it first, because it wasn't a scrap of course.'

'How was it queer?'

'This farm,' he said. 'Looks well enough, doesn't it? Prosperous enough, certainly. Man called Joe O'Leary, it's his. In the Troubles, he'd pay up his dues when we asked him, but he didn't want to be bothered with us more than that. Not if he could help it. But you know what brought O'Leary over to us lock, stock and barrel? It wasn't men being killed, imprisoned, out of his own town, not even families being burnt out, or lootings, or creameries burnt to the ground. It was the strangest thing.'

McCarthy paused his story to climb over a wall. He was nimble, which was not a talent learnt as a draper, Jude thought.

'So what brought him over to you?' she said

when they were clear and into the next field.

'They destroyed his mare.'

'They did what?'

'He'd taken his mare to be serviced by a stallion. A beautiful chestnut filly, high-spirited. He had high hopes for her. And the Tans arrived and drew their guns. Made the groom serve her with the other stallions stabled there too. All seven of them. She was ruined by it and he came home a changed man. He let us use his outbuildings as our bomb shop after that.'

'You sold bombs?'

'Made them. Incendiaries, grenades, mines. A home-made business it was. We'd two boys were the chief bomb-makers, there were weeks when they barely left the buildings. But when the heat was on, the rest of us would lend a hand.'

'Walsh?'

McCarthy shook his head. 'He hadn't the patience for it. Nor the fingers. But I was good.'

It shocked Jude, to think of the men making their own bombs, though she couldn't have said why. She looked across at the low, whitewashed buildings, hens pecking outside, wagtails courting in the afternoon.

'You made them in there?' she said, pointing.

He nodded.

'The bombs you used against . . . against the British?'

McCarthy looked at her incredulously. 'Soldiers, Auxies, Tans, yes,' he said, his voice hard. 'And they used theirs against us, against the Irish people and on our own soil.'

It had been Daniel Jude had had in mind, but

she realised she must be careful. She was walking in a minefield, she thought, smiling slightly.

'So you were good at it,' she said.

'I was,' and McCarthy looked at her, as if waiting for his cue.

'Tell me something about it,' she said, appeasing.

'All right, so I often cooked the eggs,' McCarthy said, in a voice that might have been talking about calico or tweed. 'Grenades. That's what we called them. Eggs. You were best doing the same thing each time, it got quicker that way. We'd use old Mausers to make them out of for the grenades. Clean the cartridges out with nitric acid, then cut them smaller, file them down. There was the wadding, cotton, cardboard, and the explosive. And then there was the cap last of all, drops of warm shellac for that. You had to be so careful with the explosive, gentle it in. I remember this fellow came up from Cork city to teach us, O'Faolain he was called. He told us: 'A single grain might make twenty yards of difference in the cast, so weigh out the grains, for God's sake!' And it was him told us the trick, heating the caps on a hot plate, over a Bunsen.'

'It sounds very dangerous,' Jude said.

'It was. And there were men blew themselves up, working in bomb factories. It was the care made you good at it, and I was always a careful man.'

'And you kept all these mines and grenades in those outbuildings?'

'There's a souterrain. We stored our ammunition in there. But one time I was thawing out gelignite in a pot on his stove, and the Auxies came by.' McCarthy began to laugh.

'What happened?' Jude said.

'They looked through the door, thought I'd turned into a woman of the house. Made a couple of lewd comments and left.' McCarthy was still laughing. 'What did they think I was stirring, the porridge?'

Jude laughed with him, but she thought of Peter, stirring a pot all that time in Belgium and nourishing men, not blowing them up. He must have fed Walsh, for God's sake. She shook her thoughts clear.

'And it was all because of his mare?' she said.

He nodded. 'Yes. We didn't even know what it was had brought the change of heart at first, whether to trust him right out. It was a groom at the stables told the story and it came back to us here. So then Matt asked him was it true, and O'Leary, I saw him, he was about in tears at the mention of it. Anyway, it was a great place for us because except for that once, it was never searched. Don't know why not.'

McCarthy had led Jude up around the top of the town and down again by now, across fields full of unstartled, heavy-uddered cows, along a deep boreen running with water and smelling of wild mint and manure, and finally out into some rough pasture beside the river.

'Over the river and we're there, safe,' McCarthy said, and he led Jude across a narrow hump-backed bridge no more than a quarter mile away. She could see the Protestant church from there and she wondered how Daniel was doing his waiting.

Walking quickly along the edge of the town, down one street and up another, McCarthy took Jude round the side of a tall house, one of those she'd seen on her way in with its fan-lights and tall Georgian sash windows, and the only one with impeccable woodwork and fresh pointing. Behind the house was a small, neat garden, and beside it a large, brick outbuilding.

'It's likely he'll be in there,' McCarthy said. 'It's where he runs his business from,' and he walked over to the door, turned the handle and ushered Jude before him.

20

Jude had been waiting for this moment for days, imagining it, fearing it, wanting it. She'd argued and pleaded with and yelled at the man who stood before her now, a clipboard in one hand and a fountain pen in the other, caught mid-sentence, looking over towards her, his eyebrows raised in polite query.

The last time she'd seen him, almost ten years earlier, he'd been dressed in a tattered, bloodied uniform, his skin darkened with his weeks in the trenches. He'd been gaunt then, shocked, exhausted after bringing in his friend, and for all his bravado in the day, in the dead of night he'd been no more than a boy. And Jude, who was no older than him, had done what she'd done for so many fearful, exhausted boys, holding his hand, cradling his head and stroking his hair for a time, whispering to him that it would all be all right and to sleep now. And like so many others, in the morning he behaved as though the night had never been. But she understood that, that saving of face.

Now here he was, a big, filled-out figure in a well-cut suit standing tall before her, and he'd put on weight, his face full where it had been hollow. He'd grown a moustache, a small block of orange-brown on his upper lip, and he'd lost some of his curly hair. And at a side-table, like some strange simulacrum of her old self, of the person she'd been no more than a couple of weeks earlier, sat a woman, poised before a typewriter, head turned at the intrusion, hands ready over the keys.

Jude felt McCarthy's hand on her arm, pulling her forward, heard his deep breath before he spoke. 'He's nervous,' she thought.

'Hope we've not caught you at a busy moment. This is Judith Hursten. She's a journalist, come from America to write about the Brigade.'

McCarthy stopped and waited. For a long minute Walsh didn't reply but stood looking at Jude so that she wondered whether he'd recognised her. And when he did speak, it wasn't to her, but to the typist with her hands suspended.

'Just finish off by saying that unless payment is forthcoming within the next week, and I mean that I have the money in my hand, then steps will have to be taken. And then if you'd like to make us some tea, that would be grand.'

Walsh's office was ordered and functional. Shelves of labelled files around the walls, two geraniums on the window sill, a small shelf with technical books, another with a large tape measure on its wooden reel, three spirit levels, a set of callipers and a clutch of sharpened pencils. There were some architectural drawings on the main table, and as he spoke, Walsh folded these into a tidy pile. There was no dust.

Only when the typist had left the room, glaring at Jude as she went, did Walsh speak again.

'So, Mack, a lady journalist, eh? What have

you been telling her about then?'

McCarthy had picked up one of the spirit levels and he was tipping it, this way and that, watching the bubble float its way from one end to the other.

'I told her she'd have to hear it from you,' McCarthy said. 'It was you she'd come to find. Dr Kelleher gave her your name.'

'An honourable man,' said Walsh, almost, Jude thought, as if he were crossing himself. 'And he gave you my name, did he? Have a seat then,' and he pulled out one of the chairs and motioned for Jude to sit.

She busied herself getting out notebook and pencil, pulling in her chair, writing his name at the top of a fresh sheet.

'Who sent you?'

'An American magazine.'

'Name?'

'*Griftner's Monthly*,' Jude said, straight off. 'You'll have heard of it, I expect. It's very big over there.'

Walsh nodded. He wouldn't risk losing face, Jude thought.

'And what do they want from me?'

'I'm writing an article. 'Heroes of the Irish War of Independence'. About the men behind the myths. So I've come to you. I've a photographer with me too, but perhaps we could come to that a bit later.'

There was a knock at the door and the typist came in with a tray of tea things. Jude could see she was hoping to stay, but Walsh ushered her out again quickly and nodded at McCarthy to pour the tea. Picking up the spirit level, he replaced it on the shelf, in its space between the larger and the smaller one.

'Attention to detail. Something I'm very good at. As important on the column as it is in the building trade.'

'The column?'

'Flying column.'

Jude nodded. 'Of course.'

'So, putting aside the photograph question for now, what do you want to know?' he said, jostling the papers on the table, aligning them again.

'Tell me about yourself,' Jude said. 'Childhood, family, that sort of thing.' She needed to spend more time in the room with this man, try to find his measure. He was so different from the figure in her snapshot, the boy with the dirty, tired face and the cigarette. This was a man who knew he was a leader, who knew he was in charge, in control. A man who would flick his ash on to a dead man's face, or so Daniel had said, and the thought went through her like a pulse of electricity.

'There's nothing to tell,' Walsh said. 'I'd no more than an ordinary childhood.'

'Nothing that might have told us what was to come? That you'd become a leader?'

'Commandant,' McCarthy put in. 'He was the Commandant.'

'The title doesn't matter,' Walsh said, and Jude noticed McCarthy's face widen in surprise. 'We boys were all in it together.'

'But you were the boss. We knew that from the

381

start. Still are,' McCarthy said.

'I'm no more than a simple builder,' Walsh said. 'There was demolition to be done then, and so I did it, and now there's reconstruction and I'll do that too.'

'It's really as simple as that?' Jude said wryly, and Walsh looked up at her and grinned.

'Maybe not quite,' he said, and she noticed his eyes travel down her now, as though for the first time he'd noticed she was a woman.

'So how did you get to be the boss?' Jude said. 'Were you top of the school, or captain of the hurley team?'

McCarthy laughed. 'He was as hard a nut as the Brothers had ever had to crack,' he said proudly.

Walsh picked up his cup and sipped.

'Strong enough for a mouse to trot on. I miss that from the Brigade. Stewed tea takes away hunger, Miss Hursten, did you know that?'

Jude was about to say that as a matter of fact she did, when she realised it had been a rhetorical question.

'The Christian Brothers taught me discipline, and endurance. And I needed both during those times,' and he gave a short bark of a laugh. Pulling a cigarette case from his breast pocket, he flicked it open. He offered it to Jude and, as if it were an afterthought, to McCarthy. Though she would have loved a cigarette right then, Jude shook her head. She wanted her nerves just where they were. She watched him cup the match and draw on the cigarette, sucking the glow deep into the tobacco, and because she had known so many herself, she recognised the soldier's draw. Too many cigarettes lit in the thrust of the weather.

She had thought it would be better to be circumspect, but watching Walsh, she saw that he was as eager to tell his story as she was to hear it.

'The Brothers put steel into you,' he said. 'Had me down for a vocation, and they weren't wrong. As celibate as a priest those years, and as single-minded. You had to be. Not like this little fellow, Miss Hursten,' he said, stabbing his cigarette towards McCarthy.

'Please, boss . . . ' McCarthy said, but Walsh interrupted him, leaning over to Jude, as if offering her a confidence.

'I think that's where Mack went wrong. He was a married man. Only one in the Brigade. I warned him, but he wouldn't listen. Because it softened him. He had too much to lose. You can't serve two masters.'

McCarthy was looking down at his hands. 'Please,' he said again, but Jude could tell from his voice he didn't expect Walsh to stop now.

'You tested me as much as any of my enemies,' said Walsh, relentlessly. 'Isn't that right, Mack? Very keen fellow, but squeamish. And there's no room for that in a war. You've got to be able to stomach things. Take your orders and get on with it.'

'But Miss Hursten wants to hear . . . '

'What does she want to hear?' Walsh said, interrupting. 'Not about you, anyway, Mack, with your soft heart. We'd still be under the yoke if it had been left to the likes of you.'

Jude was repulsed by Walsh, and now she pitied McCarthy, but since arriving in this room, Daniel had become strong in her mind. She saw Daniel setting fire to homes, his right hand not knowing what his left hand did, telling himself it was all legitimate, it was a fair war. And then, in that reversal, she saw him lying wounded, left for dead in the ditch, and the figure above him with his cigarette and his hard laugh. And she saw him on Horse Island standing in the roofless tower looking out beyond the current lines, and she knew she must keep her purpose in mind, not allow herself to be diverted.

'So tell me about the ambush at Clonnacook,' she said.

'What do you want to know?'

'I want to know what happened.'

'You've read about it?'

Jude shook her head. 'No. All I've done is check where it is on the map. In case of a photograph. But I was told to get it straight from the horse's mouth. No homework.'

'Maybe that's just as well,' Walsh said. 'You won't have read the English lies, then.' He pulled open a drawer in the table and drew out two worn newspaper clippings. 'The *Southern Star*, that's our local, and the *Examiner*.' He pushed them towards Jude.

She looked at the nearest one, columns of text surrounding a blurred photograph of an empty stretch of road.

'I'd prefer to hear about it from you,' she said. Yesterday she'd heard Daniel's story, seen his horror. Today, she hoped, she would hear the official Irish version, the one that didn't know there was still a survivor.

Walsh smiled. 'All right then. So the war,' he said.

'Which war?' Jude said, somewhat disingenuously.

'Our war. Of independence. Not the European one. Do you know much about it?'

Jude nodded. 'I do usually read the papers. And I have done a bit of homework,' she said.

'The Easter Rising?'

'I know about that, of course.'

'And the Black and Tans? And the Auxiliaries? Do you know what the British were getting up to by 1920?'

'I know a certain amount,' Jude said, and she saw herself again at the table in that restaurant in Cork, her fingers still sticky with lobster, reading Daniel's diary, the reprisals, the burnings. That had been the first of it, and then Dr Kelleher's story, and then Daniel yesterday, so that it was only half the truth to say she knew a certain amount, because she was brimful with those horrors.

Walsh waved his arm, sprinkling ash like favours.

'The Tans, the Auxies, they were all over the country by the time we did Clonnacook,' he said, spitting out his words. 'The country was run riot with them. They were terrorists. Thought they could get away with anything.'

'Describe them to me,' Jude said.

'They were strong, fit men, experienced soldiers. Had to have fought in the European war, that was a rule. Used to carrying all the gear: rifle, revolvers, ammo, grenades. They had that swagger soldiers get. And they were paid very well. The Auxies were on a pound a day. That's a lot of money to be given to go and beat the living daylights out of a people. They said we were barbarians, but it was them.'

'What did they do round here?'

'Drove around the countryside in their Crossleys, blind drunk often as not, firing off their guns at people. I knew men killed in the fields by stray bullets. They tore villages apart. Sometimes because they'd heard there was an IRA man there, sometimes for the hell of it. They'd drive in, two lorry loads, singing their filthy songs and do whatever they felt like. Smash up the houses, steal what they could, ornaments, livestock. Sometimes they'd burn some of the houses down. Official reprisals, they called them. They'd round up the inhabitants, women, children, and search them. Beat up the men if they felt like it.'

McCarthy was shifting a little in his seat, and Walsh turned to him now.

'What is it, Paddy? You're twitching like a man on the end of a rope. Do you not agree with me?'

'No, I do,' McCarthy said. 'It's only . . . '

'Spit it out then,' Walsh said.

'If you make them all out villains, then it lets them off more. And they weren't. Some of them did those things, but they didn't start out with black hearts.'

Walsh snorted. 'And that makes it better?'

'No. It makes it worse.'

Walsh shook his head like a man perplexed. 'You're saying they began decent men. But tell Miss Hursten what they did to you, Paddy.'

McCarthy looked down at the table. Jude thought he looked abashed, shy even.

'Will you tell me?' she said, and after a moment, he did.

'It was before I joined the Brigade. I was out visiting my sister, she's in a village three miles from here or so, and they came there and did like Matt just said. Can you imagine, Miss Hursten? The Auxies screaming obscenities, whipping me with their belts, beating me with their rifle butts, me standing there bollock-naked, excuse me, and my little nieces and nephews and my own sister watching on. That's what took me into the Brigade,' and Jude waited, pencil poised, to hear more, but Walsh was twitching his cigarette, impatient, and McCarthy bowed out. 'That's all.'

'Something had to be done,' Walsh said, his voice calm, and Jude reminded herself that he had probably told this story hundreds of times. 'They'd been terrorising our land for some seven months and there had been barely a shot fired against them in reply.'

'So who decided what it should be, and where and how?'

'I did,' Walsh said.

'Was that usual?'

He shrugged. 'We needed to stage something big. GHQ was up in Dublin, a long way away from Liscool, from these parts. It was very different in the city. They didn't know what it was like here, day in day out, and they didn't know what the boys were capable of. We couldn't wait any longer for their say-so.'

'So you were solely responsible,' Jude said. 'Is that the kind of man you are, would you say? Prepared to take those kinds of risk?'

Walsh stubbed out his cigarette. 'Sometimes you just have to get on and do it, step over the line, tread on a few toes. Somebody's got to be prepared to do it.'

'How did you know they would come that way, on that day?'

'We didn't know the time, but they always took that road. We'd been there ten hours before they came.'

'He didn't tell a soul beforehand,' McCarthy interrupted. 'Did all the reconnoitring himself. Only told us on the day.'

'I had the priest down to you all the night before, though. You must have known something big was up,' Walsh said with a laugh, but McCarthy shook his head.

'We just thought you'd got a touch of religion. Men do sometimes in a war. It was only that morning when we got the rifles and ammunition, before dawn and the birds still quiet, that we knew we were on for something.'

'And then?' Jude said.

'We waited most of the day for them.'

'D'you remember the cramps we got?' McCarthy said. 'They were wicked. I was wet through with the rain, and I had cramps in places I didn't know were possible. But the miracle of it was, how they disappeared when we were on. Just time for a quick prayer.'

'The lorries came around the bend,' Walsh said, 'and I flagged the front one down. They slowed, taking me for one of theirs, and before they knew any better, I lobbed the first bomb . . . '

A sudden bang on the door made him stop. Jude looked round to see the door handle turning this way and that and the door finally open to admit a diminutive figure holding a piece of paper before him in his fist.

'What is it, Jack?' Walsh said, his voice severe.

The boy took a step into the room.

'Sand, sir. There's a ton more needed up at the new house or the fellas can't be on with anything.'

'And what do you have there?'

The boy looked up at his hand, still carried high.

'A message,' he said.

'Give it to me then,' Walsh said, putting his hand out for it, flat on the table, and Jude saw a scar, a thin red line, that curved across his palm like a worm from his wrist to his little finger.

The boy stepped forward, gave it to Walsh, and stepped back again. Now that his task was done, he looked at Jude, a strong scrutinising glance.

'Thank you, Jack,' Walsh said, his voice gentler now. 'Tell O'Leary I'll be up in a half hour to see how things are doing. But we'll have to wait till tomorrow for the sand,' and he gave a short smile. A grin lit the boy's face, and snapping his heels like some small soldier, he turned and left.

'So I lobbed the first bomb, bang into the middle of the cab, and then it was a battle. But we had the advantage and it was clear pretty quickly we'd win this one.'

'Was it over quickly?' Jude said.

He shook his head. 'No. They were brave fighters, I'll give them that, and several of us were injured, but in the end we had them blistered with it, their men dead and dying all over the valley.'

'How did it stop? When the last man of theirs was killed?'

'They began shouting out their surrender and a couple of them threw away their rifles, so we stopped firing. It was hard to see clearly with the mist coming in, but they had their hands raised, the half dozen or so still on their feet. So I gave the ceasefire and four of our boys stood up and went to take their arms.

'It was so quiet for a minute, not even a bird cry, the Auxies with their hands above their heads, our boys walking towards them, the rest of us with our guns still raised ready. Then suddenly, no warning, they started firing again. Nearly point blank range. That's when Dom Murphy was hit.'

'God rest his soul,' McCarthy murmured, crossing himself.

'God rest his soul,' Walsh said. 'He was cheated by those bloody Auxies, and we let them know it. No more surrenders after that.'

'You killed them all,' Jude said.

'That's about the size of it. Took on the British Empire and won, and not a man of ours captured afterwards, though they had the country turned upside-down for us.'

'It was only the Colonel survived,' McCarthy said. 'He got away.'

'How did he manage that?' Jude said.

'We thought they were all killed,' Walsh said, 'so he must have been playing dead. That's all we could think of afterwards, when we heard he was alive. I checked them myself, and I know a dead man when I see one. But I got him wrong.'

Smooth as can be, Jude thought. He's like a politician. There's so much varnish, you have to scratch deep to get to the wood.

'Poked around amongst the dead men,' she said.

'That was my job.'

'And if you'd known he was alive?'

'We'd have taken him prisoner,' Walsh said, and Jude felt his eyes on her, glaring, as she took down her careful notes.

'Was he injured?' she said.

'Shoulder wound, we heard that too, later.'

'So nothing life-threatening. Couldn't he have identified some of you?'

Walsh shook his head. 'I heard he was a broken man. They took him straight off to England for his own safety.'

'You'd have hunted him down, would you?'

'All's fair in love and war, Miss Hursten.'

'But still, that many of their men killed, it was a disaster for them. Wouldn't the British have tried to have him identify you? Get a description from him at the very least?' Jude persisted.

McCarthy reached for the teapot, gave it a shake, and poured in some hot water from the jug.

'If you don't mind it poached?' he said to
Jude. She nodded her thanks and he filled her
cup, the tea as dark as blood.

'Well, they didn't,' Walsh said. 'Or he couldn't
remember. I don't know, do I? He didn't come
back to Ireland, and we had other battles to
fight. Our victory certainly didn't make the
British any gentler.'

'Must have been good for your career,
though,' Jude said.

'It was good for the cause of Irish freedom,'
Walsh said severely. 'It's become like a shrine.
Did you know that? People go there on their
wedding days, first communion. It's a place we
can be proud of.'

'But I'm interested in you, Mr Walsh,' Jude
said. And I'm interested in this ambush, because
it made your name.'

'Made him as famous as Dan Breen,'
McCarthy said proudly, and Walsh scowled.

'It's not to do with fame, Paddy,' he said, and
McCarthy's blush, his humiliation, made Jude's
anger rise. She looked at her watch.

'What do you think then, about us getting a
photograph of you?'

Walsh tapped out a cigarette. 'All right,' and
sticking the cigarette between his lips, he shook
the box of matches. 'Last match,' he said,
striking. It flared, and before he could light the
cigarette, died. 'Ah, for God's,' he said.
McCarthy's hand was already in his pocket,
rummaging to find his boss a light, but Walsh
turned to Jude. 'Would you have one?' he said.

She pulled the lighter from her pocket and

struck the flint, held it across to him. He bent his head to the flame and drew the fire. She watched him suck, the shrug of his moustache, eyes closed a moment, then blow out that first, best lungful of smoke and she waited to see if he would comment.

'You given that?' he said.

'Yes.'

'By a boyfriend? Brother?'

'By a friend I nursed with.' She put the lighter on the table.

'You were a nurse,' Walsh said, staring at the lighter.

Jude wondered how much he would ask.

'Something of a change of direction then, what you're doing now.'

'Yes, thank God,' she said, 'though I loved it.'

'Where were you?'

'Belgium. Like many others,' Jude said, keeping her voice very level, unemotional.

Walsh looked up. He stared at her, and she held his gaze.

'Whereabouts?'

This was it, Jude thought. After this, something would happen no matter what, and she wouldn't be able to prevent it. She smiled to herself. Or control it.

'A village, near the front line. Bombed out. Just about only the church tower left standing, and its bell. We were nursing in a cellar.'

Walsh drew slowly on his cigarette, then tipped his head back and made smoke rings at the ceiling. Jude waited.

'In a cellar,' he said at last. 'It was number

twenty-six, I think. The enamel plate was still beside the door.'

'Yes.'

Jude noticed that McCarthy was sitting very still, only his eyes moving, from her face to Walsh's and back again. And Walsh was staring now at somewhere beyond her left shoulder, but somewhere she imagined was not in this room. After what seemed an age, he spoke again.

'It was just you and another girl, wasn't it,' he said at last. 'Slight, with dark eyes. Two pretty girls and a young soldier playing mother at the stove.'

'Yes.'

'And I . . . ' Walsh said, his voice uncertain. He stopped, and when he spoke again, it was as though he had decided something. 'We'll do that photograph, Miss Hursten, if you're quick about it. I'll see you and your photographer in O'Connor's Hotel in fifteen minutes. And then you can be off, on your way back home where you belong,' and he stood and put out his hand.

21

It was more than two hours since Jude had left Daniel at the Protestant church, but he wasn't worried by her being late. It meant that something must have happened. Far worse, in their strange scheme, if she'd returned after fifteen minutes and empty-handed.

At first he wandered in the churchyard, counting the names on the gravestones, the bird songs. He walked with a hand in his pocket, turning and turning the smooth piece of china he'd gleaned from the tide, and tried not to check his watch. But he couldn't bear to be seen by anyone, all these people he might have had to do with back then, and people kept nodding him greetings as they walked past, so then he retreated inside.

The church was dim, the stained glass throwing out a gaudy gloom. Daniel looked at the saints, their face-forward virtue. They looked so English. And they held their swords and lances so easily. He wondered what else they might have done. Whether they fought only with dragons and the infidel, or whether they had sometimes fought the wrong man, or woman, or, God help them, child.

But he mustn't think too much because he needed to stay calm till Jude returned, so he decided to set himself small tasks. The heavy stone of the floor and walls stilled him. He would eat Mrs Murray's sandwiches very slowly, and then he'd count the number of glass pieces in St Michael and the snake, he thought, that coiled beneath. If she had still not returned, he would deadhead the flowers in their vases on either side of the altar, and look up the hymn numbers, 47 and 216, still listed on the hymn board, and after that he would count more glass. St Christopher's maybe, with his great burden. And only when each whole task was done, would he allow himself to look at his watch.

So when finally Jude pushed the heavy church door open and strode over the cold stone, all her urgency and pent excitement like a wind around her, she found Daniel standing at the far side of the aisle, his hands out, palms flat against the church wall, his head craned back, counting. And when she began to speak, he put his hand up to stop her.

'Just a moment.'

'Daniel, we're meeting him. In ten minutes' time.'

And it was only when he turned from the wall a minute later and faced her, that she saw in his eyes, in the nervous movements he made with his mouth, in his hands which twisted and turned, how much he was trying to keep at bay.

Jude found a bench in one corner of the graveyard and she sat Daniel down and talked to him, quietly, carefully, about what had happened. She even made him laugh, describing Paddy McCarthy and his bomb-making.

'He might have made the ones that got thrown at us,' Daniel said, and Jude nodded.

'And he's the gentlest-seeming fellow I ever met,' she said.

'I'll be all right now,' Daniel said, 'to go and meet Walsh.'

★ ★ ★

They walked up the steps of O'Connor's Hotel and pushed open the double doors. The air, full of cooked cabbage and old beer, assailed Daniel.

'Smells like the barracks,' he said.

The hall was gloomy, lit by a single electric light. A mahogany reception desk stretched along the wall on one side, the keys to the rooms on their pegs behind like a line of shiny soldiers, and on the other side were two doorways. A low bench ran between them and a hat stand stood at one end. The walls were a dull yellow interrupted every now and then by dusty prints of weary foxes and furious hounds. Hanging her jacket with the hats, Jude walked through a doorway. A moment later she returned and beckoned to Daniel.

'He's here,' she said. 'Don't forget who you are.'

Coming close to him, she put a hand on his shoulder, her touch so light he only knew of it when she had already stepped away again. He shouldered the camera bag and followed her in.

Daniel saw that the dining room was empty except for one table in the bay window where a man in shirtsleeves sat with a coffee and a glass of whiskey. Foxes' heads and goggle-eyed fish in glass boxes watched on. Jude walked towards him, but Daniel waited further back, leaning against an empty table, pressing his fingers into the damask, taking the weight off his leg. Things seemed to be happening very slowly, all of a sudden, like a gramophone record turning at the wrong speed.

The man was big, with ginger hair and a squat moustache, and as Jude approached, he gripped the table edge and rose, pushing his chair through the carpet pile as if it were through treacle, back till it hit the wall with a soft thunk. His mouth opened in a smile and he stretched out his hand to Jude in greeting, confident and calm. Daniel saw that the man thought Jude attractive, and he saw that Jude knew this.

Outside the window swallows were practising their tricks, and inside, two flies pressed their noses against the glass and cried. The sun came through, flashing itself about the cups and teaspoons.

Daniel stared. His body was lead, cold, the weight of the bag, the pull of his leg dragging him down. It was his man there, smiling, genial. It had to be his man. But Daniel didn't recognise him. He didn't know him. And if he didn't know him?

'Judith Hursten, I presume,' the man said with an odd smile and a glance at his watch. 'At last.'

And hearing the voice, Daniel knew and his fingers on the velvet damask burned. He saw Jude's shoulder turn to him, and, for now, he remembered his part.

The man was pulling out a chair for her, and she sat, smiling, nodding. Daniel looked down.

There were crumbs under his fingers, and a brown stain.

'Apologies for the delay,' she said. 'Mr Walsh, this is Daniel Brown, my photographer,' and she was looking at him, waiting, and so was Walsh. So he nodded, and sat in a chair at the table, then bent and grappled with the camera bag, as if to be busy about his job.

A waitress came in, a nervous girl in a tired pinny and a tight black bun like a respectable curse.

'Bring us some more coffee,' Walsh said, and she bobbed and said, 'Yes, sir.'

'So this is your photographer,' Walsh said, taking out a cigarette. 'He's looking a little peaky. I hope he'll have a steady hand with my face.'

'He'll get what he needs to,' Jude said. She passed him her lighter. 'He's good.'

'You look very different without the bandanna and cauldron of soup.'

He lit the cigarette, put it down in the ashtray and crossed his arms.

'So why are you here, Miss Hursten?'

'Do you remember all the photographs I took?' she said. Walsh looked blank. 'Or maybe you didn't notice. I was always snapping. The men liked it. It buoyed their spirits.'

'And?'

Daniel tapped gently at the ashtray. 'Don't forget your cigarette,' he said quietly, and his voice took the others by surprise, as if they'd half-forgotten he was there.

'Who is he?' Walsh said, his voice lower, darker than before.

Daniel thought he might be floating. He couldn't feel the chair beneath him. His mind was very clear. He smiled at Walsh.

'I'm not at all what you think,' he said. 'Am I, Jude? And you hold your cigarette just as I remember.'

Walsh frowned and jabbed the cigarette back in the ashtray.

'Let's get on with the job, then. I've a business to run.'

'I need to know something, Mr Walsh,' Daniel said.

'Daniel, please.'

But Daniel wouldn't catch her eye. 'Show him, Jude.'

'Daniel.'

Walsh ran a finger along his moustache. 'Show me what?'

'If you don't tell him, then I will,' Daniel said, his voice still very calm.

Jude looked back, her lips tight, resolute. 'I took a photograph of you in the war,' she said.

'Where?' Walsh was fidgeting, restless, adjusting his collar, pulling down his shirtsleeves, looking around as if something else must be more important than this.

'In Belgium.'

'So?'

'The man beside you in the photograph is clearly your friend. He's wounded and you have an arm around his shoulder. You're sharing a cigarette.'

'Why is that important? That's what happens in a war. Men stick together. You'll know that, after your time in one.'

Walsh pushed out his chair, as if getting ready to leave.

'But you met him later too,' Jude said. 'In Ireland.'

Daniel watched her with pride. She'd stopped Walsh dead in his tracks, and he wanted to applaud.

Walsh shook his head. 'You have it wrong there.'

Jude took out the photograph. 'It's a copy,' she said. She passed it across the table to Walsh. He picked it up and looked quickly, before pushing it away.

'What of it?' he said. 'They know over here that I was in the British army then. It's no great secret. And a man can't decide who his comrades are in the trenches. It's what I did afterwards that counts.'

But Daniel had watched him closely. From the other side of the table he'd felt the jump of his heart.

'The other man,' he said. 'Your friend with the cigarette. In the photograph he's a lieutenant, like you. But he was a colonel by the time I knew him.'

'And where did you know him?'

Daniel spoke as though it were nothing, this thing he was saying. 'I knew him over here. In Ireland,' he said.

'Not really a photographer, then,' Walsh said, his mouth tightening.

'No.'

'And you come asking me to give account of myself,' Walsh said. He shook his head. 'I know what you were, and I don't know how you can even look me in the eye.'

The waitress came with the coffee, her eyes on the carpet, and the three at the table were silent. When she'd gone, Walsh seemed to gather himself, as if he were about to make a bid for something.

'I'm going to tell you a story,' he said. 'If you can spare the time.'

'We've got all the time we need,' Jude said.

'All right. I was born in this place, brought up here. And when the European war broke out I was still in apprenticeship to my father. Bricklaying. I joined up in 1915 because my father told me not to. I might have been rushing to defend Belgium and the right of small nations, being as I came from one. Or I could have joined up because Redmond told us we'd get Home Rule if we did. I know all about that now, but I didn't know a thing then. Then, I could have named you the Kings and Queens of England, but I knew nothing of the history of my own country. Didn't know and didn't care. I wanted to go to a war so I could shoot my gun at something more than rabbits. And so I could get away from my father. I was seventeen and I was going to show him that I was a man.

'I was a clever boy, and after a year I got a commission. Somehow I stayed alive in that hell. And Lieutenant Whittam, he stayed alive too. That was enough to make you firm friends over there. Then he got injured, unconscious in the middle of no man's land. So I went over the top to pull him in, else he'd have been dead for sure by the morning. He'd have done the same for me.

'I was on furlough, months overdue, when we got news of the Easter Rising. I didn't know who any of them were, Connolly and Pearse and the rest, but now my head was full of questions. And when the British executed them in Kilmainham Gaol, then my blood rose and my heart turned. Now I really was in no man's land, an Irishman fighting in the British army, fighting for the country that was killing my countrymen.

'So when I got back to Ireland, I set to and schooled myself, caught up on my history. Robert Emmet and Wolfe Tone, the Potato Famine, Parnell, the Land League, and the rest. I learned what the British had done to our people. And then I joined the IRA.'

Daniel could hear Walsh, his speech, but he was seeing things again. He couldn't help it. He tried to grab hold of the room, tried to stop himself slipping. His fingers clutched at the table and the chair, at each other, he threw his glance hard at the coffee cups and the milk jug, at the wide-eyed fish, at the netted curtains. Gripping hold with all his strength, he made himself notice. The sound of the swallows outside, a small cloud high in the window, the dust ball hanging by a hair from the skirting, the paper wad beneath his table leg keeping it steady, the mole on Jude's neck, just above the collar of her blouse, a broken nail on her left hand, which she rubbed at absently with her thumb as she listened, a tendon in Walsh's neck standing proud.

Jude put up her hand, like a child in a lesson.

'But they didn't mind, that you'd fought in the British army?' she said.

Walsh laughed. 'They did mind. I had to prove myself, prove I could be trusted.'

Daniel watched Jude's face. He knew what was happening. Walsh was enchanting her. He was that kind of man, that kind of leader. Daniel could hear him that day in the rain, his voice above the ditch.

'Poor sods,' Daniel said, the words tugging themselves out of him.

Walsh looked at him. Daniel could see other tendons now. He could see his colour rise.

'What did you say?' Jude said.

Daniel wouldn't look at her. He couldn't stop himself.

'The ones you proved yourself on,' he said. 'They must have been poor sods. You know, two men from my barracks, they were buried alive. That wouldn't have been you? Proving yourself?'

'Don't,' Jude said.

'You were an Auxiliary here, weren't you?' Walsh said slowly. 'You wore that beret, you bloody mercenary. And you have the nerve to come back and accuse me of horrors. My God!'

Daniel watched him shut his eyes and shake his head.

'What did you get up to then, Mr Brown? Shall I tell your lady friend here some of the things you did?'

'It was a war,' Daniel said.

'A war. You think that excuses you, that it was a war. They were all armed, were they, the women, the old men, the children you beat and burned and killed?'

Daniel turned his head, as though to parry the blows. He couldn't think about Walsh's words or he'd have no strength for his fury. All these years he'd nursed his own injury for defence, held onto it as the truth of that time. And the question that had hung at the back of his mind had a body now and he must find out the truth. But since crossing the water he couldn't get away from the other terrible truth of what had happened over here. Which was what he had done to people. He himself, and far beyond even the awful bounds of war. And still he twisted and turned, because here was the man, and he needed to know, he needed not to break into pieces, not yet, he needed to keep his guilt at bay a little longer.

'We were under orders,' he said. 'It wasn't me. It was my leg was blasted. I tried not to.' He shook his head. He mustn't let the words in now. Not in and not out. But Walsh's voice cut into him like shrapnel, sliced between his ribs, twisted in his flesh. He could feel it sour and curdle and gather his own thoughts with it into a mess of guilt.

'I know,' Jude said, her voice breaking in. 'I know what he did. And other things were done too and that's why we're here.'

'Oh, you know. Really?' said Walsh, his voice sarcastic. 'You think it was all reported? Your newspapers didn't even want to scratch at the surface of it. Too shameful.'

'I don't know it from the newspapers,' Jude said quietly, and though Walsh didn't seem to hear her, Daniel did, and from deep inside his maze, he wondered for the first time what it was that she knew, and where from.

'What do you think you're doing anyway, coming here?' Walsh said. 'This isn't your country.'

'I'm looking for you,' Daniel said.

And when Walsh laughed, Daniel could hold himself there, in that hotel room with its coffee stains and desperate flies, no longer, and he threw off Walsh's words, blocked his ears to Jude and struck out with his own wound.

'You thought I was gone,' Daniel said. 'The mark is still on my ribs,' and his hand went to his chest as though he would show Walsh the scar. 'Where you kicked me with your muddy boot. I'd forgotten that till now, how muddy your boot was.'

'What are you talking about?' Walsh said quietly.

'But it was everybody else that was gone. You were right about them. Will and Freddie Charters and all the others. Only me and the Colonel were left, except you didn't know about me. And the raven, after you'd marched away. The raven with his horrid voice.'

'I don't know what you're talking about,' said Walsh.

'Tell me,' Daniel said, almost conversationally, 'what happened to the poor scared fellow?'

'Who?'

'He was shooting in the air and you told him not to be a coward, to get on and kill the man.'

'What are you doing, Daniel?' Jude said.

Daniel shook his head. 'Poor man,' he said, 'poor man.'

Walsh turned and looked away out of the window. 'McCarthy,' he said to himself.

'He did it, though, didn't he? He shot him in the end. 'Yerra, boy', you cried. But he did it for you, not for Ireland. Or not any more than I did it for England. Bloody hands, all of us.'

'Where did you get this from?' Walsh said. 'Because you are talking of Clonnacook, and there's nobody left alive.'

Daniel leaned across the table, his face cracked in a wide smile. 'But there is, and he wants to know something.'

Walsh shook his head. 'No.'

'You knew about one of us. You knew Colonel Whittam was alive, didn't you. And you didn't know about me. You caught me in the ribs with your boot and you flicked your cigarette on to my face, ashes to ashes. But you didn't know I was breathing.'

'I don't believe you,' Walsh said, shaking his head. 'And you better watch what you say around here, because there's a lot of men would talk of tearing you limb from limb if they knew what you were.'

'I lay doggo in that ditch and you stood above me telling your men to finish us off. We were unarmed, for Christ's sake. No weapons, and you shot us all. You shot us all dead.'

407

'It was that kind of war,' Walsh said. 'You know that.'

'It was that kind of war. But not for the Colonel. You left him alive. 'Play dead,' you told him. I can hear you say it, whispering, then more whispering I couldn't hear. You shot him carefully in the shoulder. And after you'd all gone and the raven had woken him, he walked away from us.'

Daniel saw how pale Walsh had gone.

'Is that why you've come back?' Walsh said. 'Because he walked away?'

Daniel stood up. He rolled his head round on his shoulders and flexed his fingers. Taking his stick, he walked over to the far wall and stroked the fox's head stuck proud there, its coarse fur and long nose.

'So the Kilmurphy hounds had you in 1913,' he said, reading the plaque. 'That's even before the rest of us were had.' He ran his finger down to its open mouth.

'My, what sharp teeth you have, Grandmother,' he said. 'And what beady eyes.'

He looked back towards the table in the window, towards the woman he thought, he hoped, might love him, and the man he needed to hate.

'I want to know if he betrayed us to our deaths. That's why I've come to find you. Because I don't know how to live this life until I find out, because I . . . '

He stopped, not knowing what to say.

'And why should I tell you?'

Daniel shrugged. 'Out of conscience. Or

408

because I can make you. I don't care which.'

'There had been no surrender, they weren't our prisoners,' Walsh said, looking at Jude.

Daniel lifted his hand. 'I'm leaving now. He's going to play games and I've got too old for them.'

And before Jude could reply, he had left the room.

Walsh filled Jude's cup with more coffee. He passed her the cream and the sugar. Neither of them spoke. The waitress came in, and was waved away. Jude wondered what Daniel was doing, but feeling her chest tighten with panic at the thought, she pushed it away. She sipped the lukewarm coffee. The cream was viscous, coating her mouth, smoothing her palate. This was all more frightening than she could have imagined. She didn't know where anything was going. She tried for a placatory tone.

'I'm very sorry, Mr Walsh,' she said at last. 'Maybe this was a bad idea. It's not working out as I hoped.'

Walsh shrugged, waiting.

'I thought his meeting you would exorcise something. That's why the tomfoolery about the magazine and the photograph. It was the only way I could think of to arrange it.'

'Why did you come to me first, then, if it was him all the time that needed to see me?'

'I didn't know whether he could manage it.'

'And he hasn't, has he.'

'I don't know what kind of neurasthenia he's suffering from,' she said. 'Maybe we don't have a word for it.'

'It isn't shell-shock,' Walsh said. 'Or not the kind I ever saw.'

'But he is ill. We've been hoping to find a way out of it for him.' Jude could hear herself pleading, acting the part.

'We?'

'His parents. Friends.'

'Even brutal men get sick,' Walsh said. 'This was a different war from yours, and what his lot did was indefensible. We had to meet like with like, and it was a dirty fight to free our country. Nobody has clean hands, especially not Mr Brown and his Tans. It's what he deserves, if his conscience sends him mad. You've done a dangerous thing, Miss Hursten.'

Jude nodded. 'If you play with fire, you burn your fingers. I should have listened to my mother.'

'Doesn't sound as though you've ever listened to your mother. She wouldn't have wanted you a hundred yards from the front line in Belgium either.' Walsh ran his finger over the lighter, its carved clasped hands, and looked up at Jude with a different expression.

'How is your friend? The small, pretty one.'

'Kate,' Jude said.

'Was that her name?'

Jude smiled sadly. Walsh waited.

'She got her fingers burnt,' Jude said.

'She wasn't killed?'

'She was gassed.'

'Did she die?'

'Yes.'

'I'm sorry. She's dead, and you're still acting

the heroine. What's your sweetheart going to do now, then?'

'He's not my sweetheart,' Jude said, though her heart had jumped to hear him say it. 'And I don't know. But he will do something to find out what he needs to know. He's got very little to lose. Unlike you.'

'And what will I do, Miss Hursten?'

Jude heard the steel, and she waited a moment to answer.

'I don't know that either. It depends on what you're prepared to give up.' She stood. 'I'm going to go now. I have to find him.'

Jude walked round the table and picked up the camera bag. Rising too, Walsh escorted her to the door like a proper host.

'I will very likely see you again,' he said, putting out his hand. They shook, and then, before she could prevent it, he lifted her hand to his lips and kissed it.

He watched her as she walked through the hall. She picked her jacket off the hat stand and pushed open the doors to the outside.

'Miss Hursten,' Walsh called, 'he has too much to be sorry for. He will go mad, that man. Remember it.'

'He is gone there already,' Jude said, but quietly, so he could not hear.

22

She found him beyond the church, by the river. It wasn't hard. The tall figure over its stick watching the swallows dip by the weir. They stood in silence together, and then Daniel looked at his watch.

'We should go back.'

It was only when they had reached the motorbike that he told Jude what he wanted to do, and though she was fearful of the consequences, she agreed.

'It is very nearly on our way,' Daniel said, and Jude nodded, her skin cold-pricked with apprehension. Daniel showed her the place on the map and the route was easy to plot.

Once they were clear of the town, the road was empty. Jude checked often, but there was nobody behind them. It had been dry in Liscool, but out here the ground was wet, and the air smelt of wild flowers and rain. There was nothing much to see. Just bog and hills, small twisted trees and the shine of ground water. Jude was glad of the bike beneath her, something that travelled where she wanted it to.

Too soon she felt Daniel's hand tapping on her leg. Slowing the bike into the bend, once they were round she came to a stop. She turned towards him and he nodded. He looked old suddenly, and very tired. Opening the sidecar door, she gave him her arm and, leaning heavily, he climbed out.

The clouds had cleared, leaving the sky a clear blue, and the afternoon sun was warm on their backs. Jude looked around her. This was where it had happened, in these ditches, below these rock outcrops. She turned towards Daniel.

He had walked down the road a little way and stood, hands flat to his sides, stick trailing, eyes to the ground, like one of the street-corner figures she'd grown accustomed to since the Great War.

'This is what you wanted,' she called, but he didn't reply. He was intent upon something, and as she watched she saw him look up, towards the brow of the hill, and down to the ditch, then up, then down again.

Shouldering her camera bag, Jude walked beyond him down the road. She wondered what Tom and Elsa were doing right now. She imagined them playing outside, being called in for tea, imagined their squabbling and their eagerness. She shut her eyes, homesick for the ordinary cadences. The light was milky, gentle. It was hard to imagine an ambush here. Opening them, something caught at her sight, a hard, precise line in this unruly place. Reflexively, she took out her camera and walked up closer. On one side of the road the ditch had been levelled over and against the rise of the hill, behind a flat altar of lichened rock, stood a column of dark stone. Words were carved on it in a language she didn't understand, though she recognised the name 'Dominic Murphy', and the date, 1921.

Jude crouched low to take the photograph, and the column loomed tall, monumental. She stumbled as she stood and her bag lurched out from her body, tugging at her balance so that she put her hand out for balance. There was something soft beneath it and looking down, she found a small posy of white flowers tied with a white ribbon, the petals crimped and browning at the edges, the ribbon dusty. Something about it all, about the harsh dark monument and the delicate forgotten posy, made Jude wince and she turned away and back towards Daniel. He was no longer on the road but was climbing, unsteady even with his stick, up the hillside, tripped by brambles, struggling his way through the gorse.

'Like some bloody pilgrim,' Jude said, and she laughed out loud at herself, because she understood so little of what had happened here, so little of what had happened in what was, after all, a foreign country. Then she laughed again to hear her own echo.

At the brow of the hill Daniel turned back towards Jude. She couldn't read his expression, but he called something out and pointed down the other side. Then he stepped down the far side of the hill. So she set off up the road and followed him.

By the time she reached the same point ten minutes later, Daniel was gone, but she knew where, because below her was a small cottage, one end of the roof thatched and the other sheeted in red corrugated iron. It sat snug into the hill, two small rectangles of window staring blankly up at her. She could see a track leading away from it towards the road and noted it down as an easier route back.

'There's nowhere else for him to go now,' she told herself as she scrambled down.

When she reached it, she took a photograph: a bicycle leaning beneath one window, some hens scurfing up the dust at the threshold, the turf stack piled and thatched at one end, a cart leaning on its pins at the other, and she smiled at herself, taking a picture that seemed worthy of a chocolate box, when in truth she was in the midst of something so bitter.

The door was open. Jude knocked at it, but nobody came. She called inside.

'Hello? Anybody home?'

It felt incongruous, calling out like this, but she didn't know what else to do. Still no sign of anybody. Wondering what had become of Daniel, she ducked her head through the low doorway and stepped inside. She found herself in a broad, low-ceilinged room with flitches of bacon hanging from above, a spinning-wheel on the wall above the door and a pot on the fire, banked all around with crusted, white turf embers, from which came the smell of something fresh-baked. A closed door to the left of the fire she assumed must lead through to a bedroom. The walls were whitewashed and the floor was earthen. One end of the table was laid ready for tea with plates and cups and a jug of milk brim-full. A copy of the *Irish Farmer* was spread at the other covered with dirty potatoes and a pile of peelings, and beside it a wooden doll and a bowl of peeled potatoes, shining and white in the dim light.

Jude shivered. This was eerie. Where was the woman? The child? Where was Daniel?

'Daniel?' she called.

Still there was silence, but as she listened, she thought she heard sounds from the other side of the closed door.

'Daniel?' she called again.

Dropping her bag, she walked over to the door and pushed. It was latched shut. Undecided, she put her ear against the wood and listened. There were odd noises coming from the other side, she couldn't make them out. Then, unmistakably, she heard Daniel's voice. He was speaking in a tone she'd never heard before and it made her skin go cold. She tugged down the latch and pulled open the door.

It looked as if something violent had happened in the room, a chair upturned, a rug in the middle heaped into a pile, but the figures in the corner were very still. Daniel was crouched down facing towards the far wall, like some predatory animal ready to leap, and backed up into the corner was a young woman, her eyes wide with fear or fury, turning her head this way and that as though trying to get free of his glance. The air seemed tight with static, as though any movement might provoke a fury in the gods.

She took a step closer then, wincing at the creak of the boards, and between them she saw a small child, two, perhaps three years old, sitting on the floor and playing with a pile of wooden blocks. She was chattering unconcernedly to both the adults, turning her head first to one, then to the other, a light, infant babble of sound that rose into the bright friction of the air above.

Jude watched as the child raised up a tower, each block more precarious than the last, till there were five standing proud. The child turned towards her mother, but the mother, her face bleached and tense, didn't see. So she turned back to the strange man, and Jude watched as Daniel reached out his hand and casually, as though it made no odds, swatted at the lowest block. The tower tumbled. The child looked at the blocks, then at Daniel, then at the blocks again, and her face crumpled into tears, and she let out a wail that cut like ice across Jude's skin.

The cry broke the woman's spell. She lunged forward, her pale arms flashing, and drew the little girl in close. And where before she'd been silent, motionless, now she rocked her child and spoke softly, and the child forgot her tears and smiled again and chattered.

Jude could see the woman's wedding ring, and that one of her nails was split. She could see the dirt on her fingers, no time to wipe her hands from the potatoes. She could see the thick wool of her stockings, the shape of her toes on one foot, a shoe lost on the floor, her dark skirts, her blouse, her hair somehow dragged free of its pins, falling and tumbling over her shoulders. The woman rocked her child, but still Jude saw how rigid her limbs were, as if she could make herself into something unyielding, like a hard metal, a carapace within which to keep her child safe.

When Daniel spoke, his voice was calm and cold and slow.

'Just tell me,' he said. 'Did you know he was coming? One word, and then no harm done. She can build her towers.'

'Daniel, stop,' Jude said, scared.

'Go away, Jude,' he said, his voice quiet, uninflected.

Jude felt her heart race and the sweat break down her back.

'I need the answer,' he said and he shifted slightly, moving himself closer to the woman.

Jude couldn't see what he was doing, but she saw the fear that spread itself now over the woman's face. And she saw how she hunched over her child.

'This is what you learned,' she said quietly. 'How to terrorise women and children. But it's over. You don't have to do this now.'

Daniel cuffed at his head, as though a fly were irritating him.

'For God's sake, the war's over,' Jude said. 'You're frightening her.'

'Just yes or no,' he said.

And although he had done nothing yet but knock down the tower, the violence was almost palpable, like the pressure of a storm before it breaks, and Jude was frightened that something much worse would explode through. The terrified woman would not, could not move while Daniel was crouched there. Jude looked about her for some way of distracting him, but there was nothing obvious to hand. A bed, the child's crib, a chest, a chair. So she tugged the quilt from the bed and gathered it up in her arms as best she could. It was heavy and for a moment she floundered and the floorboards groaned beneath her. But Daniel paid her no attention. He still stared at the woman. And the woman, eyes on the ground, still rocked her child. Then Jude spread her arms wide and flung the quilt over him, pushing him down onto the floorboards and gathering her arms tight around him.

Daniel struggled like a wild thing, maddened, flailing, but she held on, the muscles in her arms, her stomach, her shoulders shaking with the effort. She could feel his shoulders, bunched tight, and the force of his arms. His breath was coming in ragged bursts and he made small, fierce sounds as he fought her. She could feel the length of him, how his legs stretched just beyond hers, and how the crown of her head pressed against his cheek bone. She pushed her head harder into his face and he gave a yelp of pain. Through the clear, cotton smell of the quilt, she could smell him, a smell she didn't know she knew, and despite herself, despite her anger, her heart lurched.

She felt Daniel brace his body against hers, felt him use every ounce of his strength as he began to force her off, gaining an arm's freedom, and a shoulder's, bending his good leg beneath him for support. And then he stopped, so that for an extraordinary moment they seemed to her suspended, beyond that time and that place, for minutes, or seconds, braced each against each, till something gave way, like a wave through him. She felt his body relent and his breathing ease, as though she had brought him to quiet, and he seemed to fall across her, so that they lay with the length of each other like some strange *pietà* there on the floor.

Jude pulled herself free and as she stood up, her calm was replaced with fury, knotting her stomach.

'For Christ's sake, Daniel Brown, who the hell do you think you are?'

She was shouting, out of control. She wanted to hit him, pound her fists into him. She hadn't noticed the woman stand until she felt a hand on her arm.

'Come out of here,' the woman said, and Jude was quietened and followed her, only turning in the doorway to look back, but the bundle of quilt lay motionless, dead to the world.

In the kitchen the pot was still cooking and the potatoes were still half-peeled. The woman filled the kettle from a bucket beside the hearth, the child hoisted on one hip, and Jude sat down at the table. The child's doll looked up at her. It was a crude, wooden creature, stiff armed and legged, a smile painted on to its flat face, wool hair tied up into a bun. It wore a skirt in the same cloth as the mother's and a roughly sewn chemise. One side of the chemise was darker than the other, and damp.

Jude looked across to the woman. She was staring at the door, as if it might burst open at any moment, her eyes still wide. She was shivering.

'We could wedge it shut,' Jude said.

The woman nodded, so Jude took a chair and

propped it below the latch. There was no sound from within. Still the woman stared at the door.

'I'll sit against it too,' Jude said, and she sat beside the wedged chair on the hard ground.

Setting the child down, the woman took the pot from the fire and hung the kettle to boil. She lifted the pot lid. The smell of sweet bread was overwhelming and Jude longed above anything to be home, in her own kitchen, with the children she loved. The little girl clung to her mother's skirts. The woman set the bread on a rack at the potato end of the table and pulled out a chair, lifting the child to her lap. There was no sound from the other room.

'What's her name?' Jude asked gently.

'Nora,' the woman said.

'And you?'

'Peg Riley.'

'My name's Jude. Jude Hursten.'

The woman nodded, keeping her eyes from Jude, from the closed door. Nora buried her face in her mother's lap.

'You came here with him,' Peg said.

'Yes.'

'I thought he would kill me,' she said.

'I know,' Jude said.

'I've never met him.' She was shaking. The kettle was boiling. Lifting Nora to her hip, she got up and made a pot of tea, brought it to the table. She ran her fists across her face.

'He was a Tan?'

'Yes, he was.'

Peg looked at her. 'But Ireland is its own country now,' she said. 'They can't come and . . . ' She shook her head.

'I'm very sorry,' Jude said. 'If I'd known, I'd never have brought him here.'

'It's the ambush brought you.'

'He was one of the only two survivors.'

Peg shook her head. 'No,' she said.

'What do you mean?'

'There was only one survivor.'

'How do you know?'

Peg rubbed the teapot as if to conjure something. 'Because he came here afterwards, bloody as a clipped rabbit.'

'But not the man in there?' Jude pointed at the bedroom door. 'Not Daniel?'

'No. I never saw him before today.'

'He came to your cottage? The survivor?'

'He knocked at the door. After all the racket, the guns and grenades going off. Asked could he please trouble me for a glass of water.' She laughed grimly. 'Blood pouring from his shoulder and the rest of him filthy with mud and him troubling me for a glass of water.'

'How did he know the house was here?' Jude said. 'You can't see it from the road.'

'No.'

'It must have been Colonel Whittam,' Jude said.

'I don't know,' Peg said, shying her head away, pouring the tea into cups. 'He had a posh voice though.'

'What did you do?'

Peg shrugged. 'Took him in. Bleeding like a stuck pig. I don't know how he got up the hill. He said they were all dead behind him, and that's what I heard afterwards. That's what was printed in the papers, too. I hated them, the Tans. But I couldn't let him die.' She brought Jude over a cup, set it down on the ground.

Jude nodded. She understood this. She remembered German soldiers being brought in. She'd nursed them as carefully as any others, held their hands when they cried.

She felt it before she heard it, the sound from the next room, Daniel's voice, quiet, calm-sounding, felt his voice as a chord through the wood of the door and into her skin. She looked over at Peg. Her arms were stiff, rigid like a wall around her child. Daniel was quiet again and Jude pressed on, not knowing how long they had till he came out.

'Did you tell him this?' Jude said, 'about the bleeding man and the glass of water?'

Peg shook her head. 'Soon as he came in here, he was yelling, demanding. Shouting and mumbling. I couldn't speak to him.'

'I think he hears other voices, from that day, that time.'

Peg shivered, and crossed her arms around herself. 'I asked him to leave, and he wouldn't. He came right up to me, here, by this table, and he picked up Nora's doll, hung it from his fingers. I was so scared, I ran into the bedroom, to get her, and he followed me. She was playing, you saw, and I didn't want to alarm her, so I just crouched against the wall, and then you came.'

'So, do you know Matt Walsh?' Jude said.

Peg barely hesitated, but Jude saw it.

'You do,' she said.

'Everybody knows Matt Walsh,' Peg said finally.

'I think he will come here again,' Jude said. 'And Daniel, the man in there, was in the ambush. It's his own Colonel he's pursuing. Who's a dead man, but that doesn't stop him.'

★　★　★

Daniel was tangled in something soft, heavy. It was completely dark around him, and very warm, and he could smell all kinds of things: animals, turf smoke, soap, sweat. He lay still, didn't try to move. The struggle with Jude had left him exhausted, his limbs aching and tight.

It was quiet inside here, only the sound of his own breathing. There was something vast outside, and he'd have to look at it soon. But just for now, for these next minutes, he'd keep it at bay.

The woman had surprised him. Her fear had bothered him. He shouldn't have minded it, he knew that. He hadn't known he was speaking out loud, had thought it was just inside his head. But if she had only answered, just the one word, he would have left her be.

The air was close. He could feel the heat of it as he breathed in and out, burning his nostrils, drawing the sweat. He was angry with Jude, angry that she'd come between him and what he needed, but lying here in his dark cocoon he admitted that he'd enjoyed it when she'd held him. That despite the pain it gave to his leg, he'd resisted her for longer just to feel her body pressed so hard up against his, her arms around him. He didn't know if he was blushing at the thought, or whether it was the heat. He pulled at the heavy fabric. Now it was smothering him and there seemed no way out of it. He felt that panic he knew from his childhood when he'd got lost under the bedclothes, making his heart pound in his chest.

'Can't breathe!' he shouted, because Johnnie would help him, lifting the blankets clear, his face at the top of the well, breaking the dark, calling down comfort. Then Daniel remembered where he was and he closed his mouth and fought his way out in silence.

Free of the quilt, he curled on his side. Jude and the woman were talking in the other room, their voices adrift in the air, but he couldn't hear the words. The blocks were still where they'd fallen. He picked one up. A rough piece of painted wood, red as the red of the iron roof. With a shaky hand he placed it on the ground, perspective thrown to the winds from where he lay, and stacked the others on top, one upon one upon one, as the child had done.

His tower was lovely. Johnnie should see it. Lying with his head on the ground, he thought it might have reached to the sky. He nudged the bottom block with a finger, set it at an angle. The tower stayed true. He nudged it again, and again, till the whole height depended on a slight incidence of wood on wood. Again his finger pressed the red, and the whole tumbled around his ears, around his eyes, so that he put his hands up in defence.

The air was loud, and then it was still. A bee nuzzled and the dust motes danced their late afternoon dance at the window. Daniel lay still and grew calm. He shut his eyes and slept for a while, and when he woke, the air smelt sweet and fragrant, and the sun lay differently. He looked at the blocks all around him. There was one just near his forehead that he could see if he rolled his eyes upwards and another beside his fingers. Another lay at the edge of the quilt, and one had rolled half under the bed, beyond his reach. He sat up, his mind quite clear. He knew something at last and he needed to be out of here. Reaching for his stick, he got to his feet. The voices still murmured, but there was another one, a man's voice, added now.

Looking about him, he was shocked. It seemed as if some violence had been done in the room. So he set the chair on its feet again and straightened the rug. He put the wooden blocks in a pile together, then went to the door. One hand on the latch, he hesitated, and then he knocked.

23

The women had gone outside by the time they heard the motor car. Jude had told Peg she was a photographer and promised to take Nora's photograph and the little girl stood on the threshold, her doll still held tight to her middle, her face serious.

'There's a motor car on the road,' Peg said.

Jude lowered her camera. She heard nothing. 'Are you sure?'

'Listen,' and this time Jude could hear a low roar, a vibration almost more than a sound.

'Depends if it slows,' Peg said. 'If it's him, he'll most likely stop on the road and walk the rest. You'd damage the axle, bringing it here along the track.'

They listened as the car approached, then went quiet. A door slammed.

'Just one,' Jude said. 'So he's alone.'

'I'll fill the kettle again,' Peg said.

Jude nodded. 'Make believe, like I said.'

And in the same way Jude continued taking photographs of Nora, as though she had no idea, no thought of the man walking up the track, or of the other man still silent in the bedroom behind.

Nora had got bored of the camera and they had gone around the end of the house by the time Walsh walked up. The child's timidity was gone and she tugged Jude's hand, eager to show her some treasure. So Jude, crouched by the turf stack, gazing unseeing at some withered flowers, saw Walsh before he saw her. His face was determined, but not vengeful, and she couldn't tell for certain, but she didn't think he was armed. She watched him look through the kitchen window and raise his hand to knock, then she called out.

'Hello again, Mr Walsh.'

Holding tight to Nora's hand, she walked towards him.

He turned.

'Miss Hursten,' he said, his face unsurprised. But Jude watched it light up at the sight of Nora. Crouching down, he addressed himself in a soft tone to the little girl.

'Hello there. So you're Liam's pride and joy. Such a dote, it's no wonder.'

'I thought you'd know where to find us,' Jude said.

'Where else would he go,' Walsh said with a shrug.

'It's an elegant shrine down there at the roadside. Though I don't think Daniel saw it.'

Walsh stood up again. 'You know they've had a fair on this road each year since. The priest comes and gives his blessing, and there are songs sung, there's rejoicing.'

He took Nora's hand, and swung it as he sang.

Then here's to the boys of Clonnacook
Who feared not the might of the foe,
The day they marched into battle
And laid all the Black and Tans low.

'So you've come after us Mr Walsh.'

'As you told me earlier, I'm the only one with anything to lose. Amn't I, little princess?'

He lifted Nora up and grinned at her, eye-to-eye.

Nora stared back, then putting her hands up to his face, she pushed him away with the full force of her small arms.

The little girl's hands thrust against Walsh's eyes and nose, making him gasp and his eyes water. But he said nothing, only set her down carefully and gave a chuckle.

'Maybe I asked for that.'

'We don't always ask for what we get,' Jude said as she opened the door to the house.

Peg stood by the fire, not pretending to do anything other than wait. She gave a slight shake of the head when Jude came in, so that Jude knew Daniel was still quiet. She noticed that Peg had taken the chair from against the bedroom door and set it back at the table. Nora ran into her mother's skirts with a cry, and Peg picked her up and set her on her hip.

'Mrs Riley,' Walsh said, nodding his greeting.

'Will you have some tea?' Peg said.

'That'd be great, thank you.' Walsh glanced around the room.

'He's not in here,' Jude said.

'I can see.'

'You'll meet him soon enough.'

Walsh flashed a look at her. 'What do you mean by that?'

'No more than I said.'

Peg put the teapot on the table. 'There's fresh

brack. I must have known you'd all be arriving,' she said, and her words broke the tension and the three of them sat down.

'How much does Mrs Riley know?' Walsh said.

'She knows enough. Daniel threatened her this afternoon.'

'He did what?'

'You said he would go mad.'

'Where is he?'

Peg cut slices of the brack. It was still warm.

'This is delicious,' Jude said.

She watched Walsh pluck at his piece with his fingertips. Such delicate eating. It seemed incongruous in such a large man.

'Have you spoken with him, Mrs Riley?' he said.

Peg shook her head. 'It wasn't that kind of meeting.'

'But did he say anything about the ambush?'

'He did, but I didn't understand.'

Nora had finished her bit of brack and was becoming restive on her mother's lap. Fishing in her apron pocket, Peg brought out some beads. She gave them to the child, and Jude watched as Nora fingered through them, her small murmurs a parody of her mother's devotions.

Walsh sipped his tea and took another mouthful. He took his time, and Jude saw him regain his composure, take stock, take control. He was a powerful man. He wouldn't give his hand away easily, and certainly not to someone as lowly as Peg Riley.

'He must have been very badly wounded, or unconscious, for us to have believed him dead that day,' he said. 'And then the shellshock afterwards.' He shook his head. 'I wonder how much he can really remember.'

Jude rolled a small piece of brack between her fingers, forming it into a tight, hard ball. 'What do you mean?'

'He's an ill man, Miss Hursten. You'd agree about that. And he's making up all sorts in that sick head. And while I am equal to it, he cannot be allowed to threaten a young woman and her small child.'

'What exactly do you think he's making up?' Jude said.

'I was here that day. I directed the ambush. If it is my word against his, who is going to listen to him for a minute? An ex-Black and Tan against me?'

'But you've got something to lose, Mr Walsh,' Jude said. 'Or you wouldn't have come looking now.'

Jude took out cigarettes and lighter. She offered one to Walsh. He shook his head and took out his own, lit up and drew deeply, nodding slowly, as if he'd agreed with himself about something.

'I have a good business and a standing in the community,' he said. 'I've a part to play in building a new Ireland and I won't let it be jeopardised by a sick young Englishman pursuing some kind of crazy vendetta.'

'That's quite a speech,' Jude said.

Walsh leaned forward across the table. 'And you'd do well to remember that it was them were the enemy that day, not us. The Tans did things nobody should do, things they'd never dare confess to their mothers or their sweethearts, not even to you, Miss Hursten, and they deserved what they got that day. This is our country now, not yours, isn't that right, Mrs Riley?'

But Peg didn't reply. Cradling her daughter, making her arm strong across the little girl's chest, she was listening to the sounds from the other room. Small taps of wood on wood, the creak of floorboards, and finally something that everyone could hear, a knock on the door.

Nobody answered, so Daniel tugged down the latch and pushed the door with his stick. It swung open and he stepped into the kitchen as gently as a lamb.

The woman held her child tight to her, he could see that, and Jude sat beside her, one arm, protective, stretched across to the back of the woman's chair. Daniel thought Jude looked tense. Her eyes flicked about the room, and she was kneading what must have been a piece of bread on her plate with her free hand, pressing and turning it with her fingertips.

Walsh sat at the table too. His face was fierce. He wasn't doing anything, but Daniel had the feeling he would move very fast if he had to.

'Something smelt so good,' Daniel said. 'I couldn't stay out any longer.'

He walked further into the room and looked at Peg. 'I don't even know your name, I'm sorry.'

'Daniel,' Jude said, her voice rough, a warning.

'Mrs Riley,' Peg said.

'I must apologise, Mrs Riley,' he said, leaning over his stick. 'For my behaviour earlier. It was

432

horrible, terrible. I don't know what came over me, and I'm very sorry.'

'An apology, from the British. That'll be a first.' Walsh's voice was sarcastic, but Daniel only nodded. He carried on speaking to Peg as if she would understand everything he was saying.

'I wish I'd never come to your country. I should have thrown my coin in the well earlier. I'm a man who doesn't suffer guilt gladly, but underneath the brick tower I saw that I was a guilty man. It's been building up over me for a long while and I've kept it off, which is a terrible thing to do, . . . I've no guilt towards him,' he said, pointing to Walsh, 'but towards all of you. It's like a fever that comes over you, of righteousness and power, terrible vile, that makes you big and everyone else so small, so ugly. If I stop now, I'll never get what I came for. So I can't, I won't stop, and when I do, God knows. But at least I understand the dream, with the children and the horses.'

'What do you understand?' said Jude.

'I saw it just now, in there,' pointing to the bedroom, 'when I was putting the blocks to rights.'

'Saw what?' Jude said.

'One time we brought the wrong man in from a raid. We didn't know it of course, that he was the wrong one, and by the time we found it out, he'd been beaten up a bit, lost a tooth, some bruising. So we had a problem. We couldn't just say sorry, let him go, because it would make us look very bad and there'd be all kinds of trouble from it. So we beat him up some more, made no apology and then let him go. Because people would think he had to have done something to get that badly hurt. And besides, we knew that every Irish man was a Shinner at heart.'

'What are you telling us?' Walsh said.

'So you're lying on the floor and you build the blocks higher and higher, and nudge them further and further, till they're so high above your head and depending on so little that you know the crash is going to be very loud, and there's nothing you can do to prevent it.'

Daniel stepped forward, and the room gathered itself.

'Would you mind if I sat down?' he said to Peg. 'Being the only one standing.'

Peg nodded slightly, and he sat down at the end of the table. Cocking his head at Nora, he made a funny face, but she was still playing with the rosary and didn't see him.

'Pretty little girl,' he said, then turned to Jude. 'You see, you shouldn't have followed me out to this land.' He put his hand to his pocket. The knife was still there. He slipped his hand in his pocket and loosened the covering round the blade. 'Look what a sticky mess we've got into. And I don't have a very reliable history, when it comes to this little bit of valley.' He turned to Peg. 'Has she told you why we're here? About the picture she took? I don't think I explained myself very well.'

'Daniel, stop there,' Jude said.

'Has she told you about the photograph, and

Mr Walsh's early misdemeanours?'

The threat was naked. And his voice, which had begun in such a light tone, was now almost a growl.

Walsh was up and round the table faster than Jude would have thought possible.

'You're very eloquent all of a sudden,' he said, taking hold of Daniel's arm, 'but this conversation would be better held outside.'

And before Daniel had time to resist, Walsh had levered him up and out of his chair. Jude was on her feet too. She could feel the blood pulsing in her neck, her wrists, her forehead and she was scared. This was what they had come for, this moment, and now it was here it was terrifying. Walsh pulled on Daniel's arm, swung him round towards the door like some jointed doll, then turned back to face the room. He touched the peak of his cap to Peg.

'We've taken up more than enough of your time, and eaten more than enough of your delicious brack.' Walsh's voice was so smooth.

Peg looked down at her child. She stroked her soft hair.

'So,' Walsh went on, 'give my regards to Liam, and tell him I'll be in touch. As it happens, I have a bit of work for him.'

Daniel had opened the door and stepped outside, and Walsh followed. Jude knelt beside Peg.

'Will you be all right?' she said in a low tone. 'This is a strange business.'

Peg nodded. 'It's you should be worried,' she said.

'I can always make a getaway on my bike,' Jude said, forcing a smile. She picked up her camera bag. 'I'll send you the photographs.'

'Do that. Then I'll know you've survived.'

24

Daniel and Walsh had already walked down the track a short way by the time Jude got outside. They didn't turn or wait for her and it crossed her mind that it would be easy to let them go. She couldn't think why she'd gone this far. She'd had enough of Daniel's bloody war and of the ambush that had made this rough piece of nowhere into a famous site, and into a memory for Daniel that wouldn't leave him any peace. She'd taken the photograph that had brought them here, but it wasn't her battle. She could return to Cork and take the next boat home. Daniel was a grown man, this was his story, his past. She could leave him to it.

The sun had dropped so low that it kissed the far hill, and the men's shadows made long, unruly shapes, bucking and swinging over the gorse. She watched the swifts, high and noisy, playing to the crowd, the few sheep, and the rabbits below the house, heads up, ears pricked, till their appetite got the better of their caution. And she watched these two men who had already done each other such violence. They might be friends from where she stood, talking easily near the end of a long day.

They had stopped twenty yards away and were standing facing one another, and she didn't know exactly what it was she saw, but something in the bearing of both men had changed. They stood as if this was the place they had agreed and the time and now there was nothing for it but the combat. As if they might turn and count off the paces, except there was only bog and rock to pace into. Daniel had laid his stick against the wall and both men seemed very upright, poised, their arms held loosely by their sides. Neither moved, neither spoke.

Jude held her breath. She stood watching, rocking on the balls of her feet. The air was charged and the earth seemed too still. She thought she would scream with it. In France sometimes they would have to wait like this in the nursing station, knowing, because they had had a message, that an assault was about to take place and that soon men would be coming in dying and horribly wounded. The bandages would have been rolled, medical supplies checked, the stretchers and truckle beds laid out, the fires prepared and wood got in ready, water collected, so that all there was left to do was to wait. They could have read, or written letters, played cards, slept even, but they were able to do none of these. Instead they would strike up absurd arguments with one another, or pick the lice from one another's hair. So that it was a relief when eventually the first bodies arrived, and the pain and mess of them broke in on the strange trance of waiting.

She never knew what it was that snapped in the air finally. It might have been the small, alopecic dog that arrived from somewhere and stood between the two men barking; or the cloud that capped the slipping sun; or Walsh's reaching for a cigarette; or the flick of Daniel's eyes at a bird flying low. But suddenly both men were shouting, yelling, hurling words, English and Irish cadences crashing and feuding so fiercely in the sky that she couldn't pull them apart, and the words splintered out across the hillside. And before she knew she had moved, Jude was running down the hill, her eyes picking her way ahead of her between the loose stones and the pot-holes, over the streams and gullies of the landscape, her ears ringing with violence.

'You shot my friends . . . in cold blood . . . you killed . . . you killed . . . tortured my boys . . . children . . . innocent . . . unarmed . . . betrayed me . . . the women . . . all murderers . . . invaders . . . criminals . . . Shinners . . . British brutes . . . psychopaths . . . '

Looking back later, Jude didn't know who had said what. Now the men had moved in closer to one another, their hands making fists by their sides, their mouths wide with abuse shouted over and over, lips pulled back, shoulders lifted and tight with fury, and nothing was behind them and all was raw and bloody. A few yards from them, breathless, Jude slowed her pace. They didn't see her, they didn't see anything except each other. But she saw Daniel turn his shoulder and feel for his pocket. Draw his hand out slowly, his fingers wrapped tight around something. And then another inch and there was the dull gleam of metal.

She yelled. 'No! Daniel!'

And as he took the step towards Walsh and

lifted the knife, pulling his arm back, she lunged at him. Walsh jerked away, stepping back, stumbling, and Daniel's hand twisted. Jude felt a keen, cold line draw itself down her side and then her legs gave way and she sank and fell between the two men. She wondered what it was that had made her drop, till she put her hand to the line and felt the warm blood between her fingers. She lay, legs, arms, hands flat to the ground with weariness, and the grass was damp against her back, and her blood-sticky fingers were rough with the grit from the track, but she couldn't move, couldn't even raise an eyebrow in surprise.

Daniel was crouched beside her, his hands desperate, smoothing and touching her, his face wide with distress.

'Jude, oh God! I'm sorry, Jude, please. Jude.'

'Bit of a mess,' Jude said.

She saw Walsh kneel down, saw the shock in his face and she wondered, from inside her great weariness, why he or Daniel should be so surprised. They had seen bodies torn open enough before. The two men were still on each side of her, paralysed. She could hear their breathing. Walsh got to his feet and shook his head, rubbed his face with his hands, as if to free himself of some miasma.

'Keep her warm,' he said, his voice cheery and too sharp, spreading his jacket over Jude's chest. He leaned over her. 'We'll rig up a stretcher and get you back up to the house.' He patted her gently on the shoulder and winked. 'A turnaround, eh?' Then he was off at a half-jog up the hill.

Daniel stayed close, half-murmuring, shaking his head. The numbness was giving way to pain like a hot lance.

'Talk to me,' she said.

'Talk to you?'

'Tell me something.'

'What?'

'Anything. Something you remember. But not about this.'

He thought a moment. 'My brother, Johnnie. He had a collection of birds' eggs. Started it when he was small. Somebody gave him a clutch to get going, the commonest ones. Robin, blackbird, wren, blue tit. And after a while he had a good number. Some rare ones too.'

He paused. Jude had her eyes shut.

'And?' she said.

'My favourite is the heron's egg.'

'Must have been hard. They nest very high up.'

'There were herons on an island not a mile from our house. Towards Kew. We'd watched them often, standing in the shallows waiting. I'd seen one pounce a couple of times, bash a fish with its beak, then take it off to the bank and pick it clean. And the nests were high up in the trees, huge platforms of sticks. But this one year, I must have been about eight, and Johnnie ten, he swore there was a pair had built a nest in the reeds near the bank, where it was marshy. They'd do that occasionally. And he wanted an egg. So, one evening, dusk, we borrowed a rowing boat. It was tied up to the bank only a short way down from the island and they'd left the oars inside, foolish things. I say 'we', but it was Johnnie really. I don't remember what he bribed me with that time.'

Jude chuckled, then winced. 'What about your parents?' she said.

'We said we were off for a walk and Mother gave us sixpence for ices.'

Jude winced again. Daniel stared at her. He hadn't known how much he had come to want this woman to be part of things.

'Come on,' Jude said, her voice impatient.

'So we acted like it was our boat and, God knows how, managed to row across.'

'You hadn't rowed before?'

Daniel shook his head. 'First time. I waited, holding the boat, and Johnnie went for the egg. I stood there in the muddy water, trousers rolled up, and I knew we shouldn't be doing it. Even decided I'd tell him to put it back, if he got one.'

Daniel looked up the hillside towards the house. The door opened and Walsh and Peg appeared, carrying what looked like a door between them.

'Anyway,' he said, 'to cut a long story short, he came back with the egg and it was so beautiful, the shell like satin under your fingers, smooth, warm, I couldn't bear to say anything. Only we had to pretend to our mother that we'd had our ices.'

'That's it?' Jude said. 'That's the story?'

Daniel reached over and tucked a stray strand of hair away from Jude's face.

'We'll have you back to the house soon,' he said. 'And another day, some day, I'll show it to

442

you. It's beautiful. About two and a half inches long and a pale blue that is almost a green.'

'Like your eyes then?' Jude said.

'I can't see my own eyes,' he said.

When they carried her up to the house, Walsh took one end of the door, and Daniel and Peg the other, and they stumbled sometimes. Daniel watched Jude bite her lip to stop from crying out, the tug of her skin with her teeth.

They put her on the bed in the room with the building blocks and Peg told the men to build up the fire and to boil water. In the corner Nora was tucked asleep in a crib, and the women spoke in whispers.

'You're not squeamish?' Jude said.

'I managed it for the English man,' Peg said.

'I can tell you what to do,' Jude said. 'And I think it'll be a clean cut. Not like the things we saw in the trenches.'

'You were there?'

Jude nodded, her eyes shut.

'So tell me then.'

As Peg picked up the scissors and began, very gently, to cut away Jude's clothes, the two men next door stoked the fire and heated the water. They busied themselves as long as they could, bringing in turf, making tea, moving about in silence, alert to any sound from the bedroom. But once all was done, there was no more avoiding, and so, as if they had agreed this, they sat at the table and waited to begin.

Finally Walsh spoke.

'That would make us quits now,' he said.

Daniel looked puzzled, and Walsh went on.

'I've tried to kill you, and you've tried to kill me. Impressive for two military men, that we've both failed, and from such close quarters.'

'You got nearer to it than I did,' Daniel said.

'I didn't have an impassioned woman to contend with,' Walsh said. 'Only a few bullets.'

Daniel gave a small, serious smile.

'How do you think she is?' Walsh said.

'She's the one will know that best,' Daniel said. 'If she can stay conscious.'

They fell silent again. Daniel dropped his head to the table, his forehead against the wood. He couldn't bear what he'd done. Things were crowding in, but he needed to be lucid. A sound from the bedroom broke in the air between them. Walsh took out a packet of cigarettes and drummed them on the table top. Daniel pulled his head up, sat straight again. Walsh offered him the packet.

'No, thank you,' he said.

'You'd find one useful, a time like this,' Walsh said, tapping one out. 'Good for the nerves.' He lit up and drew, then leaned back in his chair.

'You'll break the legs, doing that.' Daniel's voice sounded sunken, as though he had dredged it up through the murkiest waters.

'Don't believe everything your mother told you,' Walsh said with a private smile.

He took a deep draw on the cigarette and blew the smoke high between them, a thin blue pall.

'Now listen to me and I'll tell you my part. I'm not going to start in on the history. Enough to say that the Irish had the right to their own country, and the right not to be occupied or ruled by England. And that we were never going to get you out except by force.

'Now, I'd been in the British army during the European war. There were thousands here joined up like I did. And I'd fought alongside Whittam. Lieutenant Whittam then. But you know that. What you don't know is how we came to meet up afterwards.'

'The ambush,' Daniel said.

'No. It was six months earlier. You might remember it. Three men brought in after a raid, caught with maps, explosives. And Whittam checked his papers and found one of them a wanted man already, up in Dublin.'

Daniel shook his head. 'I don't recall every bloody Shinner brought in,' he said. 'There were too many of you.'

Walsh drummed his feet against the floor, sucked hard on his cigarette and held his temper.

'All right. But this lot, one of them escaped. The wanted man. And so the other two . . . '

Daniel tapped a finger on the table.

'I do remember that,' he said. 'The other two got sent up to Dublin Castle in his place and one of them suffered heart failure during the interrogation. There was a bit of bother outside the barracks when they brought his body back to bury.'

Walsh snorted. 'I should bloody think so. Did you see what they'd done to him? Cigarette burns, bruising, broken fingers?'

'But you would say that,' Daniel said. 'It was your job, you insurgents, to make us seem as bad

445

as possible, so the ordinary people would side with you.'

Daniel could see them before him, the crowd of heads, the noise, stones being thrown, the women's hatred. He tapped the table again, hard, to make himself feel it. He must stay here, in the room, in the conversation. Not let himself drift, take flight.

Walsh stabbed out his cigarette. 'We didn't have to try very hard, did we?'

'Why are you telling me this?' Daniel said.

'Because I was the man who escaped. And before you ask how, I'll tell you. I was taken into an interrogation room, hands bound tight, legs hobbled, and there at the table was Whittam. I recognised him immediately. Imagine it. Imagine what that was like. For him as well as for me. The last time we'd seen each other, we'd been waving our discharge papers, arms round each other's shoulders, drunk as lords, swearing everlasting friendship. I had to bite my tongue hard, draw blood, to stop from saying anything.

'He had his head down writing, so he didn't see me at first. And when he looked up, his mouth dropped like a fish.'

'That's where his nickname came from,' Daniel said.

'What?' Walsh said frowning.

'His nickname. The Trout. Because of his face, and the fishing.'

'Not in the trenches,' Walsh said. 'But then there wasn't a lot of fishing in the trenches.'

'So what did he do then?'

'He came around the table, walked right up

close and called me a bastard. Spat in my face. Shouted at me, punched me, made my nose bleed. Said he wanted to be left alone with this one, and sent the others out.'

Daniel nodded.

'So he let you escape. It makes sense now.'

He remembered this. Whittam said he'd loosened the man's bonds because he thought he was unconscious and was worried they'd have another death in custody. He said he'd only left the room for a minute, but that somehow the prisoner had revived and jumped through the window while he was out. Whittam must have feigned fury, and he sent out patrols. Dublin Castle had demanded they have the other men in his stead, and one of them had come back dead.

'Whittam knew I'd be a dead man if he sent me to Dublin Castle, and he couldn't do it. Not after the trenches. We went through hell together and lived.'

'And so you told him about the ambush, didn't you? Said you'd make sure he'd survive.' Daniel said it casually, slipped it in.

'No!' Walsh was up from his chair, towering, raging.

Daniel spoke very calmly. 'We were unarmed. God, I can still see it so well. The lad who took my rifle, he smelt of sheep, and his hands were scratched. We'd surrendered, and then you shot us.'

'You're wrong, Mr Brown,' Walsh said.

Daniel went on, implacable. 'Whittam gave you our lives in exchange for saving his. All those men, my friends, my pals. That day you were

447

captured, you told him about the ambush. Where it would be, what day. And he led us into this valley and let you shoot us dead.'

Walsh's face was blazing. 'It was a battle, foggy, nothing was clear. No time to consider, you have to decide instantly. And I did what I thought necessary to protect my men. Whittam and I made no compact. He was an honourable man. He was fighting a dishonourable war, a repulsive war, but he would never have betrayed his men.'

'You thought I was dead, but lying in that ditch I heard you leave Whittam his life. 'Play dead,' you said, and you flicked your ash on my face.'

'I couldn't kill him,' Walsh said, his voice breathy and urgent. He was pacing the floor now, turning and turning like a dog on a chain.

'The others might have been honourable men too.' Daniel's voice was assertive, hectoring. 'Will Savage, Freddie Charters, George Spring.'

'What you did here was not honourable.'

'And Whittam?'

'I couldn't kill the man I had fought with. I'd saved his life.'

'So you shot him safely.'

'In the shoulder.'

'And this house? How did he find this house?'

'I told him . . . ' Walsh began, still pacing, and then he stopped. From the other room came the sound of cries, half-uttered and then held in. 'I sent him to it, told him to walk between the rocks. He'd have very likely died otherwise.'

Walsh sat down again, his movements leaden,

exhausted. 'That's the first time,' he said. 'And the last. The hardest part I ever had to play.'

The two men sat slumped and it seemed as if neither had the energy even to look at the other. The bedroom door opened and Peg came out with a bowl.

'I need some more water,' she said. 'Is it boiled?'

Walsh got to his feet and went over to pour it for her. 'How is she?'

'It's not bleeding so much now, and she tells me she's sure the blade didn't go into anything vital. But she's in a lot of pain.'

'Is there nothing we could give her?' Daniel said. 'Brandy? Whiskey?'

Peg shook her head. 'Not those. But I have some poteen.'

'Is it a smooth one?' Walsh said.

Peg nodded. 'It's very good. Father Michael liked it.'

'Give her some of that, then,' Walsh said. 'It'll take the edge off. I wouldn't mind a drop, either, if you've some spare. And he could do with a bit,' he said, nodding towards Daniel.

Peg found the bottle and poured some of the clear liquid into three small glasses. She took one back into the bedroom.

Daniel took a sip. It had a delicate flavour, not like anything he'd ever tasted, though it reminded him of the eau de vie he'd tried during his brief, abortive trip to war in France. The alcohol flooded his head and warmed his senses.

'That day won't let me be,' Daniel said.

'And now it has its final quarry,' Walsh said.

'So make your peace with it, and go back to your own country. Leave us to live in ours.'

'What would happen if I talked to people about you and Whittam? In your town? In the next town? Showed them the photograph?'

'You'd ruin me.'

'But you trust me not to?'

Walsh looked at Daniel. 'We've done worse in this country since then, than make friends with the wrong man. And we've done it to each other in the name of our own freedom. The blood's barely dry from the Civil War and people can bear no more wounds, old or new. They might ruin me for it, but they'd hate you more. Go home.' He looked over at the bedroom door. 'But don't lose her.'

25

Taken to the Murrays' house by a shocked McCarthy, Jude recovered quickly from her injury. She wouldn't say how she had come by it, and she asked the Murrays not to question Daniel, and she refused to see their doctor.

She had spoken to Dr Kelleher, and all being well, she and Daniel would travel to Cork as soon as she was strong enough. She told Dr Kelleher what had happened in the barest terms and faced a barrage of questions, at the end of which he said he would meet her only if he could also check her wound.

'I can't believe you're not seeing a doctor down there,' he said.

'I have your photograph, of the stones,' she said.

'I said, I can't believe you're not seeing a doctor,' he repeated.

'I don't want to give any explanations. And I saw hundreds of wounds worse than this one. I know what to do.'

'I still demand to see it when we meet,' he said, and Jude found herself smiling at the telephone, pleased by this man's fierce solicitude.

Daniel barely left her side, fetching trays of food up and down for her, adjusting the curtains if she needed to sleep, reading out details he thought would interest her from a book on Irish folklore he'd found in the bookshelf.

Mr Murray took Jude's silence over what had happened in his stride. He brought her up the *Irish Times* or a bowl of early brambles he'd found, and he told her about his fishing expeditions, or showed her the piece of wood he had salvaged from the tide.

Mrs Murray took nothing in her stride, but she made no headway against Jude's implacable refusal to explain, and so she was, by turns, solicitous and cross.

'So we have nothing to fear from Mr Walsh?' Mrs Murray said. 'You're asking me to trust you about this?'

'No,' Jude said. 'Nothing to fear from him, nor he from Daniel.'

'And Daniel's new spirit is to do with him?' Mrs Murray said, and Jude nodded. 'You know he hasn't had a nightmare since you both came back? So far as I know. And he speaks to me directly. He even thanked me the other day, for not quizzing him. He's got no shakes, no haunted looks. I'm afraid he's acting like a sane man.' And Jude laughed at this, which hurt.

When Daniel told her he was thinking of taking the day at Horse Island, before they had to return to Cork, Jude asked him a favour.

'Find me three stones,' she said. 'One like a bird, one like a fish and another,' and he smiled and brought her back exactly those.

In a reversal Jude could just about tolerate but which amused the others, Daniel rode the motorbike and she travelled in the sidecar on the return to Cork. She didn't ask how they'd retrieved the motorbike from the ambush road, but she was grateful to Mr Murray for the time he'd spent cleaning and tuning it, and most of all, teaching Daniel to ride it.

'I'll tell you one day,' Jude said to Mrs Murray, 'I promise.' And the older woman shook her head and hugged her hard, which hurt, and Jude returned it.

★ ★ ★

Jude walked up to the Whelans' house through the ordinary bustle of the weekday city, and it felt strange and hectic to her, who had seen so few people in the last two weeks, and those people with such force. She insisted she would walk in the face of Daniel's disapproval.

'Don't mollycoddle me,' she said, 'or I'll bite.'

And he stepped back, hands up in surrender.

But she felt self-protective and slow as people brushed past her, one hand on her side, sheltering her still-healing wound, and she was relieved when she had to climb uphill, because although the hill taxed her invalid strength to the limit, at least the streets emptied out. She stopped halfway up and looked back across the river. She could see the quay beside the Opera House where Dr Kelleher had faced her down. So much was changed since then.

She had Mrs Whelan sit for her photograph in the sitting room, dappled with the high thin sunlight that filtered through the trees, and between them, they worked hard to keep the conversation safe. Dr Kelleher had already delivered her excuse — a wound made while out sailing — but she knew Mrs Whelan was undeceived. Jude asked about the boys and their games, about Mary's piano-playing, about Catherine's ambition to nurse. They talked of Dr Kelleher. Jude asked why he'd never married and there was a sad tale years ago of broken promises and heartbreak. Mrs Whelan asked how Jude had found West Cork. Did she think it beautiful? And Jude told of finding the stone circle, and of the sea and the sailing. She didn't mention Horse Island.

Jude came out from behind her tripod. 'I'm going to try a few against the window, now.'

Mrs Whelan groaned. 'I didn't think it would be such a performance,' she said, 'just having my picture taken.'

'If it's to make the front pages of the *Illustrated News*, then it has to be the best,' Jude said and Mrs Whelan laughed.

'But what will we say to Martha?' she said. 'She's her heart set on that motorbike trip, and you won't be getting on a bike for some time, I'd say.'

Jude had been thinking about this, and she had a suggestion.

'I have a friend I met again in Castletowne,' she said. 'He drove me up from there. I've already asked him, and he'd be happy to take her for her ride.'

'Someone you knew already? And you happened to meet him in West Cork?'

Jude knew that Mrs Whelan didn't believe her, but that she didn't know what not to believe.

'From England, is he?'

Jude nodded.

'That's a bit of good fortune,' Mrs Whelan said in a droll voice.

'It's a long story,' Jude said. 'For another time.' She had the camera ready and her friend in the frame again.

'And English?' Mrs Whelan said, as if wanting to be sure.

'Yes.'

'Does the doctor know about him?'

'Yes.'

Mrs Whelan looked down at the floor, thinking. It was a beautiful shot, her face in profile, eyes lowered, she looked so like Kate, and Jude took it before she moved.

'That's taking advantage,' Mrs Whelan said. 'All right, she can ride out with this man. What's his name? So I know when he comes to the door?'

'Daniel. Daniel Brown.' Jude took another shot.

'And you're fond of him.'

Jude fiddled with her lens. 'I don't know,' she said. She unscrewed the lens and took her time, changing it for another, checking on the light, and the clouds outside the window. 'Tell me,' she said then, 'with your husband, were you ever anxious about what he did, in his job? Being a policeman?'

'Yes. There were times. Especially just before he died when it was becoming very ugly here. I was anxious for his safety first of all, but sometimes too I'd hear tell of things and I'd hope to God he wasn't part of them.'

'I loved a man who died in the Great War,' Jude said. 'We were barely grown up and we never had a chance. And now, I don't know, but I think perhaps I will love someone, and what about the things he's done.'

'In war?'

'Yes, I suppose. But they're not things you should ever do. Not even in a war, when you're allowed to kill.'

'I don't know, Jude. It can be hard not to forgive the people we love.'

The door-bell rang at this point, and Jude was relieved. She had said as much as she could bear to. When Dr Kelleher was shown in, both women greeted him as though he were the comic turn needed in the middle of some much graver piece of theatre.

'She has your stones, she tells me,' Mrs Whelan said.

'So I gather. But I am here first and foremost to view a wound, and will look at nothing else first.'

'I'm nothing to you except an interesting wound,' Jude said laughing. 'Not very gratifying.'

'Will you allow any liquid past your lips before you've viewed the wound, then? Will I bring in some tea, or are you set on your path?'

'I am set,' he said, and so Jude gave way and while Mrs Whelan went to see about the tea, she lay down on the sofa as ordered and Dr Kelleher examined the injury.

'You're a lucky young woman,' he said.

'I know.'

'Have you done what you came for?'

'I think so,' Jude said. 'And more.'

'And Matt Walsh?'

'He is a strong man, and a brave one, and he has my respect,' she said.

'There are some things that will not be laid to rest, not in this generation, but if they can be lived with and not died for, then perhaps we have done something,' Dr Kelleher said.

He had redressed Jude's wound and gently he eased her blouse back over her skin. Then he kissed her on the cheek and helped her sit again, before Mrs Whelan brought in the tea.

* * *

It was acknowledged by various people that they made a touching couple. And that they had suffered some grief, though people disagreed on what. Father Mulcahy's sister was sure that they were childhood sweethearts and, watching from the shore, Mr Murdoch said the exact same to his wife. Father Mulcahy thought it likely she had a child lost, though she wore no ring, or a parent. Mrs Murdoch, waving a handkerchief to her son, on his way to a good job in England, had observed the couple walking on to the ferry and said she thought that one or the other of them was not well, though she couldn't be sure who was supporting who.

'Perhaps it is a trip to rouse the spirits,' she said, 'or a last farewell.'

The water was skimmed silver and the sky was overcast, the atmosphere dense with moisture, as though, if you tipped back your head and opened your mouth, you might drink the air. And although it was chilly, Jude would not go in.

She had noticed all the others on the deck, of course. The priest and a woman with him, a man with a child, the child tugging all the time to be free of his father's hand, a group of four young men, friends, perhaps brothers, who Jude guessed were going to England to find work. It was something about their bearing, their bravado and their clothes, which were heavy for the time of year, as though they were being worn in anticipation of other kinds of weather.

But none of these others was as frail as Jude, and so, while she looked at all of them, she stood out, in a way that was new to her, that she didn't know.

Jude and Daniel sat and stared at the great expanse of Cork Harbour until the ferry slipped between the grey stone of Camden and Carlisle and the land took its leave, closing behind them, leaving them to the kindness of the sea.

Daniel went and leaned against the rail. After all that had gone on, it was strange to him that conversation between them should be so hard now. A pair of herons hunched waiting in the shallows on the far bank. He traced the current lines till they disappeared. When he turned back to Jude, he saw that she had lit a cigarette and shut her eyes, and that her mouth was set tight against something.

'Does it hurt?' he said. She gave no answer. 'It's cold out here. We should go in.' He had suggested this before and met with a refusal. But the air had become colder as they came closer to the open sea and except for two spots in her cheeks, she had gone very pale.

'Shall we go in?' he said again. 'Find a cup of coffee?'

'I'd like to live here,' Jude said.

'In Ireland?'

'I feel at home here. But then you couldn't, of course.'

'No. I couldn't.'

'Will you ever come back?'

Daniel shrugged. 'I'll miss the Murrays. And Horse Island. But it wouldn't be easy. I wouldn't be very welcome.' He looked over at Jude again, but she still had her eyes shut.

'I keep trying to fit two things together in my head,' she said at last, 'only the edges don't meet properly.'

'What?'

'It's like the bird table Tom brought home from school and the joints didn't fit quite, so the struts were at odd angles, but braced rigid.' Now she looked at Daniel. 'Do you know what I mean?'

He shook his head, smiling.

'Things grinding together that should sit smooth, snug. That are part of the same. When I returned from the war, I was out of kilter. I couldn't get the hang of what I came back to, and I couldn't bear very much of anything. Least of all people.'

Jude got to her feet. Daniel went to help her, but she shrugged him off and walked slowly towards the edge.

'It's odd, that it should have taken all this to change it for me finally.'

'This?' Daniel said.

Gripping the rail with one hand, Jude waved the other with a gesture that seemed to include not only the deck, but the whole boat, and the sea, and the lip of land they were steaming away from, and Daniel himself.

'That's not why I followed you over here, but that's what has happened. But you. After these last days, I don't know how to understand it. I don't know how to bear it.'

Daniel stared down at the churned water, the deep green-blue of it turned white and milky in the ferry's wake. Gulls rode the waves, lifting and dropping, lifting and dropping in search of flingings from the ship.

'They've been good, these few days, haven't they?' he said. 'I mean, aside from your wound.'

'I had a dream two nights ago,' Jude said. 'We were walking along a quiet road, like the valley, only more wooded. Just you and I. And we came across two dead figures, a man and a woman, who had been squashed, pressed into the patina of the road so that all that remained was the polished surface of them. We stopped and tried to clear them, remove the sight of them, but we couldn't. So we had to leave them there, visible, imprinted, to be walked on and driven over. Neither of us was happy, but we couldn't help it.'

'Do you think a place, a valley, a house, has all that written onto it?' he said. 'If something has happened? Do you think you can tell if you go there?'

460

He looked across at Jude, but she didn't meet his gaze.

'I didn't think you'd be the sort for dreams,' he said.

Still she didn't turn her head.

'Anyway, something's been laid to rest,' he said. 'I came here to know something. Colonel Whittam didn't take us to our deaths. And now,' he gestured back towards the land, 'now I can leave it behind.'

'If Britain hadn't invented you,' Jude said, 'the Black and Tans, the Auxiliaries, and set you down in Ireland, there would have been no ambush. No need. Whittam was your leader and he did lead you to your deaths that day. And I don't know how many Irish.'

'He was obeying orders. It was a war.'

Jude turned her face and met Daniel's gaze now.

'So he was,' she said, and her voice was like a cord of steel. 'And so were you, and your friends, Will and the others. Obeying orders to burn people out of their homes, kill their livestock, torture their sons. Obeying orders, so therefore it wasn't your fault that you did those things? Your fishing trips?' She paused. 'It's far, far too easy.'

'But I can't change it now, any more than I can make my leg strong again, and I have to go on living.'

'Your bloody leg,' Jude said. 'You live as though your scar tissue carried the pain of an entire army.'

'Whittam chose to die,' Daniel said, and now his voice matched hers, hard and cold. 'And I

461

don't know whether it was because of that day in the valley, or because he couldn't bear what he'd been a part of. But if you're not killed and you don't choose to die, then you have to go on living. I couldn't say it before, but now I can: I'm a guilty man, guilty of doing what I was told when I knew it went against humanity. I'd kept it at bay till coming over here, but I know it now. What I did was terrible and I have to live with it, walk on it, visible, imprinted, like the figures in your dream.'

Daniel stopped, exhausted. The deck was almost empty, only the father and child still there, the child snuggled now on his father's lap. Daniel turned back to the sea.

'How do you know about the fishing trips?' he said quietly. 'I never told you.'

Jude looked down at the bleached boards.

'I read your diary,' she said. 'Found it by mistake the day I went to your house. I was looking at your books.'

Daniel shook his head slowly. 'You thought you had the right to read a private diary?'

'You'd disappeared. Your parents were beside themselves. I was very worried. You'd been so strange when we'd met in Kew Gardens.'

'You've really made this your mission, haven't you?' he said. 'Who did you think you were rescuing? Me, or you?'

'That's how I found the Murrays.' Jude's voice was pleading. 'From the diary.'

'I should have guessed at something like that. I started to, when we were first with Walsh. If I hadn't been so lost, I'd have guessed. And so you think it makes it all right? Because you found me, and because what happened happened, it makes it all right to read somebody else's private words?'

'No,' Jude said. 'It doesn't, and I'm sorry.'

'Did you read it all? Every page, first to last?'

She nodded. 'That's how I know it all. What you did over here before.'

'And you still came to find me. Christ! After reading all that. Where?' he said.

She looked at him, puzzled.

'Where did you read it?'

'Over here. Sitting in a café in Cork. Enough to be sure you'd crossed the water.'

'And?'

'And it wasn't war, what you were doing.'

Daniel turned around and stared at her, his face slumped, his eyes puffy, his fingers twitching on the wooden rail, searching for something small to hold on to.

'I didn't want to hurt people, but I did, and I hated them for it all.'

'And Peg Riley? Was she your enemy too?'

Daniel shook his head, heavy and slow.

'Please, Jude, don't. I was mad with it,' he said. 'Poor woman, with her child. I don't know . . .'

'And then the knife? You would have killed Walsh.'

'It was to end it all. Put a stop to it. Make good finally.'

'Make good?'

Daniel raised his shoulders. 'A clean break. Colonel Whittam killed himself, and now Walsh would be dead. I'd know who my enemies were.'

'But your enemies aren't out there,' Jude said. 'And you're not innocent, any more than Whittam is, or Walsh.'

'You must despise me,' he said.

'No. Nothing as simple,' she said. She walked away from the rail, sat down on a bench and put her hands to her face as though she were taking a photograph. Daniel waited.

'A man I loved died in the Great War,' she said at last. 'I didn't know how much I loved him till he was gone. He was a friend of my brother's. He told me I should reach out, up, beyond the limit, and yet his death took away my head for heights.

'Leo used to laugh about it, but Richard always told me I should make it my business, taking pictures. It's nearly been the death of me, so now I'm going to follow his advice and go beyond the known ground and try to make it my life.'

'He was Mr Icarus wasn't he?' Daniel said. 'I'll never leap anywhere. I burned my wings badly.'

'But you're still here. Perhaps that's enough to be going on with.'

Jude reached inside her jacket and took out the worn envelope. Opening it, she pulled out the photograph, not of the leaping boy, but something much more ordinary. She stared at it.

'It was an innocent thing. Two friends sharing a cigarette, one wounded, the other still strong. One English, one Irish, fighting together in the same war.'

She thought how small the gestures were that

led to so much else — a cigarette, a snapshot, a change of mind — and shut her eyes against it all, and felt the wind and the fine salt spray on her face. If she'd hung fire, she could be pulling on her gauntlets now in that high office room, uncovering her typewriter. She could be suspended still, just wishing.

She thought how small they were, the two of them on this boat crossing the water. And how small each had been in the scheme of their different wars. Out here the sky met the sea. There was no need for the boat, or any tiny people, to fill the view.

The sun cracked through a break in the cloud lighting the water, and a few gulls crossed and re-crossed as though seeking the spotlight. Jude envied the arc of their wings, their flight, dipping and rising effortlessly in the air. She watched the bright shaft move across the sea. In a moment it would strike the boat.

Jude held out her hand, palm to the sky, and slowly Daniel put his own to it. Then, taking her hand away, Jude stood and walked back to the edge of the boat. She held the photograph over the sea and let it go. For a moment it lifted in the wind, flirting and dipping, the snapshot figures grinning and gone by turns, and then it fell to the water, caught in a scurry of foam. And she thought perhaps it was too easy an end, or beginning. But then that was how they often were.

Author's Note

Although *The Picture She Took* is entirely a work of fiction, the following books have been indispensable in the writing of it: *On Another Man's Wound* by Ernie O'Malley, *Guerilla Days* by Tom Barry, *My Fight for Freedom* by Dan Breen, *Flanders and other fields: Memoirs* by the Baroness de T'Serclaes, *The Cellar-House of Pervyse* by the Baroness de T'Serclaes and Mairi Chisolm, *Women Photographers* by Val Williams, *The Black and Tans* by Richard Bennett, *The I.R.A. and Its Enemies* by Peter Hart and *An Intimate History of Killing* by Joanna Bourke.

I would also particularly like to thank the staff in the Liddell Hart Centre for Military Archives, and in the Imperial War Museum Reading Room and the Imperial War Museum Photographic Archive for all their assistance.

Thanks to Clare Alexander, Karen Charlesworth, John Edington, Judy Giles, Lennie Goodings, Pat Palmer, Lionel Pilkington, Lawrence Rainey, Martin Riley, Fiona Shaw and Deb Taylor.

We do hope that you have enjoyed reading this large print book.

Did you know that all of our titles are available for purchase?

We publish a wide range of high quality large print books including:
Romances, Mysteries, Classics
General Fiction
Non Fiction and Westerns

Special interest titles available in large print are:
The Little Oxford Dictionary
Music Book
Song Book
Hymn Book
Service Book

Also available from us courtesy of Oxford University Press:
Young Readers' Dictionary
(large print edition)
Young Readers' Thesaurus
(large print edition)

For further information or a free brochure, please contact us at:
Ulverscroft Large Print Books Ltd.,
The Green, Bradgate Road, Anstey,
Leicester, LE7 7FU, England.
Tel: (00 44) 0116 236 4325
Fax: (00 44) 0116 234 0205

THE SWEETEST THING

Fiona Shaw

York in the late 1800s: Brought up a 'flitherlass' in a Yorkshire fishing village, Harriet escapes this harsh life and comes to York in search of a new one ... Gentle Samuel is an odd fish. He is a Quaker, a philanthropist, and he is a collector of photographs showing working-class girls in their working clothes. He wants Harriet's photograph for his collection ... From their meeting on a bridge comes an extraordinary tale: of the seductive power of photography; of the war between chocolate-makers; of the faultlines that cut through families and between friends; and of love forged and fought for across boundaries.

THE QUEEN OF SUBTLETIES

Suzannah Dunn

Lucy Cornwallis, King Henry VIII's confectioner, sculpts valuable sugar into 'subtleties', the centrepieces for royal celebrations. One day, she has an unusual visitor, someone curious to meet the creator of the famed sculptures: gorgeous Mark Smeaton, singer and musician. During a troubled year at court — the final year of Anne Boleyn's brief reign — Lucy and Mark become close. Anne Boleyn's rise has changed the history of England. Politically astute, intensely ambitious and uncompromising, she had easily caught King Henry's heart. But powerful forces are now gathering to make her pay for her prize — and Lucy Cornwallis is unwittingly in danger of giving them the means to do so . . .

BENEATH A SILENT MOON

Tracy Grant

London 1817. In the aftermath of the Napoleonic Wars, Melanie and Charles Fraser have traded the dangers of the war-ravaged Continent for the glittering world of the British ton. But Melanie soon realises how vital that spark of danger is to their partnership. She watches her husband transform into an aloof stranger as he steps back into his old life. Then, an assassination and a trail of clues plunge Charles and Melanie once more into danger. As they search for the truth in a labyrinth of lies, they discover that the answers cut shockingly close to their friends and family — and that beneath the shimmering veneer of London society, there lies an establishment that is rotten to its core . . .

Praise for
Siegfried Sassoon:
The Making of a War Poet 1886-1918:

'Based on years of research and well-fuelled by Sassoon's family and friends
who granted Wilson access to a mass of private papers, this is the first
volume of what promises to be the definitive biography of an important and
neglected poet. ... If the next volume is as careful and as compassionate, as
well as equally critical, then a long-delayed job will have been worth the
waiting for.'   Robert Nye, *The Scotsman*

'Meticulously researched, and beautifully written, this account of his early
life is thoroughly absorbing, and makes one eager for Volume Two.'
                              Charles Osborne, *Sunday Telegraph*

'Moorcroft Wilson's book will be invaluable to historians of the period.'
                              Andrew Motion, *The Times*

'Praise the Lord and pass the ammunition and the rhyming dictionary. The
canon of works on the Great War poets has finally been augmented by a
biography of the most influential of them all. ... provocative and perceptive
... Skilfully and unobtrusively, [Wilson] pieces together Sassoon's journey
from unquestioning patriot to outspoken dissident. ... Wilson has done much
to ... paint the features of a great poet who deserves much more than a
faceless obscurity.'   Hugh MacDonald, *The Herald (Glasgow)*

'Her mastery of detail is impressive, but what distinguishes her approach is
the way in which she analyses the war poetry, placing it in its biographical
context, and revealing Sassoon's progress from Brooke-like enthusiasm in
1914 ... through the angry satires, to the striking of a more prophetic note
in the poetry written towards the end of the war.'
                              Mark Bostridge, *Independent on Sunday*

'With care and courtesy, Moorcroft Wilson traces Sassoon's poetic development ... a solid and substantial foundation for further exploration.'
                              Times Educational Supplement

'Jean Moorcroft Wilson's account of all this is thorough and perceptive.
Unlike so many biographers, she takes trouble to build up subordinate
characters; she seems at home on the Western Front, in literary salons and
on the hunting field; her comments on Sassoon's poetry are both expert and
commonsensical. You long to see what she will make of the rest of Sassoon's
long and, presumably, anti-climactic career.'   Jeremy Lewis, *Observer*

'... a competent and meticulous work, sympathetic to the man and well-informed about his milieu.'   Robert O'Byrne, *The Irish Times (Dublin)*

'It is satisfyingly meaty in its detail ... but the story moves forward briskly ... As Sassoon's poetry is now read rather less than Owen's or Rosenberg's it is good to have Dr Wilson's sensitive account of his transformation into one of the great poets of protest.'   Michael Hall, *Country Life*

'... fair and reasonable; and, when it comes to talking about Siegfried's idealised passions for handsome young men, [Wilson] is sympathetic and engaged.'   Sebastian Faulks, *Literary Review*

'Jean Moorcroft Wilson has produced a biography many authors would have liked to have written ... discovering new material, pursuing hints from the Diaries and tracing relations and friends or their descendants. The result is a meticulous and enormously interesting book. ... her exhaustive research has enabled us to see a more rounded character and has explained much that previously was only hinted. ... In all this is a fascinating first volume.'
Richard Emeny, *Despatches*

'Jean Moorcroft Wilson's book provides an admirably detailed account of Sassoon's first thirty-two years; the tying-in of figures and events to specific poems is especially valuable. ... a necessary and engrossing piece of work ...'
Neil Powell, *Times Literary Supplement*

'... well written and frequently moving ... a fitting and timely reminder of all who gave their lives in those four terrible years ...'
John Knight, *Contemporary Review*

Siegfried Sassoon

Siegfried Sassoon

The Journey from the Trenches

A Biography
(1918-1967)

Jean Moorcroft Wilson

Duckworth

First published in 2003 by
Gerald Duckworth and Co. Ltd.
61 Frith Street, London W1D 3JL
Tel: 020 7434 4242
Fax: 020 7434 4420
enquiries@duckworth-publishers.co.uk
www.ducknet.co.uk

A CIP catalogue record for this book is available
from the British Library

ISBN 0 7156 2971 9

Typeset by Ray Davies
Printed in Great Britain
Biddles Ltd, www.biddles.co.uk

Contents

Contents

For Cecil

List of Plates

(Between pages 146 and 147)

1. Sassoon in a deck-chair, mid-1920s (Lady Anne Hill)
2. William ('Gabriel') Atkin (Cambridge University Library)
3. Henry ('Enrico') Festing-Jones and Augustus Theodore ('Theo') Bartholomew (Cambridge University Library)
4. Walter de la Mare (Copyright reserved)
5. Beverley Nichols (Bryan Connon)
6. Sassoon's collage of Osbert Sitwell (George Byam Shaw)
7. Cover of pamphlet announcing Sassoon's appointment as Literary Editor to the *Daily Herald*
8. Title-page of *The Old Century*
9. Sassoon's caricature of Edith, Osbert and Sacheverell Sitwell (William Reese)
10. Ralph Hodgson and W.J.Turner with a group of friends (John Harding)
11. Charlotte Mew (Copyright reserved)
12. Edmund Blunden (Claire Blunden)
13. T.E. Lawrence (from the *Daily Express*)
14. Sassoon *c.* 1920 (Claire Blunden)
15. Thomas Hardy (from the *Daily Express*)
16. The Long White Cloud, Bray-on-Thames (Cecil Woolf)
17. Frank Schuster and friends at the Long White Cloud (Renée Wylde)
18. Leslie George ('Anzie') Wylde (Renée Wylde)
19. Wendela Boreel and James Wylde (Renée Wylde)
20. Wendela Boreel's etching of Sassoon (Renée Wylde)
21. Sir Edward Elgar (Renée Wylde)
22. Prince Philipp of Hesse (Cambridge University Library)
23. Constance Collier and Glen Byam Shaw (George Byam Shaw)
24. Sassoon and Glen Byam Shaw with Ellen Terry (George Byam Shaw)
25. The New Menin Gate
26. Robert ('Bob') Gathorne-Hardy and Lord David Cecil (Lady Anne Hill)
27. Lady Ottoline Morrell (Roy Davids)
28. Sassoon with Bob Gathorne-Hardy, Kyrle Leng, Julian Morrell and Philip Morrell (Lady Anne Hill)
29. Sassoon with Stephen Tennant and Anne Tennant (George Byam Shaw)
30. Sassoon stripped to the waist (George Byam Shaw)

List of plates

Preface

The first half of this full-scale biography, *Siegfried Sassoon: The Making of a War Poet*, took Sassoon's life up to 11 November 1918, a few months past his thirty-second birthday. It opens with an account of the two very different cultures from which he came, his father's family of Jewish merchant princes from Baghdad and his mother's Thornycroft farming ancestors turned sculptors, painters and engineers. Charting his childhood in Kent as the second of three sons, it describes his father's abandonment of his family and premature death, Siegfried's late entry into the school system and failure to complete his formal education at Cambridge, together with his early determination to be a poet and his love of cricket and horses. It also reveals his growing distress as he tries to come to terms with his homosexuality in an age which had criminalized it.

Sassoon's seven years of leisure as a country gentleman, developing on the one hand his sporting skills, on the other his poetic technique, prelude his enthusiastic entry into the Army, first as a trooper with the Suffolk Yeomanry on 3 August 1914, then as a Special Reserve officer with the 1st Battalion of the Royal Welch Fusiliers in May 1915. The death of his younger brother in the Dardanelles in November 1915, his departure for the Western Front and his meeting with Robert Graves in France and Oscar Wilde's friend Robbie Ross in London are shown to be significant catalysts in his changing attitude towards the war. Initially a fervent patriot writing in the vein of Rupert Brooke, by the time his first collection of war poems is published in *The Old Huntsman* (1917) his tone has become predominantly angry, his style largely satirical, establishing him as one of the most influential and historically important poets of the First World War.

Despite his courageous, and, at times, almost foolhardy acts in the face of danger, which win him an MC and the nickname 'Mad Jack', Sassoon's opposition to the war hardens as he witnesses first the Battle of the Somme in July 1916, and then the Battle of Arras in April 1917. It is while convalescing from a war wound in mid-1917 and in close contact with Lady Ottoline Morrell and her pacifist friends that he makes his famous anti-war protest, which is read out in Parliament and published in *The Times* the following day.

Committed to a shell-shock hospital, Craiglockhart, in an attempt to silence him, Sassoon is brought into contact with Wilfred Owen, whose poetry is deeply affected by the encounter. He also meets there the eminent psychiatrist Dr Rivers, who persuades him to return to the fighting. After a few months in Palestine with the 25th Royal Welch Fusiliers, he returns to France in April 1918. Promoted to the rank of captain, he commands his company until July 1918, when he is wounded in the head while holding trenches in front of St Venant.

Sassoon's arrival back in England coincides with the publication of his second collection of war poems, *Counter-Attack* (1918), which cements his reputation. Volume One closes with his first visit to Thomas Hardy and his violent reaction to the triumphalism of the Armistice Day Celebrations of 11 November 1918.

Introduction

When the poet Charles Causley wrote to tell Sassoon how much he admired his work in 1952, Sassoon replied with the cheerful comment that most people seemed to think he had died in 1919: 'Of late years', he concluded, 'no one under forty writes to me except with inquiries concerning [Wilfred] Owen.'[1]

In a sense 'most people' were right; Sassoon had died, if only metaphorically, as a war poet in 1919, publishing just one book of war poems (only three of them new) that same year and a few isolated pieces on the subject in the ensuing decades. And so many of the First World War poets *had* died in the war – Owen, Rosenberg, Brooke, Grenfell and Sorley among them – that the assumption of his death is entirely understandable.

Even those who knew that Sassoon, like his close friends Graves, Blunden and Robert Nichols, had survived the conflict were inclined to assume during his lifetime, and especially after his death in 1967, that he was finished as a poet by 1919. One American critic, for example, declared with splendid rhetoric in 1956: 'Like a decommissioned man-of-war, he rests quietly at anchor in poetry's mothball fleet.'[2] And it is certainly true, as a later friend, Christopher Hollis, wrote in his obituary of Sassoon, that 'his earlier and in many ways less deep work is better known'.[3]

Yet Blunden, one of Sassoon's closest friends and an astute critic, was a warm admirer of much of his post-war verse, finding it 'extraordinary' that he should not have been recognized as the great pastoral and religious poet he believed him to be.[4] And Robert Nye, one of the finer poet-critics of our time, writes that 'it might not be excessive to suggest that the histories of poetry in English ... are going to have to be rewritten when the full scope and significance of Sassoon's journey begins to be realised.'[5]

For the fact is that though Sassoon did indeed stop writing war poetry – at least until the next war, in itself an interesting story – he did not stop writing poetry. There was a false start when he tried to direct the satire which had served him so well in the Great War toward the social scene. But his next volume, *The Heart's Journey* (1928), includes some of the best verse he ever wrote, which a fuller account of his life should help to illuminate – the main function of literary biography. (It was Cyril Connolly who observed in a review of Philip Spencer's book on Flaubert that 'to write a life of Flaubert which is not also a critical study of his work is

1

like presenting a film on the life of a seal with the words "Of course we shan't see what it does in the water" '.[6] Take a poem like 'When I'm Alone', for instance, a favourite of the Greek poet Cavafy. This was written at the end of a difficult five-year period trying to adjust to life in London after the First World War and also reflects his sense of isolation after a series of failed love affairs:

> *'When I'm alone'* – the words tripped off his tongue
> As though to be alone were nothing strange.
> *'When I was young,'* he said; *'when I was young ....'*
>
> I thought of age, and loneliness, and change.
> I thought how strange we grow when we're alone,
> And how unlike the selves that meet, and talk,
> And blow the candles out, and say good-night.
> *Alone* ... the word is life endured and known.
> It is the stillness where our spirits walk
> And all but inmost faith is overthrown.
>
> (CP, p. 180)

Sassoon wrote less poetry during the thirties and early forties as Europe lurched towards the Second World War, though there are a number of poems worth consideration from the three volumes published during this period. But in the late forties and fifties, years filled with extreme personal conflict, he produced some of the finest poetry of this second period as he struggled to find meaning in his life. T.E. Lawrence, who was a close friend until his premature death, argued that 'One of the good things about Sassoon is that he changes freely and completely', reflecting in his poetic development many of the dilemmas of the modern age.[7] Another sensitive judge of poetry claimed that 'as in so much else' Sassoon, in his truth to experience, 'is the mouthpiece of the common man of the twentieth century'.[8]

Sassoon himself believed that the poetry written in the later part of his life was far better than his war poems, which he saw as 'the improvisations of an impulsive, intolerant, immature young creature, under the extreme stress of experience'.[9] He grew 'ever more impatient' according to one close friend 'at the constant demand for his war poems'.[10]

And it is not only the poetry of this second period which merits closer consideration. For at the age of forty, Sassoon did what few writers in any language have successfully managed; he turned to a different medium and produced one of the prose classics of twentieth-century literature, *Memoirs of a Fox-Hunting Man* (1928). This was followed with another classic, this time of war novels, *Memoirs of an Infantry Officer* (1930), then by an equally absorbing fictionalized account of his experience at Craiglockhart Hospital for Nervous Diseases and his friendship with the remarkable Dr Rivers, *Sherston's Progress* (1936). Less commercially successful were the three volumes of straight autobiography which followed. Yet the first of these, *The Old Century* (1938), is as good if not better than *Fox-Hunting Man* in its lyrical evocations of childhood and that pre-1914 world. As autobiography, however, all three contain intriguing distortions and omissions and stop short at 1920, yet another incitement to explore his life after that in more detail.

When *Fox-Hunting Man* was published in 1928, it received largely glowing reviews, but like most authors Sassoon seems to have cared more about the few adverse ones. He was particularly irritated by Robert Graves's charge that, by writing in the guise of George Sherston, he had avoided facing the moral problems inherent in the autobiographical presentation of experience: 'He leaves the reader to decide for him', Graves argued, 'whether the book is sincere or ironical. So it has often been with him ... even with some of his war poems.'[11]

Relations between the two previously very close friends were becoming strained by 1928 when this review appeared and by 1930, the year after Graves's *Goodbye to All That* had so offended Sassoon that he had had the first edition withdrawn, their relationship was more or less at an end. But Sassoon still needed to explain to Graves why he could never entirely 'be himself' (as Graves had advised) in his work: 'Everyone wants to be himself, if he is any good ...' he wrote to Graves. 'Is it so easy when one is in my quandary – for the duration of my life – as regards "temperament" [i.e. sexuality]?'[12] Seven years earlier he had written in his diary: 'I suppose, at the back of all this smothering of my natural impulsiveness ... there is a grievance against society for refusing to allow me to write freely.'[13] And as long as 'society' continued to place homosexuality outside the law – which it did, ironically, till the year Sassoon died – he continued to suffer both as an artist and as a man.

For there is no doubting the importance of Sassoon's sexuality on him, especially in this second, less well-known period. Biographers face many problems in their work, but one of their main dilemmas seems to me the extent to which they explore this area without being thought prurient. There is, of course, no ready-made solution and the treatment will inevitably vary in each case, depending on how deeply it has affected the subject's life and work. If, as in the case of Sassoon, it has had a profound effect, then it must clearly be examined in detail. He himself, as I pointed out in my first volume, wanted to write what he called 'a Madame Bovary of sexual inversion', but had finally to accept that this would not be possible in his own lifetime.[14]

His homosexuality dominated his life, at least in the twenties and early thirties, involving him in a number of extraordinary relationships – with the German great-grandson of Queen Victoria and nephew of the Kaiser, Prince Philipp of Hesse, for instance, Ivor Novello and the Hon. Stephen Tennant among others. Though some of these connections are known, the details are not, or have been suppressed. Other equally interesting liaisons, together with their direct effect on his work, are documented here for the first time. Sassoon's love letters to Gabriel Atkin and Stephen Tennant's to Sassoon came to light just before I completed this book, as well as a number of passionate love poems, and I have recently discovered the unpublished autobiography of Atkin, all of which has enabled me to give a more rounded view. Prince Philipp's letters too, only recently placed in the public domain, have helped fill out the picture.

Unpublished material abounds. Among other things Sassoon was a prolific correspondent, regarding letter-writing as his 'safety-valve'.[15] There are letters to and from many well-known writers, such as Wells, Bennett, Hardy, de la Mare, Osbert Sitwell and Edmund Blunden, as well as virtually forgotten authors like Ralph Hodgson and Frank Swinnerton, both of whom elicited memorable replies from Sassoon.

For as T.H. White, who corresponded with Sassoon after meeting him in the thirties, claimed, Sassoon was among 'the best of contemporary letter-writers, many of his missives being small works of art in themselves'.[16] Another brilliant correspondent of the period, Walter de la Mare, believed that Sassoon was 'born to be a letter-writer' and he certainly spent a great deal of his life thus occupied.[17] And since he corresponded not only with men and women of letters, but also with artists, musicians and public figures, as well as less well-known people, the study of Sassoon is the study of an age. Since, too, he was caught up in many of the major literary and political conflicts of his time, this is as much a book for the social historian as for the lover of literature. In addition, because many of the recipients were close friends of Sassoon and wrote frankly to him about their work and their lives, a biography of Sassoon provides important insights into significant figures of the period. The letters between him and Max Beerbohm, for example, who disappeared from London life in 1910 to live in Italy, throw light as much on the elusive caricaturist as on the poet.

Even when, as is rarely the case, Sassoon's side of the correspondence is not available, it is not without interest. Edith Sitwell's letters to him, for instance, show that 'stormy spinster petrel' (as he called her) in a very different, much kinder light than the popular picture of her, as well as providing countless examples of her coruscating wit. Writing to him in 1931 about a trip to Wigan, for instance, she tells him with a satiric dig at American tourists: 'Wigan was just a great big primitive experience, and I was put to sleep on a mattress which had obviously been stuffed with the vertebrae of my hostess's defunct mother ... She died, so I was told, just after Christmas, so the vertebrae had had time to stiffen and turn cold.'[18]

More crucially for the biographer of Sassoon, since his letters – unlike his diary – cover every period, if not every day, of his life after 1918, they provide an unparalleled record of his thoughts and feelings. They also give a more reliable picture of his reactions at the time; once sent they could not be recalled or altered, in contrast to his diary, which he heavily revised and cut: useful as it is to have, it is at best a censored document. The letters undoubtedly provide a less self-conscious, less varnished account of his life. Details of his affair with Gabriel Atkin, for example, were removed from his diary (as were accounts of his other homosexual affairs) but are given passionate and explicit expression in the letters.

Such relationships reveal a rather different aspect of Sassoon's character, yet another reason for looking more closely at his life after the Great War. Whereas the trenches had brought out his daring and love of danger, as well as his kindness and sense of responsibility towards his men, his homosexual affairs highlight his generosity, a need to control and dominate verging sometimes on the sadistic, and an increasing tendency to escape into the past. The last, which he thought of as 'giv[ing] the modern world the slip', accounts to a large extent for the kind of prose he chose to write, every one of his seven prose books dealing with the past in one form or another.[19] *The Old Century*, for instance, was a loving recreation of his childhood, already described in fictional terms in *Fox-Hunting Man*, and as such gave him great pleasure: 'The delight of being back again in that other world of transmuted memory', he wrote to Beerbohm, 'is like coming to life again after – not being very much alive!'[20]

Yet his character did not basically change after 1918. Though, as Hollis noted, his life is commonly thought of in two parts – 'that of the young rebel and that of the old conservative' – the one followed logically from the other and sprang quite naturally from a character which Sassoon himself recognized as 'kaleidoscopic' as early as 1918.[21] The journalist Maurice Wiggin, who met him late in life and became a friend, confirms that it was this quality which predominated to the end:

Sassoon was a notable bundle of contradictions – and he knew it. When I photographed him in the library of Heytesbury he told me that he believed one side of his face showed the poet Siegfried Sassoon, the other George Sherston, the fox-hunting man. He was vividly aware of himself alternating between self-mockery and absorption in the minor-prophet role. He was both shy and ambitious, magnanimous and censorious, acute and simplistic, humble and disarmingly vain. Fox-hunter and poet, predator and conservationist, brave soldier and pacifist, iconoclastic radical satirist and order-loving RC convert: his many-sidedness makes him one of the most interesting literary figures of the century.[22]

To be 'interesting' is one thing, to lead an exciting life quite another. 'The life of a literary man once he has ceased to be young and enterprising, is always likely to be uneventful outwardly,' Sassoon wrote in 1948: 'He just sits there and writes his books.'[23] This was certainly not true of the first part of his own life. Nor, despite the common misconception that his life after 1918 was an 'arid desert', is it true of the second. Over and over again, just as he appears to be settling into a predictable pattern, he changes. And it is this unpredictability, together with the unfamiliarity of many of the details of this period, which makes the story of late 1918 to 1967 even more fascinating, I believe, than his development as a war poet. For example, whilst recognizing that his homosexual affairs were unlikely to lead to lasting happiness, he appeared to see no alternative in the twenties and early thirties. So that it comes as a complete shock to find him marrying very suddenly in 1933.

Perhaps the most unexpected turn in the life of the man who wrote that deeply sardonic line about the carnage in the trenches – 'And the Bishop said, "The ways of God are strange!" ' ('They', CP, p. 24) – the man who turned against his childhood Anglican faith during the First World War, is his entry into the Catholic Church at the age of seventy. Sassoon's must be among the most illustrious conversions of the twentieth century and it was my good fortune to interview the woman who started the whole process, Mother Margaret Mary, shortly before she became too ill for visitors. When she agreed to see me in 1990 at the Convent of the Assumption, Kensington Square (a place Sassoon himself had visited many times) I took a tape-recorder along and she spoke to me at length about Sassoon. A tiny, frail figure in her mid-eighties, she was nevertheless full of life and fun, helping me to understand why Sassoon had felt attracted to her faith and able to trust her at such a crucial point in his life. I particularly enjoyed her answer to my question, 'Why did you place an embargo on your correspondence with Sassoon till 1992' (an embargo she had just offered to lift for me) – 'Oh, but I thought I'd be long dead by then,' she said, merrily. For one of the advantages of dealing with this later period of Sassoon's life has been that there are (or in Mother Margaret Mary's case were) still many people alive who knew him and were happy to talk about him.

Even more importantly than the people I have been able to interview and the new material I have gathered, there is a need to look at Sassoon's life more closely in relation to his work of the post-war years, which has undoubtedly been a victim of his fame as a First World War poet and is, I believe, still undervalued. When Sassoon was diagnosed with an incurable disease in 1967, for instance, his literary executor, Rupert Hart-Davis, wrote to warn his friends that he had not long to live. The day he died – Friday, 1 September – Hart-Davis received a reply from a close admirer: 'Your warning grieves me: if Sassoon dies, the Somme is over ...'[24] Allowing for the understandable emotion, it is a revealing statement, suggesting that for many people Sassoon had come to symbolize all the heroisms and horrors of the Great War. He himself might genuinely believe in 1952 that 'most people' thought he had died in 1919, but here, only fifteen years later, is clear proof of his place in at least one man's history.

And I would argue that by the end of what we must now call 'the old century' and the beginning of the new, Sassoon's reputation should be broadened to include his later work. It was a warm admirer of that later work, Dame Felicitas Corrigan, who best expressed the full range of his achievement when she wrote to Sassoon the year before his death:

> To me you are a twentieth century portent: you have summed up in your personal experience the war-tortured, spiritually-bewildered, forsaken and blindly-seeking men of our times.[25]

1

'Pilgrimages to Poets, Post-Armistice Parties and Other Diversions' (November-December 1918)

When you were an angel and I was a god,
Earthly-fair were the paths that we trod;
You, from your heaven of Saints at the Throne,
Banished, to wander, gold-haired and alone;
And I, from my pagan Paradise hurled,
Thro' sun-shot cities of cloud to the world.

Humble you came, with your calm, clear eyes,
And parted lips; but your spirit was wise
With raptures of music and light that you'd lost ...
So we loved and were happy, nor counted the cost.
For the gates were barred, and the way was hard
Up to the bastions of Heaven proud-starred;
And I was a god no more. But you sprang
To the peace of my arms ... and an angel sang.

(Unpublished poem by
Sassoon, 'For Gabriel',
dated 20 November 1918)

Siegfried Sassoon lay in the arms of a young soldier in a Margate hotel. The 20 November 1918, it was only nine days after the end of a war which had left him with a deepened consciousness of peacetime values and enjoyments, together with a new determination to 'get the best out of life'.[1] While his years in the army had given a certain legitimacy to his love of men, his responsibilities as an officer had prevented him from expressing this in any but the most altruistic way. Once freed of such restraints, however, he had rushed headlong into a relationship which would have been unthinkable to him before the war. He was now experiencing for the first time a physical and emotional fulfilment beyond any previous imaginings. All his early romantic impulses, which had seemed out of place during the war, came flooding back as the young man left him, alone with his thoughts:

Lovers

You were glad tonight: and now you've gone away.
Flushed in the dark, you put your dreams to bed;
But as you fall asleep I hear you say
Those tired sweet drowsy words we left unsaid.

I am alone: but in the windless night
I listen to the gurgling rain that veils
The gloom with peace: and whispering of your white
Limbs, and your mouth that stormed my throat with bliss,
The rain becomes your voice, and tells me tales
That crowd my heart with memories of your kiss.

Sleep well: for I can follow you, to bless
And lull your distant beauty where you roam;
And with wild songs of hoarded loveliness
Recall you to these arms that were your home.[2]

When 'Lovers' was eventually published in *Collected Poems*, the middle stanza with its explicit physical details was omitted, and to many people, even close friends, this aspect of Sassoon's life was unknown. The more familiar image of him remained that of 'Mad Jack', the daring soldier, or the shy, impetuous poet. Only three days before 'Lovers' was written, for example, he had been sitting modestly at the feet of Walter de la Mare, full of reverence for de la Mare's poetic genius, the 'crowding enchantments of his word magic'.[3]

Sassoon's commitment to poetry had been essentially unchanged by the war, but there was yet another side to him which had been affected by it as strongly as his sexual mores. His contact in the army with working-class men, already encouraged by the great sexual pioneer Edward Carpenter in the years preceding 1914, had made him far more socially and politically aware than in his privileged youth. And his return to post-war London increased this consciousness, making him realize that it was the working classes that were bearing the brunt of the immense cost of the fighting, especially in the labour market. Jobs were scarce and wages low, the purchasing power of money being roughly one-third of what it had been in 1914. Though modest pensions and benefits were paid to war widows and war veterans, there was still a great deal of individual hardship. This was already visible in the capital, where disabled ex-servicemen begged in the streets alongside the triumphant crowds.

Sassoon's friendship with the psychiatrist Dr Rivers, who had treated him at Craiglockhart Nerve Hospital in 1917, strengthened his growing political awareness.[4] Though he had turned down the Hampstead Labour Party's invitation to become its parliamentary candidate in September 1918, less than two days after the Armistice he was consulting Rivers about a possible future in politics.

1. 'Pilgrimages to Poets ... and Other Diversions (1918)

There were, then, at least three very different sides to Sassoon at the end of 1918. And his 'reality' seemed, even to himself, 'a mere transitory and fleeting illusion', taking one form one day and another the next according to the prevailing conditions.[5]

*

The immediate post-war years were a crucial period in Sassoon's life and bear close examination, particularly his relationships. He himself told a friend in 1961 that after the Armistice his existence was 'so distracted and experimental and confused' that 'a lot of the old connections were jettisoned'.[6] What strikes the onlooker, however, is how many of them were retained.

One of his closest friends during the war had been the art connoisseur Robbie Ross, known to later generations mainly as the man who had stood by Oscar Wilde in his greatest troubles. Ross more than anyone had encouraged Sassoon's anti-war stance and had advanced his literary career by introducing him to many influential figures, such as H.G. Wells and Arnold Bennett, during their three years' friendship. And though Ross himself was no longer alive by November 1918, having died prematurely of heart failure the previous month, Sassoon's first visit on his return to London was to one of Ross's close friends, Richmond Temple, and his second to Ross's constant companion, the Treasury official Roderick Meiklejohn, who had written faithfully to Sassoon throughout the war. He also looked up Ross's oldest friend, More Adey, and his brother, Alex Ross.

Sassoon's choice of Temple for his first London contact was deliberate. Since Temple, like Ross, was an ardent admirer of his anti-war poetry, he could be relied on to share Sassoon's disgust at what he dismissed as 'the orgy of patriotic demonstrations' which met him on his arrival in the capital late on Armistice Day.[7] Temple, who was seven years younger than Sassoon's thirty-two and had served in the Air Force, seemed to the poet an 'odd character'.[8] Though he was to move in very different circles from him after the war, as director first of the Savoy and Berkeley hotels, later the Dorchester, like Ross he was anxious to help, presenting Sassoon with a new car in 1924 to encourage him to get out of London, for instance, or lending him money in emergencies. On this occasion he welcomed Sassoon to his Mayfair flat and insisted on taking him to an Armistice dinner, though of a kind calculated to annoy him with its triumphalism. By the end of an evening which both agreed had been an utter 'wash-out', Sassoon felt more than ever convinced that the war had been a 'loathsome tragedy'.[9] Flag-waving, especially by civilians, seemed to him completely out of place, as a poem written the next day but hitherto not published (ms. at Cambridge University Library), shows:

11

The Patriot
He waved his flag when War began;
A staunch and thriving English man.
And now, when fighting's finished,
He buys the Union Jack again
And demonstrates with might and main,
His ardour undiminished.

A patriot soul, I watch him stand
To shake some wounded soldier's hand.
For he's been well defended.
I see him marching with the crowd,
Cheering for Victory, flushed and proud
Because the danger's ended.

Dr Rivers, with whom Sassoon and Temple dined the next day, struck Sassoon as an 'ideal moderator of victorious agitations'.[10] His studies in anthropology and psychiatry had prepared him for a wide range of human behaviour and he was neither shocked nor surprised by the frenzied celebrations. Nor, unlike Sassoon, was he judgemental. But he was unable to share the crowd's enthusiasm, having been to some extent influenced by Sassoon's own criticisms of the war at the very moment he was persuading him to return to the fighting. Their Craiglockhart debate had brought them very close, Rivers replacing Sassoon's earlier acquaintances as a still much-needed mentor and father figure.

It was not that Sassoon felt less affectionate towards his older friends, particularly the one who had launched him on the literary scene, Sir Edmund Gosse. The day after his dinner with Rivers, he hurried to Hanover Terrace to renew contact with the earliest of his patrons. Though now less in awe of that arbiter of public taste and establishment figure and decidedly critical of Gosse's unquestioning acceptance of the war, he was still very grateful to his Uncle Hamo's old friend and ready to entertain him with accounts of his recent visits to Thomas Hardy and Robert Bridges. He found Gosse, though over seventy and in bed with bronchitis, as charming and witty as ever and was particularly amused by his suggestion that his young friend should write a long poem about rural life. (This was shrewder than Sassoon realized at the time and would form the germ of one of his most successful books, *Memoirs of a Fox-Hunting Man*.)

He was beginning to find his other early patron, Edward Marsh, a distinguished civil servant and friend of Winston Churchill, less sympathetic. He continued to admire Marsh's generous support and encouragement of young painters and writers, notably his stable of 'Georgian' poets, but was becoming increasingly critical of Marsh's need for constant social distractions. Though he had not yet arrived at his later opinion, that 'dear old Eddy was hollow inside', his experiences at the Front had made Marsh's lifestyle seem essentially frivolous.[11] Nevertheless, it was to Marsh's flat in Raymond Buildings, Grays Inn, that he lugged his suitcase next on 12 November. (The lease on his own flat in the same building had lapsed in 1917.) Armistice celebrations raged on and he longed for a quiet evening with Eddy. But Marsh was rarely without company and Sassoon found himself instead listening to an interminable reading by John Drinkwater of his latest poems.[12] He had corresponded regularly with Drinkwater since 1915, when he wrote to ask the advice of the older, more established poet about his work, but the two never became close friends. Sassoon found Drinkwater's work, like that of most of the other Georgians, insipid and by the late twenties thought him 'a (second-rate) fraud'.[13] By the early thirties he was describing Drinkwater unkindly as 'a pushful poet whom nobody needs'.[14]

He met a number of other Georgian poets during this stay at Marsh's, being taken to dine on 13 November with W.J. Turner[15] and on the 14th with Wilfrid Gibson.[16] Then on the 23rd, during his pilgrimage to de la Mare, he met Gibson again and was introduced to John Freeman.[17] Both Gibson and Freeman he dismissed as worthy but dull. Turner, who struck him as having real imagination, he wanted to know better. But it was de la Mare who most impressed him, or rather, as he himself might have put it, cast a spell on him:

> De la Mare is the most wonderful and interesting and sympathetic and mystery-haunted manuscript he has ever written. He is a human being to whom I respond with the utmost enthusiasm. I am bubbling over with excitement when I am with him ... His mind is an enchanted landscape lit by unearthly gleams and fiery auguries.[18]

There could not have been a greater contrast between de la Mare's and Marsh's worlds, though it was Marsh himself who had arranged the visit to de la Mare. During his stay with Marsh, Sassoon had been wined, dined and taken to society parties or ballets almost nightly. On 13 November, for example, Marsh had surpassed himself, not only dining his younger friend at his club, Brooks's, but afterwards whisking him off to a party given by Winston Churchill's mother. Sassoon had already met Lady Randolph while convalescing from a war wound at Lancaster Gate hospital, but was not prepared for the sheer number of distinguished guests gathered for her musical evening and listed them carefully in his diary.[19] He was even more impressed by the geniality of Winston Churchill, whom he also knew slightly through Marsh. Though threatening to have him shot as 'a bloody young Bolshevik', Churchill clearly admired his war poetry, much of which he knew by heart.

The contrast with an evening spent at de la Mare's modest suburban house in south London and his almost excessively 'ordinary' lifestyle affected Sassoon deeply. After more than a week of high life, it was a relief to be on a train clanking its way from Crystal Palace to Anerley, where de la Mare lived with his wife and four children in no very great style. Yet such was his conviction of de la Mare's magic, that he found it difficult to believe that he 'permanently existed anywhere away from the timeless province of his imagination'.[20]

It was disconcerting to discover that, like his house, there was nothing outwardly mysterious about his humorous and hospitable host. As Sassoon, Freeman, Gibson and the de la Mare family sat eating a simple supper in the small, dusky dining room, the older poet seemed to Sassoon as homely and natural as Hardy, his mind firmly on details of everyday existence. Even when the talk turned to literature, with a learned discussion of the prosody of Coventry Patmore and the problems of the later Henry James, subjects on which Sassoon felt very ignorant, de la Mare continued to be his 'everyday' self.[21] It was only when Sassoon mentioned his visit to Hardy that de la Mare became more meditative. And when they moved on to James's short stories, Sassoon finally caught a glimpse of the 'wizardry' that had so mesmerized him in de la Mare's work. Watching his host's face, half in shadow as he enthused about James's macabre masterpiece, *The Turn of the Screw*, Sassoon detected the 'haunting and haunted presence of genius' in his eyes and the 'allurement of supernatural solicitings' in his voice.[22]

Sassoon later realized that one had to be alone with de la Mare before the full extent of his 'sorcery' revealed itself. He felt the same about Hardy, whom he christened the 'Wessex wizard'.[23] Since Hardy and de la Mare were two of the three writers he most admired by the end of his life, it is reasonable to assume that his definition of genius included the notion of being 'possessed' by a force greater than the individual self. He certainly believed that some of his own best poems – 'Everyone Sang', for instance – were dictated from another, more mysterious world with which the true artist was in touch. Like de la Mare, he subscribed to the need for lucidity, order, arrangement, balance, coherence, proportion, progression, together with an evident pattern and design in a work of art; and in humour, wit and irony too.[24] But he also shared de la Mare's belief that the finest works contained something less clearly definable, imagination, even vision; and 'always profound if hidden feeling, a sentient heart, and at best magnanimity'.[25]

He had admired de la Mare's own work since 1910, when he read 'All That's Past' in the *Thrush* magazine, and had first dared to write to him after reading *The Listeners* in 1912. De la Mare's poetry had provided him, especially during the war, with an escape from 'the beastliness of life',[26] lines like the opening of 'Farewell', for example: 'Look thy last on all things lovely, / Every hour ...' Sassoon, who was suspicious of Modernist 'cleverness' in poetry, identified closely with the simplicity he found in the older man's work. When he told another poet that de la Mare was not 'clever', he meant it as praise.[27] This may help to explain why childhood played such an important part in both writers' imagination, a fact which would become more evident when Sassoon, like de la Mare, branched into prose with *Fox-Hunting Man*. They were further united by a love of nature which bordered on the mystical and a special admiration for the seventeenth-century mystic poets Vaughan and Traherne. Both were capable of great seriousness but also of an almost childish playfulness; once they got to know each other well, their conversation might range from the origins of such dialect words as 'woosh', 'gonk' and 'diddlepop' to an equally animated discussion of the poet's role in life.[28] 'To talk to another poet about poetry on a fine summer day in a green garden – could anything be better?' Sassoon was to write of a visit to de la Mare in 1927.[29]

There were other similarities – they were both shy, both essentially solitary – but it was their differences Sassoon most enjoyed. He saw de la Mare as quick and lively where he was heavy and slow, the older man's sayings 'darting away' from his 'sententious scrutinizings like trout at the edge of a pool'.[30] Their physical dissimilarity underlined the point, de la Mare's small build and almost elfin face contrasting sharply with Sassoon's taller, more muscular frame and conventionally handsome features. After a lifetime's friendship Sassoon's epitaph on de la Mare would be that he was 'unlike anyone else'.[31]

Sassoon's visits to the homes of celebrated authors in November 1918 included one different in almost every way from his trek to Anerley, and reflected his increased status in post-war England. On 3 November he had received an invitation from a leading novelist of the day, John Galsworthy, then still engaged on his *Forsyte Saga*.[32] If de la Mare epitomized the other-worldly, Galsworthy stood for the worldly, or at least worldly success. When Sassoon did finally dine with Galsworthy and his 'super-excellent' wife Ada on 15 November, it was to affluent Hampstead not the depths of south London he went. The house itself, Grove Lodge, was very beautiful and very old, unlike de la Mare's modest dwelling, and everything about it emanated signs of success, from the dark polished dining table to the vintage '87 port.[33]

Galsworthy himself, whose background included Harrow, Oxford and independent means, impressed Sassoon as 'strikingly handsome' but essentially modest and unegotistical.[34] Failing to penetrate the 'modest O.M. mask' of his host, his main memory of the evening was of 'comfort and kindness', a far cry from his magical evening with de la Mare.[35] Though he had more in common with Galsworthy on the surface, a passion for cricket and horses, for instance, he felt much closer to de la Mare and his friendship with Galsworthy would fade out. He was never quite able to accept Galsworthy as a first-rate writer, though he did find him an 'awfully nice' man and an 'admirable character'.[36] Later he would come to feel that he had underestimated him both as a writer and a man.[37]

Galsworthy had invited him to dinner ostensibly to discuss a contribution to his magazine, *Reveille*, and in that respect the evening was a complete success.[38] Sassoon had, in fact, spent the whole day promoting his work, having lunch with his publisher, Heinemann, to discuss his next volume and visiting the editor of the *Nation*, H.W. Massingham, to offer him two poems.[39] Though he later became critical of the *Nation*, possibly because of what he considered 'rude' remarks in it about Gosse, in November 1918 he was pleased to have both his poems accepted for publication.[40]

He had returned from France in July 1918 determined to pursue his ambitions as a poet. The problem was that, with the passing of the war, he was left without a subject, as he had been before its start. His horror at the carnage had resulted in some highly successful poetry, but with the arrival of peace he could no longer mine that rich vein. It was a dilemma that contributed significantly to his restlessness in the immediate post-war years.

*

Like the majority of those who have left home – and it took him far longer than most to do so – Sassoon felt comfortable neither at home nor away from it to begin with. When he finally visited his mother on 18 November, he stayed only two nights. The rambling Victorian house near Paddock Wood in Kent, where he had spent the greater part of his twenty-eight years before the war, had a neglected and melancholy feel to it. His mother, still mourning the death of the youngest of her three sons, Hamo, was far from stimulating company.[41] She continued to disagree strongly with her middle son about the war and there were few safe subjects left for them to discuss, apart from gardening, food and the weather. Still technically his 'home', Weirleigh had lost its childhood power to enchant. Though he continued trying to recreate its pre-war charm, returning for six days at the beginning of December, for instance, and spending the whole of Christmas and New Year there, Sassoon was finally separating himself emotionally from his childhood.

He made several attempts, however, to re-establish his pre-war existence, where the outward pattern of his life had been shaped round various seasonal sports. Autumn was traditionally the time he played golf, usually with one of his friends from his prep school, the New Beacon, or his crammer, Henley House. His first game after the war was with an ex-teacher from the latter, George Wilson, a 'very fine chap' who was now a stockbroker in the City.[42] The four days they spent together at Rye from 29 November were a healthy corrective, Sassoon felt, to any 'swollenhead-edness' caused by his recent literary success, since Wilson beat him soundly. (With a handicap of six Sassoon was a reasonably good player.)

Then, on 4 December, there were six days of hunting with his old pack, the Southdown. Pre-war activities inevitably brought him into contact with pre-war friends and on this occasion it was with Geoffrey ('Geoff') Harbord, the brother of his greatest sporting acquaintance, Gordon. It was the first time he had seen Geoff since Gordon's death at the Front in 1917

16

and he almost certainly suffered the kind of 'bad heartache' he had experienced in visiting Ross's close friends.[43] Hunting itself made him want to return to 'the old foolish existence of getting healthily tired four days a week' but after his war experiences he now realized that it led 'nowhere'.

Another, less strenuous, activity he had taken up just before the war, though like hunting he could not afford it, was the ballet. His intense enjoyment of the Russian Ballet in 1914 had been interrupted by the outbreak of hostilities and he now returned to it with renewed fervour, either with Marsh or a more recently acquired friend, Osbert Sitwell.

Sitwell, himself an aristocrat, moved in social circles as dazzling, if not more so, than Marsh's and there was some vying between them for Sassoon's attention. But Sitwell, unlike Marsh, had strong artistic aspirations of his own and gradually became of more interest to Sassoon. Their relationship, which had developed rapidly in the summer of 1918 during an afternoon spent with Wilfred Owen on his last leave, was to be of some significance to Sassoon during the 1920s. So, too, would his friendship with Osbert's poet-sister, Edith Sitwell. Sassoon had met Edith briefly in October 1918 and Osbert now reintroduced him to her at his house in Swan Walk, Chelsea. He shared the house with his younger brother Sacheverell ('Sachie'), who would also play a part in Sassoon's life during the twenties, though more minor than either of his siblings.

The pull of all these different worlds and his frantic rush from one to the other made Sassoon 'positively dizzy' to contemplate in later years.[44] His life became, in his own words, 'a rabble of disordered occurrences'.[45] This seemed to him acceptable in all the circumstances. What troubled him about the 'kaleidoscopic young man' he looked back on, however, was the 'remembered inconsistency' of his response to different people.[46] When he revisited friends in Cambridge, for example, especially the musicologist Edward Dent, and the University Librarian Theodore ('Theo') Bartholomew, he was drawn into an explicitly homosexual circle which would have puzzled and shocked people like his mother or Gosse.

He had first met Dent through the curator of the Fitzwilliam Museum, Sydney Carlyle Cockerell, during an army training course at Cambridge in mid-1915.[48] Cockerell would remain a good friend for forty-seven years, but Sassoon had reservations about him. While he admired the vast erudition of the man who had been secretary to William Morris at the Kelmscott Press, and was a connoisseur of great distinction, he could never fully identify with Cockerell's businesslike, sometimes calculating approach to people.

But there was another side to the man he nicknamed 'Sir Sydney Conundrum' and one he admired greatly, his determination to help struggling artists. Cockerell was to join with Sassoon in rescuing a number of penniless writers or their families in the twenties, as well as introducing his younger friend to some interesting but neglected authors. And their numerous letters to each other over the years form a valuable record of Sassoon's opinions on the arts, especially literature.

While Sassoon's friendship with Cockerell would survive, his relationship with Dent would fade out after the war. The letters with which he had inundated Dent between August 1915 and the Armistice were reduced to a trickle, then dried up completely by the mid-twenties. One reason for the correspondence had been Dent's generous help with the typing and placing of his war poems; without that motive Sassoon's interest in Dent appears to have flagged.

Even by 16 November 1918, the weekend Sassoon visited Cambridge, it is noticeable that Dent is being replaced by Theo, to whom he had originally introduced Sassoon.[49] Slightly built, with delicate features, pale complexion and dark brown eyes and hair, Theo was only four years older than Sassoon and much nearer to him in age than Dent. Strongly drawn to Sassoon, he was to become a close confidant for the next few years and to remain on good terms with him until his premature death in 1933. Beside Dent they had several friends in common, notably Edward Carpenter and E.M. Forster. Theo would also introduce Sassoon to a writer whose friendship would mean a great deal to him in the twenties, Henry ('Enrico') Festing-Jones, the former companion and literary executor of Samuel Butler.

Osbert Sitwell rather witheringly dismissed Theo as 'one of the Cambridge kittens' because he 'could not agree with the placid and well-ordered life of that backwater, nor care for his rather prim and orderly rooms in Pythagoras House, where every book and picture was chosen with great thought and deliberation'.[50] But it was precisely this aesthetic approach to life which appealed to Sassoon, particularly Theo's great interest in book design. His experience at Cambridge University Library, where he had risen to the rank of Senior Under-Librarian by 1912, had already been useful to Sassoon in the production of several poetry pamphlets during the war and he would continue to supervise his private productions throughout the twenties, together with his book-designer friend Bruce Rogers.[51] 'It is very nice of "Theo" to be interested in me,' Sassoon had written to Dent after their first meeting; 'I often think of him taking large folios from high shelves, or leaning over the noble pages of some eighteenth-century author.'[52]

An even stronger pull was their homosexuality. Theo, like Sassoon at this period, was deeply suspicious of women and moved in a largely male world. Despite his obituarist's claim that he was 'no misogynist',[53] Theo states specifically in his diary 'The longer I live the less I like women', though an infestation of body lice from one of his 'boys' in 1920 would make a settled marriage seem quite desirable for a while.[54] Like Sassoon he was drawn to younger men, with whom Cambridge was conveniently filled, and would be responsible for introducing the poet to several attractive youths, with predictable results. His one horror, of making a fool of himself and 'hanging on – oneself no longer young', may have sounded a warning note for Sassoon in the twenties.[55] They would both periodically resolve to 'give up' young men.[56]

But in November 1918 all that lay ahead of them and Theo was about to introduce Sassoon to someone who would change his life irrevocably, making him even more conscious of his divided worlds, the young army officer, Gabriel Atkin.[57]

Sassoon had already heard of Atkin from Dent, who had befriended the nineteen-year-old cadet in March 1917 when he came to Cambridge from the Durham Light Infantry on an army training course. And Dent must have mentioned Sassoon to Atkin, who next wrote to Dent from his camp at Margate to tell him how much he wanted to meet a poet he so admired. But when Dent passed this on to Sassoon in November 1917, he had replied rather off-handedly: 'Gabriel Atkins [sic] sounds all right. I wish Margate were nearer.'[58] Sassoon's posting, first to Ireland, then Palestine in the first half of 1918, had intervened and it was not until October 1918 that the subject was reintroduced. By 30 October Atkin was writing to Dent: 'I am most excited by the possibility of meeting Siegfried Sassoon. I think of him as most attractively Byronic in appearance.'[59] Clearly in awe of Sassoon, whose war poetry had made him a household name, he feels it might be 'presumptuous' of him to write or send a photograph as Dent suggests, but does hope for a few lines from the famous poet.[60] So that he is thrilled to receive a 'hectic' postcard from Sassoon on Armistice Day, though 'devastated' that it is to defer their meeting. The matchmaking is then taken up by Theo, who has himself been in and out of bed with Atkin for the past year, and it is during Sassoon's stay with Theo in mid-November that another meeting with Atkin is arranged.[61]

When Sassoon finally met Atkin for the first time at Margate station on 20 November 1918, he knew something of his background. Born in 1897 in the South Shields area, William ('Gabriel') Atkin had grown up there and was completing his education at Durham Art College when army service intervened.[62] There was little mention of a father, but many references to his mother, whom he adored. There were also three sisters, a brother and various aunts, but Gabriel was more conscious of his 'Rector uncles' whose 'domination' he was determined to escape.[63]

He was already heavily into drink and drugs by the time he left home for the army. The army did nothing to lessen his drinking and on Armistice Day, while Sassoon had been soberly eyeing the inebriated celebrators, Gabriel himself had been chief among them. (He illustrated his letter to Dent on the occasion with a sketch of his dazed self surrounded by innumerable glasses.) Sassoon attributed Gabriel's drinking to bad heredity and would try to help him curb it, but he could do little about his exhibitionist love of extraordinary clothes. This was to cause the ultra-conservative Sassoon problems, especially Gabriel's choice of his great-grandfather's red velvet dinner jacket with light blue facings and

19

gold buttons for a visit to the ballet. 'With such a face you can't afford to dress unconventionally, I assure you,' Sassoon wrote to him on 31 December 1918. 'The most I can allow will be a touch of the sportsman, and *that* is bad enough unless done with tact and sobriety.'

There was another side to Gabriel, however, which helps to explain their friends' anxiety to bring him and Sassoon together. He was not only a promising artist ('half-fledged' was how Sassoon put it),[64] which in itself would have interested Sassoon, but he was also an accomplished pianist.[65] Like Sassoon, he had yearned for a piano in the army and when he came across one, would play his favourite pieces from Puccini, Verdi and Chopin. 'I can't play Chopin or anything else. You've got to do all the ivory-tickling, please,' Sassoon wrote to him three days after their first meeting. Then, with a reference to the Russian Ballet, which they both thought 'glorious': 'Can you play Schumann's "Papillons"?'

Even more importantly Gabriel's interests included literature. (He claimed descent from the writer Leigh Hunt, whose work he presented to Sassoon.) He knew Sassoon's poetry well and the month they met was reading H.G. Wells, whom Sassoon also admired. He would complete a novel of his own, a memoir and at least two plays, though none would be published.

When Dent had first tried to interest Sassoon in 'the child "Gabriel"', he had described him as 'a pleasant and amusing lad, fearfully lonely at Margate', appealing in one stroke both to Sassoon's preference for much younger men and his protective instinct.[66] Theo found him 'very charming'.[67] They might also have added that Gabriel, despite his rackety lifestyle, was fairly thoughtful, sensitive and kind: when it came to the 'deeper things', Sassoon believed, he was 'very honest and trustworthy'.[68] Like Sassoon himself, his approach to life and art was instinctive rather than intellectual.

Gabriel's most important quality of all in relation to Sassoon was probably the one he identified himself, that he was 'very good at listening'.[69] This was a vital prerequisite for any close friend of Sassoon's, particularly in the immediate post-war years.

It is unlikely that Sassoon was thinking of Gabriel's character, however, as he made the slow journey by train from Paddock Wood to meet him on 20 November 1918. Though whether he had already decided to embark on the first physical affair of his life, or was simply intending to befriend the lonely young soldier is impossible to say. Most probably his mind was in turmoil, for he could not have been unaware of Dent's and Theo's intentions when they insisted on him meeting the attractive and promiscuous Gabriel. He had boasted to Edward Carpenter in 1911 that he was still 'unspotted' and his responsibilities during the war, together with his idealistic nature, had kept him that way.[70] But he had also told Carpenter in August 1918 of his 'craving' for something Carpenter had 'advised' him to do.[71]

1. 'Pilgrimages to Poets ... and Other Diversions (1918)

In the event Gabriel himself seems to have decided the issue. Nicknamed 'Gabriel' because of his angelic appearance, his golden hair and boyish good looks had an immediate effect on Sassoon. – 'You are all red and white roses, you darling' – and his poems to Gabriel leave little doubt as to what followed. He certainly felt, as he wrote to Theo after the first meeting, that Gabriel was one of the 'divinest' things that had ever happened to him.[72] His letters to Gabriel, recently released into the public domain, are more explicit and even more appreciative, though the same need to play on his angelic nickname is evident. 'When I got here last night', he wrote to Gabriel from Rye shortly after his letter to Theo, 'I knelt down in my dark and chilly room and said "thank God for Gabriel!" – and God said (from a long way off) – "Be good to him." It is very quiet here; there is no wind to moan around the roofs and windows. And my heart is a great golden palace full of music and your face.'[73]

Even Gabriel, who changed sexual partners frequently, thought it was 'the most wonderful thing' that had ever happened to him. 'Siegfried is the most amazing gorgeous person in the universe,' he told Dent on 24 November.[74] And in case Dent had any doubts as to the precise nature of the relationship, he added in a later letter (using a traditional euphemism for sexual intercourse) that he had been 'in the country ... bound on the N, S, E and W by Siegfried Sassoon' and 'much too busy and breathlessly happy while on leave to write at all'.[75]

Their 'lyric time', as Theo discreetly phrased it, continued the week after their first meeting, when Sassoon returned to Margate on 26 November, ostensibly to attend a concert Gabriel was organizing.[76] Sassoon's first visit had made Gabriel suddenly ashamed of his dissolute lifestyle and he had pledged himself to sobriety, vowed to give up promiscuity and resolved to work seriously at his art. He had spent the 'purest' Saturday in years after meeting Sassoon.[77] Resisting his usual visit to the pub and doing his duty by old family friends instead, he had felt rather like Dickens's pious heroine, Little Dorrit. (Dent, to whom he confided this, would have appreciated the incongruity.) Sassoon, in his first ecstasy, and possibly in an attempt to rationalize his strong sexual arousal, had quoted reams of poetry by Walt Whitman, that great exponent of 'lads-love'. This had had a powerful effect on the impressionable Gabriel, who reported in the same letter to Dent: 'Walt Whitman swarms over my horizon and makes me feel a little worm.'[78]

It is a proof of the strength of Sassoon's idealism that he could make Gabriel stop, however briefly, to consider Whitman's words. For the younger man 'falling in love' was an almost everyday occurrence and he appears to have suffered no scruples about the sexual side of the numerous relationships he carried on, often simultaneously. Nor did he seem to worry about the fact that he often drank and smoked too much and was always overdrawn, though his recklessness threatened to land him in trouble daily with his military superiors. His only real fear was, like

Dorian Gray, of getting older. 'I should like to be always nineteen,' he had told Dent and, although he was twenty-one by the time he met Sassoon, he continued to behave like an immature teenager. After one particularly drunken binge, for example, he merely thanked God that he had 'remarkably little common sense'.[79]

Like many young people from the provinces, Gabriel 'adore[d] London with a wicked foolish and childish adoration'. 'I feel a Satanic thrill when I come in sight of it', he confided to Dent, '– a wild throbbing all the time I am there. Half my life is a mad desire to be wicked – London is the Mecca of hopes.'[80] He was, therefore, thrilled when Sassoon invited him to spend five days in the capital with him, though his main motive was to introduce Gabriel to his friends rather than to new vices. Anxious to impress his young lover, Sassoon had planned an exhausting schedule. In itself a reminder of how many contacts he had made in London during his wartime visits, it puts all his previous socializing into the shade.

In the five days from 16 to 20 December he lunched, had tea and dined out with Gabriel daily, attended numerous parties and took him to three new plays, several concerts and at least one art gallery. With the notable exceptions of Gosse and Rivers, who he suspected would not approve, Gabriel met all his close friends and many of his acquaintances. And the sheer profusion of invitations the two received suggests that they all rejoiced in Sassoon's happiness, as well as being naturally concerned to meet the miracle-worker.

The first evening, after dinner with Marsh and the fashionable portrait painter Glyn Philpot, for whom Sassoon had sat in 1917,[81] they went on to a dazzling party given by one of London's best-known hostesses, Lady Colefax.[82] Gabriel was overwhelmed, as he was meant to be, by the august nature of the gathering, which included Lady Randolph Churchill, Hugh Walpole and Elizabeth Asquith. But he was equally entranced by the music, a violin recital by Jelly d'Aranyi and singing by Olga Lynn and Rosing.[83]

The next day Sassoon introduced him to two of his closest friends from the war, Vivian de Sola Pinto, who had been his second-in-command in France,[84] and Robert Graves, who came to tea and insisted that they all meet again after dinner at his Nicholson in-laws.[85] (Dinner was at the Savoy.) It was Sassoon's first encounter with Graves's wife, Nancy, of whom he was almost certainly jealous.

The highlight of the third day, 18 December, was lunch with the ex-Prime Minister Herbert Asquith and his wife Margot, who like all the other society hostesses had courted the poet after his rise to fame in 1917. As if that were not enough to convince Gabriel of his impressive connections, on their penultimate day Sassoon took him to lunch with his rich Sassoon relatives at Albert Gate.[86] Gabriel, who had felt uncharacteristically shy throughout the five days, had to be persuaded to play Chopin, but the visit went so well that they were invited back the next day. Sassoon had never been close to this side of his family, with the exception of his father's sister, Rachel Beer, who had supported her brother when he married out of the Jewish faith, and his great-aunt Mozelle, the youngest child of the dynasty founder, David Sassoon, who had befriended him in London in 1914. Now, as then, he and Mozelle went off to a matinée together, with Gabriel in tow.

But he was careful to remember Gabriel's own particular interests and on their final day they went to Philpot's Tite Street studio for tea. Though the painter was not as bowled over by Gabriel's looks as Sassoon and did not offer to paint him, as Sassoon hoped he might, he was able to advise him on resuming his art studies after demobilization. (Once settled in London studying at the Slade, Gabriel would take rooms near to Philpot's, at 122 Cheyne Walk.)

It was music, not art, however, which Gabriel found most memorable during this whirlwind visit. On the last evening, after dinner with Osbert Sitwell, Graves and Turner, Sitwell took his guests to hear the harpsichordist Violet Gordon-Woodhouse.[87] This may have been at the request of Sassoon, who had heard her play to him and Wilfred Owen at their final meeting. Like Owen, Gabriel was profoundly moved by her playing, more moved than he would admit, he told Dent: 'I wept into my cushion.'[88] He was also very nervous in the presence of an even greater musician, Delius, who was in the audience.

Gabriel had been 'more nervous' than he meant to be in London.[89] He had seen his role as looking 'ornamental', which he had tried to be, but he suspected that it 'wasn't of the type that would suit Osbert Sitwell's house', for example.[90] Though he liked Sitwell enormously, he was afraid that he and Sassoon's other friends might be 'suspicious of [his] unjustified existence'.[91]

For this initial sortie into London society Sassoon had taken lodgings, as he had during the war, with Ross's devoted landlady, Nellie Burton, in Half Moon Street. He had already visited Ross's old room the previous month, when Nellie had shown him 'the last dreadful vile attack' on Ross by Lord Alfred Douglas.[92] And, though he knew it could make no difference now to Ross, who he and other friends believed had been hounded to an early death by Douglas's persecutions, it seemed to him 'so hideous and monstrous' that he had wept all the way back to Marsh's flat on the top of a bus. But this was a happier occasion and Nellie, a gloriously Shakespearian figure according to Sassoon, welcomed one of her favourite 'boys' back with her usual gusto.

It was becoming clear to him, however, that he would need his own base in the city. The visit to Weirleigh with Gabriel which immediately followed made him more sharply conscious of this. For Gabriel was not a success with Sassoon's mother, Theresa. Though both were artists, they had little in common. Where she was religious and strictly principled, Gabriel was lax; where she, like her son, was moderate, Gabriel was excessive. 'Mother always disliked and distrusted G[abriel]', Sassoon was to write later: 'She still talks about him as "that hopeless creature" … His half-frivolous and wholly pleasure-loving temperament repelled her.'[93] Another attempt to analyse their differences helps to explain something of Gabriel's fascination for him: 'Gabriel represents green chartreuse and Epstein sculpture. Mother is G.F. Watts and holy communion. They can't be mixed.'[94] Part of Theresa's antagonism, no doubt, sprang from a suspicion that her 32-year-old son was more interested in young men than young women. Her great-niece remembered her dismissing Gabriel bitterly as 'another of Sieg's pretty boys'.[95]

*

While Theresa was trying to come to terms with her son's friend at the end of 1918, Sassoon was writing passionate love poetry to him. If, as he would argue, 'repressed sex' was behind his early romantic verse, sexual fulfilment seems equally to have inspired a burst of creativity.[96] 'I lived my poetry *physically* before I wrote it', he claimed, 'and it was written when I was feeling physically rich.'[97]

He had composed little of significance since leaving France the previous July and his work as a whole had included almost no love poetry.[98] But now, as a critic in the *Cambridge Magazine*, E.B.C. ('Topsy') Jones, noted, he becomes 'a love-poet among other things'.[99] The two poems quoted at the beginning of this chapter were the first and third poems addressed specifically to Gabriel and show Sassoon in a very different mode and mood from his war poetry. Ironic attacks on those he held responsible for the war are here replaced by tender addresses to the lover who has 'stormed [his] throat with bliss'.

But as Topsy Jones warned, romantic poems are in more danger of cliché than angry war satires and Sassoon treads warily from the start. His first poem to Gabriel, 'Parted', written while he waited impatiently for their second meeting, shows him trying to maintain what Jones called 'the extreme directness and first-handedness of his diction'. He has also learnt from his war poetry the value of presenting a 'situation', in this case a lover lying in bed alone, waiting for his 'love's release':

> Sleepless I listen to the surge and drone
> And drifting roar of the town's undertone;
> Till through quiet falling rain I hear the bells
> Tolling and chiming their brief tune that tells
> Day's midnight end. And from the day that's over
> No flashes of delight I can recover;
> But only dreary winter streets, and faces
> Of people moving in loud clanging places:
> And I in my loneliness, longing for you …
>   (CP, p. 114)[100]

24

For the fourth outpouring of his passion in 1918, 'Slumber-Song', Sassoon chooses a similar situation, but the poem is less successful, the language and thought verging frequently on cliché. Biographically, however, the work is of some interest, since its imagery recognizably reflects the poem's setting at Weirleigh and underlines the significance its garden had always had for Sassoon:

> Sleep; and my song shall build about your bed
> A paradise of dimness. You shall feel
> The folding of tired wings; and peace will dwell
> Throned in your silence: and one hour shall hold
> Summer, and midnight, and immensity
> Lulled to forgetfulness. For, where you dream,
> The stately gloom of foliage shall embower
> Your slumbering thought with tapestries of blue.
> And there shall be no memory of the sky,
> Nor sunlight with its cruelty of swords.
> But, to your soul that sinks from deep to deep
> Through drowned and glimmering colour, Time shall be
> Only slow rhythmic swaying; and your breath;
> And roses in the darkness; and my love.
>
> (CP, p. 115)[101]

Sassoon was to write a number of other poems about Gabriel as their relationship developed, but none more intriguing than the one which followed closely on 'Slumber-Song' in January 1919, 'To a Childless Woman'. This may have been sparked off by an actual encounter with such a woman, but its main interest is Sassoon's close identification with her plight:

> You think I cannot understand. Ah, but I do ...
> I have been wrung with anger and compassion for you.
> I wonder if you'd loathe my pity, if you knew.
>   * * *
> Tender, and bitter-sweet, and shy, I've watched you holding
> Another's child. O childless woman, was it then
> That, with an instant's cry, your heart, made young again,
> Was crucified for ever – those poor arms enfolding
> The life, the consummation that had been denied you?
> I too have longed for children. Ah, but you must not weep.
> Something I have to whisper as I kneel beside you ...
> And you must pray for me before you fall asleep.
>
> (CP, pp. 117-18)[102]

It may, of course, be chance that caused Sassoon to write this poem at the height of his passion for Gabriel. But it is equally possible that his first real love affair had brought home to him for the first time the full implications of a homosexual relationship. However successful it turned out to be, it could never satisfy his yearning for children, a need which the birth of Graves's first child that month may have increased. And when, more than a decade later, he decided to marry, it would not be only the strain of concealing his homosexual relationships from a society which had branded them criminal, but also a longing for children which would dictate his extraordinary volte-face.

2

'A Simpleton's Progress'[1]
(January-March 1919)

> And still they come and go: and this is all I know –
> That from the gloom I watch an endless picture-show,
> Where wild or listless faces flicker on their way,
> With glad or grievous hearts I'll never understand
> Because Time spins so fast, and they've no time to stay
> Beyond the moment's gesture of a lifted hand.
>
> And still, between the shadow and the blinding flame,
> The brave despair of men flings onward, ever the same
> As in those doom-lit years that wait them, and have been ...
> And life is just the picture dancing on a screen.
>
> (CP, p. 99)[2]

Memories of the war would continue to dominate this period of Sassoon's life. And though his passion for Gabriel blotted them out, it was for all too short a time. Only two months after their first meeting, there are signs of trouble in his Eden. 'I never asked you to be perfect – did I?' he writes in 'The Imperfect Lover' on 22 January 1919.[3] Yet the same poem strongly suggests that he misses the 'early-morning freshness' he had first found in Gabriel. He may deny having expected his beloved to be 'unsoiled, angelic and inhuman', but it is in religious terms that he describes their initial bliss:

> Oh yes, I know the way to heaven was easy.
> We found the little kingdom of our passion
> That all can share who walk the road of lovers.
> In wild and secret happiness we stumbled;
> And gods and demons clamoured in our senses.

The reference to 'gods *and* demons' (my italics) is particularly revealing. 'Neither night nor day may I escape thee oh my heavenly hell', he had written to his 'little angel-devil', Gabriel, in his first ecstasy.[4] Now, having initially idealized their physical union, he rejects it as 'lov[ing] like beasts', their 'heaven' turned to 'hell'.[5] For fundamentally he remained a puritan and would never be comfortable with what he called 'the cursed nuisance of sex'.[6] He would continue to feel guilty about his strong 'sex-cravings' and would never manage to reconcile Eros and Agape, the physical and spiritual sides of love.[7] Even in his first poem to Gabriel at the height of his passion, he had implied that lovers must be prepared to forfeit the Heaven of the Saints for the heaven of each other's bodies, a position summed up for him in a tortured poem by Charlotte Mew which he quoted to Gabriel:

> He found me, and I lost the way
> To Paradise for him. I sold
> My soul for love and not for gold.
>
> His is the only face I know,
> And in the dark church, like a screen,
> It shuts God out; it comes between.[8]

In Sassoon's case he was already looking back on his sexual gratification with Gabriel only two months after first experiencing it as 'illusions / That blossom from desire with desperate beauty'.[9] It was a pattern which would repeat itself many times in the twenties: once his physical needs had been met, he would begin to analyse his feelings, usually with negative results. 'I've grown thoughtful now', he warns Gabriel in his January 1919 poem and it is clear from the same work that Gabriel has 'learned to fear / The gloomy stricken places' in his soul and the 'occasional ghosts' that haunt him.

The last two phrases refer directly to Sassoon's experiences in the war and point to another complicating factor in his relationships in the twenties. Gabriel had helped him to forget the horrors he had witnessed – 'all the old wounds in my heart are healed for ever', Sassoon had assured him on 1 December 1918 – but it would take a stronger personality than Gabriel and many more years for him to emerge from what he called his 'devildoms'.[10] He was not, of course, alone in this. Many of those who fought in the First World War never fully recovered from its effects.

Paradoxically, then, though the war had liberated Sassoon from some of his inhibitions, it also prevented him from enjoying his new-found freedom for long. He had written, with ominous prescience, in January 1918: 'For death has made me wise and bitter and strong; / *And I am rich in all that I have lost*' (my italics).[11] And by January 1919 the living could still not compete with the memory of his dead friends.

Dame Felicitas Corrigan, in her 'spiritual' biography of Sassoon,[12] dismisses his behaviour at this period as 'post-war deviations ... unlovely but negligible', a 'backlash' against the war.[13] To me it suggests an attempt, however doomed or misguided, to find meaning in an existence turned upside down by the war.

*

Sassoon's doubts about Gabriel had started just before 'The Imperfect Lover' was written. Gabriel had returned home to Newcastle immediately after his demobilization on 20 January 1919 and, though his letters to Sassoon during this period have not survived, it is reasonable to assume that he was describing his life to him there in terms similar to those found in his letters to Dent. After lamenting the lack of good tailors or anything else civilized or beautiful in the North, he complains of being too ill to join a 'dope' party which had tempted him. Sassoon, a moderate man himself, had found Gabriel's excessive drinking difficult enough, but the idea of opium and morphia disturbed him even more. (Gabriel would later become part of the wild drug scene surrounding Jean Cocteau in Paris.)

Even before the full extent of Gabriel's dissoluteness became apparent, Sassoon suffered doubts about him. He was still close to his mother – she called him her 'second self'[14] – and her disapproval of Gabriel when he took him to visit had not been reassuring. He might think of her as old-fashioned and prejudiced, but he could not deny her essential intuitive wisdom. Rivers, who arrived at Weirleigh a week after Gabriel on 27 December 1918, had confirmed this view, telling Sassoon that he had 'seldom met anyone with a more direct and humorously simplifying intelligence or better intuitive judgement of essential human questions'.[15]

Theresa's reaction to Rivers was equally positive, making her disapproval of Gabriel all the more evident. She had a weakness for the medical profession and believed that the doctor had cured Siegfried of being 'a militant war-resister', according to her son.[16] And Rivers, a man of wide knowledge, great perception and serious purpose, was in himself such a contrast to Gabriel that he might well have caused Sassoon to wonder what position his immature young friend could occupy in his life.

Of Rivers's place there was little doubt. Sassoon depended increasingly on the man he described to Gabriel as his 'father confessor'.[17] When, after hearing of his intention to join the Labour Movement, Rivers suggested that he should study political economy at either Oxford or Cambridge, he at once agreed. He was to write a poem about Rivers called 'To a Very Wise Man',[18] but had Rivers been even wiser he would have steered his young disciple away from his choice of Oxford. Sassoon would claim in his autobiography that he chose Oxford for its nearness to his colourful friend and patron, Lady Ottoline Morrell, but that same book makes no mention of Gabriel at all, so cannot be trusted completely. To Ottoline herself he wrote that he had picked Oxford because two other close friends, Graves and Prewett, would be there. His explanation to Gabriel, who was worried that it might mean them seeing less of each other, was that living in London was 'very bad' for him since it involved 'rushing round seeing Society'.[19] 'And when you want to study anatomy', he joked coyly with him, 'you can come and stay with me.'[20]

Whatever his true motive – and none of them had much to do with political studies – Oxford was settled on and Sassoon started the new year with a much-needed sense of purpose. He was clearly hoping that his new study would give him a fresh subject for poetry: 'I am going to be an inflammatory political versifier', was how he expressed it to Dent.[21]

He had already made a modest start on his political career by agreeing to help the Labour Party in the December 1918 'Coupon' Election, so called because of the 'Coupon' (Asquith's contemptuous phrase), or letter of endorsement issued by Lloyd George and Bonar Law to sitting MPs who supported their Liberal–Conservative coalition. (Labour had withdrawn from the coalition to fight the election independently.) Sassoon's decision had been made in response to a letter from Max Plowman, another soldier-poet who, unlike himself, had been court-martialled for his pacifist stand. Plowman had asked if he would be willing to speak for another pacifist, the Labour MP for Blackburn, Philip Snowden. Playing on the public's patriotic fervour, Lloyd George's party had chosen what Sassoon succinctly called 'a Naval VC (Unionist)' to oppose Snowden and the Labour Party hoped that Sassoon's well-known war record together with his officer's uniform and MC ribbon might counteract this cynical ploy. 'I am going up to Blackburn for Snowden's Election', Sassoon announced proudly to Theo on 4 December, 'to say a few words against militarism and *Morning Post*-ishness in general ... It should be very exciting.'[22] (The *Morning Post* was a popular paper of Conservative views.)

It was with some apprehension, however, that he set out for the industrial north on 10 December.[23] His political views seemed to him a 'muddle' and, as he explained to Snowden in reply to his letter of thanks, he was completely inexperienced as a speaker.[24] A great deal, he felt, depended on whether he liked Snowden.

Fortunately he did. The politician, while very serious in his aims, had a down-to-earth Yorkshire humour which would have appealed to Sassoon as much as it did to the large audiences he addressed. Sassoon already admired Snowden's anti-war stance in Parliament and his sustained efforts on behalf of private soldiers and their families; meeting him only confirmed his view that Snowden was a 'good' man.[25] He also liked and admired Snowden's wife and a third speaker, Isabella Blow, who seemed to him 'a splendid human person'.[26] A fifth member of the team, who went on to become one of the first women MPs when she won her Northampton seat in 1923 and the very first woman Cabinet Minister, was Margaret Bondfield. The Snowdens were strong supporters of women's rights, for which Bondfield fought, and the three were close friends. Margaret Bondfield and Mrs Snowden would be responsible for Sassoon's election to the 1917 Club, which had been founded by a group of left-wing politicians in honour of the Russian Revolution. Drinking cocoa with the Blackburn team late at night after the day's exertions, Sassoon felt that they were like 'a happy family'.[27]

Snowden, who would eventually become Chancellor of the Exchequer in 1924 and 1929-31 and the first Socialist viscount, was on the right wing of the Labour Party. Described by Leonard Woolf, who veered more to the left, as 'very honest, unimaginative, conservative – fundamentally reactionary',[28] he probably appealed to the conservative Sassoon. And his lameness, which gave Woolf the impression that he was 'embittered by pain', certainly made the athletic younger man sympathetic.[29] He also understood Snowden's bitterness at being represented as 'unpatriotic': 'he has been goaded beyond endurance by the malignant hostility of his enemies', Sassoon recorded on the last day of the campaign.[30] And, in spite of Snowden's twelve-year fight to improve working-class conditions in Blackburn, it came as no surprise to any of them when he failed to be returned on this fourth occasion. Even the politically naïve Sassoon could see that the sitting MP had fought a losing battle against 'a frenzied intolerance whose catchwords were "Hang the Kaiser" and "Make the Germans Pay". "Snowden, the Arch-Pacifist" was reviled as though he were a public enemy.'[31]

Sassoon was astonished at how deeply involved he became with what he dubbed 'the Blackburn worthies', whom he carefully listed in his diary, right down to a 'fat chap' called Jon Franklin, a helper on the committee. 'These people who believe in [Snowden] are very moving,' he concluded. 'I think he is worthy of them.'[32] He was greatly relieved that all but one of his twelve speeches had been received sympathetically. (His claim that a woman in the next carriage on the way home had described him as 'a very bad speaker' for whom the King 'had no further use' was almost certainly a joke at his own expense.)[33] His remarks against conscription had gone down well, he told Ottoline Morrell, in spite of the fact that the opposition had described him as 'a stage soldier who'd never been near the war but had been got down by the pacifists'.[34] Fortunately no action had been taken about him appearing in uniform in such a context. Still technically in the army, he had already overstayed his leave by three weeks and did not want further problems. He hoped to 'bluff' the War Office a bit longer before having to join the 3rd Battalion of the Royal Welch Fusiliers in Limerick.[35]

'I shall look back on these days as a time filled with happy striving, pleasing thrills of nervousness, jolly comradeship, and rather bewildering success,' he wrote on the next-to-last evening of the campaign:

> These days are undoubtedly the beginning of a new phase of my life – I am being inflamed to an ardour which cannot fail me. I have made a strong appeal to these Blackburn people, but I must justify my words by deeds. A great vista has opened to me in the last few days, and I have escaped – for ever – those reactionary and self-indulgent influences to which I was bred and educated – I have offered myself to the people and they have accepted me – Will I live to be worthy of their trust? Who knows?[36]

These brave, somewhat high-flown words were followed almost immediately by the London whirl with Gabriel already described, which would have shown the worthy people of Blackburn a very different side to

Sassoon. Even after Gabriel's return to Margate, Sassoon was tempted into further socializing by Glyn Philpot, who insisted on taking him to a fancy-dress ball in the costume of a Tartar prince.

The ball was given by a man who could have been specially chosen to represent a set of values and way of life completely at odds with Sassoon's Blackburn vision, Frank ('Frankie') Schuster. When Sassoon had first met Schuster at Osbert Sitwell's in November 1918, he had found him 'very pleasant and congenial', but had no idea that he would become a close friend, or that they would attend innumerable concerts together until Schuster's death at eighty-seven in 1927. For Schuster, though no musician himself, was an important figure in the musical world, putting a great deal of his wealth and influence at the disposal of struggling composers and performers. His patronage of Elgar, for instance, had been a significant factor in the musician's eventual success. Sassoon, who would meet Elgar frequently at Schuster's in the twenties, thought of him as a 'godfather of musical masterpieces'.[37]

Nearly eighty when they first met, Schuster was still enjoying the good things of life with an apparent disregard for his age: a house in Old Queen Street, Westminster, in winter, with a flat in Brighton for weekends, a retreat at Bray-on-Thames for summer, a chauffeur-driven Rolls-Royce, a round of social events, and frequent trips abroad. Though unmarried, he was seldom alone and failed totally to understand Sassoon's or anyone else's need for solitude. With his bald, freckled head, his clumsy, almost malformed hands and feet, his Aberdeen terrier on a silver chain, he might have seemed a figure of fun, had it not been for his passion for music, which redeemed him in Sassoon's eyes.

Nevertheless Sassoon was at times highly critical of the man he once described as 'the Frankfurt Jew'.[38] Though his own father was Jewish, this was not intended as praise, the implication being that Schuster was vulgar. In fact he actually stated that Schuster lacked 'essential good breeding', a remark that underlines one of Sassoon's own gravest faults, his snobbishness.[39] He would also become critical of Schuster's 'carefulness' in money matters, while at the same time happy to accept Schuster's hospitality for weeks on end. Similarly, though accusing Schuster of being 'socially frothy', he was quite ready to join in with his plans if it suited him.[40]

At this first party, however, there seemed to him something magical about Schuster's world, in which his host appeared as 'a sort of party-giving Prospero'.[41]

*

When Sassoon told Rivers how he had occupied his time after returning from Blackburn, he laughed heartily: 'You'll have to decide which party you really belong to!' was his dry comment.[42] He sensibly suggested that the less Sassoon was in London the less he would be tempted by its social life and for at least a fortnight after Rivers's departure from Weirleigh on 29 December Sassoon remained soberly at home. His mother had strongly disapproved of his electioneering for the Labour Party and would probably have also disliked the Oxford plan had she known its political purpose, but Rivers could do no wrong in her eyes and he had suggested it. There was, therefore a temporary truce between mother and son.

After a fortnight, however, Sassoon was off again, this time to Garsington. His relationship with Lady Ottoline Morrell, which had started in 1916 and been partly responsible for his public protest against the war, had passed through the awkward stage, when he had had to fend off her advances, and settled down into a solid friendship. In spite of what many regarded as her pretensions, absurdities and excesses, he believed her to be a generous and loyal friend and true patron of the arts. An invitation to visit her at her Tudor manor house near Oxford was always tempting, since she gathered round her a wide variety of interesting guests and on this occasion the company was particularly intriguing. Apart from Ottoline's husband, the Liberal MP Philip Morrell, there were her ex-lover Bertrand Russell, another philosopher, George Santayana, and a young Canadian poet, Frank ('Toronto') Prewett.[43]

Sassoon himself had introduced Prewett to Garsington. He had become infatuated with him while they were both convalescing at Lennel, Coldstream, in the late summer of 1918 and, in spite of the young heterosexual's rejection of his advances, was still physically attracted to him. It was with his help that Prewett was now enrolled at Christ Church, Oxford, one of the reasons Sassoon had chosen the city as his base.

Sassoon had written to Ottoline on 4 January 1919 asking her to find him a 'modest' flat in Oxford, a place where he could meet 'a few youngish people'.[44] His excuse for accepting her invitation to visit on the 15th was to inspect her choice. Though her idea of 'modest' turned out to be a fairly luxurious apartment in Merton Street, consisting of a sitting room and two bedrooms, overlooking Christ Church meadows at a rent of almost half his income, he was unable to resist it. It was far too expensive, as he admitted to Graves (himself about to arrive in Oxford), but he had not yet learnt to live within his means. Only the advent of the war had saved him from being heavily in debt.

Setting off for Garsington after inspecting his future quarters, he looked forward to what he saw as 'home life combined with high thinking', but on this occasion he found that Russell and Santayana's philosophical heights were beyond him. His own approach to life, he insisted, was largely emotional: he had a low opinion of his intellectual powers which did not augur well for his university studies. His admiration for Russell had been increased by the philosopher's help in the wording of his anti-war protest in 1917 and when Russell had later been sent to prison for sedition he had

33

contributed to a fund for him.[45] Apart from their attitude towards war, however, they had little in common and would never become close.[46]

Prewett, on the other hand, would remain an important contact for Sassoon in Oxford and beyond, long after the sexual attraction had worn off. 'Toronto is a great man, and will be a great writer', he told Graves, who had expressed understandable reservations; '– greater than you or me, because of his simplicity of mind and freedom from intellectual prejudices.'[47] These two qualities, which Sassoon valued more than almost any other in poets, would cause him to rate several of them much higher than posterity would. Meantime, Prewett's 'simplicity of mind' must at least have provided welcome relief at Garsington from the rigorous demands of Russell's and Santayana's combined intellects. Returning to Oxford with Santayana two days later in Philip Morrell's milk-float, Sassoon had been unable to think of anything to say to the eminent philosopher.

Had Sassoon been entirely serious about avoiding social gatherings he would probably not have gone to Garsington. He would certainly not have spent the night with Eddie Marsh on his return to London, since Eddie, as usual, was busy entertaining the upper reaches of society.[48] It is a sign of Sassoon's inconsistency at this time that, having accepted the invitation to join Marsh's elaborate dinner party and having more or less apologized to him for his Blackburn activities – 'Forgive me Eddie – I'm daft' – he immediately felt hostile towards what he scornfully called Eddie's 'titled blokes and blokesses'.[49] 'On the whole', he wrote in his diary that same evening, 'I detest them and their self-indulgence and intellectual conceit.'[50] The evening papers had announced the murder of the leaders of the Communist Party, Karl Liebknecht and Rosa Luxembourg, and since Liebknecht, like Snowden, had been a pacifist member of his government, Sassoon identified with him and Luxembourg against Marsh and his guests. He stayed on to listen to Ivor Novello, who struck him as 'very charming in appearance, but really quite fifth-rate – a common little Jew snob with a pretty face and a facility for improvising taking tunes', unaware how much Novello would later make him suffer.[51] At the same time, however, he was haunted by the thought of Liebknecht and Luxembourg, 'those two anti-militarists riddled with bullets in a Berlin Hotel'.[52]

It would be interesting to know whether Sassoon confessed this particular bit of socializing to Rivers when he arrived to stay with him in Cambridge the next day. Rivers had just accepted a fellowship at his old college, St John's. As Prælector in Natural Sciences he was not obliged to provide any formal teaching but, if his obituaries are to be believed, he made a profound impact on the scientific life both of the college and the University.[53] During Sassoon's two-day stay he claimed to have met more Fellows of the Royal Society than in the whole of his previous existence, including the 91-year-old President of the College, Dr Liveing, who had made important discoveries in spectroscopy. Perhaps more to his taste was an introduction to another Fellow, the composer Cyril Rootham, who would later set some of his works to music.[54]

Famous in his own right by now, following the success of his war poetry,[55] Sassoon was persuaded on his second day at St John's to read some of his poems to a silent but seemingly appreciative circle of undergraduates. His technique on such occasions was a source of some amusement to his friends and admirers. The victim of acute shyness, he usually read very quietly and indistinctly, dropping his voice completely at the end of sentences, so that much of his performance went unheard. It is to be hoped that, as on many later occasions, his audience felt that simply meeting him and watching him read his own work was experience enough.[56]

While Sassoon was at Cambridge he also kept his promise to Theo to 'fix up' his next production.[57] Since the publication of *Counter-Attack*, which gathered together poems written between May 1917 and February 1918, he had written enough good poems, he felt, to justify a new volume and Theo was keen to produce it. So on Monday, 19 January, after leaving Rivers, he took himself and his manuscript to Cockerell, whose experience he valued greatly.[58] During the course of dinner and an overnight stay Cockerell gave his businesslike advice: if, as Sassoon claimed, he wanted to make money, he should send out prospectuses with a tear-off form, to make ordering as easy as possible – 'and on no account send the book until you've received the money!'[59] Sassoon suggested a print run of first 300, then 200 to Theo, in the hope that 150 could be subscribed at a guinea each, a wildly over-optimistic target as it turned out.

Back in London on 20 January, Sassoon had a brief meeting with his servant from his last battalion, the 25th Royal Welch Fusiliers. John Law, one of the 'best chaps' he had met during the war, had been a miner in South Wales before the army expanded his horizons. He was having problems settling back into civilian life and Sassoon wanted to help. Always generous with his money, he had sent Law at least one food parcel from Harrods after his return from France in July 1918 and was to come to his rescue financially a number of times in the twenties.[60] It was men like Law who had first made Sassoon aware of the inequalities of the social system. Perhaps meeting him on this occasion reminded him of his new-year resolution, since, resisting the lures of London, he returned straight to Weirleigh. And, apart from one visit to the ballet on 28 January, he remained there quietly until it was time to leave for Oxford.

*

While writing his own account of his life, Sassoon confessed to frequent doubts as to 'what is significant to the story',[61] a feeling many authors share. Does it really matter, for instance, that in January 1919, at the height of his resolve to help the Labour Party fight social injustice, he accepted membership of one of the most privileged gentlemen's clubs in London, the Reform?[62] It is certainly another sign of his inconsistency, which he himself attributed to 'chuckle-headed immaturity'.[63]

Sassoon had been introduced to the Reform by one of its most faithful members, Robbie Ross, and had made many friends there. With Ross dead he needed membership of his own and was grateful to Arnold Bennett for proposing him. Its Pall Mall premises would serve him as a convenient place for meeting and entertaining for the next ten years or so.

Since his introduction to Bennett at the Reform in May 1917, Sassoon had found the novelist 'always the same and always nice'.[64] 'Dear old AB', as he called him, was invariably charming and often very witty.[65] Sassoon particularly enjoyed his remark the morning after an excessively good dinner, that he was 'suffering from the four Cs: Cocktails, Caviar, Champagne and Cognac'.[66] He felt that Bennett's success as a writer had not spoilt him as a person and fully appreciated the 'genuine kindliness and interest' he showed in his work, even when it was not going well.[67] In fact, had Sassoon followed Bennett's advice to take up novel-writing in 1925, his own success with *Memoirs of a Fox-Hunting Man* might have come sooner than it did.[68] Bennett also showed a fatherly interest in Sassoon's personal life, telling him in 1921, for example, that he did not take enough interest in women. (A later remark suggests that he finally realized that Sassoon's interests lay in other directions.)[69] He also frequently invited him to dinner.

Sassoon's admiration of Bennett extended to his novels, while doubting Bennett's claim that he was on a plane with Chekhov and Flaubert, but he thought his plays very bad.[70] Overall he held him in high esteem, the most convincing sign of this being his introduction of Bennett to a man he admired even more, Dr Rivers.[71]

Sassoon often met Bennett at the Reform, but he had other friends there too. One of these was H.W. Massingham, whose continued support in the *Nation* he valued. Meeting Massingham in the club on 1 February, the evening before he planned to leave for Oxford, he was offered another chance to show his political commitment in practical terms. News had just broken of rioting in Glasgow, brought on by the prospect of unemployment following rapid demobilization and the end of war-production. The leaders of the protest, William Gallagher, David Kirkwood and Emmanuel Shinwell, were aiming at a general strike, in order to force in a forty-hour working week which would, theoretically, absorb the extra labour about to arrive on the market.

Massingham saw these riots as the first fruits of what he called the 'Khaki Election', his private sympathies lying with the demonstrators. 'I wish I could get hold of someone to go up there and find out what's happening,' he told Sassoon, adding rather pointedly, 'If I were a younger man and not tied to the office I'd go myself.'[72] Impulsive by nature, Sassoon rose to the bait and offered his services, which were quickly accepted. So, after only one day in Oxford, he set out for Glasgow by overnight train on Sunday, 2 February, with two letters of introduction from Massingham in his pocket, hoping rather ignobly that 'things wouldn't have quietened down' by the time he got there.[73]

Arriving in Glasgow on a 'dismal' Monday morning, two things immediately became clear to him: that the riots were 'all over' and that he was going to have difficulty finding anything new to report, especially in his ignorant state.[74] He was rescued by a young man called John Langdon Davies, the nephew of a well-known member of the Independent Labour Party.[75] Like most left-wingers, Davies had admired Sassoon's anti-war protest and offered to share some useful contacts he had in Glasgow, an offer which was gratefully accepted. He remembered with some amusement what happened when he took the patently middle-class Sassoon to a meeting of the Socialist Labour Party, a forerunner of the Communist Party in Britain:

> A big man said: 'We shall not see the last fight, the fight for the tools.' A very little woman in glasses with straight black hair and bitter thin lips said she did not see why, and then turned on poor Siegfried and must have surprised him very much by saying, in a Glasgow dialect, which I have no ability to imitate: 'Mr Sassoon, we are glad of your sympathy of course, but you will never understand us, Mr Sassoon. For you, Mr Sassoon, never took in Marx with your mother's milk.' She seemed to grow more bitter with every word, and Siegfried more embarrassed. It was so patently true that he had not taken in Marx with his mother's milk nor probably at any later date.[76]

Curiously, Sassoon's version of events turns his bitter little attacker into a 'warm-hearted middle-aged lady'; he may have thought the original incident too unpleasant or simply repressed it.[77] Either way, it is another warning against believing everything he wrote in his autobiography.

After three days' 'behind the scenes' activity, including a visit to the police courts, a session of the City Corporation, an engineering works and the worst of the city's slums, Sassoon realized that he was completely unqualified to produce the article Massingham needed and asked Davies to write it for him. 'It probably contained a fair number of suggestions made by me,' he explained defensively, 'but the cheque, when it arrived, went straight to Davies.[78]

*

By 7 February Sassoon was back at Oxford. He had stopped briefly in London to recover at the 1917 Club, thinking it more suitable in his 'tousled unshaven condition' than the Reform.[79] (Word of his affair with Gabriel may already have spread, since he overheard one member confessing to another that he knew very little about Sassoon except that he was said to spend a hundred pounds a year on scent.) But his main focus was

37

now Oxford. Determined to remedy his political ignorance, so apparent to him in Glasgow, he envisaged an austere but rewarding programme of study and poetry-writing. His mornings would be passed in his rooms, gazing out over Christ Church meadows while absorbing 'constructive information about Capital and Labour and how to create social equality for all'.[80] His afternoons would be occupied by healthy walks in the country and his evenings devoted to reading poetry or mixing with brilliant young dons and undergraduates, whose progressive ideas would stimulate him to further efforts. And when he needed a little home comfort combined with high-mindedness, there was Garsington only a few miles away.

He had even bought the right clothes for the occasion: 'My Bolshevik uniform here', he wrote to Graves, 'is dark-green shirt, bright-red tie and corduroy trousers.'[81] But Oxford had changed since his austere wartime convalescence at Somerville College and though there were serious, mature students there determined to make up what the war had interrupted, there were also many young men whose main purpose was to have a good time. So that instead of the earnest life he had planned, Sassoon found himself immediately caught up in a social whirl even more frenzied than his London one. His own version in *Siegfried's Journey* implies that he had no control over events, but his letters and diaries of the period make it clear that he was not being entirely honest with himself. Another letter to Graves, for instance, who was about to take up his deferred scholarship at St John's College, suggests that Sassoon was planning a busy social life among the dreaming spires; despite a passing reference to the prominent Communists, Trotsky and Liebknecht, there would clearly be little time left over for politics:

> When you come we will found a splendid debating society and dining club. Toronto and Masefield will be honorary members, and Pinto will be Portuguese representative. Eddie Marsh will preside once in 5 years and pay for dinner; Lytton Strachey will address the Club every 10 years. Liebknecht and Trotsky will be asked to subscribe. No entrance fee, and no gum-chewing. Gabriel will play the harp on Saint's Day.[82]

'My God, we'll have fun at Oxford, old frump!' Graves responded.[83] He planned to spend all his spare time in Sassoon's Merton Street rooms, but fortunately for Sassoon's good intentions, his arrival was delayed, partly by ill health and partly by the birth of his first child, Jenny. Sassoon, who still felt betrayed by Graves's marriage the previous January, and had only met his wife Nancy Nicholson after much persuasion, nevertheless agreed to be Jenny's godfather, telling Graves: 'The child will be baptized with Turtle Soup, which it will be compelled to drink.'[84]

Even without Graves there were plenty of distractions. Gabriel, for whom the second bedroom had been taken, arrived in Oxford early in the month. Lectured at by Sassoon and still full of pious resolutions – he was planning to start at the Slade School of Art as soon as possible – his lifestyle nevertheless remained essentially frivolous. And his presence alone made it difficult for Sassoon to carry out his own plan of study. He needed to be constantly looked after, his excessive drinking, smoking and late nights bringing him close to collapse on numerous occasions.

In addition to Gabriel, there were others to tempt Sassoon from this chosen path. John Masefield, for example, lived nearby in an elite artistic community on Boar's Hill.[85] Sassoon had cycled over from Garsington to meet him two days before the Armistice and had admired the man as much as he already did his work. After revisiting in February 1919, he described him to Graves as 'the nicest man on Jesu's earth'.[86] The visit in itself posed no real threat to his political studies, but its consequences did. 'We have got to write and act a 25-minute play with 5 or 6 characters ... at Masefield's ball,' Sassoon informed Graves, begging him to 'please write the play'.[87]

Sassoon was particularly impressed by Masefield's simplicity, a quality for which he had an inordinate respect. In this he may unconsciously have been justifying his own approach to life, which he believed verged on the simple-minded. Alternatively he may have been defending his work, which was largely traditional, in contrast to the deliberate difficulty, obscurity and allusiveness of many Modernist poets. T.S. Eliot, whose *Prufrock and Other Observations* had been published in America by 1919, would remain a *bête noir* all his life, with Yeats and Auden rating little better. In his 'Self-Epitaph', written in about 1953, Sassoon would write only half-jokingly:

> Though much to blame for lack of enterprise
> In metaphor, in metre, thought, and rhyme
> He still could claim to be for captious eyes,
> 'Most simple-minded poet of his time'.[88]

The other poet he admired for his 'simplicity', Prewett, also proved a distraction at Oxford. Prewett and Masefield have become 'about the best people' he has ever met by 4 March.[89] Judging from his letters to Graves, the young Canadian's poor health, lack of money and need of a holiday were of far greater concern to him than books on political theory, or even his own poetry. 'Damn you,' he expostulated with Graves, as he tried to arrange a stay at Harlech for the difficult Prewett, 'you've got to swallow Toronto whole, you sniffing childmonger'.[90]

Prewett himself led on to other diversions. By the time Sassoon arrived in Oxford, Prewett had already made friends at Christ Church and introduced at least one of them to Sassoon, William Walton. Walton and Prewett had met through a shared interest in rowing and music and it was at a concert that Prewett first brought Walton and Sassoon together: 'I went to the Musical Club last night,' Walton wrote home to his mother on

12 February 1919. 'We had a fine concert. I met John Masefield and Siegfried Sassoon, the poets. They are great men.'[91]

Walton, who had been a chorister at Christ Church Cathedral School during the war, had become an undergraduate at the college itself in October 1918 at the age of sixteen. He was determined to succeed as a composer but was still struggling to establish himself on very little money. Pale, thin and delicate-looking, he must have appealed to Sassoon's protective instincts as well as his love of music, since Sassoon would become one of his most generous patrons, his reward being the dedication of his orchestral suite, *Portsmouth Point*, to him in 1925.

His greatest favour to Walton, however, took place shortly after they met. Most lives of Walton rightly emphasize the importance of his friendship with Osbert and Sacheverell Sitwell, but none points out that it was Sassoon who introduced the young composer to them in the first place. As Osbert recalls, Sassoon took Sachie to visit Walton, who then invited both Sitwell brothers, Sassoon and Prewett to tea,[92] thus launching his own career. The Sitwells became Walton's early champions, inviting him to live in their London house with them while he worked on his early compositions. And Walton's first real success arrived with his setting of their sister Edith's poems, *Façade*.

Sassoon had contacted the Sitwell brothers when he arrived in Oxford, knowing that Sachie was studying (briefly) at Balliol, with Osbert in close attendance. Since one of his main motives in moving to the university town had been to avoid dissipating his time and energy on social occasions, it was hardly a sensible contact. But it was a highly entertaining one and the Sitwells were responsible for what Sassoon regarded as his 'oddest' encounter in Oxford.[93] With their taste for the eccentric and bizarre, Osbert and Sachie had contacted one of the most exotic writers of the day, Ronald Firbank. Firbank, who, like them, was wealthy enough to follow his own whims, had become a cult figure with his novel *Vainglory* in 1915. He had followed this up with *Inclinations* (1916) and *Caprice* (1917) and was about to publish *Valmouth* when Sassoon was taken to see him by the Sitwells in February 1919.

If the keynote to Firbank's personality and work is artificiality, then his surroundings reflected him to perfection. His novels had led Sassoon to expect 'a somewhat peculiar person' and he was not surprised by the novelist's distinctly 'orchidaceous' appearance.[94] But he was not prepared for the closely curtained room filled with countless candles and hothouse flowers. Nor did he know how to deal with Firbank's strange behaviour, which made all attempts at ordinary conversation seem farcical. The only coherent remark he made was in answer to Sassoon's polite enquiry about the origins of the exotic fruit he had ordered for tea: 'Blenheim'.

The Sitwells, more at home in such a setting, were less thrown, though even they became disconcerted when, in reply to Sachie's praise of *Caprice*, Firbank murmured in a choking voice, 'I can't bear calceolarias! Can you?'[95] As he politely ate the rich cakes and out-of-season fruits in the overheated, heavily scented room, Sassoon found it hard to believe that this 'strange being' could have any relationship with the outer world. It seemed entirely appropriate that, when he asked Firbank his favourite country, he should reply 'Lotus-land'. Altogether he made Sassoon feel very pedestrian.

Sassoon was clearly fascinated by Firbank, a prefiguring of his later obsession with Stephen Tennant's exotic lifestyle. And though at the time he was dismissive of Firbank's novels, regarding them for all their amusement value as 'the elegant triflings of a talented amateur', he was sufficiently intrigued to return his invitation to tea.[96] He also reported the occasion in his autobiography, while many apparently more significant events of his stay, such as a second visit to the poet laureate, Robert Bridges, went unrecorded. But perhaps it was simply for the pleasure of detailing Firbank's further oddities: his response, for instance, to Sassoon's well-meaning attempts to draw him out about art and literature was 'I adore italics, don't you?' And his reaction to Sassoon's hospitably generous supply of crumpets, fruit and rich chocolate cake was 'slowly [to] absorb a single grape'.[97]

Yet Sassoon was to meet the novelist several more times before his early death in 1926 and to receive copies of his later books wittily inscribed in violet ink. And at least one letter from Firbank to Sassoon survives, thanking him for his poems, which he praises. Looked at in the light of Sassoon's autobiography alone their continuing friendship is puzzling, since it omits one of the main contributory factors, Gabriel. For Gabriel, who could not be mentioned in *Siegfried's Journey*, found Firbank 'Simply too marvellous!' as Sassoon explains in his diary: '[Firbank] belongs to the life into whose fringes I am drawn by my "friendship" with G. He is the type of man that G. would have become if he'd never met me. A talented drunken freak without enough strength of character to steer him through the shoals of intellectual Bohemia.'[98]

Like Gabriel, however, for all his preciousness Firbank was fairly shrewd. 'I am Pavlova chasing butterflies,' he told Sassoon on meeting him at the Russian Ballet in 1921. 'You are Tolstoi digging for worms.'[99] It was a remark which might have been made by one of Firbank's greatest admirers, and Sassoon's future lover, Stephen Tennant, whose extraordinary behaviour was to cause the poet so much suffering. Significantly, one of Sassoon's earliest presents to Tennant would be Firbank's *Sorrow in Sunlight* (1924), a strong influence on Tennant's own, unfinished novel, *Lascar*. Though Sassoon recognized that Firbank's technique was quite deliberate and highly professional and realized 'a sort of opulent beauty and decadent gaiety' in his last novels, he was ultimately to dismiss him as a 'giggling dipsomaniac' with 'a genius for subtle silliness'.[100]

Unlike Tennant or Gabriel, Firbank, a powdered, ninetyish figure the same age as Sassoon, did not attract him physically. But another friend of

41

the Sitwells almost certainly did. Beverley Nichols, a fellow-student of Sachie at Balliol, was handsome, gifted and, crucially for Sassoon, not yet twenty-one.[101] Christened by Osbert 'the original bright young thing', he was just the kind of youth calculated to seduce Sassoon, and not just away from his work.

Sassoon may have met Nichols briefly in Cambridge in 1915 through Dent or Theo, the way in which Gabriel had got to know 'Nicolette', as his Cambridge friends called him, in 1917. This would partly explain Nichols's own interest in their relationship: 'Gabriel is now great friends with Sassoon,' he wrote euphemistically in his diary on 3 January 1919. It was a liaison which would also have signalled to him that Sassoon was finally 'available' on the sexual front.[102] The relationship began fairly formally with an invitation to tea in Nichols's rooms, which Sassoon went to, chaperoned by Gabriel, Sachie and Osbert, on 18 February. They met again at tea next day in the rooms of Graves's Charterhouse friend 'Peter' Johnstone.[103] And two days later Nichols invited Sassoon and his friends to one of his 'Society' meetings.[104] Only a day after that he was inviting Sassoon to his rooms again, with Sachie and Johnstone, this time to hear him play a scherzo on his baby grand. He played the piano well, always an attractive quality for Sassoon, who would also have appreciated his skilfully furnished rooms and well-chosen paintings. To add to the interest, Nichols was starting a new magazine, the *Oxford Outlook*, and wanted a contribution from Sassoon.

It was the magazine which provided the opportunity for their first tête-à-tête a week later, when Nichols went round to Sassoon's rooms to discuss it. Perhaps Sassoon showed him the poem he planned to submit, 'Lovers', with its explicit detail and erotic overtones.[105] He probably encouraged Nichols to approach Masefield for a contribution, which Nichols successfully did. And five days later both poets were addressing one of Nichols's many societies, Masefield having been persuaded by Sassoon to do so.

Then, on 9 March, a cryptic sentence in Nichols's diary code indicates the likely outcome of his relationship with Sassoon: 'Siegfried came up after.' For Nichols, who was cheerfully promiscuous throughout his life, the encounter seems to have meant very little: he remained friends with both Sassoon and Gabriel, the latter giving him 'two ripping cartoons' for another magazine he edited, *The Isis*, less than a month later and a cover design for a third publication, *The Topaz of Ethiopia*. But for Sassoon it was another significant step in the acceptance of his own sexuality. He had tried to idealize his physical relations with Gabriel, but there could be no denying the carnal nature of a one-night stand with an attractive, fairly casual acquaintance. Though no one would ever call him promiscuous, this liaison marked a further crumbling of his resistance to the physical side of sex, as his numerous relationships with young men in the 1920s would show.

2. 'A Simpleton's Progress' (January-March 1919)

*

By the beginning of March Sassoon was forced to admit that Rivers's plan for his education was failing. 'I am not writing anything, and find it difficult to be sufficiently alone and detached for reading much,' he told Graves.[106] Though he was happy to play on his reputation as a Labour movement personality and anti-war poet, he had done no serious political study, a fact which he rather disingenuously attributed to his unforeseen involvement in 'a series of tea parties with Oxford poets'.[107]

Even more worryingly he had written little poetry and was still no clearer as to his future direction in that area. His initial passion and subsequent despair over Gabriel had inspired at least eight poems in a very different vein from his war verses. He had also experimented with at least two poems in other poets' styles.[108] And he felt that his 'new stuff' was 'a distinct advance, in precision and economy of method, – on the old stuff'.[109] But the impetus had not lasted and by the middle of March he had added only three poems.[110] Two of these, 'The Goldsmith' and 'Devotion to Duty', look to the distant past for their inspiration, but indicate no new direction for the future.

The third poem, 'Aftermath', is more successful, though mainly as an 'effective recitation poem' according to Sassoon.[111] Its series of declamatory questions and statements may strike the modern reader as too rhetorical and much of it is highly emotive – 'Look up, and swear by the green of the spring that you'll never forget' – but it paints a vivid picture of trench warfare and conveys convincing concern for the ordinary soldier:

> ... Do you remember the dark months you held the sector at Mametz
> – The nights you watched and wired and dug and piled sandbags on parapets?
> Do you remember the rats; and the stench
> Of corpses rotting in front of the front-line trench –
> And dawn coming, dirty-white, and chill with a hopeless rain?
> Do you ever stop and ask, 'Is it all going to happen again?'
>
> Do you remember that hour of din before the attack –
> And the anger, the blind compassion that seized and shook you then
> As you peered at the doomed and haggard faces of your men?
> Do you remember the stretcher-cases lurching back
> With dying eyes and lolling heads – those ashen-grey
> Masks of the lads who once were keen and kind and gay? ...
>
> (CP, p. 119)

The main problem with 'Aftermath' for Sassoon was that it looked backwards and led him no nearer to a new path. It was almost certainly written in reaction to his demobilization on 12 March 1919.[112] He had refused to accompany Graves to Limerick for the event, but had nevertheless been officially retired with the rank of captain. Curiously, for someone who was already becoming irritated by a tendency to brand him solely as a war poet, he decided to keep his military title in civilian life, a social solecism for all but regular soldiers. And he would do so to the end of his life. Wilfred Owen's brother, Harold, whose request for 'Mr Sassoon' at the Reform Club was swiftly corrected to '*Captain* Sassoon, sir', suggests that while Sassoon repudiated war, he was snobbishly unable to resist 'empty' titles. Dame Felicitas Corrigan, on the other hand, argues that it was probably Hardy's remark to Graves, after the latter had given up his title, that dictated Sassoon's choice: '"But you have a right to it!" Hardy had said. "I should certainly keep my rank if I had one, and feel very proud to be called Captain Hardy".'[113] If so, it was probably a rationalization of a deeper urge to preserve a last link with his men who had meant so much to him. Perhaps he heard the words of Whitman in their mouths: 'O Captain, my Captain!'

This need not to forget may have stemmed from guilt that he had survived while so many had died. But there was no danger that he would ever be able to put it behind him. During the four years of war he had experienced, for the first and last time, a strong sense of purpose both in his life and his work. It was, in a strange way, a kind of 'Arcadia' (his word) to which he would constantly try to return, though 'Aftermath' was technically one of his last war poems.

Within days of writing it, he decided to leave Oxford. To his complete surprise, he had been offered the literary editorship of a new Labour paper, the *Daily Herald*. Though he had failed in his own eyes in his political efforts, he was evidently still regarded as a good socialist by the outside world. It seemed to him a heaven-sent chance to 'put an end to [his] purposeless existence at Oxford' and he accepted the post at once.[114]

By 19 March, three days before his departure, he was writing to tell Theo that he was 'rather glad to leave', because Oxford was 'no good for writing'. It was not his only motive. Apart from his failure to study, he had more practical concerns. The army had continued to pay him a modest amount, but this had come to an end with his official retirement earlier in the month. His private income was scarcely enough to cover his expenses, particularly now that he had started to make Gabriel a generous allowance.[115] And there were other obligations: his brother Michael was returning from Canada with a family and very little money. 'It is a cushy job, at £5 a week and extras,' he wrote to Graves, 'and I can't refuse it, as I've got to find at least £300 a year for my brother, who has two boys to educate as snobs at a first-class prep school ...'[116]

His most compelling reason for accepting the *Daily Herald* job, however, was the hope that it would stop him 'worrying so much about leagues of nations and conscription, etc.', the very issues one might expect to find debated in a Labour paper of the period.[117] By taking it he hoped finally to escape the war and the 'picture-show' of memories which still haunted him.

3

'Making the Book Page Memorable'[1]
(April-June 1919)

Everyone suddenly burst out singing;
And I was filled with such delight
As prisoned birds must find in freedom,
Winging wildly across the white
Orchards and dark-green fields; on – on – and out of sight.

Everyone's voice was suddenly lifted;
And beauty came like the setting sun:
My heart was shaken with tears; and horror
Drifted away ... O, but Everyone
Was a bird; and the song was wordless; the singing
    will never be done.

                ('Everyone Sang', CP, p. 124)[2]

Sassoon's acceptance of the *Daily Herald* literary editorship had a number of consequences. One of the most immediate was a sense of liberation from the war, as he had hoped. And this, in turn, inspired his popular anthology poem, 'Everyone Sang'.[3] Written during his first few weeks at the *Herald*, it expresses his powerful feeling of release from years of tension and unhappiness. Like floodwaters bursting their dam, his renewed joy in life sweeps all before it in flowing, irresistible lines.

Sassoon's description of the poem's genesis in *Siegfried's Journey* occurs, significantly, during his account of his *Herald* job. He recalls the time and place, but above all the spontaneity with which it was written: 'A few words had floated into my head as though from nowhere.'[4] There seemed to him no preliminary thinking, but rather, to repeat a phrase he would use of a later work, 'a sort of difficult remembering'.[5]

However difficult the remembering in 'Everyone Sang', it is not immediately obvious and the poem appears deceptively artless on first reading. A closer look reveals an elaborately patterned structure which makes it hard to believe that it was as spontaneous as Sassoon claimed. Though he himself described its form as 'rather free',[6] its careful rhyme-scheme and regular measure suggest the opposite. Further patterning is imposed by the emphatic repetition of 'Everyone' throughout, and the insistent alliteration of lines three and four.

Nevertheless, a sense of freedom and spontaneity is achieved, partly by the frequent running of one line into another and the visual device of an apparently irregular long last line to each stanza, but particularly by the imagery. To 'burst out singing' conveys in simple, unforced terms the uncontrollable delight of 'Everyone', including the narrator, who passes quite naturally from singing to birds, with the idea of freedom reinforced by the prison from which the birds have escaped. This set of metaphors is then expanded in stanza two, where 'Everyone' *becomes* 'a bird; and the song was wordless; the singing will never be done.'

The natural visual detail of birds 'winging wildly across white / Orchards and dark-green fields' into the 'setting sun' may also have helped to make this one of Sassoon's most popular poems, perhaps also because it is not 'thought-riddled', to use T.E. Lawrence's phrase.[7] As Sassoon put it to Walter de la Mare, 'Everyone Sang' was his 'Innisfree'.[8] And, like Yeats's poem, its popularity came to irritate its author in later life, though at the time of composition he thought it one of his best lyrics.[9] Graves was exasperated by 'Everyone Sang' from the start: '"Everybody",' he wrote, misquoting perhaps deliberately, 'did not include me.'[10]

Since 'Everyone Sang' is usually taken to refer to the Armistice, it is traditionally included with Sassoon's war poems, but he himself called it 'a peace celebration', and was proud of Masefield's recognition of it as such.[11] He was also anxious to explain that his poem was really about the social revolution he believed to be at hand in 1919.[12] And the 'singing', which many readers interpreted as a reference to soldiers on the march, really referred to this hope of social change. (It is doubtful whether his poem would have enjoyed the popularity it has if this had been made clear.)

In the light of Sassoon's gloss it becomes even more understandable why he wrote 'Everyone Sang' shortly after starting work on the *Daily Herald*, Britain's only socialist daily in 1919.[13] The *Herald*'s original founder and editor was George Lansbury, a man whom one unsympathetic contemporary described as 'one of those sentimental, muddle-headed Pecksniffian good men who mean so well in theory and do so much harm in practice'.[14]

Sassoon was almost certainly familiar with Lansbury's name, since he would have known the weekly version of the *Herald* published throughout the war, which largely reflected his own anti-war views. Its success had encouraged Lansbury to relaunch it as a daily in 1919, when he continued to make it the mouthpiece of his left-wing and markedly pro-Russian views.[15]

Lansbury would go on to be an MP and eventually leader of the Labour Party after Ramsay MacDonald's defeat in 1931. His working-class, trade-unionist background was in strong contrast to his much younger associate editor, Gerald Gould, who represented the intellectual element in the party. Only a year older than Sassoon, Gould was an ex-Fellow of Merton

College, Oxford, and much closer to him in background. It was he who had written to ask Sassoon to join the *Daily Herald* and almost certainly he who had suggested him in the first place. A poet himself, he admired not just Sassoon's anti-war protest but also his verse, offering to review it at one point if Sassoon, as literary editor, felt inhibited about asking anyone else to do so.[16]

Though Sassoon felt at home neither with intellectuals nor the working classes, a fact which contributed to his eventual rejection of socialism, he certainly felt more comfortable with fellow-poets of middle-class background like Gould and another member of the *Herald* staff, Francis Meynell. He had met Meynell briefly at Garsington in November 1918[17] and claimed to be 'very fond of him'.[18] But their mutual interest in poetry and book design would not be enough to keep their friendship alive once Sassoon had abandoned socialism.

There were other significant figures on the *Herald*'s staff; Norman Angell, for example, with what Leonard Woolf called his 'remarkable personality' and 'remarkable book', *The Great Illusion*.[19] But none of these interested Sassoon as much as the paper's music critic, W.J. Turner (of 'Chimborazo, Cotopaxi' fame).[20] Born in Australia in the 1880s, Turner had come to London as a young man determined to be a poet. He had managed to get to know Marsh, Rupert Brooke and other Georgians, with whom his own verse became identified. After serving with the Royal Artillery from 1916 to 1918 he continued with the music criticism for the *New Statesman* he had started during the war, accepted a job with the *Daily Herald* and was to become drama critic of the *London Mercury* when it was launched by his friend J.C. Squire later in 1919.

Sassoon had been reading and admiring Turner's exotic poetry since at least 1917, when he had written to Graves: 'Get *The Hunter and Other Poems* by W.J. Turner … and tell people to buy it. Some very good things in it.'[21] He reminded Graves of this when the latter, with his usual aplomb, implied that it was he who had 'discovered' Turner.[22] There seems to have been some possessiveness between them over 'Walter' – or 'Wilks', as Sassoon sometimes called him. Sassoon had first met Turner at a dinner given by Osbert Sitwell in late 1918, when their mutual commitment to poetry and music quickly drew them together. But Graves had become friends with Turner just as rapidly, asking him to be his co-editor on a new publishing venture, *The Owl*, at about the same period.

Turner must have had a magnetic personality as well as talent for neither his appearance nor voice were prepossessing. Lytton Strachey described him to Virginia Woolf with his usual cruel wit and social assumptions as 'a very small birdlike man with a desolating accent, good deal to say for himself – but punctuated by strange hesitations – impediments – rather distressing; but really a nice little fellow, when one has got over the way in which he says "count" '.[23] Anthony Powell remembers him as 'sallow, slight in build, his movements quick and nervous', a man who gave the impression of being 'eternally fed up with the human race'.[24] Powell was aware of Turner's reputation for antagonizing people by his outspokenness, especially in the musical world, but claims to have found him 'not at all unsympathetic', a careful double negative which fails to make Turner sound either interesting or appealing.

Later on, after Sassoon had grown disillusioned with Turner, he would criticize his 'general rawness and violence of opinion'[25] and other graver faults, such as his compulsive womanizing and general disloyalty to former friends. But in early 1919 he felt nothing but admiration for the small, tough, self-educated Australian. It was largely the attraction of opposites.

Sassoon particularly admired Turner's wide aesthetic taste, which included art and drama, as well as music and poetry. He found him 'if anything, more sensitive' than he was and even more involved in London's intellectual and artistic world.[26] Listening to Turner's 'stimulating and provocative talk' made him wish, uncharacteristically, to 'shake off the past'.[27] He longed to enter into Turner's world, where audacious critical opinions and adventurous ideas were the order of the day. And for a time it looked as though Turner might manage to drag him into the twentieth century.

To begin with, at least, Sassoon believed his friend to have '*real* creative imagination', though he found his work very uneven. It took him some time to understand Turner's 'extraordinary' character, his 'queer mixture of uncouthness and adventurous gusto for exquisite sensations'.[28] Though many of his ideas remained undeveloped they seemed to Sassoon highly original. His was an 'imaginative intensity', Sassoon concluded, which he had 'not learned to control or express'.[29]

Above all (and, later, in spite of all), Sassoon admired Turner's independence and seriousness. He was enormously attracted to Turner's 'quality of male independence', though not, he insisted, in a sexual way.[30] In fact, he believed that his satisfactory relationship with Turner was based on 'a complete absence of any sex feeling at all'.[31] One of Sassoon's later lovers, Prince Phillip of Hesse, would argue that Turner was a clear case of 'repressed "peculiarity" ' (i.e., homosexuality) and Sassoon felt that there was 'just enough evidence to make it barely possible ... There is something abnormal about T[urner]'s sexual organization.'[32] But there is no suggestion of any sexual relationship between the two writers. This may account for an important element in their friendship, Sassoon's ability to confide in Turner completely about his sexual problems.[33] Though Turner was to profess total ignorance on the subject of homosexuality, he was evidently able to accept Sassoon's confidences in a non-judgemental way. As a colonial and disciple of Shaw and Ibsen, whose advanced ideas caused outrage in early twentieth-century England, Turner's outlook was almost certainly less conventional and hidebound than many of Sassoon's friends. He also had a good sense of humour. All in all he was to become very important to Sassoon for a time.

*

The most important member of the *Herald*'s staff in practical terms, however, was Sassoon's secretary, Miss Irene Clephane, who ran his tiny office at 8 Carmelite Street. Since his literary columns came out initially on Wednesdays and Saturdays, she worked only part-time for him on Tuesdays and Fridays, but her help was invaluable.[34] His account in *Siegfried's Journey* stresses his own ignorance and impetuousness, both of which he exaggerated for comic effect,[35] portraying himself, as he did in the First World War, as a bungling amateur. Miss Clephane probably did contribute useful suggestions about his 'Books of To-day and To-morrow' columns, but he was not as ignorant of the technicalities of typography as he suggests, having designed at least ten privately printed volumes of his own work by 1919. And he is unlikely to have reacted to the depressing accumulation of 'unreviewable volumes' by penning a 'pungent note urging authors and publishers to cultivate continence', which he says she prevented him from doing.[36] But she would probably have known more than he did about the custom of selling review copies to nearby booksellers at half price or less, a practice which might have benefited his aunt, Rachel Beer, during her eccentric editorship of both the *Observer* and *The Sunday Times*, when Sassoon recalled books for review piling up unopened in her exotic Mayfair home.[37] And Miss Clephane almost certainly saved him from blunders in his correspondence with contributors, as he claimed. What he called his 'exuberant facetiousness' might well have displayed itself in inappropriate ways, particularly if he sensed hostility towards the paper. His secretary's judicious 'Are you sure you want to send that?' no doubt kept him out of some damaging situations.

His own attitude towards the *Daily Herald* was a mixture of resolution, excitement and pride, but he quickly realized that not everyone felt so positive about it. He knew that his mother, for example, though she 'maintained a noble reticence', privately thought of the *Herald* as 'that rabid and pestilent rag'.[38] Returning yet again to Weirleigh to live, he had found the Weald of Kent as lovely as ever, but the garden had a neglected air and there were no horses left in the stables or summer cricket matches to cheer him. Worst of all, relations between himself and his long-suffering mother were strained by her efforts to conceal her true feelings about his politics. So that it was with a sense of relief, as well as excitement, that he rode his bicycle down to Paddock Wood on Tuesdays and Fridays to take the train into London and spend the night there.

Marsh, too, disapproved of the *Daily Herald*, dismissing it as 'a very fishy try-on'.[39] His reaction came as no surprise to Sassoon, who had anticipated criticism of his socialist activities in a letter to Marsh of

January 1919 which contained a caricature of himself holding a flag with the word 'Red' on it – as he assumed he was in Marsh's ultra-conservative eyes.[40]

Marsh had also been partly responsible for the disapproval of Graves's parents, who were worried about their son reviewing books for Sassoon in a Labour daily. Far from reassuring them, Marsh had strengthened their fears by claiming that Sassoon had 'bolshevized or tried to bolshevize Robert'.[41] And though Sassoon was able to reassure Mr and Mrs Graves when he visited them at Harlech in late July 1919, it must have made him doubly conscious of the social ostracism he risked in his new position.

For, as Graves himself put it, the *Daily Herald* was 'not respectable'.[42] Its strong anti-militarism, violent criticism of the Versailles Treaty and the blockade of Russia, but above all its protest against social injustice, made uncomfortable reading for the cosy middle classes. 'The *Herald* spoilt our breakfast every morning,' Graves wrote of himself and his wife with disarming honesty.[43] Unlike his parents, however, he and Nancy 'took it to heart' and 'called [themselves] socialists'.[44] It was a great comfort to Sassoon that at least one of those closest to him approved of the paper.[45]

The most significant reaction to the *Daily Herald*, however, came not from friends and family but from publishers, who were mainly to the right of the political spectrum. And this affected Sassoon's job in a way he had not anticipated. While getting into his editorial stride, he had given no thought to what he called 'the sordid subject of advertisements'.[46] Once he understood that any paper, especially one on such a tight budget as the *Herald*, needed the money from advertising, he dutifully set out on a round of visits to publishing houses to solicit business. But, while the interviews themselves were quite agreeable, it quickly became apparent that most big publishers disliked his paper for what they considered its disruptive ideas and that smaller firms simply did not have the money to advertise. The least businesslike of people himself, it was a subject which was to mar his otherwise enjoyable time with the paper.

His own publisher, William Heinemann, considered the *Daily Herald* 'a menace to the fabric of the social system',[47] and this had one immediate and unfortunate consequence. In an effort to ensure that publishers sent in review copies to the 'Paper with its Face Towards the Future', the *Herald* had issued an eight-page pamphlet trumpeting 'A Literary Editor for the New London Daily Newspaper'. Pleasantly designed, with a border of printer's flowers enclosing each page, it included four of Sassoon's poems from *Counter-Attack*,[48] as well as a list of his impressive 'reviewing staff'.[49] Unluckily, one of the first to receive the flyer was Heinemann, the publisher of the four poems in it. Since these had been printed without his permission he was able to express his strong dislike of the *Herald* by demanding the destruction of all undistributed copies of the pamphlet. Sassoon laid the whole responsibility for its publication on Meynell's keenness to promote the new literary editor, but it is more likely that

3. 'Making the Book Page Memorable' (April-June 1919)

Sassoon had also been involved. He could be very cavalier about permissions.

At any rate, he tried to win Heinemann back by reviewing several of his publications in the following weeks and months, an attempt which explains several puzzling review choices. Heinemann was almost certainly mollified, since his firm would continue to publish Sassoon until 1928, but the main interest of the incident is that it highlights the power Sassoon's new position gave him. Not only could he choose which books to review and which not; he was also responsible for who reviewed them. On one occasion, after being lunched by W.L. George, a successful novelist of 'oily alertness' who spoke spitefully of a rival, Gilbert Cannan, and asked meaningfully to review his next book, Sassoon took evident pleasure in exercising his power.[50] Reversing the situation, he sent George's new book to Cannan for review and was not surprised when, instead of submitting the laudatory review George expected from the paper, Cannan 'slaughtered it with gusto'.[51] George's furious protest to Gould followed.

An even greater source of power for Sassoon were the 'Literary Notes' he had agreed to provide. These gave him the chance to promote his own favourites directly, which he did, writing at some length about war books in his first batch, for instance, and mentioning his friend H.G. Wells's latest book in passing.

He did not, however, exploit the potential the 'Notes' offered for developing his own prose style. Though his war experiences had inspired some memorable passages in his diary, most of his attempts at prose up to 1919 had been rather flowery, heavily influenced by Pater. But now that he had a solid platform, he seemed curiously reluctant to use it, producing only half a dozen sets of 'Notes' in over thirty issues and a few unsigned reviews. Whether this stemmed from laziness or a sense of inadequacy is not clear. His own explanation is 'diffidence and perplexity'.[52]

Whatever the reason, his first effort suggests that he was probably wise to limit these prose 'scraps', as he called them.[53] The tone is embarrassingly facetious, the irony only too obvious:

> It is easy to write literary notes. The writer need only possess the following accomplishments: a sound and comprehensive understanding of all branches of literature; a fluent and graceful style; an acute perception of what the publishing trade likes; a brilliant, creative, and facetious intellect; and an eye for the advertisement columns. The life of a literary editor is like a fairy tale. He gets up at a not unreasonable hour: on his way to work he pops in to see a few eminent and sympathetic publishers. Finally, he drifts down Fleet Street like a ray of sunshine and arrives at the office, where he finds that people have sent him presents of lovely books. After glancing at a few of these, he writes some literary notes and goes away to spend his salary.[54]

In spite of his opening claim, Sassoon clearly does *not* find it 'easy' to write prose at this point. He simply cannot settle on the right tone for the occasion and his 'cheeky jocularity', as he calls it, gives the impression he feared of 'cocksure jauntiness'.[55]

Even when he has something serious to say in his fourth set of notes on 21 May, the tone is still irritatingly jokey:

> After many hours of profound thought I have decided that literary notes ought to deal only with literature. This is a great relief; authentic literature is published so infrequently. But courage mounteth with occasion, and my obscure resolution may have extraordinary results. Who knows what disasters may fall upon the bookselling trade if this paragraph happens to catch the eyes of a few of the 'best sellers'? Oxenham may improvise a second *Paradise Lost*, and exchange the adulation of his limitless public for the more remote approbation of the professors who wage unending wars in the 'T–L–S', apparently believing that the proper study of mankind is prosody.[56]

However facetious this passage, in it Sassoon touches upon a real problem, endemic to his job: by agreeing to work for a crusading socialist daily, he is more or less obliged to review important political works, even though he may not think they have intrinsic literary merit. One such book is Professor Nicolai's *Biology of War*, which Gould makes sure is reviewed at length at the first opportunity by someone who understands its significance, Havelock Ellis. For a related, possibly even greater, problem is that Sassoon himself is not qualified to judge such books in political terms, his commitment to Labour being a largely emotional matter. His answer is to enlist a body of professionals, most of them academics or political figures, such as G.D.H. Cole, H.N. Brailsford, W.N. Ewer, Philip Guedalla and Bertrand Russell. For other specialist subjects, too, he does not hesitate to call in experts in their field, such as the philosopher C.E.M. Joad, or the Shakespearian scholar Ivor Brown.

Another problem, which threatens the space he has been allowed, is the rapid drop in advertising on his page over the first few weeks. After an impressive start it falls to virtually nothing.[57] He eventually receives a 'kindly-worded warning' from the Editorial Board that the literary side of the paper has become too expensive and must be abbreviated until it attracts more advertising, a warning he evidently takes to heart, since the advertising picks up noticeably in the twelfth number.

However unbusinesslike Sassoon affected to be, he was clearly capable of action when his own interests were threatened. Not only did he increase the advertising, but he also persuaded the Editorial Board to allow him to replace his modest twice-weekly section with a larger weekly one, as he had originally wanted.[58] Wednesday was the chosen day, though Sassoon managed to get literary articles published occasionally on Saturdays; there was a full-length column by Henry Nevinson on Walt Whitman, 'The People's Poet', on 31 May 1919, for instance, to mark the centenary of Whitman's birth. Strictly speaking, he now needed to visit London only once a week.

3. 'Making the Book Page Memorable' (April-June 1919)

With his responsibilities thus reduced, Sassoon appreciated his position even more. It seemed to him just sufficient employment to engage his interest and to provide a sense of stability destroyed by the war. The money it brought, though generous, was probably less important to him, since he paid no rent at Weirleigh and had temporarily given up one of his most expensive pre-war pursuits, hunting. He was, however, glad to be able to help with his nephews' education and he particularly enjoyed being able to pay decent rates to contributors, especially those who were still struggling to establish themselves as writers. (He managed to raise the paper's suggested rate of pay from 2 guineas to 3 guineas per 1000 words.)

His pleasure in offering work is evident in a letter he wrote to the impecunious Graves, for instance, more than a fortnight before the first issue: 'You will have to do a lot of amusing reviews for the *Herald* ... non-pompous.'[59] And the next day he added: 'Please note that you are engaged to do a brilliant signed review of 900 to 1000 words of the more important spring poetry; you ought to score heavily off Kipling, Yeats, Shanks, Binyon, etc.'[60] He also used his 'Notes' to puff both the May and November numbers of Graves's new literary venture, *The Owl*, though he was not prepared to accept everything Graves sent him, returning an article on W.H. Davies, for example, with some fairly harsh comments.[61]

Another young writer Sassoon enjoyed helping was Robert Nichols, who had been his friend since 1917.[62] Though Nichols's war poetry had been even more successful than his own, he was still finding it difficult to support himself when he returned from America in mid-1919 and appreciated the offer of review work.[63] Sassoon's readiness to help Nichols may, in part, have been a response to Nichols's extravagant praise of him in the American edition of *Counter-Attack* and his readiness to read Sassoon's poems to audiences wherever he went on his American tour.

Sassoon had not yet tired of Nichols's apparently unbounded confidence and manic energy, which bordered at times on instability. And Nichols's frequent absences abroad in the twenties would prolong the friendship beyond its natural limit.[64] In 1919 Sassoon could still believe in and enjoy the flamboyant Nichols, whom Graves (his neighbour on Boar's Hill in the early twenties) described as 'one more neurasthenic ex-soldier, with his flame-opal ring, his wide-brimmed hat, his flapping arms, and a "mournful grandeur in repose" (the phrase comes from a review by Sir Edmund Gosse).'[65]

Though the Sitwells were slightly less in need of support than Nichols, they were famously anxious to promote themselves and responded eagerly to Sassoon's invitation to contribute to his columns.[66] Osbert, in particular, benefited from Sassoon's generosity, since the four satires he submitted led directly to the publication of his first solo poetry collection, *The Winstonburg Line*.[67] The first of these, 'Corpse-Day', outdid Sassoon in its bitter condemnation of the war.[68] His three short satires on Winston Churchill, based on Sassoon's memory of Churchill telling him that 'War is the natural occupation of man', attracted so much attention that they were presented as editorial leaders.[69]

Sassoon's most interesting choice among younger writers was Alec Waugh, Evelyn's older brother. He not only invited Waugh to review a number of books for the *Herald*, but also asked Graves to write about Waugh's latest novel. Waugh's first work, *The Loom of Youth*, which dealt openly with homosexuality, had been a *succès de scandale* at its publication and Sassoon seems to have been anxious to become better acquainted with its author, which his position allowed him to do. He had a 'very jolly' lunch with Waugh and another contributor to the *Herald*, E.M. Forster, during his first month as literary editor.[70] But despite the fact that Waugh admired his war poems greatly, had published a volume of his own and shared his passion for cricket, he failed to find him anything but 'extremely uninteresting'.[71]

With Forster it was quite different. One of Sassoon's greatest achievements on the *Herald* was to persuade Forster to become a regular reviewer. Forster's wit, perception and erudition illuminate even the dullest of books and his reviews stand out in Sassoon's literary columns as small works of art. His treatment of *The Price of Things* by the popular novelist Eleanor Glyn, for example, is highly entertaining, though at her and her publisher's expense:

> *The Price of Things* is seven shillings net. I think it is too high. The paper wrapper promises well. It shows a lively young lady dancing on a heap of roses in the middle of eight snakes. Their fangs protrude; their hoods swell. She dances, she smiles and she looks absolutely topping. But when one opens the book, I'm dashed if one comes across her again. It is the most frightful swizzle.[72]

Arnold Bennett, himself a highly influential reviewer, considered Forster the best reviewer in London and Sassoon claimed to understand more about a book from Forster in a few minutes than from 'twenty volumes' of comment by other critics.[73] He felt justifiably proud of Forster's 'brilliant' reviewing for his columns.[74]

It was also an opportunity to become better acquainted with Forster. Encouraged by their mutual friend, Dent, they had corresponded in 1918, but had not yet met by March 1919 when Sassoon wrote to ask Dent for Forster's new address.[75] Their first actual meeting was in the offices of the *Daily Herald*. But the relationship, which started so warmly, would be interrupted by first Sassoon's, then Forster's prolonged absence from England and would not form a significant aspect of Sassoon's life until he had become settled in London in the early twenties.

On the whole, however, Sassoon stuck to writers he already knew well for reviews. If they were really established, like Wells, Bennett, Masefield or de la Mare, he might commission a 'special' article from them at £10 a time, or arrange for their latest book to be favourably reviewed.[76] But there were limits. He was very disappointed not to be able to review Masefield's *Reynard the Fox*, for example, in October 1919, because of the *Herald's* resolute opposition to fox-hunting. But whenever possible, he promoted his favourites, especially if they were a minority taste, like Charles Doughty, Max Beerbohm, Charlotte Mew or Wilfrid Scawen Blunt.

Though familiar with both poets' work, he had known little of Blunt and even less of Mew until Cockerell, always a champion of writers he thought unduly neglected, offered to introduce him to them. Cockerell, as Penelope Fitzgerald has pointed out in her biography of Mew, was a great 'fixer' and undoubtedly hoped that an introduction to a literary editor would help promote both poets' work.[77] He rarely wasted time and by 16 May 1919, less than two months into his new job, Sassoon found himself taking tea with Charlotte Mew at her sister Anne's studio in Charlotte Street.[78] Beside Anne there was also Mew's other great ally, Alida Klementaski, the future wife of Harold Monro and his assistant at the Poetry Bookshop. Alida and Harold had done more than anyone else to promote Charlotte's work, publishing in 1916 *The Farmer's Bride*, the collection which first brought her to Cockerell's attention in 1918.

It must have been an odd gathering that day at 6 Hogarth Studios, the tiny, mannish figure of Mew, then over fifty and white-haired, contrasting strongly with the delicate, exotic beauty of the Polish Alida, the youthful handsomeness of Sassoon and the portly respectability of Cockerell. Both Mew and Sassoon were shy and both preferred their own sex, but Cockerell, helped no doubt by Alida, appears to have succeeded in making them like each other. Whereas T.E. Lawrence, whom Cockerell also tried to enlist, declared himself 'frigid' towards women and therefore untouched by Mew, Sassoon found her 'vividly gay'.[79] He may have been influenced by the fact that Hardy, also persuaded by Cockerell to meet Mew, had given her his blessing, which would explain Sassoon's familiarity with Mew's work by the time they met.

Neither Hardy nor Sassoon could have found the proud, diffident Mew easy, but they both succumbed immediately to her poetry. Hardy, who would have identified with her strange, often tormented vision, her colloquial language and deliberately irregular rhythms, thought her 'far and away the best living woman poet'[80] and Sassoon seconded this, though he added Edith Sitwell to the claim.[81] He had probably read the whole of *The Farmer's Bride* by the time he met Mew. He certainly knew and admired one of the most daring poems in it, 'Madeleine in Church', a dramatic monologue by a much-divorced woman which at least one compositor refused to set up in type because he found it blasphemous. Sassoon admired Mew's verse for its 'complete control of form' and 'masterly speech rhythms', which seemed to him superior even to Whitman, but his greatest praise was reserved for its 'emotional magic'.[82] Her work invariably gave him 'a lump in the throat', he told de la Mare, and reduced him 'to the verge of tears'.[83] It was the raw, emotional intensity, a quality he had achieved momentarily in his own war poetry, which turned him into a lifelong admirer of this 'harper on our heartstrings'.[84]

His efforts to help Mew, until her suicide in 1928, would include introductions to influential friends like Ottoline Morrell[85] and his part in getting a Civil List Pension for her in 1923,[86] but his first act was more direct. Knowing that she and her sister had very little money with which to support themselves and their elderly mother, he offered her paid work with the *Herald*. A review by her appeared a month after their first meeting on 11 June.

The situation was reversed in the case of Blunt. Knowing that Cockerell had managed to secure an invitation for him to stay the weekend with the venerable poet, diplomat and Arabist in June, Sassoon commissioned H.W. Nevinson to write a long review of Blunt's *My Diaries* on 7 May in advance of his visit. He might well have had the book reviewed in any case, but whether at such length and so favourably by such a respected journalist is another matter.

When Sassoon eventually visited Blunt from 14 to 16 June, he was already familiar with what he described as his 'admirable sonnets and protean love-lyrics'.[87] He had also heard many stories of Blunt's colourful life, which included marriage to Byron's granddaughter, an affair in the desert with his cousin's daughter, Mary Wemyss, resulting in a child, and fights for Egyptian, Indian and Irish independence that landed him in prison. All of this, together with Blunt's famous stud of Arab horses, appealed to Sassoon's romantic imagination and he anticipated meeting a 'cultivated, picturesque and contentious character', who might not be quite so handsome as in his youth but would nevertheless be an impressive, patriarchal figure.[88]

In reality, Blunt, who was almost eighty by the time they met in the bedroom of his fine Jacobean house, Newbuildings, in West Sussex, was more fragile and less formidable than Sassoon had expected, with a surprisingly soft voice. His dark eyes appeared to observe Sassoon 'with the mournful scrutiny of a proud spirit resenting age and infirmity'.[89] But Sassoon was impressed, as he so easily was, by Blunt's aristocratic background: 'He was the most perfect example of a thoroughbred human being I had seen ...'[90]

It seems appropriate that Sassoon should have described Blunt in terms of a racehorse, since Blunt himself showed more interest in Sassoon's abilities as a horse-racer than as a poet. When they did eventually discuss poetry, Sassoon became convinced that Blunt's 'strong prejudices' against contemporary verse had stunted his development as a poet. Given Sassoon's own negative attitude towards most of the significant experimental poetry of his time, it is ironic that he should make such a charge.

He clearly preferred to think of Blunt in the context of his 'noble' Arab stallions and he ends his account of the weekend with a glowing description of Blunt, 'superb' in his white Bedouin cloak, leading his guests to the paddock in his invalid pony-carriage. The scene closes with Blunt being sung an old folksong by his ebullient neighbour, Hilaire Belloc, whom Sassoon has met the previous day:

> But what returns to me in sunset light [Sassoon writes] is the broad and bulky yet somehow boyish figure of the singer, sitting on a bench close by the old friend whom he was intent on pleasing, and Wilfrid Blunt, listening with half-closed eyes, his face touched to tenderness and regret by the power and pathos of the words. I see them thus together, and so shall always do, as though the moment could never be taken from them and might be re-enacted beyond the dream of earthly time.[91]

Cockerell, the fourth figure in the scene, thought Sassoon's rather syrupy account the 'best picture of Blunt in old age that has ever been given',[92] but it is more interesting for what it omits than what it includes. Sassoon makes no mention, for example, of having read some of his poems to Blunt, a fact which emerges only from Cockerell's diary entry for the visit. Blunt's reaction was clearly not a positive one, since Sassoon makes an oblique reference to 'suspect[ing] that he disapproved of my war poems'.[93] His unwillingness to spell out Blunt's disapproval is understandable, but it reinforces doubts about the complete reliability of his autobiography.

Blunt's failure to praise his poetry may well have contributed to Sassoon's reservations about Blunt's own work. Of all the famous writers he had visited since the end of the war Blunt was not, he felt, 'the most notable in achievement'.[94]

That position Sassoon undoubtedly reserved for Hardy and he happily exercised his new-found power to promote his hero. Not only did he commission a special article from the poet Lascelles Abercrombie to mark Hardy's seventy-ninth birthday on 2 June, but he also used his increased literary authority to organize a tribute to Hardy from the younger poets. (He realized that the traditional time to pay homage would be on Hardy's eightieth birthday but was too eager to wait.) This took the form of an anthology of poems handwritten by each contributor on special paper and beautifully bound up under Cockerell's expert supervision. With Gosse's approval, Sassoon chose a committee of influential figures, all of them friends of his by now – Gosse, Masefield, de la Mare, Newbolt and Robert Bridges, who wrote a short foreword. Sassoon himself was secretary. In all, forty-three poets contributed to the volume, which Sassoon was deputed to present to Hardy at Max Gate.

The whole project smacks of an ambitious young man's attempt to ingratiate himself, but this was almost certainly not the case. While Sassoon was quite ready to use any connection that might prove useful in the literary world, he genuinely wanted to pay tribute to the object of his worship. He had already been an admirer of Hardy's work before his first visit to him in November 1918.[95] Afterwards, it was his character which impressed him most, particularly his homely naturalness. 'It was that simplicity which made me love him,' he wrote to a friend forty-six years after their first meeting.[96]

It was probably for similar reasons that Hardy grew to love Sassoon, regarding him for the last ten years of his life as the son he had never had. And Sassoon, whose own father had left home before his fifth birthday, found in him the father-figure he craved.[97] Very few months were to pass without a meeting between them. In 1919, for example, even before his visit to present the birthday tribute, Sassoon met Hardy in London at J.M. Barrie's flat in Adelphi Terrace. Graves had persuaded Hardy to contribute a poem to *The Owl*, and had asked Sassoon, also a contributor, to take a dozen copies for the master to sign. Sassoon greatly enjoyed the occasion, particularly the sight of Hardy conscientiously monogramming the copies, while Barrie, 'almost dwarfish in a very old blue suit, stumped about the room with a big bubbling pipe in his mouth and his hands plunged deep in his pockets'.[98] Though Sassoon himself was not greatly impressed by Barrie except as a 'dramatic conjuror', he recognized that Barrie was one of Britain's most successful playwrights and was surprised to see him looking not only shabby, but also depressed.[99] In the background J.C. Squire, who knew Sassoon but not the Hardys, introduced himself to Hardy's second wife, Florence.

When, several months later, Sassoon delivered the 'Poets' Tribute' to Hardy, it seemed to him 'as good a moment as any' he had known.[100] Hardy's evident pleasure at the mark of recognition so animated him that the years dropped away from him. It was, however, the last occasion on which Sassoon could forget how old he was. 'Always, when going there again,' he wrote, 'I was in dread that he would show signs of his increasing age.'[101] When the inevitable changes occurred, gradual though they were, he became increasingly careful not to overtax Hardy. Their long discussions, like their walks in the Dorset countryside, were curtailed. And eventually, in order to avoid tiring Hardy in the evenings, Sassoon would stay, not with the Hardys themselves, but in a hotel. So that his visits became a source of some anxiety to him as well as intense pleasure. His most vivid memory of these later years was of Hardy saying, 'You'd better come again soon, or you may find me over at Stinsford churchyard.' To which Florence Hardy replied: 'Don't be so gruesome, T.H.!'[102]

When Hardy eventually died in 1928, Sassoon would find consolation in his friendship with a fellow-enthusiast, H.M. Tomlinson, a writer who appears regularly in the *Herald*'s literary columns in 1919. Hardy himself had praised Tomlinson's *Old Junk* to Sassoon in 1918, the year it was published, and Sassoon may already have met Tomlinson in the offices of the *Nation*, where he was literary editor under Massingham.[103] He may also have met him at the Reform, of which both were members, but the relationship seems to have been consolidated at the *Daily Herald*.

'No man alive,' Sassoon told the poet Charles Causley, had a 'deeper love and veneration for Hardy and his work.'[104] And when Causley persuaded Sassoon and Tomlinson to make a radio programme about Hardy in 1955, Tomlinson delighted Causley by referring to his old friend simply as 'Tom'. (Gosse had christened Hardy 'true Thomas'.) Sassoon in turn called Tomlinson 'Tommy', an affectionate echo, perhaps, of his first great love, the young army officer David Thomas. That was as far as the similarity went, however, for no one could have less resembled the handsome ex-public schoolboy than the rugged Tomlinson. Sassoon referred to his 'queer gargoyle face'[105] and Virginia Woolf saw him in terms of 'the hard knob of a walking stick carved by a boy of eight'.[106] Her husband, Leonard, remembered him more neutrally as 'gentle' and 'deaf'.[107]

Born in the dockland area of East London, Tomlinson had left school early and gone into a shipping office. He remained interested in the sea all his life, a fact which is reflected in Causley's description of him as a 'splendid sea-captainish figure'. Largely self-educated, he never quite lost his cockney accent, as Sassoon rather snobbishly noted in his diary.[108] Yet in spite of his disadvantages, he became a highly respected journalist and prose writer, producing his first successful book, *The Sea and the Jungle* (1912), at the age of thirty-nine. Sassoon thought him a 'great prose writer'.[109] He is remembered nowadays, if at all, for his novels *Gallions Reach* (1927) and *All Our Yesterdays* (1930), a powerful criticism of the First World War.

Only thirteen years older than Sassoon, Tomlinson seemed to him far more than that in experience and would go some way to replacing Hardy as a father-figure. Though he came from a very different background from Hardy, Sassoon found in him the same 'comforting voice, homeliness and profound human philosophy'.[110] He relied greatly on Tomlinson's 'simple wisdom' and 'genuineness'[111] for guidance and would consult him frequently about both work and more personal matters.

Whether Tomlinson was quite as objective a critic of Sassoon's work as he insisted is doubtful.[112] One of the things which drew them together at the start, even more than a shared love of Hardy, a critical attitude towards the First World War and a good sense of humour, was a profound distrust of Modernism. Tommy was one of the few people on whom Sassoon felt he could lean for 'support in my ignoramus pilgrimage through the mazes of modernity'.[113] It seemed to him that they both suffered a good deal from the impact of Modernist writing and he looked to Tomlinson for reassurance. In doing so, he identified with the rearguard rather than the vanguard of literature, as he had done in 1913 when he chose Gosse and Marsh as his mentors. The book of poems he dedicated to Tomlinson in 1956, *Sequences*, would demonstrate all the strengths and weaknesses of that choice.

Another writer from whom he drew 'spiritual sustenance' in his resistance to Modernism, and who also contributed regularly to his literary columns in 1919, was Frank Swinnerton.[114] Born in 1884, he was much closer in age to Sassoon than Tomlinson, but he too became a support-figure. Sassoon had a 'great respect' for his judgement, he told de la Mare, perhaps because Swinnerton confirmed his own prejudice against Modernist poets like T.S. Eliot and W.H. Auden. By 1951, he would regard Swinnerton as a 'godsend in this age of literary humbug'.[115] Swinnerton was particularly hostile to the writers of the Bloomsbury Group and Sassoon himself would become increasingly critical of them, partly under his influence, though he was loath to include Forster in his strictures.[116] He would also rely on Swinnerton for advice on his prose works later on.

When they first met, Swinnerton was one of the foremost critics of the day, according to Bennett. He would remain a literary authority until well into the fifties, writing regularly for the *Evening News* and the *Observer*, among other papers, and producing over twenty books of criticism, such as his popular *Georgian Literary Scene*. 'A complete man of letters' was how his editor at *John O'London's Weekly*, Wilson Midgley, described him. In 1919, however, Swinnerton was even better known as the author of his highly successful seventh novel, *Nocturne* (1917), a work which was to overshadow his many later efforts. Both hard-working – he produced nearly forty novels in addition to his critical books – and optimistic, he was an inspiration to Sassoon, who frequently despaired of writing anything at all. Like Tomlinson, he had overcome early hardship by sheer determination, rising from office-boy on an obscure magazine, the *Scottish Cyclist*, to become a reader at Chatto & Windus and the 'discoverer' of such classics as Daisy Ashford's *The Young Visiter* [*sic*]. Friendships with all the established writers of the day, many of whom like Wells and Bennett he met at the Reform, failed to produce the slightest sign of self-importance in him and he remained an unpretentious, kindly person to the end of his long life.

It seemed to Sassoon that one of Swinnerton's most important qualities, apart from his entertaining talk and pronounced sense of humour, was his common sense; together with his 'pluck' and 'persistent aliveness', it formed a bulwark against the forces of Modernism which so threatened him. With men like Swinnerton and Tomlinson to support him he could continue to believe in the traditional path he had chosen. It was comforting to be able to write to 'Swinny', after a particularly negative review by a young Modernist: 'We both glory in being – shall I say "a bit common"? – you know what I mean – we prefer not to be "superior persons of high intellectual attainments!" ' ...[117]

Sassoon's relationships with both Swinnerton and Tomlinson would survive a lifetime, while friendships with younger, more experimental writers, such as Graves and Osbert Sitwell, would weaken during the twenties.[118] There was one younger writer, however, also met through his *Herald* work and also a traditionalist, who would become one of his greatest friends, Edmund Blunden.

4

'Rootless Re-Beginnings'[1]
(June-December 1919)

... You charm me home to childhood and the uncouth
Cold mystery of sunrise flocked with wings,
And the inattentive field-path wanderings
   of vacant dream-led youth.

You show me a lost land
Enriched by autumn, where each wealden road
Seems winding to contentment's bourned abode ...
                ('Reading Blunden's Poems')[2]

There is a striking photograph of Edmund Blunden which shows him striding onto a cricket pitch with Rupert Hart-Davis, a friend of Blunden and Sassoon in later life. Blunden appears at least a foot shorter than Hart-Davis and looks like a child who has trespassed into an adult's world, his small, pointed face, eager expression and thin, almost stick-like arms giving him an air of extreme vulnerability.

And so, indeed, most of his close friends saw him, Sassoon in particular. 'Yes,' he wrote in June 1922, three years after their friendship started;

> ... it is the frailty of Blunden which makes him unique. Perhaps my vanity is flattered by my protective feeling for him. His spirit burns in his body with the apparent fragility of a flame. I want always to be interposing the bulk of my physical robustness between him and the brutish blustering of the winds of the outer world.[3]

Sassoon was not alone in finding Blunden's frailty appealing; Blunden would be helped and protected all his life by devoted friends of both sexes. Yet, as Sassoon implies, his 'fragility' was to some extent more apparent than real. Like Keats, to whom he was often compared, he was extremely resilient and determined, and could be almost ruthlessly single-minded on occasions. A man of fierce, if sometimes unconventional principles, he rarely hesitated to follow them, whatever complications it created.

His one burning ambition, like Keats, was to serve literature. And in that service he could also be remarkably unselfish, particularly as a teacher and correspondent, when he inspired in many students and friends a similar ambition. As Sassoon himself observed, Blunden lived 'in an atmosphere of intense devotion to the art of poetry'.[4] He was a romantic and idealist, much like Sassoon.

Blunden had first written to Sassoon at the *Daily Herald* on 3 May 1919, calling his attention to two 'chap-books' of poems, written at school but not printed until 1916 when he was out in France as a young army officer. His second letter to Sassoon fills in the details of his war career: that he had joined the army in August 1915 straight from his school, Christ's Hospital, 'in a state of singular misery', then in May 1916 been posted to the Western Front with the 11th Battalion, the Royal Sussex Regiment. 'I was stigmatized with the usual ribbon [i.e., the Military Cross] in 1916,' he continued, 'and for a few weeks was on Brigade H.Q., but my free speech secured my return to the less disgusting front line, where I kept people's spirits up by letting loose any hope of returning world sanity I could collect. Your sonnets and excerpts in the CAMBRIDGE MAG[AZINE] were the principal joy-beams.'[5] By the time of this letter he had been demobilized and was living at Plymouth with the wife he had married in 1918.

Blunden's letter was a model of literary tact, down to the well-turned compliment with which it ends:

> With gratitude not only for your vivacious critica in THE HERALD but also for your great efforts throughout the war to bring the ferocity of the trenches home to a public more disturbed about rations than Passchendaele,
> I am, sir,
> Yours truly,
> E.C. Blunden (Scholar-elect, Queen's College, Oxford)

The compliment was entirely sincere. Writing to the anti-war *Cambridge Magazine* with two of his poems in 1917, Blunden had not only begged them to 'hasten the end of the war by making the facts [about it] public' but also to 'print some more of Mr Sassoon's really fine poetry'.[6]

So that, in submitting his work to Sassoon, Blunden could have expected a positive response to his anti-war views. It was not his war poetry he sent to Sassoon, however, but some earlier pastoral verse. Perhaps he had studied Sassoon's first successful collection, *The Old Huntsman* (1917), carefully and realized that Sassoon might be even more sympathetic to poems about nature, as indeed he turned out to be:

> Within five minutes [Sassoon wrote in his autobiography] I knew that I had discovered a poet. Here was someone writing about a Kentish barn in a way I had always felt but had never been able to put into verse. I forgot that I was in a newspaper office, for the barn was physically evoked, with its cobwebs and dust and sparkling sun, its smell of cattle-cake and apples stored in hay, the sound of the breeze singing in the shattered pane and sparrows squabbling on the roof. Here too was description of mill-wheel and weir, beautifully

exact and affectionately felt, where authentic fishes basked in glades of drowsy sun.[7]

Blunden had scored a bull's eye, for not only was Sassoon a pastoral poet by inclination, like himself, but also a lover of Kent. Both had been brought up in the beautiful Weald country and reading Blunden's poetic evocations of it was for Sassoon a 'deeply consoling' experience 'strangely mingled with associations of home and childhood'.[8] As he wrote in his unpublished 'Reading Blunden's Poems', he felt as though he were actually 'watching the Kentish Weald; orchard and oast / In haze of gold, and the yellow-tufted wood / Blue-misted'.[9]

So it is not surprising that, in his reply to Blunden's first letter, he should ask to see *Pastorals*,[10] Blunden's one publication, for their shared interest in nature poetry would become one of their greatest bonds. Sassoon had strayed from his own inclinations in writing war poetry and when he returned to his more natural bent with collections like *The Heart's Journey* (1927), *Vigils* (1934) and *Rhymed Ruminations* (1939), works mainly slighted by contemporary critics, he could rely unfailingly on Blunden to approve – and to say so in print. 'I could have chosen no one except Blunden,' he told his mother after one particularly appreciative review by him, 'if I had been asked for an ideal critic of my poetry.'[11] They would be united for life by their joint devotion to an older, less fashionable mode which would brand them both traditionalists. While other friends, such as Graves, Nichols and Turner, would lecture Sassoon in the twenties about being 'old-fashioned' and try desperately to be new-fashioned themselves, Blunden would seem to Sassoon the only one who 'talked sense'.[12] He actively urged Sassoon to write more 'rural' poetry like himself, the only problem he anticipated being arguments about who got certain parts of Kent.

Sassoon and Blunden had, then, at least two interests in common when they first met, at Nellie Burton's rooms in Half Moon Street, and others would quickly emerge. Cricket, for example, a passion which arose partly out of their shared feeling for English landscape and country life, would become a frequent topic of conversation and they were to take part in many matches together well into old age. Playing cricket with Blunden, Sassoon felt, was the nearest he could get 'to sharing with beloved E.B. the essential fabric of my existence'.[13]

Book-collecting, too, a hobby Sassoon had taken up in his teens, kept them swapping stories and 'finds' from 1919 onwards.[14] It is revealing of both men that, according to Blunden, neither of them was primarily interested in costly first editions, but in the neglected by-ways, a taste which reflected their literary interests as a whole. Though both had a proper respect for the major writers of the past, it was the minor figures who intrigued them. As an ex-scholar of Christ's Hospital, Blunden was especially fond of a fellow-Bluecoat, Charles Lamb, who duly became Sassoon's staple reading. And Blunden's devotion to the eighteenth century generally and to John Clare in particular also infected Sassoon, whose poem 'To an Eighteenth Century Poet' is written in praise of another minor figure from the period, William Cowper.[15] And both were drawn to Henry Vaughan, who became the subject of a Sassoon poem greatly admired by Blunden, 'At the Grave of Henry Vaughan'.[16] Since Blunden also wrote on Vaughan, it is impossible to say now who discovered him first; what is certain is that their enthusiasms were generally shared and the influence mutual.

To begin with, however, Blunden looked to Sassoon for direction. He was ten years younger than Sassoon, as well as virtually unknown, and Sassoon felt sufficiently confident of his own position and reassured by the modesty of his letter to want to help. To this end he mentioned Blunden's work in his next set of 'Literary Notes' for the *Herald* and arranged for three influential figures from the literary world to be present at their first meeting, Squire, Turner and Edward Shanks.[17] Blunden, who felt 'at once bewildered and happy' by the swift turn of events, was accordingly launched on the literary scene by Sassoon in much the same way Sassoon himself had been through Gosse's kindness. Blunden always maintained that, if Sassoon had not encouraged him in 1919, he would probably not have continued to write poetry.

Sassoon, who took an instant personal liking to Blunden at their first meeting, made it his business from then on to introduce him to all the friends he thought might be helpful: Marsh, Gosse, Cockerell, Tomlinson, Ottoline and Graves who, as usual, tried to take Blunden over. Ottoline, too, had later to be discouraged from interfering in his personal life. But both were also of practical help, Graves asking Blunden to contribute to his second number of *The Owl* and paying him for it, Ottoline sending his work to the Poet Laureate, Robert Bridges. Marsh included him in his next volume of *Georgian Poetry* and Gosse and Cockerell pulled their usual strings. Tomlinson commissioned articles for the *Nation*.

Sassoon also introduced Blunden to Hardy, but for different reasons. In doing so he felt that he was bringing two soulmates together. Apart from superficial likenesses, such as their 'clear and graceful handwriting'[18] – a sign perhaps of pronounced aesthetic sensibilities – they shared what Sassoon most admired, 'a sort of old-fashioned seriousness about everything connected with authorship'.[19] Both seemed to him 'fundamentally countrified and homely' and loved talking about simple things.[20] (As he had anticipated, they took to each other at once.) In addition he found 'a similarly bird-like quality' in Blunden and Hardy, a reference to their quickness of perception and lightness of movement as well as their physical appearance. Blunden must surely have tired of having his 'beaky' face and diminutive stature compared to a bird, from a 'London house sparrow, that pecks and cheeps' (Virginia Woolf), to a nightjar (Barry Webb) or, less flatteringly, a crow (Virginia Woolf again). Whether he would have preferred Gosse's rather condescending though affectionate description of him as 'a dear little chinchilla', however, is doubtful.[21] The comparison had been inspired, Gosse told Sassoon, by Blunden's 'wonderful eyes', which he likened, inevitably, to Keats's.[22]

Sassoon almost always referred to his friend as '*little* Blunden' (my italics) and continued to feel protective towards him, in the way large, strong men often feel towards smaller women. He worried about Blunden's health (he was asthmatic), his finances and his complicated love life. But he insisted, as with Turner, that there was nothing sexual in the relationship: 'With Blunden I am my better self; I feel an intense sympathy and affection for him; the gross elements of sex are miraculously remote.'[23] Blunden's own powerful attraction to women probably helped.[24] It was an important factor in their relationship. With other male friendships, such as Graves and Osbert Sitwell, Sassoon's feelings were complicated by a lurking sexual element and both relationships finally foundered, whereas his friendship with Blunden would remain, in his own words, among 'the best and most fruitful' of his life.[25] It was both 'soothing and stimulating'.[26]

The flavour of that relationship comes through strongly in Sassoon's description of an early meeting between them which could stand for most of the many others that followed: 'for three days B and I talked about county cricket and the war and English poetry and our own poetry and East Anglia and our contemporaries ... He is, in fact, almost the ideal friend and fellow-craftsman.'[27] Sassoon was proud of his discovery and promotion of Blunden: 'I don't suppose anyone has done more for him than I have,' he wrote to Graves with some justification in 1920.[28] It was one of the few things that gave him any satisfaction in the immediate post-war years.

*

Sassoon's meeting with Blunden in late May or early June 1919 was the high point of his nine months with the *Daily Herald*. Until the end of June he was 'actively occupied, confident through success, and insolently healthy with youth and summer weather'.[29] His affair with Gabriel was going reasonably well, he was writing a fair amount of poetry and the literary editorship still interested him. But in early July sciatica struck, symbolizing in his own eyes 'the undoing of [his] blind belief in the beneficence of 1919'.[30] Perhaps, as he claimed, too much was expected of this first year after the war, which was for many a time of 'rootless re-beginnings and steadily developing disillusionments'.[31]

His own disillusionments started in July, as his diary records:

July 1919–January 1920   Very little poetry. Climax of bad health
and discontent with G[abriel].
Dissatisfaction with *Herald* work,
and life in town.[32]

Yet to the outside world he appeared to be going from strength to strength, Heinemann and his friends making sure that he remained firmly in the public eye.

Graves, for example, asked to include Sassoon's poems in both the first and second numbers of *The Owl* in May and October. Originated and financed by Graves's father-in-law, the artist William Nicholson, the magazine was an attractive mix of art and letters and Sassoon was flattered to be asked. Though it was never to find a popular audience and to fold after the third number, it was an honour to be seen in the company of such well-known names as John Masefield, W.H. Davies, John Galsworthy and, above all, Thomas Hardy.[33]

Both Turner and Squire had helped Graves collect material for *The Owl* and in November that same year Squire, having left the *New Statesman*, brought out the first number of his own magazine, the *London Mercury*. Again, Sassoon was included in it.[34] Harold Monro, perhaps prompted by his assistant Alida's meeting with Sassoon at Charlotte Mew's in May, also kept his name before the reading public by arranging a Poetry Bookshop appearance for him on 9 October. The audience of 145, more than five times its usual size, suggests that Sassoon's work was still very popular with lovers of poetry. Unfortunately they probably heard very little of what Sassoon read that evening, since according to Monro he was as usual 'extremely inaudible'.[35]

To his friends' efforts, Sassoon added his own, bringing out a new volume of privately printed poems, *Picture Show*, in July 1919. After leaving the manuscript with Cockerell in January and sending a copy to Theo later the same month, he had both added to and subtracted from the collection. By March he was anxious to see it out and placed advertisements for it in *Art and Letters* in April and *The Owl* in May, but was still tinkering with the typescript in late May.

Sassoon told Theo, who was helping to design *Picture Show* with Bruce Rogers, that it was a money-making venture, urging him to 'make it *look* as expensive' as possible. However, it was clearly more than money which concerned him. His endless revisions suggest that he was determined to include all his best work since January 1918, the point at which *Counter-Attack* broke off. Several pieces were written specially for the collection, notably 'Aftermath', 'Everyone Sang' and 'To a Very Wise Man', his homage to Rivers, whose anthropological background had added to his fascination with the man.[36]

One of the most ambitious poems in *Picture Show*, 'Prelude to an Unwritten Masterpiece', composed just before the book went to press, also suggests that Rivers's influence was still strong, in particular his faith in dream-analysis:

> ... Last night I dreamt an old recurring dream –
> Some complex out of childhood; (sex, of course!)

4. 'Rootless Re-Beginnings' (June-December 1919)

> I can't remember how the trouble starts;
> And then I'm running blindly in the sun
> Down the old orchard, and there's something cruel
> Chasing me; someone roused to a grim pursuit
> Of clumsy anger ...
>
> (CP, p. 120)[37]

The lack of a regular rhyme scheme, like the subject matter, is experimental, but it was not, ultimately, a direction Sassoon would take. He was to remain committed all his life to rhyme.

'Miracles', written shortly after Sassoon met Gabriel, shows a similar interest in dreams and reflects both the intense happiness and anxiety the relationship had created:

> I dreamt I saw a huge grey boat in silence steaming
> Down a canal; it drew the dizzy landscape after;
> The solemn world was sucked along with it – a streaming
> Land-slide of loveliness. O, but I rocked with laughter,
> Staring, and clinging to my tree-top. For a lake
> Of gleaming peace swept on behind. (I mustn't wake.)
>
> And then great clouds gathered ...
>
> (CP, p. 107)[38]

Less than half the pieces in *Picture Show* deal directly with war, but as the title poem suggests the whole collection was written very much in its shadow, Sassoon not having yet settled on a new direction. Heinemann's next publication of Sassoon's work in October 1919, *War Poems*, reinforces the impression that he has still not found a satisfactory alternative to the subject matter and technique which had made him famous. Like *The Old Huntsman* and *Counter-Attack*, it is, in Sassoon's own words, another 'tract against war'.[39] Exploiting his continuing popularity in the genre, Heinemann has simply gathered together his war poems, with nearly a third of the weaker ones excluded.

It was a shrewd choice on Heinemann's part, and when the first edition of 2,000 copies ran out in less than two months, it was promptly reprinted. The most significant aspect of the collection, however, is that it contains no newly written work,[40] a factor which can only have increased Sassoon's sense of unproductiveness in the second half of 1919 and added to his depression.

His most immediate cause for unhappiness, however, was his health. He had been suffering slightly from sciatica since the beginning of April but an attack in July immobilized him completely. He believed that his sciatica had been brought on by its commonest cause, a slipped disc. But conditions in the trenches had not helped either his back or his general health. He was still suffering occasional bouts of trench fever in 1918 and his teeth were already giving him trouble.

67

As he complained to Graves, sciatica was a 'rotten complaint for a comparative youth'.[41] He would apologize to readers of his autobiography for the space devoted to the 'treacherous demon'.[42] Sciatica was not, he knew, an enthralling subject but it became so much the 'autocrat' of his existence in mid-1919 that it formed almost a 'constructive element' in his life.

It led him, for example, to spend ten days with Osbert and Sachie Sitwell and, therefore, to a much closer relationship with them. This unplanned stay in their London house also turned into a whirlwind introduction to the latest trends in art and literature, a 'wholesome antidote', he believed, to his 'intolerance of the unusual' and 'instinctive preference for the traditional'.[43]

From the outside the Sitwells' house looked just like its neighbours' in pretty and privileged little Swan Walk opposite the Chelsea Physic Garden near the Thames. The inside, however, was full of challenge, especially to someone like Sassoon, brought up on the paintings of G.F. Watts – startling and experimental pictures juxtaposed with early Victorian knick-knacks, all exemplifying for Sassoon 'a new aesthetic tendency to find beauty in the barbaric'.[44] Dining with the Sitwells the previous month, with Sassoon and Atkin as fellow-guests, Bennett's reaction had been more measured, perhaps because less threatened: 'A home with much better pictures and bric-à-brac than furniture. In fact there was scarcely any what I call furniture. But lots of very modern pictures, of which I liked a number. Bright walls and bright cloths and bright glass everywhere.'[45]

Sassoon had staggered to 5 Swan Walk in a state of near collapse one fine July day and been ushered solicitously to a small bedroom at the top of the narrow house by the Sitwells' housekeeper. And when Osbert and Sachie returned home, they too behaved like 'angelic and agitated turtledoves'.[46] Sachie had quickly abandoned Oxford and both brothers now led a hectic social life, yet they found time to see Sassoon frequently during his ten-day stay and think up distractions for him, as well as arrange for a daily visit from a doctor and 'electricity' treatment.[47] And as long as Sassoon lay perfectly still, he was happy:

> Not for the first time [he wrote], I was aware that being in bed in someone else's house gives one a great pull over the problems of life and permits the mind to move with unimpeded smoothness. I have always believed in allowing things to take their course without my interference, and being in bed is the nearest one can get to invisibility ... Quietude is essential to human happiness.[48]

As Sassoon quickly discovered, it was one of the many points of difference between himself and the Sitwells, Osbert in particular. Sometimes he was so exhausted by just hearing their frequent bursts of activity below that he would pretend to be asleep when Osbert rushed up to see him – 'a blond Hanoverian apparition in a frock-coat and top-hat of immaculate grey'.[49] Was he on his way to the peace celebrations, Sassoon wondered, or off to see a printer about *Art and Letters*, the magazine he was editing with Herbert Read?

If Sassoon needed a reminder that, even in knowing the Sitwells, he had travelled a long way from his pre-war self, it arrived in the form of Norman Loder. An old hunting friend, Loder represented all that was decent, kind but essentially philistine about most of Sassoon's sporting acquaintances, a condition Sassoon had christened 'Loderism'.[50] Sassoon had been due to stay with Loder at Peterborough, where Loder was joint Master of the Fitzwilliam Hunt, but was forced to cancel when sciatica struck.[51] He had not expected Loder to visit him at Swan Walk, though was hardly surprised by his reaction when he did so. 'Whatever are you doing here?' Loder asked, eyeing a Cubist painting as if it might bite, with an air of planning to remove Sassoon from such pernicious influences as soon as possible.[52]

The dilemma was more Sassoon's than Loder's, he realized: 'Norman never actively disapproved of anyone. He was too good-natured for that.'[53] Though he had not been happy about Sassoon's public protest against the war which he regarded as 'pro-Germanism', nor his '*Daily Herald* Socialism', he had said very little. The Sitwells' pictures were also too much for his 'elementary taste in art',[54] but he merely made Sassoon promise to come and stay with him as soon as possible. His visit left Sassoon with a renewed sense of his sharply divided personality:

> ... [Loder] had dominated the sporting part of my existence. To the Sitwells, though they would probably have thought him a good joke, he was the pattern of that Philistinism against which they rebelled. And here was I, feebly attempting to be on both sides at once. For at that time I was simple-minded enough to want – and expect – all my friends to like one another.[55]

It was a dilemma he would fail to resolve for many years.

The contrast between Loder and the Sitwells became particularly obvious when Sassoon began to convalesce. Whereas Osbert took him off for a week's course of treatment to Bath, where he was 'sweepingly introduced to the eighteenth century' and forbearingly allowed to watch at least one afternoon of county cricket, Loder's reaction was more spartan.[56] Having no experience of sciatica and little imagination, his first act on Sassoon's arrival at Peterborough in late July was to take him for a ride on a bad-tempered horse, which left him lying on the ground in agony. Loder's comment – 'Old Sig lay there on his back like a crusader' – only made things worse and Sassoon resisted all further attempts to treat him like a person in robust health.

Sassoon would continue to visit Loder and his wife for another four years, realizing every time he did so the widening gap between their

ultra-bourgeois life and his increasingly chaotic ventures into the homosexual underworld. Only when he temporarily abandoned hunting in the
mid-twenties would the friendship cease.

It was not, therefore, a simple dichotomy between sport and art he faced
in 1919. His affair with Gabriel and intense relationship with Rivers at
Craiglockhart had made him aware of a number of other needs. Though
he had made Forster laugh earlier in the year with his insistence that 'You
must realize that I am *not* an intellectual,'[57] he did have intellectual needs,
which were not met at the Loders'. This may have been the reason he took
a week off during his stay with them to visit Rivers and other friends in
Cambridge.[58] And it is a sign of Rivers's stimulating effect on him that,
while with him, he wrote one of his few poems of the period, 'Early
Chronology', in which he describes an eminent colleague of Rivers's,
Professor Elliot Smith, discussing 5,000 years of 'excavated History' to a
chosen few in Rivers's rooms.[59]

Similarly, it was intellectual stimulation he hoped for when he left the
agreeable but undemanding Loders to visit Robert Graves at the end of
August. Graves, his wife Nancy and their new daughter Jenny, had gone
to stay in Nancy's father's house at Harlech in March and were still there
when Sassoon joined them. His initial resistance to Nancy seems to have
weakened after their brief meeting the previous November, but he was
evidently still jealous of her. The fact that she was pregnant again could
not have helped, underlining as it did the sexual element in her relations
with Graves. Graves, who believed Sassoon was sexually attracted to him,
would regularly accuse him of being jealous of Nancy throughout the
twenties, a charge Sassoon would just as regularly deny. But he did on one
occasion admit that he was 'afraid' of her.[60] An intriguing variation on the
theme would occur when Graves became jealous of Nancy's interest in
Sassoon.

Nevertheless, Sassoon was probably being honest when he thanked the
Graveses for an enjoyable three weeks. 'Am staying with Graves and
storing up solar energy,' he had told de la Mare a fortnight after his arrival
in Wales.[61] He was still 'passionately attached' to Graves, whom he
numbered among his pantheon of heroes and, despite a growing difference
in their approaches to literature, still needed to discuss it with him,
especially poetry.

Graves probably repeated to Sassoon what he had said to Blunden in
mid-1919, that war poetry was 'played out' and that 'the most acceptable
dope now' was 'Country Sentiment'.[62] Sassoon, whose *War Poems* were
about to be published, was, as usual, not nearly so certain as Graves about
his future direction. He was not even sure, at this point, that he would be
able to continue writing poetry at all.

*

4. 'Rootless Re-Beginnings' (June-December 1919)

So the summer passed, divided between various friends and creating its own conflicts. One struggle it did not actively involve, however, was any attempt to resolve problems with Gabriel, since Sassoon deliberately kept away from him all summer.

Drawn to Gabriel mainly by his youth and good looks, he was finding it increasingly difficult to accept his dissolute lifestyle. He had encouraged Gabriel to enrol at the Slade after their return from Oxford and had been pleased by his 'excellent drawing in the life school' during May.[63] But Gabriel could rarely sustain anything and by July Sassoon had reached his 'climax ... of discontent' with him.[64] Though he would relent later in the year, when he wrote to tell Gabriel he loved him 'more than ever I did before',[65] he intentionally avoided him during the summer in the hope of making Gabriel realize how much he could do for him.

This odd, rather unattractive behaviour may have stemmed not just from a determination to control his feckless young friend, but also from jealousy. An unguarded remark to Theo about the 'dazzling Osbert' being 'not ... much use to anyone like G[abriel]', suggests that he trusted neither Gabriel nor Osbert in the growing intimacy between the two men. He may even have been already half aware of a sexual attraction towards Osbert himself, an element which would complicate their relationship greatly in future years.[66]

At all events, the situation added greatly to his post-war moodiness. Referring to later bouts of 'self-lacerating irritability against everything', which were liable to make him do something 'stupid and regrettable', he noted that it was 'nothing new, and I suspect ... not unconnected with my animal passions'.[67] Since those 'animal passions' could never, by their socially and legally forbidden nature, be easily satisfied, he would be subject to similar 'tigerish ill-temper' and 'capricious cruelty' until the passions themselves had weakened.[68] And his relationship with Gabriel would continue to resemble a ride on a rollercoaster for the next six years.

At the same time as his trouble with Gabriel, he began to feel dissatisfied with his job at the *Daily Herald*. The literary columns were suspended for several months in August due to industrial action, and in any case he found that the literary editorship had 'simplified itself into an easy routine' and took less of his time than he would have liked.[69] The space allotted him was being cut and he suspected that no one would mind much if it were reduced to a 'mere tabloid of two half-columns'.[70] A point he fails to mention is that by November Gould was suggesting to him a more business-like approach, which may have worried him.[71] In any case, as Bennett shrewdly wrote to Nichols when he was thinking of editing a new periodical: 'I don't think this is quite your job – anymore than it is Siegfried's. You are too creative, temperamental, and wilful to be an editor.'[72]

One of Sassoon's main problems with the *Herald* remained his lack of real commitment to politics. He freely admitted that his 'projected apprenticeship to politics', set in motion by Rivers the previous Christmas, had made 'no advance whatever' by the end of 1919.[73] An invitation to become British Secretary of *Clarté*, a movement started by the French writer Henri Barbusse to help unite French and English intellectuals, ended when the extent of Sassoon's political ignorance became clear at *Clarté*'s first British meeting:

> Speeches were made by Shaw, Wells, and Zangwill. Shaw gave a brilliant and attractive demonstration of inability to be anything except a movement in himself. Wells did likewise ... When invited to voice the views of the younger generation, I rose reluctantly and made some lame and not very audible remarks which somehow ended in a suggestion that everyone ought to read Hardy's *Dynasts*.[74]

Even allowing for comic self-deprecation this is probably a fair description of Sassoon's performance and it is hardly surprising that *Clarté* dropped him. By the end of 1919, with the war behind him, he had virtually abandoned politics.[75]

He had also left Weirleigh, after a number of abortive attempts. It is ironic that, by the time he did so in October 1919, the main ground of dissent with his mother – his politics – was of little importance to him. But the cause of their other dissension – Gabriel and, behind Gabriel, Sassoon's unacknowledged homosexuality – was more important than ever and he needed freedom to explore it. A summer almost completely away from home, staying with sympathetic friends, may have prompted him to act, together with the knowledge that his brother Michael's return to Weirleigh with his family was imminent. And his growing warmth towards Turner and his wife Delphine, who lived in London, made it seem an attractive alternative to Kent.

A few weeks back at Weirleigh in October seem to have decided him and by the middle of the month he had arranged to move into 54 Tufton Street, Westminster, with the Turners. Since Walter Turner was always short of money, Sassoon had also agreed to lend him £1,300 to buy the house, a large sum which he probably borrowed against money he was expecting to inherit from his father's sister, Rachel Beer.[76] While the purchase of Tufton Street was being completed, he took temporary lodgings nearby, at 30 Hugh Street. A few minutes from the dirt, noise and crowds of Victoria Station, Hugh Street was a very different proposition from his previous lodgings, Nellie Burton's discreet apartment house in Mayfair, and he quickly realized his mistake. With winter closing in, it became apparent that the rooms he had chosen so hastily were 'sunless, stuffy-smelling, dingy and dispiriting'.[77]

*

Sassoon's unsettled state in the second half of 1919 was not due entirely to dissatisfaction with his lodgings, job, poetry or sex life. On 1 July he had received an invitation to lecture in America and, after further wooing from the lecture agent in person, had accepted. He was due to sail in January 1920, a prospect he found both exciting and disturbing.[78]

Mr Pond of Pond Lyceum Bureau, New York, had reassured him that he would not be expected to deliver 'professorial discourses';[79] he need only read his war poems and make a few informal remarks. But Sassoon doubted his ability to do even that audibly. When his offer of Osbert Sitwell as a substitute had been firmly rejected, however, he capitulated. And after his reading at the Poetry Bookshop had underlined how bad a speaker he was, he enrolled at the Central School of Speech and Drama in a panic.

His misgivings about the enterprise were equalled only by his astonishment. While he knew that Masefield's generous praise of his work during his own lecture tour a few years earlier and Nichols's effusive introduction to the American edition of *Counter-Attack* and public readings from it, as well as a temporary interest in war poets, had made him known in the States, the last thing he had expected was a eulogistic letter from a well-known lecture agency.[80] The letter may have been prompted by the first reprint of *Counter-Attack* in April 1919, in which Nichols's romantic description of 'Sassoon the Man' again appears:

> In appearance he is tall, big-boned, loosely built. He is clean-shaven, pale or with a flush; has a heavy jaw, wide mouth with the upper lip slightly protruding and the curve of it very pronounced like that of a shrivelled leaf … His nose is aquiline, the nostrils being wide and heavily arched. This characteristic and the fullness, depth and heat of his dark eyes give him the air of a sullen falcon. He speaks slowly, enunciating the words as if they pained him, in a voice that has something of the troubled thickness apparent in the voices of those who emerge from a deep grief. As he speaks, his large hands, roughened by trench toil and by riding, wander aimlessly until some emotion grips him when the knuckles harden and he clutches at his knees or at the edge of the table. And all the while he will be breathing hard like a man who has swum a distance.

Sassoon was grateful for the praise, however high-flown, but his reasons for going to America were not to gratify his ego. He had pledged himself 'to oppose war' and a lecture tour on the subject seemed an effective way of doing so.[81] He also had a 'sudden impulse and longing to escape from the postwar complexities' of his life which had involved him with a bewildering number of new people.[82] The fact that Rivers advised him to accept and would himself be lecturing in America at the same time was another deciding factor.

These were the reasons Sassoon gave for accepting Pond's invitation. The most convincing explanation for his uncharacteristic readiness to expose himself to the American public, however, was dissatisfaction with his life in post-war England and a general lack of direction.

5

'Midnight on Broadway'
(January-March 1920)

Under the fuscous canopy of heaven
Gold winking signs, façades of flickering fires,
Relentlessly proclaim the cheap-jack fame
Of Movie Stars and Chewing Gum and Tyres.

The heaped snow has an artificial look
As if impersonating sifted sugar:
Along the melting side-walks, blurred and trodden,
It clogs the feet of jostling crowds that shuffle
Through Broadway slush with faces greenish-pale,
Each face in spot-light of magnesium noon.
                  ('Midnight on Broadway', *Recreations*)[1]

If Sassoon hoped to escape his problems by leaving England for America in January 1920, it was not for long. During the voyage itself, a leisurely crossing on the Dutch liner *Rotterdam* in a first-class cabin, he had a sense of putting the complexities of the past year into some 'sort of perspective'.[2] But when he landed in New York on 28 January, he was immediately faced with a new set of complications.

His arrival was not auspicious. Met at the boat by a Pond representative, he was driven in an ancient taxi through slush and snow to the Hotel Seville, which he found 'rather depressing'.[3] A 'nasty' dinner and two uninspired newspaper interviews were followed by a sleepless night with raging toothache in an overheated room.

He started the next day with an emergency visit to the dentist, the first of nineteen hour-long appointments to deal with several decayed teeth and acute pyorrhoea. But this painful and expensive experience was not the worst of his problems. When he, next, presented himself at the Pond Lyceum Bureau at 50 East 42nd Street, he found a distinctly uneasy Mr Pond. By the terms of their contract Pond had undertaken to cover the cost of the transatlantic crossing and all rail and sleeping-car fares in America. More crucially, he had also guaranteed to pay $100 each for a minimum of twenty-five lectures. Yet by the time Sassoon was due to leave for America, he had managed to book only two paid engagements.

Pond had immediately cabled the bad news to Sassoon in England, urging him to cancel his trip. By catching an earlier boat, however, Sassoon had missed the cable, a fact he later appreciated: 'What luck that I got well away before Pond wired,' he wrote to Turner on 21 February;[4] 'no wonder he was a bit blue when I rolled up, all serene! and had to confess that he'd only got me two engagements for February, and that the market was glutted by Walpole, Dunsany ... Yeats, Cannan, Drinkwater, Housman – not to mention Sir Oliver Lodge and Coningsby Dawson!' Pond also blamed a general reaction by the American public against 'war stuff', but did not admit something Sassoon subsequently discovered, that his agency had lost a great deal of money on a recent tour by the Belgian playwright Maeterlinck, whose poor English had resulted in wholesale cancellations. The Pond Lyceum Bureau was, in fact, on the verge of bankruptcy.

Pond had, however, managed to arrange some publicity for Sassoon, who spent the afternoon being interviewed and photographed, the early evening at a reception in the National Arts Club and the evening itself at the annual dinner of the Poetry Society of America, where he had to give his first speech. Though this was unpaid, it gave him a valuable opportunity to advertise his skills and immediately brought in invitations to speak at two 'premier' ladies' clubs in the city.

His Poetry Society talk was a baptism by fire. Too busy to prepare himself mentally for the occasion and intimidated by the presence of Yeats as a fellow-speaker, Sassoon faced his first performance with dread. An absence of alcohol at the prohibition dinner itself added to his gloom. Thankful, however, for his smart new dress-suit and conscious of the fact that he was the most youthful, probably the youngest, man in the room, he decided on the 'natural' approach. Presenting himself as a 'modest, naïve sort of person, anxious to be friendly', he began in a style of 'slangy simplicity' which went down well.[5] He then worked up to a 'befitting but still boyish seriousness which declared my faith in poetry and poets'.[6] It was, as he reported to Gabriel, an 'artless mixture of cheek and pomposity', and the newspaper report of the event catches the tone well:

> Mr Sassoon, who arrived in New York from Europe recently, said he came with a toothache and would leave with a heartache. Asked by interviewers for his first impression of New York, he had replied, 'As I rode through the streets in a taxicab I kept saying to myself, Oh hell! Where's the nearest dentist?' Mr Sassoon said that if he should be asked to vote for the Prime Minister of living English poets he would cast his vote for a man whom most Americans probably knew only as a prose writer, Thomas Hardy. He read three of his own poems and gave a fourth – 'Everyone Sang' – in response to applause.[7]

The suggestion of spontaneity here is perhaps misleading. Judging from the detailed notes Sassoon made, he carefully prepared each of his presentations.[8] Though he had 'laboriously composed' a preliminary address, he quickly realized that it sounded 'didactic and unspontaneous' and subsequently adapted it to suit each audience, changing his selection of poems accordingly.[9] Between his first official 'Commemorative Reading' at Bryn Mawr Women's College on 6 February and his last performance at the People's House Auditorium on 26 May, he revised his presentation at least eight times.

A not very experienced speaker, he clearly learnt as he went along. He also gained confidence: whereas his early talks are written out in some detail – not at all the 'rough notes' he claimed they were[10] – his later ones consist of brief jottings only. And for his last two appearances he was sufficiently relaxed to note only the poems he intended to read. So that the spontaneity which he simulated at the beginning was almost certainly achieved by the end.

One example of his increasing confidence is shown in a talk he gave to the women of Smith College a month after his first engagement. Judging his prepared line (about the effects of war on the individual soldier) unsuitable for a 'Talk About Poetry', he used his more recent experience in New York to bring his presentation to life. Sydney Cockerell, whose many contacts spanned the Atlantic, had given him an introduction to Miss Belle Greene, curator of the Pierpont Morgan Library, and Sassoon had used it gratefully as a retreat from an increasingly hectic social life. And he began his talk at Smith with a description of reading a Keats manuscript in the Morgan's 'sound-proof sanctuary',[11] which enabled him to lead on quite naturally to a consideration of Keats's views on poetry. He then repeated what he had said to the undergraduates of Balliol about poetry-writing in 1919: 'when in doubt, cut it out'. He also, more seriously, emphasized the value of 'condensation', 'accuracy', 'writing with [an] eye on object' and the dangers of a 'forced poetic attitude of mind – and language'. The best modern poetry, he insisted, with obvious reference to his own work, was 'near to natural speech'. And since his talk embraced poetry in general, he included as many non-war as war poems in his reading from his own work.

Smith was only one of the disproportionately large number of women's institutions he visited at the start and, just as he had not hesitated to exploit his youthfulness at the Poetry Society dinner, so he used his masculine charms to appeal to his female audiences. The Associate Alumnae of Vassar College, the local Rochester newspaper reported, were 'frankly won by the clean-cut young Englishman, who looked a very likeable chap, the sort who might take a flier in oil stocks and know the batting average of most of the big leaguers.'[12] His evident 'lack of practice' was merely considered 'disingenuous'. Equally successful at Vassar itself, the 'intense enthusiasm' of his female audience was noted by the *Vassar Miscellany News*.[13]

Though Sassoon claimed that addressing large audiences made him feel as if his soul had been 'undressed in public', he also admitted to the 'somewhat insidious allurement of doing it'.[14] He was certainly very conscious of the charm he exercised over American women, as his parody of his own war poem 'The General' shows:

> 'Good evening; good evening!' the lecturer bowed,
> When we heard him last Monday in Carnegie Hall.
> Now the charm of his smile has caught on with the crowd,
> And he's promised to come here again in the fall.
> 'I'm afraid he's a Red!' whispered Dora to Daisy,
> As he cursed the old men who in wartime were lazy.
> * * *
> But the lilt of his eyebrow has sent them both crazy![15]

Ironically, in view of the fact that Sassoon laid the blame for the war largely on women in his preliminary address, five of Sassoon's first six engagements were at female institutions: Bryn Mawr, near Philadelphia, on 6 February was followed by Stamford's Women's Club in upstate New York on 18 February, the Cosmopolitan Club in New York City on 24 February, Smith College at Northampton, Massachusetts on 3 March (he also visited the nearby men's college, Amherst, on the 4th) and the Women's International League of Philadelphia on 10 March.[16] It was a relatively gentle introduction to the lecture circuit. And since all the engagements were either in New York or a few hours' train-ride from it, he was able to save himself the cost of hotel bills, which were not included in Pond's contract. When he did stay overnight, it was usually as a guest of the organizers. In Philadelphia, for example, he was housed at the Rittenhouse Club, a rambling, unmodernized place which reminded him of 'an elderly gentleman whose clothes are odd, old-fashioned and distinguished' and gave him a 'delightful feel of mid-Victorian comfort'.[17]

Even Philadelphia, cosily as he portrays it, was a novel event for someone who had travelled previously only under the protection of the army, and the experience helps to account for his far greater adventurousness in the twenties.

*

Most of February and early March, however, was spent in New York. Sassoon's first impressions of the city had been marred by severe toothache, but once free from pain he started to find it more interesting. Though the population of Greater New York was less than that of Greater London in 1920, its centre was far more crowded and the pace of life already much faster. A recent large increase in Italian, Irish, German and Russian immigrants, many of whom were Jewish, gave New York an exotic, cosmopolitan flavour and Sassoon found the 'strange mixture of faces' exciting.[18]

Present-day landmarks, such as the Empire State Building and Rockefeller Center, were not then part of the scenery, but there were already a number of buildings over twenty storeys, impressively high to English eyes. To Sassoon New York seemed all skyscape: the night skies, in particular, he found 'strangely attractive', 'its lights and Whistler effects, and the ceaseless drone of activity and the towering buildings'.[19]

When he moved after his first few days from the Hotel Seville to Westover Court at 210 West 44th Street, it was the night sky that dominated his impressions. Situated just off Broadway at Times Square in the heart of theatre land, his small flat looked out on the Putnam Building and a huge neon sign advertising Wrigley's chewing gum. It was a district which never slept and Sassoon was often kept awake until 3 a.m. by the sound of heavy lorries collecting the first edition of the *New York Times*, printed next door to his own building. No wonder that he described New York as 'a sort of insomnia'.[20] As he observed with some restraint, living in Westover Court was 'an acclimatizing experience'.[21]

Yet he did not really acclimatize. 'The vulgarity of the whole performance is astonishing,' he wrote to Gabriel a week after his arrival, 'and the exuberant hospitality, enormous oysters, inexhaustible supplies of ice-cream, and unfathomable beakers of clam-chowder, would tax the digestion of the King of the Hippopotami himself.' And his visit, despite the fact that it lasted nearly seven months, would do very little to alter his viewpoint. His social insecurity, which resulted partly from being born an obscure member of a well-known family, would ensure that his attitude towards Americans would remain similar to his stance towards the working classes, one of bemused condescension.

If Westover Court could not 'acclimatize' him, however, it was undeniably convenient, since he quickly found himself being invited to plays, concerts and operas in the surrounding neighbourhood. Within easy walking distance of the Pond Lyceum Bureau, Grand Central Station and most of the city's well-known clubs, such as the Century at 43rd Street, which had a reciprocal membership agreement with the Reform, it could hardly have been better placed. Part of the Vincent Astor Estate, Westover Court looked out on the Astor Hotel, where he sometimes ate – roast chicken, minute steak or, if feeling rich, a 'squab' chicken (i.e., poussin). Even in 1920, Westover Court, only four storeys high and built round a central, tree-lined court, was an unlikely place to find in Manhattan, though it probably seemed quite normal to an Englishman.[22]

Westover Court had another feature which suited Sassoon: it was a bachelor establishment, occupied largely by actors, artists and singers. He had soon tired of the constant attentions of the smart society hostesses and other well-meaning women who had welcomed him to New York. English friends, such as Masefield, Nichols and Cockerell, had supplied him, in all good faith, with numerous contacts, most of them female.[23] To begin with he had followed these up conscientiously, believing that the success of his lecture tour depended on it. Once the social machine had been set in motion, however, he began to panic and felt 'driven half off [his] head' by it. So much so that when one of his favourite hunting characters from the war years, 'The Mister', turned up from Limerick 'to see to his affairs', Sassoon was unable to appreciate him.[24] Looking just the same in a 'grand' overcoat with a bunch of violets in his buttonhole, he struck the distracted poet as an 'almost apparitional personality' and too forceful an addition to his already demanding schedule.[25] Not only was he exhausted by 'polite luncheons and distinguished dinners', but he also found them sterile and was 'frankly bored' by ladies who 'knew all the latest information from the British Embassy at Washington' and held 'superficial opinions about novels, plays and pianists'.[26]

By 1 March he had started to rebel, refusing further invitations from unknown hostesses and gravitating instead towards a small circle of liberal-minded and intelligent people, preferably male. He was fortunate enough to meet three such men in New York, all of whom would remain friends long after he returned to England.

The first of these, Louis Untermeyer, had been an admirer of his poetry since at least August 1918, when he picked Sassoon out for special praise in his review of *Georgian Poetry: 1916-1917*.[27] He had sent Sassoon a collection of his own poems shortly afterwards, followed by a glowing review of *The Old Huntsman* and *Counter-Attack* of March 1919 and a copy of his anthology *Modern American Poetry* two months later.[28] Besides arranging for some of Sassoon's more recent work to be published in America, he also planned to include him in his projected anthology, *Modern British Poetry*.

Naturally Sassoon had been appreciative and before leaving England arranged to meet Untermeyer in New York. Apart from Pond and a few English writers, whom he hoped on the whole to avoid, Untermeyer was the sole person he knew on his arrival and he was grateful for his ebullient welcome. Invited immediately to Untermeyer's apartment on the Upper West Side, an area inhabited largely by artists and intellectuals, he was to spend many enjoyable evenings there with the dynamic little German Jew and his wife, Jean. They had married young and, although Louis was only a year older than Sassoon, he already had a teenage son who added to the domesticity.[29] Sassoon felt more at home there than anywhere else in New York and considered the Untermeyers two of the 'dearest friends' he made in America.[30]

'Louis has turned out a trump,' Sassoon was writing to Turner three weeks after his arrival, 'a real nice, big-hearted little man, with a nice wife.'[31] As with Turner himself, he found Untermeyer's exuberant, extrovert personality a useful balance to his own shyness and awkwardness. Without his new friend, he would certainly not have made contact with the variety of people he did during his stay. Though still working for the family jewellery business at the age of thirty-five, Untermeyer had created a rich cultural life for himself in the city and he admitted Sassoon to it with great generosity and enthusiasm.

5. 'Midnight on Broadway' (January-March 1920)

Louis's main interest was poetry: for him, Sassoon noted, it was 'an exciting affair which had recently been invented'.[32] He and his wife, both practising poets, were proud to introduce Sassoon to some of America's most famous poets of the time at their apartment – Robert Frost, Vachel Lindsay and, later, Amy Lowell.[33] (It may also have been at the Untermeyers that Sassoon met Witter Bynner, a prolific poet who subsequently sent him five volumes of his largely undistinguished verse to read. Bynner's friendship with D.H. Lawrence and Dylan Thomas, the reason he is remembered, if at all today, still lay in the future.)

Perhaps because his own technique was nearer to Frost's than Lindsay's, Sassoon preferred Frost. While talking to him he felt that he was just as good as his poems.[34] 'Gravely humorous and obliquely commentative', he reminded Sassoon of the eighteenth-century poet Crabbe in his 'homespun strength of sobriety'.[35] Frost's philosophy of 'assertive renunciation' seemed to him attractive even then and would become more so with time.

Lindsay, on the other hand, appealed to him very little, though he was excited to meet him and hear one of his famous recitations. 'Irresistibly effective' though he found Lindsay's syncopated rhythms, as he chanted 'General William Booth Enters Heaven', Sassoon felt that his poetry was a mere *tour de force*, 'more of a dithyrambic exhibition' than, as with Frost, an 'integral expression of his inner self'.[36]

Yet it was Lindsay who appears to have made the stronger impression on him. Only two days after their meeting on 27 February he started to write a poem on the man who saw himself as 'the poet of everyone':

> Switch on the golden lights and set him going ...
> Foam-flowers and Chinese dragons; rag-time glorious;
> Visions; revivals; Vachel the uproarious,
> With chant and challenge out of gestures growing ...[37]

Untermeyer's connections in the literary world were not limited to poets. His own prodigious output had also brought him into contact with publishers, editors, playwrights and university lecturers and he made it his business to help Sassoon remedy Pond's failure. As early as 5 February he was writing to Professor Gauss at Princeton to offer Sassoon's services. With a facility which had already brought him success, and using his friendship with Vachel Lindsay as a bait, he tells Gauss that, though Sassoon has plenty of 'social' readings arranged at 'women's clubs and culture circles', he is 'anxious to speak to members of his own sex, and especially to college men'.[38] Recommending his friend as a 'fine person' as well as a 'fine poet', he concludes with an irresistible offer: though Sassoon is getting $100 a time for his 'social' readings, he is willing to 'go to the colleges for less'. It was a skilful, flattering request which Gauss did not resist and Sassoon was duly booked to speak to Princeton's Freneau Club on 11 March at the 'special' fee of $50. Untermeyer was equally successful with Yale, where Sassoon spoke to the Elizabethan Club for the same 'special' rate five days later. It is not difficult to see why Untermeyer's family were reluctant to lose his services as a jewellery salesman.

A highly practical man, Untermeyer also introduced Sassoon to several magazine and newspaper editors. One of the first of these worked for the *New York Tribune*, where Sassoon was subsequently given a blaze of publicity in an article written by – who else? – Untermeyer: 'Lilting Poet. Back from War. Speaks in Trumpet Tones'.[39] Untermeyer was also responsible for Sassoon's lucrative connection with Frank Crowninshield of *Vanity Fair*, who commissioned several articles from him and published at least eleven of his poems.[40]

Appreciative as Sassoon was of such efforts, he felt grateful above all for Untermeyer's introduction to New York's 'magnificent music'.[41] Before leaving school at fifteen, Untermeyer had wanted to be a composer and his wife shared his strong musical interests.[42] One of their earliest invitations to Sassoon was to a recital by the world-class pianist Richard Buhlig, another of Louis's protégés. Sassoon had admired Buhlig greatly in pre-war England and forty-five years after hearing him play Schumann's 'Fantastic' in C major in the Untermeyers' flat he would still be able to recall the thrill.[43] Presenting Buhlig with a copy of *Picture Show* shortly after this recital, he quoted some of his own earlier poetry to describe his excitement: 'You built cathedrals in my heart / And lit my pinnacled desire ...'

He and Buhlig quickly became close friends, lunching and dining together frequently during his stay, Sassoon attending Buhlig's concerts whenever possible. He would later have reservations about Buhlig's technique, but in 1920 he was delighted to supply a rapturous 'Tribute' for Untermeyer's promotion efforts.[44] And on his return to England he would go to some trouble to help Buhlig arrange a concert tour (subsequently cancelled).

Others in the musical world whom he met through the Untermeyers included Helen Tas, a talented violinist married to a Dutch diamond merchant, whom Sassoon would later visit in Holland in the 1920s. Such contacts, together with all the concerts and operas Louis and Jean took him to, gave him less reason than usual to miss his piano, as he often did on holiday.

Louis also took him to plays and one of these, a lavish production of *Richard III*, was responsible for a rare poem written in America, 'First Night: Richard III'.[45] Though not of great interest in itself, as Sassoon noted, it has technical significance as one of his first experiments in a genre he would explore for the next five years, social satire:

> ... The casualties were numerous: and at last
> He died (in clashing brass-ware), tired but tense;

5. 'Midnight on Broadway' (January-March 1920)

> Lord of his own undoing, crazed, aghast,
> And propertied regardless of expense.
> And the whole proud production paled and passed,
> Self-conscious, like its brilliant audience.
>
> (CP, p. 155)

A more successful attempt in the same genre, 'Storm on Fifth Avenue', written about the same time and almost certainly also inspired by an evening with Untermeyer, suggests that Sassoon was better at self-satire than satire of others:

> A sallow waiter brings me beans and pork …
> Outside there's fury in the firmament.
> Ice-cream, of course, will follow; and I'm content.
> O Babylon! O Carthage! O New York!
>
> (CP, p. 143)

There is no doubt that Sassoon appreciated Untermeyer, and not just his shrewd, practical help in the New York jungle. He particularly enjoyed his sense of humour, which was fairly similar to his own. A jokey verse-letter from him, for example, would elicit an equally witty rhymed response from his American friend.[46] Above all he loved Louis's enormous gusto for life. One of his fondest memories of New York would be 'a sudden glimpse of Louis's face behind a mound of vanilla ice-cream'.[47] Untermeyer undoubtedly valued Sassoon's friendship and continued to be an ardent admirer of his poetry.

It was, however, an admiration Sassoon could not wholeheartedly return. For theirs was largely an attraction of opposites. A certain brashness about Untermeyer – tactfully referred to as 'smart-minded immaturity' by Sassoon[48] – would prevent a deeper understanding developing. Even during his stay in New York there were things Sassoon felt unable to share with Untermeyer. He needed someone more mature, more sensitive or less worldly on occasions and was lucky enough to find it in two people who happened to be friends of Untermeyer, both, like him, of German-Jewish origin, both part of his literary and musical spheres.

He met the first of these, Ben Huebsch, directly through Untermeyer. Like Untermeyer and many other first-generation immigrants, Huebsch had had to start work young, first as an apprentice lithographer, then running a printing works with his brother, but had made up for his lack of university education by taking night classes. He had studied art at the Cooper Union and violin under Sam Franko, eventually becoming music critic for the *New York Sun*. Especially fond of chamber music, he took Sassoon to a number of performances at the Carnegie Hall among other places.

His greatest commitment, however, was to literature. By the time Sassoon arrived in New York, Huebsch had launched his own small publishing house, which had already brought out Joyce's *Dubliners*, and had also started a weekly magazine of some repute, *The Freeman*. Sassoon recognized him as 'a highly discerning publisher of good literature' and was flattered by his request to contribute to *The Freeman*.[49] And when Huebsch went on to merge his own small firm with Viking in 1925, he would become, with one exception, the sole publisher of Sassoon's poetry in America.[50] Even after Sassoon had been lured by larger advances to bigger firms for the American editions of his fictional prose trilogy, Huebsch would remain friendly and be ready to publish Sassoon's later, less popular, prose works.[51]

Sassoon had no need of the reminder by a mutual friend that Huebsch was 'a gentleman', nor that he was extremely 'lovable and kind'.[52] He himself described Huebsch as 'one of the most likeable men' in America and found his 'calmly judicious and benevolent personality' a welcome antidote to his own still occasionally juvenile behaviour.[53] Ten years older than Sassoon and about to marry, he gave him a much-needed feeling of 'serenity'.[54] 'Good and dear Ben' was how Sassoon would think of him throughout their long friendship.[55]

Another side to Huebsch that Sassoon particularly appreciated in 1920, when he was still planning to be a good socialist, was his commitment to left-wing causes. An activist in the American Civil Liberties Union, he introduced Sassoon to labour circles, which led to invitations to address the Inter-Collegiate Socialist Society, the Cooper Union and the Rand School.[56] At one point in his visit Sassoon was intending to stay on for the presidential elections. And it was probably Huebsch who introduced him to his fellow-countryman Harold Laski, then lecturing at Harvard, where Sassoon was subsequently invited to talk.[57]

Huebsch was also responsible for arranging a very different kind of engagement for him at the Free Synagogue in Carnegie Hall. 'As regards the Rabbi – I leave it to you,' Sassoon wrote to him in March 1920. Then, perhaps mindful of the Jewish reputation for striking good deals, he added, 'Make the best terms you can.'[58] The event itself, on 25 April, made him more conscious than he had previously been of his own Jewish blood. Growing up among Gentiles after his father left the family in 1890, he had known very few Jews and made no close Jewish friends until his arrival in New York. Faced with a 'prosperous and complacent' audience of over 2,000 at the Free Synagogue, he found himself behaving as though some 'angry prophet in [his] Jewish ancestry' had taken over.[59] Instead of simply reading his poems, as arranged, he delivered a blistering attack on his listeners for their ignorance of war's realities, surprising himself as well as his audience by his 'stern and dispassionate ferocity'.[60] This direct identification with Jewishness may be the most significant effect of his American visit.

It was an awareness which had been growing since his arrival in New York, one which had been stimulated unintentionally by his greatest friend of all in America, Sam Behrman.[61] Sam, the son of a rabbi from Worcester, Massachusetts, had mainly Jewish friends. Knowing Sassoon's love of music, he had taken him to visit the sister of one of them, the violinist Emily Gresser. Emily's father, a nineteenth-century Russian liberal, seemed awed at meeting a Sassoon and immediately asked him about his ancestry. When Sassoon showed little interest in it, Mr Gresser ran to the bookshelves and brought over the 'S' volume of the *Jewish Encyclopaedia*. 'He confronted Siegfried with pages about his ancestors,' Behrman recalled, 'enlivened by engravings of turbaned ancestors. One dignitary, with an immense white beard and magisterial expression, seemed to interest him particularly.'[62] This was almost certainly Sassoon's great-grandfather, the patriarch David Sassoon, an impressive reminder of all that was noblest in his father's family.

Sassoon had first met Behrman when he arrived at Westover Court to find himself living next door to 'a crashing old-young spectacled admirer who rushed in, and bored [him] at intervals'.[63] Behrman, who worked for the *New York Times*, also interviewed him for his paper.[64] Like Huebsch and Untermeyer he had strong musical interests, and would marry the sister of the Russian musician Jaffa Heifetz. One of his great friends was the Russian pianist Chotzinoff, who became another brother-in-law. And the Gershwin brothers were his close friends.

A graduate of Harvard and Columbia, Behrman was working as a freelance journalist while he struggled to establish himself as a playwright. Neither he nor Sassoon could foresee just how successful he would become and in 1920 he was the one person in New York with whom Sassoon could be what he called his 'ordinary' self.[65] Though Behrman found him far from ordinary, he had the good playwright's firm grasp of character and understood Sassoon's needs. When the flood of social invitations was at its height, he was able to reassure Sassoon and guide him through what he delighted to call his 'praeternatural popularity'.[66] Instead of dreading the letters and telephone calls that met him every time he returned to his bare little flat, Sassoon could consult Behrman, who became in essence his unpaid social secretary. Providence, it seemed to Sassoon, had been unusually co-operative in bringing Behrman into his life.

Though Behrman could be ruthless in dealing with Sassoon's social engagements, he was personally the 'nicest' of people according to Sassoon, who often used the word 'angelic' to describe him.[67] Osbert Sitwell was one of many who agreed with him: on his own visit to New York in 1929 he wrote to tell Sassoon that 'Sam B. [was] much the freshest and nicest spot in it'.[68]

Though Sassoon maintained that Sam was 'really too nice for words', he found plenty of words for him.[69] One of his favourites was 'little', a term used not just to emphasize his own superior height. As with Blunden, it indicated a strongly protective feeling. Sam was not quite as young as

Blunden, but still seven years younger than Sassoon and not nearly so successful at that point. He also lacked the good looks of Sassoon, who appeared in his eyes as 'tall, lithe and extraordinarily handsome'.[70] Ted Morgan, who knew Sam well, said that Sam believed he was physically ugly and Morgan's description certainly makes him seem so: 'On a squat body perched a large head with a high forehead and nearsighted eyes that blinked through thick-lensed glasses ... He never looked freshly shaven because his beard successfully resisted all razors. His walk was like the waddle of a penguin.'[71] Yet, as the same friend goes on to say, there was something very attractive about Behrman, 'an extraordinary warmth and charm'.[72]

Part of his charm for Sassoon lay in his humour, which insisted on assigning his friend the role of a gangling English eccentric. Sam chose to regard him as a 'quaintly trustful person on whom life was playing a series of practical jokes', a part Sassoon found himself involuntarily adopting in his company.[73] He tripped over things, forgot what he was doing and continually fulfilled Sam's idea of him. On one occasion, absent-mindedly stretching out his long legs in a very small, very ramshackle taxi, he broke the glass in the driver's partition. To Sam's glee the driver instantly leapt out, demanded 'Twenty dollars!' and advised his passenger to 'leave his legs at home next time.'[74] When particularly delighted by Sassoon's unworldliness, Sam would speak of him in the third person: 'He hasn't yet called on his publisher,' he crowed, after they had known each other about a month; 'Another example of his deeply organized business instinct!'[75] He thought one of the funniest things ever said to him by anyone was Sassoon's remark that the huge Wrigley chewing-gum advertisement which dominated his living room, instead of reading 'Don't argue but stick it in your face', should say 'Thomas Hardy's poems'.[76]

Sassoon enjoyed Behrman's humour for the same reason Behrman appreciated his, that it was so different. He loved Sam's 'wisecracking' remarks and 'smart slang phrases', which seemed so much more expressive than the conversation of the highly cultivated New York society he was trying to avoid. Only someone as unashamedly American as Sam, for example, after racking his brains for something to send Sassoon's larger-than-life friend Nellie Burton, could say, 'I'd like to send her Niagara Falls.'[77]

Sassoon's best moments were spent with Sam in modest restaurants or cafés near Times Square, eating, say, a club sandwich, while Sam lectured him on playwriting or journalism. At such times he felt he was in touch with the 'reality' of New York.[78] His own attempts to satisfy Sam's interest in the British literary scene are revealing. 'His love for some of them – Edmund Blunden and Wilfred Owen for example – was passionate,' Behrman remembered: 'He read their works aloud to me; he talked for hours about their distilled virtues.'[79]

5. 'Midnight on Broadway' (January-March 1920)

*

Behrman would ultimately become for Sassoon the 'main human fact' of his visit to America, 'superseding' all the other friends he made there.[80] And it was Behrman he turned to when trouble arose. Writing to Turner on 21 February, Sassoon had reported that he was emerging from his initial crises and beginning to find New York 'great fun'.[81] A week later he was sending Meiklejohn a hundred pounds for Gabriel to join him at the end of April and all seemed well. Though he claimed to have made the arrangement 'in a moment of emotion', he had in fact included Gabriel in his plans from the start and was evidently looking forward to it and also to a trip to California to see Gabriel's relations.[82] Only two weeks later, however, he was telling Ottoline that there were 'complications' and that he had cancelled Gabriel's visit, which would have been 'a great mistake'.[83] He was equally evasive with Gabriel himself, to whom he telegraphed on 18 March cancelling the trip. Blaming Pond's failure to find him lucrative work, he added: 'There are other complications which I can't explain now.'[84]

Clearly something dramatic had happened to account for his odd behaviour. The explanation was that he had become completely infatuated with someone else. But almost as soon as he cancelled Gabriel's visit the affair had (in his own words) 'ended disastrously'.[85]

It is possible that he had already met the young man concerned by 21 February, when he had ended a letter to Turner: 'All will be well if I can avoid falling in love!'[86] But it is more likely that he merely feared his own propensity for sudden and violent infatuations. Whatever lay behind his statement to Turner, it was a prophetic one, for by 10 March he had become deeply involved in the affair and by 16 March it was over.

Glenn Hunter was an American actor eleven years younger than Sassoon.[87] Sassoon may first have seen him on one of his many visits to the theatre with Untermeyer and Behrman. Hunter's theatre, the Hudson, was only a few blocks from Westover Court, which explains Sassoon's reference to being 'led such a devilish dance up and down West 44th Street' in March 1920.[88] Hunter was appearing in a highly successful play, *Clarence*, with three well-known actors of the day, Alfred Lunt, Helen Hayes and Maureen Boland. He had been cast as the ne'er-do-well son and his boyish good looks may have drawn Sassoon to the stage door after the performance.[89]

Judging from several later affairs, Sassoon felt a particular attraction to young male actors. It was not simply that they tended to be handsome and at least sympathetic towards homosexuals, if not homosexual themselves; they were also, he believed, involved in an important artistic profession. And, as a poem written shortly after the end of his affair with Hunter suggests, he was mesmerized by the whole theatrical experience:

87

Two Players

I,
Fumbling a few dim smouldering chords that die ...
Broken prelude, groping to find its lonely night
Of nothingness beyond love's wounded evening sky.
Blurred afterword of passion stumbling darkly by.
And you,
Lost in a fool serenade of romance, memorizing ...
Then out of the past, my dreams of the past that we knew,
With a foot-light air of mirth and mockery rising.[90]

Sassoon would later use the same image of the pianist, with his broken chords and shattered heart, to frame a short story about his sufferings over his 'foot-light' lover.

Behrman, who knew Hunter, called him 'talented, good-looking and absolutely empty ... a thoroughly commonplace young man.'[91] He had been taken into Sassoon's confidence only after the affair had run its violent course, leaving its victim humiliated and in deep despair. Though Sassoon was reluctant to give details, even in his diary, he did say that Hunter treated him 'like dirt' and that it would be years before he felt able to trust anyone again.[92] He was to experience similar sensations over another young actor in 1924.

But in 1920 there was one man he *could* trust, Behrman. (Rivers, whom he might have turned to, had just left for Baltimore after a few days in New York.) Young, inexperienced and heterosexual, Sam was at first 'bewildered, horrified and shocked' by a 'variety of love' about which he knew little.[93] But in the face of 'such suffering, such unmitigated agony' as Sassoon's, he quickly surmounted his prejudice and became, as far as Sassoon was concerned, 'an absolute darling, full of sympathy and under-standing'.[94] Though neither of them describes the affair in their autobiographies, Behrman is unable to resist an oblique reference to his friend's 'private agony'.[95] Sassoon told no one else to begin with, though Ottoline, one of his closest confidantes in England, probably guessed what he meant when he alluded to an 'amazing experience' which had brought him close to breakdown.[96]

He was saved from complete collapse by Sam's sympathy; also by his lecture itinerary, which became more demanding in mid-March, providing a much-needed distraction. By then Pond's troubles had reached crisis point and he was obliged to tell Sassoon that he was on his own. Before doing so, however, he had booked him an engagement near Chicago through his branch office there, and two days after Hunter's final, brutal rejection, Sassoon set out for the Midwest. Stopping overnight at Rochester in upstate New York to lecture to the Associate Alumnae of Vassar, he continued on to Chicago and arrived in the city on 20 March.[97]

6

Chicago and Beyond
(March-August 1920)

In a way I feel scared of returning to England. I dread seeing all the familiar faces again, and going into the same routine. – Here, at least, I am isolated, mentally, and not worried by the bickerings and jealousies of everyone.
(Sassoon to Gabriel Atkin, 17 June 1920)

When Sassoon arrived in Chicago in March 1920 it was still the most important railhead, grain market, livestock and meat-packing centre and lumber exchange in the world. Though he showed no awareness of these facts, he did know that it had a population of over two million and was second only to New York in importance. There is also a strong possibility that he had read Upton Sinclair's grim picture of the Chicago stockyards, *The Jungle* (1906). So that it would almost certainly have come as a surprise to see the beauty of the city: not just the strange beauty of a towering skyline, already encountered in New York – though Chicago was known as 'Skyscraper City' – but its dramatic architecture and the attractiveness of its waterfront setting. ('The lake is very fine,' he told his mother.[1]) Situated on the south-west corner of Lake Michigan with views protected by extensive parkland, it was also called the Garden City. And since Sassoon's first night was spent at the Auditorium Hotel, a magnificent building overlooking the lake, he might well have wondered why Chicago was mainly associated with its slaughterhouses.

Before visiting those stockyards, however, or discovering more about the city, he was obliged to leave it. His first, and only pre-booked, engagement was about thirty miles north of Chicago at Lake Forest, where he had agreed to talk to the girls of Ferry Hall School. After a successful performance in the school chapel ('Poems went well. Voice improving', he noted), he spent the night and the following week with a retired lawyer and his wife. The Horace Martins, whose low, rambling house in wooded grounds was only a few minutes' walk from the school, were ideal company for the exhausted Sassoon.[2] Quiet, elderly and devoted to English literature, they were 'graciously considerate' and allowed him the relaxation he needed.[3] Long walks by Lake Michigan and desultory reading of outdated London journals restored his energy and after a few days he was ready to follow up the contacts they kindly offered.

The first of these, an introduction to the composer John Alden Carpenter, was also Sassoon's first taste of Chicago's rich cultural life.[4] Carpenter, who was later to set several of Sassoon's poems to music, invited him to a recital by the cellist Pablo Casals, who happened to be playing some of Sassoon's favourite music by Bach the day they met.

Sassoon was deeply moved by Casals' performance and would attend other concerts during his stay, but it was the literary rather than musical life of the city which interested him most. Chicago in 1920 was associated with some of the best-known American writers of the time, such as the novelists Upton Sinclair, Theodore Dreiser, Sinclair Lewis and John Dos Passos, and the poets Carl Sandburg and Edgar Lee Masters. It was also home to Harriet Monroe's groundbreaking *Poetry* magazine, which played a prominent part in the movement known as the Chicago Renaissance.[5]

Sassoon would not have had much sympathy with *Poetry*'s Modernist aims, but he was delighted to meet one of its main contributors, Carl Sandburg.[6] Sandburg's *Chicago Poems* (1916) had already established him as a major poet, but he continued to work as labour editor for the *Chicago Daily News*. It seemed to Sassoon an appropriate setting for the man he called 'the Whitmanesque poet of the Middle West': 'Sitting in that dingy little newspaper room, with an old grey hat on his head, smoking a large companionable pipe, he appeared to have discarded inessential concerns and found his formula for arriving at the root of the matter.'[7] Sandburg was, he told Ottoline, the 'most impressive personality' he had met in America: 'forty years old, grey and tired-looking, with a deep voice and something wonderful about him – really big'.[8] His verse, when read by the poet himself, seemed 'very beautiful'.[9]

Sandburg appeared to Sassoon built on a larger scale than either Lindsay or Frost, though he shared the latter's 'deeply serious' humour.[10] Whereas Frost observed the 'minutiae of nature', Sandburg dealt in harsher realities. It was the difference between a delicate line drawing and vivid poster work. No one, Sassoon felt, had described Chicago better than Sandburg, its 'polyglot raw material', its 'teeming rudimentariness', which Sandburg had insisted on showing him. It was a side to the city he might otherwise not have seen. As he stood with Sandburg on the roof of a huge building, staring across Chicago's canyon-like streets and façades, a stormy sunset transformed the city and he noticed how it coloured not just the elegant boulevards but also the drifting clouds of factory smoke. It was indeed a place of extreme contrasts, as Sandburg had shown in his poem addressed to the city he called the 'Hog Butcher' of the world.[11]

Sassoon did not agree with Sandburg's definition of poetry as 'a series of explanations of life, fading off into horizons too swift for explanations', but he did respect his opinion in other areas.[12] It was Sandburg who made him realize that bullets, bombs, bayonets and gas were 'nothing more than words' to the majority of Americans and in doing so he provided the 'central point' of Sassoon's trip.[13] His mainly female audiences had been either too charmed or too inexperienced to question his message that 'war doesn't pay', his only challenge coming from a man whose son had been killed in the conflict.[14] But with more than half his lectures left to give, Sandburg's suggestion was an unsettling thought.

*

Sassoon's main motive in visiting Chicago had been to escape his unhappy affair in New York. He was not, however, allowed to forget it. Everywhere he went there were advertisements for Hunter's play, *Clarence*, and he was continually haunted by him. In a moment of weakness he had written to the actor from Rochester, but there was no reply. 'The whole machinery of my intellect seems to have given out,' he told Behrman on 29 March, 'and is started, on necessary occasions, by violent cranking.'[15]

This was almost certainly the reason he accepted a highly impractical invitation to lecture at the University of Toronto: it would take him almost two days to get there and two days to get back by train for less than two days' stay. Not only was it a further distraction, however, but it also meant that he could see Frank Prewett, who still seemed to him as 'sweet' and 'loveable' as ever.[16] A big dinner party was given for him by Vincent Massey on his arrival in Toronto on 30 March and he stayed the nights of 30 and 31 March with Mr and Mrs Pelham Edgars at 286 St George Street. 'Toronto' Prewett had returned home from studying English at Oxford to take an organ course at the university, but he was missing England badly. One result of Sassoon's visit would be his promise to take Prewett back on the boat with him, an offer which would delay his own return by several months.

Though Prewett failed to complete anything he undertook satisfactorily, he was clearly very able. When Sassoon learnt to his horror that, beside reading his poems at the 'benefit' for the poet Bliss Carmen, he would be expected to lecture for at least half an hour on contemporary English poets, Prewett found no difficulty in helping him 'vamp up a conspectus of living British bards'.[17] (Sassoon's firm belief that he was not an intellectual was very different from 'Toronto's' singularly confident approach in such areas.) Both the talk and the poetry-reading went well, one of the local newspapers comparing Sassoon to 'an avenging angel through whom the voice of slaughtered youth was speaking'.[18] His facility for playing on the emotions of his hearers was, he felt, becoming dangerously enjoyable.

Back in Chicago for his final fortnight he was exposed once more to the hectic social life he dreaded. His hostess on this occasion was a well-known local novelist, Janet Ayer, whom he had almost certainly met at the Cosmopolitan Club in New York.[19] She was also, through her marriage to the owner of a large meat-packing firm, Kellogg Fairbank, one of the wealthiest and most influential people in Chicago society. So that Sassoon found himself staying in an elegant town house in an expensive area of the city[20] and, besides the concerts he craved, being taken to dine with a wealthy railway director, lunch with a millionaire meat-packer and politician, attend several evening parties and take a 'regular watering-place tittup' with Mrs Fairbank along Lake Drive 'wearing ridiculous borrowed gaiters'.[21] Mrs Fairbank was also a woman of strong political concerns and he was obliged in addition to inspect two large maternity hospitals, as well as the stockyards, and meet the famous social reformer Jane Addams.[22]

His hostess's energy and connections seemed limitless and she was no doubt responsible for some of the lectures he was asked to give in his final week. He was also helped by another socialite, Mrs Vaughan Moody, wife of an English professor at Chicago University, where he was asked to lecture to both the Friday Club and the Poetry Club.[23] His flattering letter to her from Rochester suggests that, however scornful he might be about such women, he was prepared to use them without hesitation when necessary.[24] Lectures to the Winnetka Women's Club, the Council of Jewish Women and the Arts Club completed his hectic schedule.[25]

*

Sassoon's greatest problem on arrival in New York had been a lack of engagements. Now, on his return to the city, he encountered the opposite. His own and his friends' efforts to fill the gaps had been almost too successful. But they had taken time to bear fruit, so that more than half his lectures had to be crammed into April or May. And his five engagements in one week at Chicago had been followed by a rushed overnight stop at Cornell University on 15 April, with the result that he was already tired to start with.

Back in New York, even before he had time to recover from his fourth long journey in four weeks, he was on the stage of the Greenwich Village Theater, which Pond had hired on 18 April for his only public appearance. Columbia University on the 20th, Vassar College on the 23rd and appearances at both the Free Synagogue and the MacDowell Club on the 25 April concluded another exhausting week. There were times when he went onto the platform feeling so tired that he wondered whether he would get through his performance at all.

Unfortunately, his final engagement for the month, the Harvard Poetry Club, was the one he most and least looked forward to. He was delighted to be staying with Harold Laski, who had already done a great deal to help and encourage him in America, and he was anxious to meet Amy Lowell, whom he believed responsible for his invitation.[26] But he had come straight to Boston from a talk to the women of Wellesley College and was so 'thoroughly overtired' that he had to 'screw [himself] up' to appear on the platform at all.[27] He had also been told to expect some strong militarist opposition.

6. Chicago and Beyond (March-August 1920)

In the event, after a day in bed and some skilful chairing by Amy Lowell, the meeting passed off peacefully. Though he had been too exhausted to meet any of the interesting people Laski had lined up for him, he was able to enjoy an evening after his lecture with the two who most fascinated him, Lowell and Laski themselves. Sitting in Lowell's fine library, listening to them talk, he felt almost 'non-existent' in their powerful presence: 'They were a remarkably contrasted couple – he, small, boyishly brilliant, pro-vocative in argument, and essentially generous and idealistic; she, stout and masculine, jocularly downright and dogmatic, smoking a long manila cigar, and completely confident that "Imagism" was the poetry of the future.'

There was one curious footnote to Sassoon's stay in Boston which probably brought the war nearer for him than any of his talks or war poems. This was a meeting with one of his best friends from the 1st Royal Welch Fusiliers, Norman ('Birdie') Stansfield, a Canadian wool-merchant (described affectionately as 'Mansfield' in *Memoirs of a Fox-Hunting Man* and *Memoirs of an Infantry Officer*). As fat and cheerful as ever, he was doing well as a wool-broker in North America, the trenches firmly behind him.

*

Fearing himself close to breakdown at the end of April, Sassoon cancelled all further engagements with the exception of a few minor ones in New York. Thus ended what he called his 'diminutive attempt to make known to Americans an interpretation of the war as seen by the fighting man'.[28] Judging from the grateful letters he received from ex-soldiers, it seemed to him that his campaign had been moderately successful, though it is difficult to believe that it made much difference overall. Its main signifi-cance appears to have been in helping to purge his own system of the war.

He had intended to cover the presidential election in San Francisco in June for one of the big papers, a 'rather good chance of seeing something of American politics', he told his mother.[29] But when it came to it he was unable to muster the necessary interest or energy and instead stayed in New York, hoping to relax and enjoy his remaining time in America. By waiting for Prewett to make up his mind whether to return with him or not, he had forfeited the possibility of sailing home before August, which left him three whole months to fill. With Behrman's encouragement and help he moved into a larger flat at Westover Court, hired a grand piano, bought himself a straw hat and started to write again. Apart from a few poems, he had attempted nothing serious since his arrival. But Behrman, who thought it would be therapeutic, urged him to write a story about his unhappy affair with Hunter. Casting himself (with Buhlig, no doubt, in mind) as a young English pianist living in New York, Sassoon began, with some confidence and more than a little portentousness:

There are moments in the lives of men, when they are conscious only of the spirit within them, when that spirit, pausing on its journey, stands isolated between the known and the unknown, powerless to discern what shall be, yet serene in reconciliation with all that it has endured.[30]

The story opens and closes with the pianist playing Bach's Chromatic Fantasia, a fairly obvious structural device of which Sassoon was inordinately proud.

Reading Turgenev for guidance and buoyed by Behrman's confidence in him, by mid-June Sassoon was boasting to Ottoline of a 'distinct gift' for story-writing.[31] Though he knew that this particular story was 'quite unpublishable', owing to its homosexual theme, it had helped him through a bad phase: 'Work is the only anodyne.'[32] He eventually abandoned the story as 'too personal', but it is an intriguing forerunner of his later prose trilogies and indicates what he might have had in mind when he planned to write 'another Madame Bovary dealing with sexual inversion'.[33]

Even before he stopped writing his story in early July, Sassoon had found something other than 'drifting round Broadway' to fill his time.[34] Rivers had introduced him to his neurologist friend John MacCurdy, who had a country house about thirty miles north of the city.[35] As the fierce New York summer got under way Sassoon began to spend several days a week there, playing golf at the Westchester County Club among other things. After the roar of Westover Court it was wonderfully relaxing to lie in bed hearing the crickets chirp and frogs croak in the marsh below the house.

He was also invited to spend time on Staten Island with Russell Loines and his family. Loines, who was a marine-insurance lawyer, was also a devotee of poets and welcomed many of them to America. De la Mare had stayed with him in 1916 and had no doubt encouraged Sassoon to do the same. Writing to Turner from Loines's house at Dongan Hills, Sassoon tells him: 'I grow fat on ice-cream and soft shell crab, *Yep* or *Yar* do I say where I was wont to reply in the affirmative with meek and mumbled *Yes*; often I wear a sleeveless "Union suit", and green cigars have puffed beyond compute; saunter on sidewalks; breakfast on some cereal; do everything except write poetry and chew gum; am in fact $1\frac{1}{2}$% American ...'[36] Allowing for humorous exaggeration Sassoon does seem to have acclimatized somewhat to a lifestyle he would have found repugnant in England where, if he ate ice cream at all, it was at Gunter's Tea Rooms in Mayfair.

By July such escapes from New York became increasingly attractive as the city grew ever more stifling. Most of his friends were leaving for the country, Behrman for Woodstock, Vermont, and the Untermeyers for New Milford, Connecticut. So that, when an invitation arrived to stay in Maine with a man he had met briefly at Wellesley College, Edward Percy Warren, it seemed an attractive idea.

What finally convinced Sassoon to take a 300-mile train journey to stay with an almost total stranger was, as he relates in *Siegfried's Journey*, the fact that Warren had known Robbie Ross. But he fails to mention for understandable reasons that the 'freemasonry' he says this created was specifically that of fellow-homosexuals.[37] Warren, who wrote homo-erotic verse about adolescents under the pseudonym Arthur Lyon Raile, was already ten years into his life's work, *The Defence of Uranian Love*, when they met.[38] At the age of sixty he was still unmarried. A wealthy art collector, respected connoisseur and classical scholar, with degrees from both Harvard and Oxford, Warren had been made a fellow of Corpus Christi College in 1915. He was staying in Oxford when Ross visited Sassoon during his convalescence at Somerville College in 1916, but no introduction had taken place. Nor had they met at Warren's house in Lewes, a town Sassoon passed through frequently in his early hunting days. (It was at Lewes that Warren had set up a household of boys and young men, a daring experiment for the time.)[39]

Warren's American estate, Fewacres, was run by the son of one of his ex-lovers from Lewes House, Charles Murray West, who organized his life there along English country house lines, complete with a butler who served afternoon tea. (Sassoon remembered Warren's servants being inconspicuous and efficient.) Though modest in scale, Fewacres was an aesthete's delight of 'Doric porches, golden torsos, etc.', according to Sassoon.[40] Only a few miles out of the town of Westbrook, where Warren's father had founded a highly profitable paper mill, the house was surrounded by half-wild countryside, which gave Sassoon the impression that 'the landscape was its garden and the darkness of the distant wood its boundary'.[41] From the plain but perfect country food to his host's daily study of the classics, he is at pains to suggest an atmosphere of high-minded but luxurious simplicity. He does not mention something he almost certainly knew, which is that Warren's 'serenely civilized existence' centred round his still unfinished *magnum opus*, his attempt to justify what he euphemistically termed 'lad's love'.[42]

Read in this light, Sassoon's description of his visit abounds in ironies. When, for example, he wrote that Warren had a temperament 'which excels in intimacy with the young', it is difficult not to read that as an oblique reference to his paederasty.[43] Or when Sassoon claims that Warren found his stay 'memorably delightful', the reader starts to wonder exactly what kind of relationship the older man had with his attractive, still very youthful-looking guest.[44] Did he discuss his theories during the long, 'sort of one-sided platonic dialogue' he carried on with Sassoon over his four-week stay? And did Sassoon, whose only confidant in America had been the puzzled, heterosexual Behrman, find relief in telling Warren about Glenn Hunter? Such questions can only be speculative. What is more certain is the physical benefit Sassoon derived from his stay. Warren had been a keen rider in his youth and, though he no longer kept a stable of Arab horses, he did have an old grey mare which had been lodged with him for the summer. While he studied his Greek authors every morning, he encouraged his guest to go out riding. So each day, before the sun grew too hot, Sassoon enjoyed 'riding an ancient silver horse in the woods and hayfields'.[45]

It seemed to him the best antidote to the past few months of hectic city life he could imagine. Horses had played a central part in his life until the war. Even during his four years in the army he had ridden whenever possible, both in France and on leave in England. But since the Armistice and his immersion in the social whirl of London and Oxford, there had been few opportunities to ride. It was at Fewacres that he realized that he was 'one of those people on whose minds riding produces a profoundly serenifying effect'.[46] The old mare soothed him greatly, offering both mental as well as physical benefit and reminding him how much he missed the activity. One of the first things he did on returning to England a month later would be to buy himself a horse, a minor but positive result of his American trip. His mental peace was added to by Warren's resolute refusal to discuss either his lecture tour or war poetry.

A man of great physical energy and needs, Sassoon was glad of other outlets at Fewacres, from swimming and canoeing to chopping down trees. There was a river less than a mile from the house and between tea and dinner, while Warren returned to his studies, he would go swimming. Always a poor swimmer, he saw it partly as a chance to improve himself. No match for the river's deceptively strong current, however, he nearly drowned on one occasion and took to Warren's canoe with relief. Paddling up 'unfrequented, foliage-reflecting alleys' with the water 'chuckling' under his bows,[47] he may have been reminded of his canoeing trips up the Cherwell in 1916, which had provided some memorable imagery for a poem Owen had greatly admired, 'The Death-Bed'.[48]

Evenings were equally relaxing. After a plain but excellent dinner he would sit and watch the sun go down with Warren before an early bedtime. For the first time since the war, when the contrast with the trenches had made him fully appreciate the countryside behind the lines, he felt he was in 'Arcadia' and Warren had no difficulty in persuading him to remain far longer than he had intended. 'My laziness in staying on here in Arcadia', he told Untermeyer on 29 July, 'may have caused me to miss seeing you again ... [but] I am getting so much benefit from the peace of this place that I am unwilling to return to N.Y. before I am obliged to.' It was the land of the Lotus Eaters.

Sassoon felt that at Fewacres he had completed an exploration which had begun when he left England. And in a sense he had. For less than a fortnight after returning to New York, on 12 August, he was boarding the *Imperator*, an ex-German liner bound for Southampton.

*

6. Chicago and Beyond (March-August 1920)

Sassoon's journey home was very different from his voyage out. Not only was he sailing on a much larger ship, but it was one which carried a party of Hollywood stars. When he arrived at the dock, such celebrities of the silent screen as Olive Thomas, Jack Pickford and Alma Rubens were being given a high-profile send-off by their vociferous fans and an eager press. Pickford was so drunk he could hardly stand and Sassoon was amused to think how puzzled he would be when he woke the next morning to find himself at sea.

Though not the centre of this exuberant farewell, Sassoon was far from solitary, as he had been on the way out. Behrman, convinced that they would never meet again, had come to see him off and his other great friend, Huebsch, was actually travelling with him. (Prewett, when it came to it, was not.) Whereas Sassoon had spent the ten days' journey from Portsmouth contemplating his post-war problems, the eight days' journey home was passed more convivially in Huebsch's company.

He was also feeling much fitter. Expert dental treatment and a long stay in the country had left him full of physical energy, so that when the other passengers went below for their meals he often raced round the deck, jumping the railings like a hurdler. One of Huebsch's abiding memories of the trip was the sight of his unpredictable friend climbing dangerously high up a ship's mast.[49] Sassoon's impulsiveness and physical courage had earned him the name 'Mad Jack' in the army, but it would remain appropriate throughout his life. He certainly seemed a little mad to Huebsch, whose far soberer personality had probably prompted Sassoon to what he admitted was his 'extravagantly juvenile behaviour' on board.[50]

Another amusing manifestation of Mad Jack occurred in the ship's smoking room, of which the party from Hollywood had taken lordly possession. They had set up a sweepstake on the mileage of the daily run which Sassoon and others suspected was being turned to private profit. The affair ended in an unpleasant brawl, with the assistant auctioneer, for whom Sassoon felt a particular dislike, grabbing a bottle by the neck with obvious intentions. Using this as a pretext, Sassoon rushed at the man and sat so violently on his chest that his shirt collar burst off. Huebsch suggests that it was actually Sassoon, himself and another disaffected passenger who had initiated the fight by usurping the table from which Hollywood 'commanded'.[51]

The greatest difference in Sassoon's return journey, however, was not in external circumstances but in himself. For America had affected him far more than he or any of his English friends could have predicted. His seven months there, he told Behrman shortly after his arrival home, had been 'in a way the most extraordinary I shall ever experience'.[52]

They had undoubtedly broadened his still relatively limited horizons. Until the war he had never been out of England and his subsequent wartime travels to France and Palestine had been cushioned by British

Army routines. It was not until he reached America that he had been fully exposed to another culture.

This contact with a completely new, often alien, environment, which at least one of his friends could not imagine him surviving for two days, had brought him out of himself to a surprising degree. And his growing enjoyment of his 'performances' during his tour suggests a significant increase in confidence. His New York friends, Behrman, Huebsch and Untermeyer in particular, had strengthened that confidence with their firm belief in his literary powers. They had also added to his circle of close friends.

Behrman, moreover, was responsible for another important development in New York, Sassoon's first serious attempt at prose-writing. Though the affair with Hunter which inspired it had caused him enormous suffering, it had also, as he told Ottoline, 'taught [him] a little more about life'.[53] And the story itself, Behrman believed, was the first small step along the road which led to his greatest prose success, *Memoirs of a Fox-Hunting Man*.[54]

More immediately, his American stay had helped Sassoon to 'get right away from all the Georgians and their conventional poetic vocabularies', as he put it to Ottoline.[55] Distancing himself from Marsh and his friends geographically had helped him separate himself from them mentally. Though far from agreeing fully with the technical experiments of Lindsay, Sandburg and Amy Lowell, meeting them and other Modernist poets had made him realize the limitations of an increasingly effete Georgian tradition. He had written little poetry of his own during his stay and felt 'rather hopeless' about the future direction of his work,[56] but he returned to England at least knowing what he wanted to avoid. In fact his few American poems, all experiments in 'occasional' or satirical verse, suggest that his American experience would shape the course of his poetry over the next five years. It had also convinced him that what he really wanted was 'to go on being a poet'.[57] It was partly for this reason, partly because America created a distance between himself and English politics, that he had decided by the end of his stay to give up his *Daily Herald* post.

On an even more practical level his trip had provided him with a direction and the money to pursue it at a time of great personal bewilderment. Quite apart from money from magazine publications, he had earned a great deal from his tour – $2,562, at a time when the rent of a pleasant flat in central New York cost $35 per month. Despite Pond's failure, he had earned about $90 a lecture, almost twice as much as de la Mare had on a similar tour in 1917. (Like Walter Scott, Sassoon 'love[d] to be particular' and gave exact details of his engagements in *Siegfried's Journey* in the form of a batting average. He had noted them meticulously at the back of his American engagement diary.) Though it is doubtful that he arrived in England with much in his pocket, he had lived well, travelled widely and felt more sense of purpose and success than he had in post-war England.

6. Chicago and Beyond (March-August 1920)

Yet Sassoon would claim in 1924 that he was 'completely disintegrated' when he returned from America.[58] His 'ghastly cardiac enterprise', as he described his affair to Forster, his physical and mental exhaustion during a hectic lecture tour, his failure to write more than a few minor poems and his acute loneliness at times would support this interpretation of his trip. On the other hand, he told Ottoline that he felt 'stronger' for his stay.[59] By the time he arrived in England on 20 August 1920 he felt that he had 'come to the end of the journey on which [he] had set out when [he] enlisted in the army six years before'.[60]

Both statements were probably true. Only by facing extreme change and trying to purge himself completely of his war poetry could he gain the strength to continue with what still seemed to him a fairly meaningless existence.

Tufton Street Blues
(August 1920-November 1925)

I come here dull-witted and disillusioned, craving for love, craving for imaginative eloquence. Spiritual sickness overshadows me. My mind is somehow diseased and distorted. I live in myself – seek freedom in myself – self-poisoned, self-imprisoned.

(Diary entry for 29 September 1921)

Sassoon brings his published autobiography to a neat conclusion in August 1920 with the assertion that his American trip had freed him from the war. But even a cursory look at his life in the early twenties suggests that this was not so. While his frequent references to his 'fiendish' or 'vile' temper in his diary might be explained as simply a character trait, other allusions to a 'poisoned mind; an unwholesome unhappiness' pervading his 'healthy body' show that he regarded his state as an unnatural one.[1] Extending the metaphor of disease further, he writes to Graves in 1921: 'I wonder if you realise what an effort it is to me to enjoy anything. That is the trouble. Internal canker gnaws my guts.'[2]

His main problem was his failure to find a 'moral equivalent' for war.[3] Though he had stopped thinking about the war consciously, there were still times when it seemed more real than events around him. Men like Lance Corporal Gibson, whose death at Mametz Wood in July 1916 had provoked one of his most daring raids,[4] returned to haunt him, asking in effect the question Sassoon himself had posed in 'Sick Leave': 'Why are you here with all your watches ended?'[5] On such occasions Sassoon felt that he was only 'half-alive', that a part of him had 'died with all the Gibsons I used to know'.[6]

His 'sheet-anchor' in this slow recuperation from the war was Turner.[7] Together with his wife, Delphine, he formed the 'rock' on which Sassoon hoped to build his 'lighthouse'.[8] Before leaving for America Sassoon had already moved into the house they had agreed to share in Westminster, so that it was with a sense of belonging, however frail, that he returned to London. The Turners seemed to him a 'barrier' between himself and anything that threatened his gradual progress towards 'maturity and stability of mind'.[9] Turner, more than anyone he knew except Rivers, imposed 'sanity and half-humorous scrutiny' on him.[10]

One of the qualities that had attracted Sassoon to Turner initially had been his 'male independence'; he never felt Turner needed his help. In spite of which he provided it very generously. Apart from lending him the money to buy 54 Tufton Street, he paid him rent for his flat there, even after it became obvious that Turner would never be able to repay either the capital sum or the interest on it. He also handed over his literary editorship of the *Daily Herald* to Turner (who had shared it with Forster during Sassoon's absence), mainly because, he told Graves, Turner 'like[d] it and want[ed] the cash'.[11] Having done so, he was relieved to be free of the responsibility, finding it far pleasanter to write articles and reviews for Turner than organize them himself.[12]

Both Turner and Sassoon have left accounts of their relationship which suggest that it was one of more than ordinary warmth and closeness in the early twenties. Sassoon's description of their many late-night talks in Tufton Street gives the flavour:

> We discuss the arts of Music and Poetry; we arrive at the most downright and irrefutable conclusions, half-pitiful and half-contemptuous of the human race, we are infinitely thankful that we, at any rate, are not as other mortals. We do not so much *debate* as discover our own dazzling notions. Quite as often we argue about Love (or Sex).[13]

Turner's account, in the third volume of his autobiographical novel, *The Duchess of Popocatapetl*, while equally positive, is much fuller. Perhaps because he half-conceals Sassoon's identity by introducing him under two names (as himself and as the protagonist, Airbubble's great friend, Blow), it is also franker and more revealing. Portraying Blow as a strikingly handsome young man who had lived in the country, hunting, playing cricket and writing verse before 1914 (as Sassoon had), he relates how Blow had become a hero in the war but had quickly grown critical of it. Almost too daring in the front line, he was nevertheless terrified of women, with the exception of the protagonist's wife (the real-life Delphine Turner, whom Sassoon indeed trusted). Details of Sassoon's actual army career are slightly altered and something of Rupert Brooke's character added, possibly to forestall charges of libel, but he is unmistakably the model for Blow. So that it is revealing to read that he is very irritated by 'the normal attitude in English middle-class society towards homosexuality' and greatly relieved to be able to confide in Airbubble (alias Turner) with his 'completely free and unprejudiced mind'.[14] He admits to spending 'hours hanging around the stage-door of a theatre madly in love with a young actor', a reference to either Glenn Hunter or one or two other young actors with whom Sassoon became infatuated in the early twenties.[15] There is little doubt that Turner is faithfully recording something Sassoon said, or that Sassoon agreed with Airbubble's conclusion to his discussion with Blow, that 'All morality is a fraud.' This and other lightly disguised reports of their conversations not only provide an insight into Sassoon's attitude towards his sexuality at the time, but also one which is uncensored by Sassoon.

In at least one respect, then, Tufton Street was of some significance to Sassoon. It was also important as his first serious London base and the one he would live in longest. Quite different from the large and rambling country house he had inhabited most of his life, it stood on the site of a former slum and the area still retained some of the small artisan dwellings and businesses which had sprung up there in the late eighteenth and nineteenth centuries. But as the working-class houses were first abandoned, then demolished at the beginning of the twentieth century, the developers had moved in and so had the middle classes. Number 54 Tufton Street, crammed on a small plot in what had been formerly a builder's yard (Bennett's Yard), was a typical developer's attempt to pack as much as possible onto a tiny site. It had no garden and was overshadowed on three sides by larger buildings, an effect which was exacerbated by the fact that it was set several feet down from the street. (The area itself had originally been marshland and most of the roads had had to be built up considerably.) But in the first flush of enthusiasm, Sassoon could see none of the disadvantages of these conditions, referring affectionately to his new dwelling as looking 'not unlike a very large doll's house'.[16]

Fortunately his own flat was on the second floor, so was not quite as dark as the rooms below it. He had the whole floor to himself, though this consisted of only two small rooms, each measuring about twelve feet by ten feet. By most modern standards this may seem quite reasonable, but compared with his spacious flat in Raymond Buildings in 1914 or Nellie Burton's lofty rooms in Mayfair it was pokey. For Sassoon, however, Tufton Street represented independence and moving back in, after his brief stay there in December 1919 and January 1920, was an exciting moment. There were his rooms almost exactly as he had left them, his bedroom at the front, his living-cum-sitting room at the back. It is worth giving details of the latter room for, as Sassoon himself observed, 'the room in which one lives and does one's concentrated thinking is something more than cubic feet of space':

> Unknown to others, it can become saturated by the presence of its occupant and permeated by the intensity of his mind-working solitudes. And that cell-like room was indeed destined to be, for several years, the hermitage of my private self ... It represented the part of me which I had always instinctively tried to keep separate. In that room I should be a single-minded poet.[17]

Delphine Turner had added red lines to the developer's stark white walls in an effort to cheer it up, but everything else remained as basic as he had left it, 'a small writing-table, a small sofa, some shelves with a few books on them, a couple of chairs and not much else'.[18] Miniature French windows opened onto a tiny balcony which overlooked the backyards of some working-class houses. It was not quite as bleak as this description suggests, however, since he had a coal fire and a hob on which to boil a kettle. He also added more comfortable touches, such as a red-shaded reading lamp and a multi-coloured coverlet Ottoline had sent him during his army service. His one regret was the lack of space for his baby grand piano, which had to go into the Turners' much larger living room on the first floor. A minor irritation at the start, this would become a major source of grievance to Sassoon later. He had always relied on his piano for both comfort and inspiration.

Above him on the top floor were Walter's and Delphine's bedrooms, separate because, as Walter explained with characteristic frankness, their sexual relationship had been a failure due to his wife's frigidity. (This may help to explain the fact that, unusually, Sassoon felt in no way threatened by Delphine as a woman.) On the ground floor was a small kitchen, a dining room and a minute room which Turner rented to another Georgian poet, Edward Shanks, for his use on his once- or twice-weekly visits to London.

To live in someone else's house, however small, seemed to Sassoon 'an obvious way of simplifying the domiciliary problem'.[19] He did not want to live alone and was equally anxious not to take on the responsibility of organizing his own domestic arrangements. He also preferred to live as austerely as possible, his survival of the war having left him with a general sense of guilt which he tried to assuage by this means. (He was encouraged in this by Dr Rivers.) By twenty-first century standards, however, his life was far from spartan. The Turners' daily help would clean his rooms and make his breakfast, always a cooked one. He would take his lunch and dinner at the Reform, which became, in effect, an extension of his living quarters, serving as both dining and drawing room for him and his friends. His daily walk there would be part of his daily routine for many years. Writing to a friend forty years after arriving at Tufton Street he confessed that he longed for 'the comparative quiet of the 1920s, when [he] could positively potter across from Tufton Street to the Reform Club, conversing with the pelicans in Green Park'.[20] When he finally decided to leave Tufton Street, one of the things he would miss most would be his 'meal-ward walk'.[21]

Another advantage to begin with was his nearness to Chelsea, where Gabriel lived. His flat at 120 Cheyne Walk was a pleasant stroll along the Embankment. And if the evening there went well, the Thames seemed a suitable companion to Sassoon's mood as he walked back in the early hours – 'sombre and lit by silver ripples of a new understanding'.[22] He sometimes joked about the convenience of Westminster generally – if he lived there long enough, he claimed, his corpse would be within easy reach of Poets' Corner – but it was a decisive factor in the success of Tufton Street at the start. One of the most important benefits of his move had

104

been his final escape from Weirleigh. Yet it had left him feeling intensely guilty about his mother. 'She belongs now to a different life from mine,' he wrote in his diary in June 1921, 'a remote worn-out life from which I've escaped into the adventurous uncertainties and perplexities of active experience.'[23] His brother and family had arrived back from Canada in 1920 to live with her, which meant that he was no longer solely responsible for her. But he still felt obliged to visit his mother, or entertain her on her fairly frequent trips to London and it was useful to live so centrally.

The greatest advantage of all, however, was the chance to make a new start after the war:

> *I am clear about one thing* [he wrote in September 1922]: my present life (since I met Turner) has been a struggle to shake off the past (sexual fetishism, vague piano-playing, athleticism of golf, cricket and hunting, etc.). I have been trying to catch up with the intellectualism of Turner, the Sitwells, and all the rest of my post-war friends ... I have consciously repressed the past; trying to *discard* it (avoiding Weirleigh).[24]

In Turner, Sassoon had found the ideal landlord for such an experiment. As one of the younger Georgian poets and a musical, dramatic and literary critic for some of the best-known journals of the day, Turner had already created a cultural centre of sorts at Tufton Street by the time Sassoon returned from America. Sassoon often joined the Turners and their guests in the evening and even when his post-war moodiness made him slip past their door to his own room on returning from the Reform, the constant hum of discussion and debate below made him feel 'vicariously involved in the activities of the intellectual and artistic world'.[25]

One of the Turners' most regular guests and the one Sassoon identified most closely with Tufton Street, was the poet Ralph Hodgson. Sassoon calculated that, from the time Hodgson started visiting in early 1920, to July 1924, when he left to take up a professorship at Sendai University in Japan, he must at a reasonable estimate have been '150 times and have smoked at least 1,000 pipes on our premises'.[26] Though Sassoon had occasionally ignored Hodgson's old bowler hat hanging at the foot of the stairs and gone straight to his flat on returning from the Reform, his visits were very precious to him, as his diary records.

A fervent admirer of Hodgson's *The Bull* and *The Song of Honour*, the poems which had brought him to public recognition in 1913, Sassoon had been wanting to meet him since 1914. He had been particularly intrigued by Marsh's description of Hodgson as a pipe-smoking judge of bull terriers at Crufts Dog Show, who was also an expert in billiards and boxing. He felt that such a man might help him resolve his own conflict between sport and poetry. But Hodgson had been out when he called at his flat in the King's Road and shortly afterwards the threat of war had sent Sassoon first back to Weirleigh, next into the army. It was, then, with some excitement that Sassoon eventually met Hodgson in Turner's sitting room.

105

Hodgson's appearance, like everything else about him, was singular. Of only medium height and build and already forty-nine by the time Sassoon met him, he was nevertheless a physically impressive figure, with broad shoulders tapering down to narrow waist and hips. His strong, muscular features and dark, expressive eyes were set in what his friend Enid Bagnold described as a 'long-lipped lantern face'.[27] His slightly saturnine air, a reflection of what Sassoon called his 'dark side', made Blunden see him at times as 'a very dyspeptic Eagle'.[28] This may help to explain his attractiveness to women, who apparently sensed something 'passionate and sensuous' in him.[29] His own strong attraction towards them, however, was kept rigidly under control by a pronounced puritanism, which occasionally made him seem fanatical. As Sassoon noted, he was 'a passionate denouncer who would have sent you to the stake' for a cause he believed in.[30]

Hodgson was, above all, himself. From the old bowler hat he always wore, to the cheap, strong-smelling tobacco he constantly smoked in a long churchwarden pipe, or the faithful bull terrier which accompanied him and which was sorrowfully replaced when it died of old age, or his refusal to drink anything but ginger beer, or even his habit of lying down to talk in an effort to relieve the pain of chronic piles from which he suffered, he was instantly recognizable.

Hodgson is now remembered, if at all, for a striking poem or two (such as 'Time You Old Gipsy Man', 'The Bells of Heaven', or 'Eve'), in anthologies read in childhood. But to Sassoon and many others he seemed at the time 'a prodigious genius' and 'much the strongest of the Georgian poets', with whom he became connected.[31] A brilliant talker, he cast a spell over his listeners and left them with a sense of loss afterwards: 'His conversation here', Sassoon wrote in 1924, 'is a great book of prose which I shall never be able to read.'[32] Like another outstanding conversationalist of the period, Desmond MacCarthy, his friends attempted to convey this brilliance in vain. And, like MacCarthy, it is probable that much of Hodgson's energy was dissipated in talk. After *The Song of Honour* in 1913 he did not produce another work of any substance until *The Muse and the Mastiff* in 1942 and even that was a disappointment to some of his greatest admirers, though not to the loyal Sassoon.

Sassoon did, however, think it 'tragic' that Hodgson had failed to put his conversation on paper.[33] When doing so himself he tried hard to capture Hodgson's magic but, inevitably perhaps, ended by summarizing his favourite themes: the black-and-white graphic artists of the nineteenth century (Hodgson had started his career as a cartoonist), the homeliness and genius of Dickens, the callous treatment of animals, the advancement of science and the inevitability of progress. It was 'the big-visioned Hodgson, the archaeological, anthropological Hodgson, with his intensely imaginative interest in history, geography and biology, his belief in the ultimate victory of good' he wanted to convey.[34] There are moments when he manages to bring 'Hoddy' to life, lying on the sofa at Tufton Street, stabbing his pipe in the air for emphasis, bull terrier at his feet, while he rides one of his many hobby-horses into the early hours of the morning.

It is not surprising that Sassoon found Hodgson fascinating. What is less predictable is that he should have become one of his closest and lifelong friends. They were so different in many ways. Hodgson, born to a lower-middle-class family in the North, had had little formal education. He was a great believer in science and very positive about most modern developments, infuriating the drama critic Turner by arguing that 'cinema should supersede the theatre'[35] and disturbing Sassoon with his receptiveness towards Modernist poetry. (He became a friend of T.S. Eliot.) Three times married, he was flamboyantly heterosexual: for proof that the world was improving, he argued, you had only 'to look at the legs of the girls ... in the street and think what they were twenty-five years ago', not a convincing argument as far as Sassoon was concerned.[36] He was opposed to one of Sassoon's favourite sports, hunting, and worst of all did not admire Hardy, whose pessimism was a direct contradiction of his own fervent belief in progress.

And yet it was Hodgson's similarity to Hardy in some respects which attracted Sassoon to him, his 'unique quality of flavour and intensity', for example, his unworldliness and the 'startling freshness' of his poetic voice.[37] Like Hardy – and Sassoon himself – he had a great reverence for originality, which they all found in unexpected places. Blunden, Hodgson and Sassoon agreed, had more of this 'flavour' than anyone they had met. A minor writer, discovered in the old, out-of-the-way books they both loved to collect, might also have 'flavour'.[38]

What all these writers and Hodgson himself shared was an intense belief in literature, in his case poetry. 'He is a great man,' Sassoon wrote in 1938, during Hodgson's last visit to England before settling finally in America, 'and his attitude about poetry has always been an inspiration to me.'[39] More than 'any man alive' Hodgson made him want to 'serve the art of poetry faithfully'.[40] For both of them poetry was a sacred calling, the language in which they discussed it full of religious terms. 'I believe in the divinity of poets,' Hodgson told Sassoon.[41] He also argued for 'prophetic aloofness', a state in which the poet waited for the coming of the 'spell', or divine message.[42] Whereas Blunden wanted Sassoon to be more prolific, Hodgson understood his dependence on the Muse, who could be fickle.

There were other things they shared – an interest in graphic art, a love of animals, an appreciation of the absurd – but it was their strong sense of vocation as poets which kept the friendship alive. They were still writing to each other until a few years before Hodgson's death in 1962 at the age of ninety, long, enthusiastic letters about their respective lives, especially their work. Distance seems to have made no difference to their relationship, if anything increasing their closeness, affection and respect.

*

Sassoon met other people beside Hodgson at Tufton Street, the painter Mark Gertler, the poet Edgell Rickword, the novelist Romer Wilson among them, but none of them interested him as much.[43] His friends remained largely those he had made either during or just after the war. Lacking a house of his own, it seemed to him that '[his] friends [were his] house'.[44] Just as people created a home, 'furnishing it slowly and wisely', so he wanted to weave his friends into 'a tapestry of human understanding'.[45] He felt he had 'no other refuge on earth'.[46]

Living in London made it easier to cultivate his relationships, though there were exceptions. Graves, for instance, was still in Oxford and would usually turn up unannounced at Tufton Street, which meant that they sometimes missed each other. Sassoon continued to enjoy his company, in spite of their increasingly divergent views on life and art, and to rely on him for advice about his work, as Graves did on him. Graves was one of the few people, Sassoon claimed, who stimulated him intellectually and he was sad that his marriage prevented them seeing more of each other. It was not so much the geographical distance between them which mattered, for Graves frequently invited Sassoon to stay with him and his family at Islip, as Sassoon's jealousy of Nancy and hers of him. Relations would improve briefly in 1925, when Graves begged him to accompany them to Egypt for his job at Cairo University, but the friendship would never recover its early warmth.

Sassoon suffered from the marriage of a number of other friends besides Graves during this period, a situation which added to his sense of isolation. Blunden was already married when they met in 1919 and Robert Nichols became engaged before he left to work in Japan in 1921. In Blunden's case, his wife Mary appears to have handled Sassoon more tactfully than Nancy Graves and he paid several successful visits to the Blundens at their cottage near Clare in Suffolk, where Edmund was working on his edition of John Clare's poems. His appointment as Professor of English at Tokyo University in 1924 would bring an end to the visits but not the friendship which was, if anything, strengthened by the numerous letters they exchanged. (Over 500 would pass between them during their lifetimes.)

Blunden was one of a number of people Sassoon introduced to Turner. Another was Ottoline, who took Walter and Delphine under her wing, inviting them to spend several Christmases at Garsington. Not everyone liked Turner, however, as Sassoon discovered when he tried to introduce other friends to him. Gosse, for instance, 'cut' him at the Savile Club to which both men belonged; Wells 'disliked' him and the Sitwells 'loathed' him.[47]

In spite of such incompatibilities, Sassoon was nearer to the centre of the literary world at Tufton Street than he had ever been, or would be again. Though not fully aware of it at the time, he was present at the making of several important moments in literary history. This was nowhere more clearly demonstrated than in his friendships with E.M. Forster and T.E. Lawrence, both of which were cemented at the small house in Westminster.

Sassoon had met Lawrence only once before moving into Tufton Street, which was a few minutes' walk from Lawrence's London lodgings in Barton Street.[48] Over the next four years he would see him on a number of occasions. By July 1923 Lawrence was offering to let him read *Seven Pillars of Wisdom*, still at an embryonic stage. This was a rare privilege granted only to his most trusted friends and Sassoon was greatly excited when one of the eight privately printed copies arrived in November. By the time Lawrence wrote to ask on 23 November, with a diffidence Sassoon found hard to credit, 'Is any of it worthwhile?'[49] he was able to reply to the anxious author, with a sly reference to his job as a mechanic in the Royal Tank Corps: 'Damn you, how long do you expect me to go on reassuring you about your bloody masterpiece. It is a GREAT BOOK, blast you. Are you satisfied? You tank-investigating eremite.'[50]

In thanking him for his 'wonderful letter', Lawrence confessed that he still felt doubts about the book. 'Only judgements like yours and [George Bernard] Shaw's can give me any rest upon the point,' he told Sassoon, then added, alarmingly, 'It means a lot, because I'd like to act a "Nunc dimittis" ... if I were convinced.'[51] His suicide was certainly not what Sassoon intended.

Lawrence had become a 'queer figure' in the landscape of Sassoon's thoughts by 1923.[52] Reading *Seven Pillars*, even in execrably small print, had converted his feelings to hero-worship. So that when Lawrence arrived in person at Tufton Street a week after his 'Nunc dimittis' letter, it seemed like a miracle. Sassoon had been relighting the fire in the Turners' drawing room one evening, when the doorbell rang. There, standing under the porch in a new soft grey hat and light-coloured overcoat with a large brown paper parcel under his arm, was Lawrence, the last person he expected, but the one man he had been 'craving to talk to for weeks'.[53]

In town on leave from the army, to see General Trenchard about transferring back to the RAF, Lawrence had called to discuss *Seven Pillars* further. Overwhelmed by the honour and feeling 'enormous' beside his small, self-contained visitor, Sassoon remembered reacting in his usual excitable fashion, 'blundering about the room, emitting disjointed ejaculations, blurting out questions and assertions, mainly about his book and his present health and existent prospects'.[54]

While reading Lawrence's masterpiece, Sassoon had seen its author as an 'infallible superman', but watching him drink tea and nibble shortbread and sponge cakes, he felt protective towards him, in much the same way as towards Wilfred Owen and Edmund Blunden. And, as with Owen and Blunden, he wanted to be of practical help. No expert on prose himself at the time, he felt that the best reassurance he could offer was the opinion of an experienced prose-writer and brilliant critic, E.M. Forster. Forster could also be counted on to sympathize with Lawrence's mysticism, his homosexuality and his passion for the East.

By the time Sassoon asked Lawrence's permission to show Forster *Seven Pillars* in December 1923, he had come to think of Forster as one of the 'nicest' men he knew, as well as a 'real friend'.[55] Their relationship had started in earnest early in 1922 on Forster's return from a year in India. After giving him dinner at the Reform one evening, Sassoon had tried to analyse Forster's appeal for him. It was not a sexual one, though their homosexuality united them to some extent. Nor was it a complete sharing of ideas, since Forster made Sassoon feel 'youthful and impetuous and intellectually clumsy', a 'bit of a blunderbuss', as he told Graves.[56] ('You *must* realize that I am *not* an intellectual,' he warned Forster.)[57] It was partly the relation of master and pupil, Sassoon admiring Forster's 'first-class intellect' and his 'extraordinarily interesting and brilliant qualities'.[58] He found Forster so 'stimulating' that he felt he might 'explode' in his company: whenever they met he began 'chattering away in an inconsequent headlong chuckle-headed style' which Forster appeared to enjoy.[59] And he always ended by telling the older man all his secrets, even inviting him to read his most intimate diaries, a confidence Forster returned by giving him his unpublished homosexual novel, *Maurice*, to read. 'I don't see E.M.F. often enough,' Sassoon wrote in September 1925. 'No one is more sympathetic, wise and witty about the surface-subtleties of human existence.'[60] Equally importantly, he admired Forster's prose as much as Forster appreciated his poetry, concluding at their reunion in March 1922 that Forster was 'one of the very few who signify anything in our wilderness of best-sellers'.

On that same occasion he had also wished that he could help Forster to conquer the writer's block from which he was suffering, and by reintroducing him to Lawrence in a sense he did.[61] For Forster's reading of *Seven Pillars*, Lawrence's mystical response to Arabia, at a time when he was struggling to finish his own exploration of the East, had a significant effect on the last two chapters of *A Passage to India*, as well as influencing the final version of *Seven Pillars*. No wonder Lawrence found Forster's novel's ending 'breathlessly exciting'; he might almost be said to have written it himself.[62]

Like most people, Forster was as intrigued by Lawrence the man as by his work. While reading *Seven Pillars* he had felt neither emotion nor affection for its author, who seemed to him well able to look after himself. But when he met Lawrence to discuss the 'immense' letter he had written him about the book in March 1924, he had to 'stop [himself] going to pieces before him'.[63] 'I have no right to go to pieces,' he told Sassoon, 'not enough beauty.'[64]

By the end of his Dorset visit to Lawrence, when they talked 'for hours', Forster was able to be more objective about him.[65] In particular he noticed his 'flabby handshake' and his tendency to lapse into the 'close-lipped Oxford M.A.', or even 'the dashing free-booter'.[66] It seemed to him that Lawrence's chosen career as a private in the army was 'preposterous'. 'He is inside a membrane of absurdity which has worn so thin that it is amazing he cannot see the light,' he wrote to Sassoon. 'Those damned Arabs are all right and he knows it.'[67]

After another stay with Lawrence in June 1924, helping him to revise *Seven Pillars*, Forster summarized his conclusions for Sassoon:

> He is a rare, remote creature, uncanny, yet attractive. I suspect him of 'practices' – i.e. of some equivalent of yoga, otherwise I cannot understand his attitude towards the body – his own and other people's. He thinks the body dirty, and so disapproves of all voluntary physical contact with the bodies of others. Hence that flabby handshake, no doubt. I should like to know whether he held that view *before* he was tortured at Deraa.

Since Forster's sexual requirements included physical contact as well as 'beauty', he finally managed to maintain his equilibrium with Lawrence, as did Sassoon.

Sassoon's case, however, was slightly different. Like Forster, he was bowled over by Lawrence in some ways, but it is quite clear from one of his earliest descriptions that he felt scant physical attraction: 'a little man in a long, ready-made-looking, rough brown "ulster" '.[68] His description of him less than a year later, when he met Lawrence in his army mechanic's uniform, makes him seem even less physically attractive: 'a queer little figure in dark motor-overalls, his brown and grimy face framed in a fur-lined cap'.[69] There is more than a hint of snobbishness in both reactions. It is no coincidence that Sassoon's lovers, actors apart, tended to be of aristocratic or upper-middle-class origin. They were also inclined to be conspicuously 'pretty' and a great deal younger than himself, which Lawrence was not. Nevertheless, like Forster, he was intrigued by Lawrence's sexuality. When finally invited to tea with him at his cottage in Dorset, his main interest was in Lawrence's relationship to another guest, a fellow-private in the army, 'little Russell'.[70] Although he concluded that Russell was the 'Patroclus', or male lover, of the piece, both men were so discreet that he found it impossible to tell.

It would be many years before Lawrence's predilection for being flogged, sparked off by his rape at Deraa, became public knowledge. Lawrence might privately and quite rightly suspect that Sassoon had a 'savage' side to him, but it did not extend to physical violence of the kind Lawrence appeared to need.[71]

The effect, then, of the triangular relationship which developed in Tufton Street between Sassoon, Forster and Lawrence was mainly literary. And at the time it was confined largely to Forster and Lawrence, though it would eventually have a powerful influence on Sassoon.

*

Despite such distractions, Sassoon found himself with a great deal of time on his hands at Tufton Street. Turner told him that he would 'go crazy if he had so little to occupy his mind' as Sassoon, who admitted that it was 'difficult to know what actually to do with oneself if', unlike Turner, 'one feels no impulse to write plays, or reviews, or poems, and articles'.[72] He found it particularly difficult to fill his days in a town. At Weirleigh he could have weeded the lawn, or played cricket or golf, options which were denied him in London.

Part of his answer to the problem lay in an elaborate daily routine which rarely varied. While making life seem 'a very limited affair', it gave him what he needed in his fight to recover from the war, 'a grip on the details of everyday existence'.[73] His day started late, though not through any choice of his own to begin with. Since the one servant at Tufton Street did not arrive till 8.30 a.m., the Turners' breakfast was not ready until 9.30 and Sassoon had to wait until 10.30 for his. He had never been able to write poetry in the afternoon, so felt obliged to work late into the night. Eventually his first meal, taken at any time between noon and 6 p.m., became 'brunch', a rather odd affair of grilled fish and a milk or steam pudding reminiscent of the nursery or the gentlemen's clubs he frequented.

Graves, who discovered Sassoon still in bed on several afternoon calls, thought Sassoon 'lazy'[74] and Sassoon himself confessed to a tendency to 'indolence', which he blamed on his partly Oriental blood: 'Sustained efforts have always seemed impossible to me [he wrote in his diary for 10 January 1921]. At school, in games and hunting, and even in the army, I always preferred to watch other people's activities and wait for a crisis. When the crisis arrived I was usually effective; and then relapsed again into slackness.' His inertia did not extend to letter-writing and, if there was any of the morning left, he spent it writing to friends. At one point, in 1924, he was communicating regularly and at length with Nichols in Hollywood, Blunden in Tokyo and Hodgson in Sendai, as well as a host of people in England. In the period before breakfast became brunch he would walk to the Reform for lunch, sometimes inviting friends like Meiklejohn (still working nearby at the Treasury) to join him. Afterwards he might stroll through Mayfair to his barber's in Curzon Street, or visit the National Gallery, the Tate or one of the museums. Many afternoons were spent at concerts. And when the weather was particularly good, he walked in Hyde Park, or just sat and viewed the scene there.

All these activities are reflected in his poetry of the period, which suggests that he was not entirely satisfied as a gentleman of leisure. Just as he had satirized the Establishment in his war poems, so he now cast a satiric eye on the fashionable world as seen at musical performances ('Concert-Interpretation', 'Sheldonian Soliloquy', 'Hommage à Mendelssohn'), plays ('A Post-Elizabethan Tragedy'), art galleries ('In the Turner Rooms', 'In the National Gallery', 'On Some Portraits by Sargent') and museums ('The London Museum') or while promenading round London ('Observations in Hyde Park', 'Evensong in Westminster Abbey').

Unlike his war poetry, however, it was the criticism of the insider, of someone who had himself succumbed to the lure of the leisured life. While those with jobs looked forward at 4.30 p.m. to the end of the working day, for example, he would be sitting down to afternoon tea. It was often an excuse to visit Nellie Burton, after picking up strawberries and cream or a pound of fresh raspberries from nearby Fortnum and Mason. He has left a memorable description of 'great-hearted, heroic' Nellie doing justice to her own substantial teas:

> Burton was feeling bright; her cosy room was full of tulips and roses ... And she'd 'been on the bust and bought six silk jumpers' (for her bust!); with each jumper, she explained, she'd wear a different bead-necklace. 'When I change my necklace it brings me luck,' she said, helping herself to another doughnut and putting three lumps of sugar in her second cup of tea.[75]

On another occasion he took 'Dame' Nellie to Hampton Court for tea and was amply rewarded by her reactions. The flowerbeds exhausted all her superlatives ("Ow I do love flowers! They're my children') and she was thrilled to hear a cuckoo (which she 'hadn't done for years'). She was, according to Sassoon, 'in her very best form, mispronouncing the names of the flowers, dipping wildly into English History ... and remembering how she saw a white blackbird in the wistaria last time she was here. "I do love the tapestries of the Seven Deadly Sins, don't you?" she ejaculated, her voluminous face brimming over with good-humour. (She meant the Mantegna frescoes.)'[76]

Yet another trip with her to Wembley in April 1924 was the inspiration for a satirical poem on the more absurd aspects of public ceremonies (which Nellie loved), 'Afterthoughts on the Opening of the British Empire Exhibition':

> Ebullitions of Empire exulted. I listened and stared.
> Patriotic paradings with pygmy preciseness went by.
> The band bashed out bandmaster music; the trumpeters blared.
> The Press was collecting its clichés. (The cloud-covered sky
> Struck a note of neutrality, extra-terrestrial and shy.)
>
> (CP. p. 128)

Sassoon also used tea to fulfil his obligations as a nephew, sometimes visiting his Thornycroft relatives at Melbury Road, or inviting his great-aunt Mozelle to Tufton Street, duty teas which seemed to go on for ever. Nevertheless it was one of the advantages of his Westminster flat that he could entertain there, however modestly; Forster came for tea on several occasions, only afterwards complaining that the rock cakes were stale.

It was fortunate that Sassoon liked exercise since dinner, usually at the Reform, followed tea fairly quickly. He was sometimes invited to dine with friends, like the Gosses:

> Two or three times in a twelve-month I go there [he wrote in his diary in June 1922]. And Gosse is always genial ... He always sends me away with a desire to excel in the honourable craft of literature. He is a faithful servant to the distinctions and amenities of decent writing. He upholds delicacy and precision in the art of letters. And for that, as [Dr] Johnson would say, 'he is to be applauded'.[77]

If dining alone he would often follow dinner with a play or a concert, sometimes the second of the day. Occasionally he succumbed to invitations from society hostesses, such as Lady Sybil Colefax or Lady 'Ettie' Desborough, but he always regretted it. After one particularly vacuous dinner with 'nobby-snobby canary-haired' Lady Emerald Cunard, accepted (he said) with the intention of 'acquiring satirical material', he admitted his failure to achieve the 'detachment' he desired. The scorn expressed in his poem on the event, 'Breach of Decorum', is perhaps partly directed at himself for keeping such company:[78]

> I have seen a man at Lady Lucre's table
> Who stuck to serious subjects; spoke of Art
> As if he were in earnest and unable
> To ascertain its functions in the smart
> World where it shares a recreational part
> With Bridge, best-selling Fiction, and the Stable.
> * * *
> I have seen her fail, with petulant replies,
> To localize him in his social senses:
> I have observed her evening-party eyes
> Evicted from their savoir-faire defences.
> And while his intellectual gloom encroached
> Upon the scintillance of champagne chatter,
> In impotent embarrassment she broached
> Golf, Goodwood Races, and the Cowes Regatta ...
> (CP, pp.135-6)

However his evening had been spent, it usually ended at his writing desk. If poetry would not come, he filled his diary with detailed accounts of his day's activities. He had always 'seen and felt the present as material for memories' and would rely on his diary heavily when he came to write prose.[79] And because his homosexuality inhibited him from talking frankly to all but a few friends, he found it a relief to express his true feelings in its pages. Though realizing that he would probably never be able to publish such views, he was nevertheless consciously 'accumulating material' for an autobiography.[80] He would later, for various reasons, censor the material, but in the early twenties it seemed vital to record it fully. 'I have formed an inflexible resolve to reveal my real self; my inner self; my secret self; the self that never sees the light of day,' he wrote in February 1922.[81]

This need to stand back from experience even as it was taking place helps to explain why, even in the midst of his highly sociable life, he felt solitary. He frequently compared himself to Enoch Arden, Tennyson's tragic sailor-figure, who returns from a shipwreck in which he is thought to have died, and deliberately remains an onlooker when he finds his wife happily married to his best friend.[82] But as Sassoon admitted, except at Weirleigh where he had some grounds for feeling like a ghost from the past, his decision to stand apart stemmed from less noble motives than Enoch's. 'I wish I could understand why I enjoy adopting the attitude of a sort of social and slightly sinister Enoch Arden,' he wrote in 1925.[83] It had something to do with his belief that he needed to be alone to produce any poetry, though that was not the full explanation.

Forster, who understood Sassoon well, thought that his 'anti-social and self-centred life' had a 'good deal to say for it' if he would 'face its consequences and not hanker after the best of two worlds'.[84] But it would be some time, if ever, before Sassoon managed to resolve his highly ambivalent attitude towards society.

8

Satirical Poems and Other Literary Matters

Who knows what peace I might find could I but travel a little further away from the hullabaloo of social life, with its eternal menacings of ennui and its hectic struggles to 'be amused'? (Sitwellism.) In that far country my friends would be but happy shadows. Their remembered voices would be as the indefinite murmur of waters flowing under serene and austere heavens. And I should be alone with that infinite Friend who is my better Self – that microcosmic reflection of the vastness of the human spirit.

(Diary entry for 6 September 1922)

Sassoon's ambivalence and turmoil in the first half of the twenties emerges clearly from his poetry of the period. In the 'new life' he was attempting to build for himself on the 'confusion and exhaustion of 1914-19', he told Professor Lewis Chase in 1922, he needed a 'new form' and a 'new vocabulary'.[1] 'Under these circumstances, it is not surprising, is it?' he asked, 'that I find writing a little difficult.'[2] Though his whole life revolved around the determination to be a poet – '*nothing* is going to bring me peace except the struggle to achieve poetry', he told Graves[3] – he spent most of the Tufton Street years lamenting his sterility as a writer. '*Why* can't I create something?' he wailed in September 1921: 'I am as dry as a biscuit.'[4]

Since his lyric vein had temporarily dried up and would not come to order, he turned to his other talent, satire. But politics, which might once have appealed to him as a worthy substitute for war, no longer attracted him as a subject and he was a satirist without a cause.[5] He had, therefore, self-consciously to construct a subject: 'to be descriptive, critical, meditative, and satiric about the contemporary scene or anything which has social significance'.[6] His list of possible targets included various sporting events and a law court, as well as music, the theatre and art exhibitions. Such an exercise would, he hoped, enable him to 'get near to living experience'.[7] At the very least it would give scope for technical experiment and be an answer to 'any of the intellectuals (like Huxley and Murry) who have suggested that my technique is bad'.[8]

A year after taking this decision, following a trip to Rome in autumn 1921, he wrote despairingly to Graves: 'I have tried writing in clubs,

117

churches, hotels, taxis, trains de luxe, Colosseums, Vaticans, Baths of Caracalla, channel steamers, latrines, chestnut mares, Tufton Street, etc., etc. Am definitely settled down as an ex-author now.'[9] He ended his letter: 'Damn poetry, say I,' but he was unable to do so and his painful efforts to write it late into the night, combined with his inability to sleep afterwards, contributed to his 'self-lacerating irritability' at this time.[10] Wilfred Owen's younger brother, Harold, who was grateful for Sassoon's kindness and generous help as he struggled to establish himself as an artist in the early twenties, nevertheless found him moody and difficult. 'Morose', 'sardonic', 'distant', 'abstracted', 'sombre' and 'self-absorbed' are only some of the words he used to describe his contradictory benefactor.[11]

Sassoon's dissatisfaction and difficulty with his work was such that it took him nearly three years to gather sufficient material for the first of two volumes produced at Tufton Street, *Recreations*. Yet it was a collection of only twenty-four shortish poems, three of which had already appeared in *Picture Show*.[12] His lack of confidence in the work is reflected in his decision to have only seventy-five copies privately printed for friends, though he had initially intended to publish it with Heinemann.[13] The response to his gift was mainly polite praise. Gosse, Marsh, Wells, Blunden, Graves, Hodgson, Masefield, T.E. Lawrence, Lytton Strachey and others all wrote to say that they had enjoyed the book, though Strachey voiced a general concern when he tactfully wished that Sassoon could produce 'something with still more of yourself in it'.[14]

Bennett, rather more frankly, asked Sassoon when he intended to emerge from 'the carping school', for something 'more benevolent, more sublime, and more ideally beautiful?'[15] And Sassoon was even more annoyed when Vivian de Sola Pinto, *not* a poet he admired, added some equally perceptive criticism: 'As poetry, although some of it is exquisite art, it lacks something. A faith, a passion – that was what made the Shakespeares and the Donnes ... You had it for a moment during the war, but now there is only a fine technique and the languid interest of a half-amused spectator.'[16] Sassoon himself might dismiss *Recreations* as 'an unusually tidy little collection of verses',[17] 'not intended to be very exciting as poetry'[18] and admit that they were 'only a form of recreation' as the title implied; that they were 'futile – a series of disgusts'.[19] He might also tell Theo that the poems could have been written 'almost as effectively in prose'.[20] But he particularly resented criticism from Pinto, who had become a professor of English, considering it 'pedantic'.[21]

He did not need to be reminded of his lack of passion for his subject: that was what made it so difficult for him to write poetry at all. Whereas his war poems had been written compulsively and in his own voice, he now had to turn to other writers for inspiration, Byron in particular.[22]

He found it no easier to accumulate sufficient poems for a second volume at Tufton Street and, when he did, there was an element of self-mockery in the elaborate title he gave it: *Lingual Exercises for Ad-*

vanced Vocabularians (1925). The quotation from Psalms on its title-page underlines how diffident he felt about its contents: 'I am not high-minded; I have no proud looks. I do not exercise myself in great matters which are too high for me.' Again he had the book privately printed in a small edition 'for friends only'.[23] And again they responded politely but warily. Finally, however, a trade edition did appear: Heinemann, who published his *Selected Poems* in 1925, were anxious to bring out another collection of original verse and, with some cuts and a few additions, *Recreations* and *Lingual Exercises* were reprinted as *Satirical Poems* in 1926.[24]

Significantly, two of the most interesting poems in *Recreations*, 'A Fragment of Autobiography' and 'On Reading My Diary', were omitted from *Satirical Poems*. Gosse had particularly liked the first of these, perhaps because he figured in it. Looking back to his romantic 1910 self from the viewpoint of 1920, Sassoon had written:

> ... Don't you care to hear
> An outline of your future? Don't you pine
> For pale unwritten sonnets; and your name
> On a prim title-page, saluting fame? ...
> Melodious ramblings, published at a loss,
> But gracefully reviewed by Edmund Gosse?[25]

Sassoon thought 'A Fragment of Autobiography' 'too personal' for publication.[26] Yet his own favourites from *Recreations* include the highly personal 'Falling Asleep' (already printed in *Picture Show*). Together with 'Early Chronology' (also from *Picture Show*), 'Solar Eclipse', 'Fantasia on a Wittelsbach Atmosphere' and 'Storm on Fifth Avenue', his choice highlights the fact that he was not entirely committed to satire in the early twenties, since only 'Fantasia' completely fits the category. 'Solar Eclipse', a retelling of the Apollo/Daphne myth, which both Gosse and Blunden picked out for special praise, is quite out of place in a collection of satirical poems. The same applies to an even greater number of pieces in *Lingual Exercises*, as Sassoon tacitly acknowledged by excluding ten of them from *Satirical Poems* but including most of them in a later, more personal collection, *The Heart's Journey*.[27]

In calling his collection *Satirical Poems*, Blunden argued, Sassoon was suggesting a shade of meaning other than straight satire: 'A satirical person is not a satirist. He is generally as free with himself as with the rest of the spectacle of life. He does not wish things powerfully altered, and even as he grins, he is graceful. The satirist full-blown is actually angry with the world.'[28] It was an ingenious defence from a loyal friend, but most readers of *Satirical Poems* will regret the absence of the angry Sassoon of the war poems.

There are exceptions. For as Michael Thorpe points out in his excellent study of Sassoon's work, he could still be 'incisive and scathing', about social affectations in particular.[29] A poem like 'Concert-Interpretations' shows that when fully engaged (and music was something he cared about passionately) he could convey his message with some of his old verve. Contrasting the initially hostile reaction to Stravinsky's work with the later rapturous reception given to his *Rite of Spring* by polite English society, Sassoon notes another even more startling contrast between the 'vibro-atmospheric copulations' of the music celebrating fertility rites and the bland, uncomprehending audience, and the effect this has on the narrator:

> ... This matter is most indelicate indeed!
> Yet one perceives no symptom of stampede.
> The Stalls remain unruffled: craniums gleam:
> Swept by a storm of pizzicato chords,
> Elaborate ladies re-assure their lords
> With lifting brows that signify 'Supreme!'
> While orchestrated gallantry of goats
> Impugns the astigmatic programme-notes.
> * * *
> But savagery pervades Me; I am frantic
> With corybantic rupturing of laws.
> Come, dance, and seize this clamorous chance to function
> Creatively, – abandoning compunction
> To anti-social rhapsodic applause!
> Lynch the conductor! Jugulate the drums!
> Butcher the brass! Ensanguinate the strings!
> Throttle the flutes! ... Stravinsky's April comes
> With pitiless pomp and pain of sacred springs ...
> Incendiarize the Hall with resinous fires
> Of sacrificial fiddles scorched and snapping! ...
>
> Meanwhile the music blazes and expires;
> And the delighted Audience is clapping.
>
> (CP, p. 159)

The narrator's 'savagery' here makes for biting and effective satire, the ending reminiscent of war poems such as 'Blighters' or 'Fight to a Finish'. The tone varies from that of the urbane, detached onlooker, with what Sassoon described as his 'laconic, legato' voice, in the first stanza quoted,[30] to the violently committed enthusiast of the second, the message reinforced by frequent alliteration, exclamation and a deliberately absurd mixture of Latinate polysyllables with Anglo-Saxon monosyllables ('Lynch the conductor! Jugulate the drums! / Butcher the brass! Ensanguinate the strings!'). In this particular case, Sassoon's 'excessive verbal dexterity' (to quote Blunden) achieves its aim, which is (in Blunden's words) 'to illustrate brilliantly the genuine culture and the imitative clap-trap of our times'.[31]

A comparable contrast is achieved at the end of one of Forster's favourites, 'Sheldonian Soliloquy', where the narrator is listening to Bach's B minor Mass in the packed Sheldonian Theatre at Oxford on a fine summer's day:

> ... *The music's half-rococo* ... Does it matter
> While those intense musicians shout the stuff
> In Catholic Latin to the cultured mammals
> Who agitate the pages of their scores? ...
>
> Meanwhile, in Oxford sunshine out of doors,
> Birds in collegiate gardens rhapsodize
> Antediluvian airs of worm-thanksgiving.
> To them the austere and buried Bach replies
> With song that from ecclesiasmus cries
> Eternal *Resurrexit* to the living.
>
> *Hosanna in excelsis* chants the choir
> In pious contrapuntal jubilee.
> *Hosanna* shrill the birds in sunset fire.
> And Benedictus sings my heart to Me.
>
> (CP, p. 161)

Best of all, according to Edith Sitwell, is 'On Reading the War Diary of a Defunct Ambassador', which lulls the reader into a face-value acceptance of the 'fine old gentleman' through its cosy colloquialisms ('So that's your Diary – that's your private mind'), only to incite him savagely at the close with its deliberately pompous vocabulary and absurd rhymes:

> ... The world will find no pity in your pages;
> No exercise of spirit worthy of mention;
> Only a public-funeral grief-convention;
> And all the circumspection of the ages.
> But I, for one, am grateful, overjoyed,
> And unindignant that your punctual pen
> Should have been so constructively employed
> In manifesting to unprivileged men
> The visionless officialized fatuity
> That once kept Europe safe for perpetuity.
>
> (CP, p. 130)[32]

All too often, however, *Satirical Poems* reads like a series of exercises. As Desmond MacCarthy, a critic as well as a friend, observed in the *New Statesman*, the reader sometimes gets the impression that Sassoon had been 'looking round him for an occasion for satire because he [had] a satiric gift' and needed 'to vent his scorn, instead of having been provoked to utterance by the subject itself'.[33] Like Pinto, MacCarthy contrasted *Satirical Poems* with the 'memorable satiric poems' of the war: 'then there was no need to hunt for a subject ... because his subject was forced upon him, and he responded with all the rage and grief he was capable of feeling'.[34]

121

As Thorpe also points out, whatever Sassoon's original intentions as a 'satirist of materialism and privilege, he discovers a deepening vein of sympathy – approaching identification – with many of the people and things a less scrupulous Socialist would scarify unreservedly'.[35] Gone, he argues, is the 'savagery, the crushing one-sidedness of the war poems', gone the 'epigrammatic, mnemonic brevity, the succinctness of phrasing that forged whole poems amongst the war satires into weapons uniformly sharp'.[36] *Satirical Poems* is, he claims, that contradiction in terms, 'amiable satire', a statement largely if not wholly true.[37]

Sassoon himself believed that his collection was a failure owing to his 'undiscardable habit of strict versification and condensed form', which prevented him from acquiring the necessary flexibility and freedom of expression: 'I couldn't induce myself to write loosely, and my improvisations always got tidied up into neat little performances,' he wrote.[38] But his dislike of free verse was 'unconquerable' and from this time onwards he was to remain, in his own words, 'traditional'.[39]

*

Satirical Poems, as Sassoon realized, was a 'turning-point' in his career, representing his failure to escape traditional verse for something looser, freer and more modern.[40] Yet there were at least two groups of people in the early twenties who might have helped him if he had wanted, the Sitwells and Bloomsbury.

He had become friendly with several members of the Bloomsbury Group after the war. Apart from Ottoline Morrell and Forster, who hovered on its fringes, he was on good terms with at least two of its inner circle, Lytton Strachey and Desmond MacCarthy.[41] MacCarthy, who wrote as 'Affable Hawk' in the *New Statesman*, he thought 'one of the best modern critics'[42] and Strachey seemed to him a 'lovely' writer.[43] (One of his prized possessions was a small oil painting of Strachey by Henry Lamb, bought for £60 in 1923.) But Strachey also made him feel like 'a beefy young rowing blue with the intellectual equipment of a New York policeman'.[44] And, however much he enjoyed reading Strachey's historical essays, he thought that his 'pry[ing]' into his subjects' private lives was a 'bad influence' on biography.[45]

Maynard Keynes, whom he knew reasonably well by the early twenties, made him feel similarly inadequate, an effect Bloomsbury had on him generally.[46] Responding to an invitation from Virginia Woolf to dine with her and Leonard in May 1923, for example, he considered it necessary to explain, as he had to Forster: 'I am not at all intellectual – in fact I have a very cumbersome mind.'[47]

Virginia thought he exaggerated the 'horrors of our intellectuality … it does not go deep, I hope.'[48] She remembered how pleased she had been when he wrote to thank her, through Ottoline, for her review of *The Old*

Huntsman in 1917 and was gratified by his praise of her recent novel, *Jacob's Room*. And when Sassoon did eventually have dinner with the Woolfs in January 1924, it looked for a time as though he and Virginia might become close. Instead of the 'rarified intellectual atmosphere' he had feared, he found the evening 'a gossipy affair, very pleasant and unconstrained'.[49] Though Leonard struck him as 'reticent and rather weary', Virginia was 'charming', drawing him out adroitly to gossip about mutual friends and acquaintances – Hardy, Gosse, Wells, Bennett, Lady Colefax, Middleton Murry, Graves, Huxley and T.S. Eliot.[50] He was especially pleased by her attitude towards Eliot, who personified in his eyes all that Modernism represented for him, its sterility and artificiality. (He once compared Eliot to a 'dried bean'.)[51] Virginia told him that Eliot was 'rather an old prig, really', and needed to be 'chaffed out of it': otherwise, she said, he behaved 'with such absurd formality and primness'.[52] Such irreverence from another important Modernist delighted Sassoon. He was also flattered to be urged to write something for the Hogarth Press. For her part, Virginia found him 'a nice dear kind sensitive warm-hearted fellow'.[53] Coming from a group which prided itself on its frankness and sexual tolerance, she was unperturbed by his homosexuality. She also admired his work.

After a second meeting, however, the differences began to emerge, with Virginia wishing (in a misquotation of a Meredith sonnet) for 'more brain, O God, more brain!' from Sassoon.[54] And though Sassoon had agreed to write something on satire for the Woolfs' Hogarth Essays series by mid-1924, he quickly abandoned the idea and returned to less intellectual pursuits.[55] His whole philosophy of life and art was diametrically opposed to Virginia's cry for 'more brain': 'Authentic poetry [he would write to a young disciple in 1964] is, I think, the result of subconscious incubation and comes from the soil of genuine experience – in contrast to mere poeticising. Most modern verse I see seems to be entirely cerebral and therefore unsatisfying. My advice is, "look in your heart, and write!" '[56] He eventually came to believe that 'Bloomsbury lack[ed] generosity' and would refuse to be 'patronized and palavered over' by a group which seemed to think itself so superior.[57] 'They live in such a tiny world,' he wrote to Ottoline in 1928, 'and I sometimes think that they know next to nothing about life, in spite of having read all the great authors.'[58]

Osbert Sitwell believed that Sassoon's dislike of Modernism, which lay behind his antagonism to Bloomsbury, stunted his growth as a poet. He himself, together with Edith and Sachie, had enthusiastically embraced it and were another potentially modernizing influence for Sassoon in the twenties. All three wrote poetry, some of which he greatly admired, particularly the early work of Edith.

Partly because he had first met Osbert through Ross and associated him with his last meeting with Wilfred Owen, Sassoon felt almost wholly positive about him at the start. In spite of their very different attitudes towards poetry, he had been impressed by Osbert's work and published it in his *Daily Herald* columns. Osbert returned the compliment by including Sassoon's poems in the first two issues of *Art and Letters*, where he found himself in the company of Eliot and another Modernist, Wyndham Lewis. Though Osbert saw no sign of his own rebellious attitude to traditional verse technique in Sassoon, he could (and did) admire his defiance of the Establishment in making his public protest against the war.[59] Combined with his strong personal liking for Sassoon, this seems to have enabled him to accept work he might otherwise have found too traditional. In a verse-letter to Sassoon (a response to one from him) he highlights their differences, suggesting at the same time that Sassoon is afraid of anything but 'Georgian plaid'.[60] Osbert's scorn for the Georgian poets became the main cause of the rift which developed between Sassoon and Osbert in the early twenties and which lasted for a good part of his time at Tufton Street.[61] For, in attacking the Georgians, even though he carefully excluded Sassoon and Nichols, Osbert was criticizing some of Sassoon's nearest friends, particularly Turner. He made the situation worse by concentrating his fire on Squire (in his opinion the most reactionary influence on the literary scene), since Turner worked for Squire on the *London Mercury* and was very close to him and Osbert's other *bête noir*, Shanks. His worst attack on Shanks and Squire (published in Edith Sitwell's magazine, *Wheels*, under the pseudonym 'Augustine Rivers' in late 1921)[62] also included jibes at both Turner and another of Sassoon's close friends, Graves, and promised further satire on Blunden.[63] Though Osbert later exempted Turner from his criticism, in a conscious effort to placate Sassoon, the damage had been done and the battle-lines were drawn.

Osbert's first instinct under pressure was to strengthen the attack and his pamphlet, *Who Killed Cock-Robin?*, an even fiercer criticism of 'Squire-archy', followed in December 1921. Turner would eventually retaliate with a satirical play about the Sitwells, *Smaragdas Lover*, in 1924, though by that time the situation would have changed.

Sassoon always implied that his rift with the Sitwells in November 1921 was caused solely by Osbert's attack on his Georgian friends, but there were other factors at work. Sassoon himself was beginning to disassociate himself from Georgian poetry, refusing (politely) to appear in Marsh's fifth volume of 1922, and his reaction to Osbert was much more personal than he admitted at the time. In the same diary entry which records his intense annoyance at Osbert's 'doggerel satire' against Turner, Graves and Blunden, he suggests that Osbert was motivated by jealousy of their friendship with him.[64] Osbert did later admit that his 'exaggerated ideas of friendship' had made him 'jealous', but it is also likely that Sassoon was projecting his own feelings onto Osbert.[65] Only three months after the break in November 1921, Sassoon deliberately followed him out of a concert at the Wigmore Hall for the pleasure of 'cutting' him outside.

Thinking about it afterwards, he suddenly realized that his attitude towards Osbert was 'strongly sadistic': 'I saw, quite calmly, that my (supposed) stab at his feelings ... aroused in me acute sexual feelings ... (I'd never before been conscious of any sexual feelings toward him except a slight repugnance.)'[66] Osbert's comment to Sassoon on this aspect of his nature shows how shrewd an opponent he faced: 'You have a streak in your character that makes you derive a little pleasure, as well as much pain from humiliating your friends.'[67] This sadistic streak was particularly marked in the early twenties as Sassoon struggled to recover from the effects of the war and a sense of inadequacy as a poet.

His emotional instability at this time was certainly a factor in the prolonged row between himself and Osbert. 'You are a difficult friend,' Osbert wrote to him at the end of it, '– if one goes to see you, you become tired, and feel that your blood is being sucked, I believe – and if one doesn't go to see you, where are you to be found?'[68] Forster was to make a similar observation.

Differences of temperament and background also played a part. While still finding Osbert 'a tonic' in mid-1921, Sassoon had begun to think him 'frivolous, always'.[69] As early as December 1920 he had complained to Marsh: 'All this Sitwell spite and trivial charade-satire makes me tired.'[70] 'What a brilliant, disintegrating family they are!' he wrote in his diary at the height of his dissatisfaction with Osbert: 'And why can't they be just a little different, just a little more tolerant and human and free from their perennial spirit of mockery?'[71] A visit to their family home, Renishaw, in August 1921 underlined these differences, making him feel hostile, malicious and oppressed:

Blighted skies and blasted trees and blackened landscapes. Atmosphere of nerve-twitching exhaustion. Women in a gloomy room ... Ancestor-worship in oil-paintings. Who will die first? Disgruntled offspring of distrusted parents. Rich food: the house a stronghold; decayed and morose dignities fronting the encroachments of industry ...
    Harassed and skulking servants; furtive gardeners. Undoubtedly wicked influences. Crazy behaviour late at night.[72]

The Sitwells, he concluded, were 'an absolute climax! Regency relics', their trouble being 'too much taste'.[73] Staying at Renishaw with the trio and their extraordinary father, Sir George ('Ginger'), and his wife Ida, provoked Sassoon to Gothic flights of fancy: 'Restless reflections in a gilt Chippendale mirror. *Peacock en casserole* for lunch, washed down with Ginger wine: *Freaks on Ghost* for a savoury.'[74]

Osbert himself, who practised what Sassoon called 'passive resistance' throughout their feud, sending 'amiable' notes via mutual friends, claimed: 'Much mischief was made for us both before you quarrelled with me, and more, I imagine, since.'[75] His chief suspect was Gosse, who was still highly critical of the Sitwells' literary experiments in 1923, though Sassoon would later partly win him over.

What emerges most clearly from Sassoon's comments during the eighteen months' quarrel is how obsessed he was by Osbert. In May 1922 Osbert still 'angers' him and in June he vows to 'keep him at more than arms' length for several months', but he 'cannot dismiss him' from his life, try as he may.[76] By September 1922 he is 'feeling rather sad about the feud', though he cuts Osbert and Sachie pointedly when they meet in Munich that month.[77] Forced to recognize how 'fond' he is of Osbert, he remembers once more the link with Ross and Owen. Ignoring him again in Venice, where they encounter each other the following month, Sassoon attributes his stand to the 'arrogance of the artist': 'Until I have humiliated or dominated him I will not be satisfied.'[78] At the same time he realizes that he has put himself in Osbert's power 'by nourishing animosity against him': 'I wonder if he guesses it [he wrote in his diary]. What is he thinking when his pale-blue eyes watch me walking in the piazza? Why do I get myself into these tangles by my cussedness? For the original causes of my quarrel with O[sbert] have now dwindled to a mere peccadillo.'[79]

Pride, however, prevents him making any move towards reconciliation. Another seven months pass and he is still 'grim' and 'unkind' to Osbert when they meet at Nellie Burton's house in June 1923. But by the end of that month Sassoon, irritated by a favourable review of Osbert's second volume of poems, *Out of the Flames*, realizes that he is paying heavily for his feud, which by now seems to him 'futile'.[80] The end is in sight. When he meets Osbert unexpectedly the next day at the Reform, he forgets to scowl, though abstains from smiling. There is a slight hitch in the reconciliation process when he discovers that Osbert has left him a 'funny' post-card with the hall-porter and, 'infuriated', he sends a 'silly' one back.[81] But he immediately regrets it and, when Osbert then sends him a jokey Valentine in response, he finally capitulates: 'He always gets the last word and scores off me.'[82]

Defeated, he writes Osbert a 'very decent letter', explaining his position and is greatly relieved to receive a serious eight-page reply by return of post. 'Don't think for a moment', Osbert writes, 'that you are the only person who has felt pain over our differences. In spite of all the silly little things I have done since, there have been moments when I felt so miserable at it, that I hardly knew what to do.'[83] Referring to their 'different ideas of literature and art', he says that they should 'never argue about that', a tacit acceptance of the fact that he has failed to win Sassoon over to his Modernist ideas.[84]

It would take nearly another year for the relationship to settle down to its former easy amiability, but by 17 June 1924, Sassoon could write with great relief in his diary: 'Peace is signed.'[85] It was a peace which would last until 1949, when Osbert's description of him and mutual friends in *Laughter in the Next Room* would bring about a second, less dramatic withdrawal on Sassoon's part. For, as he observed to a close friend in 1927: 'What should we do without the Sitwells to amuse us, and where shall we find a more intelligent and attractive trio?'[86]

*

One benefit of his reconciliation with Osbert in 1924 was a renewal of friendship with Edith, though she had first to be convinced that Turner's skit on her family that year had nothing to do with Sassoon. She was as fiercely loyal to her brothers as they were to her and had naturally taken Osbert's side in the feud with Sassoon. Even Sassoon's generous review of her highly experimental work, *Façade*, in May 1922 had failed to win her over.[87]

Sassoon had first met Edith in October 1918, also through Ross, but it was not until late the following year that he really got to know her. Edith had published seven of Wilfred Owen's poems in her 1919 cycle of *Wheels* and hoped to bring out a wider selection of them in a separate edition. She worked hard on the difficult task of producing final texts from the several draughts in varying states of revision and was extremely disappointed when, on consulting Sassoon about the last two, he told her self-importantly that it would have been Owen's 'wish that he (Captain Sassoon) should see to the publication of the poems'.[88] It may be that Sassoon, who knew of her intentions, felt that Owen's reputation might suffer from the association with *Wheels* and the *avant-garde*, or it may simply be, as Dennis Welland suggested after talking to Sassoon, that he became jealous.[89] Whatever his motives, and they were probably a mixture of the two, Edith felt that she had to accept his claim and did so with a surprisingly good grace.

Sassoon's next move was even more difficult to take. 'Captain Sassoon has suddenly gone off to America,' she wrote to Owen's mother in late January 1920, 'leaving all your son's manuscripts with me to get ready for the printers by February 1st.'[90] As she pointed out, Sassoon had done 'nothing' at that point except arrange for Chatto & Windus to publish them. Though credited with editing the poems, which were finally published in December 1920, his sole contribution to the first edition was a short introduction.[91]

It is puzzling at first glance to find 'that stormy spinster petrel' meekly accepting such lordly behaviour from Sassoon, but there are at least two possible explanations for her uncharacteristic reaction: [92] she admired his work greatly and she was strongly attracted to him as a man.

Though she never admitted it outright, either to Sassoon or anyone else, it is more than likely that she was in love with him. Sassoon himself thought so and so did her brother Sachie.[93] As Thomas Rand suggests in his very helpful edition of Edith's letters to Sassoon, while this was almost certainly the case, it was unlikely that she would have wanted a sexual

127

relationship with him, given the opportunity: 'such a prospect', he argues, 'would have been too threatening'.[94] The very condition which prevented such a situation developing – Sassoon's homosexuality – also, ironically, made it 'safe' for Edith.

Sassoon, who had been pursued by Ottoline Morrell with much greater determination and far fewer inhibitions, would in any case have found Edith's unconventional appearance as challenging as he had Ottoline's.[95] Unfashionably tall and thin by contemporary standards, with a pronounced nose and wispy hair of indeterminate colour, Edith chose to make a feature of what she grandly called her 'Plantagenet' looks. Concealing her hair beneath highly coloured turbans but emphasizing her long, bony figure with exotic medieval robes and enormous pieces of dramatic jewellery, she deliberately attracted attention wherever she went. For Sassoon, whose aim in clothes was to dress 'correctly' and blend into the background, this in itself would have been an embarrassment.[96]

Edith's admiration for his poetry, on the other hand, he both approved and reciprocated. Her recognition of his war poems was probably more to do with their anti-Establishment content than their largely traditional technique. But her praise of *Satirical Poems* stemmed from a true appreciation of his poetic method: 'You know what we always felt about your poetry,' she wrote in 1926; 'it cuts right down to the bone – and moves one most profoundly.'[97] When he, in turn, praised one of her poems from *Rustic Elegies* (1927), she replied: 'I don't really care a toss for the insults one has to put up with, if a poet who has written some of the most magnificent poetry of the time – I mean yourself – cares for my work –'[98]

Her greatest admiration would be reserved for *The Heart's Journey* (1928), a collection of meditative poems in a more lyrical vein which Sassoon had begun accumulating alongside *Satirical Poems* in the mid-twenties. When he expressed doubt about publishing them, privately or otherwise, Edith replied firmly: 'How you can hesitate, I don't know!'[99] And after seeing the completed manuscript, she praised it in terms which indicate the point at which these two very different poets met: 'Poetry doesn't come by bellowing to attract the attention of the crowd. It is much more like taming a wild bird in a wood – one has to do it in silence. You have tamed the wild bird and no mistake.'[100] For both of them, poetry was more to do with instinct than with intellect, a patient waiting on the Muse combined with a sensitivity to words and sounds, and in this respect Edith differed as much from Eliot and other Modernists as Sassoon did. Their techniques might differ widely but their aims at this time were very similar.

Sassoon was as admiring of Edith's poetry as she was of his during the twenties. As early as July 1919 he had suggested to Marsh that Edith be included in the next *Georgian Poetry* anthology instead of Fredegond Shove, 'as her work is far stronger and quite as original'.[101] In May 1922, at the height of his quarrel with Osbert, he writes in his diary: 'Edith's poetry is original and beautiful in its modes of fantastic plumage.'[102] And a little later in the year, while dismissing the Sitwell trio as 'an excellent joke', he feels obliged to acknowledge Edith's 'originality and distinction' as a poet.[103] By June 1924, he is linking her 'genuine poetry' with that of his favourite poet of the period, Charlotte Mew.[104]

He was flattered to be sent samples of Edith's work-in-progress from 1926 onwards, almost as much as when she reassured him that he wrote 'on a big scale'.[105] One poem in particular chimed with his re-emerging lyric impulse:

> Through the long rustling branches of green eves
> The gold dust falls upon the ladies [*sic*] sleeves
> And parasols, like the gold tinkling rain
> Of spring, awakes old passion and old pain ...[106]

His admiration for Edith's poetry would continue until at least 1933, when he was instrumental in persuading the Royal Society of Literature to award her the A.C. Benson Silver Medal for Poetry.

The two of them did not always agree about poets – Eliot was a particular stumbling block – but they were generally united, and amusingly so, on those they thought frauds. When John Drinkwater, a popular contemporary poet and playwright whom Sassoon had already dismissed as 'a pompous literary humbug', dared to praise Squire's verse above Sassoon's, Edith flew to his defence with a deliberately absurd suggestion: '... would it matter if I killed Drinkwater? I'll promise not to if you say I'd better not.'[107] Her attempt to 'bump him off' in her column for the *Weekly Dispatch* was foiled by her editor, though she was given permission to say that Sassoon was 'a great poet' when she could 'work it in', a loyalty he much appreciated.[108]

Humbert Wolfe, another popular contemporary poet, was also a favourite target, Edith egging Sassoon on to write his parodies of Wolfe, *Poems by Pinchbeck Lyre* (1931).[109] (One of her favourite opening lines from the selection was 'Swing tripe, swing tosh!' though the present writer prefers 'I thought of Scotland, and somehow it was you', with 'I had often heard that Switzerland was Swiss' coming a close second.) The book itself was published by Edith's own publishers, Duckworth, and Wolfe stopped speaking to her.

Whether they were attacking poets they thought bad or praising what they found good in each other's work, Edith and Sassoon were united by their devotion to poetry. 'After all,' she wrote to him in 1927, 'that *is* our native element. And we can't really be happy outside [it].'

Altogether it was an extraordinary relationship which grew up between them in the twenties. Though it never developed into the romantic love Edith had hoped for, it was a loving relationship. When Edith's troubles, which were often numerous, became too much for her, Sassoon was ready

129

to help with advice and (though he did this indirectly through Sachie) with money.[110] He interrupted a holiday to chair her lecture on poetry at the Tomorrow Club (a 'ghastly' affair, he afterwards noted).[111] He sent flowers to her sick friends and visited them in hospital, bought paintings from her indigent protégé, Tchelitchew, invited her to the theatre, persuaded Gosse to 'puff' her in his influential *Sunday Times* column and suggested to Sir Henry Newbolt that he include Edith in his 1927 anthology, *New Paths on Helicon*. When Noël Coward's skits on Edith (under the name 'Hernia Whittlebot') made her ill, she turned to Sassoon for help, which he willingly gave.[112] He was, as she noted in an unpublished memoir written in 1930 and 1931, 'fantastically loyal' whilst his friendships lasted and 'the most generous minded man' she knew.[113] Most importantly of all, he was 'one of the very first poets', indeed 'one of the very first people', to 'uphold' her.[114]

For her part, Edith showed a side to Sassoon which is in direct contradiction to the picture often painted of her as an ascerbic personality, merciless towards all but her closest family. When that aspect of her does emerge in her letters to Sassoon, it is only in order to show him what he has escaped, as well as to amuse him. On receiving his (rare) criticism of her poetry, for example, she warns: 'My word, if it had been anyone but you who had told me to "consider and reconsider", and "sift" my poems, *I should have taken that person on a one-way journey*. Luckily, it *was* you. – But the escape has been narrow.'[115]

Usually, however, the tone is kind, concerned, almost motherly. When a mutual friend tells her he is worried that Sassoon is forgetting to eat or take care of himself, she writes to him anxiously: 'Is this so? Because if it is, do *please* turn over a new leaf about it. Neglect of meals leads to a breakdown sooner or later.'[116] She even offers to teach him to cook chops for himself: 'Do let me, please. You would feel far more independent.'[117] Her invitations to tea were endless and when, in 1928, three of his closest friends died within the year, she did her best to console him. She presented him with proofs of one of her favourite collections, *Gold Coast Customs*, and dedicated another work, *Jane Barston*, to him.

With Sassoon's switch to prose in *Memoirs of a Fox-Hunting Man* (1928), *Memoirs of an Infantry Officer* (1930) and *Sherston's Progress* (1936) and Edith's own attempts to earn money with a number of prose books during the thirties, however, their relationship began to change. Edith was noticeably less extravagant in her praise of Sassoon's prose, her greatest accolade for *Fox-Hunting Man* being that it was 'a fitting book for a *poet* to have written' (my italics).[118] (It is significant that the relationship, which had more or less finished by 1937, revived a little after Sassoon sent Edith two volumes of his poems, *Emblems of Experience* (1951) and *The Tasking* (1955).) Sassoon himself found it impossible to take Edith's prose work seriously. (She herself had told him, 'I can't write anything but poetry.')[119] His copy of her *Aspects of Modern Poetry* (1933), lavishly annotated and 'decorated', is a collage of press cuttings, cartoons and sub-headings such as 'Literary Ass' under Edith's name on the title page. And he had started a series of caricatures on the Sitwell siblings which depicts Edith in a number of absurd roles.[120] Without poetry to unite them their differences became more obvious. Other factors, such as Edith's jealousy of Stephen Tennant, also entered into it.

Distinct cracks started to appear in the relationship by the early thirties, as Sassoon retreated further into conservatism and Edith's experiments grew more pronounced. Sassoon's increasing scepticism over Edith's methods comes through wittily in his 1937 nonsense rhyme written in response to her portentous statement in *The Times*, 'I *do* risk myself … with Busoni and Paderewski':

> Miss Sitwell's like Boosoni
> What then of Butler Yeats? …
>   Go ask the telephony
>   Why Swans wear roller-skates.
>
> Miss Sitwell's Paderooski.
> Then what price Ezra Pound? …
>   The answer is 'Pooh-poohski'
>   And waltz her wildly round.[121]
>   10.1.37

By 1942 he could no longer believe in the poet he had admired so much in the twenties, responding rather ungratefully to the presentation copy she had sent of her *Street Songs*:

> Whereas Miss Sitwell's use doth stray
> 'Twixt Casiopeia and Cathay,
> One wonders – in one's humdrum way –
>   Where *is* the ruddy border-line
>   Between the foolish and the fine?
>   And does Miss Sitwell while she spins
>   Ask where Art ends and Bosh begins?

On reading an article in 1954 about Edith's career as 'a publicity personality', and her insistence on the 'rôle of a Literary Queen', he noted in his diary the differences which had finally divided them:

This reminded me of the factitiousness of contrived reputation, and made me thankful that I have chosen to isolate myself from seeking to be conspicuous. E.S.'s present prestige is upheld by an insecure fabric. Had she remained quiet and unobtrusive … she would be known and appreciated by her work as a very gifted, fantastical writer … with a highly sensitive sense of word sounds and effects. But she has assumed the robes of a prophetess and oracle – much influenced by Yeats and Eliot – and her solemnities and apocalypses will, I suspect, be found to be a pretension of powers she doesn't possess. Her earlier verse was the real E.S. – lacking in design and condensation, but exquisitely fanciful and ornamental. When reviewing *Bucolic Comedies* in 1919, I said she was in the Beardsley tradition. And I still think I was somewhere near the truth ...[122]

Edith had 'cooled off' him, he concluded, because he had resisted her influence and remained 'old-fashioned'.[123]

9

Ways of Escape

Sitting here tonight (refreshed by rest, a good dinner, and a delightful concert at the Queen's Hall) I fell into a very pleasant mood of reminiscence, while debating whether to go to Weirleigh for Easter. Although I decided in the negative, pre-war memories of Kentish landscapes and people crowded back and made a gallery of Crome-like pictures in my head. After all, the real backgrounds of my thoughts were indelibly painted before the war came and broke everything up and finally deposited me in Fleet Street, New York, and the Reform Club. And, although I never learned to understand those country places and people, as little Blunden has done, certain easy-going experiences in Kent will always mean a lot to me.

(Diary entry for 22 March 1921)

Sassoon's original feud with the Sitwells marred his Tufton Street years in a number of ways. One effect, for example, was to prevent him from continuing his visits to their family estate in Derbyshire, a decided disadvantage for someone who longed to escape from London whenever possible. The arrival of his brother and family at Weirleigh in 1920, though it helped him feel less anxious about his mother, also made him unwilling to return home, however briefly. The death of his dog Topper there in September 1920 seemed to him to symbolize the end of an era.

But even on his most enjoyable days in London, he missed the country. Though nothing would induce him to return to an existence like the one he had led in Kent until 1914, memories of it persisted. 'Brenchley [Church] bells, across the meadows, will always be music,' he wrote in 1921, 'whereas Big Ben's booming is an automatic episode in the calendar. And walking down Whitehall, or riding on a bus to Langham Place, will never be magical with the peace of bicycling to Lamberhurst for a game of golf among Squire Morland's sheep, or jogging off in the winter mornings to a meet of the Eridge Hounds at Argos Hill.'[1] Town life and social amenities, he claimed, were not 'natural' to him.[2] And though he did not share his mother's belief that Tufton Street was unhealthy because built on a former marsh, he did agree that it would be bad for him to spend all his time there. 'I do hope you will get plenty of hunting this winter,' she had remarked more than once.

Loder had urged the same thing, offering to keep a horse for him at Cirencester, where he had recently moved to be Master of the Atherstone.[3]

After only a brief struggle with his conscience – could he really afford it? and ought a socialist to hunt? – Sassoon succumbed. And when Geoffrey Harbord invited him to Weedon Equitation School for a few days' cubbing with the Grafton in October 1920, he bought himself a horse during his stay, Lady Jill, one of the best hunters he would ever ride. 'Inconsistency – double life – as usual', he noted in his diary in December 1920, '– trying to be serious about life and work – buying a horse and dreaming of winning V[ale of] W[hite] H[orse] point-to-point!'[4]

There is a myth that Sassoon abandoned hunting after the war because he was so sickened by the killing he had witnessed there. Far from rejecting the sport for its violence, however, he had actually retreated from the violence of the war *into* hunting, which for him represented a peaceful and innocent world, the continuation of a long country tradition. Whether at the Front, where he had dreamt frequently of the 'grand cry of the hounds' and 'damp, delicious smell of autumn woods',[5] or on leave, when he had hunted as often as possible, it had been his most effective antidote to war. He was describing his own state of mind at the end of a day's wartime hunting when he wrote in his unpublished poem 'The Fox-Hunter', 'So he jogged home at night a peaceful man'.[6]

Significantly, in his many personal descriptions of hunting, Sassoon rarely refers to killing foxes. As his friend and bibliographer Geoffrey Keynes noted, 'it seem[ed] to be assum[ed]' in his writing 'that the fox usually escaped'.[7] If Sassoon thought about it at all, he almost certainly shared the view of another friend and fellow-writer, T.H. White, that it was far better to give foxes a sporting chance than to trap, shoot or poison them. Like Trollope, whose *Hunting Sketches* he admired, Sassoon believed that the fox-hunter's business was, paradoxically, 'to ride to hounds and not to rush along as though he was hunting the fox himself'. In a little known essay, 'Thoughts on Horses and Hunting', he points out that 'while a fox is being hunted, very few riders are aware of what is happening … not many of the field have more than a hazy recollection of anything except the fences they have jumped'.[8]

That was certainly true of Sassoon, who thought of hunting in very different terms from its present-day opponents. His most precious memories were of 'the smell of a soft southerly wind on a dark December morning' as he opened his bedroom window onto a clouded sky.[9] His imagination would 'fondly re-create the whole day', from the time he was pulling on his boots by the light of a few candles to 'that last bit of hunting at the end of the afternoon when half the field had gone home' and his zest for jumping was only dampened by his horse being much tireder than he was.[10]

At that point, he would get off and walk, anxious to spare his mount. For he loved horses, another important factor in his feeling for the hunt. By the 1940s he believed that the world had become 'too large and unlocalised' and that 'the parish and county boundaries of personal existence [were] being obliterated'.[11] Horses, he argued, being essentially un-modernisable and 'absolutely refusing to move with the times', could redeem the situation.[12] He took equal pleasure in the English countryside, seen to such advantage on horseback. His narrator in 'The Fox-Hunter' lovingly details what is clearly Sassoon's native Kent, the sunlight over the vales, the bending trees, grey pastures and willow-lined streams.

If hunting was a way of discovering 'the secrets and manners of rural life' for Sassoon, it was also a link with a long literary tradition.[13] He loved writers like Beckford, Whyte-Melville, Trollope and Somerville and Ross. But his favourite was Surtees, whose characters reminded him of the many wonderful eccentrics, as well as good friends, he had met out hunting. His mother's accounts of 'characters' from their local Eridge Hunt had been one main reason he had become interested in the sport as a child, and his own descriptions of hunting personalities are inimitable. Who can forget 'The Mister', for example, with his Irish wit and optimism: 'In politics and religion, be pleasant to both sides. Sure, we'll all be dead drunk on the Day of Judgement'?[14]

Then there was the sheer physical thrill of hunting. 'Following the hounds, on a good horse over a good country takes ten years off me,' Sassoon once wrote to a friend.[15] Perhaps to counterbalance his dreamy, poetic side, he also had a strong need to take risks. It had earned him his nickname 'Mad Jack' in the war and in peacetime found its outlet on the hunting field, where he was recognized as a daring rider to hounds.

Naturally he was not unaware of the class connotations attached to hunting. For him it was inevitably associated with the pleasant country-house life of the past, which he knew gave it an undemocratic flavour. (There is a reference in his poem 'Reynardism Revisited' to 'Foxes Torn to Bits in Smart Society'.)[16] But was this *élitism* any worse, he wondered, than the attempts of urban-minded politicians to reduce everyone to equality and mediocrity of mind? And even if they managed to change the social system, would there not remain all the essential ingredients of hunting – 'the behaviour of the horse, the smell of a winter morning, and the sense of personal adventure and physical well-being in the rider'?[17]

Sassoon continued to hunt into the mid-thirties and his decision to stop was a practical not a moral one. He never viewed hunting as violent or morally reprehensible and, as one of his best friends in later life said, he would have been 'absolutely appalled' at the present attempt to ban the sport.[18] He believed that it was up to the individual to make up his or her own mind. Though he never wanted to shoot pheasants himself, for example, he never tried to stop others from doing so.

*

Sassoon's decision to start hunting again in 1920, though frustrated by his horse's lameness the first winter, provided him with a great deal of pleasure in the early twenties. During the season, from mid-October to April, he would leave town regularly on a Thursday afternoon for the Loders, who would take him to their Friday meet.

It was a relief to escape London for the weekend and a very real pleasure riding across country on a good hunter. He derived even greater enjoyment from competing in point-to-point races, buying a second horse, Higham Destiny, for this purpose in 1922. But, increasingly, he connected sport with 'mindlessness'.[19] In addition he began to feel uncomfortable about the 'secret life' he was forced to conceal from his 'unintellectual Loders'.[20] It was not simply his homosexuality he could not discuss with them, but a wide variety of cultural subjects. They seemed to him 'conventional grown-up children'.[21] He could see that they had their own 'solid' values and he enjoyed some aspects of his visits to them: 'But not more than once a week, please!' he begged in his diary.[22]

He had found it difficult to reconcile the two very different sides of his life before the First World War, but the problem became even more pronounced after it: 'extreme physical fitness', he argued with himself in April 1922, 'does not go with intellectual alertness and creative intensity'.[23] One might lead to the other, but they could not, in his experience, co-exist. It was one reason why, when Higham Destiny turned out a disappointment and Lady Jill had to be put down in 1923, he did not replace them. The expense of keeping two hunters also entered into it.

Another reason might have been a rare accident on the hunting field which reduced him to enforced idleness for over three weeks that same year. He had taken refuge with Ottoline at Garsington, which he often did after visiting the Loders as an antidote to their philistinism. With the threat of her romantic interest in him safely past, he was able to value Ottoline more in the twenties, and not simply as a confidante. She had done as much as any of his friends, he believed, to help him 'appreciate the best things in life and art'.[24] His visits to her manor house offered not just another escape from London but a cultural world as rich, if not richer than Turner's. After the 'genial avidity and *Tatlerism* of Loder-land and sport', Garsington and its 'ever-dear Ottoline' seemed above all 'enriching'.[25]

Another retreat both from philistinism and London was Cambridge, where he continued to visit Rivers. Of all his friends, he believed Rivers was the person who had done most to help him resolve his divided self. If anyone could guide him through the after-effects of war, it was the man he called his 'fathering friend'. The phrase comes from Sassoon's poem on Rivers, 'Revisitation', written many years after his death.[26] In lines which he ultimately omitted from the published piece, Sassoon emphasized how much he relied on Rivers' guidance after the war:

> Deep in my morning time he made his mark
> And still he comes uncalled to be my guide
> In devastated regions

9. Ways of Escape

When the brain has lost its bearings in the dark
And broken is the body's pride,
In the long campaign to which it had sworn allegiance.[27]

It was Rivers who had encouraged him to study politics at Oxford in 1919, yet had understood when he gave it up. A committed socialist himself – he agreed to stand as Labour Party candidate for the University of London in 1922 – he appeared to accept Sassoon's decreasing commitment to politics without criticism. But he made him want to be a better, more serious person.

It was under his influence, for example, that Sassoon tried hard to be 'non-acquisitive' after the war.[28] And it was almost certainly with his guidance that Sassoon made several efforts to help those less privileged than himself in the early twenties. Besides giving money to his ex-army servant, Law, he visited Wales to report on the miners' strike for the *Nation* in 1921, wrote a poem about it in 'A Case for the Miners' and started prison-visiting shortly afterwards.[29]

His 'dutiful pilgrimages' to Pentonville Gaol were harrowing but colourful, his assigned prisoners including a bigamist Yorkshire farmer and a scout-master who became '"over-enthusiastic" about some of his troops'.[30] By 1925 he was being allotted newly arrived prisoners, but most of them seemed already hardened cases. There were exceptions but, as his poem 'To One in Prison' shows, he despaired of being any real help even to those who did care. It is also clear from the same piece that he became emotionally involved with the young men he visited, an echo of his relationship with the young army private Jim Linthwaite in 1918:[31]

> And now – what use the pity that I am heaping
> Upon your head? Who knows? ... My heart, not yours, can tell.
>
> (CP, p.186)[32]

In this and his other attempts to be a 'serious' person, Sassoon was grateful for Rivers's support. He was, therefore, devastated when Rivers died suddenly on 4 June 1922 at the age of only fifty-eight.[33] But even by his death, Sassoon believed, Rivers had helped him: 'He has awakened in me a passionate consciousness of the significance of life,' he wrote in his diary the day after hearing the news. 'In a few hours I have recognized as never before the intensity of life which Rivers communicated to his friends.'[34] He now saw him 'in all his glory of selfless wisdom and human service', the inevitable effect of death, he supposed, 'when the living have loved the dead'.[35] Attending the funeral at Cambridge with one of Rivers's closest friends and colleagues, Sir Henry Head, who would to some extent replace Rivers as one of several father-figures, he felt 'profound gratitude to the dead man for all that he wrote and lived'.[36] Arnold Bennett, who had met Rivers through Sassoon, was equally appreciative of him, though he

137

declined Sassoon's invitation to write about him initially: 'I'll just keep him to myself,' he replied.[37]

Sassoon's descriptions of Rivers, even before his death, make him sound almost oppressively selfless, as though he gave everything and received nothing. But the Reverend Cyril Tompkinson, a friend of both men, was probably right to claim that Sassoon also 'did a great deal for [Rivers], bringing colour, delight and a deep affection into his life, just when it was needed'.[38]

Sassoon continued to visit Cambridge after Rivers' death, but less frequently and with less pleasure. Perhaps as a result of the withdrawal of Rivers' influence, he began to spend noticeably more time at Frankie Schuster's house on the Thames at Bray. It may have represented for him a compromise between the 'mindlessness' but physical well-being of the Loders' world and the high-mindedness of Garsington.

By the time Rivers died, Sassoon had already paid several visits to the Hut, or the Long White Cloud, as Schuster's house became known after extensive enlargement. And in 1924 and 1925 he spent virtually the whole summer in what he rechristened 'Schuster's Retreat from Reality on the river'.[39] When planning a fourth volume of autobiography which would cover some of his time at Bray, Sassoon believed that 'the Schuster material alone should make it pretty good'.[40] Though he never completed the book, he clearly enjoyed writing about his 'lotus-eating by the Thames'.[41] His descriptions are full of verbs like 'idle' and 'saunter' and leisurely accounts of days spent weeding the lawn, pulling dead wood out of poplar trees or 'lumbering up and down' on one of Schuster's several grand pianos.[42] Writing to Graves, who had followed his slow recovery from the war with fellow-feeling, he makes it clear that Bray, where he has been staying for several weeks, has helped in the healing process: 'I am,' he announced in 1925, 'in the pink, and haven't lost my temper for several weeks.'[43]

The Long White Cloud was an idyllic place to be in summer. Though less than thirty miles from London, it was surrounded by fields on three sides, with the fourth facing the Thames. Its large grounds included a tennis court bordered with lilacs and poplars, croquet grounds, a terrace for moonlit dinners, a separate garden music room and well-kept lawns running down to the river. The house itself, long, low and rambling, was architecturally undistinguished but beautifully furnished, exuding an air of tranquillity, order and civilized living.[44] There was a staff of six, including a butler, cook, housemaid and head gardener, who provided Schuster and his numerous guests with the fine food and wine he expected. Schuster, according to Sassoon, was 'a monarch among the *maîtres d'hotel* of Europe'.[45]

He was also a connoisseur of music, another source of pleasure for Sassoon at Bray. When they were not travelling up to London in Frankie's Rolls-Royce to hear an opera or concert, Schuster would often invite well-known musicians to his house for private recitals. The most famous of these and the one Sassoon came to know best was Elgar.[46]

Sassoon had admired Elgar's music long before he met him at Schuster's, particularly his Violin Concerto, about which he had written at least two poems.[47] 'He knew how to design on a big scale, as Handel so gloriously did,' he wrote to his mother after Elgar's death, 'and his feeling is so beautifully English.'[48] Elgar's appearance, that of a 'smartly dressed "military"-looking grey-haired man, with [a] carefully-trimmed moustache and curved nose', was so different from the 'magnificence' of his music that Sassoon had difficulty reconciling the two.[49] But listening to his 1st Symphony, for example, he felt he was seeing the man in his 'higher nature' and 'gloried in having known him'.[50]

He was flattered to discover that Elgar returned his admiration, asking him on one occasion to write him five or six poems to set to music, for instance.[51] Though he failed to produce the poems, he enjoyed being treated as a fellow-craftsman by the great man.

His fondest memory of the composer was an hour spent in Schuster's music room in 1924, with Elgar playing snatches from Sassoon's piano music (Mozart's A major Concerto and Bach's Fugues and Chaconne), some of his own choral works ('Death on the Hills', 'Te Deum' and 'Light of Life') and parts of Schubert's Rondo Brillante, which he loved. Watching him 'glowing with delight' in the music, Sassoon felt he was seeing the 'real' Elgar.[52] It helped him to forget the other side of Elgar, the one who told long-winded anecdotes about himself at lunch and who seemed to him 'just a type of club bore'.[53] Unfortunately, this side was never absent for long and Sassoon's overall impression was of someone 'a bit petty and disappointing'.[54] He was particularly critical of Elgar's treatment of Schuster, which was sometimes very unkind. Yet Schuster had done more than anyone, Sassoon believed, to establish Elgar's success.

Schuster's devotion to music helped Sassoon accept other aspects of him he found less attractive. His carefulness with money, for example, was completely alien to Sassoon, who found it especially irritating in someone so rich. Whilst he could see that paying for everything 'fifty-fifty' during his visits, which often lasted months, was fair and even saved him money, he disliked the calculation involved. 'What a mockery all Frankie's money and luxury is', he wrote to a friend, 'when the only thing that matters isn't here … the generosity which old Frankie lacks!'[55] He was even more critical of Schuster's social life, disliking the 'socially insincere smartly-dressed people with uninspected and protected lives' who descended on Bray at weekends.[56] 'If I were to die before one of his parties,' he wrote to Graves, 'he would have me carted away like a crate of empty bottles. And he would persuade himself that he'd enjoyed the party.'[57]

After Schuster's death, however, he came to feel that he had been unfair to him. It was true that Schuster loved a title, and if its recipient were wealthy so much the better. But he loved music more and his guests were expected either to provide it or to appreciate it. There is one group photograph taken at Bray which epitomizes the special kind of mix he created; it is of the powerful socialite Lady Randolph Churchill, Lady Maud Warrender, herself a good amateur singer, and the legendary Australian soprano Dame 'Nellie' Melba.

Sassoon would sometimes escape such gatherings. Though he was not nearly as immune to their social appeal as he suggests, he valued friendship more and preferred to visit de la Mare, for example, once he had moved to Taplow, only three miles from Bray. And there is no doubt that Sassoon felt happier in de la Mare's relatively modest house than at nearby Taplow Court, where he was sometimes invited by de la Mare's landlords, Lord and Lady Desborough.[58]

It was partly as a protest against the 'shams and insincerities of social intercourse' that Sassoon took his mother to visit Bray in 1924. Her shabby clothes, unsophisticated manner and artless appreciation of her surroundings filled him with both pride and pain. While, for him, her 'integrity withered and demolished all the "chic" associations of the Schusteristic atmosphere', he suspected that his host would ridicule her behind his back.[59] Only Schuster's much younger companion, 'Anzie' Wylde, seemed to appreciate his mother at a human level.[60]

Anzie's presence at Bray was often the only thing which stopped Sassoon leaving in disgust. A New Zealander by birth, he had acquired his nickname as a captain in the Canterbury Regiment with the ANZAC forces during the war. Wounded at Gallipoli, he was invalided back to England with severe chest wounds and a leg amputated up to the thigh. Schuster had met him while visiting the troops at Lady Astor's hospital and been attracted by the similarity of his hooded eyes, as well as name, to Oscar Wilde, whom he had known well. By the time Sassoon met Anzie he had been informally adopted by Schuster, whom he called 'Uncle', or 'Unkie'.

What struck Sassoon most about Anzie was his 'unfailing good nature and cheerfulness', his acceptance of everything that came to him, 'whether it was a leg lost at Gallipoli or the Rolls-Royce, which he'd been driving Frankie about in' since 1919.[61] Either because he did not know, or, more likely, because he was being discreet, he does not mention Wylde's recurrent drinking bouts, brought on by his depression at no longer being able to ride.[62] Anzie could, however, still swim and was a skilful yachtsman, as well as knowing a great deal about cars, as Sassoon would discover. Less predictably, he turned out to be a shrewd businessman, his speculations on the Stock Exchange bringing him in a thousand pounds in one fortnight alone in 1927. He was also to inherit Schuster's considerable fortune.

Sassoon particularly admired Anzie's 'simple wisdom', a quality he detected in all his favourite people, from the greatest, like Thomas Hardy, to the most ordinary, like Nellie Burton.[63] Anzie never elaborated or over-intellectualized problems, as 'clever' people like Forster did. At Bray

140

especially he helped Sassoon take a down-to-earth view of things. Tactful, good-humoured and witty (he referred to the fussy Schuster as '*chauffez la tasse*'), Anzie lacked nothing in Sassoon's opinion except perhaps an ability to read more than a few pages of a book at one sitting. 'Anzie's jollity has been unfailing,' Sassoon reported in his diary on a trip abroad in 1924, noting Schuster's 'occasional tiresomeness' at the same time.[64] After driving them almost non-stop from the South of France, Anzie was still ready to sit down and reminisce about the war at Abbeville. 'He would have been an ideal brother-officer,' Sassoon believed.[65]

Besides himself, Anzie introduced another redeeming feature to Bray in the woman he married in 1924, Wendela Boreel.[66] The daughter of a Dutch diplomat father and wealthy American mother, 'Wendy' as she was known, had been a neighbour of Schuster and Anzie in Tite Street before they moved to Old Queen Street. Studying art under Tonks and Sickert, she had become romantically involved with Anzie while painting his portrait in 1923. Schuster, who must have realized early on that the handsome New Zealander did not share his own preference for young men, accepted their marriage in 1924 with a good grace. Sassoon noted cynically that this was mainly because Schuster was a friend of Wendela's well-connected mother, who would leave her a 'nice little income' at her death.[67] Sassoon himself found Wendela 'delightful' and was happy to sit for her.[68] She and her painting sometimes seemed to him 'the only "serious" element' in life at Bray.[69]

By 1925 Sassoon had decided that the advantages of the Schusterian existence – 'the delicious food, the delightful riverside garden, the faultless taste in furniture', the exquisite music – were outweighed by its 'lack of serious foundations'.[70] 'Its froth-de-luxe', he wrote, rather self-righteously considering the time he had voluntarily spent there, 'conceals nothing but materialism and refusal to face life seriously.'[71] After even a few days at Bray he felt bursting with good health but 'mentally slack and sluggish'[72] and his attempts to write poetry there almost always failed.

He might long for 'austerity and solitude; to be back with Rivers at Cambridge'.[73] But he would go on visiting Bray for several years after leaving Tufton Street, a sign of his continuing lack of direction in the mid-1920s.

10

'Love is the Test'
(1921-1925)

> *Love* is the test, I suppose. One strives to keep it romantic; to make it a series
> of dramatic episodes. The breath of life will not remain in a marionette-show
> passion. In love we find salvation or shameful defeat. But O, it is difficult!
> (Diary entry for 15 August 1922)

Staying with Frankie Schuster was only one of the reasons Sassoon gave
for his difficulty in writing poetry during the Tufton Street years. Another
related to the 'cursed complication of sex', which dominated this period.[1]

While his sexual frustration before and during the war and his initial
euphoria over Gabriel had fuelled his creative urge, the restless experiments which followed had the opposite effect. Starting with his unhappy
affair with Glenn Hunter in New York, these never really satisfied him,
though it is clear from a poem written at this time that he still believed
that physical passion could inspire the artist:

> While we are sober, sage, and sane,
> We plough and plant a sterile plain.
> But passion's climax storming by
> With phallic imageries of art
> Creates in pomp along the sky
> Dazzling cloud-rhapsodies of heart.
>
> Dreaming below the stars, we spawn
> Posterity in blood-streaked dawn;
> Mocked by philosophies, we run
> Toward the secure and sexual sun;
> And till the mouths of lovers meet
> The unborn age is incomplete.[2]

Another poem written at the same time, 'A Last Judgement', orders the
protagonist to 'look for love' but, if it cannot be found, to 'look for lust', the
piece containing the despairing admission: '... mocked and maimed, he
knew, / For scrawls on dungeon walls his priapismic devils.'[3] In the light
of Sassoon's own development in the early twenties, it is difficult not to
read both poems autobiographically.

He himself believed that his best poetry was the result of 'repressed sex'

143

and the lacklustre nature of the verse written during this his period of greatest sexual activity appears to support the theory.[4] From October 1921, when he started an affair with a young German prince, to early 1925, when his disastrous relationship with a well-known actor came to a painful end, he wrote little that either he or posterity would wish to keep.

Side by side with the sexual adventures – one sometimes leading to the other – were his actual travels, which formed an important part of his routine at Tufton Street. Partly because Turner needed to let the house for extra income at times, partly because it was possible to live more cheaply abroad, but mainly because his experiences during the war and in America had given him a taste for it, Sassoon spent long periods travelling between 1920 and 1925. He also quite self-consciously set out to broaden his cultural horizons.

In many ways these trips were simply an extension of the life he lived in England, with a great deal of his time devoted to concerts, art galleries and museums. 'My travels are food for the mind,' he wrote in 1922, 'and a liberal education in arts and manners.'[5] For this reason, no doubt, his favourite countries were Italy and Germany, though he visited the South of France with Schuster on at least two occasions.[6] He particularly enjoyed Munich, where he stayed more than once during the opera season.

One reason for his restlessness was an increasing dissatisfaction with Gabriel. His first trip abroad after America, planned for April 1921, was to be with Gabriel, but only because, as he told Ottoline, there was 'no one else to go with'.[7] He was already beginning to find Gabriel 'silly and second-rate'.[8] Everything they did together now seemed to him 'flabby and sterile' and he could only 'flog' himself into emotions by having rows with him about his 'rather squalid habits and associates'.[9]

His periodic agonies about Gabriel's lifestyle were partly caused by the realization that the 'poor little soul' tried very hard to follow his sensible advice: 'but I am a hard master', Sassoon admitted, 'and my prejudice against alcohol is more than he can swallow'.[10] Turner had told him that he had 'never known anyone who had such a strong desire to dominate people's lives', a 'sort of half-paternal instinct', he called it, adding that Sassoon put 'an almost impossible strain' on the people he loved by 'demanding an intensity equal to [his] own'.[11]

Sassoon was still too attached to Gabriel to leave him completely but he was already looking for someone to replace him as a lover by 1921. And it was on his first trip abroad in September that year that he found a substitute.

He had cancelled his trip to Venice in April because of a coal strike, spending a month in Somerset instead.[12] But he still wanted to see Italy. So that when Prewett, who had returned from Canada to study at Christ Church, enthused about his own recent trip to Rome, Sassoon suggested another visit with him.[13] Though Sassoon was helping Prewett financially at Oxford and paying all the expenses for the Rome trip, Prewett made it quite clear that there would be no sex between them. Yet his very presence aroused Sassoon sexually, as did the young Italian men he saw in the streets.

> Is it my own fault [he asked after twenty-four hours in Rome] that I am under this cursed obsession of sex-cravings. If Gabriel were here it would be no better. Worse, probably. The fact is that I am not interested in the Roman Empire, or the Renaissance, or Baroque effects. My tastes are neither historical nor antiquarian, nor artistic. I am interested in the physical aspect of Italy.[14]

It was not with an Italian but with a German, however, that Sassoon was to experience the physical side of Italy. Conveniently, as it turned out, Prewett became ill on reaching Rome and had to go into a nursing home with a gastric ulcer. This left Sassoon very much to his own devices and free for what was to follow.

The one person he knew in Rome apart from Prewett was Lord Berners, who had an apartment at 6 Via Varese. Berners, born Gerald Tyrwhitt in 1883, had inherited his title in 1918 and with it the Faringdon estate, which Sassoon had already visited and would return to several times in the early twenties.[15] Monocled, bowler-hatted and urbane, the Old Etonian was a friend of the Sitwells and Morrells and rented rooms from Nellie Burton at Half Moon Street before buying his own house in Chesham Place. A colourful eccentric and aesthete, he famously had the doves on his estate dyed magenta, green and sky-blue.

There was, however, a more serious side to Berners, who was also a composer, novelist and painter.[16] Wherever he went he took with him his clavichord, strapped to the back seat of his chauffeur-driven Rolls-Royce, and Sassoon derived great pleasure from his impromptu recitals, writing at least one poem on the subject.[17] He also enjoyed Berners' wit and practical jokes, particularly the idea of a hoax telegram Berners planned to send his fellow-homosexual Osbert Sitwell in 1924, from a lady Osbert had fled to Dieppe to escape; it announced her imminent arrival there. From thinking Berners 'consistently inhuman' and 'exclusively intellectual' at the start, Sassoon would come to find him quite human and easy to get on with.[18] Whatever his criticism of Schuster and his friends, he enjoyed being with rich, titled people, especially when, unlike Schuster, they were generous with their money. Berners had an income of approximately £7,000 a year, about £254,000 by today's standards, and there was never any question of Sassoon going 'fifty-fifty' with him as Schuster demanded.

One thing Berners did have in common with Schuster, however, was a taste for fine food and wine and Sassoon was delighted to be invited to lunch with him in the Via Varese. And it was there, at the beginning of October, that he first met the young German who was to dominate his life for the next two years, Prince Philipp of Hesse. A few days later he was invited to lunch with Berners and Philipp again, this time just outside Rome at the Castel Gandolfo above Lake Albano. As the diplomat Harold Nicolson, who was also there with his wife, Vita Sackville-West, and their friends Gerald and Dorothy Wellesley, recorded in his diary, it was a romantic affair. After lunching exquisitely beneath the leaves of a vine, they all launched paper boats down a nearby waterfall and Sassoon became so excited that he threw his hat in too. He was in love again.

His attraction towards Prince Philipp was not primarily a physical one, though it would be a sexually active relationship, Philipp moving into his hotel only three days after their first meeting. 'Physically I have never been really infatuated by him,' Sassoon would note a year later.[19] Heavier than Gabriel and already balding, Philipp had none of his physical charm for Sassoon: 'Gabriel is more attractive physically,' he was to write in 1922.[20] But Philipp interested him more. Sassoon wanted a connection founded on 'a firmer basis than mere sensualism'.[21] He also hoped that Philipp would be his 'link with Europe' and a 'social experience'.[22]

Philipp's standing in society was one of his main attractions for Sassoon. His mother, Princess Margarethe of Prussia, was the daughter of Kaiser Frederick, Emperor of Germany, and granddaughter of Queen Victoria. She was also the sister of Kaiser Wilhelm II, then in exile in Holland, and of Princess Sophie who, through her marriage to the Duke of Sparta, had become Queen of Greece.[23] Philipp's father, Friedrich Karl, was next in line to become Landgrave of Hesse, when his brother died, and Philipp after him.[24] Philipp himself would marry the daughter of the King of Italy.

Though the family prestige and fortunes had suffered greatly from Germany's defeat in the war, a fact which made him not unnaturally bitter, he still carried with him the consciousness and confidence of his heritage. For Sassoon, who freely admitted that the 'main trouble' with Gabriel was that he was 'not a gentleman', it was a large part of his appeal.[25] To be intimate with the great-grandson of Queen Victoria and nephew of the King of Greece was irresistible, even if Philipp's link with his disgraced uncle, the Kaiser, was less appealing to one who had seen the carnage of the First World War.

Yet Sassoon was undoubtedly fascinated by Philipp's own role in the German army, asking specifically for a photograph of him in his cavalry uniform. His initial hatred of German soldiers had turned to a sense of identification with them after only a few months at the Front. And Philipp, like him, had seen active service in the war and lost a brother in it. But it is unlikely that he was as critical of his superiors as Sassoon, one of his less attractive traits being his acquiescence with the *status quo*. Sassoon accepted this reluctantly as 'his complacent but naturally inherited feudalism'.[26]

A more positive side to Philipp's inheritance was that it had turned him into a highly cultivated person with 'beautiful' manners.[27] And since their

146

1. SS at Garsington in the mid-1920s, photographed by Robert Gathorne-Hardy.

2. Gabriel Atkin suffering from the effects of
Armistice celebrations (self-caricature).

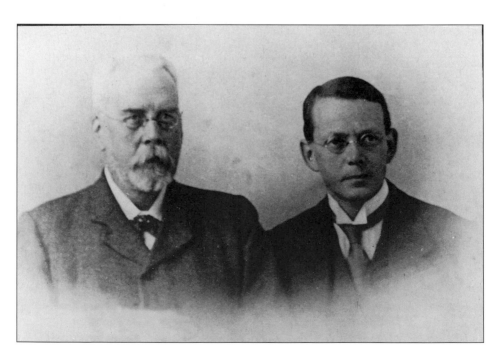

3. 'Enrico' Festing-Jones and 'Theo' Bartholomew.

4. Walter de la Mare in the 1920s.

5. Beverley Nichols in his early twenties.

6. SS's collage of Osbert Sitwell, with his manuscript verse caption.

THE OLD CENTURY

and seven more years

by

SIEGFRIED SASSOON

FABER AND FABER LIMITED
24 Russell Square
London

8. Title page of *The Old Century*.

A

LITERARY EDITOR

for the

NEW LONDON

DAILY

NEWSPAPER

7. Cover of one of the few surviving pamphlets announcing SS's appointment as Literary Editor to the *Daily Herald*, the 'paper with its Face towards the Future'.

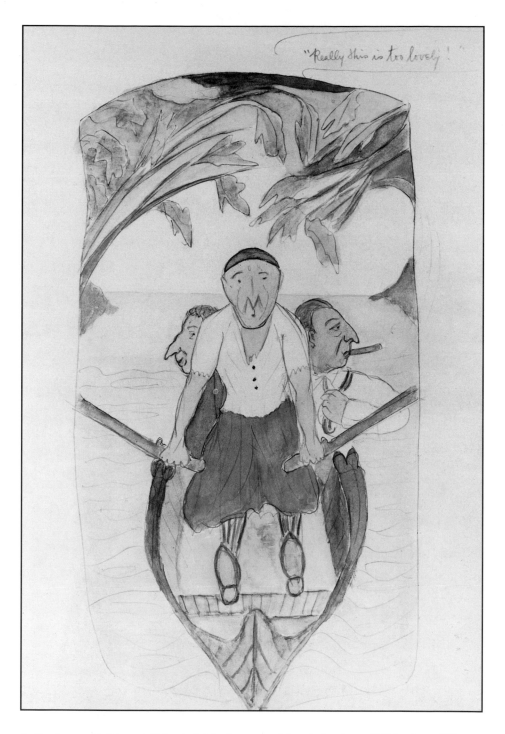

"Really this is too lovely!"

9. Sacheverell (l.) and Osbert (r.) being rowed by their sister Edith, from SS's series of caricatures of the Sitwells.

10. The 'Thursdayers': standing (l. to r.) Mark Gertler, Prof. A.S. Fulton, Walter Turner, Herbert Milne; seated: (l. to r.) Ralph Hodgson, S.S. Koteliansky, J.W.N. Sullivan.

11. Charlotte Mew in 1923.

12. Edmund Blunden at Garsington Manor in 1924.

13. T.E. Lawrence, alias Aircraftsman Shaw, *c*. 1922.

14. SS, *c*. 1920.

15. Thomas Hardy, shortly before his death in 1928.

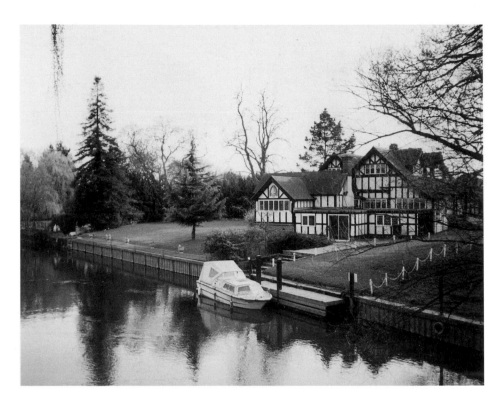

16. 'Frankie' Schuster's summer retreat, the Long White Cloud, at Bray-on-Thames, near Maidenhead.

17. Schuster (on the extreme right) at the Long White Cloud with (from l. to r.) Roger Fry, Julian Sampson and Robert Nichols.

18. Leslie George Wylde ('Anzie'), as a Captain in the Canterbury Regiment of the ANZAC forces, *c.* 1915.

19. Anzie's wife, the painter Wendela Boreel, with their son James.

20. Wendela Boreel's etching of SS, mid-1920s.

21. Sir Edward Elgar in relaxed mood at the Long White Cloud.

22. Prince Philipp of Hesse in the early 1920s.

23. Constance Collier as the Rokeby Venus, attended by the ten-year-old Glen Byam Shaw, at the Haymarket Theatre, March 1915.

24. SS and Glen Byam Shaw at the home of Ellen Terry (seated), *c.* 1926/7, shortly before her death.

25. The New Menin Gate Memorial, shortly after its opening by Field-Marshal Lord Plumer in July 1927.

26. 'Bob' Gathorne-Hardy with his monocle, together with (half of) Lord David Cecil, taken in the early 1920s at Garsington.

27. Lady Ottoline Morrell in Venice in 1926.

28. The storm clouds gather, Versailles, July 1926: (l. to r.) Julian Morrell, Bob Gathorne-Hardy, SS, Kyrle Leng and Philip Morrell.

29. SS with Stephen Tennant and his aunt, 'Nan' Tennant, on the bridge to Breitenau, Summer 1929.

30. SS preparing to chop wood at Breitenau, 1929.

31. SS with Stephen and Dr Kaltenbach at Haus Hirth.

32. The photographer photographed: Cecil Beaton in the 1920s.

33. Max and Florence Beerbohm with SS, in characteristic pose, on the Beerbohms' roof terrace at Rapallo, *c.* 1930.

34. Max's caricature of SS.

35. SS with Stephen and Poll the Parrot at Wilsford Manor.

36. SS with Edith Olivier at the Daye House, Wilton.

37. William Walton in the early 1930s.

38. Rex Whistler at 20
Fitzroy Street, London,
c. 1927.

39. Doris Westwood in the
early 1930s.

40. SS at Fitz House, Teffont Magna, in the early 1930s.

41. SS as an Elizabethan bard at the Wilton Pageant, June 1933.

42. Hester Gatty in her late twenties.

relationship coincided with Sassoon's 'grand tour in quest of culture', he fully appreciated Philipp's ability to distinguish between baroque and rococo art, for example, or his detailed knowledge of music.[28] He was later to regret the conventionality and limitations of Philipp's taste – he thought Sassoon 'wrong' to 'tolerate' Gauguin, Van Gogh and Stravinsky, for example – but at their first meeting in Rome Sassoon was very impressed by Philipp's knowledge.

He also admired Philipp's 'essential amiability' and imperturbable manner, which made it impossible for him to inflict his 'tigerish ill-temper' or 'tantrums' on Philipp as he did on Gabriel: 'he has a way of disarming me by a sort of placidity, quite different to the long-suffering flimsiness of poor G, who only takes refuge in tears and silence.'[29] Philipp's charm was his greatest asset, more than compensating for his lack of great physical appeal for Sassoon. He had only to appear with the little dog and Greek servant who always accompanied him, and any reservations Sassoon felt would vanish.

For he had begun to have reservations about Philipp within a comparatively short time, soon after their passionate ten-day idyll in Rome had ended. Philipp had returned to Germany via Venice and his first few letters were gratifyingly romantic: '[Those] days at Rome made a great change in my life [he wrote on 17 October 1921] and they have made me so happy – happier than I can say. That happiness shall remain in my heart … where I shall keep it like a precious jewel that no one can take away from me.'[30] And on 28 October 1921 he wrote: '[Your letter] brought back everything more vividly than ever; you, your voice, Rome with all its beauty, the murmuring of fountains, some vague melody of Bach played by small untrained fingers, two small rooms in a little hotel and all that happiness.'

But in his third letter, three days later, he mentions a possible visit from another English male lover. And although his next letter is full of enthusiasm for Sassoon's poems, which he has sent for Philipp's birthday, there is another reference to the English lover. A six-week silence then follows during which, it emerges, Philipp has resumed his affair with a married woman in Berlin. While describing the whole thing as a 'torture and agony', he nevertheless gives vivid details of their love-making, which has only ended because she has to leave Berlin.

It was probably at this point that Sassoon realized something he had only suspected in Rome, that Philipp was 'wholly unimaginative and rather coarsely sensual'.[31] No one of any sensitivity could have failed to understand the effect his letter would have on another lover. And after spending a much longer period with Philipp, from August to October 1922, Sassoon felt even more convinced that he lacked imagination.[32] This made Philipp far more matter-of-fact than Sassoon, who tried to keep love romantic and who wished his noble lover were not quite so 'sophisticated' about his numerous affairs.[33] Philipp made no attempt to conceal his relationship with an American woman, 'Babe', in 1922, for example, even interrupting his love-making with Sassoon to take a telephone call from her; and he seemed unembarrassed when, on several occasions, he called Sassoon by the name of yet another recent lover.

It is hardly surprising, therefore, that he failed to inspire Sassoon to write much in the way of love poetry. Apart from an indirect reference to Philipp in the 'Villa d'Este Gardens', which he had visited with the prince in October 1921, there is only one poem directly devoted to him, 'Vigil'. Written while Sassoon waited to see Philipp again in 1922, it is as conventional and formal as the man himself:

> ... Waiting you in my thought's high lonely tower
> That looks on star-lit hushed Elysian gloom,
> I know your advent certain as the flower
> Of daybreak that on breathless vales shall bloom.
>
> O never hasten now; for time's all sweet,
> And you are clad in the garment of my dreams:
> Led by my heart's enchanted cry, your feet
> Move with the murmur of forest-wandering streams
> Through earth's adoring darkness to discover
> The Paradise of your imperfect lover.[34]

Heavily derivative in general terms, the piece ends with an actual phrase taken from Sassoon's far livelier poem to Gabriel, 'The Imperfect Lover'.

Philipp's lack of imagination accounted, Sassoon felt, for most of his other faults, particularly his conventional response to the arts. This irritated Sassoon most when it concerned his own poems, which Philipp professed to admire greatly. 'His attitude towards my *work*', Sassoon noted, 'is ponderous and conventional.'[35] Gabriel, for all his limitations, was preferable in this respect.

There were, however, a number of similarities between Philipp and Gabriel: both ten years younger than Sassoon they shared an enthusiasm he did not understand for 'silly chattering smart women', cocktail bars and old brandy late at night.[36] They were both promiscuous and far less puritanical than Sassoon, Philipp, for instance, being fond of 'filthy' stories and 'obscene' statues.[37] But Sassoon was conscious mainly of Philipp's difference from Gabriel when he met him for the second time at Munich in August 1922.

To begin with the contrast was all in Philipp's favour, Sassoon finding his imperturbability a relief after Gabriel's weak and emotional nature. But by the time he moved to Venice with Philipp in October 1922, he had started to appreciate Gabriel's more creative approach to life: 'G at any rate aspires to become an artist. P is merely a cultured person.'[38]

Nevertheless, by the end of this second holiday with Philipp, he realized that his relationship with him had become very similar to that with

Gabriel. He attributed this to the fact that, as with Gabriel, he had 'all the money' and 'dole[d] it out' to his young lovers, a situation which he confessed added to his 'feeling of increased domination'.[39] He had noted early on in their relationship that Philipp's sexual attitude to him was 'identical' to Gabriel's – 'passive surrender, with hero-worship; passionate desire to be adored'.[40] But he had not yet accepted that the need to dominate people (noted by Turner), together with the sadistic streak (suspected by Osbert), made it most unlikely that he would ever achieve a successful sexual liaison. Only in relationships where, to repeat his own words, 'the gross elements of sex' were 'miraculously remote', as with Blunden, would he find genuine fulfilment.[41]

He himself explained his increasing dissatisfaction with Philipp in different terms. The young prince, he noted, had 'not got a first-class mind'.[42] And, although he doubted his own ability to handle ideas, he eventually began to think of Philipp as an 'intellectual clodpole'.[43] Worse still, he could imagine him getting 'heavier and heavier from year to year'.[44] Already too 'padded with flattery' and servile attention, he would probably become a 'bald, self-indulgent, opinionated man – living on the snobbishness of rich people'.[45] He had taught Sassoon a great deal that he 'needed to know – worldliness', but he seemed to him 'fundamentally *stupid*' and as 'heavy as a German oratorio'.[46]

Philipp made several attempts to see Sassoon again between their parting at Naples in October 1922 and his marriage to Princess Mafalda of Italy in 1925. But Sassoon, disappointed and disillusioned by Philipp and possibly repelled by his growing interest in the Nazis (which would end with collaboration with Hitler and the death of his wife in a concentration camp), had already started on a series of new relationships by early 1923.[47]

*

Sassoon had become increasingly obsessed by Walter de la Mare's son, Colin, since he had met him as a thirteen-year-old in 1918. By 1922, only a few weeks before his holiday with Philipp, he confessed that the fifteen-month break in his visits to the de la Mare family had 'probably' something to do with his attraction to Colin. 'He is an uncomfortably attractive creature – one of the most attractive I've met,' he wrote after a visit to Colin's family in July 1922: 'Instinct warns me once again to avoid seeing him often.'[48] By the following Easter, however, he was asking Ottoline if he could bring Colin with him to Garsington: 'I have seen a great deal of him lately, and I want you to share my very deep affection for him, and to help me keep it worthy of the trust which his father puts in me, (little guessing I am afraid, the perilous complications involved!)'[49]

There was a 'deep wound', he told Ottoline two months later, but it was not Colin's fault. Judging from the pages torn from his diary for mid- to late August 1924, when he spent a week with the de la Mares at Manorbier in Wales, his fascination continued to be a sexual one, fed mainly by Colin's youth and his 'queer eyes'.[50]

It was the same two qualities which attracted him to Lord David Cecil, whom he met in March 1922, just a month before Cecil's twentieth birthday. He had already heard of the precocious young man, who visited Garsington at weekends with his Oxford undergraduate friends, Eddy Sackville-West, L.P. Hartley and Robert Gathorne-Hardy, and had looked forward 'with secret curiosity and eagerness' to meeting him, his title an added incentive.[51] When they eventually did so, he found Cecil 'fragile, intellectual, and charming, with a very delicate profile' and disturbing pale-grey eyes.[52] During lunch at Garsington Cecil sat opposite him and looked at him a great deal, but Sassoon 'avoided his eyes'.[53] He felt deeply self-conscious with the youth, too aware of Cecil's attractiveness to behave naturally, and it is clear from his letters to Ottoline that he tried to become more intimate with him. He probably assumed that someone who moved in homosexual circles, as Cecil did at this time, was himself homosexual.

But by July 1923, when Cecil failed to keep an appointment for dinner with him at the Reform, Sassoon seems to have given up. 'The way he "put me through it" is not easy to forget,' he wrote subsequently to a sympathetic friend, Henry Festing-Jones, 'though excusable in one so young and wild-flower eyed.'[54] His later references to Cecil suggest that he never really forgave him, though the two remained on civil terms for the rest of Sassoon's life, meeting very occasionally once Sassoon had moved to the West Country.[55] For his part, after his first awe of the well-known poet had passed, Cecil found Sassoon 'strangely uncouth', remembering him most vividly after his death for his 'sudden laughter'.[56]

At the height of Sassoon's attempts to engage the young aristocrat more deeply, however, he was already involved with another undergraduate of a very different kind, Richardson ('Dick') Wood. Even younger than Cecil, he was an American who had come to England to study at King's College, Cambridge.[57] He had been there a year when Sassoon first met him in August 1923 and was already well known to Theo Bartholomew. From his vantage point at the University Library Theo watched each new intake of undergraduates hopefully, though resolving each autumn to resist fresh sexual adventures, which he believed bad for his health. Since Theo himself eventually succumbed to Dick's charms, in spite of his vows, it is interesting to read his reaction to him:

> Americans lack background [he wrote in his diary after less than a fortnight alone with Dick], light and shade, tradition – at all events from our point of view. They have all the goods in the shop-window – always: and some of the goods are so flimsy and some are not goods at all, but rather resemble the empty boxes which chocolate makers supply for window-dressing purposes.[58]

10. 'Love is the Test' (1921-1925)

And a few lines later he adds: 'Why is it so annoying when a person takes an intelligent interest in *everything*?' He found Dick's 'encyclopaedism' and his 'pontifical pronouncements on every subject under the sun ... irritating in the extreme'.[59]

Sassoon, who had encountered similar traits in another American, Louis Untermeyer, was more restrained in *his* diary, merely recording occasional visits to stay with 'R. Wood'. But as Theo noted, Sassoon was deeply smitten by Dick and spent many weekends with him, either in Cambridge or London. This may explain why he did not travel to the Continent at all in 1923, instead renting the whole of Tufton Street from the Turners in late September while they went to Italy.

By the following March, however, Sassoon was happy to leave England for a month in the South of France with Schuster, which suggests that his affair with Dick was over, or at least cooling. Certainly by 13 June 1924 he was 'worrying about Dick' and by the end felt in 'need of a new sexual adventure'.[60] This seems to have arrived, very conveniently, in the form of another young American, John Philbin, a friend of Schuster's. Philbin, who claimed to be a qualified mining engineer with a PhD from the University of California, arrived back in England in mid-June after a five-year absence in a poor financial state and came to stay at Bray, where he met Sassoon. (He had a charming tenor voice, which explains his attraction for Schuster.) In the same diary entry that refers to his need of a new sexual adventure, Sassoon also mentions Philbin. 'Sunburnt and wild-westerly', Philbin was physically very attractive, and his straitened circumstances added to his charms, since Sassoon 'like[d] to feel that [he could] help him'. That same summer he took Philbin to lunch at the Reform, tea with Nellie Burton and dinner at Tufton Street with the Turners and Hodgsons, as well as a visit to Rivers's friend Henry Head and his wife, and to his mother at Weirleigh, all rituals usually gone through with lovers. He also invited Philbin on a tour of the West Country and, his greatest sign of approval, took him to meet Hardy and T.E. Lawrence. The most convincing indication of a physical involvement, however, is the fact that they shared a hotel room at Bournemouth, after which Sassoon tore a page out of his diary.

It was during his tour of the West Country with Philbin that Sassoon was inspired to write one of the few poems of this period he believed showed his true poetic voice, 'Stonehenge':

> What is Stonehenge? It is the roofless past;
> Man's ruinous myth; his uninterred adoring
> Of the unknown in sunrise cold and red;
> His quest of stars that arch his doomed exploring ...
>
> (CP, p. 179)

But Philbin turned out to be 'rather a fraud', according to a disillusioned

151

Sassoon, and the relationship was short-lived. By late summer 1924 he is describing himself as a man suffering from 'sexual starvation' and by mid-September his frustration has reached the point where he finds himself attracted to almost every passably handsome youth he sees.[61] Another torn-out page in his September diary and a poem written a day later suggest that he is prepared to settle for at least one casual sexual encounter on a trip round the Midlands that month.[62] Other passing attractions appear to have included the poet Edward O'Brien, judging from his reaction to O'Brien's subsequent marriage to the novelist Romer Wilson.[63]

Though Sassoon expressed a wish to write a *Madame Bovary* of 'sexual inversion', he was not bold enough to leave an explicit account of his sexual adventures,[64] and it is significant that his diary for 1924, when his sexual frustration was at its height, has a disproportionately large number of pages torn out of it. The most intriguing of these is his destruction of entries from early October 1924 to the middle of February 1925, the period covering one of his most painful affairs of all, with Ivor Novello.

Novello had first achieved fame with his wartime song 'Keep the Home-fires Burning' and, ironically, Sassoon's initial response to him was one of intense dislike: 'Someday I will kill the man who wrote keep the home fires burning,' he had told Dent in 1916.[65] When he actually met Novello at Eddie Marsh's in January 1919, he was again critical, though at the same time acknowledging the young Welshman's talents. Partly because Sassoon identified him with Marsh, for whom Novello had become a substitute Rupert Brooke, he already regarded him as highly superficial. And when he encountered the young actor filming in Venice in October 1922, he was positively rude to him.[66] Philipp, who had witnessed the occasion, was shocked at his lack of manners, but Sassoon had justified his behaviour by arguing that he 'despise[d]' Novello and 'all he st[ood] for'.[67]

This made his infatuation with Novello, when they met for the third time in September 1924, all the more unexpected. He had been invited to tea on the 28th by the actress Constance Collier, a friend of both Marsh and Schuster. She was also close to Novello, having only recently helped him adapt his current hit, *The Rat*, from a film script to a stage play. (He, of course, played the male lead.) It was, therefore, quite natural that she should invite him to meet Sassoon, whom she had got to know that summer at Schuster's. They had sat next to each other at dinner and he may even have confided to her his need of a new sexual adventure. (There seems no reason, otherwise, for him to have torn a page out of his diary at this point.) For she not only invited Novello to meet him but another equally attractive and even younger actor, Glen Byam Shaw.

In the event Sassoon, unwisely, chose Novello, who promptly pitched him into an 'unblinking little hell', an 'inferno' far worse than that created by Glenn Hunter in New York.[68] Spoilt by his doting mother and early success and inordinately proud of his Italianate good looks, Novello deliberately cultivated a charm which concealed his essential egotism. Adored by men and women alike, he seems to have satisfied his sexual appetite with very little concern for the person involved. Though Sassoon destroyed the details of their affair, he did tell a close friend later that Novello had 'outraged and betrayed [his] decent feelings to an incredible degree'.[69]

After the first raptures of the meetings in Novello's dressing room and supper at one of his favourite restaurants, the Savoy Grill, had subsided, Sassoon began to think of him as 'something very inhuman'.[70] Sitting in the 'blinding glare of unshaded bulbs and mirrors, applying Californian sun-burn to his successful countenance', he struck Sassoon as nothing but a 'stage-self', a 'victim of his own vanity and weakness', yet he was unable to extricate himself from the affair, appearing to derive a masochistic pleasure from it. He was still suffering intensely when he went to see Novello in his dressing room for the last time alone at the beginning of May 1925. There is little doubt that it was Novello who ended the relationship and, though Sassoon denied feeling bitter about him, his subsequent references are very resentful indeed.

Sassoon perhaps found his relationship with Novello so humiliating because, for once, he was not the one in control. His usual advantages of age, fame and money did not apply.[71] Instead of 'doling out' allowances to a much younger man who worshipped him, he found himself expected to do the worshipping. He had no real power over Novello.

By late February 1925, the affair was over. Sassoon was ready to accompany Schuster to the South of France for a month again and to spend most of the summer at Bray recuperating. He even arranged to meet Gabriel during his stay in France and to take him on a tour of the West Country in mid-July.[72]

One reason for Sassoon's apparent change of heart towards Gabriel, apart from needing balm for his bruised ego, was the acquisition of a car in June 1924. By 1925 he had started to explore England in it and welcomed the chance of doing so with a companion. He was given the car, a new Gwynne Eight, by his friend Richmond Temple, who, as public relations consultant and director of the Savoy Hotel Company, received many generous but sometimes unwanted gifts. Temple thought that a car might help Sassoon 'to get more fresh air', which proved to be the case.[73] Once Anzie had taught Sassoon to drive, he left his cramped flat in Tufton Street as often as possible. And when he stayed at Bray, he was no longer dependent on Anzie to ferry him around but could come and go as he pleased.

He relished his new-found freedom and spent the summer of 1924 exploring various parts of the country with Philbin. Once he had gained confidence, he started driving alone. Turning up for weekends with H.G. Wells in Essex, Ottoline at Garsington or even the Hardys in Dorset, for instance, he would proudly offer rides in his little two-seater. Sometimes an unsuspecting friend would accept, though rarely a second time.

The problem was that Sassoon, however physically co-ordinated on the hunting field or cricket pitch, was hopeless with anything mechanical, a curious anomaly in someone related to the well-known engineering Thornycrofts. Even the telephone 'annihilated' him, according to one friend.[74] It had something to do with a general resistance to change, stemming partly from a deep reverence for the past, which also informed his attitude toward poetic techniques. Cars were a particular challenge and several witnesses have suggested that he drove them as though riding a horse.[75] Stories about his bad driving abound. His cousin Lettice, for example, said that it was a 'traumatic' experience to be driven by him.[76] She remembered replying meaningfully, when he asked her during one drive whether she liked cars, that she 'wasn't frightened that they wouldn't start, but that they wouldn't stop'.[77] Even T.E. Lawrence, who hardly knew the meaning of fear, was, by Sassoon's own account, terrified after only five minutes of his driving; 'my methods of turning from side roads into main roads were abrupt in those days', Sassoon added by way of explanation.[78]

'Abrupt' seems the right word to describe his driving. According to Dennis Silk, he never gave signals of any sort and, like most bad drivers, always blamed the other person for his numerous accidents. On one occasion he turned right into his drive without warning just as someone was overtaking him. Both cars got stuck in the gateway together and Silk remembers Sassoon reporting indignantly that the irate other driver had called him a 'b--y f-----g t--t': 'I wasn't having that [Sassoon told Silk, earnestly] and I said "Look here, sir" and I shook my fist at him and said "You can have it if you want it!" I think he'd been drinking.'[79] He was prosecuted on at least one occasion and only with great difficulty managed to have the charge changed from 'dangerous driving' to a lesser charge and to retain his licence.[80]

On his very first drive alone Sassoon had run into a dog-cart, then the next day knocked down a cyclist, but he seemed unaware of how dangerous he was and loved driving. Less than a month after being given the Gwynne he noted that his 'increasing confidence' made him 'genuinely enjoy the car. It makes me feel more human and less pathological. It is a substitute for my hunter, I suppose.'[81] Not only that but a car was also, he told Graves, 'much less trouble than a horse and much more mobile'.[82]

His preference for horses would return in due course; the Gwynne would be replaced first by a Morris Oxford, which he promptly crashed, then by a Chrysler, a Packard and, finally, by a Humber Snipe 80 Drophead Coupé; but the driving would remain completely erratic. Only in the era before the compulsory driving test would he have been allowed a licence at all.

In a curious way his car became an element in his love life in the mid-twenties. Just as he showed his renewed interest in Gabriel in the summer of 1925 by inviting him on a tour of the West Country, so when, a few months later, he started what was to become one of the most meaningful relationships of his life, the young man concerned was duly invited on a similar trip.

The only thing which worried Sassoon about owning a car was the fear of becoming dependent on material things, in his efforts of 'continually trying to escape from acquisitiveness' during this period.[83] He hoped to achieve this by sharing the Gwynne with the Turners, but suspected that, once he started to enjoy driving, his resolution might crumble. And, in any case, the situation at Tufton Street had begun to deteriorate badly by mid-1924.

*

Sassoon's first serious dissatisfaction with Tufton Street had started in late 1923, when he had rented the whole house from the Turners for several months during their visit to Italy. Much as he enjoyed this period of 'unmolested piano-playing, and using the only nice (though dark) room' in the 'poky' house, he was conscious that it must soon end and that he would be forced to revert to a routine of 'club-lunches and sitting upstairs listening to the Turners playing my piano'.[84] To his dismay he began to 'feel like a cuckoo in a linnet's nest, anxious to elbow them out of it'.[85] Back in his own rooms in December they seemed to him even more cramped by comparison. And he could scarcely fail to remember that it was his own money, still not repaid, which had bought the house originally.

Another cause for irritation was the arrival of a permanent fair on a piece of nearby waste ground in January 1924. The blaring of the hurdy-gurdy organ went on till midnight, adding considerably to the noise of tipsy singing and loud music from down the street, the booming of Big Ben and even the Turners' conversation below or above him in the poorly insulated house. Concentration became almost impossible. 'London life doesn't suit me,' he wrote to Graves later that year, but it was dark, noisy Tufton Street he meant.[86]

During the Turners' absence he had been able to eat at home, waited on happily by the one servant, Mrs Binks. Since he worked late, slept late and combined breakfast with lunch, she had a much lighter workload than usual, coming in only half a day, and was not unnaturally sorry to see the Turners arrive back. Sassoon suspected that she hoped to lure him away from Tufton Street to rooms of his own, but, if so, she did not remain long enough to succeed. By trying to make him comfortable, he believed, she brought about her own dismissal in February 1924 as well as creating a 'rift' in his relations with the Turners, who resented the extra time she devoted to him. Waited on all his life, even in the army, Sassoon could not understand the fuss: 'I never have more than one meal a day cooked here, and that's only a bit of fish and some coffee.'[87] But it was one meal more than the original agreement and with Mrs Binks's departure it stopped.

By spending most of spring and summer at Bray, Sassoon survived 1924 at Tufton Street, but by 1925 he knew he must leave what had become for him 'a poisoned house'.[88]

Turner himself, the main inducement for Sassoon to live there in the first place, had become the one problem he could not ignore. Since their successful holiday together in 1922, when Sassoon had paid for Turner to accompany him to Munich, their relationship had slowly deteriorated. To begin with Sassoon had been critical only of Turner's work but by October 1923 he was finding fault with the man himself, noting, for example, his slovenliness, so much at odds with his own 'cat-like ... enjoyment of neatness'.[89] And by April 1925 everything Turner 'says, does, and is' irritated him.[90] He also grew resentful at having given money to Turner, which he suspected made Turner resentful too. The Turners' financial obligation to him certainly exacerbated the situation, especially after Turner lost his job at the *Daily Herald* in late 1923.

Sassoon's hostility to Turner did not extend to his wife, whom he continued to admire. It was for Delphine's sake, he told Ottoline, that he tried to forget his resentment against her husband. He and Ottoline had been outraged when Walter, having visited Garsington regularly with his wife since 1920, turned up suddenly in 1925 with his current mistress, Cynthia Noble, especially since they believed he was only interested in her money. Though they successfully thwarted Turner's plans, Sassoon could not forgive him for his 'unpardonable cruelty' towards the long-suffering Delphine. He was also antagonized by Turner's lack of gratitude towards Ottoline, who had treated him with great generosity. Turner's 'insulting caricature' of her in his skit *The Aesthetes* had not been published by 1925 and Ottoline herself had not yet seen it but he had already shown it to Sassoon, who was deeply shocked.[91] It was for acts like this that Sassoon had christened Turner 'Conundrum', though Osbert Sitwell's nickname, 'Bad-Turn', might have been more appropriate.[92]

Even at this point – early August 1925 – Sassoon was prepared to try again. When Ottoline told him that the Turners would be quite happy if only they had a car, he gave them the money to buy one, though he made it clear that it was for Delphine's sake. (His self-righteous comments on Walter's bad driving make diverting reading.) And he still felt obliged to remain at Tufton Street. When friends like the Cambridge clergyman Cyril Tompkinson urged him to go and live comfortably by himself, he pointed out that if he did so the Turners would also have to leave their house, which they might then be unable to sell or let.

So things might have continued for some time longer, had it not been for Graves's intervention in mid-August. Graves had been staying at Sutton Veny in Somerset with his father-in-law, William Nicholson, who told him that the impecunious Turners were 'coming down in a car'.[93] Greatly surprised, Graves suggested that Sassoon must have bought it for them, but Nicholson rejected the idea, since Turner had told him that 'S.S.

was very mean, and never helped anyone unless it helped him to dominate them'.[94] According to Nicholson, via Graves, he had talked of Sassoon 'with great dislike' and had expressed a 'strong desire' that Sassoon should 'cease to live in *his* house' (my italics).[95] Most provokingly of all, Turner had complained that Sassoon annoyed him by playing *his* piano.

Had Sassoon not been already incensed by Turner's treatment of both Delphine and Ottoline, and sufficiently recovered from the war to contemplate independence, he might not have accepted Graves's report quite so readily. And had Graves not been jealous of Sassoon's close friendship with Turner, he might not have repeated the conversation in the first place. Delphine, who wrote a long letter of explanation to Sassoon as soon as she heard of Graves's action, believed that he was either very 'clumsy and literal-minded' or that he was deliberately trying to destroy the relationship between Sassoon and Turner.[96] Graves's biographer, Richard Perceval Graves, argues that his uncle was particularly 'anxious' about his own affairs at the time and simply being 'tactless'.[97]

Jealousy and a lack of tact were almost certainly behind Nellie Burton's actions too when, a few days later, she related her own bit of gossip to Sassoon: that Turner had told Romer Wilson that Sassoon had prevented him and Delphine from 'ever going away when they wanted to'.[98]

The result was immediate. Sassoon decided finally to leave Tufton Street, though felt unable to tell Turner so directly. Instead he asked Ottoline to explain to Delphine that he 'wanted to live more comfortably' and that he was 'deeply hurt' by Turner's reported remarks.[99] In spite of Delphine's eloquent defence – that there was something 'fine and worthwhile' in her husband under his surface roughness – Sassoon stuck to his decision and by late August was looking for other rooms.[100]

However scornful he was of most women, he relied on them heavily and the next one to help was Nellie Burton, who joined Ottoline in a search for new rooms. Delighted by his decision, they set out to find him something as different from his small, dark, noisy rooms in Tufton Street as possible. But a flat at 41 Mecklenburgh Square on the fringes of Bloomsbury fell through in late September, as did one opposite Kensington Gardens at 39 Queen's Gate a few days later. Moving slightly westwards, Sassoon next looked at rooms in Lexham Gardens in mid-October. (He had become slightly more familiar with the area when Gabriel had moved to 22 Peel Street in 1922.) But they, too, proved unsatisfactory and by late October he was beginning to despair. The Turners were actively trying to let the whole of Tufton Street and he might soon be homeless.

His anxieties about house-hunting were made worse by a growing sense of hopelessness over his love life. His long series of unsatisfactory relationships had finally made him realize that he would find 'no happiness or serenity through "falling in love" with people because they look nice'.[101] Reading J.R. Ackerley's play *The Prisoners of War* in April 1925, when he was still suffering intensely from his humiliating affair with Ivor Novello, he identified closely with Ackerley's tormented homosexual officer:

> And all today [he wrote in his diary for 22 April 1925] I have carried about with me an inward sense of homesickness for that land where I would be – that Elysium, forever deluding me with its mirage in the desert of my frustrated and distorted desires. I know that real happiness cannot be created by any sensual Elysium. But even a ramshackle Elysium is alluring, when the discredited oasis beckons me toward its disenchanted groves, though I know that the reality would leave me desolate and dissatisfied.[102]

Only six months after writing these words he was to embark on an affair which would bring him nearer to that Elysium than any he had yet experienced. It would also, in more prosaic terms, provide him with a new flat.

11

'My Glorious Angel'
(1925-1927)

> I have felt lately a new sense of proportion as regards the trivial details of
> life (which used to harass me so incessantly). My life seems to be simpler in
> construction and I realise how few are the details which are worth troubling
> about. This is an internal harmony which I have been striving for since 1918
> ... Or is it merely the complacency of middle-age?
>
> (Diary entry for 16 December 1925)

The main reason for Sassoon's optimism in December 1925, Glen Byam
Shaw, was only twenty when Sassoon started an affair with him in
October that year. Yet Glen was in many ways the wisest and most
grounded of all Sassoon's lovers and their two years together were to be
among the happiest, calmest and most productive of Sassoon's life. As
creative as Gabriel, if not more so, Glen suffered from neither his dissoluteness nor his lack of discipline. And though less well-educated than
Philipp, he had a natural intelligence and a more genuine thirst for culture
that delighted Sassoon. He was also tall, slim and good-looking.

They had been introduced in September 1924 by Constance Collier, an
old friend of the Byam Shaw family who supported Glen in his efforts to
establish himself as an actor. Had Ivor Novello not also been there on the
same occasion, Sassoon might well have escaped a year of misery and
frustration. For he had found Glen attractive from the start. Following
their first meeting, when Glen had revealed his ignorance about music,
Sassoon had immediately sent him a slightly flirtatious postcard: 'How
green of you' it opened, in green ink, 'not to have heard of Benvenuto
Cellini.' Then, in red ink, 'This is a red-letter day for you because you now
know he was ... etc., etc.'[1]

The jokiness appealed to Glen, who had a similar sense of humour. He
loved describing his actor-manager Fagan's 'huge' wife declaiming, as the
ethereal Oberon in *A Midsummer Night's Dream*, 'I am invisible', and was
delighted when Sassoon's car stuck in reverse on one occasion and had to
be driven down a street backwards. He was also greatly impressed by
Sassoon's stature as a writer, which ranked in his mind with the Russian
giants, Tolstoy and Chekhov.

Unfortunately, he was about to leave on tour when Sassoon's first

159

postcard arrived in late September 1924 and failed to respond to it. Nor did he answer a second, sent after Sassoon's affair with Novello had reached its sorry end. But when a third arrived, posted by Sassoon on his thirty-ninth birthday from the Gloucester Music Festival, Glen was sufficiently intrigued to ask Constance for Sassoon's address. And when Sassoon arrived back in Tufton Street on 10 October 1925, he found a card from Glen waiting.

It is clear from Glen's reply that Sassoon had also tried to reach him by telephone during the summer, a further sign of his interest in the young actor. Glen now seemed equally anxious to meet him and, even more gratifyingly, to read his poems. It was a promising start. But Sassoon, diffident at the best of times and especially so when dealing with someone young enough to be his son, was so vague in his invitation to dinner the following week, that Glen failed to turn up. It would be 20 October before they finally met again, more than a year after their initial encounter.

Once Glen realized his mistake over the first invitation, he had written to apologize, wanting to be reassured that Sassoon did not think he had acquired Novello's heartless 'method of treating his friends'.[2] Novello was a subject close to both their hearts, Glen having also suffered an emotional bruising at his hands, and he formed one of the main topics of conversation at their first dinner. 'It made me rather extra bitter about Ivor', Glen wrote to Sassoon the next day, 'when I heard how bloody he was to you.'[3]

Even more importantly from Sassoon's viewpoint, Glen asked for his help. Though he loved acting, which he had taken up professionally on leaving Westminster School at eighteen, he was finding actors extremely philistine and did not want to 'get like them'.[4] He knew something of art, since his father, Byam Shaw, had been a painter and run an art school until his death in 1919. But he felt almost entirely ignorant about literature and music.

Sassoon was delighted to oblige. It was reassuring to be regarded as a 'great poet', especially at a time when he felt poetry had deserted him, and a genuine pleasure to share his enthusiasms with an intelligent and imaginative young disciple. He responded at once with a book of his own poems, together with a photograph.

Best of all, it was clear from Glen's thank-you letter that he had enjoyed Sassoon's company as much as Sassoon had his. 'I felt so awfully peaceful and happy when I came home yesterday,' he wrote, unknowingly echoing Sassoon's own diary response to the event: 'Glen Byam Shaw to dinner. Very successful evening. He seems nice and straightforward, full of charm and good sense. He came back here 10-12, and I showed him various books and manuscripts. He left me with a feeling of peace.'[5]

The evening also had a practical outcome. It had seemed quite natural when they arrived back at Tufton Street from the Reform for Sassoon to refer to his increasingly pressing problem of finding alternative accommodation and Glen knew of possible rooms near his home at 18 Campden Hill

Gardens. A family friend, the painter Harold Speed,[6] had converted the top floor of his house at 23 Campden Hill Square into a flat which was still, Glen believed, empty.

Less than a week later Sassoon was viewing Speed's flat. Having meantime spent another 'happy' evening with Glen, he was already predisposed towards it, since it was only three minutes' walk away from Glen, his 'bosom's best friend'.[7] (Whether he was deterred by the fact that his 'ex-bosom friend', Gabriel, lived only a few hundred yards in the other direction across Holland Park Avenue he does not say, though he does note the fact.)[8]

Campden Hill Square rises steeply and No. 23, an elegant and spacious house, lies on the south side at its highest point. It struck Sassoon at once as the very opposite of cramped, dank Tufton Street, jammed in below street level. Instead of neighbouring tenements, the top floor of 23 looked out over the treetops of the gated central garden below, towards distant church spires. It has a 'superb view', Sassoon wrote to Graves after his first visit and, if he could not 'write an epic at that height', he told Glen, he was a very poor poet indeed.[9] The 'early morning mystery of that landscape of roofs and chimneys' would come to seem a particularly 'wonderful thing – peaceful beyond words'.[10]

In fact he wrote at least two poems based specifically on the view that, though hardly epics, suggest that his move to Campden Hill Square inspired a return to nature in his work. Looking down from his 'silent-soliloquied windows of thought' on the 'sun-slanted green of the Square' returned him to an awareness of the natural world that he had loved as a child and young man. It was an influence which would make itself strongly felt in his next collection of poems.[11]

Even on the top attic floor, the rooms at 23 Campden Hill Square were far larger than at Tufton Street, especially after Speed had agreed to remove the partition wall between the two front ones. 'It will make a perfect "apartment"', Sassoon reported to Glen, 'with stacks of room for piano, poet, armchair and an occasional visitor (from C[ampden] Hill Gardens, I hope).'[12]

Having just bought a new Bechstein, space for a grand piano was extremely important to Sassoon. So too was the fact that the flat was self-contained, with a bedroom, bathroom and small kitchen at the back. Instead of having to take all his meals out, he could look forward to eating at least one of them at home, as he had at Tufton Street in the Turners' absence. A Mrs Dingle was to replace Mrs Binks (could two domestics really have had such Dickensian names?) and supply a brunch of sole and coffee at 11 o'clock, an hour after Sassoon woke up.[13] It was a routine which would allow him time to play the piano and write some of his many letters before setting out on his daily walk. More like a marathon by modern standards, this would often last from two o'clock till five and usually take him across Kensington Gardens and Hyde Park to Mayfair, where he continued to buy his special Dunhill tobacco and Earl Grey tea.[14] If he was dining at the Reform, he would stay on in the area for tea, either at Nellie Burton's or the club itself. But more often than not he would walk all the way back to Campden Hill for dinner at one of the nearby hotels. A creature of habit, the move would shake him out of some of his most hallowed rituals but he quickly formed new ones.

On his first visit to 23 Campden Hill Square Sassoon had been gratified to learn that the previous owner, J.M. Barrie, had written *Peter Pan* there, the idea of 'the lost boy' in that play having been inspired by Barrie's predecessors in the house, the Llewellyn-Davieses, whose son had died tragically young.[15] Barrie's success with *Peter Pan* seemed a reassuring literary precedent. There were, however, a few disadvantages. The steep climb to the top floor, though no problem for someone as fit as himself, was something he felt obliged to alert his older visitors about. (He warned Sir Henry Newbolt, for example, when inviting him to tea in 1927, that he would have to climb fifty-two stairs to reach his flat.) And, a romantic at heart, he much preferred coal to the gas fires Speed had installed.

His first visit also alerted him to another possible deterrent, the character of his landlord. Speed, who struck Sassoon as a *Punch* caricature of an artist with his beard, pipe and blue smock, greeted him with ominous effusiveness, insisting that Sassoon first inspect his paintings before allowing him to see the flat. Speed's views of the rocks and streams of the Lake District seemed to his prospective tenant merely 'competent and conventional' and he was far more diverted by his breezy remark: 'I think I shall throw in a few nymphs.' (Edith Sitwell, who later received a similar reception from Speed on her way up to have tea with Sassoon, referred to him simply as 'the nymph-thrower'.)[16] Speed's greatest faults in Sassoon's eyes were his snobbishness – his commission to paint *Viscount* Grey was quickly mentioned – his bumptiousness – Sassoon's uncle, Sir Hamo Thornycroft, was dismissed condescendingly as a 'wonderful man for his age' – and his anti-socialist views, which made Sassoon identify more closely with socialism than he had for some time.[17]

He could only hope that Speed was 'sufficiently commonplace and complacent' to be no trouble to him.[18] For at a rent of £150 a year he was ready to overlook most drawbacks, rejoicing in the thought of being 'safely detached from Turner and his gloomy house and heroic wife'.[19] Moving into Campden Hill Square, an event intimately linked in his mind with his closer acquaintance with Glen, was, he believed, a 'turning-point' in his life.[20] And the 'emotional tranquillity' he would feel for at least the first two of his six years' tenancy there, was a reflection of his 'happy experience' with Glen.[21]

It seemed fitting, therefore, that his move to Campden Hill should coincide with Glen's return from a season at the Oxford Playhouse.[22] This had started in late October, shortly after their first dinner, but it had taken Speed six weeks to have the partition wall demolished and numerous bookshelves installed, so that Sassoon had had to stay on at Tufton Street until 29 November. And when it came to it, leaving Turner's gloomy house was not quite so joyful as he had anticipated. Writing up his diary 'positively for the last time' in his tiny living room, he thought back on the less negative aspects of his five years' stay. It was there that he had finally learnt to live alone, away from his mother and Weirleigh. He had also written most of *Recreations* and *Lingual Exercises* there, completing the collection of *Satirical Poems* he had first planned in 1920.[23] And once he had found alternative accommodation, Turner did not seem nearly so impossible, in fact Sassoon would voluntarily spend Christmas with him and Delphine at Garsington a month later.

Furthermore, he had loved and grown part of his room, as his nostalgic 'Farewell to a Room', written a week before his departure, shows. It is a poem which anticipates the change of style his change of situation would help develop, a move away from the detached, ironic tone he had cultivated in *Satirical Poems* to a more meditative, inward-looking verse:

> Room, while I stand outside you in the gloom,
> Your tranquil-toned interior, void of me,
> Seems part of my own self which I can see ...
>
> Light, while I stand outside you in the night,
> Shutting the door on what has housed so much,
> Nor hand, nor eye, nor intellect could touch, –
> Cell, to whose firelit walls I say farewell,
> Could I condense five winters in one thought,
> Then might I know my unknown self and tell
> What our confederate silences have wrought.
>
> (CP, p. 179)[24]

In spite of such evident nostalgia, it was finally with a sense of relief and some excitement that Sassoon left Tufton Street. After a few days with his Treasury friend, Meiklejohn, at 22 Connaught Square and a weekend at Oxford with Glen, he installed himself in his new flat on 7 December 1925. The motherly Nellie, he told Ottoline, 'flying to and fro with sticks and straws and scraps of moss in her beak', had saved one of her favourite chicks all the usual 'bother' of moving, 'bless her'.[25]

Nellie was also his first guest, having tea with him the same day; and Glen, just back from Oxford, the second. He and Sassoon celebrated both the move and his return with dinner at the Reform that same evening, retiring to his new flat afterwards. After two more evenings with Glen, both of which ended at Campden Hill Square, Sassoon could write gratefully in his diary: 'I am being compensated for much unhappiness in the past.'[26]

There is no doubt that Glen made Sassoon very happy. Yet it was a happiness which depended, curiously, on his frequent absences, either at

Oxford or on tour. Sassoon needed complete solitude to work, as well as time to savour his emotions. (He referred to 'wallowing' in his new rooms.)[27] And the pattern he established for himself in Glen's absence, of a day virtually free of human contact, goes some way to explaining his extraordinary creative productivity at Campden Hill Square. His need to be alone, yet his craving for a lasting relationship, was a problem which dominated his life after the war. One of the most perfect poems he wrote during this time centres on this crucial subject and though it has already been quoted in the introduction, I make no apology for repeating it here:

> '*When I'm alone*' – the words tripped off his tongue
> As though to be alone were nothing strange.
> '*When I was young*,' he said; '*when I was young … .*'
>
> I thought of age, and loneliness, and change.
> I thought how strange we grow when we're alone,
> And how unlike the selves that meet, and talk,
> And blow the candles out, and say good-night.
> *Alone* … The word is life endured and known.
> It is the stillness where our spirits walk
> And all but inmost faith is overthrown.
>
> (CP, p. 180)[28]

Sassoon himself believed that 'Alone' was one of the 'most successful poems' he ever wrote.[29] 'I value it', he told Dame Hildelith Cumming in 1964, 'because it was the first of my post-war poems in which I discovered my mature mode of utterance (what I call "my cello voice").'[30] It seemed to him in retrospect that he had never written a truer line than the eighth: '*Alone* … The word is life endured and known.'

Glen was not just a negative blessing, however, merely someone who allowed Sassoon freedom to work. He also brought a number of positive things to the relationship. While there was undeniably an element of the master-disciple syndrome between them – Glen almost certainly found in Sassoon the father-figure Sassoon himself had looked for – Glen gave as much as he received. And though Sassoon generally preferred the position of control that 'giving' allowed, the younger man's tact and sympathy were such that Sassoon, for once, was able to accept what he offered.

Glen's most immediate gift was to renew Sassoon's idealistic view of love, which had been badly damaged since his first idyllic venture into the world of sex with Gabriel in 1918. Sassoon's description of Glen's visit on 11 December 1925, for example, two days before his twenty-first birthday, suggests an elevated experience very different from his feelings of humiliation over Novello: 'So my new room is being blessed with happiness that fills it brimful with peace. I tell myself that this happiness has a quality unlike anything I have known before … *Thank God for him.*' [31] Glen, he believed, had made this happiness possible by his simplicity and sincerity, as well as an instinctive capacity for avoiding misunderstandings. And he would continue to maintain, long after their affair was over, that Glen was the only friend who really understood him.[32]

Glen also made Sassoon more relaxed and far more tolerant for a time, and not just with himself. When Sassoon visited the Graveses, just before they left for Cairo in November 1925, for instance, instead of finding it the usual strain, he felt 'very peaceful and happy'.[33] More remarkably he even wrote to Nancy Graves asking her to forgive him for all his 'cussedness' in the past and to allow him 'to try and be a good friend again'.[34] Glen's own equable nature enabled him to dispel the 'demons' which accumulated round Sassoon in his long periods of solitude and self-analysis.[35]

Having always looked more youthful than his years, Sassoon had found his recent thirty-ninth birthday, with its threat of a fortieth, a depressing experience and the eighteen years' age gap between himself and Glen might have made this worse. But Glen's boyish enthusiasm sent Sassoon back in time, making him feel young again. On giving him a driving lesson in the Gwynne, for instance, he had felt rejuvenated by Glen's childlike delight. Their shared jokes were often reminiscent of the game Sassoon had played with his best sporting friend, Gordon Harbord, in his early twenties. Only instead of Surtees, it was *The Diary of a Nobody* or O'Casey's controversial play *Juno and the Paycock* that supplied the humour. Sassoon became Jackie Boyle to Glen's Joxer Daley and tags from these and various other sources permeated their communications. ('Freeze on to yer collar' was a particular favourite during difficult situations.)

Sassoon had first seen *Juno and the Paycock* with Meiklejohn a few days before Glen's return from Oxford.[36] It was his seventh visit to the theatre in six weeks, clearly an attempt to draw nearer to the young actor. Only two days after their first dinner, instead of his more usual concert or opera, he had gone to *The Seagull* and Chekhov had quickly become a favourite playwright for both of them. Some of Glen's best roles in the future would be in Chekhov: Treplev in *The Seagull*, Trophimof in *The Cherry Orchard* and Baron Tusenbach in *The Three Sisters*.

Sassoon would always be grateful to Glen for his reintroduction to an area of culture that had not interested him greatly. He was thrilled when Glen introduced him to one of theatre's legendary figures, Ellen Terry, with whom they spent a whole weekend in 1927.[37] And some of their happiest times together later on would be at Stratford-upon-Avon during Glen's directorship of the Royal Shakespeare Company.[38]

When Sassoon first saw Glen act at the Oxford Playhouse in the winter of 1925, he thought him surprisingly good, especially as Oswald in Ibsen's *Ghosts*, and encouraged him to go on acting when he grew doubtful. Glen, in turn, restored Sassoon's faith in himself as a poet. For the first time in years he found himself wanting to write, rather than forcing himself to do so. Appropriately, one of the first poems to emerge was inspired by Glen, an attempt to explain the difference he had made to Sassoon's solitary existence that ends: '… But you are with me in this voiceless air; / My hands are empty, but my heart is filled.'[39]

Another more successful poem almost certainly inspired by Glen, 'The Power and the Glory', was also the first to be written in his new room. Though it would be an oversimplification to equate Glen entirely with the 'glorious angel' of the piece and the direct cause of the poet's 'rapture', there is little doubt that the renewed energy, intensity and sense of direction in it sprang mainly from their relationship:

> *Let there be life*, said God. And what He wrought
> Went past in myriad marching lives, and brought
> This hour, this quiet room, and my small thought
> Holding invisible vastness in its hands.
>
> *Let there be God*, say I. And what I've done
> Goes onward like the splendour of the sun
> And rises up in rapture and is one
> With the white power of conscience that commands.
>
> *Let life be God* … What wail of fiend or wraith
> Dare mock my glorious angel where he stands
> To fill my dark with fire, my heart with faith?
> (CP, pp. 193-4)[40]

With the move to more peaceful surroundings, the 'quiet room' becomes a central motif of his later poetry, generally used to suggest the private self looking out on the world.[41]

When Sassoon was approaching the end of his experiments with social satire, he had written to Theo on 16 December 1924: 'I have done with verbal gymnastics in future. Being smart don't suit me, really. But it was a phase which had to be worked out, and now I can be as simple, sensuous, and passionate as I please.'[42] He had already started 'escaping' into a more lyrical mode in several poems,[43] some of which had appeared in the privately printed *Picture Show* and *Lingual Exercises*.[44] But he intended to exclude these from *Satirical Poems*, since he was saving them for a separate volume of 'Love and lyrical poems' which he had been planning as early as October 1923, *The Heart's Journey*.[45] As the title implies, this would be in the nature of an exploration into his own being.

To begin with, all the pieces meant for this collection were, according to him, 'idyllic poems' deriving from the 'old days in the garden at Weirleigh', which continued to be the 'background' of his every dream.[46] And though this would not remain true for the completed book, it is remarkable how many of the poems in *The Heart's Journey* hark back to his moments of revelation at dawn in his childhood garden.[47] One of the earliest to be written, 'Song, be my Soul', which opens the sequence, shows what a powerful epiphany that had been, symbolizing a purity which the 'way-worn traveller' has lost, together with the loves that he has 'wronged and slain'. Its simplicity both of form and language reinforces the sense of the poet trying to get back to his childhood innocence through the recreation of it in his verse, or 'song'. The soul, clothed appropriately in pure white, leads the narrator through a garden full of his past ghosts at the moment when dawn is about to break. The theme and the tone set the mood for the whole collection:

> Song, be my soul; set forth the fairest part
> Of all that moved harmonious through my heart;
> And gather me to your arms; for we must go
> To childhood's garden when the moon is low
> And over the leaf-shadow-latticed grass
> The whispering wraiths of my dead selves repass.
>
> Soul, be my song; return arrayed in white;
> Lead home the loves that I have wronged and slain:
> Bring back the summer dawns that banished night
> With distant-warbling bird-notes after rain. ...
> Time's way-worn traveller I. And you, O song,
> O soul, my Paradise laid waste so long.
>
> (CP, p. 175)

This quiet, meditative sonnet of surface simplicity but some technical complexity – the insistent repetition of soft consonants (s's, l's and w's), for example, underlines the ethereal quality of the scene – heralds a poetic voice quite different from the angry tones of the war satires. The subject matter might vary, from a consideration of physical passion,[48] great men of the past,[49] the death of someone known[50] or social problems,[51] to the power of music[52] or the state of solitude,[53] and there are even two further poems on the war,[54] but the reflective voice of the poet remains constant, giving unity to the volume.

Edith Sitwell, who found the 'quiet unfaltering beginning' of 'Song, be my Soul' very 'beautiful', believed that Sassoon had finally found his true voice.[55] Even Graves 'like[d it] extremely' at first, much to the surprise of Sassoon, who had expected him to condemn it as '1902 poetry' or 'only anthology stuff'.[56] (Graves was later to dismiss the whole volume as 'lace-Valentine vulgarity', a 'monument to [Sassoon's] emotional short-coming'.)[57] Sassoon himself had been so unsure about the poem initially that he had torn it up, before writing it out again from memory. He recognized it as a new direction in which he could only with difficulty find his way. Blunden, however, believed that it belonged to a 'Sassoonian tradition older than his vision of war's realities and his subordinate satires', arguing that he 'took the mystery of things upon him in the beautiful though tentative poems of his boyhood' and that he had 'always responded in verse of great grace and significance to "invisible vastness" immanent in quiet and solitude'.[58]

The poems in *The Heart's Journey*, however, are not simply echoes of the pantheistic poems of his youth. As Thorpe argues, there is a 'lucid sense' of being on 'the threshold of a new and more vital life', which 'cannot be entered on with the old innocence: that, once lost cannot be regained by shrugging off the knowledge and experience of harsh life already under-gone'.[59] It is this conflict which lies at the centre of the collection, as one of the most successful poems in it shows:

> In me, past, present, future meet
> To hold long chiding conference.
> My lusts usurp the present tense
> And strangle Reason in his seat.
> My loves leap through the future's fence
> To dance with dream-enfranchised feet.
>
> In me the cave-man clasps the seer,
> And garlanded Apollo goes
> Chanting to Abraham's deaf ear.
> In me the tiger sniffs the rose.
>   Look in my heart, kind friends, and tremble,
>   Since there your elements assemble.
> (CP, p. 178)[60]

The echo of Shelley's *Ozymandias* in the last two lines signals only one of a number of literary influences in this sequence. Cowper's homely imagery and his tranquil, fire-lit interiors appear side by side with verbal echoes from Shakespeare's sonnets, and Graves found at least two phrases from Housman's *Shropshire Lad* in 'Conclusion'. But the greatest single debt is to the seventeenth-century devotional poets, Vaughan in particular. One of Sassoon's own favourites in *The Heart's Journey* is a Vaughan-like meditation on his visit to the poet's grave.[61] His description of the 'simply graven stone' beside a river is followed, in the last eight lines of the sonnet, by an attempt to define Vaughan's greatness and his own debt to him in suitably homely terms:

> Here sleeps the Silurist; the loved physician;
> The face that left no portraiture behind;
> The skull that housed white angels and had vision
> Of daybreak through the gateways of the mind.
>   Here faith and mercy, wisdom and humility
>   (Whose influence shall prevail for evermore)
>   Shine. And this lowly grave tells Heaven's tranquillity.
>   And here stand I, a suppliant at the door.
> ('At the Grave of Henry Vaughan', CP, p. 190)

Like Vaughan, to whom Blunden and others have compared him, in this and later collections Sassoon is trying to 'see into the heart of things'.[62] And in setting out and reflecting on a possible correspondence between this world and another, he frequently resorts to images of flowers and light, as Vaughan and his fellow-mystics had done:

> A flower has opened in my heart ...
> What flower is this, what flower of spring,
> What simple, secret thing?
> It is the peace that shines apart,
> The peace of daybreak skies that bring
> Clear song and wild swift wing. ...
>
> (CP, p. 195)[63]

Sassoon's own comment on Vaughan – that he 'seldom wrote a perfected poem' – applies equally to his own poetry of this second period.[64] As with Vaughan, the intensity comes and goes, but at its best it is so full of what Sassoon found in Vaughan – 'radiant naturalness' – that it fully justifies his belief that *The Heart's Journey* was the 'strongest work' he produced in the twenties.[65] Most of his friends agreed with him. Apart from Blunden and Edith Sitwell's endorsements, he received lavish praise from Gosse, Nichols and, even more importantly to him, Hardy, Forster and T.E. Lawrence.

Reviews were slower in coming, since Crosby Gaige, the wealthy American connoisseur who first produced *The Heart's Journey* as a limited edition in 1927, did not send out review copies.[66] It was not until Heinemann published a trade edition in 1928 that they started to appear.[67] One of the first was by a poet Sassoon despised, Humbert Wolfe, and was so lavish in its praise that, to Sassoon's embarrassment, it boosted his sales dramatically.[68] Other equally enthusiastic critics followed, Blunden and Edith Sitwell among them.[69]

*

Though Glen inspired some of the finest poems in *The Heart's Journey*, whenever he reappeared in London from his current acting engagement, Sassoon would stop writing to be with him. On his first return from Oxford in December 1925, for instance, in addition to a round of dinners and plays, Sassoon treated him to a five-day tour of the West Country for what had become a statutory visit to Hardy, his equivalent of taking a partner home for parental approval.[70] He had taken Glen's request to be educated seriously and by the time they started their trip on 18 December Glen had begun to read in earnest. Apart from the *Oxford Book of English Poetry*, he was reading Hardy's novels. And together they had been to a dramatization of *Tess of the D'Urbervilles*.[71]

Glen was therefore particularly pleased to meet the author himself. For his part Sassoon was delighted by how well they got on together. 'No one has ever been sweeter to me than G[len]' he wrote after their second tea at Max Gate on 21 December. '[Hardy] was in good fettle; and our visits were perfect ... Can't write anything about such an experience as this.'[72]

Even the death of his uncle Hamo, which he saw announced in the *Evening Standard* on the second day of their journey, could not spoil what was an almost perfect trip.[73] But it formed a sad end to it as he set off from Max Gate in wet, windy weather on 22 December with Hardy's laurel wreath to his old friend Hamo in the back of the Gwynne. Parting from Glen in Oxford the next day, he hurried out to Garsington to borrow a black suit from Philip Morrell, then made his way sombrely to his uncle's funeral at Christ Church Cathedral.

Relieved that his mother had not come to Oxford for the 'desolate business', which signified for her even more than himself the end of an era, he drove to Garsington, where he spent Christmas.[74] After the excitement of his trip with Glen it seemed a tedious period, filled with too many people, too many card games and largely trivial talk, though it was cheered up by visits to Bridges, Masefield and the painter Gilbert Spencer, a recent acquaintance.[75]

Glen spent Christmas with his family, then left shortly afterwards to join Fagan's company for a tour of the provinces. So that, apart from occasional snatched meetings with him, Sassoon was left alone once more to write, happy in the knowledge of Glen's existence and anxious to see him again but undistracted by his actual presence. 'You must come and stay with me soon or I shall die,' Glen wrote to him from the Palace Theatre, Blackpool, in March 1926, but they both survived. And at the end of April Sassoon could happily anticipate him being back in London.

He was also looking forward to the appearance of *Satirical Poems*. Publication date was set for 29 April 1926 and Heinemann had arranged maximum publicity for it. In the event both Glen's return and the launch of the book were overtaken by the General Strike, which started on 3 May.[76]

Sassoon's sympathies, which had been with the miners in their strike of 1921, were now more divided. It was not simply that the strike had killed his book 'stone-dead', but that, though he still felt for the workers, he could not fully endorse the methods they had chosen. Nor did he think much would change, a prognosis that turned out to be largely correct. In a letter of 11 May 1926 to Ottoline, Sassoon refers to his own 'clouded apprehension' of the issues, but he is clearly critical of those who call the union men 'blackmailers'. He believes that Asquith, Grey and Balfour are failing to address the situation and describes Winston Churchill, with his 'Napoleon complex', as 'the main obstruction to the reasonable settlement which can and ought to be made at once'. Referring to the Prime Minister, Baldwin, as 'a champion blurter', he jokes about 'the Sorrows of Blurter'.[77]

The strike itself, one of the most controversial and significant events of the inter-war years, was (like the previous one) brought about by the miners, who faced severe cuts in their wages. The Government, in anticipation, had set up an 'Organization for the Maintenance of Supplies', so that when the three big unions struck – the miners first, followed by the railwaymen and transport workers – it was ready for the situation. Soldiers and a large body of volunteers were brought in to staff essential services and, though life did not proceed quite as usual, it carried on.

Sassoon's own part in the strike, though hardly dramatic, was more active than his waning socialist beliefs would lead one to expect. Osbert Sitwell, now on the best of terms with Sassoon, had been drawn into a behind-the-scenes attempt to settle the dispute through his connection with the Liberal peer Lord Wimborne and his wife.[78] At a lunch organized by Lady Wimborne on 8 May for some key political figures, Osbert resolved to make his own contribution to events. Following the Labour MP and railwaymen's leader J.H. Thomas's admission that the miners were ready for a compromise, he contacted Sassoon, whose experience on the *Daily Herald* he believed might help.

'Every moment of the next few crucial days', Osbert wrote in his detailed account of the strike, 'was filled and we spent a considerable time in interviewing those who might be of aid in our endeavour to organize support for the compromise.'[79] They now 'exerted and exhausted' every possible legitimate connection they had between them, including an unsympathetic Arnold Bennett and the editor of the *Daily Express*, Beverley Baxter, who was readier to listen. Considering that he had been virtually ambushed by Sassoon and Sitwell, who lay in wait for him as he returned to his Chelsea flat at two in the morning, and that (according to his own account) the 'gallant eccentric' Sassoon had been highly excitable, pacing his sitting room and 'brandishing his fists at the ceiling' while Osbert remained 'unnaturally calm', Baxter showed exemplary fairmindedness.[80] Having accepted that Sitwell's formula for peace was 'clear, sane and wise', he agreed to approach his paper's owner, Lord Beaverbrook, in the hope of being allowed to modify the *Express*'s 'bellicose' views of the strike.[81]

While Baxter shrewdly suspected that Sassoon was 'riding some tempest of the soul that would not give him peace' – his own guilt, perhaps, at having more or less abandoned his socialist principles – Sassoon admitted no such thing to himself in his diary, merely dismissing Baxter as an enemy of the unions. He was very surprised indeed when, contrary to his gloomy predictions, the strike came to an end on 12 May. And, unlike either Baxter or Sitwell, he did not believe that it had anything to do with 'the work of two poets'.[82]

The end of the strike brought the stranded Glen home from the North. But it was only a brief interval between tours and he was soon off again. For Sassoon, meantime, the summer stretched emptily ahead. He had resisted going to Bray again, partly because Campden Hill Square seemed even lovelier in late spring and there was no longer the urgent need to escape London as there had been at Tufton Street. And he had varied his routine a little by spending several weekends at Garsington and Whitsun at 'Painshanger', the home of Lord and Lady Desborough. (He agreed with Ottoline, who was a fellow-guest, that Lady Desborough would be a remarkable woman 'if only one could unlock all the lodge-gates, front-doors, Yale locks, Chubb safes, and fire-proof despatch boxes' of her guard.)[83] By the end of June, however, he was becoming bored.

It was in this mood that Ottoline persuaded him to join her husband Philip, their daughter Julian and herself for a tour of Europe. To begin with, knowing how badly Julian was getting on with her mother, Sassoon sensibly limited his commitment to three weeks. But when another friend of the Morrells, Robert ('Bob') Gathorne-Hardy, was added to the party, he suddenly found that he could manage the full six weeks.[84]

Sassoon himself had engineered Bob's inclusion on the trip. He had first met the 'plump young undergrad. with a monocle' at Garsington in July 1924 when Bob was only twenty-two.[85] Seeing him again in November 1925, he had described him to Ottoline as a 'dear creature'.[86] And by July 1926, while he agreed with her that Bob's friend and former fellow-under-graduate at Oxford Eddy Sackville-West 'would be a help' at managing her daughter on the trip, he thought it 'a pity we can't get Bob'.[87] When he saw Bob at the opera a few days later, he insisted that he had '*got* to come'.[88] 'He would make all the difference,' Sassoon told Ottoline; Bob was quickly included.[89]

The only drawback from Sassoon's viewpoint was that Bob's partner, Kyrle Leng, was also invited. The two younger men were already living together and when, on arrival at Versailles, it became clear to Kyrle that Bob was as 'mad about' Sassoon as Sassoon was about him, he decided to return home.[90] A close friend of Bob and Kyrle, Eardley Knollys, who talked to Kyrle at the time, said that he was 'very miserable ... Bob's relations with S.S. were such that it might mean a permanent split between Kyrle and Bob.'[91] Knollys was not sure whether Bob and Sassoon actually became lovers, but he did know that it was 'a very serious matter'.[92]

It was not a subject Bob himself could refer to directly when he came to edit Ottoline's memoirs for this period, but as his sister, Lady Anne Hill, points out, there is 'clearly a disguised reference to the whole thing in Bob's introduction'.[93] Referring (truthfully) to the party's 'air of difficulty and strained feelings', he pretended that this was solely because both the cars in which the group travelled, a Buick and a Packard, had started to go wrong.[94] He also pretended that Kyrle had always meant to return home when they reached Versailles and that his own decision to accom-pany him or not depended on whether the cars could be fixed. And he was being completely disingenuous when he wrote that 'the question somehow became involved with deeper feelings than so simple a situation would in ordinary times involve'.[95]

Of course it did, because his decision rested *not* on the health of the cars, but on Sassoon's response to Bob's evident desire to have an affair. Deeply smitten himself, Sassoon had found it very difficult to resist. 'I wanted you to stay with me,' he wrote to Bob; 'the thought was Paradise.' Only the sight of Kyrle's unhappy face, 'like the troubled face of my own good angel', he told Bob, had prevented him from succumbing.[96] (If, as seems likely, the reference here is partly to Glen, it is interesting to note that his 'glorious' angel has by this time become, less excitingly, 'good'.) Instead, and at the risk of sounding 'frightfully priggish', he talked of his own 'strict moral code'.[97] As his fortieth birthday approached he was more aware than ever of the importance of forming a permanent bond: 'I have lived long enough to know that such a relationship [as yours and Kyrle's] does not happen twice in life.' Eight restless years of flitting from one relationship to another had finally convinced him that 'the paradise of the spirit is the only one worth entering'.[98] He could no longer enjoy the paradise of the flesh 'with a light heart and blinded eyes'.[99]

It seemed a mature reaction, a sign that he was finally growing up. It was also a decision which enabled him to remain friends with Bob for the rest of his life. But his infatuation with Bob in the first place suggests that he was not fully satisfied by Glen, whom he deliberately misled about Bob's reasons for returning to England.[100] Perhaps the long periods apart, forced on them by Glen's profession, had weakened his initial intensity of feeling. Whatever the explanation, when the next serious temptation came along, Sassoon would not resist a second time.

Meanwhile, feeling like the 'Sorrows of Werther', he continued 'drearily' on with the Morrells across France and Italy to Venice, as Ottoline had wished.[101] He arrived back six weeks later, exhausted, ill, underweight, but surprisingly positive about the Morrells considering the strain of trying to 'lubricate the friction between mother and daughter'.[102]

His real problem had been his usual one, the 'longing for solitude' and the desire to 'soak up the places we inspect, without being obliged to echo ejaculations of delight'.[103] He even considered returning alone by train from Milan. Yet apart from a promise to read his poems to the Literary Society of University College, London, there seemed no compelling reason to go back to England at all – 'except to see my mother'.[104]

Fortunately, filial love triumphed and Sassoon returned with the Morrells on 11 September. For it was during a short visit to his mother only a week later that the idea of his prose classic, *Memoirs of a Fox-Hunting Man*, was conceived.

12

Memoirs of a Fox-Hunting Man: 'The Testament of my Youth'

A powerful, realistic modern novel full of gloom and grandeur and tragic truthfulness – such, I had hoped, was what I had it in me to create, could I but find release for my latent abilities. The central character would probably be a poet, whose romantic emotional adventures and soul-forging frustrations would be enacted in a cosmopolitan background populated by artistic and totally unsporting persons, most of them impressively preoccupied with the future of mankind and the acceleration of sweeping social reforms. Anyhow, my magnum opus was to be about Life, (with a large L) – .

(Extract from Sassoon's fourth, unpublished, volume of autobiography.)

No one was more surprised than Sassoon himself when *Memoirs of a Fox-Hunting Man*, his nostalgic *roman à clef* so different from the prose work he had envisaged, became an instant success. 'I don't know how I wrote the book,' he told his friend Tomlinson, 'and I don't know why it is a good book.'[1] So uncertain was he of its reception that he published it anonymously to begin with,[2] but it sold 15,000 copies in three months and continued to sell year after year.[3] It also won him the prestigious James Tait Black Memorial Prize in 1928 and the Hawthornden Prize in 1929.[4] Just as importantly the book would extend his appeal to include people who might find poetry intimidating but could enjoy a simple tale of a young boy, mad about horses and cricket, growing up in rural Kent, before being catapulted into the very different landscape of the First World War. It seems extraordinary that someone who had written nothing more ambitious in prose than a handful of indifferent short stories came to equal his heroes, Hardy and Meredith, in their successful transition from one genre to another. Relatively few writers in any language have managed to excel in two different mediums. What was it that led a well-known poet with no proven record in prose to turn to novel-writing at the age of forty?

Despite his disclaimer to Tomlinson, Sassoon had a number of theories about how he came to write *Fox-Hunting Man*. In fact he planned to devote almost an entire volume of autobiography to an analysis of its composition. And though this would remain unfinished and is still unpublished, we do have his detailed notes and comments on a subject which interested him as much as it does his admirers.

The first, and very pressing, 'condition' which led him to write *Fox-Hunting Man* was his age.[5] He had an almost 'superstitious' feeling about being forty, since he had often excused any unproductiveness in the past by quoting Robert Louis Stevenson: 'Everything in a writer's life is preparation for what he does when over forty.' The realization that he was 'in his prime' and in danger of wasting it was a powerful incentive.

Rivalry also entered into it. He freely admitted to some 'discomfort' at seeing his contemporaries producing successful books. He felt particularly threatened by Osbert Sitwell, who had also started his career as a poet yet produced his first novel, *Before the Bombardment*, in 1926 to great acclaim.

The most surprising of all Sassoon's 'conditions' for writing *Fox-Hunting Man*, at first glance, is 'the fact that [he'd] given up hunting in 1923 and hadn't been on a horse since'. But he was convinced that he could not have achieved the 'detachment' necessary to describe his hunting days if he had still been mixing with horsey people. In effect, hunting, at this stage in his life, had for a time become part of his past and, therefore, fit material for reminiscence.

For nostalgia lies at the heart of *Fox-Hunting Man*, as Sassoon's last 'condition' shows. The book, he claimed, was a direct result of a weekend spent with his mother at Weirleigh from 18 to 20 September and having tea with two childhood friends there, when he made 'the discovery of the pre-1914 past as being rich literary material'. Talking to the deceased Squire Marchant's daughters, Bessie and May, who were back in Matfield on a visit as he was, he had suddenly felt himself 'invaded by all the strangeness of the past'.[6] Sparked off by two living reminders of that past, the 'little world' of his hero George Sherston's boyhood began to 'shape itself with spectroscopic distinctness'. His own childhood began to take on a peculiar intensity, 'simply because it was no longer possible for people to live in that candle and oil lamp lit, telephoneless, unmotorised Arcadia'. It is nostalgia for this world which lights up *Fox-Hunting Man* from its first to its last page.

He started the same day on his attempt to recapture that past. But his first effort, two foolscap pages of reminiscence, was far too much of a 'conscious literary performance' to satisfy him: the voice he wanted had to be a natural speaking one, innocent, even naïve, to reflect the reality of a small boy and unsophisticated young man. So the work was abandoned as quickly as it had been begun.[7]

And there his efforts might have ended, had it not been for his old rival-friend, Osbert, his new love, Glen, and two good bottles of wine. Happening to complain to Osbert about his 'urgent need for mental employment' a few weeks later over one of his host's bottles of 'lovely old Moselle', Osbert had advised him to write an essay on hunting. No lover of horses himself, he nevertheless knew how intensely Sassoon responded to them. Though Sassoon rejected the idea initially, the seed had been planted and a few days later, under the 'genial influence of Reform Club burgundy', he found himself telling Glen stories of his hunting days. Glen, like Osbert, cared little for horses,[8] but he listened with genuine enjoyment to the colourful characters and situations Sassoon described and begged him to write it all down. This, according to Sassoon, was the birth of *Fox-Hunting Man*.

Successful books are rarely the result of a single influence, however, and there were other balls in play. Sassoon had already begun to revisit his past more than a year before his weekend at Weirleigh in mid-September. The present of a car two years previously had given him the freedom to explore his childhood haunts and a nostalgic visit to his prep school, the New Beacon at Sevenoaks, with Philbin on 27 July 1924 had been followed by a solitary trip to a childhood holiday house at Edingthorpe in Norfolk less than two months later.[9] Noting in his diary various details of Edingthorpe Rectory, which his mother had rented for eight weeks in 1897, he was already subconsciously recreating the past as literature:

> Mistily I memorized an elongated old shandrydan of a vehicle with an elderly horse, in which we used to drive to North Walsham. Also I remembered the donkeys we used to ride; I rode mine in a donkey-race at a local flower-show and came in last in a 'field' mainly composed of fat farmers.
>   (That was my first race!)[10]

Though this particular episode of childhood would not be included in *Fox-Hunting Man*, it would provide one of the most successful chapters in his autobiography ten years later.

Another reminder of his past followed in February 1926, when a letter arrived from the Medical Officer of the 2nd Battalion of the Royal Welch Fusiliers, Dr Dunn, asking him to write an account of his bombing raid in the Hindenburg Trench nine years earlier.[11] (It is odd that Dunn had not been in touch before, since he had been asked to appear before a tribunal in 1922 enquiring into shell-shock, a subject on which he knew Sassoon to be knowledgeable after his experiences at Craiglockhart Hospital for shell-shock cases.)[12] Sassoon's initial response was in verse, not prose as requested, and it was to decline to contribute to Dunn's history of the 2nd RWF, *The War the Infantry Knew*:[13]

> ... What can I unbury? ...
> Seven years have crowded past me since I wrote a
> Word on a war that left me far from merry.
> And in those seven odd years I have erected
> A barrier, that my soul might be protected
> Against the invading ghosts of what I saw
> In years when Murder wore the mask of Law.[14]

Almost immediately, however, he relented and produced a twelve-page account of his experiences with the 2nd Battalion, which he sent to Dunn a month later.[15]

In the meantime, as a result of Dunn's request, no doubt, he had arranged to spend an evening with one of his closest friends from the 2nd Battalion, Ralph Greaves, resulting in a second poem about the past, 'To One Who was With Me in the War'.[16] Addressed directly to Greaves, it traces Sassoon's reluctant involvement in painful memories:

> It was too long ago – that Company which we served with …
> We call it back in visual fragments, you and I,
> Who seem, ourselves, like relics casually preserved with
> Our mindfulness of old bombardments when the sky
> With blundering din blinked cavernous.
>   * * *
>
>   Remembering, we forget
> Much that was monstrous, much that clogged our souls with clay
> When hours were guides who led us by the longest way –
> And when the worst had been endured could still disclose
> Another worst to thwart us …
>
>   We forget our fear …
> And, while the uncouth Event begins to lour less near,
> Discern the mad magnificence whose storm-light throws
> Wild shadows on these after-thoughts that send your brain
> Back beyond Peace, exploring sunken ruinous roads.
>   * * *
>
>   I'll go with you, then,
> Since you must play this game of ghosts. At listening-posts
> We'll peer across dim craters; joke with jaded men
> Whose names we've long forgotten.
>   * * *
>   What's that you said?
>
>   (CP, pp.186-7)[17]

Shortly after seeing Ralph, Sassoon spent another evening reminiscing about the war with his brother, Edward Greaves, his company commander in 'C' Company, 1st Battalion, RWF, when he first went out to France.[18] He also wrote to his old quartermaster friend from the 1st Battalion, Joe Cottrill, but was sad to learn that he had died the previous January. And though neither effort resulted in further poems, they did complete his engagement with that particular time in his past and bring into being the last section of *Fox-Hunting Man*. Just as he had needed to be detached enough from hunting to write about it, so he had required an even longer period to feel sufficiently recovered from the war to describe his part in it. Like many other writers on the First World War, it took approximately a decade for this to happen.

Once made, the decision to include his war experience in *Fox-Hunting Man* seemed to Sassoon the only way to end the book. Since it was to be the story of a young man 'being brought gradually to the reality of human experience', Sherston's confrontation of the deaths, first of his boyhood friend Stephen Colwood, then of his ex-groom, Dixon, and finally of his closest army companion, Dick Tiltwood, were essential. Not all his friends agreed; de la Mare, for instance, questioned the inclusion of any war material at all, believing that it should have been saved for a second volume.[19] But by 20 November 1926, less than six weeks after the start of the writing, the decision to include war material had been made and the germ of a sequel, *Memoirs of an Infantry Officer*, had also been planted.

Though this material is naturally quite different in tone from the childhood and hunting scenes, *Fox-Hunting Man* is unified by an equal intensity of feeling throughout, partly because of the book's autobiographical nature, partly because Sassoon is a poet even in prose. And the earlier scenes, though lying so far back in time, are as sharply realized as the later ones.

Gosse had anticipated the benefits for Sassoon in returning to his roots when he had advised him in 1918, long before Osbert's suggested use of hunting material, to draw on his 'sporting experiences for typical country figures'.[20] Though not in verse, as Gosse had envisaged, when *Fox-Hunting Man* appeared it would, Sassoon believed, be 'essentially in accordance with his advice'.[21]

Seven years after Gosse had voiced what turned out to be a sound literary intuition, another friend, Nichols, had written to Sassoon from his scriptwriting job in Hollywood with a similar suggestion: 'Why not a grim comedy of "horsey" life?'[22] He was presumably thinking of a screenplay, but Sassoon had been determined to write a novel since at least 1921, when he had planned his 'Madame Bovary dealing with sexual inversion'.[23] Though the climate of the time had made this impossible, he continued to think of his *magnum opus* as prose. He had also contemplated writing an autobiography, but in purely practical terms novels appeared to pay much better and to reach a wider audience. He had the evidence of Wells's and Bennett's affluence and fame almost daily before his eyes at the Reform. In addition, both novelists had on separate occasions 'urged' him to switch to their own medium.[24]

It was not just envy of his novelist-friends' success, however, that influenced Sassoon's choice of genre in *Fox-Hunting Man*: he also admired their achievements. Apart from Hardy, whose novels had sustained him throughout the war, he particularly respected Forster. As I have shown, Forster's own major achievement, *A Passage to India*, had been completed only two years before, partly as a result of Sassoon's mediation between Forster and T.E. Lawrence, another prose-writer he greatly admired. Identifying with Sassoon over the impossibility of publishing anything on an overtly homosexual theme, Forster had allowed him to read his own unpublished efforts in that direction.[25] He was also very helpful in guiding Sassoon's amateurish attempts at the short story.[26]

Forster, a creative but honest critic, made his reservations about Sassoon's stories clear. But he was very enthusiastic indeed about his diary, which Sassoon allowed him to read in reciprocation for *Maurice*: 'The range of incidents and of characters treated is very remarkable ... I also laugh[ed] a great deal.'[27] And it was these aspects, together with the first-person speaking voice, which Sassoon carried over from his diary to *Fox-Hunting Man*. He agreed with Forster that some 'dodge' would be needed to turn his journal material into fiction, but he relied heavily on it to create his novel. Started fairly late in his life to describe his experiences in the war, his 'descriptive diary' at the Front was an important contributory factor in his prose-writing career.[28]

Sassoon believed that the 'naturalness' of *Fox-Hunting Man* was 'entirely the result of assiduous diarising', just as the quest for self-knowledge in it derived from Rivers.[29] But the most cursory glance at his favourite novelists in the early twenties suggests that there were other significant influences. Surtees, whom he rated equal to Thackeray and Fielding, was especially appropriate for a novel on fox-hunting, as were his other favourites, Somerville and Ross.[30] Books like *Jorrocks's Jaunts and Jollities*, *Mr Sponge's Sporting Tour* and *Experiences of an Irish RM*, with their casts of eccentric hunting 'types', lie behind the creation of such 'characters' as 'Gentleman George' and Bill Jaggett in *Fox-Hunting Man*, though both are also based on real-life people.

Sassoon argued that Dickens had modelled his style partly on Surtees, which may be one reason he had started to re-read Dickens in 1922. Approaching *Bleak House* for the first time while on holiday with Prince Philipp, he had written to the Turners with great excitement: 'I had no idea that Dickens was such a *beautiful* writer.'[31] Dickens's careful choice of adjectives, the 'gusto and picturesqueness' of his kaleidoscopic scenes, together with his 'humanity' and 'fine ... descriptive writing' would all contribute to Sassoon's own creation of a teeming microcosm in *Fox-Hunting Man*.[32] Well aware that Dickens might be thought 'too sentimental' by some, Sassoon was nevertheless deeply affected by *Bleak House*, especially Esther's first-person narration. Dickens's use of this device, particularly in *Great Expectations*, which was also to influence Graham Greene more than twenty years later in *The End of the Affair*, would leave its mark on George Sherston's deliberately unpolished account of his early experiences.

Another very different writer, whom Sassoon had also been reading before starting his novel, was Proust. The first part of *A la recherche du temps perdu* had been published in 1918 but, with his fairly basic French, Sassoon had not felt able to tackle it until Scott Moncrieff's translation appeared in November 1922. While he agreed with Gosse's dismissal of the other Modernist 'giant' he had attempted to read, James Joyce, he disagreed over Proust, whom he found intensely stimulating.[33] And he was reading 'a lot of Proust' the autumn he started his own excursion into the past. In addition to certain similarities of character and background to

Proust – his homosexuality, his half-Jewishness, his love of music,[34] his sensitivity – Sassoon's work shows sufficient specific likenesses to suggest that he was directly influenced by the French writer. Proust's title alone, which Moncrieff translated as *Remembrance of Things Past*, would seem equally appropriate to Sassoon's own attempt to recreate the past. Told in the first person, both semi-autobiographical novels open with the narrator remembering himself as a young, somewhat isolated child. Both describe in highly evocative poetic prose an older social order which is brought largely to an end by the First World War. 'A few pages of Proust', Sassoon wrote in his diary before starting *Fox-Hunting Man*, 'have made me wonder whether insignificant episodes aren't the most significant,'[35] a sentiment which lies behind such revealing scenes as George Sherston losing his pony on his first ride alone and having to walk ignominiously home. It may not have been madeleines Sassoon ate at Weirleigh in September 1926, but whatever his mother provided for tea that day it had a similar effect.

Less than a year before starting *Fox-Hunting Man*, Sassoon read another novelist who reminded him strongly of Proust, his fellow-Frenchman Romain Rolland.[36] Reading Rolland's *Jean Christophe*, a monumental work in ten volumes, four of which appeared in English, Sassoon found his saga of a sensitive musician 'by far the most stimulating' book he had read since discovering Proust: 'It gives me courage and reminds me that I must learn to go my way alone as far as possible, if I am ever to be any good to the world.'[37] These are words that the 'shy and solitary' George Sherston himself might have spoken as the shrouded body of his beloved Dick Tiltwood was lowered into the ground towards the end of *Fox-Hunting Man*.

*

These were just some of the influences and events which went into the making of *Fox-Hunting Man*. But the most important of them all, Sassoon insisted, was Glen's encouragement. It was with Glen's request for hunting stories in mind that he sat down on 8 October 1926 and scribbled a few notes about a retired colonel living in Cheltenham. Though these were promptly torn up, the next day he began in earnest, producing the first four pages of his book. He had started tentatively, he remembered in his unpublished autobiography,

> but with quiet deliberation and a sense of subdued excitement, as though they were something remembered – almost as though this was the beginning of a book I had read long ago and then forgotten. Of the continuation of that book I knew nothing, for the performance was entirely unpremeditated ... I did not even know the surname of the man whom I was proposing to impersonate – in fact I had not settled on a name for him when I was more than half way through the first part ... All I knew was that I intended to write

about a shy little boy learning to ride and being taken out hunting by the family groom ... It was to begin before 1900, and end when the boy was twelve.

After another twelve days he had written nearly 14,000 words and finished Part One ('Early Days'). But in the meantime his vague scheme had 'progressively enlarged itself' and he had made a decision to take his hero's sporting experiences up to the outbreak of the First World War. A month later his scheme had expanded to include Sherston's first year and a half in the army. By 2 December he had written '41,500 unprofessional words (including about 3,000 "wrong 'uns")' in fifty-four days and had 'worked himself to a standstill'.

To begin with he had had Glen to urge him on and had read at least three instalments to him by the time he left for another season with the Oxford Rep on 16 October. Osbert, too, was most encouraging when, over yet another bottle of his fine wine, he listened to Sassoon read to him for a 'solid hour' later in the month. 'His occasional chuckles, as he sat puffing at a long cigar, were the most satisfying response I could have asked for,' Sassoon remembered, further reassured by Osbert's request for another 90,000 words. Though the final tally in *Fox-Hunting Man* would be no more than 90,000 words, he had written almost half of them by the time his first frantic onslaught came to an end at the beginning of December 1926.

His main reason for stopping, he claimed, was the arrival of his American friend Sam Behrman, whom he had not seen for six years.[38] But it is more likely that he was simply exhausted. His writing methods had always been demanding, requiring him to start work at a time when most people are going to bed and finish not long before many get up. With a pot of strong tea at his elbow, a pipe in hand and a few rough notes made earlier in the day, he would stare at the blank page of notebook on his knee 'waiting for something to happen'. (Later he learnt that an hour on the sofa with the light out made all the difference.) When inspiration did come, he would scribble it down quickly in pencil, which he found less inhibiting than typewriter or pen. His method of revision was simply to ink over what he had written, making a few alterations as he went. These amateurish practices seemed to him a crucial part of the final product. 'Had I been a more practised performer', he pointed out, 'The Fox-Hunting Man would have lacked its essential quality, which is youngness – recaptured youngness of feeling and expression. My inexpertness was appropriate to the subject matter. It was the testament of my youth.' It was also, like his relationships with much younger men, an attempt to recapture his own vanishing youth.

By the time Sam Behrman arrived in London on 18 December, Glen had been back from Oxford for nearly a fortnight and any plans Sassoon had for continuing his novel were abandoned. As usual in Sam's presence he became over-excited, unconsciously playing up to the caricature of the vague Englishman which so delighted his American friend. On being asked his telephone number, for example, he had had to confess that he did not know it, realizing even as he did so that he had added to Sam's repertoire of stories about him: 'He doesn't know his own telephone number! ...' But Sam also had a positive effect on him, encouraging him to continue *Fox-Hunting Man* and reminding him that he had prophesied in New York that he would one day produce a long, autobiographical novel. 'It was indeed', Sassoon felt, 'as though he had been sent specially to keep me up to the mark about it.'

Sam, Glen and Christmas, which he spent with his Aunt Mozelle and Schuster at Brighton, kept him busy until early January. And a visit to Dorset in the middle of the month provided a further distraction while he visited both Hardy and Rivers's colleague, Sir Henry Head. Head and his wife Ruth, having moved from London to Lyme Regis in the early twenties, had moved again and were now living only a few miles from Max Gate.[39] They were, like the Hardys, playing an increasingly parental role in Sassoon's life – even as Sir Henry himself declined into the hell of Parkinson's Disease – and Sassoon shuttled between them and the Hardys like a loving and obedient son.

When, after encouragement from Gosse, he finally got back to his writing on 27 January 1927, it was not prose but verse he produced. The first he had attempted for eight months, his poem conveys his own 'weariness' as he struggled to complete *Fox-Hunting Man*. It also reveals its ambiguous creative origins, since it can be read as either poetry or poetic prose: written originally in prose, according to Sassoon, it 'turned out, almost without alteration, to be a poem'.[40] It displays the same dependence on alliteration as the rest of his verse, the repetition of w's and p's in particular conveying the effort needed to 'climb the steepening hill':

> Everyman
> The weariness of life that has no will
> To climb the steepening hill:
> The sickness of the soul for sleep, and to be still.
> And then once more the impassioned pigmy fist
> Clenched cloudward and defiant;
> The pride that would prevail, the doomed protagonist
> Grappling the ghostly giant.
> Victim and venturer turn by turn, and then
> Set free to be again
> Companion in repose with those who once were men.
> (CP, p. 224)[41]

As 'Everyman' suggests, the beginning of 1927, except for his visits to Glen (again on tour), was a time of 'nerviness and dissatisfaction'. Without his car, which he had generously given to Glen, there was no excuse for impromptu excursions, but he was still not able to get back to work. So, on

183

April Fool's Day, he bought himself a new Morris Oxford, 'a cosy, complacent boudoir of a car'.[42] The date of his purchase turned out to be highly appropriate, since a mere fortnight later, driving along a completely empty street in Bayswater at midnight, perfectly sober according to him, he crashed into a lamppost, damaging both the car and himself. (His own explanation for the accident was not his bad driving, but irritation with a fellow-guest at the dinner party he had just left.)

The only positive aspect of the affair was the devotion of Nellie Burton, who made the most of this opportunity to 'mother her "favourite boy" '. Glen, out of town for a few days, was very alarmed when Nellie reported the incident to him, but reassured to hear that one of her most trusted tenants, and a great admirer of Sassoon, Mr Fleming, had sat up all night with him to make sure that it was only a broken rib Sassoon suffered. He was less thrilled to learn that Sassoon had, after three days, been whisked off to Bray by Schuster to convalesce.

By the time of Sassoon's accident there was already some antagonism between Glen and Schuster, stemming probably from possessiveness on both their parts. When Glen arrived to visit Sassoon at his retreat by the Thames on 24 April, Schuster made him less than welcome and Glen, normally the most easy-going of people, was deeply offended: Schuster, he declared, had 'the manners of a pig', an unfortunate choice of imagery for someone as Jewish as Frankie.[43] Caught in the middle, Sassoon tried to placate Glen, who nevertheless continued to think Schuster a 'jealous, mean vampire'.[44] It was an uneasy situation and one which was not improved by Sassoon's suggestion that the three of them should take a holiday together later in the year.

One reason for his idea was that, by the end of April, he found himself a wealthy man. His Aunt Rachel, whom he had not seen for twenty years, had died on 29 April, leaving him a quarter of her substantial fortune.[45] His father's older sister and the only Sassoon to show any kindness to Siegfried's gentile mother when she was rejected by the rest of his father's family, she had herself led an unhappy life. After her husband Frederick's death from syphilis in 1902, she had slowly declined into madness brought on by the same disease.[46] By 1927 she had been ill for so long that Sassoon claimed to have almost completely forgotten his expectation of inheriting money from her. Up to 1914 he confessed that he had been 'much addicted to conjecturings' about what he would do if he became rich. Having survived the war, however, he thought less and less about her money, he said, until by 1926 the expectation had been 'almost dismissed' from his mind. Only a few weeks before her death, he had sent a self-righteous poem to the *Labour Weekly*:

> I accuse the Rich of what they've always done before –
> Of lifting worldly faces to a diamond star,
> I accuse the Rich of being what they always are –
> The enemies of Lazarus lying at their door.[47]

Yet he was clearly still expecting to have money himself when he wrote this poem, whatever his claims to the contrary, and had ironically already inherited it by the time it was published two days after Rachel Beer's death. Three years previously he had written to the ever-needy Graves, with more honesty than sympathy: 'If my rich aunt were to die I would buy [*sic*] you and Turner and Blunden £5 a week for life; but the old creature refuses to quit the planet.'[48] And only sixteen months before her death he had joked, again with Graves:

> When Auntie Rachel hops the twig
> My friends no more will call me Sig
> But pass me with a blank look.
> My income then will be immense;
> And I'll publish, (at my own expense,)
> Not poems – but my Bank Book.[49]

He made no attempt to attend her funeral, admitting that he had used his still slightly painful rib as an excuse and that he felt virtually unmoved by the whole affair: 'The idea of being "much better off" has brought me no particular sense of pleasure,' he wrote in his diary. 'I can't see what good it will do me in my everyday life; and it certainly won't help me to write better poetry. I can be generous to my friends, and give lots of it to my mother. That seems to be about all there is in it.'[50] He had claimed to have trained himself to be 'non-acquisitive', yet his references to Graves about his aunt's possible death and his own lifestyle at this time make this seem a hollow boast. Someone who had recently bought himself both a Bechstein grand piano and a new sports car can hardly be described as 'non-acquisitive'. Edith Sitwell's comment on the subject also suggests that Sassoon was more interested in Rachel Beer's money than he admitted and comes as a relief after his own somewhat lofty diary entry. Referring to Graves's well-documented liaison with the American poetess Laura Riding, who had not only accompanied him and his wife to Cairo but also back again, she wrote to Sassoon: 'Osbert and I were so delighted to get your letter and hear the splendid news ... I only hope [it] ... won't lead Robert [Graves] to increase his harem.'[51]

Sassoon would have been less than human if he had not rejoiced in his newly acquired riches. But whether knowing, from the age of fifteen onwards, that he would one day inherit had helped or hindered him is debatable. On the one hand it had encouraged him to feel independent of the need to earn money and thus devote himself to his writing. But it had also made it more difficult for him to find a purpose in life, especially when his work was going badly. And once he actually acquired his fortune, it would, as the earlier of his two letters to Graves suggests it might, make him even more inclined to try to 'control' his friends' lives. So that when they failed to fall in with his plans, however powerful their reasons, he could become quite petulant. When Glen, for example, wrote to tell him in May 1927 that he might not be able to travel with him because of contractual commitments, Sassoon sulked like a small child. 'I think your letter most unkind,' Glen wrote in surprise, referring at one point to 'intimidation'.[52] Though the breach was quickly healed and Glen did eventually manage to join him for nearly three weeks of the planned tour, the first serious rift in their relationship had appeared, significantly because Glen had been unable to do exactly what Sassoon wanted.

The holiday itself went well. During his two months' convalescence at Bray, Sassoon had been persuaded by Anzie to spend some of his inheritance on an expensive touring car, a Chrysler.[53] After two years of marriage the Wyldes were expecting their first child, which meant that Anzie would be unable to chauffeur Schuster round Europe in his Rolls as usual that summer, and Sassoon, with some misgivings, agreed to drive him to Bayreuth for the annual music festival.[54] Crossing the Channel on 24 July with Schuster and Glen, he decided to travel by way of Ypres where, by coincidence, the New Menin Gate had been unveiled the previous day. As he studied the large white monument, covered minutely with the thousands of names of those who died there, he felt a fresh surge of bitterness about the war and the way in which one of its worst battlefields had become 'a sight-seer's centre'.[55] Who, he asked, in a sonnet written the same day, would remember the 'unheroic Dead who fed the guns?' Who would 'absolve the foulness of their fate?'

> ... Here was the world's worst wound. And here with pride
> 'Their name liveth for ever,' the Gateway claims.
> Was ever an immolation so belied
> As these intolerably nameless names?
> Well might the Dead who struggled in the slime
> Rise and deride this sepulchre of crime.
>
> (CP, p. 188)[56]

'On Passing the New Menin Gate' is among Sassoon's most vehement poems about the war, perhaps partly because one of his closest friends, Gordon Harbord, had died at Ypres. It contains some powerful imagery, 'the world's worst wound', 'the Dead ... struggl[ing] in the slime' and the 'sepulchre of crime' being particularly effective metaphors to convey his sense of outrage at the brutal way soldiers were sacrificed in their thousands in the mud of Flanders. And the paradox of 'nameless names' draws attention to his belief that no monument, however grand, could remedy the injustice done. Sassoon would later describe this poem as his 'final word about the 1914 War'.[57] While it may have been his 'final word' in poetry, however, he had still a great deal to say on the subject in prose and his visit to Ypres almost certainly strengthened his decision to continue *Fox-Hunting Man* into the war itself.

The rest of the trip was relatively uneventful, though it is clear from his letters to Glen afterwards that they had both found Schuster redundant in what Sassoon described as their 'halo of hurried happiness', which seemed to him 'as near perfection as possible'.[58] They were always 'wishing him out of the way and when he was – O heaven!'[59] Less than six months later, 'old Shuffling Shu', as Sassoon and Glen nicknamed him, was to die from a perforated ulcer and Sassoon would eventually come to feel that he had failed fully to appreciate Schuster's very real affection for him, as well as his love and knowledge of music. As it was, he said goodbye to Schuster at Munich in mid-August with some relief and, though he had had to part with Glen too, started on his long drive to Berlin in high spirits. Numerous breakdowns, flat tyres and a broken fan-belt failed to daunt him. His meetings with several attractive young hitchhikers on the way, one a sixteen-year-old sailor, more than compensated for the drawbacks of the journey and he arrived at the northern capital in good form.

He also knew that there would be friends waiting to meet him there. Partly to thank Osbert for his encouragement over *Fox-Hunting Man* the previous autumn and partly to show off his newly acquired wealth, he had invited the Sitwell brothers to join him as his guests, together with Nellie Burton. Nellie, who was delighted to be sharing a holiday with three of her favourites, already knew Berlin from previous visits to another of her 'boys', Ross's friend, the writer Max Meyerfeld.[60] Meyerfeld, who introduced the 'stately' Nellie to his friends as an 'illegal' daughter of Queen Victoria ('Can't you see it?' he asked Sassoon), was himself one of Sassoon's greatest admirers and more than a little in love with him.[61] Together they all celebrated Sassoon's forty-first birthday on 8 September and, although his *magnum opus* was still not completed and could even be said to be suffering from this prolonged holiday, Sassoon was happy. He found Osbert and Sachie 'charming and considerate companions', as well as 'very educational', especially on the baroque which surrounded them, and there were several more weeks of sightseeing to look forward to.[62]

Berlin was followed by Dresden, Dresden by Vienna and Vienna by Budapest, where they listened to gypsy music and saw the El Grecos in the Herzog Collection. Then on 29 September, more than two months after leaving England, Sassoon was home again, to see Glen off on a seven-month season in New York, an absence he was dreading.[63] With Glen gone there were no more excuses for delay and on 6 October, two days before the anniversary of his start on *Fox-Hunting Man*, he was back at work on it.

By the time he stopped the previous winter he had taken his hero, George Sherston, from his 'Early Days' as a horse-mad boy, through his adolescent cricketing triumph in 'The Flower Show Match' and his 'Fresh Start' – where he takes up hunting again after leaving Cambridge without a degree and revives a friendship with the equally horse-mad Stephen Colwood – to his 'Day with the Potsford [Hunt]'. Sassoon had always associated autumn with hunting and found the beauty of the season a 'creative stimulus'. So that he had no problems continuing Sherston's progress, describing his hero's stay with Stephen's family 'At the Rectory', where, in defiance of his guardian, he buys another hunter. Since it was all largely autobiographical, the storyline presented him with few difficulties, though he still found the actual writing an agonizing process.

He could not control external events, however, and two things conspired to bring him to a halt again only a week after he had restarted. The first was when Edmund Blunden, whom he had not seen since March 1924, returned from Japan and took him away from his work for almost a day.[64] But the second event, a weekend with a young man who was rapidly replacing the absent Glen in his affections, he could not control and on 14 October *Fox-Hunting Man* was again abandoned. It would take nearly three and a half months and the absence of the young man concerned for him to return to his writing. When he did so in January 1928, it was with a grim determination to finish it before his new lover returned in April.

By dint of avoiding almost all his friends, especially Graves, he completed the rest of the book (more than half) in less than three months. Conducting Sherston from his steeplechasing victories and further hunting experiences in the Midlands to his enlistment at the outbreak of war, he leaves him at the end on the Western Front, facing the loss of two of his closest friends, Dixon and Dick Tiltwood. Emotionally gruelling as well as hugely satisfying, the writing of *Fox-Hunting Man* was a result of both desperation and inspiration and his greatest sustained effort to date. Gratifyingly, it was an achievement friends and critics alike would recognize when it was published only four months later in September 1928.[65]

*

T.E. Lawrence told Edward Marsh that if he were 'trying to export the ideal Englishman to an international exhibition' he would choose Sassoon as his 'chief exhibit'[66] (an irony considering that Sassoon was only half English). It seems therefore appropriate that a main theme of *Fox-Hunting Man* should be Englishness. From its title-page onwards, with its reference to that most English of sports, fox-hunting, and its epigraph, taken from England's best-known writer Shakespeare's own praise of his fellow-countrymen in *Richard II* – 'This happy breed of men, this little world' – the novel is a celebration of the microcosm in which Sassoon himself grew up.

Set mainly in one of England's most beautiful landscapes, the Weald of Kent, *Fox-Hunting Man* celebrates the English countryside at the end of the nineteenth and beginning of the twentieth century in nostalgic detail:

> The air was Elysian with early summer and the shadows of steep white clouds were chasing over the orchards and meadows; sunlight sparkled on green hedgerows that had been drenched by early morning showers. As I was

carried past it all I was lazily aware through my dreaming and unobservant eyes that this was the sort of world I wanted. For it was my own countryside, and I loved it with an intimate feeling, though all its associations were crude and incoherent. I cannot think of it now without a sense of heartache, as if it contained something which I have never quite been able to discover.[67]

The young Sherston also yearningly describes such English pursuits as summer cricket matches on village greens, exhilarating hunts on crisp autumn and winter days and that dying institution, the local flower show. His description of Butley and Rotherden's cricket teams covers a wide range of English social types, from William Dodd, the saddler, with his 'Did-I-Say-Myself', to Parson Yalden, with his most 'unevangelical expression' after he has been bowled out.[68] But the more socially exclusive Packlestone Hunt is no less representative of Englishness in its own way, from the 'massive and white-moustached' Captain Harry Hinnycraft riding one of his 'magnificent weight-carriers ... with the air of a monarch' and that 'paragon of natural proficiency', Mrs Oakfield, who 'sailed over the fences in her tall hat and perfectly fitting black habit with a bunch of violets in her buttonhole', down to the pompous Sir Jocelyn Porteus-Porteous ('note the majestic variation in spelling') and the intrepid 'brothers Peppermore'.[69]

The protagonist himself, as Sassoon points out, is a 'very typical English character'. His first name, George, conjures up England's patron saint, while his surname, Sherston, refers to two typically English villages, one in the Cotswolds in an area Sassoon had hunted over with Norman Loder (the Denis Milden of the book) and the second in Wiltshire, named Sherston Magna, which Sassoon believed to be the original home of the Byam Shaws.[70] For *Fox-Hunting Man* is also a homage to Glen, especially its first half, and it is no coincidence that its hero's initials are the same as its most important, if not 'onlie begetter'.

Even the last fifth of the book, when Sherston leaves his idyllic rural surroundings for the army and the harsh conditions of wartime France, is dominated by notions of Englishness. For it is in order to defend England and Englishness that he leaves it all behind. Though he will later, in two sequels to *Fox-Hunting Man*, become disillusioned with the cause, it is in the spirit of another Shakespeare play, *Henry V*, that he sets out to defend his country.

All these aspects of Englishness are combined to produce a skilfully shaped account of Sherston's development from childhood to manhood, within a loose structure of apparently random recollections. As Sassoon told Ben Huebsch when he commented on the lack of 'fortissimo' passages in the book, he had deliberately 'strained and struggled for reticence and delicate writing' in *Fox-Hunting Man*.[71] (His early admiration for Pater had almost certainly influenced him in this direction.) Introducing the subject of cricket indirectly on the first page, by way of a contrast between

George's elderly tutor, Mr Star (real-life Mr Moon) and his aunt's robust young groom, Tom Dixon (real-life Tom Richardson), he follows this up quite naturally with a reference to Dixon teaching the boy to ride. From then on he alternates between the narrator's progress in the two sports, culminating in his triumph at cricket in 'The Flower Show Match' and his winning of 'the Colonel's Cup' at a point-to-point. Starting with a vivid recreation of George's childhood, with all its joys and woes, he ends with his realization of love and death at the Front, a conclusion which has been anticipated in Book Eight by Sherston's goodbye to his childhood drawing room at the outbreak of war, when he notes a 'fiery patch of light' resting on his aunt's reproduction of Watts's picture 'Love and Death'.[72] The book opens as it closes with a sense of Sherston's isolation.

'It is a lovely book', Forster wrote to Sassoon:

> so beautifully shaped, and full of something I often think about at present, and have to call 'tenderness', something that isn't affection though it often accompanies it, and isn't sentimentality. The death of Dixon is the 'central point', but the conception of the book is such that 'central point' is a false phrase. It's more organic than anything I've read lately. There are, as you said, things you've missed out, which would have heightened the colours and quickened the paces, but those things needn't always get put in, and you've gained other things by omitting them.[73]

Other friends and critics would be for the most part as positive as Forster, with few of the reservations that had marked their response to his poetry of the early twenties. A notable exception was Graves. Unlike Forster he believed that Sassoon had 'missed out' a great deal that mattered. By writing in the guise of George Sherston, he argued, Sassoon avoided facing the moral problems inherent in the autobiographical presentation of one's experience and left the reader 'to decide for him whether the book is sincere or ironical'.[74]

By the time Graves's review appeared the two of them were on uneasy terms and Sassoon did not respond directly to his charge. But it clearly rankled, for when he finally wrote to Graves after a gap of several years, he was still anxious to explain why he could never entirely 'be himself' as Graves had advised:

> Everyone wants to be himself, if he is any good, I imagine. Is it so easy when one is in my quandary – for the duration of my life – as regards 'temperament'.* But if you had read my diaries for the past nine years I think you would retract your remark. No one is more aware than I am that the 'Fox-Hunting Man' is mere make-believe compared with the reality of my experience. But it isn't (as your review implied) a piece of facile autobio-

---

* Both Sassoon and Graves use the word 'temperament' to mean sexuality, and the reference here is to Sassoon's homosexuality, which was making life difficult for him by the time the letter was written in March 1930.

graphic writing. Sherston is only a fifth of myself, but his narrative is carefully thought out and constructed. I don't see how it could have been done differently.[75]

As long as society continued to place homosexuality outside the law, which it did, ironically, until the year of Sassoon's death, he would continue to suffer both as an artist and a man. In *Fox-Hunting Man* it prevented him, for example, describing his true feelings for the Dick Tiltwood character and thus diminished the full impact of Sherston's loss when Tiltwood is killed.

But it was not just his homosexuality which Sassoon excluded from his first novel, however autobiographical it might first appear. He also quite deliberately omitted any literary aspirations from his hero's character, as well as any hint of Jewishness. Unlike Proust, whose narrator charts his progress towards his artistic goal, Sassoon's narrator's ambitions are sporting. (So much so that when Sassoon allows himself to describe his love of poetry in the first draft of his manuscript, he feels obliged to cross all three pages out.) Sherston's symbolic role as a typical Englishman does not allow for strong literary interests. Sherston is a deliberately 'simplified version' of himself, Sassoon explained, because he is intended to represent and speak for the generation to which he belongs and that, in his creator's opinion, did not 'typically' include a love of poetry.

When Sassoon alters any of the autobiographical material on which *Fox-Hunting Man* is based, it is never arbitrary. When, for instance, George announces in the opening paragraph that he is an only child, orphaned young and brought up by an unmarried aunt, it is partly to get round the disagreeable fact that Sassoon's own father left home before he was five, partly a reflection of his feelings of isolation from his two brothers after the age of ten and partly because he needed to keep his mother 'separate' from his emotions.[76] This can create problems. When he wants to record in *Fox-Hunting Man* his shock at hearing of the death of his real-life brother in 1915, for example, since his narrator has no brothers he has to transform it into the death of Sherston's friend, Stephen Colwood.

Another minor alteration relating to the Stephen Colwood/Gordon Harbord character suggests that some changes were made for the sake of simplification, life being generally far less shapely than art. In the novel George has already known Stephen at 'Balboro' (a thinly disguised reference to Marlborough) by the time he meets him at a point-to-point. Whereas in fact Sassoon had been at school with Gordon Harbord's brother, Kenneth, not Gordon, who went to Winchester.

Other changes are made for the sake of dramatic tension. 'The Flower Show Match', for example, is based on an actual match in which Sassoon played as a schoolboy for Brenchley ('Butley' in *Fox-Hunting Man*) against the village of Rolvenden ('Rotherden'). Whereas in the novel George scores the winning run for his team in a nail-biting finish, in real life Brenchley lost the match, with Sassoon making only a minor contribution.[77]

A more significant alteration of autobiographical material occurs towards the end of the book, when Sherston meets Dick Tiltwood, assumed by most Sassoon critics to be based exclusively on David Thomas, since Tiltwood dies in almost identical circumstances to him. It is only when one studies the original manuscript and sees a photograph of another young Welch Fusilier, Robert Hanmer, pasted in opposite the description of Tiltwood, that it becomes clear that Tiltwood is a composite character. He represents Hanmer as well as Thomas, a fact which makes sense when one knows that Sassoon became infatuated with both of them in quick succession.

The most interesting departure from autobiography in *Fox-Hunting Man* concerns another crucial structural device, the death of Dixon. As Sassoon indicated, the book 'culminates' in the deaths of Dixon and Tiltwood in order to bring its hero face to face with reality. In fact, Tom Richardson, the model for Dixon, did not die until 1928, and in rather sordid circumstances, not a suitable ending for the heroic role Sassoon created for him in his book.[78]

Some of the changes Sassoon makes are very amusing, particularly his choice of pseudonyms for real-life characters. Several are straightforward approximations – 'Barchard' for Marchant, 'Huxtable' for Ruxton, 'Packlestone' for Atherstone – but the majority involve obvious word-play. 'Dixon', for example is simply a phonetic abbreviation of 'Richard' (i.e., 'Dick') and 'son'; Mr Moon becomes another astral body, 'Mr Star', and leisurely games of golf at Lamberhurst are played at the fictional 'Amblehurst'. Many pseudonyms can only be understood with a more detailed biographical knowledge; the real-life Miss Horrocks, Gordon Harbord and Julian Dadd are given the names of the places they lived in – 'Maskall', 'Colwood' and 'Durley' respectively. And 'Mrs Oakfield', based on a well-known member of the Atherstone Hunt, Mrs Inge, derives her pseudonym from her maiden name of 'Oakeley'.[79]

Though Sassoon's primary reason for renaming his characters is to disguise their identity, like Dickens he enjoys finding names to suit his characters and often makes more than one attempt to get it right, while at the same time avoiding offence. After calling one particularly aggressive 'would-be thruster' of the Atherstone 'Bill Hoggerell', to convey his brutishness as well as echo his real name, Lindsay-Hogg, he changed it in manuscript to the even more negative but less give-away 'Bill Jaggett'. The timidity of another rider is suggested through his surname, 'Croplady'. His success at capturing the nature of his real-life models would in a few cases ('Jaggett' was one) provoke angry letters. At least with horses he did not have to worry about offending them and many of their names are taken from life. 'Cockbird', for example, remains himself, though the name of Sherston's first horse, 'Sheila', is borrowed from Sassoon's mother's hunter, and Sherston's later mount, 'Harkaway', is called after one of Norman Loder's best hunters.

Sassoon's choice of names is never random and a biographical link can usually be traced. The link to real life was clearly important to him, as the manuscript of *Fox-Hunting Man* also shows. Lovingly bound by its author in three hessian-covered notebooks, it is crammed with photographs, press cuttings and other ephemera from his own life. There are, for instance, two photographs of Richardson, looking just as Sassoon describes Dixon, one of Cockbird, another of his mother (to whom he felt obliged to explain that 'in Aunt Evelyn' he had 'only ... drawn a very faint portrait of a very small part of your character – (certainly no one could have described you as a "timid and incompetent horsewoman"!!)'), an article on and an obituary of his 'Denis Milden' figure, Norman Loder, a map of the Southdown Hunt country and an obituary of Captain Ruxton. Many of these items were added long after the book was published and all suggest how 'real' his fictional world was for him.[80]

Much of the humour of *Fox-Hunting Man* – and it is very funny indeed in parts – lies in its characterization. Like Pip in *Great Expectations*, Sherston is able to laugh at himself as he looks back on his youthful absurdities and it is a laughter the reader is invited to share. But George's superstitious methods of working out his chances of cricketing success from cricketers' names in his local paper, for example, or his attempts to become a 'hard-bitten hunting-man' in spite of several humiliations on the field, are not just amusing: they are also penetrating insights into his character and the self-deceptions of youth in general.

Aunt Evelyn, too, provides moments of rich comedy while she adds to the reader's knowledge of both Sherston and herself. Her flustered attempts to make tea on a spirit lamp in a railway carriage under the 'scandalized glances' of her fellow first-class passengers, including her craven and snobbish nephew, is one of the high points of the book. 'By the time we were home,' Sherston tells us, 'I knew quite clearly that my attitude towards the tea-making had been odious and the more I realized it the more impossible it seemed for me to make amends by behaving gently to her.'[81] It was, as he points out, 'one of those outwardly trivial episodes which one does not forget'.[82]

Though Dixon himself is not portrayed humorously, probably because like Colwood and Tiltwood he is destined to die, his relationships with both Aunt Evelyn and her nephew make for gentle comedy early on. His deft handling of his timid employer as he attempts to get her permission to take George out hunting give us the measure of the man. When she suggests that Dixon might take her nephew to the local meet in the dog-cart, his 'air of disapproval' is beautifully judged, instantly handing him the victory: '"I think, 'm, you can rely on me to take proper care of Master George," he remarked rather stiffly; the next moment he looked at me with a grin of delight followed by a solemn wink with the eye furthest away from my aunt.'[83]

As in Dickens, minor characters are generally more comical than the main ones. Virtually every member of the Butley and Rotherden cricket teams in 'The Flower Show Match' could stand as an example. This much anthologized section manages to convey the singularity of each player while, at the same time, glorying in the rich flavour of village cricket at the end of the nineteenth century.[84] Here, for example, are the two umpires:

> Tom Seamark, the Rotherden umpire, is a red-faced sporting publican who bulks as large as a lighthouse. As an umpire he has certain emphatic mannerisms. When appealed to he expresses a negative decision with a severe and stentorian 'NOT OOUT': but when adjudicating that the batsman is out, he silently shoots his right arm toward the sky – an impressive and irrevocable gesture which effectively quells all adverse criticism ...
>
> Bill Sutler, our umpire, is totally different. To begin with, he has a wooden leg. Nobody knows how he lost his leg; he does not deny the local tradition that he was once a soldier, but even in his cups he has never been heard to claim that he gave the limb for Queen and Country. It is, however, quite certain that he is now a cobbler (with a heavily waxed moustache) and Butley has ceased to deny that he is a grossly partisan umpire. In direct contrast to Tom Seamark he invariably signifies 'not out' by a sour shake of the head: when the answer is an affirmative one he bawls 'Hout' as if he'd been stung by a wasp. It is reputed that (after giving the enemy's last man out leg-before in a closely-fought finish) he was once heard to add in an exultant undertone: 'and I've won my five bob'.[85]

Comedy plays such a large part in *Fox-Hunting Man* that its near absence at the end in France points up the stark difference between the grim realities Sherston has finally to face and his earlier carefree life. It is interesting to note that when Sassoon looked back on the book forty years later, he saw it not as the comic masterpiece it undoubtedly is, but as 'a work of innocently insidious anti-war propaganda'.[86] He might complain about being branded as a war poet but he could never, even in his most light-hearted moments, escape his experiences of 1914 to 1918.

13

'The Old Earl and Little Lord Fauntleroy' (1927-1928)

> Don't be surprised if gold dust falls out of my eyelashes.
> (Sassoon to Glen Byam Shaw,
> 10 October 1927)

Sassoon always insisted that Glen was his main inspiration for *Fox-Hunting Man*.[1] Yet more than half of it was written under the influence of the person who had supplanted Glen long before its completion, Stephen Tennant. This helps to explain why the last part of the book, with its themes of love and death, is so different from the rest. For Tennant was to be the most consuming love of Sassoon's life, taking him back to his first great passion for David Thomas, which comes through thinly disguised in his book. And the TB from which Stephen suffered, then a life-threatening illness, was to make death a present reality for Sassoon as he struggled to finish *Fox-Hunting Man*.[2]

Sassoon had already met the young aristocrat and aesthete the Honourable Stephen Tennant before Glen left for America at the beginning of October 1927. The fourth son of Lord Glenconner, Stephen was a prominent member of the Bright Young Things so gleefully satirized by Evelyn Waugh. Said to be the model for Miles Malpractice in *Decline and Fall* and Sebastian Flyte in *Brideshead Revisited*, Tennant was wealthy, privileged and beautiful, his effeminate manner and provocative behaviour attracting attention wherever he went.[3] A great favourite of his fellow-exhibitionists the Sitwells, they appeared particularly keen to interest Sassoon in him. They were responsible for Stephen and Sassoon's first meeting, for example, which was at a dinner party given by Sachie and Georgia Sitwell to celebrate the christening of their son Reresby. (Sassoon had also attended the ceremony itself, which was performed by the Archbishop of Canterbury in the private chapel of Lambeth Palace, accompanied by Nellie Burton in a splendid hat.) The Sitwells had been careful to tell him in advance that Stephen was 'avid' to meet him and after the dinner, at which Sassoon found himself talking very excitably 'for the benefit of S. Tennant ... a very good audience', he was equally 'avid' to see

Stephen again.[4] 'He is 21, very affected (in a nice way), very witty and intelligent and divinely beautiful,' Sassoon told the writer Henry Festing-Jones, whom he knew would understand; 'But, alas, very fragile.'[5] Perhaps it was fear of being thought snobbish that prevented him adding the other details he noted in his diary, Stephen's 'ultra-refined voice' and 'well-bred' manner.

Despite his fascination with Stephen, however, Sassoon continued to protest his complete devotion to Glen. And while Stephen and his fashionable friends spent the summer of 1927 at increasingly wild parties, stretching aristocratic privilege and social tolerance to their limits, Sassoon passed his three weeks with Glen in Germany dreading Glen's departure for America. When Glen returned to England before him in August he 'missed him more than usual'.[6] And when he sailed for New York on 1 October Sassoon felt desolate. Yet only a fortnight later he was suffering from a bad case of what he called 'Stephenitis'.[7]

When Stephen's invitation to spend the weekend at his family house in Wiltshire arrived on 10 October, Sassoon had just started work again on *Fox-Hunting Man*. Knowing full well that it would be a distraction, he was nevertheless unable to resist. Squaring his conscience with the promise of an 'hour-by-hour' account of his visit to Glen, he set off in the Chrysler on Saturday, 15 October, for Wilsford, the large Elizabethan-style manor house designed by Detmar Blow for Stephen's mother, Pamela, shortly after her marriage to Edward Tennant.[8] Beautifully situated in a hollow of the Wiltshire Downs near Amesbury, on the banks of the Avon, it represented all that Sassoon himself had wanted from a country house in his youth and everything that Weirleigh, for all its dearness to him, did not possess – elegance, charm and distinction. But its perfection, as Stephen's niece Emma Tennant would observe, also made it seem to the critical eye rather unreal, like a stage set. 'Anyone who had spent their life in these surroundings,' she argued, '– and especially Stephen, with his adoring mother Pamela – would continue to expect a pageant, a pantomime, every time he went out of the house.'[9] Sassoon, who would live at Wilsford for extended periods, quickly began to wish that Stephen 'didn't aim so much at a Principal Boy in pantomime ideal'.[10] But he would be drawn into the performance himself for nearly six years of his own life.

The curtain went up the very night of his arrival. Coming in to dinner tired and late after losing his way in the tortuous Wiltshire lanes, he was at once transported into Stephen's fantasy world. Osbert, who had known the Tennants for years through his friendship with the eldest son, Edward ('Bim', killed in the First World War), was curious to know its effect on the puritanical Sassoon: 'Will you hate Wilsford?' he asked Sassoon just before the visit; then added as if to reassure him: 'It may be fun for two days.'[11] Stephen, whose frivolousness concealed a perceptive mind, had his own reservations about Osbert – 'extraordinary creature!! So charming!! So insincere!! How it must complicate life to be so devious – to be your own

196

mortal enemy', he was to comment to Sassoon – but found him an entertaining guest.[12]

Apart from Osbert and other people Sassoon already knew – Sachie and his wife Georgia, the Sitwells' musical protégé, William Walton, and Osbert's 'crony' Christabel McLaren[13] – Stephen had gathered together some of his most extrovert friends. If this had been done to impress Sassoon it was not entirely successful, since the first of these, the budding society photographer Cecil Beaton, had already been dismissed by Sassoon as 'clever, very affected, effeminate, *arriviste*' on the one occasion they had met.[14] And though he would agree to be photographed for *Vogue* by Beaton only a few weeks later and accept invitations to his weekend retreat at nearby Ashcombe, he was never really to change his initial opinion, counting Beaton chief among the 'dreary friends' he blamed for Stephen's silliness. He was almost equally dismissive of the Jungmann sisters, Zita and 'Baby', whose mother's second marriage to Richard Guinness had thrown them into London's fashionable set – 'two smart young ladies' was his sole comment.[15] And though he would become intimately involved with the last of Stephen's younger friends, the painter Rex Whistler (just starting out on his successful career with a commission for murals at the Tate Gallery restaurant), he scarcely registered his existence at this their first meeting.

Altogether, Sassoon felt very much out of things when he arrived at Wilsford. Exhausted from his writing efforts of the week, as well as the journey, and conscious that he was nearly twice the age of Stephen and most of his friends, he felt every inch the 'tired and middle-aged author'.[16] But as dinner progressed he found himself talking volubly to impress his host and noted with gratification that Stephen seemed to hang on his words. When it came to dressing up after dinner, however, he felt isolated again. Refusing to participate himself, he watched the young people, of both sexes, dressing up first as nuns, then in pyjamas, shocking choices in the context of the times. Even allowing for a reaction against the austerities of the war, it was the kind of deliberately provocative behaviour that was beginning to scandalize London society. Sassoon himself did 'not quite like it', though he could see that it was 'very amusing',[17] an ambivalence that would characterize his whole relationship with Stephen.

The 'high jinks' continued relentlessly the next day.[18] Stephen had ordered elaborate eighteenth-century shepherd's costumes. (With his love of cross-dressing, on this occasion the women had to wear male clothes.) It was a tribute to the fashionable painters Watteau and Lancret admired by Beaton, Whistler and himself, and Beaton was to film the various tableaux into which the actors were organized by Stephen. Whereas Sassoon had been thrilled as a child by his mother's innocent *tableaux vivants*, he was clearly uneasy at Stephen's subtle subversion of the form and again refused to join in. As a result he does not appear in Beaton's photographs, which have been described as 'the most evocative images of wealthy young England in the 1920s'.[19] One in particular, of the young people posing 'artistically' on a wooden bridge at the edge of the grounds, is very revealing. Rex, whose taste for the rococo informed his whole life, looks serious, Cecil 'poses' as he loved to, Georgia and the Jungmann sisters look fairly natural, Walton rather self-conscious and Stephen, narcissistic to the core, entirely absorbed in himself and his latest role.

It may have been in an effort to escape from this unreal world and assert his own literary authority that Sassoon suggested driving Stephen, Osbert and Christabel to see Lytton Strachey the same afternoon. Strachey lived not too far away at Ham Spray in the north-west of the county, but Sassoon got lost on the way, driving eventually into a haystack, and they arrived very late for tea. Though fascinated by this 'strange eruption of unexpected visitors from the expensive classes', Strachey resisted their pleas to accompany them back to Wilsford for more dressing up and 'shudder[ed] to think of the horrors of their return journey'.[20] 'Strange creatures', he told his friend Roger Senhouse, 'with just a few feathers where brains should be'.[21]

Strachey added as an afterthought, 'though Siegfried is rather different', and that was Sassoon's main problem. Whilst magnetized by Stephen even at his most *outré*, he could never enter unselfconsciously into his world. And it was not simply a matter of age and upbringing. For Edith Olivier, who joined them for dinner on their return from Ham Spray, was thirty-four years older than Stephen and the spinster daughter of a vicar, yet she loved being garbed and made up extravagantly for the fancy-dress dinner and charades which followed. She was to become a lifelong friend of Sassoon's, but he would never be able to share her attitude.

Edith's only complaint that Sunday evening at Wilsford was the lateness of the meal, delayed by Stephen's agonizings over his own costume – 'a white Russian suit with silver train and a bandeau round his head', she remembered.[22] But when he finally made his appearance, he seemed to her to move 'like Mercurius with winged feet'.[23] Sassoon was equally dazzled, realizing for the first time how dangerous the situation had become. Stephen, as Sassoon later recorded, was actively encouraging him 'with eyes that could persuade'.[24] Instead of withdrawing, however, as he had with Gathorne-Hardy, he made a deliberate advance, suggesting a late-night drive to Stephen, who readily agreed. It was 6.30 a.m. before they arrived back, their relationship clearly on a very different footing from when they set out.

By the time Sassoon had driven Stephen back to London and deposited him at his mother's house in Smith Square, only a few hundred yards from his old lodgings in Tufton Street, he was completely infatuated. He instantly abandoned all attempts to finish *Fox-Hunting Man*, though alternately guilty and resentful about it, and tried to put Glen out of his mind. If any proof were needed of his infidelity, he himself provided it in his diary the day he arrived back from Wilsford: 'I am torn by my sense of what Glen will [*sic*] think of me if he knew.'[25]

Two days later, after Stephen had called at Campden Hill Square and left a note for him suggesting tea,[26] he was more philosophical, already rationalizing his attraction to Stephen: 'Such is human nature!' he comforted himself: 'This doesn't mean that I don't love Glen just as much as I did four days ago.'[27] But his promised account of the Wilsford weekend for Glen was put off a whole week. And when finally dispatched it was singularly misleading, referring to Stephen only once and then simply his name. Reading it one might have thought he was falling in love with Sachie, or even Cecil Beaton, whose 'fantastic feats of female impersonation' he dwelt on.[28]

But it was Stephen he needed and who evidently needed him. Writing to Sassoon on 5 November after three tempestuous weeks together, he assured him that he was thinking 'of one vast beautiful thing that warms my heart and mind and body and soul'.[29] And though usually an assiduous diarist, he noted in his almost empty journal, with a deliberate sexual pun: 'I've been too gay to write in my diary.'[30]

Sassoon, on the other hand, scribbled copiously in his, though he knew it was *Fox-Hunting Man* he should be writing. Instead of grim midnight sessions with Sherston, however, he found himself entertaining Stephen or posing for Stephen's commissioned photographs of him in Beaton's studio, an occasion Beaton could not resist describing: 'He groaned; tears welled up into his eyes and flowed down his rugged cheeks! And when it was all over he sighed with relief and shook himself like a dog after a bath.'[31]

Beaton's account wittily pinpoints Sassoon's essential difference from Stephen, who loved posing, the more artificially the better. Stephen in a leopard skin perching on rocks, Stephen as Romeo lying on his tomb in velvet doublet and pearls, Stephen in a black, shiny mackintosh with carefully made-up face, all show the same love of the camera. Whereas he relished attracting attention to himself, Sassoon loathed it. He was already worried that their relationship would be talked about and begged Stephen to be discreet. It was a proof of Stephen's deep commitment that he agreed, since he would certainly have enjoyed flaunting their liaison for the benefit of the society gossips.

Too many people had already witnessed and talked about their evident infatuation with each other, however, and soon the only real interest of the affair for onlookers was not *whether* they were involved but *how* they could possibly have become so. It was, as Beaton observed, 'such a paradoxical combination of characters, the one so flamboyant and the other so retiring'.[32] Peter Quennell, a young Oxford graduate and aspiring poet, who knew both Stephen and Sassoon by 1927, was equally intrigued by the contrast between them: 'Sassoon was like the worthy vicar of a parish coming to town and meeting this great society beauty.'[33] And it was not simply jealousy which caused Edith Sitwell to christen the lovers 'The Old Earl and Little Lord Fauntleroy': they were conspicuously different.

To some extent this was part of their mutual attraction. Sassoon struck many people, including Anthony Powell, as 'melancholy' and 'saturnine'.[34] Ottoline had detected something '*sauvage*' in him at their first meeting, comparing him to a stag or faun, and part of his attraction for Stephen was that 'like some charming wild animal – one never felt that he was really tame (or tameable)'.[35] Though he sometimes called Sassoon 'Kangar', his army nickname derived from 'kangaroo', he thought it not quite fierce enough; a moose or grizzly bear seemed to him more appropriate.

As such similes imply, Sassoon did not always find it easy to fit into society, especially after the war. Whereas for Stephen, with what he himself called his 'light, gay nature', life was all fun.[36] He was Sassoon's obverse, his unrealized flip side. He enabled the man he once described as a 'tortured, scarred hermit' to 'remember the joy of life, to share his amazing ecstasies'.[37] Or as Beaton put it, Stephen helped Sassoon to 'enjoy ordinary things so that they [became] wildly exciting'.[38] Sassoon would later attribute Stephen's pronounced vitality, together with his wild mood-swings, to his consumptive state.

Even as Stephen grew older he retained his childlike appreciation of things, but when Sassoon first met him at twenty-one, it was at its peak. It was the age which most appealed to Sassoon, the age Gabriel and Glen had been when he first met them, the age when a youth is just turning into a man. And Sassoon found it 'impossible, or intolerable' to imagine Stephen as 'anything but young', an ominous admission for any long-term future together.[39]

Stephen's effeminate manners and appearance, his willowy slender-ness and delicate features, provided another strong contrast to Sassoon, of whom the words 'rugged', 'masculine' and 'military' were frequently used.[40] (Stephen himself thought Sassoon 'handsome in a stern rather military way'.[41]) Philip Hoare argues that Sassoon may have seen in Stephen's effeminacy 'a reaction against the masculine values of war',[42] but sexual tastes can rarely be explained in such straightforward terms. Exactly why Sassoon was attracted to Stephen's type of beauty remains largely mysterious, though it is certain he was. Just as he had been drawn to Glenn Hunter, Ivor Novello and Glen Byam Shaw, for whom make-up and fancy dress were second nature, so he found Stephen's magenta lips, necklaces and exotic scents a powerful attraction, where some might have found them repulsive.

Sassoon's mother, remembering Gabriel's golden curls and girlish fea-tures among others, would refer later to Stephen, as she had to Gabriel, as 'just another of Sieg's pretty boys'.[43] But it was more than prettiness that attracted Sassoon to Stephen. He also needed to feel protective towards his lovers and Stephen's fragile, almost ethereal beauty seems to have enhanced his own sense of dominance and control. The more vulnerable Stephen became, the deeper Sassoon's commitment. And Stephen appears to have welcomed his protectiveness at first, some of his earliest words of praise for Sassoon being 'kind and strong'.[44]

They were opposites in so many ways. While Stephen admired Sassoon's ideals and loved his earnestness, his unworldliness, his austerity, even his tidiness, his own lifestyle was frivolous, sophisticated and luxurious, his surroundings lavishly cluttered, and his morals far more relaxed. But what the two did undoubtedly share from the start was a powerful sexual attraction. A mock-Shakespearian sonnet written by Sassoon shortly after his first Wilsford visit makes this explicit:

> ... Now (swept by secret music and enslaved
> By drugged and restless raptures of desire)
> How shall we feed these flames which burn like straw?
> How shall we two be burned to death yet saved? ...
> Speak; and your mouth will set my limbs on fire.
> Ask; and my love shall break you every law.[45]

And Stephen had only to be absent from his 'Tristan and Galahad and Launcelot' to be 'hungry for the sense of [his] arms around [him] and [his] mouth'.[46]

Had sex been the only dimension to their relationship, however, it would neither have lasted as long as it did, nor survived such problems. It is significant that, on first meeting Stephen, Sassoon had not just found him 'divinely beautiful' but also 'very witty and intelligent'. Edith Olivier thought him 'the most sparkling talker' she had ever met 'and perhaps the most amusing'.[47] While Stephen appreciated Sassoon's 'funny dear clumsy' jokes, his own were more carefully orchestrated, along the lines of Oscar Wilde.[48] 'I respect you for the pride and spirit you showed in putting me in my place,' he wrote after one disagreement, 'but must I stay in it? – please no – send me a grumpy little postcard.'[49] As Sassoon noted, Stephen found 'good phrases for things'.[50]

Stephen's intelligence was largely untutored, but he delighted Sassoon with his love of literature, especially poetry. His mother had not insisted on a regular education; instead she had read to him from the poets, Hardy, Bridges and the Georgians in general, some of whom she knew. (She was a close friend of Sir Henry Newbolt, for example, who lived near Wilsford.) By the time he met Sassoon, Stephen's favourites included Shelley, Tennyson, Keats, Housman, Charlotte Mew and de la Mare, all poets Sassoon admired. Stephen wrote poetry himself, but it was perhaps fortunate that it was not very good, since the main thing Sassoon brought to their relationship was his poetic authority. Secure in his role of mentor he introduced Stephen to some of his own more recent discoveries, such as Vaughan and Landor, and revelled in his disciple's lavish praise of his own work.

Their shared interest in the other arts also drew them together, music being the one partial exception. (Sassoon never learnt to like jazz, which Stephen adored.) They both enjoyed art galleries, museums, ballet and theatre. Stephen himself was constantly drawing and painting and in this area Sassoon was happy to concede his 'delightful talent'.[51] He particularly admired Stephen's delicate and intricate designs of orchids and shells, making no public comment on his numerous sketches of sailors and missionaries, many of them indecent.[52] He arranged for Stephen to decorate three of his own works in Faber's 'Ariel' series and, when colour printing was refused on grounds of expense, paid for it himself.[53]

In a curious way Stephen was a combination of all that had attracted Sassoon to his previous lovers. Even Prince Philipp, though apparently so different from Stephen, shared one important characteristic, his social standing, which had given both of them impeccable manners and the easy charm and confidence of the privileged. Not quite so dazzling as Philipp's, Stephen's connections nevertheless impressed Sassoon greatly. In addition to his father, the 1st Baron Glenconner, there was his aunt Margot Tennant, who had married the Liberal Prime Minister Herbert Asquith, later the 1st Earl of Oxford and Asquith. And Margot's stepdaughter Violet had created yet another well-known clan, the Bonham Carters, when she married her father's private secretary. Stephen's mother's family, the Wyndhams, though not belonging to the aristocracy, moved in elevated artistic circles, and when Lord Glenconner died Pamela had married Asquith's Foreign Secretary, Lord Grey of Fallodon, a figure who inspired both awe and deep affection in Sassoon.

Stephen's was also a moneyed world and it is unlikely that Sassoon would have felt able to venture into it without his recent legacy. It is probably no coincidence that he began responding to Stephen's interest in him only two months after Rachel Beer's death. But one of the few things he regretted about Stephen at the start *was* his money. 'Do you remember you used to say you wished I was poor?' Stephen reminded him later, 'so that you could treat me.'[54] Money had often been a means of controlling relationships for Sassoon, but there was to be none of that with Stephen. Though he lived lavishly and gave generously, he had more than enough for his needs.

*

'You are the person I've most loved in my life,' Sassoon told Stephen.[55] He may not have been able to 'treat' him in the way he had indulged Gabriel, Philipp and Glen, but there were still the other rituals of courtship to enjoy. Confident that his friends would find Stephen's beauty, charm and background as irresistible as he did, he entered with even greater relish than usual on a round of introductions.

First and foremost Stephen must be taken to see the Hardys for their approval. It would be Sassoon's last visit to Hardy before his death, though nothing led him to suspect it. The octogenarian was in very good form when they arrived at Max Gate on 6 December 1927, mounting nimbly on a stool to carve the goose for lunch. (Stephen was surprised at how short the author of *Tess* was.) He also talked at length to Stephen after the meal and seemed altogether his usual observant self. Florence noted in her diary her husband's remark that Stephen was the only person he had met who walked like Swinburne, a dubious compliment *not* passed on to Sassoon. For all his powers of observation, however, Hardy apparently never suspected the nature of the relationship between Sassoon and the string of young male 'friends' he brought to visit. Florence, who (according to Hardy's biographer Robert Gittings) was half in love with Sassoon herself, may have been more sensitive to the situation. But if she had her suspicions, she kept them quiet.

Sassoon's other substitute parents, Henry and Ruth Head, also had to be introduced to Stephen, and expressed only admiration, whatever private misgivings they may have had. Even his actual mother appeared to approve of Stephen to begin with, referring to him as a 'dear boy' (though 'she very soon decided otherwise', Sassoon noted).[56] How far she had finally accepted her son's preference for young men to women is not clear, but she made no secret of her hope that 'Sieg' would one day marry.

Stephen's success with these authority figures in his life was crucial to Sassoon. It was equally important to him, however, that his younger friends should approve. It was also a chance to impress Stephen further with his literary credentials without any of the need for concealment that he experienced with the Hardys, his mother and, to some extent, the Heads. E.M. Forster, for example, could be expected to understand the situation instantly, which he did, striking up an independent friendship with Stephen in the process. T.E. Lawrence, whom Sassoon took Stephen to visit at his Dorset cottage, Cloud's Hill, also warmed to him, and continued to invite him back after Stephen's relationship with Sassoon had ended.

Even the strictly heterosexual Blunden responded to Stephen's charm when Sassoon introduced them over tea at Campden Hill Square: 'It was all Charles Lamb-like in my cosy interior,' Sassoon wrote with satisfaction in his diary at the beginning of December 1927.[57] Sam Behrman, now a great deal more sophisticated than when Sassoon had shocked him with an account of his homosexual torments in New York, was equally positive when he was introduced to Stephen the following month. And Nellie Burton, who could rarely resist young men, gave Stephen an extravagant welcome, though like Behrman and Mrs Sassoon she was to become highly critical of him later on.

The majority of these introductions took place during the first few crowded months of the relationship, which also included further visits to Wilsford to meet Stephen's own mother and stepfather. While Pamela and Sassoon, who may both have sensed competition for Stephen's affection, failed to bond, Sassoon got on well with Lord Grey, who seemed like a breath of reality in Wilsford's unreal world. What he admired most about the elderly politician was not his statesmanlike qualities but his 'perfect simplicity and kindness' or, as he would put it in a poem written nearly twenty years later, his 'native humour, human – simple yet profound'.[58] The 'strength of spirit' which was helping Grey deal with his own failing eyesight in late 1927 would convince Sassoon that he was the one member of what Ruth Head called 'that curiously hard family' whom Sassoon could trust when Stephen became seriously ill.[59]

Stephen was still free from a recurrence of his TB in January 1928 but Pamela, whose 'fussing' Edith Olivier believed was turning her son into a chronic invalid, decided that he needed to go abroad for his health. Her decision may have resulted in part from a wish to separate him from Sassoon. It is ironic if it did, since it had the opposite effect by giving Sassoon a much-needed respite.[60] At the beginning of 1928, just before Pamela announced her plan, he had reached a crisis which would have seemed unimaginable to him three months previously: 'My feelings about Stephen have changed lately', he wrote in his diary, 'owing to the conflict between my desire to get on with my book and his inability to keep away from me. This has caused me to wake out of my entrancement and to see him with the more critical eyes of commonsense. He symbolizes all that I should ordinarily regard as idle and pleasure-loving and self-indulgent.'[61] Reality was breaking through his initial enchantment. Though still charmed by the 'grace' with which Stephen performed, he was beginning to realize that he was 'essentially childish' beneath his 'veneer of sophistication'.[62] This was brought home to him sharply by Stephen's reaction, or rather lack of reaction, to Hardy's death.

Hardy, who had taken to his bed only five days after their visit the previous December, died on 11 January 1928 at the age of eighty-seven. Sassoon, who had scarcely registered Schuster's death a few weeks previously, was devastated.[63] He valued his visits to Max Gate more than anything else in his adult life and, however much he had prepared himself for the inevitable, it was a heavy blow when it came. So that Stephen's breezy announcement to him on 12 January – 'I came to tell you about darling Mr Hardy – he's dead' – can only have underlined his shallowness for Sassoon.[64] (To be fair to Stephen, he had only met Hardy once.) 'I sometimes doubt whether he is capable of feeling deeply,' Sassoon confessed on 18 January.[65] He had spent the intervening week trying to help Florence Hardy through her ordeal, shuttling between Wilsford and Max Gate on the 14th and 15th and facing his own severe trial at Hardy's funeral in Westminster Abbey on 16 January. Florence had given him a front-row seat in the Abbey but, unable to face the very public and, to him, unfeeling ceremony, he 'slunk in' and stood at a side door until he saw Hardy's ashes lowered into the ground, then rushed out overwhelmed by grief.[66]

Hardy's funeral, surrounded by publicity, controversy and outright wrangling, seemed to him the last straw. Like Hardy and Florence themselves, he believed Hardy's body should be in the family churchyard at Stinsford, near to their Dorset home, and was enraged by Cockerell's insistence, as co-executor, that it should be buried in Poets' Corner. ('Efficient but devoid of all feeling', Sassoon commented of Cockerell on this occasion.)[67] The gruesome compromise eventually reached, that Hardy's heart should go to Stinsford, his ashes to the Abbey, seemed to him lacking in any kind of dignity or appropriateness and depressed him even further. He was equally disgusted by Graves's 'presumptuous' article on Hardy in the *Sphere*, 'a vulgar and hasty exploitation', he felt, of the fact that Graves had stayed one night at Max Gate in 1920.[68] The whole affair, he told Ottoline, 'drove [him] distracted' for several weeks and made him 'hate' the world.[69]

In this context and with the added worry of his unfinished novel hanging over him, Stephen's departure for Germany a few days after the funeral was almost a relief and probably saved their relationship. Stephen would be in safe hands, since his aunt, 'Nan' Tennant, [70] had agreed to go with him to the Bavarian *pension* she had recommended for its mountain air and nursing facilities, Haus Hirth. And Sassoon would be able to devote himself to *Fox-Hunting Man*.

By 31 January he was hard at work. Avoiding most of his friends in February and March and missing Stephen during his long absence, he aimed to complete the book by his return in April. Appropriately, since *Fox-Hunting Man* ends on Easter Sunday 1916 with Sherston staring across no man's land, he finished at 5 a.m. on 8 April, another Easter Sunday, and drove out to Runnymede to gaze across the Thames. Not expecting much from his 'recreative exercise', he arranged with his new publishers, Faber and Gwyer, to have the book published anonymously later in the year and put it out of his mind.[71]

In spite of his great relief at finishing *Fox-Hunting Man* and Stephen's imminent return, the grim start to the year continued. Scarcely had he recovered from Hardy's death when another poet he greatly admired, Charlotte Mew, died in tragic circumstances, committing suicide on 24 March at the age of fifty-nine. Sassoon, who like other admirers had tried to help her, could just about rationalize her death. 'She must have wanted to be in peace very much to have done that,' he wrote to Edith Sitwell. 'And we have her magnificent poetry.'[72]

He could even accept Ottoline's cancer of the jaw, diagnosed in mid-April, since there was a reasonable chance that she would survive it. But he found it very difficult indeed to come to terms with Edmund Gosse's death on 16 May. Like Hardy's, it was not entirely unexpected: Gosse had become increasingly frail and his operation for prostate (itself a dangerous undertaking in the 1920s) at the age of nearly eighty was considered a serious risk. Nevertheless Sassoon felt almost as shocked as he had when

Hardy died. 'I am gloomy about the death of Gosse', he wrote to a mutual friend, Tomlinson, 'for I was very fond of him.'[73] He had remained grateful over the years to the man who, on his tenth birthday, sent him one of his books inscribed 'to *Mr* Siegfried Sassoon'. ('That made a man of me!' Sassoon told Tomlinson.) Gosse had always encouraged him as a writer, however harsh his criticisms at times, and though Sassoon had replaced him with other mentors, he had never forgotten his debt to him. Even in Gosse's old age, when his resolute conservatism in literature and increasing prickliness had made him seem slightly absurd to some, Sassoon went on admiring his complete devotion to letters. It seems appropriate that his epitaph on his old friend and early father-figure should echo Hamlet's description of his dead father: 'He was a man, take him for all in all, / I shall not look upon his like again.'[74]

Curiously enough, Sassoon himself had already made a link between the deaths of Hardy and Gosse, though not conscious of it at the time. After visiting Gosse's sickbed on 28 October 1927, he had written a sonnet, 'One Who Watches', which he subsequently revised for Hardy's death less than three months later:

> We are all near to death. But in my friends
> I am forewarned too closely of that nearness.
> Death haunts their days that are; in him descends
> The darkness that shall change their living dearness
>   To something different, made within my mind
>   By memories and recordings and convenings
>   Of voices heard through veils and faces blind
>   To the kind light of my autumnal gleanings.
>
> Not so much for myself I feel that fear
> As for all those in whom my loves must die;
> Thus, like some hooded death, I stand apart
> And in their happiest moments I can hear
> Silence unending, when those lives must lie
> Hoarded like happy summers in my heart.
>
> (CP, p. 191)

Without telling Gosse that it was *his* possible death which had inspired the poem, Sassoon then sent it to him 'as a consoling comment' on Hardy's death.[75] Ironically, Gosse found it 'very beautiful', little realizing that it had been written in anticipation of his own end four months on.[76]

Before Gosse died he had agreed to edit Hardy's letters as Florence had requested, in spite of Cockerell's attempts to dissuade him: 'I would be damned if anyone else should,' he told Sassoon.[77] Florence had also asked that Sassoon be approached to write the *English Men of Letters* volume on Hardy, an honour he declined. Not only did the thought of another prose book horrify him ('Verse not prose, thank God,' he jotted on one manuscript),[78] but it seemed almost disloyal to write about him publicly. 'I never

Boswellized T.H. when staying at Max Gate,' he told Tomlinson. 'When I went upstairs [to bed] I felt that it would be a sort of betrayal of the hospitality.'[79] He would later write an article in *John O'London's Weekly* for Hardy's centenary in 1940 and draw up a list of his favourite Hardy poems, first for Cockerell, then for a BBC programme in 1956.[80] He would even contemplate a book on Hardy after finishing *Meredith* in 1948, but his only sustained account of the writer he admired most in the whole of English literature would be in *Siegfried's Journey*.

*

Both Hardy's and Gosse's death had made Sassoon more conscious of his own age, an effect heightened by the return of Stephen. Whether in an attempt to make up for his own absence or, as Philip Hoare suggests, as a 'minder',[81] Sassoon had paid for William Walton to join Stephen in Bavaria and their accounts of the light-hearted holiday together on Stephen's return in mid-April underlined his own sense of mortality.[82] 'I think I am happiest, really, with elderly people', he wrote shortly afterwards, 'because they can talk about the past.' He was still deeply in love with Stephen and extremely jealous when he heard how much Stephen had enjoyed meeting Edith Sitwell's protégé the Russian painter Tchelitchew in Paris on his way home. (Stephen had almost certainly tried to make him jealous about Tchelitchew – and even the apparently safe heterosexual, Walton – maintaining that the young composer had fallen in love with him and liked it best of all when Stephen wore nothing but a 'snake skin belt'.)[83] But Sassoon was increasingly antagonized by Stephen's lifestyle, especially his society friends, who seemed to be 'silly people whose behaviour really cannot be exaggerated in its folly and extravagance'.[84] By the time Stephen left London again in late April for Preston Deanery, a health farm near Northampton, Sassoon had begun to wonder if he understood young people and their world at all.

He had agreed to attend Stephen's birthday party on 20 April, an extraordinary affair where 200 guests in fancy dress milled around drunk in two tiny rooms and the host stole the show as a sailor in huge gold earrings, but in the event he could not face it. He *was* prepared to watch Stephen posing in various elaborate society *tableaux*, such as Olga Lynn's 'Pageant of Hyde Park' in May where Stephen, reinvigorated by three weeks at the health farm, played Shelley. He was not, however, ready to accompany Stephen to any other social occasions. Though 'sighted' by one gossip columnist at the Chelsea Arts Ball on 8 June, his sole involvement was to chauffeur Stephen home in the early hours of the morning.

Temperamentally averse to dressing up, or performance of any kind, he avoided the numerous parties thrown by the Bright Young Things in that last hectic season before the Depression put an end to their cavortings. Pyjama parties, bottle parties, even swimming-bath parties, all daring innovations at the time and designed to shock, filled Stephen's diary that summer and Sassoon grew worried that people were talking about the outrageous doings of him and his friends. Like Edith Olivier, he believed Stephen's behaviour stemmed mainly from exuberance, with a little light-hearted ribaldry added. 'All that is only a mask,' he tried to reassure himself. 'All the rest of his character is lovable and witty and intelligent.'[85]

The outside world was not as tolerant, however, and eventually Stephen's own class turned against him. It was not so much the incident itself – Stephen and David Plunket-Greene bringing two uninvited guests to Lady Ellesmere's Ball on 10 July – as a refusal on the part of the soberer members of the upper classes to accept any more. As a matter of principle Lady Ellesmere complained to the press of Stephen's flouting of social etiquette, mild though it was by comparison with some of his exploits, and his name was splashed across the nation's newspapers.

Pamela Grey panicked and Sassoon's chance to win her over arrived. She and Lord Grey had been warned that it was 'the beginning of a "Round-up" of Stephen and his foppish friends', Edith Olivier wrote in her diary.[86] 'She fears he may be suspected of real immorality if he continues to be written of in the papers in this company.' Pamela, 'quite broken' by events, begged Edith to help prevent further trouble and Edith suggested writing to Sassoon.[87]

Sassoon, who had spent his summer enjoying Russian opera and ballet in Stephen's private box, a pastime which took him back to his last lonely summer in London before the outbreak of the First World War, was fully committed to Stephen by this time. His references to Glen suggest that he appreciated him more than ever, perhaps by comparison with Stephen's silliness. But he was still infatuated with Stephen and in any case Glen's return in late May had put their relationship on an entirely different footing.

Glen had been back from America a week before he contacted Sassoon at the Reform on 4 June. 'When are you coming home, my darling?' Sassoon had asked him in February, but he could not have looked forward to his return. (The hundred pounds he sent Glen in March was probably partly from a sense of guilt.) Believing that the moment of truth had now arrived and feeling very guilty indeed, he agreed to meet Glen later that evening at Glen's house in Campden Hill Gardens. But his return from the cinema with Stephen was delayed, perhaps deliberately, by Stephen, who also insisted on coming to see Glen with him. It was the last thing Sassoon wanted. Using their lateness as an excuse for not visiting Glen, he took Stephen back to his own flat in Campden Hill Square and was in the kitchen making tea when Glen announced his arrival by hooting the car horn. To his horror Sassoon heard Stephen shout airily from the window: 'Siegfried is on his way down.'[88] It was a scene either from nightmare or a Whitehall farce. 'You'll find Stephen Tennant in there,' Sassoon announced at the top of the stairs and the next hour of strained conversation and suppressed emotions may be imagined.[89]

It was only after Stephen had been driven home by a self-righteously injured Glen and they were back at Glen's house, that Sassoon attempted to explain. The irony was that, after making a 'slight scene' about Sassoon's infidelity, Glen then confessed to his own; he, too, had fallen in love with someone else.[90] The irony was strengthened by the fact that the person in question was a woman, the actress Angela Baddeley, and the sister of Stephen's brother David's new wife, Hermione.[91]

By the next day, Glen at least had adjusted to the new situation and was sending his 'love' to Stephen on a postcard to Sassoon, from his 'poor, dear, kind Speasey' (his family nickname).[92] Essentially good-natured, greatly admiring of Sassoon and indebted to him for his help in combating the philistinism of the theatrical world, he seemed determined to preserve their relationship, albeit on different terms. Unlike Sassoon's previous lovers he would become a lasting friend to him, one of the most important of his life.

The denouement with Glen behind him, Pamela's plea for help in late July encouraged Sassoon to hope for an even closer involvement with Stephen. And when he arrived at Lord Grey's Northumberland estate, Fallodon, in mid-August to spend a few days with the exiled and decidedly bored Stephen, he presented Pamela and her husband with a plan. Both he and Stephen had been invited to hear Edith Sitwell and William Walton's collaboration, *Façade*, performed at Siena on 14 September and to spend a week at Sir George Sitwell's Italian estate, Montegufoni, afterwards: Sassoon proposed to take Stephen there, then on to Venice, at his own expense. Stephen could travel by the Orient Express with his childhood nanny, Rebecca Trusler, to Munich, where Sassoon would drive to meet them and they could spend a few days at the Bavarian *pension*, Haus Hirth, for Stephen to recover from the journey.

The whole plan, like everything else in Stephen's adult life, was based on the assumption that he was still a child and still suffering from TB, neither of which was at this point true. Sassoon may have been trying to reassure Pamela, who was nevertheless only satisfied when they added another of their servants, William, to the party as Stephen's valet.

Buying a luxurious new red Packard especially for the trip, Sassoon set off in it a few days before Stephen, Nannie and William, arriving in Munich on 29 August. His drive down through France and Germany had reminded him of his trip with Glen the previous year and there were to be a number of occasions in the next few months when he would regret the exchange of Glen for Stephen.[93]

To begin with things went very well. Meeting the Wilsford trio off the train at Munich the day after his own arrival, Sassoon spent the next four days there sharing Stephen's most attractive quality, his love of art. He responded joyfully to the operas, concerts and art galleries to which

Sassoon took him, reverting to a routine he had first established during his stay in Munich with Philipp in 1922.[94] And they both read avidly, Stephen grateful for the eclectic but serious mixture of books he had asked Sassoon to bring in his car, among them Shelley's poems, Maugham's *Of Human Bondage*, Forster's *Aspects of the Novel* and Sassoon's own work.

Against this reassuring background Sassoon seems to have been happy to join in Stephen's lighter entertainments, buying 'lovely bounderish caps with long peaks and saucy patterns', tinsel paper and postcards, or simply eating pink ices in a teashop.[95] 'Dear Stephen's enjoyment of everything is infectious,' he wrote to Glen, who had quickly become a confidant. 'He is very childlike in his enthusiasms.'[96]

Their visit to Haus Hirth on 4 September also went well. Situated in the village of Untergrainau near Garmisch, a two hours' drive south-west of Munich, it was on the border of Austria and surrounded by snow-covered mountains. Set in a sheltered valley, where tinkling cow bells and fir-covered slopes created a fairy-tale atmosphere, there was something magical about it for most of its visitors. Like Stephen, Sassoon fell 'in love with everything at once ... the miraculous cleanliness of the house, the atmosphere of gaiety and happiness'.[97]

The owners of this 'holiday or rest home', as it was advertised, were Walther and Johanna Hirth. They had lost all of Walther's considerable fortune in Germany's post-war inflation, but seemed quite contented with their simple, hard-working life. Taking in guests at a very reasonable rate, they provided them with 'plain but perfect' food (according to Sassoon) and, if necessary, nursing care, as Stephen had discovered eight months earlier.

Sassoon preferred Frau Hirth, known to everyone as 'Tante Johanna', to her husband, 'Onkel Walther'. A lifelong friend of the Grand Duke of Hesse, she had been first married to a count, who had been killed in the war. It may have been her noble connections that led Sassoon to suggest that she herself could have been a grand duchess. 'Frau Hirth is tall and queenly,' he wrote to Festing-Jones on his second visit to the *pension*.[98] With her dangling earrings and tight-bodiced, full-skirted Bavarian costumes, which she changed daily, he found her 'very brisk and beautiful'.[99] He also admired her efficiency, her excellent English and her dexterity with the vacuum cleaner: '[She] is, in fact, the ideal woman,' he concluded revealingly.[100]

Walther he had less time for, dismissing him rather peremptorily as kind-hearted but stupid. (Philipp had convinced him that most Germans were stupid.) His description of a short, thick-set, ex-newspaper owner, with enormous knees poking out of perennial leather shorts is noticeably less sympathetic than his picture of Tante Johanna.

The Hirths welcomed Stephen back and made an equally great fuss of Sassoon, insisting on a special breakfast with a scarlet-candled cake and chair festooned with flowers for his birthday on 8 September. 'Their homely warm-heartedness is beyond description', Sassoon told de la Mare, 'and the air and sunshine ditto.'[101] And when he and Stephen set out for Italy in the Packard after four days' rest, it was with their laps full of dahlias from the Hirths' garden.

Tante Johanna had also supplied them with a 'divine' (Stephen's word) picnic, which they ate on a mountainside as they crossed Austria to Italy.[102] Stephen found the drive over the Brenner to Bolzano 'breathtaking' and he was not being ironic about Sassoon's handling of the car, which fortunately struck him as bold rather than erratic. 'Siegfried drove masterfully and tirelessly,' he wrote in his diary that evening, 'whisking round bend after bend, dodging touring cars and lymphatic peasants – swooping from Bavaria to Austria and finally into Italy, mellow, much warmer, *too* lovely!!'

Their second day was even more successful. Following the longer, more scenic route to Bologna, Sassoon drove over the Mendola Pass to Lake Garda, where they stayed the night at Riva, 'the most romantic place' Stephen had ever seen: 'hot, raucous, southern, slouching Italian sailors roll along the wharves and groups of giggling peasant girls cluster outside the "Ristorantes" '.[103] Dining out of doors 'beside the black waters', Stephen was at his happiest. Sassoon, too, basking in Stephen's belief that he was 'conquer[ing] the road valiantly', was content in spite of his tiredness.[104]

The tiredness, however, got worse, in spite of a much shorter drive than was planned the next day, to Gardone further down the lake. For Sassoon also found himself having to act as Stephen's valet in William's absence. So that, while Stephen strolled about the town, Sassoon did the packing of Stephen's many suitcases, all of which had to be unpacked at his insistence daily. And when Stephen brought back peaches, it was Sassoon who washed them for him to eat. Again it was Sassoon who had to prepare the car for their journey via Brescia to Cremona on their fourth day, and he who, in an attempt to make up for lost time, had the long drive from Cremona to Bologna on their fifth, followed by a last fruitless dash to reach Siena in time for *Façade* on their sixth.

But it was Stephen who complained. Having done nothing more arduous than go to the cinema, visit a few sights or eat a peach, and waited on hand and foot the whole way, he was nevertheless (in his own words) 'sulky and temperfull' by the time they reached Siena: 'We had arrived too late for *Façade* to my great grief. I thought I should die of temper. I felt eaten up with rage and hate. RAGE & HATE.'[105]

He was, however, mollified by a week at Montegufoni, an imposing eleventh-century castle with superb views of the surrounding Tuscan hills.[106] He loved gossiping with the Sitwells and their friends Walton, Constant Lambert, Christabel Aberconway, Zita Jungmann, Beryl de Zoete and Arthur Waley, all of whom he knew. It was now Sassoon's turn to react. He was in trouble with Edith for missing *Façade*, he disliked most house parties and would have much preferred to be in Florence visiting picture galleries, and he was finally beginning to 'resent the fact that Stephen never stir[red] a finger to help facilitate [their] arrangements'.[107] For the first time on their journey he longed to be alone. Having had a glimpse of just how spoilt and childish Stephen could be, he thought nostalgically of Glen.

'For really happy companionship I rely on Glen more than Stephen, who has yet to prove that his feelings for me are more than physical,' he wrote in his diary shortly after their arrival in Venice on 29 September.[108] It was the mid-point in their journey and Stephen seemed to him more physically desirable than ever. But his self-centredness and callousness could not be ignored. If Sassoon mentioned his mother's past sufferings or Blunden's growing problems, for instance, Stephen seemed indifferent, responding only with 'facile phrases and linguistic precocity – the habit of speech acquired in society, and never at a loss for an epithet'.[109] His experience of Stephen seemed to have 'worked itself through to the end of the volume' and he was now determined to try to 'influence him towards behaving sensibly'.[110] It was a re-run of his relationship with Gabriel and doomed to failure, but a resolution that would rule his life for the next three and a half years.

*

Venice marked not only a turning point in Sassoon's relations with Stephen and the journey, but also in his career as a writer. *Memoirs of a Fox-Hunting Man* had been published on 28 September, the day before his arrival in Venice, and was reviewed glowingly the day after he got there. Sitting in the sunshine with Stephen in St Mark's Square drinking hot chocolate, Sassoon was delighted to find a long and enthusiastic review by J.C. Squire in the *Observer*.[111] Humbert Wolfe's log-rolling piece on *The Heart's Journey* had reached him at Montegufoni, but this was quite different. To have his first serious attempt at prose praised so warmly and discriminatingly by someone as authoritative as Squire gave him hope for his writing future just as he had begun to despair of it.[112]

It was also a pleasure to return to a city that he had first visited with Philipp in 1922. His second stay, with the Morrells in 1926, had given him an even greater appreciation of its art and he enjoyed acting as Stephen's guide, Baedeker in hand. Stephen improved somewhat during their three-day stay, genuinely excited by the wealth of art and truly appreciative of the 'exquisite' Guardi reproductions Sassoon bought him at the Accademia.[113]

Once they had put Nannie and William, who had joined them, back on the train for Munich and started on their own return by car to Haus Hirth, however, Stephen's childishness reasserted itself. Instead of sympathizing with Sassoon's frustration when he discovered at Vicenza that he had left his case of vital travel documents in Venice, he simply escaped to the nearest cinema to see a film called *The Gorilla*. By this point in the journey Sassoon was exhausted as well as bad-tempered. The weather had also deteriorated and when they finally arrived at Haus Hirth on 4 October he was suffering from bronchitis. In an ironic reversal of what was to come, a Dr Kaltenbach was called in to examine his lungs, always his weak point. A 'few spots' were found and the return to Paris delayed while Sassoon was nursed back to health by a willing Tante Johanna. Like Florence Hardy she was more than a little in love with Sassoon.[114]

He enjoyed his convalescence. The countryside, as Stephen rather fancifully put it, was 'molten in the autumn blur', with 'dazzling days, mountains glittering like bride-cakes, gentians and the last late golden-rod'.[115] And there were 'sheaves of press-cuttings' waiting, Stephen also noted, of *Fox-Hunting Man, The Heart's Journey* and even, to his particular delight, of the Ariel poem he had illustrated, 'To My Mother'.[116] There was fresh company too, in the person of his aunt, Nan Tennant, whom Sassoon instantly liked. Nearer her age than Stephen's, he found her 'a cultivated, grey-haired, alert, well-connected woman – a cut above E.M. F[orster]'s fictional spinsters'.[117] Her habit of smoking cigarettes in a long holder and excellent imitations of American women going round the Uffizi amused him greatly, as did her nickname for him, 'pampered author' ('p.a.' for short). He would become even more appreciative of her during the next few years while she helped him deal with her difficult young nephew.

After a fortnight's peace on Tante Johanna's sunny balcony, Sassoon made the long drive back to Paris to join Stephen, Nannie and William, who had preceded him by train.[118] He arrived on 23 October with another cold, which again turned to bronchitis. Having driven approximately 2,000 miles in just under two months he longed for rest, but was once more frustrated by Stephen, who wanted to socialize. In Sassoon's absence he had been seeing several of his society acquaintances, despite his pious resolve at Haus Hirth to 'renounce society and become a recluse'.[119] It seemed to Sassoon that they exhausted Stephen, who was looking unwell. Stepping into the role which was shortly to antagonize almost all Stephen's friends, he took control, and when Brian Howard, Cynthia Mosley, Meraud Guinness and Mrs Barrymore telephoned to invite themselves to lunch, pretended to be what he had in fact become on their travels, Stephen's valet, and put them off. Eventually, at the end of October, he persuaded Stephen to move out of central Paris to Versailles. It would be even more expensive at the Hotel Trianon Palace than at the Hotel Foyot, where Stephen had run up enormous bills, but at least they would get what they both needed, 'a dose of quietude'.[120]

It should have been a successful end to a trip designed largely with Stephen's health in mind. For the rest of their stay they planned to visit only two friends, Miss Fleming-Jones and Madame Duclaux. Both of them elderly females, neither seemed likely to over-excite Stephen. But they were not calculated to cheer him either, the main topic of conversation with each being death.

Stephen's friend, Madame Duclaux, an American biographer and poet who wrote under her maiden name of A. Mary Robinson, had known Hardy during his marriage to his first wife, Emma, and it seemed natural that she should reminisce about him.[121] It was perhaps less inevitable that Sassoon's friend, Miss Fleming-Jones, should also be discussing death. When Sassoon made the arrangement to see her on 2 November, he could not have known that their mutual friend, 'Enrico' Festing-Jones, would be dead. In fact, Sassoon had mentioned his forthcoming tea with the wealthy Englishwoman to Enrico in the last letter he wrote to him. (Miss Fleming-Jones's 'interest (hobby?) for the inverted', as Sassoon put it, had attracted a number of homosexuals to her.)[122] But on 27 October, a week before his intended visit, he received news of 'dear dear Enrico's' death five days previously. 'I am haunted with suppressed sorrow,' he wrote to Glen, whom he relied on more than Stephen to understand: 'How few leave behind them such loveliness of spirit.' Enrico had been among the wisest of his friends and someone with whom, unlike Gosse or Hardy, he could discuss his homosexuality. Sassoon had used him, he admitted, as a kind of journal, writing him long, frank, confessional letters throughout the twenties. Even without the recent loss of Hardy and Gosse his death would have come as a great blow. 'They are all gone away,' he wrote bleakly at the end of 1928, echoing Vaughan's well-known lines but leaving the second of them to be inferred: 'And I alone sit lingering here.'[123]

Sad as the deaths of his three old friends were for Sassoon, none of them was entirely unexpected. A far more sudden and catastrophic loss awaited Stephen, one which would also affect Sassoon in its own way. While they had been paying a second visit to Madame Duclaux on 17 November, the day before Stephen planned to return to England with Nannie, Stephen's mother Pamela had suffered a severe stroke in the garden at Wilsford and had died four hours later. She was only fifty-seven and, though known to have a heart condition, had certainly not been expected to die.

Stephen, who had remained completely dependent on his mother and would normally have turned to her in such a situation, had no resources to deal with her death. Sassoon felt he had no choice but to take over Pamela's role. He had had almost three months' practice at the job by this point and evidently derived a certain pleasure from the control it gave him. Their holiday had made him more aware of Stephen's faults, but Pamela's death showed him, unexpectedly, a more positive side to her son: 'Stephen is … very courageous in this desolation,' Sassoon wrote to the Heads on 1 December 1928.[124] His New Year resolution for 1928 had been to see less of Stephen, but fate had intervened and by the end of the year he found himself more deeply committed than ever.

14

'The Heart's Paradise'
(November 1928-January 1931)

> I hang on to [Stephen], in thought; but no one can help me – one must just
> try and stick it out, hoping that he will become rational and human again.
> Such an illness defeats one like an interminable period of ghastly weather.
> It is death in life.
>   It has been the death of happiness for me. But one is lucky to have *known*
> happiness at all. Lots of people never do.
>   (Sassoon to Robert Nichols, 20 February 1932)

Only two things were needed to make Stephen's dependence on Sassoon
almost complete, Stephen's ill health and that of Nannie Trusler. When
both followed quickly on Pamela's death in November 1928, Sassoon took
charge, though with some apprehension. His greatest fear was that
Stephen would demand even more attention and prevent him writing
again. Ironically, it was this threat that made him write far more and more
successfully during the first three years of their relationship than either
before or after. One of his greatest problems, except in the war years, had
been motivation. Now, threatened by too little rather than too much time
for writing, he was fully motivated.

By November 1928 he was also experiencing for the first time in ten
years great popular success and enjoying the sensation. Enthusiastic
reviews of *Fox-Hunting Man* continued to pour in and Faber were so
pleased with the sales figures that they planned an illustrated edition.[1]
Sassoon was flattered to learn that the publishers Coward McCann,
having entered an unofficial auction for American rights, had offered a
much higher figure than any he had previously been paid.[2] Most gratifyingly of all, *Fox-Hunting Man* was awarded both the Hawthornden and
James Tait Black Memorial prizes.[3] Anxious to follow up his success, as
well as tap into the recent popularity of war books, Sassoon had decided
even before finishing *Fox-Hunting Man* to write a sequel. And it was this
decision which made him feel particularly anxious about Stephen's increasing demands.

Apart from Stephen's few days at Wilsford for Pamela's funeral and his
brief visit to one of her friends at Oxford, Sassoon had to be with him
'constantly' after their arrival back from France.[4] It was only when

Stephen left for Fallodon with Lord Grey on 10 December that he was able to concentrate for the first time on his new book. Relieved that Stephen's family appeared to be taking responsibility for him, at least for a few weeks, and willingly contemplating Christmas on his own, he worked hard and by the end of December had written well over 6,500 words of 'Memoirs Continued' (later retitled *Memoirs of an Infantry Officer*). But his progress was brought to an abrupt halt in the new year, first by a summons to join Stephen at Wilsford, then, more dramatically, by the news that Stephen's TB had recurred.[5] The doctors predicted that he would 'probably be dead ... within a year'.[6]

Whether Stephen's TB had been brought on by stress at losing his mother, as the doctors believed, or whether the long car journeys through Europe had affected *his* lungs as well as Sassoon's, or whether the disease had simply been missed by previous tests, the result was the same, to stop Sassoon working until Stephen was packed off to Haus Hirth again at the end of January. In an almost exact repetition of the previous year Sassoon instantly returned to his book, determined to finish at least half of it before he joined Stephen for Easter. Nan Tennant would see her nephew safely to Bavaria and Nannie, Sassoon still believed, would look after him there till his arrival.

Then the second blow fell. Tante Johanna, with whom he had been in close touch since the previous October, wrote in February 1929 to say that she was 'terribly anxious not about Stephen but about *Nannie*'.[7] Like Pamela, Nannie had a heart condition, which had started to get worse. She was also, at seventy, growing increasingly confused. For Stephen, who had depended on her since childhood and loved her as much, 'possibly more so', as his mother, the situation was grave.[8] But for Sassoon, who saw Stephen's last prop beside himself vanishing, it was extremely threatening and he redoubled what had come to seem to him his 'awful drudgery': 'My pencil crawls across the paper', he wrote to Ruth Head on 4 March 1929, 'and five hours' work seldom produces more than six- or seven-hundred words.'

As in the previous year he cut himself off from almost everyone, and by 23 February had squeezed out nearly 30,000 words, a third of the projected book. He had conducted Sherston from the point at which his adventures had ended in *Fox-Hunting Man* – on the Front opposite Mametz at Easter 1916 – through an army training course at Flixécourt and his daring rescue of Corporal O'Brien during a failed raid in May, to the Battle of the Somme and its unheroic aftermath for Sherston, trench fever, which took him back to England in July. Celebrating his achievement with a rare break, Sassoon spent the weekend with the two friends of Stephen he liked most, Edith Olivier and Rex Whistler.

Edith was not a typical parson's daughter, though she had retained her father's strong religious principles. In some ways she was a rather sad figure. Until the death of her sister, with whom she lived on the Wilton

216

estate, she had enjoyed a genteel, relatively quiet life on the fringes of the aristocracy. Then in 1925, at the age of fifty-three, everything had changed. Meeting Rex during a holiday with Stephen designed to console her for her sister's death, she had fallen deeply in love with the young art student. Rex liked her greatly but, as his friend Beaton put it, 'Rex, so romantic with his luminous face, Roman nose, and large crown to his head, exud[ing] warm-heartedness and sympathy', was nevertheless a 'strangely remote person'.[9] Quite apart from an age gap of over thirty years, he was also predominantly homosexual and Edith had to be content with the role of confidante.

It was a part she also played with Sassoon, who was already consulting her frequently about Stephen by February 1929. Her own late entry into writing, with the moderately successful romantic novels she began to produce at the age of fifty-five, gave them another interest in common. But like most of her homosexual friends he found the small, dynamic woman 'too vivacious and feminine to be a comfortable crony'.[10] (Stephen, less charitable, referred to her 'most appalling vitality'.[11]) She was to remain, nonetheless, a lifelong friend, to whom he would make a generous allowance when her own meagre income eventually failed.[12]

Edith had become very fond of Sassoon by February 1929 – he seemed to her the 'most natural, independent man' she had ever met – and probably invited him down to Wiltshire with Rex to make sure the two men did not fall out over Stephen. She may have imagined a jealousy which, according to Rex's brother, Laurence Whistler, did not exist.[13]

What did exist, however, entirely unsuspected by the rather naïve Edith, was a strong sexual attraction between Rex and Sassoon, which her innocent manoeuvre unwittingly encouraged. Their long crawl down to Wiltshire in Sassoon's car through thick fog gave them hours of intimacy together. And Rex's ardour, which Sassoon noted in his diary with some concern, was unextinguished by the icy pond Sassoon drove him into towards the end of their journey, though it caused the waiting Edith great anxiety. (The pond's owner, far from responding to their request for help, had merely erected a notice which said THIS POND IS PRIVATE.)

By the time the two men arrived back in London after their weekend together, Sassoon was actively 'worried' about Rex's evident attraction for him.[14] However careful he had been so far, he feared that Rex was 'on the verge of the precipice'.[15] He liked Rex, was grateful for his company during Stephen's absence and flattered by his delicate drawings of him. He even found him 'desirable' and thought it 'easy enough to succumb' but he knew that it would be 'no joke once it started'. It was an awkward situation and one he had faced a number of times in the twenties from both sexes. Forced to choose between two attractive young men, he picked Stephen: 'I can't divide my heart into partitions, and if I were to try the experiment I should find myself betraying [Stephen] who has given me his whole heart.'[16] It was a decision which would cause him years of unhappiness.

217

There were several other ironies in the situation. Even as Sassoon was writing these words in his diary Stephen was responding rather too warmly to two young German princes at Haus Hirth. And in later years, long after Sassoon's affair with Stephen had finished, Rex would become intimately involved in Sassoon's life again, not directly with him, but with the person who would replace Stephen. The most revealing feature of the affair, however, is the strength of Sassoon's commitment to Stephen at the very point when he might be expected to fear the effects of too great an involvement. It is characteristic of him that he found the two happiest years of their relationship those covering Stephen's deepest dependence on him.

*

Sassoon was in high spirits when he arrived at Haus Hirth on 5 April. He had written nearly 50,000 words of *Infantry Officer*, over half of its eventual 82,000.[17] Parts five, six and seven, describing Sherston's progress from his regimental depot at 'Clitherland' to the infantry base depot at Rouen, then on to the Battle of Arras, were virtually finished and the end almost in sight. Even better, he was rejoining Stephen, whom he had missed greatly. Sitting for Rex in his Fitzroy Street studio, when the artist's infatuation for him was at its height, he had had eyes only for Beaton's photographs of Stephen on the wall opposite. And during their drive down to Edith's, while Rex had longed for Sassoon, 'every milestone' had reminded Sassoon of Stephen. To be with him again gave him intense joy.

Happiness made him even more generous than usual, especially if he thought it would help Stephen. William Walton and Edith, who were there entertaining the invalid when he arrived, had both had their expenses paid by him, and when Rex turned up on 20 April it was thanks to Sassoon's money. Hearing of the Hirths' financial difficulties over a badly needed new roof, he insisted on giving them £500, a large amount matched by Stephen the next day. He also 'lent' the Hirths an even bigger sum two months later that he clearly did not expect them to repay.[18] A 'marvellous generous creature', as Edith noted,[19] it was his proud boast that he had spent none of the considerable royalties already earned from *Fox-Hunting Man* on himself, his first act being to buy Glen (now engaged to Angela Baddeley) a new car.[20] His wedding present to them when they married in September would be even more lavish, half payment for their first house.[21] He would also pay for his old friend Nellie Burton's house when her lease at Half Moon Street expired.

As Edith also noted, Sassoon was 'happy as a boy' in his generosity that spring in Bavaria.[22] His evident love for Stephen made him in turn very 'lovable'.[23] Nobody could resist him; host, hostess, servants, guests and Stephen most of all, succumbed to the extraordinary charm which nor-

218

mally lay concealed beneath a stiff, somewhat awkward, exterior. 'No one would recognize the rather grim, alarming, aloof poet of London', Edith wrote, 'in this gay creature who runs in and out of the room revelling in Tante Johanna's dishes, saying again and again how happy he is.'[24] He was also at his funniest, telling her an amusing story about a weekend at Sachie Sitwell's, 'all rather drunk and disreputable. He said "I just had to try to keep squalor at bay", picking up cigarette ends and tidying things away.'[25]

Everything delighted him during the 'month's indolence' he allowed himself, eating, drinking, sunbathing and exploring the surrounding countryside. Even Stephen's journal, a breathless, high-flown affair, seemed to him 'the revelation of a most brilliant and beautiful character and written with genius', the product of a 'unique and marvellous personality'.[26] Stephen's health especially pleased him, having improved rapidly in the hands of the specialist from Heidelberg, Dr Kaltenbach. (Sassoon would probably have approved of Kaltenbach's view of Stephen as a mixture of a Fra Angelico and Botticelli angel, but less so of Stephen's description of the doctor as 'blond, young and fascinating', a deliberate attempt to make him jealous.[27])

Kaltenbach's decision to rest Stephen's affected lung in March by collapsing it with a process known as pneumothorax, had produced hopeful results by the time Sassoon arrived in April and full recovery seemed possible. Stephen, who had been confined to his bed upstairs with visitors strictly limited, was allowed to come down on 21 April for his twenty-third birthday. This was celebrated with the usual Hirth exuberance and generosity. Sassoon's contribution was Gerard's *Herbal*, with a poem written specially for the occasion. Surrounded by such devoted attention and 'looking heavenly' in his orchid velvet dressing gown, according to Edith, Stephen was at his most appealing, making Sassoon 'wonderfully happy'.[28]

The peak of their joy was just ahead. Stephen's improvement continued and by mid-May Sassoon decided that he was well enough to move to a small house in the nearby village of Schmölz. He had reluctantly started thinking of his work again and needed more solitude than the gregarious Haus Hirth allowed. He also wanted to be alone with Stephen, or as alone as Stephen ever was. Nannie and William were still with them and an English nurse had to be added to the party to look after Stephen and the increasingly frail Nannie, but at least it meant that Sassoon was able to concentrate on revising *Infantry Officer*. They were also living less expensively than at the *pension*, though this seems not to have mattered much to either of them.

'You would love this house,' Sassoon wrote to Glen from 'Breitenau' on 22 May. 'It is approached from the main road by a plank footbridge over the river; then a path through [Himalayan cedars] and silver pines to the actual shack which is, in places, 250 years old, full of creaks and rattles and charm.'[29] For Sassoon it was the Bavarian equivalent of an enchanted house from a de la Mare poem or story and Stephen found the grounds equally fairy-tale. Five acres of lawns thickly covered with gentians and lily of the valley, they backed on to virgin pine forest, 'hot and scented in the sunshine, full of giant butterflies, snakes and lizards'.[30] 'It's paradise!' he wrote to a friend, echoing Sassoon's own word for it.

Sassoon, who had written at least two poems during his stay at Haus Hirth, now resolved to concentrate on his prose.[31] But the combination of Breitenau's exotic beauty and his passion for Stephen made verse irresistible: 'Every day we pack more wealth away – / Every night we welcome new delight', he wrote in 'Song Without Words' a week after arrival in their own house, lines he eventually rejected as perhaps too explicit.[32] On the same day, however, he wrote a poem which would be included in his *Collected Poems* and remain one of the most haunting of his non-war pieces, 'The Heart's Paradise'. In it he tried to convey the magical nature of his experience at Breitenau that summer:

> At the end of all wrong roads I came
> To the gates of the garden without a name.
> There, till the spell should fail, I found
> Sudden Elysium, strange with sound
> Of unknown birds and waters wild
> With voices unresolved for rest.
> There every flower was fancy's child,
> And every tree was glory's guest,
> And Love, by darkness undefiled,
> Went like the sun from east to west.
>
> (CP, p. 216)[33]

After the many false turnings taken since leaving his childhood garden at Weirleigh, Sassoon believed that he had finally found its equivalent, the Garden of Eden. For the first time he dared to hope that he had arrived at his goal, true love.

Yet the poem also suggests that he was aware at some level that it *was* an enchantment and unlikely to last, that the 'spell' (as he anticipates in the third line) would eventually 'fail'. Looking back on the scene three years later he remembered moments of unease, staring at the old house with its two sick inhabitants as though, in the words of another unpublished poem written there, 'halfway through some long, unhappy story'.[34]

Nevertheless, the ten weeks at Breitenau were to remain among his happiest memories. Two days after writing 'The Heart's Paradise' he was back at work on his prose, adding just one new passage to his original 50,000 words, thus bringing Sherston from his nostalgic chat with Wilmot about the Kentish Weald to his rash foray in the Hindenburg Trench, where he receives his first wound. It took the author himself to within a few hundred words of the end of Part Eight.[35] The rest of his time was spent on revision.

No greater proof of Sassoon's devotion to Stephen exists than his decision to change his working hours from night to morning to suit the invalid. So that while Stephen visited a nearby hospital for daily treatment, he sat down to work, and by the middle of June had rewritten and fair-copied almost half his manuscript in the old library on the ground floor. He had taken this for his room and, apart from hundreds of battered German books, it contained a bed, a writing table, where he also ate, and a grand piano imported from Munich especially for him. After finishing work for the day, he would relax with Bach's organ fugues adapted for piano, 'with a lot of exuberant octaves added' to reflect his mood.[36] Two floors above, Stephen would be reading or playing with several small aquaria he had set up on his balcony.

Nannie, who was confined to her room on the first floor, struggled on till mid-June, when she had to return to England for greater medical care. Stephen now became Sassoon's full responsibility and when Eddie Marsh wrote to tell him of the Hawthornden Prize-giving on 12 July, he replied, 'I must remain here with Stephen,' nominating Blunden to receive the award on his behalf as he had once done for Blunden.[37]

It was no real hardship, though Edith Olivier was sorry that Sassoon missed Lord Lonsdale's leisurely and 'very great tribute' to *Fox-Hunting Man*.[38] The skies were cloudless, the sun grew hotter and their isolated retreat even lovelier. There are photographs of Sassoon stripped to the waist, muscular, axe in hand, looking rested if a little self-conscious as he prepares to chop wood for the evening fire. ('I rather pride myself on my appearance in these photos,' he admitted to Blunden at the beginning of July; 'anyhow I look healthy and a well-preserved $42\frac{10}{12}$, don't I?', an indication of his increasing concern about ageing.)[39] Others show him with Stephen at his side, slim and girlish in a variety of fanciful outfits. They could be shots from a successful honeymoon. And the first half of *Infantry Officer*, in spite of its sombre material, reflects some of this happiness, the sections on Sherston's training at Flixécourt and convalescence at Oxford in particular.

The idyll came to an end in late July with news of Nannie's sudden deterioration and admission to hospital. Sassoon, dreading a repetition of the circumstances of Pamela's death, decided that he must take Stephen back immediately. He had difficulty in getting him through the journey.

Nannie lingered on, however, rallying slightly at the beginning of August. But by 14 August she was dead and Stephen distraught again. 'I'm crazy with unhappiness. I don't know what to do,' he announced the following day.[40] From this point on it would be Sassoon who must try to find the answers. He had become, as Strachey noted, Stephen's '*garde-malade*', the slightly sinister French word for male nurse.[41]

To this end Sassoon spent most of the next two months at Wilsford looking after Stephen. He had in any case begun to tire of 23 Campden Hill Square, which must have seemed rather modest and pedestrian after the grand hotels and romantic settings of his travels with Stephen. It was effectively the end of his time at the flat, though he would stay there occasionally on visits to London during the next few years and would not officially move out until 1932. One obvious effect of his relationship with Stephen had been to make him abandon his resolve not to let money change his way of life. Keeping up with Stephen's extravagant habits had quickly seen to that.

So instead of returning to his flat on his arrival back in England he had installed himself with Stephen in the Hyde Park Hotel, an expensive establishment he was to return to several times during the coming years. With Pamela's death Stephen's luxurious, silver-lined apartment in Smith Square had gone: Pamela had left her town house to his older brother, David, together with Wilsford. Stephen himself had been given Pamela's parents' home at Lake with its extensive grounds, but it was Wilsford he wanted. After lengthy family consultations, including plans to sell Lake to buy Wilsford from David, he succeeded in persuading his brother to rent it to him and Wilsford became his, in all but name, for life. What Stephen wanted he usually got.

It was, therefore, to Wilsford he returned when Nannie's funeral was over. And it was at Wilsford that Sassoon would spend the better part of a year, on and off, becoming in the process dependent on both Wiltshire and large houses, not to mention their grounds.

For Wilsford's grounds were enchanting and Sassoon's stay there represented a journey from one idyllic garden to another. 'This is a sort of earthly paradise', wrote Blunden on 28 September 1929 during one of several visits arranged by Sassoon, '– trees, birds, dogs, reptiles, fishes and all!'[42] Sitting just outside a small circle of trees beside a little brook, he could hear 'the call of many birds' from the large aviary Pamela had created. 'If this is autumn,' he concluded, 'what splendid flowers and bird-music must be here in spring?'[43]

But Sassoon was not to experience spring at Wilsford. Dr Kaltenbach, who had been flown over especially from Germany to inspect Stephen's lungs in late October, decreed that, though 'cured', he needed a milder climate for the next six months. Sicily was chosen.

Sassoon, possibly in anticipation, had packed all the visits he considered important into the three months since his return. His mother's health was worrying him almost as much as Stephen's and he had made the tortuous journey from Wiltshire to Kent several times to see her. He had also stayed with the Heads and the Wyldes regularly on his way to and from London, where he paid numerous visits to the dentist. He had even managed a visit, with Blunden, to the ageing poet laureate. Bridges had become very fond of Sassoon, who had organized a present of a harpsichord for him on his eightieth birthday, and Sassoon was anxious to introduce Blunden to him before it was too late.

Sassoon's only real worry about the trip to Sicily, as always with

Stephen, was his writing. He had got back to *Infantry Officer* on 21 September and carried on with it at intervals throughout October, sitting at his table on the second floor of Wilsford's thatched wing close to Stephen's open-air loggia. He was determined to keep it up and it was on the understanding that he would be allowed to complete the final half of the book in Sicily that he set off on their second long tour of the year. So that while the Great Depression of 1929 deepened into the hardships of the early 1930s the two men started for the south with Stephen's extravagant entourage, which included not only his valet and innumerable suitcases but also his pet parrot.

Their journey began in mid-November with a week in Paris to please Stephen, who was much fonder of the city than Sassoon. He also hoped to see one of his literary heroes, André Gide, there and was thrilled when Sassoon managed to arrange a meeting. Sassoon liked Gide greatly, but realized that the Frenchman was more interested in his pretty young friend than in himself.[44]

Sassoon's turn came next with a visit to one of *his* literary heroes, Max Beerbohm, at his home on the Italian Riviera. He had already met the celebrated caricaturist and writer a number of times and had been sending him copies of his privately printed books since their first meeting in 1916. But, as he told another artist, Haro Hodson, years later, 'my Max began in November 1929', that is on this visit to Rapallo, where Max had settled with his wife Florence in 1910. The invitation had come about through a chance meeting with Max on New Year's Eve 1928. Sassoon had been visiting William Nicholson at his London house in Apple Tree Yard to discuss drawings for the illustrated *Fox-Hunting Man* and Max had been staying there on one of his rare trips to England. Sassoon's admiration for him amounted to hero-worship by this time; he had read *Zuleika Dobson* and most of Beerbohm's essays and had bought eight of his caricatures in recent exhibitions. So that he was thrilled when Max accepted an invitation to tea with him at Campden Hill Square. It was during this tea on 9 January 1929 that Max and his wife urged Sassoon and his other guest, Stephen, to visit them in Rapallo. So that when planning their journey abroad later in the year Sassoon had been very careful to include Rapallo in it.

Max was almost all Sassoon looked for in a man and an artist. The wit which characterized his delicate drawings and mannered prose style made conversation with him a delight. It also, as Sassoon had noted in his diary after talking to him alone at Nicholson's, 'stimulated' others: 'I actually made an impromptu which seemed to please him. I said of Osbert Sitwell "Everything that he touches turns to publicity".'[45] Max's own epigrams, like those of Wilde (whom he had known and admired at Oxford in the early nineties), were effortlessly superior. Talking of Hardy's funeral and the interference of J.M. Barrie, who had supported the campaign to have his ashes in the Abbey while his heart went to Stinsford, he fantasized about Barrie's own death: 'The autopsy takes place, but the doctors find that – there is no heart!'[46] It was said in that 'deprecatory voice ... and manner' Sassoon loved in Max.[47]

But as another humorist, Sam Behrman, was warned when he went to pay homage to Max in Rapallo in 1952, four years before the master's death, Max did not welcome 'listeners who never talk and talkers who never listen'.[48] Like his friend Robbie Ross, he rarely allowed his own wit to dominate and Sassoon always left him feeling nourished. 'No one will ever know', Sassoon told Cockerell, 'how much he did to counteract my youthful crudities.'[49] From the start Max symbolized for him everything that was 'delightful and diverting and stimulating'.[50] Fourteen years older than Sassoon, he was in his late fifties when their 'real' friendship began, but he seemed to his disciple 'neither young nor old. Just wise, witty and sweetly civilized.'[51] As with that other dapper Edwardian dandy, Ross, he was more like a jolly bachelor uncle than a father-figure for Sassoon.

Unlike Ross, however, whose homosexuality was beyond doubt, Max was sexually ambiguous. 'The usual judgement', Anthony Powell wrote, tactfully, 'was that Beerbohm was not very active in the field of sex.'[52] And Max's biographer, Lord David Cecil, observed that he was 'of cool sexual temperament'.[53] That may well have been the case. After all, Max himself told Sassoon that 'the best thing in life is to be in bed', not with a person but 'with a book'.[54] All that can be said with certainty is that Max was not assertively heterosexual: there were no children from his marriage and his wife, though not 'self-effacing' enough for Sassoon's tastes, played a sub-servient role.[55]

Sassoon identified strongly with Max, who confirmed many of his own prejudices. Despite his wit, which Sassoon judged even greater than Ross's, Max was not 'clever' in the way Sassoon disliked so much in Modernists such as Eliot or Graves. A fellow-reactionary, Max preferred the past to the present. 'Modern writers pride themselves on being tough experts,' Sassoon wrote in notes for his description of Max in *The Weald of Youth*: 'Show that Max is faultlessly efficient in his use of words ... Let them be as *expert* as Max!'[56] Paradoxically, however, the quality which most impressed him in Max's prose and one he deliberately cultivated in his own, was its apparent amateurishness: it had, he claimed, 'the spontaneous charm of good amateur work'.[57] Max had become what he himself aimed to be, 'a completely expert amateur'.[58]

It is a highly subjective view of a writer whose style Wilde compared to a silver dagger. But there is no doubting the admiration which lies behind it. Together with Hardy and de la Mare, Max would remain one of the three writers Sassoon had known who meant more to him than any others: 'Max so different from the other two ... *gave* me something quite different.'[59] By 1952 he was to describe his visits to Max as 'the nearest thing to Paradise' he had ever experienced.[60] And after his death in 1956 he would

14. 'The Heart's Paradise' (November 1928-January 1931)

claim that his 'own Elysium would unmistakably be established at Rapallo'.[61]

The spell was cast immediately on the first visit in November 1929. Sassoon and Stephen had caught the train from Paris on 22 November, booking into the Excelsior Hotel on the 23rd. They had presented themselves for lunch the next day at the Villino Chiaro, Max's modest but dramatically situated house in the via Aurelia, just outside Rapallo on the main Genoa road. Steep stairs led up to the living quarters, then on up to a large roof terrace and Max's study. Lunch was eaten in one of the four small rooms overlooking the Bay of Genoa, and the conversation so lively that it was 6.30 p.m. before the guests left: 'An enchanting experience', Sassoon noted, 'of which one can only say that it is as enjoyable as reading [Max's] books and looking at his drawings.'[62]

They stayed a week in all, visiting the hospitable Beerbohms on alternate days for a vastly extended lunch – 'absolute bliss' to Sassoon, who spent most of his time talking to Max while Stephen engaged in stage gossip with Florence, an ex-actress. Being with Max produced in Sassoon 'a feeling of having had just enough good wine to make one happy'.[63] Less than six months after claiming that Elysium lay in Bavaria with Stephen, he was ready to relocate it to Rapallo with Max, a place which proved to be the more permanent.

Despairing of the Boswellian task of summarizing three or four six-hour sessions of sparkling conversation, Sassoon left much of it unrecorded. But he could not resist reporting his own remark about Yeats (whom he and Stephen had also visited at Rapallo), that 'he *was* a bit of a *poseur*', and Max's shrewd reply, 'that the brilliant Irishmen in London had often been *poseurs*, but had helped to keep London alive and amused – from Goldsmith, Sheridan, Burke, Tom Moore, on to Wilde, George Moore, and Bernard Shaw'.[64] He also thought Max's sharper comments worth preserving: 'Of Norman Douglas: "There is a touch of the 'codger' about him." Of Galsworthy: "He does the old uncles beautifully, but goes to pieces when describing 'the way of a man with a maid' ..." Of H.G. Wells: "His novels are like collapsed blancmanges, but always contain enjoyable passages." '[65]

Reluctant as he was to leave such 'exquisitely civilized conversation',[66] Sassoon knew that they must continue their journey south. Rapallo at the beginning of December was too cold and wet for Stephen's lungs and he himself needed to start work, as he planned to do in Sicily.

They landed at the island's capital, Palermo, on 20 December after a twelve-hour crossing from Naples. Naples had been hot and sunny and, in spite of Sassoon's good intentions, they had lingered there a fortnight. But he had not been entirely idle. In Naples, looking out over its magnificent bay to Vesuvius, his thoughts turned to Pompeii and Herculaneum, whose population the volcano had turned to stone:

... I saw them. Numberless they stood
Halfway toward heaven, that men might mark
The grandeur of their ghostlihood
Burning divinely on the dark ...
                    ('Presences Perfected', CP, p. 227)[67]

Even in Palermo, where they stayed just over a fortnight, Sassoon was unable to get on with his prose. His main problem remained Stephen. Nannie's death had upset a delicate balance, and with only William and Poll, the parrot, to distract him he was even more demanding of Sassoon's time than in Bavaria. Sassoon, who 'dread[ed] any relationship' which would 'make demands on' him, saw a conflict looming: 'I must choose', he told himself, 'between giving up my work as a writer or giving up my enslavement to Stephen's possessiveness.'[68] But he was still too infatuated to do anything about it. So for the next month he devoted himself to Stephen's entertainment, exploring the island with him, first from Palermo, then from Girgenti, where they moved on 6 January 1930.

It was a strange time for Sassoon, a mixture of intense happiness as they discovered Sicily's ancient beauties and strong foreboding as he contemplated his unfinished work. Whereas his Breitenau poem 'At the End of All Wrong Roads' had used the metaphor of the journey to lead to 'sudden Elysium', his poem 'In Sicily' uses it negatively: 'Life's one forward track' can 'never again come back.' It is also much darker in tone: 'the unreturning day must die', the word 'grave' ends the piece and the echoes from Arnold's 'Dover Beach' in line eight and Owen's 'The Unreturning' in line ten reinforce the sense of melancholy. (The poem's original title was 'Elegy in Sicily'.) Consciously or unconsciously, Sassoon is already anticipating the end of the relationship:

> Because we two can never again come back
> On life's one forward track, –
> Never again first-happily explore
> This valley of rocks and vines and orange-trees,
> Half Biblical and half Hesperides,
> With dark blue seas calling from a shell-strewn shore:
>   By the strange power of Spring's resistless green,
>   Let us be true to what we have shared and seen,
>   And as our amulet this idyll save.
>   And since the unreturning day must die,
>   Let it for ever be lit by an evening sky
>   And the wild myrtle grow upon its grave.
>   (CP, p. 214)[69]

Sassoon had spent the first two months of the trip worrying about Stephen's health, but by mid-January he knew he had to start writing again. His resolution may have been strengthened by the threat of a visit from Osbert Sitwell, who was spending the winter not far away at Amalfi.

So on 18 January, just three days before he and Stephen made their final move to Syracuse, he returned to his half-finished manuscript.

The compromise he was forced to arrive at with Stephen was less than perfect from his point of view, but it had a positive effect on his writing habits. By sitting down to his work every morning in his room at the Hotel Villa Politi while Stephen sunbathed or sketched on the balcony next to his, and abandoning it every afternoon to collect the shells Stephen loved on the beach, he established a routine he could maintain.[70]

Two and a half months and just over 30,000 words later, he had completed *Infantry Officer*; Sherston had been taken back to England, had convalesced at Nutwood (i.e., Chapelwood) Manor and, partly as a result of it, made his public protest and faced the consequences. '82,000 words all written out twice, and much of it three times, and endless hours spent revising and correcting the typescripts' had exhausted Sassoon.[71] 'I can't tell you what a relief it has been to my mind,' he wrote to Glen after finishing.[72]

The manuscript, densely written on both sides of the page, crossed out and rewritten, indicates that he had worked with a pronounced sense of urgency. And a letter to Blunden of 28 March suggests that the circumstances under which the book was written materially affected its finished form. In it he refers to his elimination of the episode with which he had originally intended to close Sherston's story, his stay at 'Slateford' (Craiglockhart). Three days after writing to Blunden, he had brought *Infantry Officer* to a slightly abrupt halt with Sherston's journey to the hospital: 'And with my arrival at Slateford War Hospital this volume can conveniently be concluded.'[73] Apart from other considerations he had been too exhausted to continue. A heavy cold in February and the constant strain of juggling his work and Stephen's pleasure had worn him out. (Towards the end he had had to work till 2 a.m. on occasions.) He himself acknowledged that if the last chapters had been written 'in strict solitude they might have been stronger'.[74]

Stephen's biographer has argued that Sicily, rather than Bavaria, was the couple's true honeymoon. If so, it was a far stricter and more prolonged test of their compatibility and Sassoon would have saved himself a great deal of suffering had he heeded the warning signs. It is clear that Stephen, beside making it difficult for him to work, could not satisfy one of his most important needs, intelligent discussion. By the end of February he was already yearning for a long talk with Blunden – 'life here – with all its compensations, – *is* a sort of exile', he confessed.[75] He was also eagerly looking forward to Max's stimulating conversation, having grown 'rusty' with Stephen.[76]

When he and Stephen had left Rapallo they had arranged to return on their way home and once his book was finished he could hardly wait. Travelling via Taormina[77] he transported Stephen and his numerous belongings by boat from Messina to Genoa and by 8 April was back in

Rapallo having tea with the Beerbohms. Florence, concerned for their comfort, had booked them into a different hotel, the Bristol, and had practically refurnished their rooms with luxuries from the Villino Chiaro.

Starved of intellectual stimulation for so long, Sassoon revelled in Max's 'delectable gossip'.[78] During the next three weeks he was to record far more of it than on his first visit, especially when it coincided with his own views. Though he maintained that Max was 'never malicious', unlike Gosse, of whom he otherwise reminded him, some of Max's judgements were decidedly astringent. T.S. Eliot, for instance, seemed to him 'a case of the Emperor wearing no clothes', D.H. Lawrence was 'a clumsy writer' with 'a diseased mind', and he 'gladdened' Sassoon by 'demolishing' Wyndham Lewis as a writer altogether.[79] Browning, he argued, was 'a gigantic and fertile continent of creative resourcefulness compared with the melancholy backyard of Tom Eliot, who sits there ironically analyzing an empty sardine-tin'.[80] The relish with which Sassoon repeats such remarks is evident. But he also enjoyed the more positive side of Max's talk, his admiration for Henry James and Walter de la Mare, for example, or his detailed knowledge of more obscure literary figures of the nineties. Strolling about his roof terrace, or darting into his little indigo-coloured study for a book, Max delighted his guest, who could only thank him 'a thousand times for restoring my faith in delicacy, and perfection of manners, mental and hospitable, in the graces of life and philosophy'.[81] Sassoon's own way of life from the mid-thirties onwards would owe much to the model he had studied so carefully at Rapallo, as his 'Memento for Max' suggests:

> Stored in my mind for life, these pacings on your roof,
> These hours detached from brawling out-of-breath existence.
> And in your 'social form' an amplitude of proof
> That modernism delights me – at a decade's distance.
> Delightful too (envisioned by Italian spring
> And belvedered above a blandly sparkling sea)
> To share your sheltered privacy of flowers, and bring
> My gratitude for conversations yet to be. ...[82]

Max's effect on Sassoon's writing was even more immediate than on his lifestyle. Sassoon had submitted *Infantry Officer* to him on arrival and was quite intoxicated by his praise of it. From this time on he was to send all his prose books to Max for him to check their style and would dedicate *The Old Century* to him in 1938. More importantly, his enthusiasm had restored Sassoon's own faith in his work, and he left for Aix-les-Bains and Biarritz at the beginning of May 'feeling very happy about my book, and quite eager to revise the proofs ... Getting my manuscript back reminds me that I am in love with it (although it has seemed such weary work) and it makes me eager to begin another book.'[83]

He was less happy with Stephen and in Paris, where they arrived in May, they had their first serious argument. 'A sad ending', Sassoon reflected, 'to our half year abroad.'[84] They were both tired and Sassoon was determined to prevent Stephen being further exhausted by friends in Paris, who only wanted to 'plunge' him into 'a vortex of silly and vicious circles of cosmopolitan cocktail consumers'.[85] Stephen, however, insisted on paying several visits to be painted by Tchelitchew, who had already made Sassoon so jealous the previous year. After six months together they were more aware of each other's faults, Sassoon oppressed by Stephen's 'possessiveness'.[86] Yet he was also conscious of his own tendency to be 'egotistical and domineering' and was still at a stage where he blamed himself for their differences.[87] He resolved to be less 'clumsy' with Stephen, to learn how to 'manage' him, terminology more appropriate in a parent or an animal-trainer than a lover.[88]

It was clearly time for a break and when they arrived back in England on 14 May, Sassoon stayed in London while Stephen went to Wilsford. But once again fate intervened and he was not free of his responsibilities for long. With the doctors' announcement on 14 June that Stephen's TB was still active, Sassoon felt obliged to take charge, installing himself at Wilsford for the rest of the summer. 'You see,' he explained to the Heads, 'unless I am here, Stephen is quite alone.'[89]

With Stephen's complete dependence on him, all his past feelings revived: 'he needs me so much and is so touchingly grateful', he told the Heads.[90] He could only be thankful that his book was 'safely off the premises of [his] mind' and that he was 'feeling rested and able to devote [him]self to the person [he] loved best in this world!'[91] His goal now was to make sure that Stephen had the best medical attention possible and to prevent him from exerting himself.

Both aims were very worthy, but in carrying them out he managed to antagonize Stephen's doctors, family and friends. Whereas someone more tactful and less impetuous might have found a smoother way of insisting on second and third opinions about Stephen's health, Sassoon bluntly declared his lack of faith in both the local doctor, Kempe, and the London consultant, Chandler, demanding that a specialist from nearer at hand should be brought in. Even he recognized that to fly Dr Kaltenbach over from Germany again, as Tante Johanna suggested, would be going too far, though he did have another German doctor, Hausen, called in. He also succeeded in getting an English lung specialist, Dr Snowden, from a neighbouring sanatorium near Cadnam, to see Stephen, and in having another X-ray taken. While all this may have been medically desirable, it did not endear him to Stephen's doctors and placed Stephen's eldest brother, Lord Glenconner, in an awkward position.[92] Only Lord Grey, won over partly by Sir Henry Head's tactful letter of professional advice, seemed to be on Sassoon's side: 'That you can be with him,' he wrote to Sassoon on 9 July 1930, 'must be a boon greater than words can express.'[93]

A similar situation developed with Stephen's friends, whom Sassoon had vowed to prevent 'descending on him in selfish shoals'.[94] Edith Olivier was exempted from this charge, but Beaton was seen as a prime suspect and became deeply offended. Even the mild and well-inclined Rex felt put out, though he would later tell Edith that 'however patronising and unfriendly' Sassoon was, he should 'always have to love him'.[95] Noting that Sassoon's own friends, like Blunden, Forster and Byam Shaw, were allowed to visit, he and Beaton believed that Stephen was deliberately being taken away from them by a possessive Sassoon. The Sitwells, who according to Edith Olivier had become increasingly jealous of the intimacy between Sassoon and Stephen, were outraged. Once again Sassoon's relationship was threatened and this time never fully recovered.

Sassoon, who referred to himself jokingly as an 'old watch-dog', ignored them all.[96] Stephen's life, he believed, 'h[ung] by a thread' and all his happiness 'depended on that thread'.[97] So from mid-June to mid-September he kept guard at Wilsford, taking time off only to visit his mother and the dentist. Stephen, terrified of a further relapse, behaved 'angelically', entertaining himself with small, daily pleasures in the garden room, and Sassoon still found it a 'great consolation' that 'he needs me and that I can help him'.[98] He quickly settled into a new routine, which combined as many elements from his past life as possible and would provide a pattern for the future. It was a balance between the physical and mental activity he had always needed.

'My salvation as regards nerves,' he told Nan Tennant, 'is due to "Bruno"; the cob who ought to be pulling the Victoria, but is ridden by me about two hours every afternoon.'[99] It was seven years since he had last ridden, but it quickly became a daily necessity that he would continue until well into his seventies. He also managed an occasional game of cricket, though not nearly as much as he would have liked. His other remedy for 'nerves' was the new piano Stephen had ordered specially for him and several more hours were passed stumbling his way through Bach.

With *Infantry Officer* at the printers he had only the proofs to deal with and was able to revert to the pre-*Memoirs* habit of more or less vegetating through the summer, saving his serious writing for autumn and winter.[100] He had longed to get back to 'the Elysium of poetry' after such a 'plodding prose expedition', but when the opportunity came it was prose not poetry he planned.[101] The story, about a man waking up in Antediluvium and creating a retrospective existence of people and episodes for himself, was never written, but the notes for it are revealing, suggesting that by the end of August he was beginning to tire of Stephen's possessiveness again.[102] The idea behind the story, as Sassoon himself recognized, expressed his 'need for solitude and reflection'. The narrator is in 'an empty house' and yearns for the 'comfortable eclectic condition' not of Wilsford but of 'Campden Hill Square-ish-ness', a 'Crusoe-like ... quiet life ... where nothing throws *habit* out of gear'. Sassoon's own longing to return to such conditions comes through unmistakably.

Stephen's need of autonomy was equally powerful, however, and by 22

September, three weeks after Sassoon's notes were written, he expressed a wish to be alone for at least ten days and a game of cat-and-mouse began. Summoned back to Wilsford in early October, Sassoon was banished for a second time at the end of that month, after an ominous entry in Stephen's diary, 'I'm better alone.'[103] And though Sassoon was recalled at short notice at the beginning of November and again in mid-December, even spending Christmas with Stephen at his request, it was in effect the end of their relationship.

A poem written on Christmas Eve at Wilsford suggests that Sassoon himself suspected as much. Entitled 'December Stillness', it is a melancholy poem, set at 'nightfall, sad and spacious' among 'loom[ing]' trees. Following a flock of birds 'in lone remote migration beating by', the poet appears to identify with their state, begging the wintry stillness to 'teach me to travel far and bear my loads'.[104] Sassoon and sympathetic friends like Edith Olivier might blame Stephen's quixotic behaviour on his physical condition and his most recent help, Nurse May, who indulged his whims, but by January 1931 it was clear that he no longer wanted Sassoon with him.

15

Memoirs of an Infantry Officer and Goodbye to Graves

> The war ... Yes – there is always a lot to be said about it, isn't there? It has been on my mind for the past sixteen months to such an extent that I can't believe I shall ever be clear of this job of putting my scrap of it on paper.
> (Sassoon to H.M. Tomlinson, 15 March 1930)[1]

Fortunately for Sassoon, Stephen's first banishment of him came a few days after the publication of *Memoirs of an Infantry Officer* on 18 September 1930, at a time when it was more convenient to be in London than Wiltshire, and he had plenty to distract him.[2] Following its serialization in the *Daily Telegraph*, Blunden had reviewed it enthusiastically in the *News Chronicle* on publication day, setting the tone for the other reviews that quickly followed.[3] During the crisis over Stephen's health Sassoon had seen much less of Blunden than he wanted and his return to London now gave him a chance to catch up on their friendship.

He had been worried about Blunden since his return from Japan in August 1927. Blunden's 'gaunt' and 'harassed' face as he had delivered a talk on Leigh Hunt to the Charles Lamb Society in November 1927 had convinced Sassoon that 'all [was] not well with him'.[4] Blunden had left for Japan in 1924 without his wife Mary, who had refused to go with him, and he returned after his long absence expecting to separate from her. She had hardly bothered to conceal her relationships with other men and he, possibly in response, had brought his Japanese mistress, Aki Hayashi, back to England with him. He had no money and no job with which to support his extended *ménage* of mistress, wife and two children. An unexpected reconciliation with Mary on his arrival home had only complicated things further and in any case had not lasted. By spring 1929 he had filed for divorce.

Sassoon, like most of Blunden's friends, felt protective of him and wanted to help, but was wary of interfering in his private life. 'I have seen too much of this discussing of other people's affairs by people who have too much time on their hands,' he wrote to Blunden, 'and I know how pernicious it can become, even when (as in O[ttoline]'s case) the original intention is a friendly anxiety to be helpful.'[5] So that when Ottoline wrote, urging him to advise Blunden to persuade Miss Hayashi to return to

Japan, he felt his 'flawless friendship' with Blunden was being threatened and refused to do so.[6] (Blunden himself would be less hesitant to take sides when Sassoon found himself in a comparable situation later on and their relationship would suffer as a result.) Sassoon did, however, offer to be guardian to Blunden's son John, a suggestion made mainly in the hope that it would help Edmund to remain close to his son.

Mary indignantly rejected Sassoon's offer[7] and he confined himself on the whole to more practical assistance. A generous present of money in October 1927 was followed by a great deal of string-pulling on Blunden's behalf with members of the Royal Literary Fund, which resulted in a grant of £500 for Blunden in February 1928. By 1930 he was offering Blunden a £50 monthly allowance and in 1933 would pay the first year's rent on a flat in Oxford for Blunden and his new wife, Sylva Norman.

But Blunden, through a mixture of unworldliness, generosity and heavy financial commitments, was never solvent for long. In spite of Sassoon's efforts, by early 1928 he was in desperate need of more money and set about earning it in the only way he knew how, by his pen. An avalanche of reviews, articles and books poured from him, including the work he had been trying to write since the war itself and by which he would become best known, *Undertones of War*.

Published in November 1928, only two months after *Fox-Hunting Man*, *Undertones* resembles it in a number of ways, though it is presented as straight autobiography not fiction. Beside being an indictment of war, it is also a celebration of the countryside and country traditions war threatens to destroy. The first-person narrators of both books share an innocence symbolized in explicit pastoral terms by Blunden in the closing words of his account, where he describes himself as 'a harmless young shepherd in a soldier's coat'. Both books are heavily nostalgic, both very poetic in their prose styles, though Sassoon does not, like Blunden, include actual poems. Both are imbued with a gently ironic humour. And both display enormous compassion for the sufferings of the ordinary soldier, a quality Sassoon had admired greatly in Barbusse's *Le feu* and Duhamel's *La vie des martyrs* when he read them during the war.

Infantry Officer, appearing two years after *Undertones*, still shows some similarities to it. Though Blunden had been in two of the worst sectors of the British Line, at Cuinchy and Passchendaele, and Sassoon had witnessed the battles of both the Somme and Arras, both writers were very careful not to sensationalize their material, as they felt Erich Remarque had done in *All Quiet on the Western Front*. 'Luckily for me', Sassoon wrote to Tomlinson, 'I had always intended to write it as unemotionally as possible, – laying stress on the contrast with ordinary peaceable conditions of life – (on £600 a year). So I am not forestalled by the horrific revelations which are now so well known and over-exploited by publishers.'[8] His main aim was not to shock, as he believed Remarque's and others' to have been, but to provide a 'warning to the generation which has no idea what the war was like for sensitive people'.[9]

Sassoon's aim affects the tone of *Infantry Officer*, which differs noticeably from *Undertones*. While Sassoon builds up to the narrator's angry public protest against the war – an incident culminating in the memorable passage where, 'outlawed, bitter and baited', he throws his MC ribbon futilely into the Mersey – Blunden's mood is more resigned and elegiac, a philosophical rather than didactic approach to the subject.

Technically, of course, *Undertones* and *Infantry Officer* are quite different, belonging to separate genres. But the divergence is far less apparent than this would suggest since, although Sassoon presents his experiences to the world as a novel, it is in reality much nearer in form to Blunden's autobiography.[10] Events and people tally almost exactly with his diary for the period, which he often quotes with only the slightest of alterations. And the factual account he wrote for Dr Dunn of his time in the Hindenburg Line appears virtually unchanged in his 'novel' eight years before Dunn published it in *The War the Infantry Knew*. Sassoon himself called his method 'fictionized reality'.

What few departures from his own life exist in *Infantry Officer* are imposed on him largely by *Fox-Hunting Man*. Having made Sherston an orphan with no siblings, a sportsman but not a writer, he cannot in his sequel change these conditions. (And given the success of *Fox-Hunting Man* and the continuing demand for war books by 1929, both he and his publishers naturally felt that a sequel was desirable.) The use of pseudonyms, also carried over from *Fox-Hunting Man*, was equally if not more necessary in a book which both explicitly and implicitly criticized individuals (some of them, like 'Leake' and 'Easby', his superior officers), institutions (the army, press and Church in particular) and the handling of the war generally. His material lay only thirteen or fourteen years back in time and many of the participants were still alive. Apart from the fear of libel, he had no wish to offend people. *Fox-Hunting Man* had shown him how careful he needed to be. In spite of his pseudonym a Mr Newgass had recognized himself as 'Tony Lewison', the man who had sold Sherston 'Cockbird' for the absurdly low price of £50 and been offended by the implication that he was a fool. Fortunately, he was easily mollified but the incident had made Sassoon realize the need for even better disguises.

He dare not, therefore, present *Infantry Officer* as autobiography, however close to the facts it might be, and it is here that his and his readers' main problem with the book lies. For himself there was the constant struggle to 'keep it inside its frame', to remember that he was describing a young man who was *not* a writer, did *not* love books.[11] The protest part, he told Ottoline, was particularly difficult to do convincingly 'while omitting everything to do with my being a writer'.[12] For his reader the difficulty lies in believing that a character like Sherston would take such a public stand against the war, a decision influenced in real life by such powerful intellectuals as Bertrand Russell.[13] Forster, who thought *Infantry Officer* 'a lovely and lovable' book, nevertheless found Sherston's protest at the end 'rather queer'; since his 'passions and brainworkings were never emphasized', he reasoned, 'he didn't (as you presented him) seem capable of more than social sulkiness – of endurance and courage inside the framework …'[14] Sassoon attempts to correct this imbalance by having the narrator look back on his protest as simply the emotional outburst of an angry and impetuous young man, but the reader's credibility is sometimes strained. Nevertheless, Forster's criticism – his only one – stands.

On the other hand, Sassoon was making the most of his strengths within the constraints imposed. Following Forster's advice he was using the 'voice' which had come through so compellingly in his war diaries, modified only by the need to make Sherston even more naïve than Sassoon felt himself to be at the time. The shape of his *roman à clef* sprang naturally from his own experience, the development of a young man from ignorance and self-absorption to greater awareness, tolerance and unselfishness. Walking round the garden with Aunt Evelyn and the kindly Captain Huxtable, for instance, having finally posted his protest to his superiors, Sherston:

> wondered whether I had exaggerated the 'callous complacency' of those at home. What could elderly people do except try and make the best of their inability to sit in a trench and be bombarded? How could they be blamed for refusing to recognize any ignoble elements in the War except those they attributed to our enemies?[15]

As with Pip in *Great Expectations*, a book Sassoon was reading while he wrote *Infantry Officer*, the distance between the narrator's experiences and his subsequent relating of them is crucial, enabling the author to preserve an ironic distance between his younger and older selves. Sherston's youthful scorn for Lady Asterisk's well-meaning patriotism is modified by the narrator's retrospective comment on her urging him to return to the Front: 'But Lady Asterisk wasn't hard-hearted. She only wanted me "to do the right thing".'[16] It was Sassoon's own 43-year-old self speaking.

Whilst this dichotomy makes at times for humour, as in *Fox-Hunting Man*, it is of the more poignant kind found towards the end of that book. Describing his foolhardy daytime sortie into no man's land to cut the enemy's wire for the coming battle, for instance, Sherston recalled that his commanding officer's ignorance of what he planned 'made it seem like an escapade, and the excitement was by no means disagreeable':

> It was rather like going out to weed a neglected garden after being warned that there might be a tiger among the gooseberry bushes. I should have been astonished if someone could have told me that I was an interesting example of human egotism. Yet such was the truth. I was cutting the wire by daylight

because common-sense warned me that the lives of several hundred soldiers might depend on it being done properly. I was excited and pleased with myself while I was doing it. And I had entirely forgotten that tomorrow six Army Corps would attack, and whatever else happened, a tragic slaughter was inevitable.[17]

The self-awareness and honesty here, which makes Sherston such an attractive character, comes entirely from an older Sherston looking back and is therefore believable.

As this example also shows, events needed little embellishment, the real-life ones being exciting enough for the most action-packed of novels. Some of them, such as Sherston's courage in bringing back the body of Corporal O'Brien after a failed raid, or capturing an enemy trench single-handed, are even played down in the interests of themes and characterization. 'My courage', Sherston writes, 'was of the cock-fighting kind. Cock-fighting is illegal in England, but in July 1916 the man who could boast that he'd killed a German in the Battle of the Somme would have been patted on the back by a bishop in a hospital ward.'[18] As the irony here indicates, Sassoon's main efforts go towards showing the evil of war together with the unimportance of the individual caught up in it. Sherston, like Sassoon, was completely peripheral to the two major battles in which he was involved, the Somme and Arras.

Sassoon's decision to end his book with Sherston's narrow avoidance of court-martial following his protest ensures that the book ends on a more dramatic note than real life generally affords, as well as bringing the action of the book to a shapely conclusion. But the narrator's ironic gloss on the event suggests that his youthful optimism is misplaced and that the war will go on: 'When we were walking back to my hotel I overheard myself whistling cheerfully, and commented on the fact. "Honestly, David, I don't believe I've whistled for about six weeks!" I gazed up at the blue sky, grateful because, at that moment, it seemed as though I had finished with the War.'[19] Sassoon has served up his own experience here with some literary skill by reinforcing at the same time one of the main themes of the book, the ineffectiveness of most human effort against the inexorability of the war machine.

The greatest advantage Sassoon saw in basing *Infantry Officer* so heavily on his own life, however, was that it enabled him to get his facts right. *All Quiet on the Western Front* had irritated him not just because of its sensationalism, but also because it gave 'no place names', left 'every-thing vague'.[20] It seemed to him the 'exact opposite' of Blunden's approach. He had been reading Remarque's book while writing *Infantry Officer* in 1929 and it undoubtedly strengthened his determination to be factually precise. Like Tolstoy's *War and Peace*, which he was also rereading while he wrote his own book, it is the combination of factual detail and direct personal experience vividly rendered that makes *Infantry Officer* a convincing and compelling picture of war. As he told Ottoline, he wanted to give 'a really truthful *inner*-narrative'.[21] He believed that this had not yet been achieved by an English writer, apart from Blunden.[22]

When Graves's autobiography, *Goodbye to All That*, was published in 1929, it did nothing to change his mind. Written at great speed to earn money, by the author's own admission, it represented all that Sassoon was anxious to avoid. (Ironically, it would become, together with *Undertones* and *Infantry Officer*, one of the three most popular war books of this period.) His criticisms of *Goodbye* are, in a sense, a reverse manifesto of what he was trying to achieve in *Infantry Officer* and are worth considering.

He had read Graves's book in November 1929, just prior to its publication and his own departure for Italy. As he pointed out to Graves a few months later in a long letter from Sicily, *Goodbye* could not have appeared at a worse moment: 'the extreme difficulty (and discomfort) of trying to recover the essentials of my war experience made me over sensitive on the subject' and the book 'landed on my little edifice like a Zeppelin bomb'.[23] Elsewhere he wrote that he felt as if Graves had 'rushed into the room and kicked my writing table over, thrown open all the windows, let in a big draught'.[24] It seemed to him that Graves had 'blurted out [his] hasty version' like a hack journalist with scant regard for accuracy, the 'antithesis' of his own method. He was particularly critical of Graves's account of his (Sassoon's) protest, which fell a long way short, he believed, of the 'impartial exactitude' required for such a sensitive topic.[25] 'He exhibits me as a sort of half-witted idealist', Sassoon complained to Louis Untermeyer and his wife, 'with a bomb in one hand and a *Daily Herald* in the other.'[26] In fact he found the whole book riddled with inaccuracies, from the number of casualties given by Graves for his last month of service and his account of a failed raid, to details about army brothels abroad. (Though Sassoon himself could hardly claim to be an expert on the last topic.)

Sassoon ended his letter to Graves by saying that he was 'extremely glad' that Graves was making a lot of money from the book and informing him that he had left him money in his new will, a provocation, intended or otherwise, that Graves dealt with in his usual robust and witty fashion: 'Signing fat cheques for your friends: the indelicate irony of it is that had you thought of signing one when you heard of "my troubles" – which left us all without money – I would not have been forced to write *Goodbye* to contribute to the work of restoration, and you would not have had the Zeppelin-bomb.'[27]

Sassoon's was a disingenuous letter in some respects. Though his unhappiness about *Goodbye* was real enough, he failed to mention the two things which had upset him most, Graves's thinly veiled description of his visit to Weirleigh, where Mrs Sassoon's desperate attempts to contact her dead son had kept him awake at night, and his inclusion of the long, disturbed verse-letter Sassoon had sent him from hospital in July 1918.

(Sassoon had insisted that this should be deleted before publication and all advance copies had had to be recalled.) Nor did he mention that it was Blunden who had drawn his attention to these facts, together with the book's inaccuracies, which Blunden, helped by Sassoon and others, had listed in exhaustive detail.[28]

Sassoon believed that Graves was jealous of his 'affinity' with Blunden,[29] but it is quite probable that the reverse was true and that Blunden was not averse to widening the growing rift between Sassoon and Graves. Graves, who was if possible even more tactless than Sassoon, had antagonized Blunden by implying that he had alcoholic tendencies and by his clumsy attempts to resolve Blunden's marital problems. To make matters worse he had written an unsympathetic review of *Undertones* in December 1928. So that by the time *Goodbye* was published eleven months later Blunden was not particularly well disposed towards him.

Even without Blunden's intervention, however, it is unlikely that Sassoon could have accepted Graves's book, which was the last of a series of irritants in their relationship. He dates his dissatisfaction as starting in November 1927 with his 'resentment' about Graves's 'behaviour to Gosse'.[30] Graves had upset Gosse by asking him point-blank to 'notice' his book *Lawrence and the Arabs* in his newspaper column, a gross breach of literary good manners as far as the old-fashioned Gosse was concerned. Gosse had appealed to Sassoon, who had first introduced him to Graves, and though Sassoon had managed to elicit an apology of sorts from the younger writer, it had left him feeling critical.

This in itself would not have been enough to end their friendship, Sassoon maintained, but a few months later Graves had again offended him with a 'crudely worded' letter after Hardy's funeral which convinced Sassoon that Graves was 'part of the vulgar uproar which attended his death'.[31] Graves's 'presumptuous' article on Hardy in the *Sphere* had added to his anger, which had gone on simmering until September 1928, when Graves's harsh review of *Fox-Hunting Man* had brought it to boiling point: as Sassoon put it, with some restraint, it was 'not helpful'.[32]

It is a convincing explanation but by no means the whole truth. For, as Sassoon admitted to several friends later, his 'quarrel' with Graves was caused almost entirely by the latter's 'subjection to Laura Riding'.[33] Graves himself had argued, in his pithy reply to Sassoon's long letter of complaint, that Sassoon's 'homosexual leanings' had already created 'several cross-currents' in their relationship before Laura's advent, notably his jealousy of Nancy and his fear of her when, according to Graves, she fell in love with him.[34] Ironically, it was just as Sassoon was finally becoming reconciled to Nancy that Laura had taken her place in Graves's life. In spite of repeated efforts to like the American poetess – he invited her to dinner with Graves and visited them several times in 1927 – Sassoon was 'finally driven away by her intense egotism and eccentricity'.[35]

He was also unable to accept Laura's extreme Modernist views and their effect on Graves, which made Sassoon feel like a lumbering 'intellectual Pickford Van'.[36] Nor could his essentially conservative nature accept the extraordinary *ménage à quatre* Laura set up with Graves, Nancy and a married Irish poet, Geoffrey Phibbs. So that when Laura, suspecting that she was losing Phibbs to Nancy, attempted suicide by swallowing poison and jumping from a fourth-floor window, he was unable to sympathize. He did not go quite as far as Nellie Burton who, on hearing incorrectly that Laura would certainly die, said 'good riddens [*sic*] to bad Rubbish'; he was simply 'appal[led]'.[37]

The most significant aspect of this interminable quarrel, which like most had two sides to it, was its effect on *Infantry Officer*. Apart from making Sassoon determined to get his own facts right, it also presented him with a problem. His mounting hostility towards Graves had already caused him to omit his meeting with him in November 1915 from *Fox-Hunting Man*, though it had been an important part of his change of attitude towards the war. And this was what he first resolved to do in *Infantry Officer*: 'I am leaving Graves out altogether,' he wrote to Ottoline on 21 January 1930. But Graves was a vital element in his plot, since it was his intervention which had convinced Sassoon to accept the army's compromise alternative to court-martial – Craiglockhart.

Another impulse provoked directly by the publication of *Goodbye* when he was halfway through writing *Infantry Officer*, was to give vent to his anger in print. One manuscript version of the latter contains a highly unsympathetic passage on Graves, whom he calls 'Robert Sarcophagus', the first name to facilitate identification, the second an easily recognizable pun on Graves's surname with unpleasant associations of decaying bodies in ancient tombs. This description, subsequently crossed through, refers to Sarcophagus's disloyalty to the narrator in a recent book, a pointed reference to *Goodbye*. The passage was almost certainly written in late November 1929, together with an unpublished poem originally entitled 'On Reading the Reminiscences of a Former Friend', which conveys the gist of it:

> Should one assume a mild magnanimous look
> When effigied and blurtingly displayed
> In a – presumably – profit-seeking book
> By someone scribbling on the downward grade?
> Resentment asks permission to protest
> Silence replies that silence answers best.
>
> I value private life; would rather read
> Revealed experience than distorted fact;
> Nor in this world, at any rate, I need
> Absence of autobiographic tact.
> Wherefore I feel impelled to write, '*Dear Blank*;
> Reviewers find your volume sanely frank;
> But I, as one among your numerous quarry,
> Am (pardon the expression) frankly sorry.'[38]

By expressing his feelings in this way Sassoon seems to have achieved the 'mild magnanimous' attitude of the poem's opening line and when he came to revise his manuscript he included a much more sympathetic though not entirely uncritical account of Graves, whom he now calls, less provocatively, 'David Cromlech'. The change is not simply to emphasize his character's Welsh connections, whilst preserving a pun on Graves's name ('Cromlech' is the Welsh word for a megalithic grave), but also to remove the ghoulish associations of 'Sarcophagus'. 'Cromlech' also half-rhymes with one of Graves's army nicknames, 'Longneck', a politer version of 'Rubberneck'. Sassoon's final portrait, as he hoped, shows no 'ill-feeling' towards Graves, a feat he accomplished apparently by trying to 'forget everything about him since 1919'.[39]

Sassoon's struggle with the Graves material is only one of a number of confrontations with his past he was forced to make in writing *Infantry Officer*. As he told Ottoline the day after completing it: 'Psychologically it has been an extraordinary tussle, but I hope it has relieved my mind.'[40] If it had relieved his mind, however, it had not done so sufficiently, since there were four more books of reminiscence to come.

The Turn of the Screw
(February 1931-May 1933)

You called me. And I never failed to come.
That is the truth. You know it. In your need
I gave days, hours, and minutes; all the sum
That unreluctant love can fit to deed.

You asked my aid. I served you with my thought
Till care for you became an added sense.
All that had been my safeguard you unwrought;
And I was glad. Your trust was my defence.

Remember this. It was my soul you took.
It is my living soul you now discard, –
You who have no compassionate word or look
For what, in mortal me, you made and marred.
So, if some day you send for me again
And I return, still hungry for our past,
My heart may yet be yours, reprieved from pain;
But not my soul. That will be mine at last.

('A Lost Soul', to Stephen Tennant) [1]

Sequels rarely sell as well as the book that spawned them and *Memoirs of an Infantry Officer* was no exception. But its sales fell very little short of *Memoirs of a Fox-Hunting Man* at the start.[2]

To some extent this was due to lucky timing on Sassoon's part. Just as his war poems had been published at a point when the public was ready to respond to their anti-war message, so his first two prose accounts of the war appeared at the height of the genre's popularity. A few years earlier and they might, like Ford Madox Ford's Tietjens tetralogy of 1924 to 1928, have attracted little attention. A few years later and they would possibly have suffered the fate of the last book in Sassoon's trilogy, *Sherston's Progress*, which was not published until 1936 and is the least well-known of the three.

Sassoon had intended to complete *Sherston's Progress* much earlier. Fired by the success of *Infantry Officer* in autumn 1930, he planned to start work at once on another volume of memoirs. Not only would this enable him to utilize the Craiglockhart material he had reluctantly abandoned at the end of *Infantry Officer* and write about Rivers, as he longed to do, but it might also distract him from the deteriorating situation at Wilsford. By late 1930 Nurse May was making life very 'uncomfortable' for him there because (he believed) the 'vixen' was 'jealous' of his relationship with Stephen. (Edith Olivier thought she had fallen in love with Sassoon, though why this should make her want to get rid of him she does not explain.) So he sat down resolutely to write a third volume of Sherston's 'Further Experiences' (later renamed *Sherston's Progress*).[3] But his efforts to work on this at Campden Hill Square in December 1930 resulted only, he told Ottoline, 'in being awake till 4 a.m. every night',[4] and by the beginning of January 1931 he had abandoned the project. The sole fruit of his midnight vigils was a poem about Rivers called 'Revisitation'.[5] It would be another two years before he returned to prose.[6]

One problem he faced in continuing Sherston's wartime experiences, which would be based like the previous two volumes on his own, was that this last phase – from the aftermath of his protest in July 1917 to his final return to England in July 1918 – was outwardly the least exciting period. It seemed to him that, though inwardly filled with great turmoil and change, there was not 'enough material for a book' in the months following his stay at Craiglockhart.[7] 'It would merely', he told the Heads, 'be a rewriting of my travel diary in Palestine and France which ended with my head-wound in July.'[8]

Even the Craiglockhart material, for all its significance in his own life, threatened to be 'flat and boring' without 'a bit of innocent fudging in places'.[9] However challenging it had been to present Sherston's protest convincingly, it had contained ready-made drama. In describing his decision to return to the fighting, Sassoon ran the risk of bathos.

One answer was suggested by William Nicholson and Max Beerbohm, who was back in London in late 1930 and anxious to complete his caricature of Sassoon for the *Spectator*.[10] Both artists urged him to extend his Sherston material to the post-war years, a possibility he had already considered. But in re-reading his diary for the period he felt that 'the part about love affairs' made 'uncomfortable reading'.[11] If, as seemed necessary, his various homosexual affairs were excluded, there would be very little left to write about. Gabriel, for example, who had been so important to him immediately after the war, could be referred to, if at all, only as an 'acquaintance' from the North. Even as he contemplated this he had, by a neat coincidence, seen Gabriel with Meiklejohn at the Reform, their first meeting in five years. Though reasonably healthy in appearance and now married, Gabriel looked 'much coarsened' by years of drink, drugs and prostitution, in itself enough to put Sassoon off the idea of recreating him as his 'angel'.[12]

Sassoon had therefore decided to stay with the war and do what he could with the limited material left to him. Not only was it meagre, however, but also difficult to write about, especially his experiences at

Craiglockhart. 'It is a description of a psychological condition about which I have practically no contemporary evidence (except my war poems),' he told the Heads.[13] Since Sherston would have to remain as innocent of poetry-writing as he had been from the start, his creator could hardly use the war poems as evidence of his hero's state of mind. 'Of course all this Craigl[ockhart] part is very incomplete without my war poems and their prestige attached,' he had written just before abandoning the material for the first time in Sicily, perhaps another reason then for not covering the period in *Infantry Officer*.[14]

Sherston's lack of literary interests may also explain another apparently odd decision made by Sassoon in relation to *Sherston's Progress*, to 'omit Owen' from the Craiglockhart chapters, since his meeting with Owen, as with Rivers, had been one of the most important events at the nerve hospital. There may, however, be another explanation. It is possible that he feared that Owen's evident infatuation with him might suggest a homosexual relationship. This was a risk he was not prepared to take, as his decision not to describe his post-war life shows. Using his own experiences was turning out to be even less straightforward than it had been in his first two volumes.

The main reason for his failure to continue with Sherston, however, was Stephen's behaviour. Sassoon's poetic sensibilities had exposed him to intense suffering in the past, but he had never felt so desperate as he did during this period. It was, he told Robert Nichols with only a little of the latter's tendency to exaggerate, 'death in life'.[15] (The echo of Coleridge's suffering Ancient Mariner was probably deliberate.) Stephen's emotional instability, which resulted in a series of harsh rebuffs followed by tearful reconciliations, would make him deeply unhappy for the next two and a half years. Sassoon was no stranger to uncertainties and he had actually enjoyed the dangers of hunting and even the perils of life at the Front, but this constant playing with his most powerful feelings was to lead him for the first time in his life to contemplate suicide:

> Just to go out and leave my life behind, –
> This writing left unsigned; click off the light,
> Close the door quietly on the house; and find
> An empty road and windless winter night.
>
> Not like a traveller starting before day,
> Who smells adventure on the early air;
> But asking only peace to be away
> From Time's mean street and those who wrangle there.
>
> Just to forget and be myself no more.
> Thus have I mused. Yet life still guards the door.[16]

And it may have been a subconscious death wish which led to his unusually high number of accidents and illnesses during this period.[17]

He had found it difficult enough to write his two previous prose books, being naturally more drawn to poetry, and had only managed to complete them when first Glen, then Stephen, had given him both the incentive and emotional stability to do so. Now, profoundly depressed by Stephen's behaviour, he could write only verse and filled his notebooks with attempts to express his desolation. Though the majority of them fall short of his best work, they are an invaluable record of his feelings:

> Angel of Heaven, be near me in my need.
> I write the words. On my dark heart I write
> Those words in letters of consoling light,
> And by that deed my frustrate soul is freed
> From inward wars of anger. Written; and I read
> 'No enemy but yourself you found to fight'.[18]

One effect of Stephen's rejection was to make him even more conscious of his age, and the passing of youth is a recurrent theme. He specifically called one poem 'Farewell to Youth' and would include it in his next-but-one volume, *Vigils*.[19] Another, untitled and unpublished, piece opens with the stark words, 'Youth gone. Midnight and winter', and closes with a clear reference to Stephen: '... and the last syllable said / Of the one love that gave him back his youth, / And then betrayed him.'[20] His most successful exploration of the theme, also published in *Vigils*, is 'The Hour-Glass', which centres round the arresting image of himself, rather than Father Time, 'holding an hourglass in his hand':

> ... Deriving intimate omens from the trickling sand:
> Intent on Time's device which casually contains
> The world's enigma in its quietly falling grains.
> Myself I see; for whom the idle moments pass
> From *is* to *was* in that *memento mori* glass; ...
> (CP, p. 224)[21]

Another powerful effect of Stephen's withdrawal was to force Sassoon to look for other meanings in life, and the poems of the early thirties reveal a search for spiritual values. In July 1932, at the height of his suffering, he told Edith Olivier that 'religion [was] the mainspring of his life and that he [thought] a Poet is a Prophet'.[22] This belief emerges in his poems not just in an increasingly religious vocabulary[23] but, more significantly, in their content. 'The mind of man environing its thought', for example, which Edith Sitwell considered among the best poems he had ever written, was originally called 'World Invisible' and ends with a plea for spiritual enlightenment:[24]

16. The Turn of the Screw (February 1931-May 1933)

> World undiscovered within us, radiant-white,
> Through miracles of sight unmastered still,
> Grant us the power to follow and to fulfil.[25]

It would be many more years before Sassoon turned fully to religion, but the process was clearly started here in the early thirties.

For the time being, however, his verse was his religion. Edith Olivier believed that he found in poetry-writing 'a complete release from the cloud over him', as he had during the war, and his output increased dramatically. So that, although Stephen may be held largely responsible for the delay and possibly the comparative failure of *Sherston's Progress*, he can also be seen as the goad which led to the writing or revising of all seven poems in *The Road to Ruin* (1933), half of the thirty-five poems in the trade edition of *Vigils* (1935) and half a dozen of the forty-two poems in *Rhymed Ruminations* (1939, 1940).

Sassoon himself was convinced that the deprivations imposed on him by Stephen resulted in some very good work between 1930 and 1933:

> I have become more and more aware that such poems [he wrote to the Heads] are the result of a sort of *physical* process, (involving sublimated sexual energy) ... it is less like writing than a physical release of something which has been stored up. Robbie Ross once told me that I only wrote well when I felt strong emotion; and he was quite right. It is not an intellectual process, and my *skill* in verse-writing is only the result of lifelong practice and much intuitive groping.[26]

However consoling he found poetry, Sassoon still needed his friends, particularly those who were close but not too close to Stephen. Edith Olivier, for example, grasped the situation better than most and proved a great comfort. Her understanding of Stephen's temperament prevented her from antagonizing Sassoon, who was still not ready to hear any real criticisms of his beloved. But she could also understand Stephen's reaction to Sassoon's zealous attempts to order his life, which had begun to 'bore him to death'.[27] (Even Sassoon realized that 'Stephen cannot be driven. He can only be led.'[28]) She needed all her tact and patience in her role as go-between. When, as a result of his dismissal, Sassoon wrote to tell Stephen 'how hurt he [was] about being banished by Nurse May', Edith received an 'agoniz[ed]' telephone call from Stephen begging for her help.[29] She agreed to write to Sassoon on his behalf, but was entirely realistic about the situation: 'The problem', she wrote in her diary on 26 February 1931, 'is really insoluble. Sieg. adores Stephen so much that he can't endure separation and is convinced that he alone can make him better ... Stephen believes only Nurse May can cure him so that he *must* stick to *her* now and [that he and Sassoon] are not compatible.'[30] On the other hand, she knew how 'wounded' Sassoon must be by Stephen's 'unkind' behaviour: 'But Stephen is quite irresponsible,' she noted a month later. 'He's like a half fairy creature – captivating and cruel.'[31] She did her best to soften each blow as it came.

One practical way in which she helped was to offer Sassoon somewhere to stay in the district now that Wilsford was closed to him, and they were to spend many evenings together in the next few years. Edith was at the centre of a large circle of people and kept Sassoon in touch with the outside world. When Rex Whistler or William Walton came to visit, for example, she would invite Sassoon too or later, when Sassoon had his own house, drive her guests over from Wilton to have dinner with him. She even persuaded him to go with her to Cecil Beaton's house, Ashcombe, on several occasions, in spite of his continuing coolness towards its host.

Another lifeline during this time was the company of two people who were even nearer to news of Stephen, being part of the Wilsford staff. They were the sisters Beryl and Eileen Hunter, who worked in the garden.

Sassoon's friendship with 'Really and Truly', as he admiringly nick-named them, had begun when he had taken up riding again in July 1930.[32] They were both horse lovers and had gladly helped him look after Bruno, the cob on which he took his daily ride. The middle-aged daughters of a Captain Hunter, who lived in the nearby village of Lake, they were better read than most of the Wilsford staff, having 'in their shy way', Sassoon told the Heads, 'a real appreciation and understanding of poetry'.[33] They had started buying Sassoon's books long before they met him and he rewarded their admiration with signed copies of his later works. The relationship meant a great deal to them and, according to Eileen Hunter, changed their lives. Like many other local people, who nicknamed him 'Don Quixote', they saw him as a valiant knight coming to the rescue of the 'young lord', their name for Stephen.

Sassoon delighted in the Hunters' devotion. His bruised ego needed all the comfort it could get after Stephen's battering. Nevertheless, it was an odd alliance that grew up between himself and the sisters during his exile from Wilsford. For a start they were unmarried and almost the same age as himself, whereas most of his female friends had previously been either safely married, like Delphine Turner, or significantly older, like Ottoline and Edith Olivier. But it is clear that for all their adoration, Beryl and Eileen were no threat to him sexually. Rather masculine in their ways, they were manual workers at a time when that was much less usual for women, they rode a motorbike together, knew all about cars and seemed more interested in animals than people on the whole. Their greatest devotion was to each other. (When Eileen died prematurely in her fifties her sister would follow shortly afterwards, unable, Sassoon believed, to live without her.)[34]

The other surprising aspect of this relationship was Sassoon's readiness to become friendly with Stephen's gardeners. The Hunters, however, were less working-class than their occupation suggested at the time and less of a challenge to Sassoon's class consciousness than might at first appear.

Impoverished circumstances had forced both their father and themselves to find work at Wilsford after the war, which had brought about great social changes. But they remained essentially middle class. Their letters to Sassoon, more than sixty of them in all, are written in an educated, witty style and full of words like 'topping', 'beastly', 'rotten', and 'top-hole', hardly the vocabulary of working-class girls. They also lived in the kind of house they could invite Sassoon to lunch or stay at, as they frequently did.

One useful aspect of Beryl and Eileen's former social standing was that it enabled them to provide Sassoon with an introduction to the local hunt. So that on 17 January 1931, after almost eight years' abstinence, he had a day out with the Wylye Valley Hounds.[35] He greatly enjoyed it, in spite of the fact that Stephen's carriage-horse, Bruno, had never seen hounds before and tried to kick both them and the other horses. Edith, who had driven over to the meet at Berwick St James with Walton's mistress, Princess Imma von Doernberg, delighted in the irony of the situation: 'The rest of the field little knew that they had the "Fox-Hunting Man" with them, but thought he and his horse were both beginners!'[36]

The experience, for all its shortcomings, left Sassoon determined to buy himself a real hunter and less than a fortnight later he was in possession of a twelve-year-old mare, Silvermane. Unfortunately, he had bought the horse while still 'under the impression that Stephen would want me to be with him a good deal', he told Nan Tennant, which added to his irritation when the opposite proved true.[37] Once again the Hunter sisters came to his help, putting Silvermane up in their own stables and doing their best to exercise the high-spirited horse, though it was well beyond their strength and control. Sassoon showed his appreciation with expensive presents from Fortnum and Mason's while in London, and by taking them for days out to local point-to-points and other attractions while in Wiltshire.

Gradually he came to rely on them heavily, especially for news of Stephen. Shrewd, outspoken and down-to-earth, with a healthy sense of humour, they were ideal informants. Anyone less sympathetic to Stephen would have angered him, anyone more so could not have identified with Sassoon as completely as they did. They were able to quieten any guilt they occasionally felt about their role as spies by telling themselves that it was for Stephen's own good. They honestly thought that the 'poor silly little tadpole', as Beryl fondly called him, was 'sick in body ... and even sicker in mind'[38] and that a reconciliation with Sassoon was his only hope.

If anything positive could be said to come out of Stephen's cruelty, Sassoon felt it was the 'golden humanity' of Beryl and Eileen.[39] They seemed to him the 'good geniuses' of Wilsford's garden and, as Ralph Hodgson put it, 'the best that England can produce'.[40] 'What I should have done without their help', Sassoon wrote to the Heads, 'I can't imagine.'[41] When it looked as though their allegiance to him might threaten their position at Wilsford, he was fully prepared to start them up in their own business, if necessary: 'Never have I felt such gratitude as I feel towards them.'[42] The Hunters were equally grateful to him. Without his support, they told him, they could 'never have stuck' Stephen's whims and all the in-fighting which went on between Wilsford's outdoor and indoor staff.[43]

Sassoon was particularly dependent on the Hunters during the first year of his exile while he was still trying to establish his own base in the district. He had moved temporarily to a nearby hotel after the sisters' attempts to find him suitable rented accommodation had failed.[44] And in March he decided to accept Walton's suggestion that he should join him and Imma in Switzerland for a break. 'I really need a change of scene badly', he wrote to his mother towards the end of March, 'as the last two months have been so full of annoyances connected with Wilsford.'[45] 'Poor Stephen', he added, was 'really only a child' and 'allowances' must be made for his 'physical condition'.[46] But for the moment his patience had run out. Still unable to live without news of Stephen, however, he was grateful for Beryl's and Eileen's promise to keep him informed of his progress, or lack of it.

Walton had written to Sassoon on 8 March from Ascona, almost certainly at Imma von Doernberg's suggestion. She had met Edith's handsome friend only very briefly before they went to see him hunt in January, but had followed Edith's report of the unfolding 'catastrophe' with Nurse May indignantly.[47] 'What a bitch,' Walton commented in his March letter, echoing no doubt both his mistress's and Sassoon's own feelings: 'I am sure she's made him ill on purpose.' Walton had to be in England on 23 March to hear his Viola Concerto played by the great Lionel Tertis and to discuss the performance of *Belshazzar's Feast* at the coming Leeds Music Festival.[48] His idea was that Sassoon should return with him to Switzerland on 29 March for an 'entire change': 'I am sure it would take your mind off all this disagreeableness and keep you quiet till it blows over.'[49] As an added incentive he argued that Sassoon would be able to settle down and do some work.

Hoping Walton was right, Sassoon agreed to his plan and duly travelled back with him to Switzerland. But in spite of Walton's industrious example – he was rushing to meet a deadline with *Belshazzar's Feast* – Sassoon wrote very little successful verse during his two months there. Apart from tinkering with old poems, he produced four new poems at Ascona, but only one ('To a Red Rose') was published.[50] He was beginning to despair of producing anything significant in poetry. His parodies of Humbert Wolfe, *Pinchbeck Lyre*, were published by Duckworth on 15 May, but they did not seem to him to count and it was two years since he had produced a serious book of poems.[51]

In spite of his inability to work well at Ascona, however, he did feel 'much more at liberty in [his] mind' and the fact that he stayed six weeks longer than his intended fortnight suggests that he enjoyed himself there.[52] Situated in southern Switzerland on Lake Maggiore, it had all the advantages of magnificent views, constant sun and mountain air. And as Walton had also pointed out, being only two miles from the Italian border it offered the amenities of ordered Swiss life without any of its drawbacks, an attractive mix of two very different cultures.

Walton was by no means the first to discover this Utopia. It had been colonized by artists and freethinkers since the end of the nineteenth century, including a wealthy Belgian, Henri Oedenkoven, who had bought a hilltop overlooking the little fishing village and named it Monte Verità, the Mountain of Truth.[53] It was here, in a hotel founded by Oedenkoven, that Sassoon stayed. Thinking his own *pension* too modest for his wealthy friend, Walton had recommended the Monte Verità as much for its extraordinary art collection of Picassos, Matisses, Braques and Chinese painters as for its dramatic views. Its only fault in Sassoon's eyes was its inability to serve a 'decent' cup of tea, a situation he quickly remedied: 'You would laugh if you could see me with my electric kettle, making myself secret cups of tea in my room,' he wrote to Ottoline towards the end of April. 'I am like an old Almsman – content with "a pinch of tea and a twist of bacca".'[54] (Already settled into lifelong routines, he was beginning to lose what youthful flexibility he had once possessed. His tea-making activities would become a familiar ritual to his friends in his old age.) Owing to the lack of other English guests at the hotel and his own linguistic shortcomings, he was in 'no danger of being talked to' during the day, but was prevented from becoming morbid by visits from Walton and Imma, who walked over from the nearby Casa Angelo most evenings for coffee and a chat.

Until this point Sassoon's relationship with Walton had consisted mainly of favours granted on his side and requests for further help on Walton's. Both of them lived mainly for themselves and their art. But with the introduction of Imma into the equation this changed and they grew closer for a time.

Imma herself became especially fond of Sassoon. Her own financial situation by 1931 was serious. Unable to return to Germany because of the Nazi persecution of the aristocracy and without any marketable skills except graphology, she lived on a modest allowance from her father, who had been forced to halve it shortly before Sassoon's visit. She was even more appreciative of Sassoon's generosity than Walton, who sometimes seemed to take it for granted. And she also liked Sassoon personally. On first meeting him she had thought him 'determined, reserved and strong-willed'; but after analysing his handwriting (at Edith's request) she recognized 'a racked, sensitive, shattered spirit'.[55] Unprompted by Edith, who knew him much better, she detected 'his uncertainty over coming to a decision, his storm-tossed soul, his naïve delight in success, his innate self-distrust combined with a passionate longing to trust, and his wish to be first – the *only* one with anyone he loves'.[56] His writing also indicated to her that, though hard to live with, he had 'a lovely nature'.[57] It was a perceptive analysis, borne out by her subsequent friendship with him.

Imma also claimed to be able to tell from his handwriting that Sassoon was homosexual 'by nature', but she was clearly attracted to him physically.[58] After he left Ascona she would write not only to wish him well with Stephen and thank him again for his financial help, but also to ask him to send a photograph of himself. And there is evidence to suggest that Sassoon felt some sexual attraction towards her. He immediately sent the photograph, and his description of her to the Heads, for instance, is much warmer than his usual response to women. A 'charming creature', he also describes her as 'pretty, sweet ... very lively and courageous with a clear ringing voice and tall, graceful figure'.[59] Imma was 'sympathetic', 'merry' and 'intelligent', according to Edith[60] and seeing how happy she made Walton may have caused Sassoon to wonder if a heterosexual relationship might not be preferable to the torments he was suffering with Stephen. There is no doubt that he envied Imma's nurturing of Walton's genius, nor that his attitude towards women began to soften at this time.

Nevertheless he was still obsessed with Stephen and waited anxiously for news of him from the Hunters at Ascona. In April Beryl reported the negative effect his leaving had had on Stephen and Nurse May's increasing domination over her patient, though she was finding it difficult to ward off Stephen's undesirable friends without Sassoon's help. (Both sisters thought Nurse May a 'demented female' and 'unscrupulous maniac'.) Beryl also promised to let him know the results of Dr Snowden's imminent visit, but since the sisters took it 'in turn' to do everything, it was Eileen who told Sassoon the good news on 23 April that Stephen had been pronounced free of TB. He had been 'worrying himself into fits' about his health and now seemed much happier, promising to show Beryl Sassoon's 'lovely' postcards from Ascona and 'murmuring about the prospect of a future that includes you'.[61]

Sassoon was not deceived. Doubly exiled as he was in Switzerland and able to rely only on Stephen's unreliability by this time, he wrote in resignation and despair:

> To all my happiness I say
> Farewell. I tell my listening heart
> 'Put all your deep desires away
> Henceforth we two must live apart.'[62]

Even when Beryl wrote to tell Sassoon on 16 May that Stephen had sent Nurse May packing – 'Oh marvellous jubilant day!' – and that her replacement, Miss Turnbull, seemed 'an awfully good sort', he was unable to rejoice.[63] He could only hope that Stephen would be led by wiser counsels to a full reconciliation with himself. Stephen's aunt, Margot Asquith, had visited Wilsford recently and talked about Sassoon to her nephew 'a great deal ... with great sympathy and perception',[64] and Edith Olivier had been sent rare invitations to tea.

Encouraged perhaps by the latter, Sassoon finally decided to return to England at the end of May[65] and was rewarded by a few days with Stephen in late June. Though the patient was 'full of affection' and invited him to return to Wilsford the following weekend, Sassoon's trust had been destroyed: 'His acts are all dictated by emotions and needs', he wrote to Nan Tennant, 'and he has no rational sense of fairness.'[66] He was by now convinced of what Stephen's new nurse had warned him, that Stephen played on his feelings about his health to an 'unfair degree', and he resolved to 'try to be more firm' and 'assert [his] independence'.[67] Feeling as useless and foolish as an 'old bus ticket' or a '*human* donkey' as he did, he suspected that it would not be easy.[68]

Stephen's invitation was, predictably, cancelled and Sassoon set about asserting his independence. Relying once more on the Hunters for news, he decided to stop hanging about Wilsford and embarked on a 'five-weeks "season" of Operas and Sitwells and asking old friends to lunch at the Hyde Park Hotel'.[69] The Sitwells' friendliness seems to have increased as his closeness to Stephen declined and June and early July passed pleasantly enough.[70]

Sassoon's next assertion of independence was to accept Anzie and Wendela's generous invitation to stay at Bray in their absence, 'the Ideal Invitation' he wrote to Max, who knew and sympathized with the Stephen situation.[71] After suggesting that Max write an essay 'On Staying with Absent Friends', he pin-pointed unintentionally what was, in fact, his own most serious bar to a close relationship: 'No one is so sociable as I am, when I am alone.' It is significant that the majority of his strongest friendships were kept up mainly by letter. Delightful as it was to be able to visit the Heads, for example, who were living near Bray by this time, he felt just as close if not closer to them in letters.

The Wyldes were another case in point, though most of the letters between them have been lost. Nevertheless, he did accept their invitation to join them at Cannes, where they had a yacht, and spent part of August with them. But by 25 August he was alone again and more depressed than ever about Stephen.

His mood was not helped by the political situation, which was at crisis point. While he had been toying with the idea of taking a luxurious holiday at Ascona in March, Britain had been facing an economic slump. Sharp rises in unemployment in July and dire warnings by the Bank of England shook national confidence further, prompting Sassoon to return briefly to his all but abandoned satiric vein:

> ... Toll for the brave
> Gold Standard sunk below the European wave.
> For Britain's Gold Redemption Policy suspended,

And the Parity of the Pound (Alas, poor Yorick!) ended,
Lament from fiscal throats,
O patriot Five-Pound Notes;
And let your dirge with Wage Reductions be well blended ...

('Mammoniac Ode', CP, p. 166)

By 23 August 1931 the entire Labour Cabinet of Ramsay MacDonald had resigned. The following day MacDonald had been invited to form a national government with the Conservatives and the Liberals to deal with the emergency.

The situation was equally precarious abroad. As Sassoon's stay with Walton and his German princess had made him aware, the Nazis were increasing their hold in Germany. Worse even than the private implications for people like Imma was the threat to international peace. As Maynard Keynes had warned at the Treaty of Versailles, the punitive treatment of Germany and her war reparations had inevitably led to great hardship and Hitler was now exploiting his countrymen's discontent. By the summer of 1931, less than thirteen years after the Armistice, Sassoon to his dismay saw war looming again.

His depression about this and his own personal situation persisted throughout September. On 25 August he had rented a pleasant country house at Ipsden near Oxford from the writer Rosamond Lehmann for five weeks. Lehmann, who had established her reputation with her first novel, *Dusty Answer*, in 1927, had been a friend of Stephen's since before her marriage to Wogan Philipps (later Baron Milford) in 1928 and Sassoon had first met her at Wilsford. 'How nice she is!' he had written to Ottoline in August 1930.[72] He also admired her books, secretly thinking her a better novelist than Edith Olivier, but it was her powers of persuasion which interested him most. 'She is one of the people who might be a really good friend to Stephen,' he had confided hopefully to Nan in July 1931.[73] One of a series of women friends he appealed to in this crisis, she tried her best to help, having reason to be grateful to him for his advice over her brother John Lehmann's first book of poems.[74] But like all his other allies, she was unable to make any headway with Stephen. Instead she suggested that Sassoon should escape to her attractive Queen Anne house while she was away in Europe with her husband.

He ought theoretically to have enjoyed his stay at Ipsden House. Though deprived of Silvermane by his determination to keep well away from Wilsford, and in spite of bad weather, he hired an old white horse locally and rode about the country lanes daily. The Heads were within visiting distance, Blunden stayed for a week in early September, Walton a little later and Osbert Sitwell came to lunch at least once. Yet he could not stop thinking about Stephen, and the prognosis was not good. In fact the situation seemed to Sassoon the worst yet. Stephen had refused to see him 'ever again', Sassoon's alleged crime having been to turn up at

Wilsford unannounced and catch Stephen without his make-up. 'I have given up expecting to see him,' Sassoon told Ottoline at the end of the month.[75]

Unfortunately this was not true. He had not yet resigned himself to the inevitable. While still at Ipsden, for example, he had asked the Hunters again about rented accommodation in their district. Yet his decision to live near Wilsford at such a time was not as perverse as it seems. He missed Wiltshire, which gave him 'a sense of freedom and untouched country life', had lived for the whole summer in large, well-appointed houses in the midst of beautiful surroundings, and returning to a small flat in London appealed to him less and less.[76] 'I get so nervy and distracted in London,' he told Hodgson.[77] He had also grown to love riding again and his horse added to the equation.

By the end of September he had made his choice from the 'wad' of house descriptions sent by Beryl at his request and two days later the Hunters obligingly went to inspect it. Reading Eileen's description of Fitz House in the village of Teffont Magna, ten miles from Salisbury, it is not difficult to understand his decision to take it. 'It looks simply topping', she wrote; 'the flagstones, lavender and mullion windows are certainly all there, to say nothing of a burbling, crystal-clear stream, and a steep little orchard at the back.'[78] The trout-filled stream ran past the front gate and the house could only be reached by a small bridge. Described (rather misleadingly to modern eyes) as a 'Gentleman's Country *Cottage* Residence', it was an impressive, stone-built, thatched edifice dating from about the fifteenth century, standing in three acres of ground. A converted barn served as a garage.[79]

The Hunters were able to see Fitz House only from the outside but Edith Olivier, who had rented it with her sister from the owner, Lord Bledisloe, just after the war, was equally enthusiastic about the interior.[80] A stone-flagged hall led to drawing room, dining room and library, all of them oak-beamed, with servants' quarters behind. Upstairs there were three good-sized bedrooms and a fourth single one, ideal for a small sitting room.

The village and its surroundings were equally 'charming' according to the romantic Eileen, who loved the streak of green sandstone up the valley and the way 'everything [grew] wild, lilies-of-the-valley, primroses and daffodils and most other things that are nice'.[81] It was also a good centre for hunting and, fourteen miles from Wilsford, was sufficiently far for Sassoon to keep away if he wished, but near enough to reach it when necessary. If Sassoon needed company Edith was only a few miles away at Wilton. A 'sort of rural Heaven', according to one of Sassoon's first guests there, Ralph Hodgson, Fitz House represented the pre-industrial England to which Sassoon was emotionally drawn, 'that "pre-lapsarian" world he so much preferred to the real one', as Hodgson's biographer puts it.[82]

After some perfunctory bargaining Sassoon agreed to the landlord's terms, which included taking on Fitz House's existing staff, a married couple named Lapworth, and a full-time gardener. Yet when Sassoon signed the lease in November 1931 he intended Fitz House only as a weekend retreat. He quickly settled down to live there, however. 'I have been here most of the winter', he wrote to Cockerell in May 1932, 'and pass the time well with books and piano, and my horse is still at Wilsford, so I go over there and ride on the downs most days.'[83]

The effect on his work is noticeable. Living permanently in the country, as he now did, hastened his return to what Blunden believed to be his true path, pastoral poetry. 'November Dusk', for example, clearly emerges from his rural situation, as well as giving some of the flavour of his life at Fitz House:

> Ruminant, while firelight glows on shadowy walls
> And dusk with the last leaves of autumn falls,
> I hear my garden thrush whose notes again
> Tell stillness after hours of gusty rain.
>   * * *
> And I've no need to travel far to find
> This bird who from the leafless walnut tree
> Sings like the world's farewell to sight and song.
>   (CP, pp. 245-6)[84]

A related effect of living in the country again was to remind him sharply of his childhood love of nature, and several of the poems written at Fitz House are a celebration of that time, like poem '6' in *Vigils*, originally entitled 'First and Last Love':

> It was the love of life, when I was young,
> Which led me out in summer to explore
> The daybreak world. A bird's first notes were sung
> For childhood standing at the garden door ...
>   (CP, p. 211)[85]

One poem was first called 'Childhood Recovered' and opens: 'Down the glimmering staircase, past the pensive clock, / Childhood creeps on tiptoe, fumbles at the lock'. Another piece, originally entitled 'Past and Present', explicitly refers to his early years at Weirleigh and mourns 'Simplicities unlearned long since and left behind'. [86]

Without Stephen to entertain, Sassoon had reverted to former habits and wrote what poems he could after dinner, leaving the mornings free for riding. The Hunters were delighted at 'Captain' Sassoon's almost daily visits to their stables and continued to report on Stephen's doings. Having become almost as critical of his new nurse as his old, they were convinced that Miss Turnbull's well-meaning intercession on Sassoon's behalf had actually made matters worse. Stephen simply felt 'coerced'.[87] After another of his aunts, Mrs Adeane, had failed to bring him to his senses, Nan Tennant had attempted, no more successfully, to plead Sassoon's cause. The only good news was that Stephen's general health had improved and that the latest X-rays still showed no recurrence of TB.

Sassoon had, with some misgivings, decided to tell Stephen of his move to Fitz House, secretly hoping that he would relent and agree to see him. When he refused (provoked again by Miss Turnbull's tactless intervention, the Hunters believed), Sassoon was forced to find other distractions. 'I have been diverting my empty mind lately with a good deal of book-buying', he wrote to Ottoline on 12 December 1931, 'and have discovered several interesting authors.'[88]

His youthful taste for book-collecting had been sharpened over the years by two fellow-enthusiasts, Blunden and Hodgson, and it was Hodgson who now stimulated his revival of interest. Since leaving for Japan in 1923, Hodgson had kept in close touch with Sassoon, responding enthusiastically to each of his poetry books as they were sent to him. He had been equally positive about Sassoon's prose, describing *Fox-Hunting Man* as 'nature (human) with a pen! A thing of glory!'[89] and urging him to continue the series.

Sassoon had been too busy with *Fox-Hunting Man* when Hodgson took his first sabbatical from the University of Sendai in 1927 for them to see as much of each other as they would have liked. But in October 1931, when he returned for his second furlough, Sassoon had almost unlimited time for him. Over dinner at the Reform they planned a tour of second-hand bookshops together and on 10 November set out in Sassoon's Packard for the north-east. Having decided to start at Hull, little as it appealed to Sassoon's romantic soul, they worked their way down through Yorkshire, Lincolnshire, Norfolk and Suffolk, visiting at least seventeen bookshops on the way.[90]

'Those five days were a joy for ever,' Sassoon told Hodgson, echoing a mutual favourite of theirs, Keats. He had loved the way Hodgson sang on the journey, 'usually without words', though on one occasion he included the lines of an old song taught to him by the poet Edward Thomas.[91] They also planned an anthology together of the 'small, neglected authors' they loved so much, like Thomas Ashe, Primovard Dugard or Charles Dalmon. This was never completed but their detailed notes for it reveal the extraordinary breadth of their reading in out-of-the-way places. One extract they intended to include from William Camden's *Remains*, 'Epitaph for a Man Killed by Falling from His Horse', is particularly interesting since it led directly to the writing of one of Sassoon's favourite poems. The words 'Betwixt the stirrup and the ground / Mercy I asked, mercy I found' haunted Sassoon from the moment Hodgson quoted them to him on their trip and lay behind the writing of 'The Merciful Knight' eight months later:

Swift, in a moment's thought, our lastingness is wrought
From life, the transient wing.
Swift, in a moment's light, he mercy found, that knight
Who rode alone in spring ...
The knight who sleeps in stone with ivy overgrown
Knew this miraculous thing.
In a moment of the years the sun, like love through tears,
Shone where the rain went by.
In a world where armoured men made swords their strength and then
Rode darkly out to die,
One heart was there estranged; one heart, one heart was changed
While the cloud crossed the sun ...
Mercy from long ago, be mine that I may know
Life's lastingness begun.

(CP, pp. 221-2)[92]

Though Graves could not see 'any use in appealing for "mercy from long ago"',[93] Sassoon seldom derived such pleasure from one of his own poems: 'I keep repeating it to myself in a quiet ecstasy', he told Hodgson, 'and loving its music and the Pre-Raphaelite pictures it evokes.'[94] The concept of 'mercy' had become even more attractive to him since Stephen's apparent lack of it had caused him so much suffering.

Hodgson was one of Sassoon's few visitors at Fitz House when he came to stay with his latest bull terrier, 'Pickwick', in June 1932. Sam Behrman, unable to entice Sassoon up to London, had visited briefly in April on his way back to America via Southampton, but other close friends were too busy. Blunden had been elected a Fellow of Merton College, Oxford, in March 1931 and was in any case preoccupied with a new collection of Owen's poems he was editing at Sassoon's suggestion. Sassoon still felt too emotionally involved with Owen to undertake it himself, as he explained to Blunden: 'I have always suffered from an obscure difficulty in clarifying my friendship with him – perhaps because the loss of him was a shock which I never faced squarely – coming as it did at the most difficult time, when I was emotionally and physically without any foundations.'[95] Blunden's own emotional involvement with the young journalist, Sylva Norman, which began in early 1932, was another reason he saw so little of Sassoon this year.

Glen also was too busy to visit Fitz House much in 1932. His first child had been born in September 1930 and christened George, partly in Sherston's honour.[96] (Sassoon had naturally been asked to be godfather.) Trying to combine his family and career left Glen little free time, but he wrote to Sassoon regularly, as he would continue to do until the latter's death. In some ways their friendship was all the stronger for being carried on by letter, but it could hardly be said to provide Sassoon with much social life at Fitz House.

For that he had to rely on Edith Olivier and other sympathetic neighbours. By mid-1932 he was already on close terms with the Bonham

Carters at nearby Stockton House. As he told Hodgson, who had been invited there during his June visit, 'Stockton House provided social life' in the summer of 1932, 'and I became very attached to Cressida and Laura and their little brother Mark.'[97] The omission of the young Bonham Carters' mother, Lady Violet, from the list is noticeable.[98] Sassoon had reason to be grateful to her, since she persuaded Stephen to see him twice that August and also took him to visit her sister-in-law, Lady Katharine Asquith, who would later become one of his most valued friends. She also introduced him to a distinguished circle of people, which clearly impressed him however blasé he appeared to be. Viscount Esher and his wife, for instance, were regular visitors and became keen collectors of his books. And Lord and Lady Desborough, whom he had not visited for seven years, managed to persuade him back to Taplow Court when they invited themselves to Stockton House with the express purpose of seeing him. Sassoon was not quite so pleased to meet Winston Churchill again at Violet's, this time dismissing Churchill as a 'fiend', presumably for his lone rearmament campaign from the back benches.

Sassoon openly admired Violet's political acumen and was very appreciative of her hospitality, but he also had serious reservations about her. For one thing he suspected that she was in love with him, a suspicion her letters to him appear to support.[99] Both Edith Olivier and Ottoline, when she came to visit him in Wiltshire, were convinced of the same thing. He also felt that, in spite of her avowed devotion to poetry, his in particular, Violet held very different values from his own and was probably no less worldly than her stepmother, Margot Asquith. (His nickname for Violet was 'Flamingo'.[100]) Like Frankie Schuster and Lady Desborough, he maintained, success was all she cared about. 'People like V.B.C. talk incessantly about Hodgson, de la Mare, etc., but they will buy anything in the world before they'll spend 5/- on one of their books.'[101] Literature, like politics, was an elaborate game to Violet and her kind, he believed.

When she left on holiday with her family for North Berwick in September 1932, however, he missed her greatly and felt lonelier than ever. It had been a bad year overall, though he had been comforted by the award of an Honorary D.Litt. from the University of Liverpool in December 1931.[102] He had been saddened by the death of his old friend 'Wirgie' (Helen Wirgmann) in March. And his mother had developed an abscess on her appendix at Christmas, which became so serious that she was encouraged to make her will early the following January.[103] 'The only good result', he told Glen, 'was that it made me realize how much she means to me and what a wonderful character she is.' Then on 21 January, the day of her operation, Stephen suffered another severe haemorrhage, suggesting a return of TB. Nellie Burton had also been very ill during the winter and was not expected to live.

As 1932 passed it became clear that Stephen's physical health was not the only problem. His mind was, in Sassoon's own words, 'as sick as his body'.[104] His family grew increasingly anxious about his behaviour, which was becoming more outrageous than ever. Not only had there been an incident with a soldier on Salisbury Station during one of his rare outings in 1931, but he was in trouble with the police again in summer 1932. They had managed to hush things up when he had got into difficulties over soliciting soldiers as a teenager, but he was now a grown man and responsible for his actions. When Sassoon took Sam Behrman to Wilsford in April 1932, in the faint hope of being allowed to see Stephen, the visit left Sam with 'an impression of evil, intensified, somehow by the surrounding beauty'.[105] Sassoon had bitterly compared this 'poisoned beauty' to Henry James's sinister setting in *The Turn of the Screw*, and as Sam watched an unsavoury 'flamboyantly dressed and arrogant young man' admitted to Stephen's quarters directly after Sassoon had been refused access, he could only agree: 'It was like that, a poisoned beauty.'[106] In this context, Sassoon's desperation and loneliness at Fitz House that summer becomes even more understandable:

> Is it not strange to haunt this tranquil house and hear
> The green months going by? Rich only in regret,
> To turn my past's loved picture to the wall, and yet
> Long that the past might speak and shine, once brave, once bright.[107]

Sassoon was beginning to believe that Stephen was 'a "dual personality". One part, vain and chic and sophisticated – behaving in terms of his abnormal temperament; the other ... as he won my devotion.'[108] Sir Henry Head was inclined to agree with him and recommended a nerve specialist, Dr George Riddoch, with whom he and Rivers had worked in 1920. Riddoch, in turn, advised treatment at the Cassel Hospital for Functional Nervous Disorders, known as 'Swaylands'. Founded in 1919 by Sir Edward Cassel, it based its treatment on experience gained from shell-shock cases during the war and was not unlike Craiglockhart. Situated at Penshurst in Kent, it was only ten miles east of Weirleigh, a factor which influenced Sassoon in its favour.

He knew better than to suggest it to the patient himself, however, and Stephen's female relatives were set to work on him instead. After a great deal of cajoling by Violet Bonham Carter and some straight talking from Nan Tennant, Stephen was persuaded to accept Riddoch's advice and left for Swaylands in the autumn of 1932. He had already started his game of cat-and-mouse again, not only allowing Sassoon his two August visits to Wilsford but encouraging fortnightly meetings with him at the hospital, then telling him 'not this week'.[109] In spite of this and his mother's scathing reference to Stephen being 'in a lunatic asylum – the best place for him',[110] Sassoon allowed himself to hope again. Stephen's new specialist, Dr Ross, had told him that Sassoon was 'good' for him and Stephen was very much under his new doctor's influence. Ross had persuaded him to talk about his 'tragic disability', Sassoon told the Heads – possibly, Stephen's biographer suggests, a coy reference to impotence, which Sassoon believed to be the source of all Stephen's difficulties. And Stephen loved talking to Ross, 'who banish[ed] bogies very cleverly', he told Sassoon: 'One thing he said I liked was – Sin – which is generally thought to be sexual aberrations, which are really unimportant – is really hate.'[111] Stephen seemed positive about his relationship with Sassoon for the first time in two years.

But Sassoon had suffered too deeply from Stephen's capriciousness ever to trust him fully again. 'I was in – 1932-33 – losing hope about my personal future,' he told T.E. Lawrence.[112] He was also conscious of the truth of Forster's shrewd analysis that Stephen might 'get much better, but … will be worried by his own behaviour to you, and will incline to see people who know nothing about it'.[113] So that when Stephen once more refused to see him, at the end of February 1933, only a week after sending him a Valentine message, 'O Siegfried, how faithful is this heart', he was not totally unprepared.[114] Though still 'loitering about in his vicinity', as he admitted to Max Beerbohm, he had already started to think of Stephen as 'a sort of idea of happiness which will not return'.[115]

He even seems to have hastened the end, consciously or not, by issuing an ultimatum. 'I have made up my mind that I will *not* submit to any more bullying, which is what S[tephen]'s behaviour amounts to,' he told the Heads in May. In his letter to Stephen he had asked more dramatically, 'Can't you hear the best thing in your life being strangled, while you lie there locked in with your obsession?'[116] He was finally prepared to 'say goodbye' if the response was negative.[117]

Nevertheless, when the end came he was devastated. In spite of having prepared himself for it and knowing that he would have cared far more six months or a year earlier, the shock of Stephen's cruel response was severe. Conveyed through an embarrassed Dr Ross, it left no room for doubt:

22 May [1933]

Dear Captain Sassoon,

Thank you for your letter. Mr Tennant told me that he had received a letter from you, but he has not read it and I do not think he intends to.

What I am now going to say is something I have nothing whatever to do with, except that I have been asked to pass it on to you as a message from him. I do not know why, but since your last visit his feelings towards you have not been what they were. He says that you upset him and make him feel ill, and that he cannot see you again. I know that he has done this before, and that you will probably feel he is a very impossible person. He is of course not well, and that is about all there is to be said for it. I know also that I encouraged you to come in the Autumn, because I thought that your visit did him good: but as he says he does not wish to see you now, I can obviously do nothing further in the matter.

Yours sincerely,
J.A. Ross[118]

It was the last turn of the screw, one of the most important turning points in Sassoon's life, and one that would lead him in directions he could never have predicted.

'O, Hester, You Must Redeem My Life'[1]
(June-December 1933)

... 'Poor ghost of murdered love, depart
In peace,' my self to selfhood said.
And then, beyond all hope you came;
With healing hands and infinite heart
Rewrote my unexpectant name
And raised my future from the dead.
                    (Unpublished poem of October 1934)[2]

Stephen had overplayed his hand and would come to regret it bitterly. In rejecting Sassoon so callously through his doctor he had underestimated Sassoon's pride and overestimated his patience. He had also made no allowance for chance – or Edith Olivier.

Edith was still sympathetic towards Stephen in 1933. Like most of his friends she believed that his mental breakdown was largely a delayed reaction to the deaths of the two people he had needed most, his mother and Nannie. But she was also shocked by the effect his behaviour had on Sassoon, who was unable to hide his suffering from her. In a deliberate attempt to distract him she insisted that he accompany her to the George Herbert Pageant at Wilton on 7 and 8 June 1933. And for it she provided him, rather optimistically, with a female partner, Hester Gatty.

Edith had known the 27-year-old all her life. Hester's mother's family, the Morrisons of nearby Fonthill Abbey, had been famous collectors and patrons of the arts and Edith had been close to two of their four children.[3] She had campaigned for their son, Hugh Morrison, when he became Conservative MP for Salisbury in 1918 and would later help their daughter (Hester's mother) Katherine, Lady Gatty, with her own mother's unfinished account of her life at Fonthill and Carlton House Terrace. Hester, like Sassoon, was suffering from the after-effects of a failed love affair and Edith undoubtedly hoped that they might help each other to recover. One of Hester's two younger brothers, Richard Gatty, was also invited to join the Wilton party, together with Glen Byam Shaw and his wife Angela.[4]

Sassoon was clearly more interested in the company of Glen and Angela, who had come to stay with him for the event, than that of a young lady, however well connected. 'Oh dear, I must go out in my motor-car and plod the lawns of Wilton House in a rehearsal of that there Pageant,' he complained to de la Mare on 4 June.[5] He was no more enthusiastic at the pageant itself, feeling both embarrassed and hot in his elaborate costume of an Elizabethan bard. Caught on camera, he stares uncomfortably into its lens, awkward in his velvet doublet, ruff and knickerbockers, frozen in time at the very moment his life is about to take one of its most unexpected turns. He is not yet aware that Hester Gatty, looking 'a dream in an oyster silk Caroline dress' according to Edith, will shortly replace Stephen in his affections and, in less than six months, become his wife.[6]

Though Sassoon afterwards claimed to have felt a 'strong affinity' with Hester, at the time she merely struck him as a charming young woman and he made no effort to see her again.[7] He was still too obsessed by Stephen: 'I simply can't escape the demon of my devotion to Stephen,' he wrote to Ottoline as late as 1 September, more than three months after Dr Ross's letter of dismissal.[8] His feelings for Stephen, he told Edith, could only 'end with [his] life'.[9] Hester herself had other ideas and took matters into her own hands. And it was almost certainly with Edith's encouragement that at the beginning of September she booked herself into the Black Horse Inn at Teffont Magna, only a few hundred yards from Sassoon's house. Her ostensible reason was artistic, to paint the village and its surroundings. Since it was still quite unusual for a well brought up young lady to take such a trip on her own, however, it is more likely that she was hoping to meet Sassoon again. Unfortunately, Sassoon failed even to recognize her when he passed her painting in the village street on 3 September, though he thought she looked vaguely familiar. It was hardly an auspicious start, but Hester was determined, and, when they exchanged pleasantries two days later, identified herself as his fellow-guest at Wilton. An invitation to Fitz House for dinner that evening duly followed. Good manners dictated that he should be hospitable to a friend of Edith's and in any case he was very lonely.

Politeness quickly turned to genuine interest and involvement. Shortly before meeting Hester for the second time, he had written in his diary: 'I need love to light up my existence. Mental friendships are not enough. Emotional companionship is what I need.' Then, after his first evening alone with her, he had confessed: 'I felt grateful for her companionship,' suggesting that she had satisfied at least one half of his needs.

Sensitive, well read and artistic (she wrote poetry, composed music and played the piano as well as painted), Hester evidently shared enough with Sassoon to make her interesting company.[10] She also had a 'good brain' and 'lovely nature', according to the admittedly partial Edith, who also enthused about her 'quiet serene beauty' and 'voice like an echo'.[11] Sassoon's first impression had been of her 'clear and gentle voice' and 'wide bluish-grey eyes'.[12] Just as importantly, like Stephen, she was twenty years younger than Sassoon, a great admirer of his work and ready to play the devoted acolyte.[13]

Love quickly followed that first evening, especially once Sassoon was convinced that, like all his previous lovers except Novello, 'she needed protecting'.[14] She herself had invited his pity when she told him of her recent recovery from a nervous breakdown after a failed love affair. 'HG has rather a sad face', he wrote in his diary after she left, 'but is attractive.'[15] Slim, dark and not unduly feminine in figure, she had a boyish look and reminded Edith, for one, of Stephen. It was not a huge transition from the young male figure to hers and Sassoon quickly found himself attracted to her. He began to entertain her daily, driving her about the Wiltshire countryside, taking her to visit the Hunter sisters (perhaps for their approval) and giving her dinner each evening at Fitz House. By the time she left she had spent more time painting in his garden than the village and they had made arrangements to meet again soon. 'Strong affection' was turning into romantic love.[16]

There was one major stumbling block in the way. Though Sassoon had mentioned his 'friendship' with Stephen, he had been unable to match her frankness about her past love life. 'What can I do?' he asked himself at the beginning of October. 'I can't say to her, "Look here, I am forty-seven, and have never had a love affair with a woman. The best thing you can do is never see me again."' After being taken home to meet her widowed mother at Ossemsley Manor near Bournemouth, however, he realized that Hester was 'gently leading' him away from Stephen.[17] For his strongest impulse had been to rescue Hester from the rather stifling atmosphere of Lady Gatty's ornate, over-furnished house.

The crisis came when they met again only five days later on 7 October in London. Sassoon now felt that he was in love with her 'physically as well as mentally' and the last obstacle crumbled.[18] That afternoon he talked to her explicitly about the past six years of his life and her sympathetic response convinced him that a future together was possible. When they travelled back to Salisbury together the next day he told her of his feelings and, on meeting her again at Edith's that evening, knew that any lingering doubts had gone. The following day, Sunday, 9 October, he formally proposed and was accepted. The white swan flying across the sky at the pageant rehearsal, he told the 'ecstatically happy' Edith, had clearly been 'Stephen passing out of his life'.[19]

It was a huge relief to Sassoon, Edith's account of him at this time suggests: 'He looks well and unnervy – laughing and chuckling and kicking up his heels. Like a young *hunter*, as well as a fox-hunting man!'[20] 'I can only sum all up', he wrote to the Heads, who had shared most of his suffering over Stephen, 'by saying it is as though my good angel had arrived in human form. My previous life seems to have been a sort of purgatory in which I was being taught to use the real happiness which has come at last with a sense of peace and security I can't describe.'[21] And elsewhere: 'All my nights are dreamless now, and I wake with a sense of limitless gratitude which is like the feeling that Bach's music gives me. My whole existence is Hester's now, and her love is something which I cannot measure or comprehend.'[22]

Sir Henry Head, he knew, would understand how extraordinary the psychological impact had been for him. For a younger man to turn from homosexuality to heterosexuality, like Robert Graves and Glen Byam Shaw, is not so unusual, but for someone of forty-seven it was a complete overturn. It is certainly one which invites speculation. Apart from the need for 'love' and 'emotional companionship' already mentioned, what was it that led Sassoon to such an abrupt change of direction?

The most obvious explanation is that he was on the rebound from Stephen and punishing him, though Stephen himself put a different, more flattering interpretation on it: 'Don't you think, Siegfried, [he asked] that it was because you and I had set such a high standard of happiness together – that when it all smashed, you had to marry in the endeavour to create a state of happiness as much like it as possible.'[23] There is no doubt that Stephen was part of the equation, if only to prepare Sassoon for the feminine, as the eunuch Bagoas brought Alexander in Mary Renault's *The Persian Boy* from being exclusively homosexual to what she considers the more usual bisexuality of Greek men.[24] It is interesting to note that when Sassoon started reading the love letters between Robert and Elizabeth Barrett Browning that summer he had been thinking of Stephen and himself, but by the time he finished them in the autumn he had come to identify the lovers with Hester and himself.

Another strong motive was undoubtedly social. The difficulties of homosexual relationships in the days before it was legalized may have attracted men like Auden, who appears to have felt it added spice to them ('heterosexual love seems so tame and easy after it', he wrote)[25] but Sassoon needed social respectability. Hester may have represented the solution. 'O Hester, you must redeem my life for me,' he had written in his diary the day before proposing to her. (As early as 1922 he had described the previously homosexual Maynard Keynes as 'lucky' to marry the Russian ballerina Lydia Lopokova.)[26]

Hester's respectable family background was an equally important factor. Solidly upper-middle class, they had some distinguished connections. Not only was her mother a Morrison of Fonthill, her mother's brother married to a lady and her mother's sister married to a viscount, but Hester's father had been knighted for his services as Chief Justice of Gibraltar.[27] Sassoon was even more impressed by the fact that Sir Stephen was the younger brother of the popular nineteenth-century children's writer Juliana Horatia Ewing, whose books he had already started collecting. Sir Stephen Gatty's mother, Margaret Gatty, also a successful children's writer, was herself the daughter of Nelson's private secretary and chaplain on the *Victory*, Alexander Scott.[28] It was a reassuring mix of the Establishment and the artistic. In addition, Hester's family had money.[29] Though that in itself is unlikely to have influenced Sassoon's choice, it would significantly affect his future.

Hester was not the first well-connected, wealthy young woman to pursue him, however, and there were other equally important considerations. Apart from the sexual frustration of a highly sexed man, he had strong needs in a different direction. 'I, too, have longed for children,' he had written at Weirleigh as long ago as January 1919, when his passion for Gabriel was at its height, and time had increased that longing. The birth of Glen's son in 1930 and his affection for the Bonham Carter children had brought it to the forefront of his mind, as had his growing reputation: sales from his work were so high that he had to pay £739 super-tax in 1933, a large amount of money for the time. But there was no one to whom he could pass on his name. A friend who knew him and Hester well later on had no hesitation in saying that 'he married to have a son' and that he viewed her mainly as 'the mother of his child'.[30] Hester not only (in his own words) 'raised [his] future from the dead' but offered him the possibility of a continuation of that future in the shape of children. And with all those 'gifted Gattys' and 'financially famous Morrisons' behind her, she promised to be good breeding stock.[31]

He was almost certainly influenced too by Glen's successful switch from a homosexual to heterosexual lifestyle. (Graves's marriage had not been so successful, but his taunt about Sassoon's 'emotional shortcomings' in October 1933 may have helped propel him towards matrimony, since his proposal followed less than a week later.)[32] And Glen's wife, Angela Baddeley, may also have contributed to his change of heart. For she was one of an increasing number of women he had grown fond of in the late twenties and early thirties. Beryl and Eileen Hunter, Imma von Doernberg, Edith Olivier and Rosamond Lehmann had all made him feel that he could trust women, and, where none of his male friends had volunteered, had tried to help him over Stephen.

There was no real question of a romantic interest with these women, though he undoubtedly found Imma physically attractive. But there was one curious relationship between 1930 and 1933 which he concealed from all his friends and which probably paved the way for Hester. It was a liaison carried on solely through letters that have only very recently come to light.[33] The person concerned was Doris Gertrude Westwood, an unmarried woman in her thirties of middle-class background and independent means, who wrote to him mainly from Digby House, Sutton Coldfield, where she lived with her mother when not staying at the Ladies International Club in Bayswater, London. A writer herself, who had studied playwriting at RADA and had had one novel published by the time she contacted Sassoon, she was intelligent, educated and cultured.[34] She was also sensitive, romantic and vaguely religious, a follower of Mahatma Gandhi and half-believer in Christian Science.

An ardent supporter of animal rights, Doris first wrote to Sassoon on 25 February 1930 after reading *Memoirs of a Fox-Hunting Man*. She admired him as a poet, particularly one who had protested publicly against the war, in which she appears to have lost her fiancé. But she was shocked to think of him hunting, a sport of which she strongly disapproved, and had refused to read the book on publication. When she eventually did so, however, she felt that 'no book could have told the story of fox-hunting with less cruelty or, perhaps, less enthusiasm for the "kill" itself', and praised its 'gentleness and humanity'. Her ostensible reason for writing was to 'apologize' for misjudging him, but it is clear that she was hoping to strike up a correspondence. When Sassoon did eventually reply from Sicily, where her letter had been forwarded, it was perhaps a sign of troubles to come with Stephen that he should describe himself during their romantic holiday together as 'a somewhat solitary person'. Her reply indicated that she, too, considered herself something of a loner, her favourite Sassoon poem being 'Alone'.

Though her letters started as fan mail, they quickly developed into something more personal. At first this centred round her sympathy for Sassoon as his relationship with Stephen deteriorated: '*Please* talk to me whenever you want to talk and there is nobody there, don't write letters in your diary. When S.T. is better and you are happy I will go back to writing to Mr Sherston once every two months, this is a promise, so you needn't be afraid.'[35] But very soon the tone becomes even more intimate: she has already requested a photograph of him and sent one of her own; now she addresses him (where he is staying in Switzerland) as 'O Kangar-among-the-mountains' and tells him that spring has refused to arrive in England in his absence.[36] By the beginning of 1932 she is assuring him of her 'love' and offering to come to Teffont Magna 'if [she] thought it would be any help to [him]'.[37] Her suggestion that she should book herself into the village inn contrasts revealingly with Hester's much bolder decision to stay at Teffont Magna *without* asking Sassoon and indicates less insight into his character.

It is at this point that Sassoon appears to panic, since shortly after his reply there is a long silence from Doris. Her next letter, on 5 November 1933, is one of shock at having read of his engagement in the newspapers, which makes it quite clear that she had still been hoping something similar would have eventually occurred in their own relationship: 'It is the last thing I ever expected to happen and feel like you did when S[tephen] shut you out. Only this is worse because I have always been outside waiting for the day when you would let me in and you have never done it.' Two more letters follow and, in July 1934, he finally has to ask her to stop writing to him now that he is married. Her final letter is one of embarrassed apology and a horrified refusal of his invitation to meet him and his wife when they are next in London.

Though Doris's letters end, however, she continues to explore her powerful feelings for Sassoon in fictional terms. In *An April Day* (1934), her third novel, almost certainly written during the most intense period of their relationship in 1933 and early 1934, the heroine falls in love with 'the lonely hermit' Kester Carmichael, who eventually rejects her advances in spite of an evident attraction to her. Not only is the allusion to 'Hester' obvious in Doris's choice of her hero's unusual first name, but Kester himself strongly resembles Sassoon. A tall, dark, fit man in his early forties with hazel eyes and rather large ears, he has a soldier's bearing and a 'strange, dignified air'. Someone who 'likes to be alone' with his beloved old books, he has himself written a number of books, at least one of them about the First World War. Even his house closely resembles Fitz House, which Doris knew from a secret pilgrimage she made to the West Country to visit all the places Sassoon had mentioned in his letters.

Fascinating as it is to discover yet another fictional representation of Sassoon, and one which precedes Turner's portrayal of him in *Blow for Balloons*, the main interest of *An April Day* lies in Doris's manipulation of a real-life situation to fit her emotional needs. Rather than have her hero end his relationship with the heroine for another woman, as Sassoon did in reality with her, she has him leave the heroine for another, much younger man resembling Stephen Tennant, though Kester's destination is the same as Sassoon's honeymoon choice, Spain.

Doris's fourth and final novel, *Humble Servant* (1936), suggests that she is still struggling with her unrequited love for Sassoon and attempting to exorcise her feelings in a more radical way. With a similar mingling of real-life details, or subversions of them, and a plot of her own invention, she makes her hero a young German prince reminiscent of Sassoon's young lover Prince Phillip of Hesse, who bears a strong physical resemblance to Sassoon as well as his unusual middle name (for a man), Loraine, with its distinctive single 'r' spelling. In this version of events, there are two main bars to a successful relationship with the novel's heroine, the prince's royal responsibilities, which he is reluctant to shoulder, and the heroine's age: at forty-two she is approximately the same age as her creator, Doris, and more than twenty years older than the hero. His attraction for her is never in question and they fall deeply in love, the problems of a future together conveniently resolved by the prince's assassination on the last page of the novel. Having killed Sassoon off in fictional terms, Doris writes no more novels.

Edith Olivier, who knew nothing of Doris Westwood, believed that Sassoon was eventually 'inspired ... to leave Stephen for Hester' by a quite different woman, whom he scarcely knew, Rachel MacCarthy.[38] She was convinced that it was seeing the newly married David Cecil, who had come to live nearby, 'watch his dear little elfin wife [Rachel] with satisfied eyes of love' that had finally persuaded him.[39] Another marriage which certainly did influence him was that of Edmund Blunden and Sylva Norman in July 1933, which appeared to make Blunden very happy.

269

An even more decisive factor in Sassoon's conversion, however, was his meeting in 1933 with Geoffrey Keynes, later an eminent surgeon and bibliophile. A friend of Theo from Cambridge and younger brother of the well-known economist and prominent member of the Bloomsbury Group, Maynard Keynes, Geoffrey appeared to have no problems with his bisexuality. Influenced perhaps by Bloomsbury's frankness on sexual matters, he made no secret of his attraction to men. Writing to Sassoon early on in their friendship, after an intimate talk about Stephen, he makes it clear that he finds men physically attractive: 'For Lifar [a lead dancer with the Russian Ballet] I cherished the Grand Passion for several years, and one of the High Spots was when I helped him take off his clothes in his dressing-room after Apollo.'[40] Sassoon would later warn a young friend about to set out on a camping trip with Keynes: 'You'd better be careful; he likes young men.'[41] And the poet Andrew Motion, who was introduced to Keynes because of his schoolboy pilgrimage to Rupert Brooke's grave on Skyros and stayed with him fairly often after that, remembers that his host's goodnights were 'fairly intimate'.[42] It was 'quite clear', Motion said, that 'I was more interested in boys than girls' at eighteen (his age at the time) and Keynes would come into his room last thing at night and sit on his bed, though not go 'beyond a certain point'.[43] For Geoffrey was 'not in the least bit camp or salacious', according to Motion, 'and there were no lunges'.

Yet Keynes was happily married and the father of four sons. Sassoon had assumed from an early age that his own sexuality was fixed for life and confined to one sex, but Keynes's attitude challenged both those assumptions when they met in June 1933, just a few months before Sassoon's second meeting with Hester. Geoffrey made marriage seem attractive as well as possible. Though one of Sassoon's most recent friends when he married, Keynes would be among the few he invited to his wedding.

Keynes had first written to Sassoon on 10 April 1933 as Theo's literary executor, to tell him of the librarian's early death at the age of fifty and to offer Sassoon his choice of book from Theo's valuable collection. In his reply Sassoon had told Keynes to 'look [him] up' sometime, a suggestion which quickly became an invitation to spend a weekend at Fitz House as soon as possible.[44] Flattered by Keynes's praise of both his poetry and prose, *Fox-Hunting Man* in particular, he also saw him as a potentially useful and interesting contact. Keynes had been the literary executor of Festing-Jones as well as Festing-Jones's great friend Samuel Butler, taking over the supervision of the Butler material at Cambridge on Theo's death. In addition he had an expert knowledge of typography and shared Sassoon's love of old books. Not only could he be relied on to prevent the sale of Sassoon's letters to Theo and the privately printed books they had produced together, but he would make an ideal replacement for Theo as a designer of any future productions by Sassoon.

Keynes's own collection of books was, to use Sassoon's word, 'scrumptious', including such priceless items as original loose plates from Blake's *Songs of Experience* printed by the poet himself, together with several of his paintings.[45] A man of enormous energy as well as enthusiasm, Keynes was an insatiable and also highly competitive collector, unable to let a bargain slip through his hands. And once he had bought one book by an author who really interested him, he might begin to collect the rest of their works, often going on to compile their bibliography, usually the first in the field.[46] His son Milo compared him not very flatteringly to a magpie,[47] but then he had a difficult relationship with his father and there was no doubting Geoffrey's love of books.

A further point of contact between him and Sassoon was the fact that Keynes had served as a major in the Royal Army Medical Corps during the war. Though frequently critical of his fellow-officers, Sassoon had always respected the regimental doctors and was still in touch with Dr Dunn. Keynes's pioneering work in blood transfusion methods with badly wounded soldiers made him seem particularly admirable. It was one more manifestation of his extraordinary range of abilities.

Like most of his friends, Sassoon found Keynes's energy both impressive and daunting. The young Dennis Silk, with the advantage of forty-four years over Keynes, felt 'stupefied' with tiredness by the end of a stay with him: 'he had the energy of ten men'.[48] The wide spread of his interests, which included entomology, woodcarving, bricklaying, croquet and mountaineering, added to his knowledge of both the arts and the sciences, made him seem out of place in the twentieth century. 'I always think of him as a seventeenth-century man,' Sassoon told de la Mare after knowing Keynes almost twenty years, but Keynes might have seemed even more at home in the Renaissance or the Victorian age. (Either would have been appropriate, Andrew Motion believed, 'so long as it emphasized his pioneering spirit'.)[49] 'How have you managed to cram into a single lifetime all your achievements?' one admirer asked Keynes as he approached his ninetieth birthday.[50]

One of Keynes's favourite roles was that of host. If he liked someone he would immediately invite them to stay, either in his London house or current weekend retreat. The poet Jon Stallworthy remembers hearing Keynes talk to the English Club at Rugby about Brooke, with whom he had attended the school, and being invited shortly afterwards to stay with him in the country. 'Hospitality at Lammas House', Stallworthy writes, 'was absolute.'[51] And, as Keynes himself did not hesitate to point out and Stallworthy discovered, everything at Lammas House, especially where guests were concerned, was 'the best'. Motion also recalls a 'fantastic sense of abundance' there, the food plain but very good. So that, while Keynes enjoyed his weekend at Fitz House on 24 June 1933, he was insistent that for their second meeting he must be host. Only a fortnight after the Wiltshire visit, therefore, Sassoon found himself staying at the Keynes's

271

family home in Arkwright Road, Hampstead, known to family and friends as 'the Ark', partly because it always contained so many people.

One of Keynes's motives in persuading Sassoon to visit him in London was to show off his library, in spite of Sassoon's fears that it would induce 'bibliographical delirium'.[52] But he also wanted to share another of his enthusiasms, the ballet. His brother Maynard, whose homosexual liaisons had been a feature of the early Bloomsbury Group, had surprised many people by marrying the Russian ballerina Lydia Lopokova in middle age and Geoffrey himself was enchanted by the Russian Ballet. He took Sassoon to see them twice during his first London visit from the 10-12 July and sympathized when Sassoon expressed interest in a male dancer called Shabelevsky – though he doubted that the information he subsequently sent him about the young Russian would 'do [him] much good'.[53] Encouraged by Keynes's own openness about his attraction to men, and having told him about his affair with Stephen at their first meeting, Sassoon arrived in London carrying his diaries for the period. 'I am afraid it is impossible that I should finish them – the story of two splendid lovers – before tomorrow,' Keynes wrote to him ten days later; 'and I mustn't carry them around the country.'[54] Sassoon also gave him photographs of himself and Stephen, whimsically captioned 'the oak and the butterfly'.[55]

Another important feature of Sassoon's first visit was his introduction to Keynes's wife, Margaret. One of the four Darwin sisters and granddaughter of Charles Darwin, she had grown up in Cambridge at the same time as Geoffrey. Though not his first choice, she had made him an ideal wife, running his busy household, bringing up their children and accepting his interest in young men.[56] Supportive but not interfering, she conformed closely to the role Sassoon believed wives should play. He had found Florence Beerbohm 'not self-effacing enough' but Margaret Keynes was not particularly self-effacing either. She simply had her own centre of existence and, following dinner, then coffee in her separate sitting room, was quite content to see her husband take his male friends off to his study, a ritual Stallworthy, Motion and Silk all remember vividly. Many of the marriages Sassoon had witnessed previously had seemed a constraining rather than enlarging influence and he had been critical of a number of his friends' wives. But the Keyneses suggested that other models existed and he found Margaret 'the kindest and best of souls'.[57]

Sassoon's second stay with the Keyneses, at a house they had rented for a family holiday in August, certainly seems to have increased his receptiveness to marriage, for it was less than a month later that he responded so positively to Hester Gatty when she presented herself at Teffont Magna.[58] And Keynes was one of the first people he told of his engagement in October, though so apologetically that Keynes was rather 'taken aback': 'Our friendship', he felt it necessary to explain in his autobiography, 'had been a sober affair, not passionate in any sense.'[59] He could see that marriage might seem a 'defection' in homosexual terms, but was personally always delighted when any of his friends, of whatever sexual persuasion, 'indulged in matrimony. It invariably meant that one friend turned into two.'[60] Two days after telling Keynes of his engagement, in what may have been a tacit acknowledgement of their influence, Sassoon took Hester to meet him and Margaret.

Keynes firmly believed that marriage would help Sassoon recover from Stephen, a relationship which could never have succeeded in his opinion. And his concern was all for Sassoon. His reverence for creative artists, which had started with Brooke, made him anxious to help Sassoon in any way possible. As Stallworthy notes: 'He had his vanity – he knew he was a good craftsman (in some crafts "the best") – but his formidable energies were directed by a deeper modesty in the service of other people: patients, friends and artists.'[61] For Keynes, Sassoon was 'Merlin', a creature of magical powers, who had every right to stay in his cave if he so wished and to demand service of himself, 'Pellinore'.[62] When Sassoon asked his advice on a limited edition of his poems in June 1933, for example, he organized the whole production of what would become *Vigils* with both taste and efficiency. He suggested presenting these 'serious and reflective poems' in a 'novel and attractive form' by having the entire book engraved on copper plates in a script based on Sassoon's own beautiful hand, with a title page by the master book designer Stephen Gooden.[63] In spite of a rather brusque manner, which went with his clipped moustache and tall, spare figure, Keynes was exceptionally kind and helpful towards Sassoon. Not only would he take charge of his privately printed books for the next twenty-five years, with one exception, but he would also deal with any medical problems that arose. And though only six months younger than Sassoon, he would frequently chauffeur him round the country in later years. He was, in Sassoon's own words, an 'unfailing friend'.[64]

Sadly, Sassoon would quickly begin to take Keynes's many good qualities for granted and fasten on his weaker points. His favourite jibe, initiated unwittingly by Keynes himself, was 'Jackdaw Keynes', a nickname Keynes had once jokingly used of himself in reference to his mania for book-collecting. Sassoon interpreted it more negatively: he might joke with a younger friend that he 'felt like a mole conversing with jackdaws' when he visited the Keyneses, adding 'such admirable jackdaws – and such an unenterprising mole', but he seriously believed that Keynes lacked 'the finer shades'.[65] The difference between Keynes and himself, he asserted, was 'the difference between a typewriter and sensitive handwriting'.[66] His evident sense of superiority was based on a belief that Keynes's 'interest in literature [was] almost entirely bibliographical. No aesthetic absorption of beauty. He loves the *look* of his books. But I doubt whether he really delights in their insides.'[67]

It was an extraordinary and unfair claim for Sassoon to make, considering how much he would profit from Keynes's counsel. That he should frequently ask Keynes's advice about which poems to include in his collections over the years is hardly the act of a man who believed that Keynes lacked literary judgement.[68] Dennis Silk, Jon Stallworthy and Andrew Motion all testify to Keynes's love of literature. Keynes had encouraged the young Stallworthy to read the poems of John Cornford (his godson), for example, and had insisted on giving an edition of them to him, together with many other books. And he loved his wife to read Jane Austen to him as they drove up to London from their weekend house.

It may be that Sassoon and Keynes were just too unlike to be really close friends. Apart from superficial differences in taste – Keynes was not remotely interested in cricket or riding, nor Sassoon in mountaineering or croquet – they were completely opposite personalities, Keynes a practical, energetic extrovert in direct contrast to the (as he saw it) 'illogical', introverted Sassoon.[69] Sassoon once described Keynes as his 'antithesis'.[70] Nevertheless they *were* friends and remained so, with only a few minor differences, until the end of Sassoon's life. And in his fairer moments Sassoon acknowledged that Keynes was 'a man of very fine quality'.[71]

*

On 9 November 1933, a month after his engagement to Hester, *The Road to Ruin* was published and Sassoon was able to show her proof of his credentials as a writer.[72] The collection, unfortunately, contains neither the best nor the most characteristic of his poetry, but it does highlight his growing concern with the international situation, an unease which might also have made the apparent security of married life seem more appealing. Five of its original seven poems appeared in the *Spectator* and the *New Statesman* in March 1933, the month Sassoon had written to Ottoline: 'The state of the world, as seen in *The Times*, alarms me. The bullying of intelligent people in Germany must be perfectly horrible.'[73] His despair is even more evident and the causes of it much clearer in a second letter to her a week later:

> The whole thing is too depressing for words. To me it is as though the powers of darkness were winning. Poor old Ramsay [MacDonald] letting off his perorations about peace, with all that cynicism and armament manufacturing in the background, and the French really believing that the Germans will bomb Paris as soon as they are strong enough. And P[hilip] Sassoon playing Winston's game at the Air Ministry (did you see that he went to see Göring on his way to Geneva!). The only hope is that the idea of war is so much in the air that people are realizing what it will mean.[74]

He found it difficult to believe that there were individuals all over England who still 'derided "pacifism"' and that the Church appeared to be supporting the idea of war. He was particularly shocked by a letter from Archbishop Temple in *The Times* and wrote to Temple himself on 19 April 1933 to argue the pacifist cause.[75] He also tried to persuade Edith Olivier to

274

tackle the Archbishop of York on the question when she visited him that spring.

His own position was virtually unchanged from 1918 and the media had used him throughout the twenties and early thirties to represent the pacifist cause. His *War Poems* had been published to mark the anniversary of Armistice in 1920, for example, and the *Daily Mail* had reprinted 'Aftermath', with its persistent question: 'Have you forgotten yet?' in November 1927 for the same purpose. As late as 1934 the *Spectator* would offer its readers 'Ex-Service', two mordant stanzas by Sassoon to mark the sixteenth anniversary of the Armistice.[76] And he would still be appearing on the Reverend 'Dick' Sheppard's Peace Pledge Union platform to read his anti-war poems as late as 1937, though that year would also see a change in his attitude.

While working on *The Road to Ruin* Sassoon had been reading *Why War? Open Letters between Albert Einstein and Sigmund Freud*, and his slim volume is prefaced with a quotation from Einstein which represents his own position in 1933 and highlights his scorn of the profiteers that had marked his position in the First World War:

> The craving for power which characterizes the governing class in every nation is hostile to any limitation of the national sovereignty. This political power-hunger is wont to batten on the activities of another group whose aspirations are on purely mercenary, economic lines. I have specially in mind that small but determined group, active in every nation, composed of individuals who, indifferent to social considerations and restraints, regard warfare, the manufacture and sale of arms, simply as an occasion to advance their personal interests and enlarge their personal authority.
>
> A. Einstein[77]

Sassoon informed Hodgson that he wrote *The Road to Ruin* to 'ease [his] spirit', but was told by most of the critics that his remarks were 'unnecessary and unlyrical, and too much of a repetition' of what he had said in 1916.[78] The latter charge was unfortunately not the case, otherwise his 1933 volume might have been more successful. Though the message of *The Road to Ruin* may be broadly similar to the anti-war polemics of *The Old Huntsman* and *Counter-Attack*, its method lacks the directness and passion of the earlier books and largely accounts for its overall failure. Instead of the concentrated vigour of attack found in poems such as 'Base Details', 'Does It Matter?' or 'They', the poems lack punch. This is partly because the targets are more general. Even when a piece has been sparked off by a specific incident, like 'At the Cenotaph', which was inspired by the German Ambassador Ribbentrop's visit to lay a wreath at the tomb of the unknown soldier (an event recorded savagely in the poem itself in the words 'The Prince of Darkness, with his Staff, / Standing bare-headed by the Cenotaph'), it usually degenerates into verbosity. The Devil's wordy and heavily ironic speech in that poem, for instance, is a far cry from the general's equally ironic but far terser '*Good* morning, *good* morning' to 'Harry and Jack' in 'The General'. What was dramatic has become melo-dramatic; references to 'the Prince of Darkness', 'Beelzebub', 'Moloch', 'Anti-Christ' and 'the Lord of Hosts', for instance, seem merely clichéd and vague. Written by an older, wearier man, the certainty of the First World War poems has gone and the language itself seems tired, the voice of a prophet crying in the void. Even the two poems which Thorpe sees as having 'real force' – 'A Premonition' and 'An Unveiling' – lack the con-densed charge of Sassoon's earlier work. In both pieces Sassoon, in his prophetic role, imagines a future where, in 'A Premonition', his 'gas-proof ghost' returns to the National Gallery after chemical warfare has destroyed the rest of the population to see how it has fared, and in 'An Unveiling' an unnamed president unveils a memorial to 'London's War-gassed Victims'. But neither poem manages the devastating finish of the earlier satires, 'A Premonition' ending with the fairly obvious message that:

> ...The claim
> Of Art was disallowed. Past locks
> And walls crass war had groped, and gas
> Was tarnishing each gilded frame.
>   (CP, p. 202)

'An Unveiling' concludes with ironic echoes of Brooke and Owen, but the irony is heavy-handed and lacks surprise:

> 'We honour here' (he paused) 'our Million Dead;
> Who, as a living poet has nobly said,
> "Are now forever London". Our bequest
> Is to rebuild, for What-they-died-for's sake,
> A bomb-proofed roofed Metropolis, and to make
> Gas drill compulsory. *Dulce et decorum est ...*'
>   (CP, p. 204)

Sassoon himself must have suspected that *The Road to Ruin*, like *Satirical Poems*, was a wrong turning since, apart from the two poems added when it was reprinted in *Collected Poems* and a few more included in *Vigils* and *Rhymed Ruminations*, it was his last concerted attempt at war poetry. This does not mean that he no longer cared about war but that the gap between the idealistic young army officer and the older, more disillusioned civilian was simply too wide to bridge, as he indicated in a poem never published in his lifetime:

> A Reunion
> Once friendly with the future, youth returned.
> Asking 'What place is this?' he stood estranged
> From harsh experience whereby I had learned
> How world behaviour, not my own, was changed.

276

'Go back', I warned, 'to where you dwelt deceived –
'You who in gradual betterment believed.'
And while the face of youth dissolved and went
I heard the drone of endless armament.[79]

The failure of *The Road to Ruin*, which Sassoon himself later described as 'just a nightmare',[80] affected him less severely than usual, since the week it was published he and Hester suddenly decided to bring forward the date of their wedding and there was a great deal to do. Any poetry he had written before he met her, he told Keynes, now felt like something he had 'discarded'.[81]

The ceremony had originally been planned for April 1934, presumably to give Hester and her mother time to organize the large society wedding a young woman in her position usually expected. But by 9 November, Sassoon was anxious on several fronts. As Nellie Burton had triumphantly reminded him the previous week, his engagement had been in 'a good many papers' and he feared further media intrusion.[82] He also wanted to get the wedding over as soon as possible: 'I begin to feel that by getting engaged and then hiding I am affronting all my (few) real friends,' he explained to Keynes in late November.[83] 'But there it is, I am a sensitive being, and I am terrified of getting nervy and then passing on my nerviness to Hester, (who, it must be remembered, was *almost* a nervous invalid last winter).'[84] Part of the strain he felt was in dealing with his friends' evident surprise at the event and answering their many letters. He was also very much in love with Hester – 'Rapture reigns over us,' he wrote a month after their engagement[85] – and may have been impatient for the consummation of their marriage. On the other hand he may have feared such a radical change and be anxious to have it behind him.

Whatever the explanation, he and Hester were married 'very quietly' by private licence at Christchurch Priory, near Bournemouth, on 18 December 1933, a Canon Gay by chance officiating.[86] The choice of church had been fairly straightforward. Christchurch was approximately five miles from Hester's family home, Ossemsley Manor, and a relatively easy drive from Fitz House; it was also convenient for the most illustrious of the wedding guests, T.E. Lawrence, who was serving as 'Aircraftsman Shaw' at Southampton, no distance at all for the powerful motorbike he liked to ride.

Lawrence was one of only five friends Sassoon invited to the wedding, the others being Glen, Geoffrey Keynes, Rex Whistler and Edith Olivier. His mother was not well enough to attend, though she had expressed complete approval of Hester when Sassoon took her to visit in late October, and the matchmaker, Edith, appropriately stood in for her. Hester, attended by her mother, two brothers and a Morrison cousin, had also invited very few friends and the wedding, as planned, was a quiet and solemn affair:

> It was a cold morning [Sassoon reported to Ralph Hodgson in America] but the sun was shining beautifully, and the bells sounded glorious. Glen Byam Shaw (best man) drove me over from Fitz House, and when we walked up to the church door the only person standing there was Aircraftsman Shaw! We were married in the choir, which seemed flooded with a celestial sort of light, and Hester looked very beautiful in her white dress.[87]

While T.E. Lawrence had his doubts about the wisdom of the marriage, Keynes rejoiced in it, though his greatest excitement was the 'heaven-sent opportunity' to meet at last with Lawrence of Arabia, who had long been one of his 'top heroes'.[88] With his customary energy he had read *Seven Pillars of Wisdom* in its uncut original form three times, making a detailed comparison of the authorized version with the whole of the linotype edition containing unpublished passages, as well as devouring everything else on Lawrence he could find. Placed opposite him in the church, he could 'gaze [his] fill at the small but strongly built man, with a pink face and a shock of yellow hair'.[89] He was even more delighted when, at the end of the ceremony, he had a long conversation with Lawrence, the two of them leaning on opposite sides of his motorbike, 'Boanerges'.

Edith was equally thrilled by the marriage, for which she felt largely responsible. But she was also worried by Stephen's reaction to the news. Cecil Beaton had lost no time in telling him of Sassoon's engagement and Stephen had burst into tears, returning to the bed he had so recently left. 'My dear Sieg,' he wrote on 14 November in a letter which may have increased Sassoon's anxiety to marry quickly, 'I thought I heard you calling me – I dreamed that you said my name urgently, tell me if you did.'[90] With a familiar mixture of romantic fancy and emotional blackmail, he concludes:

> Oh Sieg, I went to Stonehenge on Sunday! – and put my hands on the grey lichens, and somehow the happiness had the quality of terribleness that all deep emotion has, and all round the undulating downs in chilled silver air. Would you like me still to be your friend? – I always would anyway whether you wished it or not. Edith tells me how happy you are. Love, Stephen.[91]

Stephen was to remain in bed until the following April, his mental state still very precarious, as Edith realized when he appeared late and unannounced at her house one night, clothes thrown on carelessly over his pyjamas. She was shocked by the bloated appearance of the once willowy Stephen, but relieved to note that he remained 'so utterly his wayward self in spite of the disguise of the fat'.[92]

Sassoon had written Stephen a 'kindly-worded letter' about his engagement at Keynes's charitable suggestion,[93] but he found it hard to sympathize with him after his recent behaviour and had ignored his plaintive question, 'Would you like me still to be your friend?' It would be two years before Stephen wrote again, the time it took him, he claimed, to become 'unstunned' by the news of Sassoon's marriage.[94] He would continue to suffer 'a most terrible grief' periodically at the thought of it. 'I shut you out for two or three years –' he would write to Sassoon over five years after the event; 'you have shut me out forever.'[95] For the rest of his life he would swing between self-condemnation – 'This evening I am unhappy thinking how selfish I was to you' – and self-pity – 'All my friends chucked me away – as you did when you married.'[96] Rex he considered one of the worst traitors and even Edith came in for some criticism. But since no one really held him responsible for his actions, most of his friends went on humouring him and the only thing he really lost by Sassoon's marriage was Sassoon himself. 'Sometimes he is an undertone in my mind,' he wrote in his journal for 1939, 'at others a strident cry, almost unbearable, shutting out the earth and sky, blotting out everything.'[97]

Stephen's immediate reaction on first hearing of Hester had been to hope that she was not too attractive, but when he eventually met her in the early forties he quite liked her. So did Sassoon's other homosexual friends. Though they were probably all as amazed as Stephen at Sassoon's sudden change of allegiance, only Bob Gathorne-Hardy and Forster were frank enough to question it, though Forster was quick to reassure Sassoon as well:

> I didn't suppose you had acted other than rightly, [he wrote on 8 November 1933] and I shan't seek T.E. [Lawrence]'s or anyone else's opinion on her and shall like to meet her. But Siegfried, you mustn't expect me at my age to take on new intimacies. I am wonderfully pliable but I am nearly 55. You are entwined with my past and with my future so far as I can come at it with that past. To ask what doctors might call a 'certain question' and which I shouldn't ask unless I was very fond of you: – Have you had an emotional and physical overturn? Your news, though I accepted it as good news, startled me.

Once Forster met Hester, he was greatly taken with her, writing to William Plomer in March 1935 that he was 'half in love with her – she is so intelligent, simple and gentle'.[98] Marsh did not go quite so far, but he too found her 'most charming',[99] as did Osbert Sitwell, who seemed genuinely pleased at the prospect of happiness for Sassoon 'in this appalling world'.[100] And once Sassoon had explained to Gathorne-Hardy that 'only a very remarkable sort of girl could have made me feel certain that I could make her happy', he too sent his blessings.[101] Even T.E. Lawrence, who feared among other things that 'marriage would conventionalize' Sassoon, quickly succumbed to Hester's charms, though he had serious doubts about the marriage's chance of survival.[102] 'Fancy taking on SS,' he wrote to another friend, Nancy Astor, describing Hester as a 'foolhardy creature'.[103]

Sassoon's married friends were equally enthusiastic about Hester. Blunden and his new wife Sylva showed their approval with their own 'Amalgamation' of 'Prose and Verse in Honour of Siegfried and Hester', including an original poem by Blunden and some prose by Sylva, the whole written out beautifully by hand.[104] Glen and Angela, who had already met Hester at the Wilton Pageant, rejoiced for Sassoon, and the Heads were relieved and delighted. Even Graves, whose cool request for 'about £1,000' Sassoon had indignantly refused this year, sent his 'good wishes'.[105]

Sassoon's women friends, some of whom were also close to Stephen, were equally pleased for him, with one or two significant exceptions. Nan Tennant, Beryl and Eileen Hunter and even more emotionally involved friends like Ottoline and Florence Hardy, rejoiced at his escape from Stephen. Nellie Burton's loyalty to Sassoon overcame her deep-rooted suspicion of young women: 'and, above all, what a score off on [*sic*] Stephen', she wrote gleefully on receipt of the news: 'He will ... now find out who is [*sic*] true friend was.'[106] And Rosamond Lehmann was so happy at the news that she presented the Sassoons with her dog 'Sheltie', to whom Sassoon had become greatly attached while renting her house.[107]

But Violet Bonham Carter and Edith Sitwell were manifestly less happy. 'V.B.C. has been a bit odd about it,' Sassoon told Nan Tennant: 'Her only reference to Hester so far was in a long and hysterical letter asking me to go and see her – "Bring Miss Gatty". "Bring your umbrella", would have been much the same!'[108] Edith made her jealousy less obvious, telling Sassoon she was 'thrilled and delighted' at his engagement, but remarking caustically in private to her sister-in-law: 'I suppose the bridal pair will want to adopt S[tephen] T[ennant].'[109]

*

Hester and Siegfried's honeymoon in Spain completed what was, according to someone who knew them both well, 'a dream thing' – the meeting at a pageant in exotic clothes, the whirlwind courtship, the romantic marriage in a beautiful old priory, the ancient manor house they were negotiating to buy.[110] Driving out in a little carriage with jingling bells into the mountainous country behind Algeciras, populated only by goats, a few golden-brown pigs and peasants trudging behind their over-burdened donkeys, they explored magical cork woods with rocky streams running through them. In the other direction, looking towards Gibraltar and the low, humpy mountains of the African coast, they discovered sandy bays full of exquisite shells.[111] It was a 'vegetable life', Sassoon told Ottoline, and Hester made the 'perfect companion'.[112]

Algeciras had been chosen not just for its warmth, though that was 'worth every peseta we paid for it', according to Sassoon, but because it was Hester's favourite place.[113] (Her father had retired as Chief Justice of Gibraltar the year before her birth, but she knew and loved southern

Spain.) By a fortunate coincidence it was also not Germany or Italy, the two countries in which Sassoon had spent his previous 'honeymoons' with Philipp, Glen and Stephen. This did not prevent him suggesting a visit to Sicily, however, and after a few days at Malaga he and Hester passed three weeks at Syracuse, the scene of so many memories of Stephen.[114]

Then, in an almost exact repetition of that previous visit, on their way back to England, he took Hester to Rapallo to meet the Beerbohms. Staying at the same hotel (the Bristol) and following a similar routine of long lunches with Max and Florence and return dinners at their hotel, it might almost have been winter 1929 or spring 1930 again. Since, for once, Sassoon kept no record of the visit it is impossible to know how he felt about this. Nor do we know for sure how the Beerbohms regarded his change of partner. Like the rest of his married friends, they probably rejoiced for him. 'He only cares for himself,' would be Max's caustic, final word on Stephen.[115]

18

Paradise Regained and Lost
(1934-1938)

Some day, when I have 'settled down' and come into a fortune, I will buy a little manor-house in a good hunting country and keep three or four 'nailing good performers', and play on a grand piano in a room full of books, with a window looking on to an old-fashioned garden full of warbling birds and mossy apple trees. When I am forty-nine I will begin to look for that house, and when I am in it I will write wise books.

(Diary entry for 27 March 1923)

In May 1934, only a year and a few months younger than he had planned in his diary entry, Sassoon took possession of the house he had imagined in 1923 and looked forward to the lifestyle he had then envisaged. After their marriage, he and Hester had stayed for a short time at Tunbridge Wells to be near Sassoon's mother for Christmas, then spent a week in a luxurious suite at the Hyde Park Hotel, London, before returning to live in Fitz House until they left for their honeymoon at the end of January 1934. When they came back from Spain and Italy in May, however, it was to the place they had discovered together during their engagement, Heytesbury House.

Hester had liked Fitz House, but the lease was short and indefinite and in any case Sassoon had grander ideas. He wanted somewhere even more suited to the fairy-tale nature of their romance. He also still missed the luxuriousness of Wilsford Manor and may even have needed to compete with it. As a child he had looked on the gracious Queen Anne houses of his friends with envy and been secretly ashamed of Weirleigh's lack of elegance. Now, when it came to buying his own house, he was determined to put that right and, with Hester's substantial income added to his own, had more than adequate means to do so.

Neither of them wanted to leave the district, so counted themselves lucky when they discovered that Heytesbury House, two miles from Warminster and only fifteen miles from Teffont Magna, was for sale. A great yellow-grey stone mansion standing in 220 acres of park and woodland in the heart of the Wylye Valley on the edge of Salisbury Plain, it was the kind of house Sassoon had dreamed of. All his life he had been drawn, perhaps partly because of his foreign blood, to characteristically English things – hunting, cricket, English landscapes – and Heytesbury House seemed to him 'the epitome of timeless and unchangeable England'.[1] Set well back from the village of Heytesbury and the main road, it was visible only in glimpses through the magnificent trees that surrounded it, though Sassoon had already noticed the house on visits to William Nicholson at Sutton Veny about a mile away.

Heytesbury had a long and romantic history, another of its attractions for Sassoon, who had regretted Weirleigh's lack of it. Occupying the site of what was reputed to have been a manor house belonging to the twelfth-century Queen Matilda, it still retained a medieval dovecote and barn.[2] The house itself had been rebuilt several times, one such effort ending (according to another local resident, Anthony Powell) when the sixteenth-century owner, Lord Hungerford, was 'attainted for sodomy, forcing his own daughter, ... invoking devils by black magic', and 'executed for these alleged irregularities'.[3] The most recent rebuilding had been about 1700 as a red-brick house with a clock tower and garrets, which in 1780 was re-faced in Bath stone and later given other classical touches, including an imposing Grecian portico on the entrance front.[4] The last Lord Heytesbury to live there had died in Sassoon's own lifetime, another inspiration for a poem.[5]

With its seventeen bedrooms, six large reception rooms, separate service wing and numerous additions, Heytesbury House was already an anachronism in an age when servants were rapidly becoming a thing of the past. Its high ceilings, numerous large windows and long stone passages also threatened exorbitant heating bills in winter. The sale price was high, more money would have to be spent restoring the estate to its former glory and a small army of servants hired to maintain it.[6] But none of this deterred Sassoon, who clearly relished the thought of becoming lord of the manor and squire of Heytesbury, a role he would enjoy to the end of his life. 'Captain' Sassoon, ambling along on horseback, was to become a proud feature of village life, a fact Sassoon very much enjoyed. 'I always feel', he wrote to Glen a few years after moving into Heytesbury House, 'that I am being compensated for *Wilsford*. The whole feeling of the thing is so perfect, and I *am* monarch of all I survey – as well as being *liked* by everyone in the most natural and homely way.'[7]

He was not unaware of the inconsistencies of his position as a one-time socialist and his attempts to rationalize his situation are diverting. 'I must break it to you that Heytesbury is a *large* house', he wrote to the most egalitarian of his friends, Hodgson, about the fifty-two-room mansion he was about to buy, 'but you will not mind its size when you see it. We shall live very simply and quietly there, and at last I shall have a home which will be an earthly paradise for my few real friends to see me in. So don't be alarmed. Everything will be just the same, only nicer.'[8]

Sassoon did succeed in making Heytesbury what a later friend, Joe Ackerley, agreed was 'an earthly paradise' and Keynes thought a perfect setting for a writer who 'valued solitude but could no longer complain that he was lonely'.[9] He failed conspicuously, however, in his resolve to live 'very simply and quietly' and it was fortunate that Rivers was no longer alive to witness Sassoon's final abandonment of his policy of non-acquisitiveness. Seven full-time indoor staff, eight outdoor men, a groom-chauffeur and stable-boy were in place by the time Sassoon and Hester returned from their honeymoon on 18 May to a refurbished Heytesbury, and more would be added later.[10]

As if finding suitable furniture and (very importantly for Sassoon) pictures for a large mansion were not enough,[11] two new cars, more horses for the renovated stables and new plans for the walled garden had been ordered and the couple returned to a lifestyle of some grandeur, though they both denied their need for it. One of Sassoon's biggest outlays over the next few years would be the replanting of Heytesbury's sadly depleted wood. He wanted an avenue of acacia and lime and forty new bay trees, each representing one of his favourite poets, a scheme which gave rise to the opening of his next volume, *Vigils*:

> An Emblem
> Poet, plant your tree
> On the upward way;
> Aromatic bay
> Plant, that men may see
> Beauty greenly growing
> There in storm or shine,
> And through boughs divine
> Freedom bravely blowing.
> (CP, p. 209)

Sassoon also envisaged old Lord Heytesbury returning from the dead to take his favourite woodland walk and seeing:

> ... plumed acacia and the nobly tranquil bay;
> Laburnums too, now small as in the prosperous prime
> Of your well-ordered distant mid-Victorian time ...
> ('In Heytesbury Wood', CP, p. 234)

Heytesbury appears regularly in Sassoon's poetry from 1934 onwards, often as setting, sometimes as the subject itself.[12] But it is doubtful whether the move benefited his work as a whole. Representing as it did a further retreat from the modern world, it seems to have strengthened his already reactionary views on literature. For as Ackerley noted when he visited Heytesbury in the 1940s:

One could fade away here, of course, like a plant, flower and fade and never be seen. It is the enclosed eighteenth- and nineteenth-century world. In all the houses I was brought up in, when one walked out of the front door one walked smack into the life of the world, passers-by, tradesmen, cars, one jostled against life; here no, one walks into such a vast Garden of Eden of one's own, pre- or post-Eve, that one is entranced and has not the desire to go beyond, to go out of the great gates, for all one wants lies inside. No adventures, therefore, except the adventures of nature, the turn and fall of the leaves, song of birds, encounters with rabbits, squirrels and foxes – no adventures here.[13]

Sassoon's most successful poetry had arisen out of conflict; glimpses of paradise tended to slacken his verse, though he refused to accept this himself. He was convinced that Heytesbury was an ideal setting for the kind of poetry he believed he wrote best, the meditative, pastoral verse which its privileged rural calm invited. He actually felt that the house had chosen him, not vice versa:

> I have not sought these quietened cadences,
> These tragitones, these stilled interior themes,
> These vistas where imagined presences
> Lead me away from life, – loved ghosts or dreams?
> ('Tragitones', CP, p. 248)

Another effect of Heytesbury on his poetry, at least to begin with, was to dry it up. Captivated by the enchantment that the estate laid on its inhabitants, he had little time for verse in 1934 and his output dropped dramatically compared with the outpourings of his first love for Glen, or his sufferings over Stephen. He and Hester remained under its spell for the rest of the year 'like children alone in the world', as T.E. Lawrence observed.[14] One of the Sassoons' first guests in July, he felt as if he were making an invasive 'raid': 'All visitors there intrude, as yet, I think,' he told Keynes: 'The huge house ... the gardens, so lavishly kept up, the quiet sun-impregnated park: the two laughing strangers running about it, making pretence to own it. Yes, Heytesbury was rather like one of the great villas of Roman Britain, after the Legions had gone.'[15] A shrewd observer of mankind, Lawrence could not help thinking that Sassoon seemed 'abnormally' happy, though he rejoiced to see the change in his friend. 'Much of his hesitant diction has been forgotten,' he reported to Keynes. 'He speaks easily, and is full of private jests. He looks so well too.'[16]

Sassoon had also written to Keynes to tell him: 'Everything is pluperfect, like living in a cosy novel of 1870.'[17] That was in June but his feeling of almost unreal happiness continued throughout the summer. The first edition of *Vigils* had been printed in May 1934 and finished copies were ready by August, all twenty-two poems of this limited edition having been engraved on copper by Charles Sigrist. Keynes had taken immense care and Sassoon and Hester were 'enraptured' by the 'beauty' of the production.[18] It was partly to 'gloat' over *Vigils'* attractions that the equally enthusiastic bibliophile, Lawrence, had visited in July.[19] He loved the way Sigrist's engraving forced the eye to read 'slowly, almost word for word', since he believed that 'these chiselled and balancing verses of S.S. deserve to be read almost as minutely as they were made. What an iconic stillness there is about his images now! He has progressed from flesh-and-blood (in Counter-Attack) to bronze ...One of the good things about S.S. is that he changes freely and completely.'[20] Lawrence's lavish praise would not be echoed by the majority of the critics when *Vigils* appeared in a trade edition the following year, but for the moment Sassoon could enjoy a feeling of success. He was to include all twenty-two of the pieces, plus the thirteen added to the trade edition, in his *Collected Poems*, a sign of his own belief in their worth.

*

A more immediate pleasure than work was entertaining friends, who came for long weekends during the summer in a pattern that would continue throughout the thirties. With a houseful of servants, Sassoon was able to invite people he had not seen since leaving London, old friends like Marsh, de la Mare, Cockerell, Tomlinson, Lord Berners and H.G. Wells. (Bennett had died in 1931.) In their first summer at Heytesbury in 1934, besides Lawrence and Edith Olivier, he invited Ottoline, who had met and liked Edith but had still to inspect Hester. Geoffrey and Margaret Keynes also came and Sassoon's favourite nephew, Hamo, his brother's youngest child, who stayed for a few days on his way back to Sherborne School. Blunden also brought his new wife, a visit Siegfried and Hester had rather feared since Sylva Norman was reputed to be a determined, intense, somewhat neurotic woman, obsessed by physical fitness. In the event they both liked her and she became a regular visitor with Blunden for the next few years.

One reason the Blundens began to visit so often had to do with Blunden's own particular obsession, cricket. Unlike Sassoon, who had played only occasionally since his pre-war games with the Blue Mantles at Tunbridge Wells, Blunden had remained loyal to the sport and was delighted when Sassoon took it up again in earnest. One of his first tasks on returning from honeymoon had been to organize the renovation of the village cricket pitch, which lay within his own grounds a few hundred yards from the house. 'The ground belongs to ME', he wrote to his old friend Swinnerton with evident pride in 1935, 'and is believed to be the best village ground in Wilts.'[21]

Naturally he became captain of the local team, though he was by no means its best player. He could not sack any of his outdoor staff, he told Swinnerton, because 'three-quarters of the gardeners represent our two best bowlers and the wicket-keeper'.[22] One of his greatest pleasures in the game was arranging annual matches between the Heytesbury XI and Blunden's Mertonians (the Barnacles), an enjoyment unspoilt by Blunden's superiority as a cricketer. Another pleasure was the blow-by-blow analysis which followed each match, either at tea in Heytesbury's old kitchen wing, or over supper in one of Merton's lecture rooms. His later eccentricities on the cricket pitch would become the stuff of legend, but during the thirties, at least, he was still (as in the old days) a 'useful' player.[23]

As autumn approached cricket was replaced by hunting. And just as he had tried to involve Hester in his cricketing activities (she was allowed to keep the score), so he now made sure that she was included in the hunt, finding a suitable horse for her as a matter of priority. (In the one photograph we have of him in hunting gear at this period, however, it is interesting to see that Hester stands beside him dressed in ordinary clothes.) The day the opening meet of the local hunt set out from Heytesbury House marked his real 'comeback', he told the Heads, from his miseries over Stephen, 'a sort of apotheosis of my apotheosis!'[24] Like cricket, hunting was an important feature of his intense happiness at Heytesbury in 1934.

As T.E. Lawrence had predicted, however, 'the barometer [could] not always stand so high' and 1935 opened badly, with Hester suffering from 'internal troubles' following an attack of chicken pox the previous October.[25] Almost certainly a reference to gynaecological problems, this probably explains the fact that she was not yet pregnant. From Sassoon's pride in announcing her pregnancy later in the year (September), it is clear that they were both hoping for a child. The reference to her 'internal troubles' may even be a euphemism for a miscarriage, which is how her September pregnancy would end.

But it was not just Sassoon's disappointment over the 'little Sass' he had so gleefully announced to all his friends that marred 1935. Hester's problems in September also put an end for a while to visitors while she rested upstairs in a vain attempt to save the pregnancy. Hamo Sassoon, for instance, was not invited to stay as usual on his way to Sherborne School in the autumn, but had to wait until Hester was thought strong enough for visitors. When his visit did eventually take place he remembers enjoying his uncle's schoolboyish sense of humour – his sudden appearance by ladder at Hamo's bedroom window late at night, his concealment of a mint humbug at the bottom of his nephew's bedtime glass of milk. At the age of fifteen Hamo already had many interests in common with his uncle – cricket, music, art, literature, the countryside. He also formed a link for Sassoon with life at Matfield, on which he reported regularly, including the sad fact that one of Sassoon's childhood friends there, the carrier Tom Homewood, was dying of cancer and a shadow of his former self. ('Oi reckons Oi kin sit bettern what Oi kin stand nowadays!' he had told Hamo.)[26] Hamo, who became something of a substitute son at this time, would later renew an equally important era of Sassoon's life when he visited Walther and Johanna at Haus Hirth in 1938. That same year he would also start his degree studies at Merton, Oxford, under Blunden's sympathetic care – 'just one more of the things for which I owe you thanks', as he wrote to his uncle.[27]

Even during his early visits to Heytesbury, Hamo noted a curious feature of the Sassoons' marriage, which would become more significant later on: as he and his aunt prepared to retire for the night, Sassoon would sit down at his large writing table with the words 'I stay', resisting all Hester's pleas to accompany her to bed. After almost a year's rest from writing by late 1935, he felt an urgent need to get back to it. This was partly for financial reasons, since the upkeep of Heytesbury was even higher than expected, but also because writing was his *raison d'être* in a way that Hester, however miraculous she still seemed, could never be. The problem was that marriage made it even more difficult to write than living with Stephen had, mainly because of his irregular working habits. All his 'best writing', he explained to Hamo, was achieved when he stayed in bed most of the day and worked till 5 a.m.: 'I never can write "in my head" unless I am alone and one gets all the freshest ideas when just mooning about. When I sit down ... resolved to "work" nothing happens for about two hours.'[28] While explaining his habit of staying behind to write when Hamo and Hester retired to bed, this letter to Hamo did not bode well for the future of his marriage.

He had already sounded an ominous note in his diary in late 1934, less than a year after the wedding: 'Protective and possessive love can never realise that it can be a bit boring at times – lovely sweet Hester, why can't you realise this?' Hester, he was complaining to Keynes by August 1935, allowed him no time to 'relax and ruminate' and he was beginning to find her constant attention suffocating.[29] After less than two years of married life he was writing to Glen, 'I feel as if all my own vitality is needed to finish my book, and darling Hester simply *cannot* leave me alone!'[30]

The book referred to was *Sherston's Progress*, which Sassoon had taken up but quickly abandoned in the spring of 1933, shortly before his first meeting with Hester. Now, in November 1935, he was determined to complete it. Considering that Hester had just suffered a miscarriage, however, his attitude towards her was remarkably self-centred and one that would become increasingly familiar. He actually 'banished' her from Heytesbury for five weeks that same month at a time when she must have been feeling very low indeed.[31] His work was evidently more important to him even at this early stage in their marriage. For both their sakes he should probably have heeded his own words in 'Elected Silence':

> ... Allow me now much musing-space
> To shape my secrecies alone:
> Allow me life apart, whose heart
> Translates instinctive tragi-tone. ...
>
> (CP, p. 210)

This poem, which had appeared in Keynes's limited edition of *Vigils* in 1934, was also included in the trade edition, published by Faber on 4 November 1935, together with thirteen new poems. The fact that none of these additional poems were inspired by his wife is significant. Though the book was dedicated 'To Hester', it was largely inspired by Stephen, who had made him suffer but also driven him to write. The absence of love poetry from his work, which a curious fellow-soldier had noted in 1916, had been rectified after the war by a succession of male lovers, but would not return with Hester. Sassoon may even have blamed her, subconsciously, for *Vigils'* poor reception, another cause for unhappiness in 1935. Certainly its largely negative reviews help to explain his determination to finish another prose book. Unlike his poetry, which had increasingly become the target of Modernist critics after the First World War, his novels had not suffered similar Modernist strictures, perhaps because they were read more as autobiography than fiction. Since he was still regarded by many as a hero for his anti-war protest, it might have seemed churlish to attack what was a thinly veiled account of his activities in the war.

The reviewers of his poetry were restrained by no such scruples. Apart from faithful supporters like Wilfrid Gibson and Blunden, who claimed that in *Vigils'* 'fine vibration is recorded the inner experience of a modern Vaughan', the reviews seemed to Sassoon 'wicked'.[32] With the death of influential traditionalists like Gosse, he found himself exposed to the 'priggish little notes' of the 'superior intellectuals'.[33] 'Your friend D[avid] Garnett', he told Keynes, 'was responsible for a bad bit of dirty work in the *New Statesman*, and I shan't forget it. (When annoyed I keep it up for the rest of my life.)'[34] To younger critics like Garnett, brought up on Pound and Eliot and going into the thirties with poets like Auden, Spender and MacNeice, there was something outmoded and irrelevant about Sassoon's poems, however often he addressed contemporary issues, which he did. 'A new generation of critics has sprung up', he wrote mournfully to Marsh after the publication of *Vigils*, 'and they seem to regard me as a dreary back number.'[35]

Friends rallied round in private. He was comforted by Tomlinson's long letter of appreciation: 'Your *Vigils* are metaphysical,' he wrote from the coast of Dorset. 'And the music in those poems ... affected me like the wind does going through the tamarisks down by the shore after dark.'[36] Even more reassuringly Edith Sitwell, herself a pioneer of Modernism, believed that *Vigils* included 'some of the finest poems' he had ever written: 'They are so truthful, bare, controlled, and fiery, and deeply moving.'[37] She picked out for particular praise 'Presences Perfected', 'Elected Silence', 'The mind of man environing its thought', 'At the end of all wrong roads I came' and 'Ex-Service', which she declared 'magnificent'.

First published in the *Spectator* on 9 November 1934, 'Ex-Service' suggests that Sassoon was not so out of touch with political realities as the younger critics believed. In it, his reminder of the Great War is not simply a harking back to the past but a timely warning of the need to avert another world war in the face of Hitler's rise to power:

> ... The darkness of their dying
> Grows one with War recorded;
> Whose swindled ghosts are crying
> From shell-holes in the past,
> *Our deeds with lies were lauded,*
> *Our bones with wrongs rewarded.*
> Dream voices these – denying
> Dud laurels to the last.
>
> (CP, p. 217)

'All that a poet can do is warn,' Wilfred Owen had written and Sassoon did so clearly in *The Road to Ruin*, *Vigils* and, later, *Rhymed Ruminations* (1939, 1940). He also took political action. Hitler's Night of the Long Knives in July 1934 and his growing closeness to Mussolini in 1935 added to Sassoon's unease and convinced him of the need for greater commitment to the pacifist cause. By mid-1935, like 80,000 other British subjects, he had joined Canon 'Dick' Sheppard's Peace Pledge Union and appeared on the PPU platform in July that year.[38] Sheppard, a radio preacher of great popular appeal as well as former vicar of St Martin-in-the-Fields, had founded the PPU in October 1934 with the express purpose of averting another war and had attracted many well-known figures to his cause, Bertrand Russell, Vera Brittain and Aldous Huxley among them. Even Max Beerbohm, not normally drawn to idealistic clergymen with left-wing leanings, had admired him when they met in 1929, shortly after Sassoon's first visit to Rapallo, and had predisposed Sassoon towards him. So that when Sheppard wrote to ask Sassoon in 1935 to contribute to what was in effect the PPU's inaugural rally, he readily agreed.

Sassoon's contribution to the 14 July meeting at the Albert Hall was a reading of his poems which included 'Everyone Sang' and 'Credo'. He did not feel able to make a speech, but had enlisted Blunden to do so.[39] It was the first of a number of appearances by Sassoon, whose readings apparently moved Vera Brittain to tears.[40] He was to compose a poem specially for his appearance at a PPU rally on 27 November 1936, which followed the Italians' brutal invasion of Abyssinia, Hitler and Mussolini's support of Franco in the Spanish Civil War, which broke out that year, and their Rome-Berlin Axis agreement in the autumn. Not one of Sassoon's most effective anti-war poems, it nevertheless shows the strength of his pacifist commitment as late as November 1936.

> We are souls in hell; who hear no gradual music
> Advancing on the air, on wave-lengths walking.
> We are lost in life; who listen for hope and hear but
> The tyrant and the politician talking ...
>
> ('A Prayer from 1936', CP, p. 250)[41]

291

The reference to hell in this poem is, of course, meant metaphorically but by the time it was written on 20 October 1936, Sassoon could well have used it literally. For in 1935 an event had occurred which not only added to his depression that year, but also affected his whole system of beliefs. His experiences in the First World War had destroyed his faith in the simple Anglicanism of his pious mother and it was not until his period of intense suffering at Fitz House that he had been forced to look for something to replace it. While writing some of the poems in *Vigils*, he told Tomlinson, he had had the impression of 'perceiving the unseen'.[42] But it was not until the death of T.E. Lawrence in May 1935 that he had become wholly convinced of the existence of an after-life.

Lawrence was not the only close friend who died that year – Sassoon was 'much saddened' by the loss of 'Anzie' Wylde for whom he had 'a very deep affection', he told Ottoline.[43] The death of Nellie Burton left an even bigger gap. Their deaths, however, were not a complete surprise – Anzie died of complications of his old war wound and Nellie had been failing for some time – whereas Lawrence's was totally unexpected. And, while Sassoon's friendships with Anzie and Nellie had been diluted by his retirement to Wiltshire, the move had brought him closer to Lawrence. So that, when news of Lawrence's serious motorbike accident and subsequent coma reached him on 13 May 1935, he was devastated. Even before Lawrence's actual death five days later Sassoon had received a rather ghoulish request from the *Observer* for a 'personal appreciation ... in the unfortunate event of the accident proving fatal'.[44] Though he indignantly refused to oblige, he did write a poem about Lawrence a week after his death, which he sent to Marsh for *The Times*. Marsh rejected it, ostensibly as a 'technical indiscretion', but more probably because of its rather startling contents. Addressed directly to Lawrence, it was, in effect, a declaration of Lawrence's supernatural powers and his profound influence on Sassoon:

> 'Behold I show you a mystery' ...
> When I received that sign
> In the dawn of the day which followed the day when you died,
> Then was belief made mine;
> For a spirit was with me; a presence was there at my side.
>
> You came with power to amend
> A heart uncomforted, angered, impassioned by death.
> It was the living friend
> Who brought me assurance of soulhood beyond this breath.
>
> Henceforth I will believe
> In life discarnate, limitless in scope;
> And in myself perceive
> Some ghostly kinship with undying hope.[45]

18. Paradise Regained and Lost (1934-1938)

When Sassoon had first got to know Lawrence in 1923 and introduced him to Forster, he had shared neither their common attraction to the East nor their interest in mysticism. But both men were to leave their mark on him, especially Lawrence at his death. He had already impressed Sassoon directly with his 'extraordinary powers' in the autumn of 1933, when he had performed an 'act of healing' on Sassoon, who had been in danger of losing the sight in one eye after a bout of shingles.[46] His 'visitation' after death completed the process and was a significant factor in the poet's developing spirituality, the 'closest [he] had ever come to religion', he told Tomlinson.[47]

The importance of Lawrence to Sassoon emerged in the violence of his reaction at Lawrence's funeral. Sickened by its carnival-like atmosphere (as he had been at Hardy's funeral), he had knocked a camera from the hand of a man who was trying to photograph the coffin at the open grave. And his disgust at what he called Robert Graves's 'performance' after the burial resulted in a further distancing of himself from Graves and a scornful parody of Marvell's 'Coy Mistress', with not very subtle play on the word 'grave': 'The grave's a private place, I hear. / But not when Robert Graves is near.'[48] When Hester, who had quite legitimately considered herself a friend of Lawrence, tried to share his grief, he felt even more threatened by her: 'Let me have my feelings to myself,' he begged in his diary.

While Lawrence was still alive, Sassoon had declined Cape's invitation to write about him, passing the offer on to Graves,[49] but after his death he agreed to help with a script for a film planned by the Korda brothers. (Lawrence's trustees had already sold the rights for his life story to them before he died.) Though the Kordas were known to pay generously and the renovation of Heytesbury yawned like a bottomless pit, Sassoon's main motive was not mercenary: what money he did eventually earn he gave to the local almshouses on whose committee he proudly served. He simply feared that the film would be a 'travesty' and hoped to be able to 'purify' it.[50] He also liked Lawrence's brother, Arnold, who visited Heytesbury in June 1935 to discuss the project.[51]

By this point Sassoon had solemnly re-read 170 pages of *Seven Pillars of Wisdom* in preparation. Lawrence, he vowed, should say nothing in the film not said by him in his book. But if he hoped to make the film a literary one he was sadly mistaken. While his fellow-writer on the project, Colonel W.F. ('Michael') Stirling, a man for whom he had 'a great liking',[52] seemed sympathetic to his aims, it is clear from the polite but firm rejection of their initial efforts that the Kordas had quite different ideas. By the end of July Sassoon was joking to Blunden that Hester had been 'reduced to writing the scenario' for him.[53] By August a professional scriptwriter had been added to the team, it being quite obvious that both Sassoon and Stirling were too ignorant of the mechanics of film to be able to produce a workable script. Though Sassoon's involvement nominally continued into

September, his part in it had virtually ceased by the 22nd of that month. Both he and the Kordas had had enough.

A second poem about Lawrence, written by Sassoon the day the Kordas' new scriptwriter was due to visit Heytesbury, suggests why he had failed to satisfy the film-makers. His efforts to convey the real-life Lawrence he had known were not what they wanted; *they* were looking, as he points out in this second poem, for the 'unanswering myth' and 'legend mask of stone', which was precisely what Sassoon was determined to avoid.[54] Lawrence, he feared, would be turned into the most hackneyed of Hollywood heroes, 'his odd humour must become obvious "light relief", his gentleness must become sentimentality; his tortured endurance of strain and hardship an exaggerated studio gesture.'[55]

The affair in itself is of no great significance, but it does highlight Sassoon's frustration and sense of failure in 1935.

*

Lawrence himself had noted that the 'barometer cannot always stand so high', but rarely does it continue so low and by early 1936 the prospect looked distinctly more cheerful at Heytesbury. After fourteen weeks of solitary grind Sassoon had managed by 9 January to finish a first draft of *Sherston's Progress*, his shortest book at approximately 52,000 words. The speed with which he wrote it is partly explained by the fact that he had already completed the first chapter of 6,000 words by the time he took it up again in October 1935 and that the third of the four sections is lifted with very few changes from his diary for the period. Nevertheless it was a huge relief to reach the end of his trilogy, a relief which turned to joy in February when Hester announced that she was pregnant again. With his book largely behind him he was a great deal more supportive than in the previous autumn and she safely negotiated the first three critical months. Even at this happy moment, however, the warning note is still sounding in Sassoon's diary: 'I love her deeply and gratefully, but it is a love that has learnt, by previous experience, to safeguard itself – or try to.'

One indirect result of finishing his work was the opportunity to formulate a reply to the critics who had attacked *Vigils*. His first attempt, a piece called 'A Poet on Poetry' for the *Listener* in 1935, though commissioned by its editor Joe Ackerley, had been set up in proof but not published, probably because of its reactionary and aggressive tone:

> ... Small-minded critics with no intuitive understanding of what poetry really is – these wise birds have been very busy pulling the feathers out of our songsters to find out where the song comes from. The songsters themselves have grown increasingly self-conscious and cerebral about their outpourings, and 'native wood-notes wild' have been severely reprimanded. Ambiguities have been encouraged, and anybody who sang naturally has

had his licence endorsed by the pedagogues, who, in my opinion, should be forbidden to make a fool of poetry in this way ...[56]

But at the end of January 1936 Sassoon started on a series of articles for the *Spectator* which managed to strike a more reasonable note, mainly through the witty use of an imaginary 'Aunt Eudora'. By placing all his more anti-Modernist views in the mouth of a charming old lady (who strongly resembles his mother) he manages to avoid the hectoring tone of 'A Poet on Poetry'. This time all three articles were published; the first and second, 'Aunt Eudora and the Poets' and 'Educating Aunt Eudora' (ostensibly reviews of the Bodley Head's *The Year's Poetry 1935* and Walter de la Mare's *Collected Poems*, respectively), provoked a lively correspondence in the magazine between Sassoon and his critics, and the third, 'Querkes, Farmonger and Dusp', was almost certainly a response to this interest.[57] He followed it up in August with 'A Personal View on How to Write' for the *Manchester Evening News*.[58]

Then, on 3 September 1936, just two months before his first child was due, his third prose offspring, *Sherston's Progress*, was published.[59] In direct contrast to *Vigils* the previous year, the reviews were almost universally good, in some cases ecstatic, underlining the fact that his prose fared much better than his poetry in the Modernist era. Ironically, it was his poetry about which he really cared, though he was relieved at the novel's reception.

Most of the main dailies welcomed it enthusiastically on the day of publication, the *Manchester Guardian* devoting the whole of its leader page to it and the *Evening Standard* recommending it as their Book of the Month. The *Standard*'s reviewer, Howard Spring, was particularly admiring, as most readers would be, of the portrayal of Rivers, the only character in the book to keep his real name as 'a symbol of his reality and integrity in all that muddle and madness of war conditions'.[60] Spring also praised Sassoon's acute analysis of Sherston's complex emotions as he struggles to make up his mind to return to the Front and, most of all, the Irish hunting scenes. Blunden, who reviewed it anonymously the same day in the *Times Literary Supplement*, was 'perfect' according to Sassoon, understanding 'the whole mechanism of my readjustment of my simplified self of which Sherston consists'.[61] *The Times*, *Daily Telegraph* and *Church Times* were also enthusiastic. John Sparrow continued the praise the next day in the *Spectator*, Ivor Brown in Sunday's *Observer* and Basil de Selincourt the following Tuesday in the *Westminster Gazette*. H.G. Wells would recommend it a month later in the *New York Times*.

Only a few dissenting voices stood out, the fiercest of which were Graham Greene's in the *Morning Post* and John Brophy's in the *Sunday Times*.[62] Brophy, who had taken Sassoon to task for his 'bad English', was easily disposed of: the 'solemn ass', Sassoon told Gathorne-Hardy, had failed to understand his deliberate use of colloquial English to reflect 'the narrator's discomfort at having to tell such an uncomfortable story. Sherston is ... a very typical English character.'[63]

Greene's damning dismissal was harder to deal with because nearer to the book's real weakness, its poor construction. While *Fox-Hunting Man* and *Infantry Officer* have their own internal logic and structure, *Sherston's Progress* stands up in structural terms only as the concluding volume of a trilogy. Though Greene's charge, that the book gives 'a sad impression of having been thrown together without plan, without creative compulsion', is an exaggeration, it has some truth in it. Sassoon himself, as Greene points out, is his own severest critic when he refers at one point in *Sherston's Progress* to 'these apparently interminable memoirs'. 'No critic', Greene concludes, 'could describe more harshly this amorphous chronicle, this huge balloon into which the first excellent memoirs have been blown by popular breath.'

Sassoon himself had already admitted serious doubts about the interest of the period covered in this third volume of Sherston's experiences, that is, his last year of the war. Although the opening section is about Rivers, and Sherston's stay in a shell-shock hospital, the other three sections deal with his least dramatic time in the army, the months spent in Ireland, Palestine and France (again) respectively. Sassoon's justification for continuing the adventures to this point was that Sherston's is a spiritual as well as physical journey that ends only with the conclusion of the war. Events themselves are of importance mainly as they affect the protagonist's inner life. The last-minute change of title, from *Further Experiences of George Sherston* (used as late as August 1936 by *Nash's Pall Mall Magazine* to serialize the book in America) to *Sherston's Progress*, is a deliberate attempt to draw a parallel with *Pilgrim's Progress*. And the epigraph from Bunyan underlines Sassoon's symbolic intent: 'I told him that I was a Pilgrim going to the Celestial City.'[64] The book closes with Rivers's visit to Sherston as he lies recovering from his final war wound in a London hospital, an ending which emphasizes its allegorical nature as well as the centrality of Rivers to its design: 'He did not tell me that I had done my best to justify his belief in me [Sherston writes]. He merely made me feel that he took all that for granted, and now we must go on to something better still. And this was the beginning of the new life toward which he had shown me the way ...'[65]

Rivers was not alive to appreciate *Sherston's Progress* when it came out, but another of its cast list, Vivian de Sola Pinto, who appears in the last section as Sherston's second-in-command, 'Velmore', was delighted by it. He thought it much closer to the rural scenes and gentle humour of *Fox-Hunting Man*, especially in the Limerick hunting scenes of Part Two, than the grimmer realism of *Infantry Officer*. Sassoon, who had greatly enjoyed writing the hunting interlude, admitted to another admirer of that section that it was 'thrown in for the enjoyment of recreating "the Mister"',[66] whereas (he told Blunden) he had had difficulty in recovering

'Flanders' details' for *Infantry Officer*, as he had also written in 'War Experience' at the time:[67]

> Not much remains, twelve winters later, of the hater
> Of purgatorial pains. And somewhat softly booms
> A Somme bombardment: almost unbelieved-in looms
> The day-break sentry staring over Kiel Trench crater.
>
> (CP, p. 216)

Whilst there is more humour in *Sherston's Progress*, however, it also contains more pathos than *Fox-Hunting Man*, where Sherston was callower and seemed more detached from his situation until the very end of the book. Aunt Evelyn, for instance, the source of much entertainment in the earlier work, provides a more muted amusement in *Sherston's Progress* as, unable to discuss his protest of which she disapproves, she continues to fuss over her nephew:

> The pathos of her efforts needs no emphasizing, though thinking of it gives me a heartache, even now. A strong smell of frying onions greeted my arrival. This, anyhow, gave me a chance to say how fond I was of that odour – as indeed I still am. 'Steaks are quite difficult to get now, dear, so I do hope it's a tender one.' And afterwards, while we were eating it, 'Much as it disagrees with me I never can resist the merry onion.'
>
> Her tired face was just about as merry as an onion. And the steak, of course, was tough.[68]

Besides pointing to a difference in tone from *Fox-Hunting Man*, this passage also illustrates the quality Sassoon himself thought most important in *Sherston's Progress*, the 'naturalness' of its 'speaking voice'.[69]

For today's readers the portrait of Dr Rivers, which provided Pat Barker with important material for her novel *Regeneration*, is likely to be of greatest interest. Even taking this into account, however, it is impossible to agree with Sassoon's claim that *Sherston's Progress* is 'prime vintage' and the best of his three fictional works.[70] It seems, rather, a falling-off, proof perhaps that he was right to worry about the effect of marriage on his writing. It is interesting to note that Forster, the most perceptive of his prose critics, was uncharacteristically non-committal in his response to it. The book nevertheless sold very well, helping considerably towards the renovation and upkeep of Heytesbury. Together with a legacy from Hester's aunt, Lady St Cyres, it provided the Sassoons with a very healthy income in 1936.

*

If the reception of *Sherston's Progress* raised Sassoon's spirits at the beginning of September 1936, the birth of a son less than two months later carried them to unimagined heights.

'Son both well', he telegrammed to Blunden on 30 October, the day of the birth. He and Hester had rented 18 Hanover Terrace in Regent's Park, next to Gosse's old house, for October and November, to be near specialist help in London. As it turned out no complications occurred and Hester was allowed a home delivery. The baby was christened at St Martin-in-the-Fields on 28 November by its former vicar Dick Sheppard, by now a good friend. (Sassoon had appeared on his Peace Pledge Union platform only the day before the baptism and when Sheppard died less than a year later would write an elegy on him.[71]) Resisting Max's whimsical suggestion of 'Hesterus' or 'Sherston', the Sassoons nevertheless recognized Sherston's importance by christening their son George, with the 'Thornycroft' of his middle name acknowledging the English side of his father's family, but nothing to link him to Hester's. Blunden, Glen, Edith Olivier and both the Beerbohms were godparents, all but the last two being present, together with Rex Whistler, Osbert Sitwell and, in spite of increasing ill-health, Ottoline. Theresa Sassoon, suffering from severe arthritis and angina, did not attend, though she was delighted by the arrival of another grandson and would visit Heytesbury shortly afterwards to inspect him.

Most people are thrilled by the birth of their first child, awed by the realization that they have helped create another, independent life. For Sassoon, who had resigned himself to childlessness, the experience was overwhelming: it was, Glen would claim after his friend's death, 'one of the two supreme happinesses in his life'.[72] Sassoon himself said at the time that George was 'beyond anything the greatest happiness I have ever experienced', the kind of claim he had been making about Hester only a few years previously.[73] In fact his son would quickly replace Hester in his already fluctuating feelings for her. From the moment of his birth it was George, not Hester, who represented Sassoon's 'whole future'.[74]

Even before the birth it had become clear that Sassoon's suspicion of women as domineering, over-possessive creatures had not been entirely overcome. His son offered no such threat. Whether he would have been so delighted by a daughter is more doubtful. As it was, he was able to identify almost completely with a son, especially with one who resembled him closely; as he looked down at the child in his arms he saw, in the words of one of his many poems on the subject, his 'self reborn':

> Meeting and Parting
> My self reborn, I look into your eyes;
> While you, unknowing, look your first time on me.
> Thus will *you* stand when life within me dies.
> And you, full knowing, my parting presence see.
>
> Alone I stand before my new-born son;
> Alone he lies before me, doomed to live.
> Beloved, when I am dying and all is done,
> Look on my face and say that you forgive.
> (CP, p. 251)[75]

18. Paradise Regained and Lost (1934-1938)

Through George, Sassoon was transported mentally to the period when he had experienced life most intensely and it is no coincidence that he started to write about his own early childhood shortly after his birth. In addition George also represented not just the continuity Sassoon had longed for when he married, but the perpetuation of his name. Before the child was a year old he had written at least one poem about future great-grandchildren.[76] Equally importantly George seemed to him a refuge from the 'cleverness and intellectual elaboration of the modern world'.[77] From now on he would invest virtually his whole reason for living in his son. George was to be, as Hester had been, his redemption.

It was too heavy a responsibility for one child to bear. Had there been other children things might have been different, but Hester had been so traumatized by the birth, possibly also by her miscarriage, that she would refuse to have a second child until it was too late. So that George alone had to bear the weight of his father's almost idolatrous affection. And, as Ackerley would observe during his visit to Heytesbury, it was not only George who suffered. By doing what he, Ackerley, had done with his dog Queenie and becoming 'fixated' on his child, Sassoon had unwisely put 'all [his] eggs in [one] basket'.[78]

None of this was apparent at the start, however. The birth initially made Sassoon more, not less, appreciative of Hester and Christmas with her and George in 1936 seemed to him 'the happiest ... ever'.[79] But when he tried to get back to work in January 1937, the difficulties quickly resurfaced. Spurred on by the success of *Sherston's Progress*, reminded by George of his own childhood and confident that he was now sufficiently well known to justify it, he planned to start on his real autobiography, the first volume to take him to the age of thirteen in 1900 and be called *The Old Century*.

Once again he insisted that the only way he could write was to stay up half the night and sleep half the day. Whether he was using work partly as an excuse to be alone, as he had with a previous lover, Philipp,[80] or whether he was simply incapable of real adjustment, the results were the same, an increasing irritation on his part with Hester's attempts to establish a more regular married life and bewilderment and hurt on hers. There was no doubt in Sassoon's mind where the fault lay: his 'lack of freedom', as he saw his inability to live what was in effect a separate life from his wife, could 'only be resolved by Hester learning wisdom'.[81] He wanted the marriage on his own, very demanding terms. While formally acknowledging that few women of her age would be content with the large chunks of time alone he expected for his work, he resented her 'inability to control her intense devotion' to him, an extraordinary complaint considering how much he had needed it at the start.[82] It seems as if, once certain of her love, he no longer fully appreciated it and that once she had 'given' him George, his emotional fulfilment lay elsewhere. Rather than George being a 'safeguard' for their marriage, as Sassoon claimed, he was one of

299

a number of reasons for Sassoon's increasing dissatisfaction with Hester in 1937.[83]

His greatest fear remained her possessiveness. There was also her occasional 'nerviness', which had slightly marred a month's holiday with the Beerbohms at Rapallo.[84] ('Nerviness' was Sassoon's euphemism for what he was secretly beginning to believe were pronounced neurotic tendencies.) Their celebration of the coronation of King George VI in May that year was more successful, meliorated by the company of H.G. Wells, who stayed eight days at Heytesbury, and Hamo, who caught flu and stayed eighteen. Theresa Sassoon's visit in June also passed without a hitch. 'All here is peace and perfection,' Sassoon wrote to Ben Huebsch in July 1937.

So long as he and Hester did things together the calm continued. But when he tried to see Glen and Angela on his own in August, Hester felt excluded; some 'ghastly scenes' ensued and he was forced to cancel his visit.[85] And any attempt to be alone with George failed miserably. By November 1937 he reported gloomily to Glen that Hester had become 'impossibly possessive ... refusing to take her eye off [him]'.[86] In December there was a confrontation and the marriage reached crisis point.

Still struggling to finish *The Old Century*, Sassoon put his foot down at the beginning of 1938 and insisted that Hester leave him alone, even though this meant being without George, whom she took to her mother's. Another month together with the Beerbohms in the spring of 1938[87] failed to work its usual magic for Sassoon and by the beginning of July he once more banished Hester from Heytesbury. This time she was instructed to take George to the seaside for a fortnight and the situation was not improved when she returned two days later complaining of the state of the hotel. Since at that point Sassoon had not only completed *The Old Century* but also corrected the proofs, it is obvious that he simply wanted to get rid of her. While Ralph Hodgson's visit in August on his final return from Japan cheered Sassoon up, it almost certainly made Hester feel more excluded as the two old friends talked endlessly about the past and about Hodgson's future in America. A final showdown between husband and wife seems to have been averted, however, by two events of considerable importance to Sassoon in September, the publication of *The Old Century* on the 15th and Chamberlain's return from Munich on the 29th after what many would later come to regard as his appeasement of Hitler.

19

The Old Century and the New War

When sensitive readers discover [*The Old Century*], they never fail to fall in love with it (as *I* did, for it was my love affair with a vanished world and way of life) ... You realized that it was an unashamed idealization of everything that I remembered with gratitude and affection. But perhaps you missed its *mental* provenance ... I wrote it for mental release from Hitler and Mussolini – (and the war that seemed to me almost a certainty). And designed it as an anodyne for my fellow sufferers.

(Sassoon to Michael Thorpe, 14 March 1967)[1]

In one sense *The Old Century and Seven More Years* was a direct result of the threat of war. Writing to an admirer only three days after Chamberlain's return from Munich in September 1938, Sassoon told him that he created his book quite deliberately 'as an antidote to the times we live in' and that he wanted it to be 'completely harmonious and secure'.[2] Knowing that he would be accused of 'escapism' by 'sophisticated clever people' and of lack of 'realism' by the Modernists, he nevertheless believed that *The Old Century* was far more than an escape: 'It is a reassurance for decent people, that decency still exists.'[3]

It was as much to reassure himself as others, however, that he wrote it: he, too, needed 'mental release from Hitler and Mussolini' and the war that seemed to him a certainty, despite Chamberlain's soundbite, 'Peace in our time'. While admiring the Prime Minister's efforts, which he believed to be in the spirit of Dick Sheppard's passionate attempts to 'get round behind the political mechanism to the ordinary humanity of human life',[4] by mid-1937 he no longer felt that such action was enough. Influenced by Max Beerbohm's change of heart in Fascist Italy and seeing for himself the growing power of Mussolini, who had passed through Rapallo during Sassoon's stay there in spring 1937, he had finally given up the pacifist cause.[5] His visit to Max the following year had increased his awareness of the preparations for war in Europe, especially in Paris, where he and Hester had stayed with her cousin at the Embassy on their way home. He was still ready to protest against the situation, gladly allowing his name to be read out at a meeting, 'Writers Declare Against Fascism', organized by the Association of Writers for Intellectual Liberty on 8 June 1938, but his attitude had changed.[6] And as the hopes of averting a major conflict receded, it seemed to him more important than ever to provide 'some peaceful pages' within the enclosed, distant world of his book, that 'drowsy, homespun age' of long ago.[7]

It was a passive rather than an active response to the situation and in direct contrast to his strident verse-warnings of the First World War. Similarly his reluctant acceptance of the need to fight the Second World War was very different from his outspoken opposition to the continuation of the First. Like Bertrand Russell and many other eminent opponents of the earlier conflict, he felt forced to acknowledge that the only effective way of stopping Hitler was to fight him.

It was not simply as an antidote to war, however, that Sassoon wrote *The Old Century*. There were more practical motives. He needed the money to maintain Heytesbury and the success of *Sherston's Progress* encouraged him to concentrate on prose. He had already ruled out a fourth fictionalized volume covering his life in the twenties as being too sensitive, but he saw nothing to prevent him returning to his early life. ('I think I have a special gift for being in love with the past,' he told his mother.)[8] Ever since completing his account of the sporting aspect of his childhood in *Fox-Hunting Man*, he had wanted to make good his omissions by describing his other 'strange dream side'.[9] Gathorne-Hardy had once suggested, no doubt with Wordsworth's *Prelude* in mind, that this might take the form of a long poem, to be called *The Growth of a Poet's Mind*, but only three weeks after the publication of *Sherston's Progress* Sassoon was asking him: 'Could it be done, in prose, as a sort of parcelled portrait of Sherston (the "country cousin"), do you think?'.[10] From there it was only a short step to actual autobiography. With his son George as a stimulus and a daily reminder of his own childhood, it should not be difficult to recreate it.

The one real problem he faced, as he had in *Sherston's Progress*, was that of structure: 'Would "wanting to become a poet"', he asked Gathorne-Hardy, 'provide sufficient structural solidity and narrative interest?'[11] The answer, of course, was that it would depend on how he approached his material. As he knew from Proust's sensitive recreation of his past, it must appear natural, while at the same time tracing the development of the artistic consciousness. The writer must signpost the turning points – what Joyce had called 'epiphanies', Virginia Woolf 'moments of being' and Wordsworth 'spots of time' – but he or she must also supply a narrative line, however sketchy, as well as the flavour or atmosphere of the past and some sense of a philosophy or system of beliefs.

Sassoon admired Wordsworth, Proust and Woolf and appears to have been swayed by all three in his choice of method.[12] There was also the more recent influence of Dickens's handling of the first-person narrator in his account of the development of a young man from early childhood in *Great Expectations* and *David Copperfield*. And his way of looking at the past had been coloured, in more general terms, by Edmund Gosse's pioneering classic of autobiography, *Father and Son*, as well as Pater and Hardy's explorations of it. A less obvious but no less powerful influence on *The Old Century* was the Reverend James Woodforde, whose *Diary of a Country Parson* had been published between 1924 and 1931. The innocent parson's concentration on the daily minutiae of rural life in the eighteenth century gave Sassoon the same sense of authenticity which he derived from reading a very different account of the period, Defoe's *Moll Flanders*. Both lay behind his own attempt to recreate the past. It is significant that he sent the dedicatee of *The Old Century*, Max Beerbohm, Woodforde's diaries to read the year he started to write his book.

'But of course diary-writing is a technique in itself,' Sassoon replied to Max's enthusings over Woodforde's details, duckweed on the pond included. 'And, like you, I am "all for" the duck-weed method. The weather; food; details about expenditure; how one enjoys such things.'[13] They were details he had instinctively included in his own diaries and there is no doubt that one of the strongest influences on *The Old Century* was his years of diary-writing. This had alerted him to the importance of detail, in the same way that his three fictional works had given him practice in characterization, dialogue and the setting of a scene. For style he remained, even in prose, heavily dependent on his poetry. According to his fellow-versifier Walter de la Mare, *The Old Century* was 'poetry diffused into prose'.[14]

'As usual I aim at the clarity and condensation of a play (or a boiled-down diary),' he wrote in his notes to the book.[15] And, as usual, he found the solution to the problems of portraying the whole of his childhood in 'simplification': 'After all, I am under no obligation to produce a family history and psychological document.' What he aimed at was a 'pleasant outline' of his early years, a 'balanced' picture, which would be neither 'too elaborate' nor 'too introspective'.[16] His great difficulty, as he saw it, would be 'to keep poetry and sensitiveness as the narrative thread' and at the same time avoid giving an impression that he was 'a weak-kneed sort of young person'.[17] Though the emphasis must be on his 'strange dreamy side', he feared being 'too literary and artistic at the expense of conventional interests such as cricket and golf and going to dances'.[18]

Above all he wanted to avoid being 'boring and fussy':

I think the best method [he concluded] will be a series of typical scenes, showing 'home life' in 1897-8-9 (plus Edingthorpe and perhaps Broomfield [holiday homes]). And then there must be a sustained narrative about our only exciting relative – Auntie Rachel– whose background will provide contrast (and a good story).[19]

In the finished work, contrast remains an important structural principle, his account alternating between intense happiness and unhappiness in the way that memories of childhood tend to do. The 'Prelude' (and the echo of Wordsworth is probably deliberate) opens the book on a positive note with the very young Sassoon accompanying his mother to his favourite place, Watercress Well, and to watch her painting a man sowing seeds. But this is followed almost immediately in Chapter One with his misery as a five-year-old contemplating his parents' separation, which is itself (and within the same scene) contrasted with his delight in his father's weekly visits. Similarly his sadness at his father's later illness has its 'compensations' when the seven-year-old Sassoon visits him at Eastbourne, which numbers among its undeniable pleasures 'shrimps for tea'.[20] His father's death, followed by the disturbing departure of his nanny, Mrs Mitchell, and Siegfried's subsequent illness are again balanced by the eight-year-old's discovery during convalescence that he has 'a mind with which [he] liked to be alone' and the dawning of a poetic consciousness.[21] Even his unhappiness about his Uncle Beer's mysterious illness (syphilis) and his Aunt Rachel's sufferings is forgotten in the glow of recollecting childhood visits to their exotic house in Mayfair. Only towards the end of Book I, two-thirds through the story, does he fail to find any consolation in the death of his endearing Uncle Don, an event which makes him realize the inadequacy of his own immature attempts to deal with the subject in poetry. 'Very subdued and insignificant I felt, as I looked upon the reality of grief in the stricken faces of my cousins, on that quiet sunless October afternoon.'[22] Yet Book I is not allowed to end on such a sad note and its final scene is both humorous and up-beat, opening with the running argument between Sassoon's two tutors, Fräulein Stoy and Mr Hamilton, about whether the 'old century' actually ended in December 1899 or December 1900, and followed by the thirteen-year-old Sassoon reluctantly agreeing to let his younger, less sentimental brother Hamo make a bonfire of their old 'den'. Besides being a symbolic end to his childhood, it also illustrates the author's ability to see both the melancholy and the promise of life.

Sassoon had intended to finish his book at this point, with perhaps a coda on his belated departure for prep school and the death of his Uncle Beer in 1902. Its title was to be *Memoirs of Myself*, a clear allusion to the first two, and most popular, volumes of the Sherston trilogy. He had worked to this plan from late December 1936 and had completed eight of his proposed eleven chapters by the time he and Hester set out for Rapallo in early April 1937, the speed of execution suggesting how much he enjoyed writing them. Hester, delighted by the success of *Sherston's Progress* and during a temporary lull in hostilities, had typed them up for Sassoon to show to Max. Not surprisingly Max praised them lavishly, and not just because he was the book's dedicatee; for the pleasure with which Sassoon had written comes through clearly in the writing and conveys itself to most sensitive readers.

But when Sassoon returned to work on what he thought would be the final three chapters, he found the going harder, not completing his plan until late November 1937. By this time the omnibus *Complete Memoirs of*

George Sherston had been published and, possibly fearing repetition, he changed his title, *Memoirs of Myself*, to *The Old Century*.[23]

It was an excellent choice. The only problem was that it had taken him less than 40,000 words to cover the nineteenth-century period of his life, well under half the length of *Fox-Hunting Man* and barely half the 75,000 words he had agreed to deliver for his £900 advance. His publishers, Faber, were convinced that to be 'easily marketable' something more substantial was needed.[24] Rejecting Sassoon's own suggestion of an appendix of his early privately printed poems, Faber insisted that he add at least 'seven more years' to his life story.[25] Though this would make for a clumsier title, it should push the word count up to an acceptable size.

The task reduced Sassoon to near despair. Whereas he had found his early childhood a joy to recreate, much preferring it to his account in *Fox-Hunting Man*, he groaned his way through the next seven years, the period covering his formal education away from Weirleigh. Only the determination to take a completed manuscript to Max when he visited him again in late April 1938 enabled him to complete the final chapter and to bring his word count up to 63,000. All in all *The Old Century* cost him '1500 hours of dumb donkey-work', he told de la Mare, many of them concentrated into this last third of the book.[26]

The strain shows, just as clearly as his pleasure in writing the first two-thirds shines through. Book II is not without its enjoyments: Siegfried's arrival at his first prep school, the New Beacon, at the advanced age of nearly fourteen without any shirts ('It was bad enough to be ... only half educated. To be only half dressed as well was the finishing touch');[27] his determined mother's visit to Marlborough College to nurse him through a life-threatening illness with strong beef tea; the characterization of the most eccentric of his form-masters there, Mr Gould, with his final withering remark to him at eighteen, 'Try to be more sensible';[28] his doomed attempts to write a prize-winning poem for the Chancellor's Medal at Cambridge; 'Uncle's' hobby of making golf-clubs at his 'crammers', Henley House; or the final scene in the book on his twenty-first birthday, the visit of 'dear old Major Horrocks and his deaf sister, who had walked up the hill for a chat and a toddle' round Weirleigh's garden.[29]

In spite of such highlights, however, Book II lacks the poetry of Book I as well as its organic quality, giving the impression of being 'tacked on', as indeed it was. Sassoon himself believed that Book I was superior to Book II and 'the best I shall ever do'.[30]

Forster, probably Sassoon's most reliable prose critic, thought *The Old Century* as a whole very good, but it is noticeable that all the examples of excellence he chose occur in Book I – the characters of 'Wirgie' and Mrs Mitchell, the description of Farmer Ruxton 'looking only like a partridge', Aunt Rachel's extraordinarily erratic editing of both the *Observer* and *The Sunday Times*.[31] He was particularly impressed by Chapter Eight, where the adult Sassoon returns to the scene of a childhood holiday in Norfolk and remembers what stood out for his ten-year-old self. Forster recognized from his own experience how difficult it must have been to write, but believed that 'by coming off [it] increase[d] the strength of the whole fabric'.[32]

Sassoon's recreation of the shabby Norfolk rectory at Edingthorpe, where he spent two months with his mother, brothers and Gosse's daughter Tessa in 1897, shows him at his best, combining as it does all the elements Forster admired in his writing, his narrative skill, his prose style, his character-drawing, his ability to portray the pathos that often underlies a superficially comic situation, especially for the child, but, above all, his evocation of a 'drowsy, homespun age' and 'the gentleness and innocence' that went with it.[33] Forster was not ungrateful for the social progress that had been made in more recent years – 'if society hadn't broken up I should never have known Bob Buckingham [his policeman lover] except as Tom Richardson [the Sassoons' groom]'. But that 'great blessing apart', he felt that all was 'loss: smartness for comfort, pertness for gentleness, cerebral jabber for quiet easy talks about real things, movies for Tablows [*tableaux vivants*], the mechanical for the created ...'[34] Though not sure that the younger generation would understand Sassoon's book – 'they will see it in terms of park gates and servants and think we are lamenting those' – he himself valued its preservation in the pages of *The Old Century*: 'Just as a document it's important, and this is a document plus poetry.'[35]

Sassoon's opening to the Edingthorpe chapter, with his imaginary return as an adult in 1937 to his childhood home of Weirleigh in August 1897, is masterful. It enables him not only to introduce the family's absence in Norfolk on holiday but, more importantly, to draw back from the child's point of view and explore the effect of time and our inability to change one iota of the past:

> In mind-sight we return: but even if in more than mind-sight we could somehow be there in the actuality of outlived experience, we should be strangers, invisible, and powerless to avert so much as the overwinding of a clock.
> 'Don't do it; don't do it!' we should cry, discerning in some blindly enacted blunder the first step taken on some very wrong road. But the warning would be like dumb shoutings in a dream. Not by one faintest whisper could we safeguard our vanished self while he gaily or sullenly created the sorrow and bitterness of after days. Those eyes of youth would look past us even as they look past the troubled faces of those who try to help them.[36]

Sassoon then steps entirely out of his narrative to discuss his difficulties as a writer in recreating this particular section of his past, the summer holiday in Norfolk, and to take the reader with him on his return visit there, ostensibly in 1937, the year he is writing the chapter. Struck by how little has changed, he makes his way on foot to the rectory, and the past, obediently, comes flooding back with a memory of the family setting out for the seaside. 'Later on I would explore the garden for memories,' he tells his readers, shepherding them meantime to the old church and its new addition – a lychgate erected 'in loving memory of a young lance-corporal of the Norfolk Regiment' killed in 1915.[37] So that now the distant past is overlaid by the less distant past by a present-day narrator who wants to draw attention to the horrors of 1915, when his own brother, he tells us, was also killed.

It is a skilful performance but, like some other passages in Sassoon's autobiography, it is not entirely true to the facts.[38] Sassoon's first return visit to Norfolk had been on 15 September 1924, not 13 August 1937, by which time he had, in any case, already written the Edingthorpe chapter.[39] And on neither occasion was the hamlet deserted, as he claims. On the second, which actually took place in late August 1937, he was in fact accompanied by Hester, whom he omits entirely from his description.

His rewriting of events has clearly been made in the interests of atmosphere, a deserted village and isolated pilgrimage fitting in more conveniently with the mood he is trying to create, and the change is minor. Nevertheless, it is a warning against accepting *The Old Century* as entirely factual. Though he claims to have embraced conventional biography with this book, his main aim, which is to show the power of the imagination ('to trace the stream of my life back to its source')[40], leads him on occasions to reject the actual past in favour of his memory of that past.

There are also distortions brought about by his need to omit certain facts. As Forster notes, *The Old Century* carries 'the bloom of life' even more vividly than *Fox-Hunting Man*, but it cannot, as Forster himself knows, be 'something still more intimate' within the legal restrictions of the 1930s.[41] Sassoon could no more describe his adolescent misery at the realization of his homosexuality, for instance, than Forster could publish *Maurice* in his lifetime.

What Sassoon can do, however, more than compensates for what he cannot. He populates his past with characters who might, as Forster notes, have stepped straight out of *The Canterbury Tales*. Purporting to believe that the world is full of 'extremely nice people', he does a convincing job of recreating such characters – his over-protective mother, his gentle tutor, Mr Moon, the beautiful Marchant sisters, Bessie and May, the majority of his schoolteachers. As with Chaucer, however, it is the flawed people, the exceptions to his rule, who come across most vividly. His mother's friend Helen Wirgman, for instance, with her uncertain temper and passionate rendering of Beethoven, jumps directly off the page and even the treacherous Mrs Mitchell has her appeal. Likewise, in the Edingthorpe chapter, it is Sassoon's impossible Aunt Lula who triumphs.

'Magnificent' to look at, 'quite delightful' when she 'designed so to be', Aunt Lula had an 'uncontrollable temper and made scenes in tremendous style'.[42] Two of the most memorable moments, in a book full of them, involve her and highlight a central quality of *The Old Century*, its ability to embrace both high comedy and near tragedy in its vision of life. 'I like to be moved and transported by the little things of life,' Sassoon would write, '– by the humour which has a note of pathos in it, for humour is often closely allied to pathos – *sunt lacrimae rerum* [here are tears for things].'[43] Forster thought the scene where the ten-year-old Sassoon attempts to placate his cross aunt with a welcome party dressed up as monks particularly affecting (it made him want to cry), but he might just as easily have chosen Aunt Lula's premature departure from Norfolk in a rage:

> Memory now delineated Aunt Lula, sitting there in the middle of the lawn, on a wooden box which we had been using as a wicket. She was fully dressed for going away, and had just swept out of the house after a one-sided rumpus with my mother. Had Mrs Siddons been portrayed seated on a soapbox, her attitude would have resembled Aunt Lula's – majestic, aggrieved, and unbending. Watching her from behind the bushes, I had been chiefly interested in the behaviour of the box, which wasn't in a condition to stand the strain of Aunt Lula sitting, as it were, on her dignity while waiting for Lucy and the carriage to come round and convey her to the station. Needless to say, the box collapsed and with mingled agitation and derision I saw Aunt Lula with her heels in the air and her hat well over her nose. Saw, too, how haughtily she arose and made her exit, round the corner to the front door, disdaining the paltry notion that Emily Eyles might have witnessed the mishap from a window.[44]

All the comedy of the early part of *Fox-Hunting Man* is here as the small boy spies on his precariously seated aunt, but so too is the pathos of *Infantry Officer* and *Sherston's Progress* as the adult evaluates his memories of his unhappy relative, the viewpoint shifting constantly between the child's and adult's perception and the style changing accordingly (from the childish 'rumpus' to the mature man's 'disdaining the paltry notion', for example). The sly touches of humour – Aunt Lula on the frail soapbox 'sitting, as it were, on her dignity', for instance – offset any charge of sentimentalizing the past that might be levelled at the author. (Sassoon was well aware of the danger and of how the realists, in particular, would criticize his intention 'not to remember unpleasant things very clearly'.)[45]

Few readers would deny the entertainment value of *The Old Century*, but some have questioned whether it fulfils the purpose its author sets out in his 'Prelude' after describing his memories of Watercress Well and a sower at work: 'to tell whither the water journeyed from its source, and how the seed came up'.[46] Apart from the young Sassoon's convalescence on the lawn and his teenage awakening to the power of poetry through reading Thomas Hood at Marlborough College, there are no direct attempts to explain how he became a poet. Yet in its very reluctance to describe and its determination instead to 'show' the working of the young Sassoon's consciousness, *The Old Century* succeeds in conveying the slow, often jerky development of his imagination. A key scene in the book, for instance, and one chosen by him to illustrate the title-page wood-engraving by Geoffrey Keynes's sister-in-law, Gwen Raverat, is the one showing him fishing as a ten-year-old in the orchard pond. There is no direct discussion of poetry-writing here, but rather a demonstration of the future poet's imagination at work, transforming the outer world until the fairly ordinary pond becomes the banks of the Zambesi River. As Thorpe notes, Sassoon's 'refusal to exaggerate the significance of what he recalls or to moralize unduly' lends authenticity to his account of the 'growth of a poet's sensibility'.[47]

The Old Century was treated well by reviewers, with only 'three gad-flies' settling on it, according to its author.[48] Of these three Malcolm Muggeridge alone irritated Sassoon sufficiently for him to repeat Muggeridge's criticism to Keynes, that '*The Old Century* [is] like an anaemic fairy story – something belonging to a remote past and with no bearing on the so ominous present.'[49] As far as Sassoon was concerned its remoteness from the present was precisely the point, but he doubted whether younger critics like Muggeridge could understand that and was grateful to be spared the critical onslaught of *Vigils*. The previously hostile David Garnett, for example (after a rap over the knuckles by his friend Keynes, no doubt), was now full of praise. Desmond MacCarthy, whose own review in the *New Statesman* was enthusiastic, thought Garnett's 'admirable' and 'felt envious of several things he had said'.[50] And Blunden, as usual, was euphoric, calling the book 'a composition of a delicate but decisive order, a performance governed by the faith in the fine art of writing'.[51] He also drew attention to the fact that a book dedicated to Max Beerbohm (and, he might have added, proof-read by him) would naturally have a style governed by vigilance and distinctiveness. Another old friend, Tomlinson, enthused: 'The bloom on the book is as if a hand had never been on it.'[52]

Friends from the period covered by the book also wrote to congratulate Sassoon. One reason why so many of the characters in *The Old Century* emerge as 'extremely nice people' may be that its author knew that the majority of them were still alive and was afraid of offending them. (Having to use real names made him feel far more vulnerable.) He had actually sent proofs to two such friends from the past, Eustace Malden ('Uncle') and Jane Wilson (née Malden), both from his 'crammers', Henley House, but he need not have worried. Uncle was 'touchingly pleased' with the book and Jane Wilson came to stay the night at Heytesbury. Bessie Marchant, who had married a Hugh Wormald and gone to live in Norfolk, wrote to congratulate him on his vivid evocation of the past: 'She had forgotten many of the things I describe,' Sassoon boasted to a friend.[53]

Max Beerbohm was proud to have such a 'perfectly lovely thing' dedicated to him, though, like Forster, his enthusiasm was reserved mainly for Book I. 'It is like going out into a garden at 6 o'clock on a summer morning!' he told Sassoon. 'You have put the dewy cobwebs and dewdrops on to the paper without breaking a single dewdrop. You have shown childhood as it seemed to a child.'[54] Enchanted by its delicacy, he predicted that it would be an *'enormous* success'.[55] To which Sassoon, in gratitude for Max's unstinting help with proof-correcting, especially his punctuation, replied:

> Ah, what avails enormous sales!
> Ah, what unstinted praise!
> This book, with proud remembrance, hails
> Page-proof Rapallo days.
> Max, punctuation's pioneer
> The unbound *Old Century* through,
> Its every thought and cadence here
> I dedicate to you.[56]

Sassoon was not quite so lofty about sales as he affected to be, however, and by January 1939 was writing sadly to Keynes that, 'owing to the crisis' of approaching war, *The Old Century* had sold half what he and his publishers had expected.[57] It was not so much the money he minded, though the disappointing sales made domestic economy a 'drastic necessity' at Heytesbury in 1939; he was 'irked' that *The Old Century* was so little known by comparison with *Fox-Hunting Man*.[58] '*The Old Century* is a daisy of a book,' he wrote to a close friend towards the end of his life: 'I can't think how I did it.'[59] Of all his prose works, it would remain his favourite.

War Within and Without
(September 1939-October 1942)

What a comedy my career has been – in its human relationships!
(SS to Glen Byam Shaw, 15 August 1940)

By the time Britain declared war on Germany on 3 September 1939, Sassoon was already fully engaged in his own personal battle with Hester. The two conflicts would run side by side for the next five years, each affecting his attitude towards the other and both exerting a significant influence on his work.

To begin with the national emergency brought about a stand-off in his private warfare, as he and Hester faced the consequences of a second world war. Hester, who had been warned in August to expect at least twenty evacuees at Heytesbury House, was caught up in preparations for their arrival, while Sassoon braced himself to deal with the influx of army officers threatened by a visiting military man earlier in the year.

The evacuees quickly materialized and Hester, whose untidiness and lack of organization increasingly irritated her obsessively neat husband, was fully occupied trying to house and feed them. She was far more concerned about their fate than Sassoon, whose attitude was both detached and lofty, the socialism of his *Daily Herald* period now completely dead: 'The back regions are a pandemonium of squallings and peculiar smells of cooking,' he wrote to his nephew Hamo, 'while Hester, with a worried face, rushes about administering first-aid to minor ailments and settling squabbles between mothers. ... It is extraordinary how much this house can absorb without feeling the strain!'[1]

Hester was also busy helping a maid sew black-out curtains, an occupation Sassoon thought entirely appropriate to her sex: 'Nothing can alter the fact', he wrote in his diary with the full force of his male chauvinism, 'that women are only effective when they stick to their appropriate concerns.'[2] Since he regarded domestic duties as the chief of those concerns and since no army officers had presented themselves for his own attention, he himself contributed almost nothing of a practical nature during the first seven months of the war, a period which came to be known as the 'phoney' war because so little appeared to be happening. There were a few skirmishes in the Maginot Line, the series of fortifications built by the French against Germany after the First World War, and some activity at sea, but no bombing, and the war itself, which had seemed a very real threat during the year leading up to it, became rather unreal to the majority of civilian English.

Sassoon's own battle with Hester also became less prominent as she concentrated her energies elsewhere and allowed him more of the solitude he craved. Left largely to his own devices and 'sick to death' of the war after less than two months of it, he finally overcame eighteen months of writer's block to begin a second volume of autobiography, *The Weald of Youth*, on 25 October.[3]

'It was the War that did it, I think,' he wrote to Max, who had left Fascist Italy with Florence in February 1939 and settled at Abinger, Surrey, in a cottage lent to them by Sydney and Violet Schiff.[4] 'The newspapers just drove me away from *1939*; and how happy I've been during my six days' revisitation of *1909*!' By avoiding Hester, even at meal times, by sacrificing even his son's company except for his third birthday tea and, most importantly, by ignoring news of the war, he managed to write 3,200 words by 1 November 1939. It was a great deal by his standards and a sign of his complete involvement not in the present but in the past. For *The Weald of Youth*, like *The Old Century* and his fictional trilogy, would result largely from his need to 'give the present the slip' and 'escape' to what seemed in retrospect a much happier time, in this case the years covering his 'country squire' period at Weirleigh followed by an attempt to make a life for himself in London in the summer of 1914. Though the shadow of the First World War would fall across the last few pages, it was essentially a pre-war world to which he retreated. His intense nostalgia for it comes through clearly in a poem written a year previously, 'Heart and Soul', which gave *The Weald of Youth* its title and central metaphor:

> Growing older, the heart's not colder:
> Losing youngness, the eye sees clearer.
>   (Inward eye, while our sight grows blurred.)
> Living longer, the soul grows stronger.
> Looked on, the darkening weald grows dearer.
>   (Weald of youth, a remembered word.) ...
>   (CP, p. 247)[5]

A possibly subconscious reply to Gerard Manley Hopkins's lines in 'Spring and Fall' ('Ah! as the heart grows older / It will come to such sights colder'), Sassoon's poem was also a response to his own accelerated sense of ageing at this time. The outbreak of another world war reminded him that a quarter of a century had passed since his headlong entry into the previous one,[6] adding to his consciousness of the half century which lay between himself and his son.[7] And *The Weald*, like his poem, was an attempt to recapture that earlier life. He might claim that it was written with 'the deliberate purpose of providing mental relief' for his 'kind readers',[8] but it was (as with *The Old Century*) as much for his own sake as theirs that he wrote it.

His problem was that, faced with a second world war, he could not deal with it directly, either in verse or prose. It may be that he was overwhelmed by a sense of hopelessness. In 1919 he had asked, rhetorically, 'Is it all going to happen again?' and now that the answer was yes, he felt unable to comment further. During the three years he spent 'toiling, off and on' at *The Weald*, he told de la Mare, 'the muse deserted [him], except for a few snatches of contrived writing'.[9]

The verse to which he refers is very 'contrived' indeed and, fortunately for his reputation, largely unpublished.[10] The few war poems which did appear in print are mediocre efforts at best. Dismissed by Stephen Spender as 'lamentable', they are the kind of jingoistic outpourings Sassoon had challenged in the First World War. That they were published at all was due mainly to the fact that he was still thought of primarily as a war poet. The *Observer*, for instance, published two of what he called his 'duty' poems, 'The English Spirit' and 'Silent Service', in May and June 1940, when the war was entering its second, more aggressive phase.[11] 'The English Spirit', with its learned opening allusion to *Pilgrim's Progress* and word-play, its stilted vocabulary, declamatory tone and solemn, public 'message', could hardly be more of a contrast to the direct, colloquial anger of his anti-war satires in *The Old Huntsman* and *Counter-Attack*:[12]

> Apollyon having decided to employ
> His anger of blind armaments for this –
> That every valued virtue and guarded joy
> Might grieve bewildered by a bombed abyss –
>> The ghosts of those who have wrought our English Past
>> Stand near us now in unimpassioned ranks
>> Till we have braved and broken and overcast
>> The cultural crusade of Teuton tanks.
>
> (CP, p. 256)

Sassoon rightly feared that he had 'overdone the "grand style"' in this poem.[13] His few successful poems about the Second World War are those in a lower key that touch on the subject only incidentally, pieces such as 'A 1940 Memory' or 'On Scratchbury Camp', where this particular conflict is placed in the context of nature and history:

> Shadows outspread in spacious movement, always you
> Have dappled the downs and valleys at this time of year,
> While larks, ascending shrill, praised freedom as they flew.
> Now, through that song, a fighter-squadron's drone I hear
> From Scratchbury Camp, whose turfed and cowslip'd rampart seems
> More hill than history, ageless and oblivion-blurred.
>
> (CP, p. 279)[14]

It is a detached vision of events, as far from his passionate engagement of the First World War as he felt in years, but it is truer to himself as a poet in the early forties than the militant call to arms of 'The English Spirit'. He had told Tomlinson as early as March 1938 that he could no longer vent his passion about the coming war through poetry, but it would be more accurate to say that he did not feel sufficiently passionate about war this time round to deal with it effectively in verse. His own explanation was that he hated war too much to write about it. The subject which had initially brought him to life as a poet now defeated him.

He was not indifferent to the war; it was rather that the aspects which moved him most were mainly personal. Whereas from 1916 to 1918 he had been taken out of himself into a larger world of love and pity for his fellow-soldiers, so that he had daily and willingly sacrificed self-interest to a greater cause, this later war drove him deeper into himself and his own concerns, a fact he freely admitted in an unpublished poem of the period:

> ... I sometimes felt before this war broke out,
> That when it came I'd leave all else behind,
> Setting myself alight to move about
> In ardent acts, with reawakened mind.
> Yet here I ride, a landscape figure still,
> No hint of new emergence in my eyes:
> Throughout this war I've done what looks like nil;
> And no one, to my knowledge, has expressed surprise ...[15]

Where he had once rushed to enlist in the army even before war was declared, he now contemplated the situation from the sidelines. There was nothing to prevent him volunteering for meaningful war-work, such as the Home Guard. His contemporary Geoffrey Keynes, who had also served with honour in the First World War, instantly volunteered for the Second and became a consultant surgeon to the RAF. And younger friends, such as Glen Byam Shaw, Rex Whistler and his brother Laurence, all enlisted at the first opportunity. Even his nephew Hamo, whom he could still remember playing on the lawn at Weirleigh as a small child, deferred his place at Merton College, Oxford, to serve his country.

Sassoon was immensely proud of their willingness and highly critical of those he suspected of evading their responsibilities, unaware, it seems, of any irony in his own uncommitted position. 'I feel like a semi-submerged barge on a derelict canal,' he told Keynes, after congratulating him on his RAF appointment. 'No occupants except a few rats – or *ghosts* of rats – from the last great war –'[16] There were many days when he wished 'that the July 1918 bullet had finished me'.[17]

Nevertheless, apart from a half-hearted offer (through Marsh) of his services as a writer and the donation of two manuscripts illustrated by him to Red Cross sales in July 1940 and October 1942, he made no real effort to become involved.[18] He found Hester's avid following of the news just one more cause of irritation with her. 'I sometimes feel that I am living in a world which is as unreal to me as the Bronze Age,' he wrote to Blunden, whose asthma and pacifism kept him safely at Oxford. 'And Hester's mind is one hundred per cent BBC bulletins. I jog her imagination to reality occasionally; but she accepts the whole thing, and is really interested in it – not *bored* as I am!'[19]

Only when personal concerns were at stake did he take any interest in events. When Hamo, for example, who had joined his older brother Leo in the North African Campaign, narrowly escaped with his life from a burning tank, Sassoon was moved to write to Angela Baddeley: 'I sometimes feel that if it wasn't for George I should have my face lifted and enlist as a private.' And when Angela's husband Glen was posted to India, he felt equally strongly.

He was also concerned about Hitler's treatment of the Jews, again partly for personal reasons. The fact that he himself was on the Nazis' list of banned books made him more conscious of his own Jewishness and even readier to identify and sympathize. And a visit from one of T.E. Lawrence's friends, L.B. Namier, a naturalized Russian Jew who was second in command of the Zionist Federation, confirmed his belief that the Nazis' ethnic cleansing programme was 'unspeakable cold devil's work' and Hitler a 'blind fanatic and egomaniac'.[20] One of the few aspects of the war which he felt compelled to write about in verse was Belsen: 'Something has happened to the human soul / Which needs long decontamination by time', he would warn in his angriest poem of the period.[21] 'I suppose we are all callosified spiritually by the war and its procession of brutalities,' he wrote to de la Mare, confessing that he himself would enjoy seeing a few Nazis 'being told where they got off'.[22] He certainly did not feel 'genuinely humane' about the German people, though he had made good friends of the Hirths in Bavaria and still cared about them.[23] For the first time since his anti-war protest of 1917, Sassoon and his mother were united in their hatred of the Germans – 'and I *did* chase 80 Germans out of a trench by myself, didn't I?' he reminds her.[24] By April 1940 he is writing to her in the Old Testament prophet role that was growing on him with the years: 'I say that Hitler is the representative of the Evil One, and this war the final struggle between Light and Darkness.'[25]

His overwhelming feeling, however, was one of remoteness from the war, like 'a spider in his web among the weeds – at the foot of the Tower of Babel', or 'a leaning eighteenth-century gravestone in a village churchyard', fanciful conceits which nevertheless convey his strong sense of isolation.[26] Whole army camps would be built in his grounds and his house would be filled with army officers and their staff several times during the course of the war, but Heytesbury was physically distant from the main centres of action. The only real reminders of it would be the sound of planes overhead on their way to Bristol and a single, stray bomb exploding in his garden. Had he been exiled from Heytesbury as he feared, he told Blunden, he would probably have written more about the war.[27] As it was he never acquired the necessary 'mental contrast'.[28]

'All I want to do is to forget,' he wrote in his diary as 1939 turned into 1940, '– and have no arc-lights of practical-mindedness turned on to my loathing of this Second Great War, by which I am being reduced to an impotent absurdity.' His position was evidently deliberately taken and stemmed mainly from what he saw as 'a more and more intimate and personal' outlook on the world, but what looks very like self-absorption to an outsider.[29]

Looking back to the First World War, what surprised him was that he had 'had the temerity to express any opinions at all about a phenomenon which is, apparently, as uncontrollable as an earthquake'.[30] He now viewed his past self as a 'booby-trapped idealist', his present attitude to war being quite different: 'The only effective answer that a poet can make to barbarism is poetry, for the only answer to death is the life of the spirit.'[31] So that in positive moods he believed that 'we philosophers contribute something ... from our back seats'.

Such moods were rare, however, and in his more frequent negative ones he felt 'very obsolete and disregarded'.[32] 'No one has asked me to write a word about this war, or shown any awareness of my existence', he complained to a friend; '– I am merely bracketed with Rupert Brooke by the Fleet Street scribblers!'[33] If true, and there is evidence which contradicts it, the newspapers' indifference may help to explain why he failed to write more war poems, which may in turn be the reason why he was not regarded as a significant poet in the Second World War.[34] It was a horse and cart situation.

There were other pressures to explain his difficulty in writing poetry. His struggle with Hester, though temporarily in abeyance, had left him too emotionally drained for verse. 'My mental life is in ruins,' he wrote in his diary. 'I feel self-destructive and defeated.' Equally significant was his fear of the critics. Their reaction to *Vigils* in 1934 continued to discourage him. Unable to alter a technique they clearly considered out of date, he anticipated further savaging at their hands for any subsequent volumes. It was one thing to let Keynes produce a private collection of thirty-three poems, *Rhymed Ruminations*, in 1939 just two months before the war, since private editions were rarely reviewed.[35] But it was with great reluctance that he allowed Faber to publish a trade edition in October 1940, with nine poems added to make it 'a little less pamphlet-like'.[36] His motive was almost certainly money, about which he was worrying again.

Of the poems added to the trade edition, only two ('The English Spirit' and 'Silent Service') directly concern war, though the majority were written after its outbreak. The remaining seven are a similar mix to the main body of the collection, meditations on elemental human experience such as a young child at his window watching his father return home:

> Remember this, when childhood's far away;
> The sunlight of a showery first spring day;
> You from your house-top window laughing down,
> And I, returned with whip-cracks from a ride,
> On the great lawn below you, playing the clown.
> Time blots our gladness out. Let this with love abide ...
> ('The Child at the Window', CP, p. 252)[37]

The message here is simple and the appeal universal, even if the experience is particular, an effect achieved in a number of other poems in *Rhymed Ruminations*. Whether Sassoon is writing, as here, about his son,[38] his house and its history,[39] the surrounding countryside,[40] books he is reading,[41] or more abstract but equally shared human experiences, such as the ageing process,[42] his aim is to appeal to the ordinary reader through everyday events:

> A Local Train of Thought
> Alone, in silence, at a certain time of night,
> Listening, and looking up from what I'm trying to write,
> I hear a local train along the Valley. And 'There
> Goes the one-fifty', think I to myself; aware
> That somehow its habitual travelling comforts me,
> Making my world seem safer, homelier, sure to be
> The same tomorrow; and the same, one hopes, next year.
> 'There's peacetime in that train.' One hears it disappear
> With needless warning whistle and rail-resounding wheels.
> 'That train's quite like an old familiar friend,' one feels.
> (CP, p. 240)[43]

Gathorne-Hardy, who wrote to thank him for his 'enchanting little book of poems', believed that, just as verse had taught Sassoon to write prose, so his 'prose experience' had 'added' to his verse: 'Humour, irony, "commonplace", and tenderness are more completely fused and digested into these poems than in anything you have produced before.'[44] The collection held together, he argued, as 'a sort of Chinese picture – made with hints of your life'.[45] Sassoon, who himself stressed the need to read *Rhymed Ruminations* as a sequence, was deeply grateful for his friend's insight: 'I feel more and more', he replied, 'that what matters in literature is humanity.'[46]

What he also wanted, as he had defiantly stressed in his public lecture *On Poetry* to the University of Bristol in March 1939, was 'direct utterance'.[47] (The lecture, he told his mother, was 'merely a restatement of the well-known fact that poets are born – not made!)[48] In *The Weald*, which directly followed both his lecture and the publication of *Rhymed Ruminations*, he repeated the point that abstractions were 'uncongenial to his mind'.[49] He preferred poetry he could 'visualize and feel'.[50] As far as he was concerned, and as he had emphasized in his lecture, 'Intellect ... wasn't there when the thing [i.e., poetry] was being done.'[51]

A not-so-veiled attack on Modernism, it was an unpopular view to hold, as Sassoon well knew. 'My technique grows more unfashionable and obsolete every day', he wrote to de la Mare, 'and groans of disparagement from the experts will be my fate.'[52] So that he was not surprised when the reviews of *Rhymed Ruminations* proved no better than those of *Vigils*. Those that were not downright dismissive seemed to him patronizing.[53] Ignoring fairly positive praise of his 'quietened cadences' in the *Times Literary Supplement*,[54] he complained to Blunden that most of the reviewers appeared to regard him as 'a feeble haunter of the past', a 'man who lacked all intellectual grip on life'.[55] (They were 'envious' of his success, he told his mother.)[56] Even Blunden, to whom ironically *Rhymed Ruminations* was dedicated, was critical, finding it 'lacking in liveliness of epithet'.[57]

So that Sassoon was more than usually grateful for Keynes's praise of his poems' 'effective simplicity' and particularly appreciative of Christopher Hassall's enthusiasm: 'to be admired by a "younger poet"! I can hardly believe it,' he wrote to Keynes.[58] Bearing in mind how kind he had been to Hassall when he fell sick on a visit to Heytesbury, however, together with his support of Hassall for the A.C. Benson Poetry Medal in 1939[59] and Hassall's closeness to one of Sassoon's staunchest supporters, Eddie Marsh, it is hard not to question Hassall's impartiality.

Marsh, himself an astute critic of traditional verse, genuinely admired *Rhymed Ruminations*, but he could not resist a crack at its title. 'I think he rather overdoes that notion,' he wrote to Hassall, 'using the word "ruminant" three times – I don't like being forced to think of him as a cow.'[60] And, having read Sassoon's unfortunate opening lines to the collection – 'I am that man who with a luminous look / Sits up at night to write a ruminant book' – Marsh gleefully responded, with Edward Lear's absurd 'Dong' evidently in mind, 'I am the man who with a luminous nose, / Sits up at night to write voluminous prose.'[61]

But his jokes did not extend to *Rhymed Ruminations*' technique. Though Sassoon had defined poetry as 'simplified emotional experience' in his poetry lecture, he had been careful to stress the need for 'clarified construction and technical control' too: 'A man may be born a poet, but he has to make himself an artist as well. He must master the instrument.'[62] Marsh, whose classical background made him particularly sensitive to metre, greatly admired Sassoon's handling of it in *Rhymed Ruminations*. 'His mastery of the Alexandrine is astonishing,' he wrote to Hassall, quoting as proof a line from the poem he thought 'best in the book', 'In Heytesbury Wood': 'Walking, some low-lit evening in the whispering wood'.[63]

Sassoon, who continued to protest that he found the whole poetic process 'mysterious', was convinced that the 'intensity of such lines was achieved by 'an unconsciously artful alliteration and by a texture of vowels and consonants which somehow suggests control'.[64] He had long been aware that his poetry contained very little metaphor compared with that of such Modernists as Eliot (though Marsh picked out the 'neat-patterned hornet-gang' as a wonderful phrase for aeroplanes in formation, in 'Thoughts in 1932').

It was not Sassoon's lack of metaphor, however, which gave his critics ammunition in *Rhymed Ruminations*, but his diction. Increasingly he inclined towards what he called 'a sort of homespun idiom' in his verse. And though he described it fondly in terms of 'a pipe-smoker listening to someone playing an old violin in a panelled room', he also realized that the 'experts' might find it 'otiose'.[65] It is certainly very different from the direct diction of earlier poems, like 'The General'.

It was not simply the fact that he invented words, or dug up old ones which irritated the critics. Most of them would have been brought up on Hopkins and his daring compounds and many would already be familiar with the brilliant coinages of another important Modernist, Dylan Thomas. It was more that Sassoon, though an admirer of both these poets,[66] had chosen less fashionable versifiers as his models, Hardy chief among them.[67] Since 1940 was the centenary of Hardy's birth, he had been asked to write several articles on him and one of these involved a rereading of *The Dynasts*, an epic poem he argued we should all study in wartime.[68] While his perusal of Hardy's *Satires of Circumstance* in the First World War had been a beneficial influence on his poetry, however, *The Dynasts* had the reverse effect, particularly on his vocabulary. Coinages like 'contentful' and 'vintagement' join archaisms such as 'chattels', 'whence', 'unholpen' and 'symposiarch' to create a wooden, artificial feeling which his frequent alliteration does nothing to lessen. Poems which otherwise flow quite naturally, like 'Blunden's Beech', for instance, are marred by such intrusive practices:

> I named it Blunden's Beech; and no one knew
> That this – of local beeches – was the best.
> Remembering lines by Clare, I'd sometimes rest
> Contentful on the cushioned moss that grew
> Between its roots. Finches, a flitting crew,
> Chirped their concerns. Wiltshire, from east to west
> Contained my tree. And Edmund never guessed
> How he was there with me till dusk and dew.
>
> Thus, fancy-free from ownership and claim,
> The mind can make its legends live and sing
> And grow to be the genius of some place.
> And thus, where sylvan shadows held a name,
> The thought of Poetry will dwell, and bring
> To summer's idyll an unheeded grace.
>
> (CP, p. 245)

'Blunden's Beech' illustrates another problem in *Rhymed Ruminations*, prolixity of a different kind. While Gathorne-Hardy admired the poem, he rightly pointed out that it would have been even better with some judicious cutting: the last six lines merely spell out what is already obvious to most readers. And the same might be said of other poems in the book, including 'The Child at the Window'. So that while there are many memorable lines, even entire stanzas in *Rhymed Ruminations*, it contains few completely successful poems and the collection as a whole lacks the concentrated vigour of Sassoon's best verse. His resigned, at times 'prosy' tone suggests that the most appropriate epigraph for it might be 'All Passion Spent', the clearest possible indication of how unsatisfactory his relationship with Hester had become. Significantly he included none of his work after 1935 in *Poems Newly Selected*, published the same year as *Rhymed Ruminations*.[69]

It would be another eleven years before any new volume of poems appeared, and then only in a private edition. Instead he turned to prose, concentrating on it throughout the war. By February 1940, he had written 30,000 words of *The Weald* and was frankly delighted when Hester felt obliged to take George to her mother's that same month because of German measles among the evacuees. One of Sassoon's main problems with his marriage remained his inability to work with his wife in the house. If he had made any effort to accommodate her earlier on, he had now given up. By the time she returned in mid-March, far from having missed her, he could only rejoice in the 'quiet time' without her. His temporary sense of freedom had made him more determined than ever to be independent of her and in early April, with the news of Glen's posting to Yorkshire with the Royal Scots Regiment, he insisted on going to London alone to wish him goodbye. A small rebellion, it nevertheless marked the beginning of the end of their marriage.

By this point the war was entering a more threatening phase. In May 1940, when Chamberlain resigned and the more belligerent Churchill took charge of a coalition government, British troops landed in Norway but were forced to withdraw. By the end of May they had to begin their humiliating retreat from Dunkirk. The Germans had overrun the Low Countries and by mid-June had also invaded France. That same month Italy joined Germany in the fight. Only the Battle of Britain, a fierce struggle for air superiority over the Channel in July, August and September, saved Britain itself from invasion. In Churchill's famous words: 'Never in the field of human conflict was so much owed by so many to so few.'

The situation seemed to Sassoon 'too abysmal' for words, an effect reinforced by the loss of several friends in 1940.[70] The death of his old hunting companion Norman Loder coincided somewhat eerily with his attempt to recreate the period of their greatest intimacy, his six-month stay with Loder in Warwickshire during the winter of 1913-14. Though he would in any case have wanted to describe his time there, Loder's premature death seems to have added both pathos and affection to his account of him in *The Weald*. With hindsight, it reads like the obituary it was:

> He was one of those people whose strength is in their consistent simplicity and directness, and who send out natural wisdom through their mental limitations and avoidance of nimble ideas. Such characters cannot be epitomized in phrases. They are positive in their qualities and actions, getting things done instead of stopping to ask why they are doing them. He was kind, decent, and thorough, never aiming at anything beyond plain common-sense and practical ability. Tolerant and reliable, he taught me to associate easily with a varied assortment of human types. Everything that I learnt from his example was to my lasting advantage, and the amount he contributed to the Sherstonian side of my personality was incalculable.[71]

When he wrote these words, Sassoon had not seen Loder for almost twenty years and he felt sadder about the death of Ottoline, for instance, who had died in 1938.[72] But the death of a more recent friend, Sir Henry Head, seemed the greatest loss of the period. Head and his devoted wife, Ruth, who had died in 1939, had been like parents to him during his many crises with Stephen, and among the chief rejoicers when he married Hester. Theoretically Head's death was a merciful release both from the Parkinson's Disease that had rendered him completely helpless by 1940, and the misery of a life without Ruth. But his death for Sassoon meant one more blow at a deeply unhappy time. His general feeling of waste and destruction was increased by another death in the summer of 1940, that of Hester's younger brother Oliver, a brilliant physicist who had died while carrying out dangerous experiments for the Government.

During the heroisms of the Dunkirk evacuations in May and June, Sassoon had believed that 'the spirit of man is *not* going to be conquered by the abominable' and that the Nazis had 'underestimated the forces that had been built up against them', sentiments he could easily have repeated during the Battle of Britain.[73] But by the end of 1940 he had begun to despair of the situation. He longed for T.E. Lawrence to return from the dead to 'illuminate the nocturnal landscape' for him.[74] No one else seemed capable of doing so.

Dr Dunn, his former guide in military matters, had this time let him down. Dunn had visited Heytesbury that very summer, but when Sassoon wrote to him for 'elucidations' about the war later in the year, there was no response.[75] This was hardly surprising since Dunn, like Blunden, had changed roles with Sassoon and was now a pacifist, an irony completely lost on Sassoon, who merely felt abandoned. He could not agree with them that England was the real villain of the piece. He was in any case finding Dunn, now nearing his seventies, increasingly 'crotchety', and his attempts to make England responsible for the Second World War seemed to Sassoon 'a distortion of reasonableness'.[76] Though he had himself been extremely critical of Churchill's 'war-mongering' during the mid-thirties, he now entirely disagreed with Dunn's and Blunden's charge that the Prime Minister was playing into Hitler's hands on almost every occasion. In Dunn's case, at least, the profound difference of opinion between them seems gradually to have eroded their friendship.

Blunden he found harder to dismiss. Sensitive, passionate and persuasive, he was a far subtler opponent than the blunt Scotsman. To begin with, Sassoon had found it 'pleasant to hear someone talking *tolerantly* about Germany' and he agreed with Blunden to the extent that he believed war meant a world 'gone mad'.[77] But when he thought of the 'essential wickedness of the Nazi Party machine' and their determination to 'impose their will on the rest of Europe by brute force', he simply could not agree with Blunden's pacifist views.

On the other hand he did not want to lose an old and trusted friend, and one of his last explicit letters on the subject shows how anxious he was to preserve peace between them, by moving the debate to common ground: 'If only the Germans would cultivate Cricket instead of frontier expansion! We might then establish a workable human relationship.'[78] He and Blunden had already agreed that cricket and poetry were the two best things in life. The threat to both in late 1940 was one more factor in his growing unhappiness.

Not all the news was gloomy. The Italians had failed in their attempt to invade Greece, the Royal Air Force had knocked out three Italian battleships at Taranto in November and General Wavell had chased them out of Egypt, driving them 500 miles back to Benghazi in December. But 1941 brought more reverses as British troops were expelled from Greece and Crete and the Axis powers took over the whole of the Balkan peninsula, extracting a promise of neutrality from Turkey in consequence. The Royal Navy, meanwhile, was being severely challenged both in the Mediterranean and the Atlantic.

Sassoon in his Heytesbury retreat ignored the news as best he could, preferring to tell Blunden and other friends in lengthy letters of his progress (or lack of) on *The Weald*. He was trying to write chapters six to nine, covering his first formal visit to Gosse (with his mother), his musical education with Helen Wirgman and the writing of his first successful work, *The Daffodil Murderer*, which led to his introduction into the London literary scene through Gosse and Marsh. He was also rewriting Chapter Two, an attempt to make his development as a poet in his early twenties sound interesting.

As summer approached he abandoned his writing, as usual, and started to organize local cricket matches, another attempt to defy the realities of war. When he did think about the war he now felt vaguely optimistic, though there was little outward justification for it in the first five months of 1941.

The first real sign of hope came in June, when Germany attacked

Russia and the Russians entered the fighting on Britain's side; the second in December, when Japan blew up American warships at Pearl Harbor and – 'as might have been expected', according to Sassoon[79] – the Americans likewise joined the Allies. This entry of two of the world's greatest powers into the war was an important turning point. It also transformed what had been an essentially European war into a global conflict.

As public morale in Britain rose, however, Sassoon sank deeper into despair over his private troubles. Ten years later he could still vividly recall what he 'went through' with Hester in April 1941, writing to Keynes: 'All the sensitive tissues of one's writing are destroyed unless one can do it in peace.'[80] And with Hester he found no peace: 'Behind that "gentleness" there is cast-iron selfishness and lack of consideration for others.'[81] It was almost certainly how Hester saw his own behaviour by mid-1941.

The war, which had initially delayed open conflict between them, now exerted extra pressures on their crumbling relationship. By this stage every able-bodied man and woman was needed to help with the war effort and life at Heytesbury was correspondingly affected. As first the younger male staff, then the female and finally all the servants left, with only an occasional cook or charlady to help out, the situation between Sassoon and Hester deteriorated badly. The smooth running of the house by numerous servants, their very presence even, had to some extent cushioned the friction: without them things rapidly fell apart. Hester found herself, for the first time in her privileged life, having to do the housework, as well as look after George when his nanny left. Already bored by a severe reduction in her social life as a result of the war, she took her frustrations out on Sassoon – or so it seemed to him.

To begin with he simply stayed in bed, the quietest place he could find, spending six or seven hours a day there at his writing. Blunden's new love, Claire Poynting, who visited Heytesbury for the first time in the summer of 1941, remembered that Sassoon did not appear till lunchtime, spent the afternoon out riding alone, and retired to his room at night, refusing (as Claire put it) to 'go to bed with Hester'.[82]

Blunden's decision to abandon his increasingly unhappy relationship with his wife Sylva in favour of Claire in itself encouraged Sassoon to take a stand against Hester, but his greatest incentive was his work. Once he had decided that Hester prevented him from writing, their marriage was effectively over. His dread of confrontation led him first to try evasive tactics, and he began sending her away to stay with her family and friends as much as possible. He still could not concentrate, however, and spent most of 1941 struggling in vain to complete *The Weald*. He also tried going away himself, paying a visit in June to Merton College, where Blunden had arranged for him to talk on Beerbohm's prose. Then, in October, with the news of a fresh posting for Glen and, therefore, a short leave, he hurried to London to see him again, taking the opportunity to refresh his memory with a visit to his old flat in Raymond Buildings. On the point of describing the circumstances of his stay there in summer 1914, he was disturbed to find that it alone, of the many apartments at Gray's Inn, had been completely destroyed, like the leisured life it represented.

He also tried to distract himself with visitors to Heytesbury. Apart from Blunden and Claire, Hamo came from nearby Warminster Camp, and two friends from the twenties, Will Rothenstein, who wanted to draw him again, and Lord Berners.[83] By the time of Berners's stay in November 1941 music and art were among the few consolations left to Sassoon, apart from literature, and he enjoyed Berners's piano playing as much as the three large lobsters and magnum of champagne he brought with him. 'Making one's own music' rather than 'switching on the wireless' seemed more important than ever with the barbarians at the gate.[84] And with a house full of fine pictures, his own precious collection now supplemented by his solicitor Lousada's valuable paintings, which he had placed at Heytesbury for safe-keeping, he drew daily comfort from art. On the same principle that it was better to make your own, he also turned to drawing more seriously, as his several attractively illustrated Red Cross manuscripts show. And a chance meeting with the painter Edward Seago, a camouflage officer with the Southern Command, would lead to the purchase of several more pictures by Seago's teacher (and Hamo Thornycroft's old friend) Sir Arnesby Brown, as well as one by Seago himself.[85]

None of these diversions were fully effective, though he did manage to start work on his book again by December 1941. (Stimulated by the recent visit to Raymond Buildings, he broke the largely chronological sequence of composition and fast-forwarded to chapters thirteen and fourteen to describe his time at Gray's Inn, before returning to take up his story again at Chapter Ten with his visit to the Midlands.) The strain started to show itself physically. He suffered increasingly bad indigestion, not the result of Hester's inexperienced cooking, as he liked to claim, but almost certainly a reaction to the strains in their relationship and the beginning of the duodenal ulcer which would take him into hospital in 1948. He also had several bad bouts of lumbago and flu and began to feel old. He had always looked – and acted – far younger than his years; now, suddenly, he felt much older. Walking past fit young soldiers camped in Heytesbury's grounds and talking to a forty-year-old colonel about the First World War made him particularly conscious of his years, though he was still only fifty-five. It was not so much his physical infirmities as his loss of hope which made him feel that 'the fire [was] burning low'.[86]

His difficulties in writing lay at the core of the problem and the blame for this he placed firmly on Hester. To write well, he believed, he needed to be on his own, a view reflected by another novelist, Martin Amis, nearly sixty years later: 'The definition of a writer', Amis told an interviewer, 'is he or she who is happiest when alone: so much of one's character, effort and emotional energy goes into writing that the life stuff, the living, gets scrimped. If you're a writer, you're not going to be brilliant at managing your life; because that's not where you really breathe.' [87] But as another writer, Paul Theroux, asked: 'Does writing take the place of commitment?'[88] Sassoon certainly showed no sign of wanting to continue his commitment to Hester by 1941 and there is some evidence to suggest that he was using his writing as an excuse.

George was a different matter. After seven years of marriage he had replaced Hester as Sassoon's main emotional support. 'I sometimes think that nature designed me not for a successful literary man, but for a nanny pushing a pram,' he told a friend.[89] 'George has been my salvation from his earliest childhood, through the relief he gave by enabling me to escape into his childish world ...'

While George was too young to be sent to boarding school, and in the absence of anyone else to look after him, Sassoon still needed Hester, but he found the situation extremely unpleasant, as his description of Heytesbury's daily routine in 1942 shows. Writing to Keynes in September that year he complained bitterly about Hester, though he continued to do little to help himself. Her inability to control George in the mornings, he told Keynes indignantly, interrupted his peaceful reading in bed: 'Then a pandemonium lunch with Hester and George. Then shave and pull my boots on and hack ride till 5.30. Then make myself some tea; and by 6.15 G[eorge] is having his bath just outside my door, with frequent altercations, and comes in to consume the cup of cocoa which I prepare for him. I then sift wheat till dinner, and continue the process till 1 a.m., when I sometimes write a letter, as now.'[90]

The gulf between husband and wife emerges starkly from this description and though the situation improved slightly when George started attending the local school at the end of September, by that time the marriage was past saving. It lurched on, as far as Sassoon was concerned, for the sake of convenience only.

The war, too, dragged on, but with more to hope for. Sassoon reflected the opinion of most British civilians when he told Tomlinson that, however 'bedevilled' the times, he believed that 'light would prevail'.[91] There were some reverses for the Allies in 1942, such as the Japanese conquest of the Philippines and the new German Commander Rommel's capture of Tobruk in North Africa, but as the British and Americans joined forces to save Europe, the victories began to outweigh the defeats. And when General Montgomery routed Rommel's Afrika Korps at Alamein in late October and early November, Churchill declared in another of his memorable speeches that the real turning point of the war had been reached: 'Up to Alamein we survived. After Alamein we conquered.'

Since two of Sassoon's nephews, Hamo and Leo, were with the Royal Tank Regiment in North Africa and Glen was on his way to Burma by 1942, Sassoon was more involved with the war this year than at any other stage, though only the parts that concerned his nearest and dearest. Whereas he found it hard to imagine conditions in Russia, dramatic as the

Germans' attempts to defeat the Red Army were, he could only too vividly envisage the dangers faced by Glen and Hamo. As in the First World War he needed to be imaginatively engaged for war to become real to him. 'I have been much relieved to hear ... that my beloved nephew Hamo is in hospital with [only] slight burns,' he wrote to Cockerell in June 1942. 'His Tank battalion had been in the thick of the Libyan battle, and I have had three weeks of acute anxiety.'[92] A temporary lull in the Far East gave him a short respite as far as Glen was concerned.

Apart from his personal involvement in these two theatres of war, however, his greatest concern in 1942 was the completion of *The Weald*, which would be dedicated to Glen as a 'final remembrance' of their friendship.[93]

21

'The Weald of Youth,
a Remembered Word'

The book is an outline of the frustrations and delayed development of my latent abilities. The physical and emotional richness of my youth never found expression till February 1914.

(Sassoon's notes on *The Weald of Youth*)[1]

Promised to Faber for mid-1941, *The Weald of Youth* was not completed until April 1942. From conception to birth it had taken three years to write. Faber, desperate to publish, got page proofs to Sassoon in less than a month. Further delays followed, however, when Sassoon forwarded them to his 'prince of proof-readers', Beerbohm, so 'charmingly forgetful of time'.[2] It was October before *The Weald* was finally published.[3]

Sassoon predictably blamed Hester for the delay and the domestic responsibilities she had at last insisted he share. He found himself for the first time in his life having to lay the table, wash dishes, fetch food from the kitchen, make fires, scrub baths and even clean out lavatories. It was only by sending Hester and George away again in March 1942 and living on snacks that he had managed to meet his second deadline of April. His dreary living conditions at Heytesbury as he finished *The Weald* help to account for the heavily nostalgic tone of the final section, which includes the young Sassoon's excited, sole possession of his freshly decorated London flat and the solicitous care of his housekeeper, Mrs Fretter, who seems, in this context, to be everything Hester is not:

In those first days of my London summer I used to awake with a sense of freedom and exhilaration. It was the right time of year for feeling like that, and my fresh start in new surroundings seemed much the same as the outset of a holiday. I did not ask myself what I had done to deserve a holiday or what I was having a holiday from! All I knew was that the sunshine looked auspicious and the trees jubilantly green ...

I liked Mrs Fretter, who was young and pleasant-faced and did things in a shy unobtrusive way; I liked the aroma of frying bacon and well-made coffee; I liked the company of my own mind and the certainty I couldn't be interfered with. So altogether there was every reason for me to be singing while I was having a cold bath.[4]

Such passages, harking lovingly back to a leisured, pre-war England, held an obvious appeal for many readers in wartime conditions and won praise from public and critics alike. Howard Spring in the *Daily Mail* was followed by other influential reviewers, such as Blunden in the *Spectator*, Desmond MacCarthy in the *New Statesman* and an anonymous writer in the *Times Literary Supplement*.[5] Most of the reviews were 'first-rate', according to Sassoon, only a few critics, like Peter Quennell in the *Observer*, demurring.[6] An entertaining reaction came in a private letter from H.G. Wells, who managed to highlight the social difference in their backgrounds to amusing effect:

> 13, Hanover Terrace, Regent's Park, N.W.1
> Telephone, Paddington 6204
>
> Dear Siegfried,
>   *The Weald of Youth* is beautifully, finely done, and I think it will be a most valuable documentation of our age. There were you up there, free to get every drop of juice out of existence, and at the same time I was having the most ferocious struggle to have my way with life and escape frustration and falsification by the very system that floated you in your unquestioned freedom. With the comical result that here am I in old Gosse's house reading about your first encounter with Eddie Marsh – who warned Emerald Cunard that I was a very dangerous man, and so saved Nancy from my clutches. My love to the wife and son. Bless you.
>   Yours ever,
>   H.G. Wells [7]

The most gratifying praise of all for *The Weald* was from a young serviceman, later to become a literary figure in his own right, Martyn Goff. Writing from Algeria, where he was serving with the North West African Coastal Defence, Goff inadvertently pinpointed the qualities Sassoon aimed at in his prose, with a lyricism which made Sassoon suspect that he was 'one of the "younger poets" ':

> Lying in my tent, in the cool of the North African evening, all silent but for the locusts buzzing in the giant trees, I started to read your book ... I take this liberty of writing to thank you for the exquisite hours I have spent in reading and re-reading your delightful rambling recollections. For these hours I forgot the heat, the flies, the food, and the war.[8]

'Rather nice, isn't it?' Sassoon asked Keynes, '– and makes me feel that the toil was worthwhile just for that one young man in Africa.'[9] He would have been even more delighted to hear Goff's later comment, that *The Weald* was his greatest comfort in the war, transporting him mentally back to England at a time of some need. Of all the many books he read during his RAF service, Sassoon was the only author to whom he wrote.[10] It was clearly a case of the right book at the right time: the first edition of *The*

Weald sold out within a few months and a reprint was talked of before the end of the year.[11]

Delighted as he was by its reception, so different from that of his recent poetry collections, Sassoon had reservations about *The Weald*. He agreed with Tomlinson's tactful but honest opinion that it was 'a perilous sort of performance', in danger of being thought sentimental.[12] He could have written a 'bad-tempered' book about the years 1908 to 1914, Sassoon replied, but deliberately chose not to.[13] The result is undeniably anodyne, or as he himself put it, 'a syllabub of amiabilities from start to finish'.[14] 'Small beer' was another phrase he used to Marsh (and which Marsh's biographer, Christopher Hassall, may later have borrowed for his own book of reminiscences, *Ambrosia and Small Beer*).[15]

'Writing a book about "nothing much happening thirty years ago" ' was 'not easy', according to Sassoon, and by the end he had taken to calling it 'The Weald of Spoof'.[16] Though he thought it became 'quite lively' towards the finish, as the First World War loomed, he admitted that some chapters were 'all padding'.[17] Chapter Three, for instance, seemed to him little more than a celebration of the mellow Queen Anne houses and comfortingly irregular golf courses of the Kent of his youth, not 'amount[ing] to much'.[18] Nevertheless he had enjoyed recalling his life at twenty-five, with all the 'rich emptiness of immaturity ... all its gaps and impetuosities and intolerance and omniscient misapprehensions' and Chapter Three remained one of his favourite parts.[19]

Other sections which he enjoyed doing, while knowing that they were open to similar criticism, were those on sport, which he found 'easier to write than the literary part'.[20] Since he had already described his interest in cricket, golf and hunting in *Fox-Hunting Man*, he risked being repetitive, as he rather coyly acknowledges in Chapter Five of *The Weald*:

> In this 'real autobiography' of mine I have hitherto done what I could to avoid the subject of fox-hunting, for the excellent reason that it has already been monopolized by a young man named George Sherston. To tell the truth, I am a little shy of trespassing on Sherston's territory. I should not like to feel that I had in any way impaired his reality in the minds of his appreciative friends, for many of whom he is, perhaps, more alive than the present writer. And to assert that he was 'only me with a lot left out' sounds off-hand and uncivil.[21]

It was, as he otherwise put it, 'a collision between fictionized reality and essayized autobiography'.[22] But he felt that no self-portrait would be complete without the sporting details. The woodcut on the title page by Reynolds Stone is of a man on horseback, not at his writing desk.

His mother also presented him with a challenge. She was still very much alive in 1942, though nearly ninety, so that he faced not only the danger of more repetition by including a character he had already described in detail as 'Aunt Evelyn' in his fiction, but also the risk of offending her. The former obstacle he handled by making Theresa Sassoon more a point of reference than a full-blown character. Not offending her or other members of his family was more difficult and he completely rewrote his account of Aunt Rachel Beer's dementia from syphilis, for example, to this end, relying heavily on Dr Dunn's medical expertise for suitable euphemisms.[23]

Marsh was another problem, since not only had his rather fussy personality to be described tactfully, but his extreme sensitivity about anything written on his beloved Rupert Brooke had to be borne in mind. It is clear that, in the event, Sassoon was not entirely frank about his mixed feelings for Brooke in *The Weald*, where he describes their meeting in Chapter Fourteen. Osbert Sitwell, who was writing his own autobiography at the same time and knew the difficulties involved, thought that 'Eddie ought to be very happy at being shown in so favourable a light.'[24]

For these and other reasons, *The Weald* is, in its author's words, 'less spontaneous' than *The Old Century* or *Fox-Hunting Man*.[25] Like all his own favourite authors Sassoon is 'at [his] best when drawing on early experience for [his] matured performances'.[26] Not only does this 'impressionable period of youth' provide him with his 'most effective and moving material', as he argues, but there is also far less to conceal.[27] What he calls his 'frustrated erotic experience', for instance, which played such an important part in the period covered by *The Weald*, can only be hinted at 'between the lines'.[28]

He may have been thinking of such evasions when he told Blunden that he did not consider *The Weald* an autobiography in the 'proper' sense, but rather 'a poet's recreation in the winter evenings'.[29] It is certainly not a frank account of his life in the way his friend Joe Ackerley's *My Father and Myself* is, for example. (But then Ackerley's detailed account of his sexual development was not published until the year after the laws on homosexuality were changed.) Nor is *The Weald* entirely accurate in other respects, though its inaccuracies are slight and usually in the interest of literary effect. Sassoon's idea of taking a flat in London in 1914, for instance, was his own, not Marsh's, as their letters show; by making the suggestion come from Marsh, he is reinforcing one of his main themes in *The Weald*, his directionless state before the First World War.

The Weald has been criticized for other limitations, its omission of any mention of the hardships experienced by the working classes between 1908 and 1914, for example. But this appears to have been a deliberate choice on Sassoon's part, to mirror the contemporary response of his younger self to his surroundings. Nevertheless, the book is, as he claims, 'on a slightly larger scale' than his first volume of autobiography.[30] Set in a wider landscape than *The Old Century*, it takes its hero further afield, to London as well as Warwickshire, and is a vivid evocation of upper-middle-class town and country life in late Edwardian, early Georgian England.

Kent is still at the book's centre, however, as its title implies, and some of the most successful descriptions stem from it, sparked by a more intimate knowledge and fierier nostalgia, the county cricket Sassoon watched as a child at Tunbridge Wells being only one of many examples. 'The players all looked so unlike each other then', he writes wistfully, 'and there was an air of *al fresco* intimacy about their exploits which lent them a fuller flavour than seems perceptible now.'[31] His re-creation of the more 'comfortably corpulent' of the cricketers with their 'impressive untrimmed moustaches which might sometimes be seen emerging from a tankard of beer' or their highly individual outfits which ranged from Baldwin of Hampshire's 'large loose trousers' to old Walter Humphries' 'pale pink flannel shirt' with its 'artfully flapping sleeves', skilfully and humorously illustrates his point.[32]

His London scenes are also highly successful, conveying, for example, the hectic gaiety of that last, glorious pre-war summer, when the Russian Ballet was a 'must' for the young man about town he aspired to be. Entering the Drury Lane theatre, his 'sense of inexperience', he tells the reader, amounted 'almost to nervousness ... as if I had arrived uninvited at an enormous but exclusive party. Borne along by the ingoing tide ... I seemed to be surrounded by large smiling ladies with bejewelled bosoms who looked like retired prima-donnas and whose ample presences were cavaliered by suave grey-haired men who might possibly be successful impresarios.'[33]

His cast list, too, is more varied than in *The Old Century*. He still includes characters from his sheltered childhood world, such as the redoubtable 'Wirgie' (brought back, almost certainly, by popular request): 'She was getting on for seventy now, and her Beethoven playing had lost some of its passionate intensity. "I'm only a worn-out spinet," she sighed, when I asked for the "Waldstein Sonata" and lifted the piano lid full up on to its peg. So I put the lid down again and persuaded her to be a harpsichord instead.'[34] But there are also a number of splendid new characters from the wider world, like the editor of the *Academy*, T.W.H. Crosland, 'a powerful but repellently pugilistic literary journalist', who was so truculent that 'even his nose looked antagonistic to the universe'.[35] The scene where the indigent Crosland treats the mystified young Sassoon to the 'largest meal I had ever eaten', then tells him that life 'ought to be a Promethean struggle with adversity and injustice', is richly comic.[36]

The 'quiet craftsmanship' of such set pieces, their 'Flaubertian' attention to each word, was a matter of pride to Sassoon and, together with what he called its 'self-restraint', seemed to him *The Weald*'s chief merit.[37] But the 'real point' of the book, as he saw it, was his account of 'the frustration and delayed development of [his] latent abilities'.[38] Opening with his first public recognition as a poet in Crosland's *Academy* magazine, *The Weald* closes with the decision which will define him in that role, his enlistment in the army. Looked at from this angle it is easy to understand why he argued that *The Old Century* and *The Weald* were 'really *one* book', with the latter serving as a 'kind of bridge' to another instalment.[39]

He was so exhausted when he finished *The Weald* in April 1942, however, that he was unable to face starting the projected third volume for another year. Instead of feeling relieved, he became very depressed, especially about relations with Hester, as a poem written the same month shows:

> How could he think to find
> That life beloved had lied –
> Its promise undesigned
> Discordant to his dream?
> (CP, p. 265)[40]

22

'A Middle Life in Armageddon' (October 1942-May 1945)

Where are you gone, happiness that came unsought?
Lost hours, immune from scrutinies of mind,
Where's now what once you brought
In exquisite entrancement undesigned?

Heart could not hold your vanishings: you belonged
Only to freedom and illusion's grace.
Now you are unrememberable and wronged.
I hide these eyes that cannot find your face.

> (Unpublished poem of
> 2 September 1943)[1]

Sassoon could not yet free himself from Hester in October 1942, the month *The Weald of Youth* was published, but he could and did try to shut out the realities of war. His favourite literature at this time is unashamedly escapist – Jane Austen, Dickens, Trollope, Scott and Stevenson. 'I can only keep going ... by reading civilised literature,' he had written to Cockerell in 1940,[2] and as the war progressed his dependency increased. Having read many of Henry James's novels, with their 'vanished world of parties in large country houses and elaborate conversations in London drawing-rooms',[3] by 1943 he was begging Keynes to send him James's *Letters*: 'The fact is', he explained, 'I long for peace and all things autumnal.'[4] For poetry he returned to an old favourite, Fitzgerald, whose world of the 1870s seemed to him 'perpetual Sunday afternoon' by comparison with wartime England.[5]

It was, of course, impossible to escape the war for long. Rationing of food and petrol made entertaining difficult so there were far fewer visitors to distract him by 1942, and what few there were were not entirely comforting. Forster was a case in point. He had overcome at least one aspect of rationing to be at Heytesbury: 'I should very much like to come for a couple of nights', he replied to Sassoon's invitation at the beginning of June, 'if you and Hester think you could face it. It, not me; and me would try to modify it by bringing with me fortified bread, powdered milk, margarine, a processed luncheon-sausage, and a balanced egg.'[6] Forster's own answer to the horrors he anticipated in 1942 was to withdraw mentally to AD 400 and study the works of the Latin poet Ausonius, a course he advised Sassoon to follow.[7]

Sassoon found Forster as 'highly cultivated ... sensible and likeable' as ever, but was irritated by his evasiveness about 'the actualities of Armageddon', a deeply ironic charge coming from the master of escapism.[8] Evidently unaware of how inconsistent it made him seem, he told Tomlinson proudly that he had 'confronted' Forster about his friends Isherwood and Auden, who appeared to be 'avoiding military service' by remaining in America.[9] A year previously he had levelled a similar charge at T.H. White, who had visited him at Heytesbury in the mid-thirties; writing to Cockerell about White's retreat to the south of Ireland, he said he could 'only assume that his nerve failed him ... It seems to me that honour comes before life in this war for the survival of the integrity of England.'[10]

A more unexpected visit from Bobby Hanmer's sister Dorothy, to whom he had been 'rather flimsily engaged' in 1916, was another unavoidable reminder of war, since she had come to Wiltshire to visit her only son in nearby barracks.[11] Now a 'placid, plump and cosy lady with grey hair, very lame' and 'hobbling slowly on two sticks', she nevertheless took Sassoon back to the first time they had met through Loder in Warwickshire, the very period he had just finished describing in *The Weald*.[12]

His next visitor, Marsh, who had been forced to leave Gray's Inn through heavy bombing, brought further reminders of war; he had just lunched with Churchill, who told him that British reinforcements had reached Alexandria. And Cockerell, paying his first visit for three years in August, was hardly more comforting, addicted as he was to daily radio bulletins and newspapers. He and Hester between them had irritated Sassoon intensely with their discussion of war news during Cockerell's earlier stay in September 1939.[13]

The only visitor in 1942 who did not remind Sassoon of the war, though he brought many memories with him, not all of them pleasant, was Stephen Tennant. Stephen had arrived unexpectedly at Heytesbury one evening three years earlier, ostensibly in response to the copy of *Rhymed Ruminations* Sassoon had politely sent him. The visit had been constrained but not impossible, Hester behaving better than Sassoon had expected and Stephen ecstatic: 'You look so young ... Oh Sieg, – wasn't it nice meeting? ... I thought you might be rather shirty and ritzy – but all our dignity collapsed and we just giggled ... I have never laughed very much since our friendship was smashed, still, perhaps now we shall meet, and have some jokes and fun.'[14] Since then, as Sassoon's relationship with Hester deteriorated, he had actually invited Stephen to 'call' on him, an indication of how hollow their marriage had become.[15] When Stephen did eventually materialize, again unannounced, in September 1942, Sassoon was out walking with George, and Hester felt obliged to entertain him for two and a half hours. His charm undiminished, in spite of now looking like an overweight chorus boy,[16] he managed to make her feel quite sympathetic towards him. Full of 'complaints and self-pityings' about Sassoon's 'treatment' of him, according to Sassoon, he threatened to 'destroy everything [he] had built up' at Heytesbury.[17] Sassoon's reaction to Stephen sounds very similar to the accusations he was levelling at Hester by the end of 1942: 'I think his egotism and inconsiderateness have made him slightly crazy,' he wrote to Keynes shortly after this visit. 'His point of view of things doesn't fit in with normality – and other people. He complains about my heartless treatment of him. (A heart was the only thing I couldn't give him.)'[18] Hester herself seems to have identified with Stephen, urging her husband to 'be kind to him', a volte-face Sassoon found extraordinary: 'All *I* want', he told Keynes revealingly, 'is a quiet life.'[19]

It was hardly a soothing visit. Only George and his dog, Sheltie, could be guaranteed to comfort Sassoon. His old Dandie Dinmont seemed to him one of the few 'decent things' left to him by the middle of the war, as he explains in 'Man and Dog':

> ... What share we most – we two together?
> Smells, and awareness of the weather.
> What is it makes us more than dust?
> My trust in him; in me his trust.
>
> (CP, p. 268)

So that he was very sad indeed when Sheltie had to be put to sleep at the beginning of June 1942. A wedding present from Rosamond Lehmann, his end was symbolic.

'I still miss [Sheltie], and can't bear to look at his photograph,' Sassoon wrote to Hamo at the end of 1942.[20] He knew that he should have been feeling more cheerful: Montgomery's historic victory at Alamein had given heart to many. But Sassoon was still worried about Glen: by October 1942 he was undergoing jungle training in India to prepare him for Burma, which had been invaded by the Japanese in 1941. Sassoon was also anxious about the planned 'Second Front' in Europe; though he could see the need for it, he dreaded the 'loss of good men' it would cause, friends like Rex Whistler, who had been visiting Heytesbury since the end of 1941 from the nearby Welsh Guards camp.[21] 'What I really wanted to ask you', he wrote to de la Mare in March 1943, 'is do you ever feel like *stopping bothering about anything*? – even the future of the Human Race?'[22]

With Glen en route for Burma, however, 'stopping bothering' was not a choice, and he was devastated to hear in early April 1943 the news he had been dreading, that Glen had been seriously wounded.[23] (Robert Graves's son, David, was killed in the same campaign.) Only when it became certain that Glen would recover could Sassoon join in the general feeling of hope in mid-1943, that it would be only a matter of time before the Axis powers were defeated.

The complete rout of German and Italian troops in North Africa by May that year opened up Italy and the Balkans to the Allies. Italy was invaded in July, Mussolini deposed and the Italians forced to help fight the Germans by September. (Rome would fall to the Allies in June 1944, Florence two months later.) The situation in the Balkans was equally cheering and by August 1943 even Sassoon felt more 'hopeful' as the occupied countries there began to revolt against their oppressors. Meanwhile the British and Americans had started their round-the-clock 'thousand-bomber' raids on German cities, a relentless attack on industrial centres and communications. As Sassoon rightly suspected, the Nazi leaders were by this point 'in extremis', though not quite ready to 'remove' Hitler as he predicted they would.[24]

It was a buoyant and confident Sassoon, therefore, who met Field Marshal Sir Archibald Wavell on 30 June 1943 at the house of one of the few rich Sassoon relatives he would know personally, Sir Philip Sassoon's sister, Lady Sybil Cholmondeley. In 1913, Sybil Sassoon had married the 5th Marquess of Cholmondeley, to whom she brought a large dowry. It was she who had suggested this first meeting to Sassoon: 'It was always a mystery to me', she wrote to him on 2 August 1942, 'why Philip and you and I never got together – I can't help feeling that you and he *would* have been very complementary – would have got on well, but *you* never gave us a chance! Now we are likely ... to meet but such an essential vital lambent spoke of the triangle has gone.'[25]

Since Wavell's war, as the leader of the early North African Campaign, then Commander-in-Chief of India, concerned the two areas of any real interest to Sassoon, he was delighted to be introduced to the great general. But their talk was more of poetry than fighting. Wavell had specifically asked to meet Sassoon, whose work he admired, and was anxious to discuss his anthology of war poetry due out in the autumn, *Other Men's Flowers*. Sassoon was more than ready to listen and advise, in spite of his objections to being known as a war poet: he was too flattered to do otherwise.

Somewhat overawed by his 'charming and swell cousin' and her illustrious guests, who included the diplomat Sir Ronald Storrs as well as Wavell, and exhausted by his first visit to London in eighteen months, Sassoon nevertheless thoroughly enjoyed his evening at Kensington Palace Gardens.[26] It made him feel twenty years younger. By 1943, as he told Cockerell, he had stopped being able to imagine himself 'doing anything amusing or unexpected' and was frightened that he had 'got into fixed habits of carpet slipper mentality'; his evening with Wavell made him feel that he might 'come to life again some day'.[27] Not only was Wavell himself 'a very likeable modest man', but Sassoon was pleased to find that one of the other guests was the well-inclined editor of the *Observer*, Ivor Brown, another his old friend Desmond MacCarthy.[28]

An evening of great conviviality that included Sassoon uncharacteristically 'quaff[ing] champagne out of a Magnum', and 'imbib[ing] old brandy', it was midnight before he and Desmond left together, 'wandering ... along toward the Albert Memorial, signalling to already chartered taxi-cabs'.[29] He felt as if he could walk all the way back to Wiltshire.

There was to be no second talk with Wavell, Sassoon being sad to have to turn down an invitation to meet him again in 1945, but this sole meeting left a deep impression. 'On the one occasion when I met and talked with him', he told Cockerell, 'I found that we agreed completely about poetry. What a great Englishman he is.'[30] It was almost certainly in emulation of Wavell that Sassoon agreed to write an introduction to another anthology of Second World War verse, *Poems from Italy*.[31]

Ten years after the meeting, and three years after Wavell himself was dead, Cockerell would introduce Sassoon to Wavell's son, Major Earl Wavell. When, just a few months later, he was killed in action in Kenya, it left Sassoon with 'permanent heart-ache'.[32] They met only five times, but 'Archie John', as he was called, was to make Sassoon feel that he had 'gained a wonderful new friend' whose admiration for, and understanding of his work encouraged him at a time of great despair.[33] Young Wavell's sincere religious-mindedness would also influence Sassoon's own movement towards the Church a few years later.

*

Sassoon's failure to take Hester with him to meet Wavell senior was one more sign of how bad things were between them by mid-1943. After accepting his cousin Sybil's invitation for himself only in June, he had been kept up till three in the morning by Hester's 'scenes', he told Keynes, clearly wondering what all the fuss was about.[34] By this point he had dropped all pretence with his close friends and was openly accusing his wife of mental instability. (Though when his mother, who took his side completely, referred to Hester as 'sub-human', he replied: 'A lot of her behaviour is due to sheer silliness combined, of course, with her incurable possessiveness and obstinacy.')[35] From his account to Keynes of one of their many rows it is obvious not only that he was entirely unaware of her point of view, but also that she was beginning to fight back. In reply to his ironic suggestion that it would be 'better not to drink all this strong coffee and not smoke 25 cigarettes a day; and sometimes go to bed before 3 a.m.', she apparently counter-attacked: 'You are intolerable, your ill-temper is beyond endurance. I'm sick of you and your literary career. You may be very distinguished, but I want to lead my own life. You ... are wearing me out.'[36]

Her first serious act of defiance, calculated to hurt Sassoon where he was most vulnerable, was to pursue an affair with one of his close friends and former aspiring lover, Rex Whistler. Her visits to stay with him in London in the autumn of 1943 were quite blatant. She was clearly being provocative, but then she had herself been severely provoked. Though

June 1943 had been the worst month ever at Heytesbury, with no servants at all, not even a charlady, Sassoon had left most of the housework to Hester. By the end of the year he went on strike altogether, retiring to his music room and taking the handle off the outside of the door. His one concession was to help look after George: his 'sanity', he told Keynes, now depended on his son.[37] 'The worst thing of all' in the whole sorry business, he told his mother, was Hester's jealousy of his love for George: 'She made scenes whenever I tried to be alone with him.'[38]

The breaking point had been reached. Knowing that *The Weald* had been a financial success and confident that *Siegfried's Journey*, a third volume of autobiography started in October 1943, would do equally well, he believed he was now in a position to run Heytesbury independently of Hester.[39] And his first Christmas alone since his marriage reminded him of the joys of solitude. So that as soon as George started boarding at Greenways, a nearby prep school, in January 1944, he decided to act.[40] Using his need to work as his pretext and almost certainly encouraged by Blunden's decision to end his own unhappy second marriage, Sassoon insisted that Hester should go to stay with her mother and leave him entirely alone. Though not fully complying with the second edict, by the end of April 1944 she had effectively left Heytesbury. Neither the pleas of her mother, Lady Gatty, whom Sassoon liked but thought 'weak and silly' with her daughter, nor Hester's own desperate offer to have the second child she had hitherto denied him, could change his mind.[41] Had her offer come earlier, it might well have kept the marriage going, since it is clear from a poem written in 1947 that Sassoon had once longed for a second child:

The Child Denied

O Child I shall not know – heart-haunting cry
Troubling the midnight silence in a thought
That like a footstep pauses, passes by
The door that might have opened, might have brought
The face which never lived and cannot die.

Imagined presence, I have sometimes felt
You near me. In the garden I have seen
Shadow and sun delude me that you knelt
Under a beech playing at what might have been
On some such afternoon of summer sky serene.

Also it seemed you watched me with your brother,
Watched how we two together were so glad,
He unaware of an invisible other
Denied the living laughter, small and sad.
O living ghost – the child I never had.[42]

The final goad for Sassoon, as is often the case, had been an apparently trivial incident, the ultimate proof of what he called Hester's 'obtuse-

43. Mr and Mrs Siegfried Sassoon, 18 December 1933.

44. Heytesbury House.

45. The return of the fox-hunting man, Wiltshire, 1934/5.

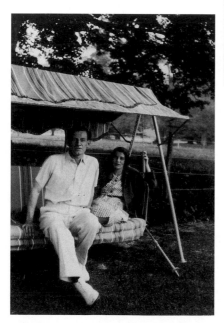

46. SS and Hester relaxing in the grounds of Heytesbury.

47. Three generations of Sassoon: Theresa, Siegfried and George.

48. George's first pony.

49. Like father, like son.

50. Hamo Sassoon in Palestine, 1945.

51. Laurence Whistler in Rifle Brigade uniform, August 1944.

52. SS seeing Dennis Silk off on his travels, Summer 1955.

53. SS alone at Heytesbury House.

54. SS, Angela Baddeley and Glen Byam Shaw at Heytesbury House, August 1952.

55. Downside Abbey.

56. Mother Margaret Mary Ross McFarlin.

SIEGFRIED

57. Dom Hubert van Zeller's impression of SS 'sitting cross-legged on the floor with his thermos and paper bag of cake-and-biscuit crumbs'.

58. 'He drove a car in the way that he rode a horse – at an uneven trot until lost in composition and then at a spanking gallop.' (Dom Hubert van Zeller)

59. Edmund Blunden and Rupert Hart-Davis opening the batting for Jonathan Cape *versus* the Alden Press, Oxford.

60. Blunden, SS and Silk listening to the Test Match results at Heytesbury in the early 1960s.

61. SS in what his friends referred to as his 'awful old hat'.

62. SS in meditative mood.

GOLDEN WEEKEND *continued*

Off again on another of the dazzling runs that have made him the most exciting player in the American Football League.

63. Haro Hodson's caricature of SS 'whizzing about in the library' with the coal scuttle in 1964. The caption reads 'GOLDEN WEEKEND. Off again on another of the dazzling runs that have made him the most exciting player in the American Football League'.

64. Haro Hodson with George Sassoon, photographed by Glen Byam Shaw at Heytesbury, *c.* 1949.

65. Old age.

ness'.[43] When Eileen Hunter died of kidney trouble in April 1944, Hester's reaction had been sympathetic: 'Ought we to ask Beryl [her sister] here for a weekend?'[44] But to Sassoon it seemed just one more example of her insensitivity. The Hunter sisters had represented for him an ideal relationship with women, warm, admiring yet emotionally undemanding – the very opposite of what he had come to expect from Hester – and he was very sad indeed when Beryl's death followed Eileen's a month later.

Whatever the reasons for the break-up, there is no doubting Sassoon's profound relief at Hester's departure. The following unpublished poem was written the month she left, after giving him 'fifteen successive days of domestic hell'[45]:

Nirvana

No need to bother ... When such thought befriends my mind,
Effort surrenders; sense of duty left behind,
Loads of vicarious experience lift; release
Signs from Nirvana's undemanding hours of peace.
Stirs the long-lost, sustaining power of poetry. Then
Head, hand, and heart unite to make me whole again,
When for unhindered being stands wide the mysteried gate
To stillness where the guardian presences await
Spirits imploring sanctuary from foiled unrest.
　　No more ingratitude there; no conflicts unconfessed.
　　Only absolvéd self; and summer daybreak breath.
　　Only the anodyne of dreams in love with death.[46]

One of the many irritants for Sassoon in the months leading up to the separation had been Hester's incessant 'grieving' about the long-awaited 'Second Front'. Since Rex Whistler was involved in the elaborate staff-work surrounding the Normandy landings, Sassoon strongly suspected that it was Rex, not the war, which concerned her. 'I worry [about Rex] just as much', he wrote to Keynes, 'but don't make a fuss about it.'[47] He was even more incensed when, after the news of Rex's death arrived in late July 1944, Hester started behaving as though she were his widow. His own grief was great, 'the worst ... I've felt since the War began. I somehow felt [Rex] would be killed,' he wrote in his diary after reading the announcement in the *Daily Telegraph*.[48] But his main concern was for Edith Olivier, who had adored Rex since the early twenties. She, if anyone, was entitled to behave like a widow, though she did no such thing. Instead she tried to carry on as normal, inviting Sassoon to dine with the Chief of Staff to the Supreme Allied Command a week after Rex's death,[49] and Sassoon did his utmost to console her: 'I am always and ever your friend,' he told her, begging her to 'be brave – *you are* – and live for us'.[50] As he and all Edith's other close friends feared, however, the loss of 'the whole happiness' of her life weakened her will to live and she would die not many years later.

'Operation Overlord', or 'D-Day' as it is popularly known, had started

339

on 6 June 1944 with the convergence of 4,000 ships on the coast of Normandy. A combined effort of British, American and Canadian troops, by the end of August the Allies had a million men in France and the Germans had been driven back to the old Siegfried Line, known so well to Sassoon and his fellow-soldiers in 1917 as the Hindenburg.

Like Hester, who had herself been driven back to Siegfried's limits, the Germans continued to harass the enemy as often as they could, their dropping of 'buzz-bombs' on London being one particularly unpleasant case in point. Hester's harassment consisted of about four visits a week and three telephone calls a day in November 1944. But in both cases the battle was essentially over. By March 1945 the Germans were forced to sign a peace treaty. The war in Europe, like Sassoon's marriage, was at an end.

It is impossible to imagine Sassoon not getting caught up to some extent in the mounting euphoria of the final struggles, but his main feeling in the case of the war was one of detachment. In his old hat and worn-out clothes, he told Blunden, he was no nearer the current conflict than the blackbirds and lilac bushes in his garden, merely a ghostly survivor from the First World War. And when Victory in Europe (VE Day) was celebrated on 8 May 1945, rather than jubilation he felt weighed down by 'mental flatness'.[51]

Instead of celebrating he spent the day quietly with his eight-year-old son, after putting his wife firmly back on a bus to Salisbury. Oppressed by thoughts of concentration camps and millions of lost lives, he was unable to satisfy the *Observer*'s request for a celebratory poem. Instead the piece which emerges is one of mourning. Could human nature ever 'escape responsibility' for such horrors, he asked Tomlinson? Added to his guilt and sorrow, there was also anger, as in the First World War, at those he believed had profited by the war:

> To Some Who Say Production Won the War
> *Won by Production, was it?* That's a fact
> We don't deny. The factories attacked
> For all they were worth; and made their profit.
> Output, impelled by minds magnificent
> To organize and – above all – invent,
> Delivered the munitions. *Well, what of it?*
>
> What now of those, on land, in air, at sea,
> Who – ardent or unafraid – went forth to be
> Defenders of the soul of man assailed
> By foul aggression and its creed of crime?
> How *their* productive fortitude prevailed,
> Ask, and be answered till the end of Time.[52]

Published in the *Observer* on 6 May 1945, this poem is the nearest Sassoon came to his bitter satires of the First World War, though it lacks their force. The two atomic bombs dropped on Hiroshima and Nagasaki later that year in a horrifying but successful effort to end the war in the Far East would pass virtually without comment from him. Perhaps beyond a certain point, as in his battle with Hester, he felt too numbed to care. From now on, he told Keynes in August 1945, 'my human existence is centred in George. I literally live for nothing else. As his concerns broaden out, mine will follow him. I have no literary ambition at all now.'[53]

It was a highly vulnerable position to be in, as the next ten years would show.

23

The Wilderness Years
(1945-1950)

How lonely – how lonely – how lifeless – how forsaken.
(Diary entry for 1947)

Once Hester had been ejected from Heytesbury, Sassoon's life quickly reverted to its pre-marital routine. Apart from school holidays devoted to George, a sacrifice he welcomed, by 1945 he was back in the round of daily rituals that had been his lifeline up to 1933. Its two main props were friends and work.

He had always valued friends highly and they now became more important than ever to him. But the break-up of a marriage can be a great divider, friends often polarizing into allies and enemies and few managing to remain convincingly neutral. Even if they try, as Keynes and his wife did, their efforts are not always appreciated. Sassoon, who had regarded Keynes as *his* property, was resentful when he and Margaret continued to visit Hester as well as himself. 'Geoffrey Keynes is no good where Hester is concerned,' he wrote in his diary: 'Admirable in his way, Geoffrey is a fair weather friend.'[1] Edith Olivier, who had known Hester from a child yet had remained open-minded about the separation, was also judged 'a disappointment over the Hester business'.[2] Sassoon demanded complete support, not fair-mindedness. He failed to appreciate the fact that no one, not even Hester's mother, condemned him outright. Lady Gatty's affectionate and admirably reasonable letter on the subject, with its concluding wish 'that you should *both* be as happy as possible under the circumstances', was firmly rejected.[3] Anyone who could see Hester's viewpoint, like Forster, for instance, was phased out as a close friend. Averse to confrontation, Sassoon went on seeing Edith and continued to write to both Forster and Keynes, but he secretly regarded them as traitors. In 1946, before the strength of Keynes's commitment to Hester as well as himself became clear, he had appointed him as his joint literary executor together with Blunden. Afterwards he very much regretted his choice of Keynes and would eventually replace him with another friend, largely because of Keynes's loyalty to Hester.

He cared even more about Blunden's 'defection' (though kept him as his literary executor), since he had regarded Blunden as his best friend. And

343

in this particular case there is probably some truth in his charge that Hester had deliberately tried to 'nobble' those closest to him.[4] She not only appealed directly to Blunden for help, but also invited him, his new wife Claire and their baby daughter to stay with her several times once she bought her own house in mid-1945.[5] Blunden's sympathetic nature disposed him to understand Hester's point of view, which was partly his own, that Sassoon's 'egotism was defeating his invention and imagination'.[6] Sassoon himself suspected that Blunden thought his behaviour unreasonable, a position he found unacceptable. So that by July 1947 Blunden was writing to regret Sassoon's apparent 'disinclin[ation] to see' him and a break of almost three years followed.[7] Whereas their letters had multiplied during Blunden's first professorship in Japan in the 1920s, by the time his second post started there in 1947 their correspondence had ceased. Blunden would later come to feel that he had been 'trapped' by Hester and relations would be resumed.[8] But the situation had hurt both men deeply and damaged what Sassoon had previously considered their 'flawless friendship' of twenty-seven years.[9] He seems conveniently to have forgotten his earlier refusal to take sides in Blunden's own marital problems.

One of the people who helped to salvage their friendship was Laurence Whistler, who visited Heytesbury more regularly after the death of his brother Rex in 1944. Both Sassoon and Hester had attended his wedding to the actress Jill Furse in 1939 and when she died tragically young, leaving Laurence with two small children, they were mutually sympathetic. 'Laurie' was one of their few friends who managed to remain neutral without endangering his relationship with Sassoon, and would continue to visit Heytesbury with his second wife, Theresa, well into the fifties, while also staying with Hester. Sydney Cockerell was another. But then neither Whistler nor Cockerell had ever been as close to Sassoon as Blunden, so it probably mattered less to him.

Fortunately, all the people he really cared about, apart from Blunden, seem to have taken his side. Friends of long standing, like Tomlinson, Hodgson, Swinnerton and de la Mare, to whom he had complained regularly and at length about Hester, made no effort to defend her and their letters continued to comfort him in the late forties and early fifties, together with those of more recent friends like Gathorne-Hardy and Nan Tennant. His family, too, were a great support, his nephew Hamo making no attempt to keep in touch with Hester after the separation and his mother telling him that she had 'sized Hester's character up' adversely years earlier.[10] Though disappointed in the failure of her son's marriage and concerned, like Lady Gatty, about its effect on George, she believed that 'a true artist should never marry'.[11]

When Sassoon first heard of Blunden's sympathy for Hester, he had written sadly in his diary: 'The curtain will come down and silence will ensue – I must cling to Glen.' Glen had been his earliest and main confidant until the war claimed him, when his wife Angela replaced him as a sympathetic listener; Sassoon's long, unhappy letters to them both make painful reading. One of Glen's first acts on his return to England in 1945 was to invite Sassoon and George to join him and his family for a seaside holiday at Minehead.[12] Seeing Glen again after three years was a high point in Sassoon's life, especially as the holiday ended with the Byam Shaws visiting Heytesbury on their way home. 'All I really want', Sassoon had written shortly before the event, 'is to see [Glen] here, and show him George. I want my friends to come here and see me at my best.'[13] The only flaw in his happiness was Glen's lameness as a result of his wound, but even that was dealt with by the ever-willing Keynes, who arranged for expert medical help.

Shortly before dividing his friends up into allies and enemies, Sassoon had told Blunden that he had only six 'real' friends left beside Blunden – Glen, Keynes, Cockerell, Edith Olivier, Sam Behrman, and his son George. (Beerbohm was excluded on the grounds that he rarely answered his letters.) By his grudge against anyone who remained in contact with Hester he eliminated at least three people from this list, leaving only Glen, Sam and George as 'real' friends. But Glen, who had been 'nothing but a blessing' since 1925,[14] returned to a busy post-war career as Director of the Old Vic Theatre Centre, which made meeting difficult; Sam was even more elusive, visiting Heytesbury only infrequently on his rare visits to England, and George was at boarding school.

That left Sassoon very much on his own. 'Without Hester this place is heaven,' he told Keynes shortly after she left. Heytesbury in the mid-1940s was a very different scene from the 1930s, however, when he and Hester had entertained almost continuously.[15] Not only had the war and loss of servants severely curtailed its social life, but Hester's departure in 1944, together with the removal of all her valuable furniture in 1945, had continued the process. By the time the full effect of Sassoon's resentment of her supporters became apparent in 1947, Heytesbury was no longer quite as inviting as it had been. And Sassoon himself was in danger of becoming almost totally isolated.

One of the few regular visitors to the 'hermit of Heytesbury', as he became known in the second half of the forties, was the owner of George's school, Vivien Hancock. Sassoon had met her shortly before deciding on a place for his son and had got to know her well on his almost daily rides to Codford St Peter to see George. Mrs Hancock had disliked Hester from the start and she and Sassoon grew particularly close after Hester left. 'He became very keen to talk about his troubles,' she remembered, 'pouring and pouring out the miseries of his life with her.'[16] He in turn was very supportive when her eldest child, Anthony, was killed on the Western Front in 1945, aged only twenty-one. He also made her a generous present of a horse when her own died.

Hester was jealous of their intimacy, though she had no cause to suspect

345

any sexual interest on either side. By 1945, when she accused them of being 'too close', Mrs Hancock was already involved with the man who would become her second husband within the year and Sassoon was still appreciating his independence.[17] But Hester persisted and, when Sassoon gave Vivien some of George's old baby clothes for a woman in the village, repeated malicious gossip about her spending too much time in the local pub drinking beer. Mrs Hancock threatened legal action and Sassoon simply ignored Hester, continuing to see Mrs Hancock at frequent intervals. When she needed money to keep her school going, he lent her a large amount to buy it outright.[18] When she found it difficult to pay the interest on the loan, low though it was, Sassoon told her to forget about it. 'He didn't really care about money as money,' she maintained.[19] But as Sassoon told Blunden, it was a case where money considerations were unimportant, since he did not want George sent to a more distant school. Hester, who wished him to go to Winchester, had announced her intention of taking him away from Greenways and sending him to a feeder-school for Winchester sixty-three miles away. Sassoon, who favoured Oundle as being more suited to George's scientific bent, was determined to thwart her at any cost. (Keynes, whose sons had attended Oundle, had strongly influenced Sassoon in this respect.) Where his son was concerned, his usual mildness deserted him: 'In me the tiger sniffs the rose,' he wrote to Keynes, quoting his own words, when he heard of Hester's scheme.[20] Mrs Hancock was an important player in his strategy to outwit her.

She was also useful in other ways. When, by coincidence, he received a letter from a master at Oundle, Rolf Barber, shortly after deciding on it for George, he passed Barber on to Mrs Hancock.[21] Though not able to provide the schoolmaster with free riding at her small stable in exchange for 'mucking out', as he wanted, she did take him as a paying guest with riding included at a very reasonable rate. In this way Sassoon hoped to establish a useful connection at the school in advance of George's arrival there. He allowed Barber to ride his own mare during his stays at Greenways. Everything he now did was with George's advancement in mind.

Despite his fairly cynical motives for cultivating the friendship initially, Sassoon learnt to enjoy Barber's company, his love of books and horses in particular. Sensitive, unmarried and prone to depression, Barber had sufficient qualities in common with him to make occasional visits and more regular letters from him pleasant. (Barber's own description of Sassoon included words like 'sensitive', 'generous' and 'spontaneous'.) The relationship would become closer once George started at Oundle, when Sassoon would, in the words of one close friend, find Barber a 'lifeline'.[22] According to the same friend Barber, who taught German, was a 'much-loved master' at the school.[23]

Another link through Mrs Hancock, and who cheered up Sassoon's life during this period, was Haro Hodson, a 24-year-old undergraduate at

Oxford and previously a wartime major in the British Army. Mrs Hancock had allowed Haro, whose parents she knew well, to use her name (Mrs Gibbons by now) to introduce himself to Sassoon in 1948. An aspiring poet and artist with a particular gift for caricature – he was already 'drawing wittily for *Punch*' – Haro greatly admired Max Beerbohm and saw Sassoon initially as a possible way of getting to know his hero on a forthcoming trip to Rapallo.[24] Having read nothing of Sassoon's own work by the time he was invited to tea at Heytesbury, he admits to bluffing his way through their first meeting, though he subsequently came to read and admire almost everything Sassoon wrote. There was only one exception and that, ironically, was the main cause of the friendship which grew up between them. Haro never learnt to like *Meredith*, the biography Sassoon had just completed when they met. Yet it was proofs of this book which Sassoon asked Haro to deliver personally to Beerbohm on his visit to Rapallo in June 1948. (Haro was so terrified of losing the proofs that he sat on them all the way to Italy in his third-class railway carriage.) Following this introduction to Max and in the years leading up to his marriage to the writer Elizabeth Mavor in 1953, Haro would stay with Sassoon seven or eight times and get to know him well. Sassoon continued his efforts to help him, introducing him to Keynes when he learnt of his passion for Blake,[25] and putting him in touch with his godson, George Byam Shaw, at Oxford. They wrote to each other frequently during this period and again in the last five years of Sassoon's life.

Sassoon's evident affection for an attractive, artistic young man in the late 1940s inevitably raises questions. He had enough in common with Haro to explain his interest in terms of straightforward friendship – poetry, art, worship of Beerbohm, a whimsical humour (he loved the idea of Haro deciding to sleep on top of his wardrobe in 1949) and a strong sense of the absurd, as well as shared army experience.[26] But Haro himself believes that it was more than simple friendship on Sassoon's part. 'As you may see,' he wrote to Rupert Hart-Davis on sending him his letters from Sassoon after his death, 'the dear old boy "fell in love" with me at the time. But I was too self-centred to know it – simply delighted that someone so civilized and humorous should treat me as an apparent equal.'[27] He had wondered why Hester, who had appeared during some of his early visits looking 'rather beautiful, like a ravaged medallion', had so evidently disliked him, but now believes that she was suspicious and jealous of any young man who visited her husband.[28]

Haro's first impression of Sassoon had been of 'a nervous being, extremely shy and kindly', who would 'talk non-stop' for several hours when his guest first appeared, never looking at him at all: 'then at one juncture the eye would quickly glance at you and, that having happened, he would calm down and conversation of a kind could occur'.[29] It was, he recalled, like catching a horse; you had to take the indirect approach. And though he found it exhausting to be talked at 'endlessly', he felt sorry for someone who seemed so very lonely. He also grew to like and admire Sassoon greatly, warning him at one point that he was becoming a 'prop' for the younger man, a sentiment Sassoon himself would repeat to Haro later on.

Sassoon's response to Haro and his attitude towards Hester and women in general suggest that his deepest instincts had not changed by 1947. But the existence of George made any further relationships with men unthinkable to him. One of his greatest fears was that George would be contaminated by his past: the 'very thought of [Stephen Tennant] being anywhere near George', for instance, horrified him.[30] His frustrated sexual needs in the late forties go some way to explain his growing sense of desolation at the time, in spite of being 'enormously happy' with George.[31]

Hester did not hesitate to use his past, which he had so trustingly confided to her in 1933, against him. When he tried to have George made a ward of court in the custody battle which developed after she left, she told him that he would stand no chance at all because of his 'association' with Stephen, of which her lawyers would make full use.[32] The threat worked and Sassoon instantly abandoned the idea. Instead he made Glen his executor, assigning him the role of George's 'personal trustee' if he died.

*

In this deeply unhappy situation Sassoon was no nearer to the peace and quiet he needed to write poetry. By the end of 1945 he had produced little of the verse he had expected to flow from him once Hester had left. Writing to Blunden in November 1945 he admitted that he had not even been able to work on the edition of his collected poems Faber planned to publish, mainly because of his preoccupation with domestic problems.

He did, however, manage to complete the third volume of his autobiography, *Siegfried's Journey*, which he had been struggling with since April 1943. His double anxiety, about Hester and the war, had almost caused him to give up, but her timely decision to take George to her mother's again in January 1944 and leave him to work in peace had saved the book. In the weeks following her departure he wrote one of his most successful sections, his first visit to Hardy in Chapter Nine. By April 1944 he had completed 15 (of 23) chapters, 56,000 of his projected 90,000 words, and had reached another of what he thought the 'best things' in *Siegfried's Journey*, his meeting with the poets Wilfrid Scawen Blunt and Hilaire Belloc in June 1919. Cockerell, who was the leading authority on Blunt and had made the introduction to him, thought Sassoon's account 'outstanding'.[33] Once he had 'vetted' it, together with the sections on Wilfred Owen in chapters six and seven, Sassoon felt free to go ahead with the final eight chapters, which largely cover his lecture tour in America. By 7 April 1945 only the revising of the book remained.

One reason it had taken almost two years to complete was that he had never written a book he 'liked so little'.[34] Perhaps because it was under-taken mainly to make money, he found it 'weary-minded drudgery'.[35] After the first 40,000 words, which took him up to his meeting with Walter de la Mare at his modest house in Anerley, he began to feel that he was 'reporting' rather than 'recreating' the past,[36] a process which is reflected in the less spontaneous writing of the second half. The account of his return to sport and subsequent electioneering with Philip Snowden in the autumn of 1918, for instance, seems self-conscious in comparison with his description of previous activities. And much of what follows concerning his decisions first to study at Oxford, then to accept the literary editorship of the *Daily Herald* in spring 1919, smacks of a conscientious rather than a vibrant reconstruction of his past. With the exception of his visit to Blunt, the same might be said of the rest of the book, particularly of the pains-taking regurgitation of the facts and figures surrounding his American tour. Sassoon believed that such patches of 'stilted writing' sprang from the fact that he was 'a poet, and not really a prose writer by inclination'.[37] It was only when writing with 'strong feeling', he told Cockerell, that he could demonstrate his full potential.[38]

The first ten chapters illustrate this, conveying a sense of recreating rather than reporting, in spite of the difficulties Sassoon had faced in dealing with the years 1916 to 1919. His chief problem was how to avoid repetition of material already covered in some detail in his 'fictionized' account in *Infantry Officer* and *Sherston's Progress*. Having exploited the more dramatic events, such as his presence at the Battle of the Somme, his trench fever, his wounding at the Battle of Arras and again in 1918, he was left with the quieter, more intimate events. His friendships with Robbie Ross, Ottoline Morrell, Wilfred Owen and Thomas Hardy, for example, or his meetings with well-known personalities of the day, like Winston Churchill and T.E. Lawrence, had not been dealt with fully, if at all, in the earlier books. Fortunately, it was material which played to his strengths, his ability to convey with warmth, sympathy and humour, in poetic prose, the importance of human relationships and, in doing so, to create a strong visual impression. The 'careworn' Robbie walking across the Somerville College lawns in his 'light grey suit', wearing his soft black hat at a 'jaunty angle',[39] Ottoline descending her studio loft-ladder back-wards in 'voluminous pale-pink trousers' expressive of her romantic temperament,[40] Owen, with his 'resolute and humorous' mouth and 'long and heavy-lidded' eyes, collapsing into 'uncontrollable hilarity' with Sas-soon at a volume of 'portentously over-elaborated verse',[41] the 'small fair-haired youthful-looking' Lawrence wanting to talk 'only about men of letters',[42] the great Winston 'pacing the room, with a big cigar in the corner of his mouth' as he tries to convert Sassoon to militarism,[43] all bring the past vividly, humorously, yet compassionately to life in concise yet sensi-tive prose. His first visit to Hardy, for instance, while full of acute observations, is drenched in the 'atmosphere' he felt lacking in the later part of *Siegfried's Journey*:

> Found little old gentleman in front of fire in candle-lit room; small wife with back turned doing something to a bookcase. Both seemed shy, and felt large and hearty. First impression of T.H. was that his voice is worn and slightly discordant, but that was only while he was nervous. Afterwards it was unstrained, gently vivacious, and – when he spoke with feeling – finely resonant. Frail and rather wizard-like in the candleshine and dim room, with his large round head, immense brow, and beaky nose, he was not unlike the 'Max' caricature, but more bird-like. He knelt by the log-fire for a bit, still rather shy. They both gained confidence, and then there was a charming little scene of 'which room is he in, dear?' 'The west room, my dear,' though of course he must have known. He lit me up the narrow staircase with a silver candlestick, quite nimble and not at all like a man of almost eighty. Already I felt at ease with him. (I think he had feared that I should be a huge swell and come down to dinner in a white waistcoat ...)[44]

As Sassoon himself realized, however, there are not enough passages of this quality in *Siegfried's Journey* to achieve the standard he had already set himself. 'I don't think it is nearly such sensitive stuff as the two previous volumes', he wrote to Keynes, 'but the material doesn't lend itself to sensitive retrospection. Much of it is a sort of news-reel of new experiences in meeting famous people ...'[45] While it is true that the book reads like a roll-call of well-known personalities (especially once the post-war Sassoon goes on to meet Masefield, Bridges, Galsworthy, de la Mare, Frost and Sandburg, among others) and lacks the frankness of Ackerley or, as Thorpe points out, the social awareness of Leonard Woolf, the opening chapters seem more like the genuine exploration of self that *Siegfried's Journey* set out to be. There, undeniably, is the humanity and power of description that Sassoon had been admiring in Scott's novels as he wrote it.

Sassoon himself believed that the strength of *Siegfried's Journey* lay in its construction. Apart from chronology, however, it is difficult to detect any firm structural principle in its composition. The final scene, where Sassoon, walking slowly across Trafalgar Square on his return from America, realizes that he has 'come to the end of the journey on which he had set out when he enlisted in the army six years before', has only too clearly been included for structural reasons.[46] But the opening scene at Somerville College, Oxford, in August 1916 seems an arbitrary beginning, dictated more by what he can include without repetition from his fiction than any conviction that this is the starting point of the 'journey' referred to in the title and on the final page. Apart from his account of his protest and what led up to it, a more satisfying analysis than the one already given in *Infantry Officer* because it can include an intellectual debate inappropriate to the Sherston character, there is little sense of progression or development in *Siegfried's Journey*. Nor is the book organized round any poetic symbols, like *The Old Century*.

As Professor B. Ifor Evans argued in his *Time and Tide* review, *Siegfried's Journey* is 'full of fascination and yet maddening'; fascinating 'in its detail, in its lively pictures of England after the war of 1914-1918' and its accounts of Owen, Hardy and Bridges; maddening 'because it has no values, no awareness that anything has happened in the world since 1920'.[47] Evans believed that this third volume of autobiography gives 'the real answer' to why Sassoon never developed into the 'great poet' promised by his 'firm and authentic' war poems: 'The artist need not write about his own age, but his heart and mind must be moved by his own times, especially when he lives in one of the crucial epochs in human history.'[48]

Other reviewers were less critical and Sassoon was relieved to be able to report to Blunden two weeks after publication that the book had been well received. An account of the First World War appearing at the end of the Second and full of famous names, it also appealed to the popular imagination. The 31,350 copies published by Faber on 7 December 1945 sold quickly and Dutch, German and Spanish rights were bought, earning Sassoon enough money to continue living independently at Heytesbury. Helped also by a Book Society Award, it had brought its author the then considerable sum of over £3,000 in royalties by March 1946, with the promise of more to come.[49] In financial terms it was by far the most successful of his three autobiographies.

Yet *Siegfried's Journey* was the least satisfactory of Sassoon's memoirs artistically and his friends' response to it was largely muted; when they praised it at all they did so for his early 'dry-point' portraits of Ross, Owen and others.[50] Edith Sitwell was more outspoken. In spite of the care Sassoon had taken over his description of her brothers, she found his account of Osbert 'detestable', dismissing the book altogether as 'one mass of treachery, fawning and snobbishness'.[51] Fortunately Sassoon never saw Edith's withering remarks, but he did read Edmund Wilson's rejection of the book in the *New Yorker* as 'narcissistic fatuity'.[52] A highly influential reviewer, Wilson's piece may help to explain the book's disappointing sales in America. For in spite of its American publisher Ben Huebsch's optimism, *Siegfried's Journey* failed to appeal in America and Viking's small edition was not reprinted.[53] Huebsch, like Sassoon, had counted on the fact that nearly a quarter of the book is situated in America but by July 1946, only four months after publication, Sassoon was forced to accept the fact that the 'Yanks' did not appear to understand him; most of them were too 'crude and provincial' to do so, he told Hodgson.[54] With Blunden he was even more critical, telling him that Americans were entirely lacking in the 'intellectual finesse' of the French: 'French letters are as far as they get.'[55]

*

Even before *Siegfried's Journey* was published in December 1945 Sassoon had been searching for something to succeed it. But the very reason he wanted to distract himself with work – the struggle over custody of George – was the same reason he found it difficult to start another book. 'I am quite unable to settle down to any fresh writing', he told Keynes in October that year, 'as Hester continues to worry me and I never feel my mind is free from her.'[56]

Once *Siegfried's Journey*, which took his life up to 1920 only, had been well received, the natural choice would have been a continuation of his life into the twenties. Quite apart from the problems of dealing with that turbulent period, however, which would mean almost certainly having to omit the most active years of his homosexual adventurings from 1920 to 1925, he had difficulty finding a focus. The material was there, as his diaries amply testify, but he was not yet able to formulate a plan for it. He needed time for it to settle in his mind.

Another idea had come from Glen, who had urged Sassoon during their holiday at Minehead to write a play for him to direct. But a reading of Chekhov's *The Cherry Orchard* convinced Sassoon that dramatic technique was beyond his powers. He also remembered Beerbohm once telling him that the theatre was 'too crude a medium' for his 'delicate prose effects'.[57]

Apart from a few desultory pieces, therefore, he had started on nothing new by January 1946 and was beginning to panic at the thought of empty days ahead. Then into this void the same month dropped an invitation from the publisher Constable to write a life of George Meredith, an offer he accepted with relief. 'It will provide literary occupation', he told de la Mare, 'while I am "filling up the cistern" for another tap-turning of "Memoirs".'[58] And it was not simply a matter of plugging a gap; he was actively 'excited', he told Blunden, at the prospect.[59]

Meredith had remained one of his favourite authors since his mother's friend, Helen Wirgman ('Wirgie'), had first introduced him to his poetry as a young man. Prompted almost certainly by his description of that conversion in *The Weald of Youth*, he had been re-reading Meredith since 1942.[60] He had also brought Meredith into *Siegfried's Journey* by describing Hardy's recollections of the older writer, together with his own post-war meeting with Meredith's daughter.[61] It may have been these references that decided Otto Kyllman, the senior director of Constable, to write to Sassoon a month after the book's publication with his offer. But it is more likely to have been his much fuller, earlier description in *The Weald*, since by January 1946 Sassoon had already been discussing the idea of a Meredith biography with another editor from Constable, Helen Waddell.[62] The *Siegfried's Journey* reference appears merely to have triggered Constable's formal approach.

However it occurred, the commission would materially affect Sassoon's life for the next few years. Though the biography itself was to lead nowhere in professional terms, the friendship it brought about with Helen Waddell would prove important to him, a very special relationship in a time of great need.

Helen Waddell, a distinguished medieval scholar, translator and novelist, whose *Wandering Scholars* had swept her to fame in 1927, would form a bridge between the long line of female confidantes of his past and those of his future. From Wirgie onwards, he had always needed a sympathetic, intelligent, preferably well-read woman friend who could be close but not too close, a role which Ottoline Morrell, Nellie Burton, Delphine Turner, Ruth Head, the Hunter sisters, Edith Olivier, Vivien Hancock and others had fulfilled with varying degrees of success. By the time his friendship with Helen Waddell started in earnest in 1946, Ottoline, Nellie, Ruth Head and the Hunter sisters were dead, Mrs Hancock had remarried and Edith Olivier had been demoted for her loyalty to Hester. He was, therefore, in need of fresh comfort, which Helen, with her ready Irish wit and abundant kindness, was able to give. They would continue to meet for several years after their Meredith transactions ended in 1948 and on every occasion Sassoon found himself '100% uplifted' by her company.[63]

He came to believe that Helen had 'one of the finest minds of any woman writer alive – possibly the finest', a reference to her scholarship in books such as *Medieval Latin Lyrics* (1929).[64] He also told a mutual friend, T.H. White, that she was the 'greatest' woman he had ever known.[65] But it was her imagination and insight rather than her intellect which enabled her to get through to him in his growing isolation, qualities which he admired in her brilliant recreation of the legendary lovers Heloise and Abelard in *Peter Abelard* (1933).[66] Her letter to him about Meredith in 1947, for example, written as he approached the end of his biographical labours, shows her insight into both biographer and subject, whom she sees as kindred spirits: 'for he had your exceedingly rare power of being completely aware of yourself and, at the same moment, of other people. For *The Egoist* is only half of Meredith. And I think you both know something of what Emily Brontë meant when she said anguish.'[67]

The daughter of a Presbyterian missionary, Helen, like Edith Olivier, had grown up with a deep respect for spiritual values and was able to give Sassoon more than understanding alone. She also reminded him of another possible element in life, one which he had begun to explore for himself in *Vigils*, anticipating by a decade the women who would become his spiritual guides and support in the last years of his life.

When accepting the invitation to write a biography of Meredith, Sassoon had made it quite clear that he was not aiming at a work of great scholarship, though he hoped it would establish him as 'quite a serious writer' with university dons.[68] All he could try to do, he felt, 'was to show what sort of a man he was, the nature of his writings, and how far they remain readable and rewarding'.[69] Based almost solely on Meredith's published *Letters* and Buxton Forman's collection of Meredithiana which

Constable had acquired, Sassoon's biography makes no attempt to be comprehensive, including few references to anything outside these two. When the scholarly Blunden suggests the need for other sources, Sassoon does not go in search of them but expects them to come to him. He complains of lack of help from Constable, but when Kyllman sends more material in mid-1947, he rejects the idea of revision and refuses to include it in his work.[70]

Even as the 'commonsense' account of Meredith's life it set out to be, *Meredith* is not altogether satisfactory.[71] At the very beginning of the book its author indicates that he will not be going into 'the details of [Meredith's] intellectual and emotional development'.[72] He also makes it clear that he does not consider himself a professional critic; 'the only critical method I feel capable of adopting is to describe my own experience when re-reading [*Evan Harrington*] after an interval of more than twenty years'.[73] In this way he hoped to get through to the '*human* interest' of the subject, whereas written in 'a professional way the book could have been thoroughly boring', he told Angela Baddeley.[74] Written in the first person, his is a frankly subjective approach, full of his own likes and dislikes – his interest in rare books and 'black and white' artists of the nineteenth century, his love of Fitzgerald and Hardy, or his suspicion of the highly analytical mind, for instance. He himself found the critical analysis of Meredith's numerous novels 'a weary game', he confessed to Blunden, and frequently wanted to tell his readers to 'Read the b——y book and decide for yourself.'[75]

As an account of Meredith's life and works, therefore, *Meredith* leaves something to be desired. In terms of Sassoon's life, however, it offers a number of fascinating insights. Sassoon told Cockerell that the writing of *Meredith* had given him great satisfaction because it had shown him 'that I can write about someone else in addition to my unworthy self'.[76] But his identification with his subject is so evident from the outset that he appears to be writing largely about himself. Meredith had been very 'much in [his] mind' when Constable approached him in 1946, as his letter to Tomlinson about his acceptance of their offer shows.[77] For he refers in the next sentence to his legal fight over George and concludes that Meredith's grim picture of the collapse of his first marriage in *Modern Love* is a 'joke' compared with what he himself has had to endure.[78] Similarities in their personal lives were reinforced in his mind by professional parallels between the two poets-turned-prose-writers.

Reading *Meredith* it becomes clear that it is not just in a general sense that Sassoon identifies with his subject; he also highlights specific coincidences, such as the fact that Meredith's first critical success was a parody, as Sassoon's was;[79] or that Meredith destroyed at least one edition of his early poems;[80] or that he was first persuaded to study law as a young man. More importantly his descriptions of Meredith's love of nature, his need for physical as well as mental activity, his dependence on a wide circle of male friends, his attitude towards journalism and his fastidious nature make clear Sassoon's similar attitude towards such things.

It is the deeper identifications that are most significant, however, since they not only dictate Sassoon's interpretation of Meredith's character, but also add to the reader's understanding of Sassoon's. When analysing the failure of Meredith's marriage, for instance, he blames the 'instability' of his wife Mary's temperament and the fact that Meredith had been 'unwarned' of it, as though he is repeating his charges against Hester and defending himself.[81] Just as he believed Hester was 'mad', so he accuses Mary of being so with no firm proof offered.[82] To anyone familiar with Sassoon's life in the forties, there is little doubt that he is justifying himself as well as Meredith when he states: 'But a writer's workshop is his head; his head has to do its work at home; and the craft of authorship demands of him an immense nervous output. The conditions imposed upon Meredith by his first marriage must, surely, have been excrutiating.'[83]

Sassoon certainly speaks from experience here. (To what extent he also identified with Meredith's realization 'that he wasn't an easy man to live with' is less sure.[84]) Refusing to condemn Meredith for what some regard as his harshness towards his dying wife, he argues: 'it is a case where the truth cannot be known'.[85] Allowing his subject the last word, he quotes in conclusion the lines from *Modern Love* that sum up the possible reasons for the failure of his own marriage as well as Meredith's:

> ... I see no sin;
> The wrong is mixed. In tragic life, God wot,
> No villain need be! Passions spin the plot:
> We are betrayed by what is false within.

The fact that Mary Meredith, like Hester, had impressive literary connections – she was the daughter of Thomas Love Peacock – undoubtedly strengthened Sassoon's sense of identification and helps to explain his strong defence of Meredith against charges of snobbishness. Sassoon's own experience of growing up as a relatively poor member of a rich and socially successful family had given him a sense of inferiority in youth and he seems to have identified with Meredith's attempts to deny his tailor-grandfather.

His identification with Meredith emerges even more powerfully in the account of Meredith's relations with the only child of his first marriage, like George a son, Arthur. Playing down the fact that Meredith had several other children later on, Sassoon describes his feelings for Arthur in words which echo his own sentiments towards George as he wrote the book: 'With deep and undeviating devotion he made Arthur the purpose of his existence and his money-earning endeavours, concentrating on him the parental love which is fathomless and immeasurable in terms of emotion, being decreed by Nature.'[86] He openly admitted that the part about

Meredith and 'little Arthur was deeply felt by me, owing to my experience with George' – so deeply, it seems, that he thought it necessary to deny that George would ever reject him, as Arthur rejected his father in later life: 'But George will never be an Arthur to me, thank God.'[87]

Sassoon's subjective approach to Meredith as husband and father to some extent damages *Meredith* as a biography. But his identification with Meredith the poet and prose-writer gives the book some value. While clearly sympathizing with Meredith's preference for poetry over prose – 'His temperament was that of a poet ... He was always an unwilling novelist'[88] – Sassoon's first-hand experience of both genres enlarges the reader's understanding of Meredith's creative processes. Discussing the fifty sixteen-line 'sonnets' of *Modern Love*, which Sassoon initially assumed had taken Meredith at least three years to write, his reaction when he discovers his mistake throws light on the way they were written:

> I was thinking of the performance in terms of a poet's technique – the intermittent periods of inspiration, the subconscious incubation of ideas, and the labour of the file. I assumed that [having outlined it in 1859, after his wife's elopement] in the autumn of 1861 he must have taken the manuscript up again and finished it at a high pressure of transfused emotion. But there was much in it which, to my mind, appeared to have been written while the drama of discord and estrangement was being enacted.
>
> In all this I was entirely wrong. I had forgotten that Meredith was also a novelist. The poem was begun immediately after his wife's death and completed in little more than three months.[89]

Not only are such pieces of analysis of Meredith's aims and methods in poetry revealing in terms of Meredith, but also of Sassoon. This is particularly true of the piece of criticism he was proudest of in *Meredith*, that of 'The Thrush in February'. Having told the reader 'why I like it so well', he continues: 'I like it also because I am myself an inveterate quietist and self-corrector of inherent excitability, and because – in the unhaltable hither and thither of human occupations – I long for something stilled and subdued to contemplation of experience. For the keynote of "The Thrush in February" is serenity.'[90] He would go on to write poems of equal serenity himself a few years later and one of them, 'Awareness of Alcuin', would make specific reference to the evening star ('a little south of coloured sky') and thrush of Meredith's poem.[91]

Though Sassoon's appreciation of Meredith's novels is limited by his own dislike of the 'experimentalism' and 'too much thought' he finds there, he can at least convey to the reader from first-hand experience the need to admire anyone 'who [has] ever tried to produce a page of decent prose ... under conditions by no means easy'.[92]

It was Sassoon's differences from Meredith the writer, as well as his 'biographical convergence' with him, which L.P. Hartley focused on in a review Sassoon found 'perceptive not only of G.M. but of my method of approaching him'.[93] His letter to Hartley shows how diffidently he had approached the biography:

> As you know, I am not a man of many ideas or an elaborate thinker. I am a writer who relies on feeling and visualising and a lucid and direct handling of word harmonies. It would have been fatal for me to attempt anything except the simplest method of treating the subject (which was, I may say, an extremely difficult one). When Constable's asked me to write the book I told them that all they would get from me would be a commonsense, unbrilliant performance. I am not a *clever* man![94]

So that he was not at all surprised when several literary professors called his book 'unscholarly'.[95] He clung to the fact that he had been helped throughout by an authority on Meredith, G.M. Trevelyan, to whom he dedicated the biography.[96]

Constable had faith in Sassoon's work and published 10,000 copies of *Meredith* in September 1948. But in spite of mainly favourable reviews, it sold slowly and there was no reprint.[97] Sassoon believed that its disappointing sales were due to the unfashionableness of Meredith's novels. A more likely explanation is that his biography falls between two stools, being neither a work of serious scholarship nor a 'popular' biography. It remains the least read of all his prose works.

It was also his last book of prose. Despite his diffidence in writing to Hartley, he had seen *Meredith* as a possible way forward and had hoped to write a similar kind of book on Hardy, believing that his personal knowledge of that poet and prose-writer, and his several articles on him and his work, gave him a head start. Once criticism of his lack of scholarship had appeared and it was clear that *Meredith* was not going to be a runaway success, however, he decided against a biography of Hardy: 'Plenty of people can do, and have done it, better than I could,' he explained to Cockerell.[98] The only published traces of this idea would be his poem on Hardy, 'At Max Gate', written at this time.[99]

He also abandoned his plans for a fourth volume of autobiography, though not without some struggle. The cistern had started to fill, as he had hoped, while he was finishing *Meredith* and his unpublished manuscript of about a hundred pages is full of lively scenes from his life in the twenties – a meeting with W.B. Yeats over 'large pink ice[s]' in Gunther's tea-shop, a weekend at H.G. Wells's with the Sitwells, a hilarious tea at Gosse's with Sam Behrman and Edith Sitwell, another visit to Thomas and Florence Hardy. But the long, false start (part of which is quoted by Rupert Hart-Davis in his Prelude to *Diaries 1920-1922*) shows the difficulties he was still experiencing. 'The vital problem is *what to try and express* by the book,' he wrote in his diary. '*The Old Century* expressed childhood and adolescence. *The Weald* – unsophisticated youth, *Siegfried's Journey* – youth finding its feet, but still undeveloped and bewildered. This one must be an adventure in the gaining of self-understanding.' Encouraged by friends like Cockerell and Keynes, who feared for the emptiness of his life, he persevered. But when it became clear that the only 'adventure' he felt free to describe in the 1920s was how he came to write *Fox-Hunting Man*, he finally gave up. He had arrived at that extraordinary moment when his writing had turned in on itself; in describing the past he had reached the point where to write about it was to write about himself writing about it. As he put it to Tomlinson, he was no longer 'writing' but merely 'editing that other self'.[100] It is hardly necessary to point out the irony of the working title of the abandoned volume, *Know Thyself*!

Otto Kyllman's explanation for Sassoon's problems with prose work in the late forties was rather different from Sassoon's. Sassoon had submitted a selection of Meredith's poems with an introduction to Constable shortly after the publication of *Meredith*, and in rejecting it in February 1949 Kyllman explained that it 'show[ed] signs that you were tired and ... under the weather'.[101] He suggested that Sassoon should return to it when he was feeling 'well and strong again'.[102]

Kyllman's rejection, however sympathetically expressed, seemed to Sassoon his death-knell as a writer. Discussing it with Keynes a few days later he concluded, 'So I suppose I am on the downward grade as an author.'[103] Yet Kyllman's analysis was perceptive; Sassoon had been both tired and physically down as he prepared his proposed selection and someone of less 'anemone-shrinking sensitiveness' (Helen Waddell's words) might have accepted Kyllman's advice rather than giving up at that point.

*

Sassoon's illness had started years before with digestive problems caused, he believed, by the stress of dealing with his failing marriage. Though the symptoms had improved temporarily after Hester's departure in 1944, her repeated visits to Heytesbury, together with the strain of being responsible for George for long periods during his school holidays and the effort of completing *Meredith*, had caused them to return in a more acute form. A four-week holiday with George on Mull in September 1948 had brought things to a head. Hester was in the process of settling down on the island, which she had known and loved since childhood, and had suggested they visit her there.[104] The combination of an unsuitable diet, the 'restless routine' of minding George and above all the daily contact with Hester had brought Sassoon to a point where he felt ready to accept medical help. 'The best treatment you can prescribe', he wrote to a concerned Keynes, 'would be to intern H[ester] in a hospital for wives who refuse to allow their better halves any peace.'[105] Since that was not possible, he agreed to bow to Keynes's and his local doctor Falk's advice and go into hospital himself. They had both diagnosed a duodenal ulcer.

Keynes, whose admiration and sympathy for Sassoon had remained unaffected by Sassoon's own cooling off, at once arranged for him to have treatment in the Central Middlesex County Hospital at Park Royal, west London. Sassoon made only one condition, that Hester should not be allowed to visit him there: 'If she does, I shall get up and come straight home. I really mean this,' he told Keynes.[106] The accumulated exhaustion and loneliness of his recent years at Heytesbury emerge in the final words of his letter: 'After all, what's wrong with reading in bed? And perhaps a few of my friends will come and see me.'[107]

Keynes was less sure about the desirability of any visitors at all for someone as excitable as Sassoon, but they came nevertheless. During Sassoon's six weeks at what he variously called, with recovered light-heartedness, 'Ovaltine Mansions' or 'Duodenal Mansion', he was entertained daily. There were not just friends of long standing like Tomlinson, the Keyneses, Nan Tennant and the Byam Shaws, but more recent ones like Haro Hodson, Helen Waddell and Joe Ackerley, literary editor of the *Listener*. Apart from a natural desire to cheer him up, it was so much easier to get to west London than Wiltshire. 'Since 1939 I have seen so few of my friends and got stuck in my silly shell, hermit crab-like,' Sassoon wrote to de la Mare, revelling in his renewed social life.[108]

De la Mare himself was too frail to travel, but Sassoon ventured out of the hospital twice towards the end of his stay to have tea with him, occasions which brought back all the old magic. He never tired of 'the dream world' to which his treasured friend admitted him.[109] Writing to thank Angela Baddeley for driving him to de la Mare's house in Twickenham, Sassoon notes that it was like seeing 'Coleridge and Lewis Carroll rolled into one'.[110] To de la Mare himself he wrote: 'Tuesday's talk was heavenly just as if we'd never missed seeing one another all those years; and you made me feel absurdly young! – by being so un-old yourself, I suppose.'[111] Nevertheless, as with Hardy and Beerbohm, he tried not to think of age creeping up on de la Mare, since the three men together had come to represent for him the greatest writers of the twentieth century.

All in all he thoroughly enjoyed his six weeks away from Heytesbury. His treatment had been gentle – luminol tablets to quieten him down, milk every two hours, bland food and a great deal of rest. Immunity from Hester had also helped him, mentally as well as physically. (Primed by Keynes, his consultant, Mr Avery Jones, had given strict instructions that she was not to be allowed to visit and her several attempts to see her husband were foiled.) He needed little encouragement to lie in bed reading and got through the complete works of Shakespeare, Lamb's *Letters*, James's *Notebooks*, *Middlemarch*, as well as some Cowper, Browning and Jane Austen. But it was the company he enjoyed most, writing to Haro only three days after his arrival at Park Royal on 19 October: 'I am becoming so popular here that I begin to feel like inviting the whole staff of the "Sick Bay" to stay at Heytesbury next summer!'[112]

It was a strong contrast to his life at Heytesbury, which seemed all the more solitary when he returned there at the end of November 1948. Still a 'paradise' to him in summer, it was at its bleakest and coldest in mid-winter, its ancient heating system quite inadequate for the demands made on it. To make matters worse his cook, Mrs Bailey, and head gardener, Gearing, had taken advantage of his absence to get rid of two members of staff they disliked, the woodman, Johnson, and his wife, who helped in the house. Sassoon arrived back to be given notice by his 'staff and prop', Johnson, and was then so furious with Gearing that his notice quickly followed: 'O for the peace of Park Royal!' he lamented.[113]

Though the domestic situation gradually improved in 1949, his loneliness grew worse. Keynes visited as frequently as possible, but that was not often; Laurence Whistler came to lunch occasionally on his way to Dorset, and George spent part of his school holidays at Heytesbury. Otherwise Sassoon was on his own for long periods. Without friends or work to distract him he became deeply depressed, the only bar to suicide being George's need of him. He could see no other meaning in life. 'Comforting and sustaining' though he found Helen Waddell's belief in the power of 'the continuity of learning and spiritual decency', by 1949 it was not enough to save him from despair.[114]

His depression had been growing on him since his sixtieth birthday in 1946, as the opening lines of his 'Solitudes at Sixty' suggest:

> Sexagenarian solitudes, I find,
> Are somewhat stagnant, motiveless and slow:
> Old friends arrive; but only to my mind,
> Since their earth-farings ended years ago ...
> (CP, p. 276)

H.G. Wells's death in August 1946 had increased his gloom, though it had been almost a decade since they had last met. 'I have been thinking a lot about H.G.,' he wrote to Angela Baddeley: 'He was a tremendous writer and gloriously human in everyday life.'[115] Critical as he had been of certain aspects of Wells's work and character, he readily acknowledged that Wells was 'a world-scale dreamer of things that might be, a breeder of big loose ideas and ideals. Vastly stimulating as he went along.'[116] One of his fondest memories was of a dinner party given by Arnold Bennett with Wells, Elgar, Rivers, Barrie, H.W. Massingham and Henry Head, all of whom were dead by the late forties.

The death of his mother the year after Wells, in July 1947, affected him even more deeply, though not immediately.[117] He had 'long prepared' himself for her death, which was hardly unexpected at the age of ninety-three, so that he 'felt very little emotion' when his brother Michael rang to tell him of it.[118] Nevertheless he 'couldn't face the funeral', or a return to Weirleigh; as he explained in his diary, it would only cause him 'the needless pain of emotion. I just resolved not to indulge in feelings (Hester has cured me of that!).'[119] And he strictly forbade Hester, who felt she ought to go in his place, to attend, possibly fearing further manipulation. As the days passed, however, his mind turned more and more to the time before his mother had become old and sick. 'Somehow she seems nearer to me than before she died,' he told Glen a week after her death: 'I can now think of her in the reality of her prime, and bring her to life in my mind with the full realisation of her qualities which were wonderful.'[120] Their earlier misunderstandings were long forgotten and her recent sympathy with him against Hester had brought them very close. Her death also eased his financial situation, releasing him from the £400 annuity he paid her and bringing the promise of money from his half-share in the sale of Weirleigh. In addition, the Weirleigh furniture would help to fill the empty spaces left by the removal of Hester's belongings from Heytesbury.

But his mother's death was also another reminder of how alone he was by 1947. Edith Olivier's death the following year and Lady Gatty's in 1949 increased this sense of being gradually abandoned. Though he had been critical of both since the break-up with Hester, they were women he had liked and respected and each had been close to him in her own way. 'I wish I didn't feel so sixtyish,' he was writing to Keynes by February 1949, the month his proposed selection of Meredith's poems had been turned down by Constable.

The award of an Order of Merit to T.S. Eliot in 1948 had made him feel even more of a back number. Though his protests were all to the effect that he thought de la Mare should have been given the coveted honour, which was limited to twenty-four holders only, it would become clear later on that he had secretly hoped for it himself. The offer of a Companion of the British Empire award in 1951 would do little to reassure him and was accepted somewhat grudgingly. 'Geoffrey is driving me to Buckingham Palace on February 28 – to be "invested",' he was to write to Haro on the occasion. 'He thinks it fun, but I am dreading it, and feel affronted by the whole affair.'[121] In the event he rather enjoyed it, writing with some complacency in his diary that evening: 'I think the King was pleased to see me, as my writings are liked by the Queen and I was undoubtedly the most famous person there. He spoke nicely with a charming, genial smile, "I am glad to see you here – I suppose you are as busy as ever?" With a strong feeling for him I said, "God bless you" in a low voice as he shook my hand.'

But a sense of slight remained. And however much he expressed horror at the idea of being nominated for the laureateship when Masefield died, he was clearly disappointed not to be asked. Though he should have been forewarned by the lukewarm to downright dismissive reception of his *Collected Poems* in 1947, he found it hard to take.

When Joe Ackerley visited him in the summer of 1949, it was his grievances, his melancholy and, above all, his isolation which struck him most forcibly. As literary editor of the *Listener*, Ackerley had been publishing poems, reviews and articles by him since 1935, and would continue to do so till 1954. But they had never been close friends and Sassoon's invitation to Ackerley to stay at Heytesbury for as long as he liked in itself smacks of loneliness. It was certainly one of the first things Ackerley noted in his diary a few days after his arrival:

> Siegfried sweet, kind, loquacious, absent-minded, lonely, dreadfully self-centred and self-absorbed. I like him very much, there is something very touching about his aged, beautiful, worn face, the light in the eyes dimmed from constant looking inwards. He scarcely ever meets one's eye – he never has, I think – but talks, talks away from one, from side to side, or into his lap or over one's head, always about himself, his life, his past fame, his present neglect, his unhappy marriage, his passionate love for his son. It is all intensely subjective (he scarcely ever asks one about oneself – a flash or two of effortful interest, but always reminding him about himself) and threnodic, it is a man who has spent years and years of loneliness, talking his thoughts at last aloud to an ear. It is all delivered in a low, mumbling, self-absorbed, almost inaudible voice, a whisper sometimes, very refined, accompanied by gestures of pain or feeling – hand on heart, clasping his face.[122]

'But why is he like this?' Ackerley asked himself.[123] His name and fame were assured, as far as this literary editor was concerned; though his poems, memoirs and heroic exploits in World War I might be 'temporarily out of mind' and a new kind of experimental poetry in fashion, he believed that Sassoon's work had 'a permanent place in our literature and his name an everlasting glory in the annals of war'.[124] His poems and books, Ackerley was convinced, would be 'rediscovered and rediscovered' because they contained 'the authentic passion that nothing can quench or stall':[125] 'Dear Siegfried, he has taken a wrong turning somewhere. There is no happiness in self, self as a permanent diet is melancholic and poisonous, it kills, one dies, as he is dying, talking, talking away about his lost fame, his loneliness, his domestic affairs – his aged, worn, fine face turned sideways, sightless, towards the window.'[126] Ackerley thought by contrast of their mutual friend, Forster, with his perennial interest in people and things, his ability to get outside himself. Ten years Sassoon's senior he seemed to Ackerley 'eternally young, eternally gay, cushioned in fat – the fat of secure love and personal esteem'.[127]

Though not, of course, intended literally, the reference to Forster's 'fat' contrasted neatly with Sassoon's physical leanness, which Ackerley shared. It was this which had made Ackerley first aware of other possible similarities between the two of them, a thought he found 'worrying'.[128] Seeing Sassoon in his hospital bed at Park Royal in an old dressing gown, he had recognized 'the same lean look, the same high imperious nose' as his own.[129] And when Sassoon began to complain of Hester and they had discussed Ackerley's sister, who played a role very similar to Hester's in his life, he was even more disturbed to hear Sassoon 'voicing my opinions as his own': 'It had the rather melancholy interest one might get out of finding that one was visiting oneself in hospital.'[130] The most disturbing similarity of all for Ackerley, however, was the way both of them looked desperately for emotional fulfilment in dangerous areas, he to his Alsatian bitch, Queenie, Sassoon to his son. Grateful for the 'lesson' and the 'warning', Ackerley resolved to help Sassoon, if he possibly could.[131]

His attempts to do so make diverting reading, particularly in view of the fact that Sassoon believed that *he* was helping Ackerley. 'He was desperately in need of a holiday and peace', Sassoon wrote in his own diary, 'owing to a bad time he's had with his sister ... I have asked J.A. to stay as long as he likes, as it is doing him so much good.'[132] While Ackerley looked pityingly on Sassoon in his threadbare clothes, his lean shank peeping through a hole in his trousers, Sassoon was feeling sorry for Ackerley, who was, he noted, going deaf. 'Ten years younger than me', he added, 'he is old and disillusioned ... Sad and used up.'[133]

By the end of a fortnight Ackerley was relieved to be going. He had started to feel resentful at what seemed to him the meanness, or at the very least carefulness, of the rich: Sassoon's evident reluctance to keep on opening his good wine for him, his unnecessary reminder to Ackerley to 'reward' the housekeeper, Miss Benn, for looking after his dog so well, his unwillingness to ask the young poet James Kirkup (whom he wanted Ackerley to meet) to stay in advance, or to invite him to do so more than one night at a time when he arrived.[134] Then there was his unawareness; when Kirkup was leaving it was Ackerley not Sassoon who realized that he needed some tea before he caught his bus to the station for the long journey home. And though Ackerley understood Sassoon's treatment of Hester, who visited daily with her 'pale, lined, ravaged face', he found the situation uncomfortable.[135] Finally, and most exhaustingly, there was Sassoon's craving for continual praise and recognition and his all-absorbing egotism.

In spite of which, Ackerley left Heytesbury with the impression that Sassoon was 'very kind and nice, and ... charming'.[136] His behaviour to both Ackerley and Kirkup overall had shown how generous he could be. Yet the overriding impression remained of a man locked up in himself, unable to find the key.

24

An Asking
(1950-1956)

Why all these enquiries about the Creator? Wouldn't it be more profitable –
and entertaining to public readers – to write something nearer everyday
reality? There is always satire, of course, which I can do with gusto when
stirred up. But I have outlived all impulse to wax indignant with the world
– the state of it has gone beyond satire. My existence consists in facing the
circumstance of growing old and teaching myself to submit to it philosophi-
cally and learn what I can from the process. This results in eliminating most
human activities as no longer worth taking seriously. One watches with
some interest; but wonders how they manage to go on believing in the urgent
occupations. *And very few themes seem worth writing about. Only one, really*
... the situation of a thoughtful human being against the background of
nature and the universe. And the achievement of faith in spiritual guidance
from beyond the apparitional existence of the flesh. Yet, most of the time, I
don't feel any confidence in myself as a spiritual person. All I can do is to
want to be spiritual minded.

(Sassoon's diary, 1949)[1]

Solitude, Sassoon realized by 1949, 'compels one to discover what one's
mental resources amount to', and his own, he concluded, were 'very
limited'.[2] Having made all the discoveries he was likely to make in poetry
and come to an end of his prose-writing, he could no longer rely on work
to give his life meaning. Nor, by 1950, could he expect George to do so; it
was becoming obvious even to his father that his departure for Oundle on
a scholarship that year was the first step towards increasing independence. Sassoon had dreaded the moment when George would leave his
nearby prep school for a public school nearly 200 miles away on the other
side of England, and it had now arrived.

Post-war Britain also filled him with gloom and foreboding. Having long
ago abandoned his socialist principles, he was positively resentful of
Clement Attlee's Labour Government and the heavy taxes it imposed on
wealthy people like himself, regardless of the benefits these might bring
to those less fortunate. Worse still was the development of the atomic
bomb, which he believed would lead to a 'suicidal conflict', a threat he
thought all the more likely because of the growing tension between Russia

and America.[3] It now seemed to him that 'nothing that one man [could] think or say / Could prove effective in the feeblest way', and that

> He, for appeasement of his tortured mind,
> Must look elsewhere to be
> Defended and befriended and resigned
> And fortified and free.[4]

Hardy's *The Dynasts*, which Sassoon re-read in 1949, had first made him ask the question that had been forming in his mind for several years: 'What *do* I really believe in?'[5] And it was this question which lay behind a series of poems written between 1946 and 1954 and privately printed in three slim volumes, *Common Chords* (1950), *Emblems of Experience* (1951) and *The Tasking* (1954).[6] Written under the same kind of intense emotions which had given rise to his First World War satires, these poems of his spiritual odyssey resemble them also in what Sassoon called 'direct utterance of dramatized emotion'.[7] As in the 1914-18 period he had again discovered a theme which inspired him. The difference is that by 1950 the drama is largely internal rather than external and that, while the earlier poems chart his gradual loss of faith when confronted with the horrors of World War I, the later pieces show his developing need to rediscover it as he faces threats of a different sort.

Reading these later poems as they were arranged by Sassoon in his private volumes and in Faber's trade edition of the three, *Sequences* (1956), it is possible to identify the various states of mind he experienced but not the precise nature of his spiritual development. Looked at chronologically, however, they provide a revealing account of his stumbling progress towards faith, particularly of its beginnings.

The first three in the series to be written, for example, 'Solitudes at Sixty', 'A Prayer to Time' and 'In Time of Decivilisation', suggest that the initial stimulus had been the pronounced sense of lost youth which followed his sixtieth birthday and an accelerated awareness of the passing of time (a theme to which later poems in the series, such as 'A Proprietor' and 'Associates', would return):

> A Prayer to Time
> Time, that anticipates eternities
> And has an art to resurrect the rose;
> Time, whose long siren song at evening blows
> With sun-flushed cloud shoreward on toppling seas;
> Time, arched by planets lonely in the vast
> Sadness that darkens with the fall of day;
> Time, unexplored elysium; and the grey
> Death-shadow'd pyramid that we name the past –
> > Magnanimous Time, patient with man's vain glory;
> > Ambition's road; Lethe's awaited guest;
> > Time, hearkener to the stumbling passionate story

24. An Asking (1950-1956)

> Of human failure humanly confessed;
> Time, on whose stair we dream our hopes of heaven,
> Help us to judge ourselves, and so be shriven.
>
> (CP, p. 275)[8]

The religious terminology with which this sonnet opens and closes indicates that, though its theme may be Shakespearian, its author, unlike Shakespeare, is looking beyond his own creative powers for answers. This terminology is taken up again in 'Praise Persistent', 'An Asking' and 'An Absentee', all three written a few months later in early 1948. And it is at this point that the concept of a living, listening God as a possibility is introduced, the first convincing sign of the birth of religious awareness. Sassoon's posing of the question in 'An Asking' – 'Primordial Cause, your creature questions why / Law has empowered him with this central I; / Asks how to carnal consciousness you brought / Spirit, the unexplained of sovereign thought;' (CP, p. 270) – shows him starting out on a spiritual quest. The reference in 'Praise Persistent' to mankind pursuing 'their one hope on earth ... / In perishable pilgrimage' suggests that he suspects that the journey will not be easy and that, in the words of 'An Absentee', he will need 'God's Mercy ... a word / Seldom in these times heard'.[9] Nevertheless, the question has been asked and the journey begun. Like St Augustine, whom he resembles in his searching and openness, Sassoon will continue to ask many questions on the way, but it is clear that he has had his first glimpse of 'the soul – a star – a gift he yet might save'.[10]

As with Christian's progress towards the Celestial City, Sassoon was to experience distractions and take false turnings on his pilgrimage. In 'Ultimate Values', for instance, written at the end of 1948, he appears to be still clinging to the memory of 'out-live[d]' friends for meaning in life, and depending for 'consolement ... / On hoarded time, enriched and redesigned'.[11]

Less than three months later he is back on track with what he describes as 'the first "spiritual" poem of the collection, which "cried out for the living God" *in me*' – 'Resurrection'.[12] It is here that he introduces another possibility, that of forgiveness for what increasingly seems to him a life misspent:

> Suppose, some quiet afternoon in spring,
> The hour of judgement came
> For me and my mistakes when journeying
> Along with that defence for nullity, my name.
> Suppose, while sauntering in the primrosed wood,
> To body and soul's dispute a voice cried *halt*,
> And I that instant stood
> Absolved of unfulfilment and essential fault ...
>
> (CP, p. 270)

Sassoon referred in the last line of this poem to 'marred and mystic me' and Blunden would make a similar point in his review of *Sequences* in the

Times Literary Supplement. In reading the collection, Blunden wrote, he had been reminded of Sassoon's 1920s sonnet 'At the Grave of Henry Vaughan', because of a 'spiritual affinity' between the twentieth-century poet and seventeenth-century mystic: 'The impression given [in *Sequences*] is of a recluse seeking some spiritual light, often under the stars, and of a solitary wayfarer pausing beneath a tree, noting the primrose, riding along the farm track.' Sassoon himself had referred in 'A Fallodon Memory' (written in March 1948) to Lord Grey's 'Wordsworthian slow self-communing',[13] a phrase that describes his own method in the poem which immediately precedes 'Resurrection', 'The Message'. 'Riding slowly homeward' on a still November day, the narrator sees 'the sky / Transfigured as by beneficence fulfilled':

> Cloud streaks and shoals, like silver wings outspread,
> Spanned innocent serenities of blue,
> As though, enharmonised with life below,
> Some heavenly minded message had been said.
> Thus, childlike, I imagined. Yet it might be true.
>
> (CP, p. 264)[14]

In 'Euphrasy', the poem which follows 'Resurrection', there is a similar sense of Nature suggesting to the poet a meaning beyond its outward appearance of 'large untidy February skies', 'low-shot sunlight' and 'cheerful starlings screeling on a tree'.[15] Though viewed at times as 'beguilements', the charms of Nature, particularly those of spring, are presented in these and other poems, such as 'An Example', 'Wren and Man' and 'Release', as a potential gateway to God.[16]

Where once Sassoon would have extended these descriptive passages, he now lets them stand as significant in themselves:

> Early March
> ... Designlessly in love with life unlived, I go
> Content with the mere fact that fields are drying fast
> And tiny beads of bud along the hedge foreshow
> The blackthorn winter that will come too late to last.
>
> Beyond that bare untidy orchard, now and then,
> One thrush half tells how in the twilight hour he'll sing
> To no one but himself his wild belief in spring.
> Meanwhile I'm thankful for this almost dusty road,
> Celandine's lowly gold, and daylight lengthening when
> The winterbournes, like time, past February have flowed.
>
> (CP, pp. 278-9)

Sassoon the nature poet has not disappeared; he has simply moved on a stage. And in concluding the first of his private volumes with 'Redemption', he makes the clearest statement to date of his transcendental yearnings by the end of 1949.[17] Its final stanza, centring round the idea of the body as a vehicle through which God's glory might shine, is Vaughan-like in its mystical acceptance of different possible ways of knowing and serving:

> ... I think; if through some chink in me could shine
> But once – O but one ray
> From that all-hallowing and eternal day,
> Asking no more of Heaven I would go hence.
>
> (CP, p. 271)

Seizing on this, one of the few but highly effective metaphors in *Common Chords*, Helen Waddell wrote to Sassoon in terms which gave him more hope than he had experienced for years: 'You do not know what you have done,' she wrote, 'and I have not the words to tell you. The soul's dark cottage in these poems has not only let in the light through chinks that time has made: it has itself become a light shining in the darkness.'[18]

Gathorne-Hardy, too, recognized the mysticism behind such poems, his chosen comparison being with Wordsworth rather than Vaughan. 'I suppose you've never again had so passionate an inspiration as you had when you wrote the War Poems', he suggested in his letter acknowledging receipt of the pieces in manuscript, '– but it seems to me that your philosophy, and your acceptance of life, with all its woes, have strengthened [these] poems.'[19] And it was Gathorne-Hardy, not Keynes, who issued the first collection of spiritual outpourings, *Common Chords*, from his private Mill House Press in 1950.[20]

Keynes, who could usually be relied on for an enthusiastic response, on this occasion failed to give one, regarding Sassoon's privately printed works as his sole domain. 'The old Jackdaw was very annoyed at my letting Bob G-H print a few poems at his amateur press', Sassoon reported to a mutual friend, 'and when Bob sent him his copy (specially done with his name printed at the end to placate his wrath) the sole comment he made to me then and thereafter, was the classic remark "The poetry is better than the printing" – (the first *new* collection of [my] verse he'd perused for more than ten years!)'[21]

The most likely explanation for Sassoon's curious departure from his usual practice of printing his private volumes with Keynes was that he felt uncertain at the new direction his poetry was taking, and suspected it was one that the rationalist Keynes would not appreciate. By the time he was ready with a second collection along similar lines, he was confident enough to return to Keynes for the production of it. Gathorne-Hardy's response to *Emblems of Experience* (1951) was more generous than Keynes's had been to his efforts. 'I was entranced', he told Sassoon, 'by that quiet, wise, ruminative music.'[22] It seemed to him that the voice was now more like another seventeenth-century mystic, George Herbert. Sassoon was gratified by the comparison, though he had been aiming at something nearer to Emily Brontë's 'Last Lines'.

It had taken him just over a year to accumulate the twenty poems for *Emblems of Experience*, a year in which he had had to come to terms with the reality of George's absence and resign himself to the fact that the CBE he received was probably the highest public acknowledgement of his achievements as a writer he could expect. He also faced increasing isolation: 'I could have known so many people so much better than I have,' he wrote in his diary. 'And now it is too late. The curtain has descended on most of them. And it doesn't rise on any new ones. I am left with my efforts to make friends with God, who doesn't appear to be a forthcoming conversationalist.'[23] Though it was not strictly speaking true that he had made no new friends,[24] there was little to lessen his despair by 1951, and the poems of *Emblems of Experience*, even more so than those of *Common Chords*, are a 'cry for salvation'.[25] ' "Take not Thy holy Spirit from us" is all they amount to,' Sassoon concluded.[26]

One of them, 'A Dream', suggests that he had been thinking a great deal about his past.[27] An account of the narrator's meeting with 'a stranger', who turns out to be himself, the poem ends: ' "Stranger," I said, "since you and I are one, / Let us go back. Let us undo what's done." ' (CP, p. 284.) The echoes of Owen's 'Strange Meeting' are more than coincidental. Owen had been much in his mind and the previous month he had written a sonnet about the two of them (never published) which underlines just how depressed he had become by January 1950, the month of its composition:

> An Incident in Literary History
> Sassoon and Owen – names that found their niche
> In literary history. Owen's dead.
> The other one survived the bullet which
> Toward that War's end just grazed him on the head.
> Yes; *his* career continued. But of late,
> His state of mind has made him wonder whether
> Sassoon's continuance was appropriate ...
> Should not these soldier poets have died together?
>
> For thirty years a person of that name
> Has done his level best to supplement
> The scraps that opportunely earned him fame.
> Yet literature's cold chronicles resent
> The existence of this ghost. He should have kept
> Silence, and out in France forever slept.[28]

'Why should anyone want such a "night of memories and sighs"?' Sassoon asked Keynes, suspecting that to the public he might have become 'rather an old bore' and to the Modernists an object of further disapproval.[29] The poems in *Emblems of Experience* seemed to him more deficient in imagery and more abstract than in *Common Chords*, more 'cerebral' as Gathorne-Hardy put it. In contrast to the numerous nature poems of the earlier volume, all but two of the pieces in *Emblems of Experience* are what Sassoon called 'indoor' poems: 'Not a breath of fresh air filters into them. Not one other human face appears in them.'[30] 'Midnight mumblings', he suggested, 'might be taken as their title.'[31]

Tomlinson's suggested 'Stellar Thoughts' would be a more appropriate title for *Emblems of Experience*. It could certainly be applied both literally and metaphorically to one of the most successful poems in the collection, 'Befriending Star'. Like Cardinal Newman's 'Lead Kindly Light', of which there are echoes, this is a plea for simple faith expressed in language which becomes progressively more direct throughout its two quatrains until the narrator's final appeal to the star.

> ... Heart-simplified, appear
> Not in ferocity of elemental fire,
> But, for my lowly faith, a sign by which to steer.
>
> (CP, p. 285)

'Such little things go to make up one's meditative existence,'[32] Sassoon noted at this time. He had been reading Helen Waddell's *Medieval Latin Lyrics* as he worked on his own poems and her translations of five poems by Alcuin had made him conscious of the similarities between men of faith in all ages. Sitting in his 'tall-windowed Wiltshire room, / (Birds overheard from chill March twilight's close)', he imagined the medieval poet undergoing a similar experience to his own, especially his comfort in the night sky:

> Alcuin, from temporalities at rest,
> Sought grace within him, given from afar;
> Noting how sunsets worked around to west;
> Watching, at spring's approach, that beckoning star;
> And hearing, while one thrush sang through the rain,
> Youth, which his soul in Paradise might regain.
>
> (CP, p. 283)

Together with his unpublished poem 'Brevis Quod Gratia Florum Est', 'Awareness of Alcuin' is Sassoon's formal tribute to Helen Waddell at the moment when, though he did not know it, she was beginning her long, slow descent into complete mental extinction.[33]

By the time he came to write the bulk of the poems in *Emblems of Experience*, like Bunyan's Christian Sassoon had already passed through the Slough of Despond, but had not yet reached the Cross, where Christian's burden rolls away. Nevertheless there is acceptance in these poems and an urgent desire for God to 'speak' to him. The irregular line lengths and changing rhythms of a poem like 'The Need' suggest that he has been pushed beyond his customary traditional forms in his effort to convey his desperation, though the careful patterning of consonants and vowels is a familiar feature:

> Nobody knows
> Whither our delirium of invention goes,
> Who turn toward time to come
> Alone with heart-beats, marching to that muffled drum.
> Nobody hears
> Bells from beyond the silence of the years
> That wait for those unborn.
> O God within me, speak from your mysterious morn.
> (CP, p. 285)

Emblems of Experience closes with two poems almost certainly written last, 'The Present Writer', where the poet describes a further step in his spiritual progress, an awareness of 'how little' the 'gnomic mind' can understand without the 'soul', and 'The Messenger':

> Mind, busy in the body's life-lit room;
> Seldom in strength, unpiloted at best;
> How ignorant you admit from outer gloom
> The soul, in all God's world, most welcome guest.
> * * *
> Poor mortal mind, when you, in me, decay –
> When once delighting faculties grow dim –
> Cry on the parting soul for power to say,
> With passion, 'I befriended was by Him.'
> (CP, pp. 286-7)

With his ingrained suspicion of the intellect, Sassoon welcomed such a revelation, which he felt he had been working his way back to all his life:

> First-found beliefs remain. I cannot free
> My thought from looking on Eternity
> As highway for the unresting soul of Man, ...
> * * *
> I see myself, one body on that invisible road;
> Brief bird on air, blind burrowing mole, dumb fish in stream.
> ('World Without End', CP, p. 286)

Ultimately it came down to a blind and trusting 'Acceptance', as his poem of that name argues. But the next step was one he was not yet able to take. For by the time *Emblems of Experience* came out in November 1951, his life had undergone a dramatic change which threatened to distract him from spiritual matters altogether.

*

It is an intriguing story. Sassoon had been corresponding since 1945 with a young Australian woman, Dorothy Wallis, who had written from Melbourne initially to say how much she admired his work. Her letters showed her to be, in his own words, 'a very nice person', of good education, who shared his love of music and ballet.[34] She also started sending fruit cake, chocolate and other luxuries, for which Sassoon was grateful, since rationing continued in England for some time after the war. So that when Glen's stepdaughter Jane planned to visit Australia in 1948, Sassoon hoped that she could 'go and be nice to that angelic young woman who has been sending me parcels of food for the last two years'.[35]

Jane duly did so and the letters continued more warmly than ever. And when Dorothy arrived in England with her mother early in 1951, Sassoon invited her to visit him at Heytesbury. The fact that he waited until December to do so and was 'somewhat hesitant' (according to Dorothy who was longing to meet him) suggests that he feared as well as wanted a further involvement, and his return to work on a fourth volume of autobiography in September that year may indicate a sense of renewed energy and hope.

When she eventually visited Heytesbury in December 1951, he insisted that she stay a whole week, 'long enough', she told Glen, 'to decide that he wanted [her] to remain in his life'.[36] Weekends followed (Dorothy worked in London during the week) until her mother, disapproving of what she suspected was more than simply friendship, made her daughter's life so 'miserable' that Dorothy temporarily stopped seeing Sassoon.[37] Once her mother returned to Australia in August 1952, however, the relationship was resumed with renewed intensity. Sassoon made it quite clear to Dorothy that he wanted her to come to live with him, though not until 1954, when George would be eighteen. He was anxious that neither George nor Hester should know of Dorothy, nor did he talk to any of his friends. He had at first wanted to tell Glen 'everything about us', Dorothy wrote, but later changed his mind.[38]

Edmund and Claire Blunden were the only ones to know of the relationship, since it was Dorothy who had brought about a reconciliation with Sassoon. Hearing him speak of Blunden and their estrangement, without telling Sassoon she had visited Blunden at the office of the *Times Literary Supplement* where he was working by early 1952 and told him how much Sassoon missed him. By August the Blundens had spent several weekends again at Heytesbury. Claire, who believed that Sassoon approved of her for Blunden in spite of a significant age difference, thought that Sassoon was subconsciously influenced by their relationship in his own with Dorothy, who was thirty-six years his junior. She also suggested that Sassoon might still secretly be hoping for more children. Dorothy, she remembered, was an attractive though not conventionally pretty woman, tallish, slim and vivacious, a 'very lively' person. Her great admiration for

Sassoon's work at a time when he felt neglected and undervalued as a poet, Claire maintained, was an important factor in the equation. [39]

By September 1952 when Dorothy resumed her visits to Heytesbury, it seemed to her that 'everything ... promise[d] well' for the future: 'I had seen Siegfried change from the man who believed there was only loneliness ahead of him to one who could say I had been "sent to deliver him" and that he could have "complete trust in my love".'[40] The fact that Blunden claimed to have witnessed the same change in his friend convinced her that she was not deluding herself.

Sassoon's poetry of that period offers strong proof of a renewed hope in life. After a significant gap in his religious questionings in the second half of 1951, when he wrote little or no poetry, the poems of 1952 (following his first meeting with Dorothy) reveal a zest for life long absent from his work. 'The Best of It', written on 27 February 1952, for instance, opens:

> Spring, surgent in the sense-delighted blood;
> In daybreak being all the burst of bud.
> This, beyond argument, was well begun.
>
> (CP, p. 298)

'Another Spring', which appeared in the *Times Literary Supplement* on 20 March 1952, shortly after it was written, conveys an even greater sense of renewal of life and hope:

> Aged self, disposed to lose his hold on life,
> Looks down, at winter's ending, and perceives
> Continuance in some crinkled primrose leaves.
>
> A noise of nesting rooks in tangled trees.
> Stillness – inbreathed, expectant. Shadows that bring
> Cloud-castled thoughts from downland distances.
> Eyes, ears are old. But not the sense of spring.
>
> *Look, listen, live*, some inward watcher warns ...
>
> (CP, pp. 296-7)[41]

Such poems alone suggest that Sassoon's relationship with Dorothy was an invigorating one, as she claimed, revealing as they do a fresh exuberance and joy in earthly things. Claire Blunden believed that the relationship had a physical side to it, though other friends questioned this.[42] After nearly a decade without a sexual relationship it is not impossible that Sassoon responded to an attractive and willing young woman, as she claims he did. A letter to Tomlinson telling him that 1952 was his 'most unworried yet' strengthens the likelihood that his life had changed significantly that year.[43] He also told Tomlinson in October 1952 that his 'inner consciousness' was prompting him with speculations about the problem of body and spirit and that his next volume of verse would be 'a series of variations on that theme'.[44] Having so recently set off on a spiritual quest, a physical relationship with Dorothy would explain why such 'speculations' as the following had raised their heads:[45]

> The Alliance
> 'You figure of flesh, abode of appetites,
> 'Duped by mean motives, frivolous in feeling,
> 'Go your own gait; enjoy those gross delights.
> 'I work elsewhere, in search of heaven-sent healing.'
>
> Thus bragged the spirit, positive in pride,
> Till from far off a wisening voice replied –
> 'Of body and soul there can be no division;
> 'Soul should embrace it, cherish and control.
> 'Our two great halves must share a single vision.
> 'Let mutual services unite them whole.' ...
>
> (CP, p. 299)

The fact that all letters between Sassoon and Blunden for this period have disappeared when almost all their others have been preserved, makes it even more likely that Sassoon felt that there was something to hide. And the clandestine nature of his relationship with Dorothy reinforces this speculation.

When things began to go wrong with Dorothy it was not because of the sexual side, she believed, but a result of her unintentional confrontation with Sassoon's housekeeper, Miss Benn. After a series of disastrous cooks, the last of whom had removed all the silver as she left, at the end of 1949 he had finally discovered Miss Kathleen Benn. An ex-kennel-maid, she brought with her her large poodle, Caesar, whom Sassoon adored. Short, squat and mannish, with cropped hair, she reminded Haro Hodson of a 'shaving brush in specs'.[46] But like all Sassoon's friends he was impressed by her excellent cooking and general efficiency. When the old housekeeper, Mrs Angus, left, Miss Benn took over the whole upkeep of Heytesbury and ran it as if it were a military operation. It was a rule of iron, as Dorothy discovered. Even Sassoon, who was abjectly grateful for a well-run house and first-class cuisine, grew tired at times of Miss Benn's bleak manner, which he complained of to Dorothy. (There was what he called 'the folded arms' situation, when Miss Benn was particularly cross.)[47]

Ostensibly a row about Dorothy daring to clean the candelabrum in the music room, when Miss Benn considered it her province, Dorothy's difference with Miss Benn was really a battle for control. Miss Benn felt her supremacy threatened and presented Sassoon with a choice between herself and Dorothy. He had become so dependent on her for the smooth running of Heytesbury by that point that he chose Miss Benn. She had not only made herself particularly obliging to him during this period, but had also managed to portray Dorothy as domineering and managerial, playing to all his deepest fears about women. (Ironically Miss Benn was much nearer to this stereotype herself and her tyranny over him would increase until he became desperate enough to dismiss her in the late 1950s.) What *he* wanted, he told Dorothy in a letter terminating their relationship, was 'another Florence Hardy; ... She would have abased herself to Miss Benn and all would have been well'.[48]

Dorothy blamed herself for playing into Miss Benn's hands, but Claire Blunden thought that she had probably built the relationship up 'to be more than it could be'.[49] Claire ultimately held Sassoon responsible for events. Though he had 'obviously enjoyed it all', she said, when the first 'glorious romance' became more ordinary, he shied away from commitment.[50] 'Such a charmer,' she remembered, 'but always dodging away from people.'[51]

Another factor which neither Claire nor Dorothy took into account was guilt, since neither was fully aware of Sassoon's spiritual searchings by 1951. While 'The Alliance' expresses the positive aspect of Sassoon's thoughts on the relationship between body and spirit, 'Human Bondage', written in October 1952 at the height of his affair, indicates that there were times when the physical seemed to him a threat to the spiritual enlightenment he had earlier glimpsed:

> I know a night of stars within me;
> Through eyes of dream I have perceived
> Blest apparitions who would win me
> Home to what innocence believed.
>
> I know a universe beyond me;
> Power that pervades the fluctuant soul,
> Signalling my brain it would unbond me
> And make heart's imperfections whole.
> * * *
> I, this blithe structure of sensation,
> Prisoned and impassioned by my clay.
> (CP, p. 300)

His longing for Dr Rivers to return from the dead to clear up his 'confusion' in January 1953 suggests that he was suffering a conflict as powerful as the one Rivers had resolved for him between his pacifism and his devotion to his soldiers. It was shortly afterwards that, according to Dorothy, he decided that she was not the answer to his problems. By the end of January he was focused once more on the 'faithful pilgrimage' on which he had embarked, 'zealous to walk the way of Henry Vaughan', though more aware than ever of the difficulties:

> ... Nature and knowledge daunt with dire denial
> The inward witness and the innocent dream.
> On such rough road must faith endure its trial,

24. An Asking (1950-1956)

Upheld by resolution to redeem
The soul, that world within an ignorant shape
One with the solar system and the ape.

('The Trial', CP, p. 296)

Dorothy did not let go without a struggle. After receiving Sassoon's letter, she wrote at length to Glen with a detailed account of events. Though she had never met him, Sassoon had described him as the only person who understood him: 'If anyone can help now you are the one,' she wrote, claiming that it was 'Siegfried's happiness ... as well as mine' that was at stake.[52] But Glen, having seen how fiercely Sassoon reacted to disloyalty in his friends, however close, refused to become involved. 'You must remember that he is one of my dearest friends', he replied to her desperate plea, 'and that I should naturally tend to see things from his point of view.'[53] Even more cogently he argued, in terms which show how well he understood Sassoon's character by 1953: 'I know he is a man who hates upsets and quarrelling. Also when he makes a decision about anything he usually sticks to it.'[54] So Dorothy was forced to accept defeat and Sassoon was faced again with a lonely life at Heytesbury.

He did not return immediately to his spiritual quest, however. His relationship with Dorothy, whatever its outcome, had given him a taste for more human pleasures, for company in particular. As he implied in a poem written at the very end of 1952, 'Retreat from Eternity', the earthly was so much less 'numbing' than the heavenly.[55] After over a year of her visits he was ready to admit that he had probably lost as well as gained by living at Heytesbury. Every year fewer friends made their way to Wilt- shire. Either they were too busy, like Glen and Keynes, or too infirm, like Tomlinson or de la Mare, or simply no longer alive, like Marsh who had died in January that year. Though too deeply rooted in Heytesbury to live elsewhere, Sassoon felt he must 'compel' himself to leave it more often.[56] Apart from other considerations Miss Benn, whose triumph over Dorothy had strengthened her hold over Sassoon, quite reasonably insisted on a holiday periodically. So, less than a fortnight after his final letter to Dorothy of 6 May 1953, he set out for a ten-day visit to Cambridge, the first of many such trips in the fifties.

His choice of Cambridge was relatively easy. Not only was it a short drive from the Keyneses' house at Brinkley near Newmarket, but also the place he expected George to attend university in a few years' time. Just as he had cultivated Rolf Barber's company initially for the sake of his son's future at Oundle, so he now planned to make Cambridge a 'centre' in advance of George's arrival there.[57] In addition most of what he dolefully called his 'few remaining connexions' were there.[58] E.M. Forster had finally accepted a post at King's after the death of his mother, and Keynes, whose company Sassoon still sought whatever his reservations, not only lived nearby but had also introduced him to a number of his friends and

377

relatives in or on the outskirts of the town. In addition Sassoon's work on
Meredith had brought him into contact with G.M. Trevelyan and his circle,
one of whom was S.C. Roberts, the Master of Pembroke. He had also by
1953 resumed relations with Edmund Gosse's son, Philip, who had retired
to Cambridge.

Sassoon had known Philip since his childhood, when Philip and his
sisters, Tessa and Sylvia, had visited Weirleigh regularly with their
mother. Seven years older than Sassoon, he had not been close to him at
that time, but later, after his father's death, they had started to write to
each other occasionally about events from their past. It was only when
Philip and his daughter Jennifer moved to Cambridge in the 1940s,
however, that he and Sassoon had become real friends. Philip, who had
served as a medic in the First World War and knew Keynes, had also
established connections with Trinity, where Trevelyan was Master. Sassoon had hoped to meet him there during his own visits to Trevelyan in
1946 and his letter to that effect was the beginning of a regular correspondence which ended only with Philip's death in 1959 at the age of eighty.

Sassoon's visits to Philip and his third wife, the Irish poet Anna Keown,
were an important feature of his Cambridge stays.[59] His affection for them
showed itself in a number of ways, from agreeing to write a foreword to
Anna's collected poems in 1952,[60] to allowing Philip to print his cricket skit
in the style of Shakespeare at his private press, the Golden Head.[61] Anna's
death in 1957 and its profound effect on Philip would not only be a great
sadness to Sassoon, but a factor in his decision against making Cambridge
his second home.

He would be similarly affected by the deaths of Gwen Raverat and
Frances Cornford in 1957 and 1960 respectively. Gwen, a painter and
fringe member of the Bloomsbury Group, had left Cambridge for France
after her marriage to another painter, Jacques Raverat, but had returned
to live there after his early death. Born Gwen Darwin, she was a sister of
Margaret Keynes and cousin of Frances Cornford. As members of the
Darwin family they were, together with the Keyneses, Huxleys and Wedg-
woods, at the centre of Cambridge life.

Sassoon had first met Frances in the 1920s, long before he got to know
the Keyneses. It seems fitting that it should have been at the house of
Walter de la Mare, since it was poetry which lay at the heart of their
friendship. Frances, who was an exact contemporary of Sassoon, was
herself (in his words) 'a classic poet, *minor* in the best sense of the word'
and fully appreciated Sassoon's work.[62] It was after reading *The Heart's
Journey* belatedly in 1931 that she first wrote inviting him to visit her and
her husband in Cambridge. Though Sassoon found her poetry 'overlaid
with Cambridge intellectualism and refinement' in places, he also thought
it 'full of lovely sensitive things, with a magical touch for the ordinary'.[63]
Her later poems, he believed, were examples of 'perfected art'.[64] By 1949
he was instructing his young friend Haro to read her, in 1959 would

nominate her for a Royal Society of Literature medal and by 1961 would declare her one of his two 'favourite women poets by a long chalk'.[65] (The other was still Charlotte Mew, Edith Sitwell having gone out of favour with him sometime in the thirties.)

Though Sassoon had met Frances independently of the Keyneses, when he started to visit Geoffrey and Margaret at Lammas House, Brinkley, where they moved in 1950, they would often make the short drive into Cambridge to have tea with Frances, taking Sassoon with them. 'Tea with Mrs Cornford' subsequently became an important component of his pilgrimages east.

One of the pleasures of visiting her was that he sometimes met Gwen Raverat at her house. He had known Gwen since at least the late thirties, when he had commissioned a small woodcut from her for the jacket and title page of *The Old Century*. Gwen had been a pioneer in the revival of wood engraving and Sassoon one of her most enthusiastic converts, decorating the title page of all three of his autobiographies in this way. He would also ask Gwen to supply a device for the title page of *The Tasking* in 1954, but she was too ill by then to oblige. Sassoon thought Gwen's own venture into autobiography, *Period Piece: A Cambridge Childhood* (1952), 'one of the most delightful and honest books ever written'.[66] He was equally admiring of her paintings and bought a number of them over the years.[67] His favourite, which hung in his bedroom, was a view of the River Cam looking towards Queen's and the boathouse of his usual stopping place in Cambridge, the Garden House Hotel.

It was at this hotel on the evening of his arrival in town from the Keyneses on 19 May 1953 that he entertained the young man who was to 'nourish and enliven' him for the next fourteen years, Dennis Silk.[68] The meeting came about through Blunden who, like all Sassoon's friends, worried about his isolation. Blunden and Silk were both old boys of Christ's Hospital and had met at a school reunion. On hearing of Sassoon's trip to Cambridge, Blunden suggested Sassoon look the young man up at the university cricket grounds. The combination of Blunden's recommendation and cricket had been irresistible and Sassoon was at Fenners within hours of his arrival. Dennis Silk, a 21-year-old history student in his second year at Sidney Sussex College, retains a vivid memory of 'the gaunt, handsome stranger in moth-eaten blue blazer and faded trilby hat who marched up to the pavilion with a long forked hazel staff in his hand'.[69] Looking up at the rows of seated spectators, he said 'in a tone of enquiry and a little awkwardly: "Dennis Silk"?'[70] When Dennis, who was playing for the university team against Worcestershire, identified himself, the reply was simply 'Siegfried Sassoon'. It was a name which, even by 1953, needed no explanation. But their talk that first afternoon was not of poetry but of Blunden and cricket.

Sassoon's enthusiasm was immediate. Not only did he invite Dennis to dinner that same evening, but also wrote the next day to Philip and Anna

Gosse, asking if he could bring 'a young gentleman' called Silk to lunch with them.[71] In addition he planned to take Dennis to tea with the Keyneses and would later introduce him to Forster at King's. In a short time Dennis would get to know all Sassoon's closest friends, becoming in the process an invaluable source of information about their relationships with Sassoon. Some he would meet at Heytesbury, where he would stay many times in the following years.

In asking to bring Dennis with him to the Gosses, Sassoon described him as 'quite exceptionally nice and intelligent' and one of 'the most successful of this year's University cricketers'.[72] And it was this mix of physical and mental prowess, together with his 'modesty' and 'gentleness', which particularly appealed to him.[73] Dennis would go on to achieve great things in sport, playing cricket for the MCC several years running, as well as rugby to county standard: Sassoon referred to him proudly as 'my splendid cricketer Silk' and when Dennis was on tour would follow his every run.[74]

Equally important to him, however, was Dennis's great love of literature. He found 'instructing young Silk about literature' just as enjoyable as discussing cricket with him, according to his diary, and talked to him at length about his own work. Dennis's public readings of Sassoon's poetry suggest that he had found a perceptive and appreciative audience in the young man. And it was not just for his work. Silk loved hearing Sassoon expound 'endlessly and unforgettably' about the First World War: '"my old war" as he called it, exorcising the ghosts of 1914-1918':

> ... His memory for the names of his men, the dates on which he went into the line, the everyday details of existence in Flanders was phenomenal. He would sometimes dart upstairs to the manuscript room and come down with little black trench notebooks. I saw the first pencil drafts of famous anthologised poems. I learnt what it had really been like to fight in France.[75]

Sometimes they would sit down in the library after dinner and, before either of them realized it, dawn had risen. Sassoon felt he was again reliving the past, particularly the time when he made his 'agonizing protest'.[76] Dennis brought back his youth to him at a time when he was feeling his age badly. 'He blossomed in the company of young people', Dennis remembered, 'and gave richly of his energy and vitality.'[77]

In a short time Dennis became indispensable to Sassoon, who would be delighted when he accepted a teaching post at Marlborough College, only thirty miles from Heytesbury. It was a decision influenced by the fact that Sassoon told him it would be a great 'boon' to him and he quickly bought Dennis a half-share in an old car so that he could come to see him more easily.[78] And as he grew less willing to drive himself, Dennis would also chauffeur him in his ancient Humber. They both looked forward to the annual visits they made to Glen and Angela at Stratford, for instance, where Glen was first co-director, then director of the Shakespeare Memorial Theatre from 1952 to 1959. Seeing stars like Lawrence Olivier and Peggy Ashcroft nightly was an unforgettable experience. They also met there the Shakespearian scholar Dover Wilson, whom Dennis charmed into addressing the Marlborough Literary Society. Sassoon was invited to the talk and would start to correspond with Wilson, whose work he greatly admired.

Being approved by Glen was one of the tests Sassoon set for new friends (a test Dorothy had almost but not quite been allowed to take), and he had no hesitation in introducing Dennis, who passed at once. 'He is one of the best characters I've known in my life,' he told Haro shortly before his death, 'and like Glen, who loves him, kind beyond computation.'[79] Dennis came to occupy a similar place to Glen and Blunden in Sassoon's affections. Dennis's heterosexuality freed Sassoon, as it had with Blunden, from what he called the 'cursed complication of sex' and when Dennis married in 1963, Sassoon's feelings for him would remain unchanged, except that they would expand to include his wife, Diana, whom he would pronounce 'quite perfect'.[80] According to Dennis, his relationship with Sassoon was entirely 'uncomplicated'.[81] He 'never sniffed any hint of homosexuality' about him and was very surprised indeed when he detected it in Sassoon's published diaries after his death.[82] The relationship seemed to him like that of father and son, a view confirmed by Claire Blunden. When in 1955, at the age of eighteen, Sassoon's own son married very suddenly and without telling his parents, Sassoon, 'bewildered, puzzled and hurt', would turn gratefully to Dennis for consolation.[83] 'He is like a son to me,' he would write to a clergyman friend, Richard Seymour, in December 1956.[84] Much as he adored George, there were times when he found himself wishing that he could be 'more like Dennis Silk in gentleness'.[85] Dennis was an ideal friend for Sassoon, bringing youth, vitality, idealism and hope to him at a crucial point in his life. After Blunden left England again for the University of Hong Kong in September 1953, Sassoon would rely increasingly on Silk for sympathy and stimulation, and his presence at Cambridge in 1953 and 1954 added greatly to its attraction during those years.

So, too, did the award of an honorary fellowship at his old college, Clare, at the end of 1953.[86] Though he claimed not to be interested in worldly honours, Sassoon was intensely gratified by the suggestion that his name should be put forward for a fellowship in October 1953. It took him completely by surprise, he told the Master of Clare, Sir Henry Thirkhill, but he had no hesitation in accepting the idea. Thirkhill's confirmation of his unanimous election on 3 November helped to make up for the long years of neglect he felt he had suffered. Whereas his CBE had seemed to him more of a 'devaluation distinction' than otherwise,[87] he agreed with S.C. Roberts, who wrote in his letter of congratulation that 'Honorary Fellowships constitute one of the few honours that remain very strictly and exclusively honourable' and that he would enjoy 'the highest possible status' at Clare.[88] He was anxious to point out to de la Mare that he was only the fifteenth Fellow to be elected since 1898. For someone who had come down from Cambridge without a degree and suffered from a sense of intellectual inferiority all his life, it was a heady moment. From this point on he would include a few days' residence at Clare in spring and autumn as part of his Cambridge season.

On one such visit in late 1954 he agreed to give an informal talk to students in the rooms of Professor John Northam, head of English. 'There was no society behind the occasion to guarantee a reasonable attendance,' Professor Northam remembers; 'I had simply let it be known that Sassoon was to speak.'[89] He therefore 'ate an anxious dinner' in Sassoon's company, 'mentally coining phrases of regret suitable to an audience of six, four, even of two'.[90] After all, as he pointed out, the Great War, to which Sassoon's name was 'riveted', had long passed:

> In the event my rooms were packed; the atmosphere was intense and it remained so throughout the evening. Not because of anything in Sassoon's performance. He did not perform. His only response to the occasion was to read from his own works in a quiet near-mumble. My recollection is that he pipe-smoked as he talked. He made few comments, none of them memorable. And yet not only did he keep the attention of his audience for the duration of the talk proper, but he mesmerized them into staying long after the talk had ended. In the end he had to be rescued.
>
> I have often wondered why he worked so powerfully upon those much younger men. Only a few, I fancy, knew his writings with any intimacy. Some, I suppose, had come out of curiosity to see a hero from a great and terrible enterprise that had become a legend. But for most, I believe, Sassoon was more than a writer or a relic. What excited their interest and admiration was his other kind of courage, the courage that made him reject war and the prestige that he had won through war. It was not the V.C. quality they had come to pay respect to, but the man who had thrown his decorations away in protest. What gripped them that evening was his integrity.[91]

One of the students present, Tim Rix, agrees that 'integrity' is 'exactly the right word' for Sassoon's appeal that evening.[92] Like the rest of the young men he found Sassoon 'mesmerizing'. It was partly because of the habit Northam noted of pipe-smoking throughout his performance – 'He lit and relit his pipe about eighty times in all and spoke in bursts in between puffs,' Rix remembers, leaving a large pyramid of used matches on the arm of his chair. But he was also riveted by Sassoon's appearance as he sat alone in the centre of the room with his 'great hawk-like head', a 'tremendous presence' in the midst of them.

*

However pleasing such public recognition of his work and however many new friends Sassoon made in the early fifties, they could not satisfy his deepest needs. By the end of 1953, without even wanting or willing it, he believed that 'creative existence as a whole is what matters to the future' and that 'the spirit of God (or good) should pervade and prevail'.[93] In spite of the fact that his own existence seemed to him 'insignificant', he felt he was being gradually compelled to believe, recording each stage of his journey in poems marking moments of illumination. Many of them seemed to him to arrive from nowhere, a process he had experienced only occasionally in his earlier life. It was, as he describes in 'The Visitant' (a poem Masefield considered one of his best), almost like being possessed:

> Someone else I know of – neither young nor old –
> Seated late at night in my accustomed chair,
> Willed to an intended thing which must be told,
> Catches intimations brought from otherwhere.
>
> Someone else invades me for an hour or two.
> Clocked occluded self wrote never lines like his.
> Me he has no need of. And I know not who
> Or from what irrational inwardness he is.
>
> (CP, p. 292)

The poems written between 1952 and 1954, published as *The Tasking*, show a greater spiritual awareness and sense of inwardness than any previous volume. 'Renewals', for instance, records an experience very close to T.S. Eliot's words in 'Ash Wednesday', 'Teach us to sit still':

> I said to downcast eyes –
> Look up; accept surprise
> Which waits, all welcomings.
> I said to shuttered ears –
> Heed how earth music nears
> On wonder's wind-swept strings.
>
> Unquesting heart I told
> To be made manifold
> Through love's resurgent will.
> I said to fitful mind –
> Put discontents behind;
> Be silent and grow still.
>
> (CP, p. 301)

Sassoon's earlier reading of the seventeenth-century mystic John Norris of Bemerton, a small parish not far from Heytesbury where another mystic, George Herbert, had also served as a priest, suggests that he was already searching for inner stillness when he quoted Norris in *Siegfried's Journey* in 1946: 'Quietude is essential to human happiness ... The solitary and contemplative man sits as safe in his retirement as of Homer's heroes in a cloud, and has this only trouble from the follies and extravagances of men, that he pities them.'[94] His own favourite poem from *The Tasking*, 'The Chord', centres on a similar theme, conveying an experience of God anticipated by his habit of sitting down to the piano for inspiration long before he started on his spiritual quest:

> On stillness came a chord,
> While I, the instrument,
> Knew long-withheld reward:
> Gradual the glory went;
> Vibrating, on and on,
> Toward harmony unheard,
> Till dark where sanctus shone;
> Lost, once a living word.
>
> But in me yet abode
> The given grace though gone;
> The love, the lifted load,
> The answered orison.
>
> (CP, p. 303)

But there are also signs of doubt and despair in *The Tasking*. These feelings may have resulted partly from outward events, such as the death of Wavell's son, Archie, at the end of 1953 just as Sassoon was getting to know him, or George's increasing independence which kept him away from Heytesbury for months at a time. But they also sprang from what Sassoon subsequently recognized as an essential stage in the spiritual process. The paradox of his position emerges most clearly in the last poem to be written in *The Tasking*, 'Faith Unfaithful':

> Mute, with signs I speak:
> Blind, by groping seek:
> Heed; yet nothing hear:
> Feel; find no one near.
>
> Deaf, eclipsed, and dumb,
> Through this gloom I come
> On the time-path trod
> Toward ungranted God ...
>
> (CP, p. 294)

The Tasking was privately printed by Keynes in November 1954.[95] Sassoon had hoped to arrange the poems as a sequence, but eventually had to accept that they were 'separate condensations or considerations ... merely an exhibition of the spiritual and intellectual shortcomings of a man trying to find things out for himself – *attempting to formulate his private religion* step by step'.[96] The 'complete absence of emotional excitement or preliminary mental chemistry' he experienced as he struggled to express each new insight may help to explain their spareness and condensed force.[97] Not a word or image is wasted. Sassoon's own description of his work in *The Tasking* is 'plainsong and essential expression'.[98] Though very different in both content and technique from his war satires, the poetry of this last period shares its muscularity and power.

Sassoon was enormously relieved at his friends' responses to *The Tasking*. 'The poems evidently do well,' he wrote to the man he claimed as the book's 'godfather', Tomlinson.[99] He was 'especially pleased' by Swinnerton saying that he found them '*refreshing* – and not depressing', since he had thought of them as 'a rather gloomy offering'.[100] And George Trevelyan, who could be 'a bit forbidding', had said he 'love[d] them and was deeply moved'.[101] John Betjeman boldly declared that the poems '*must* be immortal' and Keynes forwarded 'kind comments' from Rupert Hart-Davis, remarks that helped offset Sassoon's fears of dismissal by Modernist critics like Graves, Edith Sitwell and Geoffrey Grigson.[102]

*

The last stage of Sassoon's spiritual odyssey was the hardest. Following the composition of the final poem of *The Tasking* in March 1954, he suffered nearly three years of 'dark night'.[103] Helen Waddell's mental decline and the death of his inspirational young friend Archie Wavell in Kenya had deprived him of the two people he believed could have helped him find his way through it. The most obvious candidate, his clergyman friend Richard Seymour, 'though so holy', was 'too self-effacing and modest' to be of any use.[104] 1953 and 1954 were 'special years of frustration and discouragement and solitude' and 1955 and 1956 'little better'.[105] The deaths of two old friends who had been of particular importance to him, Max Beerbohm and Walter de la Mare, made 1956 even more of a trial.[106]

Outwardly his life followed a familiar pattern of spring and autumn breaks at Cambridge, with summer trips to Glen at Stratford beginning in 1955. There were a few new developments. In 1953, for instance, he got to know the Warden of All Soul's, Oxford, John Sparrow, and a young man Sparrow brought with him on a visit to Heytesbury that year, Colin Fenton.[107] Fenton, according to Dennis Silk, was 'very beautiful' and Sassoon welcomed his company for that and other reasons. Though Fenton, who had no private income, went on to become a director of the wine merchants Harveys in Bristol and liked to discuss wine with Sassoon, his real interests were literary. Sassoon was delighted when he decided, almost certainly at Sassoon's suggestion, to edit the works of Sassoon's old friend and one of his favourite poets, Ralph Hodgson. Fenton would also to some extent take over Dennis's role as willing chauffeur after Dennis's marriage in 1963. And it would be Fenton, rather than any of Sassoon's close friends, who would write his obituary in *The Times*.[108]

There were other distractions to break up the monotony of Sassoon's existence. He enjoyed a visit to the Whistlers at Lyme Regis in June 1954, for example, and a reunion of the Royal Welch Fusiliers at Swindon in July, when he met a number of officers he had known in the First World War and was presented to the Queen. And he was pleased to encounter Robert Graves again in October 1954 after a gap of twenty-seven years. Graves, who was delivering the Clark lectures at Cambridge, seemed to him as 'provocative' as ever, but 'personally likeable' in a way he had forgotten over the years.[109] Still as much 'half schoolboy and half schoolmaster' as when Robbie Ross had coined the phrase nearly forty years earlier, Graves would always remain for Sassoon an intriguing opposite, a 'queer fish'.[110] While he appreciated Graves's renewed admiration for his work, for instance, he felt it could only be perverseness which made Graves irreverent about Tennyson and Wordsworth and dismissive of Pope's technique in his Clark lectures. He himself turned down an invitation to deliver the lectures the following year because he felt he had nothing to say.

He was delighted, too, when George won a science scholarship to King's College, Cambridge, in 1955, though his son's sudden marriage a few months later devastated him and it was many months before he could face meeting him and his even younger wife. A disagreement with Keynes over his plans to publish an edition of Rupert Brooke's letters left him more marooned than ever at Heytesbury. By November 1956 the Suez crisis and the 'ghastly state of the world' generally added to his gloom and he began to complain once more of solitude.[111]

The publication of *Sequences*, Faber's collected trade edition of *Common Chords*, *Emblems of Experience* and *The Tasking*, on 9 November 1956 brought matters to a head. After sixteen years of 'patience and silence' on his part, he had hoped that the reviewers would at least appreciate his painful efforts to bare his soul.[112] Instead he was largely dismissed or ignored, a situation he found 'heartbreaking'.[113] As Robert Nye would point out in his review of *Siegfried Sassoon: Poet's Pilgrimage* in the *Scotsman* on 28 July 1973: 'The reviewers were not ready for the seriousness of these poems, their spiritual desolateness, their Vaughan-like hardness of language.' Blunden alone appeared to recognize his aims and achievement, arguing, as he had from the start, that Sassoon was 'essentially a religious poet'.[114]

Ironically, it was this least publicly acclaimed of all his works which was to have a more powerful effect on Sassoon's fate than anything since his First World War poetry. Not only would it win him the prestigious Queen's Gold Medal for Poetry in June 1957, but it would also lead to the complete transformation of the last ten years of his life. For it was one of *Sequences*' first readers, Mother Margaret Mary McFarlin, who recognized the spiritual darkness with which Sassoon had struggled for almost three years and who was eventually able to lead him out of it.

Doms and Dames
(1957-1960)

It seems extraordinary now, the sense of rejuvenation I experienced so intensely that summer [of 1957]. I had been telling myself in previous years that I had ceased to be capable of strong emotional aliveness, and supposed that was why my poetry had dried up. And then, for most of that year, came the greatest emotional ferment of my life, in love with the supernatural, so to speak – a kind of spiritual childhood and adolescence – and have been slowly growing up ever since. I like to think that such a transformation, at nearly 71, is evidence of the agelessness of the human spirit – anyhow, the *mind* doesn't grow old, while the brain remains in sound condition.

(Sassoon to Dame Felicitas Corrigan,
21 January 1960)[1]

Mother Margaret Mary McFarlin, according to Sassoon, was 'the greatest benefactor' of his life.[2] Mother Superior of the Convent of the Assumption in Kensington Square, London, she first wrote to him about *Sequences* at the beginning of January 1957. Reading his poems while convalescing from flu, she had felt an overwhelming urge to tell him that she was praying he might (in his own words) 'through the Darkness divine God's Presence'.[3] 'I was in a complete black-out', Sassoon remembered, '... and somehow was helped to realize that deliverance had arrived.'[4] His reply by return on 10 January was the first step in his entry into the Roman Catholic Church eight months later.

Sensitive, intelligent and devout without being in the least stuffy, Mother Margaret, as Sassoon recognized, 'never made a glimmer of mistake in her guidance and influence'.[5] Sensing that his faith sprang from emotions rather than intellect, she avoided overwhelming him with ponderous theology, appealing first to his love of literature. Her early letters deal mainly with their shared love of the Jesuit poet Gerard Manley Hopkins, Thomas Hardy and Robert Browning and the metaphysicals Henry Vaughan and George Herbert. She also suggested that he read the mystical writings of St John of the Cross and directed him towards the sermons of one of the Catholic Church's greatest converts, John Henry Newman. 'Reading Newman,' Sassoon would write in 1960, 'I wonder what effect it would have made if someone had given it to me ten years ago. Everything I needed is there, waiting for me! All clear as daylight. And as simple as falling off a log – just unconditional surrender!'[6] He longed for Newman's 'deep, silent, hidden peace ... like some well in a retired and shady place, difficult of access'.[7]

The 'unconditional surrender' was not long in coming, thanks largely to the stream of letters between the 54-year-old nun from Liverpool, who began each of hers with the confident words 'Beloved Son in Christ' and the 70-year-old poet, who addressed her as his 'Dear Mother'. (A variant on this was 'Cornucopia Mother'.)[8] His lengthy weekly reports, describing his spiritual progress and much else, quickly replaced his lonely diary musings and, unlike his diary, always produced a reply, except in Lent, when Mother Margaret was not allowed to write.

By Lent, however – more specifically by Ash Wednesday, 5 March 1957 – less than two months after his first letter to Mother Margaret, Sassoon had begun to face up to 'the proposition of becoming a Catholic'.[9] And by Easter he had regained his belief in God, an intense experience he described in a poem written the day following Good Friday:

> Deliverance
> No comfort came until I looked for light
> Beyond the darkened thickets of my brain.
> With nothingness I strove. And inward sight
> No omen but oblivion could obtain.
>
> He spoke. He held my spirit in His hand.
> Through prayer my password from the gloom was given.
> This Eastertide, absolved, in strength I stand.
> Feet firm upon the ground. My heart in heaven.[10]

Overwhelmed with relief and happiness Sassoon rushed up to London and presented himself, unannounced, at Mother Margaret's convent in Kensington Square. She would later recall the 'tall, wiry, nervy man' who talked to her in 'bursts of speech' that often seemed 'barely intelligible', and her surprise at his shabby clothing, though she recognized an 'innate elegance'.[11] Tiny, bubbly, outgoing and highly articulate herself, she was in many ways his opposite and an unlikely candidate for the sainthood he bestowed on her.[12] An inspiring teacher, she was quite ready to liven up events by unconventional means, dancing the Charleston on feast days, for example, or singing Fred Astaire and Ginger Rogers hits to hold her students' attention, behaviour which would have horrified Sassoon in earlier years.

But she was also very practical, and it was at her suggestion that he started instruction in the Catholic faith with Dom Sebastian Moore at Downside Abbey, only fifteen miles from Heytesbury. Beginning on 30 May and continuing throughout June and July, he drove there once a week to 'converse' with the Benedictine monk. Dom Sebastian, now in his eighties, still remembers Sassoon's arrival every Wednesday afternoon in his dark-green Humber, by then showing signs of its age, its antiquated hood secured not altogether effectively by yellow adhesive plaster, which 'glistened bravely in the sun' and matched Sassoon's equally ancient hat.[13]

One of the younger monks, 'dear old Sebby' (as he quickly became to Sassoon) had not been Mother Margaret's first choice. But he seemed an ideal person to instruct Sassoon, being himself a poet as well as an authority on another First World War writer, David Jones.[14] Like Mother Margaret he immediately sensed Sassoon's needs and kept things informal, holding their weekly sessions in the abbey's rock garden. He 'asked no questions', according to Sassoon, 'just let it happen through self-expression on both sides'.[15] Dom Sebastian's main memory is of how 'unorthodox' his instruction was, with only the Trinity briefly discussed, 'a bit of the Eternal Generation of the Logos and Salvation Through Christ'.[16] He knew Sassoon's war poetry well and had already thought, as a younger man, that it represented an 'attractive agnosticism'.[17] It was therefore something of a surprise to him when Sassoon failed to 'come back' at him with doubts and questions. An indirect method of instruction, it suited Sassoon perfectly and by August he felt ready to commit himself completely to what he called the 'Old Faith'.

Part of the explanation for the speed of Sassoon's conversion was that he was already well prepared when he started his instruction, having read widely on the subject under Mother Margaret's skilful direction. Dom Sebastian had also noted at their first meeting, both in Sassoon's vocabulary and his stillness, the qualities of the mystic for whom no detailed intellectual argument was needed. Sassoon had been particularly struck by Hilaire Belloc's letter to another devout Catholic, Lady Katharine Asquith:

> The Faith, the Catholic Church, is discovered, is recognized, triumphantly enters reality like a landfall at sea which first was thought a cloud. The nearer it is seen, the more it is real, the less imaginary: the more direct and external its voice, the more indubitable its representative character, its 'persona', its voice. The metaphor is not that men fall in love with it: the metaphor is that they discover home. 'This is what I sought. This was my need.' It is the very mould of the mind, the matrix to which corresponds in every outline the outcast and unprotected contour of the soul. It is Verlaine's 'Oh! Rome – oh! Mère!' And that not only to those who had it in childhood and have returned, but much more – and what a proof! – to those who come upon it from over the hills of life and say to themselves, 'Here is the town.'[18]

Belloc's 'magnificent words settled it, once and for all', Sassoon wrote: ' "That's done it," I said. My whole being was liberated.'[19]

He had also been helped by another close friend of Katharine Asquith, Monsignor Ronald Knox.[20] He had started reading Knox in 1939 when he came across the newly published *Let Dons Delight* and by 1943 was recommending it, together with *Barchester Pilgrimage* (1935), to Walter de la Mare as 'cosy' reading. He also loved Knox's essays, published posthumously in *Literary Distractions* (1958), and found one of them, 'French with Tears', so funny that he would read it, literally, with tears rolling down his cheeks. But it was Knox's more serious works, especially his sermons, that he read and re-read in the lead-up to his conversion and he found it impossible to 'measure [his] debt' to Knox's instructive writings.[21]

He had got to know Knox reasonably well in 1954 when he started revisiting Violet Bonham Carter's sister-in-law, Katharine Asquith. He had first met Katharine through Violet in the 1930s, when, ironically, he had commented unfavourably on her conversion to Roman Catholicism,[22] and had been reintroduced to her in the 1950s through Violet's daughter, Cressida, who also disapproved of her aunt's adopted faith. Knox, who was two years younger than Sassoon, had gone to live in the Asquith household after the Second World War, having by then retired as Catholic chaplain to the University of Oxford. Officially there to complete his new translation of the Bible based on the Vulgate text, he unofficially acted as private chaplain to the Asquith family and his presence reinforced Mells as a Catholic centre, its nearness to Downside (only eight miles away) adding to its attractions. Like Newman, Knox had himself been a convert, which may help to explain the appeal of both writers for Sassoon.

Though Sassoon never referred directly to his spiritual needs to Knox on his frequent visits to Mells Manor between 1954 and 1957 – 'I wouldn't dare to speak of *religion* to him!' he told a friend in 1955 – Knox reached him 'with a living voice through his writings, as no one else'.[23] Dennis Silk, who drove Sassoon to Mells on numerous occasions, believed that Knox was 'the most influential' factor in Sassoon's conversion.[24] He certainly gave intellectual respectability to Rome in Sassoon's eyes. But in addition to that, behind the 'incredibly brilliant and accomplished' front of the Old Etonian and Balliol scholar, Sassoon detected a 'creative sanctity' and 'near-saint[liness]', an 'incomparable expositor of alive religion'.[25] Above all he found that Knox '*gave* with both hands – spiritual help, scholarship, entertainment'.[26] On his last visit to the priest, shortly before Knox's death from cancer at the age of sixty-nine, he had taken Blunden to meet him and Knox had talked to them for three and a half hours 'with full enjoyment of seeing us', almost making Sassoon forget 'how heartbreaking it was, that farewell'.[27]

Knox's illness was the reason he gave Mother Margaret for not taking on Sassoon's instruction as she had suggested in 1957, though Katharine Asquith's son, Lord Oxford and Asquith, thinks that Knox was also temperamentally opposed to such 'exchange of intimacies'.[28] Mother Margaret had got to know him well during his period as chaplain to her convent at Aldenham during the Second World War. It is quite possible, even likely, that they had subsequently discussed Sassoon once he started visiting Mells in 1954 and that Mother Margaret's first letter to Sassoon had been prompted by something slightly more than a voice from above. Knox himself was far too subtle to have broached the subject of Sassoon's evident needs directly with him when it was clear that Sassoon himself was not ready to ask for help. Yet in all essential respects it was Knox who seems to have guided him towards the Catholic Church, suggesting that what might otherwise appear as a hasty conversion had been really a more gradual process over a number of years.

When Sassoon was received into the Church at Downside on 14 August 1957, the Eve of the Feast of the Assumption, it was, therefore, the culmination of years of thought and reading. Yet his inward experience during the next few days seemed to him 'something unfathomable by the mind'.[29] He 'just allowed it to happen, knowing and yet unknowing', finally at peace with himself and the world.[30]

However private the experience, Sassoon was fully aware of his news value as a high-profile convert and was greatly relieved that the Catholic papers had been persuaded to say nothing. But the 'gutter press', to his disgust, 'found out somehow and were all after [him]'.[31] Though the *News of the World* got very little from a wary abbot when they telephoned Downside, a persuasive reporter waylaying a more naïve Sassoon at Heytesbury managed to winkle a detailed account from him by reassuring him that he would not print anything he said. When the so-called 'interview' appeared Sassoon felt 'ill and utterly miserable for two solid weeks', until *The Times* published his letter explaining that the interview had been in reality his 'expostulation against [his] most sacred intimacies being exhibited as newspaper publicity'.[32] The news of his conversion, leaked so publicly, surprised almost everyone, including those closest to him, since he had told no one of his intentions, not even Glen, Blunden or Dennis. But he had no real cause for worry; his friends appeared to be delighted for him, with two exceptions: Laurence Whistler, whose violent reaction startled him – he felt that Laurie 'would quite gladly have lit the faggots at the stake'[33] – and Frank Swinnerton, a 'rational sceptic' who had 'no sympathy', he wrote, with Sassoon's 'final acceptance of clerical supervision'.[34]

Even Keynes, a confirmed agnostic married to a Darwin, responded positively to the news. Sassoon had feared ('unjustly', he later acknowledged) that he would be 'unsympathetic and insensitive',[35] but like all his true friends Keynes welcomed anything that might help offset the desolation of his life in the late forties and early fifties. Whatever his own position, he had 'always recognized Sassoon's spiritual leanings'.[36] Before long Sassoon would be taking Geoffrey and his wife to visit Mother Margaret, who had become Mother Superior at the convent school Hengrave Hall in Bury St Edmunds, not far from the Keyneses' house at Brinkley. They could 'only agree', Geoffrey wrote, that she was 'the loveliest and holiest – there is no other word for it – personality' they had ever encountered.[37] However critical he might be of Keynes, Sassoon acknowledged that he was 'good' for him and a 'truly reliable friend'.[38] By 1958, their differences over the Rupert Brooke *Letters* had been buried and Keynes was hard at work on another project to boost Sassoon's morale, a bibliography of all his verse and prose works. Though he had told Keynes that he was not particularly keen on a bibliography when Keynes first suggested it in 1950,[39] even taking a certain pleasure in concealing information from Keynes at times (according to Dennis), he was secretly reassured by this sign of his importance as a writer and eventually agreed to help Keynes compile it. To follow names like Jane Austen, Donne, Blake and Hazlitt as one of Keynes's bibliographical subjects was too great an honour to turn down.

Keynes would also be responsible for managing an even more gratifying recognition of his achievements, when he arranged to receive his own honorary doctorate from Oxford at the same time as Sassoon, 'knowing how difficult it might be to prise Sassoon out of his shell' otherwise.[40] Together with the Russian poetess Anna Akhmatova and Professor Gianfranco Contini, the two of them would be invested with their honours at a special ceremony the day before Encaenia to protect Sassoon as much as possible from the exhaustions of the more public occasion, Keynes making sure that all went smoothly.

Yet Sassoon seems never fully to have appreciated Keynes's efforts on his behalf. He would, for example, replace him as his literary executor in 1961 for a much more recent friend, continuing to imply to the very end of his life that Keynes was not really worthy of him, whereas, in reality, Keynes had single-handedly done more for his welfare and literary career over a longer period of time than anyone else. Philip Gosse was only one of a number of people who believed that Sassoon treated Keynes shabbily.[41]

Gosse's own reaction to Sassoon's conversion was less restrained than Keynes's; he sent a 'pungent reply' but not, he hoped, 'too much so', since he wanted their friendship to survive. Though happy for Sassoon, at a time when he himself was suffering greatly from his wife Anna's death, he had been antagonized by Sassoon's well-meaning attempt to help him find consolation in the Catholic Church. But he could not grudge Sassoon his 'peace beyond anything [he] could have imagined possible' and the slight awkwardness passed.[42] In his next letter to Gosse Sassoon is taking him into his confidence again, describing the 'extraordinarily kind and sympathetic letter' he has had from his son George on the matter.[43]

Hester was not quite so understanding; for her the Mass was 'only a ceremony' and 'God was mostly "out of doors".'[44] ('Hester, she has visions', 'Hester is mystical', Sassoon told one of the Downside monks, ironically.)[45] She could not begin to understand her husband's need for dogma and an organized religion. Nevertheless, she too came round when she saw how happy Sassoon's conversion had made him and was duly taken to visit

Mother Margaret, to whom she presented a huge box of Heytesbury snowdrops.

There was no such ambivalence on the part of Sassoon's three closest friends, though Blunden discovered the change only by chance, an indication that the distance between them had not been fully bridged. Sassoon had inadvertently pulled out a rosary with his handkerchief as they lunched together during Blunden's leave from Hong Kong shortly after Sassoon's reception at Downside. Claire remembered Sassoon picking it up but not saying a word. When he did finally tell Blunden, Blunden rejoiced for him and yet another visit to Mother Margaret took place. By February 1958 Sassoon was referring to his conversion quite freely, describing to Blunden, for instance, Tomlinson's 'lovely' letter on the subject shortly before he died that month.[46]

Sassoon had told Glen and Dennis almost immediately of the change during his annual trip to Stratford with Dennis, the month after his Downside reception. On arrival at their hotel, the Welcombe, Dennis had been summoned to Sassoon's room to find him sitting nervously on the edge of his bed, rosary in hand. Apparently he had feared that, as the son of an Anglican clergyman, Dennis might disapprove and was anxious to 'explain'.[47] The explanation, when it eventually emerged, was revealing: 'I'm very highly sexed, you know', he told Dennis in his abrupt way, '– had a lot of trouble down there,' pointing awkwardly at his genitals. Dennis, who knew nothing of his homosexual past, nor of his more recent affair with Dorothy Wallis, was understandably puzzled. But he was also delighted, since it was clear that Sassoon's conversion had made him 'transparently happy'.[48]

One of the most powerful attractions of the Catholic Church for Sassoon appears to have been the notion of confession and absolution. 'Could I but be absolved of what my years have wrought', he had written in an unpublished poem of 1947;[49] and two years later had argued, in a letter to Tomlinson, that the whole point of life was 'to try to rise above one's waistline'.[50] There is no doubting the sense of guilt he carried with him up to his entry into the Church. He would almost certainly have agreed with a Catholic friend's description of his homosexual lifestyle in the twenties as 'post-war deviations' and have hoped that she was right when she referred to them, rather floridly, as 'a time-deodorised dump of Dead Sea fruit by the roadside of his life's course, unlovely but negligible, its sole function to feed what medieval man called "compunction of heart" '.[51]

Glen, though suffering none of Sassoon's guilt over sex, nevertheless responded as positively as Dennis to what he recognized as Sassoon's 'infinite happiness and heart's ease'.[52] 'I shall always think of you sitting on the sofa in this room telling me that miraculous story,' he wrote from Stratford a few days after Sassoon's visit. He claimed always to have known that Sassoon could 'see further' than any other of his friends and rejoiced that he had found 'his road' and knew where he was going.[53] He felt privileged to be told about such a private matter: 'it showed me that you still love and trust me'.[54] Tactfully avoiding any reference to the failed relationship with Dorothy, or her letter to him, he nevertheless concluded with a shrewd analysis of Sassoon's frustrated needs throughout his life, sexual and otherwise:

> Above all else I have longed for you to be happy and at peace. I hoped that Hester would be able to give you that, and when she wasn't, I thought George would do so. Of course it wasn't their fault that they couldn't. You needed so much, because you are capable of so much, and I see now that you could only find supreme comfort in the way you have.[55]

It was left largely to outsiders to express doubt or disappointment. 'An old boy has sent me his pamphlet about Rational Theism,' Sassoon reported to a friend several years after his conversion: 'Says he was distressed by my becoming R.C. and can't understand how any educated man can believe in the Incarnation.'[56] Sassoon's implied criticism of Christianity during the First World War, which had helped to give his satires their shock value, had led many admirers to see him as a rationalist and some were taken aback by what seemed to them a complete volte-face. James Lees-Milne, for example, on reading a detailed account of his conversion, was 'irritated' by his 'acceptance of, swallowing of, hook line and sinker the tenets of the Catholic Church':

> When a man who all his life has been a free-thinker becomes in the eve of it a blind accepter of the Church's doctrine, I feel that this signifies weakness, a voluntary surrender of mind to spirit, no, to spiritualism, with a dash of hocus-pocus thrown in. Had he been all his life a devout believer in Christian tenets, then I should not feel suspicious of his old-age digestion of everything; I would merely think, here is a religious man who with one foot in the grave has quite properly and sensibly decided to devote all thought and energy to what throughout his life has been his dormant, but fundamental, creed, hitherto not always observed. In fact I am suspicious of 'enthusiasm', especially in the elderly convert.[57]

Lees-Milne's reaction is understandable but, according to those close to Sassoon, is based on a false premise. Vivian de Sola Pinto, who had known him since serving as his second-in-command of A Company in the 25th Battalion of the Royal Welch Fusiliers, believed that he had always been 'in a very real sense, a religious man'.[58] His condemnation of war, Pinto argued, was 'essentially religious, a protest against the maiming of the divine image in man'.[59] When, in 'The Redeemer', Sassoon had identified the English infantry soldier floundering through the mud with Christ, it was 'no mere figure of speech', Pinto maintained.[60] The later poetry of 'quiet meditation and spiritual insight' of *Sequences* seemed to him in a direct line of development from the First World War satires and he could only hope that it would one day 'come to be valued as among the most moving religious [poetry] of our time'.[61] Another close friend would trace Sassoon's spiritual leanings even further back, arguing forcibly, if a little flowerily, that it was 'not a sudden conversion: it was the movement of a straight line from the age of eight to seventy, it was the small boy arms outstretched calling to God across the Weald, it was George Sherston, the infantry officer, adding to his memoirs the curious epigraph: "I told him that I was a Pilgrim going to the Celestial City"'.[62]

A more complex question is why Sassoon chose to become a Catholic rather than simply returning to the Anglican faith of his upbringing. His conversion had been oddly anticipated twenty-eight years previously by Glen, who had dreamt of a woman in a red dress talking to Sassoon about the Church of England but a woman in a black dress insisting that he 'should uphold the Roman Catholic faith'.[63] There are, however, more than supernatural reasons to explain Sassoon's decision. In responding to Tomlinson, who sympathized with his spiritual needs but found his choice of Church puzzling, he told him that the Catholic Church gave him a 'sustenance' the Church of England could not; it seemed 'so real' and its followers so different from the 'inhibiting reticence' which characterized the average Anglican.[64] He had been particularly impressed by the warmth and uninhibitedness of Mother Margaret and the fact that the Downside Benedictines were 'not a bit monastic'.[65] In the course of tracing his spiritual needs in his long poem 'Lenten Illuminations', Sassoon had initially written in the fourth stanza of Part II:

> Why, in those Anglican churches could they find no home,
> When nothing appeared more unpredictable than this – your whole
> Influence, relief, resultancy received from Rome?[66]

Dennis Silk believed that a decisive factor in Sassoon's turning to Rome was his despair at world events, Korea and Suez in particular. He also maintained that Sassoon 'wanted to be told what to do' in his old age, and that the Catholic Church, with its claim to be the 'One True Church' and belief in the infallibility of its leader, the Pope, provided that authority. Sassoon himself, in his attempt to explain his decision, had written: 'My faith needs Authority to sustain it, I suppose. And this great traditional edifice of Catholicism makes Anglicanism seem unreal and ineffective. The faith I am now blessed with came to me through Catholic influence ...'[67] In becoming a Catholic he had found similar relief to the kind he had experienced in joining the army: he was once more 'under orders'. And as Maurice Wiggin, who met him towards the end of his life, suggested, his 'instinct for order' was very important to him.[68]

Robert Graves, who wrote to Sassoon less unsympathetically than might have been expected about his conversion, told a friend privately that it suited Sassoon 'as it suits a lot of frustrated homosexuals; but I am not one and so remain an ex-Protestant'.[69] He was almost certainly referring to the aesthetic appeal of the Catholic Church's elaborate rituals. There is no doubt that Sassoon had been influenced by these, as 'Lenten Illuminations' shows:

> The aids were manifest; but only for your eyes and ears,
> In anthems, organ music, shaft-aspiring stone,
> And jewelled windows into which your mind might melt.[70]

The appeal to Sassoon's Romantic instincts was powerful, as also to what he called his 'self-sacrificing complex'.[71] Adrian Caesar sums it up well when he describes the Catholic Church as 'an entirely appropriate mental destination for a soldier poet who had sought and seen "sacrifice" in war, who had imagined himself and others as Christ-like in their suffering and who subscribed to the Romantic view that art was also dependent upon suffering and sacrifice'.[72]

Sassoon once described Catholicism to Dennis Silk as 'so civilized', the same word Dame Felicitas Corrigan uses to describe the conversation at Mells, and there is little doubt that Lady Katharine Asquith and her circle there gave Catholicism a social as well as aesthetic appeal for Sassoon. Of Mells he wrote, 'It is all so perfect there – a survival of the old civilized life and the social graces.'[73] But it would also be true to say that Katharine meant a great deal to him personally and influenced his final decision, quite apart from her impressive connections. His visits to her became an important part of his life even before his conversion and were undiminished by Knox's death in 1957. The numerous letters between them show how precious her friendship was to him in the last ten years of his life. She is always 'dearest' or 'darling' Katharine and he her 'loving Siegfried'.[74] Dennis recalls Katharine as 'a wonderful faded beauty', a 'frail but lovely person ... just so welcoming', his most enduring memory being of her 'sitting and pouring out the tea and everyone doting on her, but she oblivious of the fact'.[75]

Like Knox, Katharine was a convert and had probably recognized the signs of Sassoon's own imminent conversion when he sent her *The Tasking* at the beginning of 1955. But, also like Knox, she had been too tactful to press him, only showing how much it meant to her by an increased warmth when he did eventually join the Catholic Church. She subsequently became one of the three most important of his female confidantes and his correspondence with her not only gives interesting side-lights on his life as a convert, but also provides illuminating details of his day-to-day existence. When she went into hospital for a serious operation in 1958, for instance, he tells her of his prayers for her and his joy when she comes through safely. At the same time he describes what is going on at Heytesbury. Though his conversion had made him noticeably more tolerant towards Hester, for example, he did not hesitate to complain of her to Katharine, nor (in 1959) of his problems with his housekeeper, Miss Benn.

His report of his relief at Miss Benn's departure is amusing as well as revealing: 'She had – bless her – become extremely autocratic – rather like a very strict Nannie, and was too touchy for words.'[76] He could not quite bring himself to confess that Miss Benn had, by 1959, reduced him at times to tears, but does happily admit to attempts to convert her, perhaps the real reason she finally agreed to leave.

Naturally Sassoon also shares all his Catholic news with Katharine. When an aspiring young Catholic poet, Ian Davie, sends him his poems in 1960, after reading one of Sassoon's in the *Tablet* ('Unfoldment'), Sassoon passes it on to her. He also sends her Davie's long poem 'Piers Prodigal', which he believes a 'masterpiece' and places with the Harvill Press. And he duly gives Katharine a full report of his successful efforts to get Davie a post at Marlborough, helped by Dennis and others.

Through Katharine Sassoon also became friends with other Catholics in the district, like the Hollises whom he first met at Mells. Christopher Hollis, an 'extraordinarily gruff' but kind man, according to Dennis, had more than his Catholic publishing and writing in common with Sassoon, being, as Dennis put it, 'mad about cricket'.[77] Hollis's obituary of Sassoon in the *Spectator* would show how well he understood his complex personality.[78]

It was cricket, too, which added to the attraction of Katharine's other good friends, the monks of Downside Abbey. Sassoon had got to know a number of the Benedictine brothers at Mells several years before his instruction at Downside in 1957; his reception into their Church only increased an existing admiration and affection for them. Apart from Dom Sebastian, who did *not* share his love of cricket, he was particularly fond of Dom Martin Salmon, who most definitely did. An ex-naval officer, Dom Martin became games master as well as a housemaster when he joined Downside in 1951. He set about reviving the school's adult cricket team, the Ravens, founded by Dom Aidan Trafford in 1921 and described by David Foot in an entertaining piece on Sassoon's cricketing as 'a worthy and esoteric team with a formidable membership'.[79] Some of the Ravens' players, such as Dennis Silk and Edmund Blunden, both 'nabbed' when they visited Downside with Sassoon, were valuable additions, others decidedly less so. Sassoon, for instance, who admitted to being 'a bit wobbly on his legs' by the early sixties, was nevertheless promptly recruited by Dom Martin, who would himself continue to play cricket into his seventies.[80] He was to keep Sassoon at it until the age of seventy-eight, a source of great pride to the poet and one very real rejuvenating effect of Downside on him. David Foot gives a number of amusing descriptions of his cricket-playing in his later years, the best perhaps being one of his last matches for the Ravens against Mells:

When it came to the fixture with Mells there was a corporate ploy of stealth to give Siegfried a valedictory lift towards the elusive double figures. Mells

introduced an excessively slow bowler of negligible merit. The ancient bats-
man played the first four deliveries with wary correctness. He tried to hit the
next for six, rather grandly, back over the bowler – and gave mid-on an
embarrassingly easy catch.

Sassoon snorted to himself and proclaimed to no one specifically as he
came in: 'The bowling was not worthy of me.'[81]

His bowling, apparently, was not risked at club level, so it was his fielding
that generated most comment and amusement. Father Martin, ever charitable and positive, described it as 'appalling but of immense courage'.[82] He
tried to make up for Sassoon's only too evident lack of mobility by acting
as his runner when he batted for the Ravens. 'I couldn't trust anyone else
for fear of a mistake,' he explained to Foot, who found his metaphor for
Sassoon's cricket-playing highly evocative: '[It was like] one of those old
gramophones with horns, a little cracked ... you felt there had been
something there at one time.'[83] It was said with great affection. Sassoon's
own affection for the Doms, as well as cricket, comes through in a few lines
of doggerel he sent to Dom Martin in 1958:

> In the First War he fooled with Mills bombs.
> After that, he just went to the Proms,
> Rode with fox-hunting dogs,
> And wrote autobiogs.
> But now he's been bowled to by Doms.[84]

Before retiring from cricket Sassoon would go regularly to Downside on
Wednesday afternoons to bat in the nets and would always stop on his way
out to visit another of his favourite monks, Dom Hubert van Zeller, at the
'stone-shed'. He had first met the sculptor in 1955 and they were already
good friends by the time of his conversion. But Dom Hubert had the
impression, in spite of having had three sculptors on his mother's side of
the family, that Sassoon was not really interested in his profession. He
seemed more intrigued by the knitted skullcap the tonsured monk wore.
It was to keep the stone-dust out of his hair, Dom Hubert explained. 'I
shouldn't have thought in your case it was necessary,' Sassoon could not
resist replying, before apologizing profusely for his 'personal' remark.[85]
After finishing his thermos of tea and paper bag of cake and biscuit
crumbs, which he consumed sitting cross-legged on the floor, Sassoon
would puff on his pipe as they discussed the relative merits of sculpture
and poetry. 'His shy, diffident, jerky manner, characteristic expressions,
movements as well as words and facial contortions' suggested to Dom
Hubert 'in equal parts a longing to get away and a longing to stop and
talk.'[86] He noted that after a short time 'the nervousness dropped away
and the essential serenity was given a chance. When one got to know him
well he was the most natural and unselfconscious person in the world,
losing himself in his conversation and blithely unaware of time, telephone

398

bells, interruptions, projecting the poet-image or creating an impression of any kind.'[87] Dom Hubert remembered taking groups of two or three senior Downside boys to Heytesbury on several visits when there was no cricket at the abbey, and how on one occasion their host became so engrossed in conversation that he went on pouring tea into a cup long after it was full, and on another absent-mindedly inscribed a book for one of the boys 'To Siegfried ... from Siegfried Siegfried'.

But for someone as frank about himself in other directions – 'endearingly ready to talk about his literary life', for example – Dom Hubert found him 'curiously reticent about his soul'.[88] He would discuss his readings among the mystics Dom Hubert had recommended to him, such as Dame Julian of Norwich and Richard Rolle, but his favourite topic was his love of Knox's work, including the simplest of his conferences to schoolgirls. Dom Hubert always felt that 'Siegfried's was an extremely simple response to grace and that he would be quite happy on a desert island – so far as his soul went – with a penny catechism and a children's prayer-book.'[89] He seemed 'instinctively [to] underst[and] a lot more about the spiritual life than he was able to explain or let on about'.[90]

This was certainly the impression of Dom Philip Jebb, son of Sassoon's friend Eleanor Jebb and grandson of Hilaire Belloc. One of the youngest monks, he was away studying at Cambridge when Sassoon first began to visit Downside regularly. But, on a trip back to the abbey shortly after Sassoon's reception into the Church, one of Dom Philip's fellow-monks announced 'Sassoon is here' and Jebb hurried to the guesthouse to see him.[91] He was not aware until then that Sassoon had known both his grandfather and mother, but had admired Sassoon's autobiographies and wanted to meet the author. It was the occasion of Sassoon's first Communion and he was in bed resting after the event, but when Dom Philip told him of his relationship to Belloc he began to talk animatedly. Their conversation, like many after it, was of 'poetry, literature, grandpapa, church and cricket', Dom Philip remembers.[92] They quickly became friends and by January 1958 Dom Philip would be visiting Heytesbury with Dom Sebastian and carrying on a regular correspondence with Sassoon,[93] in addition to meeting him at Cambridge.

With all these men Sassoon appeared to feel, more strongly than at any time since early childhood, even more than in the army, a sense of belonging. The thought of Downside was 'a sanctuary' for his mind, its 'providential nearness' having 'dissolved all the formidableness of "becoming a Catholic" ' which he had feared and offering him 'human welcomings in Father Sebastian and the gracious Benedictines'.[94] For most of his life he had felt isolated in various ways, first by his homosexuality and poetry-writing, then by his public protest and later, physically, by his retreat to Heytesbury and the breakdown of his marriage. Now, finally, he saw himself as part of a community, with no need for apology or explanation. It seemed to him one of Catholicism's most precious gifts to him.

He experienced a similar sense of belonging at Stanbrook Abbey, which he first visited in June 1960. Curiously, it was not the Downside monks who introduced him to their Benedictine sisters, but his old agnostic friend Sydney Cockerell. Cockerell's interest in medieval manuscripts and fine printing had led him, in spite of his rationalism, to Stanbrook, which had a much respected press run by the sisters under Dame Hildelith Cumming. His long correspondence with the former Abbess of Stanbrook, Dame Laurentia McLachlan, between 1907 and 1953 had been published by 1959 and was known to Sassoon, as was George Bernard Shaw's equally interesting correspondence with Dame Laurentia. Sassoon also owned and admired editions of *The Stanbrook Carols* and *The Little Breviary*.

So that when Cockerell wrote to him in October 1959 enclosing a letter from one of the Stanbrook nuns, Dame Felicitas Corrigan, he was already familiar with that remarkable collection of ladies. (He quickly came to feel, in Knox's words, that 'the interior peace of the enclosed orders is the breath of the Church's life' and that they were 'power-stations of prayer which make the materialism of principalities and worldly shows a fabric of insubstantial reality'.)[95] The letter itself pleased him greatly, being a perceptive and positive critique of *Siegfried's Journey*, which Cockerell had sent Dame Felicitas to read.[96] In it she also requested a more recent photograph than the one Cockerell had included in his collection of letters, *The Best of Friends*. Sassoon's instant response to her, with a photograph, was followed equally quickly by her reply and marked the start of a series of letters which chart his life in some detail over his last eight years. Not only does he speak to her frankly about his spiritual life and the joy he has experienced in entering the Catholic Church, he also talks to her fully about his past work and gives a running commentary on each new poem as he writes it.

They also discuss music. Dame Felicitas, a contemporary of Mother Margaret at Liverpool University, was the organist at Stanbrook Abbey and a fine musician, much to Sassoon's delight. She remembers how, on one of his visits to Stanbrook – a twice-yearly ritual from 1960 onwards – he begged her to play to him, requesting Bach's Prelude and Fugue in F. Her admiration for 'A Chord', a poem that depends on an understanding of musical technique for full effect, almost certainly explains his decision to make it the concluding poem of his revised *Collected Poems* in 1961.[97]

As her response to *Siegfried's Journey* had shown, Dame Felicitas loved words as well as music. Besides being an expert on the liturgy she had, like Mother Margaret, an extensive knowledge of English literature. And when Sassoon praised her unfailing perception it was not simply her musical interpretations or spiritual insight he meant. Though she appears to have shared Mother Margaret's reservations about some of Sassoon's more savage war poems, her appreciation of his later poetry and prose reveals shrewd critical insight. One incidental benefit of her interest in literature would be Sassoon's introduction to another poet she had come to know, Leonard Clark, also by coincidence a friend of Blunden's and an admirer of Henry Vaughan. Clark would be one of the few poets present at Sassoon's unveiling of a plaque to de la Mare in St Paul's Cathedral in December 1961 and close enough to Sassoon by April 1962 to persuade him to give a reading of his work to a group of teachers. A schools inspector, Clark organized poetry workshops, which Blunden, too, was persuaded to address.

Dame Felicitas, who had written two books herself by the time she met Sassoon, would go on to write her own formal evaluation of Sassoon based on his co-operation with her.[98] Since her focus would be more on his 'true inner biography' than his place in literary history, her otherwise authoritative account is slightly skewed by its dominating thesis – his journey to Rome. His homosexuality, for instance, is regarded as an unfortunate aberration from which he eventually recovered.

Her own deep attraction to Sassoon, both as a man as well as a writer, emerges in the detailed accounts of his visits to Stanbrook she sent Cockerell. From her first romantic description of 'a tall, spare figure with the emaciated face of an El Greco saint and the pent-up energy of a hydrogen bomb', dressed in three harmonious shades of blue which 'threw into relief his eyes and abundant silver hair', to a later one of him looking like 'some Old Testament prophet, very ascetical and world-weary' yet at the same time 'amazingly young', she is clearly fascinated by him:

> His eyes are so innocent and luminous, and he laughs so delightfully. He has a habit of shooting rapid penetrating glances which take everything in, and he misses little. But there is a striking delicacy and sensitivity about all his comments and views of life or people, which make one say with conviction, 'Yes, I like him thoroughly, even though he is an oddity like most poets.'[99]

When he asked if he might smoke his pipe in the visitors' parlour at Stanbrook, she repressed a 'What will THEY say?' and enjoyed for a short time the way the 'virginal air of the monastic parlour was polluted by the delicious aroma of tobacco', which seemed to her so masculine.[100]

Sassoon evidently basked in her admiration and that of the other nuns at Stanbrook Abbey. He was persuaded to read and give a talk to them and though both performances were complete failures in terms of audibility – his speech being more indistinct and slurred than ever – yet 'one and all were enthusiastic' according to Dame Felicitas.[101] Simply meeting him and watching him read his own poems, if only through the grille which separated them from outsiders, was, she believed, a 'memorable experience' for all.[102]

Sassoon closed his reading to the nuns on his first visit to them in June 1960 with three poems written since his conversion. The earliest of these, 'Lenten Illuminations', an 81-line account, he explained, of 'my present self telling my pre-1957 self' what had led him to the Catholic Church (written 'quite easily' in three days after only two short pieces in the previous four years), had already been published in the *Downside Review* in June 1958.[103] Though too long to recite in full, Sassoon read its final section to the assembled nuns as a testimony of his faith:

> This is the time of year when, even for the old,
> Youngness comes knocking on the heart with undefined
> Aches and announcements – blurred felicities foretold,
> And (obvious utterance) wearying winter left behind.
>
> I never felt it more than now, when out beyond these safening walls
> Sculptured with Stations of the Cross, spring-confident, unburdened, bold,
> The first March blackbird overheard to forward vision flutes and calls.
>
> You could have said this simple thing, old self, in any previous year.
> But not to that one ritual flame – to that all-answering Heart abidant here.[104]

Both these and the opening lines of 'Lenten Illuminations' ('Not properly Catholic, some might say ...') promise well. Their easy, conversational tone suits the self-examination of the subject, as do the long, irregular lines of the verse, and convinces the reader that the poem came, as Sassoon claimed, 'unbidden and spontaneous'.[105] That it is 'the real thing', as he also argued, is sadly not the case and Faber's refusal to distribute it only too understandable.[106] It quickly deteriorates, as poetry though not as devotional verse or valuable autobiographical material, into clotted, clichéd phrases. Sassoon compared it to his 1920s poem 'To One Who Was With Me in the War', but the earlier poem contained nothing as ponderous or awkward as lines like the following:

> This day twelve months ago – it was Ash Wednesday – one
> Mid-day between us two toward urgent hope fulfilled
> Strove with submission. Arduous – forbidding – then to meet
> Inflexible Authority ...[107]

Compared with the concentrated force of a Gerard Manley Hopkins or the dazzling insights of a George Herbert or Henry Vaughan, 'Lenten Illuminations' seems poetically slack, little more than a self-indulgent replay of a personally exciting period of Sassoon's life. Yet he had never written anything which gave him deeper satisfaction, he told Blunden in the letter accompanying a copy of the poem, proudly comparing its technique to that of Charlotte Mew and himself to Hardy writing 'Beeny Cliff' at the age of seventy-three. Blunden's own response, which was to give it away to a Chinese student studying to become a nun, reflects that of many of Sassoon's most perceptive admirers, that while they were delighted by the personal happiness his conversion had brought, they were unable to applaud its effect on his verse. Dennis Silk, who in 1958 supervised the printing by boys at Marlborough of his personal selection of Sassoon's verse up to 1954, went on to have one of Sassoon's specifically Catholic poems, 'Rogation', printed at the Marlborough College Press as well.[108] But it is significant that he includes none of the poems written after Sassoon's reception at Downside in his later perceptive appraisal of his friend.

Sassoon's Catholic friends were understandably less wary, encouraging him to write verses they believed helped him clarify both his thoughts and emotions about his faith. Dame Felicitas, for example, responded positively to each new poem as it was sent to her, starting with 'Sight Sufficient', which was written three months before 'Lenten Illuminations' in December 1957. Like the latter poem it had also been reproduced in the *Downside Review* and as an offprint by the time Sassoon included it in his reading to the Stanbrook nuns in June 1960. In addition it would be one of the six hitherto unpublished pieces included in Dame Felicitas's personal selection of verse tracing Sassoon's 'spiritual pilgrimage from the somewhat dreamy pantheism of youth through long years of lonely seeking to "life breathed afresh" in acceptance of the gift of faith'.[109] She 'longed' to see 'Sassoon the saint and mystic drive away the war-poet, and satirist', and hoped that their mutual friend Leonard Clark, though not himself a Catholic, would forward her aim with a suitable review.[110]

Unfortunately what Dame Felicitas's selection, *The Path to Peace*, also highlights is the inferiority on the whole of the eight specifically Catholic poems. They seem particularly weak in comparison with those charting his spiritual struggles of the late forties and early fifties, as Dame Felicitas tacitly acknowledges by choosing twelve of her twenty-nine examples from *Sequences*, significantly more than those from the post-conversion poems.

Two exceptions stand out by their simplicity and directness from the disappointing work of Sassoon's final period. Both depend for their effect on his ability to relate his new-found faith to the sense of rejuvenation spring had always brought him, the first, 'Arbor Vitae', reflecting his love of Heytesbury's heavily wooded grounds:

> For grace in me divined
> This metaphor I find:
>   A tree.
> How can that be?
>
> This tree all winter through
> Found no green work to do –
>   No life
> Therein ran rife.
>
> But with an awoken year
> What surge of sap is here –
>   What flood
> In branch and bud.

> So grace in me can hide –
> Be darkened and denied –
> Then once again
> Vesture my every vein.[111]

The change of rhythm and length in the third line of the last stanza acts out the miraculous change experienced by the narrator (now completely identified with the tree) in the final line.

The second successful poem of this last period, 'Unfoldment', centring round another Nature metaphor and also inspired by Sassoon's day-to-day life at Heytesbury, harks straight back to one of his favourite poems from a much earlier period, 'Nativity' ('A Flower has opened in my heart ...'):

> Tight buds of daffodil
> Plucked where the wind blew chill
>   In Lent begun
> Blessed by this well-warmed room
> Unsheathe themselves, for whom
>   The lamp's their sun.
>
> So, when to prayer I turn
> And my dark being discern
>   Life-locked from Thee,
> Unfold it as a flower,
> That I may know Thy power
>   Befriending me.[112]

Overjoyed by the renewal of his poetic urge, long after he had assumed it completely dead, Sassoon seems to have been untroubled by doubts as to the relative worth of his religious verse. His relief, together with his connoisseur's appreciation of the beautifully produced *Path to Peace*, which he had helped design, emerges clearly in the jokey punning of his letter to Dom Martin Salmon on the subject: 'Just fancy – *Stanbrook* is printing a super de-luxe limited selection of my verse ... in Romulus Cancelleresca Bastarda fount – so I'm not such a cancelled old bastard as some of the modern critics think!'[113]

Stanbrook Abbey Press went on to print two smaller but equally beautiful productions, a short story from Sassoon's childhood to celebrate his eightieth birthday, *Something About Myself*, and a collection of his last four poems, *Ave Atque Vale*, in 1967, but *The Path to Peace* was his last significant production. As Michael Thorpe observes, it must be left for a Catholic writer to say 'Here is the story of a soul as shapely as any poet could want his verse to be.'[114] For those more interested in his poetry than his Catholicism, the most shapely ending would have been, as Thorpe notes, *The Tasking*.

26

'It Has Been a Long Journey'
(1961-1967)

I, too, often ask whether things are worth while, for the key-word to my present existence is passivity. I submit to 'the long littleness of life' dutifully, but the central me dwells elsewhere. What Newman calls 'the accidents of life' no longer interest me, and like the late lamented Cleopatra I have immortal longings in me. The busy-mindedness of people revolves around me, and I conform to it obediently. But, O dear, I say to myself, if only things would stop happening! Not that much does happen to my seclusion. I just go on being told that I am a war poet, when all I want is to be told that I am only a pilgrim and a stranger on earth, utterly dependent on the idea of God's providence to my spiritual being. But the game goes on, so I must put my pads on and make my way to the wicket. The wicket – O please, dear St Peter, don't delay too long in opening it to me!

(Sassoon to Dame Felicitas Corrigan,
26 March 1966)[1]

Catholicism ensured that the last six years of Sassoon's life were his happiest. Rather than isolating him from people even more, as Keynes claimed, his religious belief (in the words of another close friend) 'gave him back to the world of men'.[2] Dame Felicitas, who readily acknowledged Keynes's affectionate charge of 'patent egocentricity' against Sassoon, believed that 'he tried to face up to it and at least combat it in the last years of his life' and that he '*was* endowed with a power of imaginative sympathy and compassion that rang absolutely true'.[3] She saw Sassoon's life as 'the breaking down of an immense egocentricity by the continuous hammer blows of human affliction and failure into something very like Christian holiness and humility'.[4]

Whatever the truth of her theory, there is no doubt that Sassoon was more open to people after his conversion than at almost any other period in his adult life. And they were not all Roman Catholics, though these predominated. Dennis Silk remembers with some amusement arriving at Heytesbury to the sound of Sassoon's habitual lament: ' "No one ever comes to see me," he would say rather mournfully, but gradually in the course of conversation it became apparent that Father Martin had been to tea yesterday, and three old friends had been to lunch on the day before yesterday, and Ian Balding was coming tomorrow.'[5]

Ian Balding, an outstanding amateur steeple-chaser who came into contact with Sassoon through Dennis, was only one of a number of non-Catholics to whom Sassoon responded enthusiastically in his seventies. While Balding was a pupil at Marlborough, Dennis had given him *The Complete Memoirs of George Sherston*, which he subsequently asked Sassoon to sign for the horse-mad boy. When Balding eventually met Sassoon in the spring of 1963 he had already won an important National Hunt Chase race at Cheltenham (on a horse called 'Time') and Sassoon was keen to hear all about it. Balding, who had arrived late for tea at Heytesbury and mistaken 'an old boy mooching about in an overcoat and muffler' for the gardener, when it was in fact his host, nevertheless felt immediately at ease with Sassoon, who could not resist punning about him 'not being on "Time" '.[6] Their talk was largely of horses and cricket, at which Balding also excelled. Sassoon invited him back regularly after that and Balding still recalls his visits 'very fondly'.[7] The young sportsman was, according to Dennis, 'everything Sassoon would love to have been' and it would no doubt have gratified him greatly to hear Balding's retrospective praise of his 'nice seat' on a horse.[8]

Balding remembers on one occasion taking a girlfriend, Heather Lewis, an accomplished musician, with him and how she delighted Sassoon by playing Liszt to him.[9] She pleased him even more when she asked permission to set his 'Prayer to Time' to music, a successful setting which would be followed by several others.[10]

Another friendship formed after his conversion underlines how open Sassoon's faith had made him. He had been corresponding with Rupert Hart-Davis since 1931, when Hart-Davis was a 24-year-old assistant at his first publisher's, Heinemann. The correspondence became more frequent in 1946 after Hart-Davis had returned from fighting in the Second World War and started his own small publishing house. But it was not until 1958, the year after Sassoon's conversion, that Hart-Davis felt confident enough of a warm reception to suggest lunch with Sassoon. (He was on his way to a memorial service near Salisbury for a mutual acquaintance, Edie Nicholson, widow of the painter William Nicholson.) The poet's welcoming response was the start of one of the most important friendships of his last years.

Sassoon was 'naturally nervous' to begin with and unable to look at his visitor for almost an hour, a phenomenon the actor Alec Guinness would observe when he visited the poet the following year to discuss T.E. Lawrence with him.[11] But he plied Hart-Davis with sherry and some 'terrifically good' Beycheville 1933, 'with which I washed down some fine roast duck'.[12] Sassoon himself was not drinking, but he gradually relaxed and they were soon talking 'nineteen to the dozen'.[13] Their choice of subject is particularly interesting, centring round three literary figures of some sexual ambiguity, Oscar Wilde (whose letters Hart-Davis would edit), Max Beerbohm (whose correspondence with Sassoon he would also edit) and

Edmund Gosse, whom Sassoon described to Hart-Davis as 'perfectly normal in every other way' except for 'what can only be described as a passion for my uncle, Hamo Thornycroft'.[14]

Less than a month after Hart-Davis's first visit to Heytesbury Sassoon appointed him his third literary executor, 'to defend Blunden' against Keynes, in his words.[15] And in 1961 came the dismissal of Keynes as literary executor altogether. It followed complaints from Hart-Davis of the many errors he had had to correct in Keynes's bibliography of Sassoon, which Hart-Davis was about to publish. 'I am sorry he did it', Dame Felicitas wrote frankly to Keynes about Sassoon's action after his death, 'and consider it an error of judgement on his part – but very typical.'[16] She recognized, as others did, that Keynes had done a great deal more for Sassoon, personally and professionally, than Hart-Davis, whose appointment in Keynes's place, she felt, must 'surely have been a last-minute decision'.[17]

It is not difficult to see why Sassoon found Hart-Davis more appealing than Keynes. An altogether smoother type, he was reassuringly upper-middle class. The product of Eton, Balliol and the Coldstream Guards, he was, as a near contemporary at both Eton and Balliol, Anthony Powell, suggested, 'more like a Life Guards officer than a publisher'.[18] Hart-Davis had also spent a brief spell in another world to which Sassoon was powerfully drawn, that of acting.

An equally strong appeal for Sassoon was Hart-Davis's literary acuity, particularly his admiration for and promotion of Blunden. Their correspondence of 1946 concerned Hart-Davis's 'delightful invitation' to a dinner to honour Blunden: 'Edmund has often mentioned you to me,' Sassoon concluded his first letter of the batch, 'always with affection and appreciation.'[19] Not only did he agree to write 'a few couplets' in Blunden's praise and help Hart-Davis make a selection of Blunden's poems,[20] but he also insisted on supplying the 'needful bottles of Burgundy' for the occasion.[21] Though excusing himself from attending the dinner itself by citing his work on Meredith, he very much appreciated Hart-Davis's efforts to promote his 'little' friend.[22] He was also gratified by Hart-Davis's fulsome praise of his own work.

The friendship between them developed rapidly after their first meeting in 1958 and became very important to Sassoon in the last nine years of his life. His letter to Hart-Davis on the sudden death of his third wife less than a month after he had been knighted, shows just how much the publisher had come to mean to him by February 1967. After regretting his inability to help, Sassoon continues:

> One thing I *can* offer you – my deep and devoted friendship, for you have come to be ... a source of strength and encouragement beyond anyone else, except Mother Margaret Mary, so few of my closest friends being left to me

now … All my future arrangements about literary remains etc. have come to depend on your incomparable ability to organize such things.[23]

An even greater proof of Sassoon's openness at this time, if any were needed, was his friendship with Sir Alan ('Tommy') Lascelles. Sassoon's letter to Dame Felicitas after their first meeting at Heytesbury on 2 May 1960 sets out Lascelles' appeal for him: 'Yesterday I was visited by Sir Alan Lascelles, brought here by a young friend [Colin Fenton], and new to me, though he was at Marlborough with me …'[24] After pointing out that Lascelles had been Private Secretary to the last three kings, 'so an outstanding contrast to *this* avoider of what is known as "the great world" ', Sassoon continued: 'A charming and cultivated man – drew me out about Hardy and Max Beerbohm – and was at Oxford with Ronald [Knox], and knew Katharine [Asquith]'s brother Edward Horner and her husband well – so all went easily.'[25] Other topics of conversation (not mentioned in this letter, where Lascelles' social connections are more to the fore) are likely to have been music and horses, which Lascelles also loved, and the Great War, in which he, like Sassoon, had won an MC.

Tommy, as he quickly became, was gratifyingly admiring of Sassoon's work. Even his rare reservations about it reassured Sassoon as coinciding with his own curious desire to forget the poetry which had made him famous: 'Nothing', Lascelles declared, 'will make me, who have had two wars and lost two generations, read Siegfried's war poems any more. I told him so, and he commended me.'[26] He further endeared himself to the poet by his enthusiastic response to his religious verse when Sassoon sent him *The Path to Peace* in the early 1960s:

> Nothing in literature, even in music or nature, has ever given me such a clear perception of beauty. Fifty years ago Arthur Symons wrote of Beethoven – 'to have written this is as great a thing as to have built a cathedral, in which, not more truly, the soul shelters from its grief … nor was there ever a landscape of the soul so illuminated with all the soft splendour of sunlight.' That's equally true of y[ou]r poetry and, had you never written another syllable, these poems would assure you a place among the immortals.[27]

A devout Anglican himself, Lascelles had appreciated *The Path to Peace* even though it traced Sassoon's journey to Rome. And, although Sassoon had become a great proselytizer for the Catholic Church by 1960, he made no attempt to convert either Lascelles or Hart-Davis, another staunch member of the Established Church. He was not so restrained with lapsed Catholics, like the housekeeper who followed Miss Benn at Heytesbury, Patricia Hardy, whom he finally persuaded to send her nine-year-old daughter, Julia, to a convent school. (Mrs Hardy's departure from Heytesbury shortly afterwards may, like Miss Benn's, have been not unconnected with his efforts.) Nor did he hesitate to apply pressure where he detected real spiritual need. With his niece, and god-daughter, Jessica Gatty, for instance, he quite clearly tried to win her over to Catholicism. 'I feel such concern for her spiritual welfare,' he wrote to Katharine Asquith after Jessica's stay with him in July 1960, during which he had taken her to visit both Mells and Downside: 'She was only here three nights, but I put in a lot of tip-toe influencing.'[28] There seems nothing very 'tip-toe', however, about advising her to read Ronald Knox and to visit the Convent of the Assumption in Kensington Square. Sister Jessica certainly believes that her eventual decision to join the Catholic Church was a direct result of her uncle's and Mother Margaret's guidance, an outcome which caused a rift between Sassoon and his brother-in-law, Richard Gatty, for a number of years.[29]

Lascelles, however, was left to worship as he chose and the friendship flourished, encouraged by the happy coincidence of Lascelles' grandson starting at Marlborough College in the early sixties. Lascelles' greatest achievement, which demonstrates the considerable powers of diplomacy that had led to his successful career with three successive monarchs, was to lure the 'hermit of Heytesbury' back to London after a gap of thirty years. Sassoon would be persuaded to stay with Tommy and his wife Joan at their splendid apartment in the Old Stables at Kensington Palace at least eleven times between 1960 and 1965. Equally impressive was Lascelles' success in persuading Sassoon to become a member of the Literary Society, a dining club of which he was president and Hart-Davis secretary. Its meetings at the Garrick Club were always an excuse for Lascelles to insist that Sassoon pay another visit to the Old Stables, where he made sure the company was of the best. Sassoon's description of one such stay in October 1961 gives the flavour:

Tuesday was the Literary Society [he wrote to Dame Felicitas on 12 October 1961]. Several new people there, including the Duke of Wellington, whom I sat next to. I knew him forty years ago, when he was Gerry Wellesley, but had hardly seen him since. He was very agreeable and friendly, and we had plenty in common – even Ronald and Katharine and there was general literary talk with Harold Nicolson opposite me, and Rupert Hart-Davis at the head of the table ... [and] Sir A[lan] L[ascelles] ... at the other end. What well-stocked minds they all have! They make my own repertoire seem very small. I was dazed with fatigue, and had to say half my prayers lying down. On Wednesday there was a smaller edition of it – Sir A.L. entertaining H. Nicolson, John Betjeman and George Sartoris – the latter a very nice quiet man, who greeted me by saying that *The Old Century* is one of his favourite books – he is a great-nephew of Fanny Kemble and her sister Adelaide Sartoris the famous singer – and I love Fanny K. through her friendship with Ed[ward] Fitzgerald.[30]

For all their thrill, Sassoon found these dinners in brilliant intellectual company wearying and much preferred being taken to Lords by Lascelles, who numbered cricket among his many enthusiasms. Sassoon thought of him as 'a second Geoffrey [Keynes]', though 'much more sensitive'.[31] He was quickly exhausted by the constant social events the hospitable Lascelles laid on for him, particularly when on one occasion he was taken to meet royalty.[32]

But there were some introductions he did appreciate, especially to literary figures, the most interesting of these being with another First World War writer who had also served in the Royal Welch Fusiliers, David Jones. Jones, whom Sassoon thought 'undoubtedly a man of genius', was invited to the Old Stables to meet Sassoon in July 1964. He enjoyed his talk with Sassoon – 'about Blunden and Graves and the Welch Fusiliers – Mametz, Limerick, etc. (he said that however much he tried he could never get that First War business out of his system)' – but found that he 'couldn't make much contact, if any' with Sassoon 'about poetry'.[33] Highly experimental himself, as *In Parenthesis* and his later, even more abstruse *Anathemata* show, he stood for all that Sassoon most feared in Modernism. *The Anathemata*, for example, was 'quite beyond him', he told Dame Felicitas.[34] Curiously, though Jones, who had converted to Catholicism in 1921, longed to discuss their common faith, Sassoon gently and politely evaded the topic and Jones's sad conclusion was 'that we seem *all* to live in separated worlds, and as far as I could make out, his particular literary outlook offered few openings that I could infiltrate'.[35] Jones's partial deafness combined with Sassoon's mumbling made communication even more difficult, as it had with Ackerley. Nevertheless Jones found Sassoon 'extremely nice, gentle and pleasant', if older than he expected.[36] Sassoon's own account of the working-class Jones was less charitable and rather patronizing: a 'pathetic, helpless seeming little man, ultra-sensitive', was how he described him to Dame Felicitas.[37] Any interest he felt was mainly related to himself; the fact that Jones's battalion had relieved Sassoon's 'the day after my bombing out the Prussian Guard', for instance, or that Dom Sebastian 'specialized' in *The Anathemata*.[38] While acknowledging that *In Parenthesis* was 'an important war record', he had to confess that it did not 'reach' him as Blunden's *Undertones of War* did.[39]

Sassoon's visits to the Lascelles started at a time when his attempts to make Cambridge a second 'centre' in his life had failed, mainly because so many of his friends there had died. But it was also partly because his row with Keynes over the Brooke letters had made his stays there less comfortable for a time in the late fifties, and partly because of the breakdown of his son's first marriage in 1959.[40] By 1960 his main reason for going to Cambridge, where his only remaining friend was Monsignor Alfred Gilbey, the Catholic Chaplain to the University, would be to visit Mother Margaret at her Hengrave Hall convent school. London, together with Downside, Stanbrook and Mells, would form an alternative 'centre', providing him with a more active social life than at any time since the thirties.

*

'But for what I have acquired in the past four years', Sassoon wrote to Dame Felicitas at the beginning of 1961, 'my life would be extraordinarily isolated and unpopulated.'[41] Blunden was still out in Hong Kong, 'and even he all tied up with minor literary interests', Keynes, though back in the fold, was 'totally taken up with his interests and activities' and 'dear Glen, most understanding of friends, up to his neck in theatrical productions'.[42] The one old friend who might still have been free to visit Heytesbury regularly, Morgan Forster, was now no longer as attractive to Sassoon as he had once seemed: 'O dear, I love him, but he is dreadfully anti-churchdom and needs no help from me, living as he does in an apotheosis of adulation.'[43]

Sassoon needed no help from Forster, however, to fill his life between 1960 and 1965. A typical year might start with a week's stay at Cambridge to see Mother Margaret at Hengrave Hall, followed by a few days at Stanbrook Abbey Guest House in June and, until his marriage to Diana Milton in April 1963, an extended visit from Dennis Silk in August.[44] Well timed to fit in with Dennis's long vacation from Marlborough and the height of the cricket season, much of this would be spent pursuing that sport. Even without Dennis, Sassoon would go regularly to Downside to play cricket throughout the summer and entertain the monks in turn at Heytesbury during the cricketless winter months. In September came the second of his biannual visits to Stanbrook to celebrate his birthday, which he was proud to remind people fell on the Feast Day of the Virgin Mary. By 1960, in an attempt at reconciliation with Hester, he had started inviting her to spend Christmas at Heytesbury, so that December and early January became a family affair once more. And though he found these visits exhausting he felt amply rewarded by a clearer conscience and a renewed sense of closeness to George, who was a 'great comfort' to him: 'He has realized', he wrote to Dame Felicitas in 1966, 'that I am his second self, though so far behind him in scientific ability and quickness.'[45]

If any gaps remained in this fairly full timetable, they were filled by newer friends he had made since becoming a Catholic. One of these was Muriel Galsworthy, a niece of John Galsworthy (who had died in 1933). Miss Galsworthy had been at Downside cheering her nephew on at cricket when they first saw each other, one of the meetings Sassoon felt had been 'arranged by our Lady of Consolation'.[46] She was quickly invited to Heytesbury and became a regular visitor in his last years.

The parish priest also visited, at first Father Joseph Renehan, later Father Nicholas McCarthy, arriving weekly to celebrate Mass with him. Sassoon looked forward to these occasions and the 'lovely talks' which followed.[47] He was greatly amused, even a little flattered, by Father McCarthy's adaptation of his nickname 'the hermit of Heytesbury' to 'the *Abbot* of Heytesbury'.[48]

By 1964, the year Blunden finally left Hong Kong, he too resumed visiting. He had, as usual, been in some financial difficulty trying to find the money to buy a house for his family. Just as predictably it was Sassoon who provided the bulk of it.[49] (He had intended to leave Blunden money when he died, but felt that it would be more useful in advance.) He was delighted to have Blunden back in the country again, even if he did choose to settle on the other side of England at Long Melford in Suffolk. He would also rejoice for Blunden's sake when he succeeded Robert Graves as Professor of Poetry at Oxford in 1966. 'He will now be recognized properly as what he is', Sassoon wrote to Dame Felicitas on 26 March 1966, '– the most distinguished figure in English Letters.'

The flavour of Sassoon's life at this period is captured well by Margaret Keynes in her description of lunch at Heytesbury with her husband, a less rosy description than that painted by his Catholic friends. It was an excellent meal, she remembered, but their host was unable to do justice to it. Having had all his teeth removed because of serious gum disease in 1962, he could only 'mumble his chicken ... not swallow it'.[50] She was intrigued by the fact that, though he found his false teeth too uncomfortable to wear, their absence did 'not affect his speech or make him ugly'.[51] He had spent the morning in bed, as usual, and was still in pyjamas when they arrived, for which he made no apology. Her most revealing comment – about his interminable monologue which continued long after lunch, 'punctuated ... every few words by the extraordinary grunting and groaning sounds' he uttered – suggests that the Keyneses were not as unaware as Sassoon made them out to be and that the faults were by no means all on one side.[52] In the light of Sassoon's subsequent complaints about how exhausting he had found their constant talk and barrage of questions, it is particularly amusing to read Margaret's description of Geoffrey's largely unsuccessful attempts either to stop the flood of Sassoon's monologue or divert it to new channels.

Another visitor to Heytesbury about this time has left an equally revealing account of Sassoon during his last years.[53] Anthony Powell, who met Sassoon at the Literary Society with Tommy Lascelles, was struck forcibly by the apparent contradictions in him: though he talked 'very much in the army idiom' of Powell's father, he did so 'with a gentle, remote, almost embarrassed air'.[54] He reminded the younger man, who like most people, and in spite of Dame Felicitas's efforts, associated him with his war poetry, of 'a ghost haunting the fields of Passchendaele or Bapaume', his 'unusually tall, gauntly thin' appearance making him seem 'almost transparent'.[55] (Powell rightly suspected that this 'outward unsubstantiality concealed a powerful will'.[56]) On learning that they were neighbours in the West Country, Sassoon had invited Powell and his wife Violet to tea, but when Powell rang up (as suggested) a week later, he sounded as though he was already regretting it.

A date was nevertheless agreed and the Powells arrived for tea at Heytesbury on a 'crisp luminous autumn afternoon'.[57] The house's grey façade, 'dignified and massive like its owner', and the stillness of the surrounding gardens, woods and rolling downs, made them feel that they had arrived at an enchanted castle, an effect heightened by their difficulty in gaining access.[58] When, finally, they simply stepped into the drawing room through a long, open sash window, it was as though life had 'stopped perhaps half a century before'.[59] Sassoon, who suddenly materialized from nowhere, appeared not in the least disconcerted. He seemed 'to walk in a dream through a dream world', repeating several times in response to their murmurs of Heytesbury's beauty, 'Tennysonian. Absolutely Tennysonian'.

This visit from Powell, himself a successful novelist by 1963, indicates Sassoon's own growing status as a writer. Though this second flowering of his reputation had begun as far back as 1957, when he had been awarded the Queen's Gold Medal for Poetry (ostensibly for *Sequences* but really as an acknowledgement of his life's work), his lionization proper had started with his visits to Lascelles and re-introduction to the wider world in 1960. Though Lascelles failed to get him the OM Sassoon secretly coveted (while publicly denying it), he did believe he could get Sassoon the Laureateship and might have done so, if Sassoon had not been within months of his own death when Masefield died in 1967.

It may not have been a coincidence that shortly after meeting Lascelles Sassoon was honoured by the request mentioned earlier, to unveil a plaque in St Paul's Cathedral crypt to one of his dearest friends, Walter de la Mare.[60] And it seems fitting that it was in Lascelles' best funeral overcoat that he did so on 18 December 1961. Lascelles, who thought of everything and had anticipated audibility problems, had arranged for Sassoon's tribute to de la Mare to be typed and copied for each person present and though it did not mollify de la Mare's son, Richard, it did mean that everyone knew what Sassoon had planned to say even if they could not hear it. One of those in the select audience, Harold Nicolson, neatly evaded the problem of commenting on Sassoon's inaudible speech by congratulating him on his *appearance* while he spoke, telling him that he looked magnificent, like a Homeric bard.

It is also possible that Lascelles used his considerable influence at his old university, Oxford, in 1965, when Sassoon was offered an honorary doctorate there, though a number of other friends are also reputed to have applied pressure.[61] However it was achieved and however much he denied caring about worldly distinctions, it is clear that Sassoon was very pleased indeed at this high honour.

By his eightieth birthday on 8 September 1966, therefore, Sassoon's stock had risen considerably and his long-time admirer Charles Causley had no difficulty in persuading the Literature Panel of the Arts Council on which he served to celebrate the event appropriately. After a long discussion at Heytesbury House, in which Causley and the Literature Director of the Arts Council, Eric Walter White, had urged Sassoon to allow them to print subscription copies of some of his poems along similarly lavish

413

lines to the volume marking David Jones's seventieth birthday, he agreed to let them have his last eight poems. The first six pieces from *An Octave*, as it was called, had already been printed in *The Path to Peace*.[62] Only 'Proven Purpose' and 'A Prayer in Old Age' were new and they too would appear in the final Stanbrook Abbey Press production, *Ave Atque Vale*, the following year.

The subscription list, which ran to over 200 names, suggests that by 1966 Sassoon was respected by young and old alike and that this was by no means confined to his friends. The latter were there, with the notable exception of Forster and Swinnerton, who may have objected to the wholly religious nature of the poetry, but some of the Modernists, such as Auden and Day-Lewis, and many of the younger poets of the fifties and sixties, like Roy Fuller, Ted Hughes and Philip Larkin, also subscribed, a sign of ultimate acceptance. And in his graceful introduction Causley stressed that this represented only a small section of Sassoon's 'many friends and admirers'.

Causley, who had been drawn to the 'suggestion beyond the words' in Sassoon's poetry since childhood, was also behind a BBC Bristol programme celebrating his birthday. He had already recorded two radio programmes with him at Heytesbury in 1955.[63] Though Sassoon complained of being ignored by the BBC Third Programme and 'all those clever people up in London', he was heard a number of times on radio in the last twenty years of his life and would even make a brief appearance on television, all part of his growing public recognition.[64]

The first (and until recently the only) full-length book of critical appraisal of Sassoon was also published that year, *Siegfried Sassoon* by Michael Thorpe. Its timing was wholly appropriate, as a number of reviewers pointed out, but completely coincidental, and its publisher initially Dutch.[65] It is significant, however, that though Sassoon himself was uncomfortable with an academic analysis of his work, Oxford University Press showed interest and co-published the book in England to some acclaim. It was also published in America.

'Lionized by Lords in excelsis', was how Sassoon described this late flowering of his reputation.[66] His reaction to it was as ambivalent as the phrase suggests. In the thirties, forties and fifties he had passionately wanted recognition as a poet, greatly resenting the obscurity to which he felt he had been relegated. Dennis Silk confirms that by the time he met Sassoon in 1953 he 'longed for recognition', though he always denied it and 'could not bear to hear the Modernists and younger poets praised'.[67] Yet Sassoon did not wholly enjoy the limelight, continuing to find public occasions torture. Perhaps, as he argued, it had returned to him too late. 'What you call my "high jinks" in London *are* in that category', he wrote to Dame Felicitas in 1964, 'but I sometimes feel that they are "the high that proved too high, the heroic for earth too hard" (Browning). I am submerged by a spate of admirable, worldly, literary and artistic gossip, and have to distribute my vitality in every direction. *Literary* admiration no longer means much to me.'[68]

*

Sassoon's eightieth birthday was his last. He had enjoyed reasonable good health throughout his adult life, apart from his duodenal ulcer in 1948, and when he suffered a blackout and stomach haemorrhage in late December 1964 he assumed that his old 'digestive' problems had returned. 'Exploiting the event for all [he was] worth', he indulged in 'a glorious rest cure', spending the next month in bed, with Hester allowed to fuss over him all she liked.[69] For the first time in years he genuinely welcomed her presence at Heytesbury, rather than taking it on sufferance. 'The best thing of all is Hester's happiness in ministering to my every need,' he wrote to Mother Margaret who, like Dame Felicitas, thought he owed more to his wife than he had ever acknowledged.[70] She had been seeing to the upkeep of the house for years but he had not really appreciated her efforts. ('That interminable chatter!' he would murmur to Dennis whenever she appeared.)[71] Now, with his need of her and the softening of her attitude towards his religious beliefs, something like harmony prevailed.

Though she, too, claimed to think that it was his ancient ulcer resurfacing, the episode – an alarming one in which he had lain for some time in a freezing passage unable to move – worried Hester sufficiently for her to insist on a valuation of Heytesbury. As she pointed out, they did not want George to have to sell the estate to pay off death duties. Faced with such a 'heartbreaking prospect', Sassoon agreed, but his facetious response to the estate agent's visit suggests that he was not unaware of the implications.[72] Given the main events of his career it seems appropriate that this, one of the last compositions of his life, should be a parody of Rupert Brooke and be called 'Onus of Ownership':

> Think only this: if I should hop the twig,
> Leaving to G. Sassoon some prime old pasture,
> The woodlands, and a mansion much too big,
> Will this evoke death-dutiful disaster?
> Some years, of course, may pass before they dig
> My grave; but father Time flows ever faster,
> And no one can predict when soulful Sig
> Must shift his habitat for somewhere vaster.
>
> Knight, Frank & Rutley, names of high repute,
> The whole caboodle's costliness compute,
> And, if it makes things easier for us, fudge it!
> Meanwhile with palpitations we await
> The ultimatum of your estimate.
> For God's sake get it done before the Budget![73]

Sassoon still believed he was suffering from an ulcer, even after a second 'episode' in September 1965 had prevented his usual Stanbrook visit, and it was not until the beginning of 1966, when he confessed to a noticeable loss of vitality and weight, that he began to suspect something more serious. His condition was aggravated by prostate problems, which eventually took him into the Lansdown Hospital, Bath, for an operation. It seems ironic that while the robust Keynes had suffered complications and nearly died from the same operation a month earlier, the much frailer Sassoon sailed through it, feeling much 'relieved', as he punned, after it. But his eightieth birthday and the attendant fuss three months later exhausted him again and by January 1967 he was completely housebound.

The focal point of his week now became Father McCarthy's arrival on Friday mornings to hear his confession, visits which made up, he maintained, 'for all the solitude and long littlenesses' of his invalid life.[74] Though he realized that his end was approaching, he was not afraid of death. He had found the idea of Purgatory difficult to accept and utterly rejected the notion of Hell for his non-Catholic friends, but firmly believed in Heaven. And as his physical state weakened further, he began to long for it: 'I am one of those persons who begin life by exclaiming they've "never seen anything like it before" ', he noted, 'and die in the hope that they may say the same of heaven.'[75]

It had, in his own phrase, 'been a long journey', but by July 1967 when he wrote these words, it was almost over. Incredible as it seems by today's standards, he did not learn of his inoperable stomach cancer until the month before he died from its secondaries of the liver and peritoneum. 'He knows the full facts', his GP, Dr Falk, wrote to Mother Margaret in August at Sassoon's request, 'and accepts wonderfully the truth that there is nothing we can do that can alter the outcome.'[76]

Hospital was clearly not the answer. Though he had been sent to one in Warminster as soon as the full truth was suspected, he had asked to be sent home to die 'back in his own bed and by his familiar things'.[77] Dom Philip Jebb, who had not realized that he was even ill until he was told of the situation on returning to Downside in August, had set off at once on a long bike ride to visit him. Stopping by chance to find directions in the very street where the hospital (one of three) was situated, Dom Philip felt that he had been 'led' to it:

> The cancer had got a ferocious hold upon him, and as I came into the room I thought he was dead already. But no: and the spirit was throbbing with vitality. We talked of many things, and of ... the first time I met him ... And of his son George ('a good boy George, but what could he say, poor boy? What could he say? He brought me a great bottle of water from St Columba's well on Mull ...') And he was glad that Kent were in the running for the County championship and he remembered the fun he had had with the Downside Ravens, and he gloomily held up his little stick of an arm and said, 'Is that a Raven's arm? I couldn't play with it now.' He said 'It is wonderful to know

that now it will be soon, and what an innings I have had. And all my prayer is hope and gratitude. I am right, aren't I, to be serene in my hopeful prayer?' and then he talked of [Hilaire Belloc's] Heroic Poem – Praise of Wine and quoted the ending. He was very proud of the copy HB had given him.[78]

When Dom Philip finally got up to leave, he promised that all the monks would be praying for him and asked Sassoon not to forget to pray for them. How could he *ever* forget to pray for any of them, he said indignantly, before apologizing for not being 'in better form'. To which Dom Philip replied:

... (what was true) [that] I had never known him more on top of his form, and his eyes went all bright in their deep, deep hollows and he said 'No: behind this poor little, frail little, body I am in the best of form.' And I left him to the angels as I came back through the lonely woods of Longleat.[79]

Once back at Heytesbury Sassoon settled down to die. On 15 August, the tenth anniversary to the day of his First Communion in the Catholic Church, he was anointed and given holy communion by Father McCarthy.

It was the signal for a round of last visits from close friends, with the exception of Dennis Silk, who was on a cricketing tour, and Edmund Blunden. Blunden was on a trip to Toc H (a charitable organization for servicemen) at Ypres, but it is not certain that he could have faced saying goodbye in any case. He had found his visits to Heytesbury increasingly painful, describing Sassoon as irritable, moody and difficult to bear, a rather different picture from that painted by his other friends. Blunden had dreaded the death, which he realized was imminent, and when it occurred 'there seemed little left to live for', his biographer claims.[80] Claire Blunden believed that once he heard of Sassoon's death 'he turned his face to the wall'.[81] Though not yet seventy, he would suffer a serious collapse shortly afterwards and retreat inexorably into senile dementia, dying himself at the age of seventy-eight.[82]

Mother Margaret Mary, on the other hand, made every effort to be at Sassoon's bedside. She had been in retreat in Suffolk when she heard of the diagnosis, but arrived towards the end of August with the fruits of his – and her – proselytizing, his niece Jessica Gatty. She was grateful to have been warned of his skeletal appearance and relieved to find him still lucid. He seemed to her fully prepared for death.

Hart-Davis, alerted by Mother Margaret Mary, also spent several days with him in late August, and was reminded by the gaunt figure stretched out on his large bed of a saint in a medieval painting. But Sassoon's thoughts were not all of the afterlife:

'My poems; they were all right, weren't they?' he asked his literary executor.
'Yes, Sieg, *more* than all right', Hart-Davis assured him.
'Every one a bull's-eye?'
'No, Sieg,' Hart-Davis felt compelled to reply, 'not *every* one.'[83]

Fortunately, Sassoon's humour had not deserted him and he found his friend's painful attempt at honesty immensely funny.

Hart-Davis in turn was amused by Sassoon's response to his own anxious question: 'Would you like me to get Hester down from Scotland?' 'Good Heavens no,' the dying man replied, 'we're in enough trouble as it is!'[84] Hester, in fact, was herself ill, having suffered a stroke which paralyzed her down one side. But George came as planned when Dr Falk believed the end was near. He was struck by his father's anxiety not to be 'a bore or a nuisance'.[85] Stoical to the last and buoyed up by his faith, he told his son, 'This is the final test of my endurance and I intend to put up a good show.'[86] Less than twenty-four hours later, at 8 o'clock on the evening of 1 September 1967, just a week short of his eighty-first birthday, he died.[87]

'It may not be significant, but it is perhaps worth mentioning', George wrote to Charles Causley shortly afterwards, 'that Heytesbury cricket team played their match here as usual on Saturday after a two-minute silence on the field, and soundly defeated a team from whom they usually got a hammering.'[88] Nothing, Causley felt, 'could have been more appropriate for Old Sig'.[89]

Endnotes

Abbreviations

Sources

Arkansas	University of Arkansas
Beinecke	Beinecke Rare Book Library, University of Yale
Berg	Berg Collection, New York Public Library
BL	British Library
Bodley	Bodleian Library, Oxford
Brotherton	Brotherton Library, University of Leeds
Buffalo	University of New York at Buffalo
Columbia	Columbia University Library, New York
Congress	Library of Congress, Washington DC
CUL	Cambridge University Library
Delaware	Delaware University Library
Harvard	Harvard University Library
HRHRC	Harry Ransom Humanities Research Center, University of Texas at Austin
Iowa	Iowa University Library
IWM	Imperial War Museum, London
Lilly	Lilly Library, Indiana University
Pullman	University of Washington at Pullman Library
Rutgers	Rutgers University Library
SIU	Special Collections, University of Southern Illinois at Carbondale
Syracuse	University of New York at Syracuse
Wichita	Wichita State University Library, Kansas

Main works and editions used

Works by Sassoon

CA	*Counter-Attack* (Heinemann, 1918)
CC	*Common Chords* (Mill House Press, 1950)
CP	*Collected Poems* (Faber pbk, 1961)
D1	*Diaries 1915-1918* (Faber, 1983)
D2	*Diaries 1920-1922* (Faber, 1981)
D3	*Diaries 1923-1925* (Faber, 1985)
EE	*Emblems of Experience* (Rampant Lions Press, 1951)
HJ	*The Heart's Journey* (Heinemann, 1928)
MFM	*Memoirs of a Fox-Hunting Man* (Faber, 1928; Faber Library edition, 1943, used)
MIO	*Memoirs of an Infantry Officer* (Faber, 1930; Faber 1973 pbk used)

OC	*The Old Century and Seven More Years* (Faber, 1938; Faber 1968 pbk used)
OH	*The Old Huntsman* (Heinemann, 1917)
RR	*The Road to Ruin* (Faber, 1933)
RRu	*Rhymed Ruminations* (Faber, 1940)
SJ	*Siegfried's Journey* (Faber, 1945)
SP	*Sherston's Progress* (Faber, 1936; Penguin 1948 edition used)
UV4	Unpublished and unfinished fourth volume of autobiography
WP	*The War Poems* (Faber, 1983)
WY	*The Weald of Youth* (Faber, 1942)

Works by other authors

GTAT	Graves, R., *Goodbye to All That* (Cape, 1929; Penguin 1960 edition used)
Keynes	Keynes, G., *A Bibliography of Siegfried Sassoon* (Hart-Davis, 1962)
O'Prey	O'Prey, P. (ed.), *In Broken Images: Selected Letters of Robert Graves, 1914-1946*, ed. Paul O'Prey (Hutchinson, 1982)
SS:MWP	Wilson, Jean Moorcroft, *Siegfried Sassoon: The Making of a War Poet* (Duckworth, 1998)
SS:PP	Corrigan, Dame F., *Siegfried Sassoon: Poet's Pilgrimage* (Gollancz, 1973)
Thorpe	Thorpe, M., *Siegfried Sassoon: A Critical Study* (OUP and Leiden University Press, 1966)
WIK	Dunn, J.C. (ed.), *The War the Infantry Knew* (P.S. King, 1938)

Correspondents

AB	Arnold Bennett
AL	Sir Alan Lascelles
AT	Anne Tennant
ATB	A.T. Bartholomew ('Theo')
BH	Ben Huebsch
DFC	Dame Felicitas Corrigan
DS	Dennis Silk
EB	Edmund Blunden
EG	Edmund Gosse
EJD	Edward J. Dent
EM	Edward Marsh
EH	Eileen Hunter
EMF	E.M. Forster
EO	Edith Olivier
ES	Edith Sitwell
FS	Frank Schuster
FSw	Frank Swinnerton
GA	William Atkin ('Gabriel')
GBS	Glen Byam Shaw ('Speasey')
GK	Geoffrey Keynes
GS	George Sassoon
HFJ	Henry Festing-Jones ('Enrico')
HGW	H.G. Wells
HH	Haro Hodson

HMT	H.M. Tomlinson ('Tommy')
HS	Hamo Sassoon
JA	J.R. Ackerley
JG	Sister Jessica Gatty
KA	Lady Katharine Asquith
LG	Lady Gatty
LOM	Lady Ottoline Morrell
LU	Louis Untermeyer
LW	Laurence Whistler
MB	Max Beerbohm
MMM	Mother Margaret Mary McFarlin
NB	Nellie Burton
OS	Sir Osbert Sitwell
PG	Philip Gosse
RG	Robert Graves
RGH	Robert Gathorne-Hardy ('Bob')
RH	Ralph Hodgson
RHD	Sir Rupert Hart-Davis
RN	Robert Nichols
RW	Rex Whistler
SB	S.N. Behrman ('Sam')
SCC	Sir Sydney Carlyle Cockerell
SS	Siegfried Sassoon
SSi	Sacheverell Sitwell
ST	The Rt Hon. Stephen Tennant ('Steenie')
TEL	T.E. Lawrence
TH	Thomas Hardy
TS	Theresa Sassoon ('Ash')
WdlM	Walter de la Mare
WJT	Walter James Redfern Turner ('Crikey')
WO	Wilfred Owen
WW	Sir William Walton ('Willie')

Introduction

1. 'Siegfried Sassoon', *The Author*, Winter 1989, p. 125.

2. Cohen, J., 'The Three Roles of Siegfried Sassoon', quoted by DFC in SS:PP, p. 35.

3. *Spectator*, 8 September 1967.

4. ibid.

5. 'Siegfried's Journey', a review of SS:PP, *Scotsman*, 28 July 1973.

6. Cyril Connolly, *Previous Convictions* (Hamish Hamilton, 1963), p. 184.

7. TEL to GK, 6 August 1934.

8. *Centenary Essay* on SS by DFC, 1986, sent to the author by DFC.

9. SS:PP, p. 23.

10. ibid.

11. *Daily News and Westminster Gazette*, 9 October 1928.

12. SS to RG, 2 March 1930, Buffalo.

13. D3, p. 40.

14. D2, p. 53.

15. SS to HMT, 26 February 1949, HRHRC.

16. T.H. White to SCC, [*c.* 1958], Cockerell, *The Best of Friends*, p. 166.

17. WdlM to SS, 7 February 1956, CUL.

18. ES to SS, [15?] February 1931, Pullman.

19. OC, p. 140.

20. SS to MB, 1 November 1939, Hart-Davis, *Siegfried Sassoon*, p. 81.

21. SJ, p. 105.

22. Maurice Wiggin's review of SS:PP, *The Sunday Times*, 5 August 1973.

23. SS, *Meredith*, p. 117.

24. Jackson Page to RHD, 31 August 1967, CUL.

25. DFC to SS, 30 October 1966.

Chapter 1

1. SJ, p. 26. The title quotation is from SJ, p. 109 and the epigraph poem is at the Berg and unpublished.

2. 'Lovers', written on 26 November 1918, first appeared in May 1919 in the *Oxford Outlook*, an obscure magazine started by Beverley Nichols for a small circle of aesthetes, then in Sassoon's privately printed *Picture Show* (a hyphen was later added) in June 1919, but remained largely unknown until 1947, when it was published in its censored form in CP.

3. SJ, p. 106.

4. See SS:MWP, pp. 391-5.

5. SJ, p. 106.

6. SS to DFC, 14 February 1961, SS:PP, p. 70.

7. SJ, p. 97.

8. SS to RHD, 12 December 1963, CUL.

9. D1, p. 282. SS gave Temple the manuscript notebook of *Picture Show* in April 1919 as a wedding present. Temple died in 1958. A colourful figure, he appears to have been a part-model for Arnold Bennett's hero in *Imperial Palace* (1930). The poem which follows is at CUL in an unpublished section of SS's diary.

10. SJ, p. 98.

11. SS to DFC, 28 July 1965, SS:PP, p. 66.

12. John Drinkwater (1882-1937), poet and playwright.

13. SS to HFJ, 18 June [1927], CUL.

14. Harvard MS Collection.

15. Walter James Redfern Turner (?1889-1946), poet, novelist and music critic.

16. Wilfrid Wilson Gibson (1878-1962), poet, rebel against the Tennysonian tradition.

17. John Freeman (1880-1929), a poet who died relatively young.

18. D2, p. 189.

19. i.e., Lady Leslie, Lady Essex, Princess Patricia, Sir Ian Hamilton, Lady Cranby, Sir L. Mallet, Lady Cunard and Mrs Charles Hunter.

20. SJ, p. 106.

21. ibid., p. 107.

22. ibid.

23. CP, p. 263.

24. SS to DFC, 16 February 1961, SS:PP, p. 112.

25. ibid.

26. SS to WdlM, 17 July 1919, Beinecke.

27. SS to RH, 22 July 1945, Beinecke.

28. SS to HFJ, 22 May [1927], CUL.

29. UV4, quoting diary entry for 14 May 1927, CUL.

30. SS to WdlM, 16 June 1951, Beinecke.

31. SS's address at the unveiling of a plaque to WdlM in St Paul's Cathedral on 18 December 1961, SS:PP, p. 216.

32. John Galsworthy (1867-1933), whom SS continued to visit until at least 1930.

33. SS to FSw, 17 September 1940, Arkansas.

34. SJ, p. 105.

35. SS to FSw, 17 September 1940, UA, and SJ, p. 104, respectively.

36. SS to Ruth Head, 11 March 1932, HRHRC.

37. See, for example, SS to HMT, 25 December 1942, HRHRC.

38. 'Night on the Convoy' was published in vol. III of *Reveille* in February 1919. SS had appealed to EM to help him 'tidy it up' (SS to EM, 31 October 1918, Berg).

39. H.W. Massingham (1860-1924), Liberal journalist, and editor of the *Daily Chronicle* and the *Nation*.

40. i.e., 'To Leonide Massine in "Cleopatra"' and 'Memorial Tablet', published in 15 February 1919 issue.

It would also be included in *Picture Show*.

41. Hamo Sassoon was wounded at Gallipoli in November 1915 and died at sea of wounds.

42. SS to GA, 4 January [1919], Berg. The following quotation is from SJ, p. 109. SS was to spend New Year's Eve with Wilson, his wife and two small children.

43. SS's unpublished diary for late 1918, CUL. The following quotation is from SS's letter to GA, [6 December 1918], at Berg.

44. SJ, p. 105.

45. ibid.

46. ibid.

47. Edward Joseph Dent (1876-1957) was a fellow of King's College, Cambridge, from 1902 to 1908, and from 1926 until his death. Augustus Theodore Bartholomew (1882-1933).

48. See SS:MWP, pp. 198-9.

49. ATB notes in his diary that he first met SS at the Lion in Cambridge with EJD on 25 August 1915 (Add. 8787, CUL).

50. Quoted from GA's unpublished memoirs at Wichita State University, Wichita, Kansas.

51. Famous American book designer.

52. SS to EJD, 20 March 1916, CUL.

53. Obituary by Geoffrey Keynes in the *Cambridge Review*, 28 April 1933.

54. Diary of ATB for 13 April 1920 and 9 January 1921, CUL.

55. ibid., May 1921.

56. ibid.

57. GA (1897-1937) had not been made a full lieutenant by November 1918. He was with 222nd Mixed Brigade at Margate.

58. SS to EJD, [c. November 1917], CUL.

59. GA to EJD, 30 October 1918, Dent Collection, CUL.

60. ibid.

61. ibid., [c. 11 November 1918].

62. William ('Gabriel') Park Atkin, whose uncle was the painter John Park (1880-1962), exhibited one picture at the London Salon in 1919, held an exhibition of his watercolours at the Piccadilly Gallery in 1923, and also exhibited in the Northern Counties exhibitions at the Laing Art Gallery, Newcastle, which held a loan exhibition of his work in 1940. He painted mainly watercolours but also did drawings for book illustrations and was a gifted cartoonist. The Laing Art Gallery has twelve watercolours and one oil of his and SS himself owned five of Atkin's paintings; see lot 312 in Phillip's (Bath) catalogue of the sale of the contents of Heytesbury House, 31 October 1994.

63. GA to EJD, 30 October 1918, CUL.

64. SS to EM, 4 December 1918, Berg.

65. Later on, when SS bought himself a Bechstein grand, he would give his seventeen-year-old Broadwood piano to Atkin.

66. EJD to SS, 20 February 1918, CUL.

67. Diary of ATB for 29 June 1919, CUL.

68. SS to SB, 13 December 1920, CUL.

69. GA to EJD, 30 October 1918, CUL.

70. SS to Edward Carpenter, 27 July 1911, Sheffield City Libraries.

71. ibid., 15 August 1918. Whether Sassoon is referring to a physical relationship or making a more mundane reference to taking a job as a manual worker is not certain. I have been unable to trace Carpenter's reply to SS's letter.

72. SS to ATB, 26 November 1918, CUL.

73. SS to GA, [n.d.] Berg. The following quotation occurs in a letter from GA to EJD, 24 November 1918, CUL.

74. ibid.

75. GA to EJD, 28 December 1918, CUL. SS himself refers to 'going to the country with Gabriel' (SS to GA, 1 December [1918], Berg).

76. Diary of ATB for 16 December 1918, CUL.

77. GA to EJD, 24 November 1918, CUL.

78. ibid. SS had also written to GA on 23 November 1918: 'Read *Sea-Drift* – O past, O happy life, O songs of joy! / O my darling, my darling' (Berg). He would also quote love poetry by Yeats, Milton, D.H. Lawrence, Donne, Fletcher and Charlotte Mew to Atkin, to 'garland [him] with verses' (SS to GA, 31 December 1918, Berg).

79. GA to EJD, 25 December 1917, CUL.

80. ibid., 24 October 1917, CUL.

81. Philpot was so attracted to SS that he painted his portrait in oils for only 50 guineas instead of his customary £500 fee. SS subsequently gave the portrait to Cockerell at the Fitzwilliam Museum, Cambridge, whence it passed to Clare College, which also has a drawing of him by Sir William Rothenstein of 1921.

82. SS had known Lady Sybil Colefax (known as the 'Coal box' to Osbert Sitwell who, like many, regarded her as a figure of fun) since 1917, when he had read his war poems to a society gathering at her house. They wrote to each other intermittently between 1920 and 1930.

83. Jelly d'Aranyi (b.1895) was one of two sisters, both eminent Hungarian violinists.

84. Vivian de Sola Pinto (1895-1969), poet and critic.

85. Robert von Ranke Graves (1895-1985).

86. David Sassoon's eldest son, Abdullah (Alfred), became an English baronet and was the grandfather of Sir Philip Sassoon.

87. Violet Gordon-Woodhouse (1872-1948) was highly accomplished both as a harpsichordist and clavichordist.

88. GA to EJD, 28 December 1918, CUL.

89. ibid.

90. ibid.

91. ibid.

92. This and the next quotation are from SS to GA, 23 November 1918, Berg.

93. D2, p. 71.

94. ibid., p. 72.

95. Told to me by Lady Lettice Strickland-Constable during the several interviews I had with her in 1991.

96. SS's notes on OC, CUL.

97. ibid.

98. SS explained to an American friend, Louis Untermeyer, that he had written 'fake' love sonnets by the dozen in his twenties.

99. E.B.C. Jones's review of *Picture Show*, *Cambridge Magazine*, 8 November 1919.

100. 'Parted' is dated 'Gray's Inn, 25 Nov.' in the HRHRC ms of *Picture Show*. It was first published in *Today*, April 1919.

101. Dated 'Weirleigh, Dec. 1918'. First appeared in *Picture Show* in June 1919, then was published in *Today* and the *Yale Review* in July 1919. There is also an unpublished poem, 'Love's Daybreak', among the SS mss at the Berg.

102. First published in the *Nation*, 24 May 1919, then in *Picture Show* in June 1919. SS wrote to DFC on 16 February 1962: 'As you say, I don't know how I dared to write it – but it came early in 1919, when I was in a ferment of postwar emotional release.' (SS:PP, p. 94).

Chapter 2

1. SJ, p. 127.

2. 'Picture-Show', the title poem of SS's next volume, privately printed in June 1919, was written at Weirleigh in January 1919. It was first published in the *Sphere* in April 1919.

3. CP, p. 116. This poem, described by SS as 'Donne-like', is dated in his copy at HRHRC.

4. SS to GA, [6 December 1918], Berg.

5. 'The Imperfect Lover', CP, p. 116.

6. D2, p. 86.

7. ibid.

8. 'Madeleine in Church', quoted by SS in a letter to GA of 30 November 1918, Berg.

9. CP, p. 116.

10. SS to RG, 9 February [1924], SIU.

11. 'Memory', CP, p. 105.

12. i.e., Corrigan, *Siegfried Sassoon*.

13. *Centenary Essay* on SS by DFC of 1986, sent to author by DFC.

14. SS to DFC, 25 June 1965, SS:PP, p. 48.

15. SJ, pp. 119-20.

16. ibid., p. 119.

17. SS to GA, 27 December 1918, Berg.

18. CP, p. 106.

19. SS to GA, 27 December 1918, Berg.

20. ibid., 31 December 1918, Berg.

21. SS to EJD, 27 December 1918, CUL.

22. CUL.

23. SS was at Blackburn from 10 to 15 December 1918, staying at the Old Bull Hotel.

24. SJ, p. 111.

25. Unpublished diary, entry for 10 December 1918, CUL.

26. ibid., entry for 13 December 1918, CUL.

27. ibid.

28. Woolf, L., *Downhill All the Way*, p. 84.

29. Snowden, born in 1864 to a poor weaver in Yorkshire, was knocked off his bicycle at the age of twenty-two and forced to lie on his back for nearly a year. He was handicapped for the rest of his life, unable to walk without a stick, but the event also turned him from a liberal to a socialist. He died in 1937.

30. Unpublished diary, entry for 14 December 1918, CUL.

31. SJ, p. 115. Lloyd-George's Liberal-Conservative Coalition Government was returned with an overwhelming majority of over 300 in the House of Commons, though the majority in individual votes was strikingly less – 5,000,000 for the Government, 4,600,000 against.

32. Unpublished diary, entry for 13 December 1918, CUL.

33. ibid., entry for 15 December 1918, CUL.

34. SS to LOM, [n.d.] December 1918, HRHRC.

35. SS to GA, 9 December 1918, Berg.

36. Unpublished diary, entry for 13 December 1918, CUL.

37. D2, p. 294. Schuster's sister, Adela, was similarly supportive of artists, Oscar Wilde in particular, who called her 'the lady of Wimbledon'.

38. D2, p. 294.

39. ibid.

40. SS to RN, 5 November [?1923], Berg.

41. SJ, p. 126.

42. ibid., p. 118.

43. George Santayana (1863-1952) was born in Spain but educated in America. Frank Prewett (1893-1962) published a few not very successful volumes of poetry with SS's help, including *The Rural Scene* (1924).

44. SS to LOM, 4 January 1919, HRHRC. The flat was at 14 Merton Street, which still stands. The rent was £192 p.a. and Sassoon's income approximately £600 p.a., £200 of which he had arranged to pay Gabriel.

45. See SS:MWP, p. 504.

46. Sassoon did send Russell copies of some of his books – *Recreations* in 1923, for example, and MFM in 1928, for both of which Russell thanked him. But the most interesting communication between them is part of a letter from Russell disagreeing with Sassoon's praise of Rimbaud and describing his experiences in prison. This is in the hands of a private collector.

47. SS to RG, 4 March 1919, SIU.

48. Of the dozen who came to

dinner and the eighteen who came in afterwards, Sassoon particularly noted in his diary (17 January 1919): 'General Freyburg was there – looking fat, a budding Hindenburg. Laverys, – N. Lytton, – Lady Randolph C[hurchill], – Lady Essex, – Juliet Duff, – Barbara Somerset, – Joan Capell – L[or]ds Cranbourne, Lathom, Londonderry, Sir A. Sinclair – etc.' (CUL).

49. SS to EM, letter of December 1919 re. his electioneering at Blackburn (Berg), and SJ, p. 128, respectively.

50. Unpublished diary, entry for 17 January 1919, CUL.

51. SS to GA, 20 [January 1919], Berg.

52. SJ, p. 128.

53. See, for example, the obituary by Rivers's close friend and colleague, Sir Henry Head, in the Proceedings of the Royal Society, 1922.

54. Cyril Bradley Rootham (1875-1938), who studied at Cambridge University and at the Royal College of Music, became organist at St John's College, Cambridge, and composed orchestral and choral works as well as chamber music. It is interesting to contrast Arnold Bennett's more forthright comments on the Fellows of St John's, after dining with Rivers there on 9 October 1920: 'A "short" dinner, too short, and professors etc. rather dull. Too cautious, too pedagogic.' (Bennett, *The Journals*, pp. 274-5).

55. i.e., *The Old Huntsman and Other Poems* (1917) and *Counter-Attack and Other Poems* (1918).

56. Dennis Silk, a later friend, tells the story of how during one tape-recording of his poetry, SS quite deliberately and loudly tapped his pipe out, unconcerned or unaware as to the interruption this created.

57. SS to ATB, [?16] December 1918, CUL.

58. Sassoon wrote out his poems in a lined, hessian-covered notebook, originally inscribed '1st RWF, BEF' but subsequently retitled '2nd RWF' on the front cover. He then reversed the book and copied out in his beautiful script the poems he thought possible for a new volume. Originally entitled 'The Last Word and Other Poems', this was crossed out and replaced by 'A Picture-Show', with the 'A' also subsequently crossed out. When SS presented this notebook to SCC in early 1919, it included five poems eventually omitted from the privately printed volume in July 1919: 'Great Men', 'Tariff Reform', 'Cold Steel', 'Can I Forget' and 'A Last Word', the long poem which had given its name to the original title. The manuscript notebook does not include eight poems which *were* included in the July 1919 edition of *Picture Show*: 'To a Very Wise Man', 'Devotion to Duty', 'What the Captain Said', 'Cinema Hero', 'The Imperfect Lover', 'Aftermath', 'Prelude to an Unwritten MS' and 'Everyone Sang', most of which were written or polished after SS's January 1919 visit to SCC. The notebook, now in the Berg Collection, also contains some of SS's letters to SCC on the subject, which SCC pasted into it. The final cost of the printing would be £61 8*s*. 9*d*. for 200 copies.

59. SS to ATB, 26 January 1919, CUL.

60. At one point Sassoon was planning to find £400 to start Law and his wife up with a public house (D2, p. 78); he also helped Law to buy his own lorry (D2, p. 255), though he was not so keen to lend Law another £250 after that (D2, p. 274).

61. SJ, p. 127.

62. SS was proposed by AB and seconded by His Honour Judge Hugh Murray Sturgis in November 1918, the month after Ross's death. He formally became a member in January 1919 and remained one until 1957/8, when he resigned – 'and saved 25 guineas a year', he told DFC (16

February 1961). The last time he visited the Reform Club, he continued, 'there wasn't a face there I knew and only one of the old servants left'.

63. SJ, p. 127.
64. D2, p. 32.
65. ibid., p. 143.
66. ibid., p. 129.
67. D3, p. 179.
68. ibid., p. 247.
69. ibid., p. 257.
70. D2, pp. 127-8.
71. SS introduced AB to Rivers at Cambridge in 1919 and the two men became sufficiently close by 1921 for AB to invite Rivers to spend three weeks on his yacht.
72. SJ, p. 131.
73. ibid.
74. ibid., p. 132.
75. On 22 September 1967, shortly after SS's death, John Langdon Davies (incorrectly hyphenated in *Siegfried's Journey*) wrote to the *New Statesman* letters column to describe his meeting in some detail. He claimed to have known SS slightly from Oxford when they met at Glasgow, but in fact the meeting at Oxford did not take place until shortly afterwards.
76. *New Statesman*, 22 September 1967. There is another account of SS's visit to Glasgow in Jack Lindsay's *After the Thirties*, Lawrence and Wishart, 1956, pp. 25-7.
77. SJ, p. 132.
78. ibid., p. 133 and John Langdon Davies's letter to the *New Statesman*.
79. ibid., p. 134.
80. ibid., pp. 134-5.
81. SS to RG, 2 March 1919, SIU.
82. ibid., 9 January 1919, SIU. Vivian de Sola Pinto was of Portuguese origin.
83. RG to SS, 13 January 1919, Berg.
84. SS to RG, 9 January 1919, SIU.
85. Richard Perceval Graves describes Boar's Hill at this period as a 'miniature Parnassus' in *Robert Graves: The Assault Heroic*. At

various times just after the First World War its inhabitants included John Masefield, Robert Bridges, Robert Graves, Edmund Blunden and Robert Nichols.

86. SS to RG, 2 March 1919, SIU.
87. ibid.
88. CUL.
89. SS to RG, 4 March 1919, SIU.
90. ibid.
91. Kennedy, p. 14.
92. See Osbert Sitwell's *Laughter in the Next Room*, p. 171.
93. SJ, p. 135.
94. ibid.
95. ibid., p. 136.
96. ibid., p. 137.
97. ibid.
98. D2, p. 73.
99. SJ, p. 137.
100. ibid.
101. Beverley Nichols, who had been at Balliol for a few months in 1917 but left after failing his exams, had arrived back at the college in January 1919. For further details of his life and work, see Bryan Connon's *Beverley Nichols: A Life* (Constable, 1991). I am indebted to Mr Connon for supplying me with quotations from Nichols's diary, left to him by the author.
102. Nichols's interest in Sassoon may also have been stimulated by a chance meeting the previous October with one of Sassoon's greatest friends and admirers at this time, the poet Robert Nichols (no relation). Both men were sailing to New York on the same ship, Robert on behalf of the Ministry of Information.
103. Johnstone, whose initials were G.H., had been a close friend of Graves until Graves discovered that he had been involved in homosexual activities.
104. This was probably the Psittakoi Society, which Nichols had founded for the discussion of a wide range of subjects.
105. Nichols printed Sassoon's

427

'Lovers' in full in the first issue of the *Oxford Outlook*, May 1919.

106. SS to RG, 2 March 1919, SIU.

107. SJ, p. 135.

108. See echoes of Walter de la Mare in 'The Dark House' and of Mary Coleridge in 'The Middle Ages'.

109. SS to GA, 20 [January 1919], Berg.

110. Once SS had made the decision to leave Oxford, he wrote another poem on his last day there, 'Cinema Hero', which he included in *Picture Show* after its appearance in *Land and Water* in May 1919 and *The Living Age* on 14 June 1919. But he did not believe it was good enough to include in any further collections. He also copied out twenty-eight of his poems into a book which he and other poet-friends prepared for Roderick Meiklejohn, and which Nancy Nicholson illustrated.

111. SJ, p. 141.

112. On 11 March 1919 the *London Gazette* announced: 'Lt (acting Captain) S.L. Sassoon MC relinquishes his acting rank, is placed on the retired list on account of ill-health caused by wounds 12 March 1919 and is granted the rank of Captain.'

113. SJ, p. 137.

114. SS to ATB, 19 March 1919, CUL.

115. See footnote 44.

116. SS to RG, 13 March 1919, SIU. Michael and his wife Violet had a third son, Hamo, born in England in 1920.

117. SS to RG, 13 March 1919, SIU.

Chapter 3

1. SJ, p. 138.

2. Line 3 originally read 'As prisoned birds might find in freedom' (see the periodical *Gravesiana*, vol. 1, no. 1, p. 42.).

3. Sassoon told a Mr Hillyer in a letter of 2 October 1960 (Syracuse) that 'Everyone Sang' had brought him 'several hundred pounds in anthology fees!', a large sum of money for the time.

4. Sassoon writes in SJ that 'Everyone Sang' was written in his smoking room at Weirleigh, a small room next to the front door, but Robert Nichols believed that the poem was written 'in the garden – or garden-room – of ... Frank Schuster's house on the Thames' (Bodley). He was basing this on a manuscript copy which Sassoon had sent him, headed 'The Hut, Bray, Berks.'. The most likely explanation is that Sassoon copied out the poem for Nichols at Bray some time after composing it.

5. SS to ES, 10 January 1955, HRHRC, re. *Sequences*.

6. SJ, p. 141.

7. See SS to RH, 22 July 1945, Beinecke.

8. SS to WdlM, 29 March 1943, Beinecke.

9. SS to EM, [?July] 1919, Berg.

10. GTAT, p. 228.

11. SJ, p. 141.

12. ibid.

13. The *Daily Citizen*, the official organ of the Labour Party, had folded by 1919, leaving only the *Daily Herald*. By contrast, Germany had 167 socialist dailies, Denmark 61, Sweden 15, Czechoslovakia 13, Belgium 8, Austria 7 and France 5. Sassoon states in his autobiography that the *Daily Herald* was launched as a daily on 31 March 1919. In fact, it was first published as a daily on 25 January 1911, but ran for only three months, subsequently reappearing as an unofficial Labour daily in April 1912. Though the outbreak of war put an end to it again in September 1914, it almost immediately began publication as a weekly.

14. Woolf, L., *Downhill All the Way*, p. 244.

15. The *Daily Herald* was to suffer financially from the long post-war slump and would need help from the trade unions in the early twenties.

Taken over officially by the Labour Party in 1923, it would eventually become the *Sun*.

16. Gerald Gould (1885-1936) presented Sassoon with a copy of his *The Happy Tree and Other Poems* (1919), which contained a section of war verse. It also contained, more typically, what Sassoon described as 'graceful Stevensonian lyrics' (SJ, p. 137). Earlier works include *Lyrics* (1906) and *Poems* (1911). Gould also published works of literary criticism and two collections of essays. His offer to review Sassoon's *War Poems* (1919), was written on 2 November 1919 and placed by Sassoon in a book of press-cuttings, now in the possession of William Reese.

17. See SS:MWP, p. 522.

18. SS to Harold Laski, 13 February 1920, William Reese Collection.

19. Woolf, L., *Beginning Again*, p. 223. Angell and his younger disciples, John Hilton, H.D. Henderson and Harold Wright, ran a small monthly magazine, *War and Peace*, in the later years of the war, which propagated Angell's anti-war views.

20. Turner published a number of volumes of poetry, including *The Dark Fire* (1918), *Pursuit of Psyche* (1931) and *Songs and Incantations* (1936). He also wrote some plays, including *The Man Who Ate Popomack* (1922), semi-autobiographical novels and several books on music. There is some mystery surrounding Turner's date of birth, since Sassoon claimed to have discovered from Turner's passport that, instead of being 3 years younger, Turner was 2 years *older* than he was, which suggests a birth date of 1884. See D2, p. 197.

21. SS to RG, 23 May 1917, SIU. This collection included several war poems, including 'Aeroplanes', 'In Camp' and 'Sky-Sent Death'.

22. ibid., 30 April 1919, SIU.

23. Lytton Strachey to Virginia Woolf, 19 September 1922.

24. Powell, *To Keep the Ball Rolling*, p. 312.

25. D3, p. 81.

26. D2, pp. 109 and 16.

27. ibid., p. 236.

28. ibid., p. 199.

29. ibid.

30. D2, p. 162.

31. ibid., p. 103.

32. ibid., p. 271.

33. ibid., pp. 271-2.

34. Sassoon's appreciation led him to send Irene Clephane at least two of his books after he left the paper, *Recreations* (1923) and *Lingual Exercises* (1925). Her letters of thanks of 14 October 1923 and 5 April 1925 are at CUL.

35. See SJ, p. 143. D.J. Taylor argues in one of his reviews that 'self-deprecation is, of course, the signature mark of twentieth-century literary biography'.

36. SJ, p. 143.

37. See SS:MWP, pp. 77-8.

38. SJ, p. 142.

39. Graves, R.P., *Robert Graves: The Assault Heroic*, p. 215.

40. SS to EM, 10 January 1919, Berg.

41. Graves, op. cit.

42. GTAT, p. 236.

43. ibid.

44. ibid.

45. See SS to RG, 9 April 1919, SIU.

46. SJ, p. 145.

47. ibid., p. 138.

48. 'Base Details', 'The Hawthorn Tree', 'The Investiture' and 'Together'.

49. The pamphlet claimed that the reviewing staff would include Lascelles Abercrombie, H.N. Brailsford, A. Clutton-Brock, G.D.H. Cole, W.H. Davies, Walter de la Mare, W.L. George, H.J. Massingham, Viola Meynell, H.W. Nevinson, Hon. Bertrand Russell, Evelyn Sharp, Frank Swinnerton, H.M. Tomlinson and Alec Waugh. Two interesting omissions are Robert Graves and W.J. Turner, but as Sassoon explained to Graves, he already had five Georgian poets in his list and hesitated to add two more.

50. SJ, p. 144.

51. ibid.

52. ibid., p. 139.

53. D2, p. 34.

54. *Daily Herald*, 2 April 1919.

55. SJ, pp. 139 and 145.

56. John Oxenham, born William Arthur Dunkerley (1852-1941), was a popular novelist and religious poet. He wrote about forty novels, beginning with *God's Prisoner* (1898) and many volumes of verse. His first poetry collection, *Bees in Amber*, published at his own expense in 1913, sold over 250,000 copies; his next two, *The King's Highway* (1916) and *The Vision Splendid* (1917), were among the most popular of the First World War.

57. After the first three literary pages there is no book advertising at all, apart from one small advertisement in the eighth number, until the twelfth.

58. SS told RG in a letter of 30 March 1919 (SIU): 'I only get six half-columns a week – (1,000 words to a column),' but this varied over the seven months he worked at the *Daily Herald*. It was never less than 3,000 words.

59. SS to RG, 13 March 1919, SIU.

60. ibid., 14 March 1919, SIU.

61. See SS to RG, [?July] 1919, SIU: 'I wanted a *considered article*, not a scrappy review … your stuff won't do either you or Davies any good.' This unaccustomed stand against Graves was probably made under Turner's influence, since SS refers to having 'gone through' the review with Turner.

62. Robert Nichols (1893-1944). See SS:MWP, pp. 420-3, for details of Nichols and the start of his friendship with SS.

63. Nichols reviewed *Marlborough and Other Poems* by Charles Hamilton Sorley on 4 June 1919 and a book by Max Plowman on 2 July 1919.

64. SS was to spend Christmas 1919 with RN at his family home in Essex and the two would correspond regularly (Nichols at great length) until 1926, when their letters became more infrequent. RN would write sporadically to SS until 1939.

65. GTAT, p. 241.

66. Edith Sitwell submitted a review of George Willis's *Any Soldier to his Son* on 4 June 1919.

67. This was published by the revolutionary Mr Henderson at the Bomb Shop, 66 Charing Cross Road, in 1919 and distributed at a 'Keep-hands-off-Russia' rally in the Royal Albert Hall.

68. *Daily Herald*, 19 July 1919.

69. ibid., 26 July 1919. See John Pearson's *Façades*, Fontana, 1980, pp. 136-8, for a fuller account.

70. SS to GA, [April] 1919, Berg.

71. Alec Waugh's war poems came out as *Resentment* (1918). See D2, p. 160, and D3, p. 156, for references to Waugh.

72. Review of 21 May 1919.

73. D2, p. 148.

74. SJ, p. 170.

75. See SS:MWP, pp. 458-9, for an account of the correspondence between Forster and Sassoon.

76. SS asked Lascelles Abercrombie for an article on Thomas Hardy and de la Mare for one on *Robinson Crusoe*, for example.

77. Fitzgerald, *Charlotte Mew and her Friends*.

78. This was at 6 Hogarth Studios, 64 Charlotte Street, London W1, a building which still stands.

79. TEL to SCC, 19 March 1924 ('I'm frigid towards women, so I can withstand her: so that I want to withstand her') and SS to WdlM, 30 March 1932, Beinecke.

80. Fitzgerald, *Charlotte Mew*, p. 174.

81. SS to Professor Lewis Chase, 25 January 1922, Congress. SS still believed this in 1961, though by then he had exchanged Frances Cornford's name for Edith Sitwell's.

82. SS to WdlM, 30 March 1952, Beinecke.

83. ibid.

84. ibid. There are letters from Mary Davidow in 1958 (at CUL) consulting SS about her dissertation on Mew, a source which Penelope Fitzgerald herself relied on.

85. See D3, p. 186, where SS notes that LOM sent Mew's poems to Robert Bridges.

86. See ibid., p. 46.

87. SJ, p. 151.

88. ibid.

89. ibid., p. 154.

90. ibid., p. 153.

91. ibid., pp. 158-9. SS had tried to persuade Belloc, a well-known Catholic essayist, novelist and poet, to 'write something for the literary pages of the *Daily Herald*', but Belloc evaded his request by saying that 'Lansbury's political credulities were at variance with his own convictions' (ibid., p. 157).

92. SCC to SS, 15 December 1945, Sotheby sale catalogue, July 1991.

93. SJ, p. 155.

94. ibid., p. 154.

95. See SS:MWP, pp. 517-19.

96. SS:PP, pp. 136-7.

97. SS told HMT (letter of 4 May 1949, HRHRC) that he felt as though he were Hardy's great-nephew.

98. SJ, p. 147.

99. SS to HMT, 16 August 1946, HRHRC.

100. SJ, p. 149. The tribute was delayed and delivered to Hardy in November, not June as intended.

101. SJ, p. 150.

102. ibid.

103. Henry Major Tomlinson (1873-1958). SS has *Old Junk* reviewed in the *Herald* by W.H. Davies on 9 April 1919 and quotes a paragraph of it in his 'Literary Notes' for 21 May 1919. There is a review by HMT himself in the *Herald* on 25 June 1919.

104. Causley, 'Writers Remembered: Siegfried Sassoon', *The Author*, Winter 1989.

105. D3, p. 185.

106. Diary entry for 12 March 1924.

107. Woolf, L., *Downhill All the Way*, p. 92.

108. D3, p. 189: 'Shabby little HMT with his almost cocknified accent.'

109. SS to HH, 4 November 1948, in possession of the recipient.

110. SS to HMT, 25 December 1942, HRHRC.

111. SS's notes to OC (CUL) and D3, p. 189.

112. See HMT to SS, 2 December 1927, Columbia, where HMT questions SS's charge, 'Does it matter losing your public? for Tomlinson will always be kind', with 'That was hardly just to me. I'm not kind. When it comes to poetry I'm indurated.'

113. SS to WdlM, 14 November 1948, Beinecke.

114. Frank Arthur Swinnerton (1884-1982) contributed at least four reviews to the *Daily Herald* between April and June 1919 and in November 1919 SS arranged to have Swinnerton's latest work, *September*, reviewed by E.M. Forster.

115. SS to HMT, 30 December 1951, HRHRC.

116. SS to FSw, 26 June 1931, Arkansas.

117. SS to FSw, 18 October 1935, Arkansas.

118. There would be one significant break in SS's correspondence with FSw following SS's conversion to Roman Catholicism in 1957, but the breach would be repaired in the early sixties.

Chapter 4

1. SJ, p. 160.

2. Unpublished poem in the Harvard MS Collection, dated 20 February 1924 and 25 May 1931, and 'rewritten' 26 November 1932.

3. D2, pp. 162-3.

4. ibid., p. 174.

5. EB to SS, 7 May 1919, HRHRC.

6. Letter of 2 September 1917, Iowa.

7. SJ, p. 146.

8. D3, p. 92. Born in central London in 1896, EB had moved to Kent in 1900, when his father had become headmaster of a primary school at Yalding, only six miles or so from SS's own birthplace of Matfield. EB lived at Yalding for the next nine years, until leaving to take up a scholarship at Christ's Hospital in Horsham, Sussex, and he remembered his childhood as idyllic.

9. Harvard.

10. *Pastorals* was published by Elkin Matthews in 1916.

11. SS to TS, 16 May [1929], Berg.

12. SS to WdlM, 10 February 1952, Beinecke.

13. SS to Dame Hildelith Cumming, 3 July 1962, SS:PP, p. 229.

14. See SS:MWP, pp. 103-4. The first sale alone of SS material (at Christie's on 4 June 1975) lists forty-one volumes given by EB to SS and SS was equally generous.

15. CP, p. 183.

16. ibid., p. 189. EB compared SS himself to Henry Vaughan in a review of SS's *Sequences* in the *TLS*.

17. Edward Shanks (1892-1953) was a poet, novelist and critic, and the first winner of the Hawthornden Prize in 1919. He was Assistant Editor on Squire's *London Mercury*.

18. SJ, p. 146.

19. D2, p. 177.

20. ibid.

21. EG to SS, 14 January 1923, Brotherton.

22. ibid.

23. D2, p. 171.

24. EB was married three times, divorced twice and supported an early mistress all his life. His one break with SS in the late forties would arise out of SS's treatment of his own wife, which EB considered unjust.

25. SJ, p. 146.

26. D2, p. 90.

27. ibid., p. 174.

28. SS to RG, 3 September 1920, SIU.

29. SJ, p. 160.

30. ibid.

31. ibid.

32. D2, p. 33.

33. The third issue of *The Owl* came out in 1923. SS's contributions to the first number were 'Sporting Acquaintances' and 'What the Captain Said at the Point-to-Point', and to the second 'Limitations' and 'Everyone Sang', all poems he included in *Picture Show* the same year. His contribution to the third and last number was 'Solar Eclipse'.

34. SS's contribution was 'Early Chronology', one of the few poems he wrote in the second half of 1919.

35. SJ, p. 172.

36. SS wrote 'To a Very Wise Man' shortly after his visit to Rivers at Cambridge in January 1919.

37. 'Prelude' was written at Weirleigh in April 1919.

38. 'Miracles', dated January 1918 in the ms of *Picture Show* at HRHRC, was written on 9 January 1919 at Weirleigh according to the Cockerell ms at the Berg and other evidence.

39. Keynes, *The Gates of Memory*, p. 53.

40. A note at the beginning of *War Poems* claims rather misleadingly that 'of these sixty-four poems twelve are now published for the first time'. In fact, of these twelve, nine had appeared in *Picture Show* only three months previously, but since this was a private production, they had not technically been 'published'. Even the three poems which had not already appeared in print – 'In an Underground Dressing-Station', 'Atrocities' and 'Return' – were not recent work but had been written much earlier. All three had been considered too outrageous for publication, either by Marsh,

Heinemann or even C.K. Ogden of the outspoken *Cambridge Magazine*.

41. SS to RG, 9 April 1919, SIU.

42. SJ, p. 160.

43. ibid., p. 163.

44. ibid.

45. Bennett, *The Journals*, pp. 330-1.

46. SJ, p. 161.

47. SS stayed with the Sitwells in London from 7 to 17 July 1919.

48. SJ, pp. 161-2.

49. ibid., p. 161.

50. See SS:MWP, pp. 111-12, for further details on Loder.

51. Loder had transferred from the Atherstone to the Fitzwilliam in 1914 with his new wife Phyllis, who had taken over his duties as Joint Master during the war. They lived at Longthorpe House, near Peterborough, where SS had visited Phyllis Loder several times during the war.

52. SJ, p. 165.

53. ibid.

54. ibid., p. 164.

55. ibid.

56. SS stayed at Bath from 17 to 23 July 1919.

57. ibid., p. 170.

58. SS was staying at St John's College, Cambridge, from 11 to 18 August 1919.

59. CP, p. 162.

60. SS to RG, 15 June [1924], SIU.

61. SS to WdlM, 10 September 1919, Beinecke.

62. RG to EB, 12 July 1919, SIU. *Country Sentiment* became the title of Graves's next volume of poetry, published in 1920.

63. SS to ATB, 24 May 1919, CUL.

64. D2, p. 33.

65. SS to GA, [December 1919], Berg.

66. SS to ATB, 12 November 1919, CUL.

67. D2, pp. 88-9.

68. ibid., p. 240.

69. SJ, p. 168.

70. ibid.

71. See Gerald Gould to SS, 2 November 1919, in scrapbook of press-cuttings in the William Reese Collection.

72. AB to RN, 14 August 1923, Bennett, *Letters*, p. 195.

73. SJ, p. 168.

74. ibid., p. 169. *The Dynasts* was subtitled 'An Epic-Drama of the War with Napoleon'.

75. See SS to RH, 27 June 1937, Beinecke: '... my politics ended in 1919, I think'.

76. See SS:MWP, pp. 76-9, for further details on Rachel Beer.

77. SJ, p. 167.

78. SS told GA that he had been invited to lecture in America as early as January 1919, but had turned this first invitation down.

79. SJ, p. 171.

80. *Counter-Attack* was published by Dutton in America in December 1918 and reprinted by them in April 1919 and February 1920.

81. SJ, p. 172.

82. ibid.

Chapter 5

1. 'Midnight on Broadway' appeared in the privately printed *Recreations* (1923) but was not reproduced either in *Satirical Poems* (1926) or *Collected Poems* (1947) as SS's other two poems about New York were. Written in January 1921 after SS's return from New York, it was first published in the *London Mercury* in April 1921, then in the *Literary Digest*, 7 May 1921, then in the *Living Age*, 4 June 1921. 'It is very unmusical', SS wrote in his diary (D2, p. 37), 'but gives a clear picture of the familiar scene at Times Square.'

2. SJ, p. 174. SS left Plymouth on 19 January 1920 for the ten-day crossing, according to a small diary he kept of the main events of his trip, now at CUL.

3. SJ, p. 174. The Hotel Seville functioned in mid-town New York at

Madison Avenue and 28th Street. Pond may have chosen this hotel because it was near one of the two main stations in New York, Pennsylvania Station.

4. SS to WJT, 21 February 1920, Berg. SS's reference to 'premier' ladies' clubs in the following paragraph is from a letter to GA of 5 February 1920, also at the Berg.

5. SJ, p. 177.

6. ibid.

7. ibid. The letter to GA is of 5 February 1920, Berg.

8. These are now in the hands of a private collector, with photocopies at CUL.

9. SJ, p. 180.

10. ibid.

11. ibid., p. 184. Sassoon's original notes on his talk at Smith are in the hands of a private collector.

12. ibid., p. 195. Sam Behrman, an American friend, referred to 'the women whose lives you nightly changed' (SB to SS, 23 February [1926/7]).

13. See the *Vassar Miscellany News*, 28 April 1920.

14. SJ, p. 178.

15. Included in a letter from SS to WJT, 9 July [1920], Berg. Sassoon did lecture at Carnegie Hall, to the Free Synagogue, on 25 April 1920, though it was a morning not an evening engagement.

16. Dates are taken from the small engagement diary SS kept of his trip, CUL.

17. SJ, p. 191. The Rittenhouse Club still stands, unchanged to all outward appearance.

18. SS to LOM, 17 June [1920], HRHRC.

19. SS to LU, 25 May [1921], Delaware, and SS to LOM, 15 July [1920], HRHRC.

20. SS to SCC, 24 October 1920, Berg.

21. SJ, p. 181.

22. Westover Court was demolished in 1925 to make way for a large cinema, the Paramount Building. See SB to SS, 19 April 1925, CUL: 'Westover Court is being torn down in favour of a movie-theater. Remember our summer there?'

23. Masefield, for example, wrote him a letter of introduction to Mrs Thomas Lamont, who arranged an emergency visit to her own dentist on arrival, and Nichols introduced him to Mrs Winthrop Chandler and her sister, Mrs J.J. Chapman, both influential women.

24. SS to AL, 12 May 1960, CUL. For SS's portrait of 'the Mister' see SP, pp. 66-88.

25. ibid.

26. SJ, p. 207.

27. See *The Dial*, 15 March 1918. Louis Untermeyer (1885-1980), poet, critic and parodist, was best known for his anthologies of modern American and British verse.

28. Untermeyer's review of OH and CA appeared in the *Evening Post* on 15 March 1919 and may have prompted Pond to invite him to America.

29. Louis and Jean Untermeyer were still happily married in 1920, but were later to divorce after a trial separation and the suicide of their son, Dick, at Yale. Louis married three more times and had three more sons.

30. SS to LU, 27 March [1920], Delaware.

31. SS to WJT, 21 February [1920], Berg.

32. SJ, p. 182.

33. Jean Untermeyer, who wrote under her maiden name, Jean Starr, produced at least five collections of poetry between 1918 and 1940. She and Sassoon corresponded until his death in 1967.

34. SS continued to admire Frost but by 1949 he was referring to his poems as 'unlyrical and unmusical' (SS to HMT, 8 March 1949, HRHRC).

35. SJ, p. 183.

36. ibid.

37. SS's 22-line poem, which makes witty allusions to many aspects of Lindsay's work, was finished on 1 March 1920 and published in the American *Vanity Fair* of June 1920 (no. xiv, p. 67) along with ten poems from *War Poems* and *Picture Show*, but was never reprinted. A manuscript copy of it can be found in a collection of poems centring round a cut-up copy of *Picture Show* at HRHRC.

38. Keats Memorial Volume Two, Princeton University Library.

39. SJ, p. 182.

40. SS wrote an article on war poetry, one on Thomas Hardy, a 'spoof' interview with himself and a 'Set of Parodies of the Work of Some Famous Modern Poets' in *Vanity Fair* between February and July 1920. For details of poems published in the magazine see footnote 37. Altogether he was paid $307, a large sum of money in 1920, when the rent on his two-room apartment in central New York was only $35 per month. LU may in addition have introduced Sassoon to the editor of the *New Republic*, Francis Hackett, who published several of his poems. Sassoon's satirical poem 'A Sonnet for the Celebration of Peace', which was published in the *New Republic* xxii, 28 April 1920, was written out in his hand at the beginning of the Untermeyers' complimentary copy of *Picture Show* in May 1920. Sassoon was paid $35 in all by the magazine in 1920 and published other poems with them later in the twenties.

41. SS to LU, 7 March [1921], Delaware.

42. Jean Starr Untermeyer trained professionally as a singer and tried to make a career of it in the 1920s.

43. SS to Jean Untermeyer, 23 March 1965, Buffalo.

44. SS's 'Tribute' to Buhlig can be found in the SS-LU correspondence at Lilly.

45. SS saw *Richard III* on 6 March 1919 and his poem on it followed later in the month. It is one of only two poems written during his American stay that were included in *Collected Poems*, the other being 'Storm on Fifth Avenue'.

46. See SS to LU, 2 May [1922] and LU to SS, 28 May 1922, Lilly.

47. SS to BH, 28 December 1920, Congress.

48. SJ, p. 182.

49. SJ, p. 218.

50. *Satirical Poems* (1926), *Vigils* (1936), *Rhymed Ruminations* (1941), *Collected Poems* (1949), *Sequences* (1947), but *not The Heart's Journey* (1928), which was published by Harper and Brothers.

51. MFM and MIO were published by Coward-McCann, SP and the *Complete Memoirs of George Sherston* by Doubleday, Doran and Co. Viking published OC (1938), WY (1942), SJ (1946) and *Meredith* (1948).

52. SB to SS, 21 September 1924, Sotheby catalogue, December 1994, and Behrman, *Tribulations and Laughter*, p. 13.

53. SJ, pp. 218 and 219.

54. SS to BH, 18 June 1929, Congress.

55. ibid., 29 April 1929, Congress. SS and BH remained friends until BH's death in 1964, only three years before Sassoon's own.

56. SS talked to the Inter-Collegiate Socialist Society on 7 May 1919, the Rand School on 16 May and the Cooper Union on 10 August.

57. SS spoke to the Harvard Poetry Club on 29 April 1919. Harold Laski (1893-1950) was a left-wing political theorist and university lecturer.

58. SS to BH, 27 March 1920, Congress.

59. SJ, p. 202.

60. ibid.

61. Samuel Nathaniel Behrman (1893-1973) wrote numerous successful plays, mostly social comedies, between 1923 and 1964. He also wrote more than twenty-five screenplays, two biographical works and several collections of essays and short stories. His memoir, *Tribulations and Laughter*, gives a lively but inaccurate account of his long friendship with SS.

62. *Tribulations and Laughter*, p. 14.

63. SS to GA, 5 February 1920, Berg.

64. Behrman, who was working for the book review section of the *New York Times*, was asked to interview SS by his editor, Dr Clifford Smyth, the son-in-law of Nathaniel Hawthorne.

65. SJ, p. 204.

66. ibid., p. 205.

67. e.g., SS to GBS, 25 November 1927, CUL.

68. OS to SS, 16 June 1929, Pullman.

69. SS to GBS, 23 April 1932, CUL.

70. *Tribulations and Laughter*, p. 11.

71. Morgan, T., *Somerset Maugham* (Jonathan Cape, 1980), pp. 447-8.

72. ibid. Behrman kept this quality to the end of his life. When Anthony Curtis, literary editor of the *Financial Times* for many years, went to visit him in New York on his way west, Behrman insisted that he must 'look up' his old friends Ira and George Gershwin.

73. SJ, p. 206.

74. ibid., p. 207.

75. ibid., p. 206.

76. SB to SS, 1 April [1946], Sotheby's catalogue, 13.12.93. Though Westover Court has long been replaced, a Wrigley's chewing-gum advertisement still occupies the same space in Times Square.

77. ibid.

78. SJ, p. 207.

79. *Tribulations and Laughter*, p. 13.

80. SJ, p. 207.

81. SS to WJT, 21 February 1920, Berg.

82. SS to Roderick Meiklejohn, 29 February 1920, HRHRC.

83. SS to LOM, 6 April [1920], HRHRC.

84. SS to GA, 21 March 1920, Berg.

85. SS to LOM, 6 April [1920], HRHRC.

86. SS to WJT, 21 February 1920, Berg.

87. Glenn Hunter (1897-1945) made his debut with the Washington Square Players in 1916. Between 1919 and 1926 his career was extremely successful, especially his title role in *Merton of the Movies* in 1922, but he subsequently faded out and died young.

88. D2, p. 276. SB told RHD (letter of 14 March 1969, CUL) that he did not know how SS met him.

89. *Clarence* played at the Hudson Theater from 20 September 1919 for 300 performances.

90. Published only in *To-Day* magazine, 19 November 1920. This may have been the work SS meant when he referred to 'the finest love poem I've ever done'. (SS to LOM, 15 July [1920], HRHRC.)

91. SB to RHD, 14 March 1969, CUL.

92. D2, p. 208.

93. SB to RHD, op.cit.

94. ibid. and D2, p. 209.

95. *Tribulations and Laughter*, p. 9.

96. SS to LOM, 16 March [1920], HRHRC.

97. SS stayed at Powers Hotel, Rochester, NY.

Chapter 6

1. SS to TS, 14 April 1920, Berg. The letter quoted in the epigraph to this chapter is also from the Berg collection.

2. The Ferry Hall School was at 533 North Mayflower Road, which is now a block of flats. The school itself moved its premises and was renamed Lake Forest Academy. Horace Hawes Martin was a trustee of the Newberry

Library and a member of the University Club at Chicago University, where SS subsequently spoke.

3. SJ, p. 195.

4. John Alden Carpenter (1876-1951) combined music with a successful business career. He is best known for his orchestral suite 'Adventures in a Perambulator', his two symphonies and a ballet, *Krazy Kat*.

5. There is no evidence that SS met Harriet Monroe in Chicago, but she did write to him on 27 May 1922 to ask if she could include seven of his poems in her revised edition of *The New Poetry*, originally published by Macmillan in 1917 (Regenstein Library, University of Chicago). He did meet Edgar Lee Masters, though he omits to say so in his autobiography.

6. Carl Sandburg (1878-1967) produced six major volumes of poetry and his *Complete Poems* (1950) won the Pulitzer Prize.

7. SJ, p. 196.

8. SS to LOM, 6 April 1920, HRHRC.

9. ibid.

10. SJ, p. 197.

11. 'Chicago', *Chicago Poems* (1918).

12. SJ, p. 198.

13. ibid., p. 197.

14. See SJ, pp. 185-90, for a detailed account of John Jay Chapman's violent challenge to SS during his performance at the Cosmopolitan Club. There are also several interesting letters from Chapman to SS at Harvard University Library in which he attempts, unsuccessfully, to make things up with SS.

15. SS to SB, 29 March 1920, CUL.

16. SS to LOM, 6 April [1920], HRHRC.

17. SJ, p. 199.

18. ibid., p. 200.

19. Janet Ayer (1879-1951) was a member of the Cosmopolitan Club.

Her first book, *At Home* (1910), was followed by many others, *The Cortlandts of Washington Square* (1923), *The Smiths* (1925, runner-up for the Pulitzer Prize), *The Bright Land* (1932) and *Rich Man, Poor Man* (1936) among others.

20. The Kellogg Fairbanks lived at 1244 North State Street.

21. SJ, p. 200.

22. Mrs Kellogg Fairbank had attracted national attention during the suffrage movement by riding a white charger down Michigan Boulevard and she served for twenty-four years as president of the women's board of the Chicago Lying-in Hospital, now the University of Chicago Hospital and Medical Complex. Jane Addams (1860-1935) had founded the Hull House Settlement, one of the earliest community centres, in 1889. She was vice-president of the National American Women Suffrage Alliance 1911-14 and in 1915 led the Women's Peace Party and the first Women's Peace Congress. She was joint winner of the Nobel Peace Prize in 1931.

23. SS lectured to both these clubs on 8 April 1920.

24. See letter from SS to Mrs Vaughan Moody, 18 March 1920, Regenstein Library, University of Chicago.

25. On the 9, 12 and 13 April respectively.

26. See SS to Mr Hillyer, 2 October 1960, Syracuse, where SS apologizes to Hillyer, the true organizer of the event: 'I was told by Laski that [Amy Lowell] had sponsored the lecture.' See also the minutes of the Harvard Poetry Society for 9 February 1920 at Harvard.

27. SJ, p. 202.

28. Both this and the previous quotation are from SJ, p. 203.

29. SS to TS, 14 April 1920, Berg.

30. SJ, p. 208.

31. SS to LOM, 17 June [1920], HRHRC.

32. ibid.

33. D2, p. 53. See SS:MWP, p. 2, for further details.

34. SS to RG, 1 July [1920], SIU.

35. John Thompson MacCurdy (1886-1947), who is referred to as 'that nice Canadian psychologist' by SS (D2, pp. 166-7), was a lecturer in psychopathology at Cambridge University from 1923 and was made a Fellow of Corpus Christi College, Cambridge, in 1926. He was the author of *The Psychology of Emotions* (1925) and other works.

36. SS to WJT, 30 June 1920, Berg. SS was not quite as idle as he suggests at Russell Loines' house, since he scribbled eight parodies, apparently to amuse his host, which SB then placed with *Vanity Fair*.

37. SJ, p. 213.

38. Edward Percy Warren (1860-1928); Warren's poems, which included such suggestive titles as 'Lad's Love', were published as *The Wild Rose* in 1910. The three volumes of *The Defence of Uranian Love* were published just before and just after his death in 1928. Warren himself wrote to SS with the gift of volumes 1 and 3 on 12 December 1928 – 'I send you the hand + tail of the Defence, but the body has not yet appeared' – but Warren's secretary, Frank Gearing, sent him volume 2 in 1930, following Warren's death on 28 December 1928. These letters and SS's copies of *The Defence of Uranian Love* are in the hands of a private collector.

39. Warren took the lease of Lewes House (currently the offices of Lewes District Council) in 1890 and bought it outright in 1913. He also bought School Hill House, next door to Lewes House, and 'The Shelleys', a spacious mansion further up the High Street.

40. SS to LU, 29 July 1920, Delaware.

41. SJ, p. 215.

42. ibid.

43. ibid.

44. ibid.

45. ibid., p. 214.

46. SS to LU, 29 July 1920, Delaware.

47. SJ, p. 216.

48. See SS:MWP, pp. 291-2.

49. BH to SS, 13 July 1945, Congress.

50. SJ, p. 219.

51. BH to SS, op.cit.

52. SS to SB, 3 February 1921, CUL.

53. SS to LOM, 16 March 1920, HRHRC.

54. Behrman, *Tribulations and Laughter*, p. 9.

55. SS to LOM, 15 July 1920, HRHRC.

56. SS to RG, 1 July 1920, SIU.

57. SJ, p. 219.

58. SS to RG, 13 February 1924, SIU.

59. SS to LOM, 17 June 1920, HRHRC.

60. SJ, p. 224.

Chapter 7

1. See D2, pp. 50, 52, 77-8.

2. SS to RG, 5 April 1921, SIU.

3. D2, p. 73.

4. See SS:MWP, pp. 269-70.

5. CP, p. 85.

6. D2, p. 73.

7. SS to RN, 5 November 1923, Berg.

8. D2, p. 162.

9. ibid.

10. ibid.

11. SS to RG, 3 September 1920, SIU.

12. Between October 1920 and June 1923, SS contributed at least twenty-one reviews and articles to the *Daily Herald*.

13. D2, p. 119.

14. Turner, W.J.R., *The Duchess of Popocatapetl*, Dent, 1939, p. 169.

15. ibid.

16. UV4.

17. ibid.

18. ibid.

19. ibid.

20. SS to DFC, 5 August 1960, SS:PP, p. 168.

21. D3, p. 273.

22. D2, p. 31.

23. ibid., pp. 71-2.

24. ibid., p. 236.

25. UV4.

26. D3, p. 163.

27. Bagnold's *Autobiography*, p. 82.

28. The first quotation is from my interview with Theresa Whistler on 29 March 1999, in which she described to me, among other things, her recollections of a visit to SS at Heytesbury while RH was staying there. The second quotation is from a letter of EB to SS, 8 August 1935, Columbia.

29. Interview with Theresa Whistler.

30. ibid.

31. ibid.

32. D3, p. 167.

33. SS to WdlM, 18 April 1943, Beinecke.

34. D3, p. 166.

35. ibid., p. 77.

36. ibid., p. 34.

37. SS to RN, 25 December 1941, HRHRC, and WY, p. 216.

38. SS and RH started exchanging rare books early on in their friendship and went on a book-buying tour of East Anglia together in November 1931, on one of Hodgson's sabbaticals from Japan. They also started to compile an anthology of some of their favourite passages from mainly obscure authors in the 1930s, though this was never completed.

39. SS to SCC, 29 October 1938, HRHRC.

40. SS to RH, 27 June 1937, Beinecke.

41. D3, p. 62.

42. ibid.

43. SS did, however, inscribe a copy of his *Recreations* to Romer Wilson.

44. D3, p. 253.

45. ibid.

46. ibid.

47. ibid., p. 141.

48. See SS:MWP, pp. 515-16.

49. TEL to SS, 23 November 1923, collection of Harry and Cookie Spiro.

50. SS to TEL, 26 November 1923, ibid.

51. TEL to SS, 2 December 1923, ibid.

52. D3, p. 66.

53. ibid., p. 68.

54. ibid.

55. D2, p. 148, and EMF to SS, 12 June 1922, private collection.

56. D2, p. 126, and SS to RG, 18 October 1924, SIU.

57. SJ, p. 170.

58. SS to RG, 7 June 1924, SIU, and D2, p. 126.

59. D3, p. 135, and D2, p. 149.

60. D3, p. 288.

61. EMF had met TEL only once before SS reintroduced him, and that was very briefly at a formal lunch.

62. TEL to EMF, 24 July 1924, Lawrence, *Selected Letters* (ed. David Garnett).

63. EMF to SS, 25 March 1924, private collection.

64. ibid.

65. ibid.

66. ibid.

67. ibid.

68. D2, p.151.

69. D3, p. 53.

70. ibid., p. 187.

71. D2, p. 151.

72. SS to RN, 15 May [1923], Berg.

73. D2, p. 29.

74. RG to EB, 10 March 1921, O'Prey, p. 123.

75. D3, p. 235.

76. ibid., p. 248.

77. D2, p. 165.

78. D3, pp. 101 and 102.

79. UV4.

80. D3, p. 234.

81. 'Prelude to a Self-Revealing Journal', D2, p. 104.

82. Cf. the 'Old Caspar' figure of 'The Utopian Times', CP, pp. 164-6.

83. D3, p. 251.

84. EMF to SS, 20.3.27, private collection

Chapter 8

1. SS to Professor Lewis Chase, 25 January 1922, Congress.
2. ibid.
3. SS to RG, 9 February 1924, SIU.
4. D2, p. 81.
5. 'A Case for the Miners', written on 8 April 1921 and published in the *Nation* on 16 April 1921, is one of the few exceptions in this respect.
6. UV4.
7. ibid.
8. D2, p. 254. SS knew the writers Aldous Huxley (1894-1963) and John Middleton Murry (1889-1957) quite well by the early twenties, but had reservations about both of them. See SS:MWP, pp. 522, 358, 373 and 496.
9. SS to RG, 21 November 1921, SIU.
10. D2, p. 88.
11. See Harold Owen's autobiography, *Aftermath*. SS, who wanted to help Harold for Wilfred's sake, introduced the young art student to influential friends in the art world, such as Glyn Philpot, William Rothenstein and Lady Zia Werner, invited him frequently to Tufton Street, took him to concerts and bought at least seven of his etchings. He also gave him money (See D2, pp. 88 and 89).
12. 'Limitations', 'Early Chronology' and 'Falling Asleep'.
13. *Recreations* was first printed at the Chiswick Press in January 1923, then again, with the addition of three poems, in March 1923. It was this second printing, bound by Maltby of Oxford, which SS distributed to friends in June 1923. There were seventy-five ordinary copies and six specials on large paper.
14. D3, p. 41.
15. ibid., p. 39.
16. ibid., p. 38.
17. ibid., p. 40.

18. SS to TS, 25 June 1923, Berg.
19. SS to RG, [February] 1922 and 6 June 1924, SIU.
20. SS to ATB, 27 April 1921, CUL.
21. D3, p. 38.
22. SS was reading *Don Juan* in 1921 and *Childe Harold* and Byron's letters in 1922, as well as reading books about him.
23. Ninety-nine copies were printed at the Cambridge University Press in February 1925.
24. *Selected Poems*, 2,000 copies of which were published by Heinemann on 23 April 1925, contained 67 poems from OH (1917), CA (1918) and *Picture Show* (1919). All of these had been reprinted in *War Poems* (1919) with the exception of 6 poems from *Picture Show* ('Memory', 'Wraiths', 'Ancient History', 'Idyll', 'Slumber Song' and 'Vision'). *Satirical Poems*, 2,000 of which were published by Heinemann on 29 April 1926 (500 of them for the American market), contained 32 poems: 15 from *Recreations* (1923), 11 from *Lingual Exercises*, 2 from *Picture Show*, 1 from a selection published by Ernest Benn in his *Augustan Books of Modern Poetry* series in 1926 and 3 unpublished poems. A new edition, with 5 additional poems, was published in 1933.
25. The whole of 'A Fragment of Autobiography' is reprinted in D2, pp. 21-2, and 'On Reading My Diary' in D2, pp. 34-5. Sassoon felt that the latter was 'nothing but an exercise in intellectual word-weaving' (D2, p. 35).
26. Keynes, p. 57.
27. These were 'Stonehenge', 'Alone', 'Grandeur of Ghosts', 'To an Old Lady Dead', 'To One in Prison' and 'Conclusion'.
28. Blunden, *A Selection of His Poetry and Prose*, p. 319.
29. Thorpe, *Siegfried Sassoon: A Critical Study*, p. 49.
30. SJ, p. 167.
31. Blunden, op. cit.
32. SS told RG in a letter of 5

January 1925 that the ambassador referred to was 'Lord Bertie of Thame'.

33. *New Statesman*, 23 May 1925.

34. ibid.

35. Thorpe, pp. 54-5.

36. ibid., pp. 47-8.

37. ibid., p. 58.

38. UV4.

39. ibid.

40. ibid.

41. OM had introduced SS to Desmond MacCarthy and Maynard Keynes and Keynes, in turn, had introduced him to Lytton Strachey. He often saw them at Garsington which became, in effect, an outpost of Bloomsbury during and after the First World War.

42. SS to Professor Lewis Chase, 25 January 1922, Congress.

43. SS to HH, 19 February 1949, in possession of recipient.

44. D2, p. 155.

45. SS to HH, 19 February 1949, and SS to HMT, 4 May 1949, HRHRC.

46. See SS:MWP, pp. 509-11.

47. SS to Virginia Woolf, 21 May 1923, Berg.

48. Virginia Woolf to SS, 22 May 1923, Woolf, V., *A Change of Perspective*, p. 85.

49. D3, p. 78.

50. ibid., p. 79.

51. SS to HMT, 8 March 1949, HRHRC.

52. D3, p. 79.

53. Woolf, V., *The Diary of Virginia Woolf, Vol. 2*, p. 287.

54. Woolf, V., *A Change of Perspective*, p. 85.

55. SS's ms notes for this essay are at the BL Manuscript Room.

56. SS to Mr Farmer, 24 September 1964, Berg.

57. SS to LOM, 28 March 1928, HRHRC.

58. ibid., 2 November 1928, HRHRC. SS was undoubtedly influenced by Bloomsbury's attitude to EG, which was on the whole mocking.

59. See Osbert Sitwell's *Laughter in the Next Room*, p. 112.

60. 'A Letter to S.S.', undated ms at HRHRC.

61. For two other accounts of the rift between SS and OS see Philip Ziegler's *Osbert Sitwell* and 'The Letters of Edith Sitwell to Siegfried Sassoon', edited by Thomas W. Rand, dissertation, Washington State University at Pullman.

62. *Wheels, Sixth Cycle* (C.W. Daniel, 1921), pp. 57-8.

63. This was to be called 'Hero and Blunder'.

64. D2, p. 90.

65. OS to SS, 4 July 1923, Pullman.

66. D2, p. 103.

67. OS to SS, op.cit.

68. ibid., [3/4 July 1923].

69. D2, pp. 69 and 74.

70. SS to EM, 18 December 1920, Berg.

71. D2, p. 255.

72. ibid., p. 75. Renishaw is in coal-mining country in Derbyshire, hence 'the encroachments of industry'.

73. ibid., p. 77.

74. ibid.

75. D3, pp. 39-40 and OS to SS, op. cit.

76. D2, pp. 156 and 171.

77. ibid., p. 254.

78. ibid., p. 266.

79. ibid., p. 268.

80. D3, p. 40.

81. ibid., p. 44.

82. ibid.

83. OS to SS, op.cit.

84. ibid.

85. D3, p. 141.

86. SS to GBS, 2 December 1927, CUL.

87. 'Too Fantastic for Fat-Heads', *Daily Herald*, 24 May 1922.

88. ES to Susan Owen, November 1919, Sitwell, E., *Selected Letters*, p. 20.

89. 'Sassoon on Owen', *Times Literary Supplement*, 31 May 1974, pp. 58-9.

90. Sitwell, E., p. 23.

91. SS admitted to EB in 1931, when they were working on a second edition of Owen's poems, that ES 'did most of the donkey work about the present edition of the poems, while I was in America in 1920!' (undated letter now at Columbia). He regretted that he had not taken a more active part in the book, since he was far from happy with Edith's editing. In a note made on Welland's thesis on Owen about the discrepancies between the manuscript and printed versions of Owen's Preface, he wrote: 'I had forgotten that the versions differed, though I must have been aware of it at some time ... Circumstances made it impossible for me to devote any time to studying the ms of W's Preface, and I doubt whether I noticed Edith's handling of it ... All I did was to make sure that her selection of poems was all right, (but it was only after the book was published that I was aware that she'd omitted 'The End', which I appended to the 2nd edn.)' (Welland, *Wilfred Owen: A Critical Study* (1978), p. 589).

92. SS to HH, 15 December 1964, in possession of recipient.

93. SS told DS late in life that ES was in love with him and, when the biographer Geoffrey Elborn put the idea to SSi, he confirmed it.

94. Rand, op.cit., pp. 31-2.

95. See SS:MWP, pp. 288-9. When ES read SS's description of LOM in SJ (1945) she wrote to John Lehmann: 'Have you seen Siegfried's deplorable book ... one mass of treachery, fawning and snobbishness. I didn't like the old Lady Ottoline Morrell, and she hated me – but she adored Siegfried and it is painful to see him "wishing she wouldn't look so extraordinary" ... and otherwise goring her.' (Rand, p. 49.) ES clearly identified with LOM in this respect.

96. SS occasionally admired ES's less bizarre outfits, praising her 'deeply vivid green dress', for example, in a letter to HFJ (21 June 1927,

CUL): 'If there *is* a more remarkable woman than Edith', he added ambiguously, 'I have not yet seen her.'

97. ES to SS, 4 June 1926, The Sitwell Papers, Pullman.

98. ibid., 9 November 1926.

99. ibid., 2 November 1926.

100. ibid., 14 December 1926.

101. SS to EM, 16 July 1919, Berg.

102. D2, p. 155.

103. ibid., p. 166.

104. D3, p. 134.

105. ES to SS, 11 March 1927, Pullman.

106. Untitled poem, ibid, [11 March 1927]. Nine further stanzas follow.

107. ES to SS, 2 January 1927. Drinkwater's remarks appeared in 'Some Poetry in 1926', *Observer*, 2 January 1927, together with some condescending statements on the Sitwells.

108. ES to SS, 14 January 1927, Pullman. Edith swiftly 'worked' her praise 'in' to a lecture she gave at University College, University of London, on 25 February 1927, when she compared Squire unfavourably with SS.

109. Humbert Wolfe (1885-1940), poet and critic. A thousand copies of *Poems of Pinchbeck Lyre* were published by Duckworth on 15 May 1931, with a second impression of 1,000 copies following almost immediately.

110. See SS to SSi, 12 January 1932, William Reese Collection, re SSi's repayment of a loan from SS: 'I am extremely glad to hear that you are being so generous to E[dith] (who, as you surmise, has probably been thoroughly exploited by the painter [i.e. Tchelitchew], ably assisted by his USA friend!) How I wish that E. had someone to *look after* her, instead of that mill-stone H[elen] R[ootham] round her neck.'

111. D2, p. 102.

112. See ES to SS, 3 December 1926, Pullman, and D3, p. 252.

113. Elborn, p. 98.

114. ES to SS, 3 May 1955, Pullman.

115. ibid., 22 March 1927.

116. ibid., 19 April 1928.

117. ibid., 25 October 1928.

118. ibid., 27 May 1928.

119. ibid., July 1929.

120. These caricatures, which were started *c.* 1929 and targeted mainly at Edith and Osbert, though Sachie figures in them, are now in the possession of William Reese. They were collected by SS in a folder marked 'Sitwelliana'.

121. This untitled poem, written in SS's hand and dated by him, is now in the collection of Dr Lionel Dakers. The second of his skits on Edith, which follows, was written by him into his copy of ES's *Street Songs*. It is also untitled.

122. Diary entry for 23 January 1954, quoted in SS:PP, p. 157. The article SS refers to was in the *New Statesman*.

123. SS to Dame Hildelith Cumming, 17 June 1961, quoted in SS:PP, p. 209.

Chapter 9

1. D2, p. 52.

2. ibid., p. 232.

3. The Loders moved to Cecily Hill House, Cirencester, where SS visited them frequently between 1920 and 1923.

4. D2, p. 20.

5. SJ, p. 26.

6. This poem is at CUL.

7. GK's notes on SS's career, written after his death and now at CUL.

8. 'Thoughts on Horses and Hunting', Lunn, P., *My First Horse*, 1947, p. 19.

9. SJ, p. 26.

10. ibid.

11. Lunn, op. cit., p. 14.

12. ibid.

13. ibid., p. 22.

14. See SS:MWP, p. 435, for more on 'The Mister'.

15. SS to SCC, 4 November 1919, Berg.

16. CP, p. 139.

17. Lunn, op. cit., p. 22.

18. DS, in a telephone conversation with the author in October 1999.

19. D2, p. 138.

20. ibid., p. 109.

21. ibid., p. 100.

22. ibid., p. 110.

23. ibid., p. 140.

24. ibid., p. 30.

25. ibid., p. 114. SS told DS that he felt that he had been 'very unfair' to Ottoline on the whole.

26. CP, p. 221. The first draft of this poem, now at Harvard, was written in 1930, but the completed poem was not published until 1934 in *Vigils*.

27. This was written at the height of SS's sufferings over ST, which are clearly referred to in these lines.

28. UV4.

29. See CP, p. 137, and D2, pp. 57-61.

30. D3, p. 221.

31. See SS:MWP, pp. 220, 450 and 457.

32. SS helped a number of prisoners and their wives with money during the twenties.

33. *The Times* reported on 5 June 1922 that the cause of death was 'strangulation of the intestines', but Walter Langdon Brown, in a posthumous tribute to Rivers in the *St Bartholomew Hospital Journal* of November 1936, described it as a 'perforated duodenal ulcer'.

34. D2, p. 163.

35. ibid.

36. ibid., p. 166.

37. AB to SS, 10 June 1922, Columbia. In the event, AB did write an obituary of Rivers, which appeared in the *New Statesman*, 17 June 1922. Sir Henry Head wrote one for the *British Medical Journal*, 16 June

1922 and Elliott Smith produced one for the *Lancet*, 16 June 1922.

38. Cyril Tomkinson to SS, 5 June 1922, CUL. Tomkinson (1886-1968), who was introduced to SS by RN, was curate of Little St Mary's, Cambridge, from 1923 to 1930 and later vicar of various other parishes. SS, who continued to see him well into the thirties, often referred to him as 'my prize bore'.

39. D3, p. 265.

40. SS to GBS, *c.* 1949, CUL.

41. D3, p. 129.

42. SS to HFJ, 30 May 1927, CUL, and SS to RG, 9 July 1925, SIU.

43. SS to RG, 9 July 1925, SIU.

44. The Long White Cloud still stands beside the Thames opposite Monkey Island, its situation apparently unchanged except for the development of the small hotel on the island into a major conference centre. This has resulted in the building of a large footbridge and massive car park next to the house, which has destroyed a great deal of its isolation and tranquillity.

45. D3, p. 215.

46. Edward Elgar (1857-1934) became famous when his *Enigma Variations* appeared in 1899. His choral works that followed include *The Dream of Gerontius* (1900), *The Apostles* (1903) and *The Kingdom* (1906). He also wrote many orchestral works, among them Symphony in A flat (1908), Violin Concerto (1910), Symphony in E flat (1911) and Cello Concerto (1919).

47. 'The Elgar Concerto' in 1916 and 'Philharmonic', first published in the *London Mercury*, April 1921, then in *Recreations*.

48. SS to TS, 21 October 1941, Berg.

49. D2, p. 80.

50. SS to WdlM, [20 December 1953], Beinecke.

51. See D2, pp. 124-5, where SS remembers sending Elgar his *Ode to Music* but receiving no reply.

52. D2, p. 152.

53. ibid.

54. SS to WdlM, op. cit.

55. SS to GBS, 25 April 1927, CUL. SS notes that FS's income was about £10,000 a year, 'yet he behaves as if it were £300'. (D2, p. 221), 'In money matters', he added a few pages later, 'Schuster is a knock-out.'

56. SS to RG, 9 July 1925, SIU.

57. ibid.

58. WdlM had moved by 1925 to Hill House, which, though large by modern town standards, is dwarfed by nearby Taplow Court. SS was persuaded by a desperate LOM to go to tea there in May 1925, to help her feel less out of it (D3, p. 255). Later still he would be invited to spend several weekends there.

59. D3, p. 146.

60. 'Anzie's' real name was Leslie Wylde. His wife spelt his nickname 'Anzy'.

61. UV4.

62. Catalogue of Wylie's wife Wendela Boreel's exhibition of paintings and drawings at the Parkin Gallery, London, 1980. Mrs Wylde also claims that her husband's early death in 1935 was the result of his war wounds.

63. See SS's notes on OC at CUL.

64. D3, p. 116.

65. ibid.

66. Born Edith Wandela Boreel in 1895, she was still alive in 1980, when the Parkin Gallery put on its exhibition of her work. She and Anzie had one child, James (b. 1927), who became a professor at the University of Montpellier.

67. D3, p. 101.

68. SS to HFJ, 12 July 1927, CUL.

69. SS owned four of Wendela's works, a watercolour, 'Monkey Island', and three dry-point etchings. These were sold at the Phillips sale of the contents of Heytesbury House in October 1994.

70. D3, p. 260.

71. ibid.

72. ibid., p. 148.
73. ibid.

Chapter 10

1. D2, p. 81.
2. 'The Power Ordained', unpublished poem dated '14.9.24' in one of SS's poetry notebooks at CUL.
3. CP, p. 196.
4. Notes by SS on OC, CUL.
5. D2, p. 222.
6. SS travelled to France with FS and Anzie for a month in early March 1924 and another month in late February 1925.
7. SS to LOM, 5 April 1921, HRHRC.
8. ibid.
9. D2, p. 201.
10. SS to LOM, op. cit.
11. D2, p. 214.
12. SS stayed at Porlock Weir with GA from 5 May to 6 June 1921.
13. SS stayed at the Hotel Angleterre in Rome from 28 September to the end of October 1921.
14. D2, p. 86.
15. Sir Gerald Tyrwhitt-Wilson (1883-1950) was the 5th baronet and 14th Baron Berners.
16. Berners was a composer of light divertimenti-style music, several ballets and one opera, *Le Carrosse du Saint-Sacrément* (1924). His highly autobiographical novels, like his paintings, are largely forgotten.
17. 'Clavichord Recital' was published in the *Nation*, 30 December 1922, but not in CP; it is, however, reproduced in D2, p. 246.
18. D2, pp. 119 and 121.
19. ibid., p. 280.
20. ibid., p. 223.
21. ibid., p. 201.
22. ibid., pp. 225 and 249.
23. Constantine I was King of Greece from 1913-17, then again from 1920-23.
24. Philipp's elder brother, Friedrich Wilhelm, had died at the Battle of Dobrugia in 1916, leaving

Philipp, the elder of male twins, in line for the title, which he inherited in 1940 and held until his death in 1980. The Hesse-Cassel branch, founded by an earlier Friedrich in the mid-eighteenth century, was the senior branch of the Landgrave of Hesse and had once formed the Kingdom of Westphalia under Napoleon's brother, Jerome.
25. D2, p. 270.
26. ibid., p. 260.
27. ibid., p. 225.
28. ibid., p. 272.
29. ibid., pp. 244, 240, 208 and 276.
30. Philipp's letters to SS are now at CUL. SS's letters to him have not survived according to his son, to whom I wrote.
31. D2, p. 225.
32. SS travelled down by train through France and Germany with Turner to meet Philipp in Munich, leaving Victoria Station on 20 July 1922 and arriving at Munich on 1 August 1922. It was during this journey that he wrote 'Fantasia on a Wittelsbach Atmosphere', first printed in *Recreations*, then published in the *New Statesman*, 27 October 1923, and *Lingual Exercises*, before finally being included in CP.
33. D2, p. 216.
34. Published first in the *Nation*, 30 December 1922, together with 'Clavichord Recital', the poem was inspired by the man who had introduced SS to Philipp, Lord Berners, under the pseudonym 'Simeon Hart'; it was then included in HJ as 'VI', and finally in CP (p. 177).
35. D2, p. 225.
36. ibid., p. 279.
37. ibid., p. 232.
38. ibid., p. 276.
39. ibid., p. 284.
40. ibid., p. 249.
41. ibid., p. 161.
42. ibid., p. 382.
43. ibid.
44. ibid., p. 279.
45. ibid., p. 227 and 279.

46. SS to the Heads, [April 1933], HRHRC, and D2, p. 225.

47. Philipp, according to Sarah Bradford and other reputable scholars, became the go-between for Hitler with Mussolini, but eventually put a foot wrong and was sent to Buchenwald with his wife Mafalda, who died there in 1945. Philipp was finally freed, but later arrested by the Americans for his Nazi activities.

48. D2, p. 189.

49. SS to LOM, 15 March 1923, HRHRC.

50. D2, p. 189.

51. ibid., p. 113. Lord Edward Christian David Gascoyne Cecil (1902-86), critic and biographer, was the son of the Marquess of Salisbury.

52. D2, p. 113.

53. ibid.

54. SS to HFJ, 27 April 1927, CUL. SS refers simply to 'D' here, but it is clear from the context and from other letters that he is referring to Lord David Cecil.

55. SS's confidante Ruth Head's reference to Cecil as 'the ungrateful and … the commonplace' in a letter of 3 September 1936 to SS is almost certainly a response to SS's own views on Cecil by that time.

56. Both phrases were repeated to me by Lord David Cecil's son, Jonathan Cecil, who kindly spoke to me on 4 March 2000 about his father's relations with SS.

57. Richardson King Wood (1903-76) was at King's College from 1922 to 1925, where he achieved an English, Class II, 1924; and a Modern Languages, Class II, Part Two, and a BA in 1925. He went on to become a journalist and town-planner on his return to America. For further details of his career see Wilkinson, L.P., *Kingsmen of a Century 1873-1972* (Cambridge University Press, 1980).

58. ATB's diary entry for 2 September 1925, CUL.

59. ibid.

60. D3, pp. 137 and 148. The following quotes are from D3, pp. 170 and 149.

61. See D3, p. 159, for example.

62. See D3, p. 197, and the unpublished poem quoted on the opening page of this chapter, which was written the following day, 14 September 1924.

63. See Paul O'Prey's comments in *In Broken Images*, pp. 150-5.

64. D2, p. 53.

65. SS to EJD, 18 May 1916, CUL.

66. Novello was the male lead in the film *The Bohemian Girl*, also starring Gladys Cooper and Constance Collier, which was being shot outside the Doge's Palace.

67. D2, p. 275.

68. SS to GBS, [22/23 October 1925], CUL.

69. ibid.

70. ibid.

71. There was an age difference, but only seven years, Novello being thirty-one to SS's thirty-eight in 1924.

72. SS travelled to the Riviera with FS and Anzie at the end of February 1925, staying at Cannes and the Cap d'Ail, where he was visited by GA who was living nearby. The trio also stopped at Avignon on their drive home towards the end of March. On 13 July 1925 he set off from Bray with GA, visiting Salisbury, Blandford, Exeter, then driving across Dartmoor to East Looe, Fowey and Mullion Cove before returning to London.

73. D3, p. 133.

74. Interview with DS. When SS eventually moved to his own house, he had an old-fashioned telephone on a long stem and if it rang would answer it with great reluctance and invariably speak into the wrong piece. When the caller failed to hear him, he would complain to DS: 'These modern inventions – can't they ever get it right?' (ibid.)

75. Both DS and HH have suggested this comparison to me.

76. Interview with Lady Lettice Strickland-Constable.

77. ibid.

78. SS to WdlM, 20 May 1949, Beinecke.

79. Interview with DS.

80. SS received a summons to appear at Wilton County Court Petty Sessions for 'driving without due care and attention' on 20 March 1932, which the *Salisbury Journal* reported on: 'The defendant seemed hardly responsible enough to be in charge of a car' (29 April 1932). He was fined £1, plus costs.

81. D3, p. 151.

82. SS to RG, 15 August 1924, SIU.

83. D3, p. 133.

84. ibid., p. 66.

85. ibid.

86. SS to RG, 18 October 1924, SIU.

87. D3, p. 94.

88. ibid., p. 276.

89. ibid., p. 57.

90. ibid., p. 237.

91. ibid., p. 268. *The Aesthetes*, which WJT described as a 'Philosophical Dialogue', was published in 1927. WJT was to include another caricature of LOM in *The Duchess of Popocatapetl*, p. 212ff.

92. SS refers to WJT as 'Conundrum' in several letters to LOM in the late 1920s. OS, in an undated letter from Monaco of 1925/6, denies having invented 'Bad-Turn' but thinks it amusing.

93. D3, p. 270.

94. ibid.

95. ibid.

96. ibid., p. 281.

97. Graves, R.P., *The Assault Heroic*, pp. 315-16.

98. D3, p. 272.

99. ibid., p. 281.

100. WJT tried to remain friends, asking SS if he might dedicate his play, *The Man Who Ate Potomack*, to him in 1929, since SS had inspired it. SS refused.

101. SS to RG, 9 February 1924, SIU.

102. D3, p. 235.

Chapter 11

1. SS to GBS, 17 May 1947, CUL.

2. GBS to SS, 16 October 1925, CUL.

3. ibid., 21 October 1925.

4. ibid. Glen's first professional appearance was at the Pavilion Theatre, Torquay, in 1923.

5. D3, p. 291.

6. Harold Speed (1872-1957) was known mainly as a portrait painter.

7. D3, pp. 293 and 299.

8. ibid. Holland Park Avenue forms the north end of Campden Hill Square and Gabriel lived just off it at 9 Ladbroke Grove, to which he had moved from Peel Street by 1925.

9. SS to RG, 31 October 1925, SIU, and SS to GBS, 28 October 1925, CUL.

10. SS to LOM, 30 June 1926, HRHRC.

11. 'Summer Morning in London', dated 23 June 1926, was written six months after Sassoon moved to 23 Campden Hill Square. It was never published but survived in a notebook of poems written in the 1920s, now at CUL. The second poem, written nearly three years later, 'Farewell to Youth', was first published in *Vigils* and included in CP (p. 215).

12. SS to GBS, 28 October 1925, CUL.

13. It is clear from a later reference that SS's domestic was called 'Dengel', not 'Dingle' and that he made the alteration for humorous purposes. He kept in touch with Mrs Dengel until at least the mid-forties, when he invited her to stay at Heytesbury House with her grandson during the Second World War.

14. SS shopped in Jermyn Street and when he moved permanently to the country in the 1930s, the shops there supplied the goods by post.

15. D3, p. 293.

16. ES to SS, [15 February 1931], Pullman.

17. D3, p. 293.

18. ibid., p. 299.

19. ibid.

20. SS to GBS, 4 November 1947, CUL.

21. D3, p. 303.

22. GBS was with J.B. Fagan's Repertory Company, which spent the winter at the Oxford Playhouse and the spring and early summer on tour in the provinces.

23. *Satirical Poems*, a selection from *Recreations* and *Lingual Exercises*, would be published by Heinemann in April 1926.

24. 'Farewell to a Room' was written at Tufton Street on 23 November 1925.

25. SS to LOM, 25 November 1925, HRHRC.

26. D3, p. 299.

27. SS to LOM, 9 December 1925, HRHRC.

28. SS told LOM (6 April 1925, HRHRC) that 'Alone' was written at Garsington at Christmas 1924, during the time he was seeing Novello, and was suggested by a book by Gorky which Ottoline had lent him. Graves wrote (on 2 April 1925, Berg) that it was 'a lovely thing'. RG and SS may be referring, however, to another poem opening 'Alone, I hear the wind about my walls ...' (CP, p. 182).

29. SS:PP, p. 103.

30. ibid.

31. D3, p. 300.

32. Dorothy Wallis to GBS, 7 April 1953, property of George Byam Shaw.

33. SS to RG, 19 November 1925, SIU.

34. SS to Nancy Nicholson, 11 November 1925, SIU.

35. SS to RG, 'Mon.11' [*c.* 1927], SIU.

36. *Juno and the Paycock* was first performed at the Abbey Theatre, Dublin, in 1924 and SS saw it at the Vaudeville on 1 December 1925.

37. Ellen Terry (1847-1928), leading lady to Henry Irving from 1878.

38. GBS was co-director (with Anthony Quayle) of the Shakespeare Memorial Theatre, Stratford, from 1952 to 1956, and Director from 1956 to 1959.

39. Sent in a letter from SS to GBS of 24 October 1925, the evening before GBS left for the Oxford Playhouse.

40. Written on 12 December 1925 and first published in the *London Mercury*, April 1926, then in HJ.

41. For example, compare 'Vigils', 'Farewell to Youth', 'A Local Train of Thought', 'November Dusk', 'In Time of Decivilisation', 'Old Fashioned Weather', 'Awareness of Alcuin', 'The Messenger', 'The Present Writer', 'Retreat from Eternity' and 'The Visitant'.

42. Keynes, p. 60.

43. SS to ATB, 19 November 1924, CUL.

44. 'Lovers' and 'Elegy (to R.R.)' had appeared in *Picture Show*, and 'In me past, present, future meet', 'Stonehenge', 'Alone', 'Grandeur of Ghosts', 'To an Old Lady Dead', 'To One in Prison' and 'Conclusion' in *Lingual Exercises*.

45. D3, p. 56.

46. ibid., p. 60.

47. e.g., 'Song be my soul', 'Sing bravely in my heart', 'As I was walking in the gardens', 'Strangeness of Heart', 'Alone, I hear the wind about my walls', 'Conclusion' and 'A flower has opened in my heart'.

48. 'Lovers', 'Now when we two have been apart so long', 'While I seek you'.

49. 'Grandeur of Ghosts', 'To an 18th Century Poet'.

50. 'To an Old Lady Dead', 'To One Who Watches', 'Elegy (to R.R.)'.

51. 'To One in Prison'.

52. 'From a Fugue by Bach', 'When selfhood can discern'.

53. 'Alone'.

54. 'To One Who was With Me in the War', 'On Passing the New Menin Gate'.

55. Rand, T.W. (ed.), 'The Letters

of Edith Sitwell to Siegfried Sassoon', dissertation, Washington State University at Pullman, p. 66.

56. D3, p. 90.

57. SS to RG, 3 October 1933, Buffalo.

58. 'The Watch-Tower', review of *Vigils* by EB.

59. Thorpe, M., *Siegfried Sassoon*, p. 210.

60. This poem, titled simply 'VII' in HJ, was first published as 'Apocalyptical Indiscretions' in the *Observer*, 14 September 1924, then called 'Apocalypse' in *Lingual Exercises*. EB called it 'a brief but extremely fruitful poem' and ES thought it 'particularly fine'.

61. SS visited Vaughan's grave at Llansantffraed on 27 August 1924.

62. Thorpe, DFC and Paul Moeyes (in *Siegfried Sassoon: Scorched Glory*) all make the connection on several occasions in their studies of SS.

63. This poem was first published separately as 'Nativity', No. 7 of Faber & Gwyer's 'Ariel Poems' series on 25 August 1927, before appearing simply as poem 'XXXII' in HJ *after* 'Conclusion', which suggests that it was one of the last in that collection to be written. SS told DFC that the second line of the second stanza should read 'What powers unknown your seed have sown', since it 'sounded better' when read aloud. (SS:PP, p. 108).

64. SS:PP, p. 104.

65. ibid. See also SS to ATB, 6 January [1927], CUL.

66. Crosby Gaige issued 599 copies of HJ in a limited edition (590 on rag paper and 9 on green hand-made paper) in March 1928, though it is dated 1927. The typography was by Bruce Rogers and the printer was William Edwin Rudge.

67. Heinemann published 2,000 copies of a trade edition of HJ on 19 July 1928 and reprinted it seven times from October 1928 to January 1935.

68. See SS to HFJ, 12 October

1928, CUL. By October 1928, HJ had sold 1,173 copies and was continuing to sell at the rate of approximately 40 copies a day.

69. ES's review, 'A Poet of Fiery Simplicity', appeared in *T.P.'s Weekly*, 10, no. 254, on 8 September 1928 and EB's the following June in the *London Mercury*.

70. It seems significant that SS did *not* take GA to visit TH, though he did take him to the West Country on more than one occasion.

71. SS and GBS drove from London to Godalming, then on to Winchester, Bournemouth, Blandford, Dorchester, Weymouth, back to Dorchester, Oxford. GBS tells SS in an early undated letter of autumn 1925 that he has been reading the *Oxford Book of English Poetry*, 'including Mr Thomas Treherne's [sic] effort, which I hope I appreciated'.

72. D3, p. 304.

73. SS's strong reaction to his uncle Hamo's death was not repeated when Hamo's older brother, the engineer John Thornycroft, died in 1928.

74. D3, p. 305.

75. SS described Gilbert Spencer (1893-1979) as 'good old Gil ... rubicund and charmingly simple as ever' (D3, p. 246). He had known Gilbert's brother, the painter Stanley Spencer (1891-1959), since April 1923: 'Nice little chap, and a genius, but very exhausting as he talks incessantly.' (D3, p. 28.)

76. There is a desperate telegram from Henley among GBS's communications with SS, begging SS to collect him because he was stranded there with no trains running. SS did not do so.

77. SS to LOM, 11 May 1926, HRHRC. SS wrote three poems on the General Strike which were found among his papers after his death but never published in his lifetime. One, 'Strike Me Pink', was set up in type by the *Daily Mail* but not published. All three were published in the *New Statesman*, 30 April 1976.

78. Ivor Guest, who had succeeded his father as the second Lord Wimborne in 1914, had sat in the House of Commons from 1900 to 1910, when he was raised to the Upper House as Lord Ashby St Ledgers; Paymaster-General from 1910-12 and Lord Lieutenant of Ireland from 1915-18, he was created a viscount in 1918.

79. Sitwell, O., *Laughter in the Next Room*, Macmillan, 1950, p. 222.

80. Baxter, B., *Strange Street*, p.121.

81. ibid.

82. ibid.

83. SS to LOM, 31 May 1926, HRHRC.

84. Robert Gathorne-Hardy (1902-1973), son of 3rd Earl of Cranbrook, was an author and editor of, among other books, *Ottoline at Garsington 1915–1928* (Faber and Faber, 1974). He was also secretary to and friend of Logan Pearsall Smith. The Morrells' trip, when it came to it, lasted just over seven weeks.

85. D3, p. 171.

86. SS to LOM, [*c.* November 1925], HRHRC.

87. ibid., 30 June 1926.

88. ibid., 3 July 1926.

89. ibid.

90. Letter from Eardley Knollys to Lady Anne Hill, 31 July 1990, shown to me by Lady Anne Hill, who felt that her brother, RGH, would have been 'delighted' to know that the story of his relationship with SS would be in print.

91. ibid.

92. ibid.

93. See Gathorne-Hardy, R. (ed.), *Ottoline at Garsington*, and Lady Anne Hill to Eardley Knollys, 2 August 1990, copy sent to me by Lady Anne Hill.

94. *Ottoline at Garsington*, p. 41.

95. ibid.

96. SS to RGH, 30 July 1926, Lilly.

97. ibid.

98. SS to RGH, 19 August 1926, Lilly.

99. ibid.

100. SS wrote to GBS on 29 July 1926 (CUL): 'Bob Gathorne-Hardy and his friend ... returned to London yesterday, without saying exactly why.'

101. SS to RGH, 30 July and 19 August 1926, Lilly. SS and the Morrells travelled from Versailles to Venice via Sens, Avallon, Dijon, Yverdon, Sierre, Pallenzo, Como, Bergamo, Verona, Vicenza, Padua and Bologna.

102. SS to RGH, 19 August 1926, Lilly.

103. ibid.

104. ibid.

Chapter 12

1. SS to HMT, 28 October 1928, HRHRC. 'The Testament of My Youth' is a quotation from SS's UV4.

2. The *Daily Mail* revealed SS's identity as the author of MFM on 2 October 1928.

3. MFM became an optional text on the School Certificate English Paper in 1943 and in 1954 SS was amazed to learn that it had become a set text for GCE English, a fact of which his publishers were apparently unaware.

4. The James Tait Black Prize brought a cheque for £127 6s. 2d. as well as prestige.

5. UV4. All the unattributed quotations from Sassoon in this chapter are from this source. The manuscript is owned by a private collector, but a copy of it has recently been deposited at CUL.

6. See SS:MWP, pp. 70-74.

7. 'An Enquiry', as SS called this preliminary effort, is at BL, both in original ms form and SS's transcript copy.

8. GBS's only sporting activity was rowing, which he claimed had prevented him being 'supered' (superannuated) at Westminster School.

9. See D3, pp. 172-5 and pp. 201-3.

10. ibid., p. 202.

11. J.C. Dunn to SS, 18 February 1926, CUL. See SS:MWP, pp. 347-50, for an account of this incident. RG, who had remained in touch with Dunn, had given the doctor SS's address.

12. Dunn gave evidence in 1922 to the War Office Committee Enquiry into 'Shell Shock'.

13. *The War the Infantry Knew, 1914-1919* was published by P.S. King, anonymously, in 1938.

14. 'On Being Asked to Contribute to a Regimental History', WP, p. 148.

15. This material would be incorporated into MIO, which was published long before Dunn's history of the 2nd Battalion finally appeared. SS told DS that this was his first attempt to write anything in prose about the war apart from his diary.

16. See SS:MWP, pp. 331-2.

17. First published in HJ.

18. See SS:MWP, pp. 211-12.

19. See WdlM to SS, 27 September 1928, CUL.

20. SJ, p. 100.

21. ibid., p. 101.

22. RN to SS, 16 May 1925, Berg.

23. D2, p. 53.

24. D3, p. 247. When *Lingual Exercises* was published in 1925, HGW saw it as proof that SS should be writing novels: 'Much of your verse is really prose material.' (HGW to SS, 28 April 1925, Columbia.) See also D3, pp. 131-2.

25. *Maurice* was not published until 1971, that is after EMF's death and the changes in the laws relating to homosexuality.

26. After SS's very early attempt at the form in *Celebrated Stories* (1894-5) he had concentrated on verse until May 1917, when he tried to produce some prose sketches, with the title 'Soldiers'. His next effort was his story of a young, love-sick pianist,

written in 1920 in New York with SB's encouragement. Then, also at SB's suggestion, he had made another attempt at a story in June 1921, based on his infatuation with a young private in the army, Jim Linthwaite, which he called 'Beloved Republic' (See D2, pp. 66ff). Discouraged by his friends' lukewarm response, he made several more attempts at the form between 1922 and 1926. The most interesting of these attempts is the unfinished 'A Beginning', a story featuring the Queen Anne house of his childhood friend Marjorie Forster (née Stirling), Finchhurst, which he was also to describe in OC. Centring round the Caplet family, it is narrated by a youngish, musical, homosexual narrator, Quintin Hood, who is alarmed to discover that Jill Caplet has fallen in love with him. Confiding in his 'sagacious' old friend, the psychiatrist Henry Tudeley, a figure clearly modelled on Rivers, the narrator realizes that Tudeley himself is attracted to him. The ms, together with three pages of notes, is at Rutgers.

27. EMF to SS, 23 June 1923.

28. SS's notes on OC, CUL.

29. SS to Michael Thorpe, 12 August 1966, quoted in SS, *Letters to a Critic*, privately printed (1976), p. 13.

30. There are explicit references in MFM to Surtees, whom SS continued to read till the end of his life. He also wrote introductions to editions of Surtees' *Handley Cross* and *Hillingdon Hall* (published by Harrap & Co in 1930 and 1931 respectively), and to *Hunting Scenes*, a selection from Surtees chosen by Lionel Gough and published by Rupert Hart-Davis in 1953. An old hunting friend, Geoffrey Harbord, had written to suggest that he and SS write 'a modern Jorrocks together' (CUL), but since the letter is undated, it is not possible to say whether this contributed to SS's choice of subject.

31. SS to the Turners, 13 September 1922, Berg.

32. D2, pp. 245, 256 and 286.

33. See D2, pp.113 and 165.

34. SS claimed that reading Proust sent him 'back to Debussy' (D3, p. 63).

35. D3, p. 218.

36. Romain Rolland (1866-1944) was known mainly for his *roman à fleuve, Jean Christophe*, which was published between 1904 and 1912.

37. D3, p. 301.

38. SB was in London from 18 December 1926 to 10 January 1927, as secretary to the owner-manager of the smash-hit play *Broadway*, which had transferred to England.

39. Sir Henry Head married Ruth Lawson, a headmistress, in 1904. There were no children. He received his knighthood in 1927 for his services to medicine, but he was also deeply committed to literature and published two volumes of his own verse, as well as translations of some of Heine's poems.

40. GK's notes on MFM, CUL.

41. Writing to WdlM on 24 November 1951 (Beinecke), SS told him that EG, to whom 'in despair of ever going on with it' he had lent the ms of MFM, had 'sent a glowing letter of encouragement', but that he had read the letter 'without a glimmer of elation, wishing he'd told me to stick to poetry. Then sat there with a dull empty mind for an hour or two. And then pencilled down – as though it were transmitted – a ten-line poem ...'

42. SS to LOM, 31 March 1927, HRHRC.

43. GBS to SS, 24 April 1927, CUL.

44. ibid., 31 June 1927.

45. SS writes to tell GBS on 24 October 1927 (CUL) that his solicitor has said that by Christmas he will own £43,000 in 4.5% Railway Stock – and that this is only two-thirds of what he will receive from the Beer estate. He and his brother Michael were left half of the estate between them.

46. See SS:MWP, pp. 76-7.

47. SS records 'I Accuse the Rich' as being published in the *Labour Weekly* on 1 May 1927, but Keynes records publication in the *New Leader*, xiv, on 29 April 1927, i.e. the day Rachel Beer died. It was not included in CP and reprinted only in the *Literary Digest*, 25 June 1927, and the *Indian National Herald* (Bombay), 21 July 1927.

48. SS to RG, 9 February 1924, SIU.

49. ibid., 12 December 1925.

50. Quoted from his 1927 diary in UV4.

51. ES to SS, 11 May 1927, Pullman.

52. GBS to SS, 28 May 1927, CUL.

53. Anzie was a good businessman: though the Chrysler cost £400, he managed to sell the Morris Oxford SS had smashed for £200.

54. James Wylde, who was born that summer, is no longer alive, but his widow, Mme Renée Wylde, still lives in Montpellier.

55. Diary entry for 25 July 1927.

56. Started on 25 July 1926, 'On Passing the New Menin Gate' was revised on 27 January 1928, and first published in the *London Mercury* in May 1928, then in the trade edition of HJ in July 1928, before being included in CP.

57. SS to D.J. Enright, 23 November 1960, shown to the author by the recipient.

58. SS to GBS, 23 August 1927, CUL.

59. SS to HFJ, 22 August 1927, CUL.

60. Max Meyerfeld (1875-*c.* 1952) was an editor and translater, had written an article for *Die Neue Rundschau*, November 1924, called 'Englische Menschen' ('English People'), which included individual sections on Robbie Ross, Oscar Wilde's son Vyvyan Holland, George Moore, John Galsworthy, the Sitwells, Siegfried Sassoon and 'Dame Nellie'.

SS's poem 'Concert-Interpretation' is also included in the same volume in translation as 'Konzert'. Meyerfeld had previously persuaded Ross to let him publish *Oscar Wilde* in *Die Neue Rundschau* and was the dedicatee of the English edition when it was published in England in 1908. SS had been introduced to Meyerfeld by NB in 1919 and inherited several books given to her by the German writer.

61. Max Meyerfeld to SS, 14 October 1926, CUL.

62. SS to HFJ, 17 September 1927, CUL.

63. GBS left England on 1 October 1927, arrived in New York with Fagan's Repertory Company on 9 October 1927 and was there until the end of April 1928.

64. EB had both tea and dinner with SS on 12 October 1927.

65. 1,500 copies of MFM were published on 28 September 1928 by Faber & Gwyer (later Faber and Faber), not Heinemann, who Sassoon felt had not treated him with sufficient respect in the previous few years. It was as a result of his letter to Walter de la Mare's son Richard ('Dick') at Faber & Gwyer that the firm took on publication of his prose. The firm would later buy the copyright in his poetry books from Heinemann and become Sassoon's overall British publisher. Ten impressions of MFM would be published within two years of publication and the book would be SS's best-selling work.

66. Marsh, E., *A Number of People*, p. 236.

67. MFM, p. 69.

68. ibid., pp. 52 and 60.

69. ibid., pp. 205, 206, 207 and 210. Jack and Charlie Peppermore were based on Frank and Harry Brown, both of whom were to come to sad ends, Frank in an institution and Harry destitute. The following quotation comes from a letter from SS

to RGH, 25 September 1936 (Lilly), re. reviews of SP.

70. GBS's son, George, maintains that the (Byam) Shaws came originally from Ayrshire.

71. SS to BH, 18 June 1929, Congress.

72. MFM, p. 228.

73. EMF to SS, 17 December 1928.

74. 'An Author's Secret: Mr Sassoon's Anonymous Book of Memoirs', *Daily News and Westminster Gazette*, 9 October 1928.

75. SS to RG, 2 March 1930, Buffalo.

76. SS writes in 'An Enquiry' that Weirleigh was 'all mixed up with mother, of course, but I must try to keep her separate from my emotions' (BL).

77. SS records details of this Brenchley vs Rolverden match on 27 July 1904 in a pocket diary he kept that year: 'They won the toss – made 157. Bishop 78 not out. Self bowled 5 overs, 2 maidens, 8 runs, 1 wicket. We made 132. Went in at 105 for 7 with W. Seymour took it to 120. Made 3. Caught at wkt.'

78. Tom Richardson was separated from his wife after the war and died eventually of TB.

79. When war broke out Mrs Inge became one of the first women to be a Master of Foxhounds because of the shortage of men. She went on hunting into her mid-eighties in the 1960s and died at the age of ninety.

80. There are relatively few significant changes to this ms, now at BL, which appears to be the original one. Though many words and phrases are altered, the only major change is the omission of approximately five pages from Book 3 (two introductory ones in which the narrator self-consciously discusses his aims and the three at the end where he discusses his love of poetry). The ts that is with it, containing 8 of MFM's 10 books, has no major corrections, though SS has added several paragraphs to make certain passages more vivid and occasionally deleted a few lines, such as part of a letter from Sherston's guardian, Mr Pennett. He also changed the title of Book 10 from 'At the War' to 'At the Front', which probably seemed to him more evocative. One small deletion, concerning the character 'Nigel Croplady', suggests that he was afraid of offending anyone, possibly even of libel charges. A second, later ts, covering books 1 to 4, is virtually free of corrections.

81. MFM, p. 75.

82. ibid.

83. ibid., p. 27.

84. 'The Flower Show Match' provided the title, for example, of a collection of excerpts from SS's prose published by Faber and Faber on 24 July 1941.

85. MFM, pp. 55-6.

86. SS, *Letters to a Critic*, p. 14.

Chapter 13

1. As a sign of his gratitude SS gave GBS the desk on which MFM was written. This is still in the possession of GBS's son, and SS's godson, George Byam Shaw. He also bought GBS a car and paid half the price of a house for him from the profits of the book.

2. SS was particularly aware of the possibility of death from TB, since his own father had died of the disease before he was nine.

3. See, for instance, Hoare, P., *Serious Pleasures*, p. 32.

4. SS to HFJ, 21-24 June 1927, CUL, and SS's diary entry for late June 1927.

5. SS to HFJ, op. cit.

6. SS to GBS, 18 August 1927, CUL.

7. SS's diary, *c.* 19 October 1927.

8. SS to GBS, 10 October 1927, CUL.

9. Tennant, E., *Strangers*, p. 160.

10. SS's diary, *c.* 21 January 1928.

11. OS to SS, 12 October 1927, Pullman.

12. ST to SS, 2 February 1928, Berg.

13. SS to GBS, 13 and 24 October 1927, CUL. Christabel McLaren was the wife of Henry McLaren, who became the 2nd Baronet Aberconway.

14. Cecil Beaton (1904-1980) became a highly successful and fashionable photographer. SS's diary, *c.* 7 July 1927.

15. SS to GBS, 13 and 24 October 1927, CUL.

16. SS's diary, *c.* 15 October 1927. See also Sarah Bradford's account in *Sacheverell Sitwell*, p. 170.

17. ibid.

18. SS to GBS, 13 and 24 October 1927, CUL.

19. John Culme's introduction to the catalogue *The Contents of Wilsford Manor* (Sotheby's, London, October 1987), p. 12.

20. Holroyd, M., *Lytton Strachey*, p. 953.

21. ibid.

22. Middleboe, P., *Edith Olivier*, p. 62.

23. ibid.

24. Untitled poem by SS, dated 26 October 1927, in 1920s poetry notebook, CUL.

25. SS's diary, *c.* 17 October 1927.

26. ST's note, scribbled apologetically on Sassoon's blotting paper, which has surfaced recently at the Berg, is typically charming, flattering and suggestive, as its postscript shows: 'P.S. I hope you have recovered from the exertions of the weekend. This is the most *lovely* room I have ever been in. Forgive my writing on your blotting paper.'

27. SS's diary, 19 October 1927.

28. SS to GBS, 13 and 24 October 1927, CUL.

29. ST to SS, 5 November 1927, Berg.

30. Philip Hoare notes that ST uses the word 'gay' to imply homosexuality (though the modern use of gay is seen as a recent development) citing ST's quote from *Far From the Madding Crowd* in 1936 with reference to SS: "'What kind of person is he?' 'Oh Miss – I blush to name it – a gay man.'"

31. *Vogue*, December 1927.

32. Beaton, C., *Self-Portrait with Friends*, p. 6.

33. Hoare, P., *Serious Pleasures*, p. 132. SS had met Peter Quennell (b. 1905) through LOM and owned Quennell's *Poems* (1926). He sent him his own *Lingual Exercises* in 1925. Quennell was still in touch with SS in the 1930s, when he went to teach in Japan.

34. Powell, A., *To Keep the Ball Rolling*, p. 135.

35. ST to Gilles David, 4 December 1971, Philip Hoare Collection.

36. ST to SS, [n.d.] August 1938, Berg.

37. ST to CB, 12 October 1929, Hoare, p.143 and SS to the Heads, [?1930], HRHRC.

38. Hoare, *Serious Pleasures*, p. 182.

39. SS's diary, beginning of October 1928.

40. See Bradford, S., *Sacheverell Sitwell*, p. 170.

41. Hoare, op.cit.

42. Hoare, p. 91.

43. Interview with Lady Lettice Strickland-Constable.

44. Untitled poem dated 8 November 1927 by SS (quoting ST's words) in SS's 1920s poetry notebook, CUL.

45. Untitled poem dated 26 October 1927, ibid.

46. ST to SS, 30 December and 8 May 1928, Berg.

47. Middleboe, *Edith Olivier*, p. 51.

48. ST to SS, 23 June 1942, Berg.

49. ibid., 2 May 1940.

50. SS to HH, 22 March 1950, in possession of the recipient, who kindly showed me them and told me of his knowledge of SS.

51. ibid.

52. ST's one commercially produced book, *Leaves from a Missionary's Notebook*, published by Secker & Warburg in 1937 and reprinted by Hamish Hamilton in 1986 to celebrate the author's 80th birthday, is described by Philip Hoare as 'a hilariously-drawn adult comic book, full of beefy sailor types who would gradually become part of Stephen's visual stock-in-trade'. (*Serious Pleasures*, p. 133)

53. *To My Mother*, published 24 September 1928, *In Sicily*, published 25 September 1930, and *To the Red Rose*, published 8 October 1931, nos. 14, 27 and 34 respectively in Faber's Ariel Poems series.

54. ST to SS, 19 October 1939, Berg.

55. Hoare, *Serious Pleasures*, p. 155.

56. SS's diary for 9 June 1928, with a later gloss.

57. The allusion to Lamb was partly inspired by having heard EB give a talk to the Charles Lamb Society only three days before the tea on 2 December 1927.

58. SS to TS, 26 May 1929, Berg, and 'A Fallodon Memory', CP, p.280.

59. Ruth Head to SS, 19 September 1930, CUL.

60. Middleboe, *Edith Olivier*, p. 50.

61. SS's diary, January 1928.

62. ibid.

63. FS died of a perforated ulcer on 26 December 1927.

64. SS's diary, 12 January 1928.

65. ibid., 18 January 1928.

66. SS to GBS, 17 January 1928, CUL.

67. SS to EB, 21 January 1928, HRHRC.

68. SS's diary, end of January 1928.

69. SS to LOM, 31 March 1928, HRHRC.

70. Anne Tennant (*c.* 1874-1961).

71. SS to EB, 14 April 1928, HRHRC. SS's unhappiness at Heinemann's handling of his books had been increased by their delay in publishing HJ, which came out late, in July 1928. Faber & Gwyer had already published his poem 'Nativity' as no. 7 in their Ariel Poems series in August 1927, when he wrote to Dick de la Mare about MFM.

72. SS to ES, 28 March 1928, Berg.

73. SS to HMT, 18 May 1928, HRHRC.

74. SS to HFJ, 23 May 1928, CUL.

75. SS's note on a letter from EG of 15 January 1928 (Brotherton), praising 'One Who Watches'.

76. EG to SS, 15 January 1928, Brotherton.

77. ibid., 27 March 1928.

78. Comment written on SS's 1920s poetry notebook at CUL.

79. SS to HMT, 23 March 1954, HRHRC. In the event EB wrote the 'Men of Letters' volume on Hardy.

80. See 'Writers Remembered: Siegfried Sassoon', *The Author*, Winter 1989, where Charles Causley describes persuading SS to select some TH poems for the BBC (West Regional) to broadcast. SS had made a tentative list by 7 November 1955 and sent it to HMT, who was also taking part in the programme. By 17 July 1956 this had been revised slightly as follows: 'Let Me Enjoy', 'A Church Romance', 'The Oxen', 'An August Midnight', 'The Darkling Thrush', 'The Year's Awakening', 'The Convergence of the Twain', 'In Time of the Breaking of Nations', 'When I Set Out for Lyonesse', 'Beeny Cliff' and 'Afterwords'.

81. Hoare, *Serious Pleasures*, p. 101.

82. SS gave WW £20 to visit and entertain ST at Haus Hirth, where WW arrived on 16 February 1928. The trip was also in order to help WW work on one of his compositions.

83. 25 February 1928, Berg.

84. SS's diary, April 1928.

85. ibid.

86. Middleboe, *Edith Olivier*, p. 77.

87. ibid.

88. SS's diary, 5 June 1928.

89. ibid.

90. ibid.

91. David Tennant had married the actress Hermione Baddeley on 16 April 1928 at the King's Road Register Office and Stephen had been present at the wedding.

92. GBS to SS, pc of 5 June 1928, CUL.

93. e.g., SS stayed at the same hotel in Munich, the Marienbad, as he had with GBS the previous summer.

94. SS and ST heard Elizabeth Schumann in Mozart's *The Marriage of Figaro* at the Residenz Theater, Wagner's *Meistersingers* at the Prinzregenten Theater and a Mozart quintet in the courtyard of the Residenz. They also visited the Alte Pinakothek Gallery and the Neue Staatsgalerie.

95. ST's diary, 30 August 1928, Berg.

96. SS to GBS, 30 August 1928, CUL.

97. ST's diary, 4 September 1928, Berg.

98. SS to HFJ, 12 October 1928, CUL.

99. ibid.

100. ibid.

101. SS to WdlM, 18 October 1928, Beinecke.

102. The Hirths had also provided them with an itinerary to Venice and the first day's route reads 'Garmisch, Innsbruck, Brenner, Bozen (i.e. Bolzano)'.

103. ST's diary, 10 September 1928, Berg.

104. ibid.

105. ibid., 15 September 1928. ST appears to be a day ahead in his calculations.

106. SS and ST stayed at Montegufoni from 17 to 24 September 1928, then at the Hotel Helvetia in Florence for two days.

107. SS to GBS, 3 October 1928, CUL.

108. SS and ST stayed at the Hotel d'Italie and Bauer Grunwald. Nannie and William had arrived by train from Florence to join them.

109. SS's diary, end September/beginning October 1928.

110. ibid.

111. SS had entertained J.C. Squire to lunch at the Reform on 12 June 1928.

112. Apart from the very first review in the *Irish Independent*, which dismissed MFM as 'a rather dull story', another by Raymond Mortimer in the *Nation* complaining of the lack of 'bedroom scenes' and Graves's attack in the *Westminster*, SS would continue to be reassured by MFM's reception. It was 'noticed' favourably in such disparate publications as the *Shooting Times*, the *Manchester Guardian*, *Sporting Life*, the *Times Literary Supplement*, the *Baptist Times*, *TP's Weekly* and the *London Mercury*.

113. ST's diary, 1 October 1928, Berg.

114. Edith Sitwell, who was almost certainly jealous of SS's relationship with ST, told EO that she 'had been very angry with Stephen … says that SS has two patches on his lungs and blames ST for this as he made him do rash things abroad'. (Middleboe, *Edith Olivier*, p. 85)

115. ST's diary, October 1928, Berg.

116. ibid., 6 and 10 October 1928.

117. SS to HFJ, 12 October 1928, Berg.

118. They stayed at the Hotel Foyot in Paris, as they had on the way down.

119. Hoare, *Serious Pleasures*, p. 122.

120. SS to LOM, 1 November 1928, HRHRC.

121. Madame Duclaux (1857-1944) was the sister of the novelist A. Mabel Robinson.

122. SS to HFJ, 12 July 1927, CUL. Miss Fleming-Jones, who owned a house in Paris, also went by the name of Françoise Xavier.

123. SS's own poem on HFJ, though not nearly so successful as Vaughan's, gives some idea of how much he missed him. (The ms of this is at Harvard.)

I'll go no more to Maida Vale
To dine with Henry Festing-Jones,
The friend whose friendship could not fail.

No more he'll talk in tranquil tones
Of Sicily. And sip white wine [etc.]

written 11.1.29
rev[ised] 30.10.31.

124. SS to the Heads, 1 December 1928, CUL.

Chapter 14

1. Faber & Gwyer sold 15,000 copies in less than three months. The illustrated edition was published on 29 October 1929. It contained seven full-page drawings by Graves's father-in-law, William Nicholson, and a frontispiece drawing of SS, which was suppressed at SS's demand after the binding of two or three advance copies. This may have been because, as EO put it, Nicholson's drawing made SS look like an 'Israelitish groom' (Middleboe, P., *Edith Olivier*, p. 104).

2. Coward-McCann, who published 3,175 copies in America on 25 January 1929, paid an advance of £500, a very large sum for the time.

3. The Hawthornden Prize was instituted by Miss Alice Warrender in 1919 for the best work of imaginative literature, prose or verse published during the year. Its only condition was that the author should be under forty, but SS was forty-two when he won it.

4. SS to Ruth Head, 28 February 1929, CUL.

5. ST's doctors diagnosed a recurrence of the disease on 8 January 1929.

6. SS to RG, 2 March 1930, Buffalo.

7. Johanna Hirth to SS, 24 February 1929, CUL.

8. SS to the Heads, 4 March 1929, HRHRC.

9. Beaton, C., *Self-Portrait with Friends*, p. 6.

10. SS to RGH, 26 September 1946, Lilly.

11. Middleboe, *Edith Olivier*, p. 50.

12. SS made EO an allowance of £200 a year from 1937 until her death in 1948.

13. Whistler, L., *The Laughter and the Urn*, p. 135.

14. ibid., p. 131.

15. ibid.

16. ibid.

17. The original ms of *Memoirs of an Infantry Officer*, provisionally entitled *Autobiography of an Infantry Officer*, is now at the IWM. Clearly thought of as a direct continuation of *Memoirs of a Fox-Hunting Man*, it is written in pencil in two hessian-backed notebooks, similar to the three at the British Library which contain Sassoon's first draft of the latter. The jokey, punning title, *Mem-Wars* is also perpetuated and the numbering carries on from the first three volumes, being 'IV' and 'V' respectively. The whole of notebook IV and the beginning of volume V, which represent the 50,000 words written between late November 1928 and 1 April 1929, are in a fairly advanced state of revision, suggesting that SS revised them by simply rubbing out the first draft and rewriting it, with any additions on the blank left-hand page. The later part of volume V, written mostly in early 1930 and unrevised, is far less neat and probably a genuine first draft. A corrected proof copy is in the possession of the collector William Reese.

18. When Frau Hirth sent SS interest on the loan of 10,000 marks, SS simply tore up the cheque.

19. Middleboe, *Edith Olivier*, p. 91.

20. MFM had already earned SS £1,500 by April 1929.

21. GBS and Angela Baddeley were married on 8 September 1929.

22. Middleboe, op.cit.

23. ibid.

24. ibid.

25. ibid., p. 92. SS is referring to a visit in late December 1928. It was during this visit that SS had earned Sachie and Georgia Sitwell's great gratitude by making them a generous loan to pay off the most pressing of their debts. Sachie dedicated his next book, *Dr Donne and Gargantua* (1930), to him.

26. Middleboe, *Edith Olivier*, p. 92.

27. ST's description of Kaltenbach seems to have been deliberately designed to make SS jealous: 'I cannot begin to describe him, or his strength and gentleness ... a wonderful, animal, boyish charm, utterly subjugating, he looks so deeply into my eyes ... I really felt that if Dr K. went on another minute hanging over me and drinking my eyes up I should do something really immodest ... Are you jealous?' (ST to SS, *c.* March 1929, Berg.)

28. Middleboe, *Edith Olivier*, p. 93 and SS to GBS, 15 April 1929, CUL.

29. SS to GBS, 22 May 1929, CUL. The house at Breitenau was rented from a Frau Schneider by ST, initially for a period of six weeks, though this was extended by a further month to the end of July 1929. With it came a 'very bad cook' called Thérèse, according to SS.

30. ST to Elizabeth Lowndes, 26 May 1929, Hoare, *Serious Pleasures*, p. 138.

31. SS wrote 'War Experience' and 'Childhood Recovered' ('Down the glimmering staircase ...') in April 1929, as the ms of both poems at Harvard indicates. Both were published in *Vigils* and included in CP.

32. Dated 25 May 1929 in his ms notebook of poetry and prose at the IWM.

33. Written on 25 May 1929, a few weeks after SS had joined ST in Bavaria, this poem was published first in the *Nation*, 5 April 1930, then in *Vigils*, both described by RH as 'bulls-eyes'.

34. 'At Breitenau, 23 May 1929' is dated 22 March 1932 in the Harvard ms, presumably the actual date of composition.

35. SS would finish this section on 21 September 1929, after his return to England.

36. SS to BH, 18 June 1929, Congress.

37. EB received the Hawthornden Prize for *The Shepherd* in 1922, but was in South America at the time of the prize-giving.

38. EO to SS, 13 July 1929, Columbia. SS told RH that he thought the Hawthornden Committee should have asked someone 'more literary' than Lord Lonsdale to present the prize (SS to RH, 22 June 1929, Beinecke).

39. SS to EB, 3 July 1929, HRHRC.

40. ST to Elizabeth Lowndes, 15 August 1929, Hoare, *Serious Pleasures*, p. 141.

41. Holroyd, M., *Lytton Strachey*, p. 1009.

42. EB to Aki Hayashi, 28 September 1929 (Claire Blunden).

43. ibid.

44. There is a telephone message from Gide for SS at the Hotel Plaza Athenée, where he and ST were staying, suggesting a meeting on the evening of 18 November 1929 (CUL). Gide also wrote to SS on 2 January 1931 expressing his appreciation of MFM, which had been recommended to him by their mutual friend, Arnold Bennett, and also of MIO. He asks how ST is (CUL).

45. SS's diary, 31 December 1928.

46. Hart-Davis, *Siegfried Sassoon: Letters to Max Beerbohm*, p. 4.

47. SS's diary, 31 December 1928.

48. Behrman, S., *Portrait of Max*, p. 14.

49. SS to SCC, 26 August 1952, Cockerell, S.C., *The Best of Friends*, p. 212.

50. SS to HH, 14 February 1951, in possession of the recipient.

51. ibid., 16 November 1948.

52. Powell, A., *To Keep the Ball Rolling*, p. 40.

53. Cecil, D., *Max*, p. 225.

54. SS to HH, 22 October 1948, in possession of recipient.

55. SS's diary, 31 December 1928.

56. SS wrote two pages of notes about MB in preparation for his account of him in WY. These are now at Columbia.

57. ibid.

58. ibid.

59. SS:PP, p. 137.

60. SS to SCC, 26 August 1952, Cockerell, *The Best of Friends*, p. 212.

61. Radio talk by SS on MB, recorded for the BBC Home Service on 28 June 1956 at Heytesbury House. There is a copy at CUL.

62. SS's diary for 24 November 1929.

63. ibid., 26 November 1929.

64. Hart-Davis, *Letters to Max Beerbohm*, p. 7.

65. ibid.

66. Home Service broadcast of 2 June 1952.

67. Originally called 'Spiritual Presences', then 'Servants of the Spirit', SS retitled it 'Presences Perfected' and sent it to EB, who began a year's appointment as literary editor on the *Nation* in February 1930 and arranged to have it published there on 5 April 1930. A puzzling poem, it may refer to the volcanic figures, or to ancient statues or even to his recently dead friends, TH, EG and HFJ. Or it might simply be about 'Spiritual Presences', as its original title implies. SS and ST were staying at the Hotel Bertolini in Naples.

68. SS's diary, April 1930.

69. 'In Sicily' was inspired by a valley on the way to Noto that SS and ST visited at the beginning of 1930.

The first draft was dated '23.3.30'. The poem, illustrated by ST, was published first on 25 September 1930 as No. 27 in Faber & Gwyer's 'Ariel Poem' series, then in the limited and trade editions of *Vigils* (1934 and 1935).

70. ST's passion for shells and his practice of putting them into water when he arrived back at his hotel room or Wilsford, provided SS with an elaborate simile many years later in his lecture 'On Poetry' (University of Bristol Press, 16 March 1939), p. 18: 'Imagine yourself picking up shells on a dry shingle beach: deprived of their native element they seem lifeless. But take them home and put them in a bowl of water and they revive to floral freshness and delicate aqueous colour ...'

71. SS to LOM, 2 April 1930, HRHRC.

72. SS to GBS, 20 April 1930, CUL.

73. MIO, p. 236.

74. SS's diary, *c.* April 1930.

75. SS to EB, 25 February 1930, HRHRC.

76. SS's diary, 8 April 1930.

77. SS and ST stayed at the Domenico Hotel at Taormina.

78. Hart-Davis, *Letters to Max Beerbohm*, p. 11.

79. ibid., pp. 9-11.

80. ibid., p.10.

81. ibid., p. 11.

82. ibid., p. 12.

83. SS's diary for 30 April 1930, Hart-Davis, *Letters to Max Beerbohm*, p. 13.

84. ibid., *c.* May 1930. SS and ST stayed at the Hotel Pavillon Henri IV, St Germain-en-Laye, ten miles outside Paris.

85. SS to LOM, 16 April 1930, HRHRC.

86. SS's diary, *c.* May 1930.

87. ibid.

88. ibid.

89. SS to the Heads,16 June 1930, HRHRC.

90. SS to the Heads, undated letter of 1930, HRHRC.

91. ibid.

92. Lord Glenconner would later come to appreciate SS's help, impressing upon ST's nurse in May 1931 'the family's gratitude' to him for 'all [he] had done' (EH to SS, 24 May 1931, CUL).

93. Hoare, *Serious Pleasures*, p. 162.

94. SS to Ruth Head, undated letter of 1930, CUL.

95. Middleboe, *Edith Olivier*, p. 144.

96. SS to LOM, 16 April 1930, HRHRC.

97. ibid.

98. ibid., 20 June 1930.

99. SS to AT, 2 August 1930, CUL.

100. SS had finished correcting final proofs of MIO by mid-July.

101. SS to LOM, 2 April 1930, HRHRC.

102. These notes are in the possession of a private collector, but there is now a copy at CUL.

103. ST's diary for 25 October 1930, quoted in Hoare, *Serious Pleasures*, p. 163.

104. CP, p. 211. SS had written out this poem on a card decorated with a cross and the figure of a lone person gazing at a solitary winter scene.

Chapter 15

1. SS to HMT, 15 March 1930, HRHRC.

2. Faber and Faber (formerly Faber & Gwyer) published 20,000 copies of MIO on 18 September 1930 and eight more editions in the following four years in response to its immediate popular success.

3. The *Daily Telegraph* serialized portions 6-9, 11-16, 18-23 and 25 between 6 and 26 August 1930 for the sum of £350. The *TLS* reviewed MIO (anonymously) on the day of publication and it was even reviewed, together with MFM, in *Figaro* by

Jacques-Emile Blanche ('Pitié de la Guerre') on 16 November 1930.

4. SS's diary for 30 November 1927, quoted in Blunden, E., *A Selection of his Poetry and Prose*, p. 162.

5. SS to EB, 31 October 1927.

6. ibid.

7. SS made it clear to Mary Blunden in his letter of 15 October 1929 that he was 'offering to make [himself] responsible for all expenses concerned with John's education' rather than acting *in loco parentis* to him.

8. SS to HMT, 15 March 1930, HRHRC.

9. SS to TS, 8 March 1929, Berg.

10. When Rex Whistler designed a title page for MIO he made a subconscious acknowledgement of this, calling it *Autobiography of an Infantry Officer* (see IWM). Paul Moeyes raises the question in *Scorched Glory* whether MIO is really a novel at all (p. 182ff).

11. SS to LOM, 21 January 1930, HRHRC.

12. ibid., 2 April 1930.

13. In the first ms draft of MIO at IWM, SS has crossed out several passages of apology and reflection on his writing methods with the comment 'This won't do at all' beside one of them.

14. EMF to SS, 26 September 1930, Wichita.

15. MIO, p. 221.

16. ibid., p. 188.

17. ibid., p. 51.

18. ibid., p. 68.

19. ibid., p. 236.

20. SS to RH, 15 May 1929, HRHRC.

21. SS to LOM, 9 November 1928, HRHRC.

22. By the time SS came to write MIO he had definitely read A.P. Herbert's *The Secret Battle* (1919) and Charles Edmond's *A Subaltern's War* (1929), though not R.H. Mottram's *Spanish Farm Trilogy* (1924-6). He makes no mention of *Parade's End*, a tetralogy written between 1924 and 1928 by Ford Madox Ford, who was probably too Modernist for his taste. Nor does he appear to have been influenced by Richard Aldington's *Death of a Hero* (1929). Two war books he did admire, but which came out in 1930, too late to influence him, were Frederic Manning's *Her Privates We* and H.M. Tomlinson's *All Our Yesterdays*.

23. SS to RG, 7 February 1930, Buffalo.

24. SS to HMT, 15 March 1930, HRHRC.

25. SS to RG, 7 February 1930, Buffalo.

26. SS to the Untermeyers, 6 February 1930, Lilly.

27. RG to SS, 20 February 1930, Berg. SS wrote to warn TS in February 1929: 'It is a very bad book judged by any standard of criticism, and it would only exasperate you. So I ask you not to look at it, on any account. I think he must be slightly crazy. Anyhow his sense of good taste (never very well developed!) has entirely deserted him, and my temper has been awful this evening.' (Berg.)

28. EB's annotated copy, which must be an advanced copy since it is dated 7 November 1929, is at the Berg. Its endpaper has notes by EB emphasizing its inaccuracies, such as 'Falsities for public delectation', and EB has given it a motto: 'Haply I may remember, / And haply may dismember'. On the title page he has given it an alternative title, 'The Welsh-Irish Bull in a China Shop', with a clear reference to RG's ancestry.

29. SS to EB, 20 December 1928, Columbia.

30. SS to RG, 7 February 1930, Buffalo.

31. ibid.

32. ibid.

33. SS, *Letters to a Critic*, Kent Editions, 1976, p. 21. EM (in Hassell,

C., *Ambrosia and Small Beer*, p. 29), says that he was the only pre-war friend RG had retained, owing 'entirely to [EM's] good sense in avoiding an introduction to X [Laura Riding], who has made him quarrel with *all* the others, without exception'.

34. RG to SS, 20 February 1930, Berg.

35. *Letters to a Critic*, p. 21.

36. SS to RG, 11 October 1926, SIU.

37. NB to SS, n.d., Sotheby's catalogue, 14 December 1992, and SS to GBS, 16 June 1929, CUL. RG had jumped out of a lower floor window after Laura Riding but had escaped relatively unhurt. She recovered fully, in spite of breaking her spine.

38. This poem was written in a ms notebook, now with the proofs of MIO at the IWM, with SS's comment in the margin: 'These rather deplorable lines were addressed to the author of "Goodbye to All That"!'

39. RG, however, wrote to SS in 1933 about GTAT being very complimentary about SS, whereas (he claimed) MIO was 'malicious' about himself. SS's words are from a letter to LOM of 2 April 1930, HRHRC.

40. SS to LOM, 2 April 1930, HRHRC. John Hildebidle argues in an essay entitled 'Neither Worthy Nor Capable: The War Memoirs of Graves, Blunden and Sassoon' (*Modernism Reconsidered*, ed. R. Kiely, Harvard University Press, 1983, p. 247) that *Memoirs* 'represent a polished and literary form of formulation, a way of making psychological order out of the experience of the First World War'.

Chapter 16

1. Dated 4 March 1932, this is in the Harvard poetry notebook and hitherto unpublished.

2. By 1935 MIO had sold only 7,000 less than MFM, that is 48,000. By 2001, however, MIO was selling much better than MFM in Faber's trade paperback (at £7.99).

3. 'Further Experiences' is the working title of an ms notebook containing Part 1 and virtually all of Part 4 of *Sherston's Progress*, now in the possession of William Reese. Mr Reese also owns a ts of pages 4-160 of the same book. Neither the ms nor the ts contains many corrections, though there are a few additions, made generally for purposes of elucidation, and occasional minor stylistic changes. Geoffrey Faber of Faber and Faber was still referring to the book as 'Further Experiences' in a letter of 5 March 1936 sold at Sotheby's in December 1994. Sassoon also tentatively heads his notes on SP in his IWM notebook 'Stories of My Past Life – vol. 3?'

4. SS to LOM, 17 December 1930, HRHRC.

5. CP, p. 221.

6. There would, therefore, be three years between SS's first notes on Craiglockhart of 12 February 1930 and his first serious attempt to write them up. He also abandoned another prose project, the 4,000-word piece on TH he had promised Massingham for a book he planned to put together on great Victorian writers.

7. SS to the Heads, 25 February [1933], CUL.

8. RHD states that Part III of SP consists entirely of quotations from SS's diaries, but Thorpe points out that this is not so in his review of SS's *Diaries*, 'The Road to Edinthorpe', *Focus on Robert Graves*, winter 1989-90, pp. 9-12. Thorpe also argues that 'an overall effect of [reading] the *Diaries* is to deepen one's awareness of the distinction between Sassoon's "true" self and the Sherston *persona*, which had been blurred by his allotting his war experience largely to the latter and giving it only summary treatment in *Siegfried's Journey*. From the earliest diary entries one is aware of the febrile reactions to the War of an idealist romantic poet.'

9. SS to GK, 8 September 1936, CUL.

10. MB wrote to SS on 10 December 1930: 'I have, as a matter of fact, already done a rough drawing. But I want to "check" it. I'm not sure I have your colouring right.' (Hart-Davis, *Letters to Max*, p. 15.) SS invited MB and his wife to tea at 23 Campden Hill Square on 19 December 1930, and the caricature appeared in a *Spectator* supplement on 21 March 1931. It shows SS in a very similar pose to that of a photograph taken on MB's roof-top garden in Rapallo, leaning on the balustrade with one hand on his hip.

11. SS's diary for October 1930.

12. ibid., 8 October 1930. GA married the writer Mary Butts.

13. SS to the Heads, 25 February 1933, HRHRC.

14. IWM notebook containing notes for MIO and SP.

15. SS to RN, 20 February 1932, Bodley.

16. 'Dateless oblivion and divine repose', Harvard poetry notebook, dated '18.2.32' and '28.1.33' and hitherto unpublished.

17. In one year alone, from February 1932 to February 1933, Sassoon had three driving accidents – one of which landed him in court – mumps and a broken collarbone. He also nearly set fire to the house by tossing an unextinguished match into a wastepaper basket.

18. Untitled, unpublished poem in the Harvard poetry notebook.

19. CP, p. 215. Though originally written in March 1929, this poem was revised on 17 January and 3 February 1932.

20. Harvard.

21. 'The Hour-Glass' is dated '20.9.32' and revised '9.11.32' in a 1930s poetry notebook at CUL. SS was given TH's hour-glass by his executor, SCC, and, reading the poem later, GK suggested that SS buy a skull.

22. Middleboe, P., *Edith Olivier*, p. 136.

23. e.g., 'Vigils', 'Heaven' and 'Ode' from *Vigils*.

24. ES to SS, 22 December 1934, Pullman.

25. CP, p. 225. This was dated '11.9.32' in a 1930s poetry notebook at CUL.

26. SS to the Heads, 17 April 1933, HRHRC.

27. Middleboe, *Edith Olivier*, p. 162.

28. SS to the Heads, 21 June 1931, HRHRC.

29. Middleboe, p. 122.

30. ibid., p. 123.

31. ibid., pp. 123-4.

32. Beryl appears to have been 'Really' and Eileen 'Truly', Beryl the more dominant personality, Eileen the more unworldly and passionate – the 'ardent' one according to SS.

33. SS to the Heads, 17 April [1930?], HRHRC.

34. Eileen Hunter died on 23 April 1944, Beryl on 3 May 1944.

35. SS often spells this 'Wylie'.

36. Middleboe, p. 122. The Hunters would also arrange for him to hunt with the Grafton and the South and West Wiltshire hunts, and to take part in several local point-to-points. Imma was the widow of Baron Hans-Karl von Doernberg and the daughter of Prince and Princess Alexander of Erlach-Schonberg. She was also related to both the English and Dutch royal families. Her husband, twenty-six years her senior, died ten months after their marriage in 1923. She first met WW in 1928, but got to know him properly through their mutual friend, EO.

37. SS to AT, 18 March 1931, Berg.

38. Beryl Hunter to SS, 28 July 1931, CUL.

39. SS to the Heads, 8 April 1932, HRHRC.

40. ibid., 23 May 1933.

41. ibid., 11 March 1932.

42. ibid., 23 May 1933.

43. ibid.

44. Beryl Hunter told SS of the Mill Cottage, owned by a Colonel Bailey, on 16 February 1931, after he had moved into the Avon Hotel.

45. SS to TS, 26 March 1931, Berg.

46. ibid.

47. WW to SS, 8 March 1931, William Walton Collection, Ischia.

48. WW did not arrive in England until 24 March 1931 and heard Tertis play his Viola Concerto at a Royal Philharmonic Society concert conducted by Ernest Ansermet on 26 March 1931. *Belshazzar's Feast* was first performed by the Leeds Festival Chorus on 8 October 1931 with Malcolm Sargent conducting.

49. WW to SS, op. cit.

50. SS's first poem written in Switzerland, 'Yalding Revisited! And Oxford Too!' was to celebrate EB's appointment as a fellow and tutor at Merton College, Oxford, in March 1931 and plays rather whimsically round the notion of his skill at cricket. It was never published. His second piece, also unpublished, was his brief lament about ST, 'Angel of Heaven'. The third, 'To a Red Rose', suitably musical in theme, was published in Faber's Ariel Series in October 1931 and illustrated by ST, despite their separation. His fourth was the unpublished 'To all my happiness ...' SS also revised drafts of two earlier poems, both expressing his sense of being cut off from life, 'Sometimes My Life Succeeds in Standing Still' and 'The Utopian Times', which became one of the five new poems added to the second edition of *Satirical Poems* in 1933.

51. 'Did you like *Pinchbeck Lyre*?' SS asked MB on 8 July 1931. 'Unkind; but the result of much piffle-provocation.' (Hart-Davis, *Letters to Max*, p. 167.) Humbert Wolfe told Louise Morgan in an interview that 'The only piece of criticism that has profoundly troubled me was the recent parody of my work ... [by] Siegfried Sassoon. I wasn't outraged or hurt by it; I was only appalled to discover that he felt so virulently about me, that he, a poet, troubled himself with hating.' (David Holmes Catalogue, Philadelphia.)

52. SS to LOM, 27 April 1931, HRHRC.

53. For a more detailed picture of this colony see Dominic Hibberd's excellent account in *Harold Monro: Poet of the New Age*, Palgrave, 2001.

54. SS to LOM, 27 April 1931, HRHRC.

55. Middleboe, p. 121.

56. ibid.

57. ibid.

58. ibid.

59. SS to the Heads, 10 April 1931 and 6 December 1931, HRHRC.

60. Middleboe, p. 99.

61. EH to SS, 23 April 1931, CUL.

62. Untitled, unpublished poem in Harvard poetry notebook.

63. Beryl Hunter to SS, 16 May 1931, CUL.

64. ST to SS, 6 December 1941, Berg.

65. SS stayed three days with Miss Fleming-Jones in Paris, he told his mother in a letter of 1 June 1931, at 10, place d'Henri Paté, rue François Gérard, Paris XVI – 'a kind and hospitable lady' (Berg).

66. SS to AT, 30 June 1931, Berg.

67. ibid.

68. ibid.

69. SS to MB, 8 July 1931, quoted in Hart-Davis, *Letters to Max*, p. 17.

70. Later in 1931 ES, worried about SS's own health, would arrange for him to visit her friend Dr Lydiard Wilson in Bloomsbury. (See ES to SS, 26 June 1931, Pullman.) She, in particular, had felt jealous of ST's hold over him.

71. SS to MB, 8 July 1931, Hart-Davis, *Letters to Max*, p. 16.

72. SS to LOM, 6 August 1930, HRHRC.

73. SS to AT, 22 July 1931, Berg.

74. *A Garden Revisited and Other Poems*, 1931.

75. SS to LOM, 30 September 1931, HRHRC.

76. SS to TS, 14 August 1932, Berg.

77. SS to RH, 4 December 1931, Beinecke.

78. EH to SS, 28 September 1931, CUL.

79. Details taken from the sales brochure of Fitz House at CUL.

80. SS rented Fitz House from Colonel Charles French, who had it on a long lease from Lord Bledisloe. Having failed to let it at the 'very fancy rent' he had been asking, according to EH, he had come down considerably in price by November 1931, when SS's one-year lease began. SS renewed the lease twice and was there until 1934.

81. EH to SS, 28 September 1931, CUL.

82. John Harding, in an unpublished biography of Ralph Hodgson. I am very grateful to Mr Harding for allowing me to read and quote this.

83. SS to SCC, 3 May 1932, HRHRC.

84. Dated 22/23 November 1932, Harvard.

85. Dated 13 July 1932 and 20 July 1933 in a 1930s poetry notebook at CUL.

86. 'Childhood Recovered' was written 8 April 1929 but revised at Fitz House. Both these poems are in CP, p. 213.

87. Beryl Hunter to SS, 25 July 1931, CUL.

88. Sassoon's notebook headed 'Books bought while at Fitz House' (now at Columbia) suggests that he devoted a great deal of time to book-collecting there. It lists over thirteen local bookshops he frequented and more than twenty bookshops dealt with by post. His letters to the bookseller Percy Muir between 1927 and 1962 (now in the hands of a private collector) show that his main interest lay in poetry books, including books about poetry as well as editions of poets through the ages. Seventeenth- and eighteenth-century books had a special appeal for him. He also collected anything on Wiltshire and the West Country generally, and children's books, particularly nineteenth-century ones. He would buy almost anything published by Pickering & Chatto, and was anxious to own every edition of one of Hardy's favourites, the dialect poet William Barnes.

89. Quoted in John Harding's unpublished biography of Ralph Hodgson.

90. Our Tour Book-hunting, Nov. 10-14 (1931) (Bodley).

(R.H. & S.S.)

Hull	Fitton – 34 Great Thornton Street.
	Huckle – 48a Myton-Gate. Market Place.
	Mrs Jeckells – 61 Walmsley Street.
	Lazenby – 17 Jenning Street.
	Sawyer – 56 & 58 Great Thornton Street.
Grimsby	Askew – 50 Garden Street.
	Giles (Mrs Bessie) – 154 Albert Street.
Boston	Craven – 30 Stanbow Lane.
Alford	Stephenson – Church Street.
Norfolk	Ferrow – 15a Howard Street South, Gt Yarmouth.
	Flavell – 8 St Gregory's Alley, Norwich.
	Higgins – 37 Elm Hill, Norwich.
	Hunt – 14 Orford Hill, Norwich.
	Slaughter – 7 St Peter's Street, Norwich.
	Smith – Station Road, Heacham, Lynn.
Suffolk	Green & Hatfield – Northgate Street & 70 Old Foundry Road, Ipswich.
	Read & Barrett – (new &

2nd hand; where we got the Lyrical Ballads) 8 Queen Street, Ipswich.

91. SS's notes of this journey are included in the notebook headed 'Books bought while at Fitz House' at Columbia.

92. Dated 16 July 1932 and 14 March 1933 respectively, at Harvard.

93. RG to SS, undated letter of late 1933, O'Prey, p. 232.

94. SS to RH, 5 April 1933, Beinecke.

95. SS to EB, 12 November 1931, HRHRC. SS was to contribute £100 to help the British Museum buy a collection of Owen mss in April 1933.

96. GBS's eldest brother was also called George.

97. SS to RH, 18 September 1932, Beinecke.

98. Lady Violet Bonham Carter (née Asquith, 1887-1969), very active politically in the Liberal cause, was created Baroness Asquith of Yarnbury in 1964.

99. The main collection is at CUL.

100. Hart-Davis, *Letters to Max*, p. 58.

101. SS to the Heads, 6 May 1933, HRHRC.

102. SS was awarded his Hon.D.Litt. on 18 December 1931, he maintained, because A.E. Housman had refused the honour. It was awarded by Lord Derby and followed by a dinner at the Adelphi Hotel, which he remembered from his stays at the Royal Welch Fusiliers depot at Litherland, just outside the city.

103. TS signed her will on 6 January 1932 in a nursing home at Tunbridge Wells.

104. SS to the Heads, 6 June 1932, HRHRC.

105. Behrman, S., *Tribulations and Laughter*, p. 189.

106. ibid., pp. 188-9.

107. 'The Quiet House', dated 16 July 1932, Harvard, hitherto unpublished.

108. SS to the Heads, 21 June 1932, HRHRC.

109. ST to SS, 6 March 1933, Berg. There are many more examples of ST's fluctuations in mood in this newly acquired collection.

110. SS to GBS, 12 December 1932, CUL.

111. ST to SS, 7 October 1932, Berg.

112. SS to TEL, 19 December 1934, the collection of Harry and Cookie Spiro.

113. EMF to SS, 11 April 1932, private collection.

114. ST to SS, [n.d. February 1933] Berg.

115. Hart-Davis, *Letters to Max*, p. 18, and SS to the Heads, 8 April 1933, HRHRC.

116. ibid.

117. ibid.

118. Dr Ross to SS, 22 May [1933], copied out in SS's hand and enclosed in an undated letter to the Heads, HRHRC.

Chapter 17

1. SS's diary for 8 October 1933.

2. 'Thanksgiving', an unpublished poem dated 4 October and 1 November 1934; this was included in an illustrated collection of poems (now at CUL), many of which were subsequently included in *Vigils*. In the first line 'love' was crossed out and replaced by 'faith' during revision.

3. Alfred Morrison (1821-97) and his wife Mabel (1847-1933) married in 1866; their first son, Hugh, was born in 1868 (d. 1931) and their elder daughter, Katherine, in 1869 (d. 1949). I am indebted to Philip Hoare for drawing my attention to a Morrison family tree drawn up by a local historian, Jude James.

4. Richard Gatty (1909-75) was the author of *Portrait of a Merchant Prince: James Morrison 1789-1857* (1977).

5. SS to WdlM, 4 June 1933, Beinecke.

6. EO's diary, quoted in Roberts, J.S., *Siegfried Sassoon*, p. 249.

7. SS to RH, 16 November 1933, Beinecke.

8. SS to LOM, 1 September 1933, HRHRC.

9. EO's diary for August 1933.

10. A large collection of HG's literary efforts, including a play, some stories and numerous poems, has recently been deposited at the Berg. And there is a collection of the poems she wrote specifically to SS over the years – 'My Darling Siegie, / I am giving you these because I do not want you to think I am secretive' – in the hands of a private collector. Several of her paintings were sold at Phillips' sale of the contents of Heytesbury House on 31 October 1994: unframed canvases of portraits, still lifes and landscapes. Theresa Whistler told me that HG had also composed a symphony and she had certainly planned a ballet in two acts called *The Silver Mask* (Berg).

11. EO to Ruth Head, 24 October [1933], HRHRC.

12. SS to RH, 16 November 1933, Beinecke.

13. Hester's mother approved of the age gap, which was approximately the same as that between her husband, Sir Stephen Gatty, and herself: 'That makes happiness in my eyes,' she told SS (EO to Ruth Head, 24 October [1933], HRHRC).

14. SS's diary, mid-September 1933.

15. ibid., 5 September 1933.

16. ibid., mid-September 1933.

17. ibid., *c*. October 1933.

18. ibid., 7 October 1933.

19. Middleboe, P., *Edith Olivier*, p. 145.

20. EO to Ruth Head, 24 October [1933], HRHRC.

21. SS to the Heads, 16 November 1933, HRHRC.

22. ibid., 29 October 1933.

23. ST to SS, 'January' 1942, Berg.

24. I am grateful to Kathleen Cann of CUL for this suggestion.

25. Quoted with approval in ST's journal at the Berg.

26. D2, p. 159.

27. Sir Stephen Gatty, KC, had been Chief Justice of Gibraltar from 1895 until 1905, the year he married Katherine Gatty.

28. SS noted buying 'Three books by Mrs Ewing' in his Fitz House notebook for 23 November 1931 and 'Gatty, *Legendary Tales*, 1958 3/6' (Columbia).

29. HG had an income of £2,000 p.a. of her own and would be left a large amount of money by her aunt, Lady St Cyres, in September 1936. Her mother would settle another £10,000 on her and give her £7,500 for a house of her own in the mid-1940s. When SS wrote to his mother (25 October 1933) he told her of HG's £2,000 per annum: 'A sordid detail which cannot fail to please you!' (Berg.)

30. Notes taken during an interview with Mrs Hancock on 25 April 1931. Mrs Hancock (later Clark) was the headmistress of SS's son's prep school, Greenways, in the 1940s and got to know SS well.

31. SS to HMT, 15 March 1956, Christie's catalogue, 3 April, 1992.

32. SS to RG, 3 October 1933, quoted in O'Prey, p. 230.

33. Twenty-six letters from Doris Westwood, starting on 25 February 1930 and ending in July 1934, have just been bought by the New York Public Library and are now in the Berg Collection.

34. Doris Westwood's first novel, *Starr Bladon* (Hutchinson, 1930), was not her first publication. She had already produced a slim volume of verse, *White Ash*, published by Erskine Macdonald in 1920, and a diary of her two years at the Old Vic from 1923 to 1925, published as *These Players* by Heath Cranton in 1926.

She also had three further novels published, *The Hair Shirt* (Hutchinson, 1932), *An April Day* (Hutchinson, 1934) and *Humble Servant* (Methuen, 1936).

35. Doris Westwood to SS, 12 March 1931, Berg.

36. ibid., 25 April 1931.

37. ibid., 20 February 1932.

38. Middleboe, *Edith Olivier*, p. 146.

39. ibid. Lord David Cecil and his wife went first to live at Rockbourne, about eight miles south of Salisbury.

40. GK to SS, 26 June 1933, CUL.

41. Related to me by DS during one of our many interviews.

42. Notes made during an interview with Andrew Motion on 4 July 2001. Motion had written a poem on his pilgrimage to Skyros and his headmaster at Radley, Dennis Silk, who had met GK through SS, thought that GK would be very interested to meet the young man and hear of his journey, since Brooke had been a close friend of his.

43. ibid.

44. SS's pc of Fitz House of 11 April 1933. His invitation to spend the weekend follows on 14 June 1933 (Keynes Collection, CUL).

45. SS to HH, 30 October 1948, in possession of the recipient.

46. GK compiled bibliographies of Jane Austen, Thomas Fuller, Sir Thomas Browne, Edward Gibbon, Donne, Blake, Hazlitt, and SS himself, among others.

47. Interview with Milo Keynes on 7 December 1998.

48. Interview with DS.

49. Interview with Andrew Motion, op. cit.

50. DFC to GK, 26 August 1973, CUL.

51. Stallworthy, J., *Singing School*, p. 83.

52. SS to GK, following his visit of 24 June 1933, CUL.

53. GK to SS, 16 July 1933, CUL.

54. ibid., 20 July 1933.

55. Caption on one of the photographs of SS and ST in the Keynes Collection at CUL.

56. GK had been first attracted to Margaret's sister, Gwen (later Gwen Raverat), then 'Ka' Cox, to whom he had proposed, not knowing of her affair with his close friend, Rupert Brooke.

57. SS to HH, 30 October 1948, in possession of recipient.

58. SS visited the Keynes family for a week from 8 August 1933 at Hexham, near Newcastle-upon-Tyne. He had told GK that he felt 'a bit blue' at the prospect of ST's projected return to Wilsford at the beginning of August and GK had responded with his usual practicality and kindness.

59. Keynes, G., *The Gates of Memory*, p. 234.

60. ibid.

61. Stallworthy, J., *Singing School*, p. 90.

62. These were nicknames GK used of SS and himself in his letters to SS's nephew, Hamo, who kindly lent me the letters to read. The wizard Merlin of Arthurian legend is probably linked to the bard Merlin of Welsh vernacular literature and GK may have named SS 'Merlin' in acknowledgement of his poetic calling. King Pellinore in Malory's *Morte D'Arthur* is the father of three (not four like GK) sons and has no supernatural powers.

63. Keynes, G., *The Gates of Memory*, p. 233.

64. SS to HH, 30 October 1948, in possession of recipient.

65. ibid., 30 May 1950.

66. SS to RHD, 24 September 1964, CUL.

67. SS to PG, 6 April 1955, HRHRC.

68. When, in October 1938, SS was feeling very discouraged about producing another book of poems, he told GK that if he would come to look at his poetry notebooks he might help him put another collection together. He even suggests some dates (3-5

October 1938). The result was almost certainly *Rhymed Ruminations* (privately printed 1939, trade edition 1940). Even EB had failed in his support at this time, judging SS's poems 'too simple', but GK remained very supportive.

69. GK to HS, 30 January 1950, in possession of the recipient.

70. SS to WdlM, 3 February 1952, Beinecke.

71. SS to HH, 4 November 1948, in possession of the recipient.

72. Faber and Faber published the seven poems of RR on 9 November 1933. It was not reprinted until the seven poems, plus two more – 'Asking For It' and 'The Litany of the Lost' – were reprinted in CP (1947).

73. SS to LOM, 10 March 1933, HRHRC. The poems printed in the *Spectator* on 13 March 1933 were 'Mimic Warfare', 'A Premonition', 'The Ultimate Atrocity', 'News from the War-After-Next', and in the *New Statesman* on 25 March 1933 'An Unveiling'.

74. SS to LOM, 18 March 1933, HRHRC.

75. Temple replies to SS's letter on 25 April 1933, saying that he feels that Britain must use force if the League of Nations thinks it necessary. (Sotheby's catalogue of 13 December 1993).

76. 'Ex-Service', published in the *Spectator* on 9 November 1934, was then included in the trade edition of *Vigils* (1935).

77. *Why War?* was published by the League of Nations and International Institute of Intellectual Co-operation in 1933 and was among SS's books when he died. He has marked the Einstein quotation in his copy.

78. SS to RH, 28 February 1934, Beinecke.

79. Excluded from RR before publication, but sent to HMT in a ms collection of poems he made for him at the end of 1952 (private collection).

80. SS to RHD, 3 May 1967, CUL.

81. SS to GK, 30 October 1933, CUL.

82. NB to SS, 2 November 1933, CUL.

83. SS to GK, 29 November 1933, CUL.

84. ibid.

85. ibid.

86. SS to the Heads, 29 December 1933, HRHRC.

87. SS to RH, 29 December 1933, Beinecke. The witnesses at the wedding were Katherine Gatty, Glen Byam Shaw, Richard Gatty, Oliver Gatty and J.S. Morrison.

88. Keynes, *The Gates of Memory*, p. 234.

89. ibid., p. 235.

90. ST to SS, 14 November 1933, Berg.

91. ibid.

92. Middleboe, *Edith Olivier*, p. 153.

93. SS to GK, 8 November 1933, CUL.

94. ST to SS, 31 August 1938, Berg.

95. ST to SS, pc of 13 March 1939, Berg.

96. ST to SS, January 1942 and 4 November 1941 respectively, Berg.

97. Quoted in Sotheby's catalogue 'The Contents of Wilsford Manor', 15 October 1987.

98. Furbank, P.N., *E.M. Forster*, p. 181.

99. Hassell, C., *Ambrosia and Small Beer*, p. 223.

100. OS to SS, 31 October 1933, Pullman.

101. SS to RGH, 9 December 1933, Lilly.

102. SS to the Heads, 20 October 1934, HRHRC.

103. TEL to Nancy Astor, 31 December 1933.

104. The anthology was called *The Coppice* and is now at the University of Iowa.

105. SS to RG, 24 November 1933, Buffalo: 'Many thanks for your good wishes'.

106. NB to SS, 25 October 1933, CUL.

107. This presentation of a dog encouraged SS to compare himself and Hester to the Brownings, who had a spaniel, 'Flush'.

108. SS to AT, [*c.* November 1933], Berg.

109. ES to SS, [*c.* November 1933], Pullman, and quoted in Elborn, G., *Edith Sitwell*, p. 83.

110. Notes taken during interviews with EB's third wife, Claire, on 28 September and 16 and 30 October 1990.

111. The Sassoons stayed at the Hotel Cristina, Algeciras, for the whole of February 1934.

112. SS to LOM, 8 February 1934, HRHRC.

113. SS to GK, 1 February 1934, CUL.

114. The Sassoons stayed at the Grand Hotel Miramar, Malaga, before moving on to Syracuse.

115. SS to HH, 22 March 1950, in possession of recipient.

Chapter 18

1. SS to LG, 1 April 1941, Columbia.

2. SS would later write a poem about that 'wild and warring Queen' titled 'A Remembered Queen' (CP, p. 238).

3. Powell, A., *To Keep the Ball Rolling*, p. 350.

4. This work was done in 1820 by the fashionable Bath architect John Pinch.

5. Lord Heytesbury died in 1891. The poem about him, 'In Heytesbury Wood', was written in March 1935, revised in May 1935 and included in RRu (CP, p. 234).

6. SS sold £1,300 worth of shares in February 1934 and put down a deposit of £1,290 on Heytesbury House with Jackson, Stops and Staff. By selling off other stocks and shares in March 1934, he raised the balance of £11,746. The previous owner was a Captain Henry Jump.

7. SS to GBS, 23 July 1938, CUL (the emphases are SS's). Ten years later, however, he would write to GBS and his wife (17 January 1949), 'O, these villagers and servants! They only think of themselves, and have no decent feeling for one – or gratitude.' (Letter in possession of George Byam Shaw.)

8. SS to RH, 29 December 1933, Beinecke.

9. Keynes, *The Gates of Memory*, p. 235.

10. By 1938, the servants' bill would come to over £1,000 p.a., an enormous amount of money compared with the average working man's annual income of approximately £150.

11. Even in 1955, when Heytesbury House appeared to some to wear a neglected air, the poet Charles Causley described it in glowing terms: 'There was everywhere a gleam of mahogany, walnut, delicate china. There were watercolours and oils, beautifully framed, and hundreds of books, many in leather bindings.' ('Writers Remembered: Siegfried Sassoon', *The Author*, Winter 1989.) Charles Cholmondeley, who visited Heytesbury once, remembers its wealth of fine pictures, one by Richard Dadd (which SS would present to the Tate in 1963 in memory of Dadd's nephew, Julian Dadd, and his brother, Edmund Dadd), some works by the Pre-Raphaelites, whom he collected, a portrait of Lytton Strachey by Henry Lamb, a 'beautiful picture' by William Nicholson, a 'very nice' Eric Kennington of a trooper, Pyne's 'Old Exeter', and a striking portrait of Rachel Beer.

12. Half of the thirteen poems added to GK's limited edition of *Vigils* in 1934 and 1935 make specific references to Heytesbury, though none takes it as the subject matter. In RRu, however, five of the forty-two poems are on some aspect of it – 'Property', 'Outlived by Trees', 'Eulogy of My House', 'In Heytesbury Wood' and 'A Remembered Queen' – while five more use it as their setting.

13. Ackerley, J.R., *My Sister and Myself*, p. 173.

14. TEL to GK, 6 August 1934, Lawrence, T.E., *Selected Letters*, p. 357.

15. ibid.

16. ibid.

17. SS to GK, June 1934, CUL.

18. SS to GK, 24 August 1934, CUL.

19. TEL to GK, 6 August 1934, Lawrence, *Selected Letters*, p. 357.

20. ibid., p. 358.

21. SS to FSw, 3 October 1935, Arkansas.

22. ibid.

23. EB wrote an amusing chapter on SS in *Cricket Country* (p. 44ff.), 'Among the Moderns', where he imagines SS captaining a team of his favourite literary figures.

24. SS to the Heads, 20 October 1934, HRHRC.

25. TEL to GK, 6 August 1934, in *Selected Letters*, p. 357, and SS to LG, 9 January 1935, Columbia.

26. HS to SS, *c.* 1935-36, CUL.

27. ibid., autumn 1938.

28. SS to HS, 12 December 1937, lent to me by HS.

29. SS to GK, 12 August 1935, CUL.

30. SS to GBS, 26 November 1935, CUL.

31. SS to GK, 23 December 1935, CUL.

32. EB called his review of *Vigils* 'The Watch-Tower'; SS to RH, 17 March 1936, Beinecke.

33. SS to GK, 23 December 1935, CUL.

34. ibid.

35. SS to EM, 14 January 1936, Berg.

36. HMT to SS, 17 August 1937, CUL.

37. ES to SS, 22 December 1934, Pullman.

38. The Rev. H.R.L. Sheppard (1880-1937) was vicar of St Martin-in-the-Fields 1914-27 and a canon of St Paul's Cathedral from 1934 onwards.

39. SS and EB were joined on the platform by another writer, Dr Maude Royden, and another ex-soldier, Brigadier General Crozier, the meeting chaired by Sheppard himself.

40. SS read his poems at a PPU rally at the Albert Hall on 27 November 1936, at Bristol on 13 January 1937, Salisbury on 31 January 1937 and Southend-on-Sea on 6 February 1937. (He refers to having given at least five readings in 1936.)

41. Dated 20 October 1936, this is in the original ms at CUL and was first published in the privately printed edition of RRu in 1939. SS also signed his name, with other eminent writers, to a letter in *Time and Tide* urging readers to join the International Peace Campaign. The other signatures were Aldous Huxley, C. Day-Lewis, Rose Macaulay, V.S. Pritchett, Olaf Stapledon, Sylvia Townsend Warner, Rebecca West and Leonard Woolf.

42. SS to HMT, 20 August 1937, HRHRC.

43. SS to LOM, 1 June 1935, HRHRC.

44. SS to MB, 17 May 1935, Hart-Davis, R., *Siegfried Sassoon: Letters to Max Beerbohm*, p. 27.

45. Dated 25 May 1935, a week after TEL's death on 19 May, this is in one of SS's 1930s notebooks (CUL) and was never published in SS's lifetime.

46. SS to PG, 18 March 1955, Brotherton.

47. SS to HMT, 12 November 1943, HRHRC.

48. SS to EB, 22 May 1935, HRHRC.

49. RG produced a biography, *Lawrence and the Arabs*, for Cape in 1928.

50. SS to EB, 25 June 1935, HRHRC. I am indebted to Edward

Maggs, who generously shared his research on the Korda brothers and their projected film on Lawrence with me.

51. Arnold Lawrence visited Heyesbury on 25 June 1935.

52. SS to HS, 1 September 1942, lent to me by HS. Lieutenant Colonel W.F. Stirling, DSO, MC (1880-1958) had known TEL, and SS would write a foreword to his book, *Safety Last*, in 1953.

53. SS to EB, 27 July 1935, HRHRC.

54. Dated 9 September 1935 and titled 'T.E.L.', this unpublished poem is in one of SS's 1930s poetry notebooks at CUL.

55. Quotations are taken from the ms notes of SS's work on the (as it turned out) abortive Alexander Korda film, 'Revolt in the Desert', which SS wrote in pencil in a large-format watercolour book, which he also illustrated (in possession of London booksellers Maggs Bros). Many years later, in July 1959, when GBS was Director of the Shakespeare Theatre at Stratford-upon-Avon, he sent SS Terence Rattigan's play about TEL and asked SS's opinion on it. When SS expressed approval, GBS decided to take it on and sent Sir Alec Guinness to talk to SS about TEL. Their meeting, which went well, took place at Heytesbury and Guinness subsequently appeared, to great acclaim, in Rattigan's play *Ross*.

56. *Listener*, Rack Z, 69 and 70 (1935).

57. 'Aunt Eudora and the Poets', *Spectator*, 31 January 1936; 'Educating Aunt Eudora', *Spectator*, 28 February 1936; 'Querkes, Farmonger and Dusp', *Spectator*, 19 June 1936.

58. Published on 7 August 1936 in the *Manchester Evening News*.

59. The publication of 15,720 copies of SP by Faber and Faber on 3 September 1936 was preceded by serialization from June to August in the American *Nash's Pall Mall Magazine*.

60. Ms notes on SP at IWM.

61. SS to GK, 8 September 1936, CUL.

62. *Morning Post*, 4 September 1936 and *The Sunday Times*, 6 September 1936.

63. SS to RGH, 25 September 1936, Lilly.

64. The ms notebook of part of *Sherston's Progress* has the quotation from *Pilgrim's Progress* on the page following the title page.

65. SP, p. 170.

66. SS to Mr Hardcastle, 29 October 1938, HRHRC. Hardcastle (1899-c.1972) was the vicar of St Mary's, Elsworthy Road, Primrose Hill, London. He had attended Henley House after SS and first wrote to him after reading SS's description of it in OC.

67. SS to EB, 27 December 1935, HRHRC. 'War Experience' is dated 9 April 1929 in the CUL poetry notebook and was first published in *Vigils*.

68. SP, p. 58.

69. SS to RGH, 25 September 1936, Lilly.

70. SS to RH, 17 March 1936, Beinecke.

71. 'The Heaven of Our Hearts [to H.R.L.S.]' was written on 11 August 1937 (the date on the CUL ms) and published in the *St Martin's Review* for December 1937, but nowhere else:

> Heaven is that state of which we
>   are not sure.
> Beyond this world I dare not hope
>   to endure;
> But in my heart and my
>   time-journeying head
> There's heaven on earth for friends
>   beloved and dead.
> You and your work for Christ, for
>   whom you died,
> In long remembrance live beatified.
> And your brave soul, which saw the
>   seraphim,

In hoots of heart-won heaven will
speak for him.

72. GBS to RHD, 28 April 1974
(CUL), re. an entry for SS in the
Dictionary of National Biography that
RHD was preparing.

73. SS to SCC, 18 April 1938.

74. SS's diary, quoted by J.S.
Roberts in *Siegfried Sassoon*, p. 262.

75. SS told GK that this 'grand
poem [he] wrote about seeing George
for the first time', which he believed to
be his 'very finest', was 'written in two
minutes in a state of mental release
induced by whiskey, orange juice,
sugar, and hot water' (letter of 29
August 1943 at CUL). Puzzlingly, the
poem is dated 26 October 1937 in the
CUL ms, four days before George's
first birthday, but it may represent
the date of revision rather than
composition.

76. 'Ancestral Admonition', 1930s
poetry notebook, CUL.

77. SS to HMT, 20 August 1937,
HRHRC.

78. Ackerley, J.R., *My Sister and
Myself*, p. 168.

79. SS's diary, Christmas 1936.

80. See D2, p. 240.

81. SS to the Heads, [*c.* summer
1937], HRHRC.

82. ibid.

83. ibid.

84. Hart-Davis, *Letters to Max*, p.
84.

85. SS to GBS, 11 August 1937,
CUL.

86. ibid., 28 November 1937, CUL.

87. The Sassoons stayed at the
Excelsior Hotel, Rapallo, from 21
April to 18 May 1938.

Chapter 19

1. SS to Michael Thorpe, 14 March
1967, in *Letters to a Critic*, p. 20.

2. SS to Mr Hardcastle, 2 October
1938, HRHRC.

3. ibid., 29 October 1938.

4. ibid.

5. Though SS sent no formal letter
of resignation to the PPU in 1937,
when they finally sent a 'friendly
enquiry' to him in mid-1940 about his
position, he replied with a letter
which caused the Secretary of the
PPU to record in the minutes for 7
and 8 September 1940: 'The Council
felt that under the circumstances it
would be best to regard him as no
longer wishing to be a Sponsor.' This
information was kindly sent to me by
the Honorary Archivist of the
present-day PPU, Bill Hetherington.
SS wrote to TS (10 May 1938, Berg):
'Mussolini is passing through Rapallo
on Saturday. The whole town is
plastered with enormous
white-washed inscriptions of "DUCE"
... in letters 4 ft high.'

6. 'Of course you can "read out my
name" in Queen's Hall, if it does
anyone any good! – which I doubt – to
hear the name of an obsolete amateur
writer who dislikes *all* forms of
political activity,' SS wrote to
Rosamond Lehmann (3 June 1938,
Lehmann Collection, King's College,
Cambridge), who was on the
committee of the Association of
Writers for Intellectual Liberty and
helping to organize the meeting of 8
June 1938.

7. EMF to SS, 27 January 1938,
private collection.

8. SS to TS, 8 September 1936,
Berg.

9. ST's journal, 12 October 1938,
Berg.

10. SS to RGH, 25 September 1936,
Lilly.

11. ibid.

12. It is interesting to compare
Woolf's re-creation of Jacob's life in
Jacob's Room (a novel SS praised
highly) through a series of crucial
scenes, with SS's similar approach in
OC.

13. SS to MB, 21 August 1937,
Hart-Davis, *Letters to Max*, p. 57.

14. SS to EB, 1 November 1938,
HRHRC.

15. SS's notes on OC are at CUL.

16. ibid.

17. SS to HMT, 13 February 1938, HRHRC.

18. ibid.

19. Notes on OC, CUL.

20. OC, pp. 30-31.

21. ibid., p. 65.

22. ibid., p. 189. It is significant that SS's description of his uncle Don is the only part of OC that he rewrote at his mother's suggestion: she felt that Uncle Don had not been done full justice by the Thornycroft family.

23. 4,500 copies of *The Complete Memoirs of George Sherston* were published on 4 October 1937 by Faber and Faber.

24. Hart-Davis, *Letters to Max*, p. 67.

25. Since it would bring SS to the end of his formal education, his original intention was to call this last third of the book 'Educational Experiences', a suggestion Faber rejected.

26. SS to WdlM, 15 October 1938, Beinecke. Columbia has what appears to be a fair copy of the ms of OC, which is written into three bound volumes by SS. Volume 1 contains Book 1, chapters 1-8; Volume II contains Book 1, chapters 9-11, and Book II, chapters 1-3; Volume III (which is far more untidy and contains more corrections) contains Book II, chapters 4-6. The whole is clearly a transcription, since SS notes after 'Prelude', 'Transcribing begun 20 January 1937'. Though words are changed, none of the changes are radical, but mainly stylistic: e.g., for Wirgie's 'gurgling laugh' SS has substituted 'mouth-closed laugh'. There is also a pull of the title-page vignette by Gwen Raverat and several loose items inserted into the ms, including an obituary of Tom Homewood of March 1939. There is a proof copy of the ts of OC at the Berg, but this is uncorrected and is unlikely to have been SS's copy.

27. OC, p. 197.

28. ibid., p. 243.

29. ibid., p. 300.

30. SS to HMT, 27 March 1943, HRHRC.

31. Writing to SS on 27 January 1938, EMF would almost certainly have seen all but the last chapter of OC when he made his choice. (Private collection.)

32. ibid.

33. ibid.

34. ibid.

35. ibid.

36. OC, p. 129.

37. ibid., p. 137.

38. Writing to a fellow Old Marlburian, Sir Alan Lascelles, for example, in 1961, SS admitted that he had changed his teacher Mr Gould's form from the Lower Fifth to the Middle Fifth, because the former 'looked a bit too local'. The changes are usually minor and suggest that style won over content on occasions.

39. Michael Thorpe first makes this point in his review of SS's diaries, 'The Road to Edingthorpe', *Focus on Robert Graves*, vol. 1, no. 10, Winter 1989-90, pp. 9-12.

40. OC notes, CUL.

41. EMF to SS, 27 January 1938 op. cit.

42. OC, p. 142.

43. SS:PP, p. 129, from SS's talk 'To Some Boys at Oundle'.

44. OC, p. 143.

45. ibid., p. 260.

46. ibid., p. 25. See, for example, Paul Moeyes, *Siegfried Sassoon*, p. 200, and J.S. Roberts, *Siegfried Sassoon*, pp. 265-6.

47. Thorpe, p. 121.

48. SS to RH, 15 November 1938, Beinecke.

49. SS to GK, [September 1938], CUL.

50. Desmond MacCarthy to SS, 20 September 1938, David Holmes catalogue, Philadelphia, Winter, 1991/2.

51. *London Mercury*, October 1938,

pp. 570-2. It is interesting to note that EB (as SS reports to HMT on 4 July 1938 (HRHRC)) is initially unsure what to say about OC.

52. Introduction to OC by Michael Thorpe, Faber paperback, 1968, p. 11.

53. SS to Hardcastle, 2 October 1938, HRHRC.

54. Hart-Davis, *Letters to Max*, p. 40. SS noted in a letter to TS that, while MB was 'enchanted' by OC, he found the final chapters only 'quite satisfactory' (letter of 10 May 1938, Berg).

55. Hart-Davis, *Letters to Max*, p. 40.

56. Quoted in Keynes, p. 98.

57. SS to GK, 10 January 1939, CUL. Faber had sold just over 10,000 copies by 21 January 1939.

58. SS to AL, 21 November 1961, CUL.

59. ibid.

Chapter 20

1. SS to HS, 12 October 1939.

2. SS's diary for late 1939/early 1940.

3. SS to HS, 24 September 1939.

4. SS to MB, 1 November 1939, Hart-Davis, *Letters to Max*, p. 80. The Beerbohms lived in the Schiffs' cottage until bombed out of it in August 1944. They did not return to Rapallo until 1947. Sydney Schiff was the wealthy brother-in-law of Ada Leverson, who wrote novels under the name Stephen Hudson, but was better known as a patron of other artists.

5. 'Heart and Soul' is dated 29 October 1938 in SS's 1930 notebook at CUL. SS wrote to SCC on 12 August 1939: 'I am glad you liked that poem "Heart and Soul". I think the last 2 lines of the 1st stanza have some quiet magic in them ... The line "Weald of Youth, a remembered word" ... epitomises a great deal of *The Old Century* and the intense feeling I have about the view from Weirleigh gardens.'

6. There is an unpublished poem in a 1940s notebook of SS's at CUL, written the day after war was declared, which opens: 'To-day I'm old [sic] by five and twenty years / Since 'War Declared' tolled tocsins to my ears ...'

7. Another unpublished poem in the CUL poetry notebooks, dated 23 September 1939, is titled '(Fifty Years Between Us) To a Child'.

8. SS to SCC, 24 August 1942, HRHRC.

9. SS to WdlM, 28 December 1942, Beinecke.

10. The bulk of these unpublished poems are contained in SS's poetry notebooks at CUL.

11. Published in the *Observer* on 26 May and 2 June 1940 respectively, these were reprinted in the trade edition of RRu in October 1940. The only other war poems (as such) published were 'Go, Words, on Winds of War' in the *Spectator*, 2 April 1943 (not reprinted), 'To Some Who Say Production Won the War', the *Observer*, 6 May 1945 (not reprinted), and an earlier poem, 'Litany of the Lost', the *Observer*, 18 November 1945 (reprinted from RR).

12. Apollyon is the 'foul-fiend' who assaulted Christian on his pilgrimage through the Valley of Humiliation in *Pilgrim's Progress*. The name means 'destroyer' in Greek. SS had almost certainly taken the reference from a letter written to him by HMT on 8 November 1938 about a visit to WdlM, who had 'mentioned a sensation as of hovering black pinions. Apollyon! And once it was Apollo we hoped' (CUL).

13. SS to MB, 29 May 1940, Hart-Davis, *Letters to Max*, p. 85.

14. 'On Scratchbury Camp' was first published in *Country Life*, 25 June 1943, then in EE.

15. SS's 1940s poetry notebooks, CUL.

16. SS to GK, 18 September 1939, CUL.

17. SS's diary for 3 September 1939.

18. SS wrote to GK on 18 September 1939 that the Ministry of Information had written to say that he was 'on their list of potentially useful authors', but that it signified nothing, since they just told him to go on doing what he usually did (CUL). His ironic response, in the same letter to GK, is 'that we *must* fight Hitler to the last drop of someone else's blood'. SS donated an illustrated ms of *Vigils* to the Red Cross sale of 24 and 25 July 1940 which fetched 45 guineas. His illuminated ms of RRu fetched £45 at the Red Cross sale of 13-15 October 1942.

19. SS to EB, 18 April 1943, CUL.

20. SS to HMT, 1 March 1943 and 5 February 1939 respectively.

21. Unpublished poem from 1940s notebooks, CUL.

22. SS to WdlM, 28 December 1942, Beinecke.

23. SS wrote to AT about the Hirths throughout the Second World War, saying how much he worried about them, but was unable to contact them. Johanna Hirth told HS, in a letter of 25 December 1958, that she and Walther had been through a terrible time in the war and had not dared to write to old friends in England because of the atrocities Hitler had committed.

24. SS to TS, 21 February 1940, Berg.

25. ibid., 30 April 1940.

26. SS to HMT, 1 May 1940 and 17 November 1942, HRHRC. SS also used the spider imagery in one of his few published poems of 1940, 'Ideologies': 'Meanwhile where Babels once were built we find / A spider in his web among the weeds.' (CP, p. 244.) The reference is clearly to the Second World War.

27. See SS to TS, 24 September 1939 (Berg), re. his relief at not being turned out of Heytesbury House during the war: '(Hester interviewed the Southern Command Land Agent, who called here, and he seemed to realise that we can't *quite* be treated like Jews in Germany, so I think the danger is past.) If they *had* done such a thing it would just about have finished me off.'

28. SS to EB, 18 September 1941, HRHRC.

29. SS to HMT, 21 July 1941, quoted in Christie's catalogue, 3 April 1992, p. 13.

30. SJ, p. 193.

31. ibid.

32. SS to Oliver [?Stonor], 1 September 1940, quoted by the recipient in a letter to RHD of 14 January 1981, CUL.

33. ibid.

34. SS tells TS that he *is* being asked to pronounce on the war by newspapers and magazines: 'But I am resolved to say *nothing.*'

35. Seventy-five copies of RRu were printed for SS and GK at the Chiswick Press in July 1939, with a title page designed by LW. SS's original ms ran to twenty-eight poems only, but he added five new poems at the proof stage. The book was designed by GK with the approval of SS, who found its diminutive proportions (slightly smaller than what today would be called A6) 'amusing': 'Max [Beerbohm] will be pleased,' he told GK (Keynes, *The Gates of Memory*, p. 102).

36. SS to BH, 30 August 1940, Congress. BH's firm, Viking, published RRu in America in 1941. Faber published 2,500 copies on 17 October 1940 in pale-blue cloth lettered in gold, with a yellow paper dust-jacket printed in black. The book was not reprinted.

37. HS, who knew GS well as a child, admired this poem and printed it, together with 'Wealth of Awareness', in a limited edition of not more than five copies in 1941, in a printer's shop near Wellingborough, Northants.

38. 'Meeting and Parting', 'To My Son', 'A Blessing', 'Progressions'.

39. 'Property', 'Outlived by Trees', 'Eulogy of My House', 'In Heytesbury Wood', 'A Remembered Queen', 'Pre-Historic Burials', 'Antiquities', 'A View of Old Exeter', 'Blunden's Beech', 'November Dusk', 'Wealth of Awareness'.

40. 'On Edington Hill', '878-1935', 'Thoughts in 1938', 'Gloria Mundi'.

41. 'While Reading a Ghost Story', 'Metamorphosis'.

42. 'Acceptance', 'Heart and Soul', 'Progressions', 'Old Music', 'Doggerel About Old Days'.

43. Dated 15 February 1939 in the CUL poetry notebooks, this poem was written before the official outbreak of war. It was, SS told GK in a letter of 1 May 1939 (CUL), 'specially praised' by EB.

44. RGH to SS, 11.8.39 , Lilly.

45. ibid.

46. SS to RGH, 5 December 1940, Lilly.

47. SS, *On Poetry*, p. 10 et passim. SS's lecture was published for the University of Bristol by J.W. Arrowsmith Ltd, 12 Small Street, Bristol, in 1939. SS gave his talk as the Arthur Kemp Memorial Lecture on 16 March 1939. He had also given a (private) talk, 'What Hope for Poetry', to the Bank of England Literary Society in 1935. Though this was never published, his ms notes for it survive in the hands of a private collector and an extract from it is included in SS:PP, pp. 121-3. The ideas from his unpublished *Listener* commission, 'A Poet on Poetry', were repeated in another article on the subject, 'Aliveness in Literature', *Fortnightly Review*, cxlviii, November 1940. Later, in 1951, shortly after his son became a pupil at Oundle, he would give a talk 'To Some Boys at Oundle', in which he again stressed his desire for 'aliveness and durability' in literature. (See SS:PP, pp. 128-30.)

48. SS to TS, 26 May 1939, Berg, with a copy of his lecture.

49. WY, p. 112.

50. ibid.

51. SS, *On Poetry*, p. 8.

52. SS to WdlM, 15 October 1938, Beinecke.

53. e.g., SS refers to a 'paragraph of cultured patronage by [Basil] de Selincourt in the *Observer*' (SS to EB, 23 November 1940, HRHRC).

54. See the *TLS*, 2 November 1940.

55. SS to EB, 11 January 1943, HRHRC.

56. SS to TS, 28 December 1940, Berg.

57. SS to GK, 1 May 1939, CUL.

58. ibid., 2 July 1939.

59. Hassall was eventually awarded the A.C. Benson Medal of the Royal Society of Literature jointly with John Gawsworth on 5 April 1939, but SS resigned over the muddle, mismanagement and procedural irregularities he believed had led to the inclusion of Gawsworth. SS had been a Fellow of the RSL since 1924.

60. Hassall, *Ambrosia and Small Beer*, p. 79.

61. cf. Edward Lear's 'The Dong with a Luminous Nose'.

62. SS, *On Poetry*, p. 7.

63. CP, p. 234.

64. SS to SCC, 12 August 1939, HRHRC.

65. SS to WdlM, 6 August 1939, Beinecke.

66. See SS:PP, pp. 150, 151 and 194.

67. SS was also re-reading one of TH's great loves and friend, the postman poet William Barnes, at this time and Addison, his Sir Roger de Coverley having always been 'one of [his] favourites in all literature' (SS to WdlM, 6 August 1939, Beinecke). Both writers feature archaic diction.

68. TEL's copy of *The Dynasts* was among a number of precious books and mss deposited by SCC at Heytesbury House for safety during the war and it is possible that SS's re-reading of it there preceded his decision to write about it. His 'The Dynasts in War-Time' was eventually published in the *Spectator*, 6 February 1942, though started earlier. 'Hardy as I knew Him' was published in *John O'London's Weekly*, 7 June 1940, and 'Hardy's Verse', a review of *The Selected Poems of Thomas Hardy*, in the *Spectator*, 6 September 1940.

69. Faber published 3,000 copies of *Poems Newly Selected* on 14 November 1940. It contained fifty-eight poems chosen from *Selected Poems* (1925), *Satirical Poems* (1926), *The Heart's Journey* (1928) and *Vigils* (1935). It may be that in 1940 Faber did not want to include poems from the newly published *Rhymed Ruminations* in case it spoilt sales of the latter, but even in the second issue of *Poems Newly Selected* in 1949 nothing from *Rhymed Ruminations* was added.

70. SS to HMT, 4 December 1940, HRHRC.

71. WY, p. 160.

72. 'I have felt sad about poor Lady Ottoline's sudden death,' SS wrote to TS on 26 April 1938 (Berg). 'She was a very good friend and I so much admired her courage – which she showed in ill-health, never complaining, however much pain she had to endure.'

73. SS to HMT, 28 May 1940, HRHRC.

74. ibid., 4 December 1940.

75. ibid.

76. ibid., 9 May 1941.

77. SS's diary for 22 August 1939.

78. SS to EB, 18 April 1943, CUL.

79. SS to TS, 9 December 1941, Berg.

80. SS to GK, 31 October 1951, CUL.

81. ibid., 18 July 1945.

82. Notes taken from several interviews with Claire Blunden (née Poynting) in 1990 and 1991.

83. Will Rothenstein visited with a dozen young architects serving with the Artillery Survey Companies in July 1941, to show them the pictures at Heytesbury House. Rothenstein stayed three nights with the Sassoons and he and SS had 'some fine talks' about their beloved Max Beerbohm.

84. SS to HMT, 17 November 1942, HRHRC.

85. Edward Seago, RWS, RBS (1910-1955), was a landscape painter, like his teacher, Sir John Alfred Arnesby Brown, RA (1866-1955).

86. Line from an unpublished poem, dated 27 May 1942, in SS's 1940s poetry notebooks at CUL.

87. *Reader's Digest*, February 1998, p. 65.

88. *Independent*, 3 May 2001.

89. SS to PG, 25 September 1947, Brotherton.

90. SS to GK, 25 September 1942, CUL.

91. SS to HMT, 24 August 1942, HRHRC.

92. SS to SCC, 22 June 1942, quoted in Cockerell, *The Best of Friends*, p. 88.

93. SS to GBS, 18 March 1941, CUL.

Chapter 21

1. The original ms and ts of WY (with some omissions), together with galley proofs and SS's own autograph notes and outlines for the book, are contained in seven folders at Columbia University. Both the ms and ts are heavily revised and Chapter 2 almost completely rewritten, mainly to conceal the true nature of his Aunt Rachel's dementia (which SS believed to be syphilis). The ms is written into a large, unlined notebook, with a watercolour by SS on the inside of the front cover of green trees, peacock-blue fields beyond, and lavender and cream skies, signed 'S. Fudgewell pinx$^{t.}$'

2. SS to SCC, 22 June 1942, in Cockerell, *The Best of Friends*, p. 88.

3. Though there was no serialization of WY, SS and GK had fifty copies of an extract from it printed as a pamphlet, *Early Morning Long Ago*, in March 1941. Faber published 10,000 copies of WY on 15 October 1942 and issued a reprint on 28 May 1948. The book has been out of print since 1958. The original edition was of 'war economy' standard, its blue cloth binding covered with a pale blue paper dust-jacket printed in red and brown. In addition to the dedication to GBS, it contained a frontispiece of 'THE AUTHOR' (a photograph of SS taken at Canterbury in November 1914), a wood engraving by Reynolds Stone on the title page (of a man on horseback) and the two-line quotation from SS's 'Heart and Soul' already referred to. Viking also published 2,500 copies in New York on 23 October 1942.

4. WY, pp. 206-7.

5. See *New Statesman*, xxv, 6 February 1943 and *TLS*, 31 October 1942.

6. SS to HS, 1 December 1942.

7. McMaster University Library, Hamilton, Ontario, Canada. Wells's claim to be living in Gosse's old house is not correct. Gosse had lived at 17, not 13, Hanover Terrace.

8. Quoted by SS in a letter to GK of 29 August 1943, CUL. Goff had gone straight into the RAF from Clifton College in 1941 and was subsequently posted to North Africa. Landing in Algiers with secondary reinforcements, he wrote to SS from there in 1943.

9. ibid.

10. Interview with Martyn Goff, 19 September 2001.

11. Keynes's *Bibliography* has no record of a reprint until 1948, though SS tells him of one planned quite specifically in a letter of 8 December 1942, CUL.

12. SS to HMT, 17 November 1942, HRHRC.

13. ibid.

14. SS to EM, 27 March 1941, Berg.

15. ibid., 24 February 1940.

16. SS to GK, 1 April 1941 and 22 June 1942, CUL.

17. ibid., 22 June 1942.

18. SS to Percy Muir, 16 September 1942, private collection.

19. When, on 3 October 1947, SS was asked by Mr Burnett of *Story Magazine* for an example of his work to include in his anthology, *A Hundred of the World's Greatest Living Authors*, he chose Chapter 3 of WY (letters at University of Princeton Library).

20. SS to TS, 23 September 1942, collection of HS.

21. WY, p. 70.

22. ibid., p. 73.

23. See SS:MWP, p. 77.

24. OS to SS, 27 October 1942, Pullman.

25. SS to RH, 9 July 1941, Beinecke.

26. See extract from SS's talk 'To Some Boys at Oundle', SS:PP, p. 129.

27. ibid.

28. Folder 5 of the WY material at Columbia.

29. SS to EB, 14 February 1940, HRHRC.

30. SS to GK, 6 October 1942, CUL.

31. WY, p. 60.

32. ibid., pp. 60-1.

33. ibid., p. 255.

34. ibid., p. 104.

35. ibid., pp. 11-12.

36. ibid., p. 188.

37. SS to GK, 25 September 1942, CUL.

38. Folder 5 of the WY material at Columbia.

39. SS to GK, 19 November 1942, CUL.

40. 'The Hardened Heart' is dated April 1942 in the original ms at CUL. It was first published in the *Observer* on 13 August 1944 before appearing in the privately printed *Common Chords* (1951).

Chapter 22

1. The epigraph is an unpublished

poem dated 2 September 1943 entitled 'Gone', in SS's CUL poetry notebooks. The chapter title is taken from another, untitled, CUL poem.

2. SS to SCC, 5 June 1940, Cockerell, *The Best of Friends*, pp. 78-9.

3. SS to HMT, 27 March 1943, HRHRC.

4. SS to GK, 29 August 1943, CUL.

5. SS to HMT, 4 December 1940, HRHRC.

6. EMF to SS, 3 June 1942, Columbia.

7. Ausonius (*c.* 310–*c.* 395) wrote poems on a wide variety of subjects and was particularly interested in verse catalogues.

8. SS to HMT, 20 July 1942, HRHRC.

9. ibid.

10. SS to SCC, 23 July 1941, HRHRC.

11. SS to Angela Baddeley, 12 June 1942, letter in possession of George Byam Shaw. See SS:MWP, pp. 201-2.

12. ibid.

13. SS had conflicting feelings on the subject of SCC's stay in September 1939, writing to TS on 17 September 1939, for example: 'He is a great help, as I find continuous talk about the War very trying and he does his best to discuss "something else".' (Berg.)

14. ST to SS, 22 August 1939, Berg.

15. See ST to SS, 4 November 1941, Berg.

16. See SS to GBS: 'There he sat – an artificial person – outwardly very much like "one of the chorus".' (CUL.)

17. SS to GBS, 23 September 1942, CUL.

18. SS to GK, 25 September 1942, CUL.

19. ibid.

20. SS to HS, 1 December 1942.

21. See SS to SCC, 25 December 1941 and 22 June 1942, in Cockerell, *The Best of Friends*, pp. 86 and 88.

22. SS to WdlM, 29 March 1943, Beinecke.

23. GBS, who had joined 1st Battalion, Royal Scots, in 1940 with his brother James Byam Shaw, was sent with James to join 6th Brigade in Burma. Two days after James was shot in the leg, GBS was wounded more seriously, a bullet entering through his left thigh into his scrotum, then exiting through his right thigh, damaging the sciatic nerve in his right leg as it did so. He also lost one of his testicles. Though he concealed the severity of his condition initially from his wife, he wrote to SS with full details shortly afterwards, because he was his 'best friend'. (GBS to SS, 17 May 1943, CUL.)

24. SS to GK, 29 August 1943, CUL.

25. Notes taken at Sotheby sale of December 1994. Sir Philip Sassoon (1888-1939) had died shortly before the Second World War at the age of fifty of complications of a streptococcal throat infection. His sister, the Marchioness of Cholmondeley (1894-1989) died aged ninety-five leaving £118,221,949. She and SS remained in touch until his death in 1967 and she paid at least one visit to Heytesbury House, where SS teased her by showing her his private diaries but not allowing her to read them. (Charles Cholmondeley remembers her relating this story with some amusement and I am grateful to him for it.)

26. SS to WdlM, 1 August 1943, Beinecke. This appears to have been SS's first meeting with Sir Ronald Storrs, whom he invited to visit him at Heytesbury. There are at least three letters from Storrs to SS, planning the visit and commenting on it.

27. SS to SCC, 29 December 1943, Cockerell, *The Best of Friends*, p. 115.

28. SS to WdlM, 1 August 1943, Beinecke.

29. ibid.

30. SS to SCC, 31 October 1949, Cockerell, *The Best of Friends*, p. 197.

31. Subtitled 'Verses Written by Members of the Eighth Army in Sicily and Italy, July 1943–March 1944' and with a foreword by the former Commander of the Eighth Army, Lieutenant-General Sir Oliver Leese, Bart. KCB, CBE, DSO, this was published by George G. Harrap in 1945.

32. SS to SCC, 30 December 1953, Cockerell, *The Best of Friends*, p. 228.

33. ibid.

34. SS to GK, 20 June 1943, CUL.

35. SS to TS, 5 January 1945, Berg.

36. SS to GK, 16 July 1943, CUL.

37. ibid., 14 December 1944.

38. SS to TS, 15 May 1944, Berg.

39. WY brought SS £1,374 in its first six months, with a further £80 to come from Foyle's Book Club.

40. Greenways was owned and run by a Mrs Vivien Hancock at Codford St Peter, approximately three miles from Heytesbury. It had originally been called Ashton Gifford House.

41. SS to TS, 1 May 1944, Berg.

42. Unpublished in SS's lifetime, this poem is in the CUL poetry notebooks, dated 25 December 1947. There is a slim possibility that SS is referring to HG's first miscarriage, though he does refer on a number of occasions to her unwillingness to have a second child after what she had found a traumatic first birth.

43. SS to Angela Baddeley, 10 May 1944, in possession of George Byam Shaw.

44. ibid.

45. SS to GK, 4 May 1944, CUL.

46. Unpublished poem from CUL poetry notebooks, dated 17 April 1944. See also 'A Private Peace' from the same notebooks.

47. SS to GK, 19 April 1944, CUL.

48. SS's diary for 27 July 1944.

49. i.e., Sir Frederick Morgan, Chief of Staff to the Supreme Allied Command 1943-9 and Deputy Chief of Staff to General Eisenhower 1944-5.

50. Middleboe, *Edith Olivier*, p. 201

51. SS to HMT, 16 May 1945, HRHRC.

52. Dated 3 May 1945 in the CUL poetry notebooks and published in the *Observer*, 6 May 1945.

53. SS to GK, 18 July 1945, CUL.

Chapter 23

1. Roberts, J.S., *Siegfried Sassoon*, p. 290.

2. ibid.

3. LG to SS, 27 May 1945, CUL.

4. SS to FSw, 9 August 1945, Arkansas.

5. HG was given £7,000 by her mother to buy the Grange, Winterbourne Dauntsey, in 1945. It was only five minutes' walk from Lady Gatty's current house near Salisbury and twenty-two miles from Heytesbury House. For the first few years she would regularly appear on the midday bus at Heytesbury and SS would just as regularly insist that she return on the 5 p.m. bus.

6. EB to RHD, July 1948, CUL.

7. EB to SS, 29 April 1947, HRHRC.

8. Claire Blunden to me in an interview of 28 September 1990.

9. SS to EB, 7 August 1947, HRHRC.

10. SS's diary, quoted in J.S. Roberts' *Siegfried Sassoon*, p. 285.

11. Related to me by TS's great-niece, Lady Lettice Strickland-Constable, whose great-aunt had confided in her at the time. TS herself had had to give up her painting career after marrige.

12. SS and GS stayed in lodgings shared with the Byam Shaws in Minehead from 29 August to 8 September 1945.

13. SS to GK, 18 July 1945, CUL.

14. SS's diary, quoted in Roberts, *Siegfried Sassoon*, p. 43.

15. SS to GK, op. cit.

16. Interview with Mrs Hancock on 25 April 1991.

17. ibid.

18. SS told GK that he lent Mrs Hancock £8,000 at a low interest rate, though he elsewhere refers to lending her £10,000.

19. Interview with Mrs Hancock, 25 April 1991.

20. See SS to GK, 22 November 1944, CUL; the quotation is from SS's 'In me, past, present, future meet' (CP, p. 178).

21. Barber first wrote to SS in March 1946 because he admired his work so much, he told me during an interview of 20 June 1991. In his reply SS referred him to Mrs Hancock, told him of GS being down for Oundle and said he would be 'very pleased' to see him at Heytesbury.

22. Interview with DS.

23. ibid. In the late fifties SS would lend Barber the money to restore the house he had bought in Oundle, Pain's Cottage, at a low interest rate. £500 of this was still outstanding after SS's death.

24. SS to MB, 28 June 1948, Hart-Davis, *Siegfried Sassoon: Letters to Max Beerbohm*, p. 100.

25. GK's unparalleled Blake collection, amassed largely during his work on a bibliography of the poet, included several very fine Blake paintings and some original plates from his illuminated books.

26. HH had served with the Glosters in the Second World War before becoming an official war artist.

27. HH to RHD, 29 February 1968, CUL.

28. Interview with Haro Hodson on 19 March 1991.

29. ibid.

30. SS's diary, February 1948.

31. SS to SCC, 17 December 1945, HRHRC. SS told JA in 1949 how he had once found a young soldier asleep in the ditch in front of his house: '"Wonderfully good-looking chap", said S, "most beautiful, mild, gentle sort of boy, I almost asked him back to tea." This was at a time when he was

particularly lonely.' (Ackerley, *My Sister and Myself*, p. 177.)

32. SS to GBS, 30 October 1945, CUL.

33. SCC to SS, 15 December 1945, notes taken from Sotheby's catalogue of 18 July 1991.

34. SS to GK, 14 December 1944, CUL.

35. SS to HMT, 16 May 1945, HRHRC.

36. ibid., 23 February 1944.

37. SS to SCC, 15 December 1944, HRHRC.

38. ibid.

39. SJ, p. 7.

40. ibid., p. 9. Reynolds Stone's wood engraving on the title page of a wooded and pillared entrance is of Garsington Manor.

41. ibid., pp. 63 and 62. Michael Thorpe quotes Dylan Thomas's praise of SS's 'lovely chapter about [Owen]' (*Letters to Vernon Watkins*, London, 1957, p. 103) in Thorpe, *Siegfried Sassoon*, p. 171.

42. SJ, p. 87.

43. ibid., p. 78.

44. ibid., pp. 89-90.

45. SS to GK, 19 April 1944, CUL.

46. SJ, p. 224.

47. *Time and Tide*, 2 March 1946.

48. ibid.

49. 6,000 more copies of SJ were published in October 1947, with the imprint Faber & Faber and The Book Society.

50. HMT to SS, 20 December 1945, CUL.

51. ES to John Lehmann, 21 January 1946, Dept of Mss, BL.

52. See SS to GK, 29 April 1946, CUL.

53. Viking published 3,500 on 25 March 1946, their largest edition of SS's three autobiographies. Two chapters of SJ were sold before publication for serialization in the *Atlantic Monthly*.

54. SS to RH, 21 July 1946, Beinecke.

55. SS to EB, 23 July 1946, HRHRC.

56. SS to GK, 16 October 1945, CUL.

57. See SS to EB, 21 September 1945, HRHRC.

58. SS to WdlM, 6 February 1946, Beinecke.

59. SS to EB, 17 January 1946, HRHRC.

60. See WY, p. 29ff. SS wrote to a bookseller friend, Percy Muir, on 14 April 1942, asking if he had 'any good Meredith books. I have gone back to him with gusto, and rather crave for a really fine 1862 *Modern Love* and a first edition of *Richard Feverel*.' (Private collection.)

61. SJ, pp. 122 and 123.

62. SS first met Helen Waddell on 19 July 1945 to discuss the possibility of a book on Meredith.

63. SS to HMT, 11 October 1950, HRHRC.

64. SS to GBS, 19 May 1947, CUL.

65. SS to T.H. White, 21 March 1951, HRHRC.

66. Helen Waddell presented SS with a signed copy of *Peter Abelard*.

67. Quoted by DFC in her biography, *Helen Waddell*, Gollancz, 1990, p. 347.

68. SS to SCC, 11 November 1947, HRHRC.

69. SS to L.P. Hartley, 25 September 1948, CUL.

70. See SS to EB, 24 April 1947, HRHRC, and Sotheby's sale catalogue, 18 July 1991, p. 74, for SS's Meredith collection.

71. SS to L.P. Hartley, 25 September 1948, CUL.

72. SS, *Meredith*, p. 4.

73. ibid., p. 33.

74. SS to Angela Baddeley, 8 February 1949, in possession of George Byam Shaw.

75. SS to EB, 15 December 1946, HRHRC.

76. In DFC's *Centenary Essay*, written to coincide with the SS Centenary celebrations at Weirleigh

in September 1986, a copy sent to me by the author.

77. SS to HMT, 20 February 1946, HRHRC.

78. ibid.

79. cf. Meredith's *The Shaving of Shagpat* with SS's *The Daffodil Murderer*.

80. cf. Meredith's destruction of *British Songs* and SS's burning of *Sonnets and Verses* (1909).

81. *Meredith*, p. 8.

82. ibid., p. 47.

83. ibid., p. 21.

84. ibid.

85. ibid., p. 46.

86. ibid., p. 43.

87. SS to Angela Baddeley, 8 February 1949, in possession of George Byam Shaw.

88. *Meredith*, p. 36.

89. ibid., p. 48.

90. ibid., p. 197.

91. See SS to DFC, 17 February 1960, SS:PP, p. 138.

92. *Meredith*, p. 111.

93. SS to L.P. Hartley, 25 September 1948, HRHRC. SS had first met the novelist L.P. Hartley (1895-1972) at Oxford, probably at Garsington.

94. ibid.

95. SS to R. Addyes-Scott, 4 October 1947, HRHRC.

96. G.M. Trevelyan (1876-1962) had published his influential *The Poetry and Philosophy of George Meredith* in 1906. He had also edited Meredith's *Poetical Works*.

97. SS told Patrick Lawlor in a letter of 18 February 1950 (Columbia) that Meredith had sold only about 4,500 copies. He complains elsewhere of a less favourable review of *Meredith* in the *New Statesman* by V.S. Pritchett.

98. SS to SCC, 5 December 1949, HRHRC.

99. CP, p. 263. See also SS:MWP, p. 518.

100. SS to HMT, 16 October 1951, HRHRC.

101. Otto Kyllman to SS, 18 February 1949, HRHRC. SS sent his proposed selection of Meredith's poems to Kyllman on 7 February 1949. SS's correspondence with Kyllman and Michael Sadleir of Constable is at HRHRC, together with his proposed introduction (handwritten) and list of poems.

102. Otto Kyllman to SS, 18 February 1949, HRHRC.

103. SS to GK, 23 February 1949, CUL.

104. HG's family owned land in Mull and she spent many summers there as a child.

105. SS to GK, 4 October 1948, CUL. SS and HG never divorced, nor does SS seem to have pressed for a divorce.

106. ibid., 8 October 1948.

107. ibid.

108. SS to WdlM, 14 November 1948, Beinecke.

109. ibid., 'Whitsun Day 1933'.

110. SS to Angela Baddeley, 17 January 1949, in possession of George Byam Shaw.

111. SS to WdlM, 25 November 1948, Beinecke.

112. SS to HH, 22 October 1948, in possession of recipient.

113. SS to Angela Baddeley, 1 January 1949, in possession of George Byam Shaw.

114. SS to WdlM, 7 December 1948, Beinecke, commenting on Helen Waddell's K.P. Kerr lecture.

115. SS to Angela Baddeley, 16 August 1946, in possession of George Byam Shaw.

116. SS's diary, 2 July 1953, SS:PP, p. 147.

117. TS died on 11 July 1947.

118. SS to GBS, 18 July 1947, CUL.

119. SS's diary, July 1947.

120. SS to GBS, 18 July 1947, CUL.

121. SS to HH, 14 February 1951, in possession of recipient.

122. Ackerley, J.R., *My Sister and Myself*, p. 167.

123. ibid.

124. ibid.

125. ibid.

126. ibid.

127. ibid.

128. ibid., p. 39.

129. ibid.

130. ibid.

131. ibid., p. 168.

132. SS's diary, quoted by Peter Parker in his biography *Ackerley*, p. 302.

133. Parker, p. 305.

134. James Kirkup referred to his visit to SS at Heytesbury in his autobiography, *I, of All People*, Weidenfeld & Nicolson, 1988, p. 72.

135. Ackerley, *My Sister and Myself*, p. 175.

136. ibid., p. 179.

Chapter 24

1. quoted in SS:PP, pp. 131-2.

2. ibid., p. 132.

3. 'Elsewhere', CP, p. 267.

4. ibid. 'Elsewhere' was written on 2 February 1950 and was followed shortly afterwards on 16 February by a poem in a similar vein, 'Post-Mortem' (CP, p. 267).

5. SS's diary for 26 December 1949, quoted in SS:PP, p. 132.

6. CC was dated 1950 but delayed at the binders and not issued until 1951. Though the main body of *Sequences* was written between 1946 and 1954, SS included five poems from the early forties, 'Man and Dog' (1941), 'The Hardened Heart' (1942), 'On Scratchbury Camp' (1942), 'A 1940 Memory' (1943), and 'Cleaning the Candelabrum' (1943). 'To My Mother', written much earlier in the 1920s, was added to the later trade edition incorporating the three volumes (*Sequences* (1956)), to mark his mother's death.

7. SS's diary for 29 March 1951, quoted in SS:PP, p. 140.

8. WdlM considered this sonnet 'one of the very best things' SS ever wrote (WdlM to SS, 30 June 1951,

Sotheby's catalogue, 18 July 1991) and ES thought it 'magnificent' (ES to SS, 19 April 1952, Pullman). It was the poem SS liked best from EE. He told WdlM (letter of 14 July 1951, Beinecke): 'Its history is peculiar. Looking through a 1921 diary notebook about 4 years ago, I found a rough draft of it (the first two lines caused by my having been reading Sir Thomas Browne) – so I thought, "This can be made use of," and got to work on it. How fortuitous one's successes in poetry are!'

9. CP, p. 264.

10. 'An Asking', CP, p. 270.

11. CP, p. 277.

12. SS:PP, p. 130.

13. CP, p. 280.

14. 'The Message' was first published on 3 November 1949 in *Everybody's Weekly*.

15. CP, p. 262.

16. SS uses 'beguilements' in 'Early March', CP, pp. 278-9.

17. SS thought 'Redemption' one of his 'good ones', he told HMT (letter of 11 October 1950, HRHRC). He dated it 29 December 1949.

18. Quoted in Roberts, J.S., *Siegfried Sassoon*, p. 306.

19. RGH to SS, 25 March 1950, Lilly.

20. 107 copies of CC were printed on handmade paper, of which 7 were on white parchment. Held up at the binders, CC eventually appeared in August 1951. There is a note that 'Of these [18] poems all except 4 are appearing in print for the first time.'

21. SS to PG, 18 April 1955, HRHRC.

22. RGH to SS, 29 September 1952, Lilly. Seventy-five copies of EE were printed at the Rampant Lions Press, Cambridge, in November 1951.

23. SS:PP, p. 143.

24. SS had made at least two new friends during this period, the writer Kenneth Hopkins, who published a number of SS's poems in his magazine, *Everybody's Weekly*,

between 1949 and 1952, and a clergyman from Essex, Richard Seymour, who came to stay at Heytesbury occasionally. Seymour, vicar of St Paul's, Goodmayes, Essex, wrote to SS between 1 May 1951 and 16 December 1966, but Rutgers University Library have mistakenly indexed these letters under the name of the writer Richard Church, with whom SS also corresponded.

25. SS's diary for 29 March 1951, SS:PP, p. 140.

26. ibid., p. 141.

27. 'The Dream' was written in February 1950.

28. 1950s poetry notebooks, CUL.

29. SS to GK, 19 February 1952, CUL.

30. SS's diary for 28 January 1954, SS:PP, p. 158.

31. ibid.

32. SS to DFC, 17 February 1960, SS:PP, p. 138.

33. 'Brevis Quod Gratia Florum Est' is in SS's 1950s poetry notebooks at CUL.

34. SS to GBS, 16 December 1947, CUL.

35. ibid.

36. Dorothy Wallis to GBS, 4 May 1953, in possession of George Byam Shaw.

37. ibid.

38. ibid.

39. Interview with Claire Blunden.

40. Dorothy Wallis to GBS, 4 May 1953, in possession of George Byam Shaw.

41. SS had this printed as an Easter card, which he sent out to friends. It was illustrated with a woodcut by a pupil of the artist Joan Hassall.

42. GBS's son, George, for example, doubted that there was any sexual dimension on SS's side. (Letter from George Byam Shaw to the author, 13 August 1992.)

43. SS to HMT, 1 January 1953, Christie's sale catalogue, 3 April 1992, p. 14.

44. SS to HMT, 30 October 1952, HRHRC.

45. ibid.

46. Interview with HH.

47. Interview with DS.

48. Dorothy Wallis to GBS, 4 May 1953.

49. Interview with Claire Blunden.

50. ibid.

51. ibid.

52. Dorothy Wallis to GBS, 4 May 1953.

53. GBS to Dorothy Wallis, 11 May 1953, copy in possession of George Byam Shaw.

54. ibid.

55. See last line of 'Retreat from Eternity', CP, p. 291.

56. SS to PG, 30 November 1953, Brotherton.

57. SS to DFC, 16 February 1962, quoted in SS:PP, p. 219.

58. SS to PG, 30 November 1953, Brotherton.

59. PG lived first at 256 Hills Road, Cambridge, then at Low Thatch, West Wratting, Cambridgeshire, until his death.

60. These were published with SS's foreword in 1953 as *Collected Poems* by the Caravel Press. SS owned No. 22 of 360, inscribed gratefully by the author. He thought Anna's poems 'somehow just miss being interesting, though nice in patches', he told Keynes (letter of 19 March 1952, CUL) and rather regretted having agreed to write about them.

61. See SS:MWP, Chapter 6, note 9 (p. 546), for further details.

62. SS to GK, 26 December 1960, CUL. Frances Cornford is best remembered for her triolet 'To a Fat Lady Seen from a Train' ('O Fat white lady ...') Her son, John Cornford (1915-1936), also a poet, was killed in the Spanish Civil War.

63. SS to DFC, 14 February 1961, quoted in SS:PP, p. 69, and SS to HH, 12 May 1949, in possession of recipient.

64. SS to EB, 19 November 1954, HRHRC.

65. SS to John Dreyfus, 18 February 1961, CUL.

66. SS to GK, 7 July 1953, CUL.

67. DS remembers seeing a pile of Gwen Raverat's paintings at Heytesbury House after SS's death, though there is no listing of these in the sale of the contents. SS presented one of her paintings to Clare College, Cambridge.

68. SS to HMT, 15 March 1956, Christie's sale catalogue, 3 April 1992.

69. Dennis Silk, *Siegfried Sassoon* (Compton Russell Ltd, 1975), first delivered as the Guinness Lecture at the Salisbury Festival of the Arts, July 1974, p. 27.

70. ibid.

71. SS to PG, 20 May 1953, Brotherton.

72. ibid.

73. SS to HMT, 15 August 1955, HRHRC.

74. SS to HMT, 15 March 1956, Christie's catalogue, 3 April 1992. DS got his blue three years running for Cambridge University 1st XI, captaining it on the last occasion. He went on to play thirty-three times for Somerset. He also toured with the MCC four years running from 1957, visiting East Africa, South America, Canada, North America and New Zealand with them, twice as captain. In 1992 he became President of the MCC for two consecutive years, the first President to have achieved that distinction, and in 1994-5 became President of the County Cricket Board, the governing body of cricket.

75. op. cit., p. 27.

76. SS to HMT, 5 August 1954, HRHRC.

77. op. cit., p. 28.

78. SS to GK, 23 March 1955, CUL. DS found it difficult to get to Heytesbury from Marlborough by public transport and discovered a 1936 Austin 10 for sale for £30. He persuaded his friend Martin Bushby to take a half-share and SS put up DS's £15.

79. SS to HH, 25 February 1965, in possession of recipient.

80. SS to JG, 20 July 1963, CUL.

81. Interview with DS.

82. ibid.

83. SS to PG, 6 June 1955, Brotherton.

84. SS to Richard Seymour (catalogued as 'Richard Church'), 15 December 1956, Rutgers.

85. SS to PG, 6 January 1955, Brotherton.

86. SS told GK (letter of 10 December 1953) that his cousin Oliver Thornycroft, who had also been at Cambridge, told him that the idea of the fellowship 'was mainly instigated by an F.R. named H. Godwin'.

87. SS to GK, 15 December 1950, CUL.

88. S.C. Roberts to SS, 4 November 1953, CUL.

89. Quoted in an obituary of SS in the Clare Association Annual, 1967, p. 79.

90. ibid.

91. ibid.

92. ibid.

93. SS's diary, 26 October 1953, quoted in SS:PP, p. 148.

94. SJ, p. 162.

95. 100 copies of *The Tasking* were printed for SS and GK at the University Press, Cambridge. The book was designed by John Dreyfus in consultation with Brooke Crutchley and GK. Of the thirty-seven poems SS sent GK, thirteen were omitted from the printed volume, though three of these were published elsewhere. The ms from which GK worked, very beautifully written out in SS's hand, is now in the possession of William Reese.

96. SS's diary, 27 December 1954, quoted in SS:PP, p. 154.

97. ibid., 6 December 1953, SS:PP, p. 149.

98. ibid., 13 December 1953, SS:PP, p. 151.

99. SS to HMT, 22 January 1955, HRHRC.

100. ibid.

101. ibid.

102. SS to GK, 18 January 1955, CUL.

103. SS to DFC, 5 August 1960, quoted in SS:PP, p. 167.

104. ibid.

105. SS to DFC, 22 February 1963, quoted in SS:PP, p. 169.

106. MB died on 20 March 1956 and SS delivered 'A Tribute to Max' on the BBC Home Service on 28 June 1956, shortly after WdlM's death on 22 June. His tribute to WdlM was delivered on 18 December 1961, when he unveiled WdlM's memorial tablet in the crypt of St Paul's Cathedral. His notes for his address on that occasion are given in SS:PP, pp. 215-17.

107. Colin Fenton (1929-1982), who was a student at Christ Church College, Oxford, was believed to be Sparrow's lover and for a time shared his accommodation at C1, Albany, which Harold Nicholson also shared.

108. Eton College Library have recently acquired a small archive of SS's correspondence with Colin Fenton, including one letter to John Sparrow.

109. SS to HMT, 4 December 1954, HRHRC.

110. ibid.

111. SS to PG, 5 November 1956, Brotherton.

112. SS to Michael Thorpe, 12 August 1966, *Letters to a Critic*, p. 15.

113. ibid.

114. Quoted by SS from EB's review of *Sequences* in the *TLS*. Yet SS told Mr Hillyer in a letter of 2 October 1960 (Syracuse) that 'your very gracious review of *Sequences* [was] the only good one I got ...' Charles Causley quotes another glowing review SS appears to have overlooked, by Bonamy Dobrée: 'There are pieces here as striking and as memorably moving, as full of suggestion beyond the words as in his earlier works.' (Introduction to *An Octave* (published by the Arts Council, 1966)).

Chapter 25

1. quoted in SS:PP, p. 177.
2. SS to DFC, 30 October 1959, quoted in SS:PP, p. 175. Margaret Ross McFarlin (1905-2001) died thirty-four years after SS at the age of ninety-six. She entered the religious life, to the astonishment of her family and fiancé, in 1930 at the age of twenty-five and spent the next forty-six years as an English teacher, headmistress and religious Superior (sometimes all three at once) in convent schools in Kensington, Aldenham, Exton, Hengrave, Sidmouth and Oxford.
3. Notebook of Mother Margaret Mary, CUL. Her quotation comes from SS's 'The Tasking', CP, p. 291.
4. SS to DFC, 30 October 1959, in SS:PP, p. 175.
5. ibid.
6. SS to DFC, 5 August 1960, in SS:PP, p. 167. There is some irony in SS's comments on Newman, since Newman's own conversion had been an intensely difficult and painful affair.
7. Taken from Newman's sermon on equanimity.
8. Mother Margaret Mary to RHD, 16 June 1969, CUL.
9. SS's notes on his conversion in the 1958-1964 poetry notebook at CUL.
10. Dated '19.4.57' and quoted in SS:PP, p. 173.
11. Notebook of Mother Margaret Mary, CUL.
12. SS wrote a poem dated 22/23 October 1952 entitled first 'Sainthood Sufficing', then 'Unknown Saint' (1940s and 1950s poetry notebook, CUL). In crossing out this second title he added a pencilled note, 'anticipation of Mother Margaret?':

Never encountered Saint, I know
      that you exist,
All human, all-enduring, dowered
      with what you dealt,
Carrying within you Christ: the
      crucifix you have kissed
Illumined by those deeds wherein
      your mercy knelt ...

13. Dom Hubert van Zeller to DFC, 12 March 1972, in SS:PP, p. 198, and author's telephone conversation with Dom Sebastian Moore (in 1991) and interview with him on 17 March 2002.
14. Dom Sebastian Moore, who has a First in English from Cambridge, is an authority on Jones's *The Anathemata*, an even more abstruse work than *In Parenthesis*.
15. SS to DFC, 21 January 1960, in SS:PP, p. 177.
16. Dom Sebastian Moore to author at interview on 17 March 2002.
17. ibid.
18. Read by SS in Robert Speaight's *The Life of Hilaire Belloc*, p. 377.
19. SS to DFC, 29 March 1960, in SS:PP, pp. 181-2.
20. The Rt Revd Monsignor Ronald Arbuthnott Knox (1888-1957) was educated at Eton and Balliol College, Oxford, and fellow of Trinity from 1910 to 1917, when he was received into the Church of Rome. He was Catholic chaplain at the University of Oxford from 1926 to 1939. He published a new translation of the Bible, based on the Vulgate text, between 1945 and 1949 and was the author of many works of his own, including detective stories as well as essays and sermons.
21. SS to EB, 20 February 1960, HRHRC.
22. See SS to TS, 14 August 1932 (Berg), re. his meeting with Katharine's son, 'young Lord Oxford': 'His mother became a Roman Catholic and has made him one – which the

late Lord Oxford disliked very much, and I don't blame him.'

23. SS quotes himself in a letter to DFC, 14 April 1960, in SS:PP, p. 185.

24. Interview with author.

25. SS to DFC, op. cit.

26. ibid.

27. ibid.

28. Interview with author, 19 July 2001.

29. SS to DFC, 21 January 1960, in SS:PP, p. 177. SS was received into the Catholic Church by Fr Francis Little, with Prior Duncan Pontifex assisting, in the Lady Chapel of Downside Abbey. Dom Sebastian Moore was ill and unable to attend the ceremony.

30. SS to DFC, 21 January 1960.

31. SS to PG, 14 October 1957, Brotherton.

32. ibid., and *The Times*, 1 October 1957.

33. DFC to GK, 26 August 1973, CUL. LW's second wife, Theresa, told me in my interview with her that she thought SS's reaction exaggerated and described it as 'only a slight cooling off'. LW himself, when she discussed it with him subsequently, said that he was 'really pleading' with SS, though agreeing that it had been 'unwise to do so'.

34. Swinnerton, F., *Figures in the Foreground*, p. 210. The long break between 1956 and 1963 in an otherwise faithful correspondence between SS and FSw shows how violently 'Swinny' reacted.

35. SS to PG, 14 October 1957, Brotherton.

36. GK to DFC, August 1973, quoted by her in her *Centenary Essay* of 1986.

37. Keynes, G., *The Gates of Memory*, p. 239.

38. SS to PG, 24 September 1958, Brotherton.

39. SS to GK, 15 December 1950, CUL. SS had responded in a similar fashion to the bookseller Percy Muir, who had suggested compiling a

bibliography of SS's work as early as 1927: 'I cannot say that I am particularly keen on the idea' (SS to Percy Muir, 3 February 1927, private collection).

40. Keynes, *The Gates of Memory*, p. 237. SS received his Hon. D.Litt. from Oxford on 5 June 1965.

41. DFC wrote to GK, 26 August 1973, six years after SS's death: 'I assumed … that you were SS's executor. He certainly always spoke of you as being his literary executor, and the appointment of Rupert Hart-Davis must have been surely a last-minute decision? I am sorry he did it, and consider it an error of judgement on his part – but very typical.' (CUL.)

42. SS to PG, 8 October 1957, Brotherton.

43. ibid., 14 October 1957.

44. SS to KA, 13 November 1959, in possession of Lord Oxford and Asquith.

45. Quoted by Dom Philip Jebb during an interview with the author on 17 March 2002.

46. SS to EB, 15 February 1958, HRHRC.

47. Interview with DS.

48. ibid.

49. Poem entitled 'III' and dated 28 September 1947 in the poetry notebooks at CUL.

50. SS to HMT, 4 May 1949, HRHRC.

51. DFC's *Centenary Essay* on SS.

52. GBS to SS, 11 September 1957, Columbia.

53. ibid.

54. ibid.

55. ibid.

56. SS to Dame Hildelith Cumming, 9 July 1962, in SS:PP, p. 229.

57. James Lees-Milne, *Ancient as the Hills, Diaries 1973-1974* (John Murray, 1997), pp. 99-100.

58. 'Memories of Siegfried Sassoon', *Journal of Royal Welch Fusiliers*, March 1968, vol. 17, no. 1, p. 15.

59. ibid.
60. ibid.
61. ibid.
62. DFC's *Centenary Essay* on SS.
63. GBS to SS, *c.* mid-1929, CUL.
64. SS to HMT, 10 January 1958, HRHRC.
65. ibid.
66. See SS to DFC, 29 March 1960, in SS:PP, p. 182, where 'Lenten Illuminations' is quoted in full and where SS tells DFC that the reference was specifically to King's College Chapel, where he had 'tried to say a prayer (in 1953-56). I remember kneeling alone in the choir stalls and saying one for George's career at King's; and feeling that the words went nowhere and came from nothing.'
67. Extract from the three sheets of journal entries by SS about his religious experience from April to October 1957.
68. *The Times*, 4 September 1967.
69. RG to Timothy Budd, 4 June 1971, private collection.
70. SS:PP, pp. 178-9.
71. ibid., p. 182.
72. Caesar, A., *Taking It Like a Man*, p. 102.
73. SS to AL, 17 May 1960, CUL.
74. SS's letters to KA are in the possession of KA's son, Lord Oxford and Asquith.
75. Interview with the author.
76. SS to KA, 23 November 1959.
77. Interview with author.
78. *Spectator*, 8 September 1957.
79. Foot, D., *Beyond Bat and Ball*, p. 39.
80. SS to Cecil Norman, 9 March 1963, CUL.
81. Caesar, op. cit., p. 40.
82. ibid., p. 41.
83. ibid.
84. SS added this as an annotation to a letter of 18 February 1958 sent to him by the BBC, and forwarded it to Dom Martin (CUL).
85. Dom Hubert van Zeller to DFC, 12 March 1972, in SS:PP, p. 197.
86. ibid., p. 198.

87. ibid.
88. ibid., pp. 199-200.
89. ibid., p. 200.
90. ibid.
91. Interview with the author, 17 March 2002.
92. ibid.
93. SS's letters to Dom Philip Jebb are in the latter's possession.
94. SS's journal re. his religious experiences in 1957, CUL.
95. SS:PP, p. 188.
96. DFC refers to the 'lovely prose cadences' of SJ, 'notably, his apostrophe to the dead Wilfred Owen, and his last meeting with Wilfrid Blunt', in her *Centenary Essay* on SS.
97. 3,000 copies of *Collected Poems 1908-1956* were published by Faber on 3 May 1961.
98. DFC's *Any Saint to Any Nun* was published in 1947, and *In a Great Tradition* in 1956. Her book on SS, *Siegfried Sassoon: Poet's Pilgrimage*, would be published in 1973. She would also write *George Thomas of Soho* (1970) and *Helen Waddell* (1986), as well as editing various other books.
99. SS:PP, pp. 192, 211 and 212.
100. ibid., p. 194.
101. ibid., p. 192.
102. ibid. SS's reading included 'Breach of Decorum' (DFC's request), 'Sheldonian Soliloquy', two prose passages from OC, 'The Merciful Knight', 'A Flower Has Opened in My Heart', 'Sight Sufficient', the last section of 'Lenten Illuminations' and 'A Prayer at Pentecost'.
103. *Downside Review*, lxxvi, no. 245, pp. 129-32. GK had asked to print it privately, together with 'Sight Sufficient', and thirty-five copies were printed for him and SS at Cambridge University Press, fifteen of which GK presented to SS to give to friends. Downside Review Publications also produced the two poems as an offprint, 2,000 copies in an ordinary and 200 copies in a limited edition.

But Faber refused to distribute it and its circulation was modest.

104. SS:PP, p. 181.

105. SS to Dom Martin Salmon, 16 May 1958, CUL.

106. ibid., 18 March 1958. See also note 103.

107. SS:PP, p. 180.

108. *Poems by Siegfried Sassoon* was printed at the Marlborough College Press in an edition of 150 copies, which cost £1 each, DS remembers. It contained fifty-eight poems taken from WP, *Satirical Poems*, HJ, *Vigils*, RRu and *Sequences*. 'Rogation', consisting of a single leaf, was printed in an edition of a few copies at the Marlborough College Press in 1960.

109. DFC's proposal for her selection is quoted by Keynes, *The Gates of Memory*, p. 126. An ordinary (limited) edition of 500 copies of *The Path to Peace* was printed at the Stanbrook Abbey Press, and a special (limited) edition of 20 copies, in 1960. The previously unpublished poems were 'Awaitment', 'Deliverance', 'Arbor Vitae', 'Unfoldment', 'Rogation' and 'A Prayer at Pentecost'.

110. DFC to Mrs Leonard Clark, 30 January 1961, Berg. My thanks to Steve Crook for drawing my attention to this collection, which also includes letters to Leonard Clark.

111. SS:PP, p. 188.

112. ibid., p. 189.

113. *Something About Myself,* the Stanbrook Abbey Press's first calligraphic book, was a cat story written by SS, aged eleven, that he had included in his own childhood production for his mother, *More Poems* (1897). The Stanbrook Abbey Press text was written out and illustrated in two colours by Margaret Adams. *Ave Atque Vale*, printed 'For Private Circulation Only' by the Press in 1967, contained 'Before a Crucifix' (1962), 'Compline' (1962), 'Proven Purpose' (1964) and 'A Prayer in Old Age' (1964).

114. Thorpe, *Siegfried Sassoon*, p. 250, quoting C.E. Maguire, 'Harmony Unheard: the Path of Siegfried Sassoon', *Renascence*, vol. XI, no. 5, Spring 1959.

Chapter 26

1. SS:PP, pp. 241-2. The first quotation in this letter occurs in a poem by Frances Cornford on Rupert Brooke ('A young Apollo', etc.). The chapter title is from a letter from SS to DFC, 9 July 1967, in SS:PP, p. 249.

2. DFC to GK (quoting Colin Fenton), 26 August 1973, CUL.

3. ibid.

4. DFC's *Centenary Essay* on SS.

5. op. cit., p. 28.

6. Interview with Ian Balding on 21 December 1998. SS, who wore ancient, often ragged, clothes, was mistaken for a tramp by one of George Byam Shaw's guests when he turned up for George's wedding.

7. Interview with author. Balding visited SS about a dozen times in all, he thinks.

8. Interviews with DS and Ian Balding.

9. Heather Lewis was the sister of Balding's great friend at Cambridge, 'Tony' (A.R.) Lewis, with whom he competed as full-back at rugby for Cambridge. Lewis was also a brilliant cricketer and captained England (and was recently President of the MCC). Heather Lewis was a skilled pianist, who played for the Welsh National Youth Orchestra.

10. At least thirty-five of SS's poems have been set to music, some of them more than once. 'Everyone Sang', for instance, has had twelve settings, one of them by the First World War poet Ivor Gurney.

11. See Hart-Davis, R., *The Lyttleton–Hart-Davis Letters*, p. 140. GBS was planning to direct Terence Rattigan's play *Ross*, with Alec Guinness in the lead role. He had suggested that Guinness talk to SS about TEL and SS invited him to lunch on 29 September 1959, a meeting which left both men wishing for another. But in his letter to GBS about it (30 September 1959) Guinness confesses that he thought 'it was going to be AGONY – his shifting and fidgeting and off at a tangent talk …' (private collection).

12. Hart-Davis, *The Lyttleton- Hart-Davis Letters*, p. 141.

13. ibid.

14. ibid.

15. SS to RHD, 6 October 1958, CUL.

16. DFC to GK, 26 August 1973, CUL.

17. ibid.

18. Powell, A., *To Keep the Ball Rolling*, p. 406.

19. SS to RHD, 7 April 1946, CUL.

20. This would finally appear as *Poems of Many Years*, Rupert Hart-Davis (ed.), 1956.

21. SS to RHD, 26 April and 2 May 1946, CUL.

22. RHD would subsequently help SS with his Meredith project.

23. SS to RHD, 21 February 1967, quoted in Hart-Davis, *Halfway to Heaven*, p.78.

24. SS to DFC, 3 May 1960, in SS:PP, p. 102.

25. ibid., pp. 102-3.

26. DFC's *Centenary Essay* on SS.

27. SS:PP, p. 207. Lascelles' quotation is from Arthur Symons' *Seven Studies in Art*.

28. SS to KA, 11 July 1960, in possession of Lord Oxford and Asquith.

29. There is a series of letters at CUL charting the affair.

30. SS:PP, p. 212.

31. SS to HH, 14 January 1964, in possession of recipient.

32. SS was introduced to Princess Marina on 9 June 1965 at Kensington Palace.

33. Jones, D., *Dai Greatcoat: Letters of David Jones*, p. 210: 'undoubtedly a man of genius' comes

in a letter of SS to AL, 1 July 1964, CUL.

34. SS to DFC, 5 August 1964, in SS:PP, p. 232.

35. Jones, op. cit.

36. ibid.

37. SS to DFC, 5 August 1964, quoted in full in J.S. Roberts' *Siegfried Sassoon*, p. 326, and in a silently edited version by DFC in SS:PP, p. 232.

38. SS:PP, p. 210.

39. ibid.

40. GS had settled down to live in Cambridge after taking his degree there.

41. SS to DFC, 16 February 1961, in SS:PP, p. 207.

42. ibid.

43. ibid.

44. SS did not attend DS's wedding but sent a generous wedding present of Georgian silver.

45. SS to DFC, 25 May 1966, in SS:PP, p. 242.

46. Roberts, *Siegfried Sassoon*, p. 320.

47. SS to DFC, 3 January 1967, in SS:PP, p. 248.

48. ibid., 25 October 1965, in SS:PP, p. 240.

49. SS left EB £4,000 in his will of 25 February 1946, which covered the bulk of the cost of EB's house.

50. Margaret Keynes's account of a visit to SS on 23 September 1964, CUL. SS had all his remaining teeth removed at the 'Plastic and Oral Surgery Centre', Odstock Hospital, on 17 March 1962.

51. ibid.

52. ibid.

53. Anthony Powell and his wife Violet visited SS at Heytesbury House in the autumn of 1963.

54. Powell, *To Keep the Ball Rolling*, pp. 350-1.

55. ibid.

56. ibid.

57. ibid.

58. ibid.

59. ibid., p. 351.

60. This may be a coincidence. SS told DFC that it was WdlM's son, Richard, who asked him to unveil his father's plaque.

61. John Sparrow, Lord David Cecil and Rupert Hart-Davis almost certainly joined in the campaign to have SS awarded an Hon. D.Litt. Haro Hodson also claims to have influenced matters by approaching Maurice Bowra, with whom he had been at Wadham College, where Bowra had been Warden.

62. i.e., 'Rogation', 'Sight Sufficient', 'Arbor Vitae', 'Unfoldment', 'A Prayer at Pentecost' and 'Awaitment'. *An Octave* was printed by the Shenval Press for the Arts Council and was limited to 350 copies, of which 100 were presented to SS on his eightieth birthday.

63. Causley persuaded SS to read some of his best known poems on the BBC and, together with Robert Waller, recorded this at Heytesbury House on 16 February 1955. (SS had previously had three poems broadcast on BBC West Regional on 25 March 1953, and in his description of the 1955 reading Causley has confused the two events.) SS was also persuaded to read his own selection of Hardy poems for the BBC, which Causley and Waller recorded at Heytesbury in July 1956, together with HMT's reminiscences of his old friend 'Tom'.

64. SS was interviewed for a documentary on TEL and appeared briefly in the programme, 'T.E. Lawrence, 1888-1935', which went out on the BBC on 27 November 1962.

65. *Siegfried Sassoon: A Critical Study* by Michael Thorpe was published by the University of Leiden Press and OUP in 1966 (in English).

66. Interview with DS.

67. ibid.

68. SS to DFC, 19 May 1964, in SS:PP, p. 231.

69. SS to Dame Hildelith

Cumming, 1 January 1965, in SS:PP, p. 236.

70. SS to MMM, 8 January 1965, CUL.

71. Interview with DS.

72. SS to AL, 26 February 1965, CUL.

73. 'Onus of Ownership' was enclosed in a letter of SS to RHD in February 1965 (CUL), with an equally jokey reply from John Gore, to whom RHD had shown SS's poem. In the event the estate agents Knight, Frank and Rutley valued the land and house (excluding contents) provisionally at £40,000 and SS agreed to make everything over to his son.

74. SS to DFC, 3 January 1967, in SS:PP, p. 248.

75. ibid., 9 July 1967, in SS:PP, p. 249.

76. Dr Falk to MMM, 13 August 1967, CUL.

77. Dom Philip Jebb to his parents, 7 September 1967, in possession of Dom Philip Jebb.

78. ibid.

79. ibid.

80. Webb, B., *Edmund Blunden*, p. 320.

81. Interview with the author.

82. EB did, however, write an obituary in the *Observer* on 3 September 1967, in which he dismissed as nonsense the idea of SS as a rough and ready fox-hunting man, incapable of intellectual subtleties and grandeurs: 'Despite his solitariness, he watched the world astutely!'

83. Told to DS by RHD in 1967 and related to the author by DS in an interview.

84. Jonathan Gathorne-Hardy to author, letter of 17 July 1990.

85. Charles Causley quoting GS's letter to him in 'Siegfried Sassoon', *The Author*, Winter 1989, p. 127.

86. ibid.

87. See Judith Usher to RHD, 3 September 1967, CUL: 'Captain Sassoon had a wonderful release – Dr

Falk had been in not long before and left saying that he dreaded the next few days for him – / But he seemed to have a series of small heart attacks – and finally passed, holding my hand lightly, between one breath and the next – marvellous. No struggle or fear.'

88. GS to Charles Causley, loc. cit.

89. Causley, 'Siegfried Sassoon', op. cit.

Appendix

Identification of Pseudonyms in the Sherston Trilogy

Fictional Name	Real Name	Novels in which character appears
Allgood	Goodall, M.H. (Marcus)	MIO
Asterisk, Lord & Lady	Brassey, Lord & Lady	MIO
B	Badcoe, 2nd Lt	SP
Baldock, Sergeant	Baldwin, Sergeant	MIO
Barchard family	Marchant family	MFM
Barchard, Jack	Marchant, R.E.	MFM
Barton, Captain	Greaves, Captain E. J., MC	MFM, MIO
Bates	Yates, Captain (QM) H.	MIO
Bathwick, Sam	Elphick, Sam	MFM
'Big-game hunter' at Flixécourt	Hesketh-Pearson	MIO
Blarnett, 'the Mister'	Harnett, Mr	SP
Bond, Private John (355642)	Law, Private John (355642)	SP
Brandwick	Ridsdale, Arthur	MFM
Brock	Brocklebank, R.	MIO
Brownrigg, 'Boots'	J.F. Lamont, Brigadier	MFM
'Cameronian Colonel'	Chaplin, Colonel	MIO
'Cameronian Corporal'	Smart, Corporal	MIO
Carmine, Major	Terry, Major	MFM
Clements	Cowan	SP
Colwood, Stephen	Harbord, Gordon	MFM
'Commandant' at Flixécourt	Rawlinson, Lt General Sir Henry	MIO
Cromlech, David	Graves, Robert von R.	MIO
Croplady, N.	Whitfield, G.	MFM
Dixon, Tom	Richardson, Tom	MFM
'The Doc' (of 25th RWF)	Bigger, Captain W.K.	SP
Dodd, William	Hodges, William	MFM
Dottrell, Joe	Cottrell, Captain Joe T., DSO, DCM	MFM
Duclos, Captain	Duclos, Captain	SP
Dunning	Conning, Lt T.R., MC	MIO
Dumborough, Lord	Nevill, Lord Henry	MFM

Durley, Julian	Dadd, 2nd Lt Julian	MFM, MIO
Easby, Colonel	Garnett, Lt Colonel W.B.	MIO
Eaves, Bill	Adams, J.B.P. (Bill)	MIO
Edmunds	Dadd, Edmund H., MC	MIO
Ellis, Bob	Lowes, Bob	MFM
Evans, Major	R, Major J.G., DSO	SP
Evelyn, Aunt	Sassoon, Theresa	MFM, MIO, SP
Fernby	Newton, 2nd Lt V.F.	MIO
Flook	Molyneux, Private R.	MFM, MIO
'Gentleman George'	Green, G.	MFM
Hawkes	Hawes, Captain E.G., MC	MIO
Hesmon, Colonel	Thompson, Colonel	MFM
Homeward, Tom	Homewood, Tom	MFM
Hooper	Harper, Lt S.W.	SP
Howell	Howell-Jones, Lt H.G.	SP
Howitt	Jowett, 2nd Lt W.	SP
Huxtable, Captain	Ruxton, Captain Julian H. Hay	MFM, MIO
Jaggett, Bill	Lindsay-Hogg, Bill	MFM
Jenkins	Garnon-Williams	MIO
Jones, Harry	Morgan, Harry [L]	SP
Kangaroo ('Kangar')	SS	MIO
Kendle, Lance Corporal	Gibson, Lance Corporal	MIO
Kinjack	Stockwell, Lt Colonel C.I.	MFM, MIO
Leake, Captain	Kirkby, Captain W.W.	MIO
Macartney, Major	Macartney-Filgate, Major	MIO
MacNair, Captain	Wright, Captain	MIO
Mansfield, Birdie	Stansfield, Lt N.	MFM, MIO
Markington	Massingham, H.W.	MIO
Maundle, Squire	Morland, Squire	MFM
Marshall	Robinson, Lt/Captain M.	SP
Maskall, Miss	Horrocks, Clara	MFM
Maskall, Major	Horrock, Major Edgeworth	MFM
Milden, Dennis	Loder, Norman	MFM, MIO
Mister, the	Harnett, Mr	SP
Munro, Captain	Dunn, J.C., Captain R.A.M.C.	MIO
Noakes, Ned	Lambert, Edwin	MFM
Oakfield, Mrs	Inge, Mrs	MFM
O'Donnell, Mrs	MacDonnel, Mrs	SP
Ormand	Orme, Lt E.L.	MFM, MIO
Pattons, Misses	Hollands, Misses	MFM
Peppercorn, Jack and Charlie	Brown, Frank and Harry	MFM
Perrin	Davies, 2nd Lt J.I.J.	MIO
Philipson, Tom	Atkinson, Tom	SP

Pomfret, Roger	Nevill, Rupert	MFM
Porteus-Porteous, Sir	Newdigate, Sir Francis	MFM
Puttridge, Richard	Philpot, J.G	MFM
Rees	Evans, 2nd Lt	MIO
Rivers, Dr	Rivers, Dr W.H.R.	SP
Roberts, 'Stiffy'	Phillips, 'Stiffy' [probably J.R.]	SP
Robson, Major	Compton Smith, Major	MIO
Shehan, Mike	Sheeby, Mike	SP
Sherston, 2nd Lt George	SS	MFM, MIO, SP
Shirley	Casson, 2nd Lt R.A.	MIO
Shotney, Mrs	Hussey, Mrs	MFM
Sibson	Stevenson	MFM
Star, Mr	Moon, Mr	MFM
Stonethwaite	Linthwaite, Private Jim	SP
Sutler, Bill	Butler, Will	MFM
Tiltwood, Dick	Thomas, 2nd Lt David C. ('Tommy')	MFM, MIO
	with elements of Hanmer, Lt R.H.	
Tyrell, Thornton	Russell, Bertrand	MIO
Velmore	Pinto, Captain Vivian de Sola	SP
Whincop, Major General	Pinney, Major General R.J., C.B.	MIO
Whiteway, Corporal V.C.	Whitfield, Corporal, V.C.	SP
Wilmot, Ralph	Greaves, Lt Ralph C.J.	MIO
Winchell, Colonel	Minshull Ford, Lt Colonel J.R.M.	MFM
Worgan, Private	Jordan, Private	NIO
Yalden, Parson	Leigh, Canon	MFM

Acknowledgements

My first acknowledgement must go to George Sassoon, who encouraged me to write this life of his father and has allowed me to quote extensively from his work. Other members of the family have also been extremely helpful, in particular Hamo Sassoon, the late Lady Lettice Strickland-Constable, the late Mrs Leo Sassoon, Timothy Thornycroft, Jacques Sassoon and Sister Jessica Gatty. Sassoon's godson, George Byam Shaw, and his wife Maggie have likewise contributed a great deal.

I have also been very fortunate in being able to talk to an appreciable number of Sassoon's friends, or to those who knew his friends well, and should like to express my gratitude here to Lord Oxford and Asquith, the late Lady Helen Asquith, Ian Balding, Rolf Barber, the late Claire Blunden, the late James Byam Shaw, Vivien Clarke, Haro Hodson, Dom Philip Jebb, Milo Keynes, the late Mother Margaret Mary Ross McFarlin, Dom Sebastian Moore, Andrew Motion, Dennis Silk, Jon Stallworthy and Theresa Whistler.

In addition I am grateful to those who gave me access to their collections and research or shared their expert advice with me, in particular Timothy and Angela Atkinson, Timothy d'Arch-Smith, Bryan Connon, Dame Felicitas Corrigan, Stewart Craggs, Lionel Dakers, Roy Davids, Sister Clemente Davlin, Terry Halladay, John Harding, Lady Anne Hill, Philip Hoare, William Reese, Keith Simpson, Harry and Cookie Spiro, Elizabeth Tagert, Michael Thorpe, Len Weaver and Burton Weiss.

I should also like to thank librarians and archivists throughout Britain and America: especially Kathleen Cann and Godfrey Waller at Cambridge University Library; Steve Crook, Philip Milito and Isaac Gewirtz at the Berg Collection, New York Public Library; Kenneth Lohf and his erstwhile colleagues at the Butler Library, Columbia University; Vincent Giroud at the Beinecke Rare Book Library, University of Yale; Daniel Myers of the Regenstein Library, University of Chicago; Saundra Taylor and William Cagle at the Lilly Library, University of Indiana; David Koch and Shelley Cox at Special Collections, Southern Illinois University at Carbondale; Cathy Henderson at the Harry Ransom Humanities Research Center, University of Texas at Austin; Leila Ludeking and Laila Miletic-Vejzovic, the University of Washington at Pullman; Christopher Sheppard at the Brotherton Library, University of Leeds; Ann French and Sarah Rich of

Acknowledgements

the Laing Art Gallery, Newcastle; Denison J. Beach, the Houghton Library, University of Harvard; the late Martin Taylor of the Imperial War Museum Library; Richard Sinnett and David Bowns of the Royal Welch Fusiliers Archives at Carnaervon; Margaret Clarke of the Fitzwilliam Museum, Cambridge; Colin Harris of the Bodleian Library, University of Oxford; Mrs S. Johnson of Clare College Library, University of Cambridge; Marion Baxter of Sutton Coldfield Reference Library, and the staffs of the British Library, Rutgers University Library, the State University of New York at Buffalo Library, McMaster University Library, University of Marquette Library, the Library of Congress, University of Delaware Library, University of Arkansas Library, Vassar College, King's College Library, University of Cambridge, Wichita State University Library, the Public Record Office and the National Army Museum.

My warmest thanks must also go to the following individuals who have helped me in many different ways: Gavin Beattie, Eleanor Birne, Russell Burlingham, Jonathan Cecil, Charles Cholmondeley, Anthony Curtis, Sarah Curtis, Roger Daniell, Joan Draper, Geraldine Elwes, Shu-Yiu Fenton, James Fergusson, Robert Fessenden, Jonathan Gathorne-Hardy, Martyn Goff, David Handforth, Annie Hasted, Charles Hastings, Anthony Head, Bill Hetherington, Pat and Stuart Laurence, Michael MacGarvie, Maureen Murray, John Northam, Giles Payne, Michael Pierson, Wendy Pollard, the late Anthony Powell, Lady Violet Powell, Susan Rand, Willie Reardon, Tim Rix, Rose Sanguinetti, Daphne Sayed, Winifred Stevenson, June Stubbs, Sarah Such, Gertrud Watson, Charles Wilson, Renée Wylde, Marjorie Wynne, and Gill Yudkin.

Full details have been given, either in my text or in footnotes, of sources quoted in this book, but I should like here formally to acknowledge quotations from *My Sister and Myself: The Diaries of J.R. Ackerley*, edited by Francis King (Hutchinson, 1982), *The Autobiography of Enid Bagnold* (Century, 1985), *Strange Street* by Beverley Baxter (Hutchinson, 1937), *Self-Portrait with Friends: The Selected Diaries of Cecil Beaton*, edited by Richard Buckle (Penguin, 1982), *Portrait of Max* by S.N. Behrman (Random House, 1960), *Tribulations and Laughter* by S.N. Behrman (Hamish Hamilton, 1972), *The Journals of Arnold Bennett* (Oxford University Press, 1968), *Sacheverell Sitwell: Splendours and Miseries* by Sarah Bradford (Sinclair-Stevenson, 1993), *Taking It Like a Man: Suffering, Sexuality and the War Poets* by Adrian Caesar (Manchester University Press, 1993), *Max: A Biography* by David Cecil (Atheneum, 1985), *The Best of Friends: Further Letters of Sir Sydney Carlyle Cockerell*, edited by Viola Meynell (Hart-Davis, 1956), *Previous Convictions* by Cyril Connolly (Hamish Hamilton, 1963), *Helen Waddell* by D. Felicitas Corrigan (Gollancz, 1990), *Siegfried Sassoon: Poet's Pilgrimage* by D. Felicitas Corrigan (Gollancz, 1973), *The War the Infantry Knew, 1914-1919*, edited by Dr J.C. Dunn (P.S. King, 1938), *Edith Sitwell* by Geoffrey Elborn (Sheldon, 1981), *Beyond Bat and Ball* by David Foot (Good Books, 1993), *E.M. Forster: A*

Acknowledgements

Life by P.N. Furbank (Oxford University Press, 1979), *Ottoline at Garsington, 1915-1928*, edited by Robert Gathorne-Hardy (Faber and Faber, 1974), *Robert Graves: The Assault Heroic, 1895-1926* by Richard Perceval Graves (Weidenfeld & Nicolson, 1986), *Goodbye to All That* by Robert Graves (Penguin, 1976), *Dai Greatcoat: Letters of David Jones*, edited by René Hague (Faber and Faber, 1980), *Halfway to Heaven* by Rupert Hart-Davis (Sutton, 1998), *The Lyttleton-Hart-Davis Letters*, volume two, edited by Rupert Hart-Davis (John Murray, 1986), *Praise from the Past*, by Rupert Hart-Davis (Stone Trough Books, 1996), *Siegfried Sassoon: Letters to Max Beerbohm*, edited by Rupert Hart-Davis (Faber and Faber, 1986), *Ambrosia and Small Beer*, edited by Christopher Hassall (Longmans, 1964), *Serious Pleasures: The Life of Stephen Tennant* by Philip Hoare (Penguin, 1992), *Lytton Strachey* by Michael Holroyd (Penguin, 1971), *Portrait of Walton* by Michael Kennedy (Oxford University Press, 1989), *A Bibliography of Siegfried Sassoon* by Geoffrey Keynes (Rupert Hart-Davis, 1962), *The Gates of Memory* by Geoffrey Keynes (Clarendon Press, 1981), *Modernism Reconsidered*, edited by R. Kiely (Harvard University Press, 1983), *Selected Letters of E.M. Forster, 1921-1970*, edited by M. Lago and P.N. Furbank (Collins, 1985), *Letters of T.E. Lawrence*, edited by David Garnett (World Books, 1941), *Ancient as the Hills: Diaries, 1973-1974* by James Lees-Milne (John Murray, 1997), *A Number of People* by Edward Marsh (Heinemann/Hamish Hamilton, 1939), *Edith Olivier: From her Journals, 1924-1948*, edited by Penelope Middleboe (Weidenfeld & Nicolson, 1989), *Somerset Maugham* by Ted Morgan (Jonathan Cape, 1980), *In Broken Images: Selected Letters of Robert Graves, 1914-18*, edited by Paul O'Prey (Hutchinson, 1982), *Aftermath* by Harold Owen (Oxford University Press, 1970), *Ackerley: A Life* by Peter Parker (Constable, 1989), *To Keep the Ball Rolling* by Anthony Powell (Penguin, 1983), *Siegfried Sassoon* by John Stuart Roberts (Richard Cohen Books, 1999), *Selected Letters of Edith Sitwell*, edited by Richard Greene (Virago, 1997), *Laughter in the Next Room* by Osbert Sitwell (Macmillan, 1950), *The Life of Hilaire Belloc* by Robert Speaight (Hollis & Carter, 1957), *Singing School: The Making of a Poet* by Jon Stallworthy (John Murray, 1998), *The Georgian Scene* by Frank Swinnerton (Dent, 1946), *Figures in the Foreground* by Frank Swinnerton (Hutchinson, 1963), *Strangers: A Family Romance* by Emma Tennant (Jonathan Cape, 1998), *Siegfried Sassoon: A Critical Study* by Michael Thorpe (Leiden University Press and Oxford University Press, 1966), *Blow for Balloons* by W.J.T. Turner (Dent, 1935), *Edmund Blunden: A Biography* by Barry Webb (Yale University Press, 1990), *The Laughter and the Urn* by Laurence Whistler (Weidenfeld & Nicolson, 1985), *Beginning Again* by Leonard Woolf (Chatto & Windus, 1964), *Downhill All the Way* by Leonard Woolf (Chatto & Windus, 1967), *The Letters of Virginia Woolf, 1923-1928: A Change of Perspective*, edited by Nigel Nicolson and Joanne Trautmann (Penguin, 1981), *The Diary of Virginia Woolf, Vol. 2:*

Acknowledgements

1920-1924, edited by Anne Olivier Bell and Andrew McNeillie (Penguin, 1981).

Finally, I must thank my family, who deserve medals for their encouragement, forbearance and practical help throughout this whole project: my children, Kate, Philip, Emma, Alice and Trim, and, above all, my husband, Cecil Woolf.

J.M.W.

Select Bibliography

Works by Siegfried Sassoon (in order of publication)

The Daffodil Murderer (John Richmond, 1913)
The Old Huntsman and Other Poems (Heinemann, 1917)
Counter-Attack and Other Poems (Heinemann, 1918)
Picture Show (pp, 1919)
War Poems (Heinemann, 1919)
Recreations (pp, 1923)
Lingual Exercises (pp, 1925)
Selected Poems (Heinemann, 1925)
Satirical Poems (Heinemann, 1926)
The Heart's Journey (Heinemann, 1928)
Memoirs of a Fox-Hunting Man (Faber & Gwyer, 1928)
Memoirs of an Infantry Officer (Faber and Faber, 1930)
Poems by Pinchbeck Lyre (Duckworth, 1931)
The Road to Ruin (Faber and Faber, 1933)
Vigils (Heinemann, 1935)
Sherston's Progress (Faber and Faber, 1936)
Complete Memoirs of George Sherston (Faber and Faber, 1937)
The Old Century (Faber and Faber, 1938)
On Poetry (University of Bristol Press, 1939)
Rhymed Ruminations (Faber and Faber, 1940)
Poems Newly Selected (Faber and Faber, 1940)
The Weald of Youth (Faber and Faber, 1942)
Siegfried's Journey (Faber and Faber, 1945)
Collected Poems (Faber and Faber, 1947)
Meredith (Constable, 1948)
Common Chords (pp, 1950/1951)
Emblems of Experience (pp, 1951)
The Tasking (pp, 1954)
Sequences (Faber and Faber, 1956)
Lenten Illuminations (pp, 1958)
The Path to Peace (Stanbrook Abbey Press, 1960)
Collected Poems 1908-1956 (Faber and Faber, 1961)
The War Poems (Faber and Faber, 1983)

Secondary Sources

Ackerley, J.R., *My Father and Myself* (Penguin, 1971).
———, *My Sister and Myself: The Diaries of J.R. Ackerley*, ed. Francis King (Hutchinson, 1982).

Select Bibliography

Amory, M., *Lord Berners: The Last Eccentric* (Chatto & Windus, 1998).

Bagnold, E., *Enid Bagnold's Autobiography* (Century, 1985).

Baxter, B., *Strange Street* (Hutchinson, 1935).

Beaton, C., *Self-Portrait with Friends: The Selected Diaries of Cecil Beaton*, ed. R. Buckle (Penguin, 1982).

Behrman, S., *Portrait of Max: An Intimate Memoir of Sir Max Beerbohm* (Random House, 1960).

——, *Tribulations and Laughter* (Hamish Hamilton, 1972).

Bennett, A., *The Journals of Arnold Bennett*, ed. F. Swinnerton (Penguin, 1954).

——, *The Letters of Arnold Bennett*, ed. J. Hepburn (Oxford University Press, 1968).

Blunden, E., *Edmund Blunden: A Selection of his Poetry and Prose* (Rupert Hart-Davis, 1950).

——, *Cricket Country* (Collins, 1944).

——, *Undertones of War* (Penguin, 1982).

——, *Overtones of War*, ed. M. Taylor (Duckworth, 1996).

Bradford, S., *Sacheverell Sitwell: Splendours and Miseries* (Sinclair-Stevenson, 1993).

Butcher, D., *The Stanbrook Abbey Press Bibliography* (Whittington Press, 1992).

Caesar, A., *Taking It Like a Man: Suffering, Sexuality and the War Poets* (Manchester University Press, 1993).

Cecil, D., *Max: A Biography of Max Beerbohm* (Atheneum, 1985).

Cockerell, S.C., *The Best of Friends: Further Letters of Sir Sydney Carlyle Cockerell*, ed. Viola Meynell (Hart-Davis, 1956).

Connon, B., *Beverley Nichols: A Life* (Constable, 1991).

Corrigan, D.F., *Helen Waddell* (Gollancz, 1990).

——, *Siegfried Sassoon: Poet's Pilgrimage* (Gollancz, 1973).

Coward, N., *Diaries* (Little, Brown, 1982).

Cunningham, V., *British Writers of the Thirties* (London, 1988).

Darton, J.H., *From Surtees to Sassoon* (London, 1931).

Dunn, J.C. (ed.), *The War the Infantry Knew 1914-1919: A Chronicle of Service in France and Belgium* (P.S. King, 1938).

Elborn, G., *Edith Sitwell* (Sheldon, 1981).

Fitzgerald, P., *Charlotte Mew and her Friends* (Collins, 1984).

——, *The Knox Brothers* (Macmillan, 1977).

Foot, D., *Beyond Bat and Ball* (Good Books, 1993).

Forster, E.M., *Selected Letters, 1921-1970*, ed. M. Lago and P.N. Furbank (Collins, 1985).

Furbank, P.N., *E.M. Forster: A Life* (Oxford University Press, 1979).

Gilbert, M., *Second World War* (Phoenix, 1995).

Gittings, R., *The Older Hardy* (Heinemann, 1978).

Glendinning, V., *Edith Sitwell: A Unicorn Among Lions* (Oxford University Press, 1983).

Graves, R.P., *Robert Graves: The Assault Heroic 1895-1926* (Weidenfeld & Nicolson, 1986).

——, *Robert Graves: The Years with Laura 1926-1940* (Papermac, 1991).

Graves, R., *Goodbye to All That* (Penguin, 1976).

Hardy, T., *Collected Letters*, vols 5 and 6, ed. R.L. Purdey and M. Millgate (Clarendon, 1978).

Hart-Davis, R., *Halfway to Heaven* (Sutton, 1998).

——, *The Lyttleton–Hart-Davis Letters*, Vol. II (John Murray, 1986).

——, *Praise from the Past* (Stone Trough Books, 1996).

Select Bibliography

——, *Siegfried Sassoon: Letters to Max Beerbohm* (Faber and Faber, 1986).

Hassall, C., *Edward Marsh: Patron of the Arts* (Longman, 1959).

——, (ed.), *Ambrosia and Small Beer: The Record of a Correspondence Between Edward Marsh and Christopher Hassall* (Longmans, 1964).

Hibberd, D., *Harold Monro* (Palgrave, 2001).

Hoare, P., *Serious Pleasures: The Life of Stephen Tennant* (Penguin, 1992).

Holroyd, M., *Lytton Strachey* (Penguin, 1971).

James, L., *Lawrence of Arabia: The Golden Warrior* (Weidenfeld & Nicolson, 1991).

Jones, D., *Dai Greatcoat: Letters of David Jones*, ed. René Hague (Faber and Faber, 1980).

Kennedy, M., *Portrait of Walton* (Oxford University Press, 1989).

Keynes, G., *A Bibliography of Siegfried Sassoon* (Hart-Davis, 1962).

——, *The Gates of Memory* (Clarendon Press, 1981).

Lawrence, T.E., *Selected Letters of T.E. Lawrence*, ed. D. Garnett (World Books, 1941).

——, *Seven Pillars of Wisdom* (Jonathan Cape, 1940).

Marsh, E., *A Number of People* (Heinemann/Hamish Hamilton, 1939).

Middleboe, P., *Edith Olivier: From Her Journals 1924-1948* (Weidenfeld & Nicolson, 1989).

Moeyes, P., *Siegfried Sassoon: Scorched Glory, a Critical Study* (Macmillan, 1997).

Morrell, O., *Ottoline at Garsington, 1915-1928*, ed. R. Gathorne-Hardy (Faber and Faber, 1974).

O'Prey, Paul (ed.), *In Broken Images: Selected Letters of Robert Graves, 1914-1946* (Hutchinson, 1982).

Owen, H., *Aftermath* (Oxford University Press, 1970).

Parker, P., *Ackerley: A Life* (Constable, 1989).

Pearson, J., *Façades: Edith, Osbert and Sacheverell Sitwell* (Fontana, 1980).

Pinto, V. de S., *The City That Shone* (Hutchinson, 1969).

Porter, K. and Weekes, J. (eds), *Between the Acts: Lives of Homosexual Men 1885-1967* (Routledge, 1990).

Powell, A., *To Keep the Ball Rolling* (Penguin, 1983).

Richards, H., *The Bloody Circus: The Daily Herald and the Left* (Pluto Press, 1997).

Roberts, J.S., *Siegfried Sassoon* (Richard Cohen Books, 1999).

Seymour, M., *Ottoline Morrell: Life on the Grand Scale* (Sceptre, 1992).

Seymour-Smith, M., *Robert Graves: His Life and Works* (Paladin, 1987).

Sitwell, E., *Selected Letters of Edith Sitwell*, ed. R. Greene (Virago, 1997).

Sitwell, O., *Laughter in the Next Room* (Macmillan, 1949).

Sox, D., *Bachelors of Art* (Fourth Estate, 1991).

Speight, R., *The Life of Hilaire Belloc* (Hollis & Carter, 1957).

Stallworthy, J., *Singing School: The Making of a Poet* (John Murray, 1998).

Swinnerton, F., *A London Bookman* (Secker, 1928).

——, *The Georgian Literary Scene* (Dent, 1946).

——, *Figures in the Foreground* (Hutchinson, 1963).

Tennant, E., *Strangers: A Family Romance* (Jonathan Cape, 1998).

Thorpe, M. (ed.), *Letters to a Critic* (Kent editions, 1966).

Thorpe, M., *Siegfried Sassoon: A Critical Study* (Leiden University Press/Oxford University Press, 1966).

Thwaite, A., *Edmund Gosse: A Literary Landscape* (Secker & Warburg, 1984).

Turner, W.J., *Blow for Balloons* (Dent, 1935).

——, *The Duchess of Popocatapetl* (Dent, 1939).

Webb, B., *Edmund Blunden: A Biography* (Yale University Press, 1990).

Whistler, L., *The Laughter and the Urn* (Weidenfeld & Nicolson, 1985).

Whistler, T., *Imagination of the Heart: The Life of Walter de la Mare* (Duckworth, 1993).

Woolf, L., *Beginning Again* (Chatto & Windus, 1964).

——, *Downhill All the Way* (Chatto & Windus, 1967).

Woolf, V., *A Change of Perspective: The Letters, 1923-1928*, ed. N. Nicolson and J. Trautmann (Penguin, 1981).

——, *The Diary of Virginia Woolf, Vol. 2: 1920-1924*, ed. A.O. Bell and A. McNeillie (Penguin, 1981).

Ziegler, P., *Osbert Sitwell* (Chatto & Windus, 1998).

Index

507